LAWRENCE SANDERS

FOUR COMPLETE NOVELS

ABOUT THE AUTHOR

LAWRENCE SANDERS was born in Brooklyn, New York, in 1920 and he graduated from Wabash College in 1940. During the early part of his writing career, he worked as an editor on various magazines and published numerous short stories in several genres, including men's adventure tales, war stories, and detective fiction. He also worked as an editor for *Mechanix Illustrated* and *Science and Mechanics*. It was after this editorial stint that Sanders "got to the point where a lot of editors get—I said to myself that I could write the stuff better myself. And so I wrote *The Anderson Tapes*—my first novel—at age fifty."

The Anderson Tapes became an immediate best-seller and soon after was made into a major motion picture. This inventive thriller won Sanders the Mystery Writers of America Edgar Award in 1970 for best first mystery novel. Since then the best-selling author has been writing steadily, publishing an average of one to two detective novels each year.

In addition to his crime novels, Sanders has written other titles including *The Pleasures of Helen* (1971) and *Love Songs* (1972). Sanders currently lives in Florida.

LAWRENCE SANDERS

FOUR COMPLETE NOVELS

The Anderson Tapes

The First Deadly Sin

The Sixth Commandment

The Marlow Chronicles

AVENEL BOOKS · NEW YORK

This Omnibus edition was previously published in separate volumes under the titles:
The Anderson Tapes copyright © MCMLXIX, MCMLXX by Lawrence Sanders
The First Deadly Sin copyright © MCMLXXIII by Lawrence Sanders
Excerpt on page 372 from HONEY BUNCH: HER FIRST DAYS IN CAMP. Copyright MCMXXV
by Grosset and Dunlap, Inc. Copyright renewed MCMLIII by Helen Louise Thorndyke.
Excerpt on page 464 from HONEY BUNCH: HER FIRST LITTLE GARDEN. Copyright MCMXXIV
by Grosset and Dunlap, Inc. Copyright renewed MCMLII by Helen Louise Thorndyke.
The Sixth Commandment copyright © MCMLXXIX by Lawrence Sanders
The Marlow Chronicles copyright © MCMLXXVII by Lawrence Sanders
This 1984 edition is published by Avenel Books,
distributed by Crown Publishers, Inc., by arrangement with
G.P. Putnam's Sons.

Manufactured in the United States of America

Library of Congress Cataloging in Publication Data
Sanders, Lawrence, 1920–
Lawrence Sanders: Four complete novels.
Contents: The Anderson tapes—The First deadly sin—
The Sixth commandment—The Marlow chronicles.
I. Title. II. Title: Four complete novels.
PS3569.A5125A6 1984   813'.54   83-21457
ISBN: 0-517-431483

h g f e d c b a

CONTENTS

The Anderson Tapes
1

The First Deadly Sin
151

The Sixth Commandment
549

The Marlow Chronicles
751

The Anderson Tapes

AUTHOR'S NOTE

THE FOLLOWING account of a crime committed in the City of New York on the night of 31 August and the early morning hours of 1 September, 1968, has been assembled from a variety of sources, including:

—Eyewitness reports dictated to the author, and eyewitness reports available from official sources, on tape recordings and in transcriptions.

—Records of courts, penal institutions, and investigative agencies.

—Tape recordings and transcriptions made by "bugging" and other electronic surveillance devices, by crime prevention and detection agencies of the City of New York, the State of New York, the U.S. government, and by private investigative agencies.

—Personal correspondence, speeches, and private documents of the individuals involved, made available to the author.

—Newspaper reports.

—Official reports and testimony which are a matter of public record, including deathbed statements.

—The author's personal experiences.

It would be impractical to name all the individuals, official and civilian, who provided valuable assistance to the author. However, I am especially grateful to Louis J. Girardi, Managing Editor of the Newark (N.J.) *Post-Ledger*, who granted me a leave of absence from my crime reporting duties with that newspaper in order that I might research and write the full story of this crime, as part of a continuing investigation into the uses and abuses of electronic surveillance equipment by public and private agencies.

LAWRENCE SANDERS

3

1

THE BUILDING at 535 East Seventy-third Street, New York City, was erected in 1912 as a city residence for Erwin K. Barthold, a Manhattan merchant who owned Barthold, Inc., a firm that dealt in rope, tar, ships' supplies, and marine gear of all types. On the death of Mr. Barthold in 1931, his widow, Edwina, and his son, Erwin, Jr., lived in the house until 1943. Erwin Barthold, Jr., was killed on 14 July, 1943, while engaged on a bombing mission over Bremen, Germany. This was, incidentally, the city in which his father had been born. Mrs. Barthold died six months after the death of her son, from cancer of the uterus.

The house on Seventy-third Street then passed to a brother of the original owner and builder. He was Emil Barthold, a resident of Palm Beach, Florida and shortly after the will was probated, Emil Barthold sold the house (16 February, 1946) to Baxter & Bailey, 7456 Park Avenue, New York City.

This investment company then converted the town house into eight separate apartments and two professional suites on the ground floor. A self-service elevator and central air conditioning were installed. The apartments and suites were sold as cooperatives, at prices ranging from $26,768 to $72,359.

The building itself is a handsome structure of gray stone, the architecture generally in the French chateau style. The building has been certified and listed by the New York City Landmark Society. Outside decoration is minimal and chaste; the roof is tarnished copper. The lobby is lined with veined gray marble slabs interspersed with antiqued mirrors. In addition to the main entrance, there is a service entrance reached by a narrow alleyway which stretches from the street to a back door that leads to a wide flight of concrete stairs. The two apartments on the top floor have small terraces. There is a small apartment in the basement occupied by the superintendent. The building is managed by Shovey & White, 1324 Madison Avenue, New York.

Prior to 1 September, 1967, for a period of several years, Apartment 3B at 535 East Seventy-third Street had been occupied by a married couple (childless), Agnes and David Everleigh. On or about that date, they separated, and Mrs. Agnes Everleigh remained in possession of Apartment 3B, while David Everleigh took up residence at the Simeon Club, Twenty-third Street and Madison Avenue.

On approximately 1 March, 1968 (this is an assumption), David Everleigh engaged the services of Peace of Mind, Inc., a private investigation agency located at 983 West Forty-second Street, New York. With David Everleigh's assistance—this is presumed, since he still possessed a key to Apartment 3B and was its legal owner—an electronic device was installed in the base of the telephone in Apartment 3B.

It was a microphone transmitter—an Intel Model MT-146B—capable of picking up and transmitting telephone calls as well as conversation taking place in the apartment. A sum of $25 per month was paid to the superintendent of 534 East Seventy-third Street—the building across the street—to allow Peace of Mind, Inc., to emplace a voice-actuated tape recorder in a broom closet on the third floor of that building.

Thus, it was not necessary for an investigator to be present. The voice-actuated tape recorder recorded all telephone calls and interior conversations taking place in Apartment 3B, 535 East Seventy-third Street. The tape was retrieved each morning by an operative from Peace of Mind, Inc., and a fresh tape installed.

The resulting recordings became the basis of David Everleigh's suit for divorce (Supreme Court, New York County) on the grounds of adultery (*Everleigh v Everleigh*, NYSC-148532), and transcriptions of the tapes have become a matter of public record, which allows them to be produced here. It is of some interest to note that the verdict of the trial judge, in favor of David Everleigh, has been appealed by Mrs. Everleigh's attorneys on the grounds that David Everleigh did not obtain a court order, and had no legal right, to implant an electronic surveillance device in Apartment 3B, despite the fact that he was legal owner of the premises in question.

It is expected this litigation will eventually reach the Supreme Court of the United States and will result in a landmark decision.

The following is an excerpt from the transcription made from the Peace of Mind, Inc., tape recording made at approximately 1:15 A.M. on the morning of 24 March, 1968.

This is tape POM-24MAR68-EVERLEIGH. Those present, Mrs. Agnes Everleigh and John Anderson, have been identified by voice prints and interior evidence.

[Sound of door opening and closing.]

MRS. EVERLEIGH: Here we are . . . make yourself at home. Throw your coat anywhere.

ANDERSON: How come a classy place like this don't have a doorman?

MRS. EVERLEIGH: Oh, we have one, but he's probably down in the basement with the super, sucking on a jug of muscatel. They're both a couple of winos.

ANDERSON: Oh?

[Lapse of seven seconds.]

ANDERSON: Nice place you got here.

MRS. EVERLEIGH: *So* glad you like it. Mix us a drink. The stuff's over there. Ice in the kitchen.

ANDERSON: What'll you have?

MRS. EVERLEIGH: Jameson's. On the rocks. With a little soda. What do you drink?

ANDERSON: Got any cognac? Or brandy?

MRS. EVERLEIGH: I have some Martell.

ANDERSON: That'll do fine.

[Lapse of forty-two seconds.]

ANDERSON: Here you are.

MRS. EVERLEIGH: Cheers.

ANDERSON: Yeah.

[Lapse of six seconds.]

MRS. EVERLEIGH: Sit down and relax. I'm going to take off my girdle.

ANDERSON: Sure.

[Lapse of two minutes sixteen seconds.]

MRS. EVERLEIGH: That's better. Thank God.

ANDERSON: Are all the apartments in the building like this?

MRS. EVERLEIGH: Most of them are larger. Why?

ANDERSON: I like it. Class.

MRS. EVERLEIGH: Class? Jesus, you're too much. What do you do for a living?

ANDERSON: I work on a folding machine in a printing plant. For a supermarket newspaper. A daily. Their specials and things like that.

MRS. EVERLEIGH: Aren't you going to ask me what I do?

ANDERSON: Do you do anything?

MRS. EVERLEIGH: That's a laugh. My husband owns this apartment. We're separated. He doesn't give me a cent. But I do all right. I'm the buyer for a chain of women's lingerie shops.

ANDERSON: That sounds interesting.

MRS. EVERLEIGH: Go to hell.

ANDERSON: Are you lushed?

MRS. EVERLEIGH: Some. Not enough.

[Lapse of seventeen seconds.]

MRS. EVERLEIGH: I hope you don't think I make a habit of picking men up off the street?

ANDERSON: Why me?

MRS. EVERLEIGH: You looked clean and reasonably well dressed. Except for that tie. God, I hate that tie. Are you married?

ANDERSON: No.

MRS. EVERLEIGH: Ever been?

ANDERSON: No.

MRS. EVERLEIGH: Jesus Christ, I don't even know your name. What the hell's your name?

ANDERSON: Another drink?

MRS. EVERLEIGH: Sure.

[Lapse of thirty-four seconds.]

MRS. EVERLEIGH: I thank you. What the hell's your name?

ANDERSON: John Anderson.

MRS. EVERLEIGH: That's a nice, clean, neat name. My name's Agnes Everleigh—Mrs. David Everleigh that was. What do I call you—Jack?

ANDERSON: Mostly I'm called Duke.

MRS. EVERLEIGH: Duke? Royalty, for God's sake. Jesus, I'm sleepy. . . .

[Lapse of four minutes thirteen seconds. At this point there is evidence (not admissable) that Mrs. Everleigh dozed off. Anderson wandered about the apartment (supposition). He inspected the intercom system connected to the bells and the microphone in the lobby. He inspected the locks on the windows. He inspected the lock on the front door.]

MRS. EVERLEIGH: What are you doing?

ANDERSON: Just stretching my legs.

MRS. EVERLEIGH: Would you like to stay the night?

ANDERSON: No. But I don't want to go home yet.

MRS. EVERLEIGH: Thanks a lot, bum.

[Sound of loud slap.]

MRS. EVERLEIGH [gasping]: What did you do that for?

ANDERSON: That's what you wanted, isn't it?

MRS. EVERLEIGH: How did you know?

ANDERSON: A big, beefy lady executive like you . . . it had to be.

MRS. EVERLEIGH: Does it show that plainly?

ANDERSON: No. Unless you're looking for it. Should I use my belt?

MRS. EVERLEIGH: All right.

The following is supposition, supported in part by eyewitness testimony.

When he left Apartment 3B at 3:04 A.M., John Anderson spent a few moments examining the lock on Apartment 3A, across the foyer. He then took the self-service elevator up to the fifth floor, examined the locks, and made his way slowly downward, examining doors and locks. There were no peepholes in apartment doors above the ground floor.

When he exited from the lobby—still unattended by a doorman—he was able to examine the security arrangements of the outside doors and the bell system. He then waited on the corner of East Seventy-third Street and York Avenue for a cab, and rode home to his Brooklyn apartment, arriving there at 4:26 A.M. The lights in his apartment were extinguished at 4:43 A.M. (testimony of eyewitness).

2

AT 2:35 P.M., on the afternoon of Wednesday, 17 April, 1968, a black sedan was parked on the north side of Fifty-ninth Street, New York City, between Fifth Avenue and Avenue of the Americas. The vehicle was a 1966 Cadillac Eldorado (with air conditioning), license HGR-45-9159. It was registered as a company car by the Benefix Realty Co., Inc., 6501 Fifth Avenue, New York, New York.

The chauffeur of the car—later identified as Leonard Goldberg, forty-two, a resident of 19778 Grant Parkway, the Bronx, New York—was observed lounging nearby.

The sole occupant of the parked car, seated in the back, was Frederick Simons, vice-president of the Benefix Realty Co., Inc. He was fifty-three years old; approximately 5 feet 7 inches; 190 pounds. He wore a black bowler and a double-breasted tweed topcoat. His hair and mustache were white. He was a graduate of Rawlins Law College, Erskine, Virginia, and was also licensed as a certified public accountant in the State of New York (#41-5G-1943). He had no criminal record, although he had twice been questioned—by the New York Federal District Attorney (Southern District) and by a grand jury convened by Manhattan Supreme Court—regarding the control of the Benefix Realty Co., Inc., by an organized criminal syndicate, and the role Benefix had played in the procurement of liquor licenses for several taverns and restaurants in New York City and Buffalo, New York.

Approximately five months prior to this date, on 14 November, 1967, a court order (MCC-B-189M16) had been obtained for the emplacement of an electronic transmitting device in the vehicle described. Application was made by the Frauds Division, New York State Income Tax Bureau. A Gregory MT-146-GB microphone transmitter was concealed under the dashboard of the aforesaid vehicle. It was implanted in the garage where cars registered to the Benefix Realty Co., Inc., were serviced.

At 2:38 P.M., on the afternoon of Wednesday, 17 April, 1968, a man was seen approaching this car. He was later identified by an eyewitness at the scene and by voice prints.

John "Duke" Anderson, thirty-seven, was a resident of 314 Harrar Street, Brooklyn, New York. He was 5 feet 11 inches; 178 pounds; brown hair and brown eyes; no physical scars; dressed neatly and spoke with a slight Southern accent. Anderson was a professional thief, and four months previously had been paroled after serving twenty-three months at Sing Sing

(#562-8491) after his conviction on 21 January, 1966, in Manhattan Criminal Court on a charge of breaking and entering. Although it was the first conviction on his record, he had been arrested twice before in New York State, once for burglary, once for simple assault. Both charges had been dropped with no record of trial.

Tape NYSITB-FD-17APR68-106-1A begins:

SIMONS: Duke! My Lord, it's good to see you. How you been?

ANDERSON: Mr. Simons. Mighty fine to see you. How you been?.

SIMONS: Fine, Duke, just fine. You're looking well. A little thinner, maybe.

ANDERSON: I expect so.

SIMONS: Of course, of course! We've got this little refreshment stand here. As you can see, I'm already partaking. Can I offer you something?

ANDERSON: Cognac? Or brandy?

SIMONS: How will Rémy Martin suit you?

ANDERSON: Just right.

SIMONS: Pardon the paper cups, Duke. We find it's easier that way.

ANDERSON: Sure, Mr. Simons.

[Lapse of five seconds.]

SIMONS: Well . . . here's to crime.

[Lapse of four seconds.]

ANDERSON: God . . . that's good.

SIMONS: Tell me, Duke—how have things been going for you?

ANDERSON: I got no complaints, Mr. Simons. I appreciate everything you all did for me.

SIMONS: You did a lot for us, too, Duke.

ANDERSON: Yes. But it wasn't much. I got the letters through when I could. Sometimes I couldn't.

SIMONS: We understood, I assure you. We don't expect perfection when you're inside.

ANDERSON: I'll never forget that night I got back to Manhattan. The hotel room. The money. The booze. And that cow you sent over. And the clothes! How did you know my sizes?

SIMONS: We have ways, Duke. You know that. I hope you liked the woman. I picked her out myself.

ANDERSON: Just what the doctor ordered.

SIMONS [laughing]: Exactly right.

[Lapse of nine seconds.]

ANDERSON: Mr. Simons, since I got out I been walking the arrow. I work nights on a folding machine in a printing plant. We do a daily sheet a chain of supermarkets gets out. You know—special buys for the day, things like that. And I report regular. I don't see any of the old gang.

SIMONS: We know, Duke, we know.

ANDERSON: But something came up I wanted to ask you about. A wild idea. I can't handle it myself. That's why I called.

SIMONS: What is it, Duke?

ANDERSON: You'll probably think I'm nuts, that those twenty-three months scrambled my brains.

SIMONS: We don't think you're nuts, Duke. What is it . . . a campaign?

ANDERSON: Yes. Something I came across about three weeks ago. It's been chewing at me ever since. It might be good.

SIMONS: You say you can't handle it yourself? How many will you need?

ANDERSON: More than five. No more than ten.

SIMONS: I don't like it. It isn't simple.

ANDERSON: It is simple, Mr. Simons. Maybe I could do with five.

SIMONS: Let's have another.
ANDERSON: Sure . . . thanks.
[Lapse of eleven seconds.]
SIMONS: What income do you anticipate?
ANDERSON: You want me to guess? That's all I can do—guess. I guess a minimum of a hundred thou.
[Lapse of six seconds.]
SIMONS: And you want to talk to the Doctor?
ANDERSON: Yes. If you can set it up.
SIMONS: You better tell me a little more about it.
ANDERSON: You'll laugh at me.
SIMONS: I won't laugh at you, Duke. I promise.
ANDERSON: There's a house on the East Side. Way over near the river. Used to be a privately owned town house. Now it's apartments. Doctors' offices on the ground floor. Eight apartments on the four floors above. Rich people. Doorman. Self-service elevator.
SIMONS: You want to hit one of the apartments?
ANDERSON: No, Mr. Simons. I want to hit the whole building. I want to take over the entire fucking building and clean it out.

3

ANTHONY "DOCTOR" D'Medico, fifty-four, legal residence at 14325 Mulberry Lane, Great Neck, Long Island, was identified before the U.S. Senate Special Sub-committee to Investigate Organized Crime, (Eighty-seventh Congress, first session), on 15 March, 1965 (Report of Hearings, pp. 413–19), as being the third-ranking *capo* (captain) of the Angelo family. The Angelos were one of six families controlling the distribution of illicit drugs, extortion, prostitution, loan-sharking, and other illegal activities in the New York, New Jersey, Connecticut, and eastern Pennsylvania area.

D'Medico was president of the Benefix Realty Co., Inc., 6501 Fifth Avenue, New York City. His other holdings included half-partnership in the Great Frontier Steak House, 106–372 Flatbush Avenue, Brooklyn, New York; full ownership of the New Finnish Sauna and Health Club, 746 West Forty-eighth Street, Manhattan; one-third ownership of Lafferty, Riley, Riley & D'Amato, brokers (twice fined by the Securities and Exchange Commission), of 1441 Wall Street, Manhattan; and suspected but unproved ownership or interest in several small taverns, restaurants, and private clubs on the East Side of Manhattan catering to male homosexuals and lesbians.

D'Medico was a tall man, 6 feet 5 inches, portly and he dressed conservatively (his suits were made by Quint Riddle, tailor, 1486 Saville Row, London; shirts by Trioni, 142-F Via Veneto, Rome; shoes by B. Halley, Geneva). For many years he had been the victim of a chronic and apparently incurable *tic douloureux*, an extremely painful neuralgia of the facial muscles that resulted in a spasmodic twitching of his right eye and cheek.

His criminal record was minimal. At the age of seventeen he was arrested on a charge of assault with a knife upon a uniformed officer. No injury resulted. The case was dropped by Bronx Juvenile Court on the plea of D'Medico's parents. There is no other record of charges, arrests, or convictions.

On 22 April, 1968, the premises of the Benefix Realty Co., Inc., 6501 Fifth Avenue, New York, were under electronic surveillance by three agencies: the Federal Bureau of Investigation, the Frauds Division of the New York State Income Tax Bureau, and the New York Police Department. Apparently none of these agencies was aware of the others' activities.

The following tape, dated 22 April, 1968, is NYPD-SIS-564-03.

ANDERSON: Mr. D'Medico, please. My name is John Anderson.

RECEPTIONIST: Is Mr. D'Medico expecting you?

ANDERSON: Yes. Mr. Simons set up the appointment.

RECEPTIONIST: Just a moment, please, sir.

[Lapse of fourteen seconds.]

RECEPTIONIST: You may go right in, sir. Through that door and down the hall. First door on your right.

ANDERSON: Thanks.

RECEPTIONIST: You're quite welcome, sir.

[Lapse of twenty-three seconds.]

D'MEDICO: Come in.

ANDERSON: Afternoon, Mr. D'Medico.

D'MEDICO: Duke! Good to see you.

ANDERSON: Doc . . . it's fine seeing you again. You're looking well.

D'MEDICO: Too much weight. Look at this. Too much. It's the pasta that does it. But I can't resist it. How have you been, Duke?

ANDERSON: Can't complain. I want to thank you. . . .

D'MEDICO: Of course, of course. Duke, have you ever seen the view from our roof? Suppose we go up and take a look around? Get a breath of fresh air.

ANDERSON: Fine.

[Lapse of five seconds.]

D'MEDICO: Miss Riley? I'll be out of my office for a few moments. Will you ask Sam to switch on the air conditioner? It's very stuffy in here. Thank you.

[Lapse of three minutes forty-two seconds. Remainder of recording is garbled and indistinct due to mechanical difficulties.]

D'MEDICO: . . . do we know? A guy comes in every morning . . . the place . . . but . . . You wouldn't believe . . . phones . . . gadgets that . . . The building over there, across the street . . . windows . . . long-range. . . . We try to keep . . . murder. Don't trust. . . . Over here by the air conditioner. The noise. . . . Cold for you?

ANDERSON: No. Its. . . .

D'MEDICO: Fred told me . . . campaign. . . . Interesting. About five men you figured or . . . me more.

ANDERSON: I know . . . idea . . . still. . . . Of course, I haven't even gone . . . it. So I . . . you a package, Mr. D'Medico.

D'MEDICO: [Completely garbled.]

ANDERSON: No. No, I. . . . Two months, I'd say . . . be careful . . . first investigation. Good men . . . be in . . . if we went ahead. So all I got . . . right . . . is a hustle. I hoped . . . might stake . . . piece of the action.

D'MEDICO: I see . . . much do you . . . for this initial. . . .

ANDERSON: Three grand tops I . . . most . . . good men. But no use cutting . . . like this. . . .

D'MEDICO: You've got . . . —stand, is personal. My own funds. If it . . . good, I'll have . . . bring in others. You understand? It will . . . more . . . and also we'll want . . . man in. Ours.

ANDERSON: I understand. And thanks . . . help. I really . . . can bring it. . . .

D'MEDICO: Duke . . . anyone . . . you can. You . . . think . . . Fred Simons will . . . funds . . . from him. Let's . . . downstairs. Cold . . . hell. My face . . . act up. Jesus.

End of recording. It is assumed the two men returned to the Benefix offices, but that Anderson did not reenter D'Medico's private office. He departed from the building at 2:34 P.M.

4

PATSY'S DELICIOUS Meat Market, 11901 Ninth Avenue, New York. Four months previously these premises had been placed under electronic surveillance by the Investigative Division, Food and Drug Administration. The following tape recording, labeled FDA-PMM-#198-08, is dated 24 April, 1968. Time: approximately 11:15 A.M.

ANDERSON: Are you Patsy?
PATSY: Yes.
ANDERSON: My name is Simons. I called for three of your best steaks. You said you'd have them ready when I came in.
PATSY: Sure. Here they are, all wrapped.
ANDERSON: Thanks. Add that to my bill, will you?
PATSY: A pleasure.

5

THOMAS HASKINS (alias Timothy Hawkins, Terence Hall, etc.); thirty-two; 5 feet 4 inches; 128 pounds; faint white scar on left temple; slight figure; blond hair bleached whiter; a confessed male homosexual. This man's record included two arrests on charges of molesting male juveniles. Charges dropped when parents refused to prosecute. Arrested on 18 March, 1964, during raid on bucket shop operation at 1432 Wall Street, Manhattan. Charge dropped. Arrested on 23 October, 1964, on conspiracy to defraud, complaint of Mrs. Eloise MacLevy, 41105 Central Park West, Manhattan, claiming subject had mulcted her of $10,131.56 while promising her high return on investment in porkbelly futures. Charge dropped. Last known address: 713 West Seventy-sixth Street, New York City. Subject lived with sister (see below).

Cyntia "Snapper" Haskins; thirty-six; 5 feet 8 inches; 148 pounds; red hair (dyed; frequently wore wigs); no physical scars. Four convictions for shoplifting, three for prostitution, and one for fraud, in that she charged $1,061.78 worth of merchandise against a stolen credit card of the Buy-Everything Credit Co., Inc., 4501 Marvella Street, Los Angeles, California. Subject had served a total of four years, seven months, thirteen days in the Women's House of Detention, Manhattan; Barnaby House for Women, Losset, New York; and the McAllister Home for Women, Carburn, New York. Subject was author of *I Was a B-Girl* (Smith &

Townsend, published 10 March, 1963) and *Women's Prison: A Story of Lust and Frustration* (Nu-World Publishing Corp., published 26 July, 1964).

The premises at 713 West Seventy-sixth Street, New York, were under surveillance by the Bureau of Narcotics, Department of the Treasury. The following is transcription BN-DT-TH-0018-95GT, from a tape recording of the same number (except that the final digits are 95G). Those present have been identified by voice prints and by internal and external evidence. The date and time have not been determined exactly.

HASKINS: . . . so we're on the old uppers, darling. The sad story of our lives. Would you like a stick?

ANDERSON: No. You go ahead. What about you, Snap?

CYNTHIA: We live. I boost a little, and Tommy hustles his ass. We get by.

ANDERSON: I got something for you.

CYNTHIA: Both of us?

ANDERSON: Yes.

CYNTHIA: How much?

ANDERSON: Five bills. Shouldn't take over a week. No sweat.

HASKINS: Sounds divine.

CYNTHIA: Let's hear it.

ANDERSON: I'll tell you what you need to know. After that . . . no questions.

HASKINS: Wouldn't dream, darling.

ANDERSON: There's this house on the East Side. I'll leave you the address and everything I know about the schedules of the doormen and the super. Tommy, I want a complete list of everyone who lives in the place or who works there. That includes day-only servants, doormen, and super. Anything and everything. Names, ages, business they're in, daily schedules—the whole schmear.

HASKINS: A lark, darling.

ANDERSON: Snap, there are two professional offices on the ground floor, one a doctor, one a psychiatrist. I want you to look around. Furnishings? Safes? Maybe paintings on the walls? Shoe boxes in the back closet? These fucking doctors collect a lot in cash and never declare. Look it over and decide how you'll handle it. Then let me know before you move.

CYNTHIA: Like you said—no sweat. How do we contact you, Duke?

ANDERSON: I'll call at noon every Friday until you're set. Is your phone clean?

CYNTHIA: Here . . . I'll write it down. It's a phone booth in a candy store on West End Avenue. I'll be there at twelve o'clock every Friday.

ANDERSON: All right.

CYNTHIA: A little something down?

ANDERSON: Two bills.

CYNTHIA: You're a darling.

HASKINS: He's a sweetheart, a messenger from heaven. How's your love life, Duke?

ANDERSON: All right.

HASKINS: I saw Ingrid the other night. She heard you were out. She asked about you. Do you want to see her?

ANDERSON: I don't know.

HASKINS: She wants to see you.

ANDERSON: Yes? All right. Is she still at the old place?

HASKINS: She is indeed, darling. You don't blame her . . . do you?

ANDERSON: No. It wasn't her fault. I got busted from my own stupidity. How did she look?

HASKINS: The same. The pale, white little mouse made of wire and steel. The essence of bitchery.

ANDERSON: Yes.

6

FUN CITY Electronic Supply & Repair Co., Inc., 1975 Avenue D, New York City.

The following tape recording was made by the Federal Trade Commission through a rather unusual set of circumstances. The FTC established electronic surveillance of the aforementioned premises (court order MCC-#198-67BC) following complaints from several large recording companies that the proprietor of the Fun City Electronic Supply & Repair Co., Inc., Ernest Heinrich Mann, was engaged in a criminal activity, in that he purchased expensive commercial LP's and tape recordings of classical music—operas and symphonies—recorded them onto his own tapes, and sold the tapes at a greatly reduced (but profitable) price to a large list of clients.

Tape FTC-30APR68-EHM-14.

CLERK: Yes?

ANDERSON: The owner around?

CLERK: Mr Mann?

ANDERSON: Yes. Could I see him for a minute? I want to complain about an air conditioner you people sold me.

CLERK: I'll get him.

[Lapse of nine seconds.]

ANDERSON: You installed an air conditioner in my place and it conked out after I turned it on. I tested it and it ran a few minutes, then it stopped.

MANN: Would you step into the back office for a few minutes, sir, and we'll try to solve your problem. Al, handle things.

CLERK: Yes, Mr. Mann.

[Lapse of thirteen seconds.]

ANDERSON: Professor . . . you're looking good.

MANN: All goes well. With you, Duke?

ANDERSON: Can't complain. Took me a while to track you down. Nice setup you've got here.

MANN: What I've wanted always. Radio, television, hi-fi equipment, tape recorders, air conditioners. I do good.

ANDERSON: In other words, you're making money?

MANN: Yes, that is true.

ANDERSON: In other words, it will cost me more?

MANN [laughing]: Duke, Duke, you have always been a—how do you say it?—you have always been a very sharp man. Yes, it will now cost you more. What is it?

ANDERSON: There's this house on the East Side. Not too far from here. Five floors. Service entrance to basement. I want the basement washed—telephone system, trunk lines, alarms, whatever is down there. The works.

[Lapse of nine seconds.]

MANN: Difficult. With all these terrible robberies on the East Side recently, everyone is most alert. Doorman?

ANDERSON: Yes.

MANN: Back entrance?

ANDERSON: Yes.

MANN: I would guess closed-circuit TV from the back service entrance to the doorman's cubbyhole in the lobby. He doesn't press the button that releases the service door until he sees who is ringing. Am I correct?

ANDERSON: One hundred percent.

MANN: So. Let me think. . . .

ANDERSON: Do that, Professor.

MANN: "Professor." You are the only man I know who calls me Professor.

ANDERSON: Aren't you a professor?

MANN: I *was* a professor. But please . . . let me think. Now. . . . Yes. . . . We are telephone repairmen. The authentic truck is parked in front where the doorman can see it. Uniforms, equipment, identity cards . . . everything. We are bringing a new trunk line down the block. We must inspect the telephone connections in the basement. Duke? All right so far?

ANDERSON: Yes.

MANN: The doorman insists we pull over to the service entrance. . . .

ANDERSON: It's an alleyway leading to the back of the building.

MANN: Excellent. We pull in after he has inspected my identity card. All is well. The driver stays with the truck. I go in. The doorman sees me on his TV monitor. He releases the lock. Yes, I think so.

ANDERSON: I do, too.

MANN: So? What do you want?

ANDERSON: Everything down there. How the telephone lines come in. Can we break them? How? Is it a one-trunk line? Can it be cut or bypassed? How many phones in the whole building? Extensions? Alarm systems? To the local precinct house or private agencies? I want a blueprint of the whole wiring system. And look around down there. Probably nothing, but you never can tell. Can you operate a Polaroid with flash?

MANN: Of course. Clear, complete views. Every angle. Details. Instructions on what to bridge and what to cut. Satisfaction guaranteed.

ANDERSON: That's why I looked you up.

MANN: The cost will be one thousand dollars with half down in advance.

ANDERSON: The cost will be seven hundred dollars with three in advance.

MANN: The cost will be eight with four ahead.

ANDERSON: All right.

MANN: The cost will not include telephone truck and driver. I have no one I can trust. You must provide. Telephone truck, driver, uniform, and paper. You will pay for this?

[Lapse of four seconds.]

ANDERSON: All right. You'll get your own?

MANN: Yes.

ANDERSON: I'll let you know when. Thank you, Professor.

MANN: Any time.

7

FROM TAPE recording POM-14MAY68-EVERLEIGH, Segment I, approximately 9:45 A.M.

MRS. EVERLEIGH: Jesus, you're too much. I've never met anyone like you. How did you learn to do these things?

ANDERSON: Practice.

MRS. EVERLEIGH: You turn me upside down and inside out. You know all the buttons—just what turns me on. About a half hour ago I was down to one little nerve end, red and raw. You get me out.

ANDERSON: Yes.

MRS. EVERLEIGH: For a moment there I wanted to scream.

ANDERSON: Why didn't you?

MRS. EVERLEIGH: That bitch next door—she'd probably tell the doorman to call the cops.

ANDERSON: What bitch?

MRS. EVERLEIGH: Old Mrs. Horowitz. She and her husband have Apartment Three A, across the foyer.

ANDERSON: She's home during the day?

MRS. EVERLEIGH: Of course. He is, too—most days, when he's not at his broker's. He's retired and plays the market for kicks. Why—I don't know. He's got the first buck he ever earned.

ANDERSON: Loaded?

MRS. EVERLEIGH: Loaded *and* cheap. I've seen her put dog-food cans in the incinerator, and they don't even have a dog. I was in their place once. I don't socialize with them, but he called me in one night when she fainted. He panicked and rang my bell. It was just a faint—nothing to it. But while I was in their bedroom I saw a safe that must date from Year One. I'll bet that thing is bulging. He used to be a wholesale jeweler. Do it again, baby.

ANDERSON: Do what?

MRS. EVERLEIGH: You know. . . . with your finger . . . here . . .

ANDERSON: I know something better than that. Open up a little. More. Yes. Keep your knees up, you stupid cow.

MRS. EVERLEIGH: No. Don't do that. Please.

ANDERSON: I'm just starting. It gets better.

MRS. EVERLEIGH: Please, don't. Please, Duke. You're hurting me.

ANDERSON: That's the name of the game.

MRS. EVERLEIGH: I can't . . . oh Jesus, don't . . . please . . . God . . . Duke, I beg . . . oh, oh, oh . . .

ANDERSON: What a fat slob you are. For Chrissakes, you're crying . . .

8

HELMAS JOB Printing, 8901 Amsterdam Avenue, New York; 14 May, 1968; 10:46 A.M. Electronic surveillance by the Internal Revenue Service, using a Teletek Model MT-18-48B, transmitting to a voice-actuated tape recorder in the basement of the delicatessen next door. This is tape IRS-HJB-14MAY68-106.

CLERK: Yeah?

HASKINS: Is your employer about?

CLERK: Smitty? He's in back. Hey, Smitty! Someone to see you!

[Lapse of six seconds.]

HASKINS: Hello, Smitty.

SMITTY: Where's my twenty?

HASKINS: Right here, Smitty. Sorry it took so long to pay you. I do apologize. But I assure you, I didn't forget it.
SMITTY: Yeah. Thanks, Tommy.
HASKINS: Could I speak to you for a moment, Smitty?
SMITTY: Well . . . yeah . . . all right. Come on in back.
    [Lapse of eleven seconds.]
HASKINS: I need some paper, Smitty. I've got the cash. See? Plenty of bread. Cash on delivery.
SMITTY: What do you need?
HASKINS: I typed it all out for you on Snapper's typewriter. One identification card in the name of Sidney Brevoort. I've always loved the name Sidney. The company is the New Urban Reorganization Committee, a nonprofit outfit. Any clean address. Make sure you use this phone number. Here's a snapshot of me to staple on the card. Here is what it should say: "This will identify . . ." and so forth and so forth. Then I'll want about twenty Sidney Brevoort business cards. While you're at it, better make up about ten letterheads and envelopes for the New Urban Reorganization Committee. You never know. Okay so far?
SMITTY: Sure. What else?
HASKINS: Snapper wants twenty cards. Very ladylike and elegant. Script. Here's the name and address: Mrs. Doreen Margolies, five-eight-five East Seventy-third Street. Something with taste. You know?
SMITTY: Sure. I got taste. That's it?
HASKINS: Yes, that's everything.
SMITTY: Three o'clock this afternoon. Twenty-five bucks.
HASKINS: Thanks so much, Smitty. You're a sweet. I'll see you at three.
SMITTY: With the loot.
HASKINS: Of course. Have. . . .
    [The recording was halted by mechanical failure.]

9

TAPE RECORDING POM-14MAY 68-EVERLEIGH, Segment II; approximately 11:45 A.M.

MRS. EVERLEIGH: I've got to get to the office. I've been away too long. God, I feel drained.
ANDERSON: Have another shot; you'll feel better.
MRS. EVERLEIGH: I suppose so. Do you think we should leave together?
ANDERSON: Why not? He knows I'm up here, don't he?
MRS. EVERLEIGH: Yes. He called first. Christ, I hope he doesn't shoot his mouth off to the other owners.
ANDERSON: Give him a tip. He won't talk.
MRS. EVERLEIGH: How much should I give him?
ANDERSON: Have him call you a cab and slip him two bucks.
MRS. EVERLEIGH: Two dollars? Is that enough?
ANDERSON: Plenty
MRS. EVERLEIGH: Where are you going when you leave?
ANDERSON: It's a nice day—maybe I'll walk over to Ninth and get a downtown bus to work.
MRS. EVERLEIGH: I won't be able to see you for a while. For about two weeks.

ANDERSON: How's that?

MRS. EVERLEIGH: I've got to go to Paris on a buying trip. If you'd give me your address, I'll send you a dirty French postcard.

ANDERSON: I'll wait till you get back. You go on these trips often?

MRS. EVERLEIGH: Almost every month. Either to Europe or some other place to shoot ads. I'm gone at least a week out of every month.

ANDERSON: Nice. I'd like to travel.

MRS. EVERLEIGH: It's just working in a different place. Will you miss me?

ANDERSON: Sure.

MRS. EVERLEIGH: Oh, my God. . . . Well . . . all ready?

ANDERSON: Yes. Let's go.

MRS. EVERLEIGH: Oh, by the way . . . here's something I bought for you. It's a gold cigarette lighter from Dunhill's. I hope you like it.

ANDERSON: Thanks.

MRS. EVERLEIGH: Oh my God . . .

10

APPROXIMATELY THREE weeks after the parole of John Anderson from Sing Sing Penitentiary, intermittent electronic surveillance was established on his newly rented furnished rooms at 314 Harrar Street, Brooklyn, New York. The device used has not been verified. The following tape is coded NYPD-JDA-146-09. It is not dated. Speakers have been identified by voice prints and internal evidence.

ANDERSON: Ed Brodsky?

BILLY: He ain't here.

ANDERSON: Is that you, Billy?

BILLY: Who's this?

ANDERSON: I'm the guy you went to the Peters-McCoy fight with, at the old Garden.

BILLY: Gee, this is great! Duke, how. . . .

ANDERSON: Shut up and listen to me. Got a pencil?

BILLY: Wait a sec . . . yeah . . . okay, Duke, I got a pencil.

ANDERSON: How long will it take you to get to a pay phone?

BILLY: Five minutes maybe.

ANDERSON: Call me at this number, Billy. Now write it down.

BILLY: Okay, go ahead. I'm ready.

ANDERSON: Five-five-five-six-six-seven-one. Got that?

BILLY: Yeah. Sure.

ANDERSON: Read it back.

BILLY: Five-five-five-six-six-one-seven.

ANDERSON: Seven-one. The last two numbers are seven-one.

BILLY: Seven-one. Yeah, I got it now. Five-five-five,six-six-seven-one. How you been, Duke? I sure been. . . .

ANDERSON: Just hang up and go call, Billy. I'll be here.

BILLY: Oh . . . yeah. Okay, Duke, I'll hang up now.

[Lapse of three minutes forty-two seconds.]

BILLY: Duke?

ANDERSON: How are you, Billy?

BILLY: Gee, it's good to hear from you, Duke. We heard you was out. Ed was saying just the other. . . .

ANDERSON: Where is Ed?
BILLY: He took a fall, Duke.
ANDERSON: A fall? What the hell for?
BILLY: He was a . . . he was a . . . Duke, what's that word—you know—you got a lot of traffic tickets and you throw them away?
ANDERSON: A scofflaw?
BILLY: Yeah! That's it! Ed was a scofflaw. The judge said Ed was the biggest scofflaw in Brooklyn. How about that! So he got thirty days.
ANDERSON: Beautiful. When's he springing?
BILLY: What's today?
ANDERSON: It's Friday, Billy. The seventeenth of May.
BILLY: Yeah. Let's see . . . eighteen, nineteen, twenty, twenty-one. Yeah. The twenty-oneth. That's Tuesday . . . right?
ANDERSON: That's right, Billy.
BILLY: Ed will be out on Tuesday.
ANDERSON: I'll call late Tuesday or Wednesday morning. Tell him, will you, kid?
BILLY: I sure will. Duke, you got a job for us?
ANDERSON: Something like that.
BILLY: We sure could use a job, Duke. Things ain't been so great for me since Ed's been in the can. Listen, Duke, is it something maybe I could handle? I mean, if it's something right away, I could handle it. No use waiting for Ed to spring.
ANDERSON: Well, it's really a two-man job, Billy. If it was a one-man job, I'd tell you right away because I know you could handle anything I'd give you.
BILLY: I sure could, Duke. You know me.
ANDERSON: But this is really a two-man job so I think maybe we should wait for Ed. Okay?
BILLY: Oh, yeah, sure, Duke . . . if you say so.
ANDERSON: Listen, kid, is it really bad? I mean, if you need a couple of plasters until Ed gets out, tell me right now.
BILLY: Oh, no, Duke, thanks. Gee, no. It's not that bad. I mean I can get by till Ed gets sprung. Gee, thanks, Duke, I really do appreciate it. Hey, when you mentioned about that night at the Garden it really took me back. Hey, what a night that was . . . hey? Remember that guy I decked in the restaurant? Gee, what a night that was . . . hey, Duke?
ANDERSON: A great night, Billy. I remember it. Well, listen, keep out of trouble, will you, kid?
BILLY: Oh sure, Duke. I'll be careful.
ANDERSON: And tell Ed I'll call on Tuesday night or early Wednesday.
BILLY: I won't forget, Duke. Honest I won't. Tuesday night or early Wednesday. Duke will call. When I get back to the room I'll write it down.
ANDERSON: That's a good boy, Billy. Keep your nose clean. I'll be seeing you soon.
BILLY: Sure, Duke, sure. It was real good talking to you. Thank you very much.

11

INGRID MACHT, thirty-four, a resident of 627 West Twenty-fourth Street, New York City, was of German or Polish birth (not determined); 5 feet 5 inches; 112 pounds; black hair usually worn very short. Brown eyes. Healed lash marks on left buttock. Healed knife scar in X pattern on inside of left thigh. Scar of second-degree burns on right forearm. Spoke German, English, French, Spanish, and Italian fluently. (See Interpol file #35S-M49876.) Believed to be Jewish. There is evidence (unsubstantiated) that this woman entered the United States illegally from Cuba in 1964 in a group of authentic refugees. Interpol file (see above) lists arrests in Hamburg for solicitation, prostitution, robbery, and blackmail. Served eighteen months in corrective institution in Munich. Arrested on 16 November, 1964, in Miami, Florida, charged with complicity in a scheme to extort money from Cuban refugees on the promise of getting their relatives to the United States. Charges dropped for lack of evidence. Employed as dance instructor at Fandango Dance Ballroom, 11563 Broadway, New York.

Electronic surveillance of Miss Macht's apartment had been established on 15 January, 1968, by the Investigative Branch, Securities and Exchange Commission, on application in Federal Court, claiming that Miss Macht was involved in the theft and sale of securities, including stock shares, corporate bonds, and U.S. government bonds. On the granting of court order FDC-1719M-89C, a Bottomley 956-MT microphone transmitter was installed, tapping both telephone calls and interior conversations.

By coincidence, an employee of the SEC lived in the apartment directly below Miss Macht's. With his kind permission, a voice-actuated tape recorder was installed in his linen closet.

The following transcription was made from tape SEC-21MAY68-IM-12:18PM-130C.

ANDERSON: Is your apartment clean?
INGRID: Why not? I have been living a clean life. Duke, I heard you were out. How was it?
ANDERSON: Inside? A lot of faggots. You know how it was. You've been there.
INGRID: Yes. I have been there. A brandy—as usual?
ANDERSON: Yes. I like this place now. It looks different.
      [Lapse of twenty-nine seconds.]
INGRID: Thank you. I have spent much money on it. *Prosit.*
      [Lapse of five seconds.]
INGRID: Frankly, it is a surprise to see you. I did not think you would wish to see me again.
ANDERSON: Why not?
INGRID: I thought you would blame me.
ANDERSON: No. I don't blame you. What could you have done—confessed and taken a fall? What for? How would that have helped?
INGRID: That is what I thought.
ANDERSON: I was stupid and got caught. It happens. You have to pay for stupidity in this world. You did exactly what I would have done.
INGRID: I thank you, Duke. Now . . . that makes me feel better.
ANDERSON: You've put on weight?
INGRID: Perhaps. A little. Here and there.
ANDERSON: You look good, real good. Here, I brought you something. A gold cigarette lighter from Dunhill's. You still smoke as much as ever?
INGRID: Oh, yes—more than ever. Thank you. Very handsome. Expensive—no? Are things going so good for you . . . or did a woman give it to you?
ANDERSON: You guess.

INGRID [laughing]: I don't care how you got it. It was very nice, and you were very sweet to think of me. So . . . what happens now? What do you want?
ANDERSON: I don't know. I really don't know. What do *you* want?
INGRID: Oh, *Schatzie*, I stopped wanting many years ago. Now I just accept. It is easier that way.
ANDERSON: It made no difference to you whether I looked you up or not?
INGRID: No difference . . . no. I was curious, naturally. But it makes no difference either way.
  [Lapse of fourteen seconds.]
ANDERSON: You're a cold woman.
INGRID: I have learned to be cold.
ANDERSON: Tommy Haskins said you wanted to see me.
INGRID: Did he? That's Tommy.
ANDERSON: You didn't want to see me?
INGRID: Did—didn't. What difference does it make?
ANDERSON: What time do you go to work?
INGRID: I leave here at seven. I must be at the hall by eight.
ANDERSON: I'm working. Not too far from here. I've got to be there by four.
INGRID: So?
ANDERSON: So we have three hours. I want you to make love to me.
INGRID: If you wish.
ANDERSON: That's what I like—a hot woman.
INGRID: Oh, Duke. . . . If I was a hot woman you would not bother with me.
ANDERSON: Take off your robe. You know what I like.
INGRID: All right.
ANDERSON: You have gained weight. But it looks good.
INGRID: Thank you. Do you wish to undress?
ANDERSON: Not now. Later.
INGRID: Yes.
  [Lapse of seventeen seconds.]
ANDERSON: Oh, God. A week ago a woman asked me where I learned these things. I should have told her.
INGRID: Yes. But you don't know everything, Duke. A few things I have held back. Like this. . . .
ANDERSON: I . . . oh, Jesus, don't . . . I can't . . .
INGRID: But of course you can. You will not die from this, *Schatzie*, I assure you. It can be endured. I think now you will undress.
ANDERSON: Yes. Can we go in the bedroom?
INGRID: Please, no. I have just changed the bedding. I will get the soiled sheet from the hamper and we will spread it here, on the rug.
ANDERSON: All right.
  [Lapse of twenty-three seconds.]
ANDERSON: What is that?
INGRID: A girl at the dance hall told me about it, so I went out and bought one. Less than five dollars at a discount drugstore. It is intended for massage. Would you like to try it?
ANDERSON: All right.
INGRID: Look at this shape. So obvious. It makes a buzzing noise when I switch it on. Do not be startled. You will like it. I use it on myself.
  [Buzzing sound. Lapse of eighteen seconds.]
ANDERSON: No . . . stop, I can't take that.
INGRID: From me? But Duke, you once said you could take anything from me.

ANDERSON: God . . .

INGRID: Let me get closer to you. Look at me.

ANDERSON: What? I . . . what?

INGRID: In my eyes. At me, Duke. In my eyes . . .

ANDERSON: Oh . . . oh . . .

INGRID: "Oh, oh!" What kind of love talk is that? I must punish you for that. There is a nerve near . . . ah, yes, here. Am I not clever, *Schatzie*?

ANDERSON: Uhh . . .

INGRID: Please do not become unconscious so soon. I have several new things I would like to show you. Some are old things that will be new to you. And some are truly new things I have learned since . . . since you have been away. Open your eyes; you are no longer looking at me. You must look at me, *Schatzie*. You must look into my eyes. That is very important . . .

ANDERSON: Why . . .

INGRID: It is very important to me.

ANDERSON: Ah, ah, ah, ah . . .

INGRID: Just spread yourself a little wider and I will get you out. Watch carefully, Duke, and learn. . . . And who knows? Perhaps she will give you another cigarette lighter. . . .

12

RESIDENCE OF Thomas and Cynthia Haskins, 713 West Seventy-sixth Street, New York; 24 May, 1968. Excerpt from tape recording BN-DT-TH-0018-96G.

THOMAS: . . . and then the nasty turd stiffed me. He said he only had ten dollars with him. He opened his wallet to show me.

CYNTHIA: Bastard.

THOMAS: And then he laughed and asked if I took credit cards. I swear if I had a razor with me, he'd have been a member of the castrati right then. I was just furious. I thought he was good for at least fifty. Mid-westerner, of course. Pillar of the church. PTA. Rotarians. Elks. And all that shit.

CYNTHIA: And Odd Fellows.

THOMAS: You wouldn't *believe*! He said he was in New York on a business trip—but I know better, luv. He probably comes in twice a year to get his ashes hauled. I hope the next time he meets some rough trade from uptown. They'll shove his credit cards right up his hairy ass.

CYNTHIA: Duke called today.

THOMAS: What did you say?

CYNTHIA: I said we were working on it. I said we had the paper and were working it out. He was satisfied.

THOMAS: That's good. I don't think we should appear too anxious . . . do you, luv?

CYNTHIA: No I guess not. But I really want to do a good job for him Tommy. Maybe then he'll let us in on it. I got the feeling it's something big.

THOMAS: Why do you think that?

CYNTHIA: He's being so very, very careful. And five bills is a lot of bread for what he wants us to do. Someone is behind him on this. He just got out of poke a few months ago. He wouldn't have that kind of loot.

THOMAS: We'll do a good job for him. He scares me sometimes. His eyes are so pale and they look right through you.

CYNTHIA: I know. And that Ingrid is no Mother Goose, either.
[Lapse of seven seconds.]

THOMAS: Tell me something, Snap. Did you ever swing with her?
[Lapse of five seconds.]

CYNTHIA: Twice. No more.

THOMAS: Bent—isn't she?

CYNTHIA: You have no idea. I couldn't describe it.

THOMAS: I thought so, luv. She's got the look. And I bet I can guess her hang-up. . . .

CYNTHIA: What?

THOMAS: Whips, chains, feathers . . . the whole bit.

CYNTHIA: You're warm.

THOMAS [laughing]: I bet I am. That's what I don't understand—Duke going that route. It's not like him.

CYNTHIA: Every man's got to get out sooner or later. I told him we'd be ready by next Friday. Okay?

THOMAS: Why not? I'm ready now.
[Lapse of six seconds.]

CYNTHIA: I walked past that house on Seventy-third Street this morning.

THOMAS: My God, you didn't go in, did you?

CYNTHIA: Do you think I've got shit for brains? He told us not to . . . didn't he? Until we get his go-ahead. . . . I walked by across the street.

THOMAS: How did it look? Want a stick, luv?

CYNTHIA: Yes, all right, light me one. Good-looking town house. Gray stone. Black canopy from the doorway to the curb. I saw two brass plates—the doctors' names. There was a doorman talking to the beat fuzz out in front. Rich-looking building. Smells like money. I wonder what's on Duke's mind?

THOMAS: One of the apartments, I expect. How are you going to work it?

CYNTHIA: I'm going to call the doctor-doctor for an appointment, giving the name on those cards you got me. No one recommended me; I just moved into the neighborhood and need a doctor and saw his sign. Before I go to see him, I'll bite all my nails off down to the quick. I'll ask him for something to keep me from biting my nails. If he suggests something. I'll tell him I tried all kinds of liquids and paints and they didn't work. I'll ask if he thinks it might be a mental or emotional problem. I'll get him to recommend me to the shrink next door.

THOMAS: Sounds good.

CYNTHIA: I'll stop by the shrink's office and see him or make an appointment. I'll leave another card and tell him the doctor-doctor sent me. If I don't get enough on the first visits, I'll make some excuse for going back. How does it sound? Anything wrong?

THOMAS: Well . . . one thing. You got the cards and a good address. They'll never in a billion years check to see if you actually live there—until their bills are returned. And then it'll probably be too late. But you better check with Duke to make sure. Find out how you should handle the bills. My God, if the doctor-doctor sent out a bill after the day you visited him, and it was returned, it might fuck the whole thing. You better ask Duke.

CYNTHIA: Yes, that makes sense, Tommy. Doctors usually send bills out a few weeks or a month later—but no use taking chances. I didn't think about how I was going to pay them. You know, you've got some brains in that tiny, pointed head of yours.

THOMAS: And I worship you, too, luv!

CYNTHIA: This is lousy grass . . . you know? Where did you get it?

THOMAS: I just got it. No like?

CYNTHIA: All twigs and seeds. Didn't you strain it?

THOMAS: He told me it had been strained.

CYNTHIA: Who?

THOMAS: Paul.

CYNTHIA: That little scut? No wonder it's lousy. I'd rather have a Chesterfield. Tommy, how are you going to handle your end?

THOMAS: All front. I waltz in, flash my paper, and get a complete list of everyone in the building. After all, I'm making an informal neighborhood census on behalf of the New Urban Reorganization Committee. And by the way, the day I hit you'll have to sit in that booth in the candy store most of the morning. That's the number on my ID card. In case anyone decides to check.

CYNTHIA: All right.

THOMAS: Shouldn't be more than an hour or so, at the most. I'll call as soon as I leave. After I get the list from him, I'll ask him to call individual tenants and see if they'd be willing to be interviewed. Purely voluntary. No pressure. No hard line. Easy does it. If they don't want to, they don't have to. I might get into two or three apartments. Those rich bitches get lonely in the afternoon. They want to talk to someone.

CYNTHIA: Just one visit?

THOMAS: Yes. Let's not push our luck, luv. I'll get what I can on one visit. If Duke isn't satisfied, screw him.

CYNTHIA: You'd like that, wouldn't you? Or vice versa.

THOMAS: How do you like your vice—versa? I guess I would. Maybe. I'm not sure. I told you he frightens me sometimes. He's so cold and aloof and withdrawn. Someday he's going to kill.

CYNTHIA: Do you really think so?

THOMAS: Oh, yes.

CYNTHIA: He never carries a piece.

THOMAS: I know. But he'll do it someday. Maybe he'll kick someone to death. Or with his hands or whatever is handy. That would be like him—standing there coldly kicking someone in their balls and stomping on them. Until they're dead.

CYNTHIA: Jesus, Tommy!

THOMAS: It's true. You know, I'm very psychic about people. Those are the emanations I get from him.

CYNTHIA: Then I won't even suggest it.

THOMAS: Suggest what?

CYNTHIA: Well . . . the whole deal is so interesting—I mean Duke giving us all that loot for what we're doing. I'm sure it's something big. So I thought. . . .

THOMAS: Yes?

CYNTHIA: Well, I thought that if we . . . if you and me . . . we could discover what it was, maybe we could . . . somehow, you know . . . move first and take. . . .

THOMAS [yelling]: You bloody scut! Forget it! Forget it . . . do you hear? If I ever hear you mention such a thing again I'm going right to Duke and tell him. We're getting paid for what we do. That's it! You understand? That's all we know and all we do unless Duke gives us something more. Do you have that straight?

CYNTHIA: Jesus Christ, Tommy, you don't have to scream at me.

THOMAS: Frigging cunt. You get ideas like that and we're dead. You understand what I'm saying? We're dead.

CYNTHIA: All right, Tommy, *all right*. I won't say any more about it.
THOMAS: Don't even think about it. Don't even let the idea get into your stupid little brain again. I know men better than you and. . . .
CYNTHIA: I'm sure you do, Tommy.
THOMAS: . . . and Duke isn't like you and me. If he found out what you said, he'd do things to us you wouldn't believe. And it wouldn't mean a thing to him. Not a thing. Ignorant slut!
CYNTHIA: All right, Tommy, *all right*.
[Lapse of sixteen seconds.]
CYNTHIA: When Duke calls next Friday, you want me to give him what we've got and get the go-ahead?
THOMAS: Yes. Outline it for him. Ask him how you should handle paying the doctors. He'll come up with something.
CYNTHIA: All right.
[Lapse of six seconds.]
THOMAS: Snap, I'm sorry I yelled at you. But I was frightened at what you said. Please, please, forgive me.
CYNTHIA: Sure.
THOMAS: Would you like a nice hot bath, luv? I'll get it all ready for you. With bath oil.
CYNTHIA: That would. . . .
[End of recording due to tape runout.]

13

EDWARD J. Brodsky; thirty-six; 5 feet 9½ inches; 178 pounds; black, oily hair, center part, worn long. Middle finger of right hand amputated. Faint knife scar on right forearm. Brown eyes. This man had a record of four arrests, one conviction. Arrested on charge of assault, 2 March, 1963. Case dismissed. Arrested for breaking and entering, 31 May, 1964. Case dismissed for lack of evidence. Arrested for conspiracy to defraud, 27 September, 1964. Charges withdrawn. Arrested as scofflaw, 14 April, 1968. Sentenced to thirty days in the Brooklyn jail. Completed sentence and released 21 May, 1968. Member of Brooklyn Longshoremen's Union, Local 418 (Steward, 5 May, 1965, to 6 May, 1966). Questioned in connection with fatal stabbing of union official, BLU, Local 526, 28 December, 1965. No charge. Residence: 124–159 Flatbush Avenue, Brooklyn, New York. Older brother of William K. Brodsky (see below).

William "Billy" K. Brodsky; twenty-seven; 6 feet 5 inches; 215 pounds; fair, wavy hair; blue eyes; no physical scars. Extremely muscular build. Elected "Mr. Young Brooklyn" 1963, 1964, and 1965. Arrested 14 May, 1964, on a charge of molesting a minor (female). Charge dropped. Arrested on 31 October, 1966, for assault with a deadly weapon—namely, his fists. Convicted, suspended sentence. Questioned on 16 July, 1967, in case involving attack and rape of two juveniles (female), Brooklyn, New York. Released for lack of evidence. This man dropped out of school after the seventh grade. The investigator's report leading to the suspended sentence in the assault case of 1966 states he had the mentality of a ten-year-old. Lived with his older brother at address given above.

The following meeting took place at the You-Know-It Bar & Grill, 136–943 Flatbush Avenue, Brooklyn, New York, on the afternoon of 25 May, 1968. At the time, these premises were under electronic surveillance by the

New York State Liquor Authority, on the suspicion that the owners of record were selling liquor to minors and that the premises were a gathering place for undesirables, including prostitutes and homosexuals.

This tape is coded SLA-25MAY68-146-JB.

ANDERSON: Wait'll we get our drinks, then we'll talk.

EDWARD: Sure.

BILLY: Duke, gee, it's. . . .

WAITER: Here we are, gents . . . three beers. Call me when you're ready for a refill.

EDWARD: Yeah.

ANDERSON: The old ex-con.

EDWARD: Ah, come on, Duke, don't put me on. Isn't that a pile of crap? After what I've done and I get jugged for parking in the wrong places? Honest to God, I'd laugh . . . if it happened to someone else.

BILLY: The judge said Ed was the biggest scofflaw in Brooklyn. Ain't that right, Ed?

EDWARD: *Isn't* that right. . . . You're absolutely correct, kid. That's what the judge said.

ANDERSON: Beautiful. Got anything on?

EDWARD: Not right now. I got a promise of something in October, but that's a long way away.

BILLY: Duke said he had a job for us . . . didn't you, Duke?

ANDERSON: That's right, Billy.

BILLY: Duke said it was a two-man job or I could have handled it. Ain't that right, Duke? I told him I could handle something while you were away, Edward, but Duke said he'd wait until you got out because it was a two-man job.

ANDERSON: You're right, Billy.

EDWARD: Listen, kid, why don't you drink your beer and keep quiet for a while . . . huh? Duke and I want to talk business. Don't interrupt. Just drink your beer and listen. Okay?

BILLY: Oh, yeah, sure, Edward. Can I have another beer?

EDWARD: Sure you can, kid . . . as soon as you finish that one. You got something, Duke?

ANDERSON: There's this house on the East Side in Manhattan. I need the basement swept. I got a guy to do it—a tech named Ernie Mann. You know him?

EDWARD: No.

ANDERSON: Good, solid guy. Knows his stuff. He'll be the only one to go in. But he needs a driver. He wants a telephone company truck. A Manhattan truck. Clothes and ID cards. All the equipment. I can tell you where to get the paper; you'll have to take care of the rest. It's only for a few hours. Three hours at the most.

EDWARD: Where will I be?

ANDERSON: Outside. In the truck. It's like a small van. You've seen them.

BILLY: It's a two-man job . . . right, Duke?

ANDERSON: That's up to Ed. How about it?

EDWARD: Tell me more.

ANDERSON: Converted town house on a quiet block. Doorman. Alley that leads to the service entrance. You can't get in the back door until the doorman sees you on closed-circuit TV and presses the button. You pull up in front. Ernie goes in the lobby and flashes his potsy. Real good odds that the doorman won't ask to see yours. You're sitting outside in the regulation van where he can see it. Ernie tells the doorman the telephone company is bringing a new trunk line down the block and he's got to examine the connections. All right so far?

EDWARD: So far.

ANDERSON: What could go wrong? The tech just wants to get into the basement; he doesn't want to case the apartments. The doorman says okay, that you should pull into the alley and drive to the back entrance. Like I said, only Ernie goes in. You stay with the truck.

BILLY: Me, too, Duke. Don't forget me.

ANDERSON: Yeah. How does it sound, Ed?

EDWARD: Where do we get the ID cards?

ANDERSON: There's a paper man on Amsterdam Avenue. Helmas. Ever use him?

EDWARD: No.

ANDERSON: The best. He's got the blank cards. Not copies. The real thing. You'll need snapshots to staple on—you know, the kind of four-for-a-quarter shots you get on Forty-second Street.

EDWARD: What about the truck, uniforms, equipment, and all that shit?

ANDERSON: That's your problem.

EDWARD: How much?

ANDERSON: Four bills.

EDWARD: When?

ANDERSON: As soon as you're ready. Then I'll call Ernie, and we'll set it up. This is not a hit, Ed. It's just a wash.

EDWARD: I understand, but still. . . . Can't go to five, can you, Duke?

ANDERSON: I can't, Ed. I'm on a budget. But if it works out it might be something more for you . . . for all of us. You understand?

EDWARD: Sure.

BILLY: What are you talking about? I don't understand what you're talking about.

EDWARD: Shut up a minute, kid. Let's go over it once more, Duke; I want to be sure I got it right. It's just a wash, not a hit. I don't go inside the building. I pick up a Manhattan telephone company van with all the gear. I have the uniform and crap hanging from my belt. What about the tech?

ANDERSON: He'll bring his own.

EDWARD: Good. I lift the truck. I pick up this Ernie guy somewhere. Right?

ANDERSON: Right.

EDWARD: We drive up in front of the house. He gets out, braces the doorman, and shows his ID. We drive up the alley to the back entrance. This Ernie gets out, shows on the TV, and gets let in. I stick in the truck. Have I got it?

ANDERSON: That's it.

EDWARD: How long do I stick around?

ANDERSON: Three hours tops.

EDWARD: And then . . . ?

ANDERSON: If he's not out by then, take off.

EDWARD: Good. That's what I wanted to hear. So he's out in under three hours. Then what?

ANDERSON: Drop him where he wants to go. Ditch the truck. Change back to your regular clothes. Walk away.

BILLY: Gee, that sounds easy . . . doesn't it, Edward? Doesn't that sound easy?

EDWARD: They all sound easy, kid. How do I contact you, Duke?

ANDERSON: It's on?

EDWARD: Yeah. It's on.

ANDERSON: I'll call you every day at one o'clock in the afternoon. If you miss it, don't worry; I'll call the next day. After you get it set, I'll call the tech and we'll set up a meet. Want two bills?
EDWARD: Jesus, do I? Waiter . . . another round!

14

THE PREMISES at 4678 West End Avenue, New York City, a candy and cigar store, were placed under surveillance on 16 November, 1967, by the New York Police Department, on suspicion that the store was being used as a policy (numbers racket) drop. Taps were installed on the two pay phones in booths in the rear of the store.

The following transcription was made from a tape identified as NYPD-SIS-182-BL. It is not dated definitely but is believed to have been recorded on 31 May, 1968.

CYNTHIA: . . . so that's how it shapes up, Duke. How does it sound?
ANDERSON: All right. It sounds all right.
CYNTHIA: The only hang-up we can see is that business of paying the doctors. You know doctors usually wait a few weeks or a month before they bill. But if the doctor-doctor or the shrink happens to bill within a few days, and the letter comes back from my freak address, it means I couldn't make a second visit.
ANDERSON: What does Tommy say?
CYNTHIA: He says to tell you we could handle it a couple of ways. I can tell them I'm going on a cruise or vacation or something and not to bill for a month at least because I don't want mail piling up in the mailbox because that's a tip-off to crooks that no one is home. Or, Tommy says, we can get me a book of personalized checks from Helmas. I can give them a freak check right then and there. That'll guarantee me at least three or four days before it bounces, and during that time I might be able to arrange another visit.
ANDERSON: Why not just pay cash before you leave?
CYNTHIA: Tommy says it would be out of character.
ANDERSON: Shit. That brother of yours should have been a play actor. Look, let's not get so fucking tricky. This is just a dry run. Don't take chances. Get what you can on your first visit. Pay them in cash. Then you can go back a second time whenever you like.
CYNTHIA: Okay, Duke, if you say so. How does Tommy's campaign sound?
ANDERSON: I can't see any holes, Snap. Both of you go ahead. If anything comes up, play it smart and lay off. Don't push. I'll call you next Friday, same time, and set up a meet.

15

TRANSCRIPTION FROM tape recording FTC-1JUN68-EHM-29L. Premises of Fun City Electronic Supply & Repair Co., Inc., 1975 Avenue D, New York.

ANDERSON: Professor?
MANN: Yes.
ANDERSON: Duke. Your phone clean?
MANN: Of course.
ANDERSON: I have your drivers.
MANN: Drivers? More than one?
ANDERSON: Two brothers.
MANN: This is necessary?
ANDERSON: They're a team. Professionals. No sweat. They'll sit there for three hours tops.
MANN: Plenty. More than plenty. I'll be out in one.
ANDERSON: Good. When?
MANN: Precisely nine forty-five A.M., on the morning of June fourth.
ANDERSON: That's next Tuesday morning? Correct?
MANN: Correct.
ANDERSON: Where?
MANN: On the northwest corner of Seventy-ninth Street and Lexington Avenue. I shall be wearing a light tan raincoat and carrying a small black suitcase. I shall be wearing no hat. You have that?
ANDERSON: Yes, I have it.
MANN: Duke, the two men . . . is it necessary?
ANDERSON: I told you, they're a team. The old one drives. The young one is strictly muscle.
MANN: Why should muscle be necessary?
ANDERSON: It won't be, Professor. The kid's a little light in the head. His brother takes care of him. The kid needs to be with him. You understand?
MANN: No.
ANDERSON: Professor, the two will sit in the truck and wait for you. There will be no trouble. There will be no need for muscle. Everything will go well.
    [Lapse of six seconds.]
MANN: Very well.
ANDERSON: I'll call you on Wednesday, June fifth, and we'll set up a meet.
MANN: As you wish.

16

THE FOLLOWING is a transcription of a personal tape recording made by the author on 19 November, 1968. To my knowledge, the testimony it contains is not duplicated in any official recording, transcription, or document now in existence.

AUTHOR: This will be a recording GO-1A. Will you identify yourself, please, and state your place of residence.
RYAN: My name is Kenneth Ryan. I live at one-one-nine-eight West Nineteenth Street, New York.
AUTHOR: And will you please state your occupation and where you work.
RYAN: I'm a doorman. I'm on the door at five-three-five East Seventy-third Street in Manhattan. I'm usually on eight in the morning until four in the afternoon. Sometimes we switch around, you understand. There's three of us, and sometimes we switch around, like when a guy wants to go

somewhere, like he's got a family thing to go to. Then we switch around. But generally I'm on eight to four during the day.

AUTHOR: Thank you. Mr Ryan, as I explained to you previously, this recording will be solely for my own use in preparing a record of a crime that occurred in New York City on the night and morning of August thirty-first and September first, 1968. I am not an officer of any branch of the government—city, state, or federal. I shall not ask you to swear to the testimony you are about to give, nor will it be used in a court of law or in any legal proceeding. The statement you make will be for my personal use only and will not be published without your permission, which can only be granted by a signed statement from you, giving approval of such use. In return, I have paid you the sum of one hundred dollars, this sum paid whether or not you agree to the publication of your statement. In addition, I will furnish you—at my expense—a duplicate recording of this interrogation. Is all that understood?

RYAN: Sure.

AUTHOR: Now then . . . this photograph I showed you. . . . Do you recognize him?

RYAN: Sure. That's the fly who told me his name was Sidney Brevoort.

AUTHOR: Well . . . actually this man's name is Thomas Haskins. But he told you he was Sidney Brevoort?

RYAN: That's right.

AUTHOR: When did this happen?

RYAN: It was early in June. This year. Maybe the third, maybe the fourth, maybe the fifth. Around then. This little guy comes up to me in the lobby where I work. That's five-three-five East Seventy-third Street, like I told you.

AUTHOR: About what time was this?

RYAN: Oh, I don't remember exactly. Maybe nine forty-five in the morning. Maybe ten. Around then. "Good morning," he says, and I say, "Good morning." And he says, "My name is Sidney Brevoort, and I am a field representative of the New Urban Reorganization Committee. Here is my identification card." And then he shows me his card, and it's just like he says.

AUTHOR: Did the card have his photo on it?

RYAN: Oh, sure. All printed and regular like. Official—know what I mean? So he says, "Sir . . ."—he always called me sir—he says, "Sir, my organization is making an informal census of the dwellings and popula-tion of the East Side of Manhattan from Fifth Avenue to the river, and from Twenty-third Street on the south to Eighty-sixth Street on the north. We are trying to get legislation passed by New York State allowing for a bond issue to finance the cost of a Second Avenue subway." That's as near as I can remember to what he says. He's talking very official, you know. Very impressive, it was. So I says, "You're damned right. They had the bonds for that years ago, and then they went and pissed the money away on other things. Right into the politicians' pocket." I tells him. And he says, "I can see you keep up on civic affairs." And I says to him, "I know what's going on." And he says, "I am certain you do, sir. Well, to help convince New York State legislators that this bill should be passed, the New Urban Reorganization Commit-tee is making an actual count of everyone on the East Side of Manhattan in the area I mentioned who might conceivably benefit by a Second Avenue subway. What I'd like from you are the names of people living in this building and the numbers of the apartments they occupy."

AUTHOR: And what did you say to that?

RYAN: I told him to go to hell. Well, I didn't put it in those exact words, you understand. But I told him I couldn't do it.

AUTHOR: What did he say then?

RYAN: He said it would be voluntary. He said that any tenant who wanted to volunteer information—why, that would be confidential, and their names wouldn't be given to anyone. They'd just be—you know, like statistics. What he wanted to know was who lived in what apartment, did they have servants, and how they traveled to work, and what time did they go to work and what time did they come home. Stuff like that. So I said, "Sorry, no can do." I told him Shovey and White at one-three-two-four Madison Avenue managed the house, and all us doors got strict orders not to talk to anyone about the tenants, not to give out no information, and not to let anyone into tenants' apartments unless we get the okay from Shovey and White.

AUTHOR: What was his reaction to that?

RYAN: That little shit. He said he could understand it because of all the robberies on the East Side recently, and would it be all right if he called Shovey and White and asked for permission to talk to me and interview the tenants who would volunteer to talk to him. So I said sure, call Shovey and White, and if they say it's okay, then it's okay with me. He said he'd call them and if it was okay, he'd have them call me to give me the go-ahead. He asks me who he should talk to at Shovey and White, and I told him to talk to Mr. Walsh who handles our building. I even gave him the phone number . . . oh, the filth of him! Then he asks me if I have ever seen Mr. Walsh, and I had to tell him no, I had never set eyes on the guy. I only talked to him twice on the phone. You gotta understand, these managers don't take no personal interest. They just sit on their ass behind a phone.

AUTHOR: What did the man you know as Sidney Brevoort do then?

RYAN: He said he'd call Shovey and White and explain what he wanted and have Mr. Walsh contact me. So I said if it was okay with them, it was okay with me. So he thanked me for my trouble—very polite, you understand—and walked away. The dirty little crud.

AUTHOR: Thank you, Mr. Ryan.

17

TAPE NYPD-SIS-196-BL. Premises of candy store at 4678 West End Avenue. Approximately 10:28 A.M., 3 June, 1968.

CYNTHIA HASKINS: The New Urban Reorganization Committee. May I help you?

THOMAS: It's me, Snap.

CYNTHIA: What's wrong?

THOMAS: I bombed out. The fucking Irishman on the door won't talk unless he gets a go-ahead from the management agents, Shovey and White, on Madison Avenue.

CYNTHIA: Oh, my God. Duke will kill us.

THOMAS: Don't get your balls in an uproar, luv. I thought of something on the way here. I'm calling from a pay phone on the corner of Seventy-third Street and York Avenue.

CYNTHIA: Jesus' sake, Tommy, take it easy. Duke said not to take any chances. Duke said if anything came up to lay off. Now you say you thought of something. Tommy, don't. . . .

THOMAS: You think he's paying us five bills to lay off? He wants us to use our brains, doesn't he? That's why he looked us up, isn't it? If he wanted a couple of dumdums he could have bought them for a bill. Duke wants results. If we don't blow the whole goddamned thing—whatever it is— he won't care how we did it.

CYNTHIA: Tommy, I. . . .

THOMAS: Shut up and listen. Here's how we'll work it. . . .

18

APPROXIMATELY 10:37 A.M., 3 June, 1968.

RYAN: Five thiry-five East Seventy-third Street.

CYNTHIA: Is this the doorman?

RYAN: Yeah. Who's this?

CYNTHIA: This is Ruth David at Shovey and White. Did you just talk to a man named Sidney Brevoort who said he was from the New Urban Reorganization Committee?

RYAN: Yeah. He was here a few minutes ago. He wanted a list of people in the building and wanted to talk to them. I told him to call Mr Walsh.

CYNTHIA: You did exactly right. But Mr. Walsh is out sick. The flu or something. He was out yesterday and he's out today. I'm handling his buildings while he's gone. How did this Brevoort guy look to you?

RYAN: A mousy little swish. I could chew him up and spit him over the left-field fence.

CYNTHIA: He didn't look like a thief, I mean?

RYAN: No, but that don't mean nothing. What do you want me to do if he comes back?

CYNTHIA: Well, I called the New Urban Reorganization Committee, and it's a legitimate outfit. They said yes, Sidney Brevoort was one of their field representatives. Did he have an identification card?

RYAN: Yeah. He showed it to me.

CYNTHIA: Well, I don't want to take the responsibility of giving him the names of tenants or letting him talk to them.

RYAN: You're right. I don't neither.

CYNTHIA: Tell you what . . . Mr. Walsh told me to call him at home in case something came up I couldn't handle. I've got his home phone number. If he says it's okay, you can talk to Brevoort. If Walsh says no, then to hell with Brevoort and the New Urban Reorganization Committee. Either way, you and I are out of it; we'll leave it up to Walsh.

RYAN: Yeah. That's smart.

CYNTHIA: All right. I'll hang up now and call Walsh. I'll call you back in a few minutes and tell you what he said.

RYAN: I'll be here.

19

CYNTHIA: Doorman? This is Ruth David again.
RYAN: Yeah. You talk to Mr. Walsh?
CYNTHIA: Yes. He said it was perfectly all right. He knows this New Urban Reorganization Committee. He says it's okay to give Brevoort the names of tenants. Also, he can talk to any tenants who voluntarily agree. But you ask them first on the intercom. Don't let Brevoort wander around the house. And make sure he comes down to the lobby after every interview.
RYAN: Don't worry, Miss David. I know how to handle it.
CYNTHIA: Good. Well, that's a load off my mind. I didn't want to take the responsibility.
RYAN: I didn't neither.
CYNTHIA: Mr. Walsh said to tell you that you did exactly right, making Brevoort call us. He said to tell you he won't forget how you handled this.
RYAN: Yeah. Fine. Okay, then I'll talk to Brevoort. Thanks for calling, Miss David.
CYNTHIA: Thank you, sir.

20

TRANSCRIPTION FROM tape SEC-3JUN68-IM-01:48-PM-142C. Premises of Ingrid Macht, 627 West Twenty-fourth Street, New York.

INGRID: Come in, *Schatzie*.
ANDERSON: Glasses? You're wearing glasses now?
INGRID: For perhaps a year. Only for reading. You like them?
ANDERSON: Yes. You're doing something?
INGRID: I am just finishing my breakfast. I slept late today. Coffee?
ANDERSON: All right. Black.
   [Lapse of one minute thirteen seconds.]
INGRID: A little brandy perhaps?
ANDERSON: Fine. You join me?
INGRID: Thank you, no. I will take a sip of yours.
ANDERSON: Then you'll tell me I drink too much, and meanwhile you're sipping half my booze.
INGRID: Oh, *Schatzie*, when did I ever tell you that you drank too much? When did I ever criticize anything you do?
ANDERSON: Never . . . that I can remember. I was just kidding you. Don't be so serious. You have no sense of humor.
INGRID: That is true. Is something bothering you?
ANDERSON: No. Why?
INGRID: You have a look I recognize. Something in your eyes—faraway. You are thinking very hard about something. Do I guess right?
ANDERSON: Maybe.
INGRID: Please do not tell me. I want to know absolutely nothing. I do not wish to go through all that again. You understand?

ANDERSON: Sure. Sit on my lap. No . . . leave your glasses on.

INGRID: You do like them?

ANDERSON: Yes. When I was down South I had an idea of what a big-city woman was like. I could see her. Very thin. Not too tall. Hard. Bony. Open eyes. Pale lips. And heavy, black-rimmed glasses.

INGRID: A strange dream for a man to have. Usually it is a sweet, plump little blonde with big tits.

ANDERSON: Well, that was my dream. And long, straight black hair that hung to her waist.

INGRID: I have a wig like that.

ANDERSON: I know. I gave it to you.

INGRID: So you did, *Schatzie*. I had forgotten. Shall I put it on?

ANDERSON: Yes.

[Lapse of four minutes fourteen seconds.]

INGRID: So. Am I now your dream?

ANDERSON: Close. Very close. Sit here again.

INGRID: And what have you brought me today, Duke . . . another cigarette lighter?

ANDERSON: No. I brought you a hundred dollars.

INGRID: That is nice. I like money.

ANDERSON: I know. More stocks?

INGRID: Of course. I have been doing very well. My broker tells me I have an instinct for trading.

ANDERSON: I could have told him that. Am I hurting you?

INGRID: No. Perhaps we should go into the bedroom.

[Lapse of two minutes thirty-four seconds.]

INGRID: You are thinner . . . and harder. This scar . . . you told me once but I have forgotten.

ANDERSON: Knife fight.

INGRID: Did you kill him?

ANDERSON: Yes.

INGRID: Why did you fight?

ANDERSON: I forget. At the time it seemed important. Do you want me to give you the money now?

INGRID: Do not be nasty, Duke. It is not like you.

ANDERSON: Then start. Jesus, I need it. I've got to get out.

INGRID: Getting out—that is so important to you?

ANDERSON: I need it. I'm hooked. Slowly. . . .

INGRID: Of course. No . . . I told you, don't close your eyes. Look at me.

ANDERSON: Yes. All right.

INGRID: You know, I think I shall write a book. Relax your muscles, *Schatzie*; you are too tense.

ANDERSON: All right . . . yes. Is that better?

INGRID: Much. See . . . isn't that better?

ANDERSON: Oh, God, yes. Yes. A book about what?

INGRID: About pain and about crime. You know, I think criminals—most criminals—do what they do so that they may cause pain to someone. Also, so that they may be caught and be punished. To cause pain and to feel pain. That is why they lie, cheat, steal, and kill.

ANDERSON: Yes. . . .

INGRID: Look . . . I will tie my long, black hair about you. I will pull it tight and knot it . . . like so. There. How funny you look . . . like a strange Christmas package, a gift. . . .

ANDERSON: It's starting. I can feel it. . . .

INGRID: You are getting out?

ANDERSON: Slowly. You may be right. I don't know about these things. But it makes sense. When I was inside I met a guy who drew a minimum of thirty. He would have gotten eight to ten, but he hurt the people he robbed. He didn't have to. They gave him everything he wanted. They didn't yell. But he hurt them bad. And then he left his prints all over the place.

INGRID: Yes, that is understandable. You are tensing up again, *Schatzie*. Relax. Yes, that is better. And now. . . .

ANDERSON: Oh, God, Ingrid, please . . . please don't. . . .

INGRID: First you beg me to start, and then you beg me to stop. But I must help you to get out. Is that not so, Duke?

ANDERSON: You are the only one who can do it . . . the only one. . . .

INGRID: So. . . . Now, bite down hard and try not to scream. There . . . and there . . .

ANDERSON: Your teeth . . . I can't . . . please, I . . . oh God . . .

INGRID: Just a little more. You are getting out . . . I can see it in your eyes. Just a little more. And now . . . so . . . so. . . . Oh, you are getting out now, Duke . . . are you not? Yes, now you have escaped. But not me, Duke . . . not me. . . .

21

STARTING ON 12 April, 1968, a number of letters—obviously written by a mentally deranged person—were received threatening the personal safety of the President of the United States, Justices of the Supreme Court of the United States, and certain U.S. Senators. Incredibly, the unsigned letters were typed on stationery of the Excalibur Arms Hotel, 14896 Broadway, New York, New York.

On 19 April, 1968, with the cooperation of the owners of record, the U.S. Secret Service established electronic surveillance of the premises. A master tap was placed on the main telephone line coming into the building. In addition, several rooms and suites were equipped with bugs to record interior conversations. All these devices fed into an Emplex 47-83B voice-actuated tape recorder connected to the backup Emplex 47-82B-1 in case two conversations came in simultaneously. These machines were emplaced in the basement of the Excalibur Arms.

The following tape, coded USSS-VS-901KD-432, is dated 5 June, 1968. It was recorded from Room 432. The two men present, John Anderson and Thomas Haskins, have been identified by voice prints and interior evidence.

[Knock on door.]

ANDERSON: Who is it?

HASKINS: Me . . . Tommy.

ANDERSON: Come on in. Everything look all right downstairs?

HASKINS: Clear. What a filthy fleabag, darling.

ANDERSON: I just took the room for our meet. I'm not going to sleep here. Sit down over here. I have some brandy.

HASKINS: Thanks, no. But I do believe I'll have a joint. Join me?

ANDERSON: I'll stick to brandy. How did you make out?

HASKINS: Very well, I think. I hit two days ago. Snapper will hit tomorrow.

ANDERSON: Any beef?

HASKINS: A little difficulty. Nothing important. We handled it.

ANDERSON: Get much?

HASKINS: As much as I could. Not as complete as you'd wish, I'm sure, but interesting.

ANDERSON: Tommy, I won't shit you. You've got brains. You know I can't pay out five bills for a wash if I wasn't planning a hustle. Before you give me your report, give it to me straight—would it be worth it?

HASKINS: Which apartment, darling?

ANDERSON: All of them.

HASKINS: Jesus Christ Almighty.

ANDERSON: Would it be worth it?

HASKINS: My God, yes!

ANDERSON: Guess at the income?

HASKINS: Guess? I'd guess a minimum of a hundred G's. But maybe twice that.

ANDERSON: You and I think alike. That's what I guessed. All right, let's have it.

HASKINS: I typed out a report and one carbon on Snapper's machine, so we could go over it together. Naturally you get both copies.

ANDERSON: Naturally.

HASKINS: All right . . . let's start with the doormen. Three of them: Timothy O'Leary, Kenneth Ryan, Ed Bakely. In order, they're on midnight to eight A.M., eight A.M. to four P.M., four P.M. to midnight. O'Leary, the guy on midnight to eight A.M., is the lush. An ex-cop. When one of them takes his day off, the other two work twelve-hour shifts and get paid double. Occasionally, like around Christmas, two of them are off at once, and the union sends over a temporary. Okay?

ANDERSON: Go ahead.

HASKINS: I have all this in the report in more detail, darling, but I just want to go over the highlights with you in case you have any questions.

ANDERSON: Go ahead.

HASKINS: The super. Ivan Block. A Hungarian, I think, or maybe a Pole. A wino. He lives in the basement. He's there twenty-four hours a day, six days a week. On Mondays he goes to visit his married sister in New Jersey. In case of emergency, the super next door at five-three-seven East Seventy-third Street fills in for him. He also fills in when Block takes his two-week vacation every May. Block is sixty-four years old and blind in one eye. His basement apartment is one room and bath. Ryan hinted that he's a cheap son of a bitch. He may have something under the mattress.

ANDERSON: Maybe. These Old World farts don't believe in banks. Let's get on with it. I don't want to spend too much time here. This place bugs me.

HASKINS: Literally, I'm sure. I just saw one. Suite One A, first floor, off the lobby. Dr. Erwin Leister, MD, an internist.

ANDERSON: What's that?

HASKINS: A doctor who specializes in internal medicine. One nurse, one combination secretary-receptionist. Office hours from about nine A.M. to six P.M. Occasionally he's there later. Usually the nurse and secretary are gone by five thirty. The headshrinker is Dr. Dmitri Rubicoff, Suite One B. He's got one secretary-nurse. Office hours usually from nine to nine. Occasionally later. Snapper will give you a more complete rundown on these doctors after Thursday.

ANDERSON: You're doing fine.

HASKINS: Two apartments on each floor. By the way, the lobby floor is called one. Up one flight and you're on floor two. The top floor is the fifth, where the terraces are.

ANDERSON: I know.

HASKINS: Second floor. Apartment Two A. Eric Sabine. A male interior decorator who sounds divine. His apartment got a big write-up in the *Times* last year. I looked it up. Original Picassos and Klees. A nice collection of pre-Columbian art. A gorgeous nine-by-twelve Oriental carpet that's valued at twenty G's. In the photo in the *Times* he was wearing three rings that looked legit. Not really my type, darling, but obviously loaded. I shouldn't have any trouble finding out more about him if you're interested.

ANDERSON: We'll see.

HASKINS: Apartment Two B. Mr. and Mrs. Aron Rabinowitz. Rich, young Jews. He's in a Wall Street law firm. Junior partner. They're active in opera and ballet and theater groups. Shit like that. Very liberal. This is one of the three apartments I actually cased. She was home, delighted to talk about the proposed Second Avenue subway and the plight of the poor. Modern furnishings. I didn't spot anything except her wedding ring, which looked like it had been hacked out of Mount Rushmore. Seeing he's a lawyer, I'd guess a wall safe somewhere. Good paintings, but too big to fool with. All huge, abstract stuff.

ANDERSON: Silver?

HASKINS: You don't miss a trick do you, darling? Yes, silver . . . on display and very nice. Antique, I think. Probably a wedding gift. It's on a sideboard in their dining room. Any questions?

ANDERSON: Maid?

HASKINS: Not sleep-in. She comes at noon and leaves after she serves their evening meal and cleans up. She's German. A middle-aged woman. Now then . . . up to the third floor. Apartment Three A. Mr. and Mrs. Max Horowitz. He's retired. Used to be a wholesale jeweler. She's got bad arthritis of the knees and uses a cane to walk with. She's also got three fur coats, including one mink and one sable, and drips with ice. At least, that's what the doorman says. He also says they're cheap bastards—a total of five bucks to all employees at Christmastime. But he thinks they're loaded. Apartment Three B. Mrs. Agnes Everleigh. Separated from her hubby. He owns the apartment, but she's living there. Nothing much interesting. A mink coat, maybe. She's a buyer for a chain of woman's lingerie shops. Travels a lot. Incidentally, I've been mentioning the fur coats—but of course you realize, darling, most of them will be in storage this time of year.

ANDERSON: Sure.

HASKINS: Fourth floor. Apartment Four A. Mr. and Mrs. James T. Sheldon, with three-year-old twin girls. A sleep-in maid who goes out shopping in the neighborhood every day at noon. I got into this apartment, too. I was there when the maid left. West Indian. A dish . . . if I was hungry that way. Lovely accent. Big boobs. Flashing smile. Mrs. James T. Sheldon is a perfect fright; horse face, buck teeth, skin like burlap. She must have the money. And Mr. Sheldon must be pronging the maid. He's a partner in a brokerage house, in charge of their Park Avenue branch. Lots of goodies. I caught a quick look at a wood-paneled study with glass display cases lining the walls. Then Mrs. Sheldon closed the door. A coin collection, I think. It would fit. Easy to check.

ANDERSON: Yes. You say the maid goes shopping every day at noon?

HASKINS: That's right. Like clockwork. I verified it with the doorman later. Her name's Andronica.

ANDERSON: Andronica?

HASKINS: That's right. It's in the report. Crazy. Apartment Four B. Mrs. Martha Hathway—not Hathaway but Hathway. A ninety-two-year-old widow, with an eighty-two-year-old companion-housekeeper. Somewhat nutty. Kind of a recluse.

ANDERSON: A what?

HASKINS: Recluse. Like a hermit. She rarely goes out. Watches TV all day. Has no visitors. The housekeeper shops by phone. Ryan, the doorman, said her husband was a politician, a big shit in Tammany Hall about a thousand years ago. The apartment is furnished with stuff from the original Hathway town house on East Sixty-second Street. She sold off a lot of stuff after her husband died, but kept the best. It was a big auction, so you could check it out easy enough or I could do it for you.

ANDERSON: What do you figure she's got?

HASKINS: Silver, jewelry, paintings . . . the works. It's just a feeling I have, but I think Apartment Four B might prove to be a treasure house.

ANDERSON: Could be.

HASKINS: Top floor—the fifth. Both apartments have small terraces. Apartment Five A. Mr. and Mrs. Gerald Bingham and their fifteen-year-old son, Gerald junior. The kid uses a wheelchair; he's dead from the hips down. He has a private tutor who comes in every day. Bingham has his own management consultant firm with offices on Madison Avenue. Also, he has his own limousine, chauffeur-driven, which is garaged over on Lex. He's driven to work every morning, driven home every night. Sweet. He's listed all over the place, so he won't be hard to check out. His wife has money, too. I have nothing specific on this apartment—nothing good.

ANDERSON: Go on.

HASKINS: The other is Five B. Ernest Longene and April Clifford. They're married, they say, but use their own names. He's a theatrical producer and she was a famous actress. Hasn't appeared in ten years—but she remembers. God, does she remember! Sleep-in maid. A big, fat mammy type. This was the third apartment I got into. April was on her way to a luncheon at the Plaza and was wearing her daytime diamonds. Very nice. Some good, small paintings on the walls. A very nice collection of rough gemstones in glass display cases.

ANDERSON: There's money there?

HASKINS: He's got two hits on Broadway right now. That's got to mean loose cash around the place, probably in a wall safe. Well, darling, those are just the highlights. I'm sorry I couldn't be more specific.

ANDERSON: You did better than I hoped. Give me your carbon of the report.

HASKINS: Of course. I assure you no other copy was made.

ANDERSON: I believe you. I'll pay you the balance of the five bills when I get Snapper's report.

HASKINS: No rush, no rush. Do you have any questions, or is there anything you want me to dig into further?

ANDERSON: Not right now. This is like a preliminary report. There may be some more work for you later.

HASKINS: Anytime. You know you can trust me.

ANDERSON: Sure.

[Lapse of six seconds.]

HASKINS: Tell me, darling . . . are you seeing Ingrid again?

ANDERSON: Yes.

HASKINS: And how is the dear girl?

ANDERSON: All right. I think you better leave now. I'll wait about half an hour, and then I'll take off. Tell Snapper I'll call on Friday, as usual.

HASKINS: Are you angry with me, Duke?

ANDERSON: Why should I be angry with you? I think you did a good job on this.

HASKINS: I mean because I mentioned Ingrid. . . .

[Lapse of four seconds.]

ANDERSON: Are you jealous, Tommy?

HASKINS: Well . . . maybe. A little. . . .

ANDERSON: Forget it. I don't like the way you smell.

HASKINS: Well, I guess I. . . .

ANDERSON: Yes. Better go. And don't get any ideas.

HASKINS: Ideas, darling? What kind of ideas would I get?

ANDERSON: About what I'm doing.

HASKINS: Don't be silly, darling. I know better than that.

ANDERSON: That's good.

22

TAPE NYSITB-FD-6JUNE68-106-9H. Location of car; Sixty-fifth Street near Park Avenue.

ANDERSON: Goddammit, I told the Doctor I'd contact him when I was ready. Well, I'm not ready.

SIMONS: Take it easy, Duke. Good heavens, you have the shortest fuse of any man I've ever known.

ANDERSON: I just don't like to get leaned on, that's all.

SIMONS: No one's leaning on you, Duke. The Doctor has invested three thousand dollars of his personal funds in this campaign, and quite naturally and normally he's interested in your progress.

ANDERSON: What if I told him it was a bust . . . a nothing?

SIMONS: Is that what you want me to tell him?

[Lapse of eleven seconds.]

ANDERSON: No. I'm sorry I blew, Mr. Simons, but I like to move at my own speed. This thing is big, probably the biggest thing I've ever been in. Bigger than that Bensonhurst bank job. I want everything to go right. I want to be sure. Another week or two. Three weeks at the most. I'm keeping a very careful account of those three G's. I'm not making a cent out of this. I can tell the Doctor where every cent went. I'm not trying to con him.

SIMONS: Duke, Duke, it's not the money. I assure you the money has very little to do with it. He can drop that in one day at the dogs and never notice it. But Duke, you must recognize that the Doctor is a very proud man, very jealous of his position. He is where he is today because he picked winners. You understand? He would not like the word to get around that he flushed three G's on a free-lancer and got nothing to show for it. It would hurt his reputation, and it would hurt his self-esteem. Perhaps the younger men might say he is slipping, his judgment is going, he should be replaced. The Doctor must consider these things. So, quite naturally, he is concerned. You understand?

ANDERSON: Ah . . . sure. I understand. It's just that I want to make a big

score, a *big* score . . . enough to go somewhere for a long, long time. That's why I'm wound up so tight. This one has got to be just right.
SIMONS: Are you trying to tell me it looks good . . . as of this moment?
ANDERSON: Mr. Simons, as of this moment, it looks great, just great.
SIMONS: The Doctor will be pleased.

23

ERNEST HEINRICH "Professor" Mann; fifty-three; resident of 529 East Fifty-first Street, New York City. Place of business: Fun City Electronics Supply & Repair Co., 1975 Avenue D, New York City. Five feet six inches tall; 147 pounds; almost completely bald, with gray fringe around scalp; gray eyebrows; small Van Dyke beard, also gray. Walked with slight limp, favoring left leg. Deep scar in calf of left leg (believed to be a knife wound; see Interpol file #96B-J43196). He was a technician, skilled in mechanical, electrical, and electronic engineering. Graduated from Stuttgarter Technische Hochschule, 1938, with highest honors. Assistant professor, mechanical and electrical engineering, Zurich Académie du Mécanique, 1939-46. Emigrated to the United States (with Swiss passport) in 1948. Arrested Stuttgart, 17 June, 1937, on public nuisance charge (exhibiting himself to an elderly woman). Case dismissed with warning. Arrested Paris, 24 October, 1938, for scandalous conduct (urinating on Tomb of Unknown Soldier). Deported, after case was dismissed. In Zurich, a record of three arrests for possession of a dangerous drug (opium), indecent exposure, and illegal possession of a hypodermic needle. Suspended sentences. Extremely intelligent. Speaks German, French, Italian, English, some Spanish. Not believed to be violent. Single. Record indicates intermittent drug addiction (opium, morphine, hashish). FBI file indicates no illegal activities during residence in the United States. Applied for U.S. citizenship 8 May, 1954. Rejected 16 November, 1954. (As of this date, this man's brother was a high official in the finance ministry of West Germany, and his file contained an alert tag: IN CASE OF ARREST, PLEASE CONTACT U.S. STATE DEPARTMENT BEFORE CHARGE.)

The following is the first part of a dictated, sworn, signed, and witnessed statement by Ernest Heinrich Mann. It was obtained after prolonged questioning (the complete transcription numbers fifty-six typewritten pages) from 8 October, 1968, to 17 October, 1968. The interrogator was an assistant district attorney, County of New York. The entire document is coded NYDA-FHM-101A-108B. The following section is labeled *SEGMENT* 101A.

MANN: My name is Ernest Heinrich Mann. I live at five-two-nine East Fifty-first Street, New York, New York. U.S.A. I also have a business, which I own—the Fun City Electronic Supply and Repair Co., Inc., incorporated under the laws of New York State, at one-nine-seven-five Avenue D, New York City. Am I perhaps speaking too rapidly? Good.

On April thirty, 1968, I was contacted at my place of business by a man I know as John Anderson, also known as Duke Anderson. He stated at this time that he wished to employ me to inspect the basement of a house at five-three-five East Seventy-third Street, New York City.

He said he wished me to ascertain the telephone, alarm, and security precautions of this house. At no time did he state the purpose of this.

A price was agreed upon, and it was planned that I would approach the house in the uniform of a New York City telephone repairman, arriving in an authentic truck of the telephone company. Anderson said he would supply truck and driver. I provided my own uniform and identification. May I have a glass of water, please? Thank you.

About a month later Anderson called me and said the arrangements for the telephone truck had been made. There would be two drivers. I objected, but he assured me it would be perfectly safe.

On June fourth, at nine forty-five in the morning, I met the truck at the corner of Seventy-ninth Street and Lexington Avenue. There were two men who introduced themselves to me merely as Ed and Billy. I had never seen them before. They were clad in uniforms of New York Telephone Company repairmen. We spoke very little. The actual driver, the man named Ed, seemed reasonably intelligent and alert. The other one, called Billy, was large and muscular but had a childish mentality. I believe he was mentally retarded.

We drove directly to the House on East Seventy-third Street, pulling up in front. As we had agreed, I alighted, walked into the lobby, and presented my credentials to the doorman. He inspected my identification card, glanced out to the curb where the truck was parked, and told me to pull into the alley that runs alongside the building. Do one of you gentlemen have a cigarette? I would appreciate it. Thank you very much.

[Lapse of four seconds.]

So . . . I was identified on the closed-circuit TV screen in the lobby, and the doorman pressed the button unlocking the service door and allowed me entrance into the basement. Pardon?

No, this was merely to be an inspection. There was no intent to steal or destroy. Anderson merely wanted a complete rundown of the basement plus Polaroid photos of anything interesting. You understand? If I thought there was anything illegal required, I never would have accepted the job.

So. I am now in the basement. I went first to the telephone box. Quite ordinary. I made notes of main phones and extensions. I took instant photos of the entrance of the main trunk line into the basement and where it should be cut to isolate the entire house. This was requested by Anderson, you understand. I also ascertained that there were two separate wiring systems which, by their arrangement, I judged to be alarm systems, one to the local precinct house, perhaps triggered by an ultrasonic or radio-wave alarm, and the other to a private security agency which would be, I guessed, activated by opened doors or windows. Quite unexpectedly, both systems bore small tags with the apartment numbers written on them, so I was able to note that the precinct alarm was attached to Apartment Five B, and the private agency alarm to Apartment Four B. I made notes of this, plus photos. As Anderson had requested.

At this moment a door opened into the basement and a man came in. I learned he was Ivan Block, the superintendent of the building. He asked me what I was doing, and I explained that the telephone company was intending to bring a new line down the street and I was examing the premises to see what new equipment would be required. This was the same explanation I had given to the doorman. Another glass of water, please? I thank you.

[Lapse of six seconds.]

Block appeared satisfied with my explanation. Listening to him speak, I realized he was Hungarian or perhaps a Czech. Since I speak neither of these languages, I spoke to him in German, to which he replied in very bad, heavily accented German. However, he was pleased to speak the language. I believe he was somewhat inebriated. He insisted I come into his apartment for a glass of wine. I followed him, happy at the opportunity of making a further examination.

The super's small apartment was dirty and depressing. However, I took a glass of wine with him while looking around. The only thing of value I saw was an antique triptych on his dresser. I guessed it as being at least three hundred years old, beautifully carved. The value, I estimated, might be as much as two thousand dollars. I made no reference to it.

Block continued to drink wine, and I told him I had to call my office, and I left. I then explored the main basement. The only thing of interest I found was quite odd. . . .

It appeared to be a kind of box—or rather, a small room—built into one corner of the basement. It was obviously quite old, and I judged it had been built into the basement when the building was constructed. Two walls of the basement formed two sides of the boxlike room; the two walls projecting into the basement at a right angle were constructed of fitted wooden slabs. One wood wall had a flush door, closed by an extremely heavy, old-fashioned brass lever and hasp. The big hinges were also of brass. The door was secured with a large padlock.

Closer inspection revealed that the door was also protected by a rather primitive alarm system obviously added years after the boxlike room had been built. It was a simple contact alarm that might ring a bell or flash a light when the door was opened. I traced the wire and judged it went up into the lobby area where it might alert the doorman.

I took complete Polaroid photos of this strange boxlike affair, and made notes of how the alarm might easily be bridged. Almost as an afterthought, I put my hand to the side of this unusual room and found it quite cold to the touch. It reminded me of a large walk-in refrigerator one might find in a butcher's shop in this country.

I took a final look around and decided I had everything that Anderson, my client, required. I then exited from the basement and got into the truck. The two men, Ed and Billy, had waited quite patiently. We pulled out of the driveway. The doorman was standing on the sidewalk, and I smiled and waved as we pulled away.

They dropped me on the corner of Seventy-ninth Street and Lexington Avenue, and then left. I have no knowledge of what they did after that. The entire operation consumed one hour and twenty-six minutes. John Anderson called me on June fifth. I suggested he come over to my shop on the next day. He did, and I delivered to him the photos I had taken, the diagrams, and a complete report of what I saw—which is exactly what I have reported to you gentlemen. I thank you very much for your courtesy.

24

BINKY'S BAR & Grill, 125th Street and Hannox Avenue, New York City; 12 June 1968; 1:46 P.M. On this date, these premises were under electronic surveillance by the New York State Liquor Authority, on suspicion that the owners of record were knowingly allowing gambling on the premises. The following is tape SLA-94K-KYM. Anderson's presence was verified by voice print and testimony of an eyewitness.

ANDERSON: Brandy.
BARTENDER: This place for blacks, not for whiteys.
ANDERSON: What you going to do—throw me out?
BARTENDER: You a hardnose?
ANDERSON: Hard as I gotta be. Do I get that brandy?
BARTENDER: You from the South?
ANDERSON: Not deep. Kentucky.
BARTENDER: Lexington?
ANDERSON: Gresham.
BARTENDER: I'm from Lex. Cordon Bleu okay?
ANDERSON: Fine.
     [Lapse of eight seconds.]
BARTENDER: You want a wash?
ANDERSON: Water on the side.
     [Lapse of eleven seconds.]
ANDERSON: There's a guy I want to meet. Light brown. Sam Johnson. Goes
     by the name of Skeets.
BARTENDER: Never heard of him.
ANDERSON: I know. He's got a razor scar on his left cheek.
BARTENDER: Never saw such a man.
ANDERSON: I know. My name's Duke Anderson. If such a man should come
     in, I'm going to finish this drink and go across the street and get some
     knuckles and collards. I'll be there for at least an hour.
BARTENDER: Won't do you no good. Never saw such a man. Never heard of
     him.
ANDERSON: He might come in . . . unexpected like. Here's a fin for you in
     case he does.
BARTENDER: I'll take your pound and thank you kindly. But it won't do you
     no good. I don't know the man. Never saw him.
ANDERSON: I know. The name's Duke Anderson. I'll be across the street in
     Mama's. Keep the faith, baby.
BARTENDER: Up yours, mother.

25

TAPE RECORDING NYSNB (New York State Narcotics Bureau) 48B-1061 (continuing). Taped at 2:11 P.M., 12 June, 1968, Mama's Soul Food, 125th Street and Hannox Avenue, New York City.

JOHNSON: Here's my man, and gimme your han'.
ANDERSON: Hello, Skeets. Sit down and order up.
JOHNSON: Now that I'm here, I'll have a beer.
ANDERSON: How you been?
JOHNSON: I get some jive so I'm still alive.
ANDERSON: Things going good for you?
JOHNSON: I do this and that, but I don't get fat.

ANDERSON: Cut the shit and talk straight. You got some time to do a job for me?

JOHNSON: If it's a crime, I've got the time.

ANDERSON: Jesus Christ, Skeets, there's a house on the East Side. If you're interested I'll give you the address. There's a live-in spade maid works one of the apartments. Every day at noon she comes out to do shopping.

JOHNSON: When you talk a chick, you gotta click.

ANDERSON: Light tan. West Indian. Big lungs. Pretty. I want you to get close to her.

JOHNSON: How close, oh, Lord, how close?

ANDERSON: Everything. Whatever she can tell you about her apartment. Her names Andronica. That's right—Andronica. She's from Apartment Four A. There may be a coin collection there. But I want to know about the rest of the house, too—whatever she'll spill.

JOHNSON: If she won't spill, then her sister will.

ANDERSON: There's a funny room in the basement. A cold room. It's locked. Try to find out what the hell it is.

JOHNSON: If the room is cold, then I'll be bold.

ANDERSON: You on?

JOHNSON: If you've got the loot, I've got to suit.

ANDERSON: A bill?

JOHNSON: Make it two and I'll be true.

ANDERSON: All right—two. But do a job for me. Here's a loner to get you started. I'll be back here a week from today, same time. All right?

JOHNSON: As a man you're mean, but I like your green.

26

TRANSCRIPTION OF tape recording POM-14JUN68-EVERLEIGH. Approximately 2:10 A.M.

MRS. EVERLEIGH: Did the doorman see you come in?

ANDERSON: He wasn't there.

MRS. EVERLEIGH: The bastard. We're supposed to get twenty-four-hour doorman service, and this bastard is always down in the basement drinking wine with that drunken super. Brandy?

ANDERSON: Yes.

MRS. EVERLEIGH: Yes, *please*.

ANDERSON: Go fuck yourself.

MRS. EVERLEIGH: My, we're in a pleasant mood tonight. Tired?

ANDERSON: Just my eyes.

MRS. EVERLEIGH: I think it's more than that. You look like a man who's got a lot on his mind. Money problems?

ANDERSON: No.

MRS. EVERLEIGH: If you need some money, I can let you have some.

ANDERSON: No . . . thanks.

MRS. EVERLEIGH: That's better. Drink up. I bought a case of Rémy Martin. What are you smiling about?

ANDERSON: You figure this will last for a case?

MRS. EVERLEIGH: What's that supposed to mean? You want to cut out? Then cut out.

ANDERSON: I didn't want to cut out. I just figured you might get tired of me slamming you around. Are you tired of it?

[Lapse of seven seconds.]

MRS. EVERLEIGH: No. I'm not tired of it. I think about it all the time. When I was in Paris, I missed you. One night I could have screamed, I wanted you so bad. I got a million things on my mind. Business things. Details. Pressure. I'm only as good as my last season. I work for the worst bastards in the business—the *worst*. I only relax when I'm with you. I think about you during the day, when I'm at the office. I think about what we did and what we'll do. I don't suppose I should be telling you these things.

ANDERSON: Why not?

MRS. EVERLEIGH: A girl's supposed to play hard to get.

ANDERSON: Christ, you're a stupid bitch.

[Lapse of five seconds.]

MRS. EVERLEIGH: Yes. Yes, I am. When it comes to you. You've been in prison, haven't you?

ANDERSON: Reform school. When I was a kid. I stole a car.

MRS. EVERLEIGH: And you haven't been in since?

ANDERSON: No. What makes you think so?

MRS. EVERLEIGH: I don't know. Your eyes, maybe. Those Chinese eyes. The way you talk. Or don't talk. Sometimes you frighten me.

ANDERSON: Do I?

MRS. EVERLEIGH: Here's the bottle. Help yourself. Are you hungry? I can fix you a roast beef sandwich.

ANDERSON: I'm not hungry. You going on another trip?

MRS. EVERLEIGH: Why do you ask?

ANDERSON: Just making conversation.

MRS. EVERLEIGH: I've been invited out to Southampton for the July Fourth weekend. Then, late in August and over the Labor Day weekend I'll be going to Rome. May I sit on the couch next to you?

ANDERSON: No.

MRS. EVERLEIGH: That's what I like—a romantic man.

ANDERSON: If I was a romantic man you wouldn't bother with me.

MRS. EVERLEIGH: I suppose not. Still, it would be nice to know, occasionally, that you're human.

ANDERSON: I'm human. Sit on the floor.

MRS. EVERLEIGH: Here?

ANDERSON: Closer. In front of me.

MRS. EVERLEIGH: Here, darling?

ANDERSON: Yes. Take off my shoes and socks.

[Lapse of fourteen seconds.]

MRS. EVERLEIGH: I've never seen your feet before. How white they are. Your toes look like white worms.

ANDERSON: Take off that thing.

MRS. EVERLEIGH: What are you going to do?

ANDERSON: I'm going to make you forget the bastards you work for, the business, the details, the pressure. That's what you want . . . isn't it?

MRS. EVERLEIGH: Part of it.

ANDERSON: What's the other part?

MRS. EVERLEIGH: I want to forget who I am and what I am. I want to forget you and what I'm doing with my life.

ANDERSON: You want to get out?

MRS. EVERLEIGH: Get out? Yes. I want to get out.

ANDERSON: You've got a good suntan. Take the robe off.

MRS. EVERLEIGH: Like this?
ANDERSON: Yes. God, you're big. Big tits and big ass.
MRS. EVERLEIGH: Duke . . . be nice to me . . . please.
ANDERSON: Nice to you? Is that what you want?
MRS. EVERLEIGH: Not . . . you know . . . not physically. You can do anything you want. Anything. But be nice to me as a person . . . as a human being.
ANDERSON: I don't know what the hell you're talking about. Spread out.
MRS. EVERLEIGH: Oh God, I think I'm going to be sick.
ANDERSON: Go ahead. Puke all over yourself.
MRS. EVERLEIGH: You're not human. You're not.
ANDERSON: All right. So I'm not. But I'm the only man in the world who can get you out. Spread wider.
MRS. EVERLEIGH: Like this? Is this all right, Duke?
ANDERSON: Yes.
   [Lapse of one minute eight seconds.]
MRS. EVERLEIGH: You're hurting me, you're hurting me.
ANDERSON: Sure.
MRS. EVERLEIGH: White worms.
ANDERSON: That's right. Getting out?
MRS. EVERLEIGH: Yes . . . yes . . .
ANDERSON: You've got a body like mush.
MRS. EVERLEIGH: Please, Duke. . . .
ANDERSON: You're a puddle.
MRS. EVERLEIGH: Please, Duke. . . .
ANDERSON: "Please, Duke. Please Duke." Stupid bitch.
MRS. EVERLEIGH: Please I. . . .
ANDERSON: There. Isn't that nice? Now I'm being nice to you as a person. As a human being. Right?

27

THE FOLLOWING is a Xerox copy of a handwritten report, identified by Dr. Seymour P. Ernst, president, The New Graphology Institution, 14426 Erskine Avenue, Chicago, Illinois, as being in the true handwriting of Cynthia "Snapper" Haskins (previously identified). The two sheets of un-lined paper, inscribed on both sides, revealed latent fingerprints of Cynthia Haskins, Thomas Haskins, and John Anderson. The paper itself—an inexpensive typing paper without watermark—bore miniature serrations on its upper edge (tipped with a red adhesive), indicating the sheets had been torn from a pad. The paper was identified as being a popular brand of typing paper sold in pads of twenty-five sheets. Such pads as available in many stationery and variety stores.

DUKE:

I swept the two offices, you know where. No strain, no pain. I gave both doctors freak checks instead of cash. I won't go back. No point in it.
Both big layouts. I guess they're doing all right. The doctor's got a nurse and a secretary-receptionist. I saw her opening mail. Mostly checks. No safe in outer office. Prob-

ably night bank deposits. Two rooms off the doctor's office: examination room and small supply room. Little room has drug safe in corner. Toilet is to left as you walk down corridor to doctor's private office.

Pictures on walls are cheap prints. Doctor has five silver cups in his office—for rowing a scull. Whatever that is.

Sorry I pulled a blank here—but that's all there was.

Headshrinker's office was small outer room with secretary-nurse, big private office and toilet to right of outer room.

Shrink has three nice small paintings: Picasso, Miro, and someone else. Looked like the real thing. I described them to Tommy. He estimates 20G's for the three, possibly more.

Bottom left of shrink's desk has dial lock. He was putting reel of recording tape in drawer when I came in. When I started to talk, he pressed button in desk wall. Everything I said was recorded, I'm sure. Must be some interesting things in that desk safe. Think about it.

He has small lavatory and clothes closet next to his office, at back near windows that overlook garden. Something in closet?

Nurse-secretary is young, about twenty-eight. Shrink is about fifty-five, speaks with accent. Small, fat, tired. I think he's on something. I'd guess Dexies.

That's all I got. Sorry it wasn't more.

Don't forget about those tape recordings. Hot off the couch. Know what I mean?

Rough sketches of both offices on back of this sheet. If there's anything else we can do for you, please let us know.

The rest of the $$$, Duke? We had some expenses and we're hung up. Thanks.

SNAP

28

RECORDING NYSNB-1157 (continuing). Taped at 2:17 P.M., 19 June, 1968, at Mama's Soul Food, 125th Street and Hannox Avenue, New York City. Participants John Anderson and Samuel Johnson have been identified by a paid informer present at the scene.

Samuel "Skeets" Johnson, thirty-three, was a Negro, light tan, with long black greased hair combed in a high "conk" (Pompadour). Approximately 6 feet 2 inches; 178 pounds. Deep razor scar on left cheek. Hearing impairment of 75 percent in left ear. Dressed in expensive clothing of bright hues. Wore light pink polish on fingernails. At last report, drove a 1967 Cadillac convertible (electric blue), New Jersey license plates 4CB-6732A, registered to Jane Martha Goody, 149 Hempy Street, Hackensack, New Jersey. Johnson's criminal record included arrests for loitering, petty larceny, committing a public nuisance, resisting arrest, simple assault, assault with intent to kill, threatening bodily harm, breaking parole, breaking and entering, armed robbery, and expectorating on a public sidewalk. He had served a total of six years, eleven months, fourteen days in Dawson School for Boys, Hillcrest Reformatory, and

Dannemora. This man had the unusual ability of being able to add a series
of as many as twenty dictated numbers of eight digits each in his head and
arriving at the correct sum within seconds. Frequently carried a switch-
blade knife in a small leather sheath strapped to right ankle. Frequently
spoke in rhymed slang.

ANDERSON: How you doing, Skeets?

JOHNSON: Slip me five, I'm still alive. Now that you're here, have a beer. If
   you're in the mood, make it food.

ANDERSON: Just a beer.

JOHNSON: I thought you dug this soul food crap—knuckles and hocks and
   greens?

ANDERSON: Yeah, I like it. Don't you?

JOHNSON: Shit no, man. I go for a good Chateau-briand or maybe some of
   them frogs' legs swimming in butter and garlic. That's eating. This stuff
   sucks. Just a beer? That all you want?

ANDERSON: That's all. What'd you find out?

JOHNSON: Wait for the beer, and then give ear.
   [Lapse of twenty-seven seconds.]

JOHNSON: By the way, I'm picking up the knock.

ANDERSON: Thanks.

JOHNSON: I got to thank you, lad, 'cause you made me glad.

ANDERSON: How's that.

JOHNSON: That little Andronica you put me onto. Oh, so sweet and juicy.
   You spend a night with her, all you need is a spoon and a straw. She's a
   double-dip strawberry sundae with a big whoosh of white whipped
   cream on top and then a big red cherry sticking up in the air.

ANDERSON: And the first thing you bit off was that cherry.

JOHNSON: Ask me no questions, and I tell you no lies.

ANDERSON: You pushing her?

JOHNSON: Every chance I get—which ain't often. She gets one night off a
   week. Then we fly. And we had two matinee sessions. Oh, she so cuddly
   and wiggly and squirming. I could eat her up.

ANDERSON: And I bet you do.

JOHNSON: On occasion, Great White Father, on occasion.

ANDERSON: How did you make the meet?

JOHNSON: What you want to know for?

ANDERSON: How am I going to learn to operate if you don't tell me things?

JOHNSON: Ah, Duke, Duke . . . you got more shit than a Christmas goose.
   You forgotten more than I could ever teach you. Well, I got this old
   family friend. A real coon type. But that's just front. This cat is into
   everything. I mean, he's a black Billy the Kid. Slick. You dig?

ANDERSON: Sure.

JOHNSON: So I slip him a double Z. He meets this Andronica when she
   comes out of the supermarket. My pal puts his paws on her. "You dirty
   sex fiend," I scream at him, "how dare you touch and annoy and defile
   and molest this dear, sweet, little innocent chick?"

ANDERSON: Beautiful.

JOHNSON: I feed him a knuckle sandwich—which he slips. He takes off
   down the avenue. Andronica is shook.

ANDERSON: And grateful.

JOHNSON: Yeah—and grateful. So I help her wheel her little wagon of
   groceries home. One thing leads to another.

ANDERSON: So? What did she spill?

JOHNSON: That coin collection is insured for fifty big ones. There's a wall safe behind a painting of a vase of flowers in the study. That's where Mrs. Sheldon keeps her ice. My baby think there's other goodies in there, too. Bonds. Maybe some green. Sound good?

ANDERSON: Not bad. They going to be around all summer?

JOHNSON: I regrets to report, massa, they are not. The family moves out this weekend to Montauk. Old man Sheldon will go out every weekend until after Labor Day. That means no more sweet push for pops for another three months unless we can work something out—like her coming into the city or me going out there.

ANDERSON: You'll work it out.

JOHNSON: I mean to. I really mean to. I must see Andronica so she can blow my harmonica.

ANDERSON: What about the cold room? The room in the basement. Remember?

JOHNSON: I didn't forget, white man who speaks with forked tongue. Guess what it is.

ANDERSON: I been trying to. I can't.

JOHNSON: When the house was built, that's where they kept their fruit and vegetables. Then after they had refrigerators, the old geezer who built the joint kept his wines down there. Those walls are thick.

ANDERSON: And now? What's it used for? Wine?

JOHNSON: No, indeedy. They got a little refrigerator-like in there and a machine that takes the water out of the air. It's cold and it's dry. And everyone who lives in that house—the women, that is—they puts their fur coats in there for storage come warm weather. No extra charge. They got their own fur storage locker right there on the premises. How do you like that?

ANDERSON: I like it. I like it very much.

JOHNSON: Thought you would. Duke, if you planning anything—and notice I say *if*—and you need an extra field hand, you know who's available, don't you?

ANDERSON: I give you your due; it could be you.

JOHNSON: Ah, baby, now you're singing our song!

ANDERSON: Reach under the table; it's your other bill.

JOHNSON: Your gelt I'll take, and that's no fake. But why pay me for just what's due? I should pay you for what I screw.

ANDERSON: See you around.

29

TAPE SEC-25JUN68-IM-12:48PM-139H. This is a telephone tap.

ANDERSON: Hello? It's me.

INGRID: Yes. Ah. . . .

ANDERSON: Did I wake you up? I'm sorry.

INGRID: What time is it?

ANDERSON: About a quarter to one.

INGRID: You are coming over?

ANDERSON: No. Not today. That's why I called. Is your phone clean?

INGRID: Oh, *Schatzie* . . . why should they bother with me? I am a nobody.

ANDERSON: God, how I'd like to come over. But I can't. Not today. It would put me to sleep. I have a meet tonight.

INGRID: So.
ANDERSON: It's very important. Very big men. I've got to be awake. Sharp. These are the money men.
INGRID: You know what you are doing?
ANDERSON: Yes.
INGRID: I wish you very much good luck
ANDERSON: I'll probably be through with them by two or three. It's in Brooklyn. Can I come back?
INGRID: Regretfully, no, *Schatzie*. I am busy tonight.
ANDERSON: Busy?
INGRID: Yes.
ANDERSON: Important?
INGRID: Let us say—profitable. He flies in from Fort Wayne. That is in Indiana. That is something . . . no? To fly to New York from Fort Wayne, Indiana, to see poor old Ingrid Macht.
ANDERSON: I'd fly from Hong Kong.
INGRID: Ah! Now that is romantic! I do thank you. But tomorrow perhaps?
ANDERSON: Yes. All right. I guess that would be best. I'll tell you about it then.
INGRID: As you wish. Duke. . . .
ANDERSON: Yes?
INGRID: Be careful. Be very, very careful.
ANDERSON: I will be.
INGRID: There is something in you that distresses me—a wildness, a strangeness. Think. Duke, promise me you will think . . . very clearly.
ANDERSON: I promise you I will think very clearly.
INGRID: *Das is gut*. And perhaps, tomorrow afternoon, we might get out. Together, Duke. For the first time.
ANDERSON: Together? Yes. I'll get you out. I promise.
INGRID: Good. And now I shall go back to sleep.

30

THE FOLLOWING manuscript was discovered in a search of the premises of John "Duke" Anderson on 3 September, 1968. It consisted of three sheets of yellow note paper, ruled horizontally with blue lines, and vertically by a thin triple line (red-blue-red) 1¼ inches from the left-hand margin. The sheets themselves measured approxmately 8 by 12 3/8 inches, with serrations along the top edge indicating they had been torn from a pad or tablet.

Analysis by experts disclosed that this type of paper is commonly sold in pads in stationery and notion stores and is known as legal notepaper. It is frequently used by students, lawyers, professional writers, etc.

The recovered sheets were apparently a part or section of a longer manuscript. The pages were not numbered. Analysts believe they were written approximately ten years before the date of discovery—that is, about 1958. The handwriting was determined to be definitely that of John Anderson. The writing implement used was a ballpoint pen with green ink.

The three sheets reproduced below were being used as shelf paper in a small closet in the premises of 314 Harrar Street, Brooklyn, New York, when they were discovered and submitted to analysis.

[First sheet]
it could be everything.

In other words, crime is not just a little thing, a small part of society, but is right in there, and it makes up most of what everyone calls normal, right and desent living. Let us list them.

When a woman will not give in to a man unless he marrys her, that could be called extortion or blackmail.

Or a woman who wants a fur coat, and if her husband wont give it to her, and she says no sex if he dont. This also is a kind of a crime, like blackmail.

Maybe a boss lies a secretary because she will loose her job otherwise. Extortion.

A guy says, I know you have been playing around. If you don't give me some, I will tell your husband. Blackmail.

A big grosery store comes in to a neyborhood near a small grosery store. And this big chain cuts there prices and puts the small store out of business. This is mugging. Money mugging but it is mugging all the same.

War. You say to a small country you do what we want or we will blow you up. Extortion or blackmail.

Or a big country like the USA goes into a small country and buys the kind of govt we want. This is criminal bribery.

Or we say we will give you such and so if you do this, and then the country does it, and we say thanks a lot! And don't pay off. That is fraud or conspiracy to defraud.

A business man or maybe even a professer in a collage thinks the other guy will get the job he wants. So he writes letters he dont sign and sends them to the top man. Poyson pen letters. Nothing he could get busted for but hinting.

There are many other exampels, practicaly endless that I

[Second sheet]
could give here about how much of what we say is common, ordinary human behavior is really crime.

Some of these are personel, like between a man and a woman, or two men or two women, and some are in business and some are in govt.

A man wants to shiv another guy in his company and he spreds the word hes a queer. Slander.

A guy buys gifts for his wife because he knows she won't give out if he don't. Bribery.

We teach young kids in the army what is the best way to kill people. Murder.

The local grosery store or department store jacks up the bill if they can get away with it, or maybe short-changes. Robbery.

A guy wants to go to a cheap restaurant but his woman wants to go to a fancy joint. And she hints if they don't go where she wants, its no push-push for him that night. Extortion.

A guy gives a dame a string of beads and he says there diamonds but they are really zircons or rinestones and she puts out. Fraud.

A guy in a business is taking and another guy finds out and lets the first guy know. So the first guy gets something on the second guy. Then they grin and let live. Conspiracy.

Maybe a woman likes to get beat. So her guy slaps her around. He likes it too. But whos to know? Its still assault.

A peter keeps another peter on the string by saying he will nark on him if the first guy doesn't keep playing games. Extortion.

Similar to above, anyone who says I will kill myself if you do no do like I want, that is also extortion. Or maybe blackmail

[Third sheet]
depending on how the lawyers and judges decide on it.

What I am saying is this, that crime is not just breaking laws because everyone does it. I do not know if this is something new or had been going on for many years. But we are all criminels.

We are all criminels. It is just a question of degree, like first, second and third degree. But if the laws against criminel acts are right, then almost everyone should be in the poke. If these laws are right and rigid, then it shouldn't matter what degree. The married woman who wont put out unless her husband buys her a fur coat is just as guilty as a guy whos got a million dollar extortion hustle going for him.

And the poor pop who breaks into his kids piggy bank, yes its funny, and takes out enough change to get to work, well how is he so different from a good bank man like Sonny Brooks, he died yesterday, it was in the papers. Jesus I loved that guy, he taught me all I know, he was so great. He got cut down coming out of a bank in West Va. I cant believe it he was so carefull, a real pro. Worked once a year but he planed for 6 mos. Carefull and good. Layed off for 6 mos. every year. Hit a big one once a year he said and then lay off. I worked two jobs with him and learned so much.

Oh shit, its all crime. Everything. The way we live. Everyone. We are all cons, everyone of us. So what I do is just being smart enough to make it pay.

We lie and we cheat and we steal and we kill, and if it isn't money its other people or there love or just to get some push. Whatever we get hung on. Oh Jesus its so dirty.

When I was inside I thaught those inside were cleaner then those outside. At least we were open and did our crimes in the open. But the rest think they are so normal and clean and desent and they are the biggest and dirtiest criminals of them all because they
[End of third sheet]

31

THE FOLLOWING is a transcription made from tape recodings of a conversation that took place in Elvira's, an Italian restaurant at 96352 Hammacher Street, Brooklyn, New York, during the early morning hours of 26 June, 1968.

At the time, these premises were under electronic surveillance by at least four, and possibly more, law investigation agencies. Apparently there was no cooperation between the agencies.

A great variety of miniaturized electronic devices was utilized, including telephone taps, bugs implanted beneath certain tables, in the bar, and in both the gents' and the ladies' rooms. In addition, the new Sonex Nailhead 158-JB microphone transmitters had been surreptitiously installed in the baseboards of the kitchen.

Elvira's, a popular and successful restaurant in the Flatbush section of Brooklyn, had for many years been known to law enforcement officers as an eating and meeting place for members of the Angelo family. The restaurant was fire-bombed on 15 October, 1958, during what was apparently a gang war between the Angelo family and a rival organization known as the Snipes Brothers. The bombing resulted in the death of a waiter, Pasquale Gardini.

On 3 February, 1959, Anthony "Wopso" Angelo was shot down in the front phone booth of Elvira's while making a phone call to persons unknown. His killer entered through the glass door, after apparently seeing Angelo go into the phone booth from an outside observation post. Four bullets of .32 caliber were fired into Angelo. He died instantly. His killer has not yet been apprehended.

Present at the meeting in a small, private back room at Elvira's on the morning of 26 June, 1968, were John "Duke" Anderson, Anthony "Doctor" D'Medico, and Patrick "Little Pat" Angelo. These men have been positively identified by voice prints, interior and exterior evidence, and by paid informers present at the scene.

Patrick "Little Pat" Angelo was born in 1932 in Brooklyn, New York. His father, Patsy "The Hook" Angelo, was killed in a waterfront fracas two months before Patrick's birth. Patrick's education was financed by his grandfather, Dominick "Papa" Angelo, don of the Angelo family. Patrick Angelo was 5 feet 8½ inches tall; 193 pounds; blue eyes; thick gray hair worn long, combed straight back, no part. Physical scars: scalp wound above right temple (bullet); depressed wound in left calf (shrapnel) and excised third right rib (grenade). Subject was a graduate of Walsham School of Business Administration, and had attended one year at the Rolley Law Academy. Enlisted in U.S. Army in 1950 and after training was sent to Korea with the 361st Assault Battalion, 498th Regiment, 22nd Combat Division. At war's end, he had risen to rank of major (battlefield promotions) and had earned the Purple Heart (3), Silver Star, and Distinguished Service Cross, in addition to decorations from the South Korean and Turkish governments.

Subject resigned from the Army in 1954 with letters of commendation. He then organized and became president of Modern Automanagement, 6501 Fifth Avenue, New York City, a management consultant firm. In addition, he was an officer of record for Sweeteeze Linens, 361 Forbisher Street, Brooklyn, New York; vice-president of Wrenchies Bowling Alleys, 1388 Grand Evarts, the Bronx, New York; and secretary-treasurer of the Fifth National Discount and Service Organization, Palm Credit Co., Inc., and the Thomas Jefferson Trading Corp., all of Wilmington Delaware.

Subject had no criminal record.

Subject was married (to Maria Angelo, a second cousin) and was the father of two teen-age sons currently students at Harrington Military Academy in Virginia. He also had a four-year-old daughter, Stella.

Supposition: Patrick Angelo will succeed Dominick "Papa" Angelo as don of the Angelo family upon the death of Dominick, who was ninety-four years old.

Due to mechanical difficulties and heavy external noise, no single tape recording contains the entire conversation given below. This is a transcription of parts of four different tapes made by four law enforcement agencies. (At their request, portions of the transcription have been deleted as they concern investigation currently in progress.) This is the author's transcription GO-110T-26Jun68. The time was 1:43 A.M.

D'MEDICO: . . . don't believe you've met Pat Angelo. Pat, this is Duke Anderson, the man I told you about.

ANDERSON: Pleased to make your acquaintance, Mr. Angleo.

ANGELO: Duke, I don't want you to think I'm giving you a fast shuffle, but I've got another meet tonight. Then I've got to drive home to Teaneck. So you'll understand if I make this as short as we can. Okay?

ANDERSON: Sure.

ANGELO: I'll tell you what the Doc told me. See if I got it straight. If not, you correct me. Then I'll start asking questions. You got a campaign. It's a house on the East Side of Manhattan. You want to take the whole place. He advanced you three G's. That's out of his own pocket. You been looking it over. Now we're at the point where we decide do we go ahead or do we call the whole thing off. Am I right so far?

ANDERSON: That's right, Mr. Angelo. Mr. D'Medico, I have a complete list of my expenses with me, and you have three hundred and fifty-nine dollars and sixteen cents coming back on your advance that wasn't spent.

D'MEDICO: I told you, Pat! Didn't I tell you?

ANGELO: Yes. Let's get on with it. So what have we got, Duke?

ANDERSON: I have a report here. It's a handwritten original. No copies. For you and Mr. D'Medico. I think it looks good.

ANGELO: How much?

ANDERSON: Minimum of a hundred thousand. Closer to quarter of a mil, I'd guess.

ANGELO: You'd guess? What the hell are you talking about? What? Retail value? Wholesale value? Resale value? What we can get from fences? What is it? Spell it out.

ANDERSON: It's jewelry, furs, uncut stones, a valuable coin collection, rugs, maybe drugs from two doctors, cash, negotiable securities. These people are loaded.

[Lapse of five seconds.]

ANGELO: So you're talking about original retail value?

ANDERSON: Yes.

ANGELO: So take a third of what you estimate. Maybe thirty G's if we can unload it. Or possibly eighty G's tops. Is that right?

ANDERSON: Yes.

ANGELO: Let's figure the bottom—thirty G's. How many men?

ANDERSON: Five.

ANGELO: Five? And one of ours. Six. So you want six men to put out for five G's each?

ANDERSON: No. I want my men to be paid a flat fee. Whatever I can settle for. But no share. I figure I can get the five for a total of eight thou tops. I don't know what you'll pay your man. Maybe he's on salary. But figure ten G's tops for employees. That leaves twenty G's for a split. Absolute minimum. I'm no gambler, but I still think it'll run closer to eighty G's. The total, that is.

ANGELO: Forget what you think. We're working on the minimum. So we have twenty G's left for the split. How do you figure that?

ANDERSON: Seventy-thirty.

ANGELO: Seventy to you, of course?

ANDERSON: Yes.

ANGELO: You're a hardnose, aren't you?

D'MEDICO: Pat, take it easy.

ANDERSON: Yes, I'm a hardnose.

ANGELO: Tennessee?

ANDERSON: Kentucky.

ANGELO: I thought so. Duke, put yourself in my place. You want me to okay this thing. You guarantee us about six or seven thousand if we agree to your terms. All right, all right—it may run as high as twenty G's if the take is as big as you guess it might be. I can't figure with guesses. I got to know. So I'm figuring on six G's. Anything over is gravy. All this for six thousand dollars? We can take that legit in one day from our biggest horse parlor. So what's the percentage.

ANDERSON: So what's the risk? One muscle? He's expendable, isn't he?
    [Lapse of eight seconds.]

ANGELO: You're no dumdum, are you?

ANDERSON: No, I'm not. And I got to keep repeating that seven G's is the absolute minimum. It'll run more, much more—I swear it.

ANGELO: Put your cock on the line?

ANDERSON: Goddamned right.

D'MEDICO: Jesus, Pat. . . .

ANGELO: He's a hardnose—like I said. I like you, Duke.

ANDERSON: Thanks.

ANGELO: For nothing. Have you started thinking about operations?

ANDERSON: A little. Just a beginning. It should be on a holiday weekend. Half the people will be gone to the beach or on vacation or at their summer places. July Fourth would have been good, but it's too late for that now. If you say okay, we should aim for the Labor Day weekend. We cut all communications. Isolate the house. We pull up a van. We take our time—three hours, four hours, whatever we need.

ANGELO: But you haven't thought it out?

ANDERSON: No, I haven't. I got this report here. It'll give you a rundown on who lives there and where the stuff is and where we should look and how it can be done. But if you say okay, we'll have to dig a lot deeper.

ANGELO: Like what?

ANDERSON: Habits of people in the building. Schedules of the beat fuzz and squad cars in the sector. Private watchmen. People who walk their dogs late at night. Location of call boxes and telephone booths. Bars that are open late at night. A lot of things. . . .

ANGELO: Were you ever in the military?

ANDERSON: Marine Corps. About eighteen months.

ANGELO: What happened?

ANDERSON: I got a dishonorable discharge.

ANGELO: What for?

ANDERSON: I knocked up a captain's wife—amongst other things.

ANGELO: Yes. What did you do? See any action?

ANDERSON: No. I made corporal. I was an instructor on the range at Paris Island.

ANGELO: You're a good shot?

ANDERSON: Yes.

D'MEDICO: But you've never carried a piece on a job—have you, Duke?

ANDERSON: No. I never have.

ANGELO: Christ, I'm thirsty. Doc, get us another bottle of that Volpolicella, will you? But if this campaign goes through, you'll have to pack a piece. You realize that, don't you, Duke?

ANDERSON: Yes.

ANGELO: You're willing?

ANDERSON: Yes.

ANGELO: When you were a corporal of Marines did you ever get any instructions on the technique of a raid? A quick hit-and-run?

ANDERSON: A little.

ANGELO: Did you ever hear about that campaign in Detroit on. . . . We hit the. . . . We used about. . . . What we did was to create a diversion. It pulled off all the precinct buttons to . . . and while they were. . . . And it worked perfectly. Something like that might work here.

ANDERSON: It might.

ANGELO: You don't sound very enthusiastic.

ANDERSON: I got to think about it.

D'MEDICO: Here's the wine, Pat. Chilled just a little . . . the way you like it.

ANGELO: Fine. Thank you, Doctor. So you want to think about it, do you, Duke?

ANDERSON: Yes. It's *my* cock.

ANGELO: It surely is. All right. Supposing Papa gives the go-ahead. What will you need? Have you thought of that?

ANDERSON: Yes, I thought of that. I'll need another two thousand to complete the sweep.

ANGELO: The reconnaissance?

ANDERSON: That's right. To figure how we'll handle it.

ANGELO: Operations and deployment. And then what?

ANDERSON: You'll get a final shakedown on the whole bit. Then if you okay, I'll need the loot to pay off my five men. Half in advance, half when the job's finished.

D'MEDICO: About two thousand for looking, and then another four or five for your staff?

ANDERSON: That's about it.

D'MEDICO: All advances and expenses out of the take before the split?

ANDERSON: Yes.

ANGELO: I've got to get out of here and over to Manhattan. I'm late as it is. Duke, I want to talk to the Doctor. You understand?

ANDERSON: Sure. I appreciate you giving me this time.

ANGELO: We'll get in touch with you—one way or the other—in a week or so. I've got to talk to Papa and, as you probably know, he's ailing. We should all live to be ninety-four and ailing.

D'MEDICO: Amen.

ANDERSON: Nice to meet you, Mr. Angelo. Thanks, Mr. D'Medico.

D'MEDICO: A pleasure, Duke. We'll be in touch.

[Lapse of seventeen seconds.]

D'MEDICO: How did you know he was from Kentucky, Tennessee—around there?

ANGELO: I recognized him the minute he walked in. Not him, but the type. A mountain man. God knows I saw enough of them in Korea. Kentucky, Tennessee, West Virginia. Rough boys. As rough as the Southerners . . . but they never bugged out. Sometimes you get some freaky Southerners. I never saw a freaky mountain man. They're all born piss-poor. They got nothing but their pride. I had some mountain men who never had a pair of new shoes until they got in the army. This Anderson . . . Jesus Christ, he reminds me so much of a guy I had. He was from Tennessee. Best shot I ever saw. I was a First Looey then. I had this patrol, and we were going down a dry creek bed. This mountain man was point. The target. We went through three points in three days. They fired on the point and that's how we knew where they were.

D'MEDICO: That's nice.

ANGELO: Yes. So this Tennessee mountain man was point, about twenty yards or so ahead of me. A gook comes out of the bushes and charges at him. The gook has a kitchen knife tied to a long pole with string. He was probably hopped up. He comes charging out screaming. My guy could have shot him dead—one, two, three. Like that. But he didn't. He laughed. I swear to God, he laughed. He had his blade on his rifle, and he waited for the gook to come to him. It was classic. Jesus, it was classic. I had been through all the bayonet stuff: advance, parry, thrust. Book stuff. And this was right out of the book. Classic. They could have taken pictures of it for an army manual. My guy took the position, shuffled forward, and when the gook shoved at him, he parried, got his stick in the gook's stomach, withdrew, stuck again into his balls, turned the blade, withdrew, shoved the bayonet into the ground to clean it, and turned and grinned at me. He liked it. There were guys like that. They liked it. They enjoyed it. War, I mean.

D'MEDICO: What happened to him?

ANGELO: Who?

D'MEDICO: Your guy.

ANGELO: Oh. Well, the company went back to Tokyo on leave. This Tennessee guy got caught raping a nine-year-old Japanese girl. He got racked up.

D'MEDICO: Where is he now?

ANGELO: Still in Leavenworth as far as I know. So tell me about this Anderson. What do you know?

D'MEDICO: He came out of the South about ten years ago. A helluva driver. I think he was driving alky for Solly Benedict down there. Anyway, he sliced someone and had to come north. Solly called me about him. About the same time my cousin Gino had a hustle planned. Did you ever meet Gino?

ANGELO: No, I don't believe I ever did.

D'MEDICO: Christ, my face is killing me. Well, it was a warehouse job. Drugs. Pep pills, I think they were. It was cased perfect, but someone tipped the Safe and Loft Squad. We took care of him later. Anyway, I recommended Anderson as the driver, and Gino says okay. The plan was for Gino and two muscles to pull up in his car, Anderson driving. Park a block away. Anderson is told to stay there until Gino returns. The idea is that they'll break the warehouse, the two dumdums will drive the truck out, and Gino will return to where Anderson is waiting in the car.

ANGELO: So?

D'MEDICO: So everything goes wrong. Floodlights, sirens, bullhorns, riot guns, barkers . . . the whole bit. The two muscles get cut down. Gino takes a bad one in the gut and staggers around the corner. He's told Anderson to stay there, and with all this going on, Anderson is still there.

ANGELO: A mountain man.

D'MEDICO: Yes. He didn't cut. Well, he gets Gino into the car and gets him to a sawbones. It saved his life.

ANGELO: What's he doing now?

D'MEDICO: Gino? He's got this little candy store in Newark. He takes some numbers, handles a few loans. Penny-ante stuff. He's not too good . . . but he's alive. I feed him what I can. But I never forgot. Duke sitting there while the shit hit the fan. He's some man.

ANGELO: I figured that. Then what happened with him?

D'MEDICO: He didn't want any jobs. He wanted to freelance. He cleared everything with me first, and I gave him the go-ahead. He did very well. He's a smart boy, Pat. He learned fast. He hit some East Side apartments for a bundle. Ice, mostly. Never carried a stick. Got clever. In and out so fast and so smoothly they could never figure how. He was doing all right. Maybe three or four jobs a year. Always made his contribution and never screamed. I kept track and found out he was bent, sex-wise.

ANGELO: How do you mean?

D'MEDICO: Whips . . . you know.

ANGELO: Which way is he? This is important.

D'MEDICO: Both ways, from what I hear. Then he pulled this job and was waiting on a corner for this Jew bitch he had to pass the stuff to—it was only about a block away—when some lucky probationary patrolman decided he didn't like his looks and shook him down. That kid is a Dick Two now. So Duke went up. The woman wasn't touched; he never mentioned her. I heard she was late for the meet because she was at her stockbroker's.

ANGELO: Beautiful. You been keeping in touch with her?

D'MEDICO: Oh, sure. Since Duke brought up this campaign we been checking her out. She's got a record, and she's hustling right now—shmeck, tail, abortion—the whole bit. She works in a dance hall Sam Bergman owns. We can lean on her any time we want to.

ANGELO: Good. How did Anderson get on to this thing on the East Side?

D'MEDICO: He's pronging a woman who lives there. We don't know how he met her. But he's in and out of the place at least twice a week. A big dame who looks like money.

ANGELO: All right. I guess that's about it. Christ, have we finished another bottle? My God, I've *got* to get to Manhattan.

D'MEDICO: Pat, how do you feel about it?

ANGELO: If it was up to me, I'd say no. Look, Doc, we're in restaurants, hotels, banks, linen supply, insurance, trucking, laundromats, garbage disposal—all nice, clean, legit things. And the profits are good. So why do we need this bang-bang stuff?

D'MEDICO: Still . . . you're interested?

ANGELO: Yes . . . I guess I am. It's a military problem. Look at me . . . I'm a businessman, my gut is swelling, my ass is sinking, I've got a wife and three kids, I belong to four clubs, I play golf every good weekend, I go to the PTA with my wife, I worry about crab grass, I've got a poodle with worms. In other words, I'm a solid citizen. But sometimes I look at myself in the mirror—the belly, the jowls, the fat thighs, the soft cock, and I think I was happier in Korea.

D'MEDICO: Pat, maybe you're one of those guys you were telling me about—the guys who enjoy war.

ANGELO: Maybe. I don't know. All I know is, I hear of something like this and I get all excited. My brain starts working. I'm young again. A campaign. Problems. How to figure it. It's really something. But I wouldn't decide without talking it over with Papa. First of all, I owe it to him. Second, of all, he may be bedridden with maybe a fat boy now and then to keep him warm, but his mind is still there—sharp and hard. I'll lay it out for him. He likes to feel he's still needed, still making the decisions. Jesus Christ, we got a thousand lawyers and CPA's making decisions he couldn't even understand—but a problem like this, he can understand. So I'll lay it out for him. If he says no, it's no. If he says yes, it's yes. I'll let you know within a week or so. Is that all right?

D'MEDICO: Of course. Got anyone in mind for the sixth man?

ANGELO: No. Do you?

D'MEDICO: A guy named Sam Heming. A nothing. All muscle, no brains. But he's one of Paul Washington's boys.

ANGELO: A smoke?

D'MEDICO: He is, but he passes.
ANGELO: Why him?
D'MEDICO: I owe Paul a favor.
ANGELO: Linda Curtis?
D'MEDICO: You don't miss much, do you?
ANGELO: No, Doc, not much. Heming is okay with me if he's solid.
D'MEDICO: He's solid.
ANGELO: Good. Papa will want to know. I'll tell him you go for this guy. Okay?
D'MEDICO: Yes . . . if it's necessary.
ANGELO: It's necessary. Jesus Christ, Doc, you're twitching like a maniac. Can't you do anything about that face of yours?
D'MEDICO: No. Not a thing.
ANGELO: Tough shit. I've got to run. Thanks for the dinner and vino.
D'MEDICO: My pleasure. I'll hear from you on this in a week or so?
ANGELO: Sure. Oh . . . by the way, Doc, keep an eye on Fred Simons.
D'MEDICO: Anything wrong?
ANGELO: Not yet. But he's been hitting the sauce hard lately. Maybe talking a little more than he should. Just a friendly tip.
D'MEDICO: Of course. Thanks. I'll call it to his attention.
ANGELO: You do that.

32

TAPE RECORDING POM-9JUL68-EVERLEIGH. Time is approximately 2:45 P.M.

MRS. EVERLEIGH: Let me get you a big drink. I want you to sit quietly for a while. I want to show you some pictures—my photo album.
ANDERSON: All right.
   [Lapse of sixteen seconds.]
MRS. EVERLEIGH: Here . . . just the way you like it—one ice cube. Here we go. I bought this album at Mark Cross. It's nice, isn't it?
ANDERSON: Yes.
MRS. EVERLEIGH: Here . . . this tintype. This was my great-grandfather on my father's side. He was in the Civil War. That's the uniform of a captain he's wearing. The picture was made when he came home on leave. Then he lost an arm at Antietam. But they let him keep his company. They didn't care so much about things like that in those days.
ANDERSON: I know. My great-grandpappy went through the Second Wilderness with a wooden leg.
MRS. EVERLEIGH: Then, after the war, he came home and married my great-grandmother. Here's their wedding photo. Wasn't she the tiniest, sweetest, prettiest thing you've ever seen? Raised seven children in Rockford, Illinois. Now this is the only picture I have of my mother's parents. He was an older man, had a general store near Sewickley in Pennsylvania. His wife was a real monster. I remember her vaguely. I guess I got my size from her. She was huge—and ugly. My mother was an only child. Here's my mother's graduating class. She went two years to a teachers' college. The one with the circle is her. This little fellow is my father at the age of ten. Wasn't he cute? Then he went to Yale. Look at that hat he's wearing! Isn't that a scream? He rowed for them. And he

was a great swimmer, too. Here he is in a swimsuit. This was taken during his last year at Yale.

ANDERSON: Looks like he was hung.

MRS. EVERLEIGH: Bastard. Well, I can tell you he was all man. Tall and muscular. He met my mother at a prom, and they got married right after he graduated. He started as a junior clerk in Wall Street about three years before World War One. My brother Ernest was born in 1915, but when America got into the war, Daddy enlisted. He went overseas in 1918. I don't think he ever actually saw any action. Here he is in his uniform.

ANDERSON: Those wraparound puttees must have been murder. My mother's first husband got killed with the Marines on the Marne.

MRS. EVERLEIGH: That couldn't have been your father?

ANDERSON: No. My pappy was her third husband.

MRS. EVERLEIGH: Well, here's Mom and Daddy with Ernie and Tom—he was the second-born. He was missing in action in France in World War Two. Then here's Mother holding me in her arms—the first picture ever taken of me. Wasn't I cute?

ANDERSON: Yes.

MRS. EVERLEIGH: Then here are some pictures of me growing up. Bloomers. Gym suit. Bathing suit. We went to a cabin on a lake up in Canada. Here are all the kids—Ernest and Thomas and me and Robert. All of us.

ANDERSON: You were the only girl?

MRS. EVERLEIGH: Yes. But I could keep up with them, and after a while I could outswim them all. Mother got sick and was in bed a lot, and Daddy was busy with his business. So the four of us kids were together a lot. Ernie was the leader because he was oldest, but when he went to Dartmouth, I took over. Tom and Bob never had the authority that Ernie had.

ANDERSON: How old were you when that one was taken?

MRS. EVERLEIGH: About thirteen, I think.

ANDERSON: A great pair of lungs.

MRS. EVERLEIGH: Yes, I matured early. The story of my life. I started bleeding at eleven. Look at the shoulders I had, and those thighs. I could outswim my brothers and all their friends. I think the boys resented it. They liked frail, weak, feminine things. I had this big, strong, muscular body. I thought the boys would like a girl who could swim with them and ride horses with them and wrestle and all that. . . . But when dances came along, I noticed it was the frail, weak, pale feminine things who got invited. Mother insisted I take dancing lessons, but I was never very good at it. I could dive and swim, but on the dance floor I felt like a lump.

ANDERSON: Who copped your cherry?

MRS. EVERLEIGH: My brother Ernie. Does that shock you?

ANDERSON: Why should it? I'm from Kentucky.

MRS. EVERLEIGH: Well, it happened when he was home one Easter vacation from Dartmouth. And he was drunk.

ANDERSON: Sure.

MRS. EVERLEIGH: Here I am at my high school graduation. Don't I look pretty?

ANDERSON: You look like a heifer in a nightgown.

MRS. EVERLEIGH: I guess I do . . . I guess I do. Oh, God, that hat. But then, here, when I started going to Miss Proud's school, I slimmed down. A little. Not much, but a little. I was on the swimming team, captain of the winning intramural field-hockey team, captain of the riding and golf teams, and I played a good game of tennis, too. Not clever, but strong. Here I am with the cup I got for best all-around girl athlete.

ANDERSON: Christ, what a body. I wish I could have stuck you then.

MRS. EVERLEIGH: Plenty of boys did. Maybe I couldn't dance, but I discovered the secret of how to be popular. A very simple secret. I think they called me Miss Round Heels. All you had to do was ask, and I'd roll over. So I had plenty of dates.

ANDERSON: I'd have figured you for a lez.

MRS. EVERLEIGH: Oh . . . I tried it. I never made the first advance, but I had plenty of those sweet, pale, soft, feminine things touching me up. I tried it, but it didn't take. Maybe it was because of the way they smelled. You didn't shower this morning, did you?

ANDERSON: No.

MRS. EVERLEIGH: That horsey, bitter, acid smell. It really turns me on. Then I met David. He was a friend of my youngest brother, Bob. Here's David.

ANDERSON: Looks like a butterfly.

MRS. EVERLEIGH: He was . . . but I didn't discover that until it was too late. And he drank and drank and drank. . . . But he was funny and kind and considerate. He had money, and he made me laugh and held doors open for me, and if he wasn't so great in the sack, well, I could excuse that because he always had too much to drink. You know?

ANDERSON: Yes.

MRS. EVERLEIGH: Lots of money. Cleveland coal and iron and things like that. Sometimes I wondered if he was a little Jewish.

ANDERSON: A little Jewish?

MRS. EVERLEIGH: You know . . . way back. Anyway, here we are at the beach, at the prom, at a horse show, at the engagement party, the wedding pictures, reception and so forth. I wore low heels because I was just a wee bit taller than he was. He had beautiful hair. Didn't he have beautiful hair?

ANDERSON: Beautiful. Much more of this shit?

MRS. EVERLEIGH: No, not much more. Here we are at our summer place in East Hampton. Some good times. Drunken parties. I walked in on him once when he was getting buggered by a Puerto Rican busboy. I don't have a picture of *that*! And that's about all. Some pictures of me on buying trips—Paris, Rome, London, Geneva, Vienna. . . .

ANDERSON: Who's this guy?

MRS. EVERLEIGH: A kid I bought in Stockholm.

ANDERSON: Good lay?

MRS. EVERLEIGH: Not really.

ANDERSON: What the hell are you crying for?
    [Lapse of seven seconds.]

MRS. EVERLEIGH: These pictures. A hundred years. My great-grandparents. The Civil War. My parents. The world wars. My brothers. I just think of what all these people went through. To produce me. Me. I'm the result. Ah, Jesus, Duke, what happens to us? How did we get to be what we are? I just can't stand thinking about it—it's so awful. So sad.

ANDERSON: Where's your husband now?

MRS. EVERLEIGH: David? The last time I saw him, he was wearing lipstick. That's what I mean. And look at me. Am I any better?

ANDERSON: You want me to go?

MRS. EVERLEIGH: And leave me here counting the walls? Duke, for the love of God, get me out. . . .

33

DOMINICK "PAPA" Angelo, ninety-four, don of the Angelo family, was a legal resident of 67825 Flint Road, Deal, New Jersey. Born Mario Dominick Nicola Angelo in Mareno, Sicily, 1874. His family was a "leftside" branch of the Angelo family, and for five generations had been tenant farmers in Sicily. There is no record of Dominick's early schooling.

During a New York State investigation in 1934 (see Records of the Murphy Committee, Vol I, pp. 432–35) evidence was presented that Dominick Angelo entered the United States illegally in 1891 by swimming ashore from a merchant ship on which he was working as cook. In any event, records are confused—or missing—and Dominick Angelo filed for his first citizenship papers in 1896, and became a U.S. citizen in 1903. At that time he listed his occupation as "waiter."

His criminal record includes an arrest for disturbing the peace in 1904 (no disposition) and assault with intent to kill in 1905 (charge withdrawn). In 1907 he was arrested on a charge of assault with a deadly weapon (knife) with the intent to commit grievous bodily harm (he castrated his victim). He was tried, convicted, and served two years, seven months, and fourteen days at Dannemora (#46783).

Upon his release from prison, there is inconclusive evidence that he became a "button" for the Black Hand, as the Italian criminal organization in this country was then called.

(In their treatise *Origins of American Slang*, Hawley and Butanski, Effrim Publishers Co., Inc., 1958, the authors state [pp. 38–39] that in the period of 1890–1910, the term "button" was used to describe a gangland executioner, and may have come from a description of a man who could "button the lip" of an informer or enemy. The authors point out that later, in the 1920's and 1930's, the terms "buttons" or "Mr. Buttons" came into use in criminal circles to describe a uniformed policeman.)

In 1910, Dominick Angelo, obtained employment with the Alsotto Sand & Gravel Co., of Brooklyn, New York, ostensibly as a loader. In 1917 he volunteered for service with the American Expeditionary Forces, but because of his age, his services were limited to guard duty on the docks at Bayonne, New Jersey.

In 1920 he secured employment as foreman with the Giovanni Shipping Enterprises, Inc. During this period he married Maria Florence Gabriele Angelo, a distant relative. Their first child, a boy, was born in 1923. He was subsequently killed in action on Guadalcanal Island in 1942.

During World War II, Dominick Angelo volunteered his services to the U.S. government and, according to documents on file, his assistance was "invaluable" in preparing for the invasions of Sicily and Italy. There is in existence a letter from a high official of the OSS attesting to his "magnificent and unique cooperation."

During the period of 1948–68, official records reveal his rise to a position of great prominence and power in the Italian-dominated structure controlling organized crime in the United States. From soldier to *capo* to don took him less than ten years, and by 1957 he was recognized as leader of one of the several national "families." His personal fortune was variously estimated as $20,000,000 to $45,000,000.

Students and observers of organized crime in the United States—of what has been described as the Black Hand, the Syndicate, the Mafia, the Cosa Nostra, the Family, etc.—generally agree that Dominick Angelo was the guiding spirit, brain, and power behind the conversion of the violent system to a semilegitimate cartel that increasingly avoided the strong-arm methods of previous years and invested more funds in loan companies, real estate, entertainment enterprises, brokerage houses, garbage collections, banks, linen supply companies, restaurants, laundromats, insurance companies, and advertising agencies.

In 1968,* Dominick Angelo was ninety-four; 124 pounds; 5 feet 6 inches tall; almost totally bald; almost completely bedridden from diabetes, arthritis, and the effects of two severe coronary occlusions. Very dark eyes; extraordinarily long fingers; a habit of stroking his upper lip with one finger (he wore a long mustache until 1946).

His home in Deal, New Jersey, was large, comfortable, and situated in the center of a generous acreage, without being ostentatious. The estate was surrounded by a 12-foot brick wall topped with cement into which pieces of broken glass had been studded. It is believed the staff consisted of several people—housekeeper, two or three groundsmen, a personal valet, butler, a male medical attendant, a female nurse, three maids, and two chauffeurs.

On 16 May, 1966, an explosion occurred at the locked gate leading to the Angelo estate. Officers investigating the incident reported it had been caused by several sticks of dynamite wired to a crude time fuse—a cheap alarm clock. No injuries were reported, and no arrests were made. The investigation is continuing.

Of peripheral interest are two unsubstantiated reports on Dominick Angelo: After his wife's death in 1952, he engaged in homosexual liaisons, preferring the company of very young boys; and he was the inventor of the split-level coffin, although this "credit" has since been given to others. The split-level coffin is a device to get rid of victims of gangland slayings. The coffins are built somewhat deeper than usual, and the victim is buried in a section beneath the legitimate corpse. This scheme, of course, depends upon the cooperation of funeral parlors, in which the family has a substantial financial interest.

The following transcription is from a tape recording made by agents of the New Jersey Special Legislative Subcommittee to investigate Organized Crime. The transcription is labeled NJSLC-DA-#206-IC, and is dated 10 July, 1968. The time was approximately 11:45 P.M., and the recording was made at Dominick Angelo's home at 67825 Flint Road, Deal, New Jersey. The transmitting device was a Socklet MT-Model K.

From internal evidence, the two persons present were Dominick "Papa" Angelo and Patrick "Little Pat" Angelo. Although the tape recording from which this transcription was made ran for slightly less than three hours, portions have been deleted that repeat evidence already presented. In addition, law enforcement agencies of New Jersey, New York, and Las Vegas, Nevada, have requested that certain portions be withheld, since they concern possible criminal prosecutions presently under investigation. All such deletions have been indicated by "lapse of time" notations.

[Lapse of thirty-two minutes during which Patrick Angelo inquired as to his grandfather's health and was informed that it was "as well as could be expected". Patrick Angelo then reported on the meeting with John Anderson and Anthoney D'Medico.]
PATRICK: Well, Papa, what do you think?
PAPA: What do *you* think?

---

* Dominick Angelo died on February 19, 1969.

PATRICK: I say no. Too many people involved. Too complex, considering the possible profit.

PAPA: But I see your eyes shining. I see you are interested. You say to yourself, this is action! You are excited. You say to yourself, I am getting old and fat. I need action. This is how it was in Korea. I will plan this like a military raid. To me you say no—but in yourself you want this thing.

PATRICK [laughing]: Papa, you're wonderful! You've got it all exactly right. My brain tells me this is nothing. But my blood wants it. I am sorry.

PAPA: Why be sorry? You think it is a good thing to be all brain and no blood? It is as bad as being all blood and no brain. The right mixture—that is what is important. This man Anderson—what is your feeling on him?

PATRICK: A hardnose. He has never carried a piece, but he is hard. And proud. From Kentucky. A mountain man. Everything the Doctor told me about him was good.

PAPA: Anderson? From the South? About ten years ago Gino Belli—he is the Doctor's cousin—had a thing planned. It seemed good but it went sour. He had a driver named Anderson. Is that the man?

PATRICK: The same one. What a memory you've got, Papa!

PAPA: The body grows old; the mind remains young, praise to God. This Anderson brought Gino to a doctor. I remember it all now. I met him, very briefly. Tall and thin. A long, sunken face. Proud. Yes, you are right—a very proud man. I remember.

PATRICK: So what do you want to do, Papa?

PAPA: Be quiet and let me think.
   [Lapse of two minutes thirteen seconds.]

PAPA: This Anderson—you say he has his own staff?

PATRICK: Yes. Five men. One's a smoke. One's a tech. Two are drivers, one of them a dumdum.
   [Lapse of nine seconds.]

PAPA: That is four. And the other? The fifth man?
   [Lapse of sixteen seconds.]

PAPA: Well? The fifth man?

PATRICK: He's fancy. Knows about paintings, rugs, art collections—things like that.

PAPA: I see. Is his name Bailey?

PATRICK: I don't know what his name is, Papa. I can find out.

PAPA: There was a fancy boy named Bailey out in Vegas. We did a. . . .
   [Lapse of four minutes thirty-two seconds.]

PAPA: But that is not important. Besides, I suspect it is not Bailey. I suspect Bailey is dead. And who does the Doctor recommend as our representative?

PATRICK: A man named Sam Heming. One of Paul Washington's boys.

PAPA: Another dinge?

PATRICK: Yes.

PAPA: No. That won't do.

PATRICK: Papa? You mean you approve of this campaign?

PAPA: Yes. I approve. Go ahead with it.

PATRICK: But why? The money is. . . .

PAPA: I know. The money is nothing. There are too many people involved. It will end in disaster.

PATRICK: So . . . ?
   [Lapse of seventeen seconds.]

PAPA: Little Pat is thinking why should Papa okay something like this? All these years we work hard to get legit. We deal with Wall Street bankers, Madison Avenue advertising agencies, political parties. We are in all good businesses. The profits are good. Everything is clean. We keep trouble down. And now here is Papa, ninety-four years old, and maybe his mind is getting feeble, too— here is Papa saying all right to this silly plan, this *meshugeneh* raid, where people will be hurt and probably killed. Maybe Papa is no longer to be trusted. Is that what Patrick thinks?

PATRICK: I swear to God, Papa, I never. If you say it's okay, it's okay.

PAPA: Little Pat, you will be don soon enough. Soon enough. A year. Two at the most.

PATRICK: Papa, Papa . . . you'll outlive us all.

PAPA: Two years at the most. Probably one. But if you are to be don you must learn to think . . . *think*. Not only must you think should we do this thing, can we profit from this thing, but also, what are the consequences of this thing? What will result from this thing a year, five years, ten years from now? Most men—even big executives in the best American companies—gather all the facts and make a decision. But they fail to consider the consequences of their decision. The long-term consequences. Do you understand me?

PATRICK: I think so, Papa.

PAPA: Suppose there is a man we must put down. We consider what he has done and what a danger he represents to us. On the basis of these facts, we say he must be put down. But we must also consider the consequences of his death. Does he have relatives who will be embittered? Will the blues get upset? What will the papers say? Is there a young, smart, ambitious politician who will take this man's death and get elected on it? You understand? It is not enough to consider the immediate facts. You must also project your mind and consider the future. In the long run, will it help us or hurt us?

PATRICK: Now I understand, Papa. But what has that to do with Anderson's hustle?

PAPA: Remember about four years ago in Buffalo, we. . . .

[Lapse of four minutes nine seconds.]

PAPA: So what did that teach us? The advantage of fear. We first create and then maintain an atmosphere of fear. Why do you think we have been so successful in our legitimate dealings? In real estate and garbage collection and banks and linen service? Because our rates are lower? Ah, you know our rates are higher. Higher! But they fear us. And because of their fear, we do good business. The steel fist in the velvet glove. But if this is to continue, if our legitimate enterprises are to flourish, we must maintain our reputation. We must let businessmen know who we are, of what we are capable. Not frequently, but occasionally, choosing incidents that we know will not be lost on them, we must let the public know that beneath that soft velvet glove is bright, shining steel. Only then will they fear us, and our legitimate enterprises will continue to grow.

PATRICK: And you want to use Anderson's campaign as an example? You feel it will end in failure, but you want the newspapers to play it up as ours? You want people hurt and people killed? You want businessmen who read about it in the papers to shiver, and then call us and say yes, they'll take another million yards of our rayons or use our trucking firms or our insurance business?

PAPA: Yes. That is exactly what I want.

PATRICK: Is that why you okayed Al Petty's job two years ago when. . . .

[Lapse of forty-seven seconds.]

PAPA: Of course. I knew he could never succeed. But it made headlines all over the country, and the men arrested were linked to us. Three people, one a child, were killed on that job, and our collections took a five point two percent jump in the following six months. Fear. Let others—the English and the Americans—use persuasions and business pressure. We use fear. Because we know it always works.

PATRICK: But Anderson, he's not. . . .

PAPA: I know he is not linked closely with us. So we must put a man in who is. Toast came to visit me yesterday.

PATRICK: Toast? I didn't know he was in town. Why didn't he call me?

PAPA: He asked me to apologize to you. He was between flights. He just had time for a quick trip out here by car, and then on to Palm Beach.

PATRICK: How old was she this time?

PAPA: About fifteen. A real beauty. Long blond hair. And blind.

PATRICK: Blind? That's good—for her sake.

PAPA: Yes. But Toast has a problem. Perhaps we can solve it for him with this Anderson thing.

PATRICK: What is the problem?

PAPA: Toast has a man—Vincent Parelli. You know him? They call him Socks.

PATRICK: That idiot? I've read about him.

PAPA: Yes. Parelli has gone crazy. He fights people. He runs them down in his car. He shoots them. He just doesn't care. He is a very great embarrassment to Toast.

PATRICK: I can imagine.

PAPA: Parelli is very closely linked with us, very closely. Toast wants to get him out. You understand?

PATRICK: Yes.

PAPA: But Parelli is not that easy. He has some muscle of his own. They are all crazy . . . crazy. Al Capones. Throwbacks. They cannot think. Toast asked if there is anything I can do.

PATRICK: So . . . ?

PAPA: I owe a favor to Toast. You remember last year he got Paolo's nephew into the university after the boy had been turned down all over? So here is what we do. . . . I will tell Toast to send Parelli in from Detroit to be our man on the Anderson campaign. Toast will tell Parelli that we have definite evidence of at least a million dollars' worth of jewelry in the house. Otherwise Parelli would laugh at us. Toast will tell him we want a good, trustworthy man of our own on the scene to make sure there is no chance of a cross. This Parelli is gun-happy. He will probably blast. At the same time, you tell Anderson that we approve his plan providing he carries a piece and, at the end of the action, he puts Parelli down. That is our price for financing his hustle.

[Lapse of eleven seconds.]

PATRICK: Papa, I don't think Anderson will go for it.

PAPA: I think he will. I know these amateurs. Always the big chance, the big hit, and then retirement to South America or the French Riviera for the rest of their lives. They think crime is one big lottery. They don't know what hard work it is . . . hard, grinding work, year after year. No big hits, no big chances. But a job—just like any other. Maybe the profits are larger, but so are the risks. Anderson will stall a while, but then he will go for it. He will put Parelli down. Anderson has the blood and the pride to keep a bargain. I believe the whole thing will be a madness, with innocent people hurt and killed, and Vincent Parelli, who is so closely linked with us, found dead at the scene of the crime.

PATRICK: And you think that will help us, Papa?

PAPA: It will be in headlines all over the country and, eventually, it will help us.

PATRICK: What if the campaign comes off?

PAPA: So much the better. Parelli will no longer be a nuisance to Toast, we will get credit for the grab, and we will also profit. And maybe Anderson will end up in Mexico after all. Patrick, phone me every day and tell me how this is coming. I am very interested. Explain to the Doctor only as much as he needs to know. You understand?

PATRICK: Yes, Papa.

PAPA: I will take care of Toast, and Toast will make certain that Parelli is here when needed. Do you have any questions?

PATRICK: No, Papa. I know what must be done.

PAPA: You are a good boy, Patrick . . . a good boy.

34

ON 12 July, 1968, at 2:06 P.M., a meeting took place between John Anderson and Patrick Angelo in the dispatcher's office of the Jiffy Trucking & Hauling Co., 11098 Tenth Avenue, New York, New York. This company was a subsidiary of the Thomas Jefferson Trading Corp., of which Patrick Angelo was an officer (secretary-treasurer) of record. The premises were under surveillance by the Bureau of Customs, pursuant to Federal Court Order MFC-#189-605HG, on suspicion that they were being used as a drop for smuggled merchandise. The following is tape USBC-1089756738-B2.

ANDERSON: Well?

ANGELO: It looks good. Papa okayed it.

[Lapse of four seconds.]

ANDERSON [sighing]: Jesus.

ANGELO: But you've got to do something for us.

[Lapse of six seconds.]

ANDERSON: What?

ANGELO: We've got to put our own man in. You know, that's SOP— Standard Operating Procedure.

ANDERSON: I know. I figured that. Who?

ANGELO: A man from Detroit. Vincent Parelli. They call him Socks. You know him?

ANDERSON: No.

ANGELO: You heard about him?

ANDERSON: No.

ANGELO: A good man. Experienced. He's no punk. But you'll be the boss. That's understood. He'll be told he takes orders from you.

ANDERSON: All right. That sounds all right. What else?

ANGELO: You got a brain.

ANDERSON: What else do I got to do?

ANGELO: We want you to cut down on him.

[Lapse of five seconds.]

ANDERSON: What?

ANGELO: Put him down. After it's all over. When you're ready to leave. You put him down.

[Lapse of eleven seconds.]

ANGELO: You understand?

ANDERSON: Yes.

ANGELO: You knew you'd have to carry a barker on this job?

ANDERSON: Yes.

ANGELO: So . . . you cut this Parelli down. Just before you take off.

ANDERSON: You want me to kill him.

[Lapse of seven seconds.]

ANGELO: Yes.

ANDERSON: Why?

ANGELO: You don't have to know that. It's got nothing to do with you, nothing to do with this hustle. We want him out—that's all. You get him out. That's our price.

[Lapse of sixteen seconds.]

ANGELO: Well?

ANDERSON: You want me to answer now?

ANGELO: No. Take a day or two. We'll be in touch. If it's no, then no hard feelings and we'll forget the whole thing. If it's yes, the Doctor will get the scratch to you and we'll start the operations plan. We can get you the schedules of the beat fuzz and the sector cars. But it's up to you. It's your decision.

ANDERSON: Yes.

ANGELO: You know exactly what you must do? There's no misunderstanding? I've made it plain? In things like this, it's best to make absolutely certain everyone knows what's going to happen.

ANDERSON: I know what's going to happen.

ANGELO: Good. You think about it.

ANDERSON: All right. I'll thing about it.

35

IN ADDITION to the microphone transmitter implanted at the home of Dominick Angelo, 67825 Flint Road, Deal, New Jersey, a telephone tap had been installed by the Federal Bureau of Narcotics. This portion of tape FBN-DA-10935 is dated 12 July, 1968. The time: 2:48 P.M.

ANGELO: He was shook, Papa . . . really spooked. I think you were right. I think he'll go for it. Now about this thing with Benefici in Hackensack . . . I think we should. . . .

36

TAPE SEC-13JUL68-IM-4:24PM-149H. This was a Saturday.

INGRID: So . . . how is it you are here at this hour? You are not working?

ANDERSON: No. I'm off this weekend. I get every other weekend off.

INGRID: You should have called first. I might have been busy.

ANDERSON: Are you busy?

INGRID: No. I have been doing some mending. You would like a drink?

ANDERSON: I brought some Berliner Weisse and raspberry syrup.

INGRID: You darling! How wonderful! You remembered!

ANDERSON: You have big glasses?

INGRID: I will serve it in big brandy snifters I have. How wonderful! You remembered!

[Lapse of two minutes eighteen seconds.]

INGRID: Here you are. Such a beautiful color. *Prosit.*

ANDERSON: *Prosit.*

[Lapse of fourteen seconds.]

INGRID: Ah. So good, so good. Tell me, Duke—how are things with you?

ANDERSON: All right.

INGRID: That meet you had, the last time I spoke to you . . . that turned out well?

ANDERSON: Yes . . . sort of.

INGRID: You are troubled, *Schatzie?* That is why you came? You want to get out?

ANDERSON: No. But I got to talk. I don't mean that the way it sounds. I got to talk to *you.* You're the smartest one I know. I want your opinion. Your advice.

INGRID: This is a job?

ANDERSON: Yes.

INGRID: I don't want to know about it.

ANDERSON: Please. I don't say please very often. I'm saying please to you.

[Lapse of thirteen seconds.]

INGRID: You know, Duke, I have a feeling about you. A very bad feeling.

ANDERSON: What is that?

INGRID: I have this feeling that through you I will meet my death. Just by knowing you and talking to you, I will die before my time.

ANDERSON: Does that scare you?

INGRID: No.

ANDERSON: No. Nothing scares you. Does it make you sad?

INGRID: Perhaps.

ANDERSON: Do you want me to leave?

[Lapse of twenty-two seconds].

INGRID: What do you want to tell me? Why is this thing so important you need my advice?

ANDERSON: I have this hustle planned. It's a good one. If I hit, it means a lot of money. A lot of money. If it works out, I can go to Mexico, South America, Europe—anywhere. And live for the rest of my life. I mean, *live.* I would ask you to come with me. But don't think about that. Don't let that influence what you tell me.

INGRID: I won't, *Schatzie.* I have heard that before.

ANDERSON: I know, I know. But for this hustle I need money, ready money. To pay people and plan things. You understand?

INGRID: Yes. You want money from me?

ANDERSON: No, I don't want any money from you.

INGRID: Then the people you will get money from, the people whose cooperation you need—they want something . . . *nein?*

ANDERSON: You're so goddamned smart it scares me.

INGRID: Think of what my life has been. What do they want?

ANDERSON: I have a staff. Five men I can get. But these money people must put their own man in. Okay. This is understandable. I'm a free-lance. It happens all the time with free-lancers. You get permission to operate but they must put their own man in to make sure there's no cross, so they know definitely what the take is. You understand?

INGRID: Of course. So?

ANDERSON: They want to bring a man in from Detroit. I've never met him. I've never heard of him. They tell me he's a pro. They tell me he will take orders from me. I will be the boss of this campaign.

INGRID: So?

ANDERSON: They want me to cut down on him. This is their price. After the hit is finished, I am to burn this man. They won't tell me why; it isn't my business. But this is their price.

INGRID: Ah. . . .

[Lapse of one minute twelve seconds.]

INGRID: They know you. They know you so well. They know if you agree to this, you will do it. Not from fear of what they might do if you didn't but because you are John Anderson, and when you say you will do a thing, you will do it. Am I right?

ANDERSON: I don't know what they think.

INGRID: You ask me for my advice. I am trying to give it to you. If you say yes, you will then kill this man. Tell me, *Schatzie*, if you say no, are you then in trouble?

ANDERSON: Not in trouble . . . no. They won't kill me. Nothing like that. I'm not worth it. But I couldn't free-lance anymore. I couldn't get clearance from them. I could operate, if I wanted to, but it would never be the same again. It would be very bad—penny-ante stuff. I'd have to go back home. I couldn't operate in this town.

INGRID: Home? Where is home?

ANDERSON: South. Kentucky.

INGRID: And what would you do there?

ANDERSON: Open your robe, will you?

INGRID: Yes. Like this . . . ?

ANDERSON: Yes. Just let me look at you while I'm talking. Christ, I've got to talk.

INGRID: Is this better?

ANDERSON: Yes . . . better. I don't know what I'd do. Run some alky. Gas stations maybe. A bank now and then if I could find the right men.

INGRID: That is all you know?

ANDERSON: Yes, goddammit, that's all I know. Do you think I would become a computer operator in Kentucky, or maybe an insurance salesman?

INGRID: Do not be angry with me, *Schatzie*.

ANDERSON: I'm not angry with you. I told you, I just want your advice. I'm all fucked up.

INGRID: You killed a man before.

ANDERSON: Yes. But that was in blood. I had to. You understand? he said things.

INGRID: So now it is part of a job. How is it different?

ANDERSON: Shit. You foreigners. You don't understand.

INGRID: No, I do not.

ANDERSON: This guy I cut kept pecking at me and pecking at me. We had words. Finally I had to put him down or I couldn't have lived with myself. I *had* to. I was forced into it.

INGRID: You Americans—you are so strange. You "put a man down," or you "cut him," or you "burn him," or you "put him away" or "take him for a ride." But you will never say you killed him. Why is that?

ANDERSON: Yes, you're right. It's funny. I don't know why it is. These people who want me to do this thing I told you about, I finally asked the man, "You want me to kill him?" and he finally admitted that was what they wanted. But I could tell from the way he paused and the way he looked that the word "kill" didn't taste sweet to him. When I was driving for a legger down home we had this old smoke working for us—he could turn out a mighty fine mash—and he said everybody's got to go—everybody. He said this is the one thing all men are fearful of most, and they invent all kinds of words so as not to say it. And preachers come along and say you'll be born again, and you grab at the preacher and give him money, though way down deep in your heart you know he's lying. Catholic, Baptist, Methodist, Jew—I don't care what, they all know nobody's going to be born again. When you're dead, man, you're dead. That's it. That's the end. That's what this old black kept telling me, and boy, was he right. That's the one thing in all of us—you, me, and everyone else in this world—and we're scared of dying, or even thinking about it. Look at you there, almost bare-ass naked with your cousy hanging out, and you think that's going to last forever? Baby, we're all getting out. Finally. We're all getting out. Why do you think I keep coming back to you and grabbing at you to get me out? Because you always get me out for a short time, and I always know I'm coming back. And somehow, and don't ask me how because I can't explain it or understand it, you get me out for a little while and then I come back, and it makes the big getting-out easier to take. The last getting-out. Like I might come back from that, too. I don't know. I can't figure it all—but that's what I think. I want to get out so I can forget the shit I have to eat every day, but also I want to get out like it's practice for what's coming. You know? And this poor, fat, rich East Side bitch I slap around, that's what she's looking for, too. Sure, maybe it's a kick and makes us forget how much crap we wade through every day, but maybe it convinces us that every little time we die—well, then, the big time is no different, and we'll come back from that, too. Which is a laugh. Isn't that a laugh, baby?

INGRID: Yes. That is a laugh.

ANDERSON: I didn't really come here for your advice. I came to tell you what I'm going to do. I'm going to kill this Parelli guy. I don't know who he is or what he is or how bad he needs killing. But whether I do it or a bolt of lightning strikes him tomorrow or twenty years from now, it's going to be done. But I'm going to kill him because maybe I can get a few clean years out of all this. And right now I'm so charged with blood and you sitting there with all your woman hanging out and staring at me, and I can taste the moment when I put that guy down, and what I'm going to do right now is get you out . . . maybe for the first time in your life.

INGRID: And how are you going to do that?

ANDERSON: I'll do it. I don't know how, but I'll do it. You've got all this crazy stuff around for your customers, haven't you? We'll do it with that if we have to. But we'll do it. I'm going to get you out, Ingrid. I swear it. . . .

INGRID: Yes?

37

X<small>EROX</small> <small>COPY</small> of a teletype dated 6 June, 1968.

TT-68-7946 . . . FR NYPD-PC . . . TO ALL DEP, INS, BOR AND
PRNCT CMDRS, CPTS, LTS, SGTS . . . FOR POSTING . . . REPEAT,
FOR POSTING . . . AS OF THIS DATE, NEW PCC (POLICE COMMUNI-
CATIONS CENTER) IS IN FULL OPER . . . EMRGNCY NMBR 911 . . .
KILL 440-1234 . . . ALL CMPLNTS TO 911 WILL BE FRWRD TO
PRNCT VIA TT OR TE . . . CMD OF CARS WITH PCC . . . CNFRM . . .
PC . . .

38

T<small>HIS</small> <small>IS</small> tape recording NYSITB-FD-15JUL68-437-6G; 15 JULY, 1968;
12:45 P.M.

SIMONS: Hello, Duke. Close that door quick. Let's not give any of this air
conditioning a chance to escape. Good to see you again.

ANDERSON: Hello, Mr. Simons. How you been?

SIMONS: Getting by, Duke, getting by. Can I offer you something?

ANDERSON: Not right now, Mr. Simons.

SIMONS: Well . . . you don't mind if I go ahead, do you? I have a luncheon
appointment in about half an hour, and I always find that a martini
sharpens the appetite.

ANDERSON: You go right ahead.

SIMONS: Well, now, Duke, what have you decided?

ANDERSON: Yes. It's all right.

SIMONS: You understand completely what you must do in regards to this
person from Detroit?

ANDERSON: Yes. I understand.

SIMONS: Excellent. Now then . . . let's get down to the fine print. This
person from Detroit will be our responsibility. That is, any payment to
him or to his heirs is our responsibility and its not part of any of the
financial arrangements which, I trust, you and I will soon agree upon. Is
that clear?

ANDERSON: Yes.

SIMONS: All expenses and advances will come off the top. In that
connection, if these terms are agreeable to you, I have with me and am
authorized to turn over to you the two thousand additional expense
funds you requested. Upon approval of the operational plan, we will
then turn over to you a sum sufficient for half payment of fees of the men
involved which, I understand, you estimated as four to five thousand
dollars. Is that correct?

ANDERSON: Yes. That's right. That's half their take.

SIMONS: Now then . . . when the final cash income is determined, all these
sums—advances, expenses, and salaries—will come off the top. Clear?

ANDERSON: That includes the final payment to my staff—the other half,
about four or five thousand to close them out?

SIMONS: That's correct. All such expenses will be subtracted first. We
anticipate no additional expenses other than those you have outlined. In

any event, we feel they will be so minor that they need not concern us at this time. Now then . . . we are down to the net income. We propose a fifty-fifty split.

ANDERSON: I asked for seventy-thirty.

SIMONS: I know you did, Duke. But under the circumstances, and considering the take may be considerably less than your most optimistic estimate, we feel a fifty-fifty split is justified. Especially in view of the moneys we have so far advanced.

ANDERSON: It's not right. Not when you figure what I'm going to do for you. I won't go for it.

SIMONS: Duke, we could sit here and argue for hours, but I know you don't want that any more than I do. I was instructed to offer you the fifty-fifty deal because we feel that is a fair and equitable arrangement, considering the risks involved and the cash outlay up to this point. Quite frankly, I must admit that Mr. Angelo—Little Pat, that is—he did not feel you would be satisfied with this. Therefore, I am authorized to propose a sixty-forty division. And that, Duke, I can tell you in all honesty is the best I can do. If that is not satisfactory, then you'll have to take up the entire matter with Mr. D'Medico or Mr. Angelo.

[Lapse of eighteen seconds.]

ANDERSON: Sixty for me, forty for you?

SIMONS: That is correct.

ANDERSON: And for this I put my cock on the line for a murder-one rap?

SIMONS: Duke, Duke . . . I wouldn't attempt to advise you, my boy. It's your decision to make, and you know the factors involved in it much better than I. All I can do is offer you the sixty-forty split. That's my job, and I'm doing it. Please don't be angry with me.

ANDERSON: I'm not angry with you, Mr. Simons. Or with Mr. D'Medico or Mr. Angelo. You got your job to do and I got mine. And I suppose you all got to answer to someone else.

SIMONS: We do indeed, Duke, we do indeed.

[Lapse of four seconds.]

ANDERSON: All right. I'll buy the sixty-forty.

SIMONS: Excellent. I'm sure you won't regret it. Here's the two thousand. Small bills. All clean. We'll make arrangements for Parelli to come in from Detroit. You'll be informed when he's available for planning. We think your idea of a hit on the Labor Day weekend is a good one. Meanwhile we'll see what we can do about getting you schedules of the two fifty-first Precinct and the Sector George cars. When you have your campaign firmed up, get in touch with me and I'll set up a meet for you with Mr. Angelo. I suggest you do this before you make a firm commitment to your staff. You understand? No use bringing them in until the whole thing is laid out. You agree?

ANDERSON: Yes.

SIMONS: Is everything clear now? I mean about money, and personnel, or anything else? If you have any questions, now is the time to ask them.

[Lapse of six seconds.]

ANDERSON: This Parelli—what did he do?

SIMONS: I don't know and I don't want to know. I suggest you cultivate the same attitude. Would you like something now?

ANDERSON: Yes. All right. A brandy.

SIMONS: Excellent, excellent. . . .

39

XEROX COPY of a letter dated 16 July, 1968, from United Electronics Kits, Inc., 65378 Michigan Boulevard, Chicago. Illinois, addressed to Mr. Gerald Bingham, Jr., Apartment 5A, 535 East Seventy-third Street, New York, New York.

> DEAR MR. BINGHAM:
>
> In reply to your letter of the 5th inst., please be advised that we have found your suggestion of considerable merit. Accordingly, we are modifying our Amplifier Kit 57-68A so that the back plate is easily removed (via screws) rather than soldered as at present. We are sure, as you suggest, that this will aid construction and servicing of the completed unit.
>
> We wish to express our appreciation for your interest, and we are, frankly, somewhat chagrined that our engineers did not spot this drawback to the 57-68A kit prior to its distribution. The fact that you are, as you say, fifteen years old, makes our chagrin more understandable!
>
> In any event, to express our appreciation for your suggestion in a more tangible form, we are forwarding to you (this date) a complimentary gift of our Deluxe 32-16895 Three-Speed Stereo Tape Deck Kit (no charge).
>
> Again—thank you for your kind interest in our products.
>
> Sincerely,
> [signed] DAVID K. DAVIDSON,
> *Director, Public Relations*

40

TAPE RECORDING FBN-DA-11036, Tuesday, 16 July, 1968, 2:36 P.M.

OPERATOR: I have a person-to-person call, Detroit. From Mr. Dominick Angelo of Deal, New Jersey, to Mr. Nicola D'Agostino at three-one-three, one-five-eight, eight-nine-seven-three.
OPERATOR: Just a moment, Operator.
OPERATOR: Thank you.
    [Lapse of fourteen seconds.]
OPERATOR: Is this three-one-one, one-five-eight, eight-nine-seven-three?
MALE VOICE: Yes.
OPERATOR: I have a person-to-person call for a Mr. Nicola D'Agostino from Mr. Dominick Angelo of Deal, New Jersey. Is Mr. D'Agostino there?
MALE VOICE: Just a minute, Operator.
OPERATOR: Thank you. Are you there, New Jersey?
OPERATOR: Yes, dear.
OPERATOR: Thank you. They're trying to find Mr. D'Agostino.
    [Lapse of eleven seconds.]
D'AGOSTINO: Hello?
OPERATOR: Mr. Nicola D'Agostino?
D'AGOSTINO: Yes.

OPERATOR: Just a moment, please, sir. Deal, New Jersey, calling. Go ahead, New Jersey. Mr. D'Agostino is on the line.

OPERATOR: Thank you, dear. Go ahead, Mr. Angelo. Mr. D'Agostino is on the line.

ANGELO: Hello? Hello, Toast?

D'AGOSTINO: Papa—is that you? How *nice* to hear your voice! How are you, Papa?

ANGELO: Getting along. Getting along. And how was Florida?

D'AGOSTINO: Magnificent, Papa. Gorgeous. You should move there. You'd live another hundred years.

ANGELO: God forbid. And the family?

D'AGOSTINO: Couldn't be better, Papa. Angelica asked about you. I told her you'd outlive us all.

ANGELO: And the children?

D'AGOSTINO: Fine, Papa, fine. Everyone is fine. Tony fell off his bike yesterday and broke his tooth—but it's nothing.

ANGELO: My God. You need a good dentist? I'll fly him out.

D'AGOSTINO: No, no, Papa. It's a baby tooth. We got a good dentist. He said it's nothing. Don't worry yourself.

ANGELO: Good. You have any trouble, you let me know.

D'AGOSTINO: I will, Papa. I will. Thank you for your interest. Believe me, Angelica and I, we appreciate it.

ANGELO: Toast, you remember when you were here, we discussed your problem?

D'AGOSTINO: Yes, Papa, I remember.

ANGELO: This problem, Toast—I think we can help you with it. I think we can solve it.

D'AGOSTINO: Believe me, I would appreciate that, Papa.

ANGELO: It would be a permanent solution. You understand, Toast?

D'AGOSTINO: I understand, Papa.

ANGELO: That is what you want?

D'AGOSTINO: That is what I want.

ANGELO: Good. It will work out well. You will send him to me as soon as possible. Within a week. Is that possible, Toast?

D'AGOSTINO: Of course.

ANGELO: Tell him only that it is a big job. You understand?

D'AGOSTINO: I understand, Papa. You will have him by Friday.

ANGELO: Good. Please give my love to Angelica. And to Auntie and Nick. And tell Tony I will send him a new bicycle. This one won't throw him off and break his tooth.

D'AGOSTINO [laughing]: Papa, you're too much! I love you. We all love you.

ANGELO: You keep well.

D'AGOSTINO: You too, Papa. You keep well—forever.

41

TRANSCRIPTION OF tape recording POM-20JUL68-EVERLEIGH. This recording began at 1:14 P.M., 20 July, 1968, and ended at 2:06 P.M., 21 July. It was recorded at Apartment 3B, 535 East Seventy-third Street. This tape has been heavily edited to eliminate extraneous conversations, names of innocent persons, and repetition of information already obtained from other sources. During the more than twenty-four-hour period mentioned above, it is not believed that Mrs. Agnes Everleigh and John Anderson left Apartment 3B.

SEGMENT I. 20JUL-1:48PM.
ANDERSON: . . . can't. I had last weekend off.
MRS. EVERLEIGH: You can call in sick, can't you? It's not the whole weekend. It's just tonight. You can be back at work tomorrow night. You get sick leave, don't you?
ANDERSON: Yes. Ten days a year.
MRS. EVERLEIGH: Have you taken any?
ANDERSON: No. Not since I been working there.
MRS. EVERLEIGH: So take tonight off. I'll give you fifty dollars.
ANDERSON: All right.
MRS. EVERLEIGH: You'll take the fifty?
ANDERSON: Yes.
MRS. EVERLEIGH: This is the first time you've ever taken money from me.
ANDERSON: How does it make you feel?
MRS. EVERLEIGH: You know . . . don't you?
ANDERSON: Yes. Go get the fifty. I'll make a call and tell them I'm sick.
MRS. EVERLEIGH: You'll stay with me? All night?
ANDERSON: Sure.

SEGMENT II. 20JUL-2:13PM
MRS. EVERLEIGH: I love you when you're like this—relaxed and nice and good to me.
ANDERSON: Am I good to you?
MRS. EVERLEIGH: So far. So far you've been a perfect gentleman.
ANDERSON: Like this?
MRS. EVERLEIGH: Must you? Must you do that?
ANDERSON: Sure. If I want to earn my fifty bucks.
MRS. EVERLEIGH: You're such a bastard.
ANDERSON: Honest. I'm honest.

SEGMENT III. 20JUL-5:26PM.
MRS. EVERLEIGH: . . . at least forty percent. How do you like that?
ANDERSON: Can they do it?
MRS. EVERLEIGH: You idiot, of course they can do it. This apartment is a cooperative. I'm not on the board. After my husband moved out, our lawyers got together and I agreed to pay the maintenance and he agreed to keep paying the mortgage. The apartment is in his name. Now they're going to increase the maintenance by at least forty percent.
ANDERSON: What are you going to do?
MRS. EVERLEIGH: I haven't decided yet. I'd move out tomorrow if I could find something better. But go look for an apartment on the East Side of Manhattan. These new places charge one hundred and eighty-five dollars for one room. I'll probably give them what they want and stay right here. Roll over.
ANDERSON: I've had enough.
MRS. EVERLEIGH: No you haven't.

SEGMENT IV. 20JUL-6:32PM.
MRS. EVERLEIGH: It depends on what you want. Feraccis has barbecued chicken or short ribs—stuff like that. It's a kind of a delicatessen. If we're going to cook, we can order up from Ernesto Brothers. We can get

frozen TV dinners or Rock Cornish hens or we can get a steak and pan fry or broil it—whatever you want.

ANDERSON: Let's have a chicken—a big chicken. Three pounds if they've got a fryer-broiler that size. We'll fry it. And maybe some French fried potatoes and greens.

MRS. EVERLEIGH: What kind of greens?

ANDERSON: Collards? They got collards?

MRS. EVERLEIGH: What are collards?

ANDERSON: Forget it. Just get us a big chicken we can fry and a lot of cold beer. How does that sound?

MRS. EVERLEIGH: That sounds scrumptious.

ANDERSON: Order it up. I'll pay for it. Here's fifty.

MRS. EVERLEIGH: You sonofabitch.

SEGMENT V. 20JUL-9:14PM.

ANDERSON: What are you going to do in Rome?

MRS. EVERLEIGH: The usual . . . see the new fall collections . . . visit some fag boutiques . . . buy some stuff . . . it's a drag.

ANDERSON: Like I said, I wish I could travel. All you need is money. Like this apartment house. You're going to Rome. Your neighbors are going down to the Jersey shore. I bet everyone in the house will be going somewhere on the Labor Day weekend—Rome, Jersey, Florida, France . . . somewhere. . . .

MRS. EVERLEIGH: Oh, sure. The Sheldons—they're up in Four A—they're already out in their place on Montauk. The people below me, a lawyer and his wife, will be out in East Hampton. Up on top in Five B, Longene and that bitch who's living with him—they're not married, you know—are sure to be invited some place for the Labor Day weekend. So the house will probably be about half full. That fag in Two A will probably be gone, too. What are you going to do?

ANDERSON: Work, probably. I get triple-time when I work nights on a holiday. I can make a lot of loot if I work over the Labor Day weekend.

MRS. EVERLEIGH: Will you think of me?

ANDERSON: Sure. There's one drumstick left. You want it?

MRS. EVERLEIGH: No, darling. You finish it.

ANDERSON: All right. I like drumsticks and wings and the Pope's nose. More than I do the breast. Dark meat got more flavor.

MRS. EVERLEIGH: Don't you like white meat at all?

ANDERSON: Maybe. Later.

SEGMENT VI. 21JUL-6:14AM.

ANDERSON [groaning]: Mammy . . . Mammy. . . .

MRS. EVERLEIGH: Duke? Duke? What is it, Duke?

ANDERSON: Mammy?

MRS. EVERLEIGH: Hush . . . hush. You're having a nightmare. I'm here, Duke.

ANDERSON: Mammy . . . Mammy. . . .

SEGMENT VII. 21JUL-8:56AM.

ANDERSON: Shit. You got a cigarette?

MRS. EVERLEIGH: There.

ANDERSON: Filters? Christ. These places around here—they're open on Sundays?

MRS. EVERLEIGH: Ernesto's is. What do you want?

ANDERSON: Cigarettes—to begin with. You mean this place is open on Sundays?

MRS. EVERLEIGH: Sure.

ANDERSON: Holidays too?

MRS. EVERLEIGH: They're open every day in the year, twenty-four hours a day. That's their brag. They have a sign in the window that says so. If you're pregnant you can get a dill pickle at three in the morning from Ernesto's. That's how they stay in business. They can't compete with the big supermarkets on First Avenue, like Lambreta Brothers. So they stay open every minute of the day and night.

ANDERSON: My God, don't they get held up?

MRS. EVERLEIGH: They sure do . . . about two or three times a month. But they keep open. It must pay off. Besides, doesn't insurance pay when you get robbed?

ANDERSON: I guess so. I don't know much about those things.

MRS. EVERLEIGH: Well, I'll call and have them deliver some cigarettes. It's about nine now. When do you have to go?

ANDERSON: Around two o'clock. Something like that.

MRS. EVERLEIGH: Well, suppose I order up some food for a little breakfast and some food for a dinner about noon. Like a steak and baked potatoes. How does that sound?

ANDERSON: That sounds all right.

MRS. EVERLEIGH: You're the most bubbling, enthusiastic man I've ever met.

ANDERSON: I don't understand that.

MRS. EVERLEIGH: Forget it.

42

THE FOLLOWING is labeled SEGMENT 101-B of document NYDA-EHM-101A-108B, a dictated, sworn, signed, and witnessed statement by Ernest Heinrich Mann.

MANN: So . . . we are now up to Twenty-sixth July. I remember it was on a Friday. On this date the man I know as John Anderson came to my shop and. . . .

QUESTION: What time was this?

MANN: It was perhaps one o'clock. Definitely after lunch. He came to my shop and asked to speak with me. So we went into the back room. There is a door there I can close and lock; we would not be disturbed. At this time, Anderson asked if I would be available for a job he had in mind.

QUESTION: What kind of a job?

MANN: He was most evasive. Very vague. Deliberately so, you understand. But I knew that it was to be in the apartment house I had already investigated for him. When I learned that, I asked him if he had determined the purpose of the cold room I had discovered in the basement of the house.

QUESTION: What did he say?

MANN: He said yes, he had discovered the purpose of the cold room.

QUESTION: Did he tell you what it was used for?

MANN: At this time, no. Later he told me. But at this meeting on July twenty-sixth he did not tell me and I did not ask further.

QUESTION: What kind of a job did John Anderson ask you to do for him?

MANN: Well . . . he did not actually ask me to do it. At this date he merely wanted to know if I was interested, if I would be available. He said the job would consist of cutting all telephone and alarm connections of the entire apartment house.

QUESTION: What else?

MANN: Well . . . of cutting the power supply to the self-service elevator.

QUESTION: What else?

MANN: Well . . . uh. . . .

QUESTION: Mr. Mann, you promised us complete cooperation. On the basis of that promise we agreed to offer you what assistance we could under the law. You understand, of course, we cannot offer you complete immunity?

MANN: Yes. I understand. Of course.

QUESTION: A great deal depends upon your attitude. What else did John Anderson ask you to do at this meeting on July twenty-six?

MANN: Well, as I told you, he did not actually ask. He was outlining a hypothetical situation, you understand. He was feeling me out, I believe you say. Determining my interest in an assignment.

QUESTION: Yes, yes, you've already said that. The assignment would include cutting all telephone and alarm connections of the apartment house in question, and perhaps cutting the power supply to the self-service elevator.

MANN: Yes. This is correct.

QUESTION: All right. Mr. Mann. You have now admitted to destruction of private property, a relatively minor offense. And perhaps breaking and entering. . . .

MANN: Oh no! No, no, no! Not breaking and entering. The premises were to be quite open when I arrived. I was to have nothing to do with that.

QUESTION: I see. And how much money were you offered for cutting the telephone and alarm connections, and for cutting the elevator power supply?

MANN: Well . . . we came to no definite agreement. You must realize we were talking generalities. There was no definite job, no definite assignment. This man Anderson merely wished to discover if I was interested and what my charge would be.

QUESTION: And what did you tell him your charge would be?

MANN: I suggested five thousand dollars.

QUESTION: Five thousand dollars? Mr. Mann, isn't that a rather large sum for cutting a few wires?

MANN: Well . . . perhaps . . . yes. . . .

QUESTION: All right. We've got as much time as you have. We'll try again. What else were you asked to do on this hypothetical assignment?

MANN: Well, you understand it was very indefinite. No arrangement was made.

QUESTION: Yes, yes, we understand that. What else did Anderson want you to do?

MANN: Well, there were, perhaps, some doors that would require unlocking. Also, perhaps, an upright safe and perhaps a wall safe. He wanted a technically trained man who understood those things.

QUESTION: Of course, Mr. Mann. And you understood those things?

MANN: But naturally! I am a graduate of the Stuttgarter Technische Hochschule, and served as assistant professsor in mechanical and electrical engineering at the Zurich Académie du Mécanique. I assure you, I am quite competent in my fields.

QUESTION: We are quite aware of that, sir. Now let's see if we've got all this straight. On July twenty-six, at about 1 P.M., John Anderson came to your shop at one-nine-seven-five Avenue D, New York City, and asked if you would be available for a job that might or might not materialize. This job would consist, on your part, of cutting telephone and alarm systems in a certain apartment house—location unspecified—of cutting the power supply to the self-service elevator in that house, of forcing open doors or picking the locks of doors in that house, and of opening safes of various types in the apartments of that house. Is that correct?

MANN: Well, I. . . .

QUESTION: Is that correct?

MANN: Please, may I have a glass of water?

QUESTION: Certainly. Help yourself.

MANN: Thank you. My throat is quite dry. I smoke so much. You have a cigarette perhaps?

QUESTION: Here.

MANN: Thank you again.

QUESTION: The statement I just repeated to you—is that correct?

MANN: Yes. That is correct. That is what John Anderson wanted me to do.

QUESTION: And for this you requested five thousand dollars?

MANN: Yes.

QUESTION: What was Anderson's reaction?

MANN: He said he could not pay that much, that his operating budget would not allow it. But he said, if the campaign was finalized, he was sure that he and I could get together in a mutually profitable agreement.

QUESTION: You used the term "if the campaign was finalized." Let me get this straight. Your impression is that on this date, the twenty-sixth of July, it had not yet been decided whether or not this job was actually on?

MANN: Yes, that was and is my impression.

QUESTION: Thank you. I think that's enough for today, Mr. Mann. I appreciate your cooperation.

MANN: I appreciate your kindness, sir.

QUESTION: We have much more to discuss about this affair. I'll be seeing you again, Mr. Mann.

MANN: I am at your service, sir.

QUESTION: Fine. Guard!

43

XEROX COPY of a letter dated 29 July, 1968, from the Public Information Officer, Department of Research & Development National Office of Space Studies, Washington, D.C. 20036, addressed to Mr. Gerald Bingham, Jr., Apartment 5A, 535 East Seventy-third Street, New York, New York.

DEAR SIR:

Re your letter of 16, May 1968, I have been instructed by the Director of the Department of Research & Development, National Office of Space Studies, to thank you for your interest in our activities, and for your suggestion of the use of solidified carbon dioxide ("dry ice") as an ablative material on the nose cones of rockets, space probes, and manned space vehicles during reentry into the Earth's atmosphere.

As you doubtlessly know, Mr. Bingham, a great deal of expensive research has been conducted in this area, and a wide variety of materials has been tested, ranging from metals and metal alloys to ceramics and ceramic-metal alloys. The material currently in use has been tested successfully in our Mercury, Gemini and Apollo programs.

I have been instructed to inform you that "dry ice" could not withstand the extremely high temperatures encountered during the reentry of heavy rockets and manned space vehicles.

However, your letter revealed a very high level of sophisticated scientific expertise, and the fact that you are, as you say, fifteen years old, is of great interest to us. As you probably know, the National Office of Space Studies has a number of college and university scholarship awards at its disposal. Within the next six months, a representative of our Scholarship Award Department will call upon you personally to determine your interest in this area.

Meanwhile, we wish to thank you again for your interest in our activities and your country's space program.

Cordially,
[signed] CYRUS ABERNATHY,
PIO, R&D

44

THE FOLLOWING tape recording was made on 13 August, 1968, beginning at 8:42 P.M. The participants, Patrick Angelo and John Anderson, have been identified by voice prints. The meeting was held in the upstairs study of Angelo's home at 10543 Foxberry Lane, a few miles north of Teaneck, New Jersey.

These premises were under electronic surveillance by the Federal Trade Commission, and had been for several months, in a continuing investigation of the interlocking business holdings of Patrick Angelo. The investigation concerned possible violations of the Sherman Anti-Trust Act.

There were several time gaps during the course of this recording, which technicians were unable to explain. The tape recording mechanism checked out; the experts were inclined to believe the fault lay with the SC-7, MK.II M-T, a relatively new device that may possible have been affected by atmospheric conditions. It had rained heavily prior to the meeting recorded below, and during the meeting the skies were overcast and humidity was very high.

This is recording FTC-KLL-13AUG68-1701.

ANGELO: . . . like cognac?

ANDERSON: Yes. That's all I drink—brandy.

ANGELO: Then you're going to like this. It's a small importer, maybe a thousand cases a year. I must buy two hundred of them. I drink a lot of the stuff and I give it for gifts. A guy in Teaneck orders it for me. Close to twenty a bottle. There you are. Want a wash?

ANDERSON: No. This is fine.

[Lapse of four seconds.]

ANDERSON: Jesus, that's good. I don't know whether to drink it or breathe it. That's really good.

ANGELO: Glad you like it. And no head in the morning. I keep Papa supplied. He drinks maybe a bottle a month. A thimbleful before he goes to sleep.

ANDERSON: Better than pills.

ANGELO: That's for sure. You met Parelli?

ANDERSON: Yes.

ANGELO: What do you think of him?

ANDERSON: I hardly talked to him. I hardly *saw* him. We were in the steam room of that health club the Doc's got on West Forty-eight Street.

ANGELO: I know, I know. What do you think of him?

ANDERSON: Heavy muscle. A mutt.

ANGELO: A mutt? Yeah, he's that all right. Not too much brains.

ANDERSON: I figured that.

ANGELO: Look, Duke, you're doing us a favor. So I'll do you one. The guy's crazy. Know what I mean? He likes to blast, to hurt people. He packs one of these big army automatics. What does it weigh—about ten pounds?

ANDERSON: Not that much. But it's heavy.

ANGELO: Yes, and big and mean. He loves it. You've met guys like that before. It's their cock.

ANDERSON: Yes.

ANGELO: Well, don't turn your back on him . . . you know?

ANDERSON: I know. Thanks.

ANGELO: All right . . . now what have you got for me?

ANDERSON: I got this report here. Handwritten. Just this one copy. It's how we should do it. I'm not saying it's final, but we got to start someplace. This includes what I learned since I saw you last. I've had my guys working. I know there will be changes—you'll probably want to change things—and we'll be changing things right up to the last minute . . . you know, little adjustments like. But I think the main plan is strong.

ANGELO: Did the Doctor get those police schedules to you?

ANDERSON: Yes, he did. Thanks. I had the Brodsky boys checking out the beat fuzz on my own. Everything cleared. It's all worked into the report. You want to read it now, or you want me to leave it and come back in a day or so?

ANGELO: I'll read it now. Time's getting short. We got less than three weeks.

ANDERSON: Yes.

ANGELO: Help yourself to the cognac while I read this thing. You write a nice, clear, plain hand.

ANDERSON: Thanks. Maybe my spelling ain't so great. . . .

ANGELO: It's all right. No problem. . . .

[Lapse of seven minutes twenty-three seconds, followed by sound of door opening.)

MRS. ANGELO: Pat? Oh, I'm sorry, you're busy.

ANGELO: That's all right, Maria . . . Come in, come in. Darling, this is John Anderson, a business associate. Duke, this is my wife.

MRS. ANGELO: How do you do, Mr. Anderson.

ANDERSON: Pleased to make your acquaintance, ma'am.

MRS. ANGELO: Is my husband taking care of you? I see you have a little drink. Would you like something to eat? Are you hungry? We have some cold chicken. Perhaps a sandwich?

ANDERSON: Oh, no thank you, ma'am. I'm fine.

MRS. ANGELO: Some short cookies. We have some delicious butter cookies.

ANDERSON: Ma'am, thank you kindly, I do appreciate it, but I'll just stick with this drink.

MRS. ANGELO: Pat, Stella is in bed. You want to say good night?

ANGELO: Of course. Duke, excuse me a moment, please.

ANDERSON: Sure, Mr. Angelo.

ANGELO: And when I come back, I'm bringing some of those butter cookies. My wife makes them herself. You couldn't buy them.

[Lapse of four minutes thirteen seconds.]

ANGELO: Here . . . help yourself. They're delicious. Look at the gut I got, you'll realize how many I eat.

ANDERSON: Thanks.

ANGELO: Now let's see . . . where was I. . . . Yeah, here we are. Duke, you got nice manners. I appreciate that. Now let's see. . . .

[Lapse of six minutes eighteen seconds.]

ANGELO: Duke, I got to hand it to you. Generally, I think . . . my God, no more cognac? Well, let's get rid of this dead soldier. Then we'll go over your operational plan step by step and. . . .

[Lapse of eighteen minutes nine seconds.]

ANGELO: . . . we are. Just take a sniff of that bottle.

ANDERSON: Great.

ANGELO: You're ready for another? I can see you are. So all we got is a lot of little disagreements and small details that really don't amount to much. Am I right?

ANDERSON: As long as you okay the main plan.

ANGELO: Sure. It's strong. Like I said, we can help you out with the truck. That's no problem. About the diversions—you may be right. They got these tactical squads of buttons these days—they load them into buses and before you know it, *bam*! Maybe we'd be asking for trouble. Let me talk to Papa about it.

ANDERSON: But otherwise it sounds good?

ANGELO: Yes, it sounds good. I like the idea of half the people being away on that weekend. How many on your staff?

ANDERSON: Five, With me, six. With Parelli, seven.

ANGELO: My God, you'll have them outnumbered!

ANDERSON: Just about.

ANGELO: Well, go ahead. Contact Fred Simons tomorrow and arrange to get the first half of the emolument for your personnel.

ANDERSON: Emolument?

ANGELO: It means fees or salary.

ANDERSON: Oh . . . yeah.

ANGELO: So now you can have your first real recruiting meeting. Right? You can bring them all together and get down to business. Right? This had got to include Parelli. You know how to get in touch with him?

ANDERSON: Through Simons or the Doctor. Not directly.

ANGELO: That's right. Fred will keep you in touch with him. I would also like to talk to you about once a week, at least, until D-Day. Out here. Is that a problem?

ANDERSON: I rented a car. I shouldn't be leaving the state, but I don't figure the risk is too much.

ANGELO: I agree. All right. You get the money from Simons. At the same time you contact Parelli through him and set up a meet with your other people. I'll start working on the truck. I'll talk to Papa about the diversions. You get that map to me—the one the Brodsky boys made. Come on . . . let's get rolling on this thing!

ANDERSON: Yes. We're coming down to the line. . . .
ANGELO: Jesus Christ, I'm really getting excited! Duke, I think you can pull it off.
ANDERSON: Mr. Angelo, I've been living with this thing for four months now, and I just can't see what could go wrong.

45

TAPE SEC-16AUG68-IM-11:43AM-198C. New York City. This is a telephone interception.

ANDERSON: Hello? Ingrid?
INGRID: Yes. Duke? Is that you?
ANDERSON: Can I talk?
INGRID: Of course.
ANDERSON: I got your card.
INGRID: It was a silly idea. A little-girl idea. You will laugh at me.
ANDERSON: What is it?
INGRID: Tomorrow, Saturday, do you work?
ANDERSON: Yes.
INGRID: You must be there by four o'clock you said?
ANDERSON: About.
INGRID: I would like . . . what I would like. . . . You will laugh at me, Duke.
ANDERSON: For Jesus' sake, will you tell me what it is?
INGRID: I would like us to go on a picnic.
ANDERSON: A *picnic*?
INGRID: Yes. Tomorrow, In Central Park. If the weather is nice. The radio states the weather will be nice. I will bring some cold fried chicken, potato salad, tomatoes, peaches, grapes—things like that. You will bring a bottle of wine for me and perhaps a bottle of brandy for yourself, if you so desire. Duke? What do you think?
    [Lapse of five seconds.]
INGRID: Duke?
ANDERSON: That's fine. A good idea. Let's do it. I'll bring the stuff to drink. When should I pick you up—about eleven?
INGRID: Excellent. Yes, about eleven. Then we can stay in the park and have our lunch until you must leave. You know a good place?
ANDERSON: Yes. There's a little spit of land that sticks out into the lake at Seventy-second Street. Not too crowded but easy to get to. It's really a turn-around for cars, but the grass slopes down to the lake. It's nice.
INGRID: Good. Duke, if you bring a bottle of wine for me, I would like something chilled.
ANDERSON: All right.
INGRID: And please, do not forget the corkscrew.
ANDERSON: And please, do not forget the salt.
INGRID [laughing]: Duke, it will be fun for us. I have not been on a picnic in many years.
ANDERSON: Yes. I'll see you tomorrow at eleven.

46

ACTING ON internal evidence contained in the preceding recording, the SEC requested the cooperation of the New York Parks, Recreation and Cultural Affairs Administration. With the help of this agency, a Borkgunst Telemike Mk. IV (a telescopic microphone) was concealed in wooded high ground overlooking the site of the proposed picnic of John Anderson and Igrid Macht on 17 August, 1968.

The following recording is SEC-17AUG68-#146-37A. It has been heavily edited to eliminate extraneous material and evidence currently under adjudication.

SEGMENT I. 17 AUG-11:37AM

ANDERSON: This was a great idea. Beautiful day. Clear for a change. Not too hot. Look at that sky! Looks like someone washed it and hung it out to dry.

INGRID: I remember a day like this. I was just a little girl. Eight, perhaps, or nine. An uncle took me on a picnic. My father was dead. My mother was working. So this uncle offered to take me to the country for the day. A Saturday, just like this. Sunshine. Blue sky. Cool breeze. Sweet smells. He gave me some schnapps, and then he pulled my pants down.

ANDERSON: Some uncle.

INGRID: He was all right. A widower. In his late forties. Perhaps fifty. He had a great Kaiser Wilhelm mustache. I remember it tickled.

ANDERSON: Did you like it?

INGRID: It meant nothing to me. Nothing.

ANDERSON: Did he give you something, a gift, so you wouldn't talk?

INGRID: Money. He gave me money.

ANDERSON: Was that his idea or yours?

INGRID: That was my idea. My mother and I, we were always hungry.

ANDERSON: Smart kid.

INGRID: Yes. I was a smart kid.

ANDERSON: How long did that go on?

INGRID: A few years. I took him for much.

ANDERSON: Sure. Did your mother know?

INGRID: Perhaps. Perhaps not. I think she did.

ANDERSON: What happened?

INGRID: To my uncle?

ANDERSON: Yes.

INGRID: A horse kicked him and he died.

ANDERSON: That's funny.

INGRID: Yes. But it made no difference. I was then ten, perhaps eleven. I knew then how it was done. There were others. *Schatzie*, the wine! It will be getting warm.

SEGMENT II. 17AUG-12:20PM.

ANDERSON: What then?

INGRID: You will not believe.

ANDERSON: I'll believe it.

INGRID: For an example, there was this man in Bavaria. Very rich. Very important. If I said his name, you would recognize it. Once a month, on a Friday night, his butler would assemble perhaps six, perhaps ten young girls. I was just thirteen. We would be naked. The butler would put feathers in our hair and tie belts of feathers about our waists and make us wear bracelets of feathers around our wrists and ankles. Then this man, this very important man, would sit on a chair, quite naked, and he would play with himself. You understand? And we would dance around him in a circle. We would flap our arms and caw and make bird sounds. Like chickens. You understand? And this funny butler with gray whiskers would clap his hands to mark time and chant, "One and two, and one and two," and we would dance around and caw, and this old man would look at us and our feathers and play with himself.

ANDERSON: Did he ever touch you?

INGRID: Never. When he was finished with himself, he rose and stalked out. We would remove our feathers, and we would dress. The butler stood by the door and paid us our money as we walked out. Very good money. The next month we'd be back again. Perhaps the same girls, perhaps a few new ones. Same thing.

ANDERSON: How do you figure his hangup?

INGRID: I don't. I gave up trying many years ago. People are what they are. This I can accept. But I cannot accept what they pretend to be. This man who fondled himself while I pranced about him clad in chicken feathers, this man attended church every Sunday, contributed to charities, and was—still is—considered one of the leading citizens of his city and his country. His son is also now very important. At first it all sickened me.

ANDERSON: The chicken feathers?

INGRID: The filth! The filth! Then I learned how the world is run. Who has the power. What money can do. So I declared war on the world. My own personal war.

ANDERSON: Have you won?

INGRID: I am winning, *Schatzie*.

SEGMENT III. 17 AUG-12:41PM.

ANDERSON: It could have been different.

INGRID: Perhaps. But we are mostly what has happened to us, what the world has done to us. We cannot always make the choice. By the time I was fifteen I was an accomplished whore. I had stolen, blackmailed, had been terribly beaten several times, and I had marked a pimp. Still, I was a child. I had no education. I tried only to survive, to have food, a place to sleep. At that time I wanted very little. Perhaps that is why we are so *simpatico*. You were poor also . . . *nein*?

ANDERSON: Yes. My family was white niggers.

INGRID: Understand, *Schatzie*, I make no excuses. I did what I had to do.

ANDERSON: Sure. But after you got older . . . ?

INGRID: I learned very quickly. As I told you, I learned where the money was and where the power was. Then there was nothing I would not do. It was war—total war. I hit back. Then I hit first. That is very important. The only crime in this world is to be poor. That is the only crime. If you are not poor, you can do anything.

SEGMENT IV. 17AUG-12:08PM.

ANDERSON: Sometimes you scare me.

INGRID: Why is that, *Schatzie*? I mean no bad to you.

ANDERSON: I know, I know. But you never get out. You live with it every minute.

INGRID: I have tried everything—alcohol, drugs, sex. Nothing works for me. I must live with it every minute—so I do. Now I live quietly. I have a warm home. Food. I have money invested. Safe money. Men pay me. You know that?

ANDERSON: Yes.
INGRID: I have stopped wanting. It is very important to know when to stop wanting.
ANDERSON: Don't you ever want to get out?
INGRID: It would be nice—but if I cannot, I cannot.
   [Lapse of seven seconds.]
ANDERSON: You're some woman.
INGRID: It is my occupation, *Schatzie*. It is not my sex.

SEGMENT V. 17AUG-2:14PM.
INGRID: It has been a beautiful afternoon. Are you drunk?
ANDERSON: A little.
INGRID: We must go soon. You must go to work.
ANDERSON: Yes.
INGRID: Are you sleeping?
ANDERSON: Some. . . .
INGRID: Shall I talk to you . . . the way you like?
ANDERSON: Yes. Do *you* like it?
INGRID: Of course.

SEGMENT VI. 17AUG-3:03PM.
INGRID: Please, *Schatzie*, we must go. You will be late.
ANDERSON: Sure. All right. I'll clean up. You finish the wine; I'll finish the brandy.
INGRID: Very well.
ANDERSON: I would like to tell you what I am doing.
INGRID: Please . . . no.
ANDERSON: You're the smartest woman I ever knew. I'd like to get your opinion, what you think of it.
INGRID: No . . . nothing. Tell me nothing. I do not wish to know.
ANDERSON: It's big.
INGRID: It is always big. It will do no good to tell you to be careful, I know. Just do what you must do.
ANDERSON: I can't pull out now.
INGRID: I understand.
ANDERSON: Will you kiss me?
INGRID: Now? Yes. On the lips?

47

TAPE BN-DT-TH-0018-98G; 19 August, 1968; 11:46 A.M.

HASKINS: Was that what you wanted?
ANDERSON: Fine, It was fine, Tommy. More than I expected.
HASKINS: Good. Some day I'll tell you how I got those floor plans. It was a gas!
ANDERSON: You want in?
HASKINS: In? On the whole hype?
ANDERSON: Yes.
   [Lapse of five seconds.]
HASKINS: How much?
ANDERSON: A fee. Two big ones.

HASKINS: Two? That's a bit skimpy, isn't it, darling?
ANDERSON: It's what I can go. I got six guys to think about.
HASKINS: Are you including Snapper?
ANDERSON: No.
HASKINS: I don't know . . . I don't know. . . .
ANDERSON: Make up your mind.
HASKINS: Are you anticipating . . . well, you know . . . violence?
ANDERSON: No. More than half will be out of the house.
HASKINS: You don't want me to carry . . . ?
ANDERSON: No. Just to spot for me. Finger what to take and what to leave.
The paintings, the rugs, the silver—shit like that.
[Lapse of four seconds.]
HASKINS: When would I be paid?
ANDERSON: Half before, half after.
HASKINS: I've never done anything like this before.
ANDERSON: A piece of cheese. Nothing to worry about. We'll take out time.
The whole fucking place will be ours. Two, three hours . . . whatever it
takes.
HASKINS: Will we wear masks?
ANDERSON: Are you in?
HASKINS: Yes.
ANDERSON: All right. I'll let you know later this week when we all get
together. It's going to be all right, Tommy.
HASKINS: Oh, God. Oh, Jesus.

48

21 AUGUST, 1968; 12:15 P.M. Tape NYSNB-49B-767 (continuing).

ANDERSON: You want in?
JOHNSON: Who do I bash and what's the cash?
ANDERSON: Two big ones, half in advance.
JOHNSON: Gimme your han' 'cause you're my man.
ANDERSON: I'll be in touch to tell you where and when. Keep clean for the
next two weeks. Can you do that?
JOHNSON: You gotta know. Like the driven snow.
ANDERSON: Don't fuck me up, Skeets. Or I'll have to come looking for you.
You know?
JOHNSON: Aw, now, Massa Anderson, you wouldn't be trying to skeer this
pore, ignorant ole nigguh, would you now?

49

TRANSCRIPTION NYPD-JDA-154-11; 22 August, 1968; 1:36 P.M. A telephone interception.

ANDERSON: Ed?
BRODSKY: Duke?
ANDERSON: Yes.

BRODSKY: Was everything all right? Was that what you wanted?

ANDERSON: Fine, Ed. Just right. The map was great.

BRODSKY: Jesus, that's good to hear. I mean we worked, Duke. We really sweat.

ANDERSON: I know you did, Ed. I liked it. The man liked it. Everything is set. You want in?

BRODSKY: Me? Or me and Billy?

ANDERSON: Both of you. Two G's. No shares. Just a fee. Half in advance.

BRODSKY: Yes. Christ, yes! I need it, Duke. You got no idea how I need it. The sharks are at me.

ANDERSON: I'll be in touch.

BRODSKY: Thank you very much, Duke.

50

ANDERSON'S APARTMENT; an interior conversation. Transcription NYPD-JDA-155-23; 23 August, 1968. Participants John Anderson and Vincent "Socks" Parelli have been identified by voice prints.

PARELLI: Jesus Christ, a guy could get a heart attack climbing those fucking stairs. You really live in this shit-house?

ANDERSON: That's right.

PARELLI: An you got to make a meet here? It couldn't be a nice restaurant in Times Square? A hotel room maybe?

ANDERSON: This place is clean.

PARELLI: How do you know? How does anyone know? Maybe one of your rats is wired. Maybe your cockroaches been trained. Hey! How about that! Trained bugs! Not bad, huh?

ANDERSON: Not bad.

PARELLI: What I'm saying is, why have me drag my ass all the way over here? What's so important?

ANDERSON: This is the way I wanted it.

PARELLI: All right, all right. So you're the boss. Big deal. We agreed. I take orders. Okay, boss, what's the setup?
  [Lapse of six seconds.]

ANDERSON: We have our first meet tomorrow night, eight thirty. Here's the address. Don't lose it.

PARELLI: Tomorrow? Eight thirty? For Christ's sake, tomorrow's Saturday. Who the hell works on Saturday?

ANDERSON: We meet tomorrow, like I said.

PARELLI: Not me, buster. I can't make it. I'm getting a blow-job at eight. Include me out.

ANDERSON: You want out of the whole thing?

PARELLI: No, I don't want out of the whole thing. But I. . . .

ANDERSON: I'll tell Mr. Angelo you can't make the meet tomorrow because some quiff is going to give you head. Okay?

PARELLI: You suck, you bastard. When this is all over, you and me, we'll have our own meet. Somewhere. Someday.

ANDERSON: Sure. But you be at that meet tomorrow.

PARELLI: All right, all right . . . I'll be there.

ANDERSON: I got five guys, plus you and me. There's a smart fag who can finger the good stuff. He knows paintings and jewelry and silver. His name's Haskins. I got a tech named Ernest Mann. He'll cut off the telephones and alarms, open the doors and boxes—whatever we need. Then there's a spade named Johnson, a muscle, but smart. He's no hooligan. Then there's two brothers—Ed and Billy Brodsky. Ed is an all-round man, a good driver. His young brother Billy, he's a wet-brain but he's a powerhouse. We need a guy for lifting and carrying. Billy will do what he's told.

PARELLI: Any of them panic guys?

ANDERSON: Tommy Haskins maybe. The others are solid—real pros.

PARELLI: I'll keep my eye on Haskins.

ANDERSON: You do that. Socks, I don't want no blasting. There's no need. Half the families will be gone. No one left but old women and kids. We got a plan that's been figured four ways from the middle. You'll hear it tomorrow. Everything will go like silk.

PARELLI: I carry a stick. That's definite.

ANDERSON: All right, you carry a stick. Just don't use it—that's all I'm saying.

PARELLI: I hear you work clean.

ANDERSON: That's right.

PARELLI: I still carry.

ANDERSON: I told you, that's up to you—but you'll have no call to use it. You won't need it.

PARELLI: We'll see.

ANDERSON: Another thing—I don't want these people slammed around. You understand?

PARELLI: Oh, I'll be very polite, boss.

[Lapse of five seconds.]

ANDERSON: And I don't like you, prick-nose. But I'm stuck with you. I needed another body and they gave me a sack of shit like you.

PARELLI: You fuck! You fuck! I could burn you! I should burn you right now!

ANDERSON: Go ahead, prick-nose. You're the guy who carries a stick. I got nothing. Go ahead, burn me.

PARELLI: Oh, you lousy fuck! You piece of funk! I swear to Christ, when this is over I'll get you good. But good! Nice and slow. That's what you'll get, cracker. Something nice and slow, right through the balls. Oh, are you going to get it! I can taste it. I can taste it!

ANDERSON: Sure, you can taste it. You got a big, fucking mouth—and that's all you've got. Just you be at that meet tomorrow, and at the other meets until next Saturday.

PARELLI: And after that, white trash, it'll be you and me . . . just you and me.

ANDERSON: That's right, prick-nose. How many women you screwed with that snout? Now get your ass out of here. Be careful getting a cab. We got some punks in this neighborhood—oh, maybe ten years old or so— who might take your piece away from you.

PARELLI: You mother. . . .

51

THE DRIVEWAY outside Patrick Angelo's home, 10543 Foxberry Lane, Teaneck, New Jersey; 25 August, 1968; 8:36 P.M. On this date, Angelo's "personal" car (he owned three) was under electronic surveillance by an investigative agency of the U.S. government, which cannot be named at this time, using a device which cannot be revealed. The car was a black Continental license LPA-46B-8935K. Patrick Angelo and John Anderson sat in the back seat of the parked car.

ANGELO: Sorry I can't ask you into the house, Duke. The wife's got some neighbors in tonight for bridge. I figured we could talk better out here.

ANDERSON: Sure, Mr. Angleo. This is okay.

ANGELO: But I brought out some of this cognac you like and a couple of glasses. We might as well be comfortable. Here you are. . . .

ANDERSON: Thanks.

ANGELO: Success.

ANDERSON: Luck.

[Lapse of four seconds.]

ANGELO: Beautiful. Jesus, that's like music on the tongue. Duke, I heard you leaned on our boy the other day.

ANDERSON: Parelli? Yes, I leaned on him. He tell you?

ANGELO: He told D'Medico. The Doc told me. What are you doing—setting him up?

ANDERSON: Something like that.

ANGELO: You figured he's got a short fuse as it is—and not too much brains—so you'll psych him. Now he's so sore at you he's not even using the little brains he's got. So you're that much more on top of him.

ANDERSON: I guess that's it.

[Lapse of seven seconds.]

ANGELO: Or was it you wanted to hate his guts so it would be easier to spoil him?

ANDERSON: What difference does it make?

ANGELO: None, Duke. None at all. I'm just running off at the mouth. You had your first meet yesterday?

ANDERSON: That's right.

ANGELO: How did it go?

ANDERSON: It went fine.

ANGELO: Any weak spots?

ANDERSON: The faggot, Tommy Haskins, has never done a hard job before. He's been on the con or hustling his ass or pulling paper hypes. But his job is easy. I'll keep an eye on him. Johnson—he's the dinge—and the two Brodsky boys are true blue. Hard. The tech, Ernest Mann, is so money hungry he'll do what I tell him. If he's caught, he'll spill, of course. All they'll have to do is threaten to take his cigarettes away.

ANGELO: But he's not going to be caught . . . is he?

ANDERSON: No. Parelli is stupid and vicious and kill-crazy. A bad combination.

ANGELO: You'll have to play that guy by ear. I told you . . . don't turn your back.

ANDERSON: I don't figure to. I gave my boys their advances.

ANGELO: Do they know what everyone is getting?

ANDERSON: No. I gave them sealed envelopes separately. I told each guy he was getting more than the others and to keep his mouth shut.

ANGELO: Good.

ANDERSON: Did you ask about the diversions?

ANGELO: Papa says forget it. Keep it as simple as possible. He says it's tricky enough as it is.

ANDERSON: He's right. I'm glad about that. Can you tell me about the truck now?

ANGELO: Not now. When we meet on Thursday.

ANDERSON: All right. The Brodsky boys will pick it up wherever you say. It'll be in New York, won't it?

ANGELO: Yes. In Manhattan.

ANDERSON: Fine. Then we can figure out our final timing. What about the drop?

ANGELO: I'll give you that on Thursday, too. How many men will make the drop?

ANDERSON: I was figuring on me and the Brodsky boys.

ANGELO: All right. Now let's see . . . what else did I want to ask. . . . Oh, yes . . . do you need a piece?

ANDERSON: I can get one. I don't know how good it will be.

ANGELO: Let me get you a good one. Right off the docks. When your boys pick up the truck, it'll be in the glove compartment or taped under the dash. Loaded. How does that sound?

ANDERSON: That sounds all right.

ANGELO: A .38 okay?

ANDERSON: Yes.

ANGELO: I'll see it's taken care of. Now let's see . . . oh, yes, the masks. You got all that fixed? Gloves . . . shit like that?

ANDERSON: It's all arranged, Mr. Angelo.

ANGELO: Good. Well, I can't think of anything else. I'll see you on Thursday, then. Your second meet is on Wednesday and your last on Friday?

ANDERSON: Yes.

ANGELO: How do you feel?

ANDERSON: I feel great. I'm hot with this thing but I got no doubts.

ANGELO: Duke . . . remember one thing. This is like war. Your reconnaissance and intelligence and operations plan can be the best in the world. But things go wrong. Unexpected things come up. Somebody screams. A rabbit becomes a lion. The fuzz drops by unexpected because one of them has to take a pee. Sometimes crazy things happen—things you never counted on. You know?

ANDERSON: Yes.

ANGELO: So you've got to stay loose in there. You got a good plan, but be ready to improvise, to deal with these unexpected things as they come up. Don't get spooked when something happens you didn't figure on.

ANDERSON: I won't get spooked.

ANGELO: I know you won't. You're a pro, Duke. That's why we're going along with you on this. We trust you.

ANDERSON: Thanks.

52

Dictated, signed, sworn, and witnessed statement by Timothy O'Leary, 648 Halverston Drive, Roslyn, New York. This is transcription NYPD-SIS-#146-11, dated 7 September, 1968.

"On the night of thirty-one August of this year—that is, the night it was between the last day of August and the first of September, with Labor Day to come, it was that weekend—I come on duty at 535 East Seventy-third Street where I am a doorman from midnight until eight in the morning.

"Being my usual custom, I arrived on the premises about ten minutes early, stopped to exchange the time of night with Ed Bakely, the lad I was relieving, and then I went down into the basement. There we have three lockers in the hallway that leads from the super's apartment to the back basement rooms where are the boilers and such. I changed to my uniform which, in the summer, is merely a tan cotton jacket, and as I was wearing black pants, white shirt, and a black bow tie, the time was nothing.

"I come back upstairs and Ed goes down, to change back. Whilst he was gone, I took a look at the board where it is we keep messages and such. I saw that Dr. Rubicoff, he's One B, was in his office and working late. And also there would be two friends of Eric Sabine, he's Two A, staying in his apartment for the Labor Day weekend. Ed, then, came up—he was carrying his bowling ball in a little bag—and said he was off to his alley, and would be able to get in a few games with his mates before the alleys closed.

"No sooner was he gone, with me out on the street taking a breath of air, when a truck came slowly down the street—yes, from East End Avenue since that is how the street runs. Much to my surprise it made a slow turn and pulled into our service entrance, going all the way to the back where it stopped, and turned off motor and lights. As it went past me I saw it was a moving van of some kind—I remember seeing the word 'moving' painted on the side and surmised it either had the wrong address or perhaps some of my tenants was moving or was expecting a furniture delivery of some kind which struck me as strange considering the time of night it was and also, you understand, we would have it on the board if some tenant was expecting a night delivery.

"So I strolled back to where the truck was now parked and dark, and I says, 'And what the hell do you think you are doing in my driveway?'

"No sooner was these words out of my mouth when I felt something on the back of my neck. Cool it was, metal and round. It could have been a piece of pipe, I suppose, but I surmised it was a gun. I was twenty years on the Force, and I am no stranger to guns.

"At the same time I felt the muzzle on my neck—a crawly feeling it was—the man holding the gun says, very cool, 'Do you want to die.?'

"'No,' I tells him, 'I do not want to die.' I was calm, you understand, but I was honest.

"'Then you will do just what I tell you,' he says, 'and you will not die.'

"With that he walks me back to the service door, kind of prodding me with the muzzle of the gun, if that's what it was, and I think it was, but not hurting me, you understand. All this time the truck was dark and quiet and I saw no other men. In fact, up to this time I had actually seen no one. Just felt the gun and heard the voice.

"He had me stand pressed face-up against the wall by the service door, the muzzle of the gun still in the middle of my neck. 'Not a sound from you,' he says.

"'Not a sound you'll get,' I whispers to him.

"'All right,' he calls, and I hear the doors of the truck opening. Two doors open. In a minute I hear a rattle of chain and the sound of a tailgate flopping down. I saw nothing, nothing at all. I stared at the wall and said 'Hail, Marys.' I had the feeling others were standing about, but I turned my head neither to the right nor to the left. I heard footsteps walking away. All was quiet. No one spoke. In a moment I heard the buzzer and knew that someone inside the lobby was pressing the button that released the lock on the service door.

"I was prodded forward into the service entrance, the gun still at my neck, and told to lay on the concrete floor, which I did although I was sorry for soiling my uniform jacket and my trousers which my wife Grace had pressed that very afternoon. I was told to cross my ankles and cross my wrists behind me. I did all this, just as I was told, but at this time I switched to 'Our Father, Who art in Heaven. . . .'

"They used what I guess was a wide strip of adhesive tape. I could hear that sound of sticking as it came off the reel. They taped my ankles and my wrists, and then a strip was put across my mouth.

"At this time, the man—I think he was the man with the gun—he says to me, 'Can you breathe okay? If you can breathe okay, nod your head.'

"So I nodded my head and blessed him for his consideration."

53

THE FOLLOWING is from a dictated, sworn, signed, and witnessed statement by Ernest Heinrich Mann. This is Segment NYDA-EHM-105A.

MANN: So . . . now we are at the night of August thirty-first and the morning hours of September first. The truck picked me up at the appointed place and I. . . .

QUESTION: Pardon me a moment. I believe you told us previously that the truck was to pick you up on the southeast corner of Lexington Avenue and Sixty-fifth Street. Is that correct?

MANN: Yes. Correct.

QUESTION: And that was, in fact, where you joined the others?

MANN: Yes.

QUESTION: What time was this?

MANN: It was eleven forty P.M. This was the time agreed upon. I was on time and so also was the truck.

QUESTION: Will you describe this truck for us.

MANN: It was, I would say, a medium-sized moving van. In addition to the doors to the cab, there were two large rear doors fastened with a chained tailgate, as well as a door in the middle of each side. It was by one of these doors that I entered the truck, the men inside assisting me to climb up.

QUESTION: How many men were in the truck at this time?

MANN: Everyone was there—everyone I have described to you who was at the planning meetings. The man I know as Anderson and the two men I know as Ed and Billy were in the cab. Ed was driving. The others were in the body of the truck.

QUESTION: What was painted on the side of the truck? Did you notice any words or markings?

MANN: I saw only the word "Moving." There were also several markings that appeared to be license numbers and maximum load weights—things of that sort.

QUESTION: After you boarded the truck, what happened?

MANN: The truck began to move. I assumed we were heading for the apartment house.

QUESTION: Were you standing inside the truck or were you seated?

MANN: We were seated, but not on the floor. A rough wooden bench had been provided on one side of the truck. We sat on that. Also, there was a light inside the truck body.

QUESTION: What happened then?

MANN: The man I know as John Anderson opened the sliding wooden panel between the cab and the body of the truck. He told us to put on our masks and gloves.

QUESTION: These had been provided for you?

MANN: Yes. There was a set for each of us, plus two extra sets in case of accident . . . in case the stocking masks might perhaps tear while we were putting them on.

QUESTION: And you all put them on?

MANN: Yes.

QUESTION: The men in the cab, too?

MANN: That I do not know. Anderson closed the sliding panel. I could not see what was happening up there.

QUESTION: Then what?

MANN: We drove. Then we stopped. I heard the cab door open and slam. I assumed that was Anderson getting out. As I told you, the plan required him to be waiting across the street from the apartment house when the truck arrived.

QUESTION: And then?

MANN: The truck drove on. We went around a few blocks to give Anderson time to get into position.

QUESTION: What time was this?

MANN: It was perhaps ten minutes after midnight, give or take a minute either way. Everything was precisely timed. It was an admirable plan.

QUESTION: Then what?

MANN: The truck picked up a little speed. We were all quiet. We made a very sharp turn, up a small rise. I knew we were then pulling into the driveway of the apartment house. The truck engine was switched off and the lights also.

QUESTION: Including the light in the body of the truck, where you were?

MANN: Yes. There were no lights whatsoever. In addition, we did not speak. This had been made very clear. We made no noise whatsoever.

QUESTION: Then what happened?

MANN: I heard voices outside the truck, but so low that I could not hear what was being said. Then, in a minute or two, Anderson called, "All right." At this time the side door of the truck was opened, and we all got out. Also Ed and Billy from the cab. I was assisted to descend from the truck by the man I know as Skeets, the Negro. He was very polite and helpful.

QUESTION: Go on.

MANN: The one named Tommy, the slight, boyish one, went immediately around to the front of the building. I watched him. He paused a moment to make certain there was no one on the street, no one observing—he was wearing mask and gloves, you understand—and then he slipped around to the front entrance. In a moment the release button sounded on the outside service door, and the man I know as Socks—the uncouth man I described to you before—entered first, his hand in his jacket pocket. I believe he was carrying a weapon. He went directly down to the basement. I waited until Anderson had bound and gagged the doorman, then I followed Socks down into the basement, as we had planned. Every move had been planned.

QUESTION: What was the purpose of your waiting until the doorman was tied up before following Socks down to the basement?

MANN: I don't know precisely why I was to wait, but this is what I was told to do—so I did it. I think perhaps it was to give Socks time to immobilize the superintendent. Also, it was to give Anderson time to follow me and check on my work. In any event, as I went down into the basement, Anderson was right behind me.

QUESTION: Then what?

MANN: As we entered the basement, Socks came toward us from the superintendant's apartment. He said, "What a pigsty. The slob is out cold. The place smells like a brewery. He won't wake up till Monday." Anderson said, "Good." The he turned to me. "All right, Professor," he said. So I set to work.

QUESTION: The lights in the basement were on at this time?

MANN: One dim overhead light, yes. But it was insufficient, and flashlights and a flood lantern were used in the area of my work.

QUESTION: You had brought your tools with you.

MANN: That is correct. My own personal hand and power tools. The heavy equipment, as I explained to you—the torches and the gas cylinders— had been provided and were still inside the body of the truck. So . . . I set to work on the schedule we had planned. Anderson and Socks held the lights. First of all, I cut all telephone communication, isolating the entire building. I then bridged the alarms in a manner which I have described to your technician, Mr. Browder. This was in case the alarm would sound if the current was interrupted. I then cut the power to the self-service elevator. This was simply a matter of throwing a switch. Finally, I cut the alarm to the cold box and picked the lock. I opened the door. At this time the men I know as Ed and Billy had joined us. Anderson motioned at the furs hanging inside the cold box and said to Ed and Billy, "Start loading. Everything. Clean it out. And don't forget the super's apartment." I then went back to the service entrance on the ground level and picked the lock of the door connecting the service entrance with the lobby. The Negro, Skeets, and Anderson went into the lobby. Myself and Tommy, we waited. We watched Ed and Billy carry up armloads of fur coats and put them in the truck.

54

DICTATED, SIGNED, sworn, and witnessed statement by Dr. Dmitri Rubicoff, Suite 1B, 535 East Seventy-third Street, New York City. NYPD-SIS-#146-8, dated 6 September, 1968.

"It had been my intention to spend the entire Labor Day weekend with my wife and my daughter, her husband and child, at our summer home in East Hampton. However, early Friday morning I realized the press of work facing me was so great that I could not afford the luxury of taking four of five days off away from my desk.

"Accordingly, I sent my family on ahead—they took the station wagon, my wife driving—and I told them I would be out late Saturday night or perhaps early Sunday morning. I said I would keep them informed by phone as to my plans.

"My secretary I allowed to leave early on Friday as she was planning a five-day holiday at Nassau. I worked alone in the office all day Saturday, but realized I was too tired to drive out Saturday night in the Corvair. So I determined to work late Saturday night and sleep at home—I live on East

Seventy-ninth Street—and then drive out on Sunday morning. I called my wife and informed her of my plans.

"I had a sandwich sent in at noon on Saturday. In the evening I dined at a nearby French restaurant, the Le Claire. I had an excellent poached filet of sole that was, perhaps, a trifle too salty. I returned to my office at about nine in the evening to finish up as much as I could. As usual when I am working alone in the office at night, I locked the door to the lobby and put on the chain. I then turned on my hi-fi. I believe it was something by Von Weber.

"It was perhaps twelve thirty or a little later when the lobby door chimed. I was in the process of straightening my desk and packing a briefcase with professional journals I wished to take to East Hampton with me. I went to the door and opened the peephole. The man standing there was off to one side; all I could see was his shoulder and half of his body. " 'Yes?' I said.

" 'Doctor Rubicoff,' he said, 'I'm the relief doorman for the Labor Day weekend. I have a special delivery, registered letter for you.'

"I must admit I reacted foolishly. But in my own defense, I should tell you this: First—I was ready to leave, I was about to unlock the door, and it seemed ridiculous to ask this man to slide the letter under the door. Second—frequently, you understand, on holidays and during vacations, we have relief doormen take the place of our regular employees. So I was not concerned that, on the Labor Day weekend, this was a man whose voice I did not recognize. Third—the fact that he had a special delivery, registered letter for me—or claimed he had—did not alarm me. You understand, psychiatrists are quite used to receiving letters, telegrams, and phone calls from patients, in unusual forms and at unusual hours.

"I suspected nothing. I slipped the chain and unlocked the door.

"The two men who pushed the door forcibly aside and entered were both wearing head coverings that appeared to be semiopaque women's stockings. The bottom half of the stocking had been cut off. The top half was pulled over the man's head and tied in a knot at the top. Presumably so it could not slip down or be pulled down. One of the men, I should say, was slightly under six feet tall. The other was perhaps three inches taller, and I had the feeling this man was a Negro. It was extremely difficult to judge, as only a vague shape of their features came through their masks, and both men wore white cotton gloves.

" 'Is your secretary here?' the shorter man asked me. This was the first thing he said.

"I am quite used to dealing with disturbed people, and I think I handled the situation quite calmly.

" 'No,' I told him. 'She has left for a five-day vacation, I am alone.'

" 'Good,' the man said. 'Doctor, we don't want to hurt you. Please lay down on the floor, your wrists and ankles crossed behind you.'

"Frankly, I was impressed by his air of quiet authority. I knew at once of course that this was a robbery. I though perhaps they had come for my drugs. I had been the victim twice before of robberies in which the thieves only wanted my drugs. Incidentally, I keep an extremely small supply of narcotics in my safe. I did as the man requested. My ankles and wrists were taped, and then a strip of wide tape was put across my mouth. Very painful to remove later, I might add, because of my mustache. The man asked me if I could breathe comfortably, and I nodded, I was quite impressed with him—in fact, with the whole operation. It was very professional."

55

NYPD-SIS RECORDING #146-83C; interrogation of Thomas Haskins; Segment 1A, dated 4 September, 1968. The following tape has been heavily edited to avoid repetition of material already presented and to eliminate material currently under adjudication.

QUESTION: Mr. Haskins, my name is Thomas K. Brody, and I am a detective, second grade, in the Police Department of the City of New York. It is my duty. . . .

HASKINS: Thomas! My name is Thomas, too. Isn't that sweet?

QUESTION: It is my duty to make absolutely certain that you are aware of your rights and privileges, under the laws of the United States of America, as a person accused of a crime constituting a felony under the laws of the State of New York. Now, you are. . . .

HASKINS: Oh, I'm aware, Tommy. I'm really aware! I know all that jazz about lawyers and such. You can skip it.

QUESTION: You are not required at this time to answer any questions whatsoever that may be put to you by law enforcement officials. You may request legal counsel of your choice. If you are unable to afford legal counsel, or if you have no personal counsel of your own, the court will suggest such counsel, subject to your approval. In addition, you. . . .

HASKINS: All right already! I'm willing to spiel. I want to talk! I know my rights better than you. Can't we just start talking—just you and me, two Tommies?

QUESTION: Whatever statements you may make at this time, without the presence of counsel, are of your own free will and volition. And anything you say—I repeat, *anything* you say—even that which may seem to you of an innocent nature—may possibly, in the future, be used against you. Do you understand?

HASKINS: Of course I understand.

QUESTION: Is everything clear to you?

HASKINS: Yes, Tommy baby, everything is clear to me.

QUESTION: In addition. . . .

HASKINS: Oh, Jesus Christ!

QUESTION: In addition, I have this printed statement I would like you to sign in the presence of Policewoman Alice H. Hilkins, here as witness, that you fully understand your rights and privileges as an accused person under the laws already cited, and that whatever statements you make are made with full and complete comprehension of those rights and privileges.

HASKINS: Look, Dick Two, I want to talk, I'm willing to talk, I'm eager to talk. So let's. . . .

QUESTION: Will you sign this statement?

HASKINS: Gladly, gladly. Gimme the goddamn thing.
    [Lapse of four seconds.]

QUESTION: In addition, I have a second statement that. . . .

HASKINS: Oh, oh, oh, Tommy, I just. . . .

QUESTION: This second printed statement declares that you have not been physically threatened into signing the first statement, that you signed it of your own free will and desire, that no promises have been made to you as to the extent or punishment for the accused crime. In addition, you do say, affirm, and swear that. . . .

HASKINS: Tommy, how the fuck does a guy confess these days?

[Lapse of seven minutes thirteen seconds.]

HASKINS: . . . so that the one thing that really stuck in my mind was something Duke said at our last meeting. He said crime was just war during peacetime. He said the most important thing we could learn from war was that no matter how good a plan was, it was just not humanly possible to plan *everything*. He said things can go wrong or unexpected things happen, and you must be ready to cope with them. He said—this is Duke talking, you understand—he said that he and others—that's what he said, "others"—had made our plan as foolproof as they could, but he knew unexpected things would happen they hadn't counted on. Maybe a squad car would stop by. Maybe a beat fuzz would come into the lobby to rap a little with the doorman. Maybe one of the tenants would pull a gun. He said to expect the unexpected and not get spooked by it. He said the plan was good, but things could happen that hadn't been planned for. . . .

So after we got there, I went around into the lobby and pressed the release button for the outside service door. It was right where Duke had told me it would be. While I was there, I took a look at a clipboard the doormen keep. It tells them what deliveries to expect and what tenants were away for the weekend—things like that. I saw right away that the headshrinker was in his office and working late. Also, there were two guests staying in Two A. Those were two of the unexpected things Duke had warned us about. So the moment he came through the opened door to the service entrance, I told him about them. He patted my arm. That's the first time he ever touched me. . . .

So he and the smoke took care of the doctor, just like that, and we went ahead with the plan. You see, we knew there would be several tenants still in the building who hadn't gone away for the Labor Day weekend. The idea was, instead of tying them all up in their apartments or keeping a watch on them, which we didn't have enough people to do, the idea was to assemble everyone in the building in Apartment Four B where the old widow Mrs. Hathway lived with her housekeeper. These were two really ancient dames, and Duke didn't want to risk taping them up. So it was decided we'd bring everyone in the building to Apartment Four B, scare the hell out of them, and Skeets or Socks would keep an eye on them all together. After all, what could they do? The phones were cut. They didn't know if we had guns or knives or whatever. And we had them all in one place and one guy could keep them quiet while the rest of us cleaned out the whole fucking apartment house.

It was a marvelous plan. . . .

56

THE FOLLOWING is a portion of a lengthy letter addressed to the author from Ernest Heinrich Mann, dated 28 March, 1969.

MY DEAR SIR:

I wish to thank you for your kind inquiries as to my physical health and mental stamina, as expressed in your recent missive. I am happy to tell you that, God willing, I am in good health and spirits. The food is plain but plentiful. The exercise—outdoors, that is—is sufficient, and my work in the library I find very rewarding.

You may be interested to learn that I have recently taken up the Yoga regimen, insofar as it relates to physical exercise. The philosophy does not concern me. But the physical program interests me as it requires no equipment, so that I am able to practice in my cell, at any time. Needless to say, this is much to the amusement of my cellmate whose main exercise is turning the pages of the latest comic book, detailing the adventures of Cosmic Man!

I thank you for your recent gift of books and cigarettes which arrived in good order. You ask if there is any special printed matter which you may supply that is not available in the prison library. Sir, there is. Some months ago, in an issue of the New York *Times*, I read that, for the first time, scientists had succeeded in the synthetic reproduction of an enzyme in the laboratory. This is a subject that interests me greatly, and I would be much obliged if you could obtain for me copies of the scientific papers describing this discovery. I thank you.

Now then . . . you ask me about the personality and the character traits of the man I called John Anderson.

I can tell you he was a most complex man. As you may have surmised, I had several dealings with him prior to the events of 31 August–1 September, 1968. In all our dealings, I found him a man of the highest probity, of exceptional honesty, trustworthiness, and steadfastness. I would never hesitate in giving him a character reference, if such was requested of me.

A man of very little education and very much intelligence. And the two have little in common as, I am certain, you recognize. In all our personal and business relations he radiated strength and purposefulness. As is understandable in such a relationship, I was, perhaps, a little frightened of him. Not because he ever threatened me physical harm. Not at all! But I was frightened as we all poor mortals become frightened in the presence of one we feel and sense and know is of, perhaps, almost superhuman strength and resolve. Let me say only that I felt inferior to him.

I believe that, directed into more constructive channels, his intelligence and native wit could have taken him very far. Very far indeed. Let me give you an example. . . .

Following our second planning meeting—I believe it was on August 28th—I walked with him to the subway after the meeting was concluded. Everything had gone very well. I congratulated him on the detailed planning, which I thought was superb. I told him I thought it must have taken much thought on his part. He smiled, and this is what he said—as nearly as I can remember. . . .

"Yes, I have been living with this thing for some months now, thinking of it every waking minute and even dreaming of it. You know, there is nothing like thinking. You have a problem that worries you and nags you and keeps you awake. The thing to do then is to get to the very rock bottom of that problem. First, you figure out *why* it is a problem. Once you have done that, it is half solved. For instance, what do you think was the most difficult problem in making up the plan you heard tonight?"

I suggested it might be how to handle the doorman when the truck first pulled into the driveway.

"No," he said, "there are several good ways we could handle that. The big problem, as I saw it, was how to handle the tenants who were still at home. That is, how could we get into their apartments? I figured they all had locked doors and chains also. In addition, it would be after midnight and I could figure most of them—particularly the old ladies in Four B and the family with the crippled boy in Five A— would be asleep. I thought of our possibilities. We could force the doors, of course. But even if their phones were cut, they could still scream before we broke in and maybe alert the people in the house next door. I could ask you to pick the locks—but I had no gaurantee that *everyone* would be asleep at that hour. They might hear you working and start screaming. It was a problem to know exactly what we should do. I wrestled with this thing for three days, coming up with a dozen solutions. I threw them all out because they didn't *feel* right to me. So then I went to the rock-bottom basic of the problem, just like I told you. I asked myself, Why do all these people have locks and chains on their doors? The answer was easy—because they were scared of guys like me—crooks and burglars and muggers. So then I thought, if they keep their door locked from *fear*, what can make them open up? I remembered from the first time I was in that house that the doors above the lobby didn't have peepholes. The doctors' offices on the lobby floor did, but the doors above were blind. Who needs peepholes when they have twenty-four-hour doorman service and a locked service door and all that shit? So then I thought, if *fear* makes them keep their doors locked, then a *bigger* fear will make them unlock them. And what's a bigger fear than being robbed? That was easy. It was fire."

And that, my dear sir, is something I can tell you about the man I knew as John Anderson and how intelligent he was at his job, although he was, as I have told you, un-educated. . . .

57

FOLLOWING THE events related herein, attempts were made to obtain sworn statements from all the principals involved as soon as possible, while the details were fresh in their minds. Individuals interrogated included the victims and the alleged lawbreakers. It soon became apparent that the key to the proposed plan to loot the apartment house at 535 East Seventy-third Street was Apartment 4B, owned by Mrs. Martha Hathway, widow, and occupied by her and her companion-housekeeper, Miss Jane Kaler, a spinster.

Mrs Hathway was ninety-one at the time of the crime. Miss Kaler was eighty-two. Both ladies refused to be interviewed or to make statements individually; each insisted the other be present—a rather surprising request in view of the results of their interrogation.

In any event, the statements of both ladies were taken at the same time. The following is an edited transcription of NYPD-SIS recording #146-91A.

MRS. HATHWAY: Very well. I will tell you exactly what happened. Are you taking all this down, young man?

QUESTION: The machine is, ma'am. It's recording everything we say.

MRS. HATHWAY: Hmph. Well . . . it was the morning of September first. Sunday morning. I'd say it was about one o'clock in the morning.

MISS KALER: It was about fifteen minutes to one.

MRS. HATHWAY: You shut your mouth. I'm telling this.

MISS KALER: You're not telling it right.

QUESTION: Ladies. . . .

MRS. HATHWAY: It was about one o'clock. We had been asleep for, oh, about two hours or so.

MISS KALER: You might have been asleep. I was wide awake.

MRS. HATHWAY: Oh, you were indeed! I could hear the snores!

QUESTION: Ladies, please. . . .

MRS. HATHWAY: Suddenly I woke up. There was this pounding on our front door. A man was shouting, "Fire! Fire! There is a fire in the building and everyone must vacate the premises!"

QUESTION: Were those the exact words you heard?

MRS. HATHWAY: Something like that. But of course all I heard was "Fire! Fire!" so I immediately rose and donned my dressing gown.

MISS KALER: Naturally, being awake, I was already suitably clad and standing near the front door. "Where is the fire?" I asked through the door. "In the basement, ma'am," this man said, "but it is spreading rapidly throughout the entire building and we must ask you to leave the premises until the fire is under control." So I said to him, "And who might you be?" And he said, "I am Fireman Robert Burns of the New York Fire Department, and I would—"

MRS. HATHWAY: Will you stop gabbling for just a minute? I own this apartment, and it is my right to tell what happened. Isn't that correct, young man?

QUESTION: Well, ma'am, we'd like to get both. . . .

MISS KALER: "And I would like all the occupants of this apartment to leave immediately," he said. So I said, "Is it serious?" And he said—all this was through our locked door, you understand—he said, "Well, ma'am, we hope it won't be, but for your own safety we suggest you come down to the lobby while we get the fire under control." So I said, "Well, if you're—"

MRS. HATHWAY: Will you shut your mouth, you silly, blathering creature? Just be quiet and let me tell this nice young man what happened. So, seeing we were both perfectly covered in our dressing gowns and we had on our carpet slippers, I told the girl to open the door. . . .

MISS KALER: Mrs. Hathway, I've asked you times without end not to refer to me as "the girl". If you remember, you promised to. . . .

MRS. HATHWAY: So she opened the door. . . .

QUESTION: It was locked at the time?

MRS. HATHWAY: Oh, my, yes. We have the regular lock, always double-locked whenever we're in the apartment. Then we have a chain lock which allows the door to be opened slightly but held with a powerful chain. And we also have something called a policeman's lock which had been recommended to me by Sergeant Tim Sullivan, retired now but formerly of the Twenty-first Precinct. Do you know him?

QUESTION: I'm afraid not, ma'am.

MRS. HATHWAY: A wonderful man—a very good friend of my late husband's. Sergeant Sullivan was forced to retire at an early age because of a hernia. After we had so many robberies on the East Side, I called him and he suggested we have this policeman's lock installed, which is really a steel rod that fits into the floor and is shoved against the door, and it's impossible to break in.

MISS KALER: Ask her how this "wonderful man" got his hernia.

MRS. HATHWAY: That is of no importance, I'm sure. So the man outside kept shouting, "Fire! Fire!" and naturally we were quite upset, so we opened the three locks and threw open the door. And much. . . .

MISS KALER: And there he was! A monster! He must have been seven feet tall, with this terrible mask and a big gun in his hand. And he snarled at us, "If you—"

MRS. HATHWAY: He was, perhaps, six feet tall, and he had no gun that I could see, although I believe one hand was in his pocket so he might have had a weapon. But really, he was quite polite and said, "Ladies, we must use your apartment for a short while, but if you are quiet and offer us no resistance, then we can—"

MISS KALER: And right behind him were two other monsters—sex fiends, all of them! And they had masks and revolvers. And they pushed us back into the apartment, and I said, "Then there is no fire?" And the first man to come in said, "No, ma'am, there is no fire, but we must request the use of your apartment for a while. And if you don't scream or carry on, it won't be necessary to tie you up or tape your mouth shut. And we will not tape your mouth shut if you act intelligently." And I said, "I will act intelligently." And then the first man said, "Keep an eye on them, Killer, and if they scream or act up, you may destroy them." And the second man—who, I am sure, was a darkie—he said, "Yes, Butch, if they scream or act up, I will destroy them." And then the darkie stayed and watched us through his mask, and the other two men. . . .

MRS. HATHWAY: Will you shut up? Will you just shut your mouth?

QUESTION: Ladies, ladies. . . .

58

RECORDING NYDA-#146-98B. See NYDA-#146-98BT for corrected and edited transcription.

QUESTION: The recorder has now started, Mrs. Bingham. My name is Roger Leibnitz. I am an assistant in the office of the District Attorney, County of New York, State of New York. It is the eleventh day of September, 1968. I wish to question you about events occuring during the period August thirty-first to September first of this year at your residence. If for any reason you do not wish to make a statement, or if you wish counsel of your choice to be present during this interview, or if you wish the court to appoint such counsel, will you please state at this time?

MRS. BINGHAM: No . . . that's all right.

QUESTION: Very well. You understand, it is my duty to notify you of your rights under law?

MRS. BINGHAM: Yes. I understand.

QUESTION: For the record, will you please identify yourself—your full name and your place of residence.

MRS. BINGHAM: My name is Mrs. Gerald Bingham, and I live in Apartment Five A, five-three-five East Seventy-third Street, Manhattan, New York.

QUESTION: Thank you. Before we get started—may I inquire about your husband's condition?

MRS. BINGHAM: Well . . . I feel a lot better now. At first they thought he might lose the sight of his right eye. Now they say he will be able to see, but the sight may be impaired. But he's going to be all right.

QUESTION: I'm very happy to hear that, ma'am. Your husband is a very brave man.

MRS. BINGHAM: Yes. Very brave.

QUESTION: Are you all right, Mrs. Bingham?

MRS. BINGHAM: Yes . . . I'm all right.

QUESTION: If you wish to put this questioning over to another day, or if you'd like to rest at any time, please tell me. Would you like coffee . . . a cup of tea?

MRS. BINGHAM: No . . . I'll be all right.

QUESTION: Fine. Now I want you to state in your own words exactly what happened during the period in question. I'll try to avoid interrupting. Just take your time and tell me what happened in your own words. . . .

MRS. BINGHAM: It was the thirty-first August. Most of the people in the house had left for the Labor Day weekend. We rarely go away because of my son. His name is Gerry—Gerald junior. He is fifteen years old. He was in an accident at the age of ten—he was hit by a truck—and he has lost the use of his legs. The doctors say there is no hope he will ever walk normally again. He is a good boy, very intelligent, but he must be helped. He uses a wheelchair and sometimes crutches for short periods. From the waist up he is very strong, but he can't walk without help. So we very rarely go anywhere.

QUESTION: You have no other children?

MRS. BINGHAM: No. On the night of August thirty-first, my son went to bed about midnight. He read a while, and I brought him a Coca-Cola, which he dearly loves, and then he turned out his bed lamp and went to sleep. My husband and I were in the living room. I was working on a petit point cover for a footstool, and my husband was reading something by Trollope. He dearly loves Trollope. I think it was about fifteen minutes to one. I'm not sure. It could have been fifteen minutes either way. Suddenly there was a pounding at the front door. A man's voice shouted, "Fire! Fire!" It was a very cruel thing to do.

QUESTION: Yes, Mrs. Bingham, it was.

MRS. BINGHAM: My husband said, "My God!" and jumped to his feet. He dropped his book on the floor. He rushed over to the door and unlocked it and took off the chain and opened it. There were two men standing there with masks on their faces. I could see them from where I sat. I was still in the easy chair. I hadn't reacted as fast as my husband. I could see these two men. The one in front had his hand in his jacket pocket. They were wearing these strange masks that came to a knot on the tops of their heads. I didn't know at first, but later I realized they were stockings—women's stockings. My husband looked at them and he said again, "My God!" The he . . . he struck at the man in front. He reacted very quickly. I was so proud of him, thinking about it later. He knew at once what it was and he reacted so quickly. I was just sitting there, stunned.

QUESTION: A very brave man.

MRS. BINGHAM: Yes. He is. So he hit out at this man, and this man laughed and moved his head so that my husband didn't really hit him. Then this man took a gun out of his pocket and hit my husband in the face with it. He just smashed him with it. We found out later it had broken the bones above and below my husband's right eye. My husband fell to the floor and I saw the blood. The blood just gushed out. Then this man kicked my husband. He kicked him in the stomach and in the . . . in the groin. And I just sat there. I just sat there. . . .

QUESTION: Please, Mrs. Bingham . . . please. . . . Would you like to put this over to another day?

MRS. BINGHAM: No . . . no . . . that's all right . . . no. . . .

QUESTION: Let's take a little break. What I would like you to do, if you feel you are capable of it at this time, is to come with me downstairs to another office. There we have an exhibit of many types of guns used by lawbreakers. I would like you, if you can, to identify the gun the man used when he hit your husband. Will you do that for us?

MRS. BINGHAM: It was a very big gun, very heavy. I think it was black or maybe. . . .

QUESTION: Just come with me, and let's see if you can identify the gun from our collection. I'll take the machine with us.

[Lapse of four minutes thirty-eight seconds.]

QUESTION: This is NYDA Number one-four-six, nine-eight-B, two. We are now in the gun room. Now, Mrs. Bingham, as you can see, these are cases of weapons that have been used in crimes. What I would like you to do is to examine these weapons—take all the time you need; don't hurry—and try to pick out the weapon you think that first masked man used to strike your husband.

MRS. BINGHAM: There are so many!

QUESTION: Yes . . . many. But take your time. Look at all of them and try to identify the gun the man used.

[Lapse of one minute thirty-seven seconds.]

MRS. BINGHAM: I don't see it.

QUESTION: Take your time. No hurry.

MRS. BINGHAM: It was black, or maybe dark blue. It was square.

QUESTION: Square? Come over to this case, ma'am. Something like this?

MRS. BINGHAM: Yes . . . these look more like it . . . Yes . . . yes . . . there it is! That's the one.

QUESTION: Which one is that?

MRS. BINGHAM: There it is . . . that second one from the top.

QUESTION: You're sure of that, ma'am?

MRS. BINGHAM: Absolutely. No question about it.

QUESTION: The witness has just identified a U.S. pistol, caliber .45, 1917, Colt automatic, Code number nineteen seventeen, C-A, three-seven-one-B. Thank you, Mrs. Bingham. Shall we go upstairs now? Perhaps I'll order in some coffee or tea?

MRS. BINGHAM: A cup of tea would be nice.

QUESTION: Of course.

[Lapse of seven minutes, sixteen seconds.]

MRS. BINGHAM: I feel better now.

QUESTION: Good. This is NYDA Number one-four-six, nine-eight-B, three.

Ma'am, do you think you'd like to finish up today—or should we put it off?

MRS. BINGHAM: Let's finish now.

QUESTION: Fine. Now then . . . you said your husband hit out at the masked man. The masked man drew a weapon from his pocket and struck your husband. Your husband fell to the floor. The masked man then kicked him in the stomach and in the groin. Is that correct?

MRS. BINGHAM: Yes.

QUESTION: Then what happened?

MRS. BINGHAM: It's all very hazy. I'm not sure. I think I was out of my chair by this time and moving toward the door. But I distinctly saw the second masked man push the first one aside. And the second man said, "That's enough." I remember that very clearly because it was exactly what I was thinking at the time. The second masked man shouldered the first one aside so he couldn't kick my husband anymore, and he said, "That's enough."

QUESTION: And then?

MRS. BINGHAM: I'm afraid I don't remember in what sequence things took place. I'm very hazy about it all. . . .

QUESTION: Just tell it in your own words. Don't worry about the sequence.

MRS. BINGHAM: Well, I ran over to my husband. I think I got down on my knees alongside him. I could see his eye was very bad. There was a lot of blood, and he was groaning. One of the men said, "Where's the kid?"

QUESTION: Do you remember which man said that?

MRS. BINGHAM: I'm not sure, but I think it was the second one—the one who told the first man to stop kicking my husband.

QUESTION: He said, "Where's the kid?"

MRS. BINGHAM: Yes.

QUESTION: So he knew about your son?

MRS. BINGHAM: Yes. I asked him please, not to hurt Gerry. I told him Gerry was asleep in his bedroom and that he was crippled and could only move in his wheelchair or for short distances on crutches. I asked him again, please not to hurt Gerry, and he said he wouldn't hurt him.

QUESTION: This is still the second man you're talking about?

MRS. BINGHAM: Yes, Then he went into my son's bedroom. The first man, the one who kicked my husband, stayed in the living room. After a while the second man came out of the bedroom. He was pushing my son's empty wheelchair and carrying his aluminum crutches. The first man said to him, "Where's the kid?" The other one said, "He's pretending he's asleep, but he's awake all right. I told him if he yelled I'd come back and break his neck. As long as we've got his chair and crutches, he can't move. He's a gimp. We checked this out." And the first man said, "I think we should take him." And then the second man said, "The elevator is stopped. You want to carry him down? How we going to get him down?" And then they argued a while about whether they should take the boy. Finally they agreed they would leave him in bed but they would gag him and look in on him every ten minutes or so. I asked them please not to do that. I told them that Gerry has sinus trouble, and I was afraid if they'd gag him, perhaps he wouldn't be able to breathe. The second man said they were taking my husband and me down to Mrs. Hathway's apartment on the fourth floor, and they couldn't take the chance of leaving Gerry alone in the apartment, even if he couldn't move. I told them I would make Gerry promise to keep quiet if they would let me talk to him. They argued about this for a while, and then the second man said he would come into the bedroom with me and listen to what I said to Gerry. So we went into the bedroom. I snapped on the light. Gerry was lying on his back, under the covers. His face was very white. His eyes were open. I asked him if he knew what was going on, and he said yes, he had heard us talking. My son is very intelligent.

QUESTION: Yes, ma'am. We know that now.

MRS. BINGHAM: I told him they had taken his chair and crutches, but if he promised not to yell or make any sounds, they had agreed not to tie him up. He said he wouldn't make any sounds. The man went over to the bed and looked down at Gerry. "That's a bad man out there, boy," he said to Gerry. "I think he's already put your pappy's eye out. You behave yourself or I'll have to turn him loose on your pappy again. You understand?" Gerry said yes, he understood. Then the man said there would be someone looking in on him every few minutes so not to get wise-ass. That was the expression he used. He said, "Don't get wise-ass, kid." Gerry nodded. Then we went back into the living room.

QUESTION: Did you leave the light on in the bedroom?

MRS. BINGHAM: Well, I turned it off, but the masked man turned it on again and said to leave it on. So we went back into the living room. My husband was on his feet, swaying a little. He had gotten a towel from the bathroom and was holding it to his eye. I don't know why I hadn't thought of that before. I'm afraid I wasn't behaving very well.

QUESTION: You were doing just fine.

MRS. BINGHAM: Well . . . I don't know. . . . I don't think I'm very brave. I know I was crying. I started crying when I saw my husband on the floor and the man was kicking him, and somehow I just couldn't stop. I couldn't stop. . . . I tried to stop but I just. . . .

QUESTION: Let's leave the rest of this for another day, shall we? I think we've done enough for one day.

MRS. BINGHAM: Yes . . . all right. Well, they just took us down the service staircase to the fourth floor, to Mrs. Hathway's apartment. I imagine you know what happened after that. I helped support my husband on the way down the stairs; he was still very shaky. But in Mrs. Hathway's apartment we could take care of him. They had brought everyone there, including Dr. Rubicoff, and he helped me bathe my husband's eye and put a clean towel on it. Everyone was very . . . everyone was very . . . everyone . . . oh, my God, my God!

QUESTION: Yes, Mrs. Bingham . . . yes, yes. Just relax a moment. Just sit quietly and relax. It's all over. It's all completely over.

59

THE FOLLOWING is a personal letter to the author, dated 3 January, 1969, from Mr. Jeremy Marrin, 43-580 Buena Vista Drive, Arlington, Virginia.

DEAR SIR:

In reply to your letter of recent date, requesting my personal recollections and reactions to what happened in New York City last year on Labor Day weekend, please be advised that both myself and John Burlingame have made very complete statements to the New York City police anent these events, and I'm sure our statements are a matter of public record and you may consult them. However, as a matter of common courtesy (called common, no doubt, because it is so *un*common) I will pen this very short note to you as you say it is of importance to you.

John Burlingame, a chum of mine, and I planned to spend the Labor Day weekend in New York, seeing a few shows and visiting companions. We wrote to Eric Sabine, a very dear friend of ours, who occupies Apartment 2A at 535 East Seventy-third Street, hoping to spend some time with him and his very groovy circle of acquiantances. Eric wrote back that he would be out of the city for the weekend. Fire Island, I believe he said. But he put his gorgeous apartment completely at our disposal, mailed us the key, and said he would leave instructions with the doorman that we would be staying for the weekend. Naturally, we were delighted and very grateful to kind-hearted Eric.

We started out very early Saturday morning, driving up, but with one thing and another, we did not arrive until 10:30 or so, quite worn out with the trip. The traffic was simply murder. So we bought the Sunday papers and just locked ourselves in for the night. Dear Eric had left a full refrigerator (fresh salmon in aspic, no less!) and, of course, he's got the best bar in New York—or anywhere else, for that matter. Some of his liqueurs are simply incredible. So John and I had a few drinks, soaked a while in a warm tub, and then went to bed—oh, I'd say it was 12:15, 12:30, around then. We were awake, you understand, just lying in bed and drinking and reading the papers. It was a very groovy experience.

It was about—oh, I'd say fifteen minutes after one o'clock or so, when we heard this terrible banging on the front door, and a man's voice shouted, "Fire! Fire! Everybody out! The whole house is on fire!"

So naturally, we just leaped out of bed. We had brought pj's, but neither of us had thought to bring robes. Fortunately, dear Eric has this groovy collection of dressing gowns, so we borrowed two of his gowns (I had this lovely thing in crimson jacquard silk), put them on, rushed into the living room, unlocked the door . . . and here were these two horrid men with masks over their heads. One was quite short and one quite tall. The tall one, whom I am absolutely certain was a jigaboo, said, "Let's go. You come with us and no one get hurt."

Well, we almost fainted, as you can well imagine. John shouted, "Don't hurt my face, don't hurt my face!" John is in the theater, you know—a very handsome boy. But they didn't hurt us or even touch us. They had their hands in their pockets and I suspect they had weapons. They took us up the service stairway at the back of the building. We went into Apartment 4B where there were several other people assembled. I gathered that everyone in the building, including the doorman, had been brought there. One man was wounded and bleeding very badly from his eye. His wife, the poor thing, was weeping. But as far as I could see, no one else had been physically harmed.

We were told to make ourselves comfortable, which was a laugh as this was the most old-fashioned, campy apartment I have ever seen in my life. John said it would have made a perfect set for *Arsenic and Old Lace*. They told us not to scream or make any noise or attempt to resist in any way, as they merely wished to rob the apartments and not to hurt anyone. They were polite, in a way, but still you felt that if the desire came over them, they would simply slit your throat wide open.

After a while they all left except for the man who was, I'm sure, a spade. He stood by the door with his hand in his pocket, and I believe he was armed.

I'm sure you know the rest better than I can tell it. It was a very shattering experience, and in spite of the many groovy times I have had in New York, I can assure you it will be a long time before I visit Fun City again.

I do hope this may be of help to you in assembling your account of what happened, and if you're ever down this way, do look me up.

Very cordially,
[signed] JEREMY MARRIN

60

STATEMENT NYDA-EHM-106A.

MANN: It was now twenty minutes after one. Perhaps one thirty. Everything was going very well. Everyone had been assembled in Apartment Four B except for the superintendent, drunk and asleep in his basement apartment, and the crippled boy in Apartment Five A. So then, the building secured, we moved into the second phase of the operation in which we were divided into three teams.

QUESTION: Teams?

MANN: Yes. The man I knew as John Anderson and I constituted the first team. We worked from the basement upward. He had a checklist. We would move to an apartment. I would unlock the door and. . . .

QUESTION: Pick the lock?

MANN: Well . . . ah . . . my assignment was purely technical, you understand. Then we would enter the apartment. Anderson, who carried the checklist, would point out to me what he wished me to do.

QUESTION: What did that entail?

MANN: Well . . . you understand . . . perhaps a box safe, a wall safe. Perhaps a locked closet or cabinet. Things of that sort. Then, as we left the apartment, the second team would enter. This was the very short man, Tommy—effeminate, I believe—and the two men I knew as Ed and Billy. Tommy, who apparently knew the value of things, carried a copy of Anderson's checklist. He would direct the two brothers as to what should be removed and carried down to the truck. They were merely laborers, you understand.

QUESTION: What did they remove and carry to the truck?

MANN: What did they *not* remove! Furs, the triptych from the super's apartment, a small narcotics safe from one of the doctor's offices, jewelry, paintings, silver, unset gems, *objects d'art*, even rugs and small pieces of furniture from the decorator's apartment in Two A. One unexpected treasure was discovered in the medical doctor's suite on the lobby floor. There, this man Anderson, after I had opened the door, went directly to a closet in the doctor's office and there, on a back shelf of the closet, he discovered a cardboard shoe box containing a great deal of cash. I would say at least then thousand dollars. Perhaps more. The Internal Revenue Service will be interested in that . . . *nein*?

QUESTION: Perhaps. You had no problems opening the doors or safes?

MANN: None. Very inferior. After we gained the third floor, I was confident I would have no need for the torches and tanks in the truck. Quite frankly, it was not a challenge to me. Simple. Everything went well.

QUESTION: You mentioned three teams. Who were on the third team?

MANN: They were the Negro and the uncouth man. They were detailed to guard the people assembled in Apartment Four B, and to look in on the sleeping super in the basement and the crippled boy in Apartment Five A. They were what is called muscle. They took no actual part in removing objects from the house—and, of course, I didn't either, you understand. Their duties were merely to keep the building quiet while it was being emptied.

QUESTION: And everything went well?

MANN: Beautiful. It was beautiful! A remarkable job of organization. I admired the man I knew as John Anderson.

61

THE FOLLOWING is a portion of a statement dictated to a representative of the District Attorney's Office, County of New York, by Gerald Bingham, Jr., a minor, resident of Apartment 5A, 535 East Seventy-third Street, New York, New York. His entire statement is on recordings NYDA-# 145-113A-113G, and as transcribed (NYDA-# 146-113AT-113GT) consists of forty-three typewritten pages.

The following is an excerpt covering the most crucial period of the witness' activities. Material covered in previous testimony, and that to be covered in following testimony, has been deleted.

WITNESS: I heard the front door close, and I looked at my watch on the bedside table. It was nine minutes, thirty-seven seconds past one. My watch was an Omega chronometer. I never got it back. It was a very fine machine. Very accurate. I don't believe it gained more than three minutes a year. That's very good for a wristwatch, you know. In any event, I noted the time. Of course, I wasn't certain both the thieves had left the apartment with my parents. But my hearing is very acute—possibly because of my physical debility. That is an interesting avenue for research—whether paralyzed legs might affect other senses, the way a blind man hears and smells with such sensitivity. Well, some day. . . .

I judged they would come back to check on me within ten minutes. Actually, I heard the living room door open about seven minutes after they had left. A masked man came into the apartment, came into my bedroom, and looked at me. He was not the man who had spoken to me before. This man was somewhat shorter and heavier. He just looked at me, without saying anything. Then he saw my Omega chronometer on the bedside table, picked it up, put it in his pocket, and walked out. This angered me. I was already resolved to foil their plans, but this gave me an added incentive. I do not like people to touch my personal belongings. My parents know this and respect my wishes.

I heard the living room door close, and I began counting, using the professional photographers' method of ticking off seconds: "One hundred and one, one hundred and two . . ." and so forth. While I was counting, I picked up my bedside phone extension. As I suspected, it was completely dead, and I judged they had cut the main trunk line in the basement. This did not alarm me.

I judged they would check me every ten minutes or so for one or two times. Then, when they saw I was making no effort to escape or to raise an alarm, their visits would become more infrequent. Such proved to be the case. Their first visit, as I have said, occurred about seven minutes after their initial departure from the apartment. The second visit, by the same man, was eleven minutes and thiry-seven seconds after the first. The third visit—this was by a taller, more slender, masked man—came sixteen minutes and eight seconds after the second visit.

I judged the fourth visit would be approximately twenty minutes after the third. I estimated that, conservatively speaking, I had ten minutes in which I would not be disturbed. I did not wish to take the full twenty minutes as I did not wish to endanger my parents or the other tenants of the building who endeavor to be pleasant to me.

You must understand that although the lower half of my body is paralyzed and without control, I am very well developed from the waist up. My father takes me to a private health club three times a week. I am a very good swimmer, I can perform on the horizontal bars, and Paul—he's the trainer—says he has never seen anyone as fast as I am on the rope climb. My shoulders and arms are very well muscled.

The moment I heard the outside door close, after the third visit by one of the miscreants, I threw back the sheet and began to slide to the floor. Naturally, I wanted to be as quiet as possible. I didn't want to make any heavy thumps that might alert the thieves if they happened to be in Apartment Four A, directly below. So I got my upper body onto the floor and then, lying on my shoulders and back, I lifted my legs down with my hands. All this time I was counting, you understand. I wished to accomplish everything within the ten minutes I had allotted myself and be back in bed before the next inspection.

I moved by reaching out my arms, placing my forearms flat on the floor, and dragging my body forward with my biceps and shoulder muscles. I weigh almost one hundred and seventy-five pounds, and it was slow going. I remember trying to estimate the physical coefficients involved—angles, muscles involved, power required, the friction of the rug—things like that. But that's of no importance. Within three minutes I had reached the door of my closet—the walk-in closet on the north side of my bedroom, not the clothes closet on the south side.

After I became interested in electronics, my father had the walk-in closet cleared of hooks, hangers, and poles. He had a carpenter install shelves and a desk at the right height for me when I was seated in my wheelchair. It was in this closet that I installed all my electronic equipment. This not only included my shortwave transmitter and receiver, but also hi-fi equipment wired to speakers in my bedroom and in the living room and in my parents' bedroom. I had two separate turntables so my parents could listen to one LP while I listened to another, or we could even listen to separate tapes, if so desired. This was a wise arrangement as they enjoy Broadway show tunes—original-cast recordings—while I like Beethoven, Bach, and also Gilbert and Sullivan.

You may be interested to know that I had personally assembled every unit in that closet from do-it-yourself kits. If I told you how many junctions I had soldered, you wouldn't believe me. But not only were the savings considerable—over what the cost of the completed units would be—but as I went along I was able to make certain improvements—minor ones, to be sure—they gave us excellent stereo reproduction from tape and LP's and FM radio. I am currently assembling a cassette player on the work table to the left of the control board. Well, enough of that. . . .

I opened the closet door by reaching up. However, the work table and controls of my shortwave transmitter seemed impossibly high. But fortunately, the carpenter who installed the table had built sturdily, and I was able to pull myself up by fingers, wrists, arms, and shoulders. It was somewhat painful but not unendurable. I should mention here that my antenna was on the roof of the building next door. It is an eighteen- story apartment house and towers over our five-story building. My father paid for the installation of an antenna and also pays ten dollars a month fee. The lead-in comes down the side of the tall building and into my bedroom window. It is not a perfect arrangement, but obviously better than having the anttenna on our terrace, blocked by surrounding buildings.

Supporting myself on my arms, I turned on my equipment and waited patiently for the warm-up. I was still counting, of course, and figured five minutes had elapsed since I crawled out of bed. About thirty seconds later I began broadcasting. I gave my call signal, of course, and stated that a robbery was taking place at five-three-five East Seventy-third Street, New York, New York, and please, notify the New York Police Department. I didn't have time to switch on my receiver and wait for acknowledgments. I merely broadcast steadily for two minutes, repeating the same thing over and over, hoping that someone might be on my wavelength.

When I calculated that seven minutes had elapsed from the time I got out of bed, I switched off my equipment, let myself drop to the floor, closed the closet door, dragged myself back to my bed, hauled myself up, and got beneath the sheet. I was somewhat tired.

I was glad I had not taken the full twenty minutes I had estimated I had before the fourth visit because one of the thieves came into my bedroom sixteen minutes and thirteen seconds after the third visit. It was the same tall, slender man who had made the previous inspection.

"Behaving yourself?" he asked pleasantly. Actually, he said, "Behavin' yoself," from which I judged he was colored. "Yes," I said, "I can't move, anyhow." He nodded and said, "We all got troubles." Then he left and I never saw him again.

I lay there and thought back on what I had just done. I tried to analyze the problem to see if there was anything more I could do, but I couldn't think of what it might be—without endangering my parents or the other tenants.I hoped someone had heard me, and I felt that, with luck, someone had. Luck is very important, you know. In many ways I know I am very lucky.

Also, to be quite frank, I thought these robbers were very stupid. They had obviously investigated our apartment house very well, but they had missed the one thing that might possibly negate all their efforts.

I could plan a crime much better than that.

62

NYPD-SIS RECORDING #146-83C.

HASKINS: "Oh, God, Tommy, it was beautiful. Beautiful! It's about two o'clock now, maybe a little later. The first team is working on the third floor. The second team, with me in charge, is finishing up Two A and Two B. And what we got in those places you wouldn't believe! From the fruit's apartment we took his paintings, small rugs, a few small pieces of antique furniture, his collection of unset gemstones, two original Picassos, and a Klee. From Two B, from the wall safe the tech had opened, we got a gorgeous tiara, a pearl necklace, and also a very chaste ruby choker I slipped into my pocket, figuring Snapper would flip over it. After all, she worked on this thing, too—even if the orders were that everything went into the truck. I knew we were already over our estimate when we hit the third floor. That retired jeweler in Three A had bags and bags of unset diamonds—most of them industrial but some very nice rocks as well. His little hedge against inflation. It took the tech less than three minutes to open the can—and without a torch. I was sure we'd hit a quarter of a mil at least. Maybe more. From the third, we were going to move up to the fifth, clean that out, and then come back down to the fourth where all the tenants were being held. But already I knew it was going to be great—much better than we had estimated. I knew the old biddies' apartment, Four B, would be a treasure-house. I was thinking we might hit a half a million. Jesus, what luck! Everything was coming up roses!"

63

THE FOLLOWING are the introductory paragraphs of an article appearing in *The New York Times*, Tuesday, 2 July, 1968. The story was published on the first page of the second section of that day's newspaper, was by-lined by David Burnham, and is copyrighted by *The New York Times*.

The article was entitled "Police Emergency Center Dedicated By Mayor."

Mayor Lindsay yesterday dedicated a $1.3-million police communications center that cuts in half the average time it takes the police to dispatch emergency help to the citizen.

"The miraculous new electronic communication system we inaugurate this morning will affect the life of every New Yorker in every part of our city, every hour of the day," Mr. Lindsay said during a ceremony staged in the vast, windowless, air-conditioned communications center on the fourth floor of the ponderous old Police Headquarters building at 240 Centre Street.

"This is, perhaps, the most important event of my administration as Mayor," Mr. Lindsay said. "No longer will a citizen in distress risk injury to life or property because of an archaic communications system."

The mayor dedicated the new system about four weeks after it went into operation.

In that period the police response time to emergency calls was reduced to 55 seconds from about two minutes through a number of complex inter-related changes in the police communication change.

First, the time it takes to dial the police has been shortened by changing the old seven-digit emergency number—440-1234—to a new three-digit number, 911.

Second, the time it takes the police to answer an emergency call has been reduced by increasing the maximum number of policemen receiving calls during critical periods to 48 from 38 and by putting them in one room where all are available to handle any emergency that might occur in one area. Under the old system, when a citizen dialed 440-1234, his call went to a separate communications center situated in the borough from which he was calling.

64

THE FOLLOWING section—and those of a similar nature below—are excerpts from the twenty-four-hour tape kept during the period 12:00 midnight, 31 August, 1968, to 12:00 midnight, 1 September, 1968, at the New York Police Communications Center at 240 Centre Street, Manhattan.

Tape NYPDCC-31AUG-1SEP. Time: 2:14:03 A.M.

OFFICER: New York Police Department. May I help you?
OPERATOR: Is this the New York City Police Department?
OFFICER: Yes, ma'am. May I help you?
OPERATOR: This is New York Telephone Company Operator four-one-five-six. Will you hold on a moment, please?
OFFICER: Yes.
[Lapse of fourteen seconds.]
NEW YORK OPERATOR: I have the New York City Police Department for you, Maine. Will you go ahead, please.
MAINE OPERATOR: Thank you, New York. Hello? Is this the New York City Police Department?
OFFICER: Yes, ma'am. May I help you?
MAINE OPERATOR: This is the operator in Gresham, Maine. I have a collect call for anyone in the New York City Police Department from Sheriff Jonathon Preebles of County Corners, Maine. Will you accept the charges, sir?
OFFICER: Pardon? I didn't get that.
MAINE OPERATOR: I have a call for anyone in the New York City Police Department from Sheriff Jonathon Preebles of County Corners, Maine. It is a collect call. Will you accept the charges, sir?
OFFICER: What's it about?
MAINE OPERATOR: Will you accept the charges, sir?
OFFICER: Can you hang on a minute?
MAINE OPERATOR: Yes, sir.
[Lapse of sixteen seconds.]
O'NUSKA: Sergeant O'Nuska.

OFFICER: Sarge, this is Jameson. I've got a collect call from a sheriff up in Maine. They want to know if we'll accept the charges.

O'NUSKA: A collect call?

OFFICER: That's right.

O'NUSKA: What's it about?

OFFICER: They won't tell unless we accept the charges.

O'NUSKA: Jesus Christ. Hang on a minute—I'll be right over.

OFFICER: Okay, Sarge.

[Lapse of forty-seven seconds.]

O'NUSKA: Hello? Hello? This is Sergeant Adrian O'Nuska of the New York Police Department. Who's calling?

MAINE OPERATOR: Sir, this is the operator in Gresham, Maine. I have a collect call for anyone in the New York City Police Department from Sheriff Jonathon Preebles of County Corners, Maine. Will you accept the charges, sir?

O'NUSKA: What's it about?

MAINE OPERATOR: Will you accept the charges, sir?

O'NUSKA: Hang on a minute. . . . Jameson, what can it cost to call from Maine?

JAMESON: A couple of bucks maybe. Depends on how long you talk. I call my folks down in Lakeland, Florida, every month. Costs me maybe two—three bucks, depending on how long we talk.

O'NUSKA: I'll never get it back. I'll get stuck for it. You mark my words. I'll get stuck for it. . . . Okay, Operator, put the sheriff on the line.

OPERATOR: Go ahead, sir. Sergeant Adrian O'Nuska of the New York City Police Department is on the line.

SHERIFF: Hello there! You there, Sergeant?

O'NUSKA: I'm here.

SHERIFF: Well . . . good to talk to you. What kind of weather you folks been having?

O'NUSKA: Sheriff, I. . . .

SHERIFF: I tell you, we had a rainy spell last week. Four solid days like a cow pissing on a flat rock. Let up yesterday though. Sky nice and clear tonight. Stars out.

O'NUSKA: Sheriff, I. . . .

SHERIFF: But that ain't what I called to tell you about.

O'NUSKA: I'm glad to hear that, Sheriff.

SHERIFF: Sergeant, we got a boy down the road. Smart as a whip. Willie Dunston. He's the son—the second son—of old Sam Dunston. Sam's been farming in these parts for two hundred years. His folks has, anyways. Well, Willie is the smartest kid we've had in these parts since I can remember. We're right proud of Willie. Wins all the prizes. Had a writing of his published in this here scientific journal. The kids these days—I tell you!

O'NUSKA: Sheriff, I. . . .

SHERIFF: Willie's in his last year in high school over in Gresham. He's interested in all things scientific like. He's got himself this telescope, and I saw with my own eyes this little weather station he built with his own hands. You want to know what kind of weather you'll have tomorrow down there in New York, you just ask Willie.

O'NUSKA: I'll do that. I'll surely do that. But Sheriff, I. . . .

SHERIFF: And Willie's got this ham radio setup he built in a corner of the barn old Sam let him have. You know about this shortwave radio, Sergeant?

O'NUSKA: Yes, I know. I know.

SHERIFF: Well, maybe about fifteen–twenty minutes ago, I got this call from Willie on the telephone. He said on account of it was Saturday night and he could sleep late Sunday morning, he said he was out there in his corner there in the barn, listening in and talking to folks. You know how these shortwave radio folks do.

O'NUSKA: Yes. Go on.

SHERIFF: Willie said he picked up a call from New York City. He said he logged it in real careful and he figures it was about two minutes after two o'clock. You got that, Sergeant?

O'NUSKA: I got it.

SHERIFF: He said it was from a real smart kid in New York City he had talked to before. This kid said a robbery was going on right then and there in the apartment house where he lived. The address is five-three-five East Seventy-third Street. You got that Sergeant?

O'NUSKA: I've got it. It's five-three-five East Seventy-third Street.

SHERIFF: That's right. Well, Willie said the kid wasn't receiving and didn't answer any questions. All he said was that there was a robbery going on in his house and if anyone heard him they should call the New York City Police and tell them. So then Willie called me. Got me up. I'm standing here in my skin. I figure it's probably nothing. You know how kids like to fun. But I figured I better call you anyhow and let you know.

O'NUSKA: Sheriff, thank you very much. You did exactly right, and we appreciate it.

SHERIFF: Let me know how it comes out, will you?

O'NUSKA: I'll surely do that. Thanks, Sheriff. Good-bye.

SHERIFF: Good-bye. You take care now.

[Lapse of six seconds.]

JAMESON: For God's sakes.

O'NUSKA: Were you listening in on that?

JAMESON: I sure was. That's pretty nutty—to have a Maine sheriff call us and tell us we got a crime in progress.

O'NUSKA: I think it's a lot of shit, but with all this stuff on tape, who can take a chance? Send a car. That's Sector George, isn't it? Tell them to cruise five-three-five East Seventy-third Street. Tell them not to stop—just cruise the place, take a look, and call back.

JAMESON: Will do. That was some long-winded sheriff . . . wasn't he, Sarge?

O'NUSKA: Was he? I guess so. Toward the end there he was getting to me.

2:23:41AM

DISPATCHER: Car George Three, car George Three.

GEORGE THREE: George Three here.

DISPATCHER: Proceed to five-three-five East Seventy-three. Signal nine-five. Proceed five-three-five East Seventy-three. Signal nine-five. Extreme caution. Report A-sap.

GEORGE THREE: Rodge.

2:24:13AM

OFFICER: New York Police Department. May I help you?

VOICE: This is the Wichita, Kansas, Police Department Crime Communications Center. We got a phone-call from a ham radio operator stating that he tuned in a call from New York stating that a robbery. . . .

2:25:01AM.

OFFICER: New York Police Department. May I help you?

VOICE: My name is Everett Wilkins, Junior. I live in Tulsa, Oklahoma, where I'm calling from. I'm a ham radio operator, and a little while ago I got a. . . .

2:27:23AM.
OFFICER: New York Police Department. May I help you?
VOICE: Hiya, there! This here's the chief of police down in Orange Center, Florida. We got this little boy here who's like a nut about electronics and shortwave radio, and he says. . . .

2:28:12AM.
SERGEANT O'NUSKA: Jesus Christ!

2:34:41AM.
GEORGE THREE: Car George Three reporting.
DISPATCHER: Go ahead, Three.
GEORGE THREE: On your signal nine-five. Five-story apartment house. Lobby is lighted but we couldn't see anyone in it. There's a truck pulled up in the service alley. We saw two men loading what appeared to be a rug into the truck. The men appeared to be wearing some kind of masks.
DISPATCHER: Stand by. Out of sight around the corner or some place.
GEORGE THREE: Will do.

2:35:00AM.
JAMESON: Sarge, the car says it's a five-story apartment house. No one in the lobby. Truck parked in the service entrance. Two men, maybe masked, loading what appeared to be a rug into the truck.
O'NUSKA: Yes. Who's on duty—Liebman?
JAMESON: No, Sarge, his son was Bar-Mitzvahed today—or yesterday rather. He switched with Lieutenant Fineally.
O'NUSKA: Better get Fineally down here.
JAMESON: I think he went across the street to Ready's.
O'NUSKA: Well, get him over here, God damn it! And call the phone company. Get the lobby number of that address.

2:46:15AM.
OFFICER: New York Police Department. May I help you?
VOICE: My name is Ronald Trigere, and I live at four-one-three-two East St. Louis Street, Baltimore, Maryland. I am a ham radio operator, and I heard. . . .

2:48:08AM.
OFFICER: New York Police Department. May I help you?
VOICE: This is Lieutenant Donald Brannon, Chicago. We picked up a call from New York that stated. . . .

2:49:32AM.
JAMESON: Sarge, the phone company says the lobby number of that apartment house is five-five-five, nine-oh-seven-eight.
O'NUSKA: Call it.
JAMESON: Yes, sir.

2:49:53AM.
LIEUTENANT FINEALLY: What the fuck's going on here?

65

NYPD-SIS RECORDING #146-83C.

HASKINS: Now it's a quarter to three. Maybe a smidgen before. We were all in Five B. The second team had caught up with the first. The tech was having trouble with a wall safe. This was the apartment of Longene, the theatrical producer. We already had his collection of gemstones, and the brothers had taken a very nice Kurdistan down to the truck. We figured the wall safe for Longene's cash and his wife's jewels—if she *was* his wife which I, for one, am inclined to doubt. Then Ed Brodsky came running in, breathing hard. He had just pounded up all the stairs. He told Duke a squad car had cruised by, just as he and his brother were loading the rug into the truck. Duke cursed horribly and said the cruise car for that street was supposed to be in the coop at that hour.

QUESTION: Is that the term he used—"In the coop?"

HASKINS: Yes, Tommy, it was. Definitely. Duke then asked Brodsky if he thought the fuzz had seen him. Brodsky said he couldn't tell for sure, but he thought they had. Just as the car came past, Ed and his brother were carrying the rug out the service entrance. The inside of the service entrance was lighted. We had to keep the lights on so the brothers wouldn't break their necks coming downstairs with the stuff. Brodsky said he thought he saw a white blur as the face of the driver turned towards him. Ed and his brother were still wearing their masks, of course.

QUESTION: What did Anderson say to this?

HASKINS: He just stood there a while, thinking. Then he called me over to a corner, and he said he had decided to cut the whole thing short. We would just hit the things we were sure of. So he and I went over our checklists together. We decided to do the wall safe in Five B, which the tech was still working on. We'd skip Five A completely. This was where the crippled boy was in his bedroom, but there was really nothing worth risking our necks for. Then we'd go down to Four A and get Sheldon's coin collection and also spring his wall safe. That's all we'd do there. Then we'd move all the tenants from Four B to Four A, and then we'd do as much as we could in Mrs. Hathway's Four B apartment as I anticipated a veritable treasure trove there. So we agreed on this, and Duke told everyone to move faster—we were getting out. About this time he also sent the spade down to the lobby and told him to stay there, out of sight, but to report any police activity in the street outside. That maniac from Detroit would guard the people in Four A. Just then the tech sprung Longene's wall safe, and we got a nice box of ice, some bonds, and at least twenty G's in cash. I took this as a good omen, although I didn't like the idea of a prowl car going by outside.

66

CONTINUING EXCERPTS from twenty-four-hour tape, NYPDCC-31AUG-1SEP.

2:52:21AM.

JAMESON: Sir, there's no answer from the lobby phone at five-three-five East Seventy-third Street. It's not even ringing.

LIEUTENANT FINEALLY: Get back to the phone company. Ask them if they know what's wrong. Sergeant.

O'NUSKA: Sir?

FINEALLY: The captain picked a good weekend to go to Atlantic City.

O'NUSKA: Yes, sir.

FINEALLY: Who's the standby inspector?

O'NUSKA: Abrahamson, sir.

FINEALLY: Get him up. Tell him what's happening. We'll call him as soon as we know.

O'NUSKA: Yes, sir.

FINEALLY: You . . . what's your name?

OFFICER: Bailey, sir.

FINEALLY: Bailey, get out the block map for the Two fifty-first Precinct. Find out what address is back-to-back with five-three-five East Seventy-third Street. That's on the north side of Seventy-third, so the house backing it will be on the south side of Seventy-fourth. Probably five-three-four or five-three-six. Get a description of it.

BAILEY: Yes, sir.

2:52:49AM.

FINEALLY: You want me?

JAMESON: The phone company says the lobby line is completely dead, sir. They don't know why. And they get no answer from any other phone at that address.

FINEALLY: Who told them to try the other numbers at that address?

JAMESON: I did, sir.

FINEALLY: What's your name?

JAMESON: Marvin Jameson, sir.

FINEALLY: College?

JAMESON: Two years, sir.

FINEALLY: You're doing all right, Jameson. I won't forget it.

JAMESON: Thank you, sir.

2:59:03AM.

BAILEY: Lieutenant, the house backing on five-three-five East Seventy-third Street is five-three-six East Seventy-fourth Street. It's a ten-story apartment house with a small open paved space in back.

FINEALLY: All right. Who talked to the car that saw the masked men—or thought they saw masked men?

JAMESON: I talked to the dispatcher, sir.

FINEALLY: You again? What number was it?

JAMESON: George Three, sir.

FINEALLY: Where are they now?

JAMESON: I'll find out, sir.

FINEALLY: Fast. Sergeant.

O'NUSKA: Sir?

FINEALLY: You think we ought to bring in the inspector?

O'NUSKA: Yes, sir.

FINEALLY: So do I. Call him and alert his driver.

3:01:26AM.

JAMESON: Lieutenant.

FINEALLY: Yes?

JAMESON: Car George Three is standing by on East Seventy-second Street.

FINEALLY: Tell them to proceed to five-three-six East Seventy-fourth Street. No siren. Get on the roof or any floor where they can see down onto five-three-five East Seventy-third Street. Tell them to report any activity A-sap. You got that?

JAMESON: Yes, sir.

O'NUSKA: Lieutenant, the inspector's on his way. But he's got to come in from Queens. It'll be half an hour at least.

FINEALLY: All right. It may still be nothing. Better call the Two fifty-first and talk to the duty sergeant. Tell him what's going on. Find out where his nearest beat men are. You better send three more cars. Have them stand by on East Seventy-second Street. No sirens or lights. Tell the duty sergeant of the Two fifty-first that we'll pull in two cars from Sector Harry to fill in. You take care of it. And we'll keep him informed. Now let's see—have we forgotten anything?

O'NUSKA: Tactical Patrol Force, sir?

FINEALLY: God bless you. But what have they got on for tonight? It's a holiday weekend.

O'NUSKA: One bus. Twenty men. I put them on Blue Alert.

FINEALLY: Good. Good.

O'NUSKA: And I didn't even go to college.

67

THE FOLLOWING is an additional portion of the statement dictated to a representative of the District Attorney's Office, County of New York, by Gerald Bingham, Jr., a minor, resident of Apartment 5A, 535 East Seventy-third Street, New York, New York, excerpted from recordings NYDA-#146-113A-113G, and as transcribed (NYDA-#146-113AT-113GT).

WITNESS: I estimated it was now approximately three in the morning. I heard voices and sounds of activity coming from across the hall. I judged that the thieves were ransacking Apartment Five B and would soon be into our apartment. This caused me some trepidation, as I felt certain they would discover the electronic equipment in the closet in my bedroom. However, I took comfort from the fact that it might be possible they would not recognize the nature of the equipment. They would not realize it was a shortwave transmitter. Perhaps I could convince them it was part of our hi-fi system.

In any event, you understand, although I felt some fear—I realized that my body was covered with perspiration—I did not really care what they did to me. They could not know I had used the equipment. And I did not really believe they would kill me. I felt they might hurt me if they recognized the equipment and thought I might have used it. But I am no stranger to pain, and the prospect did not alarm me unduly. But I was disturbed by the realization that they might hurt my mother and father.

However, all my fears were groundless. For reasons I did not comprehend at the time, they skipped our apartment completely. The only man who came in was the tall, slender one who had removed my wheelchair and crutches earlier. He came in, stood alongside my bed and said, "Behaving yourself, boy?"

I said, "Yes, sir."

As soon as I said it, I wondered why I called him Sir. I do not call my father Sir. But there was something about this masked man. I have thought a great deal about him since the events of that night, and I have decided that somehow—I don't know quite how—he had an air and bearing of authority. Somehow, I don't know how, he demanded respect.

In any event, he nodded and looked about. "Your room?" he asked me.

"Yes," I said.

"All yours." He nodded again. "When I was your age, I lived in a room not much bigger than this with my mammy and pappy and five brothers and sisters."

"The late John F. Kennedy said that life is unfair," I told him.

He laughed and said, "Yes, that is so. And anyone over the age of four who don't realize it ain't got much of a brain in him. What do you want to be, boy?"

"A research scientist," I said promptly. "Perhaps in medicine, perhaps in electronics, maybe in space technology. I haven't decided yet."

"A research scientist?" he asked, and by the way he said it, I knew he didn't have a very clear idea of what that was. I was going to explain to him but then I thought better of it.

"A research scientist?" he repeated. "Is there money in it?"

I told him there was, that I'd already had offers from two companies and that if you discovered something really important, you could become a multi-millionaire. I don't know why I was telling him these things except that he seemed genuinely interested. At least, that's the impression I received.

"A multimillionaire," he repeated. He said, "Mult-*eye*."

Then he looked around the room—at my books, my work table, the space maps I had pinned to the walls.

"I could—" he started to say, but then he stopped and didn't go on.

"Sir?" I said.

"I could never understand any of this shit," he said finally and laughed. Then he said, "You keep behaving yourself, y'hear? We'll be out of here soon. Try to get some sleep."

He turned around and walked out. I only saw him once after that, very briefly. I felt that if he. . . . I felt that maybe I could have been a good. . . . I felt that maybe he and I might. . . . I am afraid I am not being very precise. I do not know exactly what I felt at that moment.

68

CONTINUING EXCERPTS from the twenty-four-hour tape, NYPDCC-31AUG-1SEP.

3:14:32AM.

O'NUSKA: Lieutenant, we have a report from Officer Meyer in car George Three. He got onto the roof of the building at five-three-six East Seventy-fourth Street. He says shades are drawn in all the apartments at five-three-five East Seventy-third. Lights are on in several apartments. The service staircase in the rear of the building is also lighted. There is an unshaded window on the service staircase at each floor. Meyer says he saw masked men carrying objects down the stairs and placing them in the truck parked in the service alley.

FINEALLY: How many men did he see?

O'NUSKA: He says at least five different men, maybe more.

FINEALLY: Five men? My God, what's this going to be—the shoot-out at the O.K. Corral? Get the tactical squad moving. Red Alert. Tell them to park on Seventy-second near the river and wait further instructions. You got those three other cars?

O'NUSKA: Yes, sir. Standing by, within a block or so.

FINEALLY: Seal off East Seventy-third Street. Put one car across the street at East End Avenue and another at York Avenue.

O'NUSKA: Got it.

FINEALLY: Tell George Three to stay where they are. Send the third car around to join them.

O'NUSKA: Right.

FINEALLY: Let's see now—there's got to be tenants in there.

O'NUSKA: Yes, sir. It's the holiday weekend and some of them'll be gone, but there's got to be someone—the super, the doorman, the kid who sent out the shortwave call. Others probably.

FINEALLY: Get me the duty sergeant at the Two fifty-first. You know who he is?

O'NUSKA: Yes, sir. He's my brother.

FINEALLY: You kidding?

O'NUSKA: No, sir. He really is my brother.

FINEALLY: What kind of a precinct is it?

O'NUSKA: Very tight. Captain Delaney lived right next door in a converted brownstone. He's in and out all the time, even when he's not on duty.

FINEALLY: Don't tell me that's "Iron Balls" Delaney?

O'NUSKA: That's the man.

FINEALLY: Well, well, well. Will wonders never cease? Get him for me, will you? We need a commander on the scene.

O'NUSKA: Right away, Lieutenant.

3:19:26AM.

DELANEY: I see. . . . What is your name?

FINEALLY: Lieutenant John K. Fineally, sir.

DELANEY: Lieutenant Fineally, I shall now repeat what you have told me. If I am incorrect in any detail, please do not interrupt but correct me when I have finished. Is that understood?

FINEALLY: Yes, sir.

DELANEY: You have reason to believe that a breaking and entering, and a burglary and/or armed robbery is presently taking place at five-three-five East Seventy-third Street. A minimum of five masked men have been observed removing objects from this residence and placing them in a truck presently located in the service alleyway alongside the apartment house. Four Sector George cars are presently in the area. One is blocking Seventy-third Street at East End Avenue, and one is blocking the street at York Avenue. Two cars with four officers are on Seventy-fourth Street, in the rear of the building in question. The duty sergeant of this precinct has alerted two patrolmen to stand by their telephones and await further instructions. The Tactical Patrol Force bus is presently on its way with a complement of twenty men, under Red Alert, and has been instructed to stand by on Seventy-second Street to await further orders. Inspector Walter Abrahamson has been alerted and is on his way to the scene of the suspected crime. I will proceed to the scene and take command of the forces at my disposal until such time as the inspector arrives. I will enter the premises with the forces at my disposal and, with proper care for the life and well-being of innocent bystanders, forestall the alleged thieves from escaping, place them under arrest, and recover the reportedly stolen objects. Is that correct in every detail?

FINEALLY: You've got it right, sir. In every detail.

DELANEY: Is a tape being made of this conversation, Lieutenant?

FINEALLY: Yes, sir, it is.

DELANEY: This is Captain Edward X. Delaney signing off. I am now departing to take command of the forces available to me at the scene of the reported crime.

[Lapse of six seconds.]

FINEALLY: Jesus Christ. I don't believe it. I heard it but I don't believe it. Were you listening to that, Sergeant?

O'NUSKA: Yes, sir.

FINEALLY: I've heard stories about that guy but I never believed them.

O'NUSKA: They're all true. He's had more commendations than I've had hangovers.

FINEALLY: I still don't believe it. He's something else again.

O'NUSKA: That's what my brother says.

69

THE FOLLOWING is a typed transcription (NYDA-#146-121AT) from an original recording (NYDA-#146-121A) made on 11 September, 1968, at Mother of Mercy Hospital, New York City. The witness is Gerald Bingham, Sr., resident of Apartment 5A, 535, East Seventy-third Street, New York, New York.

QUESTION: Glad to see you looking better, Mr. Bingham. How do you feel?

BINGHAM: Oh, I feel a lot better. The swelling is down, and I received some good news this morning. The doctors say I won't lose the sight of my right eye. They say the sight may be slightly impaired, but I'll be able to see out of it.

QUESTION: Mr. Bingham, I'm glad to hear that . . . real glad. I can imagine how you felt.

BINGHAM: Yes . . . well . . . you know. . . .

QUESTION: Mr Bingham, there are just a few details in your previous statement we'd like to get cleared up—if you feel you're up to it.

BINGHAM: Oh, yes. I feel fine. As a matter of fact, I welcome your visit. Very boring—just lying here.

QUESTION: I can imagine. Well, what we wanted to clear up was the period around three thirty on the morning of 1 September, 1968. According to your previous statement, you were at that time in Apartment Four B with the other tenants and the doorman. You were being guarded by the man who struck you in the face and kicked you earlier in your own apartment. This man was carrying a weapon. Is that correct?

BINGHAM: Yes, that's right.

QUESTION: Do you know anything about handguns, Mr. Bingham?

BINGHAM: Yes . . . a little. I served with the Marines in Korea.

QUESTION: Can you identify the weapon the man was carrying?

BINGHAM: It looked to me like a government issue Colt .45 automatic pistol of the 1917 series.

QUESTION: Are you certain?

BINGHAM: Fairly certain, yes. I had range training with a gun like that.

QUESTION: At the time in question—that is, three thirty on the morning of first September—what was your physical condition?

BINGHAM: You mean was I fully conscious and alert?

QUESTION: Well . . . yes. Were you?

BINGHAM: No. My eye was quite painful, and I was getting this throbbing ache from where he had kicked me. They had put me on the couch in Mrs. Hathway's living room—it was really a Victorian love seat covered with red velvet. My wife was holding a cold, wet towel to my eye, and Dr. Rubicoff from downstairs was helping also. I think I was a little hazy at the time. Perhaps I was in mild shock. You know, it was the first time in my life I had been struck in anger. I mean, it was the first time I had ever been physically assaulted. It was a very unsettling experience.

QUESTION: Yes, Mr. Bingham, I know.

BINGHAM: The idea that a man I didn't know had struck me and injured me, and then had kicked me . . . to tell you the truth, I felt so ashamed of myself. I know this was probably a strange reaction to have, but that's the way I felt.

QUESTION: You were ashamed?

BINGHAM: Yes. That's the feeling I had.

QUESTION: But why should you feel ashamed? You had done all you could—which was, incidentally, much more than many other men would have done. You reacted very quickly. You tried to defend your family. There was no reason why you should have been ashamed of yourself.

BINGHAM: Well, that's the way I felt. Perhaps it was because the man with the gun treated me—and the others, too—with such utter, brutal contempt. The way he waved that gun around. The way he laughed. I could see he was enjoying it. He shoved us around. When he wanted the doorman to get away from the window, he didn't tell him to get away; he shoved him so that poor Tim O'Leary fell down. Then the man laughed again. I think I was afraid of him. Maybe that's why I felt ashamed.

QUESTION: The man was threatening you with a loaded gun. There was good reason to be frightened.

BINGHAM: Well . . . I don't know. I was in action in Korea. Small-scale infantry action. I was frightened then, too, but I wasn't ashamed. There's a difference but it's hard to explain. I knew this man was very sick and very brutal and very dangerous.

QUESTION: Well, let's drop that and get on. . . . Now, you said that at about three thirty—maybe a little later—four of the others came in and moved all of you to Apartment Four A across the hall.

BINGHAM: That's correct. I was able to walk, supported by my wife and Dr. Rubicoff, and they got us all out of Apartment Four B and into Four A.

QUESTION: Did they tell you why they were moving you?

BINGHAM: No. The man who seemed to be the leader just came in and said, "Everyone across the hall. Make it fast. Move." Or something like that.

QUESTION: He told you to make it fast?

BINGHAM: Yes. Perhaps I was imagining things—I was still shaky, you understand—but I thought there was a tension there. They prodded us to move faster. They seemed to be in a big hurry now. When they first came to my apartment earlier in the evening they were more controlled, more deliberate. Now they were hurrying and pushing people.

QUESTION: Why did you think that was?

BINGHAM: I thought they seemed frightened, that something was threatening them and they wanted to wind up everything and get out in a hurry. That's the impression I got.

QUESTION: You thought *they* were frightened? Didn't that make you feel better?

BINGHAM: No. I was still ashamed of myself.

70

THE FOLLOWING section (and several below) is excerpted from the final report of Captain Edward X. Delaney—a document that has become something of a classic in the literature of the New York Police Department, and that has been reprinted in the police journals of seven countries, including Russia. It's official file number is NYPD-EXD-1SEP1968.

"I arrived at the corner of East Seventy-third Street and York Avenue at approximately 3:24 A.M. I had driven over from the 251st Precinct house. My driver was Officer Aloysius McClaire. I immediately saw the squad car that had been parked across Seventy-third Street, supposedly blocking exit from the street. However, it was improperly situated. This was car George Twenty-four (See Appendix IV for complete list of personnel involved.) After identifying myself, I directed that the car be parked slightly toward the middle of the block at a point where private cars were parked on both sides of the street, thus more effectively blocking exit from the street.

"There is a public phone booth located on the northwest corner of East Seventy-third Street and York Avenue. My investigation proved this phone to be out of order. (N.B. Subsequent investigation proved all the public phone booths within a ten-block area of the crime had been deliberately damaged, apparant evidence of the careful and detailed planning of this extremely well-organized crime.)

"I thereupon directed Officer McClaire to force open the door of a cigar shop located on the northwest corner of East Seventy-third Street and York Avenue. He did so, without breaking the glass, and I entered, switched on the lights, and located the proprietor's phone. (I was careful to respect his property, although recompense should be made by the City of New York for his broken lock.)

"I then called Communications Center and spoke to Lieutenant John K. Fineally. I informed him of the location of my command post and requested that the telephone line on which I was speaking be kept open and manned every minute. He agreed. I also requested that Inspector Walter Abrahamson, on his way in from Queens, be directed to my command post. Lieutenant Fineally acknowledged. I then directed my driver, Officer McClaire, to remain at the open phone line until relieved. He acknowledged this order.

"I was dressed in civilian clothes at this time, being technically off duty. I divested myself of my jacket and carried it over one arm, after rolling up my shirt sleeves. I left my straw hat in the cigar store. I borrowed a Sunday morning newspaper from one of the officers in the car blockading Seventy-third Street. I placed the folded newspaper under my arm. Then I strolled along the south side of East Seventy-third Street, from York Avenue to East End Avenue. As I passed 535 East Seventy-third Street, across the street, I could see, without turning my head, the truck parked in the service entrance. The side doors of the truck were open, but there was no sign of human activity.

"I saw immediately that it was a very poor tactical situation for a frontal assault. The houses facing the beleaguered building offered very little in the way of cover and/or concealment. Most were of the same height as 535, being town houses or converted brownstones. A frontal assault would be possible, but not within the directives stated in NYPD-SIS-DIR-#64, dated 19 January, 1967, which states: 'In any action, the commanding officer's first consideration must be for the safety of innocent bystanders and, secondly, for the safety and well-being of police personnel under his command.'

"When I reached the corner of East Seventy-third Street and East End Avenue, I identified myself to the officers in car George Nineteen, blocking the street at this corner. Again, the car was improperly parked. After pointing out to the driver how I wished the car to be placed, I had him drive me around the block, back to my command post on York Avenue, and then directed him to return to his original post and block the street at that end in the manner in which I had directed. I then returned the newspaper to the officer from whom I had borrowed it.

"In the short drive around the block to my command post, I had formulated my plan of attack. I contacted Lieutenant Fineally at Communications Center via the open telephone line in the cigar store. (May I say at this time that the cooperation of all personnel at Communications Center during this entire episode was exemplary, and my only suggestion for improvement might be a more formalized system of communication with more code words and numbers utilized. Without these, communications tend to become personalized and informal, which just wastes valuable time.)

"I ordered Lieutenant Fineally to send to my command post five more two-man squad cars. I also requested an emergency squad—to be supplied with at least two sets of walkie-talkies; a weapons carrier, with tear gas and riot guns; two searchlight cars; and an ambulance. Lieutenant Fineally stated he would consult his on-duty roster and supply whatever was available as soon as possible. At this time—I estimate it was perhaps 3:40 or 3:45 A.M.—I also asked Lieutenant Fineally to inform Deputy Arthur C. Beatem, the standby deputy of that date, of what was going on and leave it to Deputy Beatem's judgment as to whether or not to inform the commissioner and/or the mayor.

"I then began to organize my forces. . . ."

71

NYPD-SIS RECORDING #146-83C.

HASKINS: About this time, Duke told. . . .

QUESTION: What time was it?

HASKINS: Oh, I don't know exactly, Tommy. It was getting late—or rather early in the morning. I thought the sky was getting light, or perhaps I was imagining it. In any event, I had pointed out to the Brodsky brothers what was to be taken from Apartment Four B. As I had suspected, it was a veritable treasure trove. The tech sprung a huge old-fashioned trunk, brass-bound, with a hasp and padlock on it. And he also opened a few odds and ends like jewel boxes, file cases, and even a GI ammunition box that had been fitted with a hasp and padlock. It was really hilarious what those old biddies had squirreled away. Quite obviously, they did not trust banks! There was one diamond pendant and a ruby choker—all their jewels were incredibly filthy, incidentally—and I judged those two pieces alone would bring close to fifty G's. In addition, there was cash— even some of the old-style large bills that I hadn't seen for years and years. There were negotiable bonds, scads and scads of things like Victorian tiaras, bracelets, "dog collars," headache bands, pins, brooches, a small collection of jeweled snuffboxes, loops and loops of pearls, earrings, men's stick pins—and all of it good, even if it did need a cleaning. My God, Tommy, it was like being let loose in Tiffany's about seventy-five years ago. There were also some simply yummy original glass, enamel, and cloisonné pieces that I couldn't bear to leave behind. Duke had told us to hurry it up, so we disregarded the rugs and furniture, although I saw a Sheraton table—a small one—that any museum in the city would have given an absolute fortune for, and there was a tiny little Kurdistan, no bigger than three by five, that was simply exquisite. I just couldn't bear to leave that behind, so I had Billy Brodsky—the one who had the wet brain—tuck it under his arm and take it down to the truck.

QUESTION: Where was Anderson while all this was going on?

HASKINS: Oh, he was—you know—here, there, and everywhere. He checked on the crippled boy in Apartment Five A, and then he went out on the terrace of Five B to look around. Then he checked how that monster from Detroit was doing with the tenants who had been moved across the hall to Four A, and then he helped the Brodsky boys carry some things down to the truck, and then he prowled through some of the empty apartments. Just checking, you know. He was very good, very alert. Then, after I had finished in Apartment Four B, he told me to go down to the basement and see if the super was still sleeping and also check with the spade who had been stationed in the lobby. So I went down to the basement, and the super was still snoring.

QUESTION: Did you take anything from his apartment?

HASKINS: Oh no. It had been cleaned out earlier. The only thing we got was an antique triptych.

QUESTION: The super claims he had just been paid, he had almost a hundred dollars in his wallet, and his money was taken. Did you take it?

HASKINS: Tommy, that hurts! I may be many things, but I am not a cheap little sneak thief.

QUESTION: When they searched you at the station house you had about forty dollars in a money clip. And you also had almost a hundred dollars folded into a wad and tucked into your inside jacket pocket. Was that the super's money?

HASKINS: Tommy! How could you?

QUESTION: All right. What happened next—after you checked on the super and found he was still sleeping?

HASKINS: Duke had told me to check with Skeets Johnson in the lobby on the way up. He was in the doormen's booth in the rear of the lobby so no one could see him from the street. I asked him if everything was all right.

QUESTION: And what did he say?

HASKINS: He said he hadn't seen any beat fuzz or squad cars. He said the only person he had seen was a man carrying a newspaper with his jacket over his arm go humping by on the other side of the street. He said the man hadn't turned his head when he went by so he didn't think that was anything. But I could tell something was bothering him.

QUESTION: Why do you say that?

HASKINS: Well, everything he had said up to now had been in rhymes, some of them quite clever and amusing. The man was obviously talented. But now he was speaking normally, just as you or I, and he didn't seem to have the high spirits he had earlier in the evening. Like when we were in the truck, on the way to the apartment house, he kept us laughing and relaxed. But now I could tell he was down, so I asked him why. And he said he didn't know why he was down, but he said—and I remember his exact words—he said, "Something don't smell right." I left him there and went back upstairs and reported to Duke that Skeets hadn't seen any fuzz or cars but that he was troubled. Duke nodded and hurried the Brodsky boys along. We were about ready to leave. I figured another half hour at the most and we'd be gone. I wasn't feeling down. I was feeling up. I thought it had been a very successful evening, far beyond our wildest hopes. Even though I was working for a fixed fee, I wanted the whole thing to come off because it was very exciting—I had never done anything like that before—and I thought Duke might give me some more work. Also, you know, I had pocketed a few little things— trinkets . . . really nothing of value—but the whole evening would prove very profitable for me.

72

EXCERPT FROM the final report of Captain Edward X. Delaney, NYPD-EXD-1SEP1968.

"See my memorandum No. 563 dated 21 December, 1966, in which I strongly urged that every commanding officer of the NYPD of the rank of lieutenant and above be required to attend a course in the tactics of small infantry units (up to company strength), as taught at several bases of the U.S. Army and at Quantico, Virginia, where officer candidates of the U.S. Marine corps are trained.

"During my service as patrolman in the period 1946–49, the great majority of crimes were committed by individuals, and the strategy and tactics of the NYPD were, in a large part, directed toward thwarting and frustrating the activities of individual criminals. In recent years, however, the nature of crime in our city (and, indeed, the nation—if not the world) has changed radically.

"We are now faced, not with individual criminals, but with organized bands, gangs, national and international organizations. Most of these are paramilitary or military-type organizations, be they groups of militant college students or hijackers in the garment center. Indeed, the organization variously known as Cosa Nostra, Syndicate, Mafia, etc., even has military titles for its members—don for general or colonel, *capo* for major or captain, soldier for men in the ranks, etc.

"The realization of the organized military character of crime today led me to my memo cited above in which I urged that police officers be given military training in infantry tactics, and also be required to take a two-week refresher course each year to keep abreast of the latest developments. I myself have taken such courses on a volunteer basis since my appointment as lieutenant in 1953.

"Hence, I saw the situation at 535 East Seventy-third Street, in the early morning hours of 1 September, 1968, as a classic military problem. My forces, gathered and gathering (it was now approximately 3:45 A.M.) occupied the low ground—on the street—while the enemy occupied the high ground—in a five-story apartment house. ('War is geography.') Of particular relevance to such a situation are the U.S. Army handbooks— USA-45617990-416 (*House-to-House Combat*) and USA-917835190-017 (Tactics of Street Fighting).

"I decided that, although a direct, frontal assault was possible (such an assault is *always* possible if casualties may be disregarded), the best solution would be vertical envelopment. This is a technique developed by the Germans in World War II with the dropping of paratroopers behind the enemy's lines. It was further refined during the Korean Police Action by the use of helicopters. Attack, up to this time, had been largely a two-dimensional problem. It now became three-dimensional.

"During my reconnaissance along East Seventy-third Street, I had noted that the building immediately adjacent to 535 was what I judged to be a 16- to 18-story apartment house. It was flush against the east side of the beleaguered building. I realized at once that a vertical envelopment was possible. That is, I could have combat personnel lowered from the roof of the higher building or, with luck (a very important consideration in all human activities), I could have police officers exit through the windows of the higher building at perhaps the sixth or seventh floor and merely drop or jump to the terraces of the building occupied by the enemy.

"With a noisy display of force, I judged, the police personnel on the top floors of 535 could 'spook' the criminals and drive them down onto the street. I did not desire the police personnel on the upper floor (I estimated five would be an adequate number) to enter into combat with the enemy. Their sole duty would be to frighten the criminals down to the street level without endangering any tenants of the building who might be present.

"At that time the enemy would no longer enjoy the advantage of holding the upper ground. By careful, calculated timing, I would then have emplaced in a semicircle about the front of 535, four two-man squad cars and two searchlight cars, all personnel instructed to keep behind the cover and concealment offered by their vehicles as much as possible, and not to fire until fired upon. In addition, I intended to position a force of six men in the rear of 535—that is, in the cemented open space in the rear of the Seventy-fourth Street building that backed onto 535 East Seventy-third Street. This force, I felt, would be sufficient to block a rearward escape by the enemy. The fact that one, indeed, by his extraordinary ability and good fortune, did escape (temporarily), does not, in my opinion, negate the virtues of my plan of operations.

"By this time, the tactical squad (Tactical Patrol Force) had reported to me at my command post. This unit consisted of twenty men, in a bus, commanded by a Negro sergeant. There were two additional Negroes in the squad.

"The following comments may be considered by some to be unnecessary—if not foolhardy—considering the current state of ethnic and racial unrest in New York City. However, I feel my judgments—based on twenty-two years of service in the NYPD—may be of value to other officers faced with a comparable situation, and I am determined to make them. . . .

"It is said that all men are created equal—and this may be correct, in the sight of God and frequently—but not always—under the law. However, all men are *not* created equal as to their ethnic and racial origins, their intelligence, their physical strength, and their moral commitment. Specifically, ethnic and racial groups, whatever they may be—Negro, Irish, Polish, Jewish, Italian, etc.—have certain inborn characteristics. Some of these characteristics can be an advantage to a commanding officer; some may be a disadvantage. But if the commanding officer disregards them—through a misguided belief in total equality—he is guilty of dereliction of duty, in my opinion, since his sole duty is to solve the problem at hand, using the best equipment and personnel under his command, with due regard to the potential of his men.

"It has been my experience that Negro personnel are particularly valuable when the situation calls for a large measure of élan and derring-do. And they are especially valuable when they operate as units—that is, when several Negro officers are operating together. Hence, I ordered the Negro sergeant commanding the tactical squad to select the two other Negroes in his squad, augment them by two white officers, and execute the vertical envelopment. This would be the unit that would drop onto the terrace of 535 and flush the enemy down to the street.

"He acknowledged my order, and after a short discussion we agreed his men would be armed with one Thompson submachine gun, two riot guns, service revolvers, smoke, and concussion grenades. In addition, his squad of five men (including himself) would carry a walkie-talkie radio, and they would inform me the moment they had made their drop onto the terrace of 535. The officer's name is Sergeant James L. Everson, Shield 72897537, and I hereby recommend him for a commendation. (See attached form NYPD-RC-EXD-109FGC-1968.)"

73

FROM THE official report of Sergeant James L. Everson, Shield 72897537. This is coded NYPD-JLE-1SEP68.

"I received my orders from Captain Edward X. Delaney at his command post in a cigar store on the corner of East Seventy-third Street and York Avenue. I selected the four additional officers from my squad and proceeded to the corner of East Seventy-third Street and East End Avenue. Transportation was by squad car, as directed by Captain Delaney.

"Upon arrival at the aforesaid corner, I determined it would be best if we went one at a time into the building adjoining 535 East Seventy-third Street. Therefore I ordered my men to follow me at counted intervals of sixty seconds. I went first.

"I entered the lobby of the adjoining building and found the man on duty was not the regular doorman but was the super filling in for the doorman because of the holiday weekend. He was sleeping. I awakened him and explained the situation. By the time the other four men of my squad had joined me, he had told me he thought we could drop onto the terrace of 535 by going out the windows of Apartment 6C which overlooked the apartment house where the criminals were located and operating. We had service revolvers, a submachine gun, riot guns, and grenades. The super escorted us to Apartment 6C.

"This apartment was occupied by Irving K. Mandelbaum, a single man. At the time, there was also present in the apartment a single female, Gretchen K. Strobel. I believe, if desired, a charge of unlawful fornication could be brought against Irving K. Mandelbaum under the civil laws of the

City of New York. But because of the cooperation Mr. Mandelbaum offered and provided to officers of the New York Police Department, I do not suggest this.

"Miss Strobel went into the bathroom, and me and the squad went through the bedroom window which directly overlooks the terrace of 535. It was only a two- or three-foot drop. The moment we were all on the terrace, I contacted Captain Delaney via walkie-talkie. Reception was very good. I told him we were in position, and he told me to wait two minutes, then go ahead."

74

FROM CAPTAIN Edward X. Delaney's report NYPD-EXD-1SEP1968.

"It was approximately 4:14A.M. when Sergeant Everson got through to me. I should mention here that the operation of the new 415X16C radios was excellent. Everson said he and his squad were on the terrace of 535 East Seventy-third Street. We agreed he would wait two minutes before commencing his spooking operation.

"Not all the men and equipment I had requisitioned had arrived by this time. However, I felt it better to proceed with what I had rather than await optimum conditions which rarely, if ever, seem to arrive. Hence, I directed cars George Six and George Fourteen (two officers each) to approach from York Avenue toward 535, and cars George Twenty-four and George Eight to approach from East End Avenue. Leading the two approaching from East End would be Searchlight Car SC-147 (the single one that had arrived by this time). The five vehicles would then park in a semicircle around the entrance of 535. The searchlight car would illuminate the building after all personnel had taken cover behind their vehicles. The arrival of additional squad cars, provided by the efficiency of Lieutenant John K. Fineally, NYPDCC, enabled me to station blocking cars at the exits from East Seventy-third Street at York Avenue and East End Avenue, and car George Thirty-two at York Avenue.

"I was in the first car (George Six) approaching the apartment house from York Avenue. My order, repeated several times, was that there was to be no firing until I gave the command."

75

RECORDING NYDA-#146-114A-114G. Interrogation of Gerald Bingham, Jr.

QUESTION: What time was it then?
WITNESS: I don't know exactly. It was after four in the morning.
QUESTION: What happened then?
WITNESS: Suddenly five policemen burst into my bedroom. They came in through the French doors leading to the terrace. Three of them were colored. The man in front was colored. They were all carrying weapons. The first man had a machine gun in his hands, and he said to me, "Who are you?"
I said, "I am Gerald Bingham junior, and I live in this apartment."

He looked at me and said, "You the kid that sent out the report?"

"Yes," I said, "I sent out a shortwave transmission."

He grinned at me and said, "You get yourself out on that terrace."

I told him I was crippled and couldn't move because they had taken away my wheelchair and my crutches.

He said, "Okay, you stay right where you're at. Where *they* at?"

"Down on the fourth floor," I told him. "I think they're all on the fourth floor, right below us."

"Okay," he said, "we'll take care of them. You stay right where you're at and don't make no noise."

They all started out of the apartment. I called after them, "Please don't kill him," but I don't think they heard me.

76

NYPD-SIS RECORDING #146-83C.

HASKINS: We were finishing up Apartment Four B. We were close to finishing. God, we were so *close*! Then everything came apart. Shouts from upstairs. Noise. Gunshots. A big explosion. Smoke pouring down the stairway. Men shouting, "You're surrounded! Hands up! Throw down your guns! You're dead! We've got you!" Silly things like that. I wet my pants. Yes, Tommy, I admit it freely—I soiled myself. Then we started moving. The tech went pounding down the back stairs, then the two Brodsky boys, and then me following. But before I left I saw the Detroit hooligan rush to the front window of Four A and fire his gun through the glass.

QUESTION: Was there return fire?

HASKINS: No. Well . . . I don't know for sure. I had turned away from the foyer between the two apartments. I was on my way down the service staircase. I saw and heard him fire through the window of Four A. But I didn't see or hear any return fire from the street.

QUESTION: Where was Anderson while all this was going on?

HASKINS: He was standing there in the foyer between the two apartments. He was just standing still. He just didn't move.

77

FROM THE final report of Captain Edward X. Delaney, NYPD-EXD-1SEP1968.

"My assault forces were in position. The moment I heard the envelopment squad start their mission, the searchlight car—as per my previous orders—illuminated the front of the building. We were almost immediately fired upon from a fourth-floor window. I shouted to my men to hold their fire.'

78

NYDA-EHM-108B, DICTATED, sworn, signed, and witnessed statement by Ernest Heinrich Mann.

"The moment the noise began, I realized it was all over. Therefore I walked slowly and quietly down the service staircase, took the door into the lobby, removed my mask and gloves, and seated myself on the marble floor, well out of range of the front doors. I then put my back against the wall, raised my arms above my head, and waited. I detest violence."

79

FROM THE final report of Captain Edward X. Delaney, NYPD-EXD-1SEP1968.

"We still had not yet fired a shot. Then suddenly a masked man burst through the front doors of the house, firing a revolver at the assembled cars. I thereupon gave the command to open fire, and he was cut down in short order."

80

EXCERPT FROM NYPD-SIS recording #146-83C, interrogation of Thomas Haskins by Thomas K. Brody, detective, second grade.

HASKINS: When we got down to the ground floor, the two Brodsky boys headed out to the truck through the back entrance. I took the door into the lobby. And there was the tech, sitting on the floor against the wall, without his mask, his hands raised over his head. I felt sick. Then I saw the smoke draw his gun and dash out through the front doors. I heard him say "Shit," and then he was gone out through the doors. Then I heard the guns and I knew he was dead. Frankly, I didn't know what to do. I believe I might have been somewhat hysterical. You understand, don't you, Tommy?

QUESTION: Yes. But what *did* you do?

HASKINS: Well, silly as it may seem—I wasn't thinking quite right, you understand—I turned and went back to the service staircase and started to go up. And there, at the second-floor landing, was Duke Anderson.

QUESTION: What was he doing?

HASKINS: Just standing there. Very calm. I said. "Duke, we've got—" And he said, very quiet, "Yes, I know. Don't do a thing right now. Stay right where you are. Just stand here. I've got something to do, but I'll be right down and we'll be getting out together."

QUESTION: Are those his exact words?

HASKINS: As near as I can remember.

QUESTION: And what did you do then?

HASKINS: I did exactly what he told me. I just stood there on the stairs.

QUESTION: What did he do?

HASKINS: Duke? He turned around and went back up the stairs.

81

FROM THE final report of Captain Edward X. Delaney, NYPD-EXD-1SEP1968.
"We were still receiving intermittent fire from the fourth-floor window from what, I judged, was a single gunman. I instructed my men not to return his fire. Discipline, I should say at this time, under these difficult and aggravating circumstances was excellent. At approximately three minutes after the start of the action, two men dashed from the rear service entrance, climbed aboard the truck, and began to back the truck from the service alley at high speed.
"This was, of course, a move of desperation, doomed to failure as I had arranged my cordon of squad cars to forestall such a move. As the truck backed, one man leaned from the window and fired a revolver at us as the other drove. We returned his fire.
"The truck crashed into car George Fourteen and stopped there. In the crash, Officer Simon Legrange, Shield 67935419, suffered a broken leg, and Officer Marvin Finkelstein, Shield 45670985, was slightly wounded in the upper arm by a bullet fired by the gunman in the truck. Up to this time, this was the extent of our casualties.
"When I ordered, 'Cease fire!', we determined that the gunman in the truck was dead (later certified as Edward J. Brodsky) and the driver of the truck (later certified as William K. Brodsky) suffered a broken shoulder as a result of the crash."

82

NYPD-SIS-#146-92A.

MRS. HATHWAY: Well, we were all across the hall in Apartment Four A when suddenly the shooting started. I would say it was about fifteen minutes after four in the morning.
MISS KALER: Closer to four thirty.
MRS. HATHWAY: I had my brooch watch, you silly thing, and it was almost four fifteen.
MISS KALER: Four thirty.
QUESTION: Ladies, please. What happened then?
MRS. HATHWAY: Well, this masked man who had been so mean and cruel rushed to the window and began firing his weapon. He broke the glass—and what a mess it made on the rug. And he fired his gun down into the street. And then. . . .
MISS KALER: And then there were these terrible explosions on the stairs and men shouting and everyone wondered what was happening. So I said we should all sit right where we were and not move, and that would be the best thing, and this ruffian kept shooting his gun out the window, and I was thankful we were not in our own apartment as I feared the policemen might fire an atomic rocket through the window and destroy just everything. And just about then this other masked man came through the door and he was drawing a gun from his pocket and I thought he would also fire down through the window but he didn't. . . .

83

NYDA-#146-121AT.

BINGHAM: When the firing started, I suggested everyone get down on the floor. We all did except for the old ladies from across the hall who said they wouldn't—or perhaps they couldn't. In any event, they slumped in their chairs. The man who was guarding us fired his pistol out the window.

QUESTION: Was there any return fire, Mr. Bingham?

BINGHAM: No, sir, I do not believe there was. None that I was aware of. The man just kept firing his gun and cursing. I saw him reload at least once from a clip he took from his pocket. And then a few minutes later another masked man came into the apartment. I recognized him as the second man who had been in my apartment.

QUESTION: The man who told the first masked man to stop kicking you?

BINGHAM: Yes, that's the one. Well, he came into the apartment right then and he was drawing a gun from his pocket.

QUESTION: What kind of a gun? Did you recognize it?

BINGHAM: It was a revolver, not a pistol. Big. I'd gusss a .38. I couldn't recognize the make.

QUESTION: All right. Then what?

BINGHAM: The second man, the man with the revolver who came in the door, said, "Socks."

QUESTION: Socks? That's all he said?

BINGHAM: Yes. He said, "Socks," and the man at the window turned around. And the second man shot him.

QUESTION: Shot him? How many times?

BINGHAM: Twice. I was watching this very closely and I'm sure of this. He came through the door, taking his gun from his pocket. He said, "Socks," and the man at the window turned around. And then the man coming in walked toward him and shot him twice. I could see the bullets going in. They plucked at his jacket. I think he shot him in the stomach and the chest. That's where it looked to me where the bullets went in. The man at the window dropped his own gun and went down. He went down very slowly. As a matter of fact, he grabbed at the drapes at the window and pulled down a drape and the rod. I think he said "What?"—or maybe it was something else. It sounded like "Wha" or something like that. Then he was on the floor and this maroon drape was across him and he was bleeding and twisting. Jesus. . . .

QUESTION: Shall we take a break for a few minutes, Mr. Bingham?

BINGHAM: No. I'm all right. And then my wife was sick; she up-chucked. And one of the old ladies from across the hall fainted and one screamed, and the two faggots I didn't know and had never seen before hugged each other, and Dr. Rubicoff looked like someone had sapped him. Holy God, what a moment that was.

QUESTION: And what did the killer do then?

BINGHAM: He looked at the man on the floor for a very brief moment. Then he put the gun back in his pocket, turned around, and walked out of the apartment. I never saw him again. Strange you should call him a killer.

QUESTION: That's what he was—wasn't he.

BINGHAM: Of course. But at the moment I got the feeling he was an executioner. That's the feeling I got—this man is an executioner, doing his job.

QUESTION: Then what happened?

BINGHAM: After he left? Dr. Rubicoff went over and knelt by the man who had been shot and examined his wounds and felt his pulse. "Alive," he said, "but not for long. This is very bad."

QUESTION: Thank you, Mr. Bingham.

BINGHAM: You're welcome.

84

NYPD-SIS RECORDING #146-83C.

HASKINS: It was a lifetime, an eternity. All that noise and gunfire and confusion. But I did what Duke told me and stood there on the second-floor landing.

QUESTION: You trusted him?

HASKINS: Of course, you silly! If you can't trust a man like Duke, who can you trust? So of course he came back down from the fourth floor, as I knew he would, and he said to me, "Better take your mask off, put your hands up, and go down slowly out the front door."

QUESTION: Why didn't you do that? It was good advice.

HASKINS: I know it was, I know it was. I knew it was then. But I can't explain to you how this man Anderson made me feel. He made me forget caution and made me willing to take a chance. Do you understand?

QUESTION: I'm afraid not.

HASKINS: Oh, Tommy, Tommy—he gave me balls! Well, anyway, when I didn't move, I could see him grin, and he said, "Out the back." So we took off our masks and gloves, dashed down the stairs, out the service entrance, started climbing the back wall . . . and suddenly there were eighteen million screws with flashlights in our faces and guns firing, and then I had my hands in the air as far as I could reach and I was screaming, "I surrender! I surrender!" Oh, God, Tommy, it was so *dramatic!*

QUESTION: And what happened to Anderson?

HASKINS: I really don't know. One moment he was there beside me, and the next moment he was gone. He just simply disappeared.

QUESTION: But you trusted him?

HASKINS: Of course.

85

NYDA-#146-113A-114G, INTERROGATION of Gerald Bingham, Jr.

WITNESS: The noise suddenly stopped. There was no more gunfire or shouts. It was very quiet. I thought it was all over. I was still lying in bed. I was very wet, sweating. . . . Then suddenly the front door slammed. He came running through the apartment, through my bedroom, and out onto the terrace. He didn't say anything. He didn't even look at me. But I knew it was him. . . .

86

STATEMENT OF Irving K. Mandelbaum, resident of Apartment 6C, 537 East Seventy-third Street, New York, New York. This transcription is coded NYPD-#146-IKM-123GT.

WITNESS: What a night. What a *night*! I mean, we didn't go away for the weekend. We'll stay in the city, I figured. We'll have a nice, quiet weekend. No traffic. No hang-ups. No crowds. Everything will be nice and quiet. So we're in bed. You understand? Five cops armed like the invasion of Normandy come through the bedroom and go out the window. Okay, I'm a good, law-abiding citizen. I'm with them. We get out of bed. Gretch, she goes into the bathroom while the cops pile through the window. At least one of the *shvartzes* has the decency to say, "Sorry about this, pal." So then Gretch comes out of the bathroom and says, "Back to bed." So then the fireworks start. Guns, lights, screams—the whole thing is right out of a Warner Brothers' movie of the late 1930's, which I really dig—you know, something with James Cagney and Chester Morris. We get out of bed. We're watching all this from the front windows, you understand. It's very exciting. What a weekend! Then everything dies down. No more guns. No more yells. So Gretch says, "Back to bed!" So we go. About five minutes later a guy comes through the bedroom window, hoisting himself up and climbing in. He's got a gun in his hand. Gretch and I get out of bed. He says, "One word out of you and you're dead." So naturally I didn't even agree with him. A second later and he's gone. Gretch says, "Back to bed?" And I said, "No, dear. I think at this moment I will drink a quart of Scotch." Oh boy.

87

STATEMENT OF Officer John Similar, Shield 35674262, driver of car George Nineteen. Document NYPD-#146-332S.

"I was stationed with my partner, Officer Percy H. Illingham, 45768392, in car George Nineteen closing the exit at East Seventy-third Street and East End Avenue. We had been ordered to place our car across Seventy-third Street to prevent exit from or entrance to the street. We had been informed of the action that was taking place.

"At approximately thirty minutes after four A.M. on the morning of 1 September, 1968, a male (white, about six feet, 180 pounds, black jacket and pants) approached us, walking on the sidewalk, the south sidewalk of East Seventy-third Street. Percy said, 'I better check him out.' He opened the door on his side of the car. As he emerged onto the street, the man drew a weapon from his pocket and fired directly at Officer Illingham. Officer Illingham dropped to the pavement. Later investigation proved that he had been killed.

"I thereupon got out of the car on my side and fired three times at the suspect with my service revolver (Serial Number 17189653) as he fired one shot at me which hit me in the thigh and caused me to fall to the pavement. He then began to run, and while I was trying to line up another shot at him, he disappeared around the corner of Seventy-third Street and East End Avenue.

"I did what I could."

88

THE FOLLOWING manuscript has been made available through the cooperation of its author, Dr. Dmitri Rubicoff, psychiatrist, with offices at 535 East Seventy-third Street, New York City. It is a portion of a speech Dr. Rubicoff delivered on the evening of 13 December, 1968, at a meeting of the Psychopathology Society of New York. This is an informal association of psychiatrists and psychologists in the New York area, which meets at irregular intervals to dine at one of the larger Manhattan hotels, to exchange "shop talk," and to hear an address by one of its members which then becomes the subject of a round-table discussion.

The speech from which the following remarks are excerpted (with the permission of Dr. Rubicoff) was delivered by him at the meeting of the society held in the Hunt Room of the President Fillmore Hotel. It is quoted exactly from the typed transcript of the speech made available to the author by Dr. Rubicoff.

"Madam Chairman—although I have long thought that title something of a sexual anomaly!

(Pause for laughter)

"Fellow members, and ladies and gentlemen. After such a dinner, a belch might be more in order than a speech!

(Pause for laughter)

"May I interject at this time that I feel we all owe a vote of thanks to the Entertainment Committee which arranged such a Lucullan feast.

(Pause for applause)

"Indeed, I'm certain you'll sympathize with me if I question whether their motive was to feed you well or to dull your sensibilities to my remarks that follow!

(Pause for small laughter)

"In any event, it is now my turn to offer the intellectual dessert to such a delightfully physical meal, and I shall do my best.

"As some of you, I'm sure, are aware, I was recently one of the victims of a crime which took place in the City of New York during the late evening and early morning of August 31 and September 1 of this year. My remarks this evening shall concern my thoughts about that crime, about crime in general, and what our profession can contribute to the amelioration of crime in our society.

"I can assure you my remarks will be brief—very brief!

(Possible pause for applause)

"These thoughts I offer to you are pure theory. I have done no research on the subject. I have consulted no hallowed authorities. I merely offer them as what I feel are original ideas—reactions to my experience, if you will—that will serve as subject for the discussion to follow. Needless to say, I shall be extremely interested in your reactions.

"First, let me say that it is hardly new to suggest that sexual aberrations are the underlying motivations for criminal behavior. What I would like to suggest at this time is a much closer relationship between sex and crime. In fact, I suggest that crime—in modern society—has become a substitute for sex.

"What is crime? What is sex? What have they in common? I suggest to you that both share a common characteristic—a *main* characteristic—of penetration. The bank robber forces his way into a vault. The housebreaker forces his way into a house or apartment. The mugger forces his way into your wallet or purse. Is it his intention to penetrate your body—your privacy?

"Even the more complex crimes include this motive of penetration. The confidence man invades his victim's wealth—be it wall safe or savings account. The criminal accountant rapes the firm for which he works. The public servant bent on fraud invades the body of society.

"Indeed, a term used for the most common of crimes—breaking and entering—is a perfect description of the deflowering of a virgin.

"So I suggest to you this evening that the commission of a crime is a substitute for the sexual act, committed by persons who consciously, unconsciously, or subconsciously derive extreme pleasure from this quasi-sexual activity.

"The crime having been committed—what then? The sex act having been finished—what then? In both cases, what follows the penetration is similar. Escape and withdrawal. Getting out. Frantic departure and sometimes a difficult disentangling, be it physical or emotional.

"I suggest to you that the *commission* of the sex crime—and I am convinced that *all* crimes are sex crimes—is easiest for the disturbed protagonist. The *withdrawal*, the escape, is much more difficult.

"For, considering the puritanical hang-up of most Americans, the withdrawal or escape involves recognition of guilt, an emotional desire for punishment, a terrible, nagging wish to be caught and publicly exposed.

"Sex and crime. Penetration and withdrawal. It seems to me they are all ineradicably wegded. Now, if you will allow me, I would like to expand upon. . . ."

89

FROM THE final report of Captain Edward X. Delaney, NYPD-EXD-1SEP1968.

"It was now, I would judge, approximately 4:45 A.M. We were no longer under fire from the fourth floor window. Suddenly we heard the sound of several gunshots from the vicinity of East Seventy-third Street and East End Avenue. I immediately dispatched officers Oliver J. Kronen (Shield 76398542) and Robert L. Breech (Shield 92356762) to investigate. Officer Kronen returned in a few moments to report that an officer had been slain, another wounded in the thigh. Both had been in car George Nineteen, blocking exit from Seventy-third Street at that corner.

"I thereupon contacted my command post via walkie-talkie. I instructed my driver, Officer McClaire, to send the standby ambulance around to the East End Avenue corner. He acknowledged. I also instructed him at this time to report the situation to Communications Center and request them to pass on the information to Inspector Abrahamson and Deputy Beatem. He acknowledged.

"I immediately led a squad of six armed men into the building at 535 East Seventy-third Street. We passed the body of the masked man who had been killed while trying to escape. Later investigation proved him to be Samuel 'Skeets' Johnson, a Negro. We then entered the lobby where we found a white man seated on the floor of the lobby, his back against the wall, his hands raised. He was taken into custody. Later investigation proved him to be Ernest Heinrich Mann.

"At that time my squad joined forces with the men from the Tactical Patrol Force coming down from the terrace and the men who had been stationed at the rear of the building. These men had taken an additional suspect, Thomas J. Haskins, into custody.

"We searched the building thoroughly and found the super asleep in his basement apartment. We also found some of the tenants and the doorman present in Apartment 4A. One of the tenants, Gerald Bingham, Sr., was wounded and apparently in shock. His right eye was bleeding badly. In addition to the people who had been held captive in this apartment, there was also a masked man lying on the floor, seriously wounded. I was told by eyewitnesses that he had been shot twice by another masked man.

"I thereupon instructed an officer to go outside and call for three more ambulances to facilitate the removal of the dead and wounded—officers, criminals, and innocent victims.

"Preliminary questioning of the victims revealed there had been another man (later identified as John "Duke" Anderson) who had been present during the crime and had apparently escaped. I judged he was the man responsible for the killing of Officer Illingham and the wounding of Officer Similar of car George Nineteen at the corner of Seventy-third Street and East End Avenue. I thereupon left the apartment house and, using a walktie-talkie, dictated an alert to Officer McClaire for relay to Communications Center. I described the suspect as the witnesses had described him to me. Officer McClaire acknowledged, and I stayed on the radio until he could report that Communications Center—Lieutenant Fineally in command—had acknowledged and was alerting all precincts and sectors.

"When the ambulances arrived, I sent off the wounded immediately—and later the dead. It so happened that Gerald Bingham, Sr., the wounded tenant, and the wounded suspect (later identified as Vincent 'Socks' Parelli, of Detroit) shared the ambulance going to Mother of Mercy Hospital.

"I then returned to my command post at the corner of York Avenue and East Seventy-third Street. Via Communications Center, I alerted Homicide East, the Police Laboratory, the Manhattan District Attorney's Office, and the Public Relations Division. At this time—it was shortly after 5:00 A.M.—there had been no reports on the whereabouts of the escaped suspect, John Anderson."

90

THE FOLLOWING is a transcription of a personal tape recording made by the author on 6 November, 1968. To my knowledge, the testimony it contains is not duplicated in any official recording, statement, or transcription now on record.

AUTHOR: This will be recording GO-2B. Will you identify yourself, please, and state your place of residence.
WITNESS: My name is Ira P. Mayer and I live at twelve hundred sixty East Second Street, New York.

AUTHOR: Thank you. Mr. Mayer, as I explained to you previously, this recording will be solely for my own use in preparing a record of a crime that occurred in New York City on the night and morning of August thirty-first to September first, 1968. I am not an officer of any branch of the government—city, state, or federal. I shall not ask you to swear to the testimony you are about to give, nor will it be used in a court of law or in any legal proceeding. The statement you make will be for my personal use only, and will not be published without your permission which can only be granted by a signed statement from you, giving approval of such use. In return, I have paid you the sum of fifty dollars, the sum paid whether or not you agree to the publication of your statement. Is all that understood?

WITNESS: Yes.

AUTHOR: Good. Now then, Mr. Mayer, where were you at about five o'clock on the morning of September first, 1968?

WITNESS: I was driving home. Down East End Avenue.

AUTHOR: And where had you been prior to this time?

WITNESS: Well, I was working. Ordinarily I wouldn't be working a holiday weekend, you understand, but so many of the men were off or on vacation—taking the Labor Day weekend off, you understand—that the boss asked me to work the night shift. I'm a master baker, and I work in the Leibnitz Bakery at one-nine-seven-four-oh East End Avenue. That's at One hundred fifteenth Street. My wife was expecting her seventh, and my second-youngest daughter—there was this big dental bill for her. So I needed the money, you understand, so I said I'd work. The union says we get triple time for working nights on a holiday, and also the boss said he'd slip me an extra twenty. So that's why I was working from four o'clock on August thirty-first to four o'clock the next morning.

AUTHOR: You say you're a master baker. What do you bake?

WITNESS: Bagels, bialies, onion rolls—things like that.

AUTHOR: And what did you do after you got off work at four on the morning of September first?

WITNESS: I got cleaned up and changed into my street clothes. I stopped for a beer with the boys in the locker room. No bars are open at that time, you understand, but we got a refrigerator and we keep beer in there. In the locker room. We chip in a dollar a week a man. The boss knows about it, but he don't care providing nobody gets loaded. Nobody ever does. We just have a beer or two before heading home. To relax like. You understand? So then I had one beer and got into my car and headed south on East End Avenue. I usually take First Avenue when I go uptown to work, and East End when I go downtown after work.

AUTHOR: And what happened at approximately five A.M. on the morning of September first?

WITNESS: I stopped for a red light on the corner of Seventy-fourth Street. I started to light a cigar. Then suddenly the door opened on the passenger side, and a guy was standing there. He had a gun, and he poked this gun at me. He held the gun in his right hand, and his left arm was across the front of him, like he was holding his belly.

AUTHOR: Can you describe this man?

WITNESS: Maybe six feet tall. Thin. No hat. His hair was short—like a crew cut. Sharp features. Mean looking. You understand?

AUTHOR: What was he wearing?

WITNESS: It was mostly black. A black jacket, black turtleneck sweater, black pants, black shoes. But he was a white man. You understand?

AUTHOR: And he opened the door on the passengers' side of the front seat and shoved a gun at you?

WITNESS: That's right.

AUTHOR: This was on the corner of Seventy-fourth Street and East End Avenue, while you were stopped for a light?

WITNESS: That's right. I was just lighting a cigar.

AUTHOR: And what was your reaction?

WITNESS: My reaction? Well, right away I thought it was a stickup. Why else would a guy jerk open the door of my car and point a gun at me?

AUTHOR: And how did you react?

WITNESS: How did I react? I felt sick. I had just been paid. With triple-time and the bonus I had almost four hundred bucks on me. I needed that dough. It was spent already. And I thought this guy was going to take it away from me.

AUTHOR: Would you have given it to him? If he had asked for your money?

WITNESS: Sure, I'd have given it to him. What else?

AUTHOR: But he didn't ask for your money?

WITNESS: No. He got in alongside of me and poked the gun in my side. With his left hand he slammed the door on his side, then went back to holding his belly.

AUTHOR: What did he say?

WITNESS: He said, "When the light changes, you drive south just the way you're going. Don't drive too fast and don't jump any lights. I'll tell you when to turn off." That's what he said.

AUTHOR: And what did you say?

WITNESS: I said, "You want my money? You want my car? Take them and let me go." And he said, "No, you gotta drive. I can't drive. I'm hurt." And I said, "You wanta go to a hospital? Mother of Mercy is back only five blocks. I'll drive you there." And he said, "No, you just drive where I tell you." And I said, "You gonna kill me?" And he said, "No, I won't kill you if you do what I say."

AUTHOR: And did you believe him?

WITNESS: Of course I believed him. What else am I going to do in a situation like that? You understand? Sure I believed him.

AUTHOR: What happened then?

WITNESS: I did like he said. When the light changed I headed south. I drove at the legal limit so we made all the lights.

AUTHOR: I don't imagine there was much traffic at that time on a Sunday?

WITNESS: Traffic? There was no traffic. We had the city to ourself.

AUTHOR: Did he say anything while you were driving?

WITNESS: Once. It was maybe around the Sixties. He asked me what my name was and I told him. He asked me if I was married, and I told him I was and had six kids and one on the way. I thought maybe he'd feel sorry for me and wouldn't kill me. You understand?

AUTHOR: That's all he said?

WITNESS: Yes, that's all he said. But once he kinda groaned. I looked sideways at him, just for a second, and blood was coming out from between his fingers. Where he had his left hand clamped across his belly. I could see blood coming out from between his fingers. I knew he was hurt bad, and I felt sorry for him.

AUTHOR: Then what happened?

WITNESS: At Fifty-seventh Street he told me to take a right and drive west on Fifty-seventh Street, so I did.

AUTHOR: Was his voice steady?

WITNESS: Steady? Sure, it was steady. Low, maybe, but steady. And that gun in my ribs was steady, too. So we drove across town on Fifty-seventh Street. When we got to Ninth Avenue he told me to take a left and drive downtown. So I did.

AUTHOR: What time was this?

WITNESS: Time? Oh, five thirty. About. Something like that. It was getting light.

AUTHOR: What happened then?

WITNESS: I drove very, very carefully, so I made all the signals. He told me to stop at Twenty-fourth Street.

AUTHOR: Which side?

WITNESS: The west side. On the right. I pulled over to the curb. It was on his side. He opened the door using his right hand, the hand with the gun in it.

AUTHOR: You didn't think of jumping him at this moment?

WITNESS: You crazy? Of course not. He got out, closed the door. He leaned through the window. He said, "Just keep driving. I will stand here and watch to make sure that you keep driving."

AUTHOR: And what did you do then?

WITNESS: What do you think? I kept driving. I went on south to Sixteenth Street, and I figured he couldn't see me anymore. So I stopped and went into a corner phone booth on the sidewalk. There was a sign saying you could call nine-one-one, the police emergency number, without putting a dime in. So I called the cops. When they answered, I told them what had happened. They asked me for my name and address, which I gave them. They asked where I was, which I told them. They told me to stay right where I was and a car would be right there.

AUTHOR: Then what?

WITNESS: I went back to my car. I figured I'd sit in my car and try to calm down until the cops came. I was shaky—you understand? I tried to light my cigar again—I never had got it lighted—but then I saw the seat where he had been. There was a pool of blood on the seat and it was dripping down onto the mat. I got out of the car and waited on the sidewalk. I threw my cigar away.

91

VINCENT "SOCKS" Parelli was admitted to Emergency at Mother of Mercy Hospital, Seventy-ninth Street and East End Avenue, at 5:23 A.M. 1 September, 1968. He was first declared DOA (Dead On Arrival) but a subsequent examination by Dr. Samuel Nathan revealed a faint pulse and heartbeat. Stimulants and plasma were immediately administered, and Parelli was taken to the Maximum Security Ward on the second floor. After further examination, Dr. Nathan declared the prognosis was negative. Parelli had been shot twice, one bullet apparently entering the lungs and the other rupturing the spleen.

By 5:45 A.M., the bed occupied by Parelli was surrounded by screens. In this enclosure, in addition to Dr. Nathan, were Dr. Everett Brisling (intern) and Nurse Sarah Pagent, both of the Mother of Mercy staff; Assistant District Attorney Ralph Gimble of the New York District Attorney's Office; Detective, First Grade, Robert C. Lefferts of Homicide East; Detective, Second Grade, Stanley Brown of the 251st Precinct;

Officer Ephraim Sanders (no relation to the author) of the 251st Precinct; and Security Guard Barton McCleary, also of the Mother of Mercy staff.

The following recording, made by the New York District Attorney's Office, is coded NYDA-VP-DeBeST. It is dated 6:00 A.M., 1 September 1968.

GIMBLE: What's happening?

NATHAN: He's dying. By all rights he should be dead now.

LEFFERTS: Can you do anything?

NATHAN: No. We've already done all we can.

GIMBLE: Will he regain consciousness?

NATHAN: Brisling?

BRISLING: Maybe. I doubt it.

GIMBLE: We've got to question him.

NATHAN: What do you want from me? I'm not God.

BRISLING: Let the man die in peace.

BROWN: No, goddamn it. An officer was killed. Get him up. Get him awake. We've got to find out what all this was about, why he was shot. This is important.

BRISLING: Doctor?

[Lapse of seven seconds.]

NATHAN: All right. Nurse?

PAGENT: Yes, Doctor?

NATHAN: Fifty cc's. You've got it?

PAGENT: Yes, Doctor.

NATHAN: Administer it.

[Lapse of twenty-three seconds.]

NATHAN: Pulse?

BRISLING: Maybe a little stronger. Heart is still fluttering.

GIMBLE: His eyelids moved. I saw them move.

LEFFERTS: Parelli? Parelli?

NATHAN: Don't shove him.

BROWN: He's dying, isn't he?

NATHAN: Just don't touch him. He's a patient in this hospital under my care.

PARELLI: Guh . . . guh . . .

GIMBLE: He said something. I heard him say something.

LEFFERTS: It didn't make sense. Sanders, move the mike closer to his mouth.

PARELLI: Ah . . . ah . . .

BROWN: His eyes are open.

GIMBLE: Parelli, Parelli, who shot you? Who was it, Parelli? Why did they shoot you?

PARELLI: Guh . . . guh . . .

BRISLING: This is obscene.

LEFFERTS: Who planned it, Parelli? Who put up the money? Who was behind it, Parelli? Can you hear me?

PARELLI: Climb planging. No man can ever the building. I said to bicycle of no lad can be to mother.

GIMBLE: What? What?

PARELLI: Or sake to make a lake. We see today not by gun if she does.

LEFFERTS: Can you give him another shot, Doc?

NATHAN: No.

PARELLI: Guh . . . guh . . .

BRISLING: Fibrillations.

PAGENT: Pulse weakening and intermittent.
NATHAN: He's going.
BROWN: Parelli, listen to me. Parelli, can you hear me? Who shot you, Parelli? Who put up the money? Who brought you here from Detroit? Parelli?
PARELLI: I never thought to. And then I was on the street where. Louise? We saw the car sky and what. Momma. In the sky. It was in. Never a clutch could. Some day she. Fucking bastard. I think that I should.
GIMBLE: Who, Parelli? Who did it?
PARELLI: A bird at song if even wing, the girl herself shall never sing.
NATHAN: Nurse?
PAGENT: No pulse.
NATHAN: Brisling?
BRISLING: No heartbeat.
    [Lapse of nine seconds.]
NATHAN: He's gone.
LEFFERTS: Shit.

92

MEMORANDUM (CONFIDENTIAL) EXD-794, dated 14 December, 1968, from Edward X. Delaney, Captain, NYPD, to Police Commissioner, NYPD, with confidential copies to Deputy Arthur C. Beatem and Chief Inspector L. David Whichcote.

"This document should be considered Addendum 19-B to my final report NYPD-EXD-1SEP-1969.

"It has been brought to my attention that the attempted robbery of the premises at 535 East Seventy-third Street, New York City, on 31 August-1 September, 1968, might have been prevented if there had been closer cooperation between agencies of the city, state, and federal governments, and private investigative agencies. A list of agencies involved is attached (see EXD-794-A).

"While I cannot reveal the identity of my informant *at this time*, I can state without fear of serious contradiction that for several months prior to the commission of the crime, the aforesaid agencies were in possession of certain facts (on tape recordings and in transcriptions) relating to the planned crime, obtained via bugging and other electronic surveillance devices.

"Admittedly, no *one* agency was in possession of *all* the facts or all the details regarding the proposed crime—such as address, time, personnel involved, etc. And yet, if a central pool or clearing house (computerized, perhaps?) for electronic surveillance had been in existence, I have little doubt but that the crime in question could have been forestalled.

"I strongly urge that a meeting of representatives of law-enforcement agencies of city, state, and federal governments be convened immediately to consider how such a clearing house for the results of electronic surveillance can be established. I shall hold myself ready to assist in any way I can to help organize such a project, as I have a number of very definite ideas on how it should be structured."

93

Approximately 5:45 a.m. The apartment of Ingrid Macht, 627 West Twenty-fourth Street, New York, New York. This is tape recording SEC-1SEP68-IM-5:45AM-196L.

> [Sound of doorbell.]
> [Lapse of eleven seconds.]
> [Sound of doorbell.]
> [Lapse of eight seconds.]

INGRID: Yes?

ANDERSON: Duke.

INGRID: Duke, I am sleeping. I am very tired. Please call me later in the day.

ANDERSON: You want me to shoot the lock off?

INGRID: What? What are you saying, Duke?

> [Lapse of six seconds.]

INGRID: Oh, my God.

ANDERSON: Yes. Close and lock the door. Put the chain on. Are the shades down?

INGRID: Yes.

ANDERSON: Get me something—some towels. I don't want to drip on your white rug.

INGRID: Oh, *Schatzie, Schatzie.* . . .

> [Lapse of nine seconds.]

INGRID: My God, you're soaked. Here . . . let. . . .

ANDERSON: Not so bad now. It's inside now. . . .

INGRID: Gun or knife?

ANDERSON: Gun.

INGRID: How many?

ANDERSON: Two. One high up, just below my wishbone. The other is down and on the side.

INGRID: Did they come out?

ANDERSON: What? I don't think so. Brandy. Get me some brandy.

INGRID: Yes . . . let me help you to the chair. All right. Don't move.

> [Lapse of fourteen seconds.]

INGRID: Here. Shall I hold it?

ANDERSON: I can manage. Ah Jesus . . . that helps.

INGRID: Is it bad?

ANDERSON: At first, I wanted to scream. Now it's just dull. A big blackness in there. I'm bleeding in there. I can feel it all going out . . . spreading. . . .

INGRID: I know a doctor. . . .

ANDERSON: Forget it. No use I'm getting out. . . .

INGRID: And you had to come here. . . .

ANDERSON: Yes. Ah . . . God! Yes, like a hound dragging hisself so he can die at home.

INGRID: You had to come here. Why? To pay me back for what I did?

ANDERSON: For what you did? Oh. No, I forgot that a long time ago. It was nothing.

INGRID: But you had to come here. . . .

ANDERSON: Yes. I came to kill you. See? Here . . . look. . . . Two left. I told you I'd get you out some day. I promised you. . . .

INGRID: Duke, you are not making sense.

ANDERSON: Oh, yes. Oh, yes. If I say. . . . Ah, Jesus . . . the black-ness. . . . I can hear the wind. Do you want to yell? Do you want to run into the other room, maybe jump out the window?

INGRID: Ah, *Schatzie, Schatzie* . . . you know me better than that. . . .

ANDERSON: I know you better . . . better than that. . . .

INGRID: It's worse now?

ANDERSON: It's coming in waves, like black waves. It's like the sea. I'm really getting out, I'm getting out. Ah, Jesus. . . .

INGRID: It all went bad?

ANDERSON: Yes. We were so close . . . so close. . . . But it went sour. I don't know why. . . . But for a minute there I had it. I had it all.

INGRID: Yes. You had it all. . . . Duke, I have some drugs. Some shmeck. Do you want a shot? It will make it easier.

ANDERSON: No. No, I can handle this. This isn't so bad.

INGRID: Give me the gun, *Schatzie*.

ANDERSON: I meant what I said.

INGRID: What will that do? How will that help?

ANDERSON: I promised. I gave my word. I promised you. . . .
    [Lapse of seven seconds.]

INGRID: All right. If that is what you must do. It is all over for me, anyway. Even if you died here this instant, it is all over for me.

ANDERSON: Died? Is this the end of me then? Nothing any more?

INGRID: Yes. The end of John Anderson. Nothing any more. And the end of Ingrid Macht. And Gertrude Heller. And Bertha Knobel. And all the other women I have been in my life. The end of all of us. Nothing any more.

ANDERSON: Are you scared?

INGRID: No. This is best. You are right. This is best. I am tired, and I haven't been sleeping lately. This will be a good sleep. You won't hurt me, *Schatzie*?

ANDERSON: I'll make it quick.

INGRID: Yes. Quick. In the head, I think. Here . . . see . . . I will kneel before you. You will be steady?

ANDERSON: I will be steady. You can depend on me.

INGRID: I could always depend on you. Duke, do you remember that day in the park? The picnic we had?

ANDERSON: I remember.

INGRID: For a moment there . . . for a moment. . . .

ANDERSON: I know . . . I know. . . .

INGRID: I think I will turn around now, *Schatzie*. I will turn my back to you. I find I am not as brave as I thought. I will kneel here, my back to you, and I will talk. I will just say anything that comes into my mind. And I will keep talking, and then you will. . . . You understand?

ANDERSON: I understand.

INGRID: What was it all about, Duke? Once I thought I knew. But now I am not sure. You know, the Hungarians have a saying—"Before you have a chance to look around, the picnic is over." It has all gone so fast, Duke. Like a dream. How is it the days crawl by and yet the years fly? Life for me has been a bone caught in my throat. There were little moments, like that afternoon in the park. But mostly it was hurt . . . it was hurt. . . . Duke, please . . . now . . . don't wait any longer. Please. Duke? *Schatzie*? Duke, I. . . .
    [Lapse of five seconds.]

INGRID: Ah. Ah. You are gone, Duke? You are finally out? But I am here. I am here. . . .

[Lapse of one minute fourteen seconds.]
[Sound of phone being dialed.]
VOICE: New York Police Department. May I help you?

94

THE BODY of John "Duke" Anderson was removed to the New York City Morgue at about 7:00 A.M., 1 September, 1968. Ingrid Macht was taken to the House of Detention for Women, 10 Greenwich Avenue. The premises of 627 West Twenty-fourth Street were then sealed and a police guard placed at the door.

On the morning of 2 September, 1968, at Police Headquarters, 240 Centre Street, at approximately 10:00 A.M., a meeting was held of representatives of interested authorities, including the New York Police Department; the District Attorney's Office, County of New York; the Federal Bureau of Investigation; the Internal Revenue Service; the Federal Narcotics Bureau; and the Securities and Exchange Commission. Representatives of the New York Police Department included men from the 251st Precinct, Narcotics Squad, Homicide East, Homicide West, the Police Laboratory, and the Communications Center. There was also a representative from Interpol. The author was allowed to be present at this meeting as an observer.

At this time a squad of ten men was organized and directed to search the apartment of Ingrid Macht at 627 West Twenty-fourth Street, the toss to commence at 3:00 P.M., 2 September, 1968, and to be terminated upon agreement of all representatives present. The author was allowed to attend as an observer but not active participant in the search.

The toss of the aforesaid premises commenced at approximately 3:20 P.M., and was, to my satisfaction, conducted with professional skill, speed, and thoroughness. Evidence was uncovered definitely linking Ingrid Macht with the smuggling of illicit narcotics into this country. There was also some evidence (supposition) that she had been involved in prostitution in the City of New York. In addition, there was evidence (not conclusive) that Ingrid Macht had also been involved in the theft and sale of securities, including stock shares, corporate bonds, and U.S. Government bonds.

Also, there was some evidence that Ingrid Macht was operating a loan-shark operation, lending sums to persons she met on her job at the dance hall, to pushers of narcotics, and other individuals known to law enforcement officials. In addition to all this, evidence was uncovered (not sufficient for prosecution) that she was a steerer for an abortion ring, with headquarters in a small New Jersey motel.

During the extremely painstaking search of the premises, a detective from the 251st Precinct discovered a small book concealed beneath the lowest drawer of a five-drawer chest in the bedroom. On first examination, it appeared to be merely a diary. In fact, it was a volume bound in imitation leather (in red; imprinted on the front cover: FIVE-YEAR DIARY). Closer examination proved it to be more in the nature of a commercial ledger, detailing Ingrid Macht's personal dealings in stocks and other securities.

Cursory examination of the entries, which included investments (amounts and dates) and sales (amounts, dates, and profits), showed immediately that Ingrid Macht had been successful in her financial dealings. (In a statement to the press, one of her defense attorneys has estimated her personal wealth as being "in excess of $100,000.")

The author was present when the "diary" was discovered and had an opportunity to leaf through it briefly.

On the inside back cover, in the same handwriting as the other entries in the journal, was this inscription: "Crime is the truth. Law is the hypocrisy."

The First Deadly Sin

If there was no God, how could I be a captain?
Fyodor Dostoyevsky, *The Possessed*

PART ONE

1

THERE WAS quiet. He lay on his back atop a shaft of stone called Devil's Needle, and felt he was lost, floating in air. Above him, all about him stretched a thin blue sac. Through it he could see scribbles of clouds, a lemon sun.

He heard nothing but his own strong heart, the slowly quieting of his breath as he recovered from his climb. He could believe he was alone in the universe.

Finally he stood and looked around him. Waves of foliage lapped at the base of his stone; it was a dark green ocean with a froth of autumn's russet. He could see the highway, the tarred roofs of Chilton, a steel ribbon of river uncoiling southward to the sea.

The air had the bite of Fall; it moved on a breeze that knifed lungs and tingled bare skin. He gulped this stern air like a drink; there was nothing he might not do.

He moved over to the cleft in the edge of the stone and began hauling up the nylon line clipped to his belt. At the end of the rope was his rucksack. In it were sandwiches, a thermos of black coffee, a first aid kit, spiked clamps for his climbing boots, pitons, an extra sweater and, buckled to the outside, his ice ax.

He had made the sandwiches himself, of stone-ground whole wheat said to be organically grown. The filling of one was sliced onions, of the other white radishes and plum tomatoes.

He sat on the smooth granite and ate slowly. The coffee was still warm, the sandwich bread fresh with a crunchy crust. Out of nowhere a blue jay appeared and greeted him with its two-note whistle. It landed on the stone, stared at him fearlessly. He laughed, tossed a crust. The bird took it up, then dropped it immediately and was gone in an azure flash.

Finished, he replaced sandwich wrappings and thermos in his rucksack. He lay back, using it as a pillow. He turned onto his side, bowing his spine, drawing up his knees. He determined to awake in half an hour. He was asleep almost instantly and dreamed of a woman hairless as a man's palm.

He awoke in half an hour and lighted a cigarette. The day was drawing on; he must be down and out of the park before dark. But there was time to smoke, time for silence, a final coffee, cold now and gritty with dregs.

He had been recently divorced. That was of no concern; it had happened to a stranger. But he was perplexed by what was happening to *him* since he and Gilda had parted. He was assembling a jigsaw puzzle. But he didn't have all the pieces, had no conception of what the completed picture might be.

He pulled off his knitted watch cap, exposing his shaven skull to watery sunlight. He pressed fingers to the smooth; soft skin slid on hard bone.

The divorce had just been obtained (in Mexico) but he had been separated

153

from his wife for almost two years. Shortly after they agreed to live apart, he had shaved his head completely and purchased two wigs. One ("Ivy League") he wore to the office and on formal occasions. The other ("Via Veneto") was crisp curls and ringlets. He wore it to parties or when entertaining at home. Both wigs were in the dark brown shade of his own hair.

It was true his hair had been thinning since he was 24. At the time of his separation from Gilda, when he was 33, the front hairline had receded into a "widow's peak" and there was a small tonsure at the back of his head. But he was far from bald. His remaining hair had gloss and weight.

Nevertheless, he had shaved his entire skull when he purchased the wigs, though the coiffeur assured him it was not necessary; the artificial hair could be blended ("Absolutely undetectable, sir") with his natural hair.

When climbing, or swimming, or simply alone in his apartment, he preferred the shaven pate. He had developed a habit—almost a nervous tic—of caressing it with his fingertips, probing the frail cranium and that perilous stuff that lay beneath.

He pulled on his cap, tugging it down over his ears. He prepared for the descent by donning horsehide gloves, rough side out. He then lowered his rucksack to the boulders below. The end of the line was still clipped to his belt, a wide canvas band similar to that used by professional window washers.

The cleft, by which ascents to and descents from the flat top of Devil's Needle were made, was a chimney. It was a vertical crack in the granite shaft, four feet across at the base. It narrowed as it rose until, at the top, it was barely wide enough for a climber to scrape through to the summit.

The climber braced shoulders and back against one wall of the chimney. He bent his knees, placing the soles of his boots against the opposite wall. He then, literally, walked up the cleft, depending upon the strength of buttocks, thighs and calves to maintain sufficient pressure to keep from falling.

As he took small steps, not relaxing one foot to scrape it upward until the other was firmly planted, he "walked his shoulders" slowly higher—right, left, right, left. He continued tension in his bent legs to keep himself jammed between opposing walls of the chimney.

As the cleft narrowed toward the top of the 65-foot shaft, the climber's legs became increasingly bent until his knees were almost touching his chin and gains upward were measured in inches. At the top, it was necessary to apply pressure with knees instead of feet. The climber then reached up and grabbed two heavy pitons a previous conqueror of Devil's Needle had thoughtfully left embedded in the stone. With their aid, the man ascending could pull himself out of the narrow chimney, over the lip, onto the flat top. It was a bedsheet of stone.

The descent, though more difficult, was not excessively dangerous for an experienced climber. Gripping the pitons, he allowed his body to slide down into the cleft. He started by bracing his knees against one granite wall, his back against the other. Releasing the pitons, he then slowly "walked" downward, until the crack widened sufficiently so he could put the rubber-ridged soles of his boots against the opposing wall.

At this time of day, in September, as he began the descent, the top of Devil's Needle was washed with pale sunshine. But the slit into which he lowered himself was shaded and smelled rankly.

He braced his knees, took a deep breath, released the pitons. He was suspended in gloom, emptiness below. He hung a moment in blemished light, then placed flat hands against the facing wall to take some of the tension off his knees. He started the slow wiggle downward and out.

The cleft spread until it was wide enough to press his feet against the wall. Moving faster now, he twisted, struggled, writhed, his entire body in a steady left-right rhythm, shifting from foot to foot, shoulder to shoulder, until the stretched stone thighs popped him out and he was in murk.

He rested five minutes while his breathing eased. He coiled his nylon line, slung his rucksack. He hiked across boulders, through a meadow, along a dirt road to the ranger's cabin.

The park guardian was an older man, made surly by this visitor's refusal to heed his warning about climbing alone. He shoved the register angrily across the wooden counter. The climber signed in the Out column and noted the time.

His name was Daniel Blank.

2

UNDER THE terms of the separation agreement, Gilda Blank had retained possession of their car: a four-door Buick sedan. Daniel thereupon purchased for himself a Chevrolet Corvette, a powerful machine of racy design. Since buying the sports car he had twice been arrested for speeding. He paid a fine in each case. One more similar violation would result in suspension of his license.

Now, standing beside his car to strip off canvas jacket, wool sweater and cotton T-shirt, he admired the car's clean feminine lines. He toweled off bare skull, face, neck, shoulders, arms, upper torso. The evening air was astringent as alcohol. He had a sense of healthy well-being. The hard climb, sculpted day, simple food all had left him with the exhilaration of a new start. He was beginning.

Daniel Blank was a tall man, slightly over six feet, and was now slender. In high school and college he had competed in swimming, track (220 high hurdles), and tennis, individual sports that required no teamwork. These physical activities had given his body a firm sheath of long muscle. His shoulders, pectorals and thighs were well-developed. Hands and feet were narrow fingernails and toenails long. He kept them shaped and buffed.

Shortly after his separation, he had taken a "physical inventory," inspecting his naked body minutely in the full-length mirror on the inside of his bathroom door. He saw at once that deterioration had begun, the flesh beneath his jaw had started to sag, his shoulders slumped, the lower abdomen protruded, it was soft and without tone.

He had at once begun a strict regimen of diet and exercise. In his methodical way he bought several books on nutrition and systems of physical training. He read them all carefully, making notes and devised for himself a program that appealed to him and that he felt would show almost immediate improvement in his physical appearance.

He was not a fanatic, he did not swear off drinking and smoking. But he cut his alcohol intake by half and switched to non-nicotine cigarettes made of dried lettuce leaves. He tried to avoid starches, carbohydrates, dairy products, eggs, blood meats. He ate fresh fruits, vegetables, broiled fish, salads with a dressing of fresh lemon juice. Within three months he had lost 20 pounds, his ribs and hip bones showed.

Meanwhile he had started a program of daily exercise, 30 minutes in the morning upon rising, 30 minutes in the evening before retiring.

The exercises Daniel Blank selected for himself came from a manual based on the training of Finnish gymnasts. All the movements were illustrated with photographs of young blonde women in white leotards. But Blank felt this was of no import; only the exercises counted, and these promised increased agility, pliancy, and grace.

The exercises had proved efficacious. His waist was now down to almost 32 inches. Since his hips were wide (though his buttocks were flat) and his chest enlarged from his youthful interest in running and swimming, he had developed a feminine "hourglass" figure. All his muscles regained their youthful firmness. His skin was smooth and blood-flushed. Age seemed stayed.

But the diet and exercise had also resulted in several curious side effects. His nipples had become permanently engorged and, since he ordinarily wore no undershirt, were obvious beneath the stuff of thin dress shirts or lisle pullovers. He did not find this displeasing. A heavier garment, such as a wool turtleneck sweater worn next to the skin, sometimes resulted in a not unpleasant irritation.

Another unexpected development was the change in appearance of his genitals. The testicles had become somewhat flaccid and hung lower than previously. The penis, while not growing in size (which he knew to be impossible at his age), had altered in color and elasticity. It now seemed to be slightly empurpled in a constant state of mild excitation. This also was not disagreeable. It might be caused by agitation against the cloth of the tighter trousers he had purchased.

Finally he found himself free of the diarrhea that had frequently plagued him during his marriage. He ascribed this to his new diet, exercise, or both. Whatever the reason, his bowel movements were now regular, without pain, and satisfying. His stool was firm.

He drove toward Manhattan. He had pulled on a fresh velour shirt. The radio was no more than a lulling hum. He followed an unlighted two-laner that led into the Thruway.

The speedometer climbed slowly: 50, 60, 70, 80. The car roared to catch the headlight glare. Trees flung backward; billboards and ghost houses grew out of darkness, blazed, flicked back into dark.

He loved speed, not so much for the sensual satisfaction of power as for the sense of lonely dislocation.

It was Saturday night; the Thruway was heavy with traffic pouring into the city. Now he drove with brutal hostility, switching lanes, cutting in and out. He hunched over the wheel, searching for openings to plunge through, for sudden breaks in the pattern enabling him to skin by more cautious drivers.

He came over the bridge; there were the hard edges, sharp corners, cheap lights of Manhattan. Slowed by signals, by trucks and buses, he was forced to move southward at moderate speed. He turned eastward on 96th Street; his city closed in.

It was a city sprung and lurching. It throbbed to a crippled rhythm, celebrated death with insensate glee. Filth pimpled its nightmare streets. The air smelled of ashes. In the schools young children craftily slid heroin into their veins.

A luncheonette owner was shot dead when he could not supply apple pie to a demanding customer. A French tourist was robbed in daylight, then shot and paralyzed. A pregnant woman was raped by three men in a subway station at 10:30 in the morning. Bombs were set. Acid was thrown. Explosions destroyed embassies, banks, and churches. Infants were beaten to death. Glass was shattered, leather slashed, plants uprooted, obscene slogans sprayed on marble monuments. Zoos were invaded and small animals torn apart.

His poisoned city staggered in a mad plague dance. A tarnished sun glared down on an unmeaning world. Each man, at night, locked himself within bars, hoping for survival in his iron cage. He huddled in upon himself, hoarding his sanity, and moved through crowded streets glancing over his shoulder, alert to parry the first blow with his own oiled blade.

The apartment house in which Daniel Blank lived was a raw building of glass and enameled steel. It was 34 stories high and occupied an entire city block on East 83rd Street. It was built in a U-shape; a black-topped driveway curved in front of the entrance. A stainless steel portico protruded so that tenants alighting from cars were protected from rain. The entrance step was covered with green outdoor carpeting.

Inside, a desk faced plate glass doors. Doormen were on duty 24 hours a day. They were able to inspect the underground garage, service entrances, hallways and elevators by closed-circuit TV. Behind them was a wide lobby with chairs and sofas of chrome and black plastic. There were abstract paintings on the walls and, in the center, a heavy bronze sculpture, non-representational, entitled "Birth."

Daniel Blank pulled into an alley alongside the curved driveway. It led down to the garage where tenants, for an additional rental, could park their cars, have them washed, serviced, and delivered to the main entrance when required.

He turned the Corvette over to the attendant on duty. He took his rucksack and outdoor clothes from the car, and rode the escalator to the main lobby. He went to the desk where tenants' mail was distributed, deliveries accepted, messages held.

It was almost 10:00 P.M.; no one was on duty at the mail desk. But one of the doormen went behind the counter. There was no mail in Blank's cubbyhole, but there was a small sheet of paper folded once. It said: "Brunch Sunday (tomorrow) at 11:30. Don't miss. Come early. Thousands of fantastic pipple. Love and kisses. Flo and Sam." He read the note, then tucked it into his shirt pocket.

The doorman, who had not spoken to him nor raised his eyes to Daniel's, went back behind his desk. His name was Charles Lipsky, and he had been involved with Blank in an incident that had occurred about a year previously.

Daniel had been waiting under the portico for a taxi to take him to work. He rarely drove his own car to the office since parking space near Ninth Avenue and 46th Street was almost non-existent. Doorman Lipsky had gone down to the street to whistle up a cab. He halted one and rode it up the driveway. He opened the door for Blank and held out his hand for the usual 25-cent tip.

As Daniel was about to pay him, a man he recognized as a tenant of the building came up the entrance step hauling a German shepherd pup on a long leather leash.

"Heel!" the man was shouting. "Heel!"

But the young dog hung back. Then he lay on the driveway, muzzle down between his paws, and refused to budge.

"Heel, you bastard!" the man screamed. He then struck the dog twice on the head with a folded newspaper he had been carrying under his arm. The dog cringed away. Whereupon the man kicked him heavily in the ribs.

Daniel Blank and Charles Lipsky saw all this clearly. Blank leaped forward. He could not endure the sight of an animal being mistreated; he couldn't even *think* of a horse pulling a load.

"Stop that!" he cried furiously.

The tenant turned on him in outrage. "Mind your own goddamned business!"

He then struck Daniel on the head with his folded newspaper. Blank pushed him angrily. The man staggered back, became entangled in the leather leash, stumbled off the step onto the driveway, fell awkwardly, and broke his left arm. Police were called, and the tenant insisted on charging Daniel Blank with assault.

In time, Blank and Lipsky were summoned to the 251st Precinct house to give sworn statements. Daniel said the tenant had abused his dog, and when he, Daniel, objected, the man had struck him with a folded newspaper. He had not pushed the man until after that first blow. Charles Lipsky corroborated this testimony.

The charge was eventually withdrawn, the case dropped. The dog owner moved from the building. Blank gave Lipsky five dollars for his trouble and thought no more of the matter.

But about six months after this incident, something of a more serious nature happened.

On a Saturday night, lonely and jangling, Daniel Blank put on his "Via Veneto" wig and strolled out into midnight Manhattan. He wore a Swedish blazer of black wool and a French "body shirt" in a lacy polyester weave, cut to cling to the torso. It was a style called "*Chemise de gigolo*" and had a front that opened halfway to the waist. An ornate Maltese cross hung from a silver chain about his neck.

On impulse, nothing else, he stopped at a Third Avenue tavern he had seen before but never entered. It was called "The Parrot." There were two couples at the bar and two single men. No one sat at the tiny tables. The lone waiter was reading a religious tract.

Blank ordered a brandy and lighted a lettuce cigarette. He looked up and, unexpectedly, caught the eye of one of the single men in the mirror behind the bar. Blank shifted his gaze immediately. The man was three seats away. He was about 45, short, soft, with the meaty nose and ruddy face of a bourbon drinker.

The bartender had his radio tuned to WQXR. They were playing Smetana's "The Moldau·" The bartender was reading a scratch sheet, marking his choices. The couples had their heads together and were murmuring.

"You have beautiful hair."

Daniel Blank looked up from his drink. "What?"

The porky man had moved onto the barstool next to his.

"Your hair. It's beautiful. Is it a rug?"

His first instinct was to drain his drink, pay, and leave. But why should he? The dim loneliness of The Parrot was a comfort. People together and yet apart: that was the secret.

He ordered another brandy. He turned a shoulder to the man who was hunching closer. The bartender poured the drink, then went back to his handicapping.

"Well?" the man asked.

Blank turned to look at him. "Well what?"

"How about it?"

"How about what?"

Up to now they had been speaking in conversational tones: not loud, but understandable if anyone was interested in listening. No one was.

But suddenly the man leaned forward. He thrust his flabby face close: watery eyes, trembling lips: hopeful and doomed.

"I love you," he whispered with an anxious smile.

Blank hit him in the mouth and toppled him off the stool onto the floor. When the man got up, Blank hit him again, breaking his jaw. He fell again. Blank was frantically kicking him in the groin when the bartender finally came alive and rushed around the bar to pinion his arms and drag him away.

Once again the police were summoned. This time Blank thought it best to call his lawyer, Russell Tamblyn. He came to the 251st Precinct house and, shortly before dawn, the incident was closed.

The injured man who, it was learned, had a sad record of offenses including attempts to molest a child and to proposition a plain-clothed patrolman in a subway toilet—refused to sign a complaint. He said he had been drunk, knew nothing of what had happened, and accepted responsibility for the "unfortunate accident."

The detective who took Daniel Blank's statement was the same man who had taken his testimony in the incident involving the tenant who kicked his dog.

"You again?" the detective asked curiously.

The attorney brought the signed waiver to Daniel Blank, saying, "It's all squared away. He's not making a charge. You're free to go."

"Russ, I told you it wasn't my fault."

"Oh sure. But the man has a broken jaw and possible internal injuries. Dan, you've got to learn to control yourself."

But that wasn't the end of it. Because the doorman, Charles Lipsky, found out, even though nothing had been published in the newspapers. The bartender at The Parrot was Lipsky's brother-in-law.

A week later the doorman rang the bell of Blank's apartment. After inspection through the peephole, he was admitted. Lipsky immediately launched into a long, jumbled chronicle of his troubles. His wife needed a hernia operation; his daughter needed expensive treatment for an occluded bite; he himself was heavily in debt to loansharks who threatened to break his legs, and he needed five hundred dollars at once.

Blank was bewildered by this recital. He asked what it had to do with him. Lipsky then stammered that he knew what had happened at The Parrot. It wasn't Mr. Blank's fault, certainly, but if other tenants . . . If it became known . . . If people started talking . . .

And then he winked at Daniel Blank.

That knowing wink, that smirky wink, was worse than the victim's whispered, "I love you." Daniel Blank felt attacked by a beast whose bite excited and inflamed. Violence bubbled.

Lipsky must have seen something in his eyes, for he turned suddenly, ran out, slammed the door behind him. Since then they had hardly spoken. When necessary, Blank ordered and the doorman obeyed, never raising his eyes. At Christmas, Daniel distributed the usual amounts: ten dollars to each doorman. He received the usual thank-you card from Charles Lipsky.

Blank pushed the button; the door of the automatic elevator slid silently open. He stepped inside, pushed button C (for Close door), button 21 (for his floor), and button M (for Music desired). He rode upward to the muted strains of "I Got Rhythm."

He lived at the front end of one leg of the building's U. It was an exceptionally large four-room apartment with living room windows facing north, bedroom windows east, and kitchen and bathroom windows west, or really down into the apartment house courtyard. The walk to his door from the elevator was along a carpeted tunnel. The corridor was softly lighted, the many doors blind, air refrigerated and dead.

He unlocked his door, reached in and switched on the foyer light. Then he stepped inside, looked about. He closed the door, double-locked it, put on the chain, adjusted the Police Bar, a burglar-proof device consisting of a heavy steel rod that fitted into a slot in the floor and was propped into a recess bolted to the door.

Mildly hungry, Blank dropped clothing and gear on a foyer chair and went directly to the kitchen. He switched on the blued fluorescent light. He inspected the contents of his refrigerator, selected a small cantaloupe and slived it in half, at right angles to the stem line. He wrapped half in wax paper and returned it to the refrigerator. He scooped seeds and soft pulp from the other half, then filled the cavity with Familia, a Swiss organic cereal. He squeezed a slice of fresh lemon over all. He ate it steadily, standing, staring at his reflection in the mirror over the kitchen sink.

Finished, he dumped melon rind into the garbage can and rinsed his fingers. Then he moved from room to room, turning the light on in the next before turning it off in the last. Undressing in his bedroom he found the note in his shirt pocket: ". . . Thousands of fantastic pipple . . ." He placed it on his bedside table where he'd see it upon awakening.

He closed the bathroom door tightly before taking a shower so hot it filled the air with heavy steam, clouding the mirrors and sweating the tiles. He lathered with an emollient soap of cocoa butter that slicked his skin. After rinsing in cool water and turning off the shower, he rubbed his wet body with a cosmetically treated tissue claiming to "restore natural oils to dry skin" and "smooth, soften, and lubricate the epidermis."

His twice-a-week maid had been in during the afternoon. His bed was made with fresh sheets and pillowcases. The top sheet and sateen comforter were turned down. It was hardly 11:00 P.M., but he was pleasantly weary and wanted sleep.

Naked, allowing water and tiny oil globules to dry on his exposed body, he moved about the apartment, drawing drapes, checking window latches and door locks. He stepped into the bathroom again to swallow a mild sleeping pill. He felt sure he would not need it, but he didn't want to think in bed.

The long living room was dimly lit by light from the bedroom. The end of the living room faced north, with drapes over wide plate glass windows that could not be opened. The east wall, abutting the bedroom, was almost 25 feet long and nine feet high.

This expanse, painted a flat white, Daniel Blank had decorated with mirrors. He had allowed a space four feet from the floor to accommodate a couch, chairs, end tables, lamps, a bookcase, a wheeled cart of hi-fi equipment. But above that four-foot level, the wall was covered with mirrors.

Not one mirror or fitted tiles of mirrors, but more than fifty individual mirrors adorned that wall; tiny mirrors and large mirrors, flat and beveled, true and exaggerative, round and square, oval and rectangular. The wall quivered with silver reflections.

Each mirror was framed and hung separately: frames of wood and metal, painted and bare, plain and ornate, modern and rococo, carved wood and bland plastic. Some were fogged antiques; one was a 3X4-inch sheet of polished metal: the mirror issued to Marines in World War II.

The mirrors were not arranged in a planned pattern on this nervous wall; they had been hung as they were purchased. But somehow, haphazardly, as the wall filled, frames and reflections had grown an asymmetrical composition. His city was there, sprung and lurching.

Padding back to the bedroom, naked, scented, oiled, Daniel Blank looked to his mirrored wall. He was chopped and fragmented. As he moved, his image jumped, glass to glass. A nose there. Ear. Knee. Chest.

Navel. Foot. Elbow. All leaped, were held, disappeared to be born again in something new.

He stopped, fascinated. But even motionless he was minced and snapped, all of him divided by silvered glass that tilted this way and that. He felt himself and saw twenty hands moving, a hundred fingers probing: wonder and delight.

He went into the bedroom, adjusted the air-conditioner thermostat, slid into bed. He fell asleep seeing in the dim glow of the nightlight those myriad eyes reflecting him in framed detail. Waist in steel. Shoulder in carved oak. Neck in plastic. Knee in copper. Penis in worm-eaten walnut.

Art.

3

SHE HAD been one of the first women in Manhattan to leave off her brassiere. He had been one of the first men in Manhattan to use a necktie as a belt. She had been one of the first to adopt a workman's lunch pail as a purse. He had been one of the first to wear loafers without socks. The first! A zeal for the new bedeviled them, drove them.

No notice of Florence and Samuel Morton was made in the long, detailed separation agreement signed by the Blanks. Gilda took the Buick sedan, the Waterford crystal, the Picasso print. Daniel took the apartment lease, 100 shares of U.S. Steel, and the Waring blender. No one mentioned the Mortons. It was tacitly assumed they were Daniel's "best friends," and he was to have them. So he did.

They contradicted the folk saying, "Opposites attract." Husband and wife, they were obverse and reverse of the same coin. Where did Samuel leave off and Florence begin? No one could determine. They were a bifocal image. No. They were a double image, both in focus simultaneously.

Physically they were so alike that strangers took them for brother and sister. Short, bony-thin, with helmets of black, oily hair, both had ferrety features, the quick, sharp movements of creatures assailed.

He, married, had been a converter of synthetic textiles. She, married, had been a fabric designer. They met on a picket line protesting a performance of "The Merchant of Venice," and discovered they had the same psychoanalyst. A year later they were divorced, married to each other, and had agreed to have no children because of the population explosion. Both gladly, cheerfully, joyfully, submitted to operations.

Their marriage was two magnets clicking together. They had identical loves, fears, hopes, prejudices, ambitions, tastes, moods, dislikes, despairs. They were one person multiplied by two. They slept together in a king-sized bed, entwined.

They changed their life styles as often as their underwear. They were ahead of everyone. Before it was fashionable, they bought pop art, op-art, and then switched back to realism sooner than art critics. They went through marijuana, amphetamines, barbiturates, speed, and a single, shaking trial of heroin, before returning to dry vermouth on the rocks. They were first to try new restaurants, first to wear Mickey Mouse watches, first to discover new tenors, first to see new movies, plays, ballets, first to wear their sunglasses pushed atop their heads. They explored all New York and spread the word: "This incredible little restaurant in Chinatown . . . The best belly-dancer on the West Side . . . That crazy junk shop on Canal Street . . ."

Born Jews, they found their way to Catholicism via Unitarianism, Methodism, and Episcopalianism (with a brief dabble in Marxism). After converting and confessing once, they found this groovy Evangelical church in Harlem where everyone clapped hands and shouted. Nothing lasted. Everything started. They plunged into Yoga, Zen, and Hare Krishna. They turned to astrology, took high colonics, and had a whiskered guru to dinner.

They threw themselves in the anti-Vietnam War movement and went to Washington to carry placards, parade and shout slogans. Once Sam was hit on the head by a construction worker. Once Flo was spat upon by a Wall Street executive. Then they spent three weeks in a New Hampshire commune where 21 people slept in one room.

"They did nothing but verbalize!" said Sam.

"No depth, no significance!" said Flo.

"A bad scene!" they said together.

What drove them, what sparked their search for "relevance," their hunger to "communicate," to have a "meaningful dialogue," to find the "cosmic flash," to uncover "universal contact," to, in fact, refashion the universe, was guilt.

Their great talent, the gift they denied because it was so vulgar, was simply this: both had a marvelous ability to make money. The psychedelic designs of Florence sold like mad. Samuel was one of the first men on Seventh Avenue to foresee the potential of the "youth market." They started their own factory. Money poured in.

Both, now in their middle 30's, had been the first with the new. They leeched onto the social chaos of the 1960's: the hippies, flower children, the crazy demand for denim jeans and fringed leather jackets and pioneer skirts and necklaces for men and Indian beads and granny glasses and all the other paraphernalia of the young, taken up so soon by their elders.

The Mortons profited mightily from their perspicacity, but it seemed to them a cheesy kind of talent. Without acknowledging it both knew they were growing wealthy from what had begun as a sincere and touching crusade. Hence their frantic rushing about from picket line to demonstration, from parade to confrontation. They wanted to pay their dues.

In further expiation, they sold the factory (at an enormous profit) and opened a boutique on Madison Avenue, an investment they were happily convinced would be a disaster. It was called "Erotica," based on a unique concept for a store. The idea had come to them while attending religious services of a small Scandinavian sect in Brooklyn which worshipped Thor.

"I'm bored with idleness," he murmured.

"So am I," she murmured.

"A store?" he suggested. "Just to keep busy."

"A shop?" she suggested. "A fun thing."

"A boutique," he said.

"Elegant and expensive," she said. "We'll lose a mint."

"Something different," he mused. "Not hotpants and paper dresses, miniskirts and skinny sweaters, army jackets and newsboy caps. Something really *different*. What do people want?"

"Love?" she mused.

"Oh yes," he nodded. "That's it."

Their boutique, Erotica, sold only items related, however distantly, to love and sex. It sold satin sheets in 14 colors (including black), and a "buttock pillow" advertised merely "for added comfort and convenience." It carried Valentines and books of love poetry; perfumes and incense; phonograph records that established a mood; scented creams and lotions; phallic candles; amorous prints, paintings, etchings and posters; unisex lingerie; lace pajamas for men, leather nightgowns for women; and whips for both. An armed guard had to be hired to eject certain obviously disturbed customers.

Erotica was an instant success. Florence and Samuel Morton became wealthier. Depressed, they turned to blackstrap molasses and acupuncture. Making money was their tragic talent. Their blessing was that they were without malice.

And the first thing Daniel Blank saw upon awaking Sunday morning was the note on his bedside table, the invitation to brunch from Flo and Sam. They would, he remembered fondly, serve things like hot Syrian bread, iced lumpfish, smoked carp, six kinds of herring. Champagne, even.

He padded naked to the front door, unlocked chains and bars, took in his New York *Times*. He went through the ritual of relocking, carried the newspaper to the kitchen, returned to the bedroom, began his 30 minutes of exercise in front of the mirror on the closet door.

It was the quiet Sunday routine he had grown to cherish since living alone. The day and its lazy possibilities stretched ahead in a golden glow. His extensions and sit-ups and bends brought him warm and tingling into a new world; anything was possible.

He showered quickly, gloating to see his dried skin had softened and smoothed. He stood before the medicine cabinet mirror to shave, and wondered once again if he should grow a mustache. Once again he decided against it. It would, he felt, make him look older, although a drooping Fu-Manchu mustache with his glabrous skull might be interesting. Exciting?

His face was coffin-shaped and elegant, small ears set close to the bone. The jaw was slightly aggressive, lips sculpted, freshly colored. The nose was long, somewhat pinched, with elliptic nostrils. His eyes were his best feature: large, widely spaced, with a brown iris. Brows were thick, sharply delineated.

Curiously, he appeared older full-face than in profile. From the front he seemed brooding. Lines were discernible from nose creases to the corners of his mouth. The halves of his face were identical; the effect was that of a religious mask. He rarely blinked and smiled infrequently.

But in profile he looked more alert. His face came alive. There was young expectation there: noble brow, clear eye, straight nose, carved and mildly pouting lips, strong chin. You could see the good bones of cheek and jaw.

He completed shaving, applied "Faun" after-shave lotion, powdered his jaw lightly, sprayed his armpits with a scented antiperspirant. He went back into the bedroom and considered how to dress.

The Mortons with their ". . . Thousands of fantastic pipple . . ." were sure to have a motley selection of the bizarre friends and acquaintances they collected: artists and designers; actors and writers; dancers and directors; with a spicy sprinkling of addicts, whores and arsonists. All, on a Sunday morning, would be informally and wildly costumed.

To be different—aloof from the mob, above the throng—he pulled on his conservative "Ivy League" wig, grey flannel slacks, Gucci loafers, a white cashmere turtleneck sweater, a jacket of suede in a reddish brown. He stuffed a yellow-patterned foulard kerchief in his breast pocket.

He went into the kitchen and brewed a small pot of coffee. He drank two cups black, sitting at the kitchen table and leafing through the magazine section of the Sunday *Times*. The ads proved that current male fashions had become more creative, colorful, and exciting than female.

At precisely 11:30, he locked his front door and took the elevator up to the Mortons' penthouse apartment on the 34th floor.

He was alone in the elevator, there was no one waiting for entrance at the

Mortons' door and, when he listened, he could hear no sounds of revelry inside. Perplexed, he rang the bell, expecting the door to be answered by Blanche, the Mortons' live-in maid, or perhaps by a butler hired for the occasion.

But Samuel Morton himself opened the door, stepped quickly out into the corridor, closed but did not latch the door behind him.

He was a vigorous, elfin man, clad in black leather shirt and jeans studded with steel nailheads. He twinkled when he moved. His eyes, shining with glee, were two more nailheads. He put a hand on Daniel Blank's arm.

"Dan," he pleaded, "don't be sore."

Blank groaned theatrically, "Sam, not again? You promised not to. What's *with* you and Flo? Are you professional matchmakers? I told you I can find my own women."

"Look, Dan, is it so terrible? We want you to be happy! Is that so terrible? Your happiness—that's all! All right, blame us. But we're so happy together we want everyone to be happy like us!"

"You promised," Blank accused. "Sam, your cuffs are about a half-inch too long. After that disaster with the jewelry designer, you *promised*. Who's this one?"

Morton stepped closer, whispering . . .

"You won't believe. An original! I swear to God . . ." Here he held up his right hand. ". . . an *original*! She comes into the store last week. She's wearing a sable coat down to her ankles! It's a warm day, but she's wearing an ankle-length fur. And sable! Not mink. Dan—*sable*! And she's beautiful in an off-beat, kinky way. Marilyn Monroe she's not, but she's got this thing. She scares you! Yes. Maybe not beautiful. But something else. Something better! So in she comes wearing this long sable coat. Fifty thousand that coat—at least! And with her is this kid, a boy, maybe eleven, twelve, around there. And he *is* beautiful! The most beautiful boy I've ever seen—and you know I don't swing that way! But she's not married. The kid's her brother. Anyhow, we get to talking, and Flo admires her coat, and it turns out she bought it in Russia. Russia! And she lives in a townhouse on East End Avenue. Can you imagine? East End Avenue! A townhouse! She's got to be loaded. So one thing leads to another, and we invited her up for brunch. So what's so terrible?"

"Did you also tell her you were inviting a friend—male and divorced—who is living in lonely anguish and seeking the companionship of a good woman?"

"No. I swear!"

"Sam, I don't believe you."

"Dan, would I lie to you?"

"Of course. Like your 'thousands of fantastic pipple'."

"Well . . . Flo may have casually mentioned a few neighbors might stop by."

Daniel laughed. Sam grabbed his arm, pulled him close.

"Just take a look, a quick look. Like no woman you've ever met! I swear to you, Dan—an *original*. You have simply got to meet this woman! Even if nothing comes of it—naturally Flo and I are hoping—but even if nothing happens, believe me it will be an experience for you. Here is a new human being! You'll see. You'll see. Her name is Celia Montfort. My name is Sam and her name is Celia. Right away that tells a lot—no?"

The Mortons' apartment was a shambles, thrift shop, rats' nest, charity bazaar, gypsy camp: as incoherent as their lives. They redecorated at least twice a year, and these upheavals had left a squabble of detritus: chairs in Swedish modern, a Victorian love seat, a Sheraton lowboy, a wooden

Indian, Chinese vases, chromium lamps, Persian rugs, a barber pole, a Plexiglas table, ormolu ashtrays, Tiffany glass, and paintings in a dozen trendy styles, framed and unframed, hung and propped against the wall.

And everywhere, books, magazines, prints, photographs, newspapers, posters, swatches of cloth, smoking incense, boxes of chocolates, fresh flowers, fashion sketches, broken cigarettes, a bronze screw propeller and a blue bedpan: all mixed, helter-skelter, as if giant salad forks had dug into the furnishings of the apartment, tossed them to the ceiling, allowed them to flutter down as they would, pile up, tilt, overlap, and create a setting of frenzied disorder that stunned visitors but proved marvelously comfortable and relaxing.

Sam Morton led Daniel to the entrance of the living room, tugging him along by the arm, fearful of his escaping. Blank waved a hand at Blanche, working in the kitchen, as he passed.

In the living room, Flo Morton smiled and blew a kiss to Dan. He turned from her to look at the woman who had been speaking when they entered, and who would not stop to acknowledge their presence.

"It is bad logic and worse semantics," she was saying in a voice curiously devoid of tone and inflection. "'Black is beautiful'? It's like saying, 'Down is up.' I know they mean to affirm their existence and assert their pride. But they have chosen a battlecry no one, not even themselves, can believe. Because words have more than meaning, you see. The meaning of words is merely the skeleton, almost as basic as the spelling. But words also have emotional weight. The simplest, most innocent words—as far as definition is concerned—can be an absolute horror emotionally. A word that looks plain and unassuming when written or printed can stir us to murder or delight. 'Black is beautiful'? To the human race, to whites, blacks, yellows, reds, black can *never* be beautiful. Black is evil and will always seem so. For black is darkness, and that is where fears lie and nightmares are born. Blackhearted. Black sheep of the family. Black art: the magic practised by witches. Black mass. These are not racial slurs. They spring from man's primitive fear of the dark. Black is the time or place without light, where dangers lurk, and death. Children are naturally afraid of the dark. It is not taught them; they are born with it. And even some adults sleep with a nightlight. 'Behave yourself or the boogie man will get you.' I imagine even Negro children are told that. The 'boogie'—a black monster who comes out of the dark, the perilous dark. Black is the unknowable. Black is danger. Black is evil. Black is death. But 'Black is beautiful'? Never. They'll never get anyone to believe that. We are all animals. I don't believe we've been introduced."

She raised her eyes to look directly at Daniel Blank. He was startled. He had been so engrossed with her lecture, so intent on following her thought, that he had no clear idea of what she looked like. Now, as Florence Morton hastily introduced them, as he crossed the room to take Celia Montfort's proffered hand, he inspected her closely.

She sat curled up in the softness of a big armchair that was all foam, red velvet and cigarette burns. Strangely, for a Sunday morning, she was wearing an elegant evening shift of black satin. The neckline was straight across, the dress suspended from bare shoulders by "spaghetti straps." She wore a thin choker of diamonds, and on the wrist of the hand she held out to Blank was a matching bracelet. He wondered if perhaps she had been to an all-night party and had been unable to go home to change. He thought so when he saw the silk evening slippers.

Her hair was so black it was almost purple, parted in the middle, and fell loosely below her shoulders without wave or curl. It gave her thin face a witch-like appearance, enhanced by long, slender hands, tapering fingers with stiletto nails.

Her bare arms, shoulders, the tops of her small breasts revealed by the low-cut gown: all gleamed against the red velvet. There was a peculiar, limpid *nakedness* to her flesh. The arms were particularly sensual: smooth, hairless, as seemingly boneless as tentacles: arms squeezed from tubes.

It was difficult to estimate her height or appreciate her figure while she was coiled into the armchair. Blank judged her a tall woman, perhaps five foot six or more, with a good waist, flat hips, hard thighs. But at the moment all that was of little importance to him; her face bewitched him, her eyes locked with his.

They were grey eyes, or were they a light blue? Her thin brows were arched, or were they straight? Her nose was—what? An Egyptian nose? A nose from a sarcophagus or bas-relief? And those parted lips: were they full and dry, or flat and moist? The long chin, like the toe of her silk slipper—was that enchanting or perhaps too masculine? As Sam Morton had said, not beautiful. But something there. Something better? It needed study.

He had the impression that at this time, noon on a bright Sunday, wearing Saturday night's stale finery, her face and body were smudged with weariness. There was a languor in her posture, her skin was pallid, and faint violet shadows were beneath her eyes. She had the scent of debauchery, and her toneless voice came from senses punished beyond feeling and passions spent.

Florence and Samuel immediately launched into a violent denunciation of her "Black is beautiful" comments. Daniel watched to see how she reacted to this assault. He saw at once she had the gift of repose: no twistings there, no squirmings, no fiddling with bracelet, fluffing hair, touching ears. She sat quietly, composed, and Daniel suddenly realized she was not listening to her critics. She was withdrawn from all of them.

She was gone but not, he guessed, day-dreaming. She was not floating; she had pulled back within herself, sinking deeper into her own thoughts, hungers, hopes. Those eyes, indecipherable as water, attended them, but he had a sense of her estrangement. He wanted to be in her country, if only for a visit, to look around and see what the place was like.

Flo paused for an answer to a question. But there was no answer. Celia Montfort merely regarded her with a somewhat glassy stare, her face expressionless. The moment was saved by the entrance of Blanche, pushing a big-three-shelved cart laden with hot and cold dishes, a pitcher of Bloody Marys, an iced bottle of sparkling rosé.

The food was less unconventional than Blank had hoped, but still the poached eggs were sherried, the ham was in burgundy sauce, the mushroom omelette brandied, the walnut waffles swimming in rum-flavored maple syrup.

"Eat!" commanded Flo.

"Enjoy!" commanded Sam.

Daniel had a single poached egg, a strip of bacon, a glass of wine. Then he settled back with a bunch of chilled Concord grapes, listening to the Mortons' chatter, watching Celia Montfort silently and intently devour an immense amount of food.

Afterward they had small, warmed Portuguese brandies. Daniel and the Mortons carried on a desultory conversation about Art Deco, a current fad. Celia's opinion was asked, but she shook her head. "I know nothing about it." After that she sat quietly, brandy glass clasped in both hands, eyes brooding. She had no talent for small talk. Complain of bad weather and she might, he thought, deliver you a sermon on humility. Strange woman. What was it Sam had said—"She scares you." Why on earth should he have said that—unless he was referring to her disturbing silences, her alienation: which might be nothing more than egoism and bad manners.

She rose suddenly to her feet and, for the first time, Blank saw her body clearly. As he had guessed, she was tall, but thinner and harder than he had suspected. She carried herself well, moved with a sinuous grace, and her infrequent gestures were small and controlled.

She said she must go, giving Flo and Sam a bleak smile. She thanked them politely for their hospitality. Flo brought her coat: a cape of weighted silk brocade, as dazzling as a matador's jacket. Blank was now convinced she had not been home to that East End Avenue townhouse since Saturday evening, nor slept at all the previous night.

She moved to the door. Flo and Sam looked at him expectantly.

"May I see you home?" he asked.

She looked at him thoughtfully.

"Yes," she said finally. "You may."

The Mortons exchanged a rapid glance of triumph. They waited in the hallway, in their studded jumpsuits, grinning like idiots, until the elevator door shut them away.

In the elevator, unexpectedly, she asked: "You live in this building, don't you?"

"Yes. The twenty-first floor."

"Let's go there."

Ten minutes later she was in his bedroom, brocaded cape dropped to the floor, and fast asleep atop the covers of his bed, fully clothed. He picked up her cape, hung it away, slipped off her shoes and placed them neatly alongside the bed. Then he closed the door softly, went back into the living room to read the Sunday New York *Times*, and tried not to think of the strange woman sleeping in his bed.

At 4:30, finished with his paper, he looked in upon her. She was lying face up on the pillows, her great mass of black hair fanned out. He was stirred. From the shoulders down she had turned onto her side and slept holding her bare arms. He took a light wool blanket from the linen closet and covered her gently. Then he went into the kitchen to eat a peeled apple and swallow a yeast tablet.

An hour later he was seated in the dim living room, trying to recall her features and understand why he was so intrigued by her sufficiency. The look of the sorceress, the mysterious wizard, could be due, he decided, to the way she wore her long, straight hair and the fact, as he suddenly realized, that she wore no make-up at all: no powder, no lipstick, no eye-shadow. Her face was naked.

He heard her moving about. The bathroom door closed; the toilet was flushed. He switched on lamps. When she came into the living room he noted that she had put on her shoes and combed her hair smooth.

"Don't you ever wear any make-up?" he asked her.

She stared at him a long moment.

"Occasionally I rouge my nipples."

He gave her a sardonic smile. "Isn't that in poor taste?"

She caught his lewd meaning at once. "Witty man," she said in her toneless voice. "Might I have a vodka? Straight. Lots of ice, please. And a wedge of lime, if you have it."

When he came back with identical drinks for both, she was curled up on his Tobia Scarpa sofa, her face softly illuminated by a Marc Lepage inflatable lamp. He saw at once her weariness had vanished with sleep; she was serene. But with a shock he saw something he had not noticed before: a fist-sized bruise on the bicep of her left arm: purple and angry.

She took the drink from his hand. Her fingers were cool, bloodless as plastic.

"I like your apartment," she said.

Under the terms of the separation agreement, Gilda Blank had taken most of the antiques, the overstuffed furniture, the velvet drapes, the shag rugs. Daniel was happy to see it all go. The apartment had come to stifle him. He felt muffled by all that carved wood and heavy cloth: soft things that burdened, then swaddled him.

He had redecorated the almost empty apartment in severe modern, most of the things from Knoll. There was chrome and glass, black leather and plastic, stainless steel and white enamel. The apartment was now open, airy, almost spidery in its delicacy. He kept furniture to a minimum, leaving the good proportions of the living room to make their own statement. The mirrored wall was cluttered wit, but otherwise the room was clean, precise, and exalting as a museum gallery.

"A room like this proves you don't require roots," she told him. "You have destroyed the past by ignoring it. Most people have a need for history, to live in a setting that constantly reminds of past generations. They take comfort and meaning from feeling themselves part of the flow, what was, is, will be. I think that is a weak, shameful emotion. It takes strength to break free, forget the past and deny the future. That's what this room does. Here you can exist by yourself in yourself, with no crutches. The room is without sentiment. Are you without sentiment?"

"Oh," he said, "I don't think so. Without emotion perhaps. Is your apartment in modern? As austere as this?"

"It is not an apartment. It's a townhouse. It belongs to my parents."

"Ah. They are still living then?"

"Yes," she said. "They are still living."

"I understand you live with your brother."

"His name is Anthony. Tony. He's twenty years younger than I. Mother had him late in life. It was an embarrassment to her. She and my father prefer him to live with me."

"And where do they live?"

"Oh, here and there," she said vaguely. "There is one thing I don't like about this room."

"What is that?"

She pointed to a black cast iron candelabrum with twelve contorted arms. Fitted to each was a white taper.

"I don't like unburned candles," she said tonelessly. "They seem to me as dishonest as plastic flowers and wallpaper printed to look like brick."

"Easily remedied," he said, rose and slowly lighted the candles.

"Yes," she said. "That's better."

"Are you ready for another drink?"

"Bring the vodka and a bucket of ice out here. Then you won't have to run back and forth."

"Yes," he said, "I will."

When he returned, she had snuffed three of the tapers. She added ice and vodka to her glass.

"We'll snuff them at intervals. So they will be in various lengths. I'm glad you have the dripless kind. I like candles, but I don't like leavings of dead wax."

"Memories of past pleasures?"

"Something like that. But also too reminiscent of bad Italian restaurants with candles in empty Chianti bottles and too much powdered garlic in the sauce. I hate fakery. Rhinestones and padded brassieres."

"My wife—" he started. "My ex-wife—" he amended, "wore a padded bra. The strange thing was that she didn't need it. She was very well endowed. Is."

"Tell me about her."

"Gilda? A very pleasant woman. We're both from Indiana. We met at the University. A blind date. I was a year ahead of her. We went together occasionally. Nothing serious. I came to New York. Then she came here, a year later, and we started seeing each other again. Serious, this time."

"What was she like? Physically, I mean."

"A large woman, with a tendency to put on weight. She loved rich food. Her mother is enormous. Gilda is blonde. What you'd call a 'handsome woman.' A good athlete. Swimming, tennis, golf, skiing—all that. Very active in charities, social organizations. Took lessons in bridge. Chinese cooking, and music appreciation. Things like that."

"No children?"

"No."

"How long were you married?"

"Ahh . . ." He stared at her. "My God, I can't remember. Of course. Seven years. Almost eight. Yes, that's right. Almost eight years."

"You didn't want children?"

"I didn't—no."

"She?"

"Yes."

"Is that why you divorced?"

"Oh no. No, that had nothing to do with it. We divorced because—well, why did we divorce? Incompatibility, I guess. We just grew apart. She went her way and I went mine."

"What was her way?"

"You're very personal."

"Yes. You can always refuse to answer."

"Well, Gilda is a very healthy, well-adjusted, out-going woman. She likes people, likes children, parties, picnics, the theatre, church. Whenever we went to the theatre or a movie where the audience was asked to sing along with the entertainer or music, she would sing along. That's the kind of woman she was."

"A sing-alonger with a padded brassiere."

"And plastic flowers," he added. "Well, not plastic. But she did buy a dozen roses made of silk. I couldn't convince her they were wrong."

He rose to blow out another three candles. He came back to sit in his Eames chair. Suddenly she came over to sit on the hassock in front of him. She put a light hand on his knee.

"What happened?" she whispered.

"You guessed?" he said, not surprised. "A strange story. I don't understand it myself."

"Have you told the Mortons?"

"My God, no. I've told no one."

"But you want to tell me."

"Yes I want to tell you. And I want you to explain it to me. Well, Gilda is a normal, healthy woman who enjoys sex. I do too. Our sex was very good. It really was. At the start anyway. But you know, you get older and it doesn't seem so important. To her, anyway. But I don't mean to put her down. She was good and enthusiastic in bed. Perhaps unimaginative. Sometimes she'd laugh at me. But a normal, healthy woman."

"You keep saying healthy, healthy, healthy."

"Well, she was. Is. A big, healthy woman. Big legs. Big breasts. A glow to her skin. Rubens would have loved her. Well . . . about three years ago we took a summer place for the season on Barnegat Bay. You know where that is?"

"No."

"The Jersey shore. South of Bay Head. It was beautiful. Fine beach, white sand, not too crowded. One afternoon we had some neighbors over for a cook-out. We all had a lot to drink. It was fun. We were all in bathing suits, and we'd drink, get a little buzz on, and then go into the ocean to swim and sober up, and then eat and drink some more. It was a wonderful afternoon. Eventually everyone went home. Gilda and I were alone. Maybe a little drunk, hot from the sun and food and laughing. We went back into our cottage and decided to have sex. So we took off our bathing suits. But we kept our sunglasses on."

"Oh."

"I don't know why we did it, but we did. Maybe we thought it was funny. Anyway, we made love wearing those dark, blank glasses so we couldn't see each other's eyes."

"Did you like it?"

"The sex? For me it was a revelation, a door opening. I guess Gilda thought it was funny and forgot it. I can never forget it. It was the most sexually exciting thing I've ever done in my life. There was something primitive and frightening about it. It's hard to explain. But it shook me. I wanted to do it again."

"But she didn't?"

"That's right. Even after we came back to New York and it was winter, I suggested we wear sunglasses in bed, but she wouldn't. I suppose you think I'm crazy?"

"Is that the end of the story?"

"No. There's more. Wait until I blow out more candles."

"I'll get them."

She snuffed out three more tapers. Only three were left burning, getting down close to the iron sockets. She came back to sit on the ottoman again.

"Go on."

"Well, I was browsing around Brentano's—this was the winter right after Barnegat Bay—and Brentno's, you know, carries a lot of museum-type antique jewelry and semi-precious stones, coral and native handicrafts. Stuff like that. Well, they had a collection of African masks they were selling. Very primitive. Strong and somehow frightening. You know the effect primitive African art has. It touches something very deep, very mysterious. Well, I wanted to have sex with Gilda while we both wore those masks. An irrational feeling, I know. I knew it at the time, but I couldn't resist. So I bought two masks—they weren't cheap—and brought them home. Gilda didn't like them and didn't dislike them. But she let me hang them in the hallway out there. A few weeks later we had a lot to drink—"

"You got her drunk."

"I guess. But she wouldn't do it. She wouldn't wear one of those masks in bed. She said I was crazy. Anyway, the next day she threw the masks away. Or burned them, or gave them away, or something. They were gone when I got home."

"And then you were divorced?"

"Well, not just because of the sunglasses and the African masks. There were other things. We had been growing apart for some time. But the business with the masks was certainly a contributing factor. Strange story—no?"

She got up to extinguish the three remaining candles. They smoked a bit, and she licked her fingers, then damped the wicks. She poured both of them a little more vodka, then regarded the candelabrum, head cocked to one side.

"That's better."

"Yes," he agreed. "It is."

"Do you have a cigarette?"

"I smoke a kind made from dried lettuce leaves. Non-nicotine. But I have the regular kind too. Which would you like?"

"The poisonous variety."

He lighted it for her, and she strolled up and down before the mirrored wall, holding her elbows. Her head was bent forward; long hair hid her face.

"No," she said, "I don't believe it was irrational. And I don't believe you're crazy. I'm talking now about the sunglasses and the masks. You see, there was a time when sex itself, by itself, had a power, a mystery, an awe it no longer has. Today it's 'Shall we have another martini or shall we fuck?' The act itself has no more meaning than a second dessert. In an effort to restore the meaning, people try to increase the pleasure. They use all kinds of gadgets, but all they do is add to the mechanization of sex. It's the wrong remedy. Sex is not solely, or even mainly, physical pleasure. Sex is a rite. And the only way to restore its meaning is to bring to it the trappings of a ceremony. That's why I was so delighted to discover the Mortons' shop. Probably without realizing it, they sensed that today the psychic satisfactions of sex have become more important than physical gratifications. Sex has become, or should become, a dramatic art. It was once, in several cultures. And the Mortons have made a start in providing the make-up, costumes, and scenery for the play. It is only a start, but it is a good one. Now about you . . . I think you became, if not bored then at least dissatisfied with sex with your 'healthy, normal' wife. 'Is this all there is?' you asked. 'Is there nothing more?' Of course there is more. Much, much more. And you were on the right track when you spoke about 'a revelation . . . a door opening' when you made love wearing sunglasses. And when you said the African masks were 'primitive' and 'somehow frightening.' You have, in effect, discovered the unknown or disregarded side of sex: its psychic fulfillment. Having become aware of it, you suspect—rightly so—that its spiritual satisfactions can far surpass physical pleasure. After all, there are a limited number of orifices and mucous membranes in the human body. In other words, you are beginning to see sex as a religious rite and a dramatic ceremony. The masks were merely the first step in this direction. Too bad your wife couldn't see it that way."

"Yes," he said. "Too bad."

"I must be going," she said abruptly, and marched into the bedroom to retrieve her cape.

"I'll see you home," he said eagerly.

"No. That won't be necessary. I'll take a cab."

"At least let me come down to call a cab for you."

"Please don't."

"I want to see you again. May I call you?"

"Yes."

She was out the door and gone almost before he was aware of it. The smell of snuffed candles and old smoke lingered in the room.

He turned out the lights and sat a long time in darkness, pondering what she had said. Something in him responded to it. He began to glimpse the final picture that might be assembled from the bits and pieces of his thought and behavior that had, until now, puzzled him so. That final picture shocked him, but he was neither frightened nor dismayed.

Once, late in the previous summer, he had been admiring his naked, newly slender and tanned body in the bedroom mirror. Only the nightlight was on. His flesh was sheened with its dim, rosy glow.

He noted how strange and somehow exciting the gold chain of his wrist watch looked against his skin. There was something there . . . A week later he purchased a women's belt, made of heavy, gold-plated links. He specified a chain adjustable to all sizes, and then had it gift-wrapped for reasons he could not comprehend.

Now, only hours after he had first met Celia Montfort, after she had slept in his bed, after she had listened to him and spoken to him, he stood naked again before the bedroom mirror, the room illuminated only by the caressing nightlight. About his wrist was the gold chain of his watch, and around his slim waist was the linked belt.

He stared, fascinated. Chained, he touched himself.

4

JAVIS-BIRCHAM PUBLICATIONS, Inc. owned the office building, and occupied the top fifteen floors, on 46th Street west of Ninth Avenue. The building had been erected in the late 1930s, and was designed in the massive, pyramidal style of the period, with trim and decoration modeled after that of Rockefeller Center.

Javis-Bircham published trade magazines, textbooks, and technical journals. When Daniel Blank was hired six years previously, the company was publishing 129 different periodicals relating to the chemical industry, oil and petroleum, engineering, business management, automotive, machine tools, and aviation. In recent years magazines had been added on automation, computer technology, industrial pollution, oceanography, space exploration, and a consumer monthly on research and development. Also, a technical book club had been started, and the corporation was currently exploring the possibilities of short, weekly newsletters in fields covered by its monthly and bi-monthly trade magazines. Javis-Bircham had been listed as number 216 in Fortune Magazine's most recent list of America's 500 largest corporations. It had gone public in 1951 and its stock, after a 3-1 split in 1962, showed a 20-fold increase in its Big Board price.

Daniel Blank had been hired as Assistant Circulation Manager. His previous jobs had been as Subscription Fulfillment Manager and Circulation Manager on consumer periodicals. The three magazines on which he had worked prior to his employment at Javis-Bircham had since died. Blank, who saw what was happening, had survived, in a better job, at a salary he would have considered a hopeless dream ten years ago.

His first reaction to the circulation set-up at Javis-Bircham was unequivocal. "It's a fucked-up mess," he told his wife.

Blank's immediate superior was the Circulation Manager, a beefy, genial man named Robert White, called "Bob" by everyone, including secretaries and mailroom boys. This was, Blank thought, a measure of the man.

White had been at Javis-Bircham for 25 years and had surrounded himself with a staff of more than 50 males and females who seemed, to Blank, all "old women" who smelled of lavender and whiskey sours, arrived late for work, and were continually taking up office collections for birthdays, deaths, marriages, and retirements.

The main duty of the Circulation Department was to supply to the Production Department "print-run estimates": the number of copies of each magazine that should be printed to insure maximum profit for Javis-Bircham. The magazines might be weeklies, semi-monthlies, monthlies, quarterlies, semi-annuals or annuals. They might be given away to a managerial-level readership or sold by subscription. Some were even available to the general public on newsstands. Most of the magazines earned their way by advertising revenue. Some carried no advertising at all, but were of such a specialized nature that they sold solely on the value of their editorial content.

Estimating the "press run" of each magazine for maximum profitability was an incredibly complex task. Past and potential circulation of each periodical had to be considered, current and projected advertising revenue, share of general overhead, costs of actual printing—quality of paper, desired process, four-color plates, etc.—costs of mailing and distributing, editorial budget (including personnel), publicity and public relations campaigns, etc., etc.

At the time Daniel Blank joined the organization, this bewildering job of "print-run estimation" seemed to be done "by guess and by God." Happy Bob White's staff of "old women" fed him information, laughing a great deal during their conversations with him. Then, when a recommendation was due, White would sit at his desk, humming, with an ancient slide rule in his hands, and within an hour or so would send his estimate to the Production Department.

Daniel Blank saw immediately that there were so many variables involved that the system screamed for computerization. His experience with computers was minimal; on previous jobs he had been involved mostly with relatively simple data-processing machines.

He therefore enrolled for a six months' night course in "The Triumph of the Computer." Two years after starting work at Javis-Bircham, he presented to Bob White a 30-page carefully organized and cogently reasoned prospectus on the advantages of a computerized Circulation Department.

White took it home over the weekend to read. He returned it to Blank on Monday morning. Pages were marked with brown rings from coffee cups, and one page had been crinkled and almost obliterated by a spilled drink.

White took Daniel to lunch and, smiling, explained why Blank's plan wouldn't do. It wouldn't do at all.

"You obviously put a lot of work and thought into it," White said, "but you're forgetting the personalities involved. The people. My God, Dan, I have lunch with the editors and advertising managers of those magazines almost every day. They're my friends. They all have plans for their books: an article that might get a lot of publicity and boost circulation, a new hot-shot advertising salesman who might boost revenue way over the same month last year. I've got to consider all those personal things. The human factors involved. You can't feed that into a computer."

Daniel Blank nodded understandingly. An hour after they returned from lunch he had a clean copy of his prospectus on the desk of the Executive Vice President.

A month later the Circulation Department was shocked to learn that laughing Bob White had retired. Daniel Blank was appointed Circulation *Director*, a title he chose himself, and given a free hand.

Within a year all the "old women" were gone, Blank had surrounded himself with a young staff of pale technicians, and the cabinets of AMROK II occupied half the 30th floor of the Javis-Bircham Building. As Blank had predicted, not only did the computer and auxiliary data-processing machines handle all the problems of circulation—subscription fulfillment and print-run estimation—but they peformed these tasks so swiftly that they could also be used for salary checks, personnel records, and pension programs. As a result, Javis-Bircham was able to dismiss more than 500 employees and, as Blank had carefully pointed out in his original prospectus, the annual leasing of the extremely expensive AMROK II resulted in an appreciable tax deduction.

Daniel Blank was currently earning $55,000 a year and had an unlimited expense account, a very advantageous pension and stock option plan. He was 36.

About a month after he took over, he received a very strange postcard from Bob White. It said merely: "What are you feeding the computer? Ha-ha."

Blank puzzled over this. What had been fed the computer, of course, were the past circulation and advertising revenue figures and profit and loss totals of all the magazines Javis-Bircham published. Admittedly, White had been working his worn slide rule during most of the years from which those figures were taken, and it was possible to say that, in a sense, White had programmed the computer. But still, the postcard made little sense, and Daniel Blank wondered why his former boss had bothered to send it.

It was gratifying to hear the uniformed starter say, "Good morning, Mr. Blank," and it was gratifying to ride the Executive Elevator in solitary comfort to the 30th floor. His personal office was a corner suite with wall-to-wall carpeting, a private lavatory and, not a desk, but a table: a tremendous slab of distressed walnut on a wrought-iron base. These things counted.

He had deliberately chosen for his personal secretary a bony, 28-year-old widow, Mrs. Cleek, who needed the job badly and would be grateful. She had proved as efficient and colorless as he had hoped. She had a few odd habits: she insisted on latching all doors and cabinets that were slightly ajar, and she was continually lining up the edges of the ashtrays and papers with the edges of tables and desks, putting everything parallel or at precise right angles. A picture hanging askew drove her mad. But these were minor tics.

When he entered his office, she was ready to hang away his coat and hat in the small closet. His black coffee was waiting for him, steaming, on a small plastic tray on the table, having been delivered by the commissary on the 20th floor.

"Good morning, Mr. Blank," she said in her watery voice, consulting a stenographer's pad she held. "You have a meeting at ten-thirty with the Pension Board. Lunch at twelve-thirty at the Plaza with Acme, regarding the servicing contract. I tried to confirm, but no one's in yet. I'll try again."

"Thank you," he said. "I like your dress. Is it new?"

"No," she said.

"I'll be in the Computer Room until the Pension Board meeting, in case you need me."

"Yes, Mr. Blank."

The embarrassing truth was that, as Mrs. Cleek was probably aware, he had nothing to do. It was true he was overseer of an extremely important department—perhaps *the* most important department of a large corporation. But, literally, he found it difficult to fill his working day.

He could have given the impression of working. Many executives in similar circumstances did that. He could accept invitations to luncheons easily avoided. He could stalk corridors carrying papers over which he could frown and shake his head. He could request technical literature on supplies and computer systems utterly inadequate or too sophisticated for Javis-Bircham's needs, with a heavy increase of unnecessary correspondence. He could take senseless business trips to inspect the operations of magazine wholesalers and printing plants. He could attend dozens of conventions and trade meetings, give speeches and buy the bodies of hat-check girls.

But none of that was his style. He needed work; he could not endure inaction for long. And so he turned to "empire building," plotting how he might enlarge the size of the Circulation Department and increase his own influence and power.

And in his personal life he felt the same need for action after the brief hibernation following his divorce (during which period he vowed, inexplicably, to remain continent). This desire to "do" dated from his meeting with Celia Montfort. He punched his phone for an outside line, then dialed her number. Again.

He had not seen her nor had he spoken to her since that Sunday he was introduced at the Mortons' and she had napped on his bed. He had looked her up in the Manhattan directory. There it was: "Montfort, C." at an East End address. But each time he called, a male voice answered, lisping: "Mith Montforth rethidenth."

Blank assumed it was a butler or houseman. The voice, in spite of its flutiness, was too mature to be that of the 12-year-old brother. Each time he was informed that Mith Montfort was out of town and, no, the speaker did not know when she might return.

But this time the reply was different. It was "Mith Montforth rethidenth" again, but additional information was offered: Miss Montfort had arrived, had called from the airport, and if Mr. Blank cared to phone later in the day, Mith Montforth would undoubtedly be at home.

He hung up, feeling a steaming hope. He trusted his instincts, though he could not always say *why* he acted as he did. He was convinced there was something there for him with that strange, disturbing woman: something significant. If he had energy and the courage to act . . .

Daniel Blank stepped into the open lobby of the Computer Room and nodded to the receptionist. He went directly to the large white enameled cabinet to the right of the inner doors and drew out a sterile duster and skull cap hermetically sealed in a clear plastic bag.

He donned white cap and duster, went through the first pair of swinging glass doors. Six feet away was the second pair, and the space between was called the "air lock," although it was not sealed. It was illuminated by cold blue fluorescent lights said to have a germicidal effect. He paused a moment to watch the ordered activity in the Computer Room.

AMROK II worked 24 hours a day and was cared for by three shifts of acolytes, 20 in each shift. Blank was gratified to note that all on the morning shift were wearing the required disposable paper caps and dusters. Four men sat at a stainless steel table; the others, young men and women, sexless in their white paper costumes, attended the computer and auxiliary data-processing machines, one of which was presently chattering softly and spewing out an endless record that folded up neatly into partly serrated sheets in a wire basket. It was, Blank knew, a compilation of state unemployment insurance taxes.

The mutter of this machine and the soft start-stop whir of tape reels on another were the only sounds heard when Blank pushed through the second pair of swinging glass doors. The prohibition against unnecessary noise was rigidly enforced. And this glaring, open room was not only silent, it was dust-proof, with temperature and humidity rigidly controlled and moni-tored. An automatic alarm would be triggered by any unusual source of magnetic radiation. Fire was unthinkable. Not only was smoking prohibited but even the mere possession of matches or cigarette lighters was grounds for instant dismissal. The walls were unpainted stainless steel, the lamps fluorescent. The Computer Room was an unadorned vault, an operating theatre, floating on rubber mountings within the supporting body of the Javis-Bircham Building.

And 90 percent of this was sheer nonsense, humbuggery. This was not an atomic research facility, nor a laboratory dealing with deadly viruses. The business activities of AMROK II did not demand these absurd precautions—the sterile caps and gowns, the "air lock," the prohibition against normal conversation.

Daniel Blank had decreed all this, deliberately. Even before it was installed and operating, he realized the functioning of AMROK II would be an awesome mystery to most of the employees of Javis-Bircham, including Blank's superiors: vice presidents, the president, the board of directors. Blank intended to keep the activities of the Computer Room an enigma. Not only did it insure his importance to the firm, but it made his task much easier when the annual "budget day" rolled around and he requested consistently rising amounts for his department's operating expenses.

Blank went immediately to the stainless steel table where the four young men were deep in whispered conversation. This was his Task Force X-1, the best technicians of the morning shift. Blank had set them a problem that was still "Top Secret" within this room.

From his boredom, in his desire to extend the importance of the Circulation Department and increase his personal power and influence, Blank had decided he should have the responsibility of deciding for each magazine the proportion between editorial pages and advertising pages. Years ago this ratio was dictated in a rough fashion by the limitations of printing presses, which could produce a magazine only in multiples of eight or 16 pages.

But improvements in printing techniques now permitted production of magazines of any number of pages—15, 47, 76, 103, 241: whatever might be desired, with a varied mix of paper quality. Magazine editors constantly fought for more editorial pages, arguing (sometimes correctly, sometimes not) that sheer quantity attracted readers.

But there was obviously a limit to this: paper cost money, and so did press time. Editors were continually wrangling with the Production Department about the thickness of their magazines. Daniel Blank saw a juicy opportun-ity to step into the fray and supersede both sides by suggesting AMROK II be given the assignment of determining the most profitable proportion between editorial and advertising pages.

He would, he knew, face strong and vociferous opposition. Editors would claim an infringement of their creative responsibilities; production men would see a curtailment of their power. But if Blank could present a feasible program, he was certain he could win over the shrewd men who floated through the paneled suites on the 31st floor. Then he—and AMROK II, of course—would determine the extent of the editorial content of each magazine. It seemed to him but a short step from that to allowing AMROK II to dictate the most profitable subject matter of the editorial content. It was possible.

But all that was in the future. Right now Task Force X-1 was discussing the programming that would be necessary before the computer could make wise decisions on the most profitable ratio between editorial and advertising pages in every issue of every Javis-Bircham magazine. Blank listened closely to their whispered conversation, turning his eyes from speaker to speaker, and wondering if it was true, as she had said, that she occasionally rouged her nipples.

He waited, with conscious control, until 3:00 P.M. before calling. The lisping houseman asked him to hang on a moment, then came back on the phone to tell him, "Mith Montfort requeth you call again in a half hour." Puzzled, Blank hung up, paced his office for precisely 30 minutes, ate a chilled pear from his small refrigerator, and called again. This time he was put through to her.

"Hello," he said. "How are you?" (Should he call her "Celia" or "Miss Montfort"?)

"Well. And you?"

"Fine. You said I could call."

"Yes."

"You've been out of town?"

"Out of the country. To Samarra."

"Oh?" he said, hoping she might think him clever, "you had an appointment?"

"Something like that."

"Where exactly is Samarra?"

"Iraq. I was there for only a day. Actually I went over to see my parents. They're currently in Marrakech."

"How are they?" he asked politely.

"The same," she said in her toneless voice. "They haven't changed in thirty years. Ever since . . ." Her voice trailed off.

"Ever since what?" he asked.

"Ever since World War Two. It upset their plans."

She spoke in riddles, and he didn't want to pry.

"Marrakech isn't near Samarra, is it?"

"Oh no. Marrakech is in Morocco."

"Geography isn't my strong point. I get lost every time I go south of 23rd Street."

He thought she might laugh, but she didn't.

"Tomorrow night," he said desperately, "tomorrow night the Mortons are having a cocktail party. We're invited. I'd like to take you to dinner before the party. It starts about ten."

"Yes," she said immediately. "Be here at eight. We'll have a drink, then go to dinner. Then we'll go to the Mortons' party."

He started to say "thank you" or "Fine" or "I'm looking forward to it" or "See you then," but she had already hung up. He stared at the dead receiver in his hand.

The next day, Friday, he left work early to go home to prepare for the evening. He debated with himself whether or not to send flowers. He decided against it. He had a feeling she loved flowers but never wore them. His best course, he felt, was to circle about her softly, slowly, until he could determine her tastes and prejudices.

He groomed himself carefully, shaving although he had shaved that morning. He used a women's cologne, *Je Reviens*, a scent that stirred him. He wore French underwear—white nylon bikini briefs—and a silk shirt in a geometric pattern of white and blue squares. His wide necktie was a subtly patterned maroon. The suit was navy knit, single breasted. In addition to wrist watch, cufflinks, and a heavy gold ring on his right forefinger, he wore a gold-link identification bracelet loose about his right wrist. And the "Via Veneto" wig.

He left early to walk over to her apartment. It wasn't far, and it was a pleasant evening.

His loose topcoat was a black lightweight British gabardine, styled with raglan sleeves, a fly front, and slash pockets. The pockets, in the British fashion, had an additional opening through the coat fabric so that the wearer did not have to unbutton his coat to reach his trouser or jacket pockets but could shove his hand inside the concealed coat openings for tickets, wallet, keys, change, or whatever.

Now, strolling toward Celia Montfort's apartment through the sulfur-laden night, Daniel Blank reached inside his coat pocket to feel himself. To the passer-by, he was an elegant gentleman, hand thrust casually into coat pocket. But beneath the coat . . .

Once, shortly after he was separated from Gilda, he had worn the same coat and walked through Times Square on a Saturday night. He had slipped his hand into the pocket opening, unzipped his fly, and held himself exposed beneath the loose coat as he moved through the throng, looking into the faces of passersby.

Celia Montfort lived in a five-story greystone townhouse. The door bell was of a type he had read about but never encountered before. It was a bell-pull, a brass knob that is drawn out, then released. The bell is sounded as the knob is pulled and as it is released to return to its socket. Daniel Blank admired its polish and the teak door it ornamented . . .

. . . A teak door that was opened by a surprisingly tall man, pale, thin, wearing striped trousers and a shiny black alpaca jacket. A pink sweetheart rose was in his lapel. Daniel was conscious of a scent: not his own, but something heavier and fruitier.

"My name is Daniel Blank," he said. "I believe Miss Montfort is expecting me."

"Yeth, thir," the man said, holding wide the door. "I am Valenter. Do come in."

It was an impressive entrance: marble-floored with a handsome staircase curving away. On a slender pedestal was a crystal vase of cherry-colored mums. He had been right: she did like long-stemmed flowers.

"Pleath wait in the thudy. Mith Montfort will be down thoon."

His coat and hat were taken and put away somewhere. The tall, skinny man came back to usher him into a room paneled with oak and leather-bound books.

"Would you care for a drink, thir?"

Soft flames flickering in a tiled fireplace. Reflections on the polished leather of a tufted couch. On the mantel, unexpectedly, a beautifully detailed model of a Yankee whaler. Andirons and fireplace tools of black iron with brass handles.

"Please. A vodka martini on the rocks."

Drapes of heavy brocade. Rugs of—what? Not Oriental. Greek perhaps? Or Turkish? Chinese vases filled with blooms. An Indian paneled screen, all scrolled with odd, disturbing figures. A silvered cocktail shaker of the Prohibition Era. The room had frozen in 1927 or 1931.

"Olive, thir, or a twitht of lemon?"

Hint of incense in the air. High ceiling and, between the darkened beams, painted cherubs with dimpled asses. Oak doors and window mouldings. A bronze statuette of a naked nymph pulling a bow. The "string" was a twisted wire.

"Lemon, please."

An art nouveau mirror on the papered wall. A small oil nude of a middle-aged brunette holding her chin and glancing downward at sagging breasts with bleared nipples. A tin container of dusty rhododendron leaves. A small table inlaid as a chessboard with pieces swept and toppled. And in a black leather armchair, with high, embracing wings, the most beautiful boy Daniel Blank had ever seen.

"Hello," the boy said.

"Hello," he smiled stiffly. "My name is Daniel Blank. You must be Anthony."

"Tony."

"Tony."

"May I call you Dan?"

"Sure."

"Can you lend me ten dollars, Dan?"

Blank, startled, looked at him more closely. The lad had his knees drawn up, was hugging them, his head tilted to one side.

His beauty was so unearthly it was frightening. Clear, guileless blue eyes, carved lips, a bloom of youth and wanting, sculpted ears, a smile that tugged, those crisp golden curls long enough to frame face and chiselled neck. And an aura as rosy as the cherubs that floated overhead.

"It's awful, isn't it," the boy said, "to ask ten dollars from a complete stranger, but to tell you the truth—"

Blank was instantly alert, listening now and not just looking. It was his experience that when someone said "To tell the truth—" or "Would I lie to you?" the man was either a liar, a cheat, or both.

"You see," Tony said with an audacious smile. "I saw this absolutely marvelous jade pin. I know Celia would love it."

"Of course," Blank said. He took a ten dollar bill from his wallet. The boy made no move toward him. Daniel was forced to walk across the room to hand it to him.

"Thanks so much," the youth said languidly. "I get my allowance the first of the month. I'll pay you back."

He paid then, Blank knew, all he was ever going to pay: a dazzling smile of such beauty and young promise that Daniel was fuddled by longing. The moment was saved of souring by the entrance of Valenter, carrying the martini not on a tray but in his hand. When Blank took it, his fingers touched Valenter's. The evening began to spin out of control.

She came in a few moments later, wearing an evening shift styled exactly like the black satin she had been wearing when he first met her. But this one was in a dark bottle green, glimmering. About her neck was a heavy silver chain, tarnished, supporting a pendant: the image of a beast-god. Mexican, Blank guessed.

"I went to Samarra to meet a poet," she said, speaking as she came through the door and walked steadily toward him. "I once wrote poetry. Did I tell you? No. But I don't anymore. I have talent, but not enough. The blind poet in Samarra is a genius. A poem is a condensed novel. I imagine a novelist must increase the significance of what he writes by one-third to one-half to communicate all of his meaning. You understand? But the poet, so condensed, must double or triple what he wants to convey, hoping the reader will extract from this his full meaning."

Suddenly she leaned forward and kissed him on the lips while Valenter and the boy looked on gravely.

"How are you?" she asked.

Valenter brought her a glass of red wine. She was seated next to Blank on the leather sofa. Valenter stirred up the fire, adding another small log, went to stand behind the armchair where Anthony coiled in flickering shadow.

"I think the Mortons' party will be amusing," he offered. "A lot of people. Noisy and crowded. But we don't have to stay long."

"Have you ever smoked hashish?" she asked.

He looked nervously toward the young boy.

"I tried it once," he said in a low voice. "It didn't do anything for me. I prefer alcohol."

"Do you drink a lot?"

"No."

The boy was wearing white flannel bags, white leather loafers, a white knitted singlet that left his slim arms bare. He moved slowly, crossing his legs, stretching, pouting. Celia Montfort turned her head to look at him. Did a signal pass?

"Tony," she said.

Immediately Valenter put a hand tenderly on the boy's shoulder.

"Time for your lethon, Mathter Montfort," he said.

"Oh, pooh," Tony said.

They walked from the room side by side. The lad stopped at the door, turned back, made a solemn bow in Blank's direction.

"I am very happy to have met you, sir," he said formally.

Then he was gone. Valenter closed the door softly behind them.

"A handsome boy," Daniel said. "What school does he go to?"

She didn't answer. He turned to look at her. She was peering into her wine glass, twirling the stem slowly in her long fingers. The straight black hair fell about her face: the long face, broody and purposeful.

She put her wine glass aside and rose suddenly. She moved casually about the room, and he swiveled his head to keep her in view. She touched things, picked them up and put them down. He was certain she was naked beneath the satin shift. Cloth touched her and flew away. It clung, and whispered off.

As she moved about, she began to intone another of what was apparently an inexhaustible repertoire of monologues. He was conscious of planned performance. But it was not a play; it was a ballet, as formalized and obscure. Above all, he felt *intent*: motive and plan.

"My parents are such sad creatures," she was saying. "Living in history. But that's not living at all, is it? It's an entombing. Mother's silk chiffon and father's plus-fours. They could be breathing mannequins at the Costume Institute. I look for dignity and all I find is . . . What is it I want? Grandeur, I suppose. Yes. I've thought of it. But is it impossible to be grand in life? What we consider grandeur is always connected with defeat and death. The Greek plays. Napoleon's return from Moscow. Lincoln. Superhuman dignity there. Nobility, if you like. But always rounded with death. The living, no matter how noble they may be, never quite make it, do they? But death rounds them out. What if John Kennedy had lived? No one has ever written of his life as a work of art, but it was. Beginning, middle, and end. Grandeur. And death made it. Are you ready? Shall we go?"

"I hope you like French cooking," he muttered. "I called for a reservation."

"It doesn't matter," she said.

The dance continued during dinner. She requested a banquette: they sat side by side. They ate and drank with little conversation. Once she picked up a thin sliver of tender veal and fed it into his mouth. But her free hand was on his arm, or in his lap, or pushing her long hair back so that the bottle green satin was brought tight across button nipples. Once, while they were having coffee and brandy, she crossed her knees. Her dress hiked up; the flesh of her thighs was perfectly white, smooth, glistening. He thought of good sea scallops and Dover sole.

"Do you like opera?" she asked in her abrupt way.

"No," he said truthfully. "Not much. It's so—so made up."

"Yes," she agreed, "it is. Artificial. But it's just a device: a flimsy wire coat hanger, and they hang the voices on that."

He was not a stupid man, and while they were seated at the banquette he became aware that her subtle movements—the touchings, the leanings, the sudden, unexpected caress of her hair against his cheek—these things were directorial suggestions, parts of her balletic performance. She was rehearsed. He wasn't certain of his role, but wanted to play it well.

"The voices," she went on, "the mighty voices that give me the feeling of suppressed power. With some singers I get the impression that there is art and strength there that hasn't been tapped. I get the feeling that, if they really let themselves go, they could crush eardrums and shatter stained glass windows. Perhaps the best of them, throwing off all restraint, could crush the world. Break it up into brittle pieces and send all the chunks whirling off into space."

He was made inferior by her soliloquies and made brave by wine and brandy.

"Why the hell are you telling me all this?" he demanded.

She leaned closer, pressed a satin-slicked breast against his arm.

"It's the same feeling I get from you," she whispered. "That you have a strength and resolve that could shatter the world."

He looked at her, beginning to glimpse her intent and his future. He wanted to ask, "Why me?" but found, to his surprise, it wasn't important.

The Mortons' party leavened their heavy evening. Florence and Samuel, wearing identical red velvet jumpsuits, met them at the door with the knowing smirks of successful matchmakers.

"Come in!" Flo cried.

"It's a marvelous party!" Sam cried.

"Two fights already!" Flo laughed.

"And one crying jag!" Sam laughed.

The party had a determined frenzy. He lost Celia in the swirl, and in the next few hours met and listened to a dozen disoriented men and women who floated, bumped against him, drifted away. He had a horrible vision of harbor trash, bobbing and nuzzling, coming in and going out.

Suddenly she was behind him, hand up under his jacket, nails digging into his shirted back.

"Do you know what happens at midnight?" she whispered.

"What?"

"They take off their faces—just like masks. And do you know what's underneath?"

"What?"

"Their faces. Again. And again."

She slipped away; he was too confused to hold her. He wanted to be naked in front of a mirror, making sure.

Finally, finally, she reappeared and drew him away. They flapped hands at host and hostess and stepped into the quiet corridor, panting. In the elevator she came into his arms and bit the lobe of his left ear as he said, "Oh," and the music from wherever was playing "My Old Kentucky Home." He was sick with lust and conscious that his life was dangerous and absurd. He was teetering, and pitons were not driven nor ice ax in.

There was Valenter to open the door for them, the sweetheart rose wilted. His face had the sheen of a scoured iron pot, and his lips seemed bruised. He served black coffee in front of the tiled fireplace. They sat on the leather couch and stared at blue embers.

"Will that be all, Mith Montfort?"

She nodded; he drifted away. Daniel Blank wouldn't look at him. What if the man should wink?

Celia went out of the room, came back with two pony glasses and a half-full bottle of marc.

"What is that?" he asked.

"A kind of brandy," she said. "Burgundian, I think. From the dregs. Very strong."

She filled a glass, and before handing it to him ran a long, red tongue around the rim, looking at him. He took it, sipped gratefully.

"Yes," he nodded. "Strong."

"Those people tonight," she said. "So inconsequential. Most of them are intelligent, alert, talented. But they don't have the opportunity. To surrender, I mean. To something important and shaking. They desire it more than they know. To give themselves. To what? Ecology or day-care centers or racial equality? They sense the need for something more, and God is dead. So . . . the noise and hysteria. If they could find . . ."

Her voice trailed off. He looked up.

"Find what?" he asked.

"Oh," she said, her eyes vague, "you know."

She rose from the couch. When he rose to stand alongside her, she unexpectedly stepped close, reached out, gently drew down the lower lid of his right eye. She stared intently at the exposed eyeball.

"What?" he said, confused.

"You're not inconsequential," she said, took him by the hand and led him upward. "Not at all."

Dazed by drink and wonder, he followed docilely. They climbed the handsome marble staircase to the third floor. There they passed through a tawdry wooden door and climbed two more flights up a splintered wooden stairway flecked with cobwebs that kissed his mouth.

"What *is* this?" he asked once.

"I *live* up here," she answered, turned suddenly and, being above him, reached down, pulled his head forward and pressed his face into the cool satin between belly and thighs.

It was a gesture that transcended obscenity and brought him trembling to his knees there on the dusty stairs.

"Rest a moment," she said.

"I'm a mountain climber," he said, and their whispered exchange seemed to him so inane that he gave a short bark of laughter that banged off dull walls and echoed.

"What?" he said again, and all the time he knew.

It was a small room of unpainted plank walls, rough-finished and scarred with white streaks as if some frantic beast had clawed to escape. There was a single metal cot with a flat spring of woven tin straps. On this was thrown a thin mattress, uncovered, the striped grey ticking soiled and burned.

There was one kitchen chair that had been painted fifty times and was now so dented and nicked that a dozen colors showed in bruised blotches. A bare light bulb, orange and dim, hung from a dusty cord.

The floor was patched with linoleum so worn the pattern had disappeared and brown backing showed through. The unframed mirror on the inside of the closed door was tarnished and cracked. The iron ashtray on the floor near the cot overflowed with cold cigarette butts. The room smelled of must, mildew, and old love.

"Beautiful," Daniel Blank said wonderingly, staring about. "It's a stage set. Any moment now a wall swings away, and there will be the audience applauding politely. What are my lines?"

"Take off your wig," she said.

He did, standing by the cot with the hair held foolishly in his two hands, offering her a small, dead animal.

She came close and caressed his shaven skull with both hands.

"Do you like this room?" she asked.

"Well . . . it's not exactly my idea of a love nest."

"Oh it's more than that. Much more. Lie down."

Gingerly, with some distaste, he sat on the stained mattress. She softly pressed him back. He stared up at the naked bulb, and there seemed to be a nimbus about it, a glow composed of a million shining particles that pulsed, contracted, expanded until they filled the room.

And then, almost before he knew it had started, she was doing things to him. He could not believe this intelligent, somber, reserved woman was doing those things. He felt a shock of fear, made a few muttered protests. But her voice was soft, soothing. After awhile he just lay there, his eyes closed now, and let her do what she would.

"Scream if you like," she said. "No one can hear."

But he clenched his jaws and thought he might die of pleasure.

He opened his eyes and saw her lying naked beside him, her long, white body as limp as a fileted fish. She began undressing him with practiced fingers . . . opening buttons . . . sliding down zippers . . . tugging things away gently, so gently he hardly had to move at all . . .

Then she was using him, *using* him, and he began to understand what his fate might be. Fear dissolved in a kind of sexual faint he had never experienced before as her strong hands pulled, her dry tongue rasped over his fevered skin.

"Soon," she promised. "Soon."

Once he felt a pain so sharp and sweet he thought she had murdered him. Once he heard her laughing: a thick, burbling sound. Once she wound him about with her smooth, black hair, fashioned a small noose and pulled it tight.

It went on and on, his will dissolving, a great weight lifting, and he would pay any price. It was climbing: mission, danger, sublimity. Finally, the summit.

Later, he was exploring her body and saw, for the first time, her armpits were unshaved. He discovered, hidden in the damp, scented hairs under her left arm, a small tattoo in a curious design.

Still later they were drowsing in each other's sweated arms, the light turned off, when he half-awoke and became conscious of a presence in the room. The door to the corridor was partly open. Through sticky eyes he saw someone standing silently at the foot of the cot, staring down at their linked bodies.

In the dim light Daniel Blank had a smeary impression of a naked figure or someone dressed in white. Blank raised his head and made a hissing sound. The wraith withdrew. The door closed softly. He was left alone with her in that dreadful room.

5

ONE NIGHT, lying naked and alone between his sateen sheets, Daniel Blank wondered if this world might not be another world's dream. It was conceivable: somewhere another planet populated by a sentient people of superior intelligence who shared a communal dream as a method of play. And Earth was their dream, filled with fantasies, grotesqueries, evil—all the irrationalities they themselves rejected in their daily lives but turned to in sleep for relaxation. For fun.

Then we are all smoke and drifting. We are creatures of another world's midnight visions, moving through a life as illogical as any dream, and as realistic. We exist only in a stranger's slumber, and our death is his awaking, smiling at the mad, tangled plot his sleep conceived.

It seemed to Blank that since meeting Celia Montfort his existence had taken on the quality of a dream, the vaporous quality of a dream shot through with wild, bright flashes. His life had become all variables and, just before falling asleep to his own disordered dream, he wondered if AMROK II, properly programmed, might print out the meaning in a micro-second, as something of enormous consequence.

"No, no," Celia Montfort said intently, leaning forward into the candle-light. "Evil isn't just an absence of good. It's not just omission; it's commission, an action. You can't call that man evil just because he lets people starve to put his country's meager resources into heavy industry. That was a political and economic decision. Perhaps he is right, perhaps not. Those things don't interest me. But I think you're wrong to call him evil. Evil is really a kind of religion. I think he's just a well-meaning fool. But evil he's not. Evil implies intelligence and a deliberate intent. Don't you agree, Daniel?"

She turned suddenly to him. His hand shook, and he spilled a few drops of red wine. They dripped onto the unpressed linen tablecloth, spreading out like clots of thick blood.

"Well . . ." he said slowly.

She was having a dinner party: Blank, the Mortons, and Anthony Montfort seated around an enormous, candle-lighted dining table that could easily have accommodated twice their number in a chilly and cavernous dining hall. The meal, bland and without surprises, had been served by Valenter and a heavy, middle-aged woman with a perceptible black mustache.

The dishes were being removed, they were finishing a dusty beaujolais, and their conversation had turned to the current visit to Washington of the dictator of a new African nation, a man who wore white-piped vests and a shoulder holster.

"No, Samuel," Celia shook her head, "he is not an evil man. You use that word loosely. He's just a bungler. Greedy perhaps. Or out for revenge on his enemies. But greed and revenge are grubby motives. True evil has a kind of nobility, as all faiths do. Faith implies total surrender, a giving up of reason."

"Who was evil?" Florence Morton asked.

"Hitler?" Samuel Morton asked.

Celia Montfort looked slowly around the table. "You don't understand," she said softly. "I'm not talking about evil for the sake of ambition. I'm talking about evil for the sake of evil. Not Hitler—no. I mean saints of evil—men and women who see a vision and follow it. Just as Christian saints perceived a vision of good and followed that. I don't believe there have been any modern saints, of good *or* evil. But the possibility exists. In all of us."

"I understand," Anthony Montfort said loudly, and they all turned in surprise to look at him.

"To do evil because it's fun," the boy said.

"Yes, Tony," his sister said gently, smiling at him. "Because it's fun. Let's have coffee in the study. There's a fire there."

In the upstairs room the naked bulb burned in the air: a dusty moon. There was a smell of low tide and crawling things. Once he heard a faint shout of laughter, and Daniel Blank wondered if it was Tony laughing, and why he laughed.

They lay unclothed and stared at each other through the dark sunglasses she had provided. He stared—but did she? He could not tell. But blind eyes faced his blind eyes, discs of black against white skin. He felt the shivery bliss again. It was the mystery.

Her mouth opened slowly. Her long tongue slid out, lay flaccid between dry lips. Were her eyes closed? Was she looking at the wall? He peered closer, and behind the dark glass saw a far-off gleam. One of her hands wormed between her thighs, and a tiny bubble of spittle appeared in the corner of her mouth. He heard her breathing.

He pressed to her. She moved away and began to murmur. He understood some of what she said, but much was riddled. "What is it? What is it?" he wanted to cry, but did not because he feared it might be less than he hoped. So he was silent, listened to her murmur, felt her fingertips pluck at his quick skin.

The black covers over her eyes became holes, pits that went through flesh, bone, cot, floor, building, earth, and finally out into the far, dark reaches. He floated down those empty corridors, her naked hands pulling him along.

Her murmur never ceased. She circled and circled, spiraling in, but never named what she wanted. He wondered if there was a word for it, for then he could believe it existed. If it had no name, no word to label it, then it was an absolute reality beyond his apprehension, as infinite as the darkness through which he sped, tugged along by her hungry hands.

"We've found out all about her!" Florence Morton laughed.

"Well . . . not all, but some!" Samuel Morton laughed.

They had appeared at Daniel's door, late at night, wearing matching costumes of blue suede jeans and fringed jackets. It was difficult to believe them husband and wife; they were sexless twins, with their bony bodies, bird features, helmets of oiled hair.

He invited them in for a drink. The Mortons sat on the couch close together and held hands.

"How did you find out?" he asked curiously.

"We know everything!" Florence said.

"Our spies were everywhere!" Samuel said.

Daniel Blank smiled. It was almost true.

"Lots of money there," Flo said. "Her grandfather on her mother's side. Oil and steel. Plenty of loot. But her father had the family. He didn't inherit much but good looks. They said he was the handsomest man of his generation in America. They called him 'Beau Montfort' at Princeton. But he never did graduate. Kicked out for knocking up—someone. Who was it, Samovel?"

"A dean's wife or a scullery maid—someone like that. Anyway, this was in the late Twenties. Then he married all that oil and steel. He made a big contribution to Roosevelt's campaign fund and thought he might be ambassador to London, Paris or Rome. But FDR had more sense than that. He named Montfort a 'roving representative' and got him away from Washington. That was smart. The Montforts loved it. They drank and fucked up a storm. The talk of Europe. Celia was born in Lausanne. But then things went sour. Her parents got in with the Nazis, and daddy sent home glowing reports about what a splendid, kindly gentleman Hitler was. Naturally, Roosevelt dumped him. Then, from what we can learn, they just bummed around in high style."

"What about Celia?" Daniel asked. "Is Tony really her brother?"

They looked at him in astonishment.

"You wondered?" Flo asked.

"You guessed?" Sam asked.

"We didn't get it straight," she acknowledged. "No one really knows."

"Everyone guesses," Sam offered. "But it's just gossip. No one *knows*."

"But Tony could be her son," Flo nodded.

"The ages are right," Sam nodded. "But she's never been married. That anyone knows about."

"There are rumors."

"She's a strange woman."

"And who is Valenter?"

"What's his relationship to her?"

"And to Tony?"

"And where does she go when she goes away?"

"And comes back bruised? What is she *doing*?"

"Why don't her parents want her in Europe?"

"What's *with* her?"

"Who *is* she?"

"I don't care," Daniel Blank whispered. "I love her."

He worked late in his office on Halloween night. He had a salad and black coffee sent up from the commissary. As he ate, he went over the final draft of the prospectus he was scheduled to present to the Production Board on the following day: his plan to have AMROK II determine the ratio between advertising and editorial pages in every Javis-Bircham magazine.

The prospectus seemed to him temperate, logical, and convincing. But he recognized that it lacked enthusiasm. It was as stirring as an insurance policy, as inspirational as a corporate law brief; he poked it across the table and sat staring at it.

The fault, he knew, was his; he had lost interest. Oh the plan was valid, it made sense, but it no longer seemed to him of much import.

And he knew the reason for his indifference: Celia Montfort. Compared to her, to his relations with her, his job at Javis-Bircham was a game played by a grown boy, no worse and no better than Chinese Checkers or Monopoly. He went through the motions, he followed the rules, but he was not touched.

He sat brooding, wondering where she might lead him. Finally he rose, took his trench coat and hat. He left the prospectus draft on the table, with the garbage of his dinner and the dregs of cold coffee in the plastic cup. On his way to the executive elevator he glanced through the window of the Computer Room. The night shift, white-clad, floated slowly on their crepe soles over the cork floor, drifting through a sterile dream.

The rain came in spits and gusts, driven by a hacking wind. There were no cabs in sight. Blank turned up his coat collar, pulled down the brim of his hat. He dug toward Eighth Avenue. If he didn't find a cab, he'd take a crosstown bus on 42nd Street to First Avenue, and then change to an uptown bus.

Neon signs glimmered. Porno shops offered rubdowns and body painting. From a record shop, hustling the season, came a novelty recording of a dog barking "Adeste Fidelis." An acned prostitute, booted and spurred, murmured, "Fun?" as he passed. He knew this scruffy section well and paid no heed. It had nothing to do with him.

As he approached the subway kiosk at 42nd Street, a band of young girls came giggling up, flashing in red yellow green blue party dresses, coats swinging open, long hair ripped back by the wind. Blank stared, wondering why such beauties were on such a horrid street.

He saw then. They were all boys and young men, transvestites, on their way to a Halloween drag. In their satins and laces. In evening slippers and swirling wigs. Carmined lips and shadowed eyes. Shaved legs in nylon pantyhose. Padded chests. Hands flying and throaty laughs.

Soft fingers were on his arm. A mocking voice: "Dan!"

It was Anthony Montfort, looking back to flirt a wave, golden hair gleaming in the rain like flame. And then, following, a few paces back, the tall, skinny Valenter, wrapped in a black raincoat.

Daniel Blank stood and watched that mad procession dwindle up the avenue. He heard shouts, raucous cries. Then they were all gone, and he was staring after.

She went away for a day, two days, a week. Or, if she really didn't go away, he could not talk to her. He heard only Valenter's "Mith Montforth rethidenth," and then the news that she was not at home.

He became aware that these unexplained absences invariably followed their erotic ceremonies in the upstairs room. The following day, shattered with love and the memory of pleasure, he would call and discover she was gone, or would not talk to him.

He thought she was manipulating him, dancing out her meaningful ballet. She approached, touched, withdrew. He followed, she laughed, he touched, she caressed, he reached, she pulled back, fingers beckoning. The dance inflamed him.

Once, after four days' absence, he found her weary, drained, with yellow bruises on arms and legs, and purple loops beneath her eyes. She would not say where she had been or what she had done. She lay limp, without resistance, and insisted he abuse her. Infuriated, he did, and she thanked him. Was that, too, part of her plan?

She was a tangle of oddities. Usually she was well-groomed, bathed and scented, long hair brushed gleaming, nails trimmed and painted. But one night she came to his apartment a harridan. She had not bathed, as he discovered, and played the frumpish wanton, looking at him with derisive eyes and using foul language. He could not resist her.

She played strange games. One night she donned a child's jumper, sat on his lap and called him "Daddy." Another time—and how had she guessed *that*?—she bought him a gold chain and insisted he link it about his slim waist. She bit him. He thought her mad with love for him, but when he reached for her, she was not there.

He knew what was happening and did not care. Only she had meaning. She recited a poem to him in a language he could not identify, then licked his eyes. One night he tried to kiss her—an innocent kiss on the cheek, a kiss of greeting—and she struck his jaw with her clenched fist. The next instant she was on her knees, fumbling for him.

And her monologues never ended. She could be silent for hours, then suddenly speak to him of sin and love and evil and gods and why sex should transcend the sexual. Was she training him? He thought so, and studied.

She was gone for almost a week. He took her to dinner when she returned, but it was not a comfortable evening. She was silent and withdrawn. Only once did she look directly at him. Then she looked down, and with the middle finger of her right hand lightly touched, stroked, caressed the white tablecloth.

She took him immediately home, and he followed obediently up that cobwebbed staircase. In the upstairs room, standing naked beneath the blaring orange light, she showed him the African masks.

And she told him what she wanted him to do.

6

DANIEL BLANK inched his way up the chimney of Devil's Needle. He could feel the cold of the stone against his shoulders, against his gloved palms and heavy boots. It was dark inside the cleft; the cold was damp and smelled of death.

He wormed his way carefully onto the flat top. There had been light snow flurries the day before, and he expected ice. It was there, in thin patches, and after he hauled up the rucksack he used his ice ax to chip it away, shoving splinters over the side. Then he could stand on cleated soles and search around.

It was a lowery sky, with a look of more snow to the west. Dirty clouds scummed the sun; the wind knifed steadily. This would, he knew, be his last climb until spring. The park closed on Thanksgiving; there were no ski trails, and the rocks were too dangerous in winter.

He sat on the stone, ate an onion sandwich, drank a cup of coffee that seemed to chill as it was poured. He had brought a little flask of brandy and took small sips. Warmth went through him like new blood, and he thought of Celia.

She went through him like new blood, too; a thaw he knew in heart, gut, loins. She melted him, and not only his flesh. He felt her heat in every waking thought, in his clotted dreams. His love for her had brought him aware, had made him sensible of a world that existed for others but which he had never glimpsed.

He had been an only child, raised in a large house filled with the odors of disinfectant and his mother's gin. His father was moderately wealthy, having inherited from an aunt. He worked in a bank. His mother drank and collected Lalique glass. This was in Indiana.

It was a silent house and in later years, when Daniel tried to recall it, he had an absurd memory of the entire place being tiled: walls, floors, ceilings plated with white tile, enamel on steel, exactly like a gleaming subway tunnel that went on forever to nowhere. Perhaps it was just a remembered dream.

He had always been a loner; his mother and father never kissed him on the lips, but offered their cheeks. White tiles. The happiest memory of his boyhood was when their colored maid gave him a birthday present; it was a display box for his rock collection. Her husband had made it from an old orange crate, carefully sanding the rough wood and lining it with sleazy black cloth. It was beautiful, just what he wanted. That year his mother gave him handkerchiefs and underwear, and his father gave him a savings bond.

He was a loner in college, too. But in his sophomore year he lost his virginity at the one whore house in the college town. In his last two years he had a comforting affair with a Jewish girl from Boston. She was ugly but had mad eyes and a body that didn't end. All she wanted to do was screw. That was all right with him.

He found a piece of chalcedony and polished it in his rock tumbler and on the buffing wheel. It wasn't a priceless stone, but he thought it pretty. The Jewish girl laughed when he gave it to her on graduation day. "Fucking *goy*," she said.

His graduation present from his parents was a summer in Europe, a grand tour of a dozen countries with enough time for climbing in Switzerland and visiting archeological digs in the south of France. He was waiting for his plane in New York, in a hotel bed with the Jewish girl who had flown down from Boston for a last bang, when a lawyer called to tell him his mother and father, driving home from his graduation, had gone off the highway, had been trapped in their car, and burned to death.

Daniel Blank thought less than a minute. Then he told the lawyer to sell the house, settle the estate, and bury his parents. Daniel himself would be home after his trip to Europe. The Boston girl heard him say all this on the phone. By the time he hung up, she was dressed and marching out of there, carrying her Louis Vuitton bag. He never saw her again. But it was a wonderful summer.

When he returned to his hometown late in August, no one would talk to him but the lawyer—and he as little as possible. Daniel Blank couldn't care less. He flew to New York, opened a bank account with his inheritance, then flew back to Bloomington and was finally accepted at the University of Indiana, going for an M.S. with emphasis on geology and archeology. During his second year he met Gilda, the woman he later married.

Two months before he was to get his degree, he decided it was all a lot of shit; he didn't want to spend the rest of his life shoveling dirt. He gave the best stone in his collection (a nice piece of jade) to Gilda, donated the remaining rocks to the University, and flew to New York. He played the part of a modestly moneyed bachelor in Manhattan for about six months. Then most of the cash was gone, but he hadn't sold off any of the stocks or bonds. He got a silly job in the circulation department of a national magazine. He found, to his amusement, that he was good at it. And he discovered he had an ambition unhampered by conscience. Gilda came to New York, and they were married.

He was not a stupid man; he knew the tiled emotions of his boyhood and youth had deadened him. And that house that smelled of CN and gin . . . those cheek-kisses . . . the Lalique glass. Other people fell in love and wept; he collected stones and scorned his parents' funeral.

What Celia Montfort had done for him, he decided, was to peel clean what had always been in him but had never been revealed. Now he could feel, deeply, and react to her. He could love her. He could sacrifice for her. It was *passion*, as warming as brandy on a bleak November afternoon. It was a fire in the veins, a heightened awareness, a need compounded of wild hope and fearful dread. He sought it, following the same instinct that had led him to discard his rock collection, those mementoes of dead history.

He started the climb down, still thinking of his love for Celia, of her naked and masked in the upstairs room, and of how quickly she had learned to slide her hand into his slitted pocket and fondle him as they walked in public.

Descending, he moved one boot too quickly. The heel hit the toe of the other boot, pressed against the opposite chimney wall. Then both legs dangled. For a long, stomach-turning moment he was suspended only by the pressure of his arms, clamped by shoulders and palms shoving against opposing walls. He forced himself to take a deep breath, eyes closed in the cold darkness. He would not think of the fast fall to the boulders below.

Slowly, smiling, he drew up one knee and planted a sole carefully against the opposite wall. His elbows were trembling with strain. He lifted the other boot into position and pressed. Now he could take the load off shoulders, arms, wrists, hands.

He looked up at the little patch of murky sky above the black hole he was in, and laughed with delight. He would descend safely. He could do anything. He had the strength to resist common sense.

PART TWO

1

CAPTAIN EDWARD X. DELANEY, Commanding Officer of the 251st Precinct, New York Police Department, wearing civilian clothes, pushed open the door of the doctor's office, removed his Homburg (stiff as wood), and gave his name to the receptionist.

He planted himself solidly into an armchair, glanced swiftly around the room, then stared down at the hat balanced precisely on his knees. It was the "Observation Game": originally a self-imposed duty but now a diversion he had enjoyed for almost thirty years, since he had been a patrolman. If, for any reason, he was called upon to describe the patients in the waiting room . . .

"Left: male, Negro, dark brown, about 35, approximately 5 feet 10 inches, 160 pounds. Kinky black hair cut short; no part. Wearing plaid sports jacket, fawn-colored slacks, cordovan loafers. Necktie looped but not knotted. Heavy ring on right hand. Slight white scar on neck. Smoking cork-tip cigarette held between thumb and forefinger of left hand.

"Center: female, white, about 60-65; short, plump, motherly type. Uncontrollable tremor of right hand. Wearing black coat, soiled; elastic stockings, hole in left knee; old-fashioned hat with single cloth flower. Dark reddish hair may be wig. Approximately 5 feet 1 inch, 140 pounds. Fiddles with wen on chin.

"Right: male, white, about 50, 6 feet 2 inches. Extremely thin and emaciated. Loose collar and suit jacket show recent weight loss. Sallow complexion. Fidgety. Right eye may be glass. Nicotine-stained fingers indicate heavy smoker. Gnaws on lower lip. Blinks frequently."

He raised his eyes, inspected them again. He was close. The Negro's ring was on the left hand. The old woman's hair (or wig) was more brown than reddish. The thin man wasn't quite as tall as he had estimated. But Captain Delaney could provide a reasonably accurate description and/or identify these strangers in a line-up or courtroom if needed.

He was not, he acknowledged, as exact as some men in his judgment of physical characteristics. There was, for instance, a detective second grade attached to the 251st Precinct who could glance at a man for a few seconds and estimate his height within an inch and his weight within five pounds. That was a special gift.

But Captain Delaney also had an eye. That was for the Negro's necktie that was looped but not knotted, the old woman's wen, the thin man's continual blinking. Small things. Significant things.

He saw and remembered habits, tastes, the way a man dressed, moved, grimaced, walked, spoke, lighted a cigarette or spat into the gutter. Most important, Captain Delaney—the cop—was interested in what a man did when he was alone, or thought he was alone. Did he masturbate, pick his nose, listen to recordings of Gilbert & Sullivan, shuffle pornographic photos, work out chess problems? Or did he read Nietzsche?

There was a case—Delaney remembered it well; he had been a detective in the Chelsea precinct where it happened—three young girls raped and murdered within a period of 18 months, all on the roofs of tenements. The police thought they had their man. They carefully charted his daily movements. They brought him in for questioning and got nowhere. Then they established very close surveillance. Detective Delaney watched the suspect through binoculars from an apartment across the courtyard. Delaney saw this man, who had never been known to go to church, this man who thought he was alone and unobserved, this man went each night onto his knees and prayed before a reproduction of the face of Jesus Christ—one of those monstrous prints in which the eyes seem to open, close, or wink, depending upon the angle of view.

So they took the suspect in again, but this time, on Delaney's urging, they brought in a priest to talk to him. Within an hour they had a complete confession. Well . . . that was what one man did when he thought he was alone and unobserved.

It was the spastic twitch, the uncontrollable tic that Captain Delaney had an eye for. He wanted to know what tunes the suspect whistled, the foods he ate, how his home was decorated. Was he married, unmarried, thrice-married? Did he beat his dog or beat his wife? All these things told. And, of course, what he did when he thought he was alone.

The "big things" Captain Delaney told his men—things like a man's job, religion, politics, and the way he talked at cocktail parties—these were a facade he created to hold back a hostile world. Hidden were the vital things. The duty of the cop, when necessary, was to peek around the front at the secret urges and driven acts.

"Doctor will see you now," the receptionist smiled at him.

Delaney nodded, gripped his hat, marched into the doctor's office. He ignored the hostile stares of the patients who had, obviously, been waiting longer than he.

Dr. Louis Bernardi rose from behind his desk, holding out a plump, ringed hand.

"Captain," he said. "Always a pleasure."

"Doctor," Delaney said. "Good to see you again. You're looking well."

Bernardi caressed the bulged grey flannel waistcoat, straining at its tarnished silver buttons which, Barbara Delaney had told her husband, the doctor had revealed to her were antique Roman coins.

"It's my wife's cooking," Bernardi shrugged, smiling. "What can I do? He-he! Sit down, sit down. Mrs. Delaney is dressing. She will be ready to leave soon. But we shall have time for a little chat."

A chat? Delaney assumed men had a talk or a discussion. That "chat" was Bernardi. The Captain consulted a police surgeon; Bernardi was his wife's physician, had been for thirty years. He had seen her through two successful pregnancies, nursed her through a bad bout of hepatitis, and had recommended and seen to her recovery from a hysterectomy only two months previously.

He was a round man, beautifully shaved. He was soft and, if not unctuous, he was at least a smooth article. The black silk suit put forth a sheen; the shoes bore a dulled gleam. He was not perfumed, but he exuded an odor of self-satisfaction.

Contradicting all this were the man's eyes: hard, bright. They were shrewd little chips of quartz. His glance never wavered; his toneless stare could bring a nurse to tears.

Delaney did not like the man. He did not, for a moment, doubt Bernardi's professional competence. But he mistrusted the tailored plumpness, the secret smile, the long strands of oily hair slicked across a balding pate. He was particularly incensed by the doctor's mustache: a thin, carefully clipped line of black imprinted on the upper lip as if marked by a felt-tipped pen.

The Captain knew he amused Bernardi. That did not bother him. He knew he amused many people: superiors in the Department, peers, the uniformed men of his command. Newspapermen. Investigators. Doctors of sociology and criminal pathology. He amused them all. His wife and children. He knew. But on occasion Dr. Bernardi had made no effort to conceal his amusement. Delaney could not forgive him that.

"I hope you have good news for me, doctor."

Bernardi spread his hands in a bland gesture: the dealer who has just been detected selling a ruptured camel.

"Regrettably, I do not. Captain, your wife has not responded to the antibiotics. As I told her, my first instinctive impression was of a low-grade infection. Persistent and of some duration. It accounts for the temperature."

"What kind of infection?"

Again the gesture: hands spread wide and lifted, palms outward.

"That I do not know. Tests show nothing. Nothing on X-rays. No tumor, so far as I am able to determine. But still, apparently, an infection. What do you think of that?"

"I don't like it," Delaney said stonily.

"Nor do I," Bernardi nodded. "First of all, your wife is ill. That is of most importance. Second, it is a defeat for me. What is this infection? I do not know. It is an embarrassment."

An "embarrassment," Delaney thought angrily. What kind of a thing was that to say? The man didn't know how to use the king's English. Was he an Italian, a Lebanese, a Greek, a Syrian, an Arabian? What the hell *was* he?

"Finally," Dr. Bernardi said, consulting the file open on his desk, "let us consider the fever. It has been approximately six weeks since your wife's first visit complaining of, quote, 'Fever and sudden chills.' Unquote. On that first visit, a temperature a bit above normal. Nothing unusual. Pills for a cold, the flu, a virus—whatever you want to call it. No effect. Another visit. Temperature up. Not a great increase, but appreciable. Then antibiotics. Now, third visit and temperature is up again. The sudden chills continue. It worries me."

"Well, it worries her and it worries me," Delaney said stoutly.

"Of course," Bernardi soothed. "And now she finds many loose hairs in her comb. This is undoubtedly the result of the fever. Nothing serious, but still . . . And you are aware of the rash on the insides of her thighs and forearms?"

"Yes."

"Again, undoubtedly the result of the fever stemming from the infection. I have prescribed an ointment. Not a cure, but it will take the itch away."

"She looks so healthy."

"You are seeing the fever, Captain! Don't believe the blush of health. Those bright eyes and rosy cheeks. He! It is the infection."

"What infection?" Delaney cried furiously. "What the hell *is* it? Is it cancer?"

Bernardi's eyes glittered.

"At this stage, I would guess no. Have you ever heard of a Proteus infection, Captain?"

"No. I never have. What is it?"

"I will not speak of it now. I must do some reading on it. You think we doctors know everything? But there is too much. There are young physicians today who cannot recognize (because they have never treated) typhus, small pox or poliomyelitis. But that is by the by."

"Doctor," Delaney said, wearied by all this lubricious talk, "let's get down to it. What do we do now. What are our options?"

Dr. Bernardi leaned back in his swivel chair, placed his two forefingers together, pressed them against his plump lips. He regarded Delaney for a long moment.

"You know, Captain," he said with some malevolence, "I admire you. Your wife is obviously ill, and yet you say 'What do *we* do' and 'What are *our* options.' That is admirable."

"Doctor . . ."

"Very well." Bernardi sat forward sharply and slapped the file on his desk. "You have three options. One: I can attempt to reduce the fever, to overcome this mysterious infection, by heavier doses of antibiotics or with drugs I have not yet tried. I do not recommend this out of the hospital; the side effects can be alarming. Two: Your wife can enter a hospital for five days to a week for a series of tests much more thorough than I can possibly administer in this office. I would call in other men. Specialists. Neurologists. Gynecologists. Even dermatologists. This would be expensive."

He paused, looking at the Captain expectantly.

"All right, doctor," Delaney said patiently. "What's the third choice?"

Bernardi looked at him tenderly.

"Perhaps you would prefer another physician," he said softly. "Since I have failed."

Delaney sighed, knowing his wife's faith in this oleaginous man.

"We'll go for the tests. In the hospital. You'll arrange it?"

"Of course."

"A private room."

"That will not be necessary, Captain. It is only for tests."

"My wife would prefer a private room. She's a very modest woman. Very shy."

"I know, Captain," the doctor murmured, "I know. Shall you tell her or shall I?"

"I'll tell her."

"Yes," Dr. Bernardi said. "I believe that would be best."

The Captain went back to the reception room to wait for her, and practiced smiling.

It was a doxy of a day, merry and flirting. There was a hug of sun, a kiss of breeze. Walking north on Fifth Avenue, they heard the snap of flags, saw the glister of an early September sky. Captain Delaney, who knew his city in all its moods and tempers, was conscious of a hastened rhythm. Summer over, vacation done, Manhattan rushed to Christmas and the New Year.

His wife's hand was in his arm. When he glanced sideways at her, she had never seemed to him so beautiful. The blonde hair, now silvered and fined, was drawn up from her brow and pinned in a loose chignon. The features, once precise, had been softened by time. The lips were limpid, the line of chin and throat something. Oh she was something! And the glow (that damned fever!) gave her skin a grapy youthfulness.

She was almost as tall as he, walked erect and alert, her hand lightly on his arm. Men looked at her with longing, and Delaney was proud. How she strode, laughing at things! Her head turned this way and that, as if she was seeing everything for the first time. The last time? A cold finger touched.

She caught his stare and winked solemnly. He could not smile, but pressed her arm close to his body. The important thing, he thought—the most important thing—was that . . . was that she should out-live him. Because if not . . . if not . . . he thought of other things.

She was almost five years older than he, but she was the warmth, humor, and heart of their marriage. He was born old, with hope, a secret love of beauty, and a taste for melancholy. But she had brought to their home a recipe for lentil soup, thin nightgowns with pink ribbons, and laughter. He was bad enough; without her he would have been a grotesque.

They strolled north on Fifth Avenue, on the west side. As they approached the curb at 56th Street, the traffic light was about to change. They could have made it across safely, but he halted her.

"Wait a minute," he said. "I want to catch this."

His quick eye had seen a car—a station wagon with Illinois license plates—coming southward on Fifth Avenue. It attempted to turn westward onto 56th Street, going the wrong way on a one-way street. Immediately there was a great blaring of horns. A dozen pedestrians shouted, "One-way!" The car came to a shuddering halt, nosing into approaching traffic. The driver bent over the wheel, shaken. The woman beside him, apparently his wife, grabbed his arm. In the seat behind them two little boys jumped about excitedly, going from window to window.

A young uniformed patrolman had been standing on the northwest corner of the intersection, his back against a plate glass window. Now, smiling, he sauntered slowly toward the stalled car.

"Midtown Squad," Captain Delaney muttered to his wife. "They pick the big, handsome ones."

The officer wandered around to the driver's side, leaned down, and there was a brief conversation. The couple in the out-of-state car laughed with relief. The policeman cocked thumb and forefinger at the two kids in the back and clicked his tongue. They giggled delightedly.

"He's not going to ticket them?" Delaney said indignantly. "He's going to let them go?"

The patrolman moved back onto Fifth Avenue and halted traffic. He waved the Illinois car to back up. He got it straightened out and heading safely downtown again.

"I'm going to—" Captain Delaney started.

"Edward," his wife said. "Please."

He hesitated. The car moved away, the boys in the back waving frantically at the policeman who waved back.

Delaney looked sternly at his wife. "I'm going to get his name and tin number," he said. "Those one-way signs are plain. He should have—"

"Edward," she repeated patiently, "they're obviously on vacation. Did you see the luggage in the back? They don't know our system of one-way streets. Why spoil their holiday? With two little boys? I think the patrolman handled it beautifully. Perhaps that will be the nicest thing that happens to them in New York, and they'll want to come back again. Edward?"

He looked at her. ("Your wife is obviously ill . . . the fever . . . hair in her comb . . . you have three options . . . infection that . . .") He took her arm, led her carefully across the street. They walked the next block in silence.

"Well, anyway," he grumbled, "his sideburns were too long. You won't find sideburns like that in *my* precinct."

"I wonder why?" she said innocently, then laughed and leaned sideways to touch her head against his shoulder.

He had plans for lunch at the Plaza, window-shopping, visiting the antique shops on Third Avenue—things she enjoyed doing together on his day off. It was important that she should be happy for a time before he told her. But when she suggested a walk through the Park and lunch on the terrace at the zoo, he agreed instantly. It would be better; he would find a bench where they could be alone.

As they crossed 59th Street into the Park, he looked about with wonder. Now what had been there before the General Motors Building?

"The Savoy-Plaza," she said.

"Mind-reader," he said.

So she was—where he was concerned.

The city changed overnight. Tenements became parking lots became excavations became stabbing office buildings while your head was turned. Neighborhoods disappeared, new restaurants opened, brick changed to glass, three stories sprouted to thirty, streets bloomed with thin trees, a little park grew where you remembered an old Irish bar had been forever.

It was his city, where he was born and grew up. It was home. Who could know its cankers better than he? But he refused to despair. His city would endure and grow more beautiful.

Part of his faith was based on knowledge of its past sins: all history now. He knew the time when the Five Points Gang bit off enemies' ears and noses in tavern brawls, when farm lads were drugged and shanghaied from the Swamp, when children's bordellos flourished in the Tenderloin, when Chinese hatchetmen blasted away with heavy pistols (and closed eyes) in the Bloody Triangle.

All this was gone now and romanticized, for old crime, war, and evil enter books and are leached of blood and pain. Now his city was undergoing new agonies. These too, he was convinced would pass if men of good will would not deny the future.

His city was an affirmation of life: its beauty, harshness, sorrow, humor, horror, and ecstasy. In the pushing and shoving, in the brutality and violence, he saw striving, the never-ending flux of life, and would not trade it for any place on earth. It could grind a man to litter, or raise him to the highest coppered roof, glinting in benignant sunlight.

They entered the Park at 60th Street, walking between the facing rows of benches toward the zoo. They stopped before the yak's cage and looked at the great, brooding beast, his head lowered, eyes staring at a foreign world with dull wonder.

"You," Barbara Delaney said to her husband.

He laughed, turned her around by the elbow, pointed to the cage across the way where a graceful Sika deer stood poised and alert, head proud on slim neck, eyes gleaming.

"You," Edward Delaney said to his wife.

They lunched lightly. He fretted with his emptied coffee cup: peering into it, turning it over, revolving it in his blunt fingers.

"All right," she sighed in mock weariness, "go make your phone call."

He glanced at her gratefully. "It'll just take a minute."

"I know. Just to make sure the precinct is still there."

The thick voice said, "Two hundred and fifty-first Precinct. Officer Curdy. May I help you?"

"This is Captain Edward X. Delaney," he said in his leaden voice. "Connect me with Lieutenant Dorfman, please."

"Oh. Yes, Captain. I think he's upstairs. Just a minute; I'll find him."

Dorfman came on almost immediately. "'Lo, Captain, Enjoying your day off? Beautiful day."

"Yes. What's happening?"

"Nothing unusual, sir. The usual. A small demonstration at the Embassy again, but we moved them along. No charges. No injuries."

"Damage?"

"One broken window, sir."

"All right. Have Donaldson type up the usual letter of apology, and I'll sign it tomorrow."

"It's done, Captain. It's on your desk."

"Oh. Well . . . fine. Nothing else?"

"No, sir. Everything under control."

"All right. Switch me back to the man on the board, will you?"

"Yes, sir. I'll buzz him."

The uniformed operator came back on.

"Captain?"

"Is this Officer Curdy?"

"Yes, sir."

"Curdy, you answered my original call with: 'Two hundred and fifty-first Precinct.' In my memo number six three one, dated fourteen July of this year, I gave very explicit orders governing the procedure of uniformed telephone operators on duty. I stated in that memorandum that incoming calls were to be answered: 'Precinct two five one.' It is shorter and much more understandable than 'Two hundred and fifty-first Precinct.' Did you read that memo?"

"Yes, sir. Yes, Captain, I did read it. It just slipped my mind, sir. I'm so used to doing it the old way . . ."

"Curdy, there is no 'old way.' There is a right way and a wrong way of doing things. And 'Two five one' is the right way in my precinct. Is that clear?"

"Yes, sir."

He hung up and went back to his wife. In the New York Police Department he was known as "Iron Balls"Delaney. He knew it and didn't mind. There were worse names.

"Everything all right?" she asked.

He nodded.

"Who has the duty?"

"Dorfman."

"Oh? How is his father?"

He stared at her, eyes widening. Then he lowered his head and groaned. "Oh God. Barbara, I forgot to tell you. Dorfman's father died last week. On Friday."

"Oh Edward." She looked at him reproachfully. "Why on earth didn't you tell me?"

"Well, I meant to but—but it slipped my mind."

"Slipped your mind? How could a thing like that slip your mind? Well, I'll write a letter of condolence as soon as we get home."

"Yes, do that. They took up a collection for flowers. I gave twenty dollars."

"Poor Dorfman."

"Yes."

"You don't like him, do you?"

"Of course I like him. As a man, a person. But he's really not a good cop."

"He's not? I thought you told me he does his job very well."

"He does. He's a good administrator, keeps up on his paperwork. He's one of the best lawyers in the Department. But he's not a good cop. He's a reasonable facsimile. He goes through all the motions, but he lacks the instinct."

"And tell me, oh wise one," she said, "what is this great cop's instinct?"

He was glad to have someone to talk to about such things.

"Well," he said, "laugh if you like, but it does exist. What drove me to become a cop? My father wasn't. No one in my family was. I could have gone on to law school; my marks were good enough. But all I ever wanted was to be a cop. As long as I can remember. And I'll tell you why: because when the laundry comes back from the Chinaman—as you well know, my dear, after thirty years—I insist on—"

"Thirty-one years, brute."

"All right, thirty-one years. But the first year we lived in sin."

"You *are* a brute," she laughed.

"Well, we did: the most marvelous year of my life."

She put a hand over his. "And everything since then has been anti-climax?"

"You know better than that. All right, now let me get back to the instinct of a true cop."

"And the Chinaman's laundry."

"Yes. Well, as you know, I insist on putting my own clean clothes away in the bureau and dresser. Socks are folded once and piled with the fold forward. Handkerchiefs are stacked with the open edges to the right. Shirts are stacked alternately, collar to the rear, collar to the front—so the stack won't topple, you understand. And a similar system for underwear, pajamas, and so forth. And always, of course, the freshly laundered clothes go on the bottom of each pile so everything is worn evenly and in order. That's the word: 'order.' That's the way I am. You know it. I want everything in order."

"And that's why you became a cop? To make the world neat and tidy?"

"Yes."

She moved her head back slowly and laughed. How he loved to see her laugh. If only he could laugh like that! It was such a whole-hearted expression of pure joy: her eyes squinched shut, her mouth open, shoulders shaking, and a surprisingly full, deep guffaw that was neither feminine nor masculine but sexless and primitive as all genuine laughter.

"Edward, Edward," she said, spluttering a little, taking a lace-edged hanky from her purse to wipe her eyes. "You have a marvelous capacity for deluding yourself. I guess that's why I love you so."

"All right," he said, miffed. "You tell me. Why did I become a cop?"

Again she covered his hand with hers. She looked into his eyes, suddenly serious.

"Don't you know?" she asked gently. "Don't you *really* know? Because you love beauty. Oh, I know law and order and justice are important to you. But what you really want is a beautiful world where everything is true and nothing is false. You dreamer!"

He thought about that a long time. Then they rose, and hand in hand they strolled into the park.

In Central Park, there is an inclosed carrousel that has been a delight to generations of youngsters. Some days, when the wind is right, you can hear its musical tinkle from a distance; the air seems to dance.

The animals—marvelously carved and painted horses—chase each other in a gay whirl that excites children and hypnotizes their parents. On a bench near this merry-go-round, Barbara and Edward Delaney sat to rest, shoulders touching. They could hear the music, see the giddy gyrations through trees still wearing summer's green.

They sat awhile in silence. Then she said, not looking at him, "Can you tell me now?"

He nodded miserably. As rapidly as he could, he delivered a concise report of what Dr. Bernardi had told him. He omitted only the physician's fleeting reference to a "Proteus infection."

"I see no choice," he said, and gripped her hand harder. "Do you? We've got to get this cleared up. I'll feel better if Bernardi brings in other men. I think you will, too. It only means five days to a week in the hospital. Then they'll decide what must be done. I told Bernardi to go ahead, get the room. A private room. Barbara? Is that all right?"

He wondered if she heard him. Or if she understood. Her eyes were far away, and he did not know the smile on her soft lips.

"Barbara?" he asked again.

"During the war," she said, "when you were in France, I brought the children here when the weather was nice. Eddie could walk then but Elizabeth was still in the carriage. Sometimes Eddie would get tired on the way home, and I'd put him in the carriage with Liza. How he hated it!"

"I know. You wrote me."

"Did I? Sometimes we'd sit on this very bench where we're sitting now. Eddie would ride the merry-go-round all day if I let him."

"He always rode a white horse."

"You do remember," she smiled. "Yes, he always rode a white horse, and every time he came around he'd wave at us, sitting up straight. He was so proud."

"Yes."

"They're good children, aren't they, Edward?"

"Yes."

"Happy children."

"Well, I wish Eddie would get married, but there's no use nagging him."

"No. He's stubborn. Like his father."

"Am I stubborn?"

"Sometimes. About some things. When you've made up your mind. Like my going into the hospital for tests."

"You will go, won't you?"

She gave him a dazzling smile, then unexpectedly leaned forward to kiss him on the lips. It was a soft, youthful, lingering kiss that shocked him with its longing.

And late that night she still burned with that longing, her body kindled with lust and fever. She came naked into his arms and seemed intent on draining him, exhausting him, taking all for herself and leaving nothing. He tried to contain her fury—so unlike her; she was usually languorous and teasing—but her rage defeated him. Once, thrashing about in a sweated paroxysm, she called him "Ted," which she had not done since their life together was born.

He did what he could to satisfy and soothe, wretchedly conscious that his words were not heard nor his caresses felt; the most he could do was be. Her storm passed, leaving him riven. He gnawed a knuckle and fell asleep.

He awoke a few hours later, and she was gone from the bed. He was instantly alert, pulled on his old patterned robe with its frazzled cord. Barefoot, he went padding downstairs, searching all the empty rooms.

He found her in what they still called the "parlor" of their converted brownstone, next door to the 251st Precinct house. She was on the window seat, clad in a white cotton nightgown. Her knees were drawn up, clasped. In the light from the hallway he could see her head bent forward. Her hair was down, hiding her face, drifting shoulders and knees.

"Barbara," he called.

Her head came up. Hair fell back. She gave him a smile that twisted his heart.

"I'm dying," she said.

2

Barbara Delaney's stay in the hospital for tests was longer than the five days predicted by Dr. Louis Bernardi. It became a weekend and five days, then two weekends and five days, and finally a total of fifteen days. To every inquiry by Captain Edward X. Delaney, the doctor answered only, "More tests."

From his daily—sometimes twice-daily—visits to his wife's private room, Delaney came away with the frightening impression that things were not going well at all. The fever persisted, up one day, down slightly the next. But the course was steadily upward. Once it hit almost 103; the woman was burning up.

He himself had been witness to the sudden chills that racked her body, set teeth chattering and limbs trembling. Nurses came hurrying with extra blankets and hot water bottles. Five minutes later she was burning again; blankets were tossed aside, her face rosy, she gasped for breath.

New symptoms developed during those fifteen days: headaches, urination so difficult she had to be catheterized, severe pain in the lumbar region, sudden attacks of nausea that left her limp. Once she vomited into a basin he held for her. She looked up at him meekly; he turned away to stare out the window, his eyes bleary.

On the morning he finally decided, against his wife's wishes, to dismiss Bernardi and bring in a new man, he was called at his Precinct office and summoned to an early afternoon meeting with Bernardi in his wife's hospital room. Lieutenant Dorfman saw him off with anguished eyes.

"Please, Captain," he said, "try not to worry. She's going to be all right."

Marty Dorfman was an extraordinarily tall (6'4") Jew with light blue eyes and red hair that spiked up from a squeezed skull. He wore size 14 shoes and couldn't find gloves to fit. He seemed constantly to be dribbled with crumbs, and had never been known to swear.

Nothing fitted; his oversize uniform squirmed on thin shoulders, trousers bagged like a Dutch boy's bloomers. Cigarette ashes smudged his cuffs. Occasionally his socks didn't match, and he had lost the clasp on the choker collar of his jacket. His shoes were unshined, and he reported for duty with a dried froth of shaving cream beneath his ears.

Once, when a patrolman, he had been forced to kill a knife-wielding burglar. Since then he carried an unloaded gun. He thought no one knew, but everyone did. As Captain Delaney had told his wife, Dorfman's paperwork was impeccable and he had one of the finest legal minds in the Department. He was a sloven, but when men of the 251st Precinct had personal problems, they went to him. He had never been known to miss the funeral of a policeman killed in line of duty. Then he wore a clean uniform and wept.

"Thank you, lieutenant," Delaney said stiffly. "I will call as soon as possible. I fully expect to return before you go off. If not, don't wait for me. Is that clear?"

"Yes, Captain."

Dr. Louis Bernardi, Delaney decided was perfectly capable of holding the hand of a dying man and saying, "There there." Now he was displaying the X-rays proudly, as if they were his own Rembrandt prints.

"The shadows!" he cried. "See the shadows!"

He had drawn a chair up close to the bedside of Barbara Delaney. The

Captain stood stolidly on the other side, hands clasped behind him so their tremble might not reveal him.

"What are they?" he asked in his iron voice.

"What is it?" his wife murmured.

"Kidney stones!" Bernardi cried happily. "Yes, dear lady," he continued, addressing the woman on the bed who stared at him sleepily, her head wavering slightly, "the possibility was there: a stubborn fever and chills. And more recently the headaches, nausea, difficulty in passing water, pain in the lower back. This morning, after more than ten days of exhaustive tests—which I am certain, he-he, you found exhausting as well as exhaustive—we held a conference—all the professional men who have been concerned with your condition—and the consensus is that you are, unhappily, suffering from a kidney calculus."

His tone was so triumphant that Delaney couldn't trust himself to speak. His wife turned her head on the pillow to look warningly at him. When he nodded, she turned back to Bernardi to ask weakly:

"How did I get kidney stones?"

The doctor leaned back in his chair, made his usual gesture of placing his two index fingers together and pressing them against his pouting lips.

"Who can say?" he asked softly. "Diet, stress, perhaps a predisposition, heredity. There is so much we don't know. If we knew everything, life would be a bore, would it not? He!"

Delaney grunted disgustedly. Bernardi paid no heed.

"In any event, that is our diagnosis. Kidney stones. A concretion frequently found in the bladder or kidneys. A hard, inorganic stone. Some no larger than a pinhead. Some quite large. They are foreign matter lodged in living tissue. The body, the living tissue, cannot endure this invasion. Hence, the fever, the chills, the pain. And, of course, the difficulty in urinating. Oh yes, that above all."

Once again Delaney was infuriated by the man's self-satisfaction. To Bernardi, it was all a crossword puzzle from the *Times*.

"How serious is it?" Barbara asked faintly.

A glaze seemed to come down over Bernardi's swimming eyes, a milky, translucent film. He could see out but no one could see in.

"We needed the blood tests and these sensitive plates. And then, since you have been here, the symptoms that developed gave us added indications. Now we know what we are facing."

"How serious is it?" Barbara asked again, more determinedly.

"We feel," Bernardi went on, not listening, "we feel that in your case, dear lady, surgery is indicated. Oh yes. Definitely. I am sorry to say. Surgery."

"Wait," Delaney held up his hand. "Wait just a minute. Before we start talking about surgery. I know a man who had kidney stones. They gave him a liquid, something, and he passed them and was all right. Can't my wife do the same?"

"Quite impossible," Bernardi said shortly. "When the stones are tiny, that procedure is sometimes effective. These X-rays show a large area of inflammation. Surgery is indicated."

"Who decided that?" Delaney demanded.

"We did."

"'We'?" Delaney asked. 'Who is 'we'?"

Bernardi looked at him coldly. He sat back, pulled up one trouser leg, carefully crossed his knees. "Myself and the specialists I called in," he said. "I have their professional opinions here, Captain—their written and signed opinions—and I have prepared a duplicate set for your use."

Captain Edward X. Delaney had interrogated enough witnesses and suspects in his long career to know when a man or woman was lying. The tip-off could come in a variety of ways. With the stupid or inexperienced it came with a physical gesture: a shifting away of the eyes, a nervous movement, blinking, perhaps a slight skim of sweat or a sudden deep breath. The intelligent and experienced revealed their falsehood in different ways: a too deliberate nonchalance, or an "honest" stare, eyeball to eyeball, or by a serious, intent fretting of the brows. Sometimes they leaned forward and smiled candidly.

But this man was not lying; the Captain was convinced of that. He was also convinced Bernardi was not telling the whole truth. He was holding something back, something distasteful to him.

"All right," Delaney grated, "we have their signed opinions. I assume they all agree?"

Barnardi's eyes glittered with malice. He leaned forward to pat Barbara's hand, lying limply atop the thin blue blanket. "There there," he said.

"It is not a very serious operation," he continued. "It is performed frequently in every hospital in the country. But all surgery entails risk. Even lancing a boil. I am certain you understand this. No surgery should ever be taken lightly."

"We don't take it lightly," Delaney said angrily, thinking this man—this "foreigner"—just didn't know how to talk.

During this exchange Barbara Delaney's head moved side to side, back and forth between husband and doctor.

"Very well," Delaney went on, holding himself in control, "you recommend surgery. You remove those kidney stones, and my wife regains her health. Is that it? There's nothing more you're not telling us?"

"Edward," she said. "Please."

"I want to know," he said stubbornly. "I want you to know."

Bernardi sighed. He seemed about to mediate between them, then thought better of it.

"That is our opinion," he nodded. "I cannot give you an iron-clad one hundred percent guarantee. No physician or surgeon can. You must know that. This, admittedly, will be an ordeal for Mrs. Delaney. Normal recuperation from this type of surgery demands a week to ten days in the hospital, and several weeks in bed at home. I don't wish to imply that this is of little importance. It is a serious situation, and I take it seriously, as I am certain you do also. But you are essentially a healthy woman, dear lady, and I see nothing in your medical record that would indicate anything but a normal recovery."

"And there's no choice but surgery?" Delaney demanded again.

"No. You have no choice."

A small cry came from Barbara Delaney, no louder than a kitten's mew. She reached out a pale hand to her husband; he grasped it firmly in his big paw.

"But we have no assurance?" he asked, realizing he was again repeating himself, and that his voice was desperate.

The translucent film over Bernardi's eyes seemed to become more opaque. Now it was the pearly cover on the eyes of a blind dog.

"No assurance," he said shortly. "None whatsoever."

Silence fell into the pastel room like a gentle rain. They looked at each other, all three, heads going back and forth, eyes flickering. They could hear the noises of the hospital: loudspeakers squawking, carts creaking by, murmured voices, and somewhere a radio playing dance music. But in this room the three looked into each others' eyes and were alone, swaddled in silence.

"Thank you, doctor," Delaney said harshly. "We will discuss it."

Bernardi nodded, rose swiftly. "I will leave you these documents," he said, placing a file on the bedside table. "I suggest you read them carefully. Please do not delay your decision more than twenty-four hours. We must not let this go on, and plans must be made."

He bounced from the room, light on his feet for such a stout man.

Edward X. Delaney had been born a Catholic and raised a Catholic. Communion and confession were as much a part of his life as love and work. He was married in the Church, and his children attended parochial schools. His faith was monolithic. Until 1945 . . .

On a late afternoon in 1945, the sun hidden behind a sky black with oily smoke, Captain Delaney led his company of Military Police to the liberation of a concentration camp in north Germany. The barbed wire gate was swinging wide. There was no sign of activity. The Captain deployed his armed men. He himself, pistol drawn, strode up to an unpainted barracks and threw open the door.

The things stared at him.

A moan came up from his bowels. This single moan, passing his lips, took with it Church and faith, prayer and confidence, ceremony, panoply, habit and trust. He never thought of such things again. He was a cop and had his own reasons.

Now, sensing what lay ahead, he yearned for the Church as a voluntary exile might yearn for his own native land. But to return in time of need was a baseness his pride could not endure. They would see it through together, the two of them, her strength added to his. The aggregate—by the peculiar alchemy of their love—was greater than the sum of the parts.

He sat on the edge of her bed, smiled, smoothed her hair with his heavy hand. A nurses' aide had brushed her hair smooth and tied it back with a length of thick blue knitting wool.

"I know you don't like him," she said.

"That's not important," he shook his great head. "What is important is that you trust him. Do you?"

"Yes."

"Good. But I still want to talk to Ferguson."

"You don't want to decide now?"

"No. Let me take the papers and try to understand them. Then I'll show them to Ferguson and get his opinion. Tonight, if possible. Then I'll come back tomorrow and we'll discuss it. Will that be all right?"

"Yes," she said. "Did Mary do the curtains?" She was referring to their Monday-to-Friday, 8-to-4 maid.

"Yes, she did. And she brushed and aired the living room drapes in the backyard. Tomorrow she'll do the parlor drapes if the weather holds. She wants so much to visit you but I said you weren't up to it. I've told all your friends that. Are you sure it's what you want?"

"Yes. I don't want anyone to see me like this. Maybe later I'll feel up to it. What did you have for breakfast?"

"Let's see . . ." he said, trying to remember. "A small orange juice. Cereal, no sugar. Dry toast and black coffee."

"Very good," she nodded approvingly. "You're sticking to your diet. What did you have for lunch?"

"Well, things piled up, and we had to send out for sandwiches. I had roast beef on whole wheat and a large tomato juice."

"Oh Edward," she said, "that's not enough. You must promise that tonight you'll—" Suddenly she stopped; tears flooded up to her eyes and out, down her cheeks. "Oh Jesus," she cried. "Why me?"

She lurched up to embrace him. He held her close, her wet face against his. His blunt fingers stroked her back, and he kept repeating, "I love you, I love you, I love you," over and over. It didn't seem enough.

He went back to the Precinct carrying her medical file. The moment he was at his desk he called Dr. Sanford Ferguson, but couldn't reach him. He tried the Medical Examiner's office, the morgue, and Ferguson's private office. No one knew where he was. Delaney left messages everywhere.

Then he put the medical file aside and went to work. Dorfman and two Precinct detectives were waiting to see him, on separate cases. There was a deputation of local businessmen to demand more foot patrolmen. There was a group of black militants to protest "police brutality" in breaking up a recent march. There was a committee of Jewish leaders to discuss police action against demonstrations held almost daily in front of an Egyptian embassy located in the precinct. There was an influential old woman with an "amazing new idea" for combatting drug addiction (put sneezing powder in cocaine). And there was a wealthy old man charged (for the second time) with exhibiting himself to toddlers.

Captain Delaney listened to all of them, nodding gravely. Occasionally he spoke in a voice so deliberately low his listeners had to crane forward to hear. He had learned from experience that nothing worked so well as quiet, measured tones to calm anger and bring people, if not to reason then to what was possible and practical.

It was 8:00 P.M. before his outer office had emptied. He rose and forced back his massive shoulders, stretching wide. This kind of work, he had discovered, was a hundred times more wearying than walking a beat or riding a squad. It was the constant, controlled exercise of judgment and will, of convincing, persuading, soothing, dictating and, when necessary, surrendering for a time, to take up the fight another day.

He cleaned up his desk, taking a regretful look at the paperwork that had piled up in one day and must wait for tomorrow. Before leaving, he looked in at lockups and squad rooms, at interrogation rooms and the detectives' cubbyholes. The 251st Precinct house was almost 90 years old. It was cramped, it creaked, and it smelled like all antique precinct houses in the city. A new building had been promised by three different city administrations. Captain Delaney made do. He took a final look at the Duty Sergeant's blotter before he walked next door to his home.

Even older than the Precinct house, it had been built originally as a merchant's townhouse. It had deteriorated over the years until, when Delaney bought it with the inheritance from his father's estate ($28,000), it had become a rooming house, chopped up into rat-and-roach-infested one-person apartments. But Delaney had satisfied himself that the building was structurally sound, and Barbara's quick eye had seen the original marble fireplaces and walnut paneling (painted over but capable of being restored), the rooms for the children, the little paved areaway and overgrown garden. So they had bought it, never dreaming he would one day be commanding officer of the Precinct house next door.

Mary had left the hall light burning. There was a note Scotch-taped to the handsome pier glass. She had left slices of cold lamb and potato salad in the refrigerator. There was lentil soup he could heat up if he wanted it, and an apple tart for dessert. It all seemed good to him, but he had to watch his weight. He decided to skip the soup.

First he called the hospital. Barbara sounded sleepy and didn't make much sense; he wondered if they had given her a sedative. He spoke to her for only a few moments and thought she was relieved when he said good-night.

He went into the kitchen, took off his uniform jacket and gun belt and hung them on the back of a chair. First he mixed a rye highball, his first drink of the day. He sipped it slowly, smoked a cigarette (his third of the day), and wondered why Dr. Ferguson hadn't returned his calls. Suddenly he realized it might be Ferguson's day off, in which case he had probably been out playing golf.

Carrying the drink, he went into the study and rummaged through the desk for his address book. He found Ferguson's home number and dialed. Almost immediately a jaunty voice answered:

"Doctor Ferguson."

"Captain Edward X. Delaney here."

"Hello, Captain Edward X. Delaney there," the voice laughed. "What the hell's wrong with you—got a dose of clap from a fifteen-year-old bimbo?"

"No. It's about my wife. Barbara."

The tone changed immediately.

"Oh. What's the problem, Edward?"

"Doctor, would it be possible to see you tonight?"

"Both of you or just you?"

"Just me. She's in the hospital."

"I'm sorry to hear that. Edward, you caught me on the way out. They've dragged me into an emergency cut-'em-up." (*The doctor's slang for an autopsy.*) "I won't be home much before midnight. Too late?"

"No. I can be at your home at midnight. Will that be all right?"

"Sure. What's this all about?"

"I'd rather tell you in person. And there are papers. Documents. Some X-rays."

"I see. All right, Edward. Be here at twelve."

"Thank you, doctor."

He went back into the kitchen to eat his cold lamb and potato salad. It all tasted like straw. He put on his heavy, black-rimmed glasses, and as he ate slowly, he methodically read every paper in Barbara's medical file, and even held the X-rays up to the overhead light, although they meant nothing to him. There she was, in shadows: the woman who meant everything to him.

He finished eating and reading at the same time. All the doctors seemed to agree. He decided to skip the apple tart and black coffee. But he mixed another rye highball and, in his skivvie shirt, went wandering through the empty house.

It was the first time since World War II he and his wife slept under separate roofs. He was bereft, and in all those darkened rooms he felt her presence and wanted her: sight, voice, smell, laugh, slap of slippered feet, touch . . . *her*.

The children were there, too, in the echoing rooms. Cries and shouts, quarrels and stumblings. Eager questions. Wailing tears. Their life had soaked into the old walls. Holiday meals. Triumphs and defeats. The fabric of a family. All silent now, and dark as the shadows on an X-ray film.

He climbed stairs slowly to vacant bedrooms and attic. The house was too big for the two of them: no doubt about it. But still . . . There was the door jamb where Liza's growth had been marked with pencil ticks. There was the flight of stairs Eddie had tumbled down and cut his chin and never cried. There was the very spot where one of their many dogs had coughed up his life in bright blood, and Barbara had become hysterical.

It wasn't much, he supposed. It was neither high tragedy nor low comedy.

No great heights or depths. But a steady wearing away of the years. Time evened whatever drama there may have been. Time dimmed the colors; the shouting died. But the golden monochrome, the soft tarnish that was left had meaning for him. He wandered through the dim corridors of his life, thinking deep thoughts and making foolish wishes.

Dr. Sanford Ferguson, a bachelor, was a big man, made bigger by creaseless tweed suits worn with chain-looped vests. He was broad through the shoulders and broad through the chest. He was not corpulent but his thighs were as big around as another man's waist, and his arms were meaty and strong.

No one doubted his cleverness. At parties he could relate endless jokes that had the company helpless with laughter. He knew many dialects perfectly and, in his cups, could do an admirable soft-shoe clog. He was much in demand as an after-dinner speaker at meetings of professional associations. He was an ineffectual but enthusiastic golfer. He sang a sweet baritone. He could make a soufflé. And, unknown to everyone (including his older spinster sister), he kept a mistress: a middle-aged colored lady he loved and by whom he had fathered three sons.

He was also, Delaney knew, an experienced and cynical police surgeon. Violent death did not dismay him, and he was not often fooled by the obvious. In "natural deaths" he sniffed out arsenic. In "accidental deaths" he would pry out the fatal wound in a corpus of splinters.

"Here's your rye," he said, handing the highball to Delaney. "Now sit there and keep your mouth shut, and let me read and digest."

It was after midnight. They were in the living room of Ferguson's apartment on Murray Hill. The spinster sister had greeted Delaney and then disappeared, presumably to bed. The doctor had mixed a rye highball for his guest and poured a hefty brandy for himself in a water tumbler.

Delaney sat quietly in an armchair pinned with an antimacassar. Dr. Ferguson sat on a spindly chair at a fine Queen Anne lowboy. His bulk threatened to crush chair and table. His wool tie was pulled wide, shirt collar open: wiry hair sprang free.

"That was a nice cut-'em-up tonight," he remarked, peering at the documents in the file Delaney had handed over. "A truck driver comes home from work. Greenwich Village. He finds his wife, he says, on the kitchen floor. Her head's in the oven. The room's full of gas. He opens the window. She's dead. I can attest to that. She was depressed, the truck driver says. She often threatened suicide, he says. Well . . . maybe. We'll see. We'll see."

"Who's handling it?" Delaney asked.

"Sam Rosoff. Assault and Homicide South. You know him?"

"Yes. An old-timer. Good man."

"He surely is, Edward. He spotted the cigar stub in the ashtray on the kitchen table. A cold butt, but the saliva still wet. What would you have done?"

"Ask you to search for a skull contusion beneath the dead woman's hair and start looking for the truck driver's girl friend."

Dr. Ferguson laughed. "Edward, you're wonderful. That's exactly what Rosoff suggested. I found the contusion. Right now he's out looking for the girlfriend. Do you miss detective work?"

"Yes."

"You were the best," Ferguson said, "until you decided to become Commissioner. Now shut up, lad, and let me read."

Silence.

"Oh-ho," Ferguson said. "My old friend Bernardi."

"You know him?" Delaney asked, surprised.

"I do indeed."

"What do you think of him?"

"As a physician? Excellent. As a man? A prick. No more talk."

Silence.

"Do you know any of the others?" Delaney asked finally. "The specialists he brought in?"

"I know two of the five—the neurologist and the radiologist. They're among the best in the city. This must be costing you a fortune. If the other three are as talented, your wife is in good hands. I can check. Now be quiet."

Silence.

"Oh, well," Ferguson shrugged, still reading, "kidney stones. That's not so bad."

"You've had cases?"

"All the time. Mostly men, of course. You know who get 'em? Cab drivers. They're bouncing around on their ass all day."

"What about my wife?"

"Well, listen, Edward, it could be diet, it could be stress. There's so much we don't know."

"My wife eats sensibly, rarely takes a drink, and she's the most—most serene woman I've ever met."

"Is she? Let me finish reading."

He went through all the reports intently, going back occasionally to check reports he had already finished. He didn't even glance at the X-rays. Finally he shoved back from the table, poured himself another huge brandy, freshed the Captain's highball.

"Well?" Delaney asked.

"Edward," Ferguson said, frowning, "don't bring me in. Or anyone else. Bernardi is a bombastic, opinionated, egotistical shit. But as I said, he's a good sawbones. On your wife's case he's done everything exactly right. He's tried everything except surgery—correct?"

"Well, he tried antibiotics. They didn't work."

"No, they wouldn't on kidney stones. But they didn't locate *that* until they got her in the hospital for sensitive plates, and then the trouble passing urine started. That's recent, isn't it?"

"Yes. Only in the last four or five days."

"Well, then . . ."

"You recommend surgery?" Delaney asked in a dead voice.

Ferguson whirled on him. "I recommend nothing," he said sharply. "It's not my case. But you've got no choice."

"That's what he said."

"He was right. Bite the bullet, m'lad."

"What are her chances?"

"You want betting odds, do you? With surgery, very good indeed."

"And without?"

"Forget it."

"It's not fair," Delaney cried furiously.

Ferguson looked at him strangely. "What the fuck is?" he asked.

They stared at each other a long moment. Then Ferguson went back to the table, flipped through the X-rays, selected one and held it up to the light of a tilted desk lamp. "Kidney," he muttered. "Yes, yes."

"What is it, doctor?"

"He told you and I told you: calculus in the kidneys, commonly known as stones."

"That's not what I meant. Something's bothering you."

Ferguson looked at him. "You son of a bitch," he said softly. "You should never have left the detective division. I've never met anyone as— as *attuned* to people as you are."

"What is it?" Delaney repeated.

"It's nothing. Nothing I can explain. A hunch. You have them, don't you?"

"All the time."

"It's little things that don't quite add up. Maybe there's a rational explanation. The recent hysterectomy. The fever and chills that have been going on since then. But only recently the headaches, nausea, lumbar pain, and now the difficulty passing urine. It all adds up to kidney stones, but the *sequence* of symptoms is wrong. With kidney stones, pain at pissing usually comes from the start. And sometimes it's bad enough to drive you right up a wall. No record of that here. Yet the plates show . . . You tell me she's not under stress?"

"She is not."

"Every case I've had is driven, trying to do too much, bedeviled by time, rushing around, biting fingernails and screaming at the waitress when the coffee is cold. Is that Barbara?"

"No. She's totally opposite. Calm."

"You can't tell. We never know. Still . . ." He sighed. "Edward, have you ever heard of Proteus infection?"

"Bernardi mentioned it to me."

Ferguson actually staggered back a step, as if he had been struck a blow on the chest. "He *mentioned* it to you?" he demanded. "When was this?"

"About three weeks ago, when he first told me Barbara should go into the hospital for tests. He just mentioned it and said he wanted to do some reading on it. But he didn't say anything about it today. Should I have asked him?"

"Jesus Christ," Ferguson said bitterly. "No, you shouldn't have asked him. If he wanted to tell you, he would have."

"You've treated cases?"

"Proteus? Oh yes, I have indeed. Three in twenty years. Mr. Proteus is a devil."

"What happened to them?"

"The three? Two responded to antibiotics and were smoking and drinking themselves to death within forty-eight hours."

"And the third?"

Ferguson came over, gripped Delaney by the right arm, and almost lifted him to his feet. The Captain had forgotten how strong he was.

"Go have your wife's kidney stones cut out," the doctor said brutally. "She'll either live or die. Which is true for all of us. No way out, m'lad."

Delaney took a deep breath.

"All right, doctor," he said. "Thank you for your time and your—your patience. I'm sorry to have bothered you."

"Bother?" Ferguson said gruffly. "Idiot."

He walked Delaney to the door. "I might just stop by to see Barbara," he said casually. "Just as a friend of the family."

"Yes," Delaney nodded dumbly. "Please do that. She doesn't want any visitors, but I know she'll be glad to see you."

In the foyer Ferguson took Delaney by the shoulders and turned him to the light.

"Have you been sleeping okay, Edward?" he demanded.

"Not too well."

"Don't take pills. Take a stiff shot. Brandy is best. Or a glass of port. Or a bottle of stout just before you get into bed."

"Yes. All right. Thank you. I will."

They shook hands.

"Oh wait," Ferguson said. "You forgot your papers. I'll get the file for you."

But when he returned, Delaney had gone.

He stopped at his home to put on a heavy wool sweater under his uniform jacket. Then he walked next door to the Precinct house. There was a civilian car parked directly in front of the entrance. Inside the windshield, on the passenger's side, a large card was displayed: PRESS.

Delaney stalked inside. There was a civilian talking to the Desk Sergeant. Both men broke off their conversation and turned when he tramped in.

"Is that your car?" he asked the man. "In front of the station?"

"Yes, that's mine. I was—"

"You a reporter?"

"Yes. I was just—"

"Move it. You're parked in a zone reserved for official cars only. It's clearly marked.'

"I just wanted—"

"Sergeant," Delaney said, "if that car isn't moved within two minutes, issue this man a summons. If it's still there after five minutes, call a truck and have it towed away. Is that clear?"

"Yes, sir."

"Now look here—" the man started.

Delaney walked by him and went up to his office. He took a black-painted three-cell flashlight from the top drawer of his file cabinet. He also slipped a short, hard rubber truncheon into his jacket pocket and hung a steel "come-along" on his gun belt.

When he came out into the chilly night again, the Press car had been reparked across the street. But the reporter was standing on the sidewalk in front of the Precinct house.

"What's your name?" he asked angrily.

"Captain Edward X. Delaney. You want my shield number?"

"Oh . . . Delaney. I've heard about you."

"Have you?"

"'Iron Balls.' Isn't that what they call you?"

"Yes."

The reporter stared, then suddenly laughed and held out his hand.

"The name's Handry, Captain. Thomas Handry. Sorry about the car. You were entirely right and I was entirely wrong."

Delaney shook his hand.

"Where you going with the flashlight, Captain?"

"Just taking a look around."

"Mind if I tag along?"

Delaney shrugged. "If you like."

They walked over to First Avenue, then turned north. The street was lined with stores, supermarkets, banks. Most of them had locked gates across doors and windows. All had a light burning within.

"See that?" Delaney gestured. "I sent a letter to every commercial establishment in my precinct requesting they keep at least a hundred-watt bulb burning all night. I kept after them. Now I have ninety-eight-point-two percent compliance. A simple thing, but it reduced breaking-and-entering of commercial establishments in this precinct by fourteen-point-seven percent."

He stopped in front of a shoe repair shop that had no iron gates. Delaney tried the door. It was securely locked.

"A little unusual, isn't it?" Handry asked, amused. "A captain making the rounds? Don't you have foot patrolmen for that?"

"Of course. When I first took over the 251st, discipline was extremely lax. So I started unscheduled inspections, on foot, mostly at night. It worked. The men never know when or where I may turn up. They stay alert."

"You do it every night?"

"Yes. Of course, I can't cover the entire precinct, but I do a different five or six blocks every night. I don't *have* to do it anymore, you understand; my men are on their toes. But it's become a habit. I think I enjoy it. As a matter of fact, I can't get to sleep until I've made my rounds. My wife says I'm like a householder who has to go around trying all the windows and doors before he goes to bed."

A two-man squad car came purring by. The passenger officer inspected them, recognized the Captain and threw him a salute, which he returned.

Delaney tried a few more un-gated doors and then, flashlight burning, went prowling up an alleyway, the beam flickering over garbage cans and refuse heaps. Handry stayed close behind him.

They walked a few more blocks, then turned eastward toward York Avenue.

"What were you doing in my Precinct house, Handry?" the Captain asked suddenly.

"Nosing around," the reporter said. "I'm working on an article. Or rather a series of articles."

"On what?"

"Why a man wants to become a policeman, and what happens to him after he does."

"Again?" Delaney sighed. "It's been done a dozen times."

"I know. And it's going to be done again, by me. The first piece is on requirements, screening, examination, and all that. The second will be on the Academy and probationary training. Now I'm trying to find out what happens to a man after he's assigned, and all the different directions he can go. You were originally in the detective division, weren't you?"

"That's right."

"Homicide, wasn't it?"

"For a while."

"They still talk about you, about some of your cases."

"Do they?"

"Why did you switch to patrol, Captain?"

"I wanted administrative experience," Delaney said shortly.

This time Handry sighed. He was a slender, dapper young man who looked more like an insurance salesman than a reporter. His suit was carefully pressed, shoes shined, narrow-brim hat exactly squared on his head. He wore a vest. He moved with a light-footed eagerness.

His face betrayed a certain tension, a secret passion held rigidly under control. Lips were pressed, forehead bland, eyes deliberately expressionless. Delaney had noted the bitten fingernails and a habit of stroking the upper lip downward with the second joint of his index finger.

"When did you shave your mustache?" he asked.

"You should have stayed in the detective division," Handry said. "I know I can't stop stroking my lip. Tell me, Captain—why won't policemen talk to me? Oh, they'll talk, but they won't really open up. I can't get into them. If I'm going to be a writer, that's what I've got to learn to do—how to get into people. Is it me, or are they afraid to talk for publication, or what the hell is it?"

"It isn't you—not you personally. It's just that you're not a cop. You don't belong. There's a gulf."

"But I'm trying to understand—really I am. This series is going to be very sympathetic to the police. I want it to be. I'm not out to do a hatchet job."

"I'm glad you're not. We get enough of that."

"All right, then you tell me: why *does* a man become a policeman? Who the hell in his right mind would want a job like that in this city? The pay is miserable, the hours are miserable, everyone thinks you're on the take, snot-nosed kids call you 'pig' and throw sacks of shit at you. So what the hell is the *point*?"

They were passing a private driveway alongside a luxury apartment house. Delaney heard something.

"Stay here," he whispered to Handry.

He went moving quietly up the driveway, the flashlight dark. His right hand was beneath his jacket flap, fingers on the butt of his gun.

He was back in a minute, smiling.

"A cat," he said, "in the garbage cans."

"It could have been a drug addict with a knife," Handry said.

"Yes," Delaney agreed, "it could have been."

"Well then, *why*?" Handry asked angrily.

They were strolling slowly southward on York Avenue heading back toward the Precinct house. Traffic was light at that hour, and the few pedestrians scurried along, glancing nervously over their shoulders.

"My wife and I were talking about that a few weeks ago," Delaney mused, remembering that bright afternoon in the Park. "I said I had become a cop because, essentially, I am a very orderly man. I like everything neat and tidy, and crime offends my sense of order. My wife laughed. She said I became a policeman because at heart I am an artist and want a world of beauty where everything is true and nothing is false. Since that conversation—partly because of what has happened since then—I have been thinking of what I said and what she said. And I have decided we are not so far apart—two sides of the same coin actually. You see, I became a policeman, I think, because there is, or should be, a logic to life. And this logic is both orderly and beautiful, as all good logic is. So I was right and my wife was right. I want this logic to endure. It is a simple logic of natural birth, natural living, and natural death. It is the mortality of one of us and the immortality of all of us. It is the on-going. This logic is the life of the individual, the family, the nation, and finally all people everywhere, and all things animate and inanimate. And anything that interrupts the rhythm of this logic—for all good logic does have a beautiful rhythm, you know—well, anything that interrupts that rhythm is evil. That includes cruelty, crime, and war. I can't do much about cruelty in other people; much of it is immoral but not illegal. I can guard against cruelty in myself, of course. And I can't do a great deal about war. I *can* do something about crime. Not a lot, I admit, but *something*. Because crime, *all* crime, is irrational. It is opposed to the logic of life, and so it is evil. And that is why *I* became a cop. I think."

"My God!" Handry cried. "That's great! I've got to use that. But I promise I won't mention your name."

"Please don't." Delaney said ruefully. "I'd never live it down."

Handry left him at the Precinct house. Delaney climbed slowly to his office to put away his "beat" equipment. Then he slumped in the worn swivel chair behind his desk. He wondered if he would ever sleep again.

He was ashamed of himself, as he always was when he talked too much.

And what nonsense he had talked! "Logic . . . immortality . . . evil." Just to tickle his vanity, of course, and give him the glow of voicing "deep thoughts" to a young reporter. But what did all that blathering have to do with the price of beans?

It was all pretty poetry, but reality was a frightened woman who had never done an unkind thing in her life now lying in a hospital bed nerving herself for what might come. There were animals you couldn't see gnawing away deep inside her, and her world would soon be blood, vomit, pus, and feces. Don't you ever forget it, m'lad. And tears.

"Rather her than me" suddenly popped into his brain, and he was so disgusted with himself, so furious at having this indecent thought of the woman he loved, that he groaned aloud and struck a clenched fist on the desk. Oh, life wasn't all that much of a joy; it was a job you worked at, and didn't often succeed.

He sat there in the gloom, hunched, thinking of all the things he must now do and the order in which he must do them. Brooding, he glowered, frowned, occasionally drew lips back to show large, yellowed teeth. He looked like some great beast brought to bay.

3

IN THE Metropolitan Museum of Art there is a gallery of Roman heads. Stone faces are chipped and worn. But they have a quality. Staring into those socket eyes, at those broken noses, crushed ears, splintered lips, still one feels the power of men long dead. Kill the slave who betrayed you or, if your dreams have perished, a short sword in your own gut. Edward Delaney had that kind of face; crumbling majesty.

He was seated now in his wife's hospital room, the hard sunlight profiling him. Barbara Delaney stared through a drugged dimness and saw for the first time how his features had been harshened by violence and the responsibilities of command. She remembered the young, nervy patrolman who had courted her with violets and once, a dreadful poem.

The years and duty had not destroyed him, but they had pressed him in upon himself, condensing him. Each year he spoke less and less, laughed infrequently, and withdrew to some iron core that was his alone; she was not allowed there.

He was still a handsome man, she thought approvingly, and carried himself well and watched his weight and didn't smoke or drink too much. But now there was a somber solidity to him, and too often he sat brooding. "What is it?" she would ask. And slowly his eyes would come up from that inward stare, focus on her and life, and he would say, "Nothing." Did he think himself Nemesis for the entire world?

He had not aged so much as weathered. Seeing him now, seated heavily in sharp sunlight, she could not understand why she had never called him "Father." It was incredible that he should be younger than she. With a prescience of doom, she wondered if he could exist without her. She decided he would. He would grieve, certainly. He would be numb and rocked. But he would survive. He was complete.

In his methodical way, he had made notes of the things he felt they should discuss. He took his little leather-bound notebook from his inside pocket and flipped the pages, then put on his heavy glasses.

"I called the children last night," he said, not looking up.

"I know, dear. I wish you hadn't. Liza called this morning. She wanted to come, but I told her absolutely not. She's almost in her eighth month now, and I don't want her traveling. Do you want a boy or girl?"

"Boy."

"Beast. Well, I told her you'd call as soon as it's over; there was no need for her to come."

"Very good," he nodded. "Eddie was planning to come up in two weeks anyway, and I told him that would be fine, not to change his plans. He's thinking of getting into politics down there. They want him to run for district attorney. I think they call it 'public prosecutor' in that state. What do you think?"

"What does Eddie want to do?"

"He's not sure. That's why he wants to come up, to discuss it with us."

"How do you feel about it, Edward?"

"I want to know more about it. Who'll be putting up the campaign funds. What he'll owe. I don't want him getting into a mess."

"Eddie wouldn't do that."

"Not deliberately. Maybe from inexperience. He's still a young man, Barbara. Politics is new to him. He must be careful. Those men who want him to run have their own ambitions. Well . . . we'll talk about it when he comes up. He promised not to make any decision until he talks to us. Now then . . ." He consulted his notes ". . . how do you feel about Spencer?"

He was referring to the surgeon introduced by Dr. Bernardi. He was a brusque, no-nonsense man without warmth, but he had impressed Delaney with his direct questions, quick decisions, his sharp interruptions of Bernardi's effusions. The operation was scheduled for late in the afternoon of the following day. Delaney had followed the surgeon out into the hall.

"Do you anticipate any trouble, doctor?" he asked.

The surgeon, Dr. K. B. Spencer, looked at him coldly.

"No," he said.

"Oh, I suppose he's all right," Barbara Delaney said vaguely. "What do you think of him, dear?"

"I trust him." Delaney said promptly. "He's a professional. I asked Ferguson to check him out, and he says Spencer is a fine surgeon and a wealthy man."

"Good," Barbara smiled faintly. "I wouldn't want a *poor* surgeon."

She seemed to be tiring, and there was a hectic flush in her cheeks. Delaney put his notebook aside for a moment to wring out a cloth in a basin of cold water and lay it tenderly across her brow. She was already on intravenous feeding and had been instructed to move as little as possible.

"Thank you, dear," she said in a voice so low he could hardly hear her.

He hurried through the remainder of his notes.

"Now then," he said, "what shall I bring tomorrow? You wanted the blue quilted robe?"

"Yes," she whispered. "And the fluffy mules. The pink ones. They're in the righthand corner of my closet. My feet are swollen so badly I can't get into my slippers."

"All right," he said briskly, making a note. "Anything else? Clothes, makeup, books, fruit . . . anything?"

"No."

"Should I rent a TV set?"

She didn't answer, and when he raised his head to look at her, she seemed asleep. He took off his glasses, replaced his notebook in his pocket, began to tiptoe from the room.

"Please," she said in a weak voice, "don't go yet. Sit with me for a few minutes."

"As long as you want me," he said. He pulled a chair up to the bedside and sat hunched over, holding her hand. They sat in silence for almost five minutes.

"Edward," she breathed, her eyes closed.

"Yes. I'm here."

"Edward."

"Yes," he repeated. "I'm here."

"I want you to promise me something."

"Anything," he vowed.

"If anything should happen to me—"

"Barbara."

"If anything should—"

"Dear."

"I want you to marry again. If you meet a woman . . . Someone . . . I want you to. Will you promise?"

He couldn't breathe. Something was caught in his chest. He bowed his head, made a small noise, gripped her fingers tighter.

"Promise?" she demanded.

"Yes."

She smiled, nodded, slept.

4

CAPTAIN DELANEY was detained by another demonstration at the embassy. By the time he got it squared away and the chanting marchers shunted off into side streets, it was late afternoon and almost time for Barbara's operation. He had one of the precinct squad cars rush him over to the hospital. He knew it was a breach of regulations, but he determined to make a full report on it, explaining the circumstances, and if they wanted to discipline him, they could.

He hurried up to her room, sweating under his longjohns and uniform jacket. They were wheeling her out as he arrived; he could only kiss her pale cheek and smile at her. She was on a cart, bundled up in blankets, the tube still attached to her arm, the jar of feeding fluid high on a rod clamped to the cart.

He left her on the second floor where the operating rooms were located. There was also a recovery ward, offices of physicians and surgeons, a small dispensary, and a large waiting room painted a bilious green and furnished with orange plastic couches and chairs. This brutal chamber was presided over by a handsome nurse, a woman of about 40, buxom, a blonde who kept poking tendrils of hair back under her starched cap.

Delaney gave his name, and she checked a frighteningly long list on her desk.

"Mrs. Barbara Delaney?"

"Yes."

"Captain, it will be another half-hour until the operation. Then Mrs. Delaney will go to the recovery ward. You won't be allowed to see her until she's returned to her room, and then only if her doctor approves."

"That's all right. I'll wait. I want to talk to the surgeon after the operation is finished."

"Well . . ." she said doubtfully, consulting her list. "I'm not sure you'll be able to. Dr. Spencer has two more scheduled after your wife. Captain, if you're hungry or want a cup of coffee, why don't you go downstairs to the cafeteria? Our paging system is connected there, and I can always call if you're needed."

"A good idea," he nodded approvingly. "Thank you. I'll do that. Do you happen to know if Dr. Bernardi is in the hospital?"

"I don't know, sir, but I'll try to find out."

"Thank you," he said again.

The food in the hospital cafeteria was, as he expected, wretched. He wondered how long they had to steam it to achieve that spongy texture and uniform color; the string beans were almost the same shiny hue as the mashed potatoes. And it all tasted as bad as it looked. Even liberal sprinklings of salt and pepper couldn't make the meat loaf taste like anything but wet wallboard. He thought of his wife's Italian stew, scented and spiced with rosemary, and he groaned.

He finally shoved the dishes away, hardly touched, and had a cup of black coffee and half a dish of chocolate pudding. Then he had another cup of coffee and smoked a cigarette. He was sweltering in the over-heated cafeteria, but he never considered unhooking his choker collar. It wouldn't look right in public. He reflected on how you could always spot old cops, even in a roomful of naked men. The cops had a ring of blue dye around their necks: a lifetime of wearing that damned choker collar.

He returned to the waiting room on the second floor. The nurse told him she had located Dr. Bernardi; he was gowned and observing the kidney operation on Mrs. Delaney. The Captain thanked her and went out to the public telephone in the hall. He called the precinct. Lieutenant Rizzo had the duty and reported nothing unusual, nothing that required the Captain's attention. Delaney left the extension number of the waiting room in case he was needed.

He went back in, sat down, and looked around. There was an elderly Italian couple sitting on a couch in a corner, holding hands and looking scared. There was a young man standing propped against a wall, his face vacant. He was smoking a cigarette that threatened to burn his fingers. Seated on a plastic chair was a mink-clad matron, face raddled, showing good legs and a wattled neck. She seemed to be making an inventory of the contents of her alligator handbag.

Delaney was next to an end table scattered with magazines. He picked up a six-months-old copy of "Medical Progress," flipped through it, saw he could never understand it, put it aside. Then he sat solidly, silently, and waited. It was the detectives' art. Once, on a stake-out, he had sat in a parked car for 14 hours, relieving himself in an empty milk carton. You learned to wait. You never got to like it, but you learned how to do it.

A few things happened. The big, buxom nurse went off duty and was replaced by a woman half her size: a tough, dark, surprisingly young Puerto Rican girl with glowing eyes, a brisk way of moving, a sharp way of talking. She took all their names and why they were there. She straightened magazines on the tables. She emptied ashtrays. Then, unex-pectedly, she sprayed the room with a can of deodorant and opened a window. The room began to cool; Delaney could have kissed her.

The vacant-faced young man was called and slouched out, staring at the ceiling. The mink-clad matron suddenly stood, wrapped her coat tightly about her, and pushed through the door without speaking to the nurse.

The elderly Italian couple still sat patiently in the corner, weeping quietly.

New arrivals included a stiff, white-haired gentleman leaning on a cane. He gave his name to the nurse, lowered himself into a chair, and immediately fell asleep. Then there was a pair of hippie types in faded jeans, fringed jackets, beaded headbands. They sat cross-legged on the floor and began to play some game with oversize cards whose design Delaney could not fathom.

Finally he let himself glance at the wall clock. He was shocked to see it so late. He hurried to the desk and asked the nurse about his wife. She dialed, asked, listened, hung up.

"Your wife is in the recovery ward."

"Thank you. Can you tell me where Dr. Spencer is, so I can talk to him?"

"You should have asked before. Now I have to call again."

He let her bully him. "I'm sorry," he said.

She called, asked, hung up.

"Dr. Spencer is operating and not available."

"What about Dr. Bernardi?" he said doggedly, not at all fazed by her furious glare.

Again she called, asked, spoke sharply to the person on the other end, then punched the phone down.

"Dr. Bernardi has left the hospital."

"What? What?"

"Dr. Bernardi has left the hospital."

"But he—"

At that moment the door to the waiting room slammed back. It hit the wall with the sound of a pistol shot. Thinking of it later, Delaney decided that from that moment on, the night simply exploded and went whirling away.

It was the mink-clad matron, her wrinkled face crimson.

"They're killing him!" she screamed. "They're killing him!"

The little nurse came from behind her desk. She reached for the distraught woman. The matron raised one fur-covered arm and clubbed her down.

The others in the room looked up. Dazed. Bewildered. Frightened. Delaney rose lightly to his feet.

"They're killing him!" the woman screamed.

The nurse scrambled up, rushed out the door.

Delaney moved very slowly toward the hysterical woman.

"Oh yes," he said in a voice deliberately dulled, slowed. "They're killing him. Oh yes," he nodded.

The woman turned to him. "They're killing him," she repeated, not yelling now but pulling at the loose skin beneath her chin.

"Oh yes," Delaney kept nodding. "Oh yes."

He, to whom touching a stranger was anathema, knew from experience how important physical contact was in dealing with irrational or maddened people.

"Oh yes," he kept repeating, nodding his head but never smiling. "I understand. Oh yes."

He put a hand lightly, tentatively, on her furred arm.

"Oh yes," he kept nodding. "Oh yes."

She looked down at the hand on her arm, but she didn't throw him off.

"Oh yes," he nodded. "Tell me about it. I want to know all about it. Oh yes. Tell me from the beginning. I want to hear all about it."

Now he had his arm about her shoulders; she was leaning into him. Then an intern and attendant, white-clad, came flinging in, followed by the furious nurse. Delaney, leading the matron slowly toward a couch, waved them away with his free hand. The intern had enough sense to stop in his tracks and halt the others. The old Italian couple, open-mouthed, and the hippie couple watched in silence. The white-haired gentleman slept on.

"They're killing him!" she screamed once more.

"Oh yes," he nodded, hugging her closer. "Tell me all about it. I want to know all about it."

He got her seated on a plastic couch, his arm still about her shoulders. The intern and his aides watched nervously but didn't approach.

"Tell me," Delaney soothed. "Tell me everything. Start from the beginning. I want to know."

"Shit," the woman said suddenly, and fumbled in her alligator bag for a handkerchief. She blew her nose with a tremendous fluttering blast that startled everyone in the room. "You're a beautiful man, you know that? You're not like those other mother-fuckers in this butcher shop."

"Tell me," he droned on, "tell me about it."

"Well," she said, dabbing at her nose, "it began about six months ago. Irving came home early from the office and complained about—"

Delaney heard a scuffling of feet and looked up. The room seemed filled with police uniforms. Oh God, he thought despairingly, don't tell me that stupid nurse called the cops because of one poor, sad, frightened, hysterical woman.

But it couldn't be. There was Captain Richard Boznanski of the 188th Precinct, just north of his. And he recognized a detective lieutenant and a man from the public relations section. A sergeant had his arm around Boznanski's waist and was half-supporting him.

Delaney pulled apart from the matron.

"Don't go away," she pleaded. "Please don't go away."

"Just for a minute," he whispered. "I'll be back. I promise I'll be back."

The loudspeaker was shouting: "Dr. Spencer, report to 201, please. Dr. Ingram, report to 201, please. Drs. Spencer, Ingram and Gomez, report to 201, please. Dr. Gomez, report to 201, please."

Delaney stalked over to Boznanski. He didn't like the way the man looked. His face was waxy white and covered with a sheen of sweat. His eyes seemed to move uncontrollably, and there was a tremor to his chin: his lips met and drew apart every second.

"Dick," Delaney urged, "what is it? What *is* it?"

Boznanski stared at him with dazed eyes. "Edward?" he said. "What are you doing here? Edward? How did you hear so soon?"

Delaney felt a hand on his arm and turned. It was Ivar Thorsen, Deputy Inspector, in charge of personnel in the patrol division. He drew Delaney to one side. He began to speak in a low voice, his light blue eyes never moving from Delaney's.

"It was an ambush, Edward. A call came in about a prowler. A two-man car checked it out. Jameson was black, Richmond white. It was a false alarm. At a housing project on 110th Street. They were returning to their car. Shotguns from the bushes. Jameson got his head blown off. Richmond took it in the chest and belly."

"Any chance?" Delaney asked, stone-faced.

"Well . . . no, I'd guess. I saw him. I'd guess no. But they're rounding up this team of surgeons to work on him. Listen, Edward, if Richmond dies, it'll be the fourth man Boznanski's lost this year. He's shook."

"I saw."

"Will you stay with him? The corridor's full of reporters, and they're moving in TV cameras. The Mayor and Commissioner are on their way. I've got a lot of crap to do—you know?"

"Yes."

"Just sit by him—you know."

"Sure."

Thorsen looked at him curiously, his ice eyes narrowing.

"What are you doing here, Edward?"

"My wife was operated on tonight. For kidney stones. I'm waiting to hear how she made out."

"Jesus," Thorsen breathed. "I'm sorry, Edward. I didn't know. How is she?"

"I'm trying to find out."

"Forget about Boznanski. The sergeant will stand by."

"No," Delaney said. "That's all right. I'll be here."

"They're killing him!" the matron cried, grabbing his arm. "They told me it was just a simple operation, and now they say there are complications. They're killing him!"

"Oh yes," Delaney murmured, leading her back to the couch. "I want to hear. I want to know all about it."

He lighted a cigarette for her, then started out into the hall. He fumbled in his pocket and found he had only a quarter. He was about to ask someone for change, then realized how stupid that was. He called Dr. Bernardi's office. He got an answering service. They told him they'd give the doctor his message.

He came back into the waiting room. The shaken nurse was behind her desk. He asked if Dr. Spencer was still in surgery. She said she'd check and also check on his wife in the recovery ward. He thanked her. She thanked him, softened and human.

He went back to Captain Richard Boznanski, seated now, his head thrown back, gasping for breath. He didn't look good. The sergeant was standing by, worried.

"Captain," he said, "is there any booze . . .?"

Delaney looked at the man in the chair. "I'll try," he said.

"He came home early from work about six months ago," the mink-clad matron said at his elbow, "and he complained of this pain in his chest. He's always been a heavy smoker, and I thought—"

"Oh yes," Delaney said, holding her by the arm. "And what did they say it was?"

"Well, they weren't sure, and they wanted to do this exploratory."

"Oh yes," Delaney nodded. "Just a minute now, and I'll be right back."

He asked the nurse if she had any or could find any whiskey. She explained that regulations prohibited her from giving anything like that to patients or visitors. Delaney nodded and asked if she could find Dr. Bernardi's home phone number. She said she'd try. He asked if she could change a dollar. She couldn't, but she gave him what change she had and refused to accept the dollar he offered. He gave her a grateful smile.

He called Ferguson, who wasn't home. Delaney realized he had awakened the spinster sister. He explained the situation and asked, if Ferguson returned, if he would try to reach Bernardi and find out about Mrs. Delaney's condition. Then Ferguson could call Delaney in the waiting room.

The Captain stalked to the end of the second floor corridor. The swinging doors to the elevators were guarded by two patrolmen. They drew back to let him through.

The moment he stepped out he was surrounded by reporters, all shouting at once. Delaney held up a hand until the newsmen quieted.

"Any statements will have to come from Deputy Inspector Thorsen or others. Not from me."

"Is Richmond still alive?"

"As far as I know. A team of surgeons is working. That's all I know. Now if you'll . . ."

He pushed through the crush. They were setting up small TV cameras on tripods near the elevators. Then Delaney saw Thomas Handry leaning against a wall. He was the reporter who had accompanied Delaney on his midnight rounds. He pulled Handry aside. The man's eyes seemed huge and feverish.

"I told you, I told you," he said to Delaney.

"Do you have any whiskey?" the Captain asked.

Handry looked at him, bewildered.

"Take off your hat," Delaney commanded.

Handry snatched his hat away.

"Do you have any whiskey?" Delaney repeated.

"No, I don't, Captain."

"All I need is a shot. Ask around, will you? See if any of your boys is carrying a flask. Maybe one of the TV men has a pint. I'll pay for it."

"I'll ask, Captain."

"Thank you. Tell one of the men on the door to call me. I'll be in the waiting room."

"If no one's got anything. I'll go out for it."

"Thank you."

"Is Richmond dead?"

"I don't know."

He went back into the waiting room.

"Dr. Spencer is still in surgery," the nurse told him.

"Thank you. Did Dr. Ferguson call?"

"No. But I checked recovery. Your wife is sleeping peacefully."

"Thank you."

"An exploratory," the matron said, holding onto his elbow. "They said it would just be an exploratory. Now they won't tell me anything."

"What's his name?" Delaney asked. "Maybe I can find out what's going on."

"Modell," she said. "Irving Modell. And my name is Rhoda Modell. We have four children and six grandchildren."

"I'll try to find out," Delaney nodded.

He went back to the nurse. But she had heard his conversation with the woman.

"Not a chance," she said softly. "A few hours. Before morning. They took one look and sewed him up."

He nodded and glanced at the clock. Had time speeded up? It was past midnight.

"What I'd like—" he started, but then there was a patrolman next to him.

"Captain Delaney?"

"Yes."

"There's a reporter at the door. Guy named Handry. Says you—"

"Yes, yes."

Delaney walked back with him. The door was opened wide enough for Handry to give him a wrinkled brown paper bag.

"Thank you," Delaney said, and reached for his wallet. But Handry shook his head angrily and turned away.

He peeked into the bag. It was an almost full pint bottle of bourbon. He took several paper cups from the water cooler in the hallway and went back into the waiting room. Boznanski was still lolling in the chair, his head thrown back. Delaney filled a cup with bourbon.

"Dick," he said.

Boznanski opened his eyes.

"A sip," Delaney said. "Dick, just take a little sip."

He held the cup to the policeman's lips. Boznanski tasted, coughed, bent forward in dry heaves, then leaned back. Delaney fed him slowly, sip by sip. Color began to come back into the Captain's face. He straightened in his chair. Delaney poured a cup for the sergeant who drained it gratefully, in one gulp.

"Oh my," he said.

"May I sir?" a voice asked. And there was the white-haired gentleman, finally awake and holding out a quivering hand that seemed skinned with tissue paper. And the two hippies. And the old Italian couple. Just a taste for all: the sacramental cup.

"He's not going to make it, is he?" the matron asked suddenly, looking at Delaney. "I knew you wouldn't lie to me."

"I wouldn't lie to you." Delaney nodded, pouring her the few drops remaining in the bottle. "He's not going to make it."

"Ah Jesus," she sighed, rolling a pale tongue around the inside of the waxed paper cup. "What a miserable marriage that was. But aren't they all?"

There was noise outside in the corridor. Deputy Inspector Thorsen came in, composed as ever. He stalked directly to the seated Captain Boznanski and stared at him. Then he turned to Delaney.

"Thanks, Edward."

"What about Richmond?"

"Richmond? Oh. He's gone. They tried, but it was hopeless. Everyone knew it. Five surgeons working four hours."

Delaney looked up at the clock. It couldn't be two in the morning, it *couldn't* be. What had happened to time?

"The Mayor and Commissioner are out there now," Thorsen said in a toneless voice, "giving statements about the need for gun control laws and a new moral climate."

"Yes," Delaney said. He strode over to the nurse's desk. "Where can I find Dr. Spencer?" he asked harshly.

She looked at him with tired eyes. "Try the lounge. Turn right as you go out. Then, after you go through the swinging doors, there's a narrow door on the left that says 'No Admittance.' That's the surgeons' lounge."

"Thank you," Captain Delaney said precisely.

He followed her directions. When he pushed back the narrow door without knocking, he saw a small room, one couch and two armchairs, a TV set, a card table and four folding chairs. There were five men in the room wearing surgical gowns, skull caps, and masks pulled down onto their chests. Three were dressed in light green, two in white.

One man was standing, staring out a window. One was fiddling with the knobs on the TV set, trying to bring in a clear picture. One was trimming his fingernails with a small pocket knife. One was seated at the card table, carefully building an improbable house of leaned cards. One was stretched out on the floor, raising and lowering his legs, doing some kind of exercise.

"Dr. Spencer?" Delaney said sharply.

The man at the window turned slowly, glanced at the uniform, turned back to the window.

"He's dead," he said tonelessly. "I told them that."

"I know he's dead," the Captain said. "My name is Delaney. You operated on my wife earlier this evening. Kidney stones. I want to know how she is."

Spencer turned again to look at him. The other men didn't pause in their activities.

"Delaney," Spencer repeated. "Kidney stones. Well. I had to remove the kidney."

"What?"

"I had to take out one of your wife's kidneys."

"Why?"

"It was infected, diseased, rotted."

"Infected with what?"

"It's down in the lab. We'll know tomorrow."

The man building a house of cards looked up. "You can live with one kidney," he said mildly to Delaney.

"Listen," Delaney said, choking, "listen, you said there'd be no trouble."

"So?" Spencer asked. "What do you want from me? I'm not God."

"Well, if you're not," Delaney cried furiously, "who the hell is?"

There was a knock on the door. The man on the floor, the one lifting and lowering his legs, gasped, "Come in, come in, whoever you are."

A colored nurses' aide stuck her capped head through the opened door and looked about boldly.

"Any of you gentlemen a certain Captain Delaney?" she asked saucily.

"I'm Delaney."

"You have a call, Captain. In the waiting room. They say it's very, very, very important."

Delaney took a last look around. Spencer was staring out the window again, and the others were trying to stay busy. He stalked down the hall, pushed angrily through the swinging doors, slammed back into the waiting room. The little nurse handed him the phone, not looking up.

"Captain Edward X. Delaney here."

"Captain, this is Dorfman."

"Yes, lieutenant. What is it?"

"Sorry to bother you, Captain. At this hour."

"What is it?"

"Captain, there's been a murder."

PART THREE

1

THE STREET was blocked off with sawhorses: raw yellow wood with "New York Police Department" stencilled on the sides. Below the barricades were oil lanterns, black globes with smoking wicks. They looked like 19th century anarchists' bombs.

The patrolman on duty saluted and pulled one sawhorse aside to let Delaney through. The Captain walked slowly down the center of the street, toward the river. He knew this block well; three years previously he had led a team of officers and Technical Patrol Force specialists in the liberation of a big townhouse that had been taken over by a gang of thugs and was being systematically looted. The house was near the middle of the block. A few lights were on; in one apartment the tenants were standing at the window, staring down into the street.

Delaney paused to survey the silent scene ahead of him. Understanding what was happening, he removed his cap, made the sign of the cross, bowed his head.

There were a dozen vehicles drawn up in a rough semicircle: squad cars, ambulance, searchlight truck, laboratory van, three unmarked sedans, a black limousine. Thirty men were standing motionless, uncovered heads down.

This city block had been equipped with the new street lights that cast an orange, shadowless glow. It filled doorways, alleys, corners like a thin liquid, and if there were no shadows, there was no brightness either, but a kind of strident light without warmth.

Into this brassy haze a morning mist seeped gently and collected in tears on hoods and roofs of cars and on black asphalt. It damped the hair and faces of the silent watchers. It fell as a shroud on the bundle crumpled on the sidewalk. The kneeling priest completed extreme unction and rose from his knees. The waiting men replaced their hats; there was a subdued murmur of voices.

Delaney stared at this night lithograph, then walked forward slowly. He came into a hard white beam from the searchlight truck; men turned to look at him. Lieutenant Dorfman came hurrying up, face twisted.

"It's Lombard, Captain," he gasped. "Frank Lombard, the Brooklyn councilman. You know—the one who's always talking about 'crime on the streets' and writing the newspapers what a lousy job the police are doing."

Delaney nodded. He looked around at the assembled men: patrolmen, precinct and Homicide North detectives, laboratory specialists, an inspector from the Detective Division. And a deputy commissioner with one of the Mayor's personal aides.

Now there was another figure kneeling alongside the corpse. Captain Delaney recognized the massive bulk of Dr. Sanford Ferguson. Despite the harsh glare of the searchlights, the Police Surgeon was using a penlight to examine the skull of the dead man. He stood away a moment while photographers placed a ruler near the corpse and took more flash photos. Then he kneeled again on the wet sidewalk. Delaney walked over to stand next to him. Ferguson looked up.

"Hullo, Edward," he smiled. "Wondering where you were. Take a look at this."

Before kneeling, Delaney stared down a moment at the victim. It was not difficult to visualize what had happened. The man had been struck down from behind. The back of his skull appeared crushed; thick black hair was bloodied and matted. He had fallen forward, sprawling heavily. As he fell, the left femur had snapped; the leg was now flung out at an awkward angle. He had fallen with such force that the splintered end of the bone had thrust out through his trouser leg.

As he fell, presumably his face smacked the sidewalk, for blood had flowed from a mashed nose, perhaps from a crushed mouth and facial abrasions. The pool of blood, not yet congealed, bloomed from his head in a small puddle, down into a plot of cracked earth about a scrawny plane tree at the curb.

Delaney kneeled carefully, avoiding a leather wallet lying alongside the body. The Captain turned to squint into the searchlight glare.

"The wallet dusted?" he called to men he couldn't see.

"No sir," someone called back. "Not yet."

Delaney looked down at the wallet.

"Alligator," he said. "They won't get much from that." He took a ballpoint pen from the inside pocket of his uniform jacket and gently prized open the wallet, touching only one edge. Dr. Ferguson put the beam of his penlight on it. They both saw the thick sheaf of green bills.

Delaney let the wallet fall closed, then turned back to the body. Ferguson put his light on the skull. Three men in civilian clothes came up to kneel around the corpse. The five bent over closely, heads almost touching.

"Club?" one of the detectives asked. "A pipe maybe?"

"I don't think so," Ferguson said, without looking up. "There's no crushing or depression. That's blood and matting you see. But there's a penetration. Like a puncture. A hole about an inch in diameter. It looks round. I could put my finger in it."

"Hammer?" Delaney asked.

Ferguson sat back on his heels. "A hammer? Yes, it could be. Depends on how deep the penetration goes."

"What about time, doc?" one of the other detectives asked.

"Looks to be within three hours tops. No, call it two hours. Around midnight. Just a guess."

"Who found him?"

"A cabby spotted him first but thought he was a drunk and didn't stop. The cabby caught up with one of your precinct squads on York Avenue, Captain, and they came back."

"Who were they?"

"McCabe and Mowery."

"Did they move the body or the wallet?"

"McCabe says they didn't touch the body. He says the wallet was lying open, face up, with ID card and credit cards showing in plastic pockets. That's how they knew it was Lombard."

"Who closed the wallet?"

"Mowery did that."

"Why?"

"He says it was beginning to drizzle, and they were afraid it might rain harder and ruin any latent prints on the plastic windows in the wallet. He says they could see it was a rough leather wallet and chances are there'd be a better chance of prints on the plastic than on the leather. So they closed the wallet, using a pencil. He says they didn't touch it. McCabe backs him up. McCabe says the wallet is within a quarter-inch at most from where they found it."

"When did the cabby stop them on York Avenue and tell them there was someone lying here?"

"About an hour ago. Closer to fifty minutes maybe."

"Doctor," Delaney asked, "can we roll him over now?"

"You got your pictures?" a detective roared into the darkness.

"We need the front," the reply came back.

"Careful of that leg," Ferguson said. "One of you hold it together while we roll him over."

Five pairs of hands took hold of the corpse gently and turned it face up. The five kneeling men drew back as two photographers came up for long shots and closeups of the victim. Then the circle closed again.

"No front wounds that I can see," Ferguson reported, his little flashlight beam zigzagging down the dead body. "The broken leg and facial injuries are from the fall. At least the abraded skin indicates that. I'll know better when I get him downtown. It was the skull penetration that did it."

"Dead before he hit the ground?"

"Could be if that puncture is deep enough. He's a—he was a heavy man. Maybe two twenty-five. He fell heavily." He felt the dead man's arms, shoulders, legs. "Solid. Not too much fat. Good muscle layer. He could have put up a fight. If he had a chance."

They were silent, staring down at the body. He had not been a handsome man, but his features were rugged and not unpleasant: strong jaw, full lips, a meaty nose (now crushed), thick black brows and walrus mustache. The teeth still unbroken were big, white, square—little tombstones. Blank eyes stared at the weeping sky.

Delaney leaned forward suddenly and pressed his face close to the dead man's. Dr. Ferguson grabbed him by the shoulder and pulled him back.

"What the hell are you doing, Edward?" he cried. "Kissing the poor bastard?"

"Smell him," Delaney said. "Smell the mustache. Garlic, wine, and something else."

Ferguson leaned forward cautiously, and sniffed at the thick mustache.

"Anise," he said. "Wine, garlic, and anise."

"That's an Italian dinner," one of the detectives said. "Maybe he stiffed the waiter and the guy followed him down here and offed him."

No one laughed.

"He is Italian," someone said. "His name isn't Lombard, it's Lombardo. He dropped the 'o' when he went into politics. His district in Brooklyn is mostly Jewish."

They looked up. It was Lieutenant Rizzo from the 251st.

"How do you know, lieutenant?"

"He's—was my wife's cousin. He was at our wedding. His mother lives around here somewhere. I called my wife. She's calling relatives, trying to find out the mother's address. My wife says Lombard came over from Brooklyn occasionally to have dinner with his mother. She's supposed to be a good cook."

The five men climbed shakily to their feet and brushed their damp knees. Dr. Ferguson signaled toward the ambulance, and two men came forward lugging a canvas body bag. A man came from the laboratory van with a plastic bag and a small pair of tongs to retrieve the wallet.

"Edward," Ferguson said, "I forgot to ask. How is your wife getting along?"

"She was operated on tonight. Or rather yesterday afternoon."

"And . . .?"

"They had to take out one of her kidneys."

Ferguson was silent a moment, then . . . "Infected?"

"That's what Spencer told me. Bernardi observed the operation but I can't get hold of him."

"The prick. As soon as I get to a phone I'll try to find out what the hell is going on. Where can I reach you."

"The precinct house probably. We'll have to re-shuffle schedules and figure out how many uniformed men we can spare for door-to-door questioning. They're taking our detectives away."

"I heard. Edward, I'll call if I learn anything. If I don't call, it means I haven't been able to reach Spencer or Bernardi."

Delaney nodded. Dr. Ferguson climbed into the back of the ambulance, and it went whining away. Lt. Dorfman was moving toward him, but the deputy commissioner came out of the darkness and clamped a hand on Delaney's elbow. The Captain didn't like to be touched; he tugged his arm gently away.

"Delaney?"

"Yes sir."

"My name's Broughton. B-r-o-u-g-h-t-o-n. I guess we never met."

They had, but Delaney didn't mention it. The two officers shook hands. Broughton, a thick, shapeless man, motioned Delaney toward the black limousine. He opened the back door, waved Delaney in, climbed in beside him.

"Go get a coffee, Jack," he commanded the uniformed driver.

Then they were alone. Broughton offered a cigar but Delaney shook his head. The deputy lighted up furiously, the end of the cigar flaring, the car filling with harsh smoke.

"It's a piece of shit," he said angrily. "Why the hell can't we get Havana cigars? We're defeating Communism by smoking horse shit? What kind of insanity is that?"

He sat back, staring out the window at the sidewalk where someone had chalked an outline around the corpse before it was removed.

"A lot of flak on this one, Captain," Broughton said loudly. "A *lot* of flak. The Commissioner cancelled a speech in Kansas City—Kansas *City*, for Chrissakes—and is flying back. You probably saw the Mayor's aide. His Honor is on our ass already. And don't think the fucking governor won't get in the act. You know this Lombard—the guy who got hisself killed?"

"I read his statements in the newspapers and I saw him on television."

"Yeah, he got the publicity. So you know what we're up against. 'Crime in the streets . . . no law and order . . . hoodlums and muggers running wild . . . shake up the police department . . . the Commissioner should resign . . .' You know. The shithead was running for Mayor. Now he's knocked off, and if we don't pull someone in, it proves he was right. You understand how serious this is, Captain."

"I consider every homicide serious."

"Well . . . yeah . . . sure. But the politics involved. You understand that?"

"Yes sir."

"All right. That's one thing. Now the other thing . . . This killing couldn't have happened at a worst time. You get the Commissioner's memo about precinct detectives?"

"Memorandum four six seven dash B dated eight October; subject: Detective division, reorganization of? Yes sir, I received it."

Broughton laughed shortly. "I heard about you, Delaney. Yeah, that's the memo." He belched suddenly, a ripe, liquid sound. He didn't excuse himself, but scratched in his crotch. "All right, we're pulling all the detectives out of the precinct houses. You're next on the list. You got the notification?"

"Yes."

"Starts on Monday. All detectives will be organized in special units— homicide, burglary and larceny, truck thefts, hotel thefts, and so on. Uniformed officers will make the first investigation of a crime. You're going to give your cops a crash course on what to look for. It's all spelled out in a manual you'll be getting. The investigating officers file a report. If it's a major theft, say, involving more than $1,500 in money or goods, the detective unit takes over. If it's a minor crime, say b-and-e or a mugging, the patrolman does what he can or reports it unsolvable. We tried it out in two test precincts, and we think it's going to work. What do you think?"

"I don't like it," Delaney said promptly. "It takes detectives out of the precincts and out of the neighborhoods. Sometimes they make their best busts just by knowing the neighborhood—who's missing, new hoods who have shown up, who's been flashing a roll. And of course they all have their neighborhood informers. Now, as I understand it, one specialized detective unit might be covering as many as four or five precincts. I like the idea of uniformed men getting experience in investigation work. They'll like that. They'll be functioning like detectives—which is what most of them thought police work was all about, instead of taking old people to hospitals and settling family squabbles. But while they're investigating and making out that preliminary report, they're off the beat, and I'll have less men on patrol and visible. I don't like that."

Broughton pried a fingertip roughly into one nostril, dug out some matter, rolled it into a ball between thumb and forefinger. He opened the car window and flicked it outside.

"Well, you're going to have to live with it," he said coldly. "At least for a year until we get some numbers and see what's happening to our solution rates. But now this son of a bitch Lombard gets hit right in the middle of the change-over. So we have Homicide North still in existence, the new homicide unit covering your precinct, and you still got your precinct detectives. Jesus Christ, all those guys will be walking up each other's heels, covering the same ground—and whose responsibility is it? It's going to be as fucked up as a Chinese fire drill. It is already. You got any ideas how to straighten it out?"

Delaney looked up in surprise. The final question had come so suddenly, so unexpectedly, that even though he had wondered about the reason for this private talk, he wasn't prepared for the demand.

"Can you give me twenty-four hours to think it over? Maybe I can come up with something."

"No good," Broughton said impatiently. "Right now I got to go out to the airport to pick up the Commissioner, and I got to have some suggestions on how to straighten out this mess. He'll want action. The Mayor and every councilman will be leaning on him. And if he don't produce, it's probably his ass. And if it's his ass, it's my ass too. You understand?"

"Yes."

"You agree that right now it's screwed up as far as organization goes?"

"Yes."

"Christ, you're a regular chatterbox, ain't you?" Broughton farted audibly and squirmed his buttocks on the car seat. "I been hearing how smart you are, Captain. Okay, here's your chance; give me a for-instance right now."

Delaney looked at him with distaste, recognizing the man's crude energy but angered by his bullying, disgusted by his personal habits, sensing a personality that reeked of the jungle.

"Try a temporary horizontal organization," he said tonelessly. "The Department, just like the army and most business corporations, is organized vertically. Responsibility and authority are vested in the man at the top. Orders come down the chain of command. Each division, precinct, unit, or whatever, has a definite assignment. But sometimes problems come up that can't be solved by this type of organization. It's usually a problem of limited duration that might never occur again. The Lombard homicide comes right in the middle of the re-organization of the detective division. All right, do what the army and most corporations do when they're faced with a unique situation that doesn't require a permanent organization. Set up a temporary task force. Call it 'Operation Lombard,' if you like. Appoint an overall commander. Give him full responsibility and authority to draw on any unit for personnel and equipment he needs. Detectives, patrolmen, specialists—anyone who'll help him do the job. The men are detached on a temporary basis. The whole operation is temporary. When and if Lombard's killer is found, the task force is disbanded, and the men go back to their regular units."

A light came into Broughton's muddy eyes. He laughed with glee and rubbed his palms together between his knees.

"They weren't kidding; you're a smart son of a bitch, Delaney. I like it. And I think the Commissioner will like it. A special task force: 'Operation Lombard.' It'll show we're doing something—right? That should satisfy the Mayor and the newspapers. How long do you think it'll take to break the Lombard thing?"

Delaney looked at him in astonishment.

"How would I know? How would anyone know? Maybe someone's confessing right now. Maybe it'll never be solved."

"Jesus, don't say that."

"Did you ever read solution statistics on homicides? If they're not solved within the first forty-eight hours, the solution probability drops off steeply and continues to plunge as time passes. After a month or two, solution probability is practically nil."

Broughton nodded glumly, got out of the car, spat his cold cigar into the gutter. Delaney got out too and stood there as the uniformed driver came running up. Broughton got in the front seat alongside the driver. As the limousine pulled away, the Captain saluted gravely, but it was not returned.

Delaney stood a moment, inspecting the street. The first contingent of uniformed patrolmen from his precinct came straggling up in twos and threes, to gather about the chalked outline on the sidewalk. The Captain moved over to listen to a sergeant giving them orders.

"Everyone got a flashlight?" he asked. "Okay, we spread out from here. We move slowly. Got that? slowly. We check every garbage can—" There was a groan from the massed men. "There was a pickup on this street yesterday afternoon so most of the cans should be empty. But even if they're full, spill them out. Every can has got to be searched. After you're through, try to kick most of the shit back in. We're calling for another sanitation pickup today, and the cans will be clawed through again when they're spilled into the garbage truck. Also, every area and alley, and put your light in every sewer and catch basin. This is a preliminary search. By tomorrow we'll have some sewer and street men here to take off the manhole covers and gratings and probe the sludge. Now, what we're looking for is anything that looks like a weapon. It could be a gun or a knife. But especially look for a club, a piece of pipe, an iron rod, a hammer, or maybe a rock with blood and matted hair on it. Anything with blood on it. And that includes a hat, clothing, a handkerchief, maybe a rag. If you're not sure, call me. Don't pass up anything. We do this block first. Then we cross York to the next block. Then we come back and do one block south and one block north. Got it? All right, get moving."

Delaney watched the searchlights spread out from where the dark blood still glistened in the morning mist. He knew it had to be done, but he didn't envy the men their task. It was possible they might find something. Possible. They would, he knew, also find gut-wrenching garbage, vomit, a dead cat, and perhaps the bloody body of an aborted baby.

By morning there would be more men doing the same thing, and more, and more. The search would spread farther and farther until it covered all his precinct and, finally, most of Manhattan.

Now he watched carefully as the men started their search. Then, suddenly, he realized his weariness had dropped away, or perhaps he was so exhausted he was numb. He clasped his hands behind his back and strolled down to the river fence. There he turned, faced toward York Avenue, and began to consider how the murder might have happened.

Lombard's body had been found on the sidewalk almost half-way between the river and York Avenue. If indeed he had dinner with his mother, it was reasonable to assume she lived between the river and the point where the victim was found. Lombard had fallen forward toward York. Had he, about midnight, been walking toward a bus line, a subway station, or perhaps his parked car for the trip home to Brooklyn?

Pacing slowly, Delaney inspected the buildings between the river and the spot where the body was found. They were all converted brownstones and townhouses. Fronts of the townhouses were flush; there were no areas where a killer might lurk, although it was conceivable he might have been in a lobby, ostensibly inspecting bells, his back turned to passers-by. Delaney doubted that. Too much chance of being spotted by a tenant.

But the entrances to the converted brownstones were three or four steps down from the sidewalk. There were high bushes and boxes of ivy, still green, that offered some concealment for a crouching assassin. Delaney could not believe it. No killer, even if trained and wearing crepe-soled shoes, could leap from concealment, charge up three or four steps, and rush his victim from behind without making *some* noise. And Lombard would have turned to face his attacker, perhaps throw up an arm to protect himself, or make some movement to escape. Yet apparently he was struck down suddenly and without warning.

Barely moving, Delaney stared at the building fronts across the street. It was possible, he acknowledged, that the killer had waited in an outside lobby until Lombard passed on his way to York Avenue, had then come out on the sidewalk and followed him. But again, Lombard would surely have heard him or sensed his presence. And on this block at midnight, would a man as aware of street crime as Lombard allow a man to stalk him? The councilman could have run toward the traffic on York Avenue, or even dashed across the street to seek refuge in the big townhouse lobby with the doorman.

All this theorizing, of course, assumed that Lombard was a marked target,

THE FIRST DEADLY SIN

that the killer had followed him or at least been aware that he would be on this particular street at this particular time. But the suddenness and complete success of the attack were the points that interested Delaney at the moment. He retraced his steps to the river fence, turned around, and began again a slow walk toward York.

"What's Iron Balls up to, sarge?" a uniformed patrolman asked. He was stationed at the chalked outline on the sidewalk to shoo away the curious.

The sergeant stared across the street at the slowly pacing Captain.

"Why, he's looking for clues," he explained blandly. "He's sure to find a cancelled French postage stamp, or a lefthand glove with the little finger missing, or maybe a single turkey feather. Then he'll solve the murder and make deputy inspector. What the fuck do you think he's doing?"

The patrolman didn't know, and the sergeant didn't either.

Another possibility, Delaney was thinking, was that the killer was walking along with Lombard, the two were friends. But could the killer pull out a weapon, get behind his victim, and strike him directly from the rear without Lombard turning in alarm, dodging, or trying to ward off the blow?

The sticking point was still the suddenness of the attack and the fact that Lombard, a big, muscular man, had apparently offered no resistance, had allowed the killer to come up on him from behind.

Delaney stopped a moment and reflected; he was racing ahead too fast. Perhaps the killer didn't approach from the rear. Perhaps he came directly toward Lombard from York Avenue. If he was well-dressed, walking swiftly like a resident of the block anxious to get home at midnight, chances are Lombard would have inspected him as he approached. And if the man looked all right, Lombard might have moved aside slightly to let him pass.

The weapon, of course, would have to be concealed. But if it was a pipe or a hammer, there were a number of ways that could be done—in a folded newspaper, under a coat carried on the arm, even in a trick package. Then, the instant after passing Lombard, the victim's attention now on the area in front of him, the killer could bare his weapon, whirl, crush Lombard's skull. All in an instant. Lombard would have no warning. He would topple forward, already dead. The assassin would return his weapon to its cover, and retrace his steps to York Avenue or even continue on to his own apartment, if he was a resident of the block, or to the apartment of a friend, or to a car parked for a convenient getaway.

Delaney ran through it again. The more he inspected it, the stronger it looked. It *felt* right. It assumed the killer approaching Lombard was a stranger to him. But if he was well-dressed, "legitimate" looking, and apparently hurrying home, it was doubtful if Lombard or anyone else would cross the street to escape attack. The Captain discarded the notion that after the murder the killer went on to his own apartment or that of a friend; he would surely guess that every resident of the block would be questioned and his whereabouts checked at the time of the slaying. No, the killer either went back toward York or escaped in a car parked nearby.

Delaney returned to the fence blocking off East River Drive, crossed the street, and started down the sidewalk where the body had been found, heading in the direction the victim had been walking.

Now I am Frank Lombard, soon to be dead. I have just had dinner with my mother, I have come out of her apartment house at midnight, I am in a hurry to get home to Brooklyn. I walk quickly, and I look about constantly. I even look down into the bush-surrounded entrances to the brownstones. I am acutely aware of the incidence of street assaults, and I make certain no one is lurking, waiting to bash me on the head or mug me.

I look up ahead. There is a man coming toward me from York Avenue. In the shadowless glare of the new street lights I can see that the man is well-dressed, carrying a coat over his arm. He too is hurrying, anxious to get home. I can understand that. As he approaches, our eyes lock. We both nod and smile reassuringly. "It's all right," the smile says. "We're both well-dressed. We look okay. We're not muggers." I draw aside a little to give the man room to pass. The next instant I am dead.

Delaney stopped at the chalked outline on the sidewalk. It began to seem real to him. It explained why Lombard apparently made no move to defend himself, didn't have time to make a move. The Captain walked slowly down to York Avenue. He turned, started back toward the river.

Now I am the killer, carrying a coat across my arm. Under the coat, hidden, I am grasping the handle of a hammer. I am walking quickly, with purposeful strides. Ahead of me, in the orange glare, I see the man I am to kill. I walk toward him briskly. As I come up, I nod, smile, and move to pass him. Now he is looking straight ahead. I pass, lift the hammer free, whirl, raise it high and strike. He goes down, sprawling forward. I cover the hammer again, walk quickly back to York Avenue again and escape.

Captain Delaney paused again at the chalked diagram. Yes, it could have happened that way. If the killer had nerve and resolution—and luck, of course. Always luck. No one looking out a window. No one else on the street at that hour. No cab suddenly coming down from York, its headlights picking him up the instant he struck. But assuming the killer's luck, it all— ah, Jesus! The wallet! He had forgotten that damned wallet completely!

The wallet was the folding type, the kind a man customarily carries in a hip pocket. Indeed, Delaney had noted it had acquired a slight curve, taking its shape from the buttock. He carried the same type of wallet himself, and it began to curve after several months of use.

Lombard had been wearing a three-quarter "car coat" fastened in front with wooden toggles. In back, the coat and suit jacket beneath it had been pulled up high enough to expose his hip pockets. Now why had the killer paused long enough to frisk his victim for his wallet and then leave it open beside the body, even though it was stuffed with money? Every moment he tarried, every second, the killer was in deadly peril. Yet he took the time to search the corpse and remove the wallet. And then he left it open beside the body.

Why didn't he take the money—or the entire wallet? Not because he was frightened away by someone's appearance at a window or on the street. A man with nerve enough to approach his victim from the front would have nerve enough to take his loot, even if emperiled. A man can run just as fast with a wallet as without it. No, he just didn't want the money. What did he want? To check the identification of his victim—or did he take something from the wallet, something they didn't know about yet?

Delaney went back to York Avenue, turned, started back, and ran through it again.

Now I am the killer, carrying a coat across my arm. Under the coat . . .

Delaney knew as well as any man in the Department what the chances were of solving this particular homicide. He knew that in 1971 New York City had more murders than American combat deaths in Vietnam during the same period. In New York, almost five victims a day were shot, knifed, strangled, bludgeoned, set on fire or thrown from roofs. In such a horrific bloodbath, what was one more?

But if that became the general attitude, the *accepted* attitude, society's attitude—"What's one more?"—then the murder of Frank Lombard was an incident of no significance. When plague strikes, who cares enough to mourn a single soul?

When Captain Edward X. Delaney explained to the newspaperman why he had become a cop, he said what he thought: that he believed there was an eternal harmony in the universe, in all things animate and inanimate, and that crime was a dissonance in the chiming of the spheres. That is what Delaney thought.

But now, playing his victim-killer game in the first raw attempt to understand what had happened and to begin a possible solution of this crime, he was sadly aware that he had a deeper motive, more felt than thought. He had never spoken of it to anyone, not even Barbara, although he suspected she guessed.

It was perhaps due to his Catholic nurture that he sought to set the world aright. He wanted to be God's surrogate on earth. It was, he knew, a shameful want. He recognized the sin. It was pride.

2

WHAT WAS it? He could not decipher its form or meaning. A frail thing there under white sheet and blue blanket, thin arms arranged outside. Heavy eyelids more stuck than shut, cheek bones poking, pale lips drawn back in a death's head grin, a body so frail it seemed even the blanket pressed it flat. And tubes, bandages, steel and plastic—new organs these—jars and drainage bags. He looked frantically for signs of life, stared, stared, saw finally a slow wearied rise and fall of breast no plumper than a boy's. He thought of the body of Frank Lombard and wondered, Where is the connection? Then realized he saw both through mist, his eyes damped and heavy.

"She's under heavy sedation," the nurse whispered, "but she's coming along just fine. Dr. Bernardi is waiting for you in the Surgeons' Lounge."

He searched for something he could kiss, a naked patch of skin free of tubes, needles, straps, bandages. All he wanted was to make a signal, just a signal. He bent to kiss her hair, but it was wire beneath his lips.

"I mentioned it," Bernardi said, inspecting his fingernails. Then he looked up at Delaney accusingly, daring him to deny it. "You'll remember I mentioned Proteus infection."

The Captain sat stolidly, craving sleep like an addict. They were at opposite sides of the card table in the Surgeons' Lounge. Cards were scattered across the surface, most of them face down but a queen of hearts showing, and a nine of spades.

"Proteus infection," Delaney repeated heavily. "How do you know?"

"That's what the lab tells us."

"And you think your lab is more knowledgeable than you and your associates who diagnosed my wife's illness as kidney stones?"

Again the opaque film coated the doctor's glistening eyes. His body stiffened, and he made a gesture Delaney had never seen him use before: he put the tip of his right forefinger in his right ear with the thumb stuck up in the air, exactly like a man blowing his brains out.

"Captain," he purred in his unctuous voice, "I assure you—"

"All right, all right," Delaney waved the apology away. "Let's not waste time. What is Proteus infection?"

Bernardi brightened, as he always did at an opportunity to display his erudition. Now he made his usual gesture of placing his index fingers together and pressing them against pouting lips.

"Proteus," he sang happily. "A Greek sea-god who could change his appearance at will. You should be interested in that, Captain. A million different shapes and disguises at will. That would complicate a policeman's task, would it not? He!"

Delaney grunted disgustedly. Bernardi paid no heed.

"And so the name was given to this particular infection. An infection is not an illness—but we needn't go into that. Suffice to say that Proteus infection frequently takes on the shape, appearance, form, and symptoms of a dozen other infections and illnesses. Very difficult to diagnose."

"Rare?" Delaney asked.

"Proteus rare?" the doctor said, eyebrows rising. "I would say no. But not too common. The literature is not extensive. That is what I was researching this morning, and why I did not return your calls. I was reading everything I could find on Proteus."

"What causes it?" Delaney asked, trying to keep the hatred out of his voice, to be as clinical and unemotional as this macaroni.

"I told you. Bacillus Proteus. B. Proteus. It exists in all of us. Usually in the intestinal tract. We have all kinds of good and bad little animalcules squiggling around inside us, you know. Sometimes, usually following an abdominal operation, B. Proteus goes on a rampage. Breaks loose. Sometimes in the urinary tract or in a specific organ. Rarely in the blood stream itself. The usual symptoms are high fever, chills, headaches, sometimes nausea. Which are—as I am certain you are aware—the symptoms of a dozen other infections. Proteus also causes certain changes in the blood, difficult to determine definitely. The recommended treatment for this infection is the employment of antibiotics."

"You tried that."

"True. But I assure you, Captain, I did not go through the entire spectrum. These so-called 'wonder drugs' are not all that wonderful. One of them may stifle a particular bacillus. At the same time it encourages the growth of another, more virulent bacillus. The antibiotics are not to be used lightly. In your wife's case, I believe the Proteus infection was triggered by her hysterectomy. But all the symptoms pointed to kidney stones, and there was nothing in the tests or plates to discourage that diagnosis. When Dr. Spencer got in there, we realized one kidney had to be removed. *Had* to. You understand?"

Delaney didn't answer.

"We saw there were still pockets of infection, small and scattered, that could not be removed by surgery. Now we must start again, hoping the main source of infection has been eliminated and we can clear up the remaining pockets with antibiotics."

"Hoping, doctor?"

"Yes. Hoping, Captain."

The two men stared at each other.

"She's dying, isn't she, doctor?"

"I wouldn't say that."

"No. You wouldn't."

He dragged to his feet, stumbled from the room.

Now I am the killer, Bacillus Proteus. I am in my wife's kidneys. I am . . .

He went back to the precinct house in hard afternoon sunlight. He thought he would be with her. He did not think he ought or should be with her, but that he would. He knew he could not attend her, for as long as it took, and still function efficiently as Captain Edward X. Delaney, New York

Police Department. On his old portable he typed out a letter to Deputy Inspector Ivar Thorsen, Patrol Division, asking immediate retirement. He filled out the "Request for Retirement" form and told Thorsen, in a personal note, that the request was due to his wife's illness. He asked his old friend to expedite the retirement papers. He sealed, stamped the envelope, walked down to the corner postbox and mailed it. Then he returned to his home and rolled onto his bed without undressing.

He slept for perhaps three minutes or eight hours. The brilliant ringing of the bedside phone brought him instantly awake.

"Captain Edward X. Delaney here."

"Edward, this is Ferguson. Did you talk to Bernardi?"

"Yes."

"I'm sorry, Edward."

"Thank you."

"The antibiotics might work. The main source of the infection is gone."

"I know."

"Edward, I woke you up."

"That's all right."

"I thought you might want to know."

"Know what?"

"The Lombard homicide. It wasn't a hammer."

"What was it?"

"I don't know. The skull penetration was about three to four inches deep. It was like a tapered cone. The outside hole, the entrance, was about an inch in diameter. Then it tapered down to a sharp point. Like a spoke. Do you want a copy of my report?"

"No. I've retired."

"What?"

"It's not my concern. I filed my retirement papers."

"Oh, Jesus. Edward, you can't. It's your life."

"I know."

Delaney hung up. Then he lay awake.

3

THREE DAYS later Captain Delaney received the telephone call he had been expecting: the assistant to Deputy Inspector Thorsen asked if he could meet with Thorsen that afternoon at four o'clock. Delaney went downtown via subway, wearing his uniform.

"Go right in, Captain," Thorsen's pretty secretary said when he gave his name. "They're expecting you."

Wondering who "they" might be, Delaney knocked once and pushed open the heavy oak door to Thorsen's office. The two men seated in leather club chairs rose to their feet, and the Deputy Inspector came forward smiling.

Ivar Thorsen was Delaney's "rabbi" in the Department. The term was current police slang for a superior officer or high official in city government who liked an officer personally, took an interest in his career, and generally guided and eased his advancement in rank. When a "rabbi" moved upward in the hierarchy, sooner or later his protege moved upward also.

Deputy Inspector Ivar Thorsen, a man in his late 50s, was called "The Admiral" by his subordinates, and it was easy to see why. Of relatively short stature, his body was slender and stringy, but all muscle and tendon; he bounced as he walked. His skin was fair and unblemished, features classically Nordic but without softness. His pale blue eyes could be distressingly piercing. The white hair seemed never combed but rigorously brushed until it hugged tightly the shape of his head from a leftside part that showed pink scalp.

He shook Delaney's hand, then turned to the other man in the room. "Edward, I think you know Inspector Johnson."

"I surely do. Good to see you, inspector."

"Likewise, Edward," the grinning black Buddha said. He extended a huge hand. "How you been?"

"Can't complain. Well . . . I can, but no one will listen."

"I know, I know," the big man chuckled, and his heavy belly moved up and down. "Wish we could get together more often, but they keep me chained to those damned computers, and I don't get uptown as often as I'd like."

"I read your analysis of arrest and conviction percentages."

"You did?" Johnson exclaimed with genuine pleasure. "You must be the only cop in town who did."

"Wait a minute, Ben," Thorsen protested. "I read it."

"The hell," the black scoffed. "You started it maybe, and read the last paragraph."

"I swear I read every word."

"I give you five-to-one you didn't—and I can ask questions to prove it."

"I'll take that bet."

"Misdemeanor," Delaney said promptly. "I can place you both under arrest. Gambling laws."

"Not so," Johnson shook his great head. "The courts have held a private wager between two gentlemen cannot be prosecuted under anti-gambling statutes. See *Harbiner v. the City of New York*."

"See *Plessy v. Novick*," Delaney retorted. "The court held a private unpaid wager between two persons cannot be a matter for judicial decision only because the wager itself was illegal."

"Come on," Thorsen groaned. "I didn't ask you here to argue law. Sit down." He waved them to the club chairs, then took the upholstered swivel chair behind his glass-topped desk. He flicked on his intercom. "Alice, please hold all incoming calls except emergency."

Inspector Johnson turned toward Delaney and regarded him curiously. "What did you think of my report, Edward?"

"The numbers were a shock, inspector. And the—"

"You know, Edward, if you called me Ben I really don't think I'd have you up for insolence and insubordination."

"All right, Ben. Well . . . the numbers were a shock, your analysis was brilliant, but I can't agree with your conclusion."

"What can't you agree with?"

"Suppose only five percent of felony arrests eventually produce convictions. From that you argue that we—the men on the beat—should make fewer arrests but better ones—arrests that will stand up in court. But aren't you disregarding the deterrent effect of mass arrests, even if we know the evidence will never stand up? The suspect may never be convicted, but after he goes through booking, a time in jail until he can raise bail—if he can— and the expense of a lawyer for his day in court, maybe he'll think twice before he strays again."

"Maybe, maybe not," Johnson rumbled. "I was aware of the deterrent angle when I wrote the report. As a matter of fact, I agree with it. But if I had come out recommending more arrests—whether or not they stood up in court—if I had recommended dragnet operations on prostitutes, drifters, homosexuals, gamblers—you know what would have happened? Some radical in the Department would have leaked that report to the press, and every civil liberties group would be down on our necks, and we'd be 'fascist pigs' all over again."

"You mean you tailored your convictions for the sake of public relations?"

"That's right," Johnson agreed blandly.

"Are public relations that important?"

"Got to be. For the Department. Your world is your own Precinct. My world is the Commissioner's office and, by extension, the Mayor's."

Delaney stared at the big black. Inspector Benjamin Johnson was on the Commissioner's staff, in charge of statistics and production analysis. He was an enormous man, a former All-American guard from Rutgers. He had gone to fat, but the result wasn't unpleasant; he still carried himself well, and his bulk gave him added dignity. His smile was appealing, almost childlike—a perfect disguise for what Delaney knew was a hard, complex, perceptive intelligence. A black didn't attain Johnson's rank and reputation by virtue of a hearty laugh and a mouthful of splendid teeth.

"Please," Thorsen raised a palm. "The two of you get together some night and fight it out over a beefsteak or soul food."

"Steak for me," Johnson said.

"I'll take the soul food," Delaney smiled.

"Let's get on with it," Thorsen said in his no-nonsense way. "First of all, Edward, how is Barbara feeling?"

Delaney came back to realities. He enjoyed "police talk" and could sit up all night arguing crime and punishment. But only with other cops. Civilians simply didn't *know*. Or perhaps it was like atheists arguing with priests. They were talking about different things, or in different languages. The atheist argued reason; the priest argued faith. In this case, the policeman was the atheist, the civilian the priest. Both were right and both were wrong.

"Barbara is not so good," he said steadily. "She hasn't snapped back from the operation the way she should—or at least the way I hoped she would. They've started her on antibiotics. The first didn't do a thing. They're trying another. They'll go on trying."

"I was sorry to hear your wife was ill, Edward," Johnson said quietly. "What exactly is it?"

"It's called Proteus infection. In her case it's an infection of the urinary tract. But the doctors wouldn't tell me a damned thing about how really ill she is and what her chances are."

"I know," Johnson nodded sympathetically. "The thing I hate most about doctors is when I go to one with a pain in my gut and explain exactly what the symptoms are, and the doctor says, 'That doesn't worry me.' Then I say, 'I know, goddamn it, it's *my* pain; why should it worry you'?"

Delaney smiled wanly, knowing Johnson was trying to cheer him up.

"I hate to hear about illnesses I never heard of before," Thorsen said. "There are so many things that can go wrong with the human body, it's a wonder any of us get through this life alive." Then, realizing what he had said and seeing the others' sad smiles, he added, "That's right—we don't, do we? Well, Edward, I have your application for retirement here. First of all let me confess, I haven't done a thing with it yet. It's perfectly in order. You have every right to retire if you wish. But we wanted to talk to you first. Ben, you want to take it from here?"

"No." Johnson shook his massive head. "You carry the ball."

"Edward, this concerns the Lombard homicide in your precinct. I know you know the man's reputation and the publicity he got and how important it is to the Department to come up with a quick solution and arrest. And, of course, it came in the middle of the reorganization of the Detective Division. Did you get the memo on the special task force Operation Lombard headed by Deputy Commissioner Broughton?"

Delaney paused before answering, wondering how much he should say. But Broughton was a slob—and what could the man do to him since he was retiring?

"Yes, I know," he nodded. "As a matter of fact, I suggested Operation Lombard to Broughton the morning of the murder. We had a private talk in his car."

Thorsen turned his head swiftly to look at Johnson. The two men stared at one another a moment. Then the inspector slammed a heavy palm down onto the arm of his leather chair.

"I told you," he said angrily. "I told you that stupid, racist son of a bitch didn't have the brains to come up with that idea himself. So it was you, Edward?"

"Yes."

"Well, don't expect a thank-you from brother Broughton. That bastard is strictly 'Hurray for me, fuck you.' He's flying mighty high right now."

"That's why we asked you here today, Edward," Thorsen said softly. "Broughton is flying high, and we'd like to bring him down."

Delaney looked from man to man, realizing he was getting involved in something he had vowed to avoid: the cliques and cabals that flourished in the upper echelons of the Department—and in all levels of government, and in the military, and in corporations, and in every human organization that had more than two members.

"Who is 'we'?" he asked cautiously.

"Inspector Johnson and myself, of course. And about ten or a dozen others, all of superior rank to us, who don't, for obvious reasons, want their names used at this time."

"What ranks?"

"Up to Commissioner."

"What are you trying to do?"

"First of all, we don't like Broughton. We believe he's a disgrace—hell, he's a catastrophe!—to the Department. He's amassing power, building a machine. This Operation Lombard is just another step up for him. If he can solve the murder."

"What motivates Broughton?" Delaney asked. "Ambition? What does he want? Commissioner? Mayor?"

Delaney looked at him, ready to laugh if Johnson was smiling. But he was not.

"Ben's not kidding, Edward. It's not impossible. Broughton is a relatively young man. He has an ego and hunger for power you wouldn't believe. Theodore Roosevelt went from the Commissioner's office to the White House. Why not Broughton? But even if he never gets to be President, or governor, or mayor, or even commissioner, we still want him out."

"Fascist bastard," Johnson grumbled.

"So . . .?" Delaney said.

"We have a plan. Will you listen to it?"

"I'll listen."

"I'm not even going to talk about discretion and all this being in strict confidence, etcetera. I know you too well for that. Edward, even if you retired today, you couldn't spend every waking hour with your wife. She's going to be in the hospital for the foreseeable future, isn't she?"

"Yes."

"If you retired today, you'd still have plenty of time on your hands. And I know you; after almost thirty years in the Department, you'd go nuts. All right . . . Now it's been three—no, almost four days since the Lombard homicide. It's been almost three days since the formation of Operation Lombard. Since then, Broughton has been drawing men and equipment from all over the city. He's built up a big organization, and it's still growing. I told you, the man's power-hungry. And I can also tell you that Broughton and Operation Lombard haven't come up with a thing. Not a lead, not a clue, not a single idea of how it was done, why it was done, and who did it. Believe me, Edward, they're no farther ahead at this moment than when you saw Lombard on the sidewalk."

"That doesn't mean they might not solve it tomorrow, tonight, or right now, while we're talking."

"True. And if Broughton brings it off, he'll crucify us. I mean Ben here and me and our friends. Broughton may be stupid, but he's shrewd. He knows who his enemies are. I tell you this man is capable of farming you out just because you suggested Operation Lombard from which he profited. He's the kind of man who can't stand to feel gratitude. He'll cut you down . . . somehow."

"He can't touch me. I'm retiring."

"Edward," Inspector Johnson said in a deep, throbbing voice, "suppose you didn't retire. Suppose you requested an indefinite leave of absence. We could swing it."

"Why should I do that?"

"It would relieve you of the responsibility of the Two-five-one. We'd put in an Acting Captain. An *Acting* Captain. You wouldn't be replaced. You agree it's possible your wife may recover faster than anyone expects, and then you'd want back to active duty? That's possible, isn't it?"

"Yes. It's possible."

"All right," Johnson said, seeming to look for words, to feel his way. "Now, say you're on leave of absence. You're relieved of responsibility. Now what we want you to do—" Then it all came out in rush: "Whatwewantyoutodoisfind Lombard'skiller."

"What?"

"You heard me. We want you to solve the Lombard homicide before Broughton and his Operation Lombard do it."

Delaney looked from man to man, astonished.

"Are you insane?" he finally demanded. "You want me, a single cop not even on active duty, working outside the Department like some kind of— some kind of private detective, you expect me to bring in Lombard's killer before five hundred or a thousand detectives and uniformed men and specialists with all the resources of the Department behind them? Impossible."

"Edward," Thorsen said patiently. "We think there's a chance. A small chance, true, but it's worth taking. Yes, you'd have to work in civilian clothes. Yes, you'd be by yourself; you couldn't request personnel from the Department, or equipment. But we'll set up a contact, and through the contact we'll make certain you got anything you'd need: print identification, evidence analysis, lab work, criminal records. Whatever you need, you'll get. We'll cover it somehow so Broughton doesn't get wind of it. If he does, we're all down the drain."

"Listen," Delaney said desperately, "is it only you two out to get

Broughton or are there really a dozen others all the way up to the Commissioner?"

"There are others," Thorsen said gravely, and Johnson nodded just as solemnly.

"It won't work," Delaney said definitely. He stood and began to pace back and forth, hands clasped behind him. "You know how many men you need for a homicide investigation like this? Men to search sewers. Men to dig in garbage cans. Men to ring doorbells and ask questions. Men to investigate Lombard's private life, his business life, his political life. Men to trace him back to the day he was born, trying to find an enemy. How in God's name could I—or any one man—do all that?"

"Edward," Johnson said softly, "you wouldn't have to do all that. That's what Operation Lombard is doing right now, and I swear to you, you'd get a Xerox copy of every report filed. Anytime a patrolman or detective or specialist puts anything down on paper about the Lombard off, you'll see a copy within twenty-four hours."

"That's a promise," Thorsen nodded. "Just don't ask how we'll do it."

"I won't, I won't," Delaney said hastily. "But just what more do you think I could do than Operation Lombard is doing right now?"

"Edward," Thorsen sighed, "don't put yourself down. I remember once I had dinner at your house, and we were talking about something you had done and let your division commander take the credit for—you were a lieutenant then—and Barbara got angry and told you that you should assert yourself more. She was right. Edward, you have a talent, a drive, a genius—call it whatever the hell you like—for investigative work. You know it but won't admit it. I know it and shout it every chance I get. It was my idea to bring you in on this, this way. If you say yes, fine. Then we'll go to work. If you say no, and want to go through with your retirement, okay and no hard feelings."

Delaney walked over to one of the windows and stared down into the crowded street. People were scurrying betwen honking cars in a traffic jam. There was bright movement, surge and thrust. He heard the horns, a siren, the far-off hoot of a liner putting to sea, the drone overhead of a plane slanting down to Kennedy Airport.

"No leads at all?" he asked, without turning around.

"None whatsoever," Thorsen said. "Not a thing. Not even a theory that makes sense. A blank. A complete blank. Broughton is beginning to show the strain."

Delaney turned around with a bleak smile. He looked at Inspector Johnson and spoke to him.

"Ben, I gave him the solution probability figures on homicide. You know how they drop off after forty-eight hours?"

"Yes," Johnson nodded. "It's been almost four days now, with probability dropping every minute for Broughton."

"For me too," Delaney said ruefully. "If I took this on," he added hastily.

He turned back to the window, his hands jammed into his pockets now. He wished with all his heart he could discuss this with Barbara, as he had discussed every important decision in his career. He needed her sharp, practical, aggressive, *female* intelligence to probe motives, choices, possibilities, safeguards. He tried, he strained to put himself in her place, to think as she might think and decide as she might decide.

"I'd be in civilian clothes," he said, his back to them. "Could I use my tin?"

"Yes," Johnson said immediately. "But as little as possible."

Delaney began to realize how completely they had thought this out, planned it, worried it for flaws, before they approached him.

"How often would I report?"

"As often as possible. Once a day or, if not, whenever you have something or a request for something."

"Who would I report to?"

"Me," Thorsen said promptly. "I'll give you a clean number."

"Don't tell me you think your home phone is tapped?"

"I'll give you a clean number," Thorsen repeated.

Delaney made up his mind and said what he thought Barbara would want him to say.

"If I'm on leave of absence but not retired, I can still be racked up on Departmental charges. If Broughton finds out about this, he'll fix me good. I met the man. I know what he is. I'll do what you want if I get a signed letter from either of you, or both of you, authorizing this investigation."

He turned to face them. They looked at him, then at each other.

"Edward . . ." Thorsen started, then stopped.

"Yes?"

"It's our ass."

"I know it. Without the letter, it's my ass. Mine alone. If Broughton discovers what's going on."

"Don't you trust—" Thorsen began.

"Now wait just one fat minute," Johnson held up his ham-hand. "Let's not get all riled here and start talking about trust and friendship and saying things we might be sorry for later. Just let me think a minute. Edward has a very good point, Ivar. It's something we didn't consider. Now just let me think and see if I can come up with something that will satisfy all the parties concerned."

He stared off into the middle distance, while the other two watched him expectantly. Finally Johnson grunted and heaved himself to his feet. He scrubbed his curly grey hair with knuckles, then motioned toward Thorsen. The two men went over to one corner and began to speak in low voices, Johnson doing most of the talking and gesturing frequently. Delaney took his seat again in the club chair and wished he was with his wife.

Finally the whispering ceased. The two men came over to stand before his chair.

"Edward," Johnson rumbled, "if we got a letter addressed to you personally, authorizing your unofficial or semi-official investigation into the death of Frank Lombard, and if this letter was signed by the Commissioner, would that satisfy you?"

Delaney looked up in amazement.

"The Commissioner? Why on earth would he sign a letter like that? He just appointed Broughton commander of Operation Lombard."

Inspector Johnson sighed heavily. "Edward, the Commish is a man of some ability. About a middleweight, I'd guess. And he's well-meaning and kind. All to the good. But this is the first time he's operated in New York. He's never had to keep afloat in a school of barracudas. Not the kind we got. He's learning—but the question is, will they give him time to learn? He's just beginning to realize a good executive has got to spend as much time protecting his ass as he does coping with the problems in front of him. Nine times out of ten, it's those strong, efficient executive assistants with the long knives who do a top man in. I think the Commissioner may just be starting to realize what Broughton is doing between those farts and belches. Broughton has some palsy-walsys on the Mayor's staff, you know. There's also another factor. This is something never talked about in business management manuals, but it exists in the Department, in federal, state and local government, in business, and in the military. I think the Commissioner is physically frightened of Broughton. I can't give you any evidence, but that's what I feel. It was the source of a lot of Joe McCarthy's power. Plenty of those old, frail Senators were physically afraid of Joe. Well, we've got a man, a friend—real Machiavelli type—a Deputy the Commissioner trusts who could maybe put a bug in his ear. 'Look Commissioner, Broughton is a fine fellow—a little crude for my taste but he gets things done—and maybe he'll bring off this Operation Lombard thing and find the killer. But look, Commissioner, wouldn't it be wise to have an ace in the hole? I mean if Broughton falls on his face, you really should have a back-up plan in the works. Now it just so happens I've got this smartass Captain who right now is on leave of absence, and this smart-ass Captain is the best detective this town ever saw, and if you ask him nice, Commissioner, and write him a po-lite letter, this smart-ass Captain just might be willing to smell around and find Frank Lombard's killer for you. Without Broughton knowing a thing about it, of course.'"

Delaney laughed. "Do you think he'll go for that? Do you really think he'll give me a letter of authorization?"

"If we git it, will you do it?"

"Yes."

4

THE FOLLOWING evening, as he was preparing to leave for the hospital, an envelope was delivered to his home by commercial messenger. The envelope contained a letter signed by the Commissioner, authorizing Captain Edward X. Delaney to undertake a "discreet inquiry" into the homicide of Frank Lombard. There was also a letter signed by the Chief of Patrol granting Captain Delaney an indefinite leave of absence "for personal reasons." Delaney began to appreciate the clout swung by Thorsen, Johnson, and their friends.

He was about to call Ivar Thorsen from his home, but after dialing two digits he hung up and sat a moment, staring at the phone. He remembered the Deputy Inspector had stressed that the number he had been given was "clean". He pulled on his overcoat, walked two blocks to a public phone booth and called from there. The "clean" number proved to be an answering service. He gave only his last name and the number of the phone he was calling from. Then he hung up and waited patiently. Thorsen was back to him within three minutes.

"I got the papers," Delaney said. "Quick work."

"Yes. Where are you calling from."

"A public phone booth two blocks from my house."

"Good. Keep doing that. Use different booths."

"All right. Have you made any decision on an Acting Captain?"

"Not yet. Any suggestions?"

"I have a lieutenant. Dorfman. Know him?"

"No. But a *lieutenant*? I'm not sure we can swing it. That's a boss precinct, Edward. It should have a captain or deputy inspector. I don't believe there's any precedent for a lieutenant commanding a precinct."

"Consider it, will you? Look up Dorfman's file. Four commendations. A good administrator. A fine lawyer."

"Can he hack it?"

"We'll never know until he gets the chance, will we? There's another thing."

"What's that?"

"He trusts me. More than that, he likes me. He'd make a perfect contact. The man to handle the requests I'll have for records, print identification, research, lab analysis, things like that. It could be shuffled in with the usual precinct paper. No one could spot it."

"How much would you tell him?"

"As little as possible."

There was a silence.

"There's another factor," Delaney said quickly. "I gave Broughton the idea for Operation Lombard and the homicide was in my precinct. It would be natural for him to think I was pissed-off and jealous. He'll be suspicious of any possible interference from me. I'm guessing how his mind works from what you and Johnson told me about him."

"You guess right."

"Well, he'll hear I've gone on leave of absence, and he'll relax. He'll relax even more if he hears Dorfman has been appointed Acting Captain. A *lieutenant*? And a man with no detective experience? Broughton will cross off my old Precinct as a potential trouble spot, and I'll be able to use Dorfman as a contact with little possibility of discovery."

"It's a thought," Thorsen said. "And a good one. Let me discuss it with—with others. Maybe we can swing it. I'll get back to you. Anything else?"

"Yes. I know Broughton came out of patrol. Who's strawboss of his detectives on Operation Lombard?"

"Chief Pauley."

"Oh God. He's good."

"You're better."

"Keep telling me that. I need all the reassurance I can get."

"When are you starting?"

"As of now."

"Good. You'll have the Xerox tomorrow. You understand?"

"Yes."

"Keep me informed."

The two men hung up without saying goodby.

Delaney took a cab to the hospital, pressed back into a corner of the rear seat, biting at his thumbnail. He was beginning to feel the old, familiar excitement. Forget his reasoning and emotions about police work. His gut reaction was obvious: the chase was on and he was the hunter.

He came into her room smiling determinedly, taking from his pocket a silly little thing he had bought her: a cheap, brilliant brooch, a rhinestoned penguin she could pin to her hospital gown. She held her arms out to him; he bent to embrace her.

"I was hoping you'd come."

"I told you I would. Better?"

She smiled brightly and nodded.

"Here." He handed her the penguin. "From Tiffany's. A little over a hundred thousand."

"Beautiful," she laughed. "What I've always wanted."

He helped her pin it to the shoulder of her gown. Then he took off his overcoat, pulled a chair over to the bed, sat down and took one of her hands in his.

"Truly better?"

"Truly. I think I should start seeing people. Some close friends."

"Good," he said, being careful to avoid false heartiness. "Eddie will be up next week. What about Liza?"

"No, Edward. Not in her condition. Not yet."

"All right. Shall I call your friends?"

"I'll do it. Most of them I want to see call me every day. I'll tell them I'd like to see them. You know—two or three a day. Not everyone at once."

He nodded approvingly and looked down at her smiling. But her appearance shocked him. She was so thin! The tubes and jars were gone, her face was flushed with the familiar fever, but the frailty was what tore his heart. She who had always been so active, strong, vibrant . . . Now she lay flaccid and seemed to strain for breath. The hand he was not holding picked weakly at blanket fluff.

"Edward, are you eating all right?"

"Fine."

"Sticking to your diet?"

"I swear."

"What about sleep?"

He held out a hand, palm down, then turned it over, then flipped it back and forth a few times.

"So-so. Listen, Barbara, there's something I must tell you. I want to—"

"Has something happened? Are the children all right?"

"The children are fine. This doesn't concern them. But I want to talk to you for about an hour. Maybe more. It won't tire you, will it?"

"Of course not, silly. I've been sleeping all day. I can tell you're excited. What is it?"

"Well . . . four days ago—actually early in the morning following your operation—there was a homicide in my precinct."

He described to her, as concisely and completely as he could, the discovery and appearance of Frank Lombard's body. Then he went on to tell her how important it was to solve Lombard's murder in view of the man's public criticism of the Department, and how the current reorganization of the Detective Division hampered efficient handling of the case. Then he described his private talk with Deputy Commissioner Broughton.

"He sounds like a horrible man!" she interrupted.

"Yes . . . Anyway, the next day I filed for retirement."

She came up from the bed in shock, then fell back, her eyes filling with tears.

"Edward! You didn't?"

"Yes. I wanted to spend more time with you. I thought it was the right decision at the time. But it didn't go through. This is what happened . . ."

He recounted his meeting with Deputy Inspector Thorsen and Inspector Johnson. He detailed their plan for Delaney to make an independent investigation of the Lombard homicide, in an effort to humiliate Broughton. As he spoke, he could see Barbara come alive. She propped herself on one elbow and leaned forward, eyes shining. She was the politician of the family and dearly loved hearing accounts and gossip of intra-Departmental feuding, the intrigues and squabbles of ambitious men and factions.

Delaney told her how he had demanded a letter of authorization from a superior officer before he would agree to the Lombard investigation.

"Barbara, do you think I did the wise thing?"

"You did exactly right," she said promptly. "I'm proud of you. In that jungle, the first law is 'Save yourself.'"

Then he told her about receiving the Commissioner's letter, the authorization of indefinite leave of absence, and his most recent conversation with Thorsen.

"I'm glad you recommended Dorfman," she nodded happily. "I like him. And I think he deserves a chance."

"Yes. The problem is making a lieutenant even an *acting* commander of a precinct. And of course they can't suddenly promote him without possibly alerting Broughton. Well . . . we'll see what happens. Meanwhile, I'll be getting copies of all the Operation Lombard reports tomorrow."

"Edward, it doesn't sound like you have much to go on."

"No, not much. Thorsen says that so far Operation Lombard has drawn a blank. They don't have any description of a possible suspect, how he killed, or why he killed."

"You say 'he.' Couldn't it have been a woman?"

"Possibly, but the probability percentages are against it. Women murder with gun, knife, and pistol. They rarely bludgeon. And when they do, it's usually when the victim is asleep."

"Then you're really starting from scratch?"

"Well . . . I have two things. They don't amount to much and I expect Chief Pauley has them too. Lombard was a tall man. I'd guess about six feet. Now look . . ." Delaney rose to his feet and looked around the hospital room. He found a magazine, rolled it up tightly, and gripped one end. "Now I'm the killer with a hammer, a pipe, or maybe a long spike. I'm striking down at the victim's skull." He raised the magazine above his head and brought it down viciously. "See that? I'll do it again. Watch the position of my right arm." Again he raised the magazine and brought it down in a feigned crushing blow. "What did you see?"

"Your arm wasn't extended. Your right arm was bent. The top of the magazine was only about six inches above your head."

"Correct. That's the way a man would normally strike. When you're hammering in a nail, you don't raise your arm to its full length above your head; you keep your elbow bent the better to control the accuracy of the blow. You raise your arm just high enough to provide what you estimate to be sufficient force. It's an unconscious skill, based on experience. To drive a carpet tack, you might raise a hammer only an inch or two. To drive a spike, you'd raise the hammer to your head level or higher."

"Was Lombard killed with a hammer?"

"Ferguson says no. But it was obviously something swung with sufficient force to penetrate his brain to a depth of three to four inches. I haven't seen Ferguson's report yet."

"Could the killer be lefthanded?"

"Could be. But probability is against it, unless the nature and position of the wound indicate otherwise, and then it might be due to the position of the victim at the moment of impact."

"There are so many possibilities."

"There surely are. Barbara, are you getting tired?"

"Oh no. You can't stop now. Edward, I don't understand the significance of what you just showed me—how a man strikes with his elbow bent."

"Just that Lombard was about six feet tall. If the killer raised the weapon about six inches above his own head—which is about the limit any man would raise a tool or weapon before striking downward—and the puncture was low on Lombard's skull (not so far down as to be in that hollow where the spine joins the skull, but up from that toward the crown of the skull), then I'd guess the killer to be approximately of Lombard's height or maybe a few inches taller. Yes, it's a guess. But based, it seems to me, on what little physical evidence is available. And I've got to start guessing *somewhere*."

"You said you had two things, Edward. What's the other?"

"Well . . . I worked this out the morning of the murder. While I was on the scene. Just to satisfy my own curiosity, I guess. What bothered me most about the murder was why a man of Lombard's size and strength, with his awareness of street crime, alone on a deserted street at midnight, why he would let an assailant come up behind him and chop him down without making any apparent effort to defend himself. Here's how I think it was done . . ."

He acted it out for her. First he was Lombard, in his overcoat, walking briskly around the hospital room, head turning side to side as he inspected entrances and outside lobbies. "Then I see a man coming toward me from York Avenue. Coming *toward* me." Delaney-Lombard, explaining as he performed, peeked ahead, watching the approaching figure. He slowed his steps, ready to defend himself or run to safety if danger threatened. But then he smiled, reassured by the stranger's appearance. He moved aside to let the smiling stranger pass, and then . . .

"Now I'm the killer," Delaney told a wide-eyed Barbara. He took off his overcoat and folded it over his left arm. Beneath the coat, hidden, the rolled up magazine was grasped in his left hand. His right arm swung free as he marched briskly around the hospital room. "I see the man I want to kill. I smile and continue to walk quickly like a resident of the block anxious to get home."

Delaney-killer turned his head as he passed Lombard. Then his right hand swooped under the coat. The rolled-up magazine was transferred. At the same time Delaney-killer whirled and went up on his toes. Now he was behind the victim. The magazine whistled down. The entire action took a few seconds, no longer.

"Then I bend over—"

"Get him!" Barbara cried. "Edward, get him! Get him!"

He straightened in astonishment, riven by the hatred and venom in her voice. He rushed to the bed, tried to take her in his arms, but she would not be comforted.

"Get him!" she repeated, and it was a curse. "You can do it, Edward. You're the only one who can do it. Get him! Promise me? It's not right. Life is too precious. Get him! Get him!"

And even after he calmed her, a nurse had been summoned, a sedative had been administered, Barbara was sleeping, and he left the hospital, still he heard that virulent "Get him! Get him!" and vowed he would.

5

XEROX COPIES of the Operation Lombard reports constituted a bundle of almost 500 sheets of typed papers, official forms, photostats, transcriptions of tape recordings, signed statements, etc. In addition, there was a separate envelope of more than 30 photo copies: Lombard in death and in life, his wife, mother, two brothers, political and business associates, and close friends. The dead man and his wife had been childless.

Captain Delaney, impressed with this mass of material spread out on the desk in his study, and realizing the urgency with which Operation Lombard was working, set out to organize the documents into manila folders marked Physical Evidence, Personal History, Family, Business (Lombard had been an active partner in a Brooklyn law firm), Politics, and Miscellaneous.

It took him almost two hours to get the material filed in some kind of rough order. Then he mixed a rye highball, put his feet up on the desk, and began reading. By two in the morning he had read every report and stared at every photo in every file. He was doubly impressed with the thoroughness of Broughton's investigation, but as far as first impressions went, Ivar Thorsen was right: there was nothing—no leads, no hints, no mysteries at all—except who killed Frank Lombard.

He started his second reading, going slower this time and making notes on a pad of long yellow legal notepaper. He also set aside a few documents for a third reading and study. Dawn was lightening the study windows when he closed the final folder. He rose to his feet, stretched and yawned, put his hands on his hips and bent his torso backward until his spine cracked.

Then he went into the kitchen and drank a large glass of tomato juice with a lemon wedge squeezed into it. He made a carafe of three cups of instant coffee, black, and carried that into the study along with a dry and stale bagel.

He consulted his notes and, sipping coffee, read for the third time Dr. Sanford Ferguson's medical report. It was one of Ferguson's usual meticulous autopsies; the eight-page statement included two sketches showing the outside wound in actual size and a profile outline of the human skull showing the location and shape of the penetration. It looked like an elongated isosceles triangle. The outside wound was roughly circular in shape, slightly larger than a quarter.

The essential paragraph of the report was as follows:

"The blow caused a penetrating wound, fracturing the right occipital bone, lacerating the dura, piercing the right occipital lobe. Laceration of the cerebellum caused hemorrhaging with resultant rupture into the posterior fossa and 4th ventrical causing acute compression of the brain stem with subsequent death."

Delaney made several additional notes on the autopsy report. He had questions he knew could only be answered in a personal interview with Ferguson. How he would explain to the doctor his interest in the Lombard homicide was a problem he'd face when he came to it.

His other notes concerned the interviews with the widow, Mrs. Clara Lombard. She had been interviewed five times by three different detectives. Delaney nodded approvingly at Chief Pauley's professionalism. It was standard detective procedure: you send three different detectives for the first three interviews. Then the three get together with their chief, discuss the subject's personality, and select the detective who has established the closest rapport with her, the one she feels most *simpatico* with. He returns for the two final interviews.

Delaney began to get a picture of the widow from the typed reports. (The first three were transcriptions made from tape recordings.) Mrs. Clara Lombard seemed to be a flighty, feather-brained woman, trying hard to appear devastated by the tragedy of her husband's violent death, but still capable of infantile laughter, jokes of a dubious nature, sudden inquiries about insurance money, questions about probating the will, illlogical threats of legal action against New York City, and statements that could only be construed as outright flirtation.

Delaney wasn't interested in all that; careful investigation showed that although Clara was a very social woman—a happy party-goer with or without her husband—she had no boyfriend, and no one, not even her women friends, even hinted she might have been unfaithful.

The portion of her testimony that interested Delaney most was concerned with Frank Lombard's wallet. That damned wallet irritated the Captain . . . its position near the body . . . the fact that it had been deliberately removed from the hip pocket . . . it was lying open . . . it was still full of money . . .

To Delaney's surprise, in only one interview had Mrs. Lombard been handed a detailed inventory of the wallet. This document was included in the Physical Evidence file. Clara had been asked if, to her knowledge, anything was missing. She had replied no, she thought all her late husband's identification and credit cards were there, and the sum of money—over two hundred dollars—was what he customarily carried. Even two keys, one to his home, one to his office—in a "secret pocket" in the wallet—were there.

Delaney didn't accept her statement. How many wives could tell you exactly what their husbands carried in their wallets? How many husbands could list exactly what their wife's purse contained? As a matter of fact, how many men knew exactly how much money they had in their own wallets? To test this, Delaney thought a moment and guessed he had fifty-six dollars in the wallet in his hip. Then he took it out and counted. He had forty-two— and wondered where his money was going.

The only other Operation Lombard report that interested him was an interview with the victim's grieving mother. Delaney read this transcription again. As he had suspected, Mrs. Sophia Lombard lived in a converted brownstone between the East River and the point where her son's body had been found.

Mrs. Lombard had been questioned— and very adroitly, Delaney acknowledged; that was Chief Pauley's doing—on the circumstances of her son's visits to her. Did he come every week? The same night every week? The same time every night? In other words, was it a regular, established routine? Did he call beforehand? How did he travel over from Brooklyn?

The answers were disappointing and perplexing. Frank Lombard had no regular schedule for dining with his mother. He came to see her when he could. Sometimes two weeks, sometimes a month would elapse before he could make it. But he was a good boy, Mrs. Sophia Lombard assured her interrogator; he called every day. On the day he could come to dinner, he would call before noon so Mrs. Lombard could go out and shop in the markets along First Avenue for the things he liked.

Lombard didn't drive his car over from Brooklyn because parking space was hard to find near his mother's apartment. He would take the subway, and a bus or taxi from the subway station. He didn't like to walk on the streets at nights. He always left for his Brooklyn home before midnight.

Did Mrs. Clara Lombard ever accompany her husband to his mother's home for dinner?

"No," Mrs. Sophia Lombard said shortly. And reading that reply, Delaney smiled, understanding the discord that must have existed in *that* family.

Delaney replaced the reports in their folders, and put all the Operation Lombard file in a small safe in the corner of the study. As he well knew, an experienced "can man" could be into that in one minute flat. And two inexperienced thieves could carry it out between them to sledge it open later.

His eyes were sandy and his bones ached. It was almost seven A.M. He dumped the cold coffee, went upstairs, undressed and rolled into bed. Something was nagging at his mind, something he had read in the Operation Lombard reports. But that had happened to him frequently: a lead sensed but not recognized. It didn't worry him; he tried not to think about it. He knew from experience that it would come to him eventually, sliding into his mind like a remembered name or a tune recalled. He set the alarm for eight-thirty, closed his eyes and was instantly asleep.

He arrived at the precinct house a little after nine A.M. The Desk Sergeant was a policewoman, the second of her rank in New York to be assigned to such duty. He went over to the log with her, and asked questions. She was a tall, powerfully built woman with what he termed to himself, without knowing why, a *thunderous* body. In truth, he was intimidated by her, but could not deny her efficiency. The book was in order; nothing had been neglected that could have been done – a sad, sad list of drunks, missing persons, beaten wives, stolen welfare checks, mistreated children, burglaries, Peeping Toms, prostitutes, dying oldsters, homosexuals, breaking-and-entering, exhibitionists . . . People. But the moon was full, and Delaney knew what that meant.

He climbed the creaking wooden steps to his office and, on the landing, met Detective Lieutenant Jeri Fernandez who was, or had been, in command of detectives assigned to the 251st.

"Morning, Captain," Fernandez said glumly.

"Good morning, lieutenant," Delaney said. He looked at the man sympathetically. "Having a rough time, aren't you?"

"Oh shit!" Fernandez burst out. "Half my men are gone already. The others will be gone within a week. Okay, that's one thing. But the paper work! All our open cases have to be transferred to the proper unit covering this precinct. Jesus, it's a mess."

"What did you get?"

"I drew a Safe, Loft and Truck Division in midtown," Fernandez said disgustedly. "It covers four precincts including the Garment Center. How does that grab you? I'm second in command, and we'll be getting dicks from all over Manhattan. It'll take us at least a year to set up our snitches. What great brain dreamed up this idea?"

Delaney knew how Fernandez felt. The man was a conscientious, efficient, but unimaginative detective. He had done a good job in the 251st, training his men, being hard when he had to be hard and soft when he had to be soft. Now they were breaking up his crew and farming them out to specialized divisions. And Fernandez himself would now be number two man under a detective captain. He had a right to his anger.

"I would have guessed Broughton would have grabbed you for Operation Lombard," Delaney said.

"Not me," Fernandez said with a sour grin. "I ain't white enough."

They nodded and separated. Delaney went on to his office, marveling how quickly a man's prejudices and record spread throughout the Department. More fool Broughton, he thought; Fernandez could have been a big help. Unimaginative he might have been, but when it came to dull, foot-flattening routine, he was excellent. The important thing was to know how to use men, to take advantage of their particular talents and the best in them.

The moment he was at his desk he called the hospital. The head floor nurse told him his wife was down in the lab, having more X-ray plates taken, but she was doing "as well as can be expected." Trying to conceal his distaste for that particular phrase, Delaney thanked her and said he'd call later.

Then he called Dr. Sanford Ferguson and, unexpectedly, was put through to him immediately at his office.

"That you, Edward?"

"Yes. Can we get together?"

"How's Barbara?"

"Doing as well as can be expected."

"I seem to recognize the words. Is it about Barbara you want to see me?"

"No. The Lombard homicide."

"Oh? I was glad to hear you hadn't retired. Now it's an indefinite leave of absence."

"News travels fast."

"It was on the Telex about ten minutes ago. Edward, what's this about Lombard? I thought Broughton was handling it."

"He is. But I want to see you, to talk to you. Can you make it?"

"Well . . ." Ferguson was cautious, and Delaney didn't blame him. "Look, I've got to go up to 34th Street today. It's my sister's birthday, and I want to get her something. At Macy's. Any suggestions?"

"When in doubt, a gift certificate."

"Won't work. I know her. She wants something personal."

"A silk scarf. That's what I always buy for Barbara. She's got enough silk scarves to make a parachute."

"Good idea. Well then, how about lunch?"

"Fine."

"I know a good chop house near Macy's. Do you like mutton chops?"

"Hate them."

"Idiot. That heavy, gamy taste . . . nothing like it."

"Can I get a broiled kidney?"

"Of course."

"Then let's have lunch at your chop house."

"Good. You get there at twelve-thirty. I'll be finished shopping by then and will be there before you. Ask the head waiter for my table. He knows me. It will be in the bar, not the main dining room. All right?"

"Of course. Thank you."

"For what? I haven't done anything for you yet."

"You will."

"Will I? In that case you're paying for the lunch."

"Done," Captain Edward X. Delaney said.

Ferguson gave him the address of the chop house and they hung up.

"Oysters!" Ferguson boomed happily. "I definitely recommend the oysters. The horse-radish is freshly ground. Then I'll have the mutton chop."

"Very good, sir," the waiter said.

"Oysters for me also," Delaney nodded. "Then I'll have the broiled kidney. What comes with that?"

"Home-fries and salad, sir."

"Skip the potatoes, please. Just the salad. Oil and vinegar."

"I'll have everything," Ferguson cried, and drained half his martini.

"What did you buy your sister?" Delaney asked.

"A silk scarf. What else? Come on, Edward, what's this all about? You're on leave of absence."

"Do you really want to know?"

Dr. Sanford Ferguson was suddenly sober and quiet. He stared at Delaney a long moment. "No," he said finally. "I really don't want to know. Except . . . will my name be brought into it?"

"I swear to you—no."

"That's good enough for me."

Their oysters were brought, and they looked down at them, beaming. They went through the business with the horse-radish sauce and the hot stuff. They swallowed, looked at each other, groaned with pleasure.

"All right," Ferguson said. "What do you want?"

"About your report on the Lombard—"

"How did you get my report?"

Delaney looked at him steadily. "You said you didn't want to know."

"That's right; I don't. All right, what about the report?"

"I have a few questions." Delaney took a short list out of his side pocket, put it on the cloth before him, donned his heavy glasses, consulted it, then leaned toward Ferguson.

"Doctor," he said earnestly, "your official reports are most complete. I don't deny it. But they're couched in medical language. As they should be, of course," he added hastily.

"So?"

"I have some questions about what your medical terms mean."

"Edward, you're jiving me."

"Well . . . really what the significance is."

"That's better," Ferguson smiled. "You can read a PM as well as a third-year medical student."

"Yes. Also, I happen to know, doctor, that you include in your official reports only that which you objectively observe and which could be substantiated by any other capable surgeon doing the identical post-mortem. I also know that in an autopsy—in *any* investigation—there are impressions, feelings, hunches—call them what you like—that can never be part of an official report because the physical evidence doesn't exist. And it's those impressions, feelings and hunches that I want from you."

Ferguson slipped a dipped oyster into his mouth, swallowed, rolled his eyes.

"You're a bastard, Edward," he said amiably. "You really are a bastard. You'll use anyone, won't you?"

"Yes," Delaney nodded. "I'll use anyone. Any time."

"Let's start from word one," Ferguson said, busily stirring his oyster sauce. "Let's start with head wounds. Much experience?"

"No. Not much."

"Edward, the human skull and the human brain are tougher beyond your comprehension. Ever read a detective novel or see a movie where a man has a single bullet fired into his head and dies instantly? Practically impossible. I've had cases of victims with five bullets in their heads who lived. They were vegetables, true, but they lived. Three years ago I had a would-be suicide who fired a bullet at his head with a low calibre revolver. Twenty-two, I think. The slug bounced off his skull and hit the ceiling. Literally. Commit suicide by firing a bullet into your temple? Forget it. The slug could pass completely through, come out the other side, and you still wouldn't be dead. You might live hours, weeks, or years. Maybe you couldn't talk, or move, or control your bowels, but you'd be alive. How are your oysters, Edward?"

"Very good. Yours?"

"Marvelous. There's only one way of committing sure suicide—instan-taneous suicide—by a gunshot to the head. That's by using a pistol or revolver of reasonably heavy calibre, say a thirty-eight at least—a rifle or shotgun would do as well, of course—put the muzzle deep into your mouth aimed at the back of your head, close your lips and teeth firmly about the barrel, pull the trigger, and splatter your brains onto the opposing wall. Some of these little oysterettes, Edward?"

"Yes, thank you."

"Now about the Lombard homicide. The entry was made from the back, low on the crown. About halfway to where the spine joins the skull. The only other spot where death might be instantaneous."

"You think the killer had a surgeon's knowledge?"

"Oh God, no," Ferguson said, signaling the waiter to remove their emptied oyster plates. "Yes, to hit that spot deliberately would require a surgeon's experience. But the victim would have to be on an operating table. No killer swinging a weapon violently could hope to hit it. It was luck. The killer's luck, not Lombard's luck."

"Was death instantaneous?" Delaney asked.

"Close to it. If not instant, then within a few seconds. A half-inch to the right or left and the man might have lived for hours or weeks."

"It was that close?"

"I told you the human skull and brain are much tougher than most people realize. Do you know how many ex-soldiers are walking around today with hunks of shrapnel in their brains? They live normally, except for occasional crushing headaches, but we can't operate. And they'll live out their normal lives and die from smoking too many cigarettes or eating too much cheese."

The mutton chop, broiled kidney, and salads were served. Ferguson got his home-fries, a big plate with plenty of onions. After consultation with the head waiter, who was 343 years old, they ordered a bottle of heavy burgundy.

"To get back to Lombard," Delaney said, digging into his broiled kidney, "was it really a circular wound?"

"Oh you're so smart," Ferguson said without rancor. "You're so fucking smart. My report stated it *appeared* to be a circular penetration. But I had the impression it could have been triangular. Or even square. Look, Edward, you've never probed a brain penetration. You think it's like pounding a spike into modeling clay, and then you pull out the spike and you've got a nice, clean perfect cavity? It's nothing like that. The wound fills up. Brain matter presses in. There is blood. Bits of bone. Hair. All kinds of crap. And you expect me to— How's the kidney?"

"Delicious," Delaney said. "I've been here before, but I forgot how much bacon they give you."

"The mutton chop is fine," Ferguson said, dipping into his little dish of applesauce. "I'm really enjoying this. But about that Lombard wound . . . In addition to the impression I had that the opening was not necessarily circular in shape, I also had the feeling that the penetration curved downward."

"Curved?"

"Yes. Like a limp cone. The tip of the weapon lower than the shaft. A curve. Like a hard-on just beginning to go soft. You understand?"

"Yes. But why are you so uncertain about the shape of the wound and the shape of the penetration? I know what you wrote, but what do you guess?"

"I think, I *guess* that Lombard fell forward with such force that it wrenched the weapon out of the killer's hand. And that the killer then bent forward and twisted his tool or weapon to remove it from Lombard's skull. If the spike was triangular or square, the twisting would result in a roughly circular shape."

"And it would mean the weapon was valuable to the killer," Delaney said. "He took the time to recover it. It was valuable intrinsically, or valuable because it might be traced to the killer. Murderers who use a hammer or pipe or rock usually wear gloves and leave the weapon behind."

"Beautiful," Dr. Ferguson said, draining his wine. "I love to listen to you think."

"I'm glad it wasn't a hammer," Delaney said. "I never really believed it was."

"Why not?"

"I've handled three hammer cases. In two of them the handle broke. In the third, the head snapped off."

"So you knew how tough the human skull is? But you let me talk."

"That's the name of the game. Anything else?"

"What else? Nothing else. It's all smoke. On the evidence, the penetration was circular, but it might have been triangular. It might have been square. It hit the one spot that killed the man instantly. Do I think the killer has surgical knowledge? No. It was a lucky hit."

"Dessert?" Delaney asked.

"Just coffee for me, thanks."

"Two coffees, please," Delaney ordered. "Any ideas, any guesses, any wild suggestions at all as to what the weapon might have been?"

"None whatsoever."

"Was there anything inside the wound you didn't expect to find? Anything that wasn't in your report?"

Ferguson looked at him sternly a moment, then relaxed and laughed. "You never give up, do you? There were traces of oil."

"Oil? What kind of oil?"

"Not enough for analysis. But undoubtedly hair oil. The rest of his hair was heavily oiled, so I assume the oil in the wound came from the hair driven into it."

"Anything else?"

"Yes. Since you're paying, I'll have a brandy."

After Ferguson took a cab back to his office, Delaney walked slowly toward Sixth Avenue. He realized he was only a few blocks from the flower market and sauntered down there. He was in no hurry. He knew from experience that each investigation had a pace of its own. Some shouted of a quick solution and were wrapped-up in hours. Others had the feel of slow growth and the need for time. The Lombard homicide was one of those. He consoled himself that Broughton, who *was* in a hurry, was getting nowhere. But was he doing any better? As Dr. Ferguson had said, it was all smoke.

He found what he was looking for in the third flower shop he visited: violets, out of season. They were the flowers with which he had courted Barbara. They were sold by street vendors in those days, old ladies with baskets next to old men selling chestnuts. He would buy a bunch for Barbara and ask, "Fresh roasted violets, lady?" She was always kind enough to laugh. Now he bought the last two bunches the store had and took a cab to the hospital.

But when he tiptoed into her room she was sleeping peacefully and he didn't have the heart to awaken her. He unwrapped the violets and looked around the room for something to put them in, but there was nothing. Finally he sat in the straight chair, his uniformed bulk overflowing it. He grasped the tender violets in his big fist and waited quietly, watching his wife sleep. He glanced once at the dusty windows. The sharp November sunlight was diluted and softened.

Perhaps, the sad, hunkering man wondered, a marriage was like one of those stained glass windows he had seen in a modest village church in France. From the outside, the windows were almost opaque with the dirt and grime of centuries. But when you went inside, and saw the sunlight leaping through, diffused by the dust, the colors struck into your eye and heart with their boldness and purity, their youth and liveliness.

His marriage to Barbara, he supposed, must seem dull and dusty to an outsider. But seen from within, as father of a family, it was all bright and beguiling, touching and, finally, holy and mysterious. He watched his wife sleep and *willed* his strength to her, making her whole and laughing again. Then, unable to endure his thoughts, he stood and placed the violets on her bedside table with a scribbled note: "Fresh roasted violets, lady?"

When he got back to his office, Dorfman was waiting for him with a sheet of paper torn from the Telex.

"Captain," he said in a choked voice, and Delaney was afraid he might weep, "is this—"

"Yes, lieutenant, it's correct. As of now, I'm on leave of absence. Come on in and let's talk about it."

Dorfman followed him inside and took the scarred chair next to Delaney's desk.

"Captain, I had no idea your wife was so ill."

"Well, as far as I can guess, it's going to be a long haul, and I wanted to spend as much time with her as possible,"

"Is there anything I can do?"

"Thank you, no. Well, perhaps there is something. You might call her. I have a feeling she'd like to see you. Whenever you can spare the time."

"I'll call her right away," Dorfman cried.

"Wait a few hours. I've just come from there, and she's sleeping."

"I'll call just before my watch ends. Then if she wants to see me, I can go right over. What can I bring—flowers, candy, what?"

"Oh nothing, thanks. She has everything she needs."

"Maybe a cake?" Dorfman said. "A nice cake. She can share it with the nurses. Nurses love cake."

"Fine," Delaney smiled. "I think she'd like a cake from you."

"Captain," Dorfman mourned, his long horse-face sagging again, "I suppose this means we'll be getting an Acting Captain?"

"Yes."

"Do you have any idea who it will be, sir?"

Delaney debated a moment, briefly ashamed of manipulating a man so honest and sincere. But it was the sensible thing to do, to cement Dorfman's trust and affection.

"I recommended you for the job, lieutenant," he said quietly.

Dorfman's pale blue eyes widened in shock.

"Me?" he gasped. Then, "Me?" he repeated with real pleasure.

"Wait a minute," Delaney held up his hand. "I recommended you, but I don't think you'll get it. Not because your file isn't good enough or you couldn't handle the job, but your rank is against you. This precinct calls for a captain or deputy inspector. You understand that?"

"Oh sure, Captain. But I certainly do appreciate your recommending me."

"Well, as I said, I don't think, you're going to get it. So if I were you, I wouldn't mention it to a soul. Particularly your wife. Then, if they turn you down, it'll just be your disappointment, and no one will think they considered you and passed you over, for one reason or another."

"I won't mention it, sir."

Delaney considered whether or not to hint to Dorfman the services as a contact he might be asked to provide in the Captain's investigation of the Lombard homicide. Then he decided against it. This wasn't the right time, and he had given the man enough to think about.

"In any event," Delaney said, "if you get the job or don't get it, remember I'm still living next door and if there is ever anything I can help you with, don't hesitate to give me a call or ring my bell. I mean that. Don't get the idea you'll be bothering me or annoying me. You won't. As a matter of fact, I'd appreciate knowing what's going on over here. This is my precinct and, with luck, I hope to be back in command some day."

"I hope so too, Captain," Dorfman said fervently. "I really do hope so." He rose and stuck out a hand. "Best of luck, sir, and I hope Mrs. Delaney is feeling better real soon."

"Thank you, lieutenant."

After Dorfman left, Delaney sat swinging back and forth slowly in his swivel chair. Was a man as gentle and sensitive as the lieutenant capable of administering a busy precinct in the New York Police Department? It was a job that occasionally demanded ruthlessness, a certain amount of Broughton-type insensibility. But then, Delaney reflected, ruthlessness could be an acquired trait. Even an assumed trait. He certainly hoped *he* had not been born with it. Dorfman could learn to be ruthless when necessary, just as he, Delaney, had learned. He did it, but he didn't enjoy it. Perhaps that was the essential difference between Broughton and him: he didn't enjoy it.

Then he slammed his swivel chair level and reached into his bottom desk drawer to haul out a long card file. The grey metal box was dented and battered. Delaney opened it and began searching for what he wanted. The cards were filed by subject matter.

Soon after Patrolman Edward X. Delaney was promoted to detective third grade—more years ago than he cared to remember—he became aware that despite the enormous resources of the New York Police Department, he frequently came up against problems that could only be solved, or moved toward solution, by civilian experts.

There was, for instance, a retired detective, delighted to cooperate with his former colleagues, who had established and maintained what was probably the world's largest collection of laundry marks. There was an 84-year-old spinster who still operated a shop on Madison Avenue. She could glance at an unusual button you showed her, and name the material, age, and source. There was a Columbia University professor whose specialty was crickets and grasshoppers. There was an amateur archeologist, all of whose "digs" had been made within city limits. He could examine rocks and soil and place them within a few blocks of their origin. A Bronx recluse was one of the world's foremost authorities on ancient writing, and could read hieroglyphics as quickly as Delaney read English.

All these experts were willing—nay, *eager* to cooperate with police investigations. It was a welcome interruption of their routine, gave them a chance to exhibit their expertise in a good cause. The only problem was shutting them up; they all did seem to talk excessively, like anyone whose hobby is his vocation. But eventually they divulged the information required.

Delaney had them all in his card file, carefully added to and maintained for almost twenty years. Now he flipped through the cards until he found the one he was looking for. It was headed: "Weapons, antique and unusual." The man's name was Christopher Langley, an assistant curator of the Arms and Armor Collection of the Metropolitan Museum of Art. (The card following his was "Weapons, modern," and that man was a retired colonel of Marines.)

Delaney called the Metropolitan (the number on the card), asked for the Arms and Armor Section, and then asked for Christopher Langley.

"I'm sorry, sir," a young, feminine voice replied. "Mr. Langley is no longer with us. He retired about three years ago."

"Oh. I'm sorry to hear that. Do you happen to know if he's living in New York?"

"Yes sir, I believe he is."

"Then he'll be in the phone book?"

There was a moment's silence.

"Well . . . no sir. I believe Mr. Langley has an unlisted number."

"Could you tell me what it is? I'm a personal friend."

"I'm sorry, sir. We cannot reveal that information."

He was tempted to say, "This is Captain Edward X. Delaney, New York Police Department, and this is official business." Or, he could easily get the number from the phone company, as an official police inquiry. But then he thought better of it. The fewer people who knew of his activities, the better.

"My name is Edward Delaney," he said. "I wonder if you'd be kind enough to call Mr. Langley at the number you have, tell him I called, and if he wishes to contact me, he can reach me at this number." He then gave her the phone number of the 251st Precinct.

"Yes sir," she said. "I can do that."

"Thank you."

He hung up, wondering what percentage of his waking hours was spent on the telephone, trying to complete a call, or waiting for a call. He sat patiently, hoping Langley was in. He was: Delaney's desk phone rang within five minutes.

"Delaney!" Christopher Langley cried in his remarkably boyish voice (the man was pushing 70). "Gosh, I asked for *Lieutenant* Delaney and your operator said it was *Captain* Delaney now. Congratulations! When did that happen?"

"Oh, a few years ago. How are you, sir?"

"Physically I'm fine but, gee, I'm bored."

"I heard you had retired."

"Had to do it, you know. Give the young men a chance—eh? The first year I dabbled around with silly things. I've become a marvelous gourmet cook. But my gosh, how many *Caneton à l'Orange* can you make? Now I'm bored, bored, bored. That's why I was so delighted to hear from you."

"Well, I need your help, sir, and was wondering if you could spare me a few hours?"

"As long as you like, dear boy, as long as you like. Is it a big caper?"

Delaney laughed, knowing Langley's fondness for detective fiction.

"Yes sir. A very big caper. The biggest. Murder most foul."

"Oh gosh," Langley gasped. "That's marvelous! Captain, can you join me for dinner tonight? Then afterwards we can have brandy and talk and you can tell me all about it and how I can help."

"Oh I couldn't put you to that—"

"No trouble at all!" Langley cried. "Gee, it'll be wonderful seeing you again, and I can demonstrate my culinary skills for you."

"Well . . ." Delaney said, thinking of his evening visit to Barbara, "it will have to be a little later. Is nine o'clock too late?"

"Not at all, not at all! I much prefer dining at a late hour. As soon as I hang up, I'll dash out and do some shopping." He gave Delaney his home address.

"Fine," the Captain said. "See you at nine, sir."

"Gosh, this is keen!" Langley said. "We'll have frogs' legs sauteed in butter and garlic, *petite pois* with just a hint of bacon and onion, and *gratin de pommes de terre aux anchois*. And for dessert, perhaps a *crème plombières pralineé*. How does that sound to you?"

"Fine," Delaney repeated faintly. "Just fine."

He hung up. Oh God, he thought, there goes my diet, and wondered what happened when sauteed frogs' legs met broiled kidney.

A young woman was walking toward Central Park, between Madison and Fifth Avenues, pushing a baby carriage. Suddenly a wooden rod, about nine inches long, was projecting from her breast. She slumped to her knees, falling forward, and only the fast scramble of a passerby prevented the baby carriage from bouncing into Fifth Avenue traffic.

Delaney, who was then a detective lieutenant working out of Homicide East (as it was then called) arrived on the scene shortly after the woman died. He joined the circle of patrolmen and ambulance attendants staring down incredulously at the woman with the wooden spike driven through her breast, like some modern vampire.

Within an hour they had the missile identified as a quarrel from a crossbow. Delaney went up to the Arms and Armor Department of the Metropolitan Museum of Art, seeking to learn more about crossbows, their operation, range, and velocity of the bolts. That was how he met Christopher Langley.

From the information supplied by the assistant curator, Delaney was able to solve the case, to his satisfaction at least, but it was never prosecuted. The boy responsible, who had shot the bolt at a stranger from a townhouse window across the street, was the son of a wealthy family. They got him out of the country and into a school in Switzerland. He had never returned to the United States. The District Attorney did not feel Delaney's circumstantial evidence was sufficiently strong to warrant extradition proceedings. The case was still carried as open.

But Delaney had never forgotten Christopher Langley's enthusiasic cooperation, and his name was added to the detective's "expert file." Delaney frequently recalled a special memory of the skinny little man. Langley was showing him through a Museum gallery, deserted except for a grinning guard who evidently knew what to expect.

Suddenly the assistant curator plucked a two-handed sword from the wall, a XVI Century German sword as long as he was tall, and fell into a fighting stance. The blade whirled about his head in circles of flashing steel. He chopped, slashed, parried, thrust.

"That's how they did it," he said calmly, and handed the long sword to Delaney.

The detective took it, and it almost clattered to the floor. Delaney estimated its weight as thirty pounds. The wiry Christopher Langley had spun it like a feather.

When he opened the door to his apartment on the fifth floor of a converted brownstone on East 89th Street, he was exactly as Delaney remembered him. In another age he would have been called a fop or dandy. Now he was a well-preserved, alert, exquisitely dressed 70-year-old bachelor with the complexion of a maiden and a small yellow daisy in the lapel of his grey flannel Norfolk jacket.

"Captain!" he said with pleasure, holding out both hands. "Gosh, this *is* nice!"

It was a small, comfortable apartment the ex-curator had retired to. He occupied the entire top floor: living room, bedroom, bath, and a remarkably large kitchen. There was a glass skylight over the living room which, Delaney was glad to see, had been fitted with a guard of iron bars.

Langley took his hat and overcoat and hung them away.

"Not in uniform tonight, Captain?"

"No. As a matter of fact, I am not on active duty. I'm on leave of absence."

"Oh?" Langley asked curiously. "For long?"

"I don't know."

"Well . . . do sit down. There—that's a comfortable chair. Now what can I bring you? Cocktail? Highball?"

"Oh, I don't—"

"I have a new Italian aperitif I'm trying for the first time. It's quite dry. Very good on the rocks with a twist of lemon."

"Sounds fine. Are you having one?"

"Of course. Just take me a minute."

Langley bustled into the kitchen, and the Captain looked around. The walls of the living room were almost solid book-cases with deep, high shelves to accommodate volumes on antique weaponry, most of them outsize "art books" illustrated with color plates.

Only two actual weapons were on display: an Italian arquebus of the 17th century with exquisitely detailed silver-chasing, and an African warclub. The head was intricately carved stone. Delaney rose to his feet and went over to inspect it. He was turning it in his hands when Langley came back with their drinks.

"Mongo tribe," he said. "The Congo. A ceremonial ax never used in combat. The balance is bad but I like the carving."

"It's beautiful."

"Isn't it? Dinner in about ten minutes. Meanwhile, let's relax. Would you like a cigarette?"

"No, thank you."

"Good. Smoking dulls the palate. Do you know what the secret of good French cooking is?"

"What?"

"A clear palate and butter. Not oil, but butter. The richest, creamiest butter you can find."

Delaney's heart sank. The old man caught his look of dismay and laughed.

"Don't worry, Captain. I've never believed you had to eat a lot of one dish to enjoy it. Small portions and several dishes—that's best."

He was as good as his word; the portions were small. But Delaney decided it was one of the best dinners he had ever eaten and told the host so. Langley beamed with pleasure.

"A little more dessert? There is more, you know."

"Not for me. But I'll have another cup of coffee, if you have it."

"Of course."

They had dined at a plain oak table covered with a black burlap cloth, a table, Delaney was sure, doubled as Langley's desk. Now they both pushed back far enough to cross their legs, have a cigarette, drink coffee, sip the strong Portuguese brandy Langley had served.

"About this—" Delaney had started, but just then the apartment doorbell rang, in the familiar "shave and a haircut, two bits" rhythm, and the Captain was surprised to see Langley's face go white.

"Oh gracious," the old man whispered. "It's her again. The Widow Zimmerman! She lives right below me."

He bounced to his feet, trotted across the room, looked through the peephole, then unlocked and opened the door.

"Ahh," he said. "Good evening, Mrs. Zimmerman."

Delaney had a clear view of her from where he sat. She was perhaps 60, taller than Langley by about six inches, certainly heavier than he by fifty pounds. She balanced a beehive of teased brassy hair above her plump face, and her bare arms looked like something you might see on a butcher's block. She was so heavily girdled that her body seemed hewn from a single chunk of wood; when she walked, her legs appeared to move only from the knees down.

"Oh, I do hope I'm not disturbing you," she simpered, looking at the Captain boldly over Langley's shoulder. "I know you've got company. I heard you go out to shop and then come back. I heard your bell ring and your guest arrive. One of your fantastic foreign dinners, I'm sure. Now I just happened to bake a fresh prune strudel today, and I thought you and your guest might enjoy a nice piece for dessert, and here it is."

She held out the napkin-covered dish to Langley; he took it with the tips of his fingers.

"That's very kind of you, Mrs. Zimmerman. Won't you come—"

"Oh, I won't interrupt. I wouldn't think of it."

She waited expectantly, but Langley did not repeat his invitation.

"I'll just run along," the Widow Zimmerman said, pouting at Delaney. "Thank you for the strudel."

"My pleasure. Enjoy."

She gave him a little-girl smile. He closed the door firmly behind her, bolted and chained it, then put his ear to the panel and listened as her steps receded down the stairs. He came back to the table and whispered to Delaney . . .

"A dreadful woman! Continually bringing me food. I've asked her not to, but she does. I'm perfectly capable of cooking for myself. Been doing it for fifty years. And the food she brings! Strudel and chopped liver and stuffed derma and pickled herring. Gracious! I can't throw it away because she might see it in the garbage cans and be insulted. So I have to wrap it like a gift package and carry it three or four blocks away and dump it into a litter basket. She's such a problem."

"I think she's after you," Delaney said solemnly.

"Oh my!" Christopher Langley said, blushing. "Her husband—her late husband—was such a nice, quiet man. A retired furrier. Well, let me put this in the kitchen, and then please go on with what you were saying."

"Did you read in the papers about the murder of Frank Lombard?" the Captain asked when Langley had rejoined him.

"Goodness, I certainly did. Everything I could find. A fascinating case. You know, whenever I read about a real-life murder or assault, I always look for a description of the weapon. After all, that was my life for so many years, and I'm still interested. But in all the accounts of the Lombard killing, the description of the weapon was very vague. Hasn't it been identified yet?"

"No. It hasn't. That's why I'm here. To ask your help."

"And as you know, I'll be delighted to give you every assistance I can, dear boy."

Delaney held up his hand like a traffic cop.

"Just a minute, sir. I want to be honest with you. As I told you, I am not on active duty. I am on leave of absence. I am not part of the official investigation into the death of Frank Lombard."

Christopher Langley looked at him narrowly a moment, then sat back and began to drum his dainty fingers against the table top.

"Then what is your interest in the Lombard case?"

"I am conducting a—a private investigation into the homicide."

"I see. Can you tell me more?"

"I would prefer not to."

"May I ask the purpose of this—ah—private investigation?"

"The main purpose is to find the killer of Frank Lombard as quickly as possible."

Langley stared at him a long, additional moment, then let off his finger drumming and slapped the table top with an open palm.

"All right," he said briskly. "Was it a striking weapon or a swinging weapon? That is: do you visualize it as a knife, a dagger, a dirk, a poniard—something of that sort—or was it a sword, pole, battleax, club, mace—something of that sort?"

"I'd say the percentages would be in favor of the swinging weapon."

"The percentages!" Langley laughed. "I had forgotten you and your percentages. This is a business to you, isn't it?"

"Yes. It's a business. And sometimes the only things you have to work with are the percentages. But what you said about a striking weapon—a knife or dagger—surely a blade couldn't penetrate a man's skull?"

"It could. And has. If blade and handle are heavy enough. The Marines' combat knife in World War Two could split a man's skull. But most blades would glance off, causing only superficial wounds. Besides, Lombard was struck on the head from behind, was he not?"

"That's correct."

"Then that would probably rule out a striking weapon. An assailant using a blade and coming from behind would almost certainly go in between the shoulder blades, into the ribs, sever the spine, or try for the kidneys."

Delaney nodded, marveling at the gusto with which this impish man ticked off these points on his fingers, an enthusiasm made all the more incredible by his age, diminutive physique, elegant appearance.

"All right," Langley went on, "let's assume a swinging weapon. One-hand or two-hand?"

"I'd guess one-hand. I think the killer approached Lombard from the front. Then, as he passed, he turned and struck him down. During the approach the weapon could have been concealed beneath a coat on the killer's arm or in a newspaper folded under his arm."

"Yes, that certainly rules out a halberd! You're talking about something about the size of a hatchet?"

"About that."

"Captain, do you believe it was an antique weapon?"

"I doubt that very much. Once again, the percentages are against it. In my lifetime I've investigated only two homicides in which antique weapons were used. One was the crossbow case in which you were involved. The other was a death caused by a ball fired from an antique duelling pistol."

"Then we'll assume a modern weapon?"

"Yes."

"Or a modern tool. You must realize that many modern tools have evolved from antique weapons. The reverse is also true, of course. During hand-to-hand combat in Korea and Vietnam, there were several cases of American soldiers using their Entrenching tool, shovel, or Entrenching tool, pickmattock, as a weapon both for offense and defense. Now let's get to the wound itself. Was it a crushing, cutting, or piercing blow?"

"Piercing. It was a penetration, about three to four inches long."

"Oh my, that *is* interesting! And what was the shape of the penetration?"

"Here I'm going to get a little vague," Delaney warned. "The official autopsy of the examining surgeon states that the outside wound was roughly circular in shape, about one inch in diameter. The penetration dwindled rapidly to a sharp point, the entire penetration being round and, as I said, about three or four inches deep."

"Round?" Langley cried, and the Captain was surprised at the little man's expression.

"Yes, round," he repeated. "Why—is anything wrong?"

"Is the surgeon certain of this? The roundness, I mean?"

"No, he is not. But the wound was of such a nature that precise measurements and analysis were impossible. The surgeon had a feeling— just a guess on his part—that the spike that penetrated was triangular or square, and that the weapon became stuck in the wound, or the victim in falling forward, wrenched the weapon out of the killer's hand, and that the killer then had to twist the weapon back and forth to free it. And this twisting motion, with a square or triangular spike, would result in—"

"Ah-ha!" Langley shouted, slapping his thigh. "That's exactly what happened! And the surgeon believes the spike could have been triangular or square?"

"Believes it *could* have been—yes."

"*Was*," Langley said definitely. "It was. Believe me, Captain. Do you know how many weapons there are with tapering round spikes that could cause the kind of wound you describe? I could name them on the fingers of one hand. You will find round spikes on the warclubs of certain Northwest Coast Indian tribes. There is a Tlingit warclub with a jade head that tapers to a point. It is not perfectly round, however. Thompson Indians used a warclub with a head of wood that was round and tapered: a perfect cone. The Tsimshian Indians used horn and bone, again round and tapered. Esquimo tribes used clubs with spikes of bone or narwhale or walrus tusks. Do you understand the significance of what I am saying, Captain?"

"I'm afraid not."

"The materials used in weapons that had a cone spike were almost always *natural* materials that tapered naturally—such as teeth or tusks—or were soft materials, such as wood, that could be tapered to a cone shape easily. But now let's move on to iron and steel. Early metal weapons were made by armorers and blacksmiths working with a hammer on a hot slug held on an anvil. It was infinitely easier and faster to fashion a flat spike, a triangular spike, or a square spike, than a perfect cone that tapered to a sharp point. I can't recall a single halberd, partison or *couteaux de brèche* in the Metropolitan that has a round spike. Or any war hammer or war hatchet. I seem to remember a mace in the Rotterdam museum that had a round spike, but I'd have to look it up. In any event, early weapons almost invariably were fashioned with flat sides, usually triangular or square, or even hexagonal. A perfectly proportioned round spike was simply too difficult to make. And even after dies and stamping of iron and steel came into existence, the same held true. It is cheaper, faster, and easier to make blades and spikes with flat sides than round ones that taper to a point. I think your surgeon's 'guesses' are correct. Using your famous 'percentages.'"

"Interesting," Delaney nodded, "and exactly what I came to you for. But there's another thing I should tell you. I don't know what it means, if anything, but perhaps you will. The surgeon has a feeling that the sharp tip of the penetration was lower than the opening wound. You understand? It was not a straight, tapered penetration, but it curved gently downward. Maybe I should make a little drawing."

"Oh gosh," Langley chortled, "that's not necessary. I know exactly what you mean." He leaped to his feet, rushed to a bookcase, ran his fingers over the bindings, grabbed out a big book, and hustled it back to the table. He turned to the List of Illustrations, ran his finger down, found what he was looking for, and flipped pages. "There," he said. "Take a look at that, Captain."

Delaney stared. It was a one-handed club. The head had a hatchet blade on one side, a spike on the other. The spike was about an inch across at the head, tapered to a sharp point and, as it tapered, curved downward.

"What is it?" he asked.

"Iroquois tomahawk. Handle of ash. Those are feathers tied to the butt. The head is iron, probably cut out of a sheet of hot metal with shears or hammered out with a chisel and then filed sharp. White traders carried them and sold them for pelts."

"Are you suggesting . . . ?"

"Heavens, no. But note how that flat spike curves downward? I could show you that same curve in warclubs and war-axes and halberds of practically every nation, tribe, and race on earth. Very effective; very efficient. When you hack down on a man, you don't want to hit his skull with a horizontal spike that might glance off. You want a spike that curves downward, pierces, penetrates, and kills."

"Yes," Delaney said. "I suppose you do."

The two men sat in silence a few moments, staring at the color photo of the Iroquois tomahawk. How many had *that* killed, Delaney wondered, and then, leafing slowly through the book, was suddenly saddened by the effort, art, and genius that the human race had expended on killing tools, on powder and shot, sword and stiletto, bayonet and bludgeons, crossbow and Centurion tank, blowpipe and cannon, spear and hydrogen bomb. There was, he supposed, no end to it.

But what was the need, or lust, behind all this interest, ingenuity, and vitality in the design and manufacture of killing tools? The lad with his slingshot and the man with his gun: both showing a dark atavism. Was killing then a passion, from the primeval slime, as valid an expression of the human soul as love and sacrifice?

Suddenly depressed, Delaney rose to his feet and tried to smile at his host.

"Mr. Langley," he said brightly, "I thank you for a pleasant evening, a wonderful dinner, and for your kind cooperation. You've given me a lot to think about."

Christopher Langley seemed as depressed as his guest. He looked up listlessly.

"I haven't helped, and you know it. You're no closer to identifying the weapon that killed Frank Lombard than you were three hours ago."

"You *have* helped, sir," Delaney insisted. "You've substantiated the surgeon's impressions. You've given me a clearer idea of what to look for. In a case like this, every little bit helps."

"Captain . . ."

"Yes, Mr. Langley?"

"In this 'private investigation' of yours, the weapon isn't the only thing. I know that. You're going to interview people and check into past records and things like that. Isn't that true?"

"Yes."

"Well, gosh, then you can only spend so much time trying to identify the weapon. Isn't that so?"

"Yes."

"Captain, let me do it. Please. Let me *try*."

"Mr. Langley, I can't—"

"I know you're not on active duty. I know it's a private investigation. You told me. But still . . . you're trying. Let me help. Please. Look at me. I'm seventy. I'm retired. To tell you the truth, Captain, I'm sick of gourmet cooking. My whole life was . . . Oh God, what am I supposed to do—sit up here and wait to die? Captain, please, let me *do* something, something important. This man Lombard was murdered. That's not right. Life is too precious."

"That's what my wife said," Delaney said wonderingly.

"She knew," Langley nodded, his eyes glistening now. "Let me do some work, some *important* work. I know weapons. You know that. I might be a help to you. Truly. Let me try."

"I don't have any funds," Delaney started. "I can't—"

"Forget it," the old man waved him away. "This will cost nothing. I can pay for cabs and books, or whatever. But let me work. At an important job. You understand, Captain? I don't want to just drift away."

The Captain stared, wondering if the ex-curator was prey to his own gloomy thoughts. Langley was far from being stupid, and how did an intelligent man justify a lifetime devoted to killing tools? Perhaps it was true, as he had said, that he was simply bored with retirement and wanted to work again. But his insistence on something "important," "important" work, an "important" job led Delaney to wonder if the old man, his life drawing to a close, was not, in a sense, seeking a kind of expiation, or at least hungering to make a sunny, affirmative gesture after a career celebrating shadows and the bog.

"Yes," Captain Delaney said, clearing his throat. "I understand. All right. Fine. I appreciate that, sir. If I find out anything more relating to the weapon, I'll make sure you know of it. Meanwhile, see what you can come up with."

"Oh!" Langley cried, effervescent again. "I'll get on it right away. There are some things I want to check in my books tonight, and tomorrow I'll go to the museums. Maybe I'll get some ideas there. And to hardware stores. To look at tools. Captain, am I a detective now?"

"Yes," Delaney smiled. "You're a detective."

He moved toward the door, and Langley scampered to get his coat and hat from the closet. He gave his unlisted phone number to the Captain, and Delaney carefully copied it into his pocket notebook. Langley unlocked the door, then leaned close.

"Captain," he whispered, "one final favor . . . When you go down the stairs, please try to tiptoe past the Widow Zimmerman's door. I don't want her to know I'm alone."

6

THE HOME of the late Frank Lombard was on a surprisingly pastoral street in the Flatbush section of Brooklyn. There were trees, lawns, barking dogs, shrieking children. The house itself was red brick, two stories high, its ugliness hidden in a tight cloak of ivy that was still green and creeped to the eaves.

There was an asphalt driveway leading to a two-car garage. There were four cars, bumper to bumper, on the driveway, and more in front of the house, two double-parked. Captain Delaney observed all this from across the street. He also observed that one of the double-parked cars was a three-year-old, four-door Plymouth, and had the slightly rusted, slightly dusty, nondescript appearance of an unmarked police car. Two men in civilian clothes were in the front seat.

Delaney approved of a guard being stationed for the protection of the widow, Mrs. Clara Lombard. It was very possible, he thought, there was also a personal guard inside the house; Chief Pauley would see to that. Now the problem was, if Delaney went through with his intention to interview the widow, would one of the cops recognize him and report to Broughton that Captain Delaney had been a visitor.

The Captain pondered this problem a few minutes on the next corner, still watching the Lombard home. While he stood, hands shoved deep in his civilian overcoat pockets, he saw two couples leave the house, laughing, and another car double-park to disgorge two women and a man, also laughing.

Delaney devised a cover story. If the guards made him, and he was eventually braced by Broughton, he would explain that because the homicide occurred in his precinct, he felt duty-bound to express his condolences to the widow. Broughton wouldn't buy it completely; he'd be suspicious and have the widow checked. But that would be all right; Delaney did feel duty-bound to express his condolences, and would.

As he headed up the brick-paved walk to the door, he heard loud rock music, screams of laughter, the sound of shattering glass. It was a party, and a wild one.

A man answered his ring, a flush-faced, too-handsome man wearing not one, but two pinkie rings.

"Come in come in come in," he burbled, flourishing his highball glass and slopping half of it down the front of his hand-tailored, sky-blue silk suit. "Always room for one more."

"Thank you," Delaney said. "I'm not a guest. I just wanted to speak to Mrs. Lombard for a moment."

"Hey, Clara!" the man screamed over his shoulder. "Get your gorgeous ass out here. Your lover is waiting."

The man leered at Delaney, then plunged back into the dancing, drinking, laughing, yelling mob. The Captain stood patiently. Eventually she came weaving toward him.

A *zoftig* blonde who reminded him of Oscar Wilde's comment about the widow "whose hair turned quite gold from grief." She overflowed an off-the-shoulder cocktail dress that seemed capable of standing by itself, so heavily encrusted was it with sequins, rhinestones, braid, a jeweled peacock brooch and, unaccountably, a cheap tin badge, star-shaped, that said "Garter Inspector." She looked down at him from bleary eyes.

"Yeah?"

"Mrs. Clara Lombard?"

"Yeah."

"My name is Delaney, Captain Edward X. Delaney. I am the former commanding officer of the—"

"Jesus," she breathed. "Another cop. Haven't I had enough cops?"

"I would like to express my condolences on the death—"

"Five," she said. "Or six times. I lost count. What the hell is it now? Can't you see I've got a houseful of people? Will you stop bugging me?"

"I just wanted to tell you how sorry I—"

"Thanks a whole hell of a lot," she said disgustedly. "Well, screw all of you. This is a going-away party. I'm shaking New York, and the whole lot of you can go screw."

"You're leaving New York?" he asked, amazed that Broughton would let her go.

"That's right, buster. I've sold the house, the cars, the furniture—everything. By Saturday I'll be in sunny, funny Miami and starting a new life. A brand new life. And then you can all go screw yourselves."

She turned away and went rushing back to her party. Delaney replaced his hat, walked slowly down to the corner. He watched the traffic, waiting for the light to change. Cars went rushing by, and the odd thing that had nagged him since his reading of the Operation Lombard reports whisked into his mind, as he knew it would. Eventually.

In the interview with the victim's mother, Mrs. Sophia Lombard, she had stated he never drove over from Brooklyn because he couldn't find parking space near her apartment; he took the subway.

Delaney retraced his steps, and this time the outside guards stared at him.

He rang the bell of the Lombard home again. The widow herself threw open the door, a welcoming smile on her puffy face—a smile that oozed away as she recognized Delaney.

"Jesus Christ, you again?"

"Yes. You said you're selling your car?"

"Not car—cars. We had two of them. And forget about getting a bargain; they're both sold."

"Your husband—your late husband drove a car?"

"Of course he drove a car. What do you think?"

"Where did he usually carry his driver's license, Mrs. Lombard?"

"Oh God," she shouted, and immediately the pinkie-ringed man was at her shoulder.

"Wassamatta, honey?" he inquired. "Having trouble?"

"No trouble, Manny. Just some more police shit. In his wallet," she said to Delaney. "He carried his driver's license in his wallet. Okay?"

"Thank you," Delaney said humbly. "I'm sorry to bother you. It's just that the license wasn't in his wallet when we found him." He refrained from mentioning that she had stated nothing was missing from the wallet. "It's probably around the house somewhere."

"Yeah, yeah," she said impatiently.

"If you come across it while you're packing, will you let us know? We've got to cancel it with the State."

"Sure, sure. I'll look, I'll look."

He knew she wouldn't. But it didn't make any difference; she'd never find it.

"Anything else?" she demanded.

"No, nothing. Thank you very much, Mrs. Lombard, for your kind cooperation."

"Go screw yourself," she said, and slammed the door in his face.

He went back to his home and methodically checked the inventory of personal effects taken from the body of Frank Lombard, and Mrs. Sophia Lombard's statement about her son's visiting habits. Then he sat a long time in the growing darkness. Once he rose to mix a weak rye highball and sat nursing that, sipping slowly and still thinking.

Finally he pulled on his overcoat and hat again and went out to find a different phone booth. He had to wait almost fifteen minutes before Deputy Inspector Ivar Thorsen got back to him, a period during which three would-be phone users turned away in disgust. One of them kicked the phone booth in anger before he left.

"Edward?" Thorsen asked.

"Yes. I've got something. Something I don't think Broughton has."

He heard Thorsen's swift intake of breath.

"What?"

"Lombard was a licensed driver. He owned two cars. His wife has sold them, incidentally. She's leaving town."

"So?"

"She says he carried his driver's license in his wallet. That makes sense. The percentages are for it. The license wasn't in the wallet when it was found. I checked the inventory."

There was a moment's silence.

"No one would kill for a driver's license," Thorsen said finally. "You can buy a good counterfeit for fifty bucks."

"I know."

"Identification?" Thorsen suggested. "A hired killer. He takes the license to prove to his employer he really did hit Lombard."

"What for? It was in all the papers the next day. The employer would know the job had been done."

"Jesus, that's right. What do you think? Why the driver's license?"

"Identification maybe."

"But you just said—"

"Not a hired killer. I have two ideas. One, the killer took the license as a souvenir, a trophy."

"That's nuts, Edward."

"Maybe. The other idea is that he took the license to prove to a third party that he had killed. Not killed *Lombard*, but killed someone, *anyone*. If the stories were in the papers, and the killer could present the victim's driver's license, that would prove *he* was the killer."

The silence was longer this time.

"Jesus, Edward," Thorsen said finally. "That's wild."

"Yes. Wild." (And suddenly he remembered a sex killing he had investigated. The victim's eyelids had been stitched together with her own hairpins.)

Thorsen came on again: "Edward, are you trying to tell me we're dealing with a crazy?"

"Yes. I think so. Someone like Whitman, Speck, Unruh, the Boston Strangler, Panzram, Manson. Someone like that."

"Oh God."

"If I'm right, we'll know soon enough."

"How will we know?"

"He'll do it again."

PART FOUR

1

HE THOUGHT she was wearing a loose-fitting dress of black crepe with white cuffs. Then he saw the cuffs were actually bandages about both wrists. But he was so inflamed with what he wanted to tell her that he didn't question the bandages, knowing. Instead, he merely held up before her eyes Frank Lombard's driver's license. She would not look at it, but took him by the arm and drew him slowly, step by step, to the upstairs room. Where he was impotent.

"It's all right," she soothed. "I understand. Believe me, I understand and love you for it. I told you sex should be a ritual, a ceremony. But a rite has no consummation. It's a celebration of a consummation. Do you understand? The ritual celebrates the climax but does not encompass it. It's all right, my darling. Don't think you've failed. This is best. That you and I worship the fulfillment—a continuing celebration of an unknowable finality. Isn't that what prayer is all about?"

But he was not listening to her, so livid was he with the need to talk. He snapped on that cruel overhead light and showed her the driver's license and newspaper headlines, proving himself.

"For you," he said. "I did it for you." Then they both laughed, knowing it was a lie.

"Tell me everything," she said. "Every detail. I want to know everything that happened."

His soft scrotum huddled in her hand, a dead bird.

He told her, with pride, of the careful planning, the long hours of slow thought. His first concern, he said, had been the weapon.

"Did I want a weapon that could be discarded?" he asked rhetorically. "I decided not, not to leave a weapon that might be traced to me. So I chose a weapon I would take with me when I left."

"To be used again," she murmured.

"Yes. Perhaps. Well . . . I told you I'm a climber. I'm not an expert; just an amateur. But I have this ice ax. It's a tool of course, but also a very wicked weapon. All tempered steel. A hammer on one side of the head for pitons, and a tapered steel pick on the other. There are hundreds just like it. Also, it has a leather-wrapped handle and a rawhide thong hanging from the butt. Heavy enough to kill, but small and light enough to carry concealed. You know that coat I have with slits in the pockets, so that I can reach inside?"

"Do I not!" she smiled.

"Yes," he smiled in reply. "I figured I could wear that coat, the front unbuttoned and hanging loose. My left hand would be through the slit, and I could carry the ice ax by the leather thong, dangling from my fingers but completely concealed. When the time came to use it, I could reach inside the unbuttoned coat with my right hand and take the ax by the handle."

265

"Brilliant," she said.

"A problem," he shrugged. "I tried it. I practised. It worked perfectly. If I was calm and cool, unhurried, I could transfer the ax to my right hand in seconds. *Seconds!* One or two. No more. Then, after, the ax would disappear beneath my coat again. Held by my left hand through the pocket slit."

"Did you see his eyes?" she asked.

"His eyes?" he said vaguely. "No. I must tell you this in my own way."

She leaned forward to put her lips on his left nipple; his eyes closed with pleasure.

"I didn't want to travel too far," he said. "The farther I went, carrying the concealed ice ax, the greater the danger. It had to be in my own neighborhood. Near. Why not? The murder of a stranger. A crime without motive. What difference if it was next door or a hundred miles away? Who could connect me?"

"Yes," she breathed. "Oh yes."

He told her how he had walked the streets for three nights, seeking the lonely blocks, noting the lighting, remembering bus stops and subway stations, lobbies with doormen, deserted stretches of unattended stores and garages.

"I couldn't plan it. I decided it would have to be chance. Pure chance. 'Pure.' That's a funny word, Celia. But it was pure. I swear to you. I mean, there was no sex connected with it. I mean, I didn't walk around with an erection. I didn't have an orgasm when I did it. Nothing like that. Do you believe me?"

"Yes."

"It really was pure. I swear it. It was religious. I was God's will. I know that sounds insane. But that's how I felt. Maybe it is mad. A sweet madness. I was God on earth. When I looked at people on shadowed streets . . . Is *he* the one? Is *he* the one? My God, the *power!*"

"Oh yes. Darling, oh yes."

He was so tender with her in that awful room . . . so tender. And then, the memory of the two times he had been unfaithful to his wife . . . He had enjoyed both adventures; both women had been his wife's superior in bed. But he had not loved her the less for that. Instead, unaccountably, his infidelity had increased his affection for and kindness toward his wife. He touched her, kissed her, listened to her.

And now, telling this woman of murder, he felt the same thaw: not increased sexuality but heightened sweetness because he had a new mistress. He touched Celia's cheek, kissed her fingertips, murmured, saw to her comfort, and in all things acted the gentle and *parfait* lover, loving her the more because he loved another most.

"It was not someone else doing it," he assured her. "You've read these stories where the killer blames it on someone else. Another *him*. Someone who took over, controlled his mind and guided his hand. It was nothing like that. Celia, I have never had such a feeling of being myself. You know? It was a sense of *oneness*, of *me*. Do you understand?"

"Oh yes. And then?"

"I hit him. We smiled. We nodded. We passed, and I transferred the ax to my right hand. Just as I had rehearsed. And I hit him. It made a sound. I can't describe it. A sound. And he fell forward so heavily that it pulled the ax out of my hand. I didn't know that might happen. But I didn't panic. Jesus, I was cool. Cold! I bent down and twisted the ax to pull it free. Tough. I had to put my foot on the back of his neck and pull up on the ax with both hands to free it. I did that. I did it! And then I found his wallet and took his driver's license. To prove to you."

"You didn't have to do that."

"Didn't I?"

"Yes. You did."

They both laughed then, and rolled on the soiled bed, holding.

He tried, again, to enter into her and did not succeed, not caring, for he had already surpassed her. But he would not tell her that since she knew. She took his penis into her mouth, not licking or biting, but just in her mouth: a warm communion. He was hardly conscious of it; it did not excite him. He was a god; she was worshipping.

"One other thing," he said dreamily. "When, finally, on the night, I looked down the street and saw him walking toward me through that orange glow, and I thought yes, now, he is the one, I loved him so much then, *loved* him."

"Loved him? Why?"

"I don't know. But I did. And respected him. Oh yes. And had such a sense of gratitude toward him. That he was giving. So much. To me. Then I killed him."

2

"GOOD-MORNING, Charles," Daniel called, and the doorman whirled around, shocked by the friendly voice and pleasant smile. "Looks like a sunny day today."

"Oh. Yes sir," Lipsky said, confused. "Sunny day. That's what the paper said. Cab, Mr. Blank?"

"Please."

The doorman went down to the street, whistled up a taxi, rode it back to the apartment house entrance. He got out and held the door open for Daniel.

"Have a good day, Mr. Blank."

"You too, Charles," and handed him the usual quarter. He gave the driver the address of the Javis-Bircham Building.

"Go through the park, please. I know it's longer but I've got time."

"Sure."

"Looks like a nice sunny day today."

"That's what the radio just said," the driver nodded. "You sound like you feel good today."

"Yes," Blank smiled. "I do."

"Morning, Harry," he said to the elevator starter. "A nice sunny morning."

"Sure is, Mr. Blank. Hope it stays like this."

"Good-morning, Mrs. Cleek," Blank said to his secretary as he hung away his hat and coat. "Looks like it's going to be a beautiful day."

"Yes sir. I hope it lasts."

"It will." He looked at her closely a moment. "Mrs. Cleek, you seem a bit pale. Are you feeling all right?"

She blushed with pleasure at his concern. "Oh yes, Mr. Blank, I feel fine."

"How's that boy of yours?"

"I got a letter from him yesterday. He's doing very well. He's in a military academy, you know."

Blank didn't, but nodded. "Well, you do look a bit weary. Why don't you plan on taking a few Fridays off? It's going to be a long winter. We all need relaxation."

"Why . . . thank you very much, Mr. Blank. That's very kind of you."

"Just let me know in advance and arrange for someone from the pool to fill in. That's a pretty dress."

"Thank you very much, Mr. Blank," she repeated, dazed. "Your coffee is on your desk, and a report came down from upstairs. I put it next to your coffee."

"What's it about?"

"Oh, I didn't read it, sir. It's sealed and confidential."

"Thank you, Mrs. Cleek. I'll buzz when I want to do letters."

"Thank you again, Mr. Blank. For the days off, I mean."

He smiled and made a gesture. He sat down at his bare table and sipped coffee, staring at the heavy manila envelope from the president's office, stamped CONFIDENTIAL. He didn't open it, but taking his plastic container of coffee walked to the plate glass windows facing west.

It was an extraordinarily clear day, the smog mercifully lifted. He could see tugboats on the Hudson, a cruise liner putting out to sea, traffic on the Jersey shore, and blue hills far away. Everything was bright and glittering, a new world. He could almost peer into a distant future.

He drained his coffee and looked into the plastic cup. It was white foam, stained now, and of the consistency of cottage cheese. It bulged in his grip and felt of soap. He flicked on his intercom.

"Sir?" Mrs. Cleek asked.

"Would you do me a favor?"

"Of course, sir."

"On your lunch hour—well, take your usual hour, of course, but then take some more time—grab a cab over to Tiffany's or Jensen's—someplace like that—and buy me a coffee cup and saucer. Something good in bone China, thin and white. You can buy singles from open stock. If it's patterned, pick out something attractive, something you like. Don't be afraid to spend money."

"A coffee cup and saucer, sir?"

"Yes, and see if you can find a spoon, one of those small silver French spoons. Sometimes they're enameled in blue patterns, flowered patterns. That would be fine."

"One coffee cup, one saucer, and one spoon. Will that be all, sir?"

"Yes—no. Get the same thing for yourself. Get two sets."

"Oh, Mr. Blank, I couldn't—"

"Two sets," he said firmly. "And Mrs. Cleek, from now on when the commissary delivers my coffee, will you pour it into my new cup and leave it on my desk that way?"

"Yes, Mr. Blank."

"Keep track of what you spend, including cab fares there and back. I'll pay you personally. This is not petty cash."

"Yes, Mr. Blank."

He clicked off and picked up the president's envelope, having no great curiosity to open it. He searched the outside. Finally, sighing, he tore open the flap and scanned the two-sheet memo swiftly. It was about what he had expected, considering the lack of zeal in his prospectus. His suggestion of having AMROK II compute the ratio between editorial and advertising in all Javis-Bircham magazines was approved to this extent: it would be tried on an experimental basis on the ten magazines listed on the attached page, and would be limited to a period of six months, after which time a production management consultant would be called in to make an independent evaluation of the results.

Blank tossed the memo aside, stretched, yawned. He couldn't, he realized, care less. It was a crock of shit. Then he picked up the memo again and wandered out of the office.

"I'll be in the Computer Room," he said as he passed Mrs. Cleek's desk. She gave him a bright, hopeful smile.

He went through the nonsense of donning the sterile white skull cap and duster, then assembled Task Force X-1 about the stainless steel table. He passed around the second sheet of the president's memo, deeming it wise, at this time, not to tell them of the experimental nature and limited duration of the project.

"We've got the go-ahead," he said, with what he hoped they would think was enthusiasm. "These are the magazines we start with. I want to draw up a schedule of priorities for programming. Any ideas?"

The discussion started at his left and went around the table. He listened to all of them, watching their pale, sexless faces, not hearing a word that was said.

"Excellent," he said occasionally. Or, "Very good." Or, "I'll take a raincheck on that." Or, "Well . . . I don't want to say no, but . . ." It didn't make any difference: what they said or what he said. It had no significance.

Significance began, I suppose, when my wife and I separated. Or when she wouldn't wear the sunglasses to bed. Oh, it probably began much sooner, but I wasn't aware of it. I was aware of the glasses, the masks. And then, later, the wigs, the exercises, the clothes, the apartment . . . the mirrors. And standing naked in chains. I was aware of all that. I mean, I was conscious of it.

What was happening to me—*is* happening to me—is that I am feeling my way—*feeling*: that's a good word—feeling in the sense of emotion rather than the tactile sense—*feeling* my way to a new perception of reality. Before that, before the sunglasses, I perceived and reasoned in a masculine, in-line way, vertical, just like AMROK II. And now . . . and now I am discovering and exploring a feminine, horizontal perception of reality.

And what that requires is to deny cold order—logical, intellectual order, that is—and perceive a deeper order, glimpsing it dimly now, somewhere, an order much deeper and broader because . . . The order I have known up to now has been narrow and restricted, tight and disciplined. But it cannot account for . . . for all.

This feminine, horizontal perception applies to breadth, explaining the apparent illogic and seeming madness of the universe—well, this perception does not deny science and logic but offers something more—an emotional consciousness of people and of life.

But is it only emotional? Or is it spiritual? At least it demands a need to accept chaos—a chaos outside the tight, disciplined logic of men and AMROK II, and seeks a deeper, more fundamental order and logic and significance within that chaos. It means a new way of life: the truth of lies and the reality of myths. It demands a whole new way to perceive a—

No, that's not right. Perception implies a standing aside and observing. But this new world I am now in requires participation and sharing. I must strip myself naked and plunge—if I hope to know the final logic. If I have the courage . . .

Courage . . . When I told Celia of the power I felt when selecting my victim, and the love I had for him when he was selected—all that was true. But I didn't mention the fear—fear so intense it was all I could do to control my bladder. But isn't that part of it? I mean emotion—*feeling*. And from emotion to a spiritual exaltation, just as Celia is always speaking of ceremony and ritual and the beauty of evil. That is *her* final logic. But is it mine? We shall see. We shall see.

I must open myself, to everything. I grew in a tiled house of Lalique glass and rock collections. Now I must become warm and tender and accept everything in the universe, good and evil, the spread and the cramped. But not just accepting. Because then I'd be a victim. I must plunge to the heart of life and let its heat sear me. I must be moved.

To *experience* reality, not merely to perceive it: that is the way. And the final answer may be dreadful to divine. But if I can conquer fear, and kill, and feel, and learn, I will bring a meaning out of the chaos of my new world, give it a logic few have ever glimpsed before, and then I'll know.

Is there God?

3

HE PULLED that brass plunger, standing at her teak door, grasping the bundle of long-stemmed roses, blood-colored, and feeling as idiotic and ineffectual as any wooer come to call upon his lady-love with posies, vague hope, a vapid smile.

"Good-afternoon, Valenter."

"Good-afternoon, thir. Do come in."

He was inside, the door closed behind him, when the tall, pale houseman spoke in tones Daniel was certain were a burlesque, a spoof of sadness. That long face fell, the muddy eyes seemed about to leak, the voice was suited for a funeral chapel.

"Mither Blank, I am thorry to report Mith Montfort hath gone."

"Gone? Gone where?"

"Called away unexthpectedly. She athked me to prethent her regreth."

"Oh shit."

"Yeth thir."

"When will she be back? Today?"

"I do not know, thir. But I thuthpect it may be a few dayth."

"Shit," Blank repeated. He thrust the flowers at Valenter. "Put these in some water, will you? Maybe they'll last long enough for her to see them."

"Of course, thir. Mather Tony ith in the thtudy and would like you to join him, thir."

"What? Oh. All right."

It was a Saturday noon. He had imagined a leisurely lunch, perhaps some shopping, a visit to the Mortons' Erotica, which was always crowded and entertaining on a Saturday afternoon. And then, perhaps, a movie, a dinner, and then . . . Well, anything. Things went best, he decided, when they weren't too rigidly programmed.

The boy languished on the tufted couch—a beauty!

"Dan!" he cried, holding out a hand.

But Blank would not cross the room to touch that languid palm. He sat in the winged armchair and regarded the youth with what he believed was amused irony. The roses had cost twenty dollars.

"About Celia," Tony said, looking down at his fingernails. "She wanted me to make her apologies."

"Valenter already has."

"Valenter? Oh pooh! Have a drink."

And suddenly, Valenter was there, leaning forward slightly from the waist.

"No, thank you," Blank said. "It's a little early for me."

"Oh come," Tony said. "Vodka martini on the rocks with a twist of lemon. Right?"

Daniel considered a moment. "Right," he smiled.

"What will your son have?" the waiter asked, and they both laughed.

"My son?" Blank said. He looked to Tony. "What will my son have?"

They were in a French restaurant, not bad and not good. They didn't care.

Tony ordered oysters and frogs' legs, a salad doused with a cheese dressing. Blank had a small steak and endives with oil and vinegar. They smiled at each other. Tony reached forward to touch his hand. "Thank you," he said humbly.

Daniel had two glasses of a thick burgundy, and Tony had something called a "Shirley Temple." The boy's knee was against his. He didn't object, wanting to follow this plot to its denouement.

"Do you drink coffee?" he asked. They flirted.

"How is school?" he asked, and Tony made a gesture, infinitely weary.

They were strolling then, hands brushing occasionally, up Madison Avenue, and stopped to smile at a display of men's clothing in a boutique.

"Oh," Tony said.

Daniel Blank glanced at him. The lad was in sunlight, brazen. He gleamed, a gorgeous being.

"Let's look," Blank said. They went inside.

"Ooh, thank you," Tony said later, giving him a dazzling smile. "You spent so much money on me."

"Didn't I though?"

"Are you rich, Dan?"

"No, I'm not rich. But not hurting."

"Do you think the pink pullover was right for me?"

"Oh yes. Your coloring."

"I would have loved those fishnet briefs, but I knew even the small size would be too large for me. Celia buys all my underwear in a women's lingerie shop."

"Does she?"

They sat on a park bench unaccountably planted in the middle of a small meadow. Tony fingered the lobe of Dan's left ear; they watched an old black man stolidly fly a kite.

"Do you like me?" Tony asked.

Daniel Blank would not give himself time to fear, but twisted around and kissed the boy's soft lips.

"Of course I like you."

Tony held his hand and made quiet circles on the palm with a forefinger.

"You've changed, Dan."

"Have I?"

"Oh yes. When you first started seeing Celia, you were so tight, so locked up inside yourself. Now I feel you're breaking out. You smile more. Sometimes you laugh. You never did that before. You wouldn't have kissed me three months ago, would you?"

"No, I wouldn't have, Tony, perhaps we should get back. Valenter is probably—"

"Valenter," Tony said in a tone of great disgust. "Pooh! Just because he—" Then he stopped.

But Valenter was nowhere about, and Tony used his own key to let them in. Daniel's roses were arranged in a Chinese vase on the foyer table. And in addition to the roses' sweet musk, he caught another odor: Celia's perfume, a thin, smoky scent, Oriental. He thought it odd he had not smelled it in this hallway at noon.

And the scent was there in the upstairs room to which Tony led him by the hand, resolute and humming.

He had vowed not only to perceive but to experience, to strip himself bare and plunge to the hot heart of life. The killing of Frank Lombard had been a cataclysm that left him riven, just as an earthquake leaves the tight, solid earth split, stretched open to the blue sky.

Now, alone and naked with this beautiful, rosy lad, the emotions he sought came more quickly, easily, and fear of his own feelings was already turning to curiosity and hunger. He sought new corners of himself, great sweetness and great tenderness, a need to sacrifice and a want to love. Whatever his life had lacked to now, he resolved to find, supply, to fill himself up with things hot and scented, all the emotions and sentiments which might illume life and show its mystery and purpose.

The boy's body was all warm fabric: velvet eyelids, silken buttocks, the insides of his thighs a sheeny satin. Slowly, with a deliberate thoughtfulness, Daniel Blank put mouth and tongue to those cloths, all with the fragrance of youth, sweet and moving. To use youth, to pleasure it and take pleasure from it, seemed to him now as important as murder, another act of conscious will to spread himself wide to sentient life.

The infant moved moaning beneath his caresses, and that incandescent flesh heated him and brought him erect. When he entered into Tony, penetrating his rectum, the boy cried out with pain and delight. Dimly, far off, Blank thought he heard a single tinkle of feminine laughter, and smelled again her scent clinging to the soiled mattress.

Later, when he held the lad in his arms and kissed his tears away—new wine, those tears—he thought it possible, probable even, that they were manipulating him, for what reason he could not imagine. But it was of no importance. Because whatever the reason, it must certainly be a selfish one.

Suddenly he *knew*; her slick words, her lectures on ritual, her love of ceremony and apotheosis of evil—all had the stench of egotism; there was no other explanation. She sought, somehow, to set herself apart. Apart and above. She wanted to conquer the world and, perhaps, had enlisted him in her mandarin scheme.

But, enlisted or not, she had unlocked him, and would find he was moving beyond her. Whatever her selfish motive, he would complete his own task: not to conquer life, but to become one with it, to hug it close, to feel it and love it and, finally, to know its beautiful enigma. Not as AMROK II might know it, but in his heart and gut and gonads, to become a secret sharer, one with the universe.

4

AFTER WRENCHING his ice ax from the skull of Frank Lombard, he had walked steadily homeward, looking neither to the right nor to the left, his mind resolutely thoughtless. He had nodded in a friendly fashion to the doorman on duty, then ascended to his apartment. Only after he was inside, the battery of chains and locks in place, did he lean against the wall, still coated, close his eyes, drew a deep breath.

But there was still work to be done. He put the ax aside for the moment. Then he stripped naked. He examined coat and suit for stains, of any kind. He could see none. But he placed coat and suit in a bundle for the drycleaner, and shirt, socks and underclothing in the laundry hamper.

Then he went into the bathroom and held the ice ax so that the head was under water in the toilet bowl. He flushed the toilet three times. Practically all the solid matter—caked blood and some grey stuff caught in the saw-tooth serrations on the bottom point of the pick—was washed away.

Then, still naked, he went into the kitchen and put a large pot of water on to boil. It was the pot he customarily used for spaghetti and stew. He waited patiently until the water boiled, still not reflecting on what he had done. He wanted to finish the job, then sit down, relax, and savor his reactions.

When the water came to a rolling boil he immersed the ice ax head and shaft up to the leather around the handle. The tempered steel boiled clean. He dunked it three times, swirling it about, then turned the flame off under the pot, and held the ax head under the cold water tap to cool it.

When he could handle it, he inspected the ax carefully. He even took a small paring knife and gently pried up the top edge of the blue leather-covered handle. He could see no stains that might have leaked beneath. The ax smelled of steel and leather. It shone.

He took the little can of sewing machine oil from his kitchen closet and, with his bare hands, rubbed oil into the exposed steel surfaces of the ax. He applied a lot of oil, rubbing strongly, then wiped off the excess with a paper towel. He started to discard the towel in his garbage can, then thought better of it and flushed it down the toilet. The ice ax was left with a thin film of oil. He hung it away in the hall closet with his rucksack and crampons.

Then he showered thoroughly under very hot water, using a small brush on hands and fingernails. After he dried, he used cologne and powder, then donned a short cotton kimono. It was patterned with light blue cranes stalking across a dark blue background. Then he poured himself a small brandy, went into the living room, sat on the couch before the mirrored wall, and laughed.

Now he allowed himself to remember, and it was a beloved dream. He saw himself walking down that oranged street toward his victim. He was smiling, coat rakishly open, left hand inside the slit pocket, right arm swinging free. Was he snapping the fingers of his right hand? He might have been.

The smile. The nod. The hot surge of furious blood when he whirled and struck. The sound. He remembered the sound. Then the victim's incredible plunge forward that pulled the ice ax from his grasp, toppled him forward. Then, quickly pulling the ax free, search, wallet, and the steady walk homeward.

Well then . . . what did he feel? He felt, he decided, first of all an enormous sense of pride. That was basic. It was, after all, an extremely difficult and dangerous job of work, and he had brought it off. It was not too unlike a difficult and dangerous rock climb, a technical assignment that demanded skill, muscular strength and, of course, absolute resolve.

But what amazed him, what completely amazed him, was the *intimacy*! When he spoke to Celia about his love for the victim, he only hinted. For how could she understand? How could anyone understand that with one stroke of an ice ax he had *plundered* another human being, knowing him in one crushing blow, his loves, hates, fears, hopes—his *soul*.

Oh! It was something. To come so close to another. No, not close, but *in* another. Merged. Two made one. Once, he had suggested in a very vague, laughing, roundabout fashion to his wife that it might be fun if they sought out another woman, and the three might be naked together. In his own mind he had visualized the other woman as thin and dark, with enough sense to keep her mouth shut. But his wife didn't understand, didn't pick up on what he was suggesting. And if she had, she would have attributed it to his depraved appetites—a man naked in bed with two women.

But sex had nothing to do with it. That was the whole point! He wanted another woman both he and his wife could love because that would be a new, infinitely sweet intimacy between them. If he and his wife had gone to bed with a second woman, simultaneously sucked her hard nipples, caressed her, and their lips—his and his wife's—perhaps meeting on foreign flesh, well then . . . well then that would be an intimacy so sharp, so affecting, that he could hardly dream of it without tears coming to his eyes.

But now. Now! Recalling what he had done, he felt that sense of heightened intimacy, of entering into another, merging, so far beyond love that there was no comparison. When he killed Frank Lombard, he had become Frank Lombard, and the victim had become Daniel Blank. Linked, swooning, they swam through the endless corridors of the universe like two coupling astronauts cast adrift. Slowly tumbling. Turning. Drifting. Throughout all eternity. Never decaying. Never stopping. But caught in passion. Forever.

5

WHENEVER DANIEL Blank saw Florence and Samuel together, he remembered a film he had once seen on the life of sea otters. The pups! They nuzzled each other, touched, frolicked and frisked. And the Mortons' close-fitting helmets of black oily hair were exactly like pelts. He could not watch them without amused indulgence.

Now, seated in the couch in his apartment, they insisted on sharing one Scotch-on-the-rocks—which he had replenished four times. They were clad in their black leather jumpsuits, sleek as hides, and their bright eyes and ferrety features were alive and curious.

Since they were so ready—ready? eager!—to reveal intimate details of their private lives, they assumed all their friends felt the same. They wanted to know how his affair with Celia Montfort was coming along. Had they been physically intimate? Was it a satisfying sex relationship? Had he discovered anything more about her they should know? What was Anthony's role in her household? And Valenter's?

He answered in generalities and tried to smile mysteriously. After awhile, balked by his reticence, they turned to each other and began to discuss him as if they were alone in their own apartment. He had endured this treatment before (as had all their silent friends), and sometimes he found it entertaining. But now he felt uncomfortable and, he thought, perhaps fearful. What might they not stumble on?

"Usually," Sam said, speaking directly to Flo, "when a man like Dan is asked point-blank if his sex relations with a particular woman are satisfactory, he will say something like, 'How on earth would I know? I haven't been to bed with her.' That means, A, he is telling the truth and has not been to bed with her. Or B, he has been to bed with her and is lying to protect the lady's reputation."

"True," Flo nodded solemnly. "Or C, it was so bad he doesn't want to mention it because he has failed or the lady has failed. Or D, it was absolutely marvelous, so incredible he doesn't want to talk about it; he wants to keep this wonderful memory for himself."

"Hey, come on," Dan laughed. "I'm not—"

"Ah yes," Sam interrupted. "But when a man like Dan replies to the question, 'How was sex with this particular woman?' by answering, 'It was all right,' what are we to understand from that? That he has been to bed with the lady but the experience was so-so?"

"I think that is what Dan would like us to believe," Flo said thoughtfully. "I think he is concealing something from us, Samovel."

"I agree," he nodded. "What could it be? That he has not yet made the attempt?"

"Yes," Flo said. "That makes psychological sense. Dan is a man who was married several years to a woman his physical and mental inferior. Correct?"

"Correct. And during that time sex became a routine, a habit. Suddenly separated and divorced, he looks around for a new woman. But he feels uncertain. He has forgotten how to operate."

"Exactly," Flo approved. "He is unsure of himself. He fears he may be rejected. After all, the boy isn't a mad rapist. And if he is rejected, then he will think the failure of his marriage was his fault. And his ego can't accept that. So in Dan's approach to this new woman, he is careful. He is wary. Did you ever know a wary lover to succeed?"

"Never," Sam said definitely. "Successful sex always demands aggression, either attack on the man or surrender on the part of the woman."

"And surrender on the part of the woman is as valid a method of aggression as attack on the part of the man."

"Of course. You remember reading—"

But at this point, tiring of their game, Daniel Blank went into the kitchen to pour himself a fresh vodka. When he returned to the living room, they were still at it, their voices louder now, when the bell of the hall door rang so stridently they were shocked to silence. Daniel Blank, to whom an unexpected knock or ring now came as a heart flutter or spasm of the bowels, behaved, he assured himself later, with nonchalant coolness.

"Now who on earth can that be?" he inquired of no one.

He rose and moved to the hallway door. Through the peephole he caught a glimpse of a woman's hair—long, blonde hair—and a padded coat shoulder. Oh my God, he thought, it's Gilda. What's she doing here?

But when he unhooked the chain and opened the door, it wasn't Gilda. It was and it wasn't. He stared, trying to understand. She stared back just as steadily. It wasn't until his mouth opened in astonishment that she broke into a laugh, and then he saw it was Celia Montfort.

But what a Celia! Wearing a blonde wig down to her shoulders, with the tips curled upward. Thick makeup including scarlet lip rouge. A tacky tweed suit with a ruffled blouse. A necklace of oversize pearls. Crimson nail polish. And, obviously, a padded brassiere.

She had never seen his ex-wife, never seen a photo of her, but the resemblance was startling. The physical bulk was there, the gross good health, high color, muscular swagger, a tossing about of elbows and shoulders.

"My God," Daniel said admiringly, "you're marvelous."

"Am I like her?"

"You wouldn't believe. But why?"

"Oh . . . just for fun, as Tony would say. I thought you'd like it."

"I do. I really do, My God, you're so like her. You really should have been an actress."

"I am," she said. "All the time. Aren't you going to ask me in?"

"Oh, of course. Listen, the Mortons are here. I'll announce you as Gilda. I want to see their reactions."

He preceded her to the doorway of the living room.

"It's Gilda," he called brightly, then stepped aside.

Celia came to the doorway and stood posed, sweeping the Mortons with a beaming smile.

"Gilda!" Sam cried, bouncing to his feet. "This is—" He stopped.

"Gilda!" Florence cried, waving. "How nice that—" She stopped.

Then Celia and Daniel burst out laughing, and within a moment the Mortons were laughing too.

Flo came over to embrace Celia, then patted the padded shoulders of her suit and the tweed behind.

"A padded ass," she reported to the men. "And sponge rubber tits. My God, sweetie, you thought of everything."

"Do you think I'm like?"

"Like?" Sam said. "A dead ringer. Even the makeup."

"Perfect," Flo nodded. "Even to the fingernails. How did you do it?"

"Guessed," Celia said.

"You guessed right," Daniel said. "Now would you like to take off your jacket and get comfortable?"

"Oh no. I'm enjoying this."

"All right. Vodka?"

"Please."

He went into the kitchen to prepare new drinks for all of them. When he came back, Celia had turned off all the lights except for one standing lamp, and in the gloom she looked even more like his ex-wife. The resemblance was shattering, even to the way she sat upright in the Eames chair, her back straight, feet firmly planted on the floor, knees slightly spread as if the thickness of her thighs prevented a more modest pose. He felt . . . something.

"Why the disguise?" Flo asked.

"What's the point?" Sam asked.

Celia Montfort fluffed her blonde wig, smiled her secret smile.

"Haven't you ever wanted to?" she asked them all. "Everyone wants to. Walk away from yourself. Quit your job, desert wife or husband and family, leave your home and all your possessions, strip naked if that is possible, and move to another street, city, country, world, and become someone else. New name, new personality, new needs and tastes and dreams. Become someone entirely different, entirely new. It might be better or it might be worse, but it would be *different*. And you might have a chance, just a chance, in your new skin. Like being born again. Don't you agree, Daniel?"

"Oh yes," he nodded eagerly. "I do agree."

"I don't," Sam said. "I like who I am."

"And I like who I am," Flo said. "Besides, you can never change, really."

"Can't you?" Celia asked lazily. "What a drag."

They argued the possibility of personal change, *essential* change. Blank listened to the Mortons' hooted denials and sensed the presence of an obscene danger: he was tempted to refute them, calmly, a cool, sardonic smile on his lips, by saying, "I have changed. I killed Frank Lombard." He resisted the temptation, but toyed with the risk a moment, enjoying it. Then he contented himself with an unspoken, "I know something you don't know," and this childish thought, for reasons he could not comprehend, made them immeasurably dear to him.

Eventually, of course, they were all talked out. Daniel served coffee, which they drank mostly in silence. At an unseen signal, Flo and Sam Morton rose to their feet, thanked Daniel for a pleasant evening, congratulated Celia Montfort on her impersonation, and departed. Blank locked and chained his door behind them.

When he returned to the living room, Celia was standing. They embraced and kissed, his mouth sticking to the thick rouge on her lips. He felt her padded ass.

"Shall I take it off?" she asked.

"Oh no. I like it."

They emptied ashtrays, carried glasses to the kitchen sink.

"Can you stay?" he asked.

"Of course."

"Good."

She went into the bathroom. He moved around the apartment, checking windows, turning off lights, putting the iron bar on the hallway door. When he walked across the living room he saw his ghostly reflection jump from mirror to mirror, bits and pieces.

When he came back into the bedroom she was sitting quietly on the bed, staring.

"What do you want?" she asked, looking up at him.

"Oh, leave the wig on," he said quickly. "And the brassiere and girdle. Or whatever it is. You'll want to take off the suit and blouse."

"And slip? And stockings?"

"Yes."

"The pearls?"

"No, leave them on. Would you like a robe? I have a silk robe."

"All right."

"Is it too warm in here?"

"A little."

"I'll turn down the heat. Are you sleepy?"

"More tired than sleepy. The Mortons tire me. They never stop moving."

"I know. I showered this morning. Shall I shower now?"

"No. Let me hold you."

"Naked?"

"Yes."

Later, under a single light blanket, she held him, and through her silk robe he felt padded brassiere and girdle.

"Mommy," he said.

"I know," she murmured. "I know."

He curled up in her arms, began weeping quietly.

"I'm trying," he gasped. "I really am trying."

"I know," she repeated. "I know."

The thought of fucking her, or attempting it, offended him, but he could not sleep.

"Mommy," he said again.

"Turn over," she commanded, and so he did.

"Ahh," she said. "There."

"Oh. Oh."

"Am I hurting you?"

"Oh yes! Yes."

"Am I Gilda now?"

"Yes. But she never would."

"More?"

"Slowly. Please."

"What is my name?"

"Celia."

"What?"

"Gilda."

"What?"

"Mommy."

"That's better. Isn't that better?"

He slept, finally. It seemed to him he was awake a moment later.

"What?" he said. "What is it?"

"You were having a nightmare. You screamed. What was it?"

"A dream," he said, snuggling into her. "I had a bad dream."

"What did you dream?"

"All confused."

He moved closer to her, his hands on cotton batting and sponge rubber.

"Do you want me to do it again?" she asked.

"Oh yes," he said thankfully. "Please."

In the morning when he awoke, she was lying beside him, sleeping naked, having sometime during the night taken off her wig, robe, costume. But she still wore the pearls. He touched them. Then he moved stealthily down beneath the blanket until he was crouched, completely covered, and smelled her sweet warmth. He spread her gently. Then he drank from her, gulping from the fountain, greedy he, until he felt her come awake. Still he persisted, and she moved, reaching down under the blanket to press the back of his head. He groaned, almost swooning, fevered with the covered heat. He could not stop. Afterwards she licked his mouth.

And still later, when they were dressed and at the kitchen table, she said, "You'll do it again?"—more of a statement than a question.

He nodded wordlessly, knowing what she meant, and beginning to comprehend the danger she represented.

"From the front?" she asked. "Will you? And look into his eyes, and tell me?"

"Difficult," he said.

"You can do it," she said. "I know you can."

"Well . . ." He glowed. "It needs planning. And luck, of course."

"You make your own luck."

"Do I? Well. I'll think about it. It's an interesting problem."

"Will you do something for me?"

"Of course. What?"

"Come to me immediately afterwards."

He thought a moment.

"Perhaps not immediately afterwards. But soon. That night. Will that do?"

"I may not be home."

He was instantly suspicious. "Do you want to know the night? I don't know that myself. And won't."

"No, I don't want to know the night, or the place. Just the week. Then I'll stay home every night, waiting for you. Can you tell me the week?"

"Yes. I'll tell you that. When I'm ready."

"My love," she said. "The eyes," she said.

6

BERNARD GILBERT took life seriously—and he had a right to be mournful. Orphaned at an early age he had been *schlepped* around from uncle to aunt, cousin to cousin, six months at each, and always assured that the food he was eating, his bed, his clothes—all this came from the labor of his benefactors, at their expense.

At the age of eight he was shining shoes on the street, then delivering for a delly, then waiting on table, then selling little pieces of cloth, then bookkeeper in a third-rate novelty store. And all the time going to school, studying, reading books. All joylessly. Sometimes, when he had saved enough money, he went to a woman. That, too, was joyless. What could he do?

Through high school, two miserable years in the army, City College, always working, sleeping four or five hours a night, studying, reading, making loans and paying them back, not really thinking of *why*? but obeying an instinct he could not deny. And suddenly, there he was, Bernard Gilbert, C.P.A., in a new black suit, a hard worker who was good with numbers. This was a life?

There was a spine in him. Hard work didn't daunt him, and when he had to, he grovelled and shrugged it away. Much man. Not a swaggering, hairy-chested conqueror, but a survivor. A special kind of bravery; hope never died.

It came in his 32nd year when a distant cousin unexpectedly invited him for dinner. And there was Monica. "Monica, I'd like you to make the acquaintance of Bernard Gilbert. He's a C.P.A."

And so they were married, and his life began. Happy? You wouldn't believe! God said, "Bernie, I've been shitting on you for 32 years. You can take it, and it's time you deserve a break. Enjoy, kid, enjoy!"

First of all, there was Monica. Not beautiful, but handsome and strong. Another hard worker. They laughed in bed. Then came the two children, Mary and Sylvia. Beautiful girls! And healthy, thank God. The apartment wasn't much, but it was home. *Home!* His home, with wife and children. They all laughed.

The bad memories faded. It all went away: the cruelties, the hand-me-down clothes, the insults and crawling. He began, just began, to understand joy. It was a gift, and he cherished it. Bernard Gilbert: a melancholy man with sunken cheeks always in need of a shave, stooped shoulders, puzzled eyes, thinning hair, a scrawny frame: a man who, if he had his life to live over again, would have been a violinist. Well . . .

He had a good job with a large firm of accountants, where his worth was recognized. In the last few years he had started to moon-light, doing the tax returns of self-employed people like doctors, dentists, architects, artists, writers. He made certain his employers knew about it; they didn't object, since he was doing it on his own time and it didn't conflict with their own commercial accounts.

His private business grew. It was hard, putting in an eight-hour day and then coming home for another two- to four-hours' work. But he talked it over with Monica—he talked *everything* over with Monica—and they agreed that if he stuck to it, maybe within five to ten years he might be able to cut loose and start his own business. It was possible. So Monica took a course in accounting, studied at home, and after awhile she could help him at night, in addition to cooking and cleaning and taking care of Mary and Sylvia. They were both hard workers, but they never thought of it, would have been surprised if someone had told them they worked hard. What else?

So there they were in a third-floor walk-up on East 84th Street. It wasn't a fancy apartment, but Monica had painted it nice, and there were two bedrooms and a big kitchen where Monica made matzoh brie like he couldn't believe, it was so good, and a record player with all of Isaac Stern's recordings, and a card table where he could work. It wasn't luxury, he acknowledged, but he wasn't ashamed of it, and sometimes they had friends or neighbors in and laughed. Sometimes they even went out to eat, with the children, at an expensive restaurant, and were very solemn, giggling inside.

But the best times were when he and Monica would finish their night's work, and would sit on the couch, after midnight, the children asleep, and they just were there, listening to Vivaldi turned down low, just together. He would have worked his ass off for the rest of his life for moments like that. And when Monica brushed her lips across his sunken cheek . . . Oh!

He was thinking of moments like that when he got off the First Avenue bus. It wasn't even midnight. Well, maybe a little later. He had been downtown, working on the books of a medical clinic. It was a possible new account, a good one and a big one. The meeting with the doctors had taken longer than he had expected. Patiently he explained to them what the tax laws said they could do and what they could not do. He felt he had impressed them. They said they'd discuss it and let him know within a week. He felt good about it, but resolved not to be too optimistic when he discussed it with Monica. In case . . .

He turned into his own block. It had not yet been equipped with the new street lights, and far ahead, in the gloom, he saw a man walking toward him. Naturally, he was alerted—at that hour, in this city. But as they drew closer he saw the other man was about his age, well-dressed, coat flapping wide. He was striding along jauntily, left hand in his pocket, right arm swinging free.

They came close. Bernard Gilbert saw the other man was staring at him. But he was smiling. Gilbert smiled in return. Obviously the man lived in the neighborhood and wanted to be friendly. Gilbert decided he would say, "Good-evening."

They were two steps apart, and he had said, "Good—" when the man's right hand darted beneath the open flap of his coat and came out with something with a handle, something with a point, something that gleamed even in the dull street light.

Bernard Gilbert never did say, "—evening." He knew he halted and drew back. But the thing was in the air, swinging down. He tried to lift a defending arm, but it was too heavy. He saw the man's face, handsome and tender, and there was no hate there, nor madness, but a kind of ardor. Something struck high on Bernard Gilbert's forehead, slamming him down, and he knew he was falling, felt the crash of sidewalk against his back, wondered what had happened to his new-found joy, and heard God say, "Okay, Bernie, enough's enough."

PART FIVE

1

THREE TIMES a week a commercial messenger arrived at Captain Delaney's home with copies of the most recent Operation Lombard reports. Delaney noted they were becoming fewer and shorter, and Chief Pauley was sending his detectives back to recheck matters already covered: Lombard's private life and political career; possible links with organized crime; any similar assaults or homicides in the 251st Precinct, neighboring precincts, and eventually all of Manhattan, then all of New York; and then queries to the FBI and the police departments of large cities asking for reports of homicides of a similar nature.

Delaney admired Chief Pauley's professional competence. The Chief had assembled a force of almost 500 detectives brought in from all over the city. Many of these men Delaney knew personally or by reputation, and they included assault specialists, weapons technicians, men familiar with the political jungle, and detectives whose success was based on their interrogative techniques.

The result was nil: no angle, no handle, no apparent motive. Chief Pauley, in a confidential memo to Deputy Commissioner Broughton, had even suggested a possibility that Delaney himself had considered: the snuff had been committed by a policeman angered by Lombard's public attacks on the efficiency of the Department. Pauley didn't believe it.

Captain Delaney didn't either. A policeman would probably kill with a gun. But most career cops, who had seen mayors, commissioners, and politicians of all ranks come and go, would shrug off Lombard's criticism as just some more publicity bullshit, and go about their jobs.

The more Delaney pondered the killing, the more Operation Lombard reports he studied, the more firmly he became convinced that it was a motiveless crime. Not motiveless to the killer, of course, but motiveless to any rational man. Lombard had been a chance victim.

Delaney tried to fill up his hours. He visited his wife in the hospital twice a day, at noon and in the early evening. He did some brief interrogations of his own, visiting Frank Lombard's partner, his mother, and a few of his political associates. For these interviews Delaney wore his uniform and badge, risking Broughton's wrath if he should somehow discover what Delaney was up to. But it was all a waste of time; he learned nothing of value.

One evening, despairing of his failure to make any meaningful progress, he took a long pad of legal notepaper, yellow and ruled, and headed it "The Suspect." He then drew a line down the center of the page. The lefthand column he headed "Physical," the righthand column "Psychological." He resolved to write down everything he knew or suspected about the killer.

Under "Physical" he listed:

"Probable male, white."

"Tall, probably over six feet."

"Strong and young. Under 35?"

"Of average or good appearance. Possibly well-dressed."

"Very quick with good muscular coordination. An athlete?" Under "Psychological" he listed:

"Cool, determined."

"Driven by unknown motive."

"Psychopath? Unruh type?"

At the bottom of the page he made a general heading he called "Additional Notes." Under this he listed:

"Third person involved? Because of stolen license as 'proof of homicide.'"

"Resident of 251st Precinct?"

Then he reread his list. It was, he admitted, distressingly skimpy. But just the act of writing down what he knew—or guessed, rather; he *knew* nothing—made him feel better. It was all smoke and shadows. But he began to feel someone was there. Someone dimly glimpsed . . .

He read the list again, and again, and again. He kept coming back to the notation "Driven by unknown motive."

In all his personal experiences with and research on psychopathic killers he had never come across or read of a killer totally without motive. Certainly the motive might be irrational, senseless, but in every case, particularly those involving multiple murders, the killer had a 'motive.' It might be as obvious as financial gain; it might be an incredible philosophical structure as creepy and cheap as an Eiffel Tower built of glued toothpicks.

But however mad the assassin, he had his reasons: the slights of society, the whispers of God, the evil of man, the demands of political faith, the fire of ego, the scorn of women, the terrors of loneliness . . . whatever. *But he had his reasons.* Nowhere, in Delaney's experience or in his readings, existed the truly motiveless killer, the quintessentially evil man who slew as naturally and casually as another man lighted a cigarette or picked his nose.

There was no completely good man alive upon this earth and, Delaney believed—hoped!—there was no completely evil man. It was not a moral problem; it was just that no man was complete, in any way. So the killer of Frank Lombard had crushed his skull for a reason, a reason beyond logic and sense, but for a purpose that had meaning to him, twisted and contorted though it might be.

Sitting there in the gloom of his study, reading and rereading his sad little "Portrait of a Killer," Edward Delaney thought of this man existing, quite possibly not too far from where he now sat. He wondered what this man might be thinking and dreaming, might be hoping and planning.

In the morning he made his own breakfast, since it had been arranged that their day-only maid, Mary, would go directly from her home to the hospital, bringing Barbara fresh nightgowns and an address book she had requested. Delaney drank a glass of tomato juice, doggedly ate his way through two slices of unbuttered whole wheat toast, and drank two cups of black coffee. He scanned the morning paper as he ate. The Lombard story had fallen back to page 14. It said, in essence, there was nothing to say.

Wearing his winter overcoat, for the November day was chill, and the air smelled of snow, Delaney left the house before ten a.m. and walked over to Second Avenue, to a phone booth in a candy store. He dialed Deputy Inspector Thorsen's answering service, left his phone booth number, hung up, waited patiently. Thorsen was back to him within five minutes.

"I have nothing to report," Delaney said flatly. "Nothing."

Thorsen must have caught something in his tone, for he attempted to soothe.

"Take it easy, Edward. Broughton doesn't have anything either."

"I know."

"But I have some good news for you."

"What's that?"

"We were able to get your Lieutenant Dorfman a temporary appointment as Acting Commander of the Two-five-one Precinct."

"That's fine. Thank you."

"But it's only for six months. After that, either you'll be back on the job or we'll have to put in a captain or deputy inspector."

"I understand. Good enough. It'll help with the problem of Lombard's driver's license."

"What's the problem?"

"I'm on leave of absence, but I'm still on the Department list. I've got to report the license is missing."

"Edward, you worry too much."

"Yes. I do. But I've got to report it."

"That means Broughton will learn about it."

"Possibly. But if there is another killing, and I think there will be, and Chief Pauley's boys find the victim's license is missing—or anything like it—they'll check back with Lombard's widow down in Florida. She'll tell them I asked about the license and she couldn't find it. Then my ass will be in a sling. Broughton will have me up for withholding evidence."

"How do you want to handle it?"

"I've got to check the book, but as I recall, precinct reports of lost or stolen drivers' licenses are sent to Traffic Department personnel who then forward the report to the New York State Department of Motor Vehicles. I'll tell Dorfman about it and ask him to file the usual form. But Broughton might learn about it from Traffic. If they get a report that Frank Lombard's license is missing, someone will start screaming."

"Not to worry. We have a friend in Traffic."

"I thought you might have."

"Tell Dorfman to make out the usual form, but to call me before he sends it in. I'll tell him the man to send it to in Traffic. It will get to the State, but no one will tip Broughton. Does that satisfy you?"

"Yes."

"You're playing this very cautiously, Edward."

"Aren't you?"

"Yes, I guess we are. Edward, tell me . . ."

"What?"

"Are you making any progress at all? Even if it's something you don't want to talk about yet?"

"Yes," Delaney lied, "I'm making progress."

He walked back to his home, head bent, hands deep in overcoat pockets, trundling through the damp, gloomy day. His lie to Thorsen depressed him. It always depressed him when it was necessary to manipulate people. He would do it, but he would not enjoy it.

Why was it necessary to keep Thorsen's morale high? Because . . . because, Delaney decided, the Lombard homicide was more than just an intramural feud between the Broughton forces and the Thorsen-Johnson forces. In fact, he acknowledged, he had accepted their offer, not because he instinctively disliked Broughton and wanted him put down, or had any interest in Departmental politics, but because . . . because . . . because . . .

He groaned aloud, knowing he was once again at the bone, gnawing. Was it the intellectual challenge? The atavistic excitement of the chase? The belief he was God's surrogate on earth? Why did he do it! For that universe of harmony and rhythm he had described so glowingly to Thomas Handry? Oh shit! He only knew, mournfully, that the time, mental effort and creative energy spent exploring his own labyrinthine motives might better be spent finding the man who sent a spike smashing into the skull of Frank Lombard.

He came up to his own stoop, and there was Lieutenant Dorfman ringing his bell. The lieutenant turned as he approached, saw Delaney, grinned, came bouncing down the steps. He caught up Delaney's hand, shook it enthusiastically.

"I got it, Captain!" he cried. "Acting Commander for six months. I thank you!"

"Good, good," Delaney smiled, gripping Dorfman's shoulder. "Come in and have a coffee and tell me about it."

They sat in the kitchen, and Delaney was amused to note that Dorfman was already assuming the prerogatives of his new rank; he unbuttoned his uniform blouse and saw sprawled, his long, skinny legs thrust out. He would never have sat in such a position in the Captain's office, but Delaney could understand, and even approve.

He read the teletype Dorfman had brought over and smiled again.

"All I can tell you is what I said before: I'm here and I'll be happy to help you any way I can. Don't be shy of asking. There's a lot to learn."

"I know that, Captain, and I appreciate anything you can do. You've already done plenty recommending me."

Delaney looked at him closely. Here it was again: using people. He forced ahead.

"I was glad to do it," he said. "In return, there is something you can do for me."

"Anything, Captain."

"Right now, I am going to ask you for two favors. In the future, I will probably ask for more. I swear to you I will not ask you to do anything that will jeopardize your record or your career. If you decide my word is not sufficient—and believe me, I wouldn't blame you if you thought that—then I won't insist. All right?"

Dorfman straightened in his chair, his expression puzzled at first, then serious. He stared at Delaney a long moment, their eyes locked.

"Captain, we've worked together a long time."

"Yes. We have."

"I can't believe you'd ask me to do anything I shouldn't do."

"Thank you."

"What is it you want?"

"First, I want you to file a report with the Traffic Department of a missing driver's license. I want it clearly stated on the report that I was the one who brought this matter to your attention. Before the report is sent in, I ask you to call Deputy Inspector Thorsen. He will give you the name of the man in the Traffic Department to send the report to. Thorsen has assured me the report will be forwarded to the New York State Department of Motor Vehicles in the usual manner."

Dorfman was bewildered.

"That's not much of a favor, Captain. That's just routine. Is it your license?"

"No. It's Frank Lombard's."

Dorfman stared at him again, then slowly began to button up his uniform jacket.

"Lombard's?"

"Yes. Lieutenant, if you want to ask questions, I'll try to answer them. But please don't be insulted if I say that in this matter, the less you know, the better."

The tall, red-headed man stood, began to pace about the kitchen, hands thrust into his trouser pockets. He counted the walls, didn't look at Delaney.

"I've been hearing things," he said. "Rumors."

"I imagine you have," Delaney nodded, knowing there was scarcely a man in the Department, down to the lowliest probationary patrolman, who wasn't dimly aware of the feuds and schisms amongst high-level commanders. "You don't want to get involved in it, do you?"

Dorfman stopped and gripped the top rail of a kitchen chair with reddish hands, knuckles bulging. Now he looked directly at Delaney.

"No, Captain, I don't want to get involved at all."

"What I've asked so far is pure routine, is it not? I'm asking you to report a missing driver's license. That's all."

"All right. I'll call Thorsen, get the name of the man at the Traffic Department, and file a report. Do you know the license number?"

"No."

"What is the second favor you want, Captain?"

There was something in his voice, something sad. The Captain knew Dorfman would do as he, Delaney, requested. But somehow, subtly, their relationship had changed. Dorfman would pay his debt as long as he was not compromised. But once he paid what he felt was enough, they would no longer be mentor and student, captain and lieutenant. They would no longer be friends. They would be professional associates, cautious, pleasant but reserved, watchful. They would be rivals.

Delaney had, he acknowledged, already destroyed a cordial relationship. In some small way he had corrupted faith and trust. Now, to Dorfman, he was just another guy who wanted a favor. But there was no help for it, no turning back.

"The second favor," Delaney said, accenting the word "favor" somewhat ironically, "is that I would appreciate it, lieutenant—" and again he deliberately accented the word "lieutenant"—"if you would keep me personally informed of any assaults or homicides in the Two-five-one Precinct in which the circumstances and particularly the wound are similar to the Lombard homicide."

"That's all?" Dorfman asked, and now the irony was his.

"Yes."

"All right, Captain," Dorfman nodded. He hooked his collar, tugged his jacket straight. The stains and crumbs were missing now. He was Acting Commander of the 251st Precinct.

He strode to the door without another word. Then, hand on the knob, he paused, turned to face Delaney, and seemed to soften.

"Captain," he said, "in case you're interested, I already have orders to report any assault or homicide like that to Chief Pauley."

"Of course," Delaney nodded. "He couldn't do anything else. Report to him first."

"Then to you?"

"Then to me. Please."

Dorfman nodded, and was gone.

Delaney sat without moving. Then he held out his right hand. It was trembling, a bit. It had not gone as well as he had hoped or as badly as he had feared. But, he assured himself again, it had to be done—and perhaps it would have happened in the ordinary course of events. Dorfman was a natural worshipper, almost a hanger-on, and if he was to make anything of himself, eventually he would have to be cast adrift, sink or swim. And Delaney laughed ruefully at his own rationalizing. There was, he admitted disgustedly, too goddamn much Hamlet in him.

It was almost time to leave for the hospital. He consulted his little pocket notebook and checked off the items Mary had taken care of. He had already donned his overcoat and hard Homburg, his hand reaching for the outside doorknob, when the phone rang. He picked up the extension in the hall and said, "Captain Edward X. Delaney here."

"Captain, this is Christopher Langley."

"Mr Langley. Good to hear from you. How are you, sir?"

"Very well, and you?"

"Fine. I've been intending to call, but I didn't want you to feel I was pressuring you. So I thought it best to say *nothing*. You understand?"

There was silence for a moment, then Langley said, "I think I do understand. Gee, this is great! But it's been over a week since we met. Could we have lunch today, Captain? There's something I'd like your advice on."

"Oh?" Delaney said. "I'm afraid I can't make lunch. My wife is in the hospital, and I'm just leaving to visit her."

"I'm sorry to hear that, Captain. Nothing serious, I hope?"

"Well . . . we don't know. But it will take time. Listen, Mr Langley, what you wanted to talk me about—is it important?"

"It might be, Captain," the thin, flutey voice came back, excited now. "It's not anything final, but it's a beginning. That's why—"

"Yes, yes," Delaney interrupted. "Mr Langley, would it be possible for you to meet me at the hospital? I do want to see you. Unfortunately, I can't have lunch with you, but we'll have a chance to talk and discuss your problem."

"Excellent!" Christopher Langley chortled, and Delaney knew he was enjoying this cloak-and-dagger conversation. "I'll be glad to meet you there. I hope you may be able to help me. At least it will give me an opportunity to meet your wife."

Delaney gave him the address and room number, and then rang off. The Captain stood a moment, his hand still on the dead phone, and hoped, not for the first time, that he had acted correctly in entrusting the important job of weapon identification to this elderly dandy. He started to analyze his motives for enlisting Langley's aid: the man's expertise; the need to recruit a staff, however amateur; Langley's plea for "important" work; Delaney's need—

He snorted with disgust at his own maunderings. He wanted to *move* on the Lombard homicide, and it seemed to him he had spent an unconscionable amount of time interrogating himself, probing his own motives, as if he might be guilty of—of what? Dereliction of duty? He resolved to be done, for this day at least, with such futile searchings. What was necessary was to *do*.

Barbara was seated in a wheelchair at the window, and she turned her head to give him a dazzling smile when he entered. But he had come to dread that appearance of roseate good health—the bright eyes and flushed cheeks— knowing what it masked. He crossed the room swiftly, smiling, kissed her cheek, and presented her with what might have been the biggest reddest Delicious apple ever grown.

"An apple for the teacher," he said.

"What did I ever teach you?" she laughed, touching his lips.

"I'd tell you, but I don't want to get you unnecessarily excited."

She laughed again and turned the enormous apple in her slim fingers, stroking it. "It's beautiful."

"But probably mealy as hell. The big ones usually are."

"Maybe I won't eat it," she said faintly. "Maybe I'll just keep it next to my bed and look at it."

He was concerned. "Well . . . yes," he said finally. "Why not? Listen, how *are* you? I know you must be bored with me asking that, but you know I *must* ask it."

"Of course." She reached out to put a hand on his. "They started the new injections this morning. Two days before they know." *She* was comforting *him*.

He nodded miserably. "Is everything all right?" he asked anxiously. "I mean the food? The nurses?"

"Everything is fine." .

"I asked for Temples at that stand on First Avenue. They expect them next week. I'll bring them over then."

"It's not important."

"It *is* important," he said fiercely. "You like Temples, you'll get Temples."

"All right, Edward," she smiled, patting his hand. "It's important, and I'll get Temples."

Then she was gone. It had happened several times recently, and it frightened him. Her body seemed to stiffen, her eyes took on an unfocused stare. She ceased speaking but her lips moved, pouting and drawing apart, kissing, over and over, like a babe suckling, and with the same soft, smacking sound.

"Listen," he said hurriedly, "when Eddie was here last week, I thought he looked thin. Didn't you think he looked thin?"

"Honey Bunch," she said.

"What?" he asked, not understanding and wanting to weep.

"My Honey Bunch books," she repeated patiently, still looking somewhere. "What happened to them?"

"Oh," he said. "Your Honey Bunch books. Don't you remember? When Liza told us she was pregnant, we packed up all the children's books and sent them off to her."

"Maybe she'll send them back," she murmured, turning her head to look at him with blind eyes. "My Honey Bunch books."

"I'll get some for you."

"I don't want new ones. I want the old ones."

"I know, I know," he said desperately. "The old ones with the red covers and the drawings. I'll get them for you, Barbara. Barbara? Barbara?"

Slowly the focus of her eyes shortened. She came back. He saw it happen. Then she was looking at him.

"Edward?"

"Yes," he smiled, "I'm here."

She smiled, gripped his hand. "Edward," she repeated.

"Listen, Barbara, there is someone coming here to meet me. Christopher Langley. He's an ex-curator of the Metropolitan. I told you about him."

"Oh, yes," she nodded. "You told me. He's trying to identify the weapon in the Lombard case."

"Exactly!" he cried delightedly, and leaned forward to kiss her cheek.

"What was that for?" she laughed.

"For being you."

"Edward, when Eddie was here last week, didn't you think he looked a little thin?"

"Yes," he nodded. "I thought he looked a little thin."

He lurched his chair closer, clasping her hands, and they talked of little things: the drapes in the study, whether or not to draw out accumulated dividends on his insurance policy to help pay hospital costs, what he had for breakfast, a rude attendant in the X-ray lab, a nurse who had unaccountably broken into tears while taking Barbara's temperature. He told her about Dorfman's promotion. She told him about a pigeon that came to her windowsill every morning at the same time. They spoke in low, droning voices, not really hearing each other, but gripping hands and singing a lovely duet.

They came out of it, interrupted by a timid but persistent rapping on the hospital room door. Delaney turned from the waist. "Come in," he called.

And into the room came dashing the dapper Christopher Langley, beaming. And behind him, like a battle-ship plowing into the wake of a saucy corvette, came the massive Widow Zimmerman, also beaming. Both visitors carried parcels: brown paper bags of curious shape.

Delaney sprang to his feet. He shook Langley's little hand and bowed to the Widow. He introduced his wife to both. Barbara brightened immediately. She liked people, and she particularly liked people who knew what they were and could live with it.

There was talk, laughter, confusion. Barbara insisted on being moved back to the bed, knowing Edward would want to talk to Langley privately. The Widow Zimmerman planted her monumental butt in a chair alongside the bed and opened her brown paper bag. Gefilte fish! And homemade at that. The two men stood by, nodding and smiling, as the Widow expounded on the nutritive and therapeutic qualities of gefilte fish.

Within moments the good Widow had leaned forward over the bed, grasped one of Barbara's hands in her own meaty fists, and the two women were deep in a whispered discussion of such physical intimacy that the men hastily withdrew to a corner of the hospital room, pulled up chairs, leaned to each other.

"First of all, Captain," the little man said, "let me tell you immediately that I have not identified the weapon that killed Frank Lombard. I went through my books, I visited museums, and I saw several weapons—antique weapons—that could have made that skull puncture. But I agree with you: it was a modern weapon or tool. Gosh, I *thought* about it! Then, last week, I was walking down my street, and a Con Edison crew was tearing up the pavement. To lay a new cable, I suppose. They do it all the time. Anyway, they had a trench dug. There was a man in the trench, a huge black, and even in this weather he was stripped to the waist. A magnificent torso. Heroic. But Captain. An ordinary pick. A wooden handle as long as a woodman's ax, and then a steel head with a pick on each side, tapering to a point. Much too large to be the Lombard weapon, of course. And I remembered you felt the killer carried it concealed. Extremely difficult to carry a concealed pick."

"Yes," Delaney nodded, "it would be. But the pick idea is interesting."

"The shape!" Langley said, hunching forward. "That's what caught my eye. A square spike tapering to a sharp point. More than that, each spike of the pick curved downward, just as your surgeon described the wound. So I began wondering if that pick, customarily used in excavation and construction work, might have a smaller counterpart—a one-handed pick with a handle no longer than that of a hatchet."

Delaney brooded a moment. "I can't recall ever seeing a tool like that."

"I don't think there is one," Langley agreed. "At least, I visited six hardware stores and none of them had anything like what I described. But at the seventh hardware store I found this. It was displayed in their window."

He opened his brown paper bag and withdrew a tool: magician and rabbit. He handed it to Delaney. The Captain took it in his blunt fingers, stared, turned it over and over, hefted it, gripped it, swung it by the handle, peered at the head. He sniffed at the wood handle.

"What the hell *is* it?" he asked finally.

"It's a bricklayer's hammer," Langley said rapidly. "Handle of seasoned hickory. Head of forged steel. Notice the squared hammer on one side of the head? That's for tapping bricks into place in the mortar. Now look at the spike. The top surface curves downward, but the bottom side is horizontal. The spike itself doesn't curve downward. In addition, the spike ends in a sharp, chisel point, used to split bricks. I knew at once it wasn't the weapon we seek. But it's a start, don't you think?"

"Of course it is," Delaney said promptly. He swung the hammer in short, violent strokes. "My God, I never knew such a tool existed. You could easily split a man's skull with this."

"But it isn't what we want, is it?"

"No," Delaney acknowledged, "it isn't. The spike doesn't curve downward, and the end comes to a chisel edge about—oh, I'd guess an inch across. Mr Langley, there's something else I should have mentioned to you. This has a wooden handle. I admit Lombard might well have been killed with a wood-handle weapon, but my experience has been that with wood-handled implements, particularly old ones, the handle breaks. Usually at the point where it's been compressed into the steel head. I'd feel a lot better if we could find a tool or weapon that was made totally of steel. This is just a feeling I have, and I don't want to inhibit your investigation, sir."

"Oh, it won't, it won't!" the little man cried, bouncing up and down on his chair in his excitement. "I agree, I agree! Steel would be better. But I haven't told you everything that happened. In the store where I found this bricklayer's hammer, I asked the proprietor why he stocked them and how many he sold. After all, Captain, how many bricklayers are there in this world? And how many hammers would they need? Look at that tool. Wouldn't you judge that an apprentice bricklayer, buying a tool as sturdy as that, would use it for the rest of his professional career?"

Delaney hefted the hammer again, swinging it experimentally.

"Yes," he nodded, "I think you're right. The handle might possibly break, but this thing could last fifty, a hundred years."

"Exactly. Well, the hardware store owner said—and it's amazing how willing and eager men are to talk about their jobs and specialities—"

"I know," Delaney smiled.

"Well, he said he stocked those hammers because he sold twenty or thirty a year. And not only to bricklayers! He sold them he said, to 'rock hounds'—a term, as he explained it, that applies to the people who search for precious and semi-precious stones—gemmologists and others of their ilk. In addition, he sold a few hammers to amateur archeologists. I then asked if he knew of a smilar hammer on which the spike, instead of ending in a wide chisel edge, came to a sharp, tapered point. He said he had heard of such a hammer but had never seen it—a hammer made especially for rock hounds, prospectors, and archeologists. And this hammer had a spike, a pick, that tapered to a sharp point. I asked him where it might be available, but he couldn't say, except that I might try hobby and outdoor stores. What do you think, Captain?"

Delaney looked at him. "First of all," he said, "I think you have done remarkably well. Much better than I could have done." He was rewarded by

Langley's beam of pleasure. "And I hope you will be willing to track this thing down, to try to find the rock hound's hammer with a spike that curves downward and tapers to a point."

"Willing?" Christopher Langley shouted delightedly. "Willing?" And the two women at the bed, still speaking softly, broke off their conversation and looked over inquiringly.

"Willing?" Langley asked in a quieter voice. "Captain, I cannot stop now. I never knew detective work could be so fascinating."

"Oh yes," Delaney nodded solemnly, "fascinating."

"Well, I haven't had so much fun in my life. After we leave here, Myra and I—"

"Myra?" Delaney interrupted.

"The Widow Zimmerman," the old dandy said, casting his eyes downward and blushing. "She has several admirable qualities."

"I'm sure."

"Well, I made a list of hobby shops from the Yellow Pages. We're going to have lunch in the Times Square area, and then we're going around to all the addresses I have and try to locate a rock hound's hammer. Is that the right way, Captain?"

"Exactly the right way," Delaney assured him. "It's just what I'd do. Don't be discouraged if you don't find it in the first four or five or dozen or fifty places you visit. Stick to it."

"Oh, I intend to," Langley said stoutly, straightening up. "This is important, isn't it, Captain?"

Delaney looked at him strangely. "Yes," he nodded, "it *is* important. Mr Langley, I have a feeling about you and what you're doing. I think it's *very* important."

"Well," Christopher Langley said, "then I better get to it."

"May I keep this hammer?"

"Of course, of course. I have no use for it. I'll keep you informed as to our progress."

"*Our?*"

"Well . . . you know. I must take the Widow Zimmerman to lunch. She has been very kind to me."

"Of course."

"But I've told her nothing, Captain. *Nothing*. I swear. She thinks I'm looking for a rock hammer for my nephew."

"Good. Keep it that way. And I must apologize for my phone conversation this morning. I'm probably being overcautious. I doubt very much if my phone is being tapped, but there's no point in taking chances. When you want to reach me from now on, just dial my home phone and say something innocuous. I'll get back to you within ten or fifteen minutes from an outside phone. Will that be satisfactory?"

Then the ex-curator did something exceedingly curious. He made an antique gesture Delaney had read about in Dickens' novels but had never seen. Langley laid a forefinger alongside his nose and nodded wisely. Captain Delaney was delighted.

"Exactly," he nodded.

Then they were gone, waving goodby to Barbara and promising to visit her again. When the door closed behind them, Barbara and Edward looked at each other, then simultaneously broke into laughter.

"I like her," Barbara told him. "She asked very personal questions on short acquaintance, but I think it was from genuine interest, not just idle curiosity. A very warm, out-going, good-hearted woman."

"I think she's after Langley."

THE FIRST DEADLY SIN

"So?" she challenged. "What's wrong with that? She told me she's been very lonely since her husband died, and he's all alone, too. It's not good to be alone when you get old."

"Look at this," he said, changing the subject hastily. "It's a bricklayer's hammer. This is what Langley's come up with so far."

"Is that what killed Lombard?"

"Oh no. But it's close. It's an ugly thing, isn't it?"

"Yes. Evil-looking. Put it away, please, dear."

He put it back in the brown paper sack and placed it atop his folded overcoat, so he wouldn't forget it when he left. Then he drew up a chair alongside her bed.

"What are you going to do with the gefilte fish?" he smiled.

"I may try a little. Unless you'd like it, Edward?"

"No, thank you!"

"Well, it was nice of her to bring it. She's one of those women who think food solves all problems and you can't be miserable on a full stomach. Sometimes they're right."

"Yes."

"You're discouraged, aren't you, Edward?"

He rose and began to stalk up and down at the foot of her bed, hands shoved into his hip pockets.

"Nothing is happening!" he said disgustedly. "I'm not *doing* anything."

"You're convinced the killer is crazy?"

"It's just an idea," he sighed, "but the only theory that makes any sense at all. But if I'm right, it means we have to wait for another killing before we learn anything more. That's what's so infuriating."

"Isn't that hammer Langley brought a lead?"

"Maybe. Maybe not. But even if Lombard had been murdered with a hammer exactly like that, I'd be no closer to finding the killer. There must be hundreds—thousands!—of hammers exactly like that in existence, and more sold every day. So where does that leave me?"

"Come over here and sit down." She motioned toward the chair at the bedside. He slumped into it, took her proffered hand. She lifted his knuckles to her face, rubbed them softly on her cheek, kissed them. "Edward," she said. "Poor Edward."

"I'm a lousy cop," he grumbled.

"No," she soothed. "You're a good cop. I can't think of anything you could have done that you haven't done."

"Operation Lombard did it all," he said dispiritedly.

"You discovered his driver's license was missing."

"Oh sure. Whatever the hell that means."

After 30 years of living with this man, she was almost as familiar with police procedure as he. "Did they check license numbers of parked cars?" she asked.

"Of course. Chief Pauley saw to that. The license number of every parked car in a five-block area was taken down on three successive nights. Then the owners were looked up and asked if they saw anything on the night of the murder. What a job that must have been! But Broughton has the manpower to do it, and it had to be done. They got nothing. Just like the questioning of residents in the neighborhood. Zero."

"Occam's Razor," she said, and he smiled, knowing what she meant.

Several years ago he had come across the unfamiliar phrase "Occam's Razor" in a criminologist's report dealing with percentages and probabilities in homicide cases in the Boston area. Delaney trusted the findings since the percentages quoted were very close to those then current in New York: the great majority of homicides were committed by relatives or "friends" of the victim—mothers, fathers, children, husbands, wives, uncles, aunts, neighbors . . . In other words, most killings involved people who knew each other.

In light of these findings, the Boston criminologist had stated, it was always wise for investigating officers to be guided by the principle of "Occam's Razor."

Intrigued by the phrase, Delaney had spent an afternoon in the reading room of the 42nd Street library, tracking down Occam and his "Razor." Later he told Barbara what he had discovered.

"Occam was a fourteenth century philosopher," he reported. "His philosophy was 'nominalism,' which I don't understand except that I think he meant there are no universal truths. Anyway, he was famous for his hard-headed approach to problem solving. He believed in shaving away all extraneous details. That's why they call his axiom 'Occam's Razor.' He said that when there are several possible solutions, the right one is probably the most obvious. In other words, you should eliminate all the unnecessary facts."

"But you've been doing that all your life, Edward."

"I guess so," he laughed, "but I call it 'Cut out the crap.' Anyway, it's nice to know a fourteenth century philosopher agrees with me. I wish I knew more about philosophy and could understand it."

"Does it really bother you that you can't?"

"Nooo . . . it doesn't bother me, but it makes me realize the limitations of my intelligence. I just can't think in abstractions. You know I tried to learn to play chess three times and finally gave up."

"Edward, you're more interested in people than things, or ideas. You have a very good intelligence for people."

Now, in the hospital room, when Barbara mentioned Occam's Razor, he knew what she meant and smiled ruefully.

"Well," he said, rubbing his forehead, "I wonder if old Occam ever tried solving an irrational problem by rational means. I wonder if he wouldn't begin to doubt the value of logic and deductive reasoning when you're dealing with—"

But then the door to the hospital room swung open, and Dr Louis Bernardi glided in, olive skin gleaming, his little eyes glittering. A stethoscope was draped about his neck.

He offered Delaney a limp hand, and with the forefinger of his left hand lovingly caressed his ridiculous stripe of a mustache.

"Captain," he murmured. "And you, dear lady," he inquired in a louder voice, "how are we feeling today?"

Barbara began to explain that her feet continued to be swollen uncomfortably, how the rash had reappeared on the insides of her thighs, that the attack of nausea had seemed to worsen with the first injection of the antibiotic.

To each complaint Bernardi smiled, said, "Yes, yes," or "That doesn't bother me."

Why should it bother you, Delaney thought angrily. It's not happening to you, you little prick.

Meanwhile the doctor was taking her pulse, listening to her heart, gently pushing up eyelids to peer into her staring eyes.

"You're making a fine recovery from surgery," he assured her. "And they tell me your appetite is improving. I am so very happy, dear lady."

"When do you think—" Delaney began, but the doctor held up a soft hand.

"Patience," he said. "You must have patience. And I must have patients. He!"

Delaney turned away in disgust, not understanding how Barbara could trust this simpering popinjay.

Bernardi mumured a few more words, patted Barbara's hand, smiling his oleaginous smile, then turned to go. He was almost at the door when Delaney saw he was leaving.

"Doctor," he called, "I want to talk to you a minute." He said to Barbara, "Be right back, dear."

In the hall, the door of the room closed, he faced Bernardi and looked at him stonily. "Well?" he demanded.

The doctor spread his hands in that familiar bland gesture that said nothing. "What can I tell you? You can see for youself. The infection still persists. That damned Proteus. We are working our way through the full spectrum of antibiotics. It takes time."

"There's something else."

"Oh? What is that?"

"Recently my wife has been exhibiting signs of—well, signs of irrationality. She gets a curious stare, she seems suddenly withdrawn, and she says things that don't make too much sense."

"What kind of things?"

"Well, a little while ago she wanted some children's books. I mean books she owned and read when she was a child. She's not under sedation, is she?"

"Not now, no."

"Pain-killers? Sleeping pills?"

"No. We are trying to avoid any possibility of masking or affecting the strength of the antibiotics. Captain, this does not worry me. Your wife has undergone major surgery. She is under medication. The fever is, admittedly, weakening her. It is understandable that she might have brief periods of—oh, call it wool-gathering. He! I suggest you humor her insofar as that is possible. Her pulse is steady and her heart is strong."

"As strong as it was?"

Bernardi looked at him without expression. "Captain," he said softly—and Delaney knew exactly what was coming—"your wife is doing as well as can be expected."

He nodded, turned, glided away, graceful as a ballet dancer. Delaney was left standing alone, impotent fury hot in his throat, convinced the man knew something, or suspected something, and would not put it into words. He seemed blocked and thwarted on all sides: in his work, in his personal life. What was it he had said to Thomas Handry about a divine order in the universe? Now order seemed slipping away, slyly, and he was defeated by a maniacal killer and unseen beasts feeding on his wife's flesh.

From the man on the beat to the police commissioner—all cops knew what to expect when the moon was full: sleep-walkers, women who heard voices, men claiming they were being bombarded by electronic beams from a neighbor's apartment, end-of-the-world nuts, people stumbling naked down the midnight streets, urinating as they ran.

Now Delaney, brooding on war, crime, senseless violence, cruel sickness, brutality, terror, and the slick, honeyed words of a self-satisfied physician, wondered if this was not The Age of the Full Moon, with order gone from the world and irrationality triumphant.

He straightened, set his features into a smile, reentered his wife's hospital room.

"I suddenly realized why solving the Lombard killing is so important to me," he told her. "It happened in the Two-five-one Precinct. That's my world."

"Occam's Razor," she nodded.

Later, he returned home and Mary fixed him a baked ham sandwich and brought that and a bottle of cold beer into his study. He propped the telephone book open on his desk, and as he ate he called second-hand bookstores, asking for original editions of the Honey Bunch books, the illustrated ones.

Everyone he called seemed to know immediately what he wanted: the Grossett & Dunlap editions published in the early 1920s. The author was Helen Louise Thorndyke. But no one had any copies. One bookseller took his name and address and promised to try to locate them. Another suggested he try the chic "antique boutiques" on upper Second and Third Avenues, shops that specialized in nostalgic Americana.

Curiously, this ridiculous task seemed to calm him, and by the time he had finished his calls and his lunch, he was determined to get back to work, to work steadily and unquestioningly, just doing.

He went to his book shelves and took down every volume he owned dealing, even in peripheral fashion, with the histories, analyses and detection of mass murderers. The stack he put on the table alongside his club chair was not high: literature on the subject was not extensive. He sat down heavily, put on his thick, horn-rimmed reading glasses, and began to plow through the books, skipping and skimming as much as he could of material that had no application to the Lombard case.

He read about Gille de Raix, Verdoux, Jack the Ripper and in more recent times, Whitman, Speck, Unruh, the Boston strangler, Panzram, Manson, the boy in Chicago who wrote with the victim's lipstick on her bathroom mirror, "Stop me before I kill more." It was a sad, sad chronicle of human aberration, and the saddest thing of all was the feeling he got of killer as victim, dupe of his own agonizing lust or chaotic dreams.

But there was no pattern—at least none he could discern. Each mass killer, of tens, hundreds, reputedly thousands, was an individual and had apparently acted from unique motives. If there was any pattern it existed solely in each man: the *modus operandi* remained identical, the weapon the same. And in almost every case, the period between killings became progressively shorter. The killer was caught up in a crescendo: more! more! faster! faster!

One other odd fact: the mass killer was invariably male. There were a few isolated cases of women who had killed several times; the Ohio Pig Woman was one, the Beck-Fernandez case involved another. But the few female mass murderers seemed motivated by desire for financial gain. The males were driven by wild longings, insane furies, mad passions.

The light faded; he switched on the reading lamp. Mary stopped by to say good-night, and he followed her into the hall to double-lock and chain the front door behind her. He returned to his reading, still trying to find a pattern, a repeated cause-effect, searching for the percentages.

It was almost five in the evening when the front doorbell chimed. He put aside the article he was reading—a fascinating analysis of Hitler as a criminal rather than a political leader—and went out into the hallway again. He switched on the stoop light, peered out the etched glass panel alongside the door. Christopher Langley was standing there, a neat white shopping bag in one hand. Delaney unlocked the door.

"Captain!" Langley cried anxiously. "I hope I'm not disturbing you? But I didn't want to call, and since it was on my way home, I thought I'd take the chance and—"

"You're not disturbing me. Come in, come in."

"Gee, what a marvelous house!"

"Old, but comfortable."

They went into the lighted study.

"Captain, I've got—"

"Wait, just a minute. Please, let me get you a drink. Anything?"

"Sherry?"

"At the moment, I'm sorry to say, no. But I have some dry vermouth. Will that do?"

"Oh, that's jim-dandy. No ice. Just a small glass, please."

Delaney went over to his modest liquor cabinet, poured Langley a glass of vermouth, took a rye for himself. He handed Langley his wine, got him settled in the leather club chair. He retreated a few steps out of the circle of light cast by the reading lamp and stood in the gloom.

"You health, sir."

"And yours. And your wife's."

"Thank you."

They both sipped.

"Well," Delaney said, "how did you make out?"

"Oh, Captain, I was a fool, *such* a fool! I didn't do the obvious thing, the thing I should have done in the first place."

"I know," Delaney smiled, thinking of Occam's Razor again. "I've done that many times. What happened?"

"Well, as I told you at the hospital, I had gone through the Yellow Pages and made a list of hobby shops in the midtown area, places that might sell a rock hound's hammer with a tapered pick. The Widow Zimmerman and I had lunch—I had stuffed sole: marvelous—and then we started walking around. We covered six different stores, and none of them carried rock hammers. Some of them didn't even know what I was talking about. I could tell Myra was getting tired, so I put her in a cab and sent her home. She is preparing dinner for me tonight. By the by, she's an awful cook. I thought I'd try a few more stores before calling it a day. The next one on my list was Abercrombie & Fitch. And of course they carried a rock hound's hammer. It was so obvious! It's the largest store of its kind in the city, and I should have tried them first. That's why I say I was a fool. Anyway, here it is."

He leaned over, pulled the tool from his white shopping bag, handed it to Captain Delaney.

The hammer was still in its vacuum-packed plastic coating, and the cardboard backing stated it was a "prospector's ax recommended for rock collectors and archeologists." Like the bricklayers' hammer, it had a wood handle and steel head. One side of the head was a square hammer. The other side was a pick, about four inches long. It started out as a square, then tapered to a sharp point. The tool came complete with a leather holster, enabling it to be worn on a belt. The whole thing was about as long as a hatchet: a one-handed implement.

"Notice the taper of the pick," Langley pointed out. "It comes to a sharp point, but still the pick itself does not curve downward. The upper surface curves, but the lower surface is almost horizontal, at right angles to the handle. And, of course, it has a wooden handle. But still, it's closer to what we're looking for—don't you think?"

"No doubt about it," Delaney said definitely. "If that pick had a downward curve, I'd say this is it. May I take off the plastic covering?"

"Of course."

"You're spending a lot of money."

"Nonsense."

Delaney stripped off the clear plastic covering and hefted the ax in his hand.

"This is almost it," he nodded. "A tapered spike coming to a sharp point. About an inch across at the base of the pick. And with enough weight to crush a man's skull. Easily. Maybe this really is it. I'd like to show it to the police surgeon who did the Lombard autopsy.

"No, no," Christopher Langley protested. "I haven't told you the whole story. That's why I stopped by tonight. I bought this in the camping department, and I was on my way out to the elevators. I passed through a section where they sell skiing and mountain climbing gear. You know, rucksacks and crampons and pitons and things like that. And there, hanging on the wall, was something very interesting. It was an implement I've never seen before. It was about three feet long, a two-handed tool. I ruled it out immediately as our weapon: too cumbersome to conceal. And the handle was wood. At the butt end was a sharp steel spike, about three inches long, fitted into the handle. But it was the head that interested me. It was apparently chrome-plated steel. On one side was a kind of miniature mattock coming to a sharp cutting edge, a chisel edge. And the other side was exactly what we're looking for! It was a spike, a pick, about four or five inches long. It started out from the head as a square, about an inch on each side. Then it was formed into a triangle with a sharp edge on top and the base an inch across. Then the whole thing tapered, and as it thinned, it curved downward. Captain, *the whole pick curved downward,* top and bottom! It came to a sharp point, so sharp in fact that the tip was covered with a little rubber sleeve to prevent damage when the implement wasn't being used. I removed the rubber protector, and the underside of the tip had four little saw teeth. It's serrated, for cutting. I finally got a clerk and asked him what this amazing tool was called. He said it's an ice ax. I asked him what it was used for, and he—"

"What?" Delaney cried. "What did you say?"

"I asked the clerk what it was used—"

"No, no," the Captain said impatiently. "What did the clerk say it was called?"

"It's an ice ax."

"Jesus Christ," Delaney breathed. "Leon Trotsky. Mexico City. Nineteen-forty."

"What? Captain, I don't understand."

"Leon Trotsky. He was a refuge from Stalin's Russia—or perhaps he escaped or was deported; I don't remember exactly; I'll have to look it up. Trotsky and Lenin and Stalin were equals at one time. Then Lenin died. Then Stalin wanted to be Numero Uno. So Trotsky got out of Russia, somehow, and made his way to Mexico City. They caught up with him in nineteen-forty. At least it was said the assassin was an agent of the Russian Secret Police. I don't recall the details. But he killed Trotsky with an ice ax."

"Surely you don't think there's any connection between that and Frank Lombard's death?"

"Oh no. I doubt that very much. I'll look into it, of course, but I don't think there's anything there."

"But you think Lombard may have been killed with an ice ax?"

"Let me freshen your drink," Delaney said. He went over to the liquor cabinet, came back with new drinks for both of them. "Mr Langley, I don't know whether being a detective is a job, a career, a profession, a talent or an art. There are some things I do know. One, you can't teach a man to be a *good* detective, anymore than you can teach him to be an Olympic miler or a great artist. And two, no matter how much talent and drive a man starts out with, he can never become a *good* detective without experience. The more years, the better. After you've been at it awhile, you begin to see the patterns. People repeat, in motives, weapons, methods of entrance and escape, alibis. You keep finding the same things happening over and over again; forced windows, kitchen knives, slashed screens, tire irons, jammed locks, rat poison—the lot. It all becomes familiar. Well, what bugged me about the Lombard killing, nothing *familiar* in it. Nothing! The first reaction, of course, going by percentages, was that it had been committed by a relative or acquaintance, someone known to Lombard. Negative. The next possibility was that it was an attempted robbery, a felony-homicide. Negative. His money hadn't even been touched. And worst of all, we couldn't even identify the weapon. But now you walk in here and say, 'Ice ax.' Magic words! Click! Trotsky was killed with an ice ax. Suddenly I've got something *familiar*. A murder weapon that's been used before. It's hard to explain, I know, Mr Langley, but I feel better about this than I've felt since it started. I think we're moving now. Thanks to you."

The man glowed.

"But I'm sorry," Delaney said. "I interrupted you. You were telling me what the clerk at Abercrombie & Fitch said when you asked him what the ice ax was used for. What did he say?"

"What?" Langley asked again, somewhat dazed. "Oh. Well, he said it was used in mountain climbing. You could use it like a cane, leaning on the head. The spike on the butt of the handle bites into crusty snow or ice, if you're hiking across a glacier, for instance. He said you could get this ice ax with different ends on the butt—a spike, the way I saw it, or with a little wheel, like a ski pole, for soft snow, and so forth. So then I asked him if there was a shorter ice ax available, a one-handed tool, but with the head shaped the same way. He was very vague; he wasn't sure. But he thought there was such an implement, and he thought the whole thing might be made of steel. Think of that, Captain! A one-handed tool, all steel, with a spike that curves downward and tapers to a sharp point as it curves. How does that strike you?"

"Excellent!" Captain Delaney crowed. "Just excellent! It's now a familiar weapon, used in a previous homicide, and I feel very good about it. Mr Langley, you've done wonders."

"Oh," the old man smiled, "it was mostly luck. Really."

"You make your own luck," Delaney assured him. "And my luck. Our luck. You followed through. Did the clerk tell you where you can buy a one-handed ice ax?"

"Well . . . no. But he did say there were several stores in New York that specialized in camping and mountain climbing equipment—axes, hatchets, crampons, special rucksacks, nylon rope and things of that sort. The stores must be listed somewhere. Probably in the Yellow Pages. Captain, can I stick with this?"

Delaney took two quick steps forward, clapped the little man on both arms.

"Can you?" he declaimed. "*Can* you? I should think you can! You're doing just fine. You try to pin down that one-handed, all-steel ice ax, who sells them, who buys them. Meanwhile, I want to dig into the Trotsky murder, maybe get a photo of the weapon. And I want to get more information on mountain climbers. Mr. Langley, we're moving. We're really *doing* now! I'll call you or you call me. The hell with security. I just feel—I *know*—we're heading in the right direction. Instinct? Maybe. Logic has nothing to do with it. It just *feels* right."

He got Langley out of there, finally, bubbling with enthusiasm and plans of how he intended to trace the ice ax. Delaney nodded, smiled, agreeing to everything Langley said until he could, with decency, usher him out, lock the front door, and come back into the study. He paced up and down in front of his desk, hands shoved into hip pockets, chin on chest.

Then he grabbed up the telephone directory, looked up the number, and dialed Thomas Handry's newspaper. The switchboard operator gave him the City Room where they told him Handry had left for the day. He asked for Handry's home phone number, but they wouldn't give it to him.

"Is it an unlisted number?" he asked.

"Yes, it is."

"This is Captain Edward X. Delaney, New York Police Department," the Captain said in his most pontifical tones. "I'm calling on official business. I can get Handry's phone number from the telephone company, if you insist. It would save time if you gave it to me. If you want to check on me, call your man at Centre Street. Who is he—Slawson?"

"Slawson died last year."

"I'm sorry to hear that. He was a good reporter."

"Yes. Just a minute, Captain."

The man came back and read off Handry's home phone number. Delaney thanked him, hung up, waited a few seconds, then lifted the receiver again and dialed. No answer. He waited ten minutes and called again. Still no answer.

There wasn't much in the refrigerator: half of that same baked ham he had had for lunch and some salad stuff. He sliced two thick slices of ham, then sliced a tomato and cucumber. He smeared mustard on the ham, and salad dressing on the rest. He ate it quickly, crunching on a hard roll. He glanced several times at his watch as he ate, anxious to get back to the hospital.

He slid plate and cutlery into the sink, rinsed his hands, and went back into his study to call Handry again. This time he got through.

"Hello?"

"Thomas Handry?"

"Yes."

"Captain Edward X. Delaney here."

"Oh. Hello, Captain. How are you?"

"Well, thank you. And you?"

"Fine. I heard you're on leave of absence."

"Yes, that's true."

"I understand your wife is ill. Sorry to hear that. I hope she's feeling better."

"Yes. Thank you. Handry, I want a favor from you."

"What is it, Captain?"

"First of all, I want some information on the murder of Leon Trotsky in Mexico City in nineteen-forty. I thought you might be able to get it from your morgue."

"Trotsky in Mexico City in nineteen-forty? Jesus, Captain, that was before I was born."

"I know."

"What do you want?"

"Nothing heavy. Just what the newspapers of the time reported. How he was killed, who killed him, the weapon used. If there was a photograph of the weapon published, and you could get a photostat, that would help."

"What's this all about?"

"The second thing," Delaney went on, ignoring the question, "is that I'd like the name and address of the best mountain climber in New York—the top man, or most experienced, or most skillful. I thought you might be able to get it from your Sports Desk."

"Probably. Will you please tell me what the hell this is all about?"

"Can you have a drink with me tomorrow? Say about five o'clock?"

"Well . . . sure. I guess so."

"Can you have the information by then?"

"I'll try."

"Fine. I'll tell you about it then." Delaney gave him the address of the chop house where he had lunched with Dr. Ferguson. "Is that all right, Handry?"

"Sure. I'll see what I can do. Trotsky and the mountain climber. Right?"

"Right. See you tomorrow."

Delaney hurried out and got a cab on Second Avenue. He was at the hospital within fifteen minutes. When he gently opened the door of his wife's room he saw at once she was sleeping. He tiptoed over to the plastic armchair, switched off the floor lamp, then took off his overcoat. He sat down as quietly as he could.

He sat there for two hours, hardly moving. He may have dozed off a few minutes, but mostly he stared at his wife. She was sleeping calmly and deeply. No one came into the room. He heard the corridor sounds dimly. Still he sat, his mind not so much blank as whirring, leaping, jumping about without order or connection: their children, Handry, Langley, Broughton, the Widow Zimmerman, the ice ax, Thorsen and Johnson, a driver's license—a smear of thoughts, quick frames of a short movie, almost blending, looming, fading . . .

At the end of the two hours he scrawled a message in his notebook, tore the page out, propped it on her bedside table. "I was here. Where were you? Love and violets. Ted." He tiptoed from the room.

He walked back to their home, certain he would be mugged, but he wasn't. He went back into his study and resumed his readings of the histories, motives and methods of mass murderers. There was no one pattern.

He put the books aside, turned off the study lights shortly after midnight. He toured the basement and street floor, checking windows and locks. Then he trudged upstairs to undress, take a warm shower, and shave. He pulled on fresh pajamas. The image of his naked body in the bathroom mirror was not encouraging. Everything—face, neck, breasts, abdomen, ass, thighs— seemed to be sinking.

He got into bed, switched off the bedside lamp, and lay awake for almost an hour, turning from side to side, his mind churning. Finally he turned on the lamp, shoved his feet into wool slippers, went padding down to the study again. He dug out his list, the one headed "The Suspect." Under the "Physical" column he had jotted "An athlete?" He crossed this out and instead inserted "A mountain climber?" At the bottom, under "Additional Notes," he wrote "Possesses an ice ax?"

It wasn't much, he admitted. In fact, it was ridiculous. But when he turned out the study lights, climbed once more to the empty bedroom, and slid into bed, he fell asleep almost instantly.

2

"You didn't give me much time," Thomas Handry said, unlocking his attache case. "I guessed you'd be more interested in the assassination itself rather than the political background, so most of the stuff I've got is on the killing."

"You guessed right," Captain Delaney nodded. "By the way, I read all your articles on the Department. Pretty good, for an outsider."

"Thanks a whole hell of a lot!"

"You want to write poetry, don't you?"

Handry was astonished, physically. He jerked back in the booth, jaw dropping, took off his Benjamin Franklin reading glasses.

"How did you know that?"

"Words and phrases you used. The rhythm. And you were trying to get inside cops. It was a good try."

"Well . . . you can't make a living writing poetry."

"Yes. That's true."

Handry was embarrassed. So he looked around at the paneled walls, leather-covered chairs, old etchings and play-bills, yellowed and filmed with dust.

"I like this place," he said. "I've never been here before. I suppose it was created last year, and they sprayed dirt on everything. But they did a good job. It really does look old."

"It is," Delaney assured him. "Over a hundred years. It's not a hype. How's your ale?"

"Real good. All right, let's get started." He took handwritten notes from his attache case and began reading rapidly.

"Leon Trotsky. Da-dah da-dah da-dah. One of the leaders of the Russian Revolution, and after. A theorist. Stalin drives him out of Russia, but still doesn't trust him. Trotsky, even overseas, could be plotting. Trotsky gets to Mexico City. He's suspicious, naturally. Very wary. But he can't live in a closet. A guy named Jacson makes his acquaintance. It's spelled two ways in newspaper reports: J-a-c-s-o-n and J-a-c-k-s-o-n. A white male. He visits Trosky for at least six months. Friends. But Trotsky never sees *anyone* unless his secretaries and bodyguards are present. August twentieth, nineteen-forty, Jacson comes to visit Trotsky, bringing an article he's written that he wants Trotsky to read. I couldn't find what it was about. Probably political. Jacson is invited into the study. For the first time the secretaries aren't notified. Jacson said later that Trotsky started reading the article. He sat behind his desk. Jacson stood at his left. He had a raincoat, and in the pockets were an ice ax, a revolver, and a dagger. He said—"

"Wait a minute, wait a minute," Delaney protested. "Jacson had an ice ax in his raincoat pocket? Impossible. It would never fit."

"Well, one report said it was in the raincoat pocket. Another said it was concealed by Jacson's raincoat."

"'Concealed.' That's better."

"All right, so Trotsky is reading Jacson's article. Jacson takes the ice ax from under his raincoat, or out of the pocket, and smashes it down on Trotsky's skull. Trotsky shrieks and throws himself on Jacson, biting his left hand. Beautiful. Then he staggers backward. The secretaries come running in and grab Jacson."

"Why the revolver and dagger?"

"Jacson said they were to be used to kill himself after he killed Trotsky."

"It smells. Did Trotsky die then, in his study?"

"No. He lived for about twenty-six hours. Then he died."

"Any mention of the direction of the blow?"

"On top of Trotsky's head, as far as I can gather. Trotsky was seated, Jacson was standing."

"What happened to him?"

"Jacson? Imprisoned. One escape try failed, apparently planned by the GPU. That's what the Russian Secret Police was called then. I don't know where Jacson is today, or even if he's alive. There was a book published on Trotsky last year. Want me to look into it?"

"No. It's not important. Another ale?"

"Please. I'm getting thirsty with all this talking."

They sat silently until another round of drinks was brought. Delaney was drinking rye and water.

"Let's get back to the weapon," he said, and Handry consulted his notes.

"I couldn't locate a photo, but the wonderful old lady who runs our morgue, and who remembers *everything*, told me that a magazine ran an article on the killing in the 1950s and published a photo of the ice ax used, so apparently a photo does exist, somewhere."

"Anything else?"

"It was the kind of ice ax used in mountain climbing. First, Jacson said he bought it in Switzerland. Now the testimony gets confused. Jacson's mistress said she had never seen it in Paris or New York, prior to their trip to Mexico. Then Jacson said he liked mountaineering and had bought the ax in Mexico and used it when climbing—wait a minute; I've got it here somewhere—when climbing the Orizaba and Popo in Mexico. But then later it turned out that Jacson had lived in a camp in Mexico for awhile, and the owner's son was an enthusiastic mountaineer. He and Jacson talked about mountain climbing several times. This son owned an ice ax, purchased four years previously. The day following the attack on Trotsky, and Jacson's arrest, the camp owner went looking for his son's ice ax, but it had disappeared. Confusing, isn't it?"

"It always is," Delaney nodded. "But Jacson could have purchased the ax in Switzerland, Paris, New York, or stolen it in Mexico. Right?"

"Right."

"Great," Delaney sighed. "I didn't know you could buy the damned thing like a candy bar. Was Jacson really a GPU agent?"

"Apparently no one knows for sure. But the ex-chief of the Secret Service of Mexican Police says he was. Says it in a book he wrote about the case anyway."

"You're sure Jacson hit Trotsky only once with the ice ax?"

"That's one thing everyone seems to agree on. One blow. You need anything else on this?"

"Nooo. Not right now. Handry, you've done excellently in such a short time."

"Sure. I'm good. I admit it. Now let's get to New York's best mountain climber. Two years ago—about eighteen months, to be exact—that would have been an easy question to answer. Calvin Case, thirty-one, married, internationally recognized as one of the most expert, bravest, most daring mountaineers in the world. Then, early last year, he was the last man on the rope of a four-man team climbing the north wall of the Eiger. That's supposed to be the most difficult climb in the world. The guy I spoke to on our Sports Desk said Everest is pure technology, but the north wall of the Eiger is pure guts. It's in Switzerland, in case you're wondering, and apparently it's practically sheer. Anyway, this guy Calvin Case was tail-end Charlie on the rope. He either slipped or an outcrop crumbled or a piton pulled free; my informant didn't remember the details. But he did remember that Case dangled, and finally had to cut himself loose from the others, and fell."

"Jesus."

"Yes. Incredibly, he wasn't killed, but he crushed his spine. Now he's paralyzed from the waist down. Bed-ridden. Can't control his bladder or bowels. My man tells me he's on the sauce. Won't give any interviews. And he's had some good offers for books."

"How does he live?"

"His wife works. No children. I guess they get along. But anyway, I got another guy, active, who's now the number one New York climber. But right now he's in Nepal, preparing for some climb. Who do you want?"

"Do I have a choice? I'll take this Calvin Case. Do you have his address?"

"Sure. I figured you'd want him. I wrote it down. Here." He handed Delaney a small slip of paper. The Captain glanced at it briefly.

"Greenwich Village," he nodded. "I know that street well. A guy took a shot at me on a rooftop on that street, years ago. It was the first time I had ever been shot at."

"He didn't hit?" Handry asked.

"No," Delaney smiled. "He didn't hit."

"Did you?"

"Yes."

"Kill him?"

"Yes. Another ale?"

"Well . . . all right. One more. You having another drink?"

"Sure."

"But I've got to go to the john first. My back teeth are floating."

"That door over there, in the corner."

When Handry came back, he slid into the booth and asked, "How did you know I want to write poetry?"

Delaney shrugged. "I told you. Just a guess. Don't be so goddamned embarrassed about it. It's not shameful."

"I know," Handry said, looking down at the table, moving his glass around. "But still . . . All right, Captain, now you talk. What the hell is this all about?"

"What do you think it's about?"

"You ask me for a run-down on Trotsky, killed with an ice ax. A mountaineer's tool. Then you ask me for the name of the top mountain climber in New York. It's something to do with mountain climbing, obviously. The ice ax is the main thing. What's it all about?"

Delaney, knowing he would be asked, had carefully considered his answers. He had prepared three possible replies, of increasing frankness, still not certain how far he could trust the reporter. But now that Handry had made the Trotsky-ice ax-mountain climbing connection, he went directly to his second reply.

"I am not on active duty," he acknowledged. "But Frank Lombard was killed in my precinct. You may think it's silly, but I consider that my responsibility. The Two-five-one Precinct is my home. So I'm conducting what you might call an unofficial investigation. Operation Lombard is handling the official investigation. I'm sure you know that. Whatever I do, whatever I ask you to do, is outside the Department. As of the date of my leave of absence, I have no official standing. Whatever you do for me is a personal favor—you to me."

Thomas Handry stared at him a long moment. Then he poured himself a full glass of ale and drained off half of it. He set the glass down, a white foam mustache on his upper lip.

"You're full of shit," he informed Captain Edward X. Delaney.

"Yes," Delaney nodded miserably. "That's true. I think Lombard was killed with an ice ax. That's why I asked you for background on Trotsky and mountain climbers. That's all I've got. I asked you to look into it because I trust you. All I can promise you is first whack at the story—if there is a story."

"Do you have a staff?"

"A staff? No, I don't have a staff. I have some people helping me, but they're not in the Department. They're civilians."

"I'll get the story? Exclusively?"

"You'll get it. If there is a story."

"I could get a story published right now. Leave-of-absence police captain personally investigating a murder in his old precinct. Harmonicas and violins. 'I want revenge,' states Captain Edward X. Delaney. Is that what you want?"

"No. What do you want?"

"To be in on it. Okay, Captain? Just to know what's going on. You can use me as much as you want. I'm willing. But I want to know what you're up to."

"It may be nothing."

"Okay, it's nothing. I'll take the gamble. A deal?"

"You won't publish anything without my go-ahead?"

"I won't."

"I trust you, Handry."

"The hell you do. But you've got no choice."

3

IT WAS a faint dream. He followed a man down a misted street. Not a man, really, but something there, a bulk, in the gilded gloom. Like the night when Frank Lombard was killed: orange light and soft rain.

The figure stayed ahead of him, indecipherable, no matter how fast he moved to see what it was he chased. He never closed. He felt no fear nor panic; just a need, a want for the shadow moving through shadows.

Then there was a ringing; not the siren of a squad car or the buffalo whistle of a fire engine, but the ringing of an ambulance, coming closer, louder; he drifted up from sleep and fumbled for the telephone.

Before he could identify himself he recognized Dorfman's voice.

"Captain?"

"Yes."

"Dorfman. There's been an assault on East Eighty-fourth. About halfway between First and Second. Sounds like the Lombard thing. A man tentatively identified as Bernard Gilbert. He's not dead. They're waiting for the ambulance now. I'm on my way."

"Did you call Chief Pauley?"

"Yes."

"Good."

"You want to meet me there?"

"No. You can handle it. Go by the book. Where they taking him?"

"Mother of Mercy."

"Thank you for calling, lieutenant."

"You're welcome."

Then he switched on the light, stepped into slippers, pulled on a robe. He went down to the study, flipping wall switches as he went, and finally lighted the lamp on his desk. The house was cold and damp; he pulled his overcoat on over his bathrobe. Then he consulted his desk calendar: 22 days since the Frank Lombard homicide. He made careful note of this on a fresh sheet of paper, then called Deputy Inspector Thorsen's answering service. He left his name and number.

Thorsen called him in minutes, sounding sleepy but not angry.

"What is it, Edward?"

"I'm calling from my home, but it's important. There's been a Lombard-type assault in the Two-five-one. Eight-fourth Street. A man tentatively identified as Bernard Gilbert. He's still alive. They're taking him to Mother of Mercy. That's all I've got."

"Jesus," Thorsen breathed. "Sounds like you were right."

"No comfort in that. I can't go over there."

"No. That wouldn't be wise. Is it certain it's a Lombard-type thing?"

"I told you all I know."

"All right, assuming it is, what will Broughton do now?"

"If the wound is similar to the one that killed Lombard, Chief Pauley will try to establish a link between Lombard and this Bernard Gilbert. If he can't, and I don't believe he will, unless it's pure coincidence, he'll realize they were both chance victims, and he's faced with a crazy. Then he'll check every mental institution in a five-state area. He'll have men checking private doctors and psychiatrists and recently released inmates. He'll pull in every known nut in the city for questioning. He'll do what he has to do."

"Do you think it'll work?"

"No. Broughton has had about five hundred dicks working for him. Figure each detective has a minimum of three or four snitches on his wire. That means about two thousand informers, all over the city, and they've come up with zilch. If there was a crazy running wild—a crazy with a record—*someone* would know about it, or notice something weird, or hear some talk. Our man is new. Probably no record. Probably normal-appearing. I've already got him on my list as a good appearance, possibly well-dressed."

"What list?"

Delaney was silent a moment, cursing his lapse. That list was *his*.

"A stupid list I made out of things I suspect about the guy. It's all smoke. I don't *know* anything."

Now Thorsen was silent a moment. Then . . .

"I think maybe you and Johnson and I better have a meeting."

"All right," Delaney said glumly.

"And bring your list."

"Can it wait until I see the reports on this Bernard Gilbert assault?"

"Sure. Anything I can do?"

"Will you have a man at the scene—or involved in the investigation?"

"Well . . ." Thorsen said cautiously, "maybe."

"If you do, a couple of things . . . Is anything missing from the victim's wallet? Particularly identification of any kind? And second, does he—or did he—use hair oil of any kind?"

"Hair oil? What the hell is that all about?"

Delaney frowned at the telephone. "I don't know. I honestly don't know. Probably not important. But can you check?"

"I'll try. Anything else?"

"One more thing. If this Bernard Gilbert dies, and it's proved similar to the Lombard snuff, the papers are going to get hold of it, so you better be prepared for 'Maniacal Killer on Loose' type of thing. It's going to get hairy."

"Oh God. I suppose so."

"Most of the pressure will be on Broughton."

"And the Commish."

"Him, too, of course. But it will affect Chief Pauley most. He's sure to get hundreds of phony leads and false confessions. They'll all have to be checked out, of course. And there's a good possibility there may be imitative assaults and homicides in other parts of the city. It usually happens. But don't be spooked by them. Eventually they'll be weeded out . . ."

He had more conversation with Deputy Inspector Thorsen. They agreed that since Dorfman was recently appointed Acting Commander of the 251st Precinct, and since Thorsen was head of personnel of the patrol division, it would be entirely logical and understandable if Thorsen went to the scene of the Gilbert assault, ostensibly to check up on how Dorfman was handling things. Thorsen promised to call Delaney back as soon as possible, and he would, personally, try to check out the questions of missing identification from Bernard Gilbert's wallet and whether or not the victim used hair oil.

The moment he hung up, Delaney dialed the home number of Dr. Sanford Ferguson. It was getting on to 2:00 a.m., but the doctor was awake and cheerful.

"Edward!" he said. "How's by you? I just came in from an on-the-spot inspection of a luscious young piece. Couldn't have been over twenty-six or seven. Oh so lovely."

"Dead?"

"Oh so dead. Apparently cardiac arrest. But doesn't that strike you as odd, Edward? A luscious young piece with a shattered heart?"

"Married?"

"Not legally."

"Is the boy friend a doctor or a medical student?"

There was silence a moment.

"You bastard," Ferguson said finally, "you scare me, you know that? In case you're interested, the boy friend is a pharmacist."

"Beautiful," Delaney said. "Well, he probably found a younger, more luscious piece. But doctor, why I called . . . There's been an assault in the Two-five-one Precinct. Tonight. Preliminary reports are that the wound and weapon used are similar to the Lombard homicide. The victim in this case, still alive, a man named Bernard Gilbert, will be taken or has been taken to Mother of Mercy."

"Dear old Mother."

"I wonder if you've been assigned to this?"

"No, I have not."

"I wondered if you could call the attending doctors and surgeons at Mother of Mercy and find out if it really is a Lombard-type penetration, and whether he'll live or not, and—you know—whatever they'll tell you."

Again there was silence. Then . . .

"You know, Edward, you want a lot for one lousy lunch."

"I'll buy you another lousy lunch."

Ferguson laughed. "You treat everyone differently, don't you?"

"Don't we all?"

"I guess so. And you want me to call you back with whatever I can get?"

"If you would. Please. Also, doctor, if this man should die, will there be an autopsy?"

"Of course. On every homicide victim. Or suspected victim."

"With or without next-of-kin's consent?"

"That's correct."

"If this man dies—this Bernard Gilbert—could you do the autopsy?"

"I'm not the Chief Medical Examiner, Edward. I'm just one of the slaves."

"But could you wangle it?"

"I might be able to wangle it."

"I wish you would. If he dies."

"All right, Edward. I'll try."

"One more thing . . ."

Ferguson's laughter almost broke his eardrum; Delaney held the phone up in the air until the doctor stopped spluttering.

"Edward," Ferguson said, "I love you. I really do. With you it's always 'I want two things' or 'I'd like three favors.' But then you always say, 'Oh, just one more thing.' You're great. Okay, what's your 'one more thing'?"

"If you should happen to talk to a doctor or surgeon up at Mother of Mercy, or if you should happen to do the postmortem, find out if the victim used hair oil, will you?"

"Hair oil?" Ferguson asked. "Hair oil," Ferguson said. "Hair oil!" Ferguson cried. "Jesus Christ, Edward, you never forget a thing, do you?"

"Sometimes," Captain Delaney acknowledged.

"Nothing important, I'll bet. All right, I'll keep the hair oil in mind if I do the cut-'em -up. I'm certainly not going to bother the men in emergency at Mother of Mercy with a thing like that right now."

"Good enough. You'll get back to me?"

"If I learn anything. If you don't hear from me, it means I've drawn a blank."

Delaney rejected the idea of sleep, and went into the kitchen to put water on for instant coffee. While it was heating, he returned to the study and from a corner closet he dragged out a three-by-four ft. bulletin board to which he had pinned a black-and-white street map of the 251st Precinct. The map was covered with a clear plastic flap that could be wiped clean. In the past, while on active duty, Delaney had used the map to chart location and incidence of street crimes, breaking-and-entering, felonious assaults, etc. The map was a miniature of the big one on the wall of the commander's office in the precinct house.

Now he wiped the plastic overlay clean with a paper tissue, returned to the kitchen to mix his cup of black coffee, brought it back with him and sat at the desk, the map before him. He sharpened a red grease pencil and carefully marked two fat dots: on East 73rd Street where Lombard had been killed and on East 84th Street where Gilbert had been assaulted. Alongside each dot he wrote the last name of the victim and the date of the attack.

Two red dots, he acknowledged, hardly constituted a pattern, or even a crime wave. But from his experience and reading of the histories of mass murders, he was convinced additional assaults would be confined to a limited area, probably the 251st Precinct, and the assailant was probably a resident of the area. (Probably! Probably! Everything was probably.) The assassin's success in the Lombard killing would certainly make him feel safe in his home territory.

Delaney sat back and stared at the red dots. He gave Chief Pauley about three days to acknowledge there was no connection between the victims. Then Pauley would opt for a psychopathic killer and would do all those things Delaney had mentioned to Deputy Inspector Thorsen.

In addition, Delaney guessed, Chief Pauley, with no announcement and no publicity, would put on 10 or 20 decoys on the streets of the 251st Pre- cinct, from about ten p.m. till dawn. In civilian clothes, newspapers clutched under one arm, the detectives would scurry up one street and down the next, appar- ently residents hurrying home in the darkness, but actually inviting attack. That's what Delaney would do. He was certain, knowing Pauley's thorough- ness, that the Chief would do it, too. It might work. And it might only serve to drive the killer farther afield if he recognized the decoys for what they were. But you took your chances and hoped. You had to do *something*.

He was still staring at the red dots on the map overlay, sipping cooled black coffee and trying to compute percentages and probabilities, when the desk phone rang. He snatched it up after one ring.

"Captain Edward X. Delaney here."

"Thorsen. I'm calling from a tavern on Second Avenue. They had taken Gilbert to the hospital by the time I arrived. Broughton and Pauley are with him, hoping he'll regain consciousness and say something."

"Sure."

"Gilbert's wallet was on the sidewalk next to him, just like in the Lombard case. Someone's at his home now, trying to find out what, if anything, is missing."

"Was there money in it?"

"Dorfman tells me yes. He thinks it was about fifty dollars."

"Untouched?"

"Apparently."

"How is Dorfman managing?"

"Very well."

"Good."

"He's a little nervous."

"Naturally. Any prediction on whether Gilbert will live?"

"Nothing on that. He is a short man, about five-six or five-seven. He was hit from the front. The penetration went in high up on the skull, about an inch or so above where the hair line would have been."

"'Would have been'?"

"Gilbert is almost completely bald. Dorfman says just a fringe of thin, grey hair around the scalp, above the ears. But not in front. He was wearing a hat, so I assume some of the hat material was driven into the wound. Jesus, Edward, I don't like this kind of work. I saw the blood and stuff where he lay. I want to get back to my personnel records."

"I know. So you have nothing on whether or not he used hair oil?"

"No, nothing. I'm a lousy detective, I admit."

"You did all you could. Why don't you go home and try to get some sleep?"

"Yes. I'll try. Anything else you need?"

"Copies of the Operation Lombard reports as soon as you can."

"I'll put the pressure on. Edward . . ."

"Yes?"

"When I saw the pool of blood there, on the sidewalk, I got the feeling . . ."

"What?"

"That this business with Broughton is pretty small potatoes. You understand?"

"Yes," Delaney said gently. "I know what you mean."

"You've got to get this guy, Edward."

"I'll get him."

"You sure?"

"I'm sure."

"Good. I think I'll go home now and try to get some sleep."

"Yes, you do that."

After he hung up, Delaney drew his list, "The Suspect," from his top drawer and went through it, item by item. None of his notations had been negated by what Thorsen had told him. If anything, his supposition had been strengthened. Certainly a swinging blow high on the skull of a short man would indicate a tall assailant. But why the attack from the front when the rear attack on Lombard had been so successful? And couldn't Gilbert see the blow coming and dodge or throw up an arm to ward it off? A puzzle.

He was almost ready to give it up for the night, to try to grab a few hours of sleep before dawn, when the phone rang. He reached for it, wondering again how much of his life was spent with that damned black thing pressing his ear flat and sticky.

"Captain Edward X. Delaney here."

"Ferguson. I'm tired, I'm sleepy, I'm irritable. So I'll go through this fast. And don't interrupt."

"I won't."

"You just did. Bernard Gilbert. White male, About forty years old. Five feet six or seven. About one-fifty. Around there. I'll skip the medical lingo. Definitely a Lombard-type wound. Struck from the front. The penetration went in about two inches above the normal hair line. But the man is almost totally bald. That answers your hair oil question."

"The hell it does. Just makes the cheese more binding."

"I'll ignore that. Foreign matter in the wound from the felt hat he was wearing. Penetration to a depth of four or five inches. Curving downward. He's in a deep coma. Paralyzed. Prognosis: negative. Any questions?"

"How long do they figure?"

"From this instant to a week or so. His heart isn't all that strong."

"Will he recover consciousness?"

"Doubtful."

Delaney could tell Ferguson's patience was wearing thin.

"Thank you, doctor. You've been a great help."

"Any time," Ferguson assured him. "Any two o'clock in the morning you want to call."

"Oh, wait a minute," Delaney said.

"I know," Ferguson sighed. "'One more thing.'"

"You won't forget about the autopsy."

Ferguson began to swear—ripe, sweaty curses—and Delaney hung up softly, smiling. Then he went to bed, but didn't sleep.

It was something he hated and loved: hated because it kept his mind in a flux and robbed him of sleep; loved because it was a challenge: how many oranges could he juggle in the air at one time?

All difficult cases came eventually to this point of complexity: weapon, method, motives, suspects, alibis, timing. And he had to juggle them all, catching, tossing, watching them all every second, relaxed and laughing.

It had been his experience that when this point came in a difficult, involved investigation, when the time arrived when he wondered if he could hold onto all the threads, keep the writhings in his mind, at that point, at that time of almost total confusion, if he could just endure, and absorb more and more, then somehow the log jam loosened, he could see things beginning to run free.

Right now it was a jam, everything caught up and canted. But he began to see key logs, things to be loosened. Then it would all run out. Now the complexity didn't worry him. He could accept it, and more. Pile it on! There wasn't anything one man could do that a better man couldn't undo. That was a stupid, arrogant belief, he admitted. But if he didn't hold it, he really should be in another line of business.

4

FOUR DAYS later Bernard Gilbert died without regaining consciousness. By that time Chief Pauley had established, to his satisfaction, that there was no link between Lombard and Gilbert, except the nature of the attack, and he had set in motion all those things Captain Delaney had predicted: the check-up of recent escapes from mental institutions, investigation of recently released inmates, questioning of known criminals with a record of mental instability, the posting of decoys in the 251st Precinct.

Delaney learned all this from copies of Operation Lombard reports supplied by Deputy Inspector Thorsen. Once again there were many of them, and they were long. He studied them all carefully, reading them several times. He learned details of Bernard Gilbert's life. He learned that the victim's wife, Monica Gilbert, had stated she believed the only thing missing from her husband's wallet was an identification card.

The accountants for whom Bernard Gilbert worked audited the books of a Long Island manufacturer doing secret work for the U. S. government. To gain access to the premises of the manufacturer, it was necessary for Bernard Gilbert to show a special identification card with his photo attached. It was this special identification card that was missing. The FBI had been alerted by Chief Pauley but, as far as Delaney could determine, the federal agency was not taking any active role in the investigation at this time.

There was a long memo from Chief Pauley to Deputy Commissioner Broughton speculating on the type of weapon used in the Lombard and Gilbert assaults. The phrase "a kind of ax or pick" was used, and Delaney knew Pauley was not far behind him.

At this point the news media had not yet made the Lombard-Gilbert connection. In fact, Gilbert's attack earned only a few short paragraphs on inside pages. Just another street crime. Delaney considered a few moments whether to tip off Thomas Handry, then thought better of it. He'd learn soon enough, and meanwhile Chief Pauley would be free of the pressures of screaming headlines, crank calls, false confessions, and imitative crimes.

It was the timing of his own activities that concerned Captain Delaney most. He wanted to keep up with the flood of Operation Lombard reports. He wanted desperately to interrogate Monica Gilbert himself. He needed to visit Calvin Case, the crippled mountain climber, and learn what he could about ice axes. He wanted to check the progress of Christopher Langley without giving the sweet old man the feeling that he, Delaney, was leaning on him. And, of course, the two visits a day to Barbara in the hospital—that came first.

Two days after the Gilbert attack, while the victim floated off somewhere, living and not living, but still breathing, Delaney thought long and hard on how to approach Monica Gilbert. She was sure to be spending many hours at her husband's bedside. And it was certain she would be guarded by Operation Lombard detectives, probably a two-man team outside her house, although there might be an interior man, too.

The Captain considered and rejected several involved plans for a clandestine meeting with her, unobserved by Operation Lombard. They all seemed too devious. He decided the best solution would be the obvious: he would call for an appointment, give his name, and then walk right up to her door. If he was braced or recognized by Broughton's dicks he would use the same cover story he had prepared when he had gone to question the widow of Frank Lombard: as ex-commander of the 251st Precinct he had come to express his sympathy.

It worked—up to a point. He phoned, identified himself, made an appointment to see her at her home at 4:00 p.m., when she returned from Mother of Mercy. He thought it likely she would repeat the conversation to her guard, as she had been instructed. Or perhaps her phone was tapped. Anything was possible. So, when he walked over a few minutes before four, and one of the dicks in the unmarked police car parked outside her brownstone cranked down his window, waved, and called, "Hi, Captain," he wasn't surprised. He waved back, although he didn't recognize the man.

Monica Gilbert was a strong, handsome woman, hairy, wearing a shapeless black dress that didn't quite conceal heavy breasts, wide hips, pillar thighs. She had been brewing a pot of tea, and he accepted a cup gratefully. There were two little girls in the room, peeking out from behind their mother's skirts. They were introduced to him as Mary and Sylvia, and he rose to bow gravely. They ran giggling from the room. He saw no sign of an interior guard.

"Milk?" she asked. "Sugar?"

"Thank you, no. I take it straight. How is your husband?"

"No change. Still in a coma. They don't hold out much hope."

She said all that in a flat monotone, not blinking, looking at him directly. He admired her control, knowing what it cost.

Her thick black hair, somewhat oily, was combed back from a wide, smooth brow, and fell almost to her shoulders. Her large eyes appeared blue-grey, and were her best feature. The nose was long but proportionate. All of her was big. Not so much big as assertive. She wore no makeup, had made no effort to pluck heavy eyebrows. She was, he decided, a complete woman, but he knew instinctively she would respond to soft speech and a gentle manner.

"Mrs. Gilbert," he said in a low voice, leaning forward to her, "I know you must have spent many hours with the police since the attack on your husband. This is an unofficial visit. I am not on active duty; I'm on leave of absence. But I was commander of this precinct for many years, and I wanted to express my regrets and sympathy personally."

"Thank you," she said. "That's very kind of you. I'm sure everything is being done . . ."

"I assure you it is," he said earnestly. "A great number of men are working on this case."

"Will they get the man who did it?"

"Yes," he nodded. "They will. I promise you that."

She looked at him strangely a moment.

"You're not involved in the investigation?"

"Not directly, no. But it did happen in my precinct. What was my precinct."

"Why are you on leave of absence?"

"My wife is ill."

"I'm sorry to hear that. You live in the neighborhood?"

"Yes. Right next door to the precinct house."

"Well, then you know what it's like around here—robberies and muggings, and you can't go out at night."

"I know," he nodded sympathetically. "Believe me, I know, and hate it more than you do."

"He never hurt anyone," she burst out, and he was afraid she might weep, but she did not.

"Mrs. Gilbert, will it upset you to talk about your husband?"

"Of course not. What do you want to know?"

"What kind of a man is he? Not his job, or his background—I've got all that. Just the man himself."

"Bernie? The dearest, sweetest man who ever lived. He wouldn't hurt a fly. He worked so hard, for me and the girls. I know that's all he thinks about."

"Yes, yes."

"Look around. Does it look like we're rich?"

Obediently he looked around. In truth it was a modest apartment: linoleum on the floor, inexpensive furniture, paper drapes. But it was clean, and there were some touches: a good hi-fi set, on one wall an original abstraction that had color and flash, a small wooden piece of primitive sculpture that had meaning.

"Comfortable," he murmured.

"Paradise," she said definitely. "Compared to what Bernie had and what I had. It's not right, Captain. It's just not right."

He nodded miserably, wondering what he could say to comfort her. There was nothing. So he got on with it, still speaking in a quiet, gentle voice, hoping to soothe her.

"Mrs. Gilbert," he asked, remembering Ferguson's comment about the victim's heart, "was your husband an active man?" Realizing he had used the past tense, he switched immediately to the present, hoping she hadn't caught it. But the focus of her eyes changed; he realized she had, and he cursed himself. "I mean, is he active physically? Does he exercise? Play games?"

She stared at him without answering. Then she leaned forward to pour him another cup of tea. The black dress left her arms bare; he admired the play of muscle, the texture of her skin.

"Captain," she said finally, "for a man not involved in the investigation, you're asking a lot of unusual questions."

He realized then how shrewd she was. He could try lying to her, but was convinced she'd know.

"Mrs. Gilbert," he said, "do you really care how many men are working on this, or who they are, or what their motives are? The main thing is to catch the man who did it. Isn't that true? Well, I swear to you, I want to find the man who struck down your husband more than you do."

"No!" she cried. "Not more than I do." Her eyes were glittering now, her whole body taut. "I want the one who did it caught and punished."

He was astonished by her fury. He had thought her controlled, perhaps even phlegmatic. But now she was twanging, alive and fiery.

"What do you want?" he asked her. "Vengeance?"

Her eyes burned into his.

"Yes. That's exactly what I want. Vengeance. If I answer your questions, will it help me get it?"

"I think so."

"Not good enough, Captain."

"Yes, if you answer my questions it will help find the man who did this thing to your husband."

"Your husband" were the key words, as he had hoped they would be. She started talking.

Her husband was physically weak. He had a heart murmur, arthritis of the left wrist, intermittent kidney pains, although examinations and X-rays showed nothing. His eyes were weak, he suffered from periodic conjunctivitis. He did not exercise, he played no games. He was a sedentary man.

But he worked hard, she added in fierce tones; he worked so hard.

Delaney nodded. Now he had some kind of answer to what had been bothering him: why hadn't Bernard Gilbert made a response to a frontal attack, dodged or warded off the blow? It seemed obvious now: poor musculature, slow physical reactions, the bone-deep weariness of a man working up to and beyond his body's capacity. What chance did he have against a "strong, young, cool, determined psychopath with good muscular coordination"?

"Thank you, Mrs. Gilbert," Captain Delaney said softly. He finished his tea, rose to his feet. "I appreciate your giving me this time, and I hope your husband makes a quick recovery."

"Do you know anything about his condition?"

This time he did lie. "I'm sure you know more than I do. All I know is that he's seriously injured."

She nodded, not looking at him, and he realized she already knew.

She walked him to the door. The delightful little girls came scampering out, stared at him, giggled, and pulled at their mother's skirt. Delaney smiled at them, remembering Liza at that age. The darlings!

"I want to do something," she said.

"What?" he asked, distracted. "I don't understand."

"I want to *do* something. To help."

"You have helped."

"Isn't there anything else I can do? You're doing something. I don't know what you're up to, but I trust you. I really feel you're trying to find who did it."

"Thank you," he said, so moved. "Yes, I'm trying to find who did it."

"Then let me help. Anything! I can type, take shorthand. I'm very good with figures. I'll do anything. Make coffee. Run errands. Anything!"

He couldn't trust himself to speak. He tried to nod brightly and smile. He left, closing the door firmly behind him.

Out on the street the unmarked police car was still parked in the same position. He expected a wave. But one of the detectives was sleeping, his head thrown back, his mouth open. The other was marking a racing sheet. They didn't even notice him. If they had been under his command he'd have reamed their ass out.

5

THE NEXT day started well, with a call from a book dealer informing Captain Delaney that he had located two volumes of the original Honey Bunch series. The Captain was delighted, and it was arranged that the books would be mailed to him, along with the invoice.

He took this unexpected find as a good omen, for like most policemen he was superstitious. He would tell others, "You make your own luck," knowing this wasn't exactly true; there was a good fortune that came unexpectedly, sometimes unasked, and the important thing was to recognize it when it came, for luck wore a thousand disguises, including calamity.

He sat at his study desk and reviewed a list of "Things to Do" he had prepared. It read:

"Interrogate Monica Gilbert.

"Calvin Case re ice ax.

"Ferguson re autopsy.

"Call Langley.

"Honey Bunch."

He drew a line through the final item. He was about to draw a line through the first and then, for a reason he could not understand, left it open. He searched, and finally found the slip of paper Thomas Handry had given him, bearing the name, address and telephone number of Calvin Case. He realized more and more people were being drawn into his investigation, and he resolved to set up some kind of a card file or simple directory that would list names, addresses, and phone numbers of all the people involved.

He considered what might be the best way to handle the Calvin Case interview. He decided against phoning; an unexpected personal visit would be better. Sometimes it was useful to surprise people, catch them off guard with no opportunity to plan their reaction.

He walked over to Lexington Avenue, shoulders hunched against the raw cold, and took the IRT downtown. It seemed to him each time he rode the subway—and his trips were rare—the graffiti covered more and more of interior and exterior surfaces of cars and platforms. Sexual and racist inscriptions were, thankfully, relatively rare, but spray cans and felt-tipped markers had been used by the hundreds for such records as: "Tony 168. Vic 134. Angie 127. Bella 78. Iron Wolves 127." He knew these to be the first names of individuals and the titles of street gangs, followed by their street number—evidence: "I was here."

He got off at 14th Street and walked west and south, looking about him constantly, noting how this section had changed and was changing since he had been a dick two in this precinct and thought he might leave the world a better place than he found it. Now if he left it no worse, he'd be satisfied.

The address was on West 11th Street, just off Fifth Avenue. The rents here, Delaney knew, were enormous, unless Case was fortunate enough to have a rent-controlled apartment. The house itself was a handsome old structure in the Federal style. All the front windows had white-painted boxes of geraniums or ivy on the sills. The outside knob and number plate were polished brass. The garbage cans had their lids on; the entryway had been swept. There was a little sign that read "Please curb your dog." Under it someone had written, "No shit?"

Calvin Case lived in apartment 3-B. Delaney pushed the bell and leaned down to the intercom. He waited, but there was no answer. He pushed the bell again, three long rings. This time a harsh masculine voice said, "What the hell. Yes?"

"Mr Calvin Case?"

"Yes. What do you want?"

"My name is Captain Edward X. Delaney. Of the New York Police Department. I'd like to talk to you for a few minutes."

"What about?" The voice was loud, slurred, and the mechanics of the intercom made it raucous.

"It's about an investigation I'm conducting."

There was silence. It lasted so long that Delaney was about to ring again when the door lock buzzed, and he grabbed the knob hastily, opened the door, and climbed carpeted steps to 3-B. There was another bell. He rang, and again he waited for what he thought was an unusually long time. Then another buzzer sounded. He was startled and did nothing. When you rang the bell of an apartment door, you expected someone to inquire from within or open the door. But now a buzzer sounded.

Then, remembering the man was an invalid, and cursing his own stupidity, Delaney rang again. The answering buzz seemed long and angry. He pushed the door open, stepped into the dark hallway of a small, cluttered apartment. Delaney shut the door firmly behind him, heard the electric lock click.

"Mr Case?" he called.

"In here." The voice was harsh, almost cracked.

The captain walked through a littered living room. Someone slept in here, on a sofa bed that was still unmade. There were signs of a woman's presence: a tossed nightgown, a powder box and makeup kit on an end table, lipsticked cigarette butts, tossed copies of "Vogue" and "Bride." But there were a few plants at the windows, a tall tin vase of fresh rhododendron leaves. Someone was making an effort.

Delaney stepped through the disorder to an open door leading to the rear of the apartment. Curiously, the door frame between the cluttered living room and the bedroom beyond had been fitted with a window shade with a cord pull. The shade, Delaney guessed, could be pulled down almost to the floor, shutting off light, affording some kind of privacy, but not as sound-proof as a door. And, of course, it couldn't be locked.

He ducked under the hanging shade and looked about the bedroom. Dusty windows, frayed curtains, plaster curls from the ceiling, a stained rag rug, two good oak dressers with drawers partly open, newspapers and magazines scattered on the floor. And then the bed, and on the opposite wall a shocking big stain as if someone had thrown a full bottle, watched it splinter and the contents drip down.

The smell was . . . something. Stale whiskey, stale bedclothes, stale flesh. Urine and excrement. There was a tiny log of incense smoking in a cast iron pot; it made things worse. The room was rotting. Delaney had smelled odors more ferocious than this—was there a cop who had not?—but it never got easier. He breathed through his mouth and turned to the man in the bed.

It was a big bed, occupied at some time in the past, Delaney imagined, by Calvin Case and his wife. Now she slept on the convertible in the living room. The bed was surrounded, by tables, chairs, magazine racks, a telephone stand, a wheeled cart with bottles and an ice bucket, on the floor an open bedpan and plastic "duck." Tissues, a half-eaten sandwich, a sodden towel, cigarette and cigar butts, a paperback book with pages torn out in a frenzy, and even a hard-cover bent and partly ripped, a broken glass, and . . . and everything.

"What the fuck do you want?"

Then he looked directly at the man in the bed.

The soiled sheet, a surprising blue, was drawn up to the chin. All Delaney saw was a square face, a square head. Uncombed hair was spread almost to the man's shoulders. The reddish mustache and beard were squarish. And untrimmed. Dark eyes burned. The full lips were stained and crusted.

"Calvin Case?"

"Yeah."

"Captain Edward X. Delaney, New York Police Department. I'm investigating the death—the murder—of a man we believe—"

"Let's see your badge."

Delaney stepped closer to the bed. The stench was sickening. He held his identification in front of Case's face. The man hardly glanced at it. Delaney stepped back.

"We believe the man was murdered with an ice ax. A mountain climber's ax. So I came—"

"You think I did it?" The cracked lips opened to reveal yellowed teeth: a death's head grin.

Delaney was shocked. "Of course not. But I need more information on ice axes. And as the best mountain climber—you've been recommended to me—I thought you might be—"

"Fuck off," Calvin Case said wearily, moving his heavy head to one side.

"You mean you won't cooperate in finding a man who—"

"Be gone," Case whispered. "Just be gone."

Delaney turned, moved away two steps, stopped. There was Barbara, and Christopher Langley, and Monica Gilbert, and all the peripheral people: Handry and Thorsen and Ferguson and Dorfman, and here was this . . . He took a deep breath, hating himself because even his furies were calculated. He turned back to the cripple on the soiled bed. He had nothing to lose.

"You goddamned cock-sucking mother-fucking son-of-a-bitch," he said steadily and tonelessly. "You shit-gutted ass-licking bastard. I'm a detective, and I detect *you*, you punky no-ball frigger. Go ahead, lie in your bed of crap. Who buys the food? Your wife—right? Who tries to keep a home for you? Your wife—right? Who empties your shit and pours your piss in the toilet? Your wife—right? And you lie there and soak up whiskey. I could smell you the minute I walked in, you piece of rot. It's great to lie in bed and feel sorry for yourself, isn't it? You corn-holing filth. Go piss and shit in your bed and drink your whiskey and work your wife to death and scream at her, you crud. A man? Oh! You're some man, you lousy ass-kissing turd. I spit on you, and I forget the day I heard your name, you dirt-eating nobody. You don't exist. You understand? You're no one."

He turned away, almost out of control, and a woman was standing in the bedroom doorway, a slight, frail blonde, her hair brushing the window shade. Her face was blanched; she was biting on a knuckle.

He took a deep breath, tried to square his shoulders, to feel bigger. He felt very small.

"Mrs. Case?"

She nodded.

"My name is Edward X. Delaney, Captain, New York Police Department. I came to ask your husband's help on an investigation. If you heard what I said, I apologize for my language. I'm very sorry. Please forgive me. I didn't know you were there."

She nodded dumbly again, still gnawing her knuckle and staring at him with wide blue eyes.

"Good-day," he said and moved to pass her in the doorway.

"Captain," the man in the bed croaked.

Delaney turned back. "Yes?"

"You're some bastard, aren't you?"

"When I have to be," Delaney nodded.

"You'll use anyone, won't you? Cripples, drunks, the helpless and the hopeless. You'll use them all."

"That's right. I'm looking for a killer. I'll use anyone who can help."

Calvin Case used the edge of his soiled blue sheet to wipe his clotted eyes clear.

"And you got a big mouth," he added. "A *biiig* mouth." He reached to the wheeled cart for a half-full bottle of whiskey and a stained glass. "Honey," he called to his wife, "we got a clean glass for Mister Captain Edward X. Delaney, New York Police Department?"

She nodded, still silent. She ran out, then came back with two glasses. Calvin Case poured a round, then set the bottle back on the cart. The three raised glasses in a silent toast, although what they were drinking to they could not have said.

"Cal, are you hungry?" his wife asked anxiously. "I've got to get back to work soon."

"No, not me. Captain, you want a sandwich?"

"Thank you, no."

"Just leave us alone, hon."

"Maybe I should just clean up a—"

"Just leave us alone. Okay, hon?"

She turned to go.

"Mrs. Case," Delaney said.

She turned back.

"Please stay. Whatever your husband and I have to discuss, there is no reason why you can't hear it."

She was startled. She looked back and forth, man to man, not knowing.

Calvin Case sighed. "You're something," he said to Captain Delaney. "You're really something."

"That's right," Delaney nodded. "I'm something."

"You barge in here and you take over."

"You want to talk now?" Delaney asked impatiently. "Do you want to answer my questions?"

"First tell me what it's all about."

"A man was killed with a strange weapon. We think it was an ice ax and—"

"Who's 'we'?"

"*I* think it was an ice ax. I want to know more about it, and your name was given to me as the most experienced mountaineer in New York."

"Was," Case said softly. "*Was.*"

They sipped their drinks, looked at each other stonily. For once, there were no sirens, no buffalo whistles, no trembles of blasting or street sounds, no city noises. It was on this very block, Delaney recalled, that a fine old town house was accidentally demolished by a group of bumbling revolutionaries, proving their love of the human race by preparing bombs in the basement. Now, in the Case apartment, they existed in a bubble of silence, and unconsciously they lowered their voices.

"A captain comes to investigate a crime?" Case asked quietly. "Even a murder? No, no. A uniformed cop or a detective, yes. A captain, no. What's it all about, Delaney?"

The Captain took a deep breath. "I'm on leave of absence. I'm not on active duty. You're under no obligation to answer my questions. I was commander of the Two-five-one Precinct. Uptown. A man was killed there about a month ago. On the street. Maybe you read about it. Frank Lombard, a city councilman. A lot of men are working on the case, but they're getting nowhere. They haven't even identified the weapon used. I started looking into it on my own time. It's not official; as I told you, I'm on leave of absence. Then, three days ago, another man was attacked not too far from where Lombard was killed. This man is still alive but will probably die. His wound is like Lombard's: a skull puncture. I think it was done with an ice ax."

"What makes you think so?"

"The nature of the wound, the size and shape. And an ice ax has been used as a murder weapon before. It was used to assassinate Leon Trotsky in Mexico City in nineteen-forty."

"What do you want from me?"

"Whatever you can tell me about ice axes, who makes them, where you buy them, what they're used for."

Calvin Case looked at his wife. "Will you get my axes, hon? They're in the hall closet."

While she was gone the men didn't speak. Case motioned toward a chair, but Delaney shook his head. Finally Mrs. Case came back, awkwardly clutching five axes. Two were under an arm; she held the handles of the other three in a clump.

"Dump 'em on the bed," Case ordered, and she obediently let them slide onto the soiled sheet.

Delaney stood over them, inspected them swiftly, then grabbed. It was an all-steel implement, hatchet-length, the handle bound in leather. From the butt of the handle hung a thong loop. The head had a hammer on one side, a pick on the other. The pick was exactly like that described by Christopher Langley; about five inches long, it was square-shaped at the shaft, then tapered to a thinning triangle. As it tapered, the spike curved downward and ended in a sharp point. On the underside were four little saw teeth. The entire head was a bright red, the leather-covered handle a bright blue. Between was a naked shaft of polished steel. There was a stamping on the side of the head: a small inscription. Delaney put on his glasses to read it: "Made in West Germany."

"This—" he began.

"That's not an ice ax," Calvin Case interrupted. "Technically, it's an ice hammer. But most people call it an ice ax. They lump all these things together."

"You bought it in West Germany?"

"No. Right here in New York. The best mountain gear is made in West Germany, Austria and Switzerland. But they export all over the world."

"Where in New York did you buy it?"

"A place I used to work. I got an employees' discount on it. It's down on Spring Street, a place called 'Outside Life.' They sell gear for hunting, fishing, camping, safaris, mountaineering, back-packing—stuff like that."

"May I use your phone?"

"Help yourself."

He was so encouraged, so excited, that he couldn't remember Christopher Langley's phone number and had to look it up in his pocket notebook. But he would not put the short ice ax down; he held it along with the phone in one hand while he dialed. He finally got through.

"Mr Langley? Delaney here."

"Oh, Captain! I should have called, but I really have nothing to report. I've made a list of possible sources, and I've been visiting six or seven shops a day. But so far I—"

"Mr Langley, do you have your list handy?"

"Why yes, Captain. Right here. I was just about to start out when you called."

"Do you have a store named Outside Life on your list?"

"Outside Life? Just a minute . . . Yes, here it is. It's on Spring Street."

"That's the one."

"Yes, I have it. I've divided my list into neighborhoods, and I have that in the downtown section. I haven't been there yet."

"Mr Langley. I have a lead they may have what we want. Could you get there today?"

"Of course. I'll go directly."

"Thank you. Please call me at once, whether you find it or not. I'll either be home or at the hospital."

He hung up, turned back to Calvin Case, still holding the ice ax. He didn't want to let it go. He swung the tool in a chopping stroke. Then he raised it high and slashed down.

"Nice balance," he nodded.

"Sure," Case agreed. "And plenty of weight. You could kill a man easily."

"Tell me about ice axes."

Calvin Case told him what he could. It wasn't much. He thought the modern ice ax had evolved from the ancient Alpinestock, a staff as long as a shepherd's crook. In fact, Case had seen several still in use in Switzerland. They were tipped with hand-hammered iron spikes, and used to probe the depth of snow, try the consistency of ice, test stone ledges and overhangs, probe crevasses.

"Then," Case said, "the two-handed ice ax was developed." He leaned forward from the waist to pick up samples from the foot of his bed. Apparently he was naked under the sheet. His upper torso had once been thick and muscular. Now it had gone to flab: pale flesh matted with reddish hair, smelling rankly.

He showed the long ice axes to Delaney, explaining how the implement could be used as a cane, driven into ice as a rope support, the mattock side of the head used to chop foot and hand holds in ice as capable of load-bearing as granite. The butt end of the handle varied. It could be a plain spike for hiking on glaciers, or fitted with a small thonged wheel for walking on crusted snow, or simply supplied with a small knurled cap.

"Where did you get all these?" Delaney asked.

"These two in Austria. This one in West Germany. This one in Geneva."

"You can buy them anywhere?"

"Anywhere in Europe, sure. Climbing is very big over there."

"And here?"

"There must be a dozen stores in New York. Maybe more. And other places too, of course. The West Coast, for instance."

"And this one?" Delaney had slipped the thong loop of the short ice ax over his wrist. "What's this used for?"

"Like I told you, technically it's an ice hammer. If you're on stone, you can start a hole with the pick end. Then you try to hammer in a piton with the other side of the head. A piton is a steel peg. It has a loop on top, and you can attack a line to it or thread it through."

Delaney drew two fingers across the head of the ax he held. Then he rubbed the tips of the two fingers with his thumb and grinned.

"You look happy," Case said, pouring himself another whiskey.

"I am. Oiled."

"What?"

"The ax head is oiled."

"Oh . . . sure. Evelyn keeps all my stuff cleaned and oiled. She thinks I'm going to climb again some day. Don't you, hon?"

Delaney turned to look at her. She nodded mutely, tried to smile. He smiled in return.

"What kind of oil do you use, Mrs Case?"

"Oh . . . I don't know. It's regular oil. I buy it in a hardware store on Sixth Avenue."

"A thin oil," Calvin Case said. "Like sewing machine oil. Nothing special about it."

"Do all climbers keep their tools cleaned and oiled?"

"The good ones do. And sharp."

Delaney nodded. Regretfully he relinquished the short-handled ice ax, putting it back with the others on the foot of Case's bed.

"You said you worked for Outside Life, where you bought this?"

"That's right. For almost ten years. I was in charge of the mountaineering department. They gave me all the time off I wanted for climbs. It was good publicity for them."

"Suppose I wanted to buy an ice ax like that. I just walk in and put down my money. Right?"

"Sure. That one cost about fifteen dollars. But that was five years ago."

"Do I get a cash register receipt, or do they write out an itemized sales check?"

Case looked at him narrowly. Then his bearded face opened into a smile; he showed his stained teeth again.

"Mr. Detective," he grinned. "Thinking every minute, aren't you? Well, as far as Outside Life goes, you're in luck. A sales slip is written out—or was, when I worked there. You got the customer's name and address. This was because Sol Appel, who owns the place, does a big mail order business. He gets out a Summer and Winter catalogue, and he's always anxious to add to his list. Then, on the slip, you wrote out the items purchased."

"After the customer's name and address were added to the mailing list, how long were the sales slips kept? Do you know?"

"Oh Jesus, years and years. The basement was full of them. But don't get your balls in an uproar, Captain. Outside Life isn't the only place in New York where you can buy an ice ax. And most of the other places just ring up the total purchase. There's no record of the customer's name, address, or what was bought. And, like I told you, most of these things are imported. You can buy an ice ax in London, Paris, Berlin, Vienna, Rome, Geneva, and points in between. And in Los Angeles, San Francisco, Boston, Portland, Seattle, Montreal, and a hundred other places. So where does that leave you?"

"Thank you very much," Captain Delaney said, without irony. "You have really been a big help, and I appreciate your cooperation. I apologize for the way I spoke."

Calvin Case made a gesture, a wave Delaney couldn't interpret.

"What are you going to do now, Captain?"

"Do now? Oh, you mean my next step. Well, you heard my telephone call. A man who is helping me is on his way to Outside Life. If he is able to purchase an ice ax like yours, then I'll go down there, ask if they'll let me go through their sales slips and make a list of people who have bought ice axes."

"But I just told you, there'll be thousands of sales checks. *Thousands!*"

"I know."

"And there are other stores in New York that sell ice axes with no record of the buyer. And stores all over the world that sell them."

"I know."

"You're a fool," Calvin Case said dully, turning his face away. "I thought for awhile you weren't, but now I think you are."

"Cal," his wife said softly, but he didn't look at her.

"I don't know what you think detective work is like," Delaney said, staring at the man in the bed. "Most people have been conditioned by novels, the movies and TV. They think it's either exotic clues and devilishly clever deductive reasoning, or else they figure it's all rooftop chases, breaking down doors, and shoot-outs on the subway tracks. All that is maybe five percent of what a detective does. Now I'll tell you how he mostly spends his time. About fifteen years ago a little girl was snatched on a street out on Long Island. She was walking home from school. A car pulled up alongside her and the driver said something. She came over to the car. A little girl. The driver opened the door, grabbed her, pulled her inside, and took off. There was an eyewitness to this, an old woman who 'thought' it was a dark car, black or dark blue or dark green or maroon. And she 'thought' it had a New York license plate. She wasn't sure of anything. Anyway, the parents got a ransom note. They followed instructions exactly: they didn't call the cops and they paid off. The little girl was found dead three days later. *Then* the FBI was called in. They had two things to work on: it *might* have been a New York license plate on the car, and the ransom note was handwritten. So the FBI called in about sixty agents from all over, and they were given a crash course in handwriting identification. Big blowups of parts of the ransom note were pasted on the walls. Three shifts of twenty men each started going through every application for an automobile license that originated on Long Island. They worked around the clock. How many signatures? Thousands? Millions, more likely. The agents set aside the possibles, and then handwriting experts took over to narrow it down."

"Did they get the man?" Evelyn Case burst out.

"Oh, sure," Delaney nodded. "They got him. Eventually. And if they hadn't found it in the Long Island applications, they'd have inspected every license in New York State. Millions and millions and millions. I'm telling you all this so you'll know what detective work usually is: common sense; a realization that you've got to start somewhere; hard, grinding, routine labor; and percentages. That's about it. Again, I thank you for your help."

He was almost at the shaded doorway to the living room when Calvin Case spoke in a faint, almost wispy voice.

"Captain."

Delaney turned. "Yes?"

"If you find the ax at Outside Life, who'll go through the sales slips?"

Delaney shrugged. "I will. Someone will. They'll be checked."

"Sometimes the items listed on the sales slips are just by stock number. You won't know what they are."

"I'll get identification from the owner. I'll learn what the stock numbers mean."

"Captain, I've got all the time in the world. I'm not going any place. I could go through those sales checks. I know what to look for. I could pull out every slip that shows an ice ax purchase faster than you could."

Delaney looked at him a long moment, expressionless. "I'll let you know," he nodded.

Evelyn Case saw him to the outside door.

"Thank you," she said softly.

When he left the Case home he walked directly over to Sixth Avenue and turned south, looking for a hardware store. Nothing. He returned to 11th Street and walked north. Still nothing. Then, across Sixth Avenue, on the west side, he saw one.

"A little can of oil," he told the clerk. "Like sewing machine oil."

He was offered a small, square can with a long neck sealed with a little red cap.

"Can I oil tools with this?" he asked.

"Of course," the clerk assured him. "Tools, sewing machines, electric fans, locks . . . anything. It's the biggest selling all-purpose oil in the country."

Thanks a lot, Delaney thought ruefully. He bought the can of oil.

He shouldn't have taken a cab. They still had sizable balances in their savings and checking accounts, they owned securities (mostly tax-exempt municipal bonds) and, of course, they owned their brownstone. But Delaney was no longer on salary, and Barbara's medical and hospital bills were frightening. So he really should have taken the subway and changed at 59th Street for a bus. But he felt so encouraged, so optimistic, that he decided to buy a cab to the hospital. On the way uptown he took the little red cap off the oil can and squeezed a few drops of oil onto his fingertips. He rubbed it against his thumb. Thin oil. It felt good, and he smiled.

But Barbara wasn't in her room. The floor nurse explained she had been taken down to the lab for more X-rays and tests. Delaney left a short note on her bedside table: "Hello. I was here. See you this evening. I love you. Edward."

He hurried home, stripped off overcoat and jacket, loosened his tie, rolled up his cuffs, put on his carpet slippers. Mary was there and had a beef stew cooking in a Dutch oven. But he asked her to let it cool after it was done; he had too much to do to think about eating.

He had cleaned out the two upper drawers of a metal business file cabinet in the study. In the top drawer he had filed the copies of the Operation Lombard reports. Methodically, he had divided this file into two: Frank Lombard and Bernard Gilbert. Under each heading he had broken the reports down into categories: Weapon, Motive, Wound, Personal History, etc.

In the second drawer he had started his own file, a thin folder that consisted mostly, at this time, of jotted notes.

Now he began to expand these notes into reports, to whom or for what purpose he could not say. But he had worked this way on all his investigations for many years, and frequently found it valuable to put his own instinctive reactions and questions into words. In happier times Barbara had typed out his notes on her electric portable, and that was a big help. But he had never solved the mysteries of the electric, and now would have to be content with handwritten reports.

He started with the long-delayed directory of all the people involved, their addresses and telephone numbers, if he had them or could find them in the book. Then he wrote out reports of his meeting with Thorsen and Johnson, of his interviews with Lombard's widow, mother, and associates, his talks with Dorfman, with Ferguson. He wrote as rapidly as he could, transcribing scribbles he had made in his pocket notebook, on envelopes of letters, on scraps of paper torn from magazines and newspaper margins.

He wrote of his meeting with Thomas Handry, with Christopher Langley, with Calvin Case. He described the brick-layers' hammer, the rock hounds' hammer, and Case's ice ax—where they had been purchased, when, what they cost, and what they were used for. He wrote a report of his interrogation of Monica Gilbert, his purchase of the can of light machine oil, his filing of a missing driver's license report.

He should have done all this weeks ago, and he was anxious to catch up and then to keep his file current with daily additions. It might mean nothing, it probably meant nothing, but it seemed important to him to have a written record of what he had done, and the growing mass of paper was, somehow, reassuring. At the rear of the second file drawer he placed the bricklayers' hammer, the rock hounds' hammer, and the can of oil: physical evidence.

He worked steadily, stopping twice just long enough to get bottles of cold beer from the kitchen. Mary was upstairs, cleaning, but she had turned the light out under the stew. He lifted the lid and sniffed experimentally. The steam smelled great.

He wrote as clearly and as swiftly as he could, but he admitted his handwriting was miserable. Barbara could read it, but who else could? Still, his neat manila file folders grew: "The Suspect," Weapon, Motive, Interrogations, Timing, Autopsies, etc. It all looked very official and impressive.

Late in the afternoon, still writing as fast as he could, Mary departed, with a firm command to eat the stew before he collapsed from malnutrition. He locked the door behind her, went back to his reports and then, a few minutes later, the front door bell chimed. He threw his pen down in anger, thought, then said aloud, "Please, God, let it be Langley. With the ax."

He peered through the narrow glass side panels, and it was Langley. Bearing a paper-wrapped parcel. And beaming. Delaney threw open the door.

"Got it!" Langley cried.

The Captain could not tell him he had held the same thing in his hands a few hours previously; he would not rob this wonderful little man of his moment of triumph.

In the study they inspected the ice ax together. It was a duplicate of the one Calvin Case owned. They went over it, pointing out to each other the required features: the tapering pick, the downward curve, the sharp point, the all-steel construction.

"Oh yes," Delaney nodded. "Mr. Langley, I think this is it. Congratulations."

"Oh . . ." Langley said, waving in the air. "You gave me the lead. Who told you about Outside Life?"

"A man I happened to meet," Delaney said vaguely. "He was interested in mountain climbing and happened to mention that store. Pure luck. But you'd have gotten there eventually."

"Excellent balance," Langley said, hefting the tool. "Very well made indeed. Well . . ."

"Yes?" Delaney said.

"Well, I suppose my job is finished," the old man said. "I mean, we've found the weapon, haven't we?"

"What we think is the weapon."

"Yes. Of course. But here it is, isn't it? I mean, I don't suppose you have anything more for me to do. So I'll . . ."

His voice died away, and he turned the ice ax over and over in his hands, staring at it.

"Nothing more for you to do?" Delaney said incredulously. "Mr. Langley, I have a great deal more I'd like you to do. But you've done so much already, I hesitate to ask."

"What?" Langley interrupted eagerly. "What? Tell me what. I don't want to stop now. Really I don't. What's to be done? Please tell me."

"Well . . ." Delaney said, "we don't know that Outside Life is the only store in New York that sells this type of ice ax. You have other stores on your list you haven't visited yet, don't you?"

"Oh my yes."

"Well, we must investigate and make a hard list of every place in New York that sells this ice ax. This one or one like it. That involves finding out how many American companies manufacture this type of ax and who they wholesale to and who the wholesalers retail to in the New York area. Then—you see here? On the side of the head? It says 'Made in West Germany.' Imported. And maybe from Austria and Switzerland as well. So we must find out who the exporters are and who, over here, they sell to. Mr Langley, that's a hell of a lot of work, and I hesitate to ask—"

"I'll do it!" Christopher Langley cried. "My goodness, I had no idea detective work was so—so involved. But I can understand why it's necessary. You want the source of every ice ax like this sold in the New York area. Am I correct?"

"Exactly," Delaney nodded. "We'll start with the New York area, and then we'll branch out. But it's so much work. I can't—"

Christopher Langley held up a little hand.

"Please," he said. "Captain, I *want* to do it. I've never felt so *alive* in my life. Now what I'll do is this: first I'll check out all the other stores on my list to see if they carry ice axes. I'll keep a record of the ones that do. Then I'll go to the library and consult a directory of domestic tool manufacturers. I'll query every one of them, or write for their catalogues to determine if they manufacture a tool like this. At the same time I'll check with European embassies, consulates and trade commissions and find out who's importing these implements to the U.S. How does that sound?"

Delaney looked at him admiringly. "Mr. Langley, I wish I had had you working with me on some of my cases in the past. You're a wonder, you are."

"Oh . . ." Langley said, blushing with pleasure, "you know . . ."

"I think your plan is excellent, and if you're willing to work at it—and it's going to be a lot of hard, grinding work—all I can say is 'Thank you' because what you'll be doing is important."

Key word.

"Important," Langley repeated. "Yes. Thank you."

They agreed Delaney could retain possession of the Outside Life ice ax. He placed it carefully in the rear of the second file cabinet drawer. His "exhibits" were growing. Then he walked Langley to the door.

"And how is the Widow Zimmerman?" he asked.

"What? Oh. Very well, thank you. She's been very kind to me. You know . . ."

"Of course. My wife thought very well of her."

"Did she!"

"Oh yes. Liked her very much. Thought she was a very warm hearted, sincere, out-going woman."

"Oh yes. Oh yes. She is all that. Did you eat any of the gefilte fish, Captain?"

"No, I didn't."

"It grows on you. An acquired taste, I suspect. Well . . ."

The little man started out. But the Captain called, "Oh, Mr. Langley, just one more thing," and he turned back.

"Did you get a sales check when you bought the ice ax at Outside Life?"

"A sales check? Oh, yes. Here it is."

He pulled it from his overcoat pocket and handed it to Delaney. The Captain inspected it eagerly. It bore Langley's name and address, the item ("Mountain ax—4B54C") and the price, $18.95, with the city sales tax added, and the total.

"The clerk asked for my name and address because they send out free catalogues twice a year and want to add to their mailing list. I gave my right name. That was all right, wasn't it, Captain?"

"Of course."

"And I thought their catalogue might be interesting. They do carry some fascinating items."

"May I keep this sales check?"

"Naturally."

"You're spending a lot of money on this case, Mr. Langley."

He smiled, tossed a hand in the air, and strutted out, the debonair boulevardier.

After the door was locked behind him, the Captain returned to his study, determined to take up his task of writing out the complete reports of his investigation. But he faltered. Finally he gave it up; something was bothering him. He went into the kitchen. The pot of stew was on the cold range. Using a long-handled fork, he stood there and ate three pieces of luke-warm beef, a potato, a small onion, and two slices of carrot. It all tasted like sawdust but, knowing Mary's cooking, he supposed it was good and the fault was his.

Later, at the hospital, he told Barbara what the problem was. She was quiet, almost apathetic, lying in her bed, and he wasn't certain she was listening or, if she was, if she understood. She stared at him with what he thought were fevered eyes, wide and brilliant.

He told her everything that had happened during the day, omitting only the call from the bookseller about the Honey Bunch books. He wanted to surprise her with that. But he told her of Langley buying the ice ax and how he, Delaney, was convinced that a similar tool had been used in the Lombard and Gilbert attacks.

"I know what should be done now," he said. "I already have Langley working on other places where an ice ax can be bought. He'll be checking retailers, wholesalers, manufacturers and importers. It's a big job for one man. Then I must try to get a copy of Outside Life's mailing list. I don't know how big it is, but it's bound to be extensive. Someone's got to go through it and pull the names and addresses of every resident of the Two-five-one Precinct. I'm almost certain the killer lives in the neighborhood. Then I want to get all the sales slips of Outside Life, for as many years as they've kept them, again to look for buyers of ice axes who live in the Precinct. And that checking and cross-checking will have to be done at every store where Langley discovers ice axes are sold. And I'm sure some of them won't have mailing lists or itemized sales checks, so the whole thing may be a monumental waste of time. But I think it has to be done, don't you?"

"Yes," she said firmly. "No doubt of it. Besides, it's your only lead, isn't it?"

"The only one," he nodded grimly. "But it's going to take a lot of time."

She looked at him a few moments, then smiled softly.

"I know what's bothering you, Edward. You think that even with Mr. Langley and Calvin Case helping you, checking all the lists and sales slips will take too much time. You're afraid someone else may be wounded or killed while you're messing around with mailing lists. You're wondering if perhaps you shouldn't turn over what you have right now to Operation Lombard, and let Broughton and his five hundred detectives get on it. They could do it so much faster."

"Yes," he said, grateful that she was thinking clearly now, her mind attuned to his. "That's exactly what's worrying me. How do you feel about it?"

"Would Broughton follow up on what you gave him?"

"Chief Pauley sure as hell would. I'd go to him. He's getting desperate now. And for good reason. He's got *nothing*. He'd grab at this and really do a job."

They were silent then. He came over to sit by her bedside and hold her hand. Neither spoke for several minutes.

"It's really a moral problem, isn't it?" she said finally.

He nodded miserably. "It's my own pride and ambition and ego . . . And my commitment to Thorsen and Johnson, of course. But if I don't do it, and someone else gets killed, I'll have a lot to answer for."

She didn't ask to whom.

"I could help you with the lists," she said faintly. "Most of the time I just lie here and read or sleep. But I have my good days, and I could help."

He squeezed her hand, smiled sadly. "You can help most by telling me what to do."

"When did you ever do what I told you to do?" she scoffed. "You go your own way, and you know it."

He grinned. "But you help," he assured her. "You sort things out for me."

"Edward, I don't think you should do anything immediately. Ivar Thorsen is deeply involved in this, and so is Inspector Johnson. If you go to Broughton, or even Chief Pauley, and tell them what you've discovered and what you suspect, they're sure to ask who authorized you to investigate."

"I could keep Thorsen and Johnson out of it. Don't forget, I have that letter from the Commissioner."

"But it would still be a mess, wouldn't it? And Broughton would probably know Thorsen is involved; the two of you have been so close for so long. Edward, why don't you have a talk with Ivar and Inspector Johnson? Tell them what you want to do. Discuss it. They're reasonable men; maybe they can suggest something. I know how much this case means to you."

"Yes," he said, looking down, "it does. More ever day. And when Thorsen went to the scene of the Gilbert attack, he was really spooked. He as much as said that this business of cutting Broughton down was small stuff compared to finding the killer. Yes, that's the best thing to do. I'll talk to Thorsen and Johnson, and tell them I want to go to Broughton with what I've got. I hate the thought of it—that shit! But maybe it has to be done. Well, I'll think about it some more. I'll try to see them tomorrow, so I may not be over at noon. But I'll come in the evening and tell you how it all came out."

"Remember, don't lose your temper, Edward."

"When did I ever lose my temper?" he demanded. "I'm always in complete control."

They both laughed.

6

HE SHAVED with an old-fashioned straight razor, one of a matched pair his father had used. They were handsome implements of Swedish steel with bone handles. Each morning, alternating, he took a razor from the worn, velvet-lined case and honed it lightly on a leather strop that hung from the inside knob of the bathroom door.

Barbara could never conceal her dislike of the naked steel. She had bought him an electric shaver one Christmas and, to please her, he had used it a few times at home. Then he had taken it to his office in the precinct house where, he assured her, he frequently used it for a "touch-up" when he had a meeting late in the afternoon or evening. She nodded, accepting his lie. Perhaps she sensed that the reason he used the straight razors was because they had belonged to his father, a man he worshipped.

Now, this morning, drawing the fine steel slowly and carefully down his lathered jaw, he listened to a news broadcast from the little transistor radio in the bedroom and learned, from a brief announcement, that Bernard Gilbert, victim of a midnight street attack, had died without regaining consciousness. Delaney's hand did not falter, and he finished his shave steadily, wiped off excess lather, splashed lotion, powdered lightly, dressed in his usual dark suit, white shirt, striped tie, and went down to the kitchen for breakfast, bolstered and carried along by habit. He stopped in the study just long enough to jot a little note to himself to write a letter of condolence to Monica Gilbert.

He greeted Mary, accepted orange juice, one poached egg on unbuttered toast, and black coffee. They chatted about the weather, about Mrs.

Delaney's condition, and he approved of Mary's plan to strip the furniture in
Barbara's sewing room of chintz slipcovers and send them all to the dry
cleaner.

Later, in the study, he wrote a pencilled rough of his letter of condolence
to Mrs. Gilbert. When he had it the way he wanted—admitting it was stilted,
but there was no way of getting around *that*—he copied it in ink, addressed
and stamped the envelope and put it aside, intending to mail it when he left
the house.

It was then almost 9:30, and he called the Medical Examiner's office.
Ferguson wasn't in yet but was expected momentarily. Delaney waited
patiently for fifteen minutes, making circular doodles on a scratch pad, a thin
line that went around and around in a narrowing spiral. Then he called again
and was put through to Ferguson.

"I know," the doctor said, "he's dead. I heard when I got in."

"Did you get it?"

"Yes. The lump is on the way down now. The big problem in my life,
Edward, is whether to do a cut-'em-up before lunch or after. I finally decided before is better. So I'll probably get to him about eleven or eleven-
thirty."

"I'd like to see you before you start."

"I can't get out, Edward. No way. I'm tied up here with other things."

"I'll come down. Could you give me about fifteen minutes at eleven
o'clock?"

"Important?"

"I think so."

"You can't tell me on the phone?"

"No. It's something I've got to show you, to give you."

"All right, Edward. Fifteen minutes at eleven."

"Thank you, doctor."

First he went into the kitchen. He tore a square of paper towel off the
roller, then a square of wax paper from the package, then a square of
aluminium foil. Back in the study he took from the file drawer the can of light
machine oil and the ice ax Christopher Langley had purchased at Outside
Life.

He removed the cap from the oil can and impregnated the paper towel
with oil. He folded it carefully into wax paper, then wrapped the whole thing
in aluminum foil, pressing down hard on the folds so the oil wouldn't seep
out. He put the package in a heavy manila envelope.

Then he sharpened a pencil, using his penknife to scrape the graphite to a
long point. He placed the ice ax head on a sheet of good rag stationery and
carefully traced a profile with his sharpened pencil, going very slowly, taking
particular care to include the four little saw teeth on the underside of the
point.

Then he took out his desk ruler and measured the size of the spike where it
left the head, as a square. Each of the four sides, as closely as he could
determine, was 15/16th of an inch. He then drew a square to those
dimensions on the same sheet of paper with the silhouette of the pick. He
folded the sheet, tucked it into his breast pocket. He took the envelope with
the oil-impregnated paper towel and started out. He pulled on his overcoat
and hat, shouted upstairs to Mary to tell her he was leaving, and heard her
answering shout. At the last minute, halfway out of the door, he
remembered his letter of condolence to Monica Gilbert and went back into
the study to pick it up. He dropped it in the first mailbox he passed.

●　　　●　　　●

"Better make this quick, Edward." Dr. Ferguson said. "Broughton is sending one of his boys down to witness the autopsy. He wants a preliminary verbal report before he gets the official form."

"I'll make it fast. Did the doctors at Mother of Mercy tell you anything?"

"Not much. As I told you, Gilbert was struck from the front, the wound about two inches above the normal hair line. The blow apparently knocked him backward, and the weapon was pulled free before he fell. As a result, the penetration is reasonably clean and neat, so I should be able to get a better profile of the wound than on the Lombard snuff."

"Good." Delaney unfolded his paper. "Doctor, this is what I think the penetration profile will look like. It's hard to tell from this, but the spike starts out as a square. Here, in this little drawing, are the dimensions, about an inch on each side. If I'm right, that should be the size of the outside wound, at scalp and skull. Then the square changes to a triangular pick, and tapers, and curves downward, coming to a sharp point."

"Is this your imagination, or was it traced from an actual weapon?"

"It was traced."

"All right. I don't want to know anything more. What are these?"

"Four little saw teeth on the underside of the point. You may find some rough abrasions on the lower surface of the wound."

"I may, eh? The brain isn't hard cheddar, you know. You want me to work with this paper open on the table alongside the corpse?"

"Not if Broughton's man is there."

"I didn't think so."

"Couldn't you just take a look at it, doctor? Just in case?"

"Sure," Ferguson said, folding up the paper and sliding it into his hip pocket. "What else have you got?"

"In this envelope is a folded packet of aluminum foil, and inside that is an envelope of wax paper, and inside that is a paper towel soaked in oil. Light machine oil."

"So?"

"You mentioned there were traces of oil in the Lombard wound. You thought it was probably Lombard's hair oil, but it was too slight for analysis."

"But Gilbert was bald—at least where he was hit he was bald."

"That's the point. It couldn't be hair oil. But I'm hoping there will be oil in the Gilbert wound. Light machine oil."

Ferguson pushed back in his swivel chair and stared at him. Then the doctor pulled his wool tie open, unbuttoned the neck of his flannel shirt.

"You're a lovely man, Edward," he said, "and the best detective in town, but Gilbert's wound was X-rayed, probed and flushed at Mother of Mercy."

"If there was any oil in it, there couldn't be any now?"

"I didn't say that. But it sure as hell cuts down on your chances."

"What about the Olfactory Analysis Indicator?"

"The OAI? What about it?"

"How much do you know about it, doctor?"

"About as much as you do. You read the last bulletin, didn't you?"

"Yes. Sort of inconclusive, wasn't it?"

"It surely was. The idea is to develop a sniffer not much larger than a vacuum cleaner. Portable. It could be taken to the scene of a crime, inhale an air sample, and either identify the odors immediately or store the air sample so it could be taken back to the lab and analyzed by a master machine. Well, they're a long way from that right now. It's a monstrous big thing at this point, very crude, but I saw an impressive demonstration the other day. It correctly identified nine smokes from fifteen different brands of cigarettes. That's not bad."

"In other words, it's got to have a comparison to go by? Like the memory bank in a computer?"

"That's right. Oh-ho. I see what you're getting at. All right, Edward. Leave me your machine oil sample. I'll try to get a reading on tissue from Gilbert's wound. But don't count on it. The OAI is years away. It's just an experiment now."

"I realize that. But I don't want to neglect any possibility."

"You never did," Dr. Ferguson said.

"Should I wait around?"

"No point in it. The OAI analysis will take three days at least. Probably a week. As far as your drawing goes, I'll catch you this afternoon or this evening. Will you be home?"

"Probably. But I may be at the hospital. You could reach me there."

"How's Barbara?"

"Getting along."

Ferguson nodded, stood, took off his tweed jacket, hung it on a coat tree, began to shrug into a stained white coat.

"Getting anywhere, Edward?" he asked.

"Who the hell knows?" Captain Delaney grumbled. "I just keep going."

"Don't we all?" the big man smiled.

Delaney called Ivar Thorsen from a lobby phone. The answering service got back to him a few minutes later and said Mr. Thorsen was not available and would he please call again at three in the afternoon.

It was the first time Thorsen had not returned his call, and it bothered Delaney. It might be, of course, that the deputy inspector was in a meeting or on his way to a precinct house, but the Captain couldn't shake a vague feeling of unease.

He consulted his pocket notebook in which he had copied the address of Outside Life. He took a taxi to Spring Street, and when he got out of the cab, he spent a few minutes walking up and down the block, looking around. It was a section of grimy loft buildings, apparently mostly occupied by small manufacturers, printers, and wholesalers of leather findings. It seemed a strange neighborhood for Outside Life.

That occupied the second and third floors of a ten-story building. Delaney walked up the stairs to the second floor, but the sign on the solid door said "Offices and Mailing. Store on third floor." So he climbed another flight, wanting to look about before he talked to—to— He consulted his notebook again: Sol Appel, the owner.

The "store" was actually one enormous, high-ceilinged loft with pipe racks, a few glass showcases, and with no attempts made at fashionable merchandizing. Most of the stock was piled on the floor, on unpainted wooden shelves, or hung from hooks driven into the whitewashed walls.

As Langley had said, it was a fascinating conglomeration: rucksacks, rubber dinghies, hiking boots, crampons, dehydrated food, kerosene lanterns, battery-heated socks, machetes, net hammocks, sleeping bags, outdoor cookware, hunting knives, fishing rods, reels, creels, pitons, nylon rope, boating gear—an endless profusion of items ranging from five-cent fishhooks to a magnificent red, three-room tent with a mosquito-netted picture window, at $1,495.00.

Outside Life seemed to have its devotees, despite its out-of-the-way location; Delaney counted at least 40 customers wandering about, and the clerks were busy writing up purchases. The Captain found his way to the mountaineering department and inspected pitons, crampons, web belts and harnesses, nylon line, aluminum-framed backpacks, and a wide variety of ice axes. There were two styles of short-handled axes: the one purchased by Langley and another, somewhat similar, but with a wooden handle and no saw-tooth serrations under the spike. Delaney inspected it, and finally found "Made in U.S.A." stamped on the handle butt.

He halted a scurrying clerk just long enough to ask for the whereabouts of Mr. Appel. "Sol's in the office," the departing clerk called over his shoulder. "Downstairs."

Delaney pushed open the heavy door on the second floor and found himself in a tiny reception room, walled with unfinished plywood panels. There was a door of clear glass leading to the open space beyond, apparently a combination warehouse and mailing room. In one corner of the reception room was a telephone operator wearing a wired headset and sitting before a push-pull switchboard that Delaney knew had been phased out of production years and years ago. Outside Life seemed to be a busy, thriving enterprise, but it was also obvious the profits weren't going into fancy offices and smart decoration.

He waited patiently until the operator had plugged and unplugged half-a-dozen calls. Finally, desperately, he said, "Mr. Appel, please. My name is—"

She stuck her head through the opening into the big room beyond and screamed, "Sol! Guy to see you!"

Delaney sat on the single couch, a rickety thing covered with slashed plastic. He was amused to note an overflowing astray on the floor. The single decoration in the room was a plaque on the plywood wall attesting to Mr. Solomon Appel's efforts on behalf of the United Jewish Appeal.

The glass door crashed back, and a heavy, sweating man rushed in. Delaney caught a confused impression of a round, plump face (the man in the moon), a well-chewed, unlit cigar, a raveled, sleeveless sweater of hellish hue, unexpectedly "mod" jeans of dark blue with white stitching and a darker stain down one leg, and Indian moccasins decorated with beads.

"You from Benson & Hurst?" the man demanded, talking rapidly around his cigar. "I'm Sol Appel. Where the hell are those tents? You promised—"

"Wait, wait," Delaney said hastily. "I'm not from Benson & Hurst. I'm—"

"Gatters," the man said positively. "The fiberglass rods. You guys are sure giving me the rod—you know where. You said—"

"Will you wait a minute," Delaney said again, sighing. "I'm not from Gatters either. My name is Captain Edward X. Delaney. New York Police Department. Here's my identification."

Sol Appel didn't even glance at it. He raised his hands above his head, palms outward, in mock surrender.

"I give up," he said. "Whatever it was, I did it. Take me away. Now. Please get me out of this nuthouse. Do me a favor. Jail will be a pleasure."

"No, no," Delaney laughed. "Nothing like that. Mr. Appel, I wanted—"

"You're putting on a dance? A dinner? You want a few bucks? Of course. Why not? Always. Any time. So tell me—how much?"

He was already reaching for his wallet when Delaney held out a restraining hand and sighed again.

"Please, Mr. Appel, it's nothing like that. I'm not collecting for anything. All I want is a few minutes of your time."

"A few minutes? Now you're really asking for something valuable. A few minutes!" He turned back to the opened glass door. "Sam!" he screamed. "You, Sam! Get the cash. No check. The cash! You understand?"

"Is there any place we can talk?" the Captain asked.

"We're talking, aren't we?"

"All right," Delaney said doubtfully, glancing at the switchboard operator. But she was busy with her cords and plugs. "Mr. Appel, your name was given to me by Calvin Case, and I—"

"Cal!" Appel cried. He stepped close and grabbed Delaney's overcoat by the lapels. "That dear, sweet boy. How is he? Will you tell me?"

"Well . . . he's—"

"Don't tell me. He's on the booze. I know. I heard. I wanted him back. 'So you can't walk,' I told him. 'Big deal. You can think. No? You can work. No?' That's the big thing—right, Captain—uh, Captain—"

"Delaney."

"Captain Delaney. That's Irish, no?"

"Yes."

"Sure. I knew. The important thing is to work. Am I right?"

"You're right."

"Of course I'm right," Sol Appel said angrily. "So any time he wants a job, he's got it. Right here. We can use him. Tell him that. Will you tell him that?" Suddenly Appel struck his forehead with the heel of his hand. "I should have been to see him," he groaned. "What kind of *schmuck* am I? I'm really ashamed. I'll go to see him. Tell him that, Chief Delaney."

"Captain."

"Captain. Will you tell him that?"

"Yes, certainly, if I speak to him again. But that isn't the—"

"You're taking up a collection for him? You're making a benefit, Captain? It will be my pleasure to take a table for eight, and I'll—"

Delaney finally got him calmed down, a little, and seated on the plastic couch. He explained he was involved in an investigation, and the cigar-chomping Sol Appel asked no questions. Within five minutes Delaney had discovered that Outside Life had a mailing list of approximately 30,000 customers who were sent Summer and Winter catalogues. The mailings were done with metal addressing plates and printed labels. There was also a typed master list, and Sol Appel would be happy to provide a copy for Captain Delaney whenever he asked.

"I assure you, it'll be held in complete confidence," the Captain said earnestly.

"Who cares?" Appel shouted. "My competitors can meet my prices? Hah!"

Delaney also learned that Outside Life kept sales checks for seven years. They were stored in cardboard cartons in the basement of the loft building, filed by month and year.

"Why seven years?" he asked.

"Who the hell knows?" Appel shrugged. "My father—God rest his soul—he only died last year—I should live so long—Mike Appel—a *mensch*. You know what a *mensch* is, Captain?"

"Yes. I know. My father was an Irish *mensch*."

"Good. So he told me, 'Sol,' he said a hundred times, 'always keep the copies of the sales checks for seven years.' Who the hell knows why? That's the way he did it, that's the way I do it. Taxes or something; I don't know. Anyway, I keep them seven years. I add this year's, I throw the oldest year's away."

"Would you let me go through them?"

"Go through them? Captain, there's got to be like a hundred thousand checks there."

"If I have to, can I go through them?"

"Be my guest. Sarah!" Sol Appel suddenly screamed. "You, Sarah!"

An elderly Jewish lady thrust her head through the switchboard operator's window.

"You called, Sol?" she asked.

"Tell him 'No!'" Appel screamed, and the lady nodded and withdrew.

Now that Delaney wanted to leave, Appel wouldn't let him depart. He shook his hand endlessly and talked a blue streak . . .

"Go up to the store. Pick out anything you like. Have them call me before you pay. You'll get a nice discount, believe me. You know, you Irish and us Jews are much alike. We're both poets—am I right? And who can talk these days? The Irish and the Jews only. You need a cop, you find an Irishman. You need a lawyer, you find a Jew. Thus stuff I sell, you think I understand it? Hah! For me, I go camping on Miami Beach or Nassau. You float on the pool there in this plastic couch with a nice, tall drink and all around these girlies in their little bitty bikinis. That, to me, is outside life. Captain, I like you. Delaney—right? You in the book? Sure, you're in the book. Next month, a Bar-Mitzvah for my nephew. I'll call you. Bring nothing, you understand? Nothing! I'll go see Calvin Case. I swear I'll go. You've got to work. Sarah! Sarah!"

Delaney finally got out of there, laughing aloud and shaking his head, so that people he passed on the stairway looked at him strangely. He didn't think Appel would remember to invite him to the Bar-Mitzvah. But if he did, Delaney decided he would go. How often do you meet a *live* man?

Well, he had found out what he wanted to know—and, as usual, it wasn't as bad as he had feared or as good as he had hoped. He walked west on Spring Street and, suddenly, pierced by the odor of frying sausage and peppers, he joined a throng of Puerto Ricans and blacks at an open luncheonette counter and had a slice of sausage pizza and a glass of sweet cola, resolutely forgetting about his diet. Sometimes . . .

He took two subways and a bus back to his home. Mary was having coffee in the kitchen, and he joined her for a cup, telling her he had already eaten lunch, but not saying what it was.

"Whatever it was, it had garlic in it," she sniffed, and he laughed.

He worked in his study until 3:00 P.M., bringing his reports up to date. The file of his own investigation was becoming pleasingly plump. It was nowhere near as extensive as the Operation Lombard reports, of course, but still, it had width to it now, it had width.

At 3:00 P.M., he called Deputy Inspector Thorsen. This time the answering service operator asked him to hold while she checked. She was back on again in a few minutes and told him Thorsen asked him to call again at seven in the evening. Delaney hung up, now convinced that something was happening, something was awry.

He put the worry away from him and went back to his notes and reports. If "The Suspect" was indeed a mountain climber—and Delaney believed he was—weren't there other possible leads to his identity other than the mailing list of Outside Life? For instance, was there a local or national club or association of mountain climbers whose membership list could be culled for residents of the 251st Precinct? Was there a newsletter or magazine devoted to mountaineering with a subscription list that could be used for the same purpose? What about books on mountain climbing? Should Delaney inquire at the library that served the 251st Precinct and try to determine who had withdrawn books on the subject?

He jotted down notes on these questions as fast as they occurred to him. Mountain climbing was, after all, a minor sport. But could you call it a *sport*? It really didn't seem to be a pastime or diversion. It seemed more of a—of a—well, the only word that came to his mind was "challenge." He also thought, for some reason, of "crusade," but that didn't make too much sense, and he resolved to talk to Calvin Case about it, and carefully made a note to himself to that effect.

Finally, almost as a casual afterthought, he came back to the problem that had been nagging him for the past few days, and he resolved to turn over everything he had to Broughton and Chief Pauley. They could follow through much faster than he could, and their investigation might, just might, prevent another death. He would have liked to stick to it on his own, but that was egotism, just egotism.

He was writing out a detailed report of his meeting with Sol Appel when the desk phone rang. He lifted the receiver and said absently, "Hello."

"'Hello'?" Dr Sanford Ferguson laughed. "What the hell kind of a greeting is that—'Hello?' Whatever happened to 'Captain Edward X. Delaney here'?"

"All right. Captain Edward X. Delaney here. Are you bombed?"

"On my way, m'lad. Congratulations."

"You mean the drawing was accurate?"

"Right on. The outside wound—I'm talking about the skull now—was a rough square, about an inch on each side. For the probe I used glass fiber. You know what that is?"

"A slender bundle of glass threads, flexible and transmitting light from a battery-powered source."

"You know everything, don't you, Edward? Yes, that's what I used. Tapering, curving downward to a sharp point, and I even found some evidence of heavier abrasions on the lower surface, a tearing. That could be accounted for by those little saw teeth. Not definite enough to put in my official report, but a possible, Captain, a possible."

"Thank you, doctor. And the oil?"

"No obvious sign of it. But I sent your rag and a specimen of tissue to the lab. I told you, it'll take time."

"They won't talk?"

"The lab boys? Only to me. It's just a job. They know from nothing. Happy, Edward?"

"Yes. Very. Why are you getting drunk?"

"He was so small. So small, so frail, so wasted and his heart wasn't worth a damn and he had a prick about the size of a thimble. So I'm getting drunk. Any objections?"

"No. None."

"Get the bastard, Edward."

"I will."

"Promise?"

"I promise," Captain Edward X. Delaney said.

He got to the hospital shortly after 5:30, but the visit was a disaster. Barbara immediately started talking of a cousin of hers who had died twenty years ago, and then began speaking of "this terrible war." He thought she was talking about Vietnam, but then she spoke of Tom Hendricks, a lieutenant of Marines, and he realized she was talking about the Korean War, in which Tom Hendricks had been killed. Then she sang a verse of "Black is the color of my true love's hair," and he didn't know what to do.

He sat beside her, tried to soothe her. But she would not be still. She gabbled of Mary, of the drapes in the third-floor bedrooms, Thorsen, violets, a dead dog—and who had taken her children away? He was frightened and close to weeping. He pushed the bell for the nurse, but when no one came, he rushed into the corridor and almost dragged in the first nurse he saw.

Barbara was still babbling, eyes closed, an almost-smile on her lips, and he waited anxiously, alone, while the nurse left for a moment to consult her medication chart. He listened to a never-ending stream of meaningless chatter: Lombard and Honey Bunch and suddenly, "I need a hundred dollars," and Eddie and Liza, and then she was at the carrousel in the park, describing it and laughing, and the painted horses went round and round, and then the nurse came back with a covered tray, removed a hypodermic, gave Barbara a shot in the arm, near the wrist. In a few moments she was calm, then sleeping.

"Jesus Christ," Delaney breathed, "what happened to her? What was that?"

"Just upset," the nurse smiled mechanically. "She's all right now. She's sleeping peaceably."

"Peacefully," the Captain said.

"Peacefully," the nurse repeated obediently. "If you have any questions, please contact your doctor in the morning."

She marched out. Delaney stared after her, wondering if there was any end to the madness in the world. He turned back to the bed. Barbara was, apparently, sleeping peacefully. He felt so goddamned frightened, helpless, furious.

It wasn't 7:00 p.m., so he couldn't call Thorsen. He walked home, hoping, just hoping, he might be attacked. He was not armed, but he didn't care. He would kick them in the balls, bite their throats—he was in that mood. He looked around at the shadowed streets. "Try me," he wanted to shout. "Come on! I'm here."

He got inside, took off his hat and coat, treated himself to two straight whiskies. He calmed down, gradually. What a thing that had been. He was home now, unhurt, thinking clearly. But Barbara . . .

He sat stolidly sipping his whiskey until 7:00 p.m. Then he called Thorsen's number, not really caring. Thorsen called him back almost immediately.

"Edward?"

"Yes."

"Something important?"

"I think so. Can you get Johnson?"

"He's here now."

Then Delaney became aware of the tone of the man's voice, the tightness, urgency.

"I've got to see you," the Captain said. "The sooner the better."

"Yes," Thorsen agreed. "Can you come over now?"

"Your office or home?"

"Home."

"I'll take a cab," Captain Delaney told him. "About twenty minutes, at the most."

He hung up, then said, "Fuck 'em all," in a loud voice. But he went into the kitchen, found a paper shopping bag in the cabinet under the sink, brought it back to the study. In it he placed the three hammers and the can of machine oil—all his "physical evidence." Then he set out.

Mrs. Thorsen met him at the door, took his coat and hat and hung them away. She was a tall silver-blonde, almost gaunt, but with good bones and the most beautiful violet eyes Delaney had ever seen. They chatted a few moments, and she asked about Barbara. He mumbled something.

"Have you eaten tonight, Edward?" she asked suddenly.

He tried to think, not remembering, then shook his head.

"I'm making some sandwiches. Ham-and-cheese all right? Or roast beef?"

"Either or both will be fine, Karen."

"And I have some salad things. In about an hour or so. The others are in the living room—you know where."

There were three men in the room, all seated. Thorsen and Inspector Johnson rose and came forward to shake his hand. The third man remained seated; no one offered to introduce him.

This man was short, chunky, swarthy, with a tremendous mustache. His hands lay flat on his knees, and his composure was monumental. Only his dark eyes moved, darting, filled with curiosity and a lively intelligence.

It was only after he was seated that Delaney made him: Deputy Mayor Herman Alinski. He was a secretive, publicity-shy politico, reputed to be the mayor's trouble-shooter and one of his closest confidants. In a short biographical sketch in the *Times,* the writer, speculating on Alinski's duties, had come to the conclusion that, "Apparently, what he does most frequently is listen, and everyone who knows him agrees that he does that very well indeed."

"Drink, Edward?" Thorsen asked. "Rye highball?"

Delaney looked around. Thorsen and Johnson had glasses. Alinski did not.

"Not right now, thank you. Maybe later."

"All right. Karen is making up some sandwiches for us. Edward, you said you had something important for us. You can talk freely."

Again Delaney became conscious of the tension in Thorsen's voice, and when he looked at Inspector Johnson, the big black seemed stiff and grim.

"All right," Delaney said. "I'll take it from the top."

He started speaking, still seated, and then, in a few moments, rose to pace around the room or pause with his elbow on the mantel. He thought and spoke better, he knew, on his feet, and could gesture freely. None of the three men interrupted, but their heads or eyes followed him wherever he strode.

He began with Lombard's death. The position of the body. His reasons for thinking the killer had approached from the front, then whirled to strike Lombard down from behind.The shape and nature of the wound. Oil in the wound. The missing driver's license. His belief that it was taken as evidence of the kill. Then Langley, his expertise, and the discovery of the bricklayers' hammer which led to the rock hounds' hammer which led to the ice ax.

At this point he unpacked his shopping bag and handed around the tools. The three men examined them closely, their faces expressionless as they tested edges with thumbs, hefted the weight and balance of the tools.

Delaney went on: the Bernard Gilbert attack. The missing ID card. His belief that the assailant was psychopathic. A resident of the 251st Precinct. And would kill again. The information supplied by Handry: the Trotsky assassination and the name of Calvin Case. Then the interview with Case. The oil on the ice ax heads. He handed around the can of oil.

He had them now, and the three were leaning forward intently, Thorsen and Johnson neglecting their drinks, the Deputy Mayor's sharp eyes darting and glittering. There wasn't a sound from them.

Delaney told them about the interview with Sol Appel at Outside Life. The mailing list and itemized sales checks. Then he related how he had traced a profile of the ice ax head. How he had given that and a sample of machine oil to the surgeon who did the autopsy on Gilbert. How the profile on the wound checked out. How the oil would be analyzed on the OAI.

"Who did the post?" Inspector Johnson asked.

Alinski's head swivelled sharply, and he spoke for the first time. "Post?" he asked. "What's post?"

"Post-mortem," Delaney explained. "I promised to keep the surgeon's name out of it."

"We could find out," Alinski said mildly.

"Of course," the Captain said, just as mildly. "But not from me."

That seemed to satisfy Alinski. Thorsen asked how much Delaney had told the surgeon, had told Langley, Handry, Case, Mrs. Gilbert, Sol Appel.

Only as much as they needed to know, Delaney assured him. They knew only that he was engaged in a private investigation of the deaths of Lombard and Gilbert, and they were willing to help.

"Why?" Alinski asked.

Delaney shrugged. "For reasons of their own." There was silence for a few minutes, then Alinski spoke softly:

"You have no proof, do you, Captain?"

Delaney looked at him in astonishment.

"Of course not. It's all smoke, all theory. I haven't told you or shown you a single thing that could be taken into court at this time."

"But you believe in it?"

"I believe in it. For one reason only—there's nothing else to believe in. Does Operation Lombard have anything better?"

The three men turned heads to stare wordlessly at each other. Delaney could tell nothing from their expressions.

"That's really why I'm here," he said, addressing Thorsen. "I want to turn—"

But at that moment there was a kicking at the door; not a knocking, but three sharp kicks. Thorsen sprang up, stalked over, opened the door and relieved his wife of a big tray of food.

"Thank you dear," he smiled.

"There's plenty more of everything," she called to the other men. "So don't be polite if you're hungry; just ask."

Thorsen put the loaded tray on a low cocktail table, and they clustered around. There were ham-and-cheese sandwiches, roast beef sandwiches, chunks of tomato, radishes, dill pickles, slices of Spanish onions, a jar of hot mustard, olives, potato chips, scallions.

They helped themselves, all standing, and Thorsen mixed fresh drinks. This time Delaney had a rye and water, and Deputy Mayor Alinski took a double Scotch.

Unwilling to sacrifice the momentum of what he had been saying, and the impression he had obviously made on them, Delaney began talking again, speaking between bites of his sandwich and pieces of scallion. This time he looked at Alinski as he spoke.

"I want to turn over everything I've got to Chief Pauley. I admit it's smoke, but it's a lead. I've got three or four inexperienced people who can check sources of the ax and the Outside Life mailing list and sales checks. But Pauley's got five hundred dicks and God knows how many deskmen if he needs them. It's a question of time. I think Pauley should take this over; he can do it a lot faster than I can. It might prevent another kill, and I'm convinced there will be another, and another, and another, until we catch up with this nut."

The other three continued eating steadily, sipping their drinks and looking at him. Once Thorsen started to speak, but Alinski held up a hand, silencing him. Finally the Deputy Mayor finished his sandwich, wiped his fingers on a paper napkin, took his drink back to his chair. He sat down, sighed, stared at Delaney.

"A moral problem for you, isn't it, Captain?" he asked softly.

"Call it what you like, " Delaney shrugged. "I just feel what I have is strong enough to follow up on, and Chief Pauley is—"

"Impossible," Thorsen said.

"Why impossible?" Delaney cried angrily. "If you—"

"Calm down, Edward," Inspector Johnson said quietly. He was on his third sandwich. "That's why we wanted to talk to you tonight. You obviously haven't been listening to radio or TV in the last few hours. You can't turn over what you have to Chief Pauley. Broughton canned him a few hours ago.

"Canned him?"

"Whatever you want to call it. Relieved him of command. Kicked him off Operation Lombard."

"Jesus Christ!" Delaney said furiously. "He can't do that."

"He did it," Thorsen nodded. "And in a particularly—in a particularly brutal way. Didn't even tell the Chief. Just called a press conference and announced he was relieving Pauley of all command responsibilities relating to Operation Lombard. He said Pauley was inefficient and getting nowhere."

"But who the hell is—"

"And Broughton is going to take over personal supervision of all the detectives assigned to Operation Lombard."

"Oh God," Delaney groaned. "That tears it."

"You haven't heard the worst," Thorsen went on, staring at him without expression. "About an hour ago Pauley filed for retirement. After what Broughton said, Pauley knows his career is finished, and he wants out."

Delaney sat down heavily in an armchair, looked down at his drink, swirling the ice cubes.

"Son of a bitch," he said bitterly. "Pauley was a good man. You have no idea how good. He was right behind me. Only because I had the breaks, and he didn't. But he would have been on to this ice ax thing is another week or so. I know he would; I could tell it by the reports. God damn it! The Department can't afford to lose men like Pauley. Jesus! A good brain and thirty years' experience down the drain. It just makes me sick!"

None of them said anything, giving him time to calm down. Alinski rose from his chair to go over to the food tray again, take a few radishes and olives. Then he came over to stand before Delaney's chair, popping food.

"You know, Captain," he said gently, "this development really doesn't affect your moral problem, does it? I mean, you can still take what you have to Broughton."

"I suppose so," Delaney said morosely. "Canning Pauley, for God's sake. Broughton's out of his mind. He just wanted a goat to protect his own reputation."

"That's what we think," Inspector Johnson said.

Delaney looked up at Deputy Mayor Alinski, still standing over him.

"What's it all about?" he demanded. "Will you please tell me what the hell this is all about?"

"Do you really want to know, Captain?"

"Yeah, I want to know," Delaney grunted. "But I don't want you to tell me. I'll find out for myself."

"I think you will," Alinski nodded. "I think you are a very smart man."

"Smart? Shit! I can't even find one kill-crazy psychopath in my own precinct."

"It's important to you, isn't it, Captain, to find the killer? It's the most important thing."

"Of course it's the most important thing. This nut is going to keep killing, over and over and over. There will be shorter intervals between murders. Maybe he'll hit in the daytime. Who the hell knows? But I can guarantee one thing: he won't stop now. It's a fever in his blood. He can't stop. Wait'll the newspapers get hold of this. And they will. Then the shit will hit the fan."

"Going to take what you have to Broughton?" Thorsen asked, almost idly.

"I don't know. I don't know what I'll do. I have to think about it."

"That's wise," Alinski said unexpectedly. "Think about it. There's nothing like thought—long, deep thought."

"I just want all of you to know one thing," Delaney said angrily, not understanding why he was angry. "The decision is mine. Only mine. What I decide to do, I'll do."

They would have offered him something, but they knew better.

Johnson came over to put a heavy hand on Delaney's shoulders. The big black was grinning. "We know that, Edward. We knew you were a hard-nose from the start. We're not going to lean on you."

Delaney drained his drink, rose, put the empty glass on the cocktail table. He repacked his paper shopping bag with hammers and the can of oil.

"Thank you," he said to Thorsen. "Thank Karen for me for the food. I can find my own way out."

"Will you call and tell me what you've decided, Edward?"

"Sure. If I decide to go to Broughton, I'll call you first."

"Thank you."

"Gentlemen," Delaney nodded around, and marched out. They watched him go, all of them standing.

He had to walk five blocks and lost two dimes before he found a public phone that worked. He finally got through to Thomas Handry.

"Yes?"

"Captain Edward X. Delaney here. Am I interrupting you?"

"Yes."

"Working?"

"Trying to."

"How's it coming?"

"It's never as good as you want it to be."

"That's true," Delaney said, without irony and without malice. "True for poets and true for cops. I was hoping you could give me some help."

"The photo of the ice ax that killed Trotsky? I haven't been able to find it."

"No, this is something else."

"You're something else too, Captain—you know that? All for you and none for me. When are you going to open up?"

"In a day or so."

"Promise?"

"I promise."

"All right. What do you want?"

"What do you know about Broughton?"

"Who?"

"Broughton, Timothy A., Deputy Commissioner."

"That prick? Did you see him on TV tonight?"

"No, I didn't."

"He fired Chief Pauley. For inefficiency and, he hinted, dereliction of duty. A sweet man."

"What does he want?"

"Broughton? He wants to be commissioner, then mayor, then governor, then President of these here You-nited States. He's got ambition and drive you wouldn't believe."

"I gather you don't approve of him."

"You gather right. I've had one personal interview with him. You know how most men carry pictures of their wives and children in their wallets? Broughton carries pictures of himself."

"Nice. Does he have any clout? Political clout?"

"Very heavy indeed. Queens and Staten Island for starters. The talk is that he's aiming for the primary next year. On a 'law and order' platform. You know, 'We must clamp down on crime in the streets, no matter what it costs.'"

"You think he'll make it?"

"He might. If he can bring off his Operation Lombard thing, it's bound to help. And if Lombard's killer turns out to be a black heroin addict on welfare who's living with a white fifteen-year-old hippie with long blonde hair, there'll be no stopping Broughton."

"You think the mayor's worried?"

"Wouldn't you be?"

"I guess. Thank you, Handry. You've made a lot of things a lot clearer."

"Not for me. What the hell is going on?"

"Will you give me a day—or two?"

"No more. Gilbert died, didn't he?"

"Yes. He did."

"There's a connection, isn't there?"

"Yes."

"Two days," Handry said. "No more. If I don't hear from you by then, I'll have to start guessing. In print."

"Good enough."

He walked home, the shopping bag bumping against his knee. Now he could understand something of what was going on—the tension of Thorsen, Johnson's grimness, Alinski's presence. He really didn't want to get involved in all that political shit. He was a cop, a professional. Right now, all he wanted to do was to catch a killer, but he seemed bound and strangled by this maze of other men's ambitions, feuds, obligations.

What had happened, he realized, was that his search for the killer of Lombard and Gilbert had become a very personal thing to him, a private thing, and he resented the intrusion of other men, other circumstances, other motives. He needed help, of course—he couldn't do everything himself—but essentially it was a duel, a two-man combat, and outside advice, pressures, influence were to be shunned. You knew what you could do, and you respected your opponent's ability and didn't take him lightly. Whether it was a fencing exhibition or a duel to the death, you put your cock on the line.

But all that was egotism he admitted, groaning aloud. Stupid male *machismo*, believing that nothing mattered unless you risked your balls. It should not, it *could* not affect his decision which, as Barbara and Deputy Mayor Alinski had recognized, was essentially a moral choice.

Thinking this way, brooding, his brain in a whirl, he turned into his own block, head down, *schlepping* along with his heavy shopping bag, when a harsh voice called, "Delaney!"

He stopped slowly. Like most detectives in New York—in the world!—he had helped send men up. To execution, or to long or short prison terms, or to mental institutions. Most of them vowed revenge—in the courtroom, in threats phoned by their friends, in letters. Very few of them, thankfully, ever carried out their threats. But there were a few . . .

Now, hearing his name called from a dark sedan parked on a poorly lighted street, realizing he was unarmed, he turned slowly toward the car.

He let the shopping bag drop to the sidewalk. He raised his arms slightly, palms turned forward.

But then he saw the uniformed driver in the front seat. And in the back, leaning toward the cranked-down window, the bulk and angry face of Deputy Commissioner Broughton. The cigar, clenched in his teeth, was burning furiously.

"Delaney!" Broughton said again, more of a command than a greeting. The Captain stepped closer to the car. Broughton made no effort to open the door, so Delaney was forced to bow forward from the waist to speak to him. He was certain this was deliberate on Broughton's part, to keep him in a supplicant's position.

"Sir?" he asked.

"Just what the fuck do you think you're doing?"

"I don't understand, sir."

"We sent a man to Florida. It turns out that Lombard's driver's license is missing. The widow says you spoke to her about it. You were seen entering her house. You knew the license was missing. I could rack you up for withholding evidence."

"But I reported it, sir."

"You reported it? To Pauley?"

"No, I didn't think it was that important. I reported it to Dorfman, Acting Commander of the Two-five-one Precinct. I'm sure he sent a report to the Traffic Department. Check the New York State Department of Motor Vehicles, sir. I'm certain you'll find a missing license report was filed with them."

There was silence for a moment. A cloud of rank cigar smoke came billowing out the window, into Delaney's face. Still he stooped.

"Why did you go see Gilbert's wife?" Broughton demanded.

"For the same reason I went to see Mrs. Lombard," Delaney said promptly. "To present my condolences. As commander and ex-commander of the precinct in which the crimes occurred. Good public relations for the Department."

Again there was a moment's silence.

"You got an answer for everything, you wise bastard," Broughton said angrily. He was in semi-darkness. Delaney, bending down, could barely make out his features. "You been seeing Thorsen? And Inspector Johnson?"

"Of course I've been seeing Deputy Inspector Thorsen, sir. He's been a friend of mine for many years."

"He's your 'rabbi'—right?"

"Yes. And he introduced me to Johnson. Just because I'm on leave of absence doesn't mean I have to stop seeing old friends in the Department."

"Delaney, I don't trust you. I got a nose for snots like you, and I got a feeling you're up to something. Just listen to this: you're still on the list, and I can stomp on you any time I want to. You know that?"

"Yes, sir."

"Don't fuck me, Delaney. I can do more to you than you can do to me. You *coppish?*"

"Yes. I understand."

So far he had held his temper under control and now, in a split-second, he made his decision. His anger wasn't important, and neither was Broughton's obnoxious personality. He brought the shopping bag closer to the car window.

"Sir," he said, "I have something here I'd like to show you. I think it may possibly help—"

"Go fuck yourself," Broughton interrupted roughly, and Delaney heard the belch. "I don't need your help. I don't want your help. The only way you can help me is to crawl in a hole and pull it in over your head. Is that clear?"

"Sir, I've been—"

"Jesus Christ, how can I get through to you? Fuck off, Delaney. That's all I want from you. Just fuck off, you shit-head."

"Yes, sir," Captain Edward X. Delaney said, almost delirious with pleasure. "I heard. I understand."

He stood and watched the black sedan pull away. See? You worry, brood, wrestle with "moral problems" and such crap and then suddenly a foul-mouthed moron solves the whole thing for you. He went into his own home happily, called Deputy Inspector Thorsen and, after reporting his meeting with Broughton, told Thorsen he wanted to continue the investigation on his own.

"Hang on a minute, Edward," Thorsen said. Delaney guessed Inspector Johnson and Deputy Mayor Alinski were still there, and Ivar was reepeating the conversation to them. Thorsen was back again in about two minutes.

"Fine," he said. "Go ahead. Good luck."

7

HE SEEMED to be spending a lot of time doodling, staring off into space, jotting down almost incomprehensible notes, outlining programs he tore up and discarded as soon as they were completed. But he was, he knew, gradually evolving a sensible campaign in the two weeks following the meeting in Thorsen's home.

He sat down with Christopher Langley in the Widow Zimmerman's apartment and, while she fussed about, urging them to more tea and crumbcake, they went over Langley's firm schedule for his investigation. The little man had already discovered two more stores in Manhattan that sold ice axes, neither of which had mailing lists or kept a record of customers' purchases.

"That's all right," Delaney said grimly. "We can't be lucky all the time. We'll do what we can with what we have."

Langley would continue to look for stores in Manhattan where the ice ax was sold, then broadening his search to the other boroughs. Then he would check tool and outdoor equipment jobbers and wholesalers. Then he would try to assemble a list of American manufacturers of ice axes. Then he would assemble a list of names and addresses of foreign manufacturers of mountaineering gear who exported their products to the U.S., starting with West Germany, then Austria, then Switzerland.

"It's a tremendous job," Delaney told him.

Langley smiled, seemingly not at all daunted by the dimensions of his task.

"More crumbcake?" the Widow Zimmerman asked brightly. "It's homemade."

Langley had told the truth; she was a lousy cook.

Delaney had another meeting with Calvin Case, who announced proudly that he was now refraining from taking his first drink of the day until his bedside radio began the noon news broadcast.

"I have it prepared," Case said, "but I don't touch it until I hear that chime. Then . . ."

Delaney congratulated him, and when Case repeated his offer of help, they began to figure out how to handle the Outside Life sales checks.

"We got a problem," Case told him. "It'll be easy enough to pull every sales slip that shows a purchase of an ice ax during the past seven years. But what if your man bought it ten years ago?"

"Then his name should show up on the mailing list. I'll have someone working on that."

"Okay, but what if he bought the ice ax some place else but maybe bought some other mountain gear at Outside Life?"

"Well, couldn't you pull every slip that shows a purchase of mountain climbing gear of any type?"

"That's the problem," Case said. "A lot of stuff used in mountaineering is used by campers, back-packers, and a lot of people who never go near a mountain. I mean stuff like rucksacks, lanterns, freeze-dried foods, gloves, web belts and harnesses. Hell, ice fishermen buy crampons, and yachtsmen buy the same kind of line mountaineers use. So where does that leave us?"

Delaney thought a few minutes. Case took another drink.

"Look," Delaney said, "I'm not going to ask you to go through a hundred thousand sales checks more than once. Why don't you do this: why don't you pull every check that has anything at all to do with mountain climbing? I mean *anything*. Rope, rucksacks, food—whatever. That will be a big stack of sales checks—right? And it will include a lot of non-mountain climbers. That's okay. At the same time you make a separate file of every sales check that definitely lists the purchase of an ice ax. After you've finished with all the checks, we'll go through your ice ax file first and pull every one purchased by a resident of the Precinct from your general file of mountaineering equipment purchases. And if that doesn't work, we'll branch out and take in everyone in that file."

"Jesus Christ. And if that doesn't work, I suppose you'll investigate every one of those hundred thousand customers in the big file?"

"There won't be that many. There have got to be people who bought things at Outside Life several times over the past seven years. Notice that Sol Appel estimates a hundred thousand sales checks in storage, but only thirty thousand on his mailing list. I'll check with him, or you can, but I'd guess he's got someone winnowing out repeat buyers, and only *new* customers are added to the mailing list."

"That makes sense. All right, suppose there are thirty thousand individual customers. If you don't get anywhere with the sales checks I pull, you'll investigate all thirty thousand?"

"If I have to," Delaney nodded. "But I'll cross that bridge when I come to it. Meanwhile, how does the plan sound to you—I mean your making two files: one of ice ax purchases, one of general mountaineering equipment purchases?"

"It sounds okay."

"Then can I make arrangements with Sol Appel to have the sales checks sent up here?"

"Sure. You're a nut—you know that, Captain?"

"I know."

The meeting with Monica Gilbert called for more caution and deliberation. He walked past her house twice, on the other side of the street, and could see no signs of surveillance, no uniformed patrolmen, no unmarked police cars. But even if the guards had been called off, it was probable that her phone was still tapped. Remembering Broughton's threat to "stomp" him, he had no desire to risk a contact that the Deputy Commissioner would learn about.

Then he remembered her two little girls. One of them, the older, was surely of school age—perhaps both of them. Monica Gilbert, if she was sending her children to a public school, and from what Delaney had learned of her circumstances she probably was, would surely walk the children to the nearest elementary school, three blocks away, and call for them in the afternoon.

So the next morning, he stationed himself down the block, across the street, and waited, stamping his feet against the cold and wishing he had worn his earmuffs. But, within half an hour, he was rewarded by the sight of Mrs. Gilbert and her two little girls, bundled up in snowsuits, exiting from the brownstone. He followed them, across the street and at a distance, until she left her daughters at the door of the school. She started back, apparently heading home, and he crossed the street, approached her, raised his hat.

"Mrs. Gilbert."

"Why, it's Captain . . . Delaney?"

"Yes. How are you?"

"Well, thank you. And thank you for your letter of condolence. It was very kind of you."

"Yes, well . . . Mrs. Gilbert, I was wondering if I could talk to you for a few minutes. Would you like a cup of coffee? We could go to a luncheonette."

She looked at him a moment, debating. "Well . . . I'm on my way home. Why don't you come back with me? I always have my second cup after the girls are in school."

"Thank you. I'd like that."

He had carefully brought along the Xerox copy of the Outside Life mailing list, three packs of 3x5 filing cards, and a small, hand-drawn map of the 251st Precinct, showing only its boundaries.

"Good coffee," he said.

"Thank you."

"Mrs. Gilbert, you told me you wanted to help. Do you still feel that way?"

"Yes. More than ever. Now . . ."

"It's just routine work. Boring."

"I don't care."

"All right."

He told her what he wanted. She was to go through the 30,000 names and addresses on the mailing list, and when she found one within the 251st Precinct, she was to make out a typed file card for each person. When she had finished the list, she was then to type out her own list, with two carbons, of her cards of the Precinct residents.

"Do you have any questions?" he asked her.

"Do they have to live strictly within the boundaries of this Precinct?"

"Well . . . use your own judgment on that. If it's only a few blocks outside, include them."

"Will this help find my husband's killer?"

"I think it will, Mrs. Gilbert."

She nodded. "All right. I'll get started on it right away. Besides, I think it's best I have something to keep me busy right now."

He looked at her admiringly.

Later, he wondered why he felt so pleased with himself after his meetings with Calvin Case and Mrs. Gilbert. He realized it was because he had been discussing names and addresses. Names! Up to now it had all been steel tools and cans of oil. But now he had names—a reservoir, a Niagara of names! And addresses! Perhaps nothing would come of it. He was prepared for that. But meanwhile he was investigating *people,* not things, and so he was pleased.

The interview with Thomas Handry was ticklish. Delaney told him only as much as he felt Handry should know, believing the reporter was intelligent enough to fill in the gaps. For instance, he told Handry that both Lombard and Gilbert had been killed with the same weapon—had *apparently* been killed with the same weapon. He didn't specify an ice ax, and Handry, writing notes furiously, nodded without asking more questions on the type of weapon used. As a newspaperman he knew the value of such qualifiers as "apparently," "allegedly," and "reportedly."

Delaney took complete responsibility for his own investigation, made no mention of Thorsen, Johnson, Alinski or Broughton. He said he was concerned because the crimes had occurred in his precinct, and he felt a personal responsibility. Handry looked up from his notebook to stare at Delaney a long time, but made no comment. Delaney told him he was convinced the killer was a psychopath, that Lombard and Gilbert were chance victims, and that the murderer would slay again. Handry wrote it all down and, thankfully, didn't inquire why Delaney didn't take what he had to Operation Lombard.

Their big argument involved when Handry could publish. The reporter wanted to go at once with what he had been told; the Captain wanted him to hold off until he got the go-ahead from him, Delaney. It developed into a shouting match, louder and louder, about who had done more for whom, and who owed whom what. Finally, realizing simultaneously how ridiculous they sounded, they dissolved into laughter, and the Captain mixed fresh drinks. They came to a compromise; Handry would hold off for two weeks. If he hadn't received the Captain's go-ahead by then, he could publish anything he liked, guess at anything he liked, but with no direct attribution to Delaney.

His biggest disappointment during this period came when he happily, proudly brought Barbara the two Honey Bunch books he had received in the mail. She was completely rational, apparently in flaming good health. She inspected the books, and gave a mirthful shout, looking at him and shaking his head.

"Edward," she said, "what on *earth?*"

He was about to remind her she had requested them, then suddenly realized she obviously didn't remember. He hid his chagrin.

"I thought you'd like them," he smiled. "Just like the ones you sent to Liza."

"Oh, you're such an old dear," she said, holding up her face to be kissed.

He leaned over the hospital bed eagerly, hoping her cheerfulness was a presage of recovery. When he left, the two books were alongside her bed, on the floor. When he returned the next day, one was opened, spread, pages down, on her bedside table. He knew she had been reading it, but he didn't know if this was a good sign or a bad sign. She made no reference to the book, and he didn't either.

So his days were spent mostly on plans, programs, meetings, interviews, and there was absolutely no progress to report when he called Thorsen twice a week. Having assigned his amateur "staff" their tasks, he called each of them every other day or so, not to lean on them, but to talk, assure them of the importance of what they were doing, answer their questions, and just let them know that he was there, he knew it would take time, and not to become discouraged. He was very good at this, because he liked these people, and he knew or sensed their motives for helping him.

But when all his plans and programs were in progress, when all his amateurs were busy at their tasks, he found himself with nothing to do. He went back through his own notes and reports, and found the suggestions about a mountain climbers' magazine, an association or club of mountain climbers, a mention to check the local library on withdrawals of books on mountaineering.

Then he came across his list. "The Suspect." He had not made an addition to it in almost six weeks. He looked at his watch. He had returned from his evening visit to the hospital; it was almost 8:00 p.m. Had he eaten? Yes, he had. Mary had left a casserole of shrimp, chicken, rice, and little pieces of ham. And walnuts. He didn't like the walnuts, but he picked them out, and the rest was good.

He called Calvin Case.

"Captain Edward X. Delaney here. How are you?"

"Okay."

"And your wife?"

"Fine. What's on your mind?"

"I'd like to talk to you. Now. It's not about the sales checks. I know you're working away at them. It's something else. If I can find a cab, I could be at your place in half an hour."

"Sure. Come ahead. I've got something great to show you."

"Oh? I'll be right down."

Evelyn Case met him at the door. She was flushed, happy, and looked about 15 years old, in faded jeans, torn sneakers, one of her husband's shirts tied about her waist. Unexpectedly, she went up on her toes to kiss his cheek.

"Well!" he said. "I thank you."

"We're working on the sales checks, Captain," she said breathlessly. "Both of us. Every night. And Cal taught me what the stock numbers mean. And sometimes I come home during my lunch hour and help him."

"Good," he smiled, patting her shoulder. "That's fine. And you look just great."

"Wait till you see Cal!"

The apartment was brighter now, and smelled reasonably clean. The windows of Case's bedroom were washed, there were fresh paper drapes, a pot of ivy on his cart, a new rag rug on the floor.

But the cartons of Outside Life sales checks were everywhere, stacked high against walls in the hallway, living room, bedroom. Delaney had to thread his way through, walking sideways in a few places, sidling through the open bedroom doorway from which, he noted, the window shade had been removed.

"Hi," Calvin Case called, gesturing around. "How do you like this?"

He was waving at an incredible contraption, a framework of two-inch iron pipe that surrounded his bed and hung over it, like the bare bones of a canopy. And there were steel cables, weights, handles, pulleys, gadgets.

Delaney stared in astonishment. "What the hell *is* it?" he asked.

Cal laughed pleased at his wonderment.

"Sol Appel gave it to me. He came up to see me. The next day a guy showed up to take measurements. A few days later three guys showed up with the whole thing and just bolted it together. It's a gym. So I can exercise from the waist up. Look at this . . ."

He reached up with both hands, grabbed a trapeze that hung from wire cables. He pulled his body off the bed. The clean sheet dropped away to his waist. His naked torso was still flaccid, soft muscles trembling with his effort. He let go, let himself fall back onto the bed.

"That's all," he gasped. "So far. But strength is coming back. Muscle tone. I can feel it. Now look at this . . ."

Two handles hung above his head. They were attached to steel cables that ran over pulleys on the crossbar above him. The cables ran down over the length of the bed, across pulleys on the lower crossbar, and then down. They were attached to stainless steel weights.

"See?" Case said, and demonstrated by pulling the handles down to his chest alternately: right, left, right, left. "I'm only raising the one-pound weights now," he admitted. "But you can add up to five pounds on each cable."

"And when he started he couldn't even raise the one-pound weights," Evelyn Case said eagerly to Captain Delaney. "Next week we're going to two-pound weights."

"And look at this," Case said, showing what appeared to be a giant steel hairpin hanging from his pipe cage. "It's for your grip. For biceps and pectorals."

He grasped the hairpin in both hands and tried to squeeze the two arms together, his face reddening. He barely moved them.

"That's fine," Delaney said. "Just fine."

"The best thing is this," Case said, and showed how a steel arm was hinged to swing out sideways from the gym. "I talked to the guys who put this thing together. They're from some physical therapy outfit that specializes in stuff like this. Well, they sell a wheelchair with a commode built into it. I mean, you sit on a kind of a potty seat. You wheel yourself around, and when you've got to shit, you shit. But Jesus Christ, you're mobile. I'm too heavy for Ev to lift me into a chair like that, but when I get my strength back, I'll be able to move this bar out and swing onto that potty chair by myself, and swing back into bed whenever I want to. I know I'll be able to do it. My arms and shoulders were always good. I've hung from my hands lots of times, and then pulled myself up."

"That sounds great," Delaney said admiringly. "But don't overdo it. I mean, take it easy at first. Build your strength up gradually."

"Oh sure. I know how to do it. We ordered one of those chairs, but it won't be delivered for a couple of weeks. By that time I hope I'll be able to flip myself in and out of bed with no sweat. The chair's got a brake you can set so it won't roll away from you while you're getting into it. You realize what that means, Delaney? I'll be able to sit up at that desk while I'm going through the sales checks. That'll help."

"It surely will," the Captain smiled. "How you doing with the booze?"

"Okay. I haven't stopped, but I've cut down—haven't I, hon?"

"Oh yes," his wife nodded happily. "I know because I'm only buying about half the bottles I did before."

The two men laughed, and then she laughed.

"Incidentally," Case said, "the sales checks are going a lot faster than I expected."

"Oh? Why is that?"

"I hadn't realized how much of Outdoor Life's business was in fishing and hunting gear, tennis, golf, even croquet and badminton and stuff like that. About seventy-five percent, I'd guess. So I can just take a quick glance at the sales slip and toss it aside if it has nothing to do with mountaineering."

"Good. I'm glad to hear that. Can I talk to you a few minutes? Not about the sales checks. Something else. Do you feel up to it?"

"Oh sure. I feel great. Hon, pull up a chair for the Captain."

"I'll get it," Delaney told her, and brought the straight-backed desk chair over to the bedside and sat where he could watch Case's face.

"A drink, Captain?"

"All right. Thank you. With water."

"Hon?"

She went out into the kitchen. The two men sat in silence a few moments.

"What's it all about?" Case asked finally.

"Mountain climbers."

Later, in his own study, Captain Delaney took out his list, "The Suspect," and began to add what Calvin Case had told him about mountain climbers while it was still fresh in his mind. He extrapolated on what Case had said, based on his own instinct, experience, and knowledge of why men acted the way they did.

Under "Physical" he added items about ranginess, reach, strength of arms and shoulders, size of chest, resistance to panic. It was true Case had said mountain climbers come "in all shapes and sizes," but he had qualified that later, and Delaney was willing to go with the percentages.

Under "Psychological" he had a lot to write: love of the outdoors, risk as an addiction, a disciplined mind, no obvious suicide compulsion, total egotism, pushing to—what was it Case had said?—the "edge of life," with nothing between you and death but your own strength and wit. Then, finally, a deeply religious feeling, becoming one with the universe—"one with everything." And compared to that, everything else was "just mush."

Under "Additional Notes" he listed "Probably moderate drinker" and "No drugs" and "Sex relations probably after murder but not before."

He read and reread the list, looking for something he might have forgotten. He couldn't find anything. "The Suspect" was coming out of the gloom, looming. Delaney was beginning to get a handle on the man, grabbing what he was, what he wanted, why he had to do what he did. He was still a shadow, smoke, but there was an outline to him now. He began to exist, on paper and in Delaney's mind. The Captain had a rough mental image of the man's physical appearance, and he was just beginning to guess what was going on in the fool's mind. "The poor, sad shit," Delaney said aloud, then shook his head angrily, wondering why he should feel any sympathy at all for this villain.

He was still at it, close to 1:00 a.m. when the desk phone rang. He let it ring three times, knowing—*knowing*—what the call was, and dreading it. Finally he picked up the receiver.

"Yes?" he asked cautiously.

"Captain Delaney?"

"Yes."

"Dorfman. Another one."

Delaney took a deep breath, then opened his mouth wide, tilted his head back, stared at the ceiling, took another deep breath.

"Captain? Are you there?"

"Yes. Where was it?"

"On Seventy-fifth Street. Between Second and Third."

"Dead?"

"Yes."

"Identified?"

"Yes. His shield was missing but he still had his service revolver."

"What?"

"He was one of Broughton's decoys."

PART SIX

1

"I DIDN'T want him to suffer," he said earnestly, showing her Bernard Gilbert's ID card. "Really I didn't."

"He didn't suffer, dear," she murmured, stroking his cheek. "He was unconscious, in a coma."

"But I wanted him to be happy!" Daniel Blank cried.

"Of course," she soothed. "I understand."

He had waited for Gilbert's death before he had run to Celia, just as he had run to her after Lombard's death. But this time was different. He felt a sense of estrangement, withdrawal. It seemed to him that he no longer needed her, her advice, her lectures. He wanted to savor in solitude what he had done. She said she understood, but of course she didn't. How could she?

They were naked in the dreadful room, dust everywhere, the silent house hovering about them. He thought he might be potent with her, wasn't sure, didn't care. It was of no importance.

"The mistake was in coming from in front," he said thoughtfully. "Perhaps the skull is stronger there, or the brain not as frail, but he fell back, and he lived for four days. I won't do that again. I don't want anyone to suffer."

"But you saw his eyes?" she asked softly.

"Oh yes."

"What did you see?"

"Surprise. Shock. Recognition. Realization. And then, at the final moment, something else . . ."

"What?"

"I don't know. I'm not sure. Acceptance, I think. And a kind of knowing calm. It's hard to explain."

"Oh!" she said. "Oh, *yes!* Finitude. That's what we're all looking for, isn't it? The last word. Completion. Catholicism or Zen or Communism or Meaninglessness. Whatever. But Dan, isn't it true we need it? We all need it, and will abase ourselves or enslave others to find it. But is it one for all of us, or one for each of us? Isn't that the question? I think it's one absolute for all, but I think the paths differ, and each must find his own way. Did I ever tell you what a beautiful body you have, darling?"

As she spoke she had been touching him softly, arousing him slowly.

"Have you shaved a little here? And here?"

"What?" he asked vaguely, drugged by her caresses. "I don't remember. I may have."

"Here you're silk, oiled silk. I love the way your ribs and hip bones press through your skin, the deep curve from chest to waist, and then the flare of your hips. You're so strong and hard, so soft and yielding. Look how long your arms are, and how wide your shoulders. And still, nipples like buds and your sweet, smooth ass. How dear your flesh is to me. Oh!"

She murmured, still touching him, and almost against his will be responded and moved against her. Then he lay on his back, pulled her over atop him, spread his legs, raised his knees.

"How lovely if you could come into me," he whispered and, knowing, she made the movements he desired. "If you had a penis, too . . . Or better yet, if we both had both penis and vagina. What an improvement on God's design! So that we both might be inside each other, simultaneously, penetrating. Wouldn't that be wonderful?"

"Oh yes," she breathed. "Wonderful."

He held her weight down onto him, calling her "Darling" and "Honey" and saying, "Oh love, you feel so good," and it seemed to him the fabric of his life, like a linen handkerchief laundered too often, was simply shredding apart. Not rotting, but pulling into individual threads; light was coming through.

In her exertions, sweat dripped from her unshaven armpits onto his shoulders; he turned his head to lick it up, tasting salty life.

"Will you kill someone for me?" she gasped.

He pulled her down tighter, elevating his hips, linking his ankles around her slender back.

"Of course not," he told her. "That would spoil everything."

2

HE GREW up in that silent, loveless, white-tiled house and, an only child, had no sun to turn to and so turned inward, becoming contemplative, secretive even. Almost all he thought and all he felt concerned himself, his wants, fears, hates, hopes, despairs. Strangely, for a young boy, he was aware of this intense egoism and wondered if everyone else was as self-centered. It didn't seem possible; there were boys his age who were jolly and out-going, who made friends quickly and easily, who could tease girls and laugh. But still . . .

"Sometimes it seemed I might be two persons: the one I presented to my parents and the world, and the one I *was*, whirling in my own orbit. The outward me was the orderly, organized boy who was a good student, who collected rocks and stowed them away in compartmented trays, each specimen neatly labeled: 'Blank, Daniel: Good boy.'

"But from my earliest boyhood—from my infancy, even—I have dreamed in my sleep, almost every night: wild, disjointed dreams of no particular meaning: silly things, happenings, people all mixed up, costumes, crazy faces, my parents and kids in school and historical and literary characters—all in a churn.

"Then—oh, perhaps at the age of eight, but it may have been later—I began to lose myself in daytime fantasies, as turbulent and incredible as my nighttime dreams. This daydreaming had no effect on my outward life, on the image I presented to the world. I could do homework efficiently, answer up in class, label the stones I collected, kiss my parents' cold cheeks dutifully . . . and be a million miles away. No, not away, but down inside myself, dreaming.

"Gradually, almost without my being aware of it, daytime fantasies merged with nighttime dreams. How this developed, or exactly when, I cannot say. But daytime fantasies became extensions of nighttime dreams, and it happened that I would imagine a 'plot' that continued, day and night, for perhaps a week. And then, having been rejected in favor of a new 'plot,' I might come back to the old one for a day or two, simply recalling it or perhaps embellishing it with fanciful details.

"For instance, I might imagine that I was actually not the child of my mother and father, but was a foster child placed with them for romantic reasons. My true father was, perhaps, a well-known statesman, my mother a great beauty who had sinned for love. For various reasons, whatever, they were unable to acknowledge me, and had placed me with this dull, putty-faced, childless Indiana couple. But the day would come . . .

"There was something else I became aware of during my early boyhood, and this may serve to illustrate my awareness of myself. Like most young boys of the same age—I was about twelve at the time—I was capable of certain acts of nastiness, even of minor crimes: wanton vandalism, meaningless violence, 'youthful high spirits,' etc. Where I differed from other boys of that age, I believe, was that even when caught and punished, I felt no guilt. No one could make me feel guilty. My only regret was in being caught.

"Is it so strange that someone can live two lives? No, I honestly believe most people do. Most, of course, play the public role expected of them: they marry, work, have children, establish a home, vote, try to keep clean and reasonably law-abiding. But each—man, woman, and child—has a secret life of which they rarely speak and hardly ever display. And this secret life, for each of us, is filled with ferocious fantasies and incredible wants and suffocating lusts. Not shameful in themselves, except as we have been taught so.

"I remember reading something a man wrote—he was a famous author—and he said if it was definitely announced that the world would end in one hour, there would be long lines before each phone booth, with people waiting to call other people to tell them how much they loved them. I do not believe that, I believe most of us would spend the last hour mourning, 'Why didn't I do what I *wanted* to do?'

"Because I believe each of us is a secret island ('No man is an island'? What shit!) and even the deepest, most intense love cannot bridge the gap between individuals. Much of what we feel and dream, that we cannot speak of to others, is shameful, judged by what society says we are allowed to feel and dream. But if humans are capable of it, how can it be shameful? Rather do as our natures dictate. It may lead to heaven or it may lead to hell—what does 'heaven' mean or 'hell'?—but the most terrible sin is to deny. *That* is inhuman.

"When I fucked that girl in college, and later with my wife, and all those in between, I found it exciting and pleasurable, naturally. Satisfying enough to ignore the grunts, coughs, farts, belches, bad breath, blood and . . . and other things. But a moment later my mind would be on my collection of semi-precious stones or the programming of AMROK II. I had enjoyed masturbation as much, and began to wonder how much so-called 'normal sex' is really masturbation *à deux*. All the groans and protestations of love and ecstasy are the public face; the secret reactions are hidden from the partner. I once fucked a woman, and all the time I was thinking of—well, someone I had seen at a health club I belonged to. God knows what *she* was thinking of. Island lives.

"Celia Montfort was the most intelligent woman I had ever met. Much more intelligent than I was, as a matter of fact, although I think she lacked my sensitivity and understanding. But she was complex, and I had never met a complex woman before. Or perhaps I had, but could not endure the complexity. But in Celia's case, it attracted me, fascinated me, puzzled me—for a time.

"I wasn't certain what she wanted from me, if she wanted anything at all. I enjoyed her lectures, the play of her mind, but I could never quite pin down who she was. Once, when I called for a dinner date, she said, 'There is something I want to ask you.'

"'Yes?' I said.

"There was a pause.

"'I'll ask you tonight,' she said finally. 'At dinner.'

"So, at dinner, I said, 'What did you want to ask me?'

"She looked at me and said, 'I think I better put it in a letter. I'll write you a letter, asking it.'

"'All right,' I nodded, not wanting to push.

"But, of course, she never wrote me a letter asking anything. She was like that. It was maddening, in a way, until I began to understand . . .

"Understand that she was as deep and moiling as I, and subject, as I was, to sudden whims, crazy passions, incoherent longings, foolish dreams . . . the whole bit. Irrational, I suppose you might say. If I didn't lie to myself— and it's extremely difficult not to lie to yourself—I had to recognize that some of my hostility toward her—and I recognized I was beginning to feel a certain hostility, because she *knew*—well, some of this was because I was a man and she was a woman. I am not a great admirer of the women's liberation movement, but I agree men are victims of a conditioning difficult to recognize and analyze.

"But once I stopped lying to myself, I could acknowledge that she upset me because she had a secret life of her own, an intelligence greater than mine and, when it pleased her, a sexuality more intense than mine.

"I could realize that and admit it to myself: she was the first woman I had been intimate with who existed as an individual, not just as a body. The Jewish girl from Boston had been a body. My wife had been a body. Now I knew a person—call it a 'soul' if it amuses you—as unfathomable as myself. And it was no more logical for me to expect to understand her than to expect her to understand me.

"Item: We have come from a sweated bed where we have been as intimate as man and woman can be physically intimate. I have tasted her. Then, dressed, composed, on our way to dinner, I grab her arm to pull her out of the way of a careening cab. She looks at me with loathing. 'You touched me!' she gasps.

"Item: She has been tender, sympathetic, but somewhat withdrawn all evening. We returned to her home and, only because I need to use the john, does she allow me inside the door. I know there will be no sex that night. That's all right with me. It is her prerogative; I am not a mad rapist. But, from the bathroom, I return to the study. She is seated in the leather armchair and, standing behind her, Valenter is softly massaging her neck and bare shoulders with loving movements. Curled in a corner, Tony is watching them curiously. What am I to make of all this?

"Item: She disappears, frequently and without notice, for hours, days, a week at a time. She returns without explanation or excuse, usually weary and bruised, sometimes wounded and bandaged. I ask no questions; she volunteers no information. We have an unspoken pact: I will not pry; she will not ask. Except about the killing. She can't get enough of *that!*

"Item: She buys an imported English riding crop, but I refuse. Either way.

"In fact, there is no end to her.

"Item: She treats a cab driver shamefully for taking us a block out of our way, and tells me loudly not to tip him. Three hours later she insists I give money to a filthy, drunken panhandler who smells of urine. Well . . .

"I think what was happening was this: we had started on one level, trying to find a satisfactory relationship. Then, sated or bored, the wild sex had calmed and we began to explore the psychic part of sex in which she, and I, believed so strongly. After that—it proving not completely satisfactory—we went on digging deeper, inserting ourselves into each other, yet remaining essentially strangers. I tried to tell her: to achieve the final relationship, you must penetrate. Is that not so?

"I must not see her again. I would resolve that, unable to cope with her *humanity*, and, at the last moment, when I was certain our affair was over, she would call and say things to me on the phone. Oh! So we would once again have lunch or dinner, and under the table cloth, beneath our joined napkins, she would touch me, looking into my eyes. And it would start again.

"I do owe her one thing: the killings. You see, I can acknowledge them openly. The murders. Daniel, I love you! I know what I have done, and will do, and I feel no guilt. It is not someone else doing them. It is I, Daniel Blank, and I do not deny them, apologize or regret. Any more than when I stand naked before a dim mirror and once again touch myself. To deny your secret, island life and die unfulfilled—that is the worst.

"I need, most of all, to go deeper and deeper into myself, peeling layers away—the human onion. I am in full possession of my faculties. I know most people would think me vicious or deranged. But is that of any importance? I don't think so. I think the important thing is to fulfill yourself. If you can do that, you come to some kind of completion where both of you, the two you's, become one, and that one merges and becomes part of and adds to the Cosmic One. What *that* might be, I do not know—yet. But I am beginning to glimpse its outlines, the glory it is, and I think, if I continue on my course, I will know it finally.

"With all this introspection, all this intent searching for the eternal verity, which may make you laugh—do *you* have the courage to try it?—the incredible thing, the amazing thing is that I have been able to keep intact the image I present to the world. That is, I function: I awake each morning, bathe and dress, in a fashion of careless elegance, take a cab to my place of work, and there, I believe, I do my job in an efficient and useful manner. It is a charade, of course, but I perform well. In all honesty, perhaps not as I did before . . . Am I going through the movements, marching out the drill? It's probably my imagination but, a few times, I thought members of my X-1 computer team looked at me a bit queerly.

"And one day my secretary, Mrs. Cleek, was wearing a pants suit—it's allowed at Javis-Bircham—and I complimented her on how well it looked. Actually, it was much too snug for her. But later in the day, while she was standing by me, waiting while I signed some letters, I suddenly reached to stroke her pudendum, obvious beneath the crotch of her pants. I didn't grab or squeeze; I just stroked. She drew away, making a small cry. I went back to signing letters; neither of us spoke of what had happened.

"There was one other thing, but since nothing came of it, it hardly seems worth mentioning. I had a dream, a nighttime dream that merged into a daytime fantasy, of doing something to the computer, AMROK II. That is, I wanted to—well, I suppose in some way I wanted to destroy it. How, I didn't know. It was just a vagrant thought. I didn't even consider it. But the thought did come to me. I think I was searching for more humanity, not less. For more *human*-ness, with all its terrible mystery.

"Now we must consider why I killed those men and why (Sigh! Sob!

Groan!) I suppose I will kill again. Well . . . again, it's *human*-ness, isn't it? To come close, as close as you can possibly come. Because love—I mean physical love (sex) or romantic love—isn't the answer, is it? It's a poor, cheap substitute, and never quite satisfactory. Because, no matter how good physical love or romantic love may seem, the partners still have, each, their secret, island life.

"But when you kill, the gap disappears, the division is gone, you are one with the victim. I don't suppose you will believe me, but it is so. I assure you it is. The act of killing is an act of love, ultimate love, and though there is no orgasm, no sexual feeling at all—at least in my case—you do, you really do, enter into another human being, and through that violent conjunction—painful perhaps, but just for a split-second—you enter into all humans, all animals, all vegetables, all minerals. In fact, you become one with everything: stars, planets, galaxies, the great darkness beyond, and . . .

"Oh. Well. What this is, the final mystery, is what I'm searching for, isn't it? I'm convinced it is not in books or beds or conversation or churches or sudden flashes of inspriation or revelation. It must be worked for, and it will be, in me.

"What I'm saying is that I want to go into myself, penetrate myself, as deeply as I possibly can. I know it will be a long and painful process. It may prove, eventually, to be impossible—but I don't believe that. I think that I can go deep within myself—I mean *deep!*—and there I'll find it.

"Sometimes I wonder if it's a kind of masturbation, as when I stand naked before my full-length mirror, golden chains about wrist and waist, and look at my own body and touch myself. The wonder! But then I come back, always come back, to what I seek. And it has nothing to do with Celia or Tony or the Mortons or my job or anything else but me. Me! That's where the answer lies. And who can uncover it but me? So I keep trying, and it is not too difficult, too painful or exhausting. Except, in all truth, I must tell you this: If I had my life to live over again, I would want to lie naked in the sun and watch women oil their bodies. That's all I've ever wanted."

He should have stopped there; it was a logical end to his musings. But he would not, could not. He thought of Tony Montfort, what they had done, what they might do. But the dream was fleeting, flicking away a mosquito or something else that might bite. He thought of Valenter, and of a professor in his college who had smelled of earth, and of going into a women's lingerie shop to buy a white bikini panties for himself. Because they fit better? Once a man on a Fifth Avenue bus had smiled at him.

He still had the nighttime dreams, the daytime fantasies, but he was aware that the images were becoming shorter. That is, they no longer overlapped from night to day, the "plots" were abbreviated, visions flickered by sharply. His mind was so charged, so jumping, that he became vaguely alarmed, went to a doctor, received a prescription for a mild tranquilizer. They worked on him as a weak sleeping pill. But his mind still jumped.

He could not penetrate deeply enough into himself. He lied to himself; he admitted it; he caught himself at it. It was difficult not to lie to himself. He had to be on guard, not every day or every hour but every minute. He had to question every action, every motive. Probing. Penetrating. If he wanted to discover . . . what?

He soothed an engorged penis in a Vaselined hand, probed his own rectum with a stiff forefinger pointing toward Heaven, opened his empty mouth to a white ceiling and waited for bliss. Throbbing warmth engulfed him, eventually, but not what he sought.

There was more. He knew there was more. He had experienced it, and he set out to find it again, bathing, dusting, perfuming, dressing, preparing for an assignation. We all—all of us—must fulfill our island life. Oh yes, he thought, we must. Taking up the ice ax . . .

"Blood is thicker than water," he said aloud, "and semen is thicker than blood."

He laughed, having no idea what that meant, or if, indeed, it meant anything at all.

3

A WEEK or so after the death of Bernard Gilbert, Daniel Blank went on the stalk. It was not too unlike learning to climb. You had to master the techniques, you had to test your strength and, of course, you had to try your nerve, pushing it to its limit, but not beyond. You did not learn how to murder by reading a book, anymore than you could learn how to swim or ride a bicycle by looking at diagrams.

He had already acquired several valuable techniques. The business of concealing the ice ax under his top coat, holding it through the pocket slit by his left hand, then transferring it swiftly to his right hand shoved through the opened fly of his coat—that worked perfectly, with no fumbling. The death of Lombard had been, he thought, instantaneous, while Gilbert lingered four days. He deduced from this that a blow from the back apparently penetrated a more sensitive area of the skull, and he resolved to make no more frontal attacks.

He was convinced his basic method of approach was sound: the quick, brisk step; the eye-to-eye smile; the whole appearance of ease and neighborliness. Then the fast turn, the blow.

He had, of course, made several errors. For instance, during the attack on Frank Lombard, he had worn his usual black calfskin shoes with leather soles. At the moment of assault his right foot had slipped on the pavement, leather sliding on cement. It was not, fortunately, a serious error, but he had been off-balance, and when Lombard fell backward the ice ax was pulled from Blank's grasp.

So, before the murder of Bernard Gilbert, Blank had purchased a pair of light-weight crepe-soled shoes. It was getting on to December, with cold rain, sleet, snow flurries, and the rubber-soled shoes gave much better traction and stability.

Similarly, in the attack on Lombard, the leather handle of the ice ax had twisted in his sweated hand. Reflecting on this, he had, before the Gilbert assault, roughed the leather handle by rubbing it gently with fine sand-paper. This worked well enough, but he still was not satisfied. He purchased a pair of black suede gloves, certainly a common enough article of apparel in early winter weather. The grip between suede glove and the roughened leather of the ice ax handle was all that could be desired.

These were details, of course, and those who had never climbed mountains would shrug them off as of no consequence. But a good climb depended on just such details. You could have all the balls in the world, but if your equipment was faulty, or your technique wasn't right, you were dead.

There were other things to consider; you just didn't go out and murder the first man you met. He cancelled out rainy and sleety nights; he needed a reasonably dry pavement for that quick whirl after he had passed his victim. A cloudy or moonless night was best, with no strong wind to tug at his unbuttoned coat. And he carried as few objects and as little identification as possible; less to drop accidentally at the scene.

He went to his health club twice a week and worked out, and he did his stretch exercises at home every night, so strength was no problem. He was, he knew, in excellent physical condition. He could lift, turn, bend, probably better than most boys half his age. He watched his diet; his reactions were still fast. He meant to keep them that way, and looked forward to climbing Devil's Needle again in the spring, or perhaps taking a trip to the Bavarian Alps for more technical climbs. That would be a joy.

So there was the passion—just as in mountain climbing—and there was also the careful planning, the mundane details—weapon, shoes, gloves, smile—just as any great art is really, essentially, a lot of little jobs. Picasso mixed paints, did he not?

He took the same careful and thoughtful preparation in his stalk after Gilbert's death. A stupid assassin might come home from his job and eat, or dine out and then come home, and return to his apartment house at the same time. Sooner or later, the apartment house doorman on duty would become aware of his routine.

So Daniel Blank varied his arrivals and departures, carefully avoiding a regular schedule, knowing one doorman went off duty at 8:00 p.m., when his relief arrived. Blank came and he went, casually, and usually these departures and arrivals went unobserved by a doorman busy with cabs or packages or other tasks. He didn't prowl every night. Two nights in a row. One night in. Three out. No pattern. No formal program. Whatever occurred to him; irregularity was best. He thought of everything.

There was, he admitted, something strange that to this enterprise that meant so much to him emotionally, privately, he should bring all his talents for finicky analysis, careful classifying, all the cold, bloodless skills of his public life. It proved he supposed, he was still two, but in this case it served him well; he never made a move without thinking out its consequences.

For instance, he debated a long time whether or not, during an actual murder, he should wear a hat. At this time of year, in this weather, most men wore hats.

But it might be lost by his exertions. And, supposing he made a murder attempt and was not successful—the possibility had to be faced—and the intended victim lived to testify. Surely he would remember the presence of a hat more strongly than he would recall the absence of a hat.

"Sir, did he wear a hat?"

"Yes, he wore a black hat. A soft hat. The brim was turned down in front."

That would be more likely than if Blank wore no hat at all.

"Sir, did he wear a hat?"

"What? Well . . . I don't remember. A hat? I don't know. Maybe. I really didn't notice."

So Daniel Blank wore no hat on his forays. He was that careful.

But his cool caution almost crumbled when he began his nighttime reconnaissance following the death of Bernard Gilbert. It was on the third night of his aimless meanderings that he became aware of what seemed to be an unusual number of single men, most of them tall and well proportioned, strolling through the shadowed streets of his neighborhood. The pavements were alive with potential victims!

He might have been mistaken, of course; Christmas wasn't so far away, and people were out shopping. Still . . . So he followed a few of these single males, far back and across the street. They turned a corner. He turned a corner. They turned another corner. He turned another corner. But none of them, none of the three he followed cautiously from a distance, ever entered a house. They kept walking steadily, not fast and not slow, up one street and down another.

He stopped suddenly, half-laughing but sick with fear. Decoys! Policemen. Who else could they be? He went home immediately, to think.

He analyzed the problem accurately: (1) He could cease his activities at once. (2) He could continue his activities in another neighborhood, even another borough. (3) He could continue his activities in his own neighborhood, welcoming the challenge.

Possibility (1) he rejected immediately. Could he stop now, having already come so far, with the final prize within recognizable reach? Possibility (2) required a more reasoned dissection. Could he carry a concealed weapon—the ice ax—by taxi, bus, subway, his own car, for any distance without eventual detection? Or (3), might he risk it?

He thought of his options for two whole days, and the solution, when it came, made him smack his thigh, smile, shake his head at his own stupidity. Because, he realized, he had been analyzing, thinking along in a vertical, in-line, masculine fashion—as if such a problem could be solved so!

He had come so far from this, so far from AMROK II, that he was ashamed he had fallen into the same trap once again. The important thing here was to trust his instincts, follow his passions, do as he was compelled, divorced from cold logic and bloodless reason. If he was finally to know truth, it would come from heart and gut.

And besides, there was risk—the sweet attraction of risk.

There was a dichotomy here that puzzled him. In the planning of the crime he was willing to use cool and formal reason: the shoes, the gloves, the weapon, the technique—all designed with logic and precision. And yet when it came to the *reason* for the act, he deliberately shunned the same method of thought and sought the answer in "heart and gut."

He finally came to the realization that logic might do for method but not for motive. Again, to use the analogy of creative art, the artist thought out the techniques of his art, or learned them from others and, with patience, became a skilled craftsman. But where craft ended and art began was at the point where the artist had to draw on his own emotions, dreams, fervors and fears, penetrating deep into himself to uncover what he needed to express by his skill.

The same could be said of mountain climbing. A man might be an enormously talented and knowledgeable mountaineer. But it was just a specialized skill if, within him, there was no drive to push himself to the edge of life and know worlds that the people of the valley could not imagine.

He spent several evenings attempting to observe the operations of the decoys. So far as he could determine, the detectives were not being followed by "back-up men" or trailed by unmarked police cars. It appeared that each decoy was assigned a four-block area, to walk up one street and down the next, going east to west, then west to east, then circling to cover the north-south streets. And unexpectedly, hurrying past a decoy who had stepped into a shadowed doorway, he saw they were equipped with small walkie-talkies and were apparently in communication with some central command post.

It was, he decided, of little significance.

Sixteen days after the attack on Bernard Gilbert, Daniel Blank returned home directly from work. It was a cold, dry evening with a quarter moon barely visible through a clouded sky. There was some wind, a hint of rain or snow in a day or so. But generally it was a still night, cold enough to tingle nose, ears, ungloved hands. There was one other factor: the neighborhood theatre was showing a movie Daniel Blank had seen a month ago when it opened on Times Square.

He mixed himself a single drink, watched the evening news on TV. Americans were killing Vietnamese. Vietnamese were killing Americans. Jews were killing Arabs. Arabs were killing Jews. Catholics were killing Protestants. Protestants were killing Catholics. Pakistani were killing Indians. Indians were killing Pakistani. There was nothing new. He fixed a small dinner of broiled calves' liver and an endive salad. He brought his coffee into the living room and had that and a cognac while he listened to a tape of the Brandenburg Concerto No.3. Then he undressed, got into bed, took a nap.

It was a little after nine when he awoke. He splashed cold water on his face, dressed in a black suit, white shirt, modestly patterned tie. He put on his crepe-soled shoes. He donned his topcoat, pulled on the black suede gloves, held the ice ax under the coat by his left hand, through the pocket slit. The leather thong attached to the handle butt of the ax went around his left wrist.

In the lobby, doorman Charles Lipsky was at the desk, but he rose to unlock and hold the outer door for Blank. The door was kept locked from 8:00 p.m., when the shift of doormen changed, to 8:00 a.m. the following morning.

"Charles," Blank asked casually, "do you happen to know what movie's playing at the Filmways over on Second Avenue?"

"Afraid, I don't, Mr. Blank."

"Well, maybe I'll take a walk over. Nothing much on TV tonight."

He strolled out. It was that natural and easy.

He actually did walk over to the theatre, to take a look at the movie schedule taped to the ticket seller's window. The feature film would begin again in 30 minutes. He had the money ready in his righthand trouser pocket. He bought a ticket with the exact sum, receiving no change. He went into the half-empty theatre, sat in the back row without removing his coat or gloves. When the movie ended and at least fifty people left, he left with them. No one glanced at him, certainly not the usher, ticket taker, or ticket seller. They would never remember his arrival or departure. But, of course, he had the ticket stub in his pocket and had already seen the film.

He walked eastward, toward the river, both hands now thrust through the coat's pocket slits. On a deserted stretch of street he carefully slipped the leather loop off his left wrist. He held the ax by the handle with his left hand. He unbuttoned his coat, but he didn't allow the flaps to swing wide, holding them close to his body with hands in his pockets.

Now began the time he liked best. Easy walk, a good posture, head held high. Not a scurrying walk, but not dawdling either. When he saw someone approaching, someone who might or might not have been a police decoy, he crossed casually to the other side of the stret, walked to the corner and turned, never looking back. It was too early; he wanted this feeling to last.

He *knew* it was going to be this night, just as you know almost from the start of a climb that it will be successful, you will not turn back. He was confident, alert, anxious to feel once again that moment of exalted happiness when the eternal was in him and he was one with the universe.

He was experienced now, and knew what he would feel before that final moment. First, the power: should it be you or shall it be you? The strength and glory of the godhead fizzing through his veins. And second, the pleasure that came from the intimacy and the love, soon to be consummated. Not a physical love, but something much finer, so fine indeed that he could not put it into words but only felt it, knew it, floated with the exaltation.

And now, for the first time, there was something else. He had been frightened and wary before, but this night, with the police decoys on the streets, held a sense of peril that was almost tangible. It was all around him, in the air, in the light, on the mild wind. He could almost *smell* the risk; it excited him as much as the odor of new-fallen snow or his own scented body.

He let these things—power, pleasure, peril—grow in him as he walked. He opened himself to them, cast off all restraint, let them flood and engulf him. Once he had "shot the rapids" in a rubber dinghy, on a western river, and then and now he had the not unpleasant sensation of helplessness, surrender, in the hands of luck or an unknown god, swept along, this way, that, the world whirling, and, having started, no way to stop, no way, until passion ran its course, the river finally flowed placid between broad banks, and risk was a happy memory.

He turned west on 76th Street. Halfway down the block a man was also walking west, at about the same speed, not hurrying but not dallying either. Daniel Blank immediately stopped, turned around, and retraced his steps to Second Avenue. The man he had seen ahead of him had the physical appearance, the *feel,* of a police decoy. If Blank's investigations and guesses were accurate, the man would circle the block to head eastward on 75th Street. So Blank walked south on Second Avenue and paused on the corner, looking westward toward Third Avenue. Sure enough, his quarry turned the corner a block away and headed toward him.

"I love you," Daniel Blank said softly.

He looked about. No one else on the block. No other pedestrians. All parked cars dark. Weak moon behind clouds. Pavement dry. Oh yes. Walk toward the approaching man. Pacing himself so they might meet about halfway between Second and Third Avenues.

Ice ax gripped lightly in fingertips of left hand, beneath his unbuttoned coat. Right arm and gloved hand swinging free. Then the hearty tramp down the street. The neighborly smile. That smile! And the friendly nod.

"Good evening!"

He was of medium height, broad through the chest and shoulders. Not handsome, but a kind of battered good looks. Surprisingly young. A physical awareness, a tension, in the way he walked. Arms out a little from his sides, fingers bent. He stared at Blank. Saw the smile. His whole body seemed to relax. He nodded, not smiling.

They came abreast. Right hand darting into the open coat. The smooth, practised transfer of the ax to the free right hand. Weight on left foot. Whirl as smooth as a ballet step. An original art form. Murder as a fine art: all sensual kinetics. Weight onto the right foot now. Right arm rising. Lover sensing, hearing, pausing, beginning his own turn in his dear *pas de deux.*

And then. Oh. Up onto his toes. His body arching into the blow. Everything: flesh, bone, sinew, muscle, blood, penis, kneecaps, elbows and biceps, whatever he was . . . giving freely, completely, all of him. The crunch and sweet thud that quivered his hand, wrist, arm, torso, down into his bowels and nuts. The penetration! And the ecstasy! Into the grey wonder and mystery of the man. Oh!

Plucking the ax free even as the body fell, the soul soaring up to the cloudy sky. Oh no. The soul entering into Daniel Blank, becoming one with his soul, the two coupling even as he had imagined lost astronauts embracing and drifting through all immeasurable time.

He stooped swiftly, not looking at the crushed skull. He was not morbid. He found the shield and ID card in a leather folder. He no longer had to prove his deeds to Celia, but this was for him. It was not a trophy, it was a gift from the victim. I love you, too.

So simple! It was incredible, his luck. No witnesses. No shouts, cries, alarms. The moon peeped from behind clouds and withdrew again. The mild wind was there. The night. Somewhere, unseen, stars whirled their keening courses. And tomorrow the sun might shine. Nothing could stop the tides.

"Good movie, Mr Blank?" Charles Lipsky asked.

"I liked it," Daniel Blank nodded brightly. "Very enjoyable. You really should see it."

He went through the now familiar drill: washing and sterilizing the ice ax, then oiling the exposed steel. He put it away with his other climbing gear in the front hall closet. The policeman's badge represented a problem. He had tucked Lombard's driver's license and Gilbert's ID card under a stack of handkerchiefs in his top dresser drawer. It was extremely unlikely the cleaning woman, or anyone else, would uncover them. But still . . .

He wandered through the apartment, looking for a better hiding place. His first idea was to tape the identification to the backs of three of the larger mirrors on the living room wall. But the tape might dry, the gifts fall free, and then . . .

He finally came back to his bedroom dresser. He pulled the top drawer out and placed it on his bed. There was a shallow recess under the drawer, between the bottom and the runners. All the identification fitted easily into a large white envelope, and this he taped to the bottom of the drawer. If the tape dried, and the envelope dropped, it could only drop into the second drawer. And, while taped, it was a position where he could easily check its security every day, if he wanted to. Or open the envelope flap and look at his gifts.

Then he was home free—weapon cleansed, evidence hidden, all done that reason told him should be done. He even saved the ticket stub for the neighborhood movie. Now was the time for reflection and dreaming, for pondering significance and meaning.

He bathed slowly, scrubbing, then rubbing scented oil onto his wet skin. He stood on the bathroom mat, staring at himself in the full-length mirror, unaccountably, he began to make the gyrations of a strip-tease dancer: hands clasped behind his head, knees slightly bent, pelvis pumping in and out, hips grinding. He became excited by his own mirror image. He became erect, not fully but sufficiently to add to his pleasure. So there he stood, pumping his turgid shaft at the mirror.

Was he mad? he wondered. And, laughing, thought he might very well be.

4

THE FOLLOWING morning he was having breakfast—a small glass of apple juice, a bowl of organic cereal with skim milk, a cup of black coffee—when the nine o'clock news came on the kitchen radio and a toneless voice announced the murder of Detective third grade Roger Kope on East 75th Street the previous midnight. Kope had been promoted from uniformed patrolman only two weeks previously. He left a widow and three small children. Deputy Commissioner Broughton, in charge of the investigation, stated several important leads were being following up, and he hoped to make an important statement on the case shortly.

Daniel Blank put his emptied dishes into the sink, ran hot water into them, went off to work.

When he left his office in the evening, he purchased the afternoon *Post,* but hardly glanced at the headline: "Killer Loose on East Side." He carried the paper home wth him and collected his mail at the lobby desk. He opened envelopes in the elevator: two bills, a magazine subscription offer, and the winter catalogue from Outside Life.

He fixed himself a vodka on the rocks with a squeeze of lime, turned on the television set and sat in the living room, sipping his drink, leafing through the catalogue, waiting for the evening news.

The coverage of Kope's murder was disappointingly brief. There was a shot of the scene of the crime, a shot of the ambulance moving away, and then the TV reporter said the details of the death of Detective Kope were very similar to those in the murder of Frank Lombard and Bernard Gilbert, and police believed all three killings were the work of one man. "The investigation is continuing."

Later that evening Blank walked over to Second Avenue to buy the early morning editions of the *News* and the *Times.* "Mad Killer Strikes Again," the *News'* headline screamed. The *Times* had a one-column story low on the front page: "Detective Slain on East Side." He brought the papers home, added them to the afternoon *Post* and settled down with a kind of bored dread to read everything that had been printed on Kope's death.

The most detailed, the most accurate report, Blank acknowledged, appeared under the byline "Thomas Handry." Handry, quoting "a high police official who asked that his name not be used," stated unequivocally that the three murders wers committed by the same man, and that the weapon used was "an ax-like tool with an elongated spike." The other papers identified the weapon as "a small pick or something similar."

Handry also quoted his anonymous informant in explaining how a police decoy, an experienced officer, could be struck down from behind without apparently being aware of the approach of his attacker or making any effort to defend himself. "It is suggested," Handry wrote, "the assailant approached from the front, presenting an innocent, smiling appearance to his victim, then, at the moment of passing, turned and struck him down. It is believed by the usually reliable source that the killer carried his weapon concealed under a folded newspaper or under his coat. Although Gilbert died from a frontal attack, the method used in Kope's murder closely parallels that in the Lombard killing."

Handry's report ended by stating that his informant feared there would be additional attacks unless the killer was caught. Another paper spoke of an unprecedented assignment of detectives to the case, and the third paper stated that a curfew in the 251st Precinct was under consideration.

Blank tossed the papers aside. It was disquieting, he admitted, that the term 'ax-like tool" had been used in Handry's report. He had to assume the police knew exactly what the weapon was, but were not releasing the information. He did not believe they could trace the purchase of an ice ax to him; his ax was five years old, and hundreds were sold annually all over the world. But it did indicate he would be wise not to underestimate the challenge he faced, and he wondered what kind of a man this Deputy Commissioner Broughton was who was trying so hard to take him by the neck. Or, if not Broughton, who Handry's anonymous "high police official" was. That business of approaching from the front, then whirling to strike— who had guessed *that?* There were probably other things known or guessed, and not released to the newspapers—but *what?*

Blank went over his procedures carefully and could find only two obvious weak links. One was his continued possession of the victims' identification. But, after pondering, he realized that if it ever came to a police search of his apartment, they would already have sufficient evidence to tie him to the murders, and the identification would merely be the final confirmation.

The other problem was more serious: Celia Montfort's knowledge of what he had done.

5

EROTICA, THE sex boutique owned by Florence and Samuel Morton was located on upper Madison Avenue, between a gourmet food shop and a 100-year-old store that sold saddles and polo mallets. Erotica's storefront had been designed by a pop-art enthusiast and consisted of hundreds of polished automobile hubcaps which served as distorting mirrors of the street scene and passing pedestrians.

"It boggles the mind," Flo nodded.

"It blows the brain," Sam nodded.

Between them, they had come up with this absolutely marvy idea for decorating their one window for the Christmas shopping season. They had, at great expense, commissioned a display house to create a naked Santa Claus. He had the requisite tasseled red cap and white beard, but otherwise his plump and roseate body was nude except for a small, black patent leather bikini equipped with a plastic codpiece, an item of masculine attire Erotica was attempting to revive in New York, with limited success.

The naked Santa was displayed in the Madison Avenue window for one day. Then Lieutenant Marty Dorfman, Acting Commander of the 251st Precinct, paid a personal visit to Erotica and politely asked the owners to remove the display, citing a number of complaints he had received from local churches, merchants, and outraged citizens. So the bikini-clad Saint Nicholas was moved to the back of the store, the window filled with miscellaneous erotic Christmas gifts, and Flo and Sam decided to inaugurate the extended-hours shopping season with an open house; free Swedish glug for old and new customers and a dazzling buffet that included such exotic items as fried grasshoppers and chocolate-covered ants.

Daniel Blank and Celia Montfort were specifically invited to this feast and asked to return to the Morton' apartment later for food and drink of a more substantial nature. They accepted.

The air was overheated—and scented. Two antique Byzantine censers hung suspended in corners; from their pierced shells drifted fumes of musky incense called "Orgasm," one of Erotica's best sellers. Customers checked their coats and hats with a dark, exquisite, sullen Japanese girl clad in diaphanous Arabian Nights pajamas beneath which she wore no brassiere—only sheer panties imprinted with small reproductions of Mickey Mouse. Incredibly, her pubic hair was blond.

Celia and Daniel stood to one side, observing the hectic scene, sipping small cups of spiced, steaming glug. The store was crowded with loud-voiced, flush-faced customers, most of them young, all wearing the kinky, trendy fashions of the day. They weren't clothed; they were costumed. Their laughter was shrill, their movements jerky as they pushed through the store, examining phallic candles, volumes of Aubrey Beardsley prints, leather brassieres, jockstraps fashioned in the shape of a clutching hand.

"They're so excited," Daniel Blank said. "The whole world's excited."

Celia looked up at him and smiled faintly. Her long black hair, parted in the middle, framed her witch's face. As usual, she was wearing no makeup, though her eyes seemed shadowed with a bone-deep weariness.

"What are you thinking?" she asked him, and he realized once again how ideas, abstract ideas, aroused her.

"About the world," he said, looking around the frantic room. "The ruttish world. About people today. How stimulated they all are."

"Sexually stimulated?"

"That, of course. But in other ways. Politically. Spiritually, I guess. Violence. The new. The terrible hunger for the new, the different, the 'in thing.' And what's in is out in weeks, days. In sex, art, politics, everything. It all seems to be going faster and faster. It wasn't always like this, was it?"

"No," she said, "it wasn't."

"The in thing," he repeated. "Why do they call it 'in'? Penetration?"

Now she looked at him curiously. "Are you drunk?" she asked.

He was surprised. "On two paper cups of Swedish glug? No," he laughed, "I am not drunk."

He touched her cheek with warm fingers. She grabbed his hand, turned her head to kiss his fingertips, then slid his thumb into her wet mouth, tongued it, drew it softly out. He looked swiftly about the room; no one was staring.

"I wish you were my sister," he said in a low voice.

She was silent a moment, then asked, "Why did you say that?"

"I don't know. I didn't think about it. I just said it."

"Are you tired of sex?" she asked shrewdly.

"What? Oh no. No. Not exactly. It's just . . ." He waved at the crowded room. "It's just that they're not going to find it this way."

"Find what?"

"Oh . . . you know. The answer."

The evening had that chopped, chaotic tempo that now infected all his hours: life speeding in disconnected scenes, a sharply cut film, images and distortions in an accelerating frenzy: faces, places, bodies, speech and ideas swimming up to the lens, enlarging, then dwindling away, fading. It was difficult to concentrate on any one experience; it was best simply to open himself to sensation, to let it all engulf him.

"Something's happening to me," he told her. "I see these people here, and on the street, and at work, and I can't believe I belong with them. The same race, I mean. They seem to me dogs, or animals in a zoo. Or perhaps I am. But I can't relate. But if they are human, I am not. And if I am, they are not. I just don't recognize them. I'm apart from them."

"You *are* apart from them," she said softly. "You've done something so meaningful that it sets you apart."

"Oh yes," he said, laughing happily. "I have, haven't I? If they only knew . . ."

"How does it feel?" she asked him. "I mean . . . knowing? Satisfaction? Pleasure?"

"That, of course," he nodded, feeling an itch of joy at talking of these things in a crowded, noisy room (he was naked but no one could see). "But mostly a feeling of—of gratification that I've been able to accomplish so much."

"Oh yes, Dan," she breathed, putting a hand on his arm.

"Am I mad?" he asked. "I've been wondering."

"Is it important?"

"No. Not really."

"Look at these people," she gestured. "Are they sane?"

"No," he said. "Well . . . maybe. But whether they're sane or mad, I'm different from them."

"Of course you are."

"And different from you," he added, smiling.

She shivered, a bit, and moved closer to him.

"Do we have to go to the Mortons?" she murmured.

"We don't have to. I think we should."

"We could go to your place. Or my place. Our place."

"Let's go to the Mortons," he said, smiling again and feeling it on his face.

They waited until Flo and Sam were ready to leave. Then they all shared a big cab back to the Mortons' apartment. Flo and Sam gabbled away in loud voices. Daniel Blank sat on the monkey seat, smiled and smiled.

Blanche had prepared a roast duckling garnished with peach halves. And there were small roasted potatoes and a tossed salad of romaine and Italian water cress. She brought the duckling in on a carving board to show it around for their approval before returning it to the kitchen to quarter it.

It looked delicious, they agreed, with its black, crusty skin and gleaming peach juice. And yet, when Daniel Blank's full plate was put before him, he sat a moment and stared; the food offended him.

He could not say why, but it happened frequently of late. He would go into a familiar restaurant, alone or with Celia, order a dish that he had had before, that he knew he liked, and then, when the food was put before him, he had no appetite and could scarcely toy with it.

It was just so—so *physical*. That steaming mixture to be cut into manageable forkfuls and shoved through the small hole that was his mouth, to emerge, changed and compounded, a day later via another small hole. Perhaps it was the vulgarity of the process that offended him. Or its animality. Whatever, the sight of food, however well prepared, now made him queasy. It was all he could do, for politeness' sake, to eat a bit of his duckling quarter, two small potatoes, dabble in the salad. He wasn't comfortable until, finally, they were seated on sofas and in soft chairs, having black coffee and vodka stingers.

"Hey, Dan," Samuel Morton said abruptly, "you got any money to invest?"

"Sure," Blank said amiably. "Not a lot, but some. In what?"

"First of all, this health club you belong to—what does it cost you?"

"Five hundred a year. That doesn't include massage or food, if you want it. They have sandwiches and salads. Nothing fancy."

"Liquor?"

"You can keep a bottle in your locker if you like. They sell set-ups."

"A swimming pool?"

"A small one. And a small sundeck. Gymnasium, of course. A sauna. What's this all about?"

"Can you swim naked in the pool?"

"Naked? I don't know. I suppose you could if you wanted to. It's for men only. I've never seen anyone do it. Why do you ask?"

"Sam and I had this marvy idea," Florence Morton said.

"A natural," Sam said. "Can't miss."

"There's this health club on East Fifty-seventh Street," Flo said. "It started as a reducing salon, but it's not making it. It's up for grabs now."

"Good asking price." Sam nodded. "And they'll shave."

"It's got a big pool," Flo nodded. "A gym with all the machines, two saunas, locker room, showers. The works."

"And a completely equipped kitchen," Sam added. "A nice indoor-outdoor lounge with tables and chairs."

"The decor is hideous," Flo added. "Hideous. But all the basic stuff is there."

"You're thinking of opening a health club?" Celia Montfort asked.

"But different," Flo laughed.

"Totally different," Sam laughed.

"For men *and* women," Flo grinned.

"Using the same locker room and showers," Sam grinned.

"With nude sunbathing on the roof," Sam noted.

Blank looked from one to the other. "You're kidding?"

They shook their heads.

"You'd take only married couples and families for members?"

"Oh no," Flo said. "Swinging singles only."

"That's just the point," Sam said. "That's where the money comes from. Lonely singles. And it won't be cheap. We figure five hundred members at a thousand a year each. We'll try to keep the membership about sixty-forty."

"Sixty percent men and forty percent women," Flo explained.

Blank stared at them, shook his head. "You'll go to jail," he told them. "And so will your members."

"Not necessarily," Flo said. "We've had our lawyers looking into it."

"There are some encouraging precedents," Sam said. "There are beaches out in California set aside for swimming in the nude. All four sexes. The courts have upheld the legality. The law is very hazy in New York. No one's ever challenged the right to have mixed nude bathing in a private club. We think we can get away with it."

"It all hinges on whether or not you're 'maintaining a public nuisance,'" Flo explained.

"If it's private and well-run and no nudity in public, we think we can do it," Sam explained.

"No nudity in public?" Daniel Blank asked. "You mean fornication in the sauna or in a mop closet or underwater groping is okay?"

"It's all private," Flo shrugged.

"Who's hurting whom?" Sam shrugged. "Consenting adults."

Daniel looked at Celia Montfort. She sat still, her face expressionless. She seemed waiting for his reaction.

"We're forming a corporation," Flo said.

"We figure we'll need a hundred thousand tops," Sam said, "for lease, mortgage, conversion, insurance, etcetera."

"We're selling shares," Flo said.

"Interested?" Sam asked.

Daniel Blank patted his Via Veneto wig gently.

"Oh," he said. "No," he said. "I don't think so. Not my cup of tea. But I think, if you can get around the legal angle, it's a good idea."

"You think it'll catch on?" Sam asked.

"Profitable?" Flo asked.

"No doubt about it," Blank assured them. "If the law doesn't close you down, you'll make a mint. Just walk down Eighth Avenue, which I do almost every day. Places where you can get a woman to give you a rub-down, or you can paint her body, or watch films, or get tickled with feathers. And ordinary prostitution too, of course. Mixed nude bathing in a private pool? Why not? Yes, I think it's a profitable idea."

"Then why don't you want to invest?" Celia asked him.

"What? Oh . . . I don't know. I told you—not my style. I'm tired of it all. Maybe just bored. Anyway, it puts me off. I don't like it."

They stared at him, the three of them, and waited. But when he said nothing more, Celia spurred him on.

"What don't you like?" she asked quietly. "The idea of men and women swimming naked together? You think it's immoral?"

"Oh God no!" he laughed loudly. "I'm no deacon. It's just that . . ."

"It's just what?"

"Well," he said, showing his teeth, "sex is so—so inconsequential, isn't it? I mean, compared to death and—well, virginity. I mean, they're so absolute, aren't they? And sex never is. Always something more. But with death and virginity you're dealilng with absolutes. Celia, that word you used? Finitudes. Was that it? Or finalities. Something like that. It's so nice to—it's so warm to—I know life is trouble, but still . . . What you're planning is wrong. Not in the moral sense. Oh no. But you're skirting the issue. You know? You're wandering around and around, and you don't see the goal, don't even glimpse it. Oh yes. Profitable? It will surely be profitable. For a year or two. Different. New. The in-thing. But then it will fall away. Just die. Because you're not giving them the answer, don't you see? Fucking underwater or in a sauna. And then. No, no! It's all so—so superficial. I told you. Those people tonight. Well, there you are. What have they learned or won? Maybe masturbation is the answer. Have you ever considered that? I know it's ridiculous. I apologize for mentioning it. But still . . . Because, you see, in your permissive world they say porn, perv and S-M. That's how much it means, that you can abbreviate it. So there you are. And it offends me. The vulgarity. Because it might have been a way, a path, but is no longer. Sex? Oh no. Shall we have another martini or shall we fuck? That important. I knew a girl once . . . Well. So you've got to go beyond. I tell you, it's just not enough. So, putting aside sex, you decide what comes next. What number bus to the absolute. And so you—"

Celia Montfort interrupted swiftly.

"What Daniel is trying to say," she told the astounded Mortons, "is that in a totally permissive society, virginity becomes the ultimate perversion. Isn't that what you wanted to say, dear?"

He nodded dumbly. Finally, they got out of there. She was trembling but he was not.

6

HE PROPPED himself on his left elbow, let his right palm slide lightly down that silky back.

"Are you awake?"

"Yes."

"Tell me about this woman, Celia Montfort."

Soft laughter.

"What do you want to know about 'this woman, Celia Montfort'?"

"Who is she? What is she?"

"I thought you knew all about her."

"I know she is beautiful and passionate. But so mysterious and with-drawn. She's so locked up within herself."

"Yes, she is, luv. Very deep, is our Celia."

"When she goes away, unexpectedly, where does she go?"

"Oh . . . places."

"To other men?"

"Sometimes. Sometimes to other women."

"Oh."

"Are you shocked, darling?"

"Not really. I guess I suspected it. But she comes back so weary. Sometimes she's been hurt. Does she want to be? I mean, does she deliberately seek it?"

"I thought you knew. You saw those bandages on her wrists. I saw you staring at them. She tried to slash her veins."

"My God."

"She tried it before and will probably try it again. Pills or driving too fast or a razor."

"Oh sweetheart, why does she do it?"

"Why? She really doesn't know. Except life has no value for her. No real value. She said that once."

He kissed those soft lips and with his fingertips touched the closed eyes gently. The limpid body moved to him, pressed sweetly; he smelled again that precious flesh, skin as thin, as smooth as watered silk.

"I thought I made her happy."

"Oh you did, Dan. As much as any man can. But it's not enough for her. She's seen everything, done everything, and still nothing has meaning for her. She's run through a dozen religions and faiths, tried alcohol and all kinds of drugs, done things with men and women and children you wouldn't believe. She's burned out now. Isn't it obvious? Celia Montfort. Poor twit."

"I love her."

"Do you? I think it's too late for her, Dan. She's—she's beyond love. All she wants now is release."

"Release from what?"

"From living, I suppose. Since she's trying so hard to kill herself. Perhaps her problem is that she's too intelligent. She's painted and written poetry. She was very good but couldn't endure the thought of being just 'very good.' If she didn't have the talent of a genius, she couldn't settle for second-best. Always, she wants the best, the most, the final. I think her problem is that she wants to be *sure*. Of something, anything. She wants final answers. I think that's why she was attracted to you, darling. She felt you were searching for the same thing."

"You're so old for your age."

"Am I? I'm ancient. I was born ancient."

They laughed gently, together, and moved together, holding each other. Then kissing, kissing, with love but without passion, wet lips clinging. Blank stroked webbed hair and with a fingertip traced convolution of delicate ear, slender throat, thrust of rib beneath satin skin.

Finally they drew apart, lay on their backs, side by side, inside hands clasped loosely.

"What about Valenter?"

"What about him?"

"What is his role in your home?"

"His *role?* He's a servant, a houseman."

"He seems so—so sinister."

Mocking: "Do you think he's sleeping with brother or sister? Or both?"

"I don't know. It's a strange house."

"It may be a strange house, but I assure you Valenter is only a servant. It's your imagination, Dan."

"I suppose so. That room upstairs. Are there peepholes where other people can watch? Or is the place wired to pick up conversation?"

"Now you're being ridiculous."

"I suppose so. Perhaps I was believing what I wanted to believe. But why that room?"

"Why did I take you there? Because it's at the top of the house. No one ever goes there. It's private, and I knew we wouldn't be interrupted. It's shabby, I know, but it was fun, wasn't it? Didn't you think it was fun? Why are you laughing?"

"I don't know. Because I read so much into it that doesn't exist. Perhaps."

"Like what?"

"Well, this woman—"

"I know, 'this Celia Montfort.'"

"Yes. Well, I thought this Celia Montfort might be manipulating me, using me."

"For what?"

"I don't know. But I feel she wants something from me. She's waiting for something. From me. Is she?"

"I don't know, Dan. I just don't know. She is a very complex woman. I don't know too much about women; most of my experience has been with men, as you very well know. But I don't think Celia Montfort knows exactly what she wants. I think she senses it and is fumbling toward it, making all kinds of false starts and wrong turnings. She's always having accidents. Slipping, upsetting things. Knocking things over, falling and breaking this or that. But she's moving toward something. Do you have that feeling?"

"Yes. Oh yes. Are you rested now?"

"Yes, darling, I'm rested."

"Can we make love again?"

"Please. Slowly."

"Tony, Tony, I love you."

"Oh pooh," Tony Montfort said.

7

THE STRANGE thing, the strange thing, Daniel Blank decided, was that the world, his world, was expanding at the same time he, himself, was contracting. That is, Tony and Mrs. Cleek and Valenter and the Mortons—everyone he knew and everyone he saw on the streets—well, he loved them all. So sad. They were all so sad. But then, just as he had told Celia that night at the Erotica, he felt apart from them. But still he could love them. That was curious and insolvable.

At the same time his love and understanding were going out to encompass all living things—people, animals, rocks, the whirling skies—he pulled in within himself, chuckling, to nibble on his own heart and hug his secret life. He was condensing, coiling in upon himself, penetrating deeper and deeper. It was a closed life of shadow, scent, and gasps. And yet, and yet there were stars keening their courses, a music in the treacherous world.

Well, it came to this: should he or should he not be a hermit? He could twirl naked before a mirrored wall and embrace himself in golden chains. That was one answer. Or he could go out into the clotted life of the streets, and mingle. Join. Penetrate, and know them all. Loving.

He opted for the streets, the evil streets, and openness. The answer, he decided, was there. It was not in AMROK II; it was in Charles Lipsky, and all the other striving, defeated clods. He hated them for their weaknesses and vices, and loved them for their weaknesses and vices. Was he a Christ? It was a vagrant thought. Still, he acknowledged, he could be. He had Christ's love. But, of course, he was not a religious man.

So, Daniel Blank on the prowl. Grinning at the dull winter sky, determined to solve the mystery of life.

This night he had bathed, oiled and scented his slender body, dressed slowly and carefully in black suit, black turtle-neck sweater, crepe-soled shoes, the slit-pocket topcoat with the ice ax looped over his left wrist within. He sauntered out to search for his demon lover, a Mongol of a man, so happy, so happy. It was eleven days after the murder of Detective third grade Roger Kope.

It had become increasingly difficult, he acknowledged. Since the death of the detective, the neighborhood streets at night were not only patrolled by plain-clothes decoys, but two-man teams of uniformed officers appeared on almost every block and corner, wary and not at all relaxed after what happened to Kope. In addition, the assignment of more squad cars to the area was evident, and Daniel Blank supposed that unmarked police cars were also being used.

Under the circumstances he would have been justified in seeking another hunting ground, perhaps another borough. But he considered it more challenge than risk. Did you reject a difficult climb because of the danger? If you did, why climb at all? The point, the whole point, was to stretch yourself, probe new limits of your talent and courage. Resolution was like a muscle: exercised it grew larger and firmer: unused it became pale and flabby.

The key, he reasoned, might be the time factor. His three killings had all taken place between 11:30 p.m. and 12:30 a.m. The police would be aware of this, of course, and all officers warned to be especially alert during the midnight hour. They might be less vigilant before and after. He needed every advantage he could find.

He decided on an earlier time. It was the Christmas shopping season. It was dark by seven p.m. but the stores were open until nine, and even at ten o'clock people were scurrying home, laden with parcels and bundles. After 12:30 the streets were almost deserted except for the decoys and uniformed patrols. Neighborhood residents had read the newspaper reports following Kope's death; few ventured out after midnight. Yes, earlier would be best: any time from nine to ten-thirty. Mountain climbers judged carefully the odds and percentages; they were not deliberate suicides.

He needed camouflage, he decided, and after long consideration determined what he must do. The previous evening, on his way home from work, he stopped in a store on 42nd Street that sold Christmas cards, artificial trees, ornaments, wrapping paper, and decorations. The store had opened six weeks before Christmas and would go out of business on Christmas Eve. He had seen it happen frequently, all over the city.

He purchased two boxes, one about the size of a shoe box, the other flat and long, designed for a man's necktie or a pair of gloves. He bought a roll of Christmas wrapping paper, the most conventional he could find: red background with reindeer pulling Santa's sled imprinted on it. The roll itself was wrapped in cellophane. He bought a small package of stickers and a ball of cord that was actually a length of knitting yarn wound about a cardboard square.

He wore his thin, black suede gloves while making the purchase. The store was mobbed; the clerk hardly glanced at him. At home, still wearing the gloves, he prepared the two empty boxes as Christmas packages, wrapping them neatly in the reindeer paper, sticking down the end flaps with the gummed Santa Claus heads, then tying them up with red yarn, making very attractive bows on top. Finished, he had what were apparently two Christmas gifts, handsomely wrapped. He intended to leave them at the scene; the chances of their being traced to him, he believed, were absolutely minimal. He then shoved excess wrapping, stickers, cord and paper bag into his garbage can, took it to the incinerator room down the hall, and dumped it all down. Then he came back to his apartment and took off his gloves.

As he had expected, the doorman on duty when he left the following evening—it was not Charles Lipsky—hardly looked up when Daniel Blank passed, carrying his two empty Christmas boxes; he was too busy signing for packages and helping tenants out of cabs with shopping bags stuffed with bundles. And if he had noted him, what of that? Daniel Blank on his way to an evening with friends, bringing them two gaily wrapped presents. Beautiful.

He was so elated with his own cleverness, so surprised by the number of shoppers still on the streets, that he decided to walk over to The Parrot on Third Avenue, have a leisurely drink, kill a little time. "Kill time." He giggled, the ax clasped beneath his coat, the Christmas packages in his right arm.

The Parrot was almost empty. There was one customer at the bar, a middle-aged man talking to himself, making wide gestures. The lone waiter sat at a back table, reading a religious tract. The bartender was marking a racing form. They were the two who had been on duty when he had had the fight with the homosexual the previous year. They both looked up when he came in, but he saw no recognition in their faces.

He ordered a brandy, and when it was brought he asked the bartender if he'd have something, too.

"Thanks," the man said with a cold smile. "Not while I'm working."

"Quiet tonight. Everyone Christmas shopping, I suppose."

"It ain't that," the man said, leaning toward him. "Other Christmases we used to get a crowd when the stores closed. This year, no one. Know why?"

"Why?"

"This nutty killer on the loose," the man said angrily, his reddish wattles wagging. "Who the hell wants to be out on the streets after dark? I hope they catch him soon and cut his balls off. The son-of-a-bitch, he's ruining our business."

Blank nodded sympathetically and paid for his drink. The ax was still under his coat. He sat at the bar, coated, gloved, although the room was warm, and sipped his brandy with pleasure. The Christmas boxes were placed on the bar next to him. It was quiet and restful. And amusing, in a way, to learn that what he was doing had affected so many people. A stone dropped in a pool, the ripples going out, spreading . . .

He had the one drink, left a modest tip, walked out with his packages. He turned at the door to see if he should make a half-wave to the bartender or waiter, but no one was looking at him. He laughed inwardly; it was all so easy. No one cared.

The shoppers were thinning out; those still on the streets were hurrying homeward, packages under their arms or shopping bags swinging. Blank imitated their appearance: his two Christmas presents under one arm, his head and shoulders slightly bent against the cruel wind. But his eyes flicked everywhere. If he couldn't finish his business before 11:00, he would give it up for another night; he was determined on that.

He lost one good prospect when the man suddenly darted up the stairway of a brownstone and was gone while Daniel Blank was still practicing his smile. He lost another who stopped to talk to the doorman of an apartment house. A third looked promising, but too much like a detective decoy; a civilian wouldn't be walking *that* slowly. Another was

lost because a uniformed patrol turned the corner after him unexpectedly
and came sauntering toward Blank.

He would not be frustrated and tried to keep his rage under control. But
still . . . what were they doing to him? He pulled his left wrist far enough
from his coat pocket to read the time under a street lamp. It was almost
10:30. Not much left. Then he'd have to let it go for another night. But he
couldn't. *Couldn't.* The fever was in his blood, blazing. The hell with . . .
Damn the . . . Fix bayonets, lads, and over . . . Now or . . . It had to be. His
luck was so good. A winning streak. Always ride a winning streak.

And so it was. For there—incredibly, delightfully, free of prowling cars
and uniformed patrols—the block was empty and dim, and toward him
came striding a single man, walking swiftly, under one arm a package in
Christmas wrapping. And in the buttonhole of his tweed overcoat, a small
sweetheart rose. Would a police decoy carry a Christmas package? Wear a
rose? Not likely, Daniel Blank decided. He began his smile.

The lover passed under a street lamp. Blank saw he was young, slender,
mustached, erect, confident and, really, rather beautiful. Another Daniel
Blank.

"Good evening!" Daniel called out, a pace away, smiling.

"Good evening!" the man said in return, smiling.

At the moment of passing, Blank transferred the ax and started his turn.
And even as he did he was aware that the victim had suddenly stopped and
started *his* turn. He had a dim feeling of admiration for a man whose
instincts, whose physical reactions were so right and so swift, but after that it
was all uncertain.

The ax was raised. The Christmas packages dropped to the sidewalk.
Then there were two hands clamped on his lifted wrist. The man's package
fell also. But his grip didn't loosen. Blank was pulled tight. Three arms were
high in the air. They stood a second, carved in sweet embrace, breathing
wintry steam into each other's open lips, close. The physical contact was so
delicious that Daniel was fuddled, and pressed closer. Warmth. Lovely
warmth and strength.

Sense came flooding back. He hooked a heel behind the man's left knee,
pulled back and pushed. It wasn't enough. The man staggered but would not
go down. But his grip on Blank's wrist loosened. He hooked again and
shoved again, his entire body against the other body. Oh. He thought he
heard a distant whistle but wasn't sure. They fell then, and Daniel Blank,
rolling, heard and felt his bent left elbow crack against the pavement and
wondered, idly, if it was broken, and thought perhaps it was.

Then they were flat, Blank lying on top of the man whose eyes were dull
with a kind of weariness. His hands fell free from Blank's wrist. So he
brought the ice ax up and down, up and down, up and down, hacking
furiously, in an ecstasy, pressing close, for this was the best yet, and hardly
aware of weak fingers and nails clawing at his face. Something warm there.

Until the young man was still, black eyes glaring now. Blank laid the ax
aside a moment to snatch at the lapel rose, picked up the ax again, staggered
to a snarling crouch, looked about wildly. There were whistles now,
definitely. A uniformed cop came pounding down from the far corner, hand
fumbling at his hip, and his partner across the avenue, blowing and blowing
at that silly whistle. Blank watched a few seconds, looping the ax about his
dead left wrist under his coat.

He was suddenly conscious of the pain, in his left elbow, in his bleeding
face. Then he was running, holding his injured left elbow close to his body,
calculating possibilities and probabilities, but never once considered casting
aside the sweetheart rose.

The body on the sidewalk should stop them for a moment, one of them at least, and as he turned onto First Avenue he stopped running, shoved the rose into his righthand coat pocket, fished out a handkerchief from the breast pocket of his jacket and held it across his bleeding face, coughing and coughing. He went into a luncheonette, two doors down from the corner. Still coughing, his bleeding face concealed by his handkerchief, he walked steadily to the phone booth in the rear. He actually clamped the handkerchief with his shoulder and took a coin from his righthand pocket to put in and dial the weather service. He was listening to a disembodied voice say, "Small craft warnings are in effect from Charleston to Block Island," when, watching, he saw a uniformed cop run by the luncheonette with drawn gun. Blank left the phone booth immediately, still coughing, handkerchief to face. There was an empty cab stopped for a light at 81st Street. Luck. Wasn't it all luck?

He asked the driver, politely, to take him to the west side bus terminal. His voice—to his own ears, at least—was steady. When the light changed and the cab started off, he pushed to the far left corner where the driver couldn't see him in his rear view mirror without obvious craning. Then Blank held out his right hand, fingers spread. They didn't seem to be trembling.

It was almost a twenty-minute trip to the bus terminal and he used every one of them, looking up frequently to make certain the driver wasn't watching. First he swung open his topcoat, unbuttoned his jacket, unhooked his belt. Then he gently slid the loop of the ice ax off his nerveless left wrist, put his belt through the loop, and buckled it again. Now the ax would bump against his thigh as he walked, but it was safe. He buttoned his jacket.

Then he spit onto his handkerchief and softly rubbed his face. There was blood, but much less than he had feared. He put the handkerchief beside him on the seat and, gripping his left hand in his right, slowly bent his left arm. It hurt, it ached, but the pain was endurable, the elbow seemed to be functioning, and he hoped it was a bad bruise, not a break or a chip. He bent his left elbow and put the forwarm inside his jacket, resting on the buttons, like a sling. It felt better that way.

He spit more into his handkerchief, wiped his face again, and there was hardly any fresh blood. The shallow wounds were already clotting. Blank pushed his reddened handkerchief into his breast pocket. He dragged out his wallet with one hand, glanced at the taxi meter, then extracted three one-dollar bills, replaced his wallet, sat back in the seat, drew a deep breath and smiled.

The bus station was mobbed. No one stared at him, and he didn't even bother covering his face with his handkerchief. He went directly to the men's room. It, too, was crowded, but he was able to get a look at himself in the mirror. His wig was awry, his left cheek scratched deeply—they'd surely scab—his right cheek roughened but not cut. Only one scratch on his left cheek was still welling blood, but slowly.

There was a man washing his hands in the basin alongside. He caught Blank's eye in the mirror.

"Hope the other guy looks as bad," he said.

"Never laid a hand on him," Blank said ruefully, and the man laughed.

Daniel moistened two paper towels under the tap and went into one of the pay toilets. When he had locked the door, he used one wet towel to wipe his face again, then plastered toilet paper onto his scratched, wet cheek. He used the other dampened towel to sponge his coat and suit. He discovered an abrasion on the left knee of his trousers; the cloth had been scraped through and skin showed. He would have to throw away the entire suit, wrap it in brown paper and dump it in a trash basket on his way to work. Chances were a derelict would fish it out before the sanitation men got to the basket. In any event, Blank could tear out the labels and burn them. It wasn't important.

He tried his left arm again. The elbow joint worked but painfully—no doubt about that. He took off his jacket and rolled up his sleeve. A lovely swelling there, already discolored. But the elbow worked. He adjusted all his clothes and managed his topcoat so that it hung from his shoulders, continental style, both his arms inside, the ax swinging from his belt. He peeled the toilet paper carefully from his face and looked at it. Faintly pinkish. He flushed paper and towels down the drain, tugged his clothing smooth, and opened the toilet door, smiling faintly.

In the mirror over the basin he adjusted his wig and combed it slowly with his right hand.

Another man, a hatless bald-headed man, was drying his hands nearby. He stared at Blank. Daniel turned to stare back.

"Looking at something?" he asked.

The man gestured apologetically. "Your hair," he said, "it's a rug. Right?"

"Oh yes."

"I've been thinking," the man said. "You recommend?"

"Absolutely. No doubt about it. But get the best you can afford. I mean, don't skimp."

"It don't blow off?"

"Not a chance. I never wear a hat. You can swim in it. Even shower in it if you like."

"You really think so?"

"Definitely," Blank nodded. "Change your whole life."

"No kidding?" the man breathed, enthused.

He took a cab back to his apartment house, his coat hanging loosely from his shoulders.

"Hey, Mr. Blank," the doorman said. "Another guy got killed tonight. Not two blocks from here."

"Is that right?" Daniel said, and shook his head despairingly. "From now on I'm takings cabs *everywhere*."

"That's the best way, Mr. Blank."

He drew a hot tub, poured in enough scented bath oil to froth the water and spice the bathroom. He undressed and slid in carefully, leaving the cleaning of the ice ax until later. But atop the sudsy water, he floated the sweetheart rose. He watched it, immersed to his chin in the steaming tub, soaking his sore elbow. After awhile his erection came up until the flushed head of his penis was above the surface, and the small rose bobbed about it. He had never been so happy in his life. He dreamed.

PART SEVEN

1

"THEY HAD stopped at a wharf painted white, and now Honey Bunch followed her daddy and her mother up this and found herself at the steps of the cunningest bungalow she had ever seen. It was painted white and it had green window boxes and green shutters with little white acorns painted on them. Honey Bunch had never seen a white acorn, but she thought they looked very pretty on the shutters. There was a little sign over the porch of his bungalow and on it were the words 'Acorn house.'"

Captain Edward X. Delaney stopped. At his wife's request he had been reading aloud from "Honey Bunch: Her First Days in Camp," but when he glanced up at the hospital bed Barbara seemed asleep, breathing heavily, thin arms and white hands lying limply atop the single blanket. She never got out of bed any more, not even to sit in a wheelchair.

He had arrived in time to help her with the evening meal. She nibbled a muffin, ate a little mashed potatoes, a few string beans, but wouldn't taste the small steak.

"You've got to eat, dear," he said, as firmly as he could, and she smiled wanly as he took the spoon and held some custard to her lips. She ate almost all the custard, then pushed his hand away, averted her face; he didn't have the heart to insist.

"What have you been doing, Edward?" she asked weakly.

"Oh . . . you know; trying to keep myself busy."

"Is there anything new on the case?"

"What case?" he asked, and then was ashamed and dropped his eyes. He did not want to dissemble but it seemed cruel, in her condition, to speak of violent death.

"What is it, Edward?" she asked, guessing.

"There's been another one," he said in a low voice. "A detective. One of Broughton's decoys."

"Married?"

"Yes. Three small children."

Her eyes closed slowly, her face took on a waxen hue. It was then she asked him to read aloud to her from one of the "Honey Bunch" books he had brought her. He took it up gladly, eager to change the subject, opened the book at random and began reading aloud in a resolute, expressive voice.

But now, after only two pages, she seemed to be sleeping. He put the book aside, pulled on his overcoat, took his hat, started to step quietly from the room. But she called, "Edward," and when he turned, her eyes were open, she was holding a hand out to him. He returned immediately to her bedside, pulled up a chair, sat holding her hot, dry fingers.

"That makes three," she said.

"Yes," he nodded miserably. "Three."

372

"All men," she said vaguely. "Why all men? It would be so much easier to kill women. Or children. Wouldn't it, Edward? Not as dangerous for the killer."

He stared at her, the import of what she was saying growing in his mind. It could be nothing, of course. But it could be something. He leaned forward to kiss her cheek softly.

"You're a wonder, you are," he whispered. "What would I ever do without you?"

Back in his study, a rye highball in his big fist, he forgot about the chicken pie Mary had left on the kitchen table, and thought only of the significance of what his wife had suggested.

It certainly wasn't unusual for a psychopathic killer to be uninterested in or fearful of sex before killing (or even impotent) and then, during or after the murder, to become an uncontrollable satyr. There had been many such cases, but all, to his knowledge, involved women or children as victims.

But now the three victims were men, and Lombard and Kope had been big, muscular men, well able to defend themselves, given half a chance. Still, so far the killer had selected only men, slaying with an ice ax. As Barbara had said, it was a dangerous way to kill—dangerous for the assassin. How much easier to strike down a woman or use a gun against a man. But he had not. Only men. With an ax. Did that mean anything?

It might, Delaney nodded, it just might. Of course, if the next victim was a woman, the theory would be shot to hell, but just consider it a moment. The killer, a male, had killed three other men, risking. Playing amateur psychologist, Delaney considered the sexual symbolism of the weapon used: a pointed ice ax, an ax with a rigid spike. Was that so far-fetched? An ice ax with a drooping spike! Even more far-fetched?

He took his "Expert File" from the bottom drawer of his desk and found the card he wanted: "PSYCHIATRIST-CRIMINOLOGIST. Dr. Otto Morgenthau." There were short additional notes in Delaney's handwriting on the card, recalling the two cases in which Dr. Morgenthau had assisted the Department. One involved a rapist, the other a bomber. Delaney called the number listed: The doctor's office on Fifth Avenue in the 60s, not in the 251st Precinct.

A feminine voice: "Dr. Morgenthau's office."

"Could I speak to Dr. Morgenthau, please? This is Captain Edward X. Delaney, New York Police Department."

"I'm sorry, Captain, the doctor is unavailable at the moment."

That meant Morgenthau had a patient.

"Could he call me back?" Delaney asked.

"I'll try, sir. May I have your number?"

He gave it to her, hung up, then went into the kitchen. He tried some of the chicken pie; it was good but he really wasn't hungry. He covered the remainder carefully with plastic wrap and put it into the refrigerator. He mixed another rye highball and sat hunched in the swivel chair behind his study desk, sipping his drink, staring blankly at the telephone. When it rang, half an hour later, he let it ring three times before he picked it up.

"Captain Edward X. Delaney here."

"And here is Dr. Otto Morgenthau. How are you, Captain?"

"Well, thank you, doctor. And you?"

"Weary. What is it, Captain?"

"I'd like to see you, sir."

"*You*, Captain? Personally? Or Department business?"

"Department."

"Well, what is it?"

"It's difficult to explain over the phone, doctor. I was wondering—"

"Impossible," Morgenthau interrupted sharply. "I have patients until ten o'clock tonight. And then I must—"

"The three men who were axed to death on the east side," Delaney interrupted in his turn. "You must have read about it."

There was a moment of silence.

"Yes," Dr. Morgenthau said slowly, "I havé read about it. Interesting. The work of one man?"

"Yes, sir. Everything points to it."

"What do you have?"

"Bits and pieces. I hope you could fill in some of the gaps."

Dr. Morgenthau signed. "I suppose it must be immediately?"

"If possible, sir."

"Be here promptly at ten o'clock. Then I will give you fifteen minutes. No more."

"Yes, sir. I'll be there. Thank you, doctor."

Delaney arrived five minutes early. The morose, matronly nurse was pulling on an ugly cloth coat, fastened in front with wooden toggles.

"Captain Delaney?"

"Yes."

"Please to doublelock the door after I leave," she said. "Doctor will call you when he is ready."

Delaney nodded, and after she marched out, he obediently turned the latch, then sat down in a straight chair, his hat hooked over one knee, and waited patiently, staring at nothing.

When the doctor finally appeared from his consulting room, Delaney rose to his feet, shocked at the man's appearance. The last time the Captain had seen him, Morgenthau was somewhat corpulent but robust, alert, with erect posture, healthy skin tone, clear and active eyes. But now Delaney was confronted by a wheyfaced man shrunken within clothing that seemed three sizes too large in all dimensions. The eyes were dull and hooded, the hair thinning and uncombed. There was a tremor to the hands and, Delaney noted, fingernails were dirty and untrimmed.

They sat in the consulting room, Morgenthau slumped behind his desk, Delaney in an armchair at one side.

"I'll be as brief as possible, doctor," he began. "I know how busy—"

"Just a moment," Morgenthau muttered, gripping the edge of the desk to pull himself upright. "Sorry to interrupt you, Captain, but I have just remembered a phone call I must make at once. A disturbed patient. I shall only be a few minutes. You wait here."

He hurried out, not to the reception room but to an inner office. Delaney caught a quick glimpse of white medical cabinets, a stainless steel sink. Morgenthau was gone almost ten minutes. When he returned, his walk was swift and steady, his eyes wide and shiny. He was rubbing his palms together, smiling.

"Well now," he said genially, "what have we got, Captain?"

Not pills, Delaney thought; the reaction was too swift for pills. Probably an amphetamine injection. Whatever it was, it had worked wonders for Dr. Otto Morgenthau; he was relaxed, assured, listened closely, and when he lighted a cigar his hands were unhurried and steady.

Delaney went through it all: the deaths of the three victims, the ice ax, what he had learned about mountaineers, the way he believed the crimes were committed, the missing identification—everything he felt Morgenthau needed to know, omitting the fact, naturally, that he, Delaney, was not on active duty and was not in charge of the official investigation.

"And that's about all we've got, doctor."

"No possible link between the three men?"

"No, sir. Nothing we've been able to discover."

"And what do you want from me?"

"What you were able to provide us before—a psychiatric profile of the criminal. They were of great help, doctor."

"Oh yes," Morgenthau nodded. "Rape and bombing. But they are sufficiently popular pastimes so that there is a large history available, many similar cases. So it is possible to analyze and detect a pattern. You understand? Make a fairly reasonable guess as to motivation, *modus operandi*, perhaps even physical appearance and habits. But in this case— impossible. Now we are dealing with multiple murder. It is, fortunately for all of us, a relatively rare activity. I am now eliminating political assassination which, I would guess, does not apply here."

"No sir. I don't believe it does."

"So . . . the literature on the subject is not extensive. I tried my hand at a short monograph but I do not believe you read it."

"No, doctor, I didn't."

"No wonder," Morgenthau giggled. "It was published in an obscure German psychiatric journal. So then, I cannot, regretfully, provide you with a psychiatric profile of the mass murderer."

"Well, listen," Delaney said desperately, "can you give me *anything?* About motivation, I mean. Even general stuff might help. For instance, do you think this killer is insane?"

Dr. Morgenthau shook his head angrily. "Sane. Insane. Those are legal terms. They have absolutely no meaning in the world of mental health. Well, I will try . . . My limited research leads me to believe mass murderers are generally one of three very broad, indefinite types. But I warn you, motivations frequently overlap. With multiple killers, we are dealing with individuals; as I told you, there are no definitive patterns I can discern. Well, then . . . the three main types . . . One: biological. Those cases in which mass murder is triggered by a physical defect, although the killer may have been psychologically predisposed. As an example, that rifleman up in the Texas tower who killed—how many people? I understand he had a brain tumor and had been trained as a skilled marksman and killer in the military service. Two: psychological. Here the environment in general is not at fault, but the specific pressures—usually familial or sexual—on the individual are of such an extreme nature that killing, over and over again, is the only release. Bluebeard might be such a case, or Jack the Ripper, or that young man in New Jersey—what was his name?"

"Unruh."

"Yes, Unruh. And then the third cause: sociological. This might be when the killer, in a different environment, might live out his days without violence. But his surroundings are so oppressive that his only recourse is fighting back, by killing, against a world he never made, a world that grinds him down to something less than human. This sociological motivation involves not only the residents of ghettoes, the brutalized minorities. There was a case a few years ago—again in New Jersey, I believe—where a 'solid citizen,' a middle-aged, middle-class gentleman who worked for a bank or insurance company—something like that—and passed the collection—"

The fifteen minutes Dr. Morgenthau had allotted Delaney had long since passed. But the doctor kept talking, as Delaney knew he would. It was hard to stop a man riding his hobby.

"—and passed the collection plate at his church every Sunday," Morgenthau was saying. "And then one day this fine, mild, upstanding citizen kills his wife, children, and his mother. Mark that—his mother! And then he takes off."

"I remember that case," Delaney nodded.

"Have they caught him yet?"

"No, I don't think so."

"Well, anyway, Captain, in the investigation, according to newspaper reports, it was discovered this pillar of the community was living in a much larger house than he could afford; it was heavily mortgaged and he was deeply in debt: insurance, cars, clothes, furniture, his children's education—all the social pressures to consider. A sociological motivation here, obviously, but as I told you, mass killers do not fit into neat classifications. What of the man's personality, background, childhood, his crimes considered as a part of the nation's or the world's social history? Charles Manson, for instance. What I am trying to prove to you is that despite these three quite loose classifications, each case of mass murder is specific and different from the others. Men who kill children and the man who killed all those nurses in Chicago and Panzram all seem to have had a similar childhood: physical abuse and body contact at an early age. Sexual pleasure at an infantile level. And yet, of the three I just mentioned, one kills children, one kills young women, and one kills young boys—or buggers them. So where is the pattern? Well, there is a superficial one perhaps. Most mass murderers tend to be quiet, conservative, neat. They attract no attention until their rampage. Often they wear the same suit or the same cut and color suit for days on end."

Delaney had been taking notes furiously in his pocket notebook. Now he looked up, eyes gleaming.

"That's interesting, doctor. But Manson wasn't like that."

"Exactly!" Morgenthau cried triumphantly. "That's just what I've been telling you: in this field it is dangerous to generalize. Here is something else interesting . . . Wertham says mass murderers are not passionless; they only appear to be so. But—and this is what is significant—he says that when their orgy of killing is finished, they once again become apparently passionless and are able to describe their most blood-curdling acts in chilling detail, without regret and without remorse. You know, Captain, my field has its own jargon, just as yours does. And the—the—what do you call it?—the lingo changes frequently, just like slang. Five or ten years ago we spoke of 'CPI's.' These were 'Constitutional Psychopathic Inferiors.' Apparently normal, functioning effectively in society, the CPI's feel no guilt, apparently are born without conscience, have no remorse, and cannot understand what the fuss is all about when the law objects to them holding a child's hand over a gas flame, throwing a puppy out of a ten-story window, or giving apples studded with razor blades and broken glass to a Halloween trick-or-treat visitor. Most mass murderers are CPI's, I would guess. Was that lecture of any help to you, Captain?"

"A very great help," Delaney said gravely. "You've made a number of things clear. But doctor . . . well, the fault is mine, I suppose, in asking you about 'motives.' You spoke mostly about causes. But what about *motives?* I mean, how does the killer justify to himself what he has done or is doing?"

Dr. Morgenthau stared at him a moment, then laughed shortly. His exhilaration was wearing off, his body seemed to be shrinking as he slumped down into his swivel chair. "Now I know why they call you 'Iron Balls,'" he said. "Oh yes, I know your nickname. During our first—ah—cooperation —I believe it was that Chelsea rapist—I made certain inquiries about you. You interested me."

"Did I?"

"You still do. The nickname is a good one for you, Captain."

"Is it?"

"Oh yes. You are surprisingly intelligent and perceptive for a man in your position. You are remarkably well-read, and you ask the right questions. But do you know what you are, Captain Edward X. Delaney? I mean beneath the intelligence, perception, patience, understanding. Do you know what you are, really?"

"What am I?"

"You are a cop."

"Yes," Delaney agreed readily. "That's what I am all right: a cop." The doctor was drifting away from him; he better finish it up fast.

"Iron balls," Dr. Morgenthau muttered. "Iron soul."

"Yes," Delaney nodded. "Let's get back to this problem of motives. How does the killer justify himself what he is doing?"

"Highly irrational," Morgenthau said in a slurred voice. "Highly. Most fascinating. They all have elaborate rationalizations. It allows them to do what they do. It absolves them. It makes no sense to so-called 'normal' men, but it relieves the killer of guilt. What they are doing is *necessary*."

"Such as?"

"What? Well, now we are getting into metaphysics, are we not? Have some ideas. Do a monograph some day. Captain, will you excuse . . ."

He started to lift himself from his chair, but Delaney held out an arm, the palm of his hand turned downward.

"Just a few more minutes," he said firmly, "and then I'll be out of your hair."

Morgenthau fell back into his chair, looked at the Captain with dull, weary eyes.

" 'Iron Balls,' " he said. "The mass killer seeks to impose order on chaos. Not the kind of order you and I want and welcome, but *his* kind of order. World in a ferment. He organizes it. He can't cope. He wants the security of prison. That dear, familiar prison. 'Catch me before I kill again.' You understand? He wants the institution. And if not that, order in the universe. Humanity is disorderly. Unpredictable. So he must work for order. Even if he must kill to attain it. Then he will find peace, because in an ordered world there will be no responsibility."

Delaney wasn't making notes now, but leaning forward listening intently. Dr. Morgenthau looked at him and suddenly yawned, a wide, jaw-cracking yawn. Delaney, unable to help himself, yawned in return.

"Or," Dr. Morgenthau went on, and yawned again (and Delaney yawned in reply), "we have the graffiti artist. Pico 137. Marv 145. Slinky 179. Goddamn it, world, I exist. I am Pico, Marv, Slinky. I have made my mark. You are required to acknowledge my existence. You mother-fuckers, *I am!* So he kills fifteen people or assassinates a President so the world says, 'Yes, Pico, Marv, Slinky, you do exist!' "

Delaney wondered if the man would last. Puffed lids were coming down over dulled eyes, the flesh was slack, swollen fingers plucked at folds of loose skin under the chin. Even the voice had lost its timbre and resolve.

"Or," Morgenthau droned, "or . . ."

Eyes rolled up into his skull until all Delaney could see were clotted whites. But suddenly, pulling himself partly upright, the doctor shook his head wildly, side to side, tiny drops of spittle splattering the glass top of his desk.

"Or alienation," he said thickly. "You cannot relate. Worse. You cannot feel. You want to come close. You want to understand. Truly you do. Come close. To another human being and through him to all humanity and the secret of existence. Captain? Iron Balls? You want to enter into life. Because emotion, feeling, love, ecstasy—all that has been denied you. I said metaphysical. But. That's what you seek. And you cannot find, except by killing. To find your way. And now, Captain Iron Balls, I must . . ."

"I'm going," Delaney said hastily, rising to his feet. "Thank you very much, doctor. You've been a big help."

"Have I?" Morgenthau said vaguely. He staggered upward, made it on the second try, headed toward his inner office.

Delaney paused with his hand on the knob of the reception room door. Then he turned.

"Doctor," he said sharply.

Morgenthau turned slowly, staggered, looked at him through unseeing eyes.

"Who?" he asked.

"Captain Delaney. One more thing . . . This killer we've been discussing has snuffed three men. No women or children. He kills with an ice ax, with a pointed pick. A phallus. I know I'm talking like an amateur now. But could he be a homosexual? Latent maybe? Fighting it. Is it possible?"

Morgenthau stared at him, and before Delaney's eyes he melted into his oversize clothes, his face decayed and fell, the light vanished from his eyes.

"Possible?" he whispered. "Anything is possible."

2

DELANEY WATCHED, with anger and dismay, as Operation Lombard fell apart. It had been a viable concept—a temporary horizontal organization cutting across precinct lines and the chain of command—and under Chief Pauley, with his talent for oganization and administrative genius, it had had a good chance of succeeding. But Pauley had been fired, and under the direction of Deputy Commissioner Broughton, Operation Lombard was foundering.

It was not for lack of energy; Broughton had plenty of that—too much. But he simply didn't have the experience to oversee a manhunt of this size and complexity. And he didn't know the men working for him. He sent weapons specialists halfway across the country to interrogate a recaptured escapee from a mental institution, and he used interrogation experts to check birth and marriage records in musty libraries. He dispatched four men in a car with screaming siren to question a suspect, where one man on foot would have obtained better results. And his paper work was atrocious; from reading the Operation Lombard reports, Delaney could tell it was getting out of hand; Broughton was detailing men to tasks that had been checked out weeks ago by Chief Pauley; reports were in the file, if Broughton knew where to look.

It was Thomas Handry, now calling Delaney at least twice a week, who described another of Broughton's failures: his ineptitude at handling the news media. Broughton made the fatal error of continually promising more than he could deliver, and newsmen became disillusioned with his "An arrest is expected momentarily" or "I'll have a *very* important announcement tomorrow" or "We have a suspect in custody who looks very hot." According to Handry, few reporters now bothered to attend Broughton's daily news briefings; he had earned the sobriquet of "Deputy Commissioner Bullshit."

Medical Examiner Sanford Ferguson also called. He wanted to tell Delaney that the Olfactory Analysis Indicator report on tissue taken from Bernard Gilbert's wound had been inconclusive. There could have been trace elements of a light machine oil; it could also have been half a dozen similar substances. Ferguson was trying again with scrapings from the fatal wound of Detective Roger Kope.

"Did you tell Broughton anything about this?"

"That son of a bitch? Don't be silly. He's caused us more trouble—I can't begin to tell you. It's not the work we mind, it's the bastard's *manner*."

Then Ferguson detailed some Departmental gossip:

Broughton was in real trouble. Demands from wealthy east side residents of the 251st Precinct for a quick solution to the three street murders were growing. A citizens' group had been formed. The Mayor was leaning on the Commissioner, and there were even rumors of the Governor appointing a board of inquiry. The murder of Frank Lombard was bad enough—he had wielded a lot of political clout—but the killing of a police officer had intensified editorial demands for a more productive investigation. Broughton, said Ferguson, had a lighted dynamite stick up his ass.

"It couldn't happen to a nicer guy," he added cheerfully.

Delaney wasted no time savoring the comeuppance of Deputy Commissioner Broughton. Nor did he dwell too long on his own personal guilt in the death of Detective third grade Roger Kope. He had done all he could to alert Broughton to the weapon used and the method of attack. And besides, if the truth be known, he blamed Kope; no officer on decoy should have allowed himself to be taken that way. Kope knew what he was up against and what the stakes were. You could feel horror and sympathy for a man shot down from ambush. But Kope had failed—and paid for it.

Delaney had enough on his plate without guilt feelings about Detective Kope. His amateurs needed constant mothering: telephone calls, personal visits and steady, low-key assurance that what they were doing was of value. So when Christopher Langley called to invite him to dinner with the Widow Zimmerman, and to discuss Langley's progress and future activities later, Delaney accepted promptly. He knew Langley's business could be decided in that phone conversation, but he also knew his physical presence was important to Langley, and he gave up the time gladly.

The dinner, thankfully, was prepared by the dapper little gourmet and served in his apartment, although the Widow Zimmerman had provided an incredibly renitent cheese cake. Delaney brought two bottles of wine, white and red, and they drank them both with Langley's *poulet en cocotte du midi*, since he assured them the business of red for meat and white for fish was pure poppycock.

After the meal, the Widow Zimmerman cleaned up, moving about Christopher Langley's apartment as if she was already mistress—as indeed she probably was, Delaney decided, having intercepted their affectionate glances, sly touchings, and sudden giggles at comments the humor of which he could not detect.

Langley and Delaney sat at the cleared table, sipped brandy, and the ex-curator brought out his lists, records, and notes, all beautifully neat, written out in a scholar's fine hand.

"Now then," he said, handing a paper over to Delaney, "here is a list of all stores and shops in the New York area selling the ice ax. Some call it 'ice ax' and some call it 'ice hammer.' I don't think that's important, do you?"

"No. Not at all."

"Of the five, the three I had checked in red itemize their sales checks, so that the purchase of an ice ax would be on record. Of these three, one does no mail order business and hence has no mailing list. The other two do have mailing lists and send out catalogues."

"Good," Delaney nodded. "I'll try to get copies of the mailing lists and their sales checks."

"I should warn you," Langley said, "not all these stores carry the same ax I found at Outside Life. The axes are similar in design, but they are not identical. I found one from Austria, one from Switzerland, and one made in America. The other two were identical to the Outside Life ax made in West Germany. I've marked all this on the list."

"Fine. Thank you. Well . . . where do we go from here?"

"I think," Christopher Langley said thoughtfully, "I should first concentrate on the West German ax, the one Outside Life sells. They're by far the largest outlet for mountaineering equipment in this area—and the least expensive, incidentally. I'll try to identify the manufacturer, the importer, and all retail outlets in this country that handle that particular ax. How does that sound?"

"Excellent. Just right. You're doing a marvelous job on this, Mr. Langley."

"Oh well, you know . . ."

When he left them, the Widow Zimmerman was washing dishes, and Christopher Langley was drying.

Delaney spent the next two days checking on Langley's list of stores in the New York area that sold ice axes and kept itemized sales checks. The one that did no mail order business and had no mailing list was willing to cooperate and lend Delaney the sales slips. He made arrangements to have them delivered to Calvin Case. The Captain wasn't optimistic about results; this particular store kept the checks for only six months.

Of the other two stores, Delaney was able to obtain checks and mailing lists from only one. The owner of the other simply refused to cooperate, claiming his mailing list was a carefully guarded business secret, of value to competitors, and Delaney couldn't have it without a court order. The Captain didn't push it; he could always come back to it later.

So he now had two more shipments of itemized sales checks for Calvin Case and another mailing list for Monica Gilbert. He decided to tackle Case first. He called, then subwayed down about noon.

The change in Calvin Case was a delight. He was clean, his hair cut and combed, his beard trimmed. He sat in pajamas in his aluminum and plastic wheelchair at his desk, flipping through Outside Life sales checks. Delaney had brought him a bottle, the same brand of whiskey Case had been drinking when Delaney first met him. The crippled mountaineer looked at the bottle and laughed.

"Thanks a lot," he said, "but I never touch the stuff now until the sun goes down. You?"

"No. Thanks. It's a bribe. I've got bad news for you."

"Oh?"

"We've found two more stores that sell ice axes. Ice hammers, I guess you'd say. Anyway, these stores have itemized sales checks."

Unexpectedly, Calvin Case smiled. "So?" he asked.

"Will you be willing to go through them?"

"Is it going to help?"

"Damned right," Delaney said fervently.

"Pile it on," Case grinned. "I ain't going no place. The more the merrier."

"Very few receipts," Delaney assured him. "I mean," he added hastily, "compared to Outside Life. One store keeps them for six months, and the other store for a year. How you coming?"

"Okay. Another three days, I figure. Then what happens?"

"Then you'll have a file of all ice ax purchases made at Outside Life in the past seven years. Right? Then I'll give you a map of the Two-five-one Precinct, and you'll go through your file and pull every sales check for an ice ax in the precinct."

Case stared at him a long moment, then shook his head.

"Delaney," he said, "you're not a detective; you're a fucking bookkeeper. You know that?"

"That's right," the Captain agreed readily. "No doubt about it."

He was going down the stairs when he met Evelyn Case coming up. He took off his hat, nodded, and smiled. She put down her shopping bag to grab him in her arms, hug him, kiss his cheek.

"He's wonderful," she said breathlessly. "Just the way he used to be. And it's all your doing."

"Is it?" Delaney asked wonderingly.

His next meet had to be with Monica Gilbert, for he now had another mailing list for her to check. But she called him first and told him she had completed the Outside Life mailing list, had made out a file card for every resident of the 251st Precinct on the list, and had a typed record of those residents, a master and two carbon copies, just as he had instructed.

He was amazed and delighted she had completed her job so quickly . . . and a little worried that she had not been as meticulous as he wanted her to be. But he had to work with what he had, and he arranged to meet her at her home the following evening. She asked him if he would care to come for dinner but he declined, with thanks; he would dine early (he lied) before he visited his wife at the hospital, and then be over later. Though why he had accepted Christopher Langley's dinner invitation and not Monica Gilbert's, he could not have said.

He bought two stuffed toys for the young daughters: a black and a white poodle. When you pressed their stomachs, they made a funny barking, squeaking sound. When he arrived, Mary and Sylvia were already in their little nightgowns, but Mrs. Gilbert allowed them out of the bedroom to say hello to the visitor. They were delighted with their presents and finally retired (pushed) to their bedroom, arguing about which poodle had the more ferocious expression. For a half-hour afterwards the adults heard the squeal of pressed toys. But the sounds gradually grew more infrequent, then ceased, and then Monica Gilbert and Edward Delaney were alone, in silence.

Finally: "Thank you for thinking of the girls," she said warmly.

"My pleasure. They're lovely kids."

"It was very kind of you. You like children?"

"Oh yes. Very much. I have a son and a daughter."

"Married?"

"My daughter is. She's expecting. Any day now."

"Her first?"

"Yes."

"How wonderful. You'll be a grandfather."

"Yes," he laughed with delight. "So I will."

She served coffee and almond-flavored cookies, so buttery he knew immediately they were homemade. His mother had made cookies like that. He put on his heavy glasses to inspect what she had done, while he sipped black coffee and nibbled cookies.

He saw immediately he needn't have doubted her swift efficiency. There had been 116 residents of the 251st Precinct on the Outside Life mailing list. She had made out a file card for each one: last name first in capital letters, followed by the given name and middle initial. Beneath the name was typed the address, in two lines. Then she had made a master list and two carbons from the cards, now neatly filed alphabetically in a wooden box.

"Very good," he nodded approvingly. "Excellent. Now I have some bad news for you; I have another mailing list from another store." He smiled at her. "Willing?"

She smiled in return. "Yes. How many names?"

"I estimate about a third of the number of the Outside Life list; maybe less. And you'll probably find duplications. If you do, don't make out a separate card, just note on the Outside Life card that the individual is also on this list. Okay?"

"Yes. What happens now?"

"To your typed list, you mean? You keep one carbon. Just stick it away somewhere as insurance. I'll keep the other carbon. The original will go to friends in the Department. They'll check the names with city, state, and federal files to see if anyone listed has a criminal record."

"A record?"

"Sure. Been charged, been convicted of any crime. Been sentenced. Fined, on probation, or time in jail."

She was disturbed; he could see it.

"Will this help find the man who killed my husband?"

"Yes," he said decisively, paused a moment, staring at her, then asked, "What's bothering you?"

"It seems so—so unfair," she said faintly.

He became suddenly aware of her as a woman: the solid, warm body beneath the black dress, the strong arms and legs, the steady look of purpose. She was not a beautiful woman, not as delicate as Barbara nor as fine. But there was a peasant sensuality to her; her smell was deep and disturbing.

"What's unfair?" he asked quietly.

"Hounding men who have made one mistake. You do it all the time I suppose."

"Yes," he nodded, "we do it all the time. You know what the recidivist rate is, Mrs. Gilbert? Of all the men present in prison, about eighty percent have been behind bars at least once before."

"It still seems—"

"Percentages, Mrs. Gilbert: We've got to use them. We know that if a man rapes, robs, or kills once, the chances are he'll rape, rob, or kill again. We can't deny that. We didn't create that situation, but we'd be fools to overlook it."

"But doesn't police surveillance, the constant hounding of men with records, contribute to—"

"No," he shook his great head angrily. "If an ex-con wants to go straight, really wants to, he will. I'm not going to tell you there have never been frames of ex-cons. Of course there have. But generally, when a man repeats, he wants to go back behind bars. Did you know that? There's never been a study of it, to my knowledge, but my guess is that most two-and-three-time losers are asking for it. They need the bars. They can't cope on the outside. I'm hoping a check on your list will turn up a man or men like that. If not, it may turn up *something*. A similar case, a pattern of violence, *something* that may give me a lead."

"Does that mean if you get a report that some poor man on this list forged a check or deserted his wife, you'll swoop down on him and demand to know where he was on the night my husband and those other men were killed?"

"Of course not. Nothing like that. First of all, criminals can be classified.

they have their specialities, and rarely vary. Some deal strictly in white-collar crime: embezzlement, bribery, patent infringement—things like that. Crimes against property, mostly. Then there's a grey area: forgery, swindling, fraud, and so forth. Still crimes against property, but now the victim tends to be an individual rather than the government or the public. And then there's the big area of conventional crime: homicide, kidnapping, robbery, and so forth. These are usually crimes of violence during which the criminal actually sees and has physical contact with his victim; and infliction of injury or death usually results. Or, at least, the potential is there. I'm looking for a man with a record in this last classification, a man with a record of violence, physical violence."

"But—but how will you *know?* What if one of the men on that list was arrested for beating his wife? That's certainly violent, isn't it? Does that make him the killer?"

"Not necessarily, though I'd certainly check him out. But I'm looking for a man who fits a profile."

She stared at him, not understanding. "A profile?"

He debated if he should tell her, but felt a need to impress her, couldn't resist it, and wondered why that was.

"Mrs. Gilbert, I have a pretty good idea—a pretty good *visualization* of the man who's doing these killings. He's young—between thirty-five and forty—tall and slender. He's in good health and strong. His physical reactions are very fast. He's probably a bachelor. He may be a latent homosexual. He dresses very well, but conservatively. Dark suits. If you passed him on the street at night, you'd feel perfectly safe. He probably has a good job and handles it well. There's nothing about him that would make people suspect him. But he's addicted to danger, to taking risks. He's a mountain climber. He's cool, determined, and I'm positive he's a resident of this neighborhood. Certainly of this precinct. And tall. Did I say he was tall? Yes, I did. Well, he's probably six feet or over."

Her astonishment was all he could have asked, and he cursed his own ego for showing off in this fasion.

"But how do you know all this?" she said finally.

He rose to his feet and began to gather his papers together. He was so disgusted with himself.

"Sherlock Holmes," he said sourly. "It's all guesswork, Mrs. Gilbert. Forget it. I was just shooting off my mouth."

She followed him to the door.

"I'm sorry about what I said," she told him, putting a strong hand on his arm. "I mean about how cruel it is to check men with records. I know you've got to do it."

"Yes," he nodded. "I've got to do it. Percentages."

"Captain, please do everything you think should be done. I don't know anything about it. This is all new to me."

He smiled at her without speaking.

"I'll get on the new list tonight. And thank you, Captain."

"For what?"

"For doing what you're doing."

"I haven't done anything yet except give you work to do."

"You're going to get him, aren't you?"

"Listen," Delaney said, "could we—"

He stopped suddenly and was silent. She was puzzled. "Could we what?" she asked finally.

"Nothing," he said. "Good-night, Mrs. Gilbert. Thank you for the coffee and cookies."

He walked home, resolutely turning his mind from the thought of what a fool he had made of himself—in his own eyes if not in hers. He stopped at a phone booth to call Deputy Inspector Thorsen, and waited five minutes until Thorsen called him back.

"Edward?"

"Yes."

"Anything new?"

"I have a list of a hundred and sixteen names and addresses. I need them checked out against city, state, and federal records."

"My God."

"It's important."

"I know, Edward. Well . . . at least we've got some names. That's more than Broughton has."

"I hear he's in trouble."

"You hear right."

"Heavy?"

"Not yet. But it's growing. Everyone's leaning on him."

"About this list of mine—I'll get it to your office tomorrow by messenger. All right?"

"Better send it to my home."

"All right, and listen, please include the State Department of Motor Vehicles and the NYPD's Special Services Branch. Can you do that?"

"We'll have to do it."

"Yes."

"Getting close, Edward?"

"Well . . . closer."

"You think he's on the list?"

"He better be," Delaney said. Everyone was leaning on him, too.

He was weary now, wanting nothing but a hot shower, a rye highball, perhaps a sleeping pill, and bed. But he had his paper work to do, and drove himself to it. What was it Case called him—a fucking bookeeper.

He finished his writing, his brain frazzled, and filed his neat folders away. He drained his highball, watery now, and considered the best way to handle results from the search of records of those 116 individuals, when they began to come in on printouts from city, state, and federal computers.

What he would do, he decided, was this: he would ask Monica Gilbert to make notations of any criminal history on the individual cards. He would buy five or six packages of little colored plastic tabs, the kind that could be clipped on the upper edge of file cards. He would devise a colour code: a red tab attached to a card would indicate a motor vehicle violation, a blue tab would indicate a New York City criminal record . . . and so forth. When reports were in from all computers, he could then look at Monica Gilbert's file box and, without wasting time flipping through 116 cards, see at a glance which had one, two, three or more plastic tabs attached to their upper edges. He thought it over, and it seemed an efficient plan.

His mind was working so sluggishly that it was some time before he wondered why he hadn't brought Monica Gilbert's card file home with him, to keep in his own study. The computer printouts Thorsen would obtain would be delivered to him, Delaney. He could make handwritten notations on individual cards himself and attach the color-coded plastic tabs. It wasn't necessary for him to run over to Mrs. Gilbert's apartment to consult the file every time he needed to. So why . . . Still . . . She *was* efficient and he couldn't do everything . . . Still . . . Had he angered her? If she . . . Barbara . . .

He dragged himself up to bed, took no shower and no sleeping pill, but lay awake for at least an hour, trying to understand himself. Not succeeding, he finally slid into a thin sleep.

3

IT BEGAN to come together. Slowly. What he had set in motion. The first report on the 116 names came from the New York State Department of Motor Vehicles: a neatly folded computer printout, an original and six copies. Delaney took a quick look, noted there were 11 individuals listed, tore off a carbon for his own file, and took the report over to Monica Gilbert. He explained what he wanted:

"It's easy to read once you get the hang of it. It's computer printing—all capitals and no punctuation—but don't let that throw you. Now the first one listed is AVERY JOHN H on East Seventy-ninth Street. You have Avery's card?"

Obediently she flipped through her file and handed him the card.

"Good. Now Avery was charged with going through a unattended toll booth without tossing fifty cents in the hopper. Pleaded guilty, paid a fine. It's printed here in a kind of official lingo, but I'm sure you can make it out. Now I'd like you to make a very brief notation on his card. If you write, 'Toll booth—guilty—fine,' it will be sufficient. I'd also like you to note his license number and make of car, in this case a blue Mercury. All clear?"

"I think so," she nodded. "Let me try the next one myself. 'BLANK DANIEL G on East Eighty-third Street; two arrests for speeding, guilty, fined. Black Corvette and then his license number.' Is that what you want on this card?"

"Right. In case you're wondering, I'm not going to lean on these particular people. This report is just possible background stuff. The important returns will come from city and federal files. One more thing . . ."

He showed her the multicolored plastic tabs he had purchased in a stationery store, and explained the color code he had written out for her. She consulted it and clipped red tabs onto the top edges of the AVERY and BLANK cards. It looked very efficient, and he was satisfied.

Calvin Case called to report he had finished going through the Outside Life sales checks and had a file of 234 purchases of ice axes made in the past seven years. Delaney brought him a hand-drawn map of the 251st Precinct, and by the next day Case had separated those purchases made by residents of the Precinct. There were six of them. Delaney took the six sales checks, went home, and made two lists. One was for his file, one he delivered to Monica Gilbert so she could make notations on the appropriate cards and attach green plastic tabs. He had hardly returned home when she called. She was troubled because one of the six ice ax purchasers was not included in her master file of Outside Life customers. She gave him the name and address.

Delaney laughed. "Look," he said, "don't let it worry you. We can't expect perfection. It was probably human error; it usually is. For some reason this particular customer wasn't included on the mailing list. Who knows—maybe he said he didn't want their catalogue; he doesn't like junk mail. Just make out a card for him."

"Yes, Edward."

He was silent. It was the first time she had used his given name. She must have realized what she had done for suddenly she said, in a rush, "Yes, Captain."

"Edward is better," he told her, and they said goodby.

Now he could call her Monica.

Back to his records, remembering to start a new list for Thorsen headed by the single ax purchaser not included on the original list. Two days later Monica Gilbert had finished going through the new mailing list he had given her, and 34 more names were added to her master file and to the new list for Thorsen. And two days after that, Calvin Case had finished flipping through sales checks of the two additional New York stores that sold ice axes, and the names of three more purchasers in the 251st Precinct were added to Monica's file, green plastic tabs attached, and the names also added to the new Thorsen list. Delaney had it delivered to the Deputy Inspector.

Meanwhile computer printouts were coming in on the original 116, and Monica Gilbert was making notations on her cards, attaching colored tabs to indicate the source of the information. Meanwhile Calvin Case was breaking down his big file of Outside Life receipts of sales of any type of mountaineering equipment, to extract those of residents of the 251st Precinct. Meanwhile Christopher Langley was visiting official German agencies in New York to determine the manufacturer, importer, jobbers and retail outlets that handled the ice ax in the U.S. Meanwhile, Captain Edward X. Delaney was personally checking out the six people who had purchased ice axes at the other two stores. And reading "Honey Bunch" to his wife.

Ever since he had been promoted from uniformed patrolman to detective third grade, Delaney, following the advice of his first partner—an old, experienced, and alcoholic detective who called him "Buddy Boy"—had collected business cards. If he was given a card by a banker, shoe salesman, mortician, insurance agent, private investigator—whatever—he hung onto it, and it went into a little rubber-banded pack. Just as his mentor had promised, the business cards proved valuable. They provided temporary "cover." People were impressed by them; often they were all the identification he needed to be banker, shoe salesman, mortician, insurance agent, private investigator—whatever. That little bit of pasteboard was a passport; few people investigated his identity further. When he passed printing shops advertising "100 Business Cards for $5.00" he could understand how easily conmen and swindlers operated.

Now he made a selection of his collected cards and set out to investigate personally the nine residents of the 251st Precinct who had purchased ice axes in the past seven years. He had arranged the nine names and addresses according to location, so he wouldn't have to retrace his steps or end the day at the other end of the Precinct. This was strictly a walking job, and he dug out an old pair of shoes he had worn on similar jobs in the past. They were soft, comfortable kangaroo leather with high laced cuffs that came up over his ankles.

He waited until 9:00 a.m., then began his rounds, speaking only to doormen, supers, landlords, neighbors . . .

"Good morning. My name's Barrett, of Acme Insurance. Here's my card. But I don't want to sell you anything. I'm looking for a man named David Sharpe. He was listed as beneficiary on one of our policies and has some money coming to him. He live here?"

"Who?"

"David Sharpe."

"I don't know him."

"This is the address we have for him."

"Nah, I never—wait . . . What's his name?"

"David Sharpe."

"Oh yeah. Chris', he move away almost two years ago."

"Oh. I don't suppose you have any forwarding address?"

"Nah. Try the post office."

"That's a good idea. I'll try them."

And plucking his business card back, Delaney trudged on.

"Good morning. My name's Barrett, of Acme Insurance. Here's my card. But I don't want to sell you anything. I'm looking for a man named Arnold K. Abel. He was listed as beneficiary on one of our policies and has some money coming to him. He—"

"Tough shit. He's dead."

"Dead?"

"Yeah. Remember that plane crash last year? It landed short and went into Jamaica Bay."

"Yes, I remember that."

"Well, Abel was on it."

"I'm sorry to hear that."

"Yeah, he was a nice guy. A lush but a nice guy. He always give me a tenner at Christmas."

And then something happened he should have expected.

"Good morning," he started his spiel, "I'm—"

"Hell, I know you, Captain Delaney. I was on that owners' protective committee you started. Don't you remember me? The name's Goldenberg."

"Of course, Mr. Goldenberg. How are you?"

"Healthy, thank God. And you, Captain?"

"Can't complain."

"I was sorry to hear you retired."

"Well . . . not retired exactly. Just temporary leave of absence. But things piled up and I'm spending a few hours a day helping out the new commander. You know?"

"Oh sure. Breaking him in—right?"

"Right. Now we're looking for a man named Simmons. Walter J. Simmons. He's not wanted or anything like that, but he was a witness to a robbery about a year ago, and now we got the guy we think pulled the job, and we hoped this Simmons could identify him."

"Roosevelt Hospital, Captain. He's been in there almost six months now. He's one of these mountain climbers, and he fell and got all cracked up. From what I hear, he'll never be the same again."

"I'm sorry to hear that. But he still may be able to testify. I better get over there. Thank you for your trouble."

"My pleasure, Captain. Tell me the truth, what do you think about this new man, this Dorfman?"

"Good man," Delaney said promptly.

"With these three murders we've had in the last few months and the dingaling still running around free? What's this Dorfman doing about that?"

"Well, it's out of his hands, Mr. Goldenberg. The investigation is being handled personally by Deputy Commissioner Broughton."

"I read, I read. But it's Dorfman's precinct—right?"

"Right," Delaney said sadly.

So the day went. It was a disaster. Of the nine ice ax purchasers, three had moved out of the precinct, one had died, one was hospitalized, and one had been on a climbing tour in Europe for the past six months.

That left three possibles. Delaney made a hurried visit to Barbara, then spent the evening checking out the three, this time questioning them personally, giving his name and showing his shield and identification. He didn't tell them the reason for his questions, and they didn't ask. The efforts of Delaney, New York Police Department, were no more productive than those of Barrett, Acme Insurance.

One purchaser was an octogenarian who had bought the ax as a birthday present for a 12-year-old great-grandson.

One was a sprightly, almost maniacal young man who assured Delaney he had given up mountain climbing for skydiving, "Much more *machismo*, man!" At Delaney's urging, he dug his ax out of a back closet. It was dusty, stained, pitted with rust, and the Captain wondered if it had ever been used, for anything.

The third was a young man who, when he answered Delaney's ring, seemed at first sight to fit the profile: tall, slender, quick, strong. But behind him, eyeing the unexpected visitor nervously and curiously, was his obviously pregnant wife. Their apartment was a shambles of barrels and cartons; Delaney had interrupted their packing; they were moving in two days since, with the expected new arrival, they would need more room. When the Captain brought up the subject of the ice ax, they both laughed. Apparently, one of the conditions she had insisted on, before marrying him, was that he give up mountain climbing. So he had, and quite voluntarily he showed Delaney his ice ax. They had been using it as a general purpose hammer; the head was scarred and nicked. Also, they had tried to use the spike to pry open a painted-shut window and suddenly, without warning, the pick of the ice ax had just snapped off. And it was supposed to be steel. Wasn't that the damndest thing? they asked. Delaney agreed despondently it was the damndest thing he ever heard.

He walked home slowly, thinking he had been a fool to believe it would be easy. Still, it was the obvious thing to trace weapon to source to buyer. It had to be done, and he had done it. Nothing. He knew how many other paths he could now take, but it was a disappointment; he admitted it. He had hoped—just hoped—that one of those cards with the green plastic tab would be the one.

His big worry was time. All this checking of sales receipts and list making and setting up of card files and questioning innocents—time! It all took days and weeks, and meanwhile this nut was wandering the streets and, as past histories of similar crimes indicated, the intervals between murders became shorter and shorter.

When he got home he found a package Mary had signed for. He recognized it as coming from Thorsen by commercial messenger. He tore it open and when he saw what it was, he didn't look any further. It was a report from the Records Division, New York Police Department, including the Special Services Branch. That completed the check on criminal records of the original 116 names.

He had been doing a curious thing. As reports came in from federal, state, and local authorities, he had been tearing off a carbon for his files, then delivering the other copies to Monica Gilbert for notation and tabbing in her master file. He didn't read the reports himself; he didn't even glance at them. He told himself the reason for this was that he couldn't move on individuals with criminal records until *all* the reports were in and recorded on Monica's file cards. Then he'd be able to see at a glance how many men had committed how many offenses. That's what he told himself.

He also told himself he was lying—to himself.

The real reason he was following this procedure was very involved, and he wasn't quite sure he understood it. First of all, being a superstitious cop, he had the feeling that Monica Gilbert had brought him and would bring him luck. Somehow, through her efforts, solely or in part, he'd find the lead he needed. The second thing was that he hoped these computer printouts of criminal records would lead to the killer and thus prove to Monica he had merely been logical and professional when he had requested them. He had seen it in her eyes when he told her what he was about to do; she had thought him a brutal, callous—well, a *cop*, who had no feeling or sympathy for human frailty. That was, he assured himself, simply not true. ·

Unlacing his high shoes, peeling off his sweated socks, he paused a moment, sock in hand, and wondered why her good opinion of him was so important to him. He thought of her, of her heavy muscular haunches moving slowly under the thin black dress, and he realized to his shame that he was beginning to get an erection. He had had no sex since Barbara became ill, and his "sacrifice" seemed so much less than her pain that he couldn't believe what he was dreaming: the recent widow of a murder victim . . . while Barbara . . . and he . . . He snorted with disgust at himself, took a tepid shower, donned fresh pajamas, and got out of bed an hour later, wide-eyed and frantic, to gulp two sleeping pills.

He delivered the new report to her the next morning refused her offer to stay for coffee and Danish. Did she seem hurt? He thought so. Then, sighing, he spent a whole day—time! time!—doing what he had to do and what he knew would be of no value whatsoever: he checked those purchasers of ice axes who had moved, died, were abroad, or hospitalized. The results, as he knew they would, added up to zero. They really had moved, died, were abroad, or hospitalized.

Mary had left a note that Mrs. Gilbert had called, and would the Captain please call her back. So he did, immediately, and there was no coolness in her voice he could detect. She told him she had completed noting all the reported criminal records in her master file, and had attached appropriately colored plastic tabs. He asked her if she'd care to have lunch with him at 1:00 p.m. the following day, and she accepted promptly.

They ate at a local seafood restaurant and had identical luncheons: crabmeat salads with a glass of white wine. They spent a pleasant hour and half together, talking of the pains and pleasures of life in the city. She told him of her frustrated efforts to grow geraniums in window boxes; he told her of how, for years, Barbara and he had tried to grow flowers and flowering shrubs in their shaded backyard, had finally surrendered to the soot and sour soil, and let the ivy take over. Now it was a jungle of ivy and, surprisingly, rather pretty.

He told her about Barbara while they sipped coffee. She listened intently and finally asked:

"Do you think you should change doctors?"

"I don't know what to do," he confessed. "He's always been her physician, and she has great faith in him. I couldn't bring someone else in without her permission. He's trying everything he can, I'm sure. And there are consultants in on this. But she shows no improvement. In fact, it seems to me she's just wasting away, just fading. My son was up to visit a few weeks ago and was shocked at how she looked. So thin and flushed and drawn. And occasionally now she's irrational. Just for short periods of time."

"That could be the fever, or even the antibiotics she's getting."

"I suppose so," he nodded miserably. "But it frightens me. She was always so—so sharp and perceptive. Still is, when she isn't floating off in never-never land. Well . . . I didn't invite you to lunch to cry on your shoulder. Tell me about your girls. How are they getting along in school?"

She brightened, and told him about their goodness and deviltry, things they had said and how different their personalities were, one from the other. He listened with interest, smiling, remembering the days when Eddie and Liza were growing up, and wondering if he was now paying for that happiness.

"Well," he said, after she finished her coffee, "can we go back to your place? I'd like to take a look at that card file. All the reports finished?"

"Yes," she nodded, "everything's entered. I'm afraid you're going to be disappointed."

"I usually am," he said wryly.

"Oh well," she smiled, "these are only the unsuccessful criminals."

"Pardon?" he asked, not realizing at first that she was teasing him.

"Well, when a man has a record, it proves he was an inefficient criminal, doesn't it? He got caught. If he was good at his job, he wouldn't have a record."

"Yes," he laughed. "You're right."

They stood and moved to the cashier's desk, Delaney had his wallet out, but the manager, who had apparently been waiting for this moment, moved in close, smiling, and said to the cashier, "No check for Captain Delaney."

He looked up in surprise. "Oh . . . hello, Mr. Varro. How are you?"

"Bless God, okay, Captain. And you?"

"Fine. Thanks for the offer, but I'm afraid I can't accept it, I'm not on active duty, you know. Leave of absence. And besides—" He gestured towards Monica Gilbert who was watching this scene closely. "—this young lady is a witness, and I wouldn't want her to think I was accepting a bribe."

They all laughed—an easy laugh.

"Tell you what," Delaney said, paying his bill, "next time I'll come in alone, order the biggest lobster in the house, and let you pick up the tab. Okay?"

"Sure, okay," Varro smiled. "You know me. Anytime, Captain."

They walked toward Monica's apartment, and she looked up at him curiously. "Will you?" she asked. "Stop in for a free meal, I mean?"

"Sure," he said cheerfully. "He'd be hurt if I didn't. Varro is all right. The best men stop in for coffee almost every day. The squad car men do, too. Not all of them take, but I'd guess most of them do. It doesn't mean a thing. Happens in a hundred restaurants and bars and hotdog stands and pizza parlors in the Precinct. Are you going to say, 'Petty graft'? You're right, but most cops are struggling to get their kids to college on a cop's pay, and a free lunch now and then is more important than you think. When I said it doesn't mean a thing, I meant that if any of these generous owners and managers get out of line, they'll be leaned on like anyone else. A free cup of coffee doesn't entitle them to anything but a friendly hello. Besides, Varro owes me a favor. About two years ago he discovered he was losing stuff from his storeroom. It wasn't the usual pilferage—a can or package now and then. This stuff was disappearing in *cases*. So he came to me, and I called in Jeri Fernandez who was lieutenant of our precinct detective squad at that time. Jeri put a two-man stakeout watching the back alley. The first night they were there—the *first* night!—this guy pulls up to the back door in a station wagon, unlocks the door cool as you please, and starts bringing up cases and cartons and bags from the basement and loading his wagon. They waited until he had the wagon full and was locking the back door. Then they moved in."

"What did they do?" she asked breathlessly.

Delaney laughed. "They made him unload his station wagon and carry all that stuff back down to the basement again and store it neatly away. They said he was puffing like a whale by the time he got through. He was one of the assistant chefs there and had keys to the back door and storeroom. It really wasn't important enough to bring charges. It would have meant impounding evidence, a lot of paperwork for everyone, time lost in court, and the guy probably would have been fined and put on probation if it was his first offense. So after he finished putting everything back the way it was, Jeri's boys worked him over. Nothing serious. I mean he didn't have to go to the hospital or anything like that, but I suppose they marked him up some—a few aches and pains. And of course he was fired. The word got around, and Varro hasn't lost a can of salad oil since. That's why he wanted to buy our lunch."

He looked at her, smiling, and saw her shiver suddenly.

"It's a whole different world," she said in a low voice.

"What is?"

But she didn't answer.

She was right; the criminal records were a disappointment. What he had been hoping was that when the computer printouts were collated and entered on the file cards, there would be a few or several cards with a perfect forest of multicolored plastic tabs clipped to their upper edges, indicating significant criminal records that might show a pattern of psychopathic and uncontrollable violence.

Instead, the card file was distressingly bare. There was one card with three tabs, two with two tabs, and 43 with one tab. None of the nine purchasers of ice axes, who Delaney had already checked out, had a criminal record.

While he went through the tabbed cards, slowly, working at Monica's kitchen table, she had brought in mending, donned a pair of rimless spectacles, and began making a hem on one of the girl's dresses, working swiftly, making small stitches, a thimble and scissors handy. When he had finished the cards, he pushed the file box away from him, and the sound made her look up. He gave her a bleak smile.

"You're right," he said. "A disappointment. One rape, one robbery, one assault with a deadly weapon. And my God, have you ever seen so many income tax frauds in your life!"

She smiled slightly and went back to her sewing. He sat brooding, tapping his pencil eraser lightly on the table top.

"Of course, this is a good precinct," he said, thinking aloud as much as he was talking to her. "I mean 'good' in the sense of better than East Harlem and Bedford-Stuyvesant. The per capita income is second highest of all the precincts in the city, and the rates of crimes of violence are in the lower third. I'm speaking of Manhattan, Bronx, and Brooklyn now. Not Queens and Staten Island. So I should have expected a high preponderance of white-collar crime. Did you notice the tax evasions, unscrupulous repair estimates, stock swindles—things like that? But still . . . What I didn't really consider is that all these cards, all these individuals—by the way, did you see that there are only four women in the whole file?—these individuals are all presumably mountain climbers or have bought gifts for mountain climbers or are outdoorsmen of one type or another: hunters, fishermen, boat owners, hikers, campers, and so forth. That means people with enough money for a leisure hobby. And lack of money is usually the cause of violent crime. So what we've got is a well-to-do precinct and a file of people who can afford to spend money, heavy money, on their leisure-time activities. I guess I was foolish to expect mountain climbers and deep-sea fishermen to have the same percentage of records as people in the ghettos. Still . . . it is a disappointment."

"Discouraged?" she asked quietly, not looking up.

"Monica," he said, and at this tone of voice she did look up to find him smiling at her. "I'm never discouraged," he said. "Well . . . hardly ever. I'll check out the rape, the robbery, and the assault. If nothing comes of that, there's a lot more I can do. I'm just getting started."

She nodded, and went back to her mending. He took notes on the three records of violent crimes included on the file cards. For good measure, although he thought the chances were nil, he added the names and addresses of men convicted of vandalism, extortion, and safe-breaking. He glanced at his watch, a thick hunter his grandfather had owned, and saw he had time to check out three or four of the men with records.

He rose, she put aside her sewing and stood up, and they took off their glasses simultaneously, and laughed together, it seemed like such an odd thing.

"I hope your wife is feeling better soon," she said, walking him to the door.

"Thank you."

"I'd—I'd like to meet her," she said faintly. "That, if you think it's all right. I mean, I have time on my hands now that the file is finished, and I could go over and sit with—"

He turned to her eagerly. "Would you? My God, that would be wonderful! I know you two will get along. She'll like you, and you'll like her. I try to get there twice a day, but sometimes I don't. We have friends who come to see her. At least at first they did. But—you know—they don't come too often anymore. I'll go over with you and introduce you, and then if you could just stop by occasionally . . ."

"Of course. I'll be happy to."

"Thank you. You're very kind. And thank you for having lunch with me. I really enjoyed it."

She held out her hand. He was surprised, a second, then grasped it, and they shook. Her grip was dry, her flesh firm, the hand unexpectedly strong.

He went out into the dull winter afternoon, the sky tarnished pewter, and glanced at his list to see who he should hit first. But curiously he was not thinking of the list, nor of Monica Gilbert, nor of Barbara. Something was nibbling at the edge of his mind, something that had to do with the murders. It was something he had heard recently; someone had said something. But what it was he could not identify. It hovered there, tantalizing, teasing, until finally he shook his head, put it away from him, and started tramping the streets.

He got home a little after ten that evening, his feet aching (he had not worn his "cop shoes"), and so soured with frustration that he whistled and thought of daffodils—anything to keep from brooding on false leads and time wasted. He soaked under a hot shower and washed his hair. That made him feel a little better. He pulled on pajamas, robe, slippers, and went down to the study.

During the afternoon and evening he had checked out five of the six on his list. The rapist and the robber were still in prison. The man convicted of assault with a deadly weapon had been released a year ago, but was not living at the address given. It would have to be checked with his parole officer in the morning. Of the other three, the safe-breaker was still in prison, the vandal had moved to Florida two months ago and considerately left a forwarding address, and Delaney was just too damned tired to look for the extortionist, but would the next day.

He stolidly wrote out reports on all his activities and added them to his files. Then he made his nightly tour of inspection, trying locks on all windows and outside doors. Lights out and up to bed. It wasn't midnight, but he was weary. He was really getting too old for this kind of nonsense. No pill tonight. Blessed sleep would come easily.

While he waited for it, he wondered if it was wise to introduce Monica Gilbert to his wife. He had said they would hit it off, and they probably would. Barbara would certainly feel sympathy for a murder victim's widow. But would she think . . . would she imagine . . . But she had asked him to . . . Oh, he didn't know, couldn't judge. He'd bring them together, once at least, and see what happened.

Then he turned his thoughts to what had been nagging his brain since he left Monica's apartment that afternoon. He was a firm believer in the theory that if you feel asleep with a problem on your mind—a word you were trying to remember, an address, a name, a professional or personal dilemma—you would awake refreshed and the magic solution would be there, the problem solved in your subconscious while you slept.

He awoke the next morning, and the problem still existed, gnawing at his memory. But now it was closer; it was something Monica had said at their luncheon. He tried to remember their conversation in every detail: she had talked about her geraniums, he had talked about his ivy; she had talked about her children, he had talked about Barbara. Then Varro tried to pick up the check, and he, Delaney, told her about the break-in at the restaurant. But what the hell did all that have to do with the price of eggs in China? He shook his head disgustedly and went in to shave.

He spent the morning tracking down the extortionist, the last man of the six in Monica Gilbert's file with a record of even mildly violent crime. Delaney finally found him pressing pants in a little tailor shop on Second Avenue. The extortionist was barely five feet tall, at least 55 and 175 lbs., pasty-faced, with trembling hands and watery eyes. What in God's name did he ever extort? Delaney muttered something about "mistaken identity" and departed as fast as he could, leaving the fat little man in a paroxysm of trembling and watering.

He went directly to the hospital, helped feed Barbara her noon meal, and then read to her for almost an hour from "Honey Bunch: Her First Little Garden." Strangely, the reading soothed him as much as it did her, and when he returned home he was in a somber but not depressed mood—a mood to work steadily without questioning the why's or where-fore's.

He spent an hour on his personal affairs: checks, investments, bank balances, tax estimates, charitable contributions. He cleaned up the month's accumulated shit, paid what he had to pay, wrote a letter to his accountant, made out a deposit for his savings account and a withdrawal against his checking account for current expenses.

Envelopes were sealed, stamped, and put on the hall table where he'd be sure to see them and pick them up for mailing the next time he went out. Then he returned to the study, drew the long legal pad toward him, and began listing his options.

1. He could begin personally investigating *every* name in Monica's card file. He estimated there were about 155.

2. He could wait for Christopher Langley's report, and then contact, by mail or phone, every retail outlet for the West German ice ax in the U.S.

3. He could wait for Calvin Case's file of everyone in the 251st Precinct who had bought any kind of mountaineering equipment whatsoever from Outside Life and that other store that had supplied a mailing list, and then he could ask Monica to double-check her file to make certain she had a card for every customer.

4. He could go back to the store that refused to volunteer sales checks

and mailing list, and he could lean on them. If that didn't work, he could ask Thorsen what the chances were for a search warrant.

5. He could recheck his own investigations of the nine ice ax purchases and the six men in the file with a record of violent crime.

6. He could finally get to his early idea of determining if there was a magazine for mountain climbers and he could borrow their subscription list; if there was a club or society of mountain climbers and he could borrow their membership list; and if it was possible to check the local library on residents of the 251st Precinct who had withdrawn books on mountaineering.

7. If it came to it, he would personally check out every goddamn name of every goddamn New Yorker on the goddamn Outside Life mailing list. There were probably about 10,000 goddamn New Yorkers included, and he'd hunt down every goddamn one of them.

But he was just blathering, and he knew it. If he was commanding the 500 detectives in Operation Lombard he could do it, but not by himself in much less than five years. How many murder victims would there be by then? Oh? . . . probably not more than a thousand or so.

But all this was cheesy thinking. One thing was bothering him, and he knew what it was. When Monica called him to report that one of the ice ax purchasers in Calvin Case's file hadn't been included on her Outside Life mailing list, he had laughed it off as "human error." No one is perfect. People do make mistakes, errors of commission or omission. Quite innocently, of course.

What if Calvin Case, late at night and weary, flipped by the sales check of an ice ax purchaser?

What if Christopher Langley had missed a store in the New York area that sold axes?

What if Monica Gilbert had somehow skipped a record of violent crime on one of the computer reports she noted on her file cards?

And what if he, Captain Edward X. Delaney, had the solution to the whole fucking mess right under his big, beaky nose and couldn't see it because he was stupid, stupid, stupid?

. Human errors. And professionals were just as prone to them as Delaney's amateurs. That was why Chief Pauley sent different men back to check the same facts, why he repeated interrogations twice, sometimes three times. My God, even computers weren't perfect. But was there anything he could do about it? No.

So the Captain read over his list of options again and tossed it aside. A lot of shit. He called Monica Gilbert.

"Monica? Edward. Am I disturbing you?"

"Oh no."

"Do you have a few minutes?"

"Do you want to come over?"

"Oh no. I just want to talk to you. About our lunch yesterday. You said something, and I can't remember what it was. I have a feeling it's important, and it's been nagging at me, and I can't for the life of me remember it."

"What was it?"

He broke up: a great blast of raucous laughter. Finally he spluttered. "If I knew, I wouldn't be calling, would I? What did we talk about?"

She wasn't offended by his laughter. "Talk about?" she said. "Let's see . . . I told you about my window boxes, and you told me about your backyard. And then you spoke about your wife's illness, and then we talked about my girls. Going out, the manager tried to pick up the check, and you wouldn't let him. On the way home you told me about the assistant chef who was robbing him."

"No, no," he said impatiently. "It must have been something to do with the case. Did we discuss the case while we were eating?"

"Nooo . . ." she said doubtfully. "After we finished coffee you said we'd come back to my place and you'd go over the cards. Oh yes. You asked if I had finished entering all the reports on the cards, and I said I had."

"And that's all?"

"Yes. Edward, what is this— No, wait a minute. I was teasing you. I said something about the records from the computers just showing unsuccessful criminals, because if they were good at their jobs, they wouldn't have any record, and you laughed and said that was so."

He was silent a moment.

"Monica," he said finally.

"Yes, Edward?"

"I love you," he said, laughing and keeping it light.

"You mean *that's* what you wanted?"

"That's *exactly* what I wanted."

His erratic memory flashed back now, and he recalled talking to Detective Lieutenant Jeri Fernandez on the steps leading up to the second floor of the precinct house. That was when they were breaking up the precinct detective squads.

"What did you get?" Delaney asked.

"I drew a Safe, Loft, and Truck Division in midtown," Fernandez had said disgustedly.

Now Delaney called Police Information, identified himself, told the operator what he wanted: the telephone number of the new Safe, Loft and Truck Division in midtown Manhattan. He was shunted twice more—it took almost five minutes—but eventually he got the number and, carefully crossing his fingers, dialed and asked for Lieutenant Fernandez. His luck was in; the detective picked up the phone after eight rings.

"Lieutenant Fernandez."

"Captain Edward X. Delaney here."

There was a second of silence, then a jubilant, "Captain! Jesus Christ! This is great! How the hell are you, Captain?"

"Just fine, lieutenant. And you?"

"Up to my ears in shit. Captain, this new system just ain't working. I can tell you. It's a lot of crap. You think I know what's going on? I don' know what's going on. No one knows what's going on. We got guys in here from every precinct in town. They set us all down here, and we're supposed to know all about the garment business. Pilferage, hijacking, fraud, arson, safecracking, the mob—the whole bit. Captain, it's wicked. I tell you, it's *wicked!*"

"Take it easy," Delaney soothed. "Give it a little time. Maybe it'll work out."

"Work out my ass," Fernandez shouted. "Yesterday two of my boys caught a spade taking packages out of the back of a U.S. Mail parcel post truck. Can you imagine that? In broad daylight. It's parked at Thirty-fourth and Madison, and this nut is calmly dragging out two heavy packages and strolling off with them. The U.S. Mail!"

"Lieutenant," Delaney said patiently, "the reason I called, I need some help from you."

"Help?" Fernandez cried. "Jesus Christ, Captain, you name it you got it. You know that. What is it?"

"I remember your telling me, just before the precinct squad was broken up, that you had been working on your open files and sending them to the new detective districts, depending on the nature of the crime."

"That's right, Captain. Took us weeks to get cleaned out."

"Well, what about the garbage? You know—the beef sheets, reports on squeals, tips, diaries, and so forth?"

"All the shit? Most of it was thrung out. What could we do with it? We was sent all over the city, and maybe only one or two guys would be working in the Two-five-one. It was all past history anyway—right? So I told the boys to trash the whole lot and—"

"Well, thanks very much," Delaney said heavily. "I guess that—"

"—except for the last year," Fernandez kept talking, ignoring the Captain's interruption. "I figured the new stuff might mean something to somebody, so we kept the paper that came in the last year, but everything else was thrung out."

"Oh?" Delaney said, still alive. "What did you do with it?"

"It's down in the basement of the precinct house. You know when you go down the stairs and the locker room is off to your right and the detention cells on your left? Well, you go past the cells and past the drunk tank, then turn right. There's this hallway that leads to a flight of stairs and the back door."

"Yes, I remember that. We always closed off that hallway during inspections."

"Right. Well, along that hallway is the broom closet where they keep mops and pails and all that shit, and then farther on toward the back door there's this little storage room with a lot of crap in it. I think it used to be a torture chamber in the old days."

"Yes," Delaney laughed. "Probably was."

"Sure, Captain. The walls are thick and the room's got no windows, so who could hear the screams? Who knows how many crimes got solved in there—right? Anyways, that's where we dumped all the garbage files. But just for the last year. That any help?"

"A lot of help. Thank you very much, lieutenant."

"My pleasure, Captain. Listen, can I ask you a favor now?"

"Of course."

"It's a one-word favor: HELP! Captain, you got influence and a good rep. Get me out of here, will you? I'm dying here. I don't like the spot and I don't like the guys I'm with. I shuffle papers around all day like some kind of Manchurian idiot, and you think I know what I'm doing? I don' know my ass from my elbow. I want to get out on the street again. The street I know. Can you work it, Captain?"

"What do you want?"

"Assault-Homicide or Burglary," Fernandez said promptly. "I'll even take Narcotics. I know I can't hope for Vice; I ain't pretty enough."

"Well . . ." Delaney said slowly, "I can't promise you anything, but let me see what I can do. Maybe I can work something."

"That's good enough for me," Fernandez said cheerfully. "Many thanks, Captain."

"Thank *you*, lieutenant."

He hung up and stared at the telephone, thinking of what Fernandez had told him. It was a long shot, of course, but it shouldn't take more than a day, and it was better than resigning himself to one of those seven options on his list, most of which offered nothing but hard, grinding labor with no guarantees of success.

When Monica Gilbert had repeated her teasing remark about successful criminals having no record, he had to recognize its truth. But Monica wasn't aware that between a criminal's complete freedom and formal charges against him existed a half-world of documentation: of charges dismissed, of arrests never made because of lack of adequate evidence, of suits settled out of court, of complaints dropped because of dollar bribery or physical threats, of trials delayed or rejected simply because of the horrific backlog of court cases and the shortage of personnel.

But most of these judicial abortions had a history, a written record that existed *somewhere*. And part of it was in detectives' paperwork: the squeals and beef sheets and diaries and records of "Charge dropped," "Refused to press charges," "Agreed to make restitution," "Let off with warning,"—all the circumlocutions to indicate that the over-worked detective, using patient persuasion in most cases, with or without the approval of his superior officer, had kept a case off the court calendar.

Most judicial adjustments were of a minor nature, and a product of the investigating officer's experience and common sense. Two men in a bar, both liquored up, begin beating on each others' faces with their fists. The police are called. Each antagonist wants the other arrested on charges of assault. What is the cop to do? If he's smart, he gives both a tongue-lashing, threatens to arrest both for disturbing the peace, and sends them off in opposite directions. No pain, no strain, no paperwork with formal charges, warrants, time lost in court—an ache in the ass to everyone. And the judge would probably listen incredulously for all of five minutes and then throw both plaintiff and defendant out of his court.

But if the matter is a little more serious than a barroom squabble, if damage has been done to property or someone has suffered obvious injury, then the investigating officer might move more circumspectly. It can still be settled out of court, with the cop acting as judge and jury. It can be settled by voluntary withdrawal of charges, by immediate payment of money to the aggrieved party by the man who has wronged him, by mutual consent of both parties when threatened with more substantial charges by the investigating officer, or by a bribe to the cop.

This is "street justice," and for every case that comes to trial in a walnut-paneled courtroom, a hundred street trials are held every hour of every day in every city in the country, and the presiding magistrate is a cop—plainclothes detective or uniformed patrolman. And honest or venal, he is the kingpin of the whole ramshackle, tottering, ridiculous, working system of "street justice," and without him the already overclogged formal courts of the nation would be inundated, drowned in a sea of pettifoggery, and unable to function.

The conscientious investigating officer will or will not make a written report of the case, depending on his judgement of its importance. But if the investigating officer is a plainclothes detective, and if the case involves people of an obviously higher social status than sidewalk brawlers, and if formal charges have been made by *anyone,* and one or more visits to the precinct house have been made, then the detective will almost certainly make a written report of what happened, who did what, who said what, how much injury or damage resulted. Even if the confrontation simply dissolves—charges withdrawn, no warrants issued, no trial—the detective, sighing, fills out the forms, writes his report, and stuffs all the paper in the slush heap, to be thrown out when the file is overflowing.

Knowing all this, knowing how slim his chances were of finding anything meaningful in the detritus left behind by the Precinct's detective squad when it was disbanded, Delaney followed his cop's instinct and phoned Lt. Marty Dorfman at the 251st Precinct, next door.

Their preliminary conversation was friendly but cool. Delaney asked after the well-being of Dorfman's family, and the lieutenant inquired as to Mrs. Delaney's health. It was only when the Captain inquired about conditions in the Precinct that Dorfman's voice took on a tone of anguish and anger.

It developed that Operation Lombard was using the 251st Precinct house as command headquarters. Deputy Commissioner Broughton had taken over Lt. Dorfman's office, and his men were filling the second floor offices and bull pen formerly occupied by the Precinct detective squad. Dorfman himself was stuck at a desk in a corner of the sergeants' room.

He could have endured this ignominy, he suggested to Delaney, and even endured Broughton's slights that included ignoring him completely when they met in the hallway and commandeering the Precinct's vehicles without prior consultation with Dorfman. But what really rankled was that apparently residents of the Precinct were blaming him, Dorfman, personally for not finding the killer. In spite of what they read in the papers and saw on television about Operation Lombard, headed by Deputy Commissioner Broughton, they knew Dorfman was commander of their precinct, and they blamed him for failing to make their streets safe.

"I know," Delaney said sympathetically. "They feel it's your neighborhood and your responsibility."

"Oh yes," Dorfman sighed. "Well, I'm learning. Learning what you had to put up with. I guess it's good experience."

"It is," Delaney said definitely. "The best experience of all—being on the firing line. Are you going to take the exam for captain?"

"I don't know what to do. My wife says no. She wants me to get out, get into something else."

"Don't do that," Delaney said quickly. "Hang in there. A little while longer anyway. Things might change before you know it."

"Oh?" Dorfman asked, interested now, curious, but not wanting to pin Delaney down. "You think there may be changes?"

"Yes. Maybe sooner than you think. Don't make any decisions now. Wait. Just wait."

"All right, Captain. If you say so."

"Lieutenant, the reason I called—I want to come into the Precinct house around eight or nine tomorrow morning. I want to go down to that storage room in the basement. It's off the hallway to the back door. You know, when you pass the pens and drunk tank and turn right. I want to go through some old files stored in there. It's slush left by the detective squad. It'll probably take me all day, and I may remove some of the files. I want your permission."

There was silence, and Delaney thought the connection might have been cut.

"Hello? Hello?" he said.

"I'm still here," Dorfman said finally in a soft voice. "Yes, you have my permission. Thank you for calling first, Captain. You didn't have to do that."

"It's your precinct."

"So I've been learning. Captain . . ."

"What?"

"I think I know what you've been doing. Are you getting anywhere?"

"Nothing definite. Yet. Coming along."

"Will the files help?"

"Maybe."

"Take whatever you need."

"Thank you. If I meet you, just nod and pass by. Don't stop to talk. Broughton's men don't have to—"

"I understand."

"Dorfman . . ."

"Yes, Captain?"

"Don't stop studying for the captain's exam."

"All right. I won't."

"I know you'll do fine on the written, but on the oral they ask some tricky questions. One they ask every year, but it takes different forms. It goes something like this: You're a captain with a lieutenant, three sergeants, and maybe twenty or thirty men. There's this riot. Hippies or drunks off a Hudson River cruise or some kind of nutty mob. Maybe a hundred people hollering and breaking windows and raising hell. How do you handle it?"

There was silence. Then Dorfman said, not sure of himself, "I'd have the men form a wedge. Then, if I had a bullhorn, I'd tell the mob to disperse. If that didn't work, I'd tell the men to—"

"No," Delaney said. "That isn't the answer they want. The right answer is this: you turn to your lieutenant and say. 'Break 'em up.' Then you turn your back on the mob and walk away. It might not be the *right* way. You understand? But it's the right answer to the question. They want to make sure you know how to use command. Watch out for a question like that."

"Thank you, Captain," Dorfman said, and Delaney hoped they might be easing back into their earlier, closer relationship.

He thought it out carefully in his methodical way. He would wear his oldest suit, since the basement storeroom was sure to be dusty. It was probably adequately lighted with an overhead bulb, but just in case he would take along his flashlight.

Now, the room itself might be locked, and then he'd be forced to make a fuss until he found someone with the proper key. But he had never turned in his ring of master keys which, his predecessor had assured him, opened every door, cell and locker in the Precinct house. So he'd take his ring of keys along.

He didn't know how long it would take to go through the detectives' old files, but he judged it might be all day. He wouldn't want to go out to eat; the less chance of being seen by Broughton's men, or by Broughton himself, moving around the stairs and corridors, the better for everyone. So he would need sandwiches, two sandwiches, that he would ask Mary to make up for him in the morning, plus a thermos of black coffee. He would carry all this, plus the flashlight and keys in his briefcase, which would also hold the typed lists of the cards included in Monica Gilbert's file.

Anything else? Well, he should have some kind of cover story just in case, by bad luck, Broughton saw him, braced him, and wanted to know what the fuck he was up to. He would say, he decided, that he had just stopped by to reclaim some personal files from the basement storeroom. He would keep it as vague as possible; it might be enough to get by.

He awoke the next morning, resolutely trying not to hope, but attempting to treat this search as just another logical step that had to be taken, whether it yielded results or not. He ate an unusually large breakfast for him: tomato juice, two poached eggs on whole wheat toast, a side order of pork sausages, and two cups of black coffee.

While Mary was preparing his luncheon sandwiches and his thermos, he went into the study to call Barbara, to explain why he would be unable to see her that day. Thankfully, she was in an alert, cheery mood, and when he told her exactly what he planned to do, she approved immediately and made him promise to call her as soon as his search was completed, to report results.

His entry into the 251st Precinct house went easily, without incident. That intimidating woman, the blonde sergeant, was on the blotter when he walked in. She was leaning across the desk, talking to a black woman who was weeping. The sergeant looked up, recognized the Captain, and flapped him a half-salute. He waved in return and marched steadily ahead, carrying his briefcase like a salesman. He went down the worn wooden staircase and turned into the detention area.

The officer on duty—on limited duty since his right arm had been knifed open by an eleven-year-old on the shit—was tilted back against the wall in an ancient armchair. He was reading a late edition of the *Daily News*; Delaney could see the headline: MANIAC KILLER STILL ON LOOSE. The officer glanced up, recognized the Captain, and started to scramble to his feet. Delaney waved him down, ashamed of himself for not remembering the man's name.

"How you coming along?" he asked.

"Fine, Captain. It's healing real good. The doc said I should be mustering in a week or so."

"Glad to hear it. But don't hurry it; take all the time you need. I'm going to that storeroom in the back hallway. I've got some personal files there I want to get."

The officer nodded. He couldn't care less.

"I don't know how long it'll take, so if I'm not out by the time you leave, please tell your relief I'm back here."

"Okay, Captain."

He walked past the detention cells: six cells, four occupied. He didn't look to the right or to the left. Someone whispered to him; someone screamed. There were three men in the drunk tank lying in each others' filth and moaning. It wasn't the noise that bothered him, it was the smell; he had almost forgotten how bad it was: old urine, old shit, old blood, old vomit, old puss—90 years of human pain soaked into floors and walls. And coming through the miasma, like a knife thrust, the sharp, piercing carbolic odor that stung his nostrils and brought tears to his eyes.

The storeroom was locked, and it took him almost five minutes to find the right key on the big ring. And when the latch snapped open, he paused a few seconds and wondered why he hadn't turned that ring of keys over to Dorfman. Officially, they should be in the lieutenant's possession; it was his precinct.

He shoved the door open, found the wall switch, flipped on the overhead light, closed the door behind him and looked around. It was as bad as he had expected.

The precinct house had opened for business in 1882 and, inspecting the storeroom, Delaney guessed that every desk blotter for every one of those 90 years was carefully retained and never looked at again. They were stacked to the ceiling. An historian might do wonders with them. The Captain was amused by the thought: "A Criminal History of Our Times"—reconstructing the way our great-grandparents, grandparents, and parents lived by analyzing the evidence in those yellowing police blotters. It could be done, he thought, and it might prove revealing. Not the usual history, not the theories of philosophers, discoveries of scientists, programs of statesmen; not wars, explorations, revolutions, and new religions.

Just the petty crimes, misdemeanors, and felonies of a weak and sinning humanity. It was all there: the mayhem, frauds, child-beating, theft, drug abuse, alcoholism, kidnapping, rape, murder. It would make a fascinating record, and he wished an historian would attempt it. Something might be learned from it.

He took off his coat, hat and jacket and laid them on the least dusty crate he could find. The windowless room had a single radiator that clanked and hissed constantly, spitting out steam and water. Delaney opened the door a few inches. The air that came in was carbolic-laden, but a little cooler.

He put on his glasses and looked at what else the room held.

Mostly cardboard cartons, overflowing with files and papers.

The cartons bore on their sides the names of whiskies, rums, gins, etc., and he knew most of them came from the liquor store on First Avenue, around the corner. There were also rough wooden cases filled with what appeared to be physical evidence of long forgotten crimes: a knitted woolen glove, moth-eaten; a rusted cleaver with a broken handle; a stained upper denture; a child's Raggedy-Ann doll; a woman's patent leather purse, yawning empty; a broken crutch; a window-weight with black stains; a man's fedora with one bullet hole through the crown; sealed and bulging envelopes with information jotted on their sides; a bloodied wig; a corset ripped down with a knife thrust.

Delaney turned away and found himself facing a carton of theatrical costumes. He fumbled through them and thought they might have been left from some remote Christmas pageant performed in the Precinct house by neighborhood children, the costumes provided by the cops. But beneath the cheap cotton—sleazy to begin with and now rotting away—he found an ancient Colt revolver, at least 12 inches long, rusted past all usefulness, and to the trigger guard was attached a winkled tag with the faded inscription: "Malone's gun. July 16, 1902." Malone. Who had he been— cop or killer? It made no difference now.

He finally found what he was looking for: two stacks of relatively fresh cardboard cartons containing the last year's garbage from the detective squad's files. Each carton held folders in alphabetical order, but the cartons themselves were stacked helter-skelter, and Delaney spent almost an hour organizing them. It was then past noon, and he sat down on a nailed wooden crate (painted on the top: "Hold for Capt. Kelly") and ate one of his sandwiches, spiced salami and thickly sliced Spanish onion on rye bread thinly spread with mayonnaise—which he dearly loved—and drank half his thermos of coffee.

Then he got out his list of names from Monica's cards and went to work. He had to compare list to files, and had to work standing up or kneeling or crouching. Occasionally he would spread his arms wide and bend back his spine. Twice he stepped out into the hallway and walked up and down a few minutes, trying to shake the kinks out of his legs.

He felt no elation whatsoever when he found the first file labeled with a name on his list. The address checked out. He merely put the file aside and went on with the job. It was lumbering work, like a stake-out or a 24-hour shadow. You didn't stop to question what you were doing; it was just something that had to be done, usually to prove the "no" rather than discover the "yes."

When he finished the last file in the last cardboard carton, it was nearly 7:00 p.m. He had long ago finished his second sandwich and the remainder of his coffee. But he wasn't hungry; just thirsty. His nostrils and throat seemed caked with dust, but the radiator had never stopped clanking, hissing steam and water, and his shirt was plastered to armpits, chest, and back; he could smell his own sweat.

He packed carefully. Three files. Three of the people on Monica's cards had been involved in cases of "street justice." He tucked the files carefully in his brief case, added the empty thermos and wax paper wrappings from the sandwiches. He pulled on jacket and overcoat, put on his hat, took a final look around. If he ever came back to the Two-five-one, the first thing he'd do was have this room cleaned up. He turned off the light, stepped out into the hallway, made certain the spring lock clicked. He walked past the drunk tank and detention cells. Two of the drunks were gone, and only one cell was occupied. There was no uniformed officer about, but he might have gone upstairs for coffee. Delaney walked up the rickety staircase and was surprised to feel his knees tremble from tiredness. Lt. Dorfman was standing near the outside door, talking to a civilian Delaney didn't recognize. When he passed, the Captain nodded, smiling slightly, and Dorfman nodded in return, not interrupting his conversation.

In his bedroom, Delaney stripped down to his skin as quickly as he could, leaving all his soiled clothing in a damp heap on the floor. He soaked in a hot shower and soaped his hands three times but was unable to get the grime out of the pores or from under his nails. Then he found a can of kitchen cleanser in the cabinet under the sink; that did the trick. After he dried, he used cologne and powder, but he still smelled the carbolic.

He dressed in pajamas, robe, slippers, then glanced at the bedside clock. Getting on . . . He decided to call Barbara, rather than wait until he went through the retrieved files. But when she answered the phone, he realized that she had drifted away. Perhaps it was sleep or the medication, perhaps the illness; he just didn't know. She kept repeating his name. Laughing: "Edward!" Questioning: "Edward?" Demanding: "Edward!" Loving: "Ed-d-w-ward . . ."

Finally he said, "Good-night, dear," hung up, took a deep breath, tried not to weep. In his study, moving mechanically, he mixed a heavy rye highball, then unpacked his briefcase. Flashlight back to the drawer in the kitchen cabinet. Crumpled wax paper into the garbage can. Thermos rinsed out, then filled with hot water and left to soak on the sink sideboard. Ring of keys into his top desk drawer, to be handed over to Lt. Dorfman. Delaney knew now, in some realization, he would never again command the Two-five-one.

And the three files stacked neatly in the center of his desk blotter. He got a square of paper towel, wiped off their surface dust, stacked them neatly again. He washed his hands, sat down behind his desk, put on his glasses. Then he just sat there and slowly, slowly sipped away half his strong highball, staring at the files. Then he leaned forward, began to read.

The first case was amusing, and the officer who had handled the beef, Detective second grade Samuel Berkowitz, had recognized it from the start; his tart, ironic reports understated and heightened the humor. A man named Timothy J. Lester had been apprehended shortly after throwing an empty garbage can through the plate glass window of a Madison Avenue shop that specialized in maternity clothes. The shop was coyly called "Expectin'." Berkowitz reported the suspect was "apparently intoxicated on Jamesons"—a reasonable deduction since next door to "Expectin'" was a tavern called "Ye Olde Emerald Isle." Detective Berkowitz had also determined that Mr. Lester, although only 34, was the father of seven children and had, that very night, been informed by his wife that it would soon be eight. Timothy had immediately departed for "Ye Olde Emerald Isle" to celebrate, had celebrated, and on his way home had paused to toss the garbage can through the window of "Expectin'." Since Lester was, in Berkowitz' words, "apparently an exemplary family man," since he had a good job as a typesetter, since he offered to make complete restitution for the shattered window, Detective Berkowitz felt the cause of justice would be best served if Mr. Lester was allowed to pay for his mischievous damage and all charges dropped.

Captain Edward X. Delaney, reading this file and smiling, concurred with the judgment of Detective Berkowitz.

The second file was short and sad. It concerned one of the few women included on Monica Gilbert's list. She was 38 years old and lived in a smart apartment on Second Avenue near 85th Street. She had taken in a room-mate, a young woman of 22. All apparently went well for almost a year. Then the younger woman met a man, they became engaged, and she announced the news to her roommate and was congratulated. She returned home the following evening to discover the older woman had slashed all her clothes to thin ribbons with a razor blade and had trashed all her personal belongings. She called the police. But after consultation with her fiancé, she refused to press charges, moved out of the apartment, and the case was dropped.

The third file, thicker, dealt with Daniel G. Blank, divorced, living alone on East 83rd Street. He had been involved in two separate incidents about six months apart. In the first he had originally been charged with simple assault in an altercation involving a fellow tenant of his apartment house who apparently had been beating his own dog. Blank had intervened, and the dog owner had suffered a broken arm. There had been a witness, Charles Lipsky, a doorman, who signed a statement that Blank had merely pushed the other man after being struck with a folded newspaper. The man had stumbled off the curb and fell, breaking his arm. Charges were eventually dropped.

The second incident was more serious. Blank had been in a bar, The Parrot on Third Avenue, and was allegedly solicited by a middle-aged homosexual. Blank, according to testimony of witnesses, thereupon hit the man twice, breaking his jaw with the second blow. While the man was helpless on the floor, Blank had kicked him repeatedly in the groin until he was dragged away and the police were called. The homosexual refused to sign a complaint, Blank's lawyer appeared, and apparently the injured man signed a release.

The same officer, Detective first grade Ronald A. Blankenship, had handled both beefs. His language, in his reports, was official, clear, concise, colorless, and implied no judgments.

Delaney read through the file slowly, then read it through again. He got up to mix another rye highball and then, standing at his desk, read it through a third time. He took off his glasses, began to pace about his chilly study, carrying his drink, sipping occasionally. Once or twice he came back behind his desk to stare at the Daniel Blank manila folder, but he didn't open the file again.

Several years previously, when he had been a Detective lieutenant, he had contributed two articles to the Department's monthly magazine. The first monograph was entitled "Common Sense and the New Detective." It was a very basic, down-to-earth analysis of how the great majority of crimes are solved: good judgment based on physical evidence and experience—the ability to put two and two together and come up with four, not three or five. It was hardly a revolutionary argument.

The second article, entitled "Hunch, Instinct, and the New Detective," occasioned a little more comment. Delaney argued that in spite of the great advances in laboratory analysis, the forensic sciences, computerized records and probability percentages, the new detective disregarded his hunches and instinct at his peril, for frequently they were not a sudden brainstorm, but were the result of observation of physical evidence and experience of which the detective might not even be consciously aware. But stewing in his subsconscious, a rational and reasonable conclusion was reached, thrust into his conscious thought, and should never be allowed to wither unexplored, since it was, in many cases, as logical and empirical as common sense.

(Delaney had prepared a third article for the series. This dealt with his theory of an "adversary concept" in which he explored the Dostoevskian relationship between detective and criminal. It was an abstruse examination of the "sensual" (Delaney's word) affinity between hunter and hunted, of how, in certain cases, it was necessary for the detective to penetrate and assume the physical body, spirit, and soul of the criminal in order to bring him to justice. This treatise, at Barbara's gentle persuasion, Delaney did not submit for publication.)

Now, thinking over the facts included in the Daniel Blank file, Captain Delaney acknowledged he was halfway between common sense and instinct. Intelligence and experience convinced him that the man involved in the two incidents described was worth investigating further.

The salient point in the second incident was the raw savagery Blank had displayed. A normal man—well, an average man—might have handled the homosexual's first advance by merely smiling and shaking his head, or moving down the bar, or even leaving The Parrot. The violence displayed by Blank was excessive. Protesting too much?

The first incident—the case of the injured dog-owner—might not be as innocent as it appeared in Detective Blankenship's report. It was true that the witness, the doorman—what was his name? Delaney looked it up. Charles Lipsky—it was true that Lipsky stated that Blank had been struck with a folded newspaper before pushing his assailant. But witnesses can be bribed; it was hardly an uncommon occurrence. Even if Lipsky had told the truth, Delaney was amazed at how this incident fit into a pattern he had learned from experience; men prone to violence, men too ready to use their fists, their feet, even their teeth, somehow became involved in situations that were obviously not their fault, and yet resulted in injury or death to their antagonist.

Delaney called Monica Gilbert.

"Monica? Edward. I'm sorry to disturb you at this hour. I hope I didn't wake the children."

"Oh no. That takes more than a phone ring. What is it?"

"Would you mind looking at your card file and see if you have anything on a man named Blank. Daniel G. He lives on East Eighty-third Street."

"Just a minute."

He waited patiently. He heard her moving about. Then she was back on the phone.

"Blank, Daniel G.," she read. "Arrested twice for speeding. Guilty and fined. Do you want the make of car and license number?"

"Please."

He took notes as she gave him the information.

"Thank you," he said.

"Edward, is it—anything?"

"I don't know. I really don't. It's interesting. That's about all I can say right now. I'll know more tomorrow."

"Will you call?"

"Yes, if you want me to."

"Please do."

"All right. Sleep well."

"Thank you. You, too."

Two arrests for speeding. Not in itself significant, but within the pattern. The choice of car was similarly meaningful. Delaney was glad Daniel Blank didn't drive a Volkswagen.

He called Thomas Handry at the newspaper office. He had left for home. He called him at home. No answer. He called Detective Lieutenant Jeri

Fernandez at his office. Fernandez had gone home. Delaney felt a sudden surge of anger at these people who couldn't be reached when he needed them. Then he realized how childish that was, and calmed down.

He found Fernandez' home phone number in the back of his pocket notebook where he had carefully listed home phone numbers of all sergeants and higher ranks in the 251st Precinct. Fernandez lived in Brooklyn. A child answered the phone.

"Hello?"

"Is Detective Fernandez there, please?"

"Just a minute. Daddy, it's for you!" the child screamed.

In the background Delaney could hear music, shouts, loud laughter, the thump of heavy dancing. Finally Fernandez came to the phone.

"Hello?"

"Captain Edward X. Delaney here."

"Oh. Howrya, Captain?"

"Lieutenant, I'm sorry to disturb you at this hour. Sounds like you're having a party."

"Yeah, it's the wife's birthday, and we have some people in."

"I won't keep you long. Lieutenant, when you were at the Two-five-one, you had a dick one named Blankenship. Right?"

"Sure. Ronnie. Good man."

"What did he look like? I can't seem to remember him."

"Sure you do, Captain. A real tall guy. About six-three or four. Skinny as a rail. We called him 'Scarecrow.' Remember now?"

"Oh yes. A big Adam's apple?"

"That's the guy."

"What happened to him?"

"He drew an Assault-Homicide Squad over on the West Side. I think it's up in the Sixties-Seventies-Eighties—around there. I know it takes in the Twentieth Precinct. Listen, I got his home phone number somewhere. Would that help?"

"It certainly would."

"Hang on a minute."

It was almost five minutes, but eventually Fernandez was back with Blankenship's phone number. Delaney thanked him. Fernandez seemed to want to talk more, but the Captain cut him short.

He dialed Blankenship's home phone. A woman answered. In the background Delaney could hear an infant wailing loudly.

"Hello?"

"Mrs. Blankenship?"

"Yes. Who is this?"

"My name is Delaney, Captain Edward X. Delaney, New York Police Depart—"

"What's happened? What's happened to Ronnie? Is he all right? Is he hurt? What—"

"No, no, Mrs. Blankenship," he said hurriedly, soothing her fears. "As far as I know, your husband is perfectly all right."

He could sympathize with her fright. Every cop's wife lived with that dread. But she should have known that if anything had happened to her husband, she wouldn't learn of it from a phone call. Two men from the Department would ring her bell. She would open the door and they would be standing there, faces twisted and guilty, and she would know.

"I'm trying to contact your husband to get some information, Mrs. Blankenship," he went on, speaking slowly and distinctly. This was obviously not an alert woman. "I gather he's not at home. Is he working?"

"Yes. He's on nights for the next two weeks."

"Could you give me his office phone number, please?"

"All right. Just a minute."

He could also have told her not to give out any information about her husband to a stranger who calls in the middle of the night and claims he's a captain in the NYPD. But what would be the use? Her husband had probably told her that a dozen times. A dull woman.

He got the number and thanked her. It was now getting on toward eleven o'clock; he wondered if he should try or let it go till morning. He dialed the number. Blankenship had checked in all right, but he wasn't on the premises. Delaney left his number, without identifying himself, and asked if the operator would have him call back.

"Please tell him it's important," he said.

"'Important'?" the male operator said. "How do you spell that, Mr. Important?"

Delaney hung up. A wise-ass. The Captain would remember. The Department moved in involved and sometimes mysterious ways. One day that phone operator in that detective division might be under Delaney's command. He'd remember the high, lilting, laughing voice. It was stupid to act like that.

He started a new file, headed BLANK, Daniel G., and in it he stowed the Blankenship reports, his notes on Blank's record of arrests for speeding, the make of car he drove and his license number. Then he went to the Manhattan telephone directory and looked up Blank, Daniel G. There was only one listing of that name, on East 83rd Street. He made a note of the phone number and added that to his file.

He was mixing a fresh rye highball—was it his second or third?—when the phone rang. He put down the glass and bottle carefully, then ran for the phone, catching it midway through the third ring.

"Hello?"

"This is Blankenship. Who's this?"

"Captain Edward X. Delaney here. I was—"

"Captain! Good to hear from you. How are you, sir?"

"Fine, Ronnie. And you?" Delaney had never before called the man by his first name, hadn't even known what it was before his call to Fernandez. In fact, he couldn't remember ever speaking to Blankenship personally, but he wanted to set a tone.

"Okay, Captain. Getting along."

"How do you like the new assignment? Tell me, do you think this reorganization is going to work?"

"Captain, it's great!" Blankenship said enthusiastically. "They should have done it years ago. Now I can spend some time on important stuff and forget the little squeals. Our arrest rate is up, and morale is real good. The case load is way down, and we've got time to think."

The man sounded intelligent. His voice was pleasingly deep, vibrant, resonant. Delaney remembered that big, jutting Adam's apple.

"Glad to hear it," he said. "Listen, I'm on leave of absence, but something came up and I agreed to help out on it."

He let it go at that, keeping it vague, waiting to see if Blankenship would pick up on it and ask questions. But the detective hesitated a moment, then said, "Sure, Captain."

"It concerns a man named Daniel Blank, in the Two-five-one. He was involved in two beefs last year. You handled both of them. I have your reports. Good reports. Very complete."

"What was that name again?"

"Blank, B-l-a-n-k, Daniel G. He lives on East Eighty-third Street. The first thing was a pushing match with a guy who was allegedly beating his dog. The second—"

"Oh sure," Blankenship interrupted. "I remember. Probably because his name is Blank and mine is Blankenship. At the time I thought it was funny I should be handling him. Two beefs in six months. In the second, he kicked the shit out of a faggot. Right?"

"Right."

"But the victim wouldn't sign a complaint. What do you want to know, Captain?"

"About Blank. You saw him?"

"Sure. Twice."

"What do you remember about him?"

Blankenship recited: Blank, Daniel G. White, male, approximately six feet or slightly taller, about—"

"Wait, wait a minute," Delaney said hastily. "I'm taking notes. Go a little slower."

"Okay, Captain. You got the height?"

"Six feet or a little over."

"Right. Weight about one seventy-five. Slim build but good shoulders. Good physical condition from what I could see. No obvious physical scars or infirmities. Dark complexion. Sunburned, I'd say. Long face. Sort of Chinese-looking. Let's see—anything else?"

"How was he dressed?" Delaney asked, admiring the man's observation and memory.

"Dark suits," Blankenship said promptly. "Nothing flashy, but well-cut and expensive. Some funny things I remember. Gold link chain on his wrist watch. Like a bracelet. The first time I saw him I think it was his own hair. The second time I swear it was a rug. The second time he was wearing a real crazy shirt open to his *pipik*, with some kind of necklace. You know—hippie stuff."

"Accent?" Delaney nodded.

"Accent?" Blankenship repeated, thought a moment, then said, "Not a native New Yorker. Mid-western, I'd guess. Sorry I can't be more specific."

"You're doing great," Delaney assured him, elated. "You think he's strong?"

"Strong? I'd guess so. Any guy who can break another man's jaw with a punch has got to be strong. Right?"

"Right. What was your personal reaction to him? Flitty?"

"Could be, Captain. When they punish an obvious faggot like that, it's got to mean something. Right?"

"Right."

"I wanted to charge him, but the victim refused to sign anything. So what could I do?"

"I understand," Delaney said. "Believe me, this has nothing to do with that beef."

"I believe you, Captain."

"Do you know where he works, what he does for a living?"

"It's not in my reports?"

"No, it isn't."

"Sorry about that. But you've got his lawyer's name and address, haven't you?"

"Oh yes, I have that. I'll get it from him," Delaney lied. It was Blankenship's first mistake, and a small one. No use going to the lawyer;

he'd simply refuse to divulge the information, then surely mention to Blank that the police had been around asking questions.

"That just about covers it," Delaney said. "Thanks very much for your help. What are you working on now?"

"It's a beaut, Captain," Blankenship said in his enthusiastic way. "This old dame got knocked off in her apartment. Strangled. No signs of forcible entry. And as far as we can tell, nothing stolen. A neighbor smelled it; that's how we got on to it. A poor little apartment, but it turns out the old dame was loaded."

"Who inherits?"

"A nephew. But we checked him out six ways from the middle. He's got an alibi that holds up. He was down in Florida for two weeks. We checked. He really was there. Every minute."

"Check his bank account, back for about six months or a year. See if there was a heavy withdrawal—maybe five or ten big ones."

"You mean he hired—? Son of a bitch!" Blankenship said bitterly. "Why didn't I think of that?"

"Stick around for twenty-five years," Delaney laughed. "You'll learn. Thanks again. If there's ever anything I can do for you, just let me know."

"I'll hold you to that, Captain," Blankenship said in his deep, throaty voice.

"You do that," Delaney said seriously.

After he hung up, he finished mixing his highball. He took a deep swallow, then grinned, grinned, grinned. He looked around at walls, ceiling, floor, furniture, and grinned at everything. It felt good. It had gone beyond his first article on common sense: the value of personally observed evidence and experience. It had even gone beyond the second article that extolled the value of hunch and instinct. Now he was in the realm of the third, unpublished article which Barbara had convinced him should never be printed. Quite rightly, too. Because in that monograph, exploring the nature of the detective-criminal relationship—his theory of the adversary concept—he had rashly dwelt on the "joy" of the successful detective.

That was what he felt now—*joy!* He worked at his new file—BLANK, Daniel G.—adding to it everything Detective Blankenship had reported, and not a thing, not one single thing, varied in any significant aspect from his original "The Suspect" outline. He gained surety as he amplified his notes. It was beautiful, beautiful, all so beautiful. And, just as he had written in his unpublished article, there was sensuous pleasure—was it sexual?—in the chase. So intent was he on his rapid writing, his reports, his new, beautiful file, that the phone rang five times before he picked it up. As a matter of fact, he kept writing as he answered it.

"Captain Edward X. Delaney here."

"Dorfman. There's been another one."

"Captain—*what?*"

"Lieutenant Dorfman, Captain. Sorry to wake you up. There's been another killing. Same type, with extras."

"Where?"

"Eighty-fifth. Between First and York."

"A man?"

"Yes."

"Tall?"

"Tall? I'd guess five ten or eleven."

"Weight?"

There was silence, then Dorfman's dull voice: "I don't know what he weighed, Captain. Is it important?"

"Extras? You said 'Extras.' What extras?"

"He was struck at least three times. Maybe more. There are signs of a struggle. Christmas packages, three of them, thrown around. Scuff marks on the sidewalk. His coat was torn. Looks like he put up a fight."

"Identified?"

"A man named Feinberg. Albert Feinberg."

"Anything missing? Identification of any kind?"

"We don't know," Dorfman said wearily. "They're checking with his wife now. His wallet wasn't out like in the Lombard kill. We just don't know."

"All right," Delaney said softly. "Thank you for calling. Sounds like you could use some sleep, lieutenant."

"Yes, I could. If I could sleep."

"Where was it again?"

"Eighty-fifth, between First and York."

"Thank you. Good-night."

He looked at his desk calendar and counted carefully. It had been eleven days since the murder of Detective Kope. His research was proving out; the intervals between killings were becoming shorter and shorter.

He got out his Precinct map with the plastic overlay and, with a red grease pencil, carefully marked in the murder of Albert Feinberg, noting victim's name, date of killing, and place. The locations of the four murders formed a rough square on the map. On impulse, he used his grease pencil and a ruler to connect opposite corners of the square, making an X. It intersected at 84th Street and Second Avenue, right in the middle of the crossing of the two streets. He checked Daniel Blank's address. It was on 83rd Street, about a block and a half away. The map didn't say yes and it didn't say no.

He was staring the map, nodding, and awoke fifteen minutes later, startled, shocked that he had been sleeping. He pulled himself to his feet, drained the watery remains of his final highball, and made his rounds, checking window locks and outside doors.

Then the bed, groaning with weariness. What he really wanted to do . . . what he wanted to do . . . so foolish . . . was to go to Daniel Blank . . . go to him right now . . . introduce himself and say, "Tell me all about it."

Yes, that was foolish . . . idiotic . . . but he was sure . . . well, maybe not sure, but it was a chance, and the best . . . and just before he fell asleep he acknowledged, with a sad smile, that all this shitty thinking about patterns and percentages and psychological profile was just that—a lot of shit. He was following up on Daniel Blank because he had no other lead. It was as simple and obvious as that. Occam's Razor. So he fell asleep.

4

HIS BEDSIDE alarm went off at 8:00 a.m. He slapped it silent, swung his legs out from under the blankets, donned his glasses, consulted a slip of paper he had left under the phone. He called Thomas Handry at home. The phone rang eight times. He was about to give up when Handry answered.

"Hello?" he asked sleepily.

"Captain Edward X. Delaney here. Did I wake you up?"

"Why no," Handry yawned. "I've been up for hours. Jogged around the reservoir, wrote two deathless sonnets, and seduced my landlady. All right, what do you want, Captain?"

"Got a pencil handy?"

"A minute . . . okay, what is it?"

"I want you to check a man in your morgue file."

"Who is he?"

"Blank, Daniel G. That last name is Blank, B-l-a-n-k."

"Why should he be in our morgue?"

"I don't know why. It's just a chance."

"Well, what has he done? I mean, has he been in the news for any reason?"

"Not to my knowledge."

"Then why the hell should we have him in the morgue?"

"I told you," Delaney said patiently, "it's just a chance, but I've got to cover every possibility."

"Oh, Jesus. All right. I'll try. I'll call you around ten, either way."

"No, don't do that," the Captain said quickly. "I may be out. I'll call you at the paper around ten."

Handry grunted and hung up.

Afer breakfast he went in to the study. He wanted to check the dates of the four murders and the intervals between them. Lombard to Gilbert: 22 days. Gilbert to Kope: 17 days. Kope to Feinberg: 11 days. By projection, the next murder should occur during the week between after Christmas and New Year's Day, and probably a few days after Christmas. He sat suddenly upright. Christmas! Oh God.

He called Barbara immediately. She reported she was feeling well, had had a good night's sleep, and ate all her breakfast. She always said that.

"Listen," he said breathlessly, "it's about Christmas . . . I'm sorry, dear. I forgot all about gifts and cards. What are we to do?"

She laughed. "I knew you were too busy. I've mailed things to the children. I saw ads in the newspapers and ordered by phone. Liza and John are getting a nice crystal ice bucket from Tiffany's, and I sent Eddie a terribly expensive sweater from Saks. How does that sound?"

"You're a wonder," he told her.

"So you keep saying," she teased, "but do you *really* mean it? Give Mary some money, as usual, and maybe you can get her something personal, just some little thing, like a scarf or handkerchief or something like that. And put the check in the package."

"All right. What about the cards?"

"Well, we have some left over from last year—about twenty, I think—and they're in the bottom drawer of the secretary in the living room. Now if you buy another three boxes, I'm sure it'll be enough. Are you coming over today?"

"Yes. Definitely. At noon."

"Well, bring the cards and the list. You know where the list is, don't you?"

"Bottom drawer of the secretary in the living room."

"Detective!" she giggled. "Yes, that's where it is. Bring the list and cards over at noon. I feel very good today. I'll start writing them. I won't try to do them all today, but I should have them finished up in two or three days, and they'll get there in time."

"Stamps?"

"Yes, I'll need stamps. Get a roll of a hundred. A roll is easier to handle. I make such a mess of a sheet. Oh Edward, I'm sorry . . . I forgot to ask. Did you find anything in the old files?"

"I'll tell you all about it when I see you at noon."

"Does it look good?"

"Well . . . maybe."

She was silent, then sighed, "I hope so,"she said. "Oh, how I hope so."

"I do, too. Listen dear . . . what would you like for Christmas?"

"Do I have a choice?" she laughed. "I know what I'm going to get—perfume from any drugstore you find that's open on Christmas Eve."

He laughed too. She was right.

He hung up and glanced at his watch. It was a little past 9:00 a.m., later than he wanted it to be. He dug hurriedly through his pack of business cards and found the one he was looking for: Arthur K. Ames. Automobile Insurance.

Blank's apartment house occupied an entire block on East 83rd Street. Delaney was familiar with the building and, standing across the street, looking up, thought again of how institutional it looked. All steel and glass. A hospital or a research center, not a place to live in. But people did, and he could imagine what the rents must be.

As he had hoped, men and women were still leaving for work. Two doormen were constantly running down the driveway to flag cabs and, even as he watched, a garage attendant brought a Lincoln Continental to the entrance, hopped out and ran back to the underground garage to drive up another tenant's car.

Delaney walked resolutely up the driveway, turned right and walked down a short flight of steps to the underground garage. A light blue Jaguar came roaring by him, the garage man at the wheel. Delaney waited patiently at the entrance until the black attendant came trotting back.

"Good morning," he said proffering his business card. "My name is Ames, of Cross-Country Insurance."

The attendant glanced at the card. "You picked a bad time to sell insurance, man."

"No, no," Delaney said quickly, smiling. "I'm not selling anything. One of the cars we cover was involved in an accident with a nineteen-seventy-one Chevy Corvette. The Corvette took off. The car we cover was trashed. The driver's in the hospital. Happened over on Third Avenue. We think the Corvette might be from the neighborhood, so I'm checking all the garages around here. Just routine."

"A nineteen-seventy-one Corvette?"

"Yes."

"What color?"

"Probably dark blue or black."

"When did this happen?"

"Couple of days ago."

"We got one Corvette. Mr. Blank. But it couldn't be him. He hasn't had his car out in weeks."

"The police found glass at the scene and pieces of fiberglass from the left front fender."

"I'm telling you it couldn't be Mr. Blank's Corvette. There's not a scratch on it."

"Mind if I take a look?"

"Help yourself," the man shrugged. "It's back there in the far corner, behind the white Caddy."

"Thank you."

The man took a phone call, hopped into a Ford station wagon, began to back out into the center of the garage so he could turn around. He was busy, which was why Delaney had picked this time. He walked slowly over to the black Corvette. The license number was Blank's.

The door was unlocked. He opened it and looked in, sniffing. A musty, closed-window smell. There was an ice-scraper for the windshield, a can of defogger, a dusty rag, a pair of worn driving gloves. Between the two seats was tucked a gasoline station map that had been handled, unfolded and refolded several times. Delaney opened it far enough to look. New York State. With a route marked on it in heavy black pencil: from East 83rd Street, across town, up the West Side Highway to the George Washington Bridge, across to New Jersey, up through Mahwah into New York again, then north to the Catskill Mountains, ending at a town called Chilton. He reshuffled the map, put it back where he found it.

He closed the car door gently and started out. He met the attendant coming back.

"It sure wasn't that car," he smiled.

"I told you that, man."

Delaney wondered if the attendant would mention the incident to Blank. He thought it likely, and he tried to guess what Blank's reaction would be. It wouldn't spook him but, if he was guilty, it might start him thinking. There was an idea there, Delaney acknowledged, but it wasn't time for it . . . yet.

Back in his study, he looked up Chilton in his world atlas. All it said was "Chilton, N.Y. Pop.: 3,146." He made a note about Chilton and added it to the Daniel Blank file. He looked at his watch. It wasn't quite ten, but close enough. He called Handry at his office.

"Captain? Sorry. No soap."

"Well . . . It was a long shot. Thank you very much for—"

"Hey, wait a minute. You give up too easily. We got other files of people. For instance, the sports desk keeps a file of living personalities and so does the theatre and arts section. Could your boy be in either?"

"Maybe in the sports file, but I doubt it."

"Well, can you tell me *anything* about him?"

"Not much. He lives in an expensive apartment house and drives an expensive car, so he must be loaded."

"Thanks a lot," Handry sighed. "Okay, I'll see what I can do. If I have something, I'll call you. If you don't hear from me, you'll know I didn't turn up a thing. Okay?"

"Yes. Sure. Fine," Delaney said heavily, feeling this was just a polite kiss-off.

He got over to the hospital as Barbara's noon meal was being served and he watched, beaming, as she ate almost all of it, feeding herself. She really was getting better, he told himself happily. Then he showed her the Christmas cards he had purchased, in three different price ranges; the most expensive for their "important" friends and acquaintances, the least expensive for—well, for people. And the twenty cards left over from last year, the list, the stamps.

Then he told her about Daniel Blank, stalking about the room, making wide gestures. He told her the man's history, what he had been able to dig up, what he suspected.

"What do you think?" he asked finally, eager for her opinion.

"Yes," she said thoughtfully. "Maybe. But you've really got nothing, Edward. You know that."

"Of course."

"Nothing definite. But certainly worth following up. I'd feel a lot better if you could tie him up with an ice ax purchase."

"I would too. But right now he's all I've got."

"Where do you go from here?"

"Where? Checking out everything. Charles Lipsky. The Parrot, where he had that fight. Trying to find out who he is and what he is. Listen, dear, I won't be over this evening. Too much to do. All right?"

"Of course," she said. "Are you sticking to your diet?"

"Sure," he said, patting his stomach. "I'm up only three pounds this week."

They laughed, and he kissed her on the lips before he left. Then they kissed again. Soft, clinging, wanting kisses.

He clumped down to the lobby, dug out his pocket notebook, looked up the number. Then he called Calvin Case from the lobby booth.

"How you coming?"

"All right," Case said. "I'm still working on the general mountaineering equipment sales checks, pulling those in the Two-five-one Precinct."

Delaney was amused at Case's "Two-five-one Precinct." His amateur was talking officialese.

"Am I doing any good?" Case wanted to know.

"You are," Delaney assured him. "I've got a lead. Name is Daniel Blank. Know him?"

"What's it?"

"Blank. B-l-a-n-k. Daniel G. Ever hear of him?"

"Is he a climber?"

"I don't know. Could be."

"Hey, Captain, there're two hundred thousand climbers in the country and more every year. No, I don't know any Daniel G. Blank. What does the G. stand for?"

"Gideon. All right, let me try this one on you: Ever hear of Chilton? It's a town in New York."

"I know. Up in the Catskills. Sleepy little place."

"Would a mountain climber go there?"

"Sure. Not Chilton itself, but about two miles out of town is a state park. A small one, but nice. Benches, tables, barbecues—crap like that."

"What about climbing?"

"Mostly for hiking. There are some nice outcrops. There's one good climb, a monolith. Devil's Needle. It's a chimney climb. As a matter of fact, I left two pitons up there to help whoever came after me to crawl out onto the top. I used to go up there to work out."

"Is it an easy climb?"

"Easy? Well . . . it's not for beginners. I'd say an intermediate climb. If you know what you're doing, it's easy. Does that help?"

"At this point everything helps."

Back home, he added the information Calvin Case had given him about Chilton and the Devil's Needle to the Daniel Blank file. Then he checked the address of The Parrot in Blankenship's report. He went through his pack of business cards found one that read: "Ward M. Miller. Private Investigations. Discreet—Reliable—Satisfaction Guaranteed." He began to plan his cover story.

He was still thinking it out an hour later, so deeply engrossed with the deception he was plotting that the phone must have rung several times without his being aware of it. Then Mary, who had picked up the hall extension, came in to tell him Mr. Handry was on the phone.

"Got him," Handry said.

"What?"

"I found him. Your Daniel G. Blank."

"Jesus Christ!" Delaney said excitedly. "Where?"

Handry laughed. "Our business-finance keeps a personality file, mostly on executives. They get tons of press releases and public relations reports every year. You know, Joe Blow has been promoted from vice president to executive vice president, or Harry Hardass has been hired as sales manager at Wee Tots Bootery, or some such shit. Usually it's a one-page release with a small photo, a head-and-shoulders-shot. You know what the business desk calls that stuff?"

"What?"

"The 'Fink File.' And if you got a look at those photos, you'd understand why. You wouldn't believe! They print about one out of every ten releases they get, depending on the importance of the company. Anyway, that's where I found your pigeon. He got a promotion a couple of years ago, and there's a photo of him and a few paragraphs of slush."

"Where does he work?"

"Ohhh no," Handry said. "You haven't a bloody chance. I'll have a Xerox made of the release and a copy of the photo. I'll bring them up to your place tonight if you'll tell me why you're so interested in Mr. Blank. It's the Lombard thing, isn't it?"

Delaney hesitated. "Yes," he said finally.

"Blank a suspect?"

"Maybe."

"If I bring the release and photo tonight, will you tell me about it?"

"There isn't much to tell."

"Let me be the judge of that. Is it a deal?"

"All right. About eight or nine."

"I'll be there."

Delaney hung up, exultant. Information *and* a photo! He knew from experience the usual sequence of a difficult case. The beginning was long, slow, muddled. The middle began to pick up momentum, pieces coming together, fragments fitting. The end was usually short, fast, frequently violent. He judged he was in the middle of the middle now, the pace quickening, parts clicking into place. It was all luck. It was all fucking luck.

The Parrot was no worse and no better than any other ancient Third Avenue bar that served food (steak sandwich, veal cutlet, beef stew; spaghetti, home fries, peas-and-carrots; apple pie, tapioca pudding, chocolate cake). With the growth of high-rise apartment houses, there were fewer such places every year. As he had hoped, the tavern was almost empty. There were two men wearing yellow hardhats drinking beer at the bar and matching coins. There was a young couple at a back table, holding hands, dawdling over a bottle of cheap wine. One waiter at this hour. One bartender.

Delaney sat at the bar, near the door, his back to the plate glass window. He ordered a rye and water. When the bartender poured it, the Captain put a ten-dollar bill on the counter.

"Got a minute?" he asked.

The man looked at him. "For what?"

"I need some information."

"Who are you?"

Delaney slid the "Ward M. Miller—Private Investigations" business card across the bar. The man picked it up and read it, his lips moving. He returned the card.

"I don't know nothing," he said.

"Sure you do," the Captain smiled genially. He placed the card atop the ten-dollar bill. "It's a matter of public record. Last year there was a fight in here. A guy kicked the shit out of a faggot. Were you on duty that night?"

"I'm on duty every night. I own the joint. Part of it anyways."

"Remember the fight?"

"I remember. How come you know about it?"

"I got a friend in the Department. He told me about it."

"What's it got to do with me?"

"Nothing. I don't even know your name, and I don't want to know it. I'm interested in the guy who broke the other guy's jaw."

"That sonofabitch!" the bartender burst out. "That guy should have been put away and throw away the key. A maniac!"

"He kicked the faggot when he was down?"

"That's right. In the balls. He was a wild man. It took three of us to pull him away. He would have killed him. I came close to sapping him. I keep a sawed-off pool cue behind the bar. He was a raving nut. How come you're interested in him?"

"Just checking up. His name is Daniel Blank. He's about thirty-six, thirty-seven—around there. He's divorced. Now he's got the hots for this young chick. She's nineteen, in college. This Blank wants to marry her, and she's all for it. Her old man is loaded. He thinks this Blank smells. The old man wants me to check him out, see what I can dig up."

"The old man better kick his kid's tail or get her out of the country before he lets her marry Blank. That guy's bad news."

"I'm beginning to think so," Delaney agreed.

"Bet your sweet ass," the bartender nodded. He was interested now, leaned across the bar, his arms folded. "He's a wrongo. Listen, I got a young daughter myself. If this Blank ever came near her, I'd break his arms and legs. He was in trouble with the cops before, you know."

Delaney took back his business card, moved the ten-dollar bill closer to the man's elbow.

"What happened?" he asked.

"He got in trouble with some guy who lives in his apartment house. Something about the guy's dog. Anyway, this guy got a busted arm, and this Blank was hauled in on an assault rap. But they fixed it up somehow and settled out of court."

"No kidding?" the Captain said. "First I heard about it. When did this happen?"

"About six months before he had the fight in here. The guy's a trouble-maker."

"Sure sounds like it. How did you find out about it—the assault charge I mean?"

"My brother-in-law told me. His name's Lipsky. He's a doorman in the apartment house where this Blank lives."

"That's interesting. You think your brother-in-law would talk to me?"

The bartender looked down at the ten-dollar bill, slid it under his elbow. The two construction workers down at the other end of the bar called for more beer; he went down there to serve them. Then he came back.

"Sure," he said. "Why not? He thinks this Blank stinks on ice."

"How can I get in touch with him?"

"You can call him on the lobby phone. You know where this Blank lives?"

"Oh sure. That's a good idea. I'll call Lipsky there. Maybe this Blank is shacking up or something and is playing my client's daughter along for kicks or maybe he smells money."

"Could be. Another drink?"

"Not right now. Listen, have you seen Blank since he got in that fight in here?"

"Sure. The bastard was in a few nights ago. He thought I didn't recognize him, the shit, but I never forget a face."

"Did her behave himself?"

"Oh sure. He was quiet. I didn't say word one to him. Just served him his drink and left him alone. He had some Christmas packages with him so I guess he had been out shopping."

Christmas packages. It could be the night Albert Feinberg was killed. But Delaney didn't dare press it.

"Thanks very much," he said, sliding off the stool. He started toward the door, then stopped and came back. The ten-dollar bill had disappeared.

"Oh," he said, snapping his fingers, "two more things . . . Could you call your brother-in-law and tell him I'm going to call him? I mean, it would help if I didn't just call him cold. You can tell him what it's all about, and there'll be a couple of bucks in it for him."

"Sure," the bartender nodded, "I can do that. I talk to him almost every day anyway. When he's on days, he usually stops by for a brew when he gets off. But he's on nights this week. You won't get him before eight tonight. But I'll call him at home."

"Many thanks. I appreciate that. The other thing is this: if Blank should stop in for a drink, tell him I was around asking questions about him. You don't have to give him my name; just tell him a private investigator was in asking questions. You can describe me." He grinned at the bartender. "Might put the fear of God in him. Know what I mean?"

"Yeah," the man grinned back, "I know what you mean."

He returned home to find a packet of Operation Lombard reports Mary had signed for. He left them on the hallway table, went directly to the kitchen, still wearing his stiff Homburg and heavy, shapeless overcoat. He was so hungry he was almost sick, and realized he had eaten nothing since breakfast. Mary had left a pot of lamb stew on the range. It was still vaguely warm, not hot, but he didn't care. He stood there in Homburg and overcoat, and forked out pieces of lamb, a potato, onions, carrots. He got a can of beer from the refrigerator and drank deeply from that, not bothering with a glass. He gulped everything, belching once or twice. After awhile he began to feel a little better; his knees stopped trembling.

He took off hat and coat, opened another can of beer, brought that and the Operation Lombard reports into the study. He donned his glasses, sat at his desk. He began writing an account of his interview with the bartender at The Parrot.

He filed away his account, then opened the package of Operation Lombard reports dealing with the murder of the fourth victim, Albert Feinberg. There were sketchy preliminary statements from the first uniformed patrolmen on the scene, lengthier reports from detectives, temporary opinion of the Medical Examiner (Dr. Sanford Ferguson again), an inventory of the victim's effects, the first interview with the victim's widow, photos of the corpse and murder scene, etc., etc.

As Lt. Dorfman had said, there were "extras" that were not present in the three previous homicides. Captain Delaney made a careful list of them:

1. Signs of a struggle. Victim's jacket lapel torn, necktie awry, shirt pulled from belt. Scuff marks of heels (rubber) and soles (leather) on the sidewalk.

2. Three Christmas packages nearby. One, which contained a black lace negligee, bore the victim's fingerprints. The other two were empty—dummy packages—and bore no prints at all, neither on the outside wrapping paper nor the inside boxes.

3. Drops of blood on the sidewalk a few feet from where the victim's battered skull rested. Careful scrapings and analysis proved these several drops were not the victim's blood type and were presumed to be the killer's. (Delaney made a note to call Ferguson and find out exactly what blood types were involved.)

4. The victim's wallet and credit card case appeared to be intact in his pockets. His wife stated that, to her knowledge, no identification was missing. However, pinned behind the left lapel of the victim's overcoat and

poking through the buttonhole, examiners had found a short green stem. The forensic men had identified it as genus *Rosa*, family *Rosaceae*, order *Rosales*. Investigation was continuing to determine, if possible, exactly what type of rose the victim had been sporting on his overcoat lapel.

He was going over the reports once again when the outside door bell rang. Before he answered it, he slid the Operation Lombard material and his own notes into his top desk drawer and closed it tightly. Then he went to the door, brought Thomas Handry back into the study, took his coat and hat. He poured a Scotch on the rocks for Handry, drained the warm dregs of his own beer, then mixed himself a rye and water, sat down heavily behind the desk. Handry slumped in the leather club chair, crossed his knees.

"Well . . ." Delaney said briskly. "What have you got?"

"What have *you* got, Captain? Remember our deal?"

Delaney stared at the neatly dressed young man a moment. Handry seemed tired; his forehead was seamed, diagonal lines that hadn't been there before now ran from the corners of his nose down to the sides of his mouth. He bit continually at the hard skin around his thumbnails.

"Been working hard?" Delaney asked quietly.

"Handry shrugged. "The usual. I'm thinking of quitting."

"Oh?"

"I'm not getting any younger, and I'm not doing what I want to do."

"How's the writing coming?"

"It's not. I get home at night and all I want to do is take off my shoes, mix a drink, and watch the boob tube."

Delaney nodded. "You're not married, are you?"

"No."

"Got a woman?"

"Yes."

"What does she think about your quitting?"

"She's all for it. She's got a good job. Makes more than I do. She says she'll support us until I can get published or get a job I can live with."

"You don't like newspaper work?"

"Not anymore."

"Why not?"

"I didn't know there was so much shit in the world. I can't take much more of it. But I didn't come here to talk about my problems."

"Problems?" the Captain said, surprised. "That's what it's all about. Some you have to handle. Some there's nothing you can do about. Some go away by themselves if you wait long enough. What were you worrying about five years ago?"

"Who the hell knows."

"Well . . . there you are. All right, here's what I've got . . ."

Handry knew about the Captain's amateurs, of the checkings of mailing lists and sales slips, of the setting up of Monica Gilbert's master file of names, the investigation of their criminal records.

Now the Captain brought him up-to-date on Daniel Blank, how he, Delaney, had found the year-old beef sheets in the Precinct house basement, the search of Blank's car, the interview with the bartender at The Parrot.

" . . . and that's all I've got," he concluded. "So far."

Handry shook his head. "Pretty thin."

"I know."

"You're not even sure if this guy is a mountain climber."

"That's true. But he was on the Outside Life mailing list, and that map in his car could be marked to a place where he climbs in this area."

"Want to go to the D.A. with that?"

"Don't be silly."

"You don't even know if he owns an ice ax."

"That's true; I don't."

"Well, what I've got isn't going to help you much more."

He drew an envelope from his breast pocket, leaned forward, scaled it onto Delaney's desk. The envelope was unsealed. The Captain drew out a 4x5 glossy photo and a single Xerox sheet that he unfolded and smoothed out on his desk blotter. He tilted his desk lamp to cast a stronger beam, took up the photo. He stared at it a long time. There. You. Are.

It was a close-up. Daniel Blank was staring directly at the lens. His shoulders were straight and wide. There was a faint smile on his lips, but not in his eyes.

He seemed remarkably youthful. His face was smooth, unlined. Small ears set close to the skull. A strong jaw. Prominent cheek bones. Large eyes, widely spaced, with an expression at once impassive and brooding. Straight hair, parted on the left, but combed flatly back. Heavy brows. Sculpted and unexpectedly tender lips, softly curved.

"Looks a little like an Indian," Delaney said.

"No," Handry said. "More Slavic. Almost Mongol. Look like a killer to you?"

"Everyone looks like a killer to me." Delaney said, not smiling. He turned his attention to the copy of the press release.

It was dated almost two years previously. It was brief, only two paragraphs, and said merely that Daniel G. Blank had been appointed Circulation Director of all Javis-Bircham Publications and would assume his new duties immediately. He was planning to computerize the Circulation Department of Javis-Bircham and would be in charge of the installation of AMROK II, a new computer that had been leased and would occupy almost an entire floor of the Javis-Bircham Building on West 46th Street.

Delaney read through the release again, then pushed it away from him. He took off his heavy glasses, placed them on top of the release. Then he leaned back in his swivel chair, clasped his hands behind his head, stared at the ceiling.

"I told you it wouldn't be much help," Handry said.

"Oh . . . I don't know," Delaney murmured dreamily. "There are some things. . .Fix yourself a fresh drink."

"Thanks. You want some more rye?"

"All right. A little."

He waited until Handry was settled back in the club chair again. Then the Captain sat up straight, put on his glasses, read the release again. He moved his glasses down on his nose, stared at Handry over the rims.

"How much do you think the Circulation Director of Javis-Bircham earns?"

"Oh, I'd guess a minimum of thirty thousand. And if it ran to fifty, I wouldn't be a bit surprised."

"That much?"

"Javis-Bircham is a big outfit. I looked it up. It's in the top five hundred of all the corporations in the country."

"Fifty thousand? Pretty good for a young man."

"How old is he?" Handry asked.

"I don't know exactly. Around thirty-five I'd guess."

"Jesus. What does he do with his money?"

"Pays a heavy rent. Keeps an expensive car. Pays alimony. Travels, I suppose. Invests. Maybe he owns a summer home; I don't know. There's a lot I don't know about him."

He got up to add more ice to his drink. Then he began to wander about the room, carrying the highball.

"The computer," he said. "What was it—AMROK II?"

Handry, puzzled, said nothing.

"Want to hear something funny?" Delaney asked.

"Sure. I could use a good laugh."

"This isn't funny-haha; this is funny strange. I was a detective for almost twenty years before I transferred to the Patrol Divison. In those twenty years I had my share of cases involving sexual aberrations, either as a primary or secondary motive. And you know, a lot of those cases—many more than could be accounted for by statistical averages—involved electronic experts, electricians, mechanics, computer programmers, bookkeepers and accountants. Men who worked with things, with machinery, with numbers. These men were rapists or Peeping Toms or flashers or child molesters or sadists or exhibitionists. This is my own experience, you understand. I have never seen any study that breaks down sex offenders according to occupation. I think I'll suggest an analysis like that to Inspector Johnson. It might prove valuable."

"How do you figure it?"

"I can't. It might just be my own experience with sex offenders, too limited to be significant. But it does seem to me that men whose jobs are—are mechanized or automated, whose daily relations with people are limited, are more prone to sex aberrations than men who have frequent and varied human contacts during their working hours. Whether the sex offense is due to the nature of the man's work, or whether the man unconsciously sought that type of work because he was already a potential sex offender and feared human contact, I can't say. How would you like to go talk to Daniel Blank in his office?"

Handry was startled. His drink slopped over the rim of the glass.

"What?" he asked incredulously. "What did you say?"

Delaney started to repeat his question, but the phone on his desk shrilled loudly.

"Delaney here."

"Edward? Thorsen. Can you talk?"

"Not very well."

"Can you listen a moment?"

"Yes."

"Good news. We think Broughton's on the way out. This fourth killing did it. The Mayor and Commissioner and their top aides are meeting tonight on it."

"I see."

"If I hear anything more tonight, I'll let you know."

"Thank you."

"How are you coming?"

"So-so."

"Got a name?"

"Yes."

"Good. Hang in there. Things are beginning to break."

"All right. Thank you for calling."

He hung up, turned back to Handry. "I asked how you'd like to go talk to Daniel Blank in his office."

"Oh sure," Handry nodded. "Just waltz in and say, "Mr. Blank, Captain Edward X. Delaney of the New York Police Department thinks you axed four men to death on the east side. Would you care to make a statement?"

"No, not like that," Delaney said seriously. "Javis-Bircham will have a publicity or public relations department, won't they?"

"Bound to."

"I'd do this myself, but you have a press card and identifications man. Identify yourself. Make an appointment. The *top* man. When you go see him, flash your buzzer. Say that your paper is planning a series of personality profiles on young, up-and-coming executives, the—"

"Hey, wait a minute!"

"The new breed of young executives who are familiar with computers, market sampling, demographic percentages and all that shit. Ask the public relations man to suggest four or five young, progressive Javis-Bircham executives who might fit the type your paper is looking for."

"Now see here—"

"Don't—repeat, *do not*—ask for Blank by name. Just come down hard on the fact that you're looking for a young executive familiar with the current use and future value of computers in business operations. Blank is certain to be one of the four or five men he suggests to you. Ask a few questions about each man he suggests. Then you pick Blank. See how easy it is?"

"Easy?" Handry shook his head. "Madness! And what if the Javis-Bircham PR man checks back with the finance editor of my paper and finds out no such series of articles is planned?"

"Chances are he won't. He'll be happy to get the publicity for Javis-Bircham, won't he?"

"But what if he does check? Then I'll be out on my ass."

"So what? You're thinking of quitting anyway, aren't you? So one of your problems is solved right there."

Handry stared at him, shaking his head. "You really are a special kind of bastard," he said in wonderment.

"Or," Delaney went on imperturbably, "if you like, you can give the finance editor on your paper a cover story. Tell him it's a police case—which it is—and if he asks questions, tell him it involves a big embezzlement or fraud or something like that. Don't mention the Lombard case. He'd probably cover for you if the Javis-Bircham PR man called and say, yes, the paper was planning a series of articles on young, progressive executives. He'd do that for you, wouldn't he?"

"Maybe."

"So you'll do it?"

"Just one question: why the fuck should I?"

"Two answers to that. One, if Blank turns out to be the killer, you'll be the only reporter in the world who had a personal interview with him. That's worth something, isn't it? Two, you want to be a poet, don't you? Or some kind of writer other than a reporter or a rewrite man. How can you expect to be a good writer if you don't understand people, if you don't know what makes them tick? You've got to learn to get inside people, to penetrate their minds, their hearts, their souls. What an opportunity this is—to meet and talk to a man who might have slaughtered four human beings!"

Handry drained his drink in a gulp. He rose, poured himself another, stood with his back to Delaney.

"You really know how to go for the jugular, don't you?"

"Yes."

"Aren't you ever ashamed of the way you manipulate people?"

"I don't manipulate people. Sometimes I give them the chance to do what they want to do and never had the opportunity. Will you do it, Handry?"

There was silence. The reporter took a deep breath, then blew it out. He turned to face Delaney.

"All right," he said.

"Good," the Captain nodded. "Set up the appointment with Blank the way I've outlined it. Use your brains. I know you've got a good brain. The day before your interview is scheduled, give me a call. We'll have a meet and I'll tell you what questions to ask him. Then we'll have a rehearsal."

"A rehearsal?"

"That's right. I'll play Blank, to give you an idea of how he might react to your questions and how you can follow up on things he might or might not say."

"I've interviewed before," Handry protested. "Hundreds of times."

"None as important as this. Handry, you're an amateur liar. I'm going to make you a professional."

The reporter nodded grimly. "If anyone can, you can. You don't miss a trick, do you?"

"I try not to."

"I hope to Christ if I ever commit a crime you don't come after me, Iron Balls."

He sounded bitter.

After Handry left, Delaney sat at his study desk, staring again at the photo of Daniel Blank. The man was handsome, no doubt about it: dark and lean. His face seemed honed; beneath the thin flesh cover the bones of brow, cheeks and jaw were undeniably there. But the Captain could read nothing from that face: neither greed, passion, evil nor weakness. It was a closed-off mask, hiding its secrets.

On impulse, not bothering to analyze his own motive, he took out the Daniel G. Blank file, flipped through it until he found Blank's phone number and dialed it. It rang four times, then:

"Hello?"

"Lou?" Delaney said. "Lou Jackson?"

"No, I'm afraid you've got the wrong number," the voice said pleasantly.

"Oh. Sorry."

Delaney hung up. It was an agreeable voice, somewhat musical, words clearly enunciated, tone deep, a good resonance. He stared at the photo again, matching what his eyes saw to what his ears had heard. He was beginning, just beginning, to penetrate Daniel Blank.

He worked on his records and files till almost 11:00 p.m., then judged the time was right to call Charles Lipsky. He looked up the apartment house number and called from his study phone.

"Lobby," a whiny voice answered.

"Charles Lipsky, please."

"Yeah. Talking. Who's this?" Delaney caught the caution, the suspicion in that thin, nasal voice. He wondered what doom the doorman expected from a phone call at this hour.

"Mr. Lipsky, my name is Miller, Ward M. Miller. Did your brother-in-law speak to you about me?"

"Oh. Yeah. He called." Now Delaney caught a note of relief, of catastrophe averted or at least postponed.

"I was hoping we might get together, Mr. Lipsky. Just for a short talk."

"Yeah. Well, listen . . ." Now the voice became low, conspiratorial. "You know I ain't supposed to talk to anyone about the tenants. We got a very strict rule against that."

Delaney recognized this virtuous reminder for what it was: a ploy to drive the price up.

"I realize that, Mr. Lipsky, and believe me, you don't have to tell me a thing you feel you shouldn't. But a short talk would be to our mutual advantage. You understand?"

"Well . . . yeah."

"I have an expense account."

"Oh, well, okay then."

"And your name will be kept out of it."

"You're sure?"

"Absolutely. When and where?"

"Well, how soon do you want to make it?"

"As soon as possible. Wherever you say."

"Well, I get off tomorrow morning at four. I usually stop by this luncheonette on Second and Eighty-fifth for coffee before I go home. It's open twenty-four hours a day, but it's usually empty at that hour except for some hackies and hookers."

Delaney knew the place Lipsky referred to, but didn't mention he knew it.

"Second Avenue and Eighty-fifth," he repeated. "About four-fifteen, four-thirty tomorrow morning?"

"Yeah. Around there."

"Fine. I'll be wearing a black Homburg and a double-breasted black overcoat."

"Yeah. All right."

"See you then."

Delaney hung up, satisfied. Lipsky sounded like a grifter, and penny ante at that. He jotted a note to have Thorsen check Department records to see if there was a sheet on Charles Lipsky. Delaney would almost bet there was.

He went immediately to bed, setting his alarm for 3.30 a.m. Thankfully, he fell asleep within half an hour, even as he was rehearsing in his mind how to handle Lipsky and what questions to ask.

The luncheonette had all the charm and ambience of a subway station. The walls and counter were white linoleum tiles, dulled with grease. Counter and table tops were plastic, scarred with cigarette burns. Chairs and counter stools were molded plastic, unpadded to reduce the possibility of vandalism. Rancid grease hung in the air like a wet sheet, and signs taped to the walls would have delighted a linguist: "Turky and all the tremens: $2.25" "Fryed Shrims—$1.85 with French pots and cold slaw." "Our eggs are strickly fresh."

Down at the end of the counter, two hookers, one white, one black, both in orange wigs, were working on plates of steak and eggs, conversing in low voices as fast as they were eating. Closer to the door, three cabbies were drinking coffee, trading wisecracks with the counterman and the black short order cook who was scraping thick rolls of grease off the wide griddle.

Delaney was early, a few minutes after four. When he entered, talk ceased, heads swivelled to inspect him. Apparently he didn't look like a holdup man; when he ordered black coffee and two sugared doughnuts, the other customers went back to their food and talk.

The Captain carried his coffee and doughnuts to a rear table for two. He sat where he could watch the door and the plate glass window. He didn't remove his hat but he unbuttoned his overcoat. He sat patiently, sipping the bitter coffee that had a film of oil glinting on the surface. He ate half a doughnut, then gave up.

His man came in about ten minutes later. Short, almost stunted, but heavy through the waist and hips, like an old jockey gone to seed. His eyes drifted, seemed to float around the room. The other customers glanced at him, but didn't stop eating or talking. The newcomer ordered a cup of light coffee, a piece of apple pie, and brought them over to Delaney's table.

"Miller?"

Delaney nodded. "Mr. Lipsky?"

"Yeah."

The doorman sat down opposite the Captain. He was still wearing his doorman's overcoat and uniform but, incongruously, he was wearing a beaked cap, a horseman's cap, in an horrendous plaid. He looked at Delaney briefly, but then his yellowish eyes floated off, to his food, the floor, the walls, the ceiling.

A grifter. Delaney was sure of it now. And seedy. Always with the shorts. On the take. A sheet that might include gambling arrests, maybe some boosting, receiving stolen property, bad debts, perhaps even an attempted shakedown. Cheap, dirty stuff.

"I ain't got much time," Lipsky said in his low, whiny voice. "I start on days again at noon." He shoveled pie into his surprisingly prim little mouth. "So I got to get home and catch a few hours of shuteye. Then back on the door again at twelve."

"Rough," Delaney said sympathetically. "Did your brother-in-law tell you what this is all about?"

"Yeah," Lipsky nodded, gulping his hot coffee. "This Blank is after some young cunt and her father wants to break it up. Right?"

"That's about it. What can you tell me about Blank?"

Lipsky scraped pie crust crumbs together on his plate with his fingers, picked them up, tossed them down his throat like a man downing a shot of liquor neat.

"Thought you was on an expense account."

Delaney glanced at the other customers. No one was observing them. He took his wallet from his hip pocket, held it on the far side of the table where only Lipsky could see it. He opened it wide, watched Lipsky's hungry eyes slide over and estimate the total. The Captain took out a ten, proffered it under the table edge. It was gone.

"Can't you do better than that?" Lipsky whined. "I'm taking an awful chance."

"Depends," Delaney said. "How long has Blank been living there?"

"I don't know exactly. I been working there four years, and he was living there when I started."

"He was married then?"

"Yeah. A big zoftig blonde. A real piece of push. Then he got divorced."

"Know where his ex-wife is living?"

"No."

"Does he have any woman now? Anyone regular who visits him?"

"Yeah. What does this young cunt look like? The one her father doesn't want her to see Blank?"

"About eighteen," Delaney said smoothly. "Long blonde hair. About five-four or five. Maybe one-twenty. Blue eyes. Peaches-and-cream complexion. Big jugs."

"Yum-yum," the doorman said, licking his lips. "I ain't seen anyone like that around."

"Anyone else? Any woman?"

"Yeah. A rich bitch. Mink coat down to her feet. About thirty, thirty-five. No tits. Black hair. White face. No makeup. A weirdo."

"Know her name?"

"No. She comes and she goes by cab."

"Sleep over?"

"Sure. Sometimes. What do you think?"

"That's interesting."

"Yeah? How interesting?"

"You're getting there," Delaney said coldly. "Don't get greedy. Anyone else?"

"No women. A boy."

"A boy?"

"Yeah. About eleven, twelve. Around there. Pretty enough to be a girl. I heard Blank call him Tony."

"What's going on there?"

"What the hell do you think?"

"This Tony ever sleep over?"

"I never seen it. One of the other doors tells me yes. Once or twice."

"This Blank got any close friends? In the building, I mean?"

"The Mortons."

"A family?"

"Married couple. No children. You want a lot for your sawbuck, don't you?"

Sighing, Delaney reached for his wallet again. But he looked up, saw a squad car roll to a stop just outside the luncheonette, and he paused. A uniformed cop got out of the car and came inside. The cabbies had gone, but the two hookers were picking their teeth, finishing their coffee. The cop glanced at them, then his eyes slid over Delaney's table.

He recognized the Captain, and Delaney recognized him. Handrette. A good man. Maybe a little too fast with his stick, but a good, brave cop. And smart enough not to greet a plainclothesman or superior officer out of uniform in public unless spoken to first. His eyes moved away from Delaney. He ordered two hamburgers with everything, two coffees, and two Danish to go. Delaney gave Charles Lipsky another ten.

"Who are the Mortons?" he asked. "Blank's friends."

"Loaded. Top floor penthouse. They own a store on Madison Avenue that sells sex stuff."

"Sex stuff?"

"Yeah," Lipsky said with his wet leer. "You know, candles shaped like pricks. Stuff like that."

Delaney nodded. Probably the Erotica. When he had commanded the 251st, he had made inquiries about the possibility of closing the place down and making it stick. The legal department told him to forget it; it would never hold up in court.

"Blank got any hobbies?" he asked Lipsky casually. "Is he a baseball or football nut? Anything like that?"

"Mountain climbing," Lipsky said. "He likes to climb mountains."

"Climb mountains?" Delaney said, with no change of expression. "He must be crazy."

"Yeah. He's always going away on weekends in the Spring and Fall. He takes all this crap with him in his car."

"Crap? What kind of crap?"

"You know—a knapsack, a sleeping bag, a rope, things you tie on your shoes so you don't slip."

"Oh yes," Delaney said. "Now I know what you mean. And an ax for chipping away ice and rocks. Does he take an ax with him on these trips?"

"Never seen it. What's this got to do with cutting him loose from the young cunt?"

"Nothing," Delaney shrugged. "Just trying to get a line on him. Listen, to get back to this woman of his. The skinny one with black hair. You know her name?"

"No."

"She come around very often?"

"She'll be there like three nights in a row. Then I won't see her for a week or so. No regular schedule, if that's what you're hoping." He grinned shrewdly at Delaney. Two of his front teeth were missing, two were chipped; the Captain wondered what kind of bet he had welshed on.

"Comes and goes by cab?"

"That's right. Or they walk out together."

"The next time you're on duty, if she comes or goes by cab, get the license number of the hack, the date, and the time. That's all I need—the date, the time, the license number of the cab. There's another tenner in it for you."

"And then all you got to do is check the trip sheets. Right?"

"Right," Delaney said, smiling bleakly. "You're way ahead of me."

"I could have been a private eye," Lipsky bragged. "I'd make a hell of a dick. Listen, I got to go now."

"Wait. Wait just a minute," Delaney said. making up his mind that moment. He watched the cop pay for the hamburgers, coffee, Danish and carry the bag out to his partner in the parked squad. He wondered idly if the copy insisted on paying because he, the Captain, was there.

"In your apartment house," Delaney said slowly, "you keep master keys? Or dupes to all the door locks on tenants' doors, locks they put on themselves?"

"Sure we got dupes," Lipsky frowned. "What do you think? I mean, in case of fire or an emergency, we got to get in—right?"

"And where are all these keys kept?"

"Right outside the assistant manager's office we got—" Lipsky stopped suddenly. His lips drew back from his chipped teeth. "If you're thinking what I think you're thinking," he said, "forget it. Not a chance. No way."

"Look, Mr. Lipsky," Delaney said earnestly, sincerely, hunching forward on the table. "It's not like I want to loot the place. I wouldn't take a cigarette butt out of there. All I want to do is look around."

"Yeah? For what?"

"This woman he's been sleeping with. Maybe a photo of them together. Maybe a letter from her to him. Maybe she's keeping some clothes up there in his closet. Anything that'll help my client convince his daughter that Blank has been cheating on her all along."

"But if you don't take anything, how . . ."

"You tell me," Delaney said. "You claim you could have been a private eye. How would you handle it?"

Lipsky stared at him, puzzled. Then his eyes widened. "Camera!" he gasped. "A miniature camera. You take pictures!"

Delaney slapped the table top with his palm. "Mr. Lipsky, you're all right," he chuckled. "You'd make a hell of a detective. I take a miniature camera. I shoot letters, photos, clothes, any evidence at all that Blank has been shacking up with this black-haired twist or even this kid Tony. I put everything back exactly where it was. Believe me, I know how to do it. He'll never know anyone's been in there. He leaves for work around nine and comes back around six. Something like that—correct?"

"Yeah."

"So the apartment's empty all day?"

"Yeah."

"Cleaning woman?"

"Two days a week. But she comes early and she's out by noon."

"So . . . what's the problem? It'll take me an hour. No more, I swear. Would anyone miss the keys?"

"Nah. That board's got a zillion keys."

"So there you are. I come into the lobby. You've already got the keys off the board. You slip them to me. I'm up and down in an hour. Probably less. I pass the keys back to you. You replace them. You're going on duty days starting today—right? So we make it about two or three in the afternoon. Right?"

"How much?" Lipsky said hoarsely.

Got him, Delaney thought.

"Twenty bucks," the Captain said.

"Twenty?" Lipsky cried, horrified. "I wouldn't do it for less than a C. If I'm caught, it's my ass."

Five minutes later they had agreed on fifty dollars, twenty immediately, thirty when Delaney returned the keys, and an extra twenty if Lipsky could get the license number of the cab used by Blank's skinny girl friend.

"If I get it," Lipsky said, "should I call your office?"

"I'm not in very much," Delaney said casually. "In this business you've got to keep moving around. I'll call you every day on the lobby phone. If you go back on nights, leave a message with your brother-in-law. I'll find out from him when to call. Okay?"

"I guess," Lipsky said doubtfully. "Jesus, if I didn't need the dough so bad, I'd tell you to go suck."

"Sharks?" the Captain asked.

"Yeah," Lipsky said wonderingly. "How did you know?"

"A guess," Delaney shrugged. He passed twenty under the table to the doorman. "I'll see you at two-thirty this afternoon. What's the apartment number?"

"Twenty-one H. It's on a tag attached to the keys."

"Good. Don't worry. It'll go like silk."

"Jesus, I hope so."

The Captain looked at him narrowly. "You don't like this guy much, do you?"

Lipsky began to curse, ripe obscenities spluttering from his lips. Delaney listened awhile, serious and unsmiling, then held up a hand to cut off the flow of invective.

"One more thing," he said to Lipsky. "In a few days, or a week from now, you might mention casually to Blank that I was around asking questions about him. You can describe me, but don't tell him my name. You forgot it. Just say I was asking personal questions, but you wouldn't tell me a goddamned thing. Got that?"

"Well . . . sure," Lipsky said, puzzled. "But what for?"

"I don't know," Captain Delaney said. "I'm not sure. Just to give him something to think about, I guess. Will you do it?"

"Yeah. Sure. Why not?"

They left the luncheonette together. There were early workers on the streets now. The air was cold, sharp. The sky was lightening in the east; it promised to be a clear day. Captain Delaney walked home slowly, leaning against the December wind. By the time he unlocked his door he could hardly smell the rancid grease.

The projected break-in had been a spur-of-the-moment thing. He hadn't planned that, hadn't even considered it. But Lipsky had tied Daniel Blank to mountain climbing: the first time that was definitely established. And that led to the ice ax. That damned ax! Nothing so far had tied Blank to the purchase or possession of an ice ax. Delaney wanted things tidy. Possession would be tidy enough; purchase could be traced later.

He wasn't lying when he told Lipsky he'd be in and out of Blank's apartment in an hour. My God, he could find an ice ax in Grand Central Station in that time. And why should Blank hide it? As far as he knew, he wasn't suspected. He owned rucksack, pitons, crampons, ice ax. What could be more natural? He was a mountaineer. All Delaney wanted from that break-in was the ice ax. Anything else would be gravy on the roast.

He wrote up his reports and noted, gratified, how fat the Daniel G. Blank file was growing. More important, how he was beginning to pentrate his man. Tony, a twelve-year-old boy pretty enough to be a girl. A thin, black-haired woman with no tits. Friends who owned a sex boutique. Much, much there. But if the ice ax didn't exist in Blank's apartment, it was all smoke. What would he do then? Start in again—someone else, another angle, a different approach. He was prepared for it.

He worked on his reports until Mary arrived. She fixed him coffee, dry toast, a soft-boiled egg. No grease. After breakfast, he went into the living room, pulled the shades, took off his shoes and jacket, unbuttoned his vest. He lay down on the couch, intending to nap for only an hour. But when he awoke, it was almost 11.30, and he was angry at himself for time wasted.

He went into the downstairs lavatory to rub his face with cold water and comb his hair. In the mirror he saw how he looked, but he had already felt it: blueish bags swelling down beneath his eyes, the greyish unhealthy complexion, lines deeper, wrinkled forehead, bloodless lips pressed tighter, everything old and troubled. When all this was over, and Barbara was well again, they'd go somewhere, groan in the sun, stuff until their skins were tight, eyes clear, memories washed, blood pure and pumping. And they'd make love. That's what he told himself.

He called Monica Gilbert.

"Monica, I'm going over to visit my wife. I was wondering if—if you're not busy—if you'd like to meet her."

"Oh, yes, I would. When?"

"Fifteen minutes or so. Too soon? Would you like lunch first?"

"Thank you, but I've had a salad. That's all I'm eating these days."

"A diet?" he laughed. "You don't need that."

"I do. I've been eating so much since—since Bernie died. Just nerves, I guess. Edward . . ."

"What?"

"You said you'd call me about Daniel Blank, but you didn't. Was it anything?"

"I think so. But I'd like my wife to hear it, too. I trust her judgment. She's very good on people. I'll tell you both at the same time. All right?"

"Of course."

"Be over in fifteen minutes."

Then he called Barbara and told her he was bringing Monica Gilbert to meet her, the widow of the second victim. Barbara said of course. She was happy to talk to him and told him to hurry.

He had thought about it a long time—whether or not to bring the two women together. He recognized the dangers and the advantages. He didn't want Barbara to think, even to suspect, that he was having a relationship—even an innocent relationship—with another woman while she, Barbara, was ill, confined to a hospital room, despite what she had said about his marrying again if anything happened to her. That was just talk, he decided firmly; an emotional outburst from a woman disturbed by her own pain and fears of the future. But Barbara would enjoy company—that he knew. She really did like people, much more than he did. He could tell her of a man arrested for molesting women—there was one crazy case: this nut would sneak into bedrooms out in Queens, always coming through unlocked windows, and he would kiss sleeping women and then run away. He never put his hands on them or injured them physically, He just kissed them. When he told Barbara about it, she gave a troubled sigh and said, "Poor fellow. How lonely he must have been."—and her sympathies were frequently with the suspect, unless violence was involved.

Monica Gilbert needed a confidante as well. Her job was finished, her file complete. He wanted to continue giving her a feeling of involvement. So, finally, he had decided to bring them together.

It wasn't a disaster, as he had feared, but it didn't go marvelously well, as he had hoped. Both women were cordial, but nervous, guarded, reserved. Monica had brought Barbara a little African violet, not from a florist's shop but one she had nurtured herself. That helped. Barbara expressed her condolences in low tones on the death of Monica's husband. Delaney stayed out of it, standing away from Barbara's bed, listening and watching anxiously.

Then they began speaking about their children, exchanging photographs and smiling. Their talk became louder than sickroom tones; they laughed more frequently; Barbara touched Monica's arm. Then he knew it was going to be all right. He relaxed, sat in a chair away from them, listening to their chatter, comparing them: Barbara so thin and fine, wasted and elegant, a silver sword of a woman. And Monica with her heavy peasant's body, sturdy and hard, bursting with juice. At that moment he loved them both.

For awhile they leaned close, conversing in whispers. He wondered if they might be talking about women's ailments, women's plumbing—a complete mystery to him—or perhaps, from occasional glances they threw in his direction, he wondered if they might be discussing him, although what there was about him to talk about he couldn't imagine.

It was almost an hour before Barbara held out a hand to him. He came over to her bedside, smiling at both of them.

"Daniel Blank?" Barbara asked.

He told them about the interviews with the bartender, with Handry, with Lipsky. He told them everything except his plan to be inside Blank's apartment within two hours.

"Edward, it's beginning to take form," Barbara nodded approvingly. As usual, she went to the nub. "At least now you know he's a mountain climber. I suppose the next step is to find out if he owns an ice ax?"

Delaney nodded. She would never even consider asking him how he might do this.

"Can't you arrest him now?" Monica Gilbert demanded. "On suspicion or something?"

The Captain shook his head. "Not a chance," he said patiently. "No evidence at all. Not a shred. He'd be out before the cell door was slammed behind him, and the city would be liable for false arrest. That would be the end of that."

"Well, what can you do then? Wait until he kills someone else?"

"Oh . . ." he said vaguely, "there are things. Establish his guilt without a doubt. He's just a suspect now, you know. The only one I've got. But still just a suspect. Then, when I'm sure of him, I'll—well, at this moment I'm not sure what I'll do. Something."

"I'm sure you will," Barbara smiled, taking Monica's hand. "My husband is a very stubborn man. And he's neat. He doesn't like loose ends."

They all laughed. Delaney glanced at his watch, saw he had to leave. He offered to take Monica Gilbert home, but she wanted to stay awhile and said she'd leave when it was time to pick up her girls at school. Delaney glanced at Barbara, realized she wanted Monica's company a while longer. He kissed Barbara's cheek, nodded brightly at both, lumbered from the room. Outside in the hall, adjusting his Homburg squarely atop his head, he heard a sudden burst of laughter from inside the room, quickly suppressed. He wondered if they could be laughing at him, something he had done or said. But he was used to people finding him amusing; it didn't bother him.

He had never, of course, had any intention of taking a camera to Blank's apartment. What would a photograph of an ice ax prove? But he did take a set of locksmith's picks, of fine Swedish steel, fitted into individual pockets in a thin chamois case. Included in the set were long, slender tweezers. The case went into his inside jacket pocket. In the lefthand pocket he clipped a two-battery penlite. Into his overcoat pocket he folded a pair of thin black silk gloves. Barbara called them his "undertaker's gloves."

At 2:30, Captain Delaney walked steadily up the driveway, pushed through the lobby door. Lipsky saw him almost at once. His face was pale, sheeny with sweat. His hand dipped into his lefthand jacket pocket. Brainless idiot, Delaney thought mournfully. The whole idea had been to transfer the keys during a normal handshake. Well, it couldn't be helped now . . .

He advanced, smiling, holding out his right hand. Lipsky grabbed it with a damp palm and only then realized the keys were gripped in his left fist. He dropped Delaney's hand, transferred the keys, almost losing them in the process. Delaney plucked them lightly from Lipsky's nerveless fingers. The Captain slid them into his overcoat pocket, still smiling slightly, and said, "Any trouble, give me three fast rings on the intercom."

Lipsky turned even paler. It was a warning Delaney had deliberately avoided giving the doorman at the luncheonette; it might have queered the whole thing right then.

He sauntered slowly toward the elevator banks, turning left to face the cars marked 15–34. Two other people were waiting: a man flipping through a magazine, a woman with an overflowing Bloomingdale's shopping bag. A door slid open on a self-service elevator; a young couple with a small child came out. Delaney hung back a moment, then followed the other two into the elevator. The man punched 16, the woman pushed 21—Blank's floor. Delaney pressed 24.

Both men removed their hats. They rode up in silence. The magazine reader got off at 16. The woman with the shopping bag got off at 21. Delaney rode up to 24 and stepped out. He killed a few minutes pinpointing the direction of apartment H, assuming it was in the same location on every floor.

He came back to the elevators to push the Down button. Thankfully, the elevator that stopped for him a moment later was empty. He pushed 21, suddenly became aware of the soft music. He didn't recognize the tune. The door opened at 21. He pushed the Lobby button, then stepped out quickly before the doors closed.

The 21st Floor corridor was empty. He took off his fleece-lined leather gloves, stuffed them in an overcoat pocket, pulled on his "undertaker's gloves." As he walked the carpeted corridor, he scraped soles and heels heavily, hoping to remove whatever mud or dog shit or dust or dirt that had accumulated, possibly to show up in Blank's apartment. And he noted the peephole in every door.

He rang the bell of apartment 21-H twice, heard it peal quietly inside. He waited a few moments. No answer. He went to work.

He had no trouble with two of the keys, but the third lock, the police bar, took more time. His hands were so large that he could not slip his fingers inside the partly opened door to disengage the diagonal rod. He finally took the tweezers from his pick case and, working slowly and without panic, moved the bar up out of its slot. The door swung open.

He stepped inside, closed the door gently behind him but did not lock it. He moved through the apartment swiftly, opening closet doors, glancing inside, closing them. He peeked behind the shower curtain in the bathroom, went down on his knees to peer under the bed. When he was satisfied the apartment was unoccupied, he returned to the front door, locked it, set the police bar in place.

The next step was silly, but basic. But perhaps not so silly. He remembered the case of a dick two who had spent four hours tossing the wrong apartment. Delaney went looking for subscription magazines, letters . . . anything. He found a shelf of books on computer technology. Each one, on the front end paper, bore an engraved bookplate neatly pasted in place. A nude youth with bow and arrow leaping through a forest glade. "Ex Libris. Daniel G. Blank." Good enough.

He returned to the front door again, put his back against it, then began to stroll, to wander through the apartment. Just to absorb it, to try to understand what kind of a man lived here.

But did anyone live here? Actually breathe, sleep, eat, fart, belch, defecate in these sterile operating rooms? No cigarette butts, no tossed newspapers, no smells, no photos, personal mementoes, vulgar little geegaws, souvenirs, no unwashed glass or chipped paint or old burns or a cracked ceiling. It was all so antiseptic he could hardly believe it; the cold order and cleanliness were overwhelming. Furniture in black leather and chrome. Crystal ashtrays precisely arranged. An iron candelabra with each taper carefully burned down to a different length.

He thought of his own home: his, Barbara's, their family's.

Their home sang their history, who they were, their taste and lack of taste, worn things, used things, roots, smells of living, memories everywhere. You could write a biography of Edward X. Delaney from his home. But who was Daniel G. Blank? This decorator's showroom, this model apartment said nothing. Unless . . .

That heavy beveled mirror in the foyer, handsomely framed. That long wall in the living room bearing at least 50 small mirrors of various shapes, individually framed. A full-length mirror on the bedroom door. A double medicine cabinet, both sliding doors mirrored. Did that plethora of mirrors say anything about the man who lived there?

There was another sure tip-off, to anyone's life style: the contents of the refrigerator, kitchen cabinets, the bathroom cabinet. In the refrigerator, a bottle of vodka, three bottles of juice—orange, grapefruit, tomato. Salad fixings. Apples, tangerines, plums, peaches, dried apricots and dried prunes. In the cabinets, coffee, herbal teas, spices, health foods, organic cereals. No meats anywhere. No cheese. No coldcuts. No bread. No potatoes. But sliced celery and carrots.

In the bathroom, behind the sliding cabinet doors, he found the scented soaps, oils, perfumes, colognes, lotions, unguents, powders, deodorants, sprays. One bottle of aspirin. One bottle of pills, almost full, he recognized as Librium. One envelope of pills he could not identify. One bottle of vitamin B-12 pills. Shaving gear. He closed the doors with the tips of his gloved fingers. Was the toilet paper scented? It was. He glanced at his watch. About ten minutes so far.

Once again he returned to the entrance, trying to walk softly in case the tenant in the apartment below might hear footsteps and wonder who was in Mr. Blank's apartment at this hour.

He switched on the overhead light, opened the door of the foyer closet.

On the top shelf: six closed hatboxes and a trooper's winter hat of black fur.

On the rod: two overcoats, three topcoats, two raincoats, a thigh-length coat of military canvas, olive-drab, fleece-lined, with an attached hood, a waist-length jacket, fur-lined, two light-weight nylon jackets.

On the floor: a sleeping bag rolled up and strapped, heavy climbing boots with ridged soles, a set of steel crampons, a rucksack, a webbed belt, a coil of nylon line, and . . .

One ice ax.

There it was. It was that easy. An ice ax. Delaney stared at it, feeling no elation. Perhaps satisfaction. No more than that.

He stared at it for almost a minute, not doubting his eyes but memorizing its exact position. Balanced on the handle butt. The head leaning against two walls in the corner. The leather thong loop from the end of the handle curved to the right, then doubled back upon itself.

The Captain reached in, picked it up in his gloved hand. He examined it closely. "Made in West Germany." Similar to those sold by Outside Life. He sniffed at the head. Oiled steel. The handle darkened with sweat stains. Using one of his lock picks, he gently prized the leather covering away from the steel shaft, just slightly. No stains beneath the leather. But then, he hadn't expected to find any.

He stood gripping the ax, loath to put it down. But it could tell him nothing more; he doubted very much if it could tell the forensic men anything either. He replaced it as carefully as he could, leaning it into the corner at the original angle, arranging the leather thong in its double-backed loop. He closed the closet door, looked at his watch. Fifteen minutes.

The living room floor was a checkerboard pattern, alternating black and white tiles, 18 inches square. Scattered about were six small rugs in bright colors and modern design. Scandinavian, he guessed. He lifted each rug, looked underneath. He didn't expect to find anything; he didn't.

He wasted a few minutes staring at that long mirrored wall, watching his image jerk along as he moved. He would have liked to search behind each mirror but knew it would take forever, and he'd never get them back in their precise pattern. He turned instead to a desk near the window. It was a slim, elegant spider of chrome and glass. One center drawer, one deep file drawer on the left side.

The top drawer was marvelously organized with a white plastic divider: paper clips (two sizes), sharpened pencils, stamps, built-in Scotch tape dispenser, scissors, ruler, letter opener, magnifying glass—all matching. Delaney was impressed. Not envious, but impressed.

There were three documents. One was a winter catalogue from Outside Life; the Captain smiled, without mirth. One, in a back corner, was obviously half a salary check, the half that listed taxes, pension payment, hospitalization, and similar deductions. Delaney put on his glasses to read it. According to his calculations, Blank was earning about $55,000 a year. That was nice.

The third document was an opened manila envelope addressed to Mr. Daniel G. Blank from something called Medical Examiners Institute. Delaney drew out the stapled report, scanned it quickly. Apparently, six months ago, Blank had undergone a complete physical checkup. He had had the usual minor childhood illnesses, but the only operation noted was a tonsillectomy at the age of nine. His blood pressure was just slightly below normal, and he had a 20 percent impairment of hearing in his left ear. But other than that, he seemed to be in perfect physical condition for a man his age.

Delaney replaced this document and then, recalling something, drew it out again. In his pocket notebook, he made a notation of Blank's blood type.

The deep file drawer contained one object: a metal document box. Delaney lifted it out, placed it atop the desk, examined it. Grey steel. Locked, with the lock on top. White plastic handle in front. About 12 inches long, eight inches wide, four inches deep. He could never understand why people bought such boxes for their valuables. It was true the box might be fire-resistant, but no professional thief would waste time forcing or picking the lock; he'd just carry the entire box away by its neat plastic handle, or slip it into a pillowcase with his other loot.

Delaney took a closer look at the lock. Five minutes at the most, but was it worth it? Probably checkbooks, bank books, maybe some cash, his lease, passport, a few documents not valuable enough to put in his safe deposit box. Blank, he was certain, would have a safe deposit box. He was that kind of a man. He replaced the document box in the desk, closed the drawer firmly. If he had time, he'd come back to it. He glanced at his watch; almost 25 minutes.

He moved toward the bedroom. But he paused before an ebony and aluminum liquor cabinet. He could not resist it, and opened the two doors. Matching glassware on one side: Baccarat crystal, and beautiful. What was it Handry had asked? What does Blank do with his money? He could tell Handry now: he buys Baccarat crystal.

The liquor supply was curious; one gin, one Scotch, one rye, one bourbon, one rum, and at least a dozen bottles of brandies and cordials. Curiouser and curiouser. What did a grown man want with an ink-colored liqueur called "Fleur d'Amour"?

There was a technique to a good search; some dicks were better at it than others. It was a special skill. Delaney knew he was good at it, but he knew others who were better. There was an old detective—the Captain thought he was probably retired by now—who could go through a six-room house in an hour and find the cancelled stamp he was looking for, or a single earring, or a glassine envelope of shit. You simply could not hide anything with absolute certainty that it could never be found. Given enough time, enough men, anything could be found, anywhere. Swallow a metal capsule? Stick a microfilm up your ass? Put a microdot in a ground-out tooth and have it capped? Tattoo your skull and let the hair grow over? Forget it. Anything could be found.

But those methods were rare and exotic. Most people with something to hide—documents, money, evidence, drugs—hid it in their own home or apartment. Easy to check its safety. Easy to destroy fast in an emergency. Easy to get when needed.

But within their homes—as the cops good at tossing well knew—most people had two tendencies: one rational, one emotional. The rational was that, if you lived a reasonably normal life, you had visitors: friends and neighbors dropping in, sometimes unexpectedly. So you did not hide your secret in the foyer, living room, or dining room: areas that were occupied by others at various times, where the hidden object might, by accident, be uncovered or be discovered by a drunken and/or inquisitive guest. So you selected bathroom or bedroom, the two rooms in your home indisputably *yours*.

The emotional reason for choosing bathroom *or* bedroom was this: they were intimate rooms. You were naked there. You slept there, bathed, performed your bodily functions. They were your "secret places." Where else would you conceal something secret, of great value to you alone, something you could not share?

Delaney went directly to the bathroom, removed the top of the toilet tank. An old trick but still used occasionally. Nothing in there except, he was amused to note, a plastic daisy and a bar of solid deodorant that kept Daniel Blank's toilet bowl sweet-smelling and clean. Beautiful.

He tapped the wall tiles rapidly, lifted the tufted bathmat from the floor and looked underneath, made a closer inspection of the medicine cabinets, used his penlite to tap the length of the shower curtain rod. All hollow. What was he looking for? He knew but would not admit it to himself. Not at this moment. He was just looking.

Into the bedroom. Under the rug again. A long wiggle under the bed to inspect the spring. A careful hand thrust between spring and mattress. Under the pillows. Then the bed restored to its taut neatness. Nothing in the Venetian blinds. Base of the lamp? Nothing. Two framed French posters on the walls. Nothing on their backs. The paper appeared intact. That left the wall-length closet and the two dressers in pale Danish wood. He looked at his watch. Coming up to forty minutes. He was sweating now; he had not removed hat or overcoat or taken anything from his pockets that he did not immediately replace.

He tried the closet first. Two wide, hinged, louvred doors that could be folded back completely. So he did, and gazed in astonishment. He himself was a tidy man, but compared to Daniel Blank he was a lubber. Delaney liked his personal linen folded, softly, neatly stacked with fold forward, newly laundered to the bottom. But this display in Blank's closet, this was—was mechanized!

The top shelf, running the length of both closets, held linen: sheets, pillowcases, beach towels, bath towels, bathmats, hand towels, dish towels, washcloths, napkins, tablecloths, mattress covers, mattress pads, and a stack of heavy things whose function Delaney could only guess at, although they might have been dustcloths for covering furniture during an extended absence.

But what was so amazing was the precision with which these stacks had been arranged. Was it a militaristic cleaning woman or Blank himself who had adjusted these individual stacks, and then aligned all stacks as if with a stretched string? And the colors! No white sheets and pillowcases here, no dull towels and washcloths, but bright, jumping colors, floral designs, abstract patterns: an eye-jarring display. How to reconcile this extravagance with the white-and-black sterility of the living room, the architectural furniture?

On the floors of both closets were racks of shoes. In the left-hand closet, summer shoes—whites, sneakers, multi-colors—each pair fitted with trees, encased in clear plastic bags. In the other closet, winter shoes, also with trees but not bagged. Practically all blacks these, mostly slip-ons, moccasin styles, two pair of buckled Guccis, three pairs of boots, one knee-high.

Similarly, hanging from the rod, summer clothing on the left, winter on the right. The summer suits were bagged in clear plastic, jackets on wooden hangers, trousers suspended from their cuffs on clamps. The uncovered winter suits were almost all black or midnight blue. There was a suede sports jacket, a tartan, a modest hound's tooth. Four pairs of slacks: two grey flannel, one tartan, one a bottle-green suede. Two silk dressing gowns, one in a bird print, one with purple orchids.

Delaney did the best he could in a short time, feeling between and under the stacks of linen, shaking the shoes heels downward, pressing between his palms the bottoms of the plastic bags that protected the summer suits. He went into the living room, removed a small metal mirror from its hook on the wall, and by stretching, using the mirror and his penlite, he was able to see behind the stacks of linen on the top shelf. It was, he admitted, a cursory search, but better than nothing. That's just what he found—nothing. He returned the mirror to its hook, adjusted it carefully.

That left the two dressers. They were matching pieces, each with three full drawers below and two half-drawers on top. He looked at his watch. About 46 minutes gone now. He had promised Lipsky an hour, no more.

He started on the dresser closest to the bedroom window. The first half-drawer he opened was all jewelry, loose or in small leather cases: tie pins, cufflinks, studs, tie tacks, a few things he couldn't immediately understand—a belt of gold links, for instance, and a gold link wristwatch band, three obviously expensive identification bracelets, two heavy masculine necklaces, seven rings, a hand-hammered golden heart strung on a fine chain. He cautiously pried under everything.

The other half-drawer contained handkerchiefs, and how long had it been since he had seen Irish linen laundered to a silken feel? Nothing underneath.

Top full drawer: hosiery, at least fifty pair, from black silk formal to knee-length Argyle-patterned knits. Nothing there.

Second and third full drawers: shirts. Obviously business shirts in the second: white and light blue in a conservative cut. In the third drawer, sports shirts, wilder hues, patterns, knits, polyesters. Again he thrust his hand carefully between and beneath the neat piles. His silk-covered fingers slid on something smooth. He drew it out.

It was, or had been originally, an 8x10 glossy photo of Daniel Blank taken in the nude. Not recently. He looked younger. His hair was thicker. He was standing with his hands on his hips, laughing at the camera. He had, Delaney realized, a beautiful body. Not handsome, not rugged, not especially muscular. But beautiful: wide shoulders, slender waist, good arms. It was impossible to judge his legs since the photograph had been cut across just above the pubic hair, by scissors, razor, or knife. Blank stood smiling at Delaney, hands on hips, prick and balls excised and missing. The Captain carefully slid the mutilated photo back beneath the knitted sports shirts.

He went to the second dresser now, feeling certain he would find little of significance, but wanting to learn this man. He had already observed enough to keep him pondering for weeks, but there might be more.

One half-drawer of the second dresser contained scarves: mostly foulard ascots, squares, a formal white silk scarf, a few patterned handkerchiefs. The second half-drawer contained a miscellany: two crushable linen beach hats, two pairs of sunglasses, a bottle of suntan lotion in a plastic bag, a tube of "Cover-All" sunscreen cream, and timetables of airline flights to Florida, the West Indies, Britain, Brazil, Switzerland, France, Italy, Sweden—all bound together with a rubber band.

The top full drawer was underwear. Delaney looked at the assortment, oddly moved. It was a feeling he had had before when searching the apartment of a stranger: secret intimacy. He remembered once sitting around in a squad room, just relaxing with two other detectives, gossiping, telling stories about their cases and experiences. One of the dicks was telling about a recent toss he had made of the premises of a hooker who had been beaten to death by one of her customers.

"My God," the cop said, "I handled all her underwear and that frilly stuff, her garter belt and that thing they pin their napkins on and blue baby-doll pajamas she had, and the smell of it all, and I damned near came in my pants."

The others laughed, but they knew what he meant. It wasn't only that she had been a whore with lacy things that smelled sexy. It was the secret sharing, entering into another's life as a god might enter—unseen, unsuspected, but penetrating into a human being and knowing.

That was something of what Captain Edward X. Delaney felt, staring at Blank's precise stacks of briefs, bikinis, shorts, stretch panties, trimmed garments in colors he could not believe were sold anywhere but in women's lingerie shops. But stolidly he felt beneath each stack after flipping them through, replaced everything meticulously, and went on.

The second drawer was pajamas: jackets and pants in nylon, cotton, flannel. Sleep coats. Even a bright red nightshirt.

The bottom drawer was bathing suits—more than one man could use in a lifetime: everything from the tiniest of bikinis to long-legged surfing trunks. Three jockstraps, one no larger than an eyepatch. And in with it all, unexpectedly, six pairs of winter gloves: thin, black leather; rough cowhide; fleece-lined; bright yellow suede; grey formal with black stitching along the knuckles; etc. Nothing. Between items or underneath.

Delaney closed the final drawer, drew a deep breath. He looked at his watch again. Five minutes to go. He might stretch it a minute or two, but no more. Then, he was certain, he'd hear three frantic intercom rings from a spooked Charles Lipsky.

He could open that document case in the living room desk. He could take a look at the bottom kichen cabinets. He could try several things. On impulse, nothing more, he got down on his hands and knees, felt beneath the bottom drawer of one of the dressers. Nothing. He crawled on hands and knees, felt beneath the other. Nothing. But as he felt about, the wood panel pressed slightly upward.

Now that was surprising. In chests of drawers as expensive and elegant as these appeared to be, he would have guessed a solid piece of wood beneath the bottom drawer, and between each pair of drawers another flat layer of wood. They were called "dust covers," he remembered. Good furniture had them. Cheaply made chests had no horizontal partitions between the bottom of one drawer and the open top of the one beneath.

He climbed to his feet, brushed his overcoat, knees, and trouser cuffs free of carpet lint. There was lint; he picked it off carefully, put it into a vest pocket. Then he opened a few dresser drawers at random. It was true; there were no wooden partitions between drawers; they were simply stacked. Well, it would only take a minute . . .

He pulled out the first drawer of one dresser, reached in and felt the bottom surfaces of the two half-drawers above it. Nothing. He closed the first full drawer, opened the second and ran his fingers over the bottom surface of the first full drawer. Nothing. He continued in this fashion. It only took seconds. Seconds of nothing.

He started on the second dresser. Closed the drawer containing Blank's incredible underwear, opened the drawer containing pajamas, thrust his hand in to feel the undersurface of the drawer above. And stopped. He withdrew his hand a moment, wiped his silk-clad fingertips on his overcoat, reached in again, felt cautiously. Something there.

"Please, God," he said aloud.

Slowly, with infinite caution, he closed the pajama drawer and then drew out the one above it, the underwear drawer. He drew it halfway out of the dresser. Then, fearful there might be wood splinters on the runners, sawdust, stains, anything, he took off his overcoat and laid it out on Daniel Blank's bed, lining side up. Then he carefully removed the underwear drawer completely from the chest, placed it softly on his overcoat. He didn't look at his watch now. Fuck Charles Lipsky.

He removed the stacks of underwear, placing them on the other side of the bed in the exact order in which he removed them. Four stacks across, two stacks back to front. They'd be returned to the drawer in the same order. When the drawer was empty, he slowly turned it upside down and placed it on his opened overcoat. He stared at the taped envelope. He could appreciate Blank's reasoning: if the tape dried out and the envelope dropped, it could only drop into the next drawer down.

He pressed the envelope gently with his fingertips. Things stiffer than paper, and something hard. Leather maybe, wood or metal. The envelope was taped to the wooden bottom of the drawer on all its four sides. He put on his glasses again, bent over it. He used one of his lock picks, probed gently at the corners of the envelope where the strips of tape didn't quite meet.

He wanted to avoid, if possible, removing the four strips of tape completely. He finally determined, to his satisfaction, the top of the envelope. Using a pick, he lifted a tiny corner of the top tape. Then he switched to tweezers. Slowly, slowly, with infinite caution, he peeled the tape away from the wood, making certain he did not pull the tape away from the paper envelope. Tape peeled off the rough wood stickily; he tried to curl it back without tearing it or folding it. He heard, dimly, three sharp rings on the intercom, but he didn't pause. Screw Lipsky. Let him sweat for his fifty bucks.

When the top tape was free of the wood, he switched back to a locksmith's pick, slender as a surgeon's scalpel. He knew the envelope flap would be unsealed, he *knew* it! Well, it wasn't just luck or instinct. Why should Blank want to seal the envelope? He'd want to gloat over his goodies, and add more to them later.

Gently Delaney prized out the envelope flap, lifted it. He leaned forward to smell at the open envelope. A scent of roses. Back to the tweezers again, and he carefully withdrew the contents, laying them out on his overcoat lining in the order in which they had been inserted in the envelope: Frank Lombard's driver's license. Bernard Gilbert's ID card. Detective Kope's shield and identification. And four withered rose petals. From Albert Feinberg's boutonniere. Delaney turned them over and over with his tweezers. Then he left them alone, lying there, walked to the window, put his hands in his pockets, stared out.

It really was a beautiful day. Crisp, clear. Everyone had been predicting a mild winter. He hoped so. He'd had his fill of snow, slush, blizzards, garbage-decked drifts—all the crap. He and Barbara would retire to some warm place, some place quiet. Not Florida. He didn't enjoy the heat that much. But maybe the Carolinas. Some place like that. He'd go fishing. He had never fished in his life, but he could learn. Barbara would have a decent garden. She'd love that.

God damn it, it wasn't the murders! He had seen the results of murder without end. Murders by gun, by knife, by strangling, by bludgeoning, by drowning, by stomping, by—by anything. You name it; he had seen it. And he had handled homicides where the corpse was robbed: money taken, fingers cut off to get the rings, necklaces wrenched from a dead neck, even shoes taken and, in one case, gold teeth pulled out with pliers.

He turned back to that display on his overcoat. This was the worst. He could not say exactly why, but this was an obscenity so awful he wasn't certain he wanted to live, to be a member of the human race. This was despoiling the dead, not for vengeance, want, or greed, but for—For what? A souvenir? A trophy? A scalp? There was something godless about it, something he could not endure. He didn't know. He just didn't know. Not right now. But he'd think about it.

He cleaned up fast. Everything back in to the envelope with tweezers, in the exact order in which they had originally been packed. The envelope flap tucked under with no bend or crease. The top tape pressed down again upon the wood. It held. The drawer turned rightside up. Underwear back in neat stacks in the original order. Drawer slid into the dresser. He inspected the lining of his overcoat. Some wood dust there, from the drawer runners. He went in to the bathroom, moistened two sheets of toilet paper at the sink, came back into the bedroom, sponged his overcoat lining clean. Back into the bathroom, used tissues into the toilet. But before he flushed, he used two more squares to wipe the sink dry. Then those went into the toilet also; he flushed all away. He would, he thought sardonically—and not for the first time—have made a hell of a murderer.

He made a quick trip of inspection through the apartment. All clean. He was at the front door, his hand on the knob, when he thought of something else. He went back into the kitchen, opened the lower cabinets. A plastic pail, detergents, roach spray, floor wax, furniture polish. And, what he had hoped to find, a small can of light machine oil.

He tore a square of paper towel from the roll hanging from the kitchen wall. Could this man keep track of pieces of toilet paper or sections of paper towel? Delaney wouldn't be a bit surprised. But he soaked the paper towel in the machine oil, folded it up, put it inside one of his fleece-lined gloves in his overcoat pocket. Machine oil can return to its original position.

Then back to the outside door, unlocking, a quick peer outside at an empty corridor. He stepped out, locked up, tried the knob three times. Solid. He walked toward the elevators, stripping off his black silk gloves stuffing them away into an inside pocket. He rang the Down button and while he waited, he took three ten-dollar bills from his wallet, folded them tightly about the keys, held them in his right hand.

There were six other people in the elevator. They stood back politely to let him get on. He edged slowly toward the back. Music was playing softly. In the lobby, he let everyone else off first, then walked out, looked about for Lipsky. He finally saw him, outside, helping an old woman into a cab. He waited patiently until Lipsky came back inside. Lipsky saw him, and the Captain thought he might faint. Delaney moved forward smiling, holding out his right hand. He felt Lipsky's wet palm as keys and money were passed.

Delaney nodded, still smiling, and walked outside. He walked down the driveway. He walked home. He was thinking a curious thought: that his transfer to the Patrol Division had been a mistake. He didn't want administrative experience. He didn't want to be Police Commissioner. This was what he did best. And what he liked best.

He called Thorsen from his home. It was no time to be worrying about tapped phones, if that ever had any validity to begin with. But Thorsen did not return his call, not for 15 minutes. Delaney then called his office. The Deputy Inspector was "in conference" and could not be disturbed.

"Disturb him," Delaney said sharply. "This is Captain Edward X. Delaney. It's an emergency."

He waited a few moments, then:

"Jesus Christ, Edward, what's so—"

"I've got to see you. At once."

"Impossible. You don't know what's going on down here. All hell is breaking loose. It's the showdown."

Delaney didn't ask what "showdown." He wasn't interested. "I've got to see you," he repeated.

Thorsen was silent a minute. Then: "Will it wait till six o'clock? There's another meeting with the Commissioner at seven, but I'll be able to see you at six. Can it hold till then?"

Delaney thought. "All right. Six o'clock. Where?"

"Uptown. The seven o'clock meeting's at the Mansion. Better make it my house at six."

"I'll be there."

He pressed the phone prongs just long enough to break the connection, then dialed Dr. Sanford Ferguson.

"Captain Edward X. Delaney here."

"Neglect, neglect, neglect," Ferguson said sorrowfully. "You haven't called me for 'two more things' in weeks. Not sore at me, are you, Edward?"

"No," Delaney laughed, "I'm not sore at you."

"How you coming along?"

"All right. I read your preliminary report on the Feinberg kill, but I didn't see the final PM."

"Completed it today. The usual. Nothing new."

"The preliminary report said that blood found on the sidewalk was not the victim's type."

"That's correct."

"What type was it?"

"You're *asking* me? Edward, you're losing your grip. I thought you'd be telling me."

"Just a minute." Delaney took his notebook from his inside coat pocket. "All right, I'll tell you. AB-Rh negative."

There was a swift intake of breath. "Edward, you *are* getting somewhere, aren't you? You're right. AB-Rh negative. A rare type. Who has it?"

"A friend of mine," Delaney said tonelessly. "A close friend."

"Well, when you take him, make it clean, will you?" the Medical Examiner said. "I'm getting bored with crushed skulls. A single pop through the heart would be nice."

"Too good for him," Delaney said savagely.

Silence then. Finally: "Edward, you're not losing your cool, are you?" Ferguson asked, concern in his voice.

"I've never been colder in my life."

"Good."

"One more thing. . ."

"Now I know you're normal."

"I'm mailing you a sample of a light machine oil. It's a different brand from the one I gave you before. Will you try to get a match with oil in the tissue from Feinberg's wounds?"

"I'll try. Sounds like you're close, Edward."

"Yes. Thank you, doctor."

"He looked at his watch. Almost two hours to kill before his meeting with Thorsen. He sat down at his study desk, put on his glasses, picked up a pencil, drew a pad toward him. He began to head the page "Report on—" then stopped, thinking carefully. Was it wise to have an account of that illegal break-in, in his handwriting? He pushed pad and pencil away, rose, began to pace around the room, hands jammed in his hip pockets.

If, for some reason he could not yet foresee, it came to a court trial or the taking of sworn depositions, it was Lipsky's word against his. All Lipsky could swear to was that he had passed the keys. He had not seen Delaney in Blank's apartment. He could not honestly swear to that, only that he had given Delaney the keys and *presumed* he was going to search the apartment. But presumptions had no value. Still, the Captain decided, he would not make a written report of the search. Not at this moment, at any rate. He continued his pacing.

The problem, he decided—the *essential problem*—was not how to take Blank. That had to wait for his meeting with Thorsen at six o'clock. The essential problem was Blank, the man himself, who he was, what he was, what he might do.

That apartment was a puzzle. It displayed a dichotomy (the Captain was familiar with the word) of personality difficult to decipher. There was the incredible orderliness, almost a fanatical tidiness. And the ultramodern furnishings, black and white, steel and leather, no warmth, no softness, no personal "give" to the surroundings.

Then there were the multi-hued linens, luxurious personal belongings, the excess of silk and soft fabrics, feminine underwear, the perfumes, oils, scented creams, the jewelry. That mutilated nude photograph. And, above all, the mirrors. Mirrors everywhere.

He went over to the cabinet, flipped through the Daniel G. Blank file, pulled out the thick report he had written after his interview with Dr. Otto Morgenthau. Delaney stood at his desk, turning pages until he found the section he wanted, where Morgenthau, having discussed causes, spoke about motives, how the mass murderer, justified his actions to himself. The Captain had jotted short, elliptic notes:

"Elaborate rationalizations. No guilt. Killings necessary . . .

"1. Impose order on chaos. Cannot stand disorder or the unpredictable. Needs rules of institution: prison, army, etc. Finds peace, because no responsibility in completely ordered world.

"2. Graffiti artist. Make his mark by murder. I exist! Statement to world.

"3. Alienation. Cannot relate to anyone. Cannot feel. Wants to come close to another human being. To love? Through love to all humanity and secret of existence. God? Because (in youth?) emotion, feeling, love have been denied to him. Cannot find (feel) except by killing. Ecstasy."

Delaney reread these notes again, and recalled Dr. Morgenthau's warning that in dealing with multiple killers, there were no precise classifications. Causes overlapped, and so did motives. These were not simple men who killed from greed, lust or vengeance. They were a tangled complex, could not recognize themselves where truth ended and fantasy began. But perhaps in their mad, whirling minds there were no endings and no beginnings. Just a hot swirl, with no more outline than a flame and as fluid as blood.

He put the notes away, no closer to Dan's heart. The thing about Dan was—He stopped suddenly. Dan? He was thinking of him as "Dan" now? Not Blank, or Daniel G. Blank, but Dan. Very well, he would think of him as Dan. "A friend," he had told Dr. Ferguson. "A close friend." He had smelled his soap, handled his underwear, felt his silken robes, heard his voice, seen a photo of him naked. Discovered his secrets.

The trouble with Dan, the trouble with understanding Dan, was the question he had posed to Barbara: Was it possible to solve an irrational problem by rational means? He hadn't the answer to that. Yet. He glanced at his watch, hurriedly emptied his pockets of penlite, black silk gloves, case of lock picks. He wrapped the oil-soaked wad of paper towel in a square of aluminum foil, put it into an envelope addressed to Dr. Sanford Ferguson, and mailed it on his way to the home of Deputy Inspector Thorsen.

It was strange, he could smell cigar smoke on the sidewalk outside Thorsen's brownstone. He walked up the stoop; the smell was stronger. He hoped to hell Karen was visiting or up in her bedroom; she hated cigars.

He rang. And rang. Rang. Finally Thorsen pulled open the door.

"Sorry, Edward. Lots of noise."

Thorsen, he noted, was under pressure. The "Admiral' was hanging on tight, but the fine silver hair was unbrushed, blue eyes dimmed, the whites bloodshot, lines in his face Delaney had never seen before. And a jerkiness to his movements.

The door of the living room was closed. But the Captain heard a loud, angry babble. He saw a pile of overcoats, at least a dozen, thrown over hallway chairs. Civilian and uniform coats, civilian hats and cop hats. One cane. One umbrella. The air was hot and swirling—cigar smoke, and harsh. Thorsen didn't ask for his hat and coat.

"Come in here," he commanded.

He led Delaney down a short hall to a dining room, flicked on a wall switch. There was a Tiffany lampshade over the heavy oak dining table. Thorsen closed the door, but the Captain could still hear the voices, still smell the coarse cigars.

"What is it?" Thorsen demanded.

Delaney looked at him. He could forgive that tone; the man was obviously exhausted. Something was happening, something big.

"Ivar," he said gently—perhaps the second or third time in his life he had used the Deputy Inspector's given name—"I've found him."

Thorsen looked at him, not comprehending.

"Found him?"

Delaney didn't answer. Thorsen, staring at him, suddenly knew.

"Oh Jesus," he groaned. "Now of all times. Right now. Oh, God. No doubt at all?"

"No. No doubt. It's absolute."

Thorsen took a deep breath.

"Don't—" he started to say, then stopped, smiled wanly at the Captain. "Congratulations, Edward."

Delaney didn't say anything.

"Don't move from here. Please. I want Johnson and Alinski in on this. I'll be right back."

The Captain waited patiently. Still standing, he ran his fingers over the waxed surface of the dining table. Old, scarred oak. There was something about wood, something you couldn't find in steel, chrome, aluminum, plastic. The wood had lived, he decided; that was the answer. The wood had been seedling, twig, trunk, all pulsing with sap, responding to the seasons, growing. The tree cut down eventually, and sliced, planed, worked, sanded, polished. But the sense of life was still there. You could feel it.

Inspector Johnson seemed as distraught as Thorsen; his black face was sweated, and Delaney noted the hands thrust into trouser pockets. You did that to conceal trembling. But Deputy Mayor Herman Alinski was still expressionless, the short, heavy body composed, dark, intelligent eyes moving from man to man.

The four men stood around the dining table. No one suggested they sit. From outside, Delaney could still hear the loud talk going on, still smell the crude cigar smoke.

"Edward?" Thorsen said in a low voice.

Delaney looked at the other two men. Then he addressed himself directly to Alinski.

"I have found the killer of Frank Lombard, Bernard Gilbert, Detective Kope, and Albert Feinberg," he said, speaking slowly and distinctly. "There is no possibility of error. I know the man who committed the four homicides."

There was silence. Delaney looked from Alinski to Johnson to Thorsen.

"Oh Jesus," Johnson said. "That tears it."

"No possibility of error?" Alinski repeated softly.

"No, sir. None."

"Can we make a collar, Edward?" Thorsen asked. "Now?"

"No use. He'd be out in an hour."

"Run him around the horn?" Johnson said in a cracked voice.

Delaney: "What for? A waste of time. He'd float free eventually."

Thorsen: "Search warrant?"

Delaney: "Not even from a pet judge."

Johson: "Anything for the DA?"

Delaney: "Not a thing."

Thorsen: "Will he sweat in the slammer?"

Delaney: "No."

Johnson: "Break-in?"

Delaney: "What do you think?"

Thorsen: "You left it?"

Delaney: "What else could I do?"

Thorsen: "But it was there?"

Delaney: "Three hours ago. It may be gone by now."

Johnson: "Witnesses to the break-in?"

Delaney: "Presumption only."

Thorsen: "Then we've got nothing?"

Delaney: "Not right now."

Johnson: "But you can nail him?"

Delaney (astonished): "Of course. Eventually."

Deputy Mayor Herman Alinski had followed this fast exchange without interrupting. Now he held up a hand. They fell silent. He carefully relighted a cold cigar he had brought into the room with him.

"Gentlemen," he said quietly, "I realize I am just a poor pole, one generation removed from the Warsaw ghetto, but I did think I had mastered the English language and the American idiom. But I would be much obliged, gentlemen, if you could inform me just what the fuck you are talking about."

They laughed then. The ice was broken—which was, Delaney realized, exactly what Alinski had intended. The Captain turned to Thorsen.

"Let me tell it my way?"

Thorsen nodded.

"Sir," the Captain said, addressing the Deputy Mayor directly, "I will tell you what I can. Some things I will not tell you. Not to protect myself. I don't give a damn. But I don't think it wise that you and these other men should have guilty knowledge. You understand?"

Alinski, smoking his cigar, nodded. His dark eyes deepened even more; he stared at Delaney with curious interest.

"I know the man who committed these homicides," the Captain continued. "I have seen the evidence. Conclusive, incontrovertible evidence. You'll have to take my word for that. The evidence exists, or did exist three hours ago, in this man's apartment. But the evidence is of such a nature that it doesn't justify a collar—an arrest. Why not? Because it exists in his apartment, his home. How could I swear to what I have seen? Legally, I have seen nothing. And if, by any chance, a sympathetic judge issued a search warrant, what then? Served on the man while he was at home, he could stall long enough to destroy the evidence. Somehow. Then what? Arrest him on a charge—any charge? And run the risk of a false arrest suit? What for? Run him around the horn? That's probably some of our cop talk you didn't understand. It means collaring a suspect, keeping him in a precinct house detention cell, trying to sweat him—getting him to talk. He calls his lawyer. We're required to let him do that. His lawyer gets a release. By the time the lawyer shows up with the paper, we've moved him to another precinct house tank. No one knows where. By the time the lawyer finds out, we've moved him again. We waltz him "around the horn." It's an old routine, not used much these days, originally used when cops needed to keep an important witness in the slammer, or needed another day or two days or three days to nail the guy good. It wouldn't work here. Sweating him wouldn't work either. Don't ask me how I know—I just know. He won't talk. Why should he? He makes fifty-five thousand a year. He's an important business executive with a big corporation in the city. He's no street ponce with a snoot full of shit. We can't lean on him. He's got no record. He's got a good lawyer. He's got friends. He carries weight. Got it now?"

"Yes. . ." Alinski said slowly. "I've got it now. Thank you, Captain."

"Fifty-five thousand a year?" Inspector Johnson said incredulously. "Jesus H. Christ!"

"One thing," the Deputy Mayor said. "Inspector Johnson asked if you could nail him, and you said yes. How do you propose to do that?"

"I don't know," Delaney admitted. "I haven't thought it through yet. That's not why I came here tonight."

"Why did you come?"

"This crazy's coming up to another kill. I figure it should be in the week between Christmas and New Year's. But it may be sooner. I can't take the chance."

Strangely, no one asked him how he had estimated the killer's schedule. They simply believed him.

"So," Delaney went on, "i came here tonight for three men, plainclothes, on foot, and one unmarked car, with two men, to cover this guy tonight. I either get this cover or I'll have to dump what I have in Broughton's lap, let him own it, and take my lumps. Before, I just had a lead to offer him. Now I've got the guy he's bleeding for."

His demand came so suddenly, so abruptly, that the other three were startled. They looked at each other; the noise and smells from outside, men talking, arguing, smoking in the living room, seemed to invade this quiet place and envelop them all.

"Now," Thorsen said bitterly. "It would have to be tonight."

"You can do it," Delaney said stonily, staring at the Deputy Inspector. "I don't give a fuck where you get them. Bring them in from Staten Island. This guy has got to be covered. Tonight and every night until I can figure out how to take him."

Silence then, in the dining room, the four men standing. Only Delaney looked at Thorsen; the other men's eyes were turned downward, unseeing.

Was it a minute, or five, or ten? The Captain never knew. Finally Deputy Mayor Alinski sighed deeply, raised his head to look at Thorsen and Johnson.

"Would you excuse us?" he asked gently. "I would like to speak to Captain Delaney privately. For just a few moments. Would you wait outside, please?"

Wordlessly, they filed out, Johnson closing the door behind them.

Alinski looked at Delaney and smiled. "Could we sit down?" he asked. "It seems to me we have been standing much too long."

Delaney nodded. They took padded armchairs on opposite sides of the oak table.

"You don't smoke cigars?" Alinski asked.

"No more. Oh, occasionally. But not very often."

"Filthy habit," Alinski nodded. "But all enjoyable habits are filthy. I looked up your record. 'Iron Balls.' Am I right?"

"Yes."

"In my younger days I was called 'Bubble Head.'"

Delaney smiled.

"Good record," Alinski said. "How many commendations?"

"I don't know."

"You've lost count. Many. You were in the Army in World War Two. Military Police."

"That's correct."

"Yes. Tell me something, Captain: Do you feel that the military—the Army, Navy, Air Force—should be, at the top, under control of civilian authority—President, Secretary of Defense, and so forth?"

"Of course."

"And do you also believe that the Police Department of the City of New York should also, essentially, be under civilian control? That is, that the Commissioner, the highest ranking police officer, should be appointed by the Mayor, a civilian politician?"

"Yes . . . I guess I believe that," Delaney said slowly. "I don't like civilian interference in Department affairs anymore than any other cop. But I agree the Department should be subject to some civilian control authority, not be a totally autonomous body. Some form of civilian control is the lesser of two evils."

Alinski smiled wryly. "So many decisions in this world come down to that," he nodded. "The lesser of two evils. Thorsen and Johnson tell me you are an apolitical man. That is, you have very little interest in Department politics, in feuds, cliques, personality conflicts. Is that correct?"

"Yes."

"You just want to be left alone to do your job?"

"That's right."

The Deputy Mayor nodded again. "We owe you an explanation," he said. "It won't be a complete explanation because there are some things you have no need to know. Also, time is growing short. We must all be at the Mansion by seven. Well then . . .

"About three years ago it became apparent that there was a serious breach of security in the Mayor's 'Inner Circle.' This is an informal group, about a dozen men—the Mayor's closest personal friends, advisors, various media experts, campaign contributors, labor leaders, and so forth—on whom he depends for advice and ideas. Meetings are held once a month, or more often when needed. Well, someone in that group was leaking. Newspapers were getting rumors they shouldn't get, and some individuals were profiting from plans still in the discussion stage, before the public announcement was made. The problem was dumped in my lap; one of my responsibilities is internal security. It wasn't hard to discover who was leaking—his name's of no importance to you."

"How did you do it?" Delaney asked. "I'm just interested in the technique you used."

"The most obvious," Alinski shrugged. "Various fictitious documents planted with every man in the Inner Circle. Only one was leaked. It was that easy. But before we kicked this bastard downstairs to a job inspecting monuments or potholes—you don't fire a man like that; the public scandal helps no one—I put him under twenty-four hour surveillance and discovered something interesting. Once a week he was having dinner with five men, always the same five men. They were meeting at one of their homes or in a hotel room or renting a private dining room in a restaurant. It was a curious group. Chairman of the Board of a downtown bank, real estate speculator, editor of a news magazine, a corporation VP, our squealer, and Deputy Commissioner Broughton. I didn't like the smell of it. What did those men have in common? They didn't even all belong to the same political party. So I kept an eye on them. A few months later, the six had grown to twelve, then to twenty. And they were entertaining occasional guests from Albany, and once a man from the Attorney-General's office in Washington. By this time there were almost thirty members, dining together ever week."

"Including the man you infiltrated," Delaney said.

Alinski smiled distantly but didn't answer. "It took me a while to catch on," he continued. "As far as I could determine, they had no name, no address, no letterhead, no formal organization, no officers. Just an informal group who met for dinner. That's what I called them in my verbal reports to the Mayor—the 'Group.' I kept watching. It was fascinating to see how they grew. They split into three divisions; three separate dinners every week: one of the money men; one of the editors, writers, publishers, TV producers; one of cops—local, state, a few federal. Then they began recruiting. Nothing obvious, but a solid cadre. Still no name, no address, no program—nothing. But odd things began happening: certain editorials, hefty campaign contributions to minor league pols, pressure for or against certain bills, some obviously planned and extremely well organized demonstrations, heavy clout that got a certain man off on probation of a tax evasion rap that should have netted him five years. The Group was growing, fast. And the members were Democrats, Republicans, Liberals, Conservatives—you name it, they had them. Still no public announcements, no formal program, no statement of principles—nothing like that. But it came increasingly clear what they were after: an authoritarian city government, 'law and order,' let the cops use their sticks, guns for everyone. Except the blacks. More muscle in government. Tell people, don't ask them. Because people really want to be told, don't they? All they need or want is a cold six-pack and a fourth rerun of 'I Love Lucy.'"

Alinski glanced at his watch. "I've got to cut this short," he said. "Time's running out. But I get carried away. Half my family got made into soup at Treblinka. Anyway, Deputy Commissioner Broughton began to throw his weight around. The man is good; I don't deny it. Shrewd, strong, active. And loud. Above all, loud. So when Frank Lombard was killed, the Group's agit-prop division went to work. It was a natural. After all, Frank Lombard was a member of the Group."

Delaney looked at him, astounded. "You mean these four victims had something in common after all—a political angle? Were the other three members of the Group, too?"

"No, no," Alinski shook his head. "Don't get me wrong. Detective Kope couldn't have been a member because the Group doesn't recruit cops under the rank of lieutenant. And Bernard Gilbert and Albert Feinberg couldn't have been members because there are no Jews in the Group. No, Lombard's death was just a coincidence, a chance killing, and I guess the man you've found has never even heard of the Group. Not many people have. But Lombard's murder was a marvelous opportunity for the Group. First of all, he was a very vocal advocate of 'law and order.' 'Let us crush completely crime in our city streets.' Broughton saw his opportunity. He got command of Operation Lombard. With the political pressures the Group organized he got everything he wanted—men, equipment, unlimited funds. You've met Broughton?"

"Yes."

"Don't underestimate him. He has the confidence of the devil. He thought he'd wrap up the Lombard murder in record time. Score one for his side, and an important step toward becoming the next Commissioner. But in case he didn't find Lombard's killer, the Group would be left with their thumbs up their assholes. So I asked Thorsen and Johnson who were the best detectives in New York. They named you and Chief Pauley. Broughton took Pauley. Thorsen and Johnson asked for you, and we went along with them."

"Who is 'we'?"

"Our Group," Alinski smiled. "Or call it our 'Anti-Group.' Anyway, here is the situation of this moment. At the meeting tonight, we think we can get Broughton dumped from Operation Lombard. No guarantee, but we think we can do it. But not if you go to him now and give him the killer."

"Fuck Broughton," Delaney said roughly. "I couldn't care less about his ambitions, political or otherwise. I won't go to him if you'll just give me my three plainclothesmen on foot and two in an unmarked car."

"But you see," Alinski explained patiently, "we cannot possibly do that. How could we? From where? You don't realize how big the Group has grown, how powerful. They are everywhere, in every precinct, in every special unit in the Department. Not the men; the officers. How can we risk alerting Broughton that we have the killer and want to put a watch on him? You know exactly what would happen. He would come galloping with sirens screaming, flashing lights, a hundred men and, when all the TV cameras were in place, he'd pull your man out of his apartment in chains."

"And lose him in the courts," Delaney said bitterly. "I'm telling you, at this moment you couldn't even indict this man, let alone convict him."

The Deputy Mayor looked at his watch again and grimaced, "We're going to be late," he said. H strode to the door, yanked it open. Thorsen and Johnson were waiting outside, in hats and overcoats. Alinski waved them into the dining room, then closed the door behind them. He turned to Delaney. "Captain," he said. "Twenty-four hours. Will you give us that? Just twenty-four hours. After that, if Broughton still heads Operation Lombard, you better go to him and tell him what you have. He'll crucify you, but he'll have the killer—and the headlines—whether or not the man is ever convicted."

"You won't give the guards?" Delaney asked.

"No. I can't stop you from going to Broughton right now, if that's what you want to do. But I will not cooperate in 'iis triumph by furnishing the men you want."

"All right," the Captain said mildly. He pushed by Alinski, Thorsen, Johnson, and pulled open the door. "You can have your twenty-four hours."

He made his way through the hallway, crowded now with men pulling on hats and coats. He looked at no one, spoke to no one, although one man called his name.

Back in the dining room, Alinski looked at the two officers in astonishment. "He agreed so easily," he said, puzzled. "Maybe he was exaggerating. Perhaps there is no danger tonight. He certainly didn't fight very hard for the guards he wanted."

Thorsen looked at him, then looked out into the hallway where the others were waiting.

"You don't know Edward," he said, almost sadly.

"That's right," Inspector Johnson agreed softly. "He's going to freeze his ass off tonight."

●　　●　　●

He wasn't furious, wasn't even angry. They had their priorities, and he had his. They had the "Group" and "Anti-Group." He had Daniel G. Blank. It was interesting, listening to the Deputy Mayor, and he supposed their concern was important. But he had been in the Department a long time, had witnessed many similar battles between the "Ins" and the "Outs," and it was difficult for him to become personally involved in this political clash. Somehow the Department always survived. At the moment, his only interest was Dan, his close friend Dan.

He walked home rapidly, called Barbara immediately. But it was Dr. Louis Bernardi who answered the phone.

"What's wrong?" Delaney demanded. "Is Barbara all right?"

"Fine, fine, Captain," the doctor soothed. "We're just conducting a little examination."

"So you think the new drug is helping?"

"Coming along," Bernardi said blithely. "A little fretful, perhaps, but that's understandable. It doesn't worry me."

Oh you bastard, Delaney thought again. Nothing worries *you*. Why the hell should it?

"I think we'll give her a little something to help her sleep tonight," Bernardi went on in his greasy voice. "Just a little something. I think perhaps you might skip your visit tonight, Captain. A nice, long sleep will do our Barbara more good."

"Our Barbara." Delaney could have throttled him, and cheerfully. "All right," he said shortly. "I'll see her tomorrow."

He looked at his watch: almost seven-thirty. He didn't have much time; it was dark outside; the street lights were on, had been since six. He went up to the bedroom, stripped down to his skin. He knew, from painful experience, what to wear on an all-night vigil in winter.

Thermal underwear, a two-piece set. A pair of light cotton socks with heavy wool socks over them. An old winter uniform, pants shiny, jacket frayed at the cuffs and along the seams. But there was still no civilian suit as warm as that good, heavy blanket wool. And the choker collar would protect his chest and throat. Then his comfortable "cop-shoes" with a pair of rubbers over them, even though the streets were dry and no rain or snow predicted.

He unlocked his equipment drawer in the bedroom taboret. He owned three guns: his .38 service revolver, a .32 "belly gun" with a two-inch barrel, and a .45 automatic pistol which he had stolen from the U.S. Army in 1946. He selected the small .32, slid it from its flannel bag and, flicking the cylinder to the side, loaded it slowly and carefully from a box of ammunition. He didn't bother with an extra gun belt. The gun was carried on his pants belt in a black leather holster. He adjusted it under his uniform jacket so the gun hung down over his right groin, aimed toward his testicles: a happy thought. He checked the safety again.

His identification into his inside breast pocket. A leather-covered sap slid into a special narrow pocket alongside his right leg. Handcuffs into his righthand pants pocket and, at the last minute, he added a steel-linked "come-a-long"—a short length of chain, just long enough to encircle a wrist, with heavy grips at both ends.

Downstairs, he prepared a thick sandwich of bologna and sliced onion, wrapped it in waxed paper, put it into his civilian overcoat pocket. He filled a pint flask with brandy; that went into the inside overcoat breast pocket. He found his fleece-lined earmuffs and fur-lined leather gloves; they went into outside overcoat pockets.

Just before he left the house, he dialed Daniel Blank. He knew the number by heart now. The phone rang three times, then that familiar voice said, "Hello?" Delaney hung up softly. At least his friend was home, the Captain wouldn't be watching an empty hole.

He put on his stiff Homburg, left the hall light burning, double-locked the front door, went out into the night. He moved stiffly, hot and sweating under his layers of clothing. But he knew that wouldn't last long.

He walked over to Daniel Blank's apartment house, pausing once to transfer the come-along to his lefthand pants pocket so it wouldn't clink against the handcuffs. The weighted blackjack knocked against his leg as he walked, but he was familiar with that feeling; there was nothing to be done about it.

It was an overcast night, not so much cold as damp and raw. He pulled on his gloves and knew it wouldn't be long before he clamped on the earmuffs. It was going to be a long night.

Plenty of people still on the streets; laden Christmas shoppers hurrying home. The lobby lights of Dan's apartment house were blazing. Two doormen on duty now, one of them Lipsky. They were hustling tips. Why not—it was Christmas, wasn't it? Cabs were arriving and departing, private cars were heading into the underground garage, tenants on foot were staggering up with shopping bags and huge parcels.

Delaney took up his station across the street, strolling up and down the length of the block. The lobby was easily observable during most of his to-and-from pacing, or could be glimpsed over his shoulder. When it was behind him, he turned his head frequently enough to keep track of arrivals and departures. After every five trips, up and down, he crossed the street and walked along the other side once, directly in front of the apartment house, then crossed back again and continued his back-and-forth vigil. He walked at a steady pace, not fast, not slow, stamping each foot slightly with every step, swinging his arms more than he would ordinarily.

He could perform this job automatically, and he welcomed the chance it gave him to consider once again his conversation with Thorsen, Johnson, Deputy Mayor Alinski.

What disturbed him was that he was not positive he had been entirely accurate in his comments regarding the admissibility of evidence and the possibility of obtaining a search warrant. Ten years ago he would have been absolutely certain. But recent court decisions, particularly those of the Supreme Court, had so confused him—and all cops—that he no longer comprehended the laws of evidence and the rights of suspects.

Even such a Philadelphia lawyer as Lt. Marty Dorfman had admitted his confusion. "Captain," he had said, "they've demolished the old guidelines without substituting a new, definite code. Even the DA's men are walking on eggs. As I see it, until all this gets straightened out and enough precedents established, each case will be judged on its own merits, and we'll have to take our chances. It's the old story: 'The cop proposes, the judge disposes.' Only now even the judges aren't sure. That's why the percentage of appeals is way, way up."

Well, start from the beginning . . . His search of Dan's apartment had been illegal. Nothing he saw or learned from that search could be used in court. No doubt about that. If he had taken away Dan's "trophies," it would have served no purpose other than to alert Blank that his apartment had been tossed, that he was under suspicion.

Now what about a search warrant? On what grounds? That Dan owned an ice ax of a type possibly used to kill four men? And, of course, of a type owned by hundreds of people all over the world? That blood of Dan's type had been found at the scene of the most recent homicide? How many people had that blood type? That he possessed a can of light machine oil that a thousand other New Yorkers owned? And all of these facts established only by an illegal break-in. Or tell the judge that Daniel G. Blank was a known mountaineer and was suspected of carrying two dummy Christmas packages the night Albert Feinberg was slain? Delaney could imagine the judge's reaction to request for a search warrant on those grounds.

No, he *had* been correct. As of this moment, Dan was untouchable. Then why hadn't he taken the whole mess to Broughton and dumped it on him? Because Alinski had been exactly right, knowing his man. Broughton would have said, "Fuck the law," would have come on like Gang Busters, would have collared Blank, got the headlines and TV exposure he wanted.

Later, when Blank was set free, as he was certain to be, Broughton would denounce "permissive justice," "slack criminal laws," "handcuffing the cops, not the crooks." The fact that Blank walked away a free man would have little importance to Broughton compared to the publicity of the suspect's release, the public outcry, the furtherance of exactly what the Group wanted.

But if Dan couldn't legally—

Delaney ceased pondering, his head crooked over his shoulder. There was a man standing in the lighted lobby, talking to one of the doormen. The man was tall, slender, wearing a black topcoat, no hat. Delaney stopped midstride, took a sham look at a nonexistent wristwatch, made a gesture of impatience, turned in his tracks, walked toward the lobby. He should apply for an Actors Equity card, he thought; he really should.

He came abreast of the lobby, across the street, just as Daniel Blank exited from the glass doors and stood a moment. It was undeniably him: wide shoulders, slim hips, handsome with vaguely Oriental features. His left hand was thrust into his topcoat pocket. Delaney glanced long enough to watch him sniff the night air, button up his coat with his right hand, turn up the collar. Then Blank walked down the driveway, turned west in the direction Delaney was moving across the street.

Ah there, the Captain thought. Out for a stroll, Danny boy?

"Danny Boy." The phrase amused him; he began to hum the tune. He matched Blank's speed, and when Dan crossed Second Avenue, Delaney crossed on his side, keeping just a little behind his target. He was good at tailing, but not nearly as good as, say, Lt. Jeri Fernandez, known to his squad as the "Invisible Man."

The problem was mainly one of physical appearance. Delaney was obvious. He was tall, big, stooped, lumbering, with a shapeless black overcoat, a stiff homburg set squarely atop his heavy head. He could change his costume but not the man he was.

Fernandez was average and middle. Average height, middle weight, no distinguishing features. On a tail, he wore clothes a zillion other men wore. More than that, he had mastered the rhythm of the streets, a trick Delaney could never catch. Even within a single city, New York, people moved differently on different streets. In the Garment District they trotted and shoved. On Fifth Avenue they walked at a slower tempo, pausing to look in shop windows. On Park Avenue and upper eastside cross streets they sauntered. Wherever he tailed, Fernandez picked up the rhythm of the street, unconsciously, and moved like a wraith. Set him down in Brussels, Cairo, or Tokyo, the Captain was convinced, and Lt. Jeri Fernandez would take one quick look around and become a resident. Delaney wished he could do it.

But he did what he could, performed what tricks he knew. When Blank turned the corner onto Third Avenue, Delaney crossed the street to move up behind him. He increased his speed to tail from in front. The Captain stopped to look in a store window, watched the reflection in the glass as Blank passed him. Delaney took up a following tail again, dropping behind a couple, dogging their heels closely. If Blank looked back, he'd see a group of three.

Dan was walking slowly. Delaney's covering couple turned away. He continued in his steady pace, passing his quarry again. He was conscious that Blank was now close behind him, but he felt no particular fear. The avenue was well-lighted; there were people about. Danny Boy might be crazy, but he wasn't stupid. Besides, Delaney was certain, he always approached his victims from the front.

Delaney walked another half-block and stopped. He had lost him. He knew it, without turning to look. Instinct? Something atavistic? Fuck it. He just knew it. He turned back, searched, cursed his own stupidity. He should have known, or at least wondered.

Halfway down the block was a pet shop, still open, front window brilliantly lighted. Behind the glass were pups—fox terriers, poodles, spaniels—all frolicking on torn newspaper, and gumming each other, pissing, shitting up a storm, pressing noses and paws against the window where at least half a dozen people stood laughing, tapping the glass, saying things like "Kitchy-koo." Daniel Blank was one of them.

He should have guessed, he repeated to himself. Even the dullest dick three learned that a high percentage of killers were animal lovers. They kept dogs, cats, parakeets, pigeons, even goldfish. They treated their pets with tender, loving care, feeding them at great expense, hustling them to the vet at the first signs of illness, talking to them, caressing them. Then they killed a human being, cutting off the victim's nipples or slicing open the abdomen or shoving a beer bottle up the ass. Captain Edward X. Delaney really didn't want to know the explanation of this predilection of animal lovers for homicide. It was difficult enough, after years of experience, to assimilate the facts of these things happening. The facts themselves were hard enough to accept; who had the time or stomach for explanations?

Then Blank moved off, crossed the street, dodging oncoming traffic. Delaney tailed him on his side of the avenue, but when Dan went into a large, two-window liquor store, the Captain crossed and stood staring at the shop's window display. He was not alone; there were two couples inspecting Christmas gift packages, wicker baskets of liqueurs, cases of imported wine. Delaney inspected them, too, or appeared to. His head was tilted downward just enough so that he could observe Daniel Blank inside the store.

Dan's actions were not puzzling. He took a paper from his righthand pocket, unfolded it, handed it to the clerk. The clerk glanced at it and nodded. The clerk took a bottle of Scotch from a shelf, showed it to Blank. The bottle was in a box, gift-wrapped, a red plastic bow on top. Blank inspected it and approved. The clerk replaced the bottle on the shelf. Blank took several sealed cards from his pocket. They looked to Delaney, standing outside, like Christmas cards. The clerk ran off a tape on an electric adding machine, showed it to Blank. Dan took a wallet from his pocket, extracted some bills, paid in cash. The clerk gave him change. The clerk kept the sheet of paper and the envelopes. They smiled at each other. Blank left the store. It wasn't difficult to understand; Dan was sending several bottles of holiday-wrapped Scotch to several people, several addresses. He left his list and identical cards to be enclosed with each gift. He paid for the liquor and the delivery fee. So?

Delaney tailed him away from the store, south three blocks, east two blocks, north four blocks. Dan walked steadily, alertly; the Captain admired the way he moved: balls of feet touching before the heels came down. But he didn't dawdle, apparently wasn't inspecting, searching. Just getting a breath of air. Delaney was back and forth, across, behind, in front, quartering like a good pointer. Nothing.

In less than a half-hour, Dan was back in his apartment house, headed for the bank of elevators, and eventually disappeared. Delaney, across the street, took a swallow of brandy, ate half his bologna and onion sandwich as he paced, watching. He belched suddenly. Understandable. Brandy and bologna and onion?

Was Dan in for the night? Maybe, maybe not. In any event, Delaney would be there until dawn. Blank's stroll had been—well, inconclusive. It made sense, but the Captain had a nagging feeling of having missed something. What? The man had been under his direct observation for—oh, well, say 75 percent of the time he had been out on the street. He had acted like any other completely innocent evening stroller, out to buy some Christmas booze for his friends, doormen, acquaintances. So?

It did nag. Something. Delaney re-wrapped his half-sandwich, continued his routine pacing. Now the thing to do was to take it from the start, the beginning, and remember everything his friend had done, every action, every movement.

He had first glimpsed him inside the lobby, talking to a doorman. Blank came outside, looked up at the sky, buttoned his coat, turned up the collar, started walking west. Nothing in all that.

He recalled it all again. The slow walk along Third Avenue, Blank's stop outside the pet shop, the way—

Suddenly there was a car pulling up alongside Delaney at the curb. A dusty, four-door, dark blue Plymouth. Two men in the front seat in civilian clothes. But the near man, not the driver, turned a powerful flashlight on Delaney.

"Police," he said. "Stop where you are, please."

Delaney stopped. He turned slowly to face the car. He raised his arms slightly from his body, turned his palms outward. The man with the flashlight got out of the car, his right hand near his hip. His partner, the driver, dimly seen, was cuddling something in his lap. Delaney admired their competence. They were professionals. But he wondered, not for the first time, why the Department invariably selected three-year-old, dusty, four-door, dark blue Plymouths for their unmarked cars. Every villain on the streets could spot one a block away.

The detective with the flashlight advanced two steps, but still kept a long stride away from Delaney. The light was directly in the Captain's eyes.

"Live in the neighborhood?" the man asked. His voice was dry gin, on the rocks.

"Yes," the Captain nodded.

"Do you have identification?"

"Yes," Delaney said. "I am going to reach up slowly with my left hand, open my overcoat, then my jacket. I am going to withdraw my identification from the inside right breast pocket of my jacket with my left hand and hand it to you. Okay?"

The detective nodded.

Delaney, moving slowly, meticulously, handed over his buzzer and ID card in the leather folder. It was a long reach to the detective. The flashlight turned down to the badge and photo, then up again to Delaney's face. Then it was snapped off.

"Sorry, Captain," the man said, no apology in his voice. He handed the leather back.

THE FIRST DEADLY SIN

"You did just right," Delaney said. "Operation Lombard?"

"Yeah," the detective said, and asked no unnecessary questions. "You'll be around awhile?"

"Until dawn."

"We won't roust you again."

"That's all right," Delaney assured him. "What's your name?"

"You're not going to believe it, Captain, but it's William Shakespeare."

"I believe it," Delaney laughed. "There was a football player named William Shakespeare."

"You remember him?" the dick said with wonder and delight. "He probably had the same trouble I have. You should see the looks I get when I register at a motel with my wife."

"Who's your partner?"

The dick turned his flashlight on the driver. He was black, grinning. "A spook," the man on the sidewalk said. "Loves fried chicken and watermelon. Sam Lauder."

The black driver nodded solemnly. "Don't forget the pork chops and collard greens," he said in a marvelously rich bass voice.

"How long you two been partners?" Delaney asked.

"About a thousand years," the driver called.

"Naw," the sidewalk man said. "A year or two. It just *seems* like a thousand."

They all laughed.

"Shakespeare and Lauder," Delaney repeated, "I'll remember. I owe you one."

"Thanks, Captain," Shakespeare said. He got back in the car; they drove away. Delaney was pleased. Good men.

But to get back to Dan . . . He resumed his pacing, the lobby never out of his glance for more than 30 seconds. It was quiet in there now. One doorman.

After the stop at the pet shop, Dan had crossed to the liquor store, presented his Christmas list, paid for his purchases, then sauntered home. So what was bugging Delaney? He reached into his inner overcoat pocket for a swig of brandy from the flask. Reached into his outer pocket for a bit of sandwich. Reached—

Ah. Ah. Now he had it.

Blank had been talking to a doorman inside the lobby when Delaney first spotted him. Unbuttoned black topcoat, left hand thrust into topcoat pocket. Then Dan had come out under the portico, buttoning up his topcoat, turning up the collar with his right hand. No action from the left hand so far—correct?

Then the stroll. Both hands jammed into topcoat pockets. The walk, the tail, the stop at the pet shop—all that was nothing. But now Delaney, from under the brim of his wooden Homburg, is observing Blank inside the liquor store. The right hand dips into the righthand topcoat pocket and comes out with a folded list. The right hand unfolds it on the counter. The right hand holds it out to the clerk. The clerk offers a Christmas-wrapped bottle of Scotch to Blank. Dan takes it in his right hand, inspects it, approves, hands it back to the clerk. Still no action from that left hand. It's dead. Right hand goes back to the topcoat pocket. Out come a half-dozen Christmas cards to be taped to the gifts of liquor. The right hand comes out again with a wallet. The tape is run off. Money paid. The change goes back into the righthand pocket of the topcoat. Left hand, where are you?

Captain Delaney stopped, stood, remembering and suddenly laughing. It was so beautiful. The details always were. What man would carry his

Christmas list, Christmas cards and wallet in the outer pocket of his topcoat? Answer: no man. Because Delaney owned a handsome, custom-made, uniform overcoat that had flapped slits just inside the pocket openings so that he could reach inside to equipment on his gun belt without unbuttoning the overcoat. During World War II he had a lined trench coat with the same convenience, and for his birthday in 1953, Barbara had given him an English raincoat with the identical feature; it could be raining cats and dogs, but you didn't have to unbutton your coat, you just reached through those flapped slits for wallet, tickets, identification—whatever.

Sure. That's how Dan had paid for his liquor purchase. He had reached *through* his topcoat pocket for the list in his jacket pocket. *Through* his topcoat pocket to take the wallet off his hip. *Through* his topcoat pocket to find, somewhere, in some jacket or trouser pocket, the addressed and sealed Christmas cards to be taped to the bottles he was sending. Beautiful.

Beautiful not because this was how Daniel G. Blank was sending Christmas gifts, but because this was how Danny Boy was killing men. Slit pockets. Left hand in pocket, through the slit, holding the ice ax handle. Coat unbuttoned. Right hand swinging free. Then, at the moment of meeting, the quick transfer of the ax to the right hand—that innocent, open, swinging right hand—and then the assault. It was slick. Oh God, was it slick.

Delaney continued his patrol. He knew, he *knew*, Blank would not come out again this night. But that was of no consequence. Delaney would parade until dawn. It gave him time to think things out.

Time to consider The Case of the Invisible Left Hand. What was the solution to that? Two possibilities, Delaney thought. One: The left hand was through the slit of the topcoat pocket and was actually holding the ax under the coat by its handle or leather loop. But the Captain didn't think it likely. Dan's coat had been open when Delaney first saw him in the brightly lighted lobby. Would he risk the doorman or another tenant glimpsing the ax beneath his open coat? From then on, the topcoat was buttoned. Why would Dan carry an ice ax beneath a buttoned coat? He obviously wasn't on the prowl for a victim.

Possibility Two: The left hand was injured or incapacitated in some way. Or the wrist, arm, elbow, or shoulder. Danny Boy couldn't use it normally and tucked it away into the topcoat pocket as a kind of sling. Yes, that was it and it would be easy to check. Thomas Handry could do it in his interview or, better yet, when Delaney called Charles Lipsky tomorrow, he'd ask about any sign of injury to Blank's left arm. The Captain planned to call Lipsky every day to ask if the doorman had been able to get the taxi license number of Dan's dark, skinny girl friend.

All Delaney's interest in a possible injury to Dan's left arm was due, of course, to the evidence of a scuffle, a fight, at the scene of the most recent homicide. Albert Feinberg had made his killer bleed a few drops on the sidewalk. He might have done more.

What time was it? Getting on toward midnight, Delaney guessed. On a long stake-out like this he very deliberately avoided looking at his watch. Start watching the clock, and you were dead; time seemed to go backwards. When the sky lightened, when it was dawn, then he could go home and sleep. Not before.

He varied his patrol, just to keep himself alert. Three up-and-downs on the apartment side. Crossing at different corners. Stopping in the middle of the block to retrace his steps. Anything to keep from walking in a dream. But always watching the lobby entrance. If his friend came out again, he'd come through there.

He finished his sandwich but saved the remainder of the brandy for later.

It must be in the low 40's or high 30's by now; he put on his earmuffs. They were cops' style, connected with a strip of elastic that went entirely around his head, and they fitted snugly. No metal band clamping them to his ears. That clamp could get so cold you thought your skull was coming off.

So what was this business about right hand, left hand, and slit pockets? He knew—no doubt at all—that Daniel Blank was guilty of four homicides. But what he needed was hard evidence, good enough to take to the DA and hope for an indictment. That was the reason for the Handry interview, and the follow-ups he'd have to make on Blank's girl friend, the boy Tony, the Mortons. They were leads that any detective would investigate. They might peter out—probably would—but one of them might, just might, pay off. Then he could nail Danny Boy and bring him to trial. And then?

Then Delaney knew exactly what would happen. Blank's smart, expensive lawyer would cop an insanity plea—"This sick man killed four complete strangers for no reason whatsoever. I ask you, Your Honor, were those the acts of a sane man?"—and Dan would be hidden away in an acorn academy for a period of years.

It would happen, and Delaney couldn't object too strongly; Blank *was* sick, no doubt of that. Hospitalization, in his case, was preferable to imprisonment. But still . . . Well, what was it he, Delaney, wanted? Just to get this nut out of circulation? Oh no. No. More than that.

It wasn't only Dan's motives he couldn't understand; it was his own as well. His thoughts about it were nebulous; he would have to do a lot more pondering. But he knew that never in his life had he felt such an affinity for a criminal. He had a sense that if he could understand Dan, he might better understand himself.

Later in the morning, the sky lightening now, Delaney continued his patrol, swinging his arms, stamping his feet because the brandy had worn off; it was goddamned cold. He got back to the problem of Daniel G. Blank, and to his own problems.

The truth came to him slowly, without shock. Well, it was *his* "truth." It was that he wanted this man dead.

What was in Daniel Blank, what was in him, what he hoped to demolish by putting Dan to death was evil, all evil. Wasn't that it? The idea was so irrational that he could not face, could not consider it.

He looked up to the sky again; it was once again black. It had been a false dawn. He resumed his patrol, flinging his arms sideways to smack his own shoulders, slapping his feet on the pavement, shivering in the darkness.

The phone awoke him. When he looked at the bedside clock it was almost 11.00 a.m. He wondered why Mary hadn't picked it up downstairs, then remembered it was her day off. And he had left a note for her on the kitchen table. He really hadn't been functioning too well when he came off that patrol, but he felt okay now. He must have slept "fast"—as they said in the Army; those four hours had been as good as eight.

"Captain Edward X. Delaney here."

"This is Handry. I got that interview set up with Blank."

"Good. When's it for?"

"The day after Christmas."

"Any trouble?"

"Noo . . . not exactly."

"What happened?"

"I did just what you said, contacted the Javis-Bircham PR man. He was all for it. So I went to see him. You know the type: a big laugh and lots of teeth. I showed him my press pass but he didn't even look at it. He'll never check with the paper. He can't believe anyone could con him. He's too bright—he thinks."

"So what went wrong?"

"Nothing went wrong . . . exactly. He suggested the names of four young, up-and-coming J-B executives—that's the way he kept referring to the corporation, J-B, like IBM, GE and GM—but none of the four names was Blank's."

"Did you tell him you wanted to interview a guy familiar with the uses and future of the computer in business?"

"Of course. But he didn't mention Blank. That's odd—don't you think?"

"Mmm. Maybe. So how did you handle it?"

"Told him I was particularly interested in AMROK II. That's the computer mentioned in that release about Blank I dredged out of the Fink File. Remember?"

"I remember. What did he say to that?"

"Well, then, he mentioned Blank, and agreed when I said I wanted to interview him. But he wasn't happy about it, I could tell."

"It might be personal animosity. You know—office politics. Maybe he hates Blank's guts and doesn't want him to get any personal publicity."

"Maybe," Handry said doubtfully, "but that's not the impression I got."

"What impression did you get?"

"Just a crazy idea."

"Let's have it," Delaney said patiently.

"That maybe Blank's stock is falling. That maybe he hasn't been doing a good job. That maybe the rumor is around that they're going to get rid of him. So naturally the PR man wouldn't want an article in the paper that says what a great genius Blank is, and a week later J-B ties a can to him. Sound crazy?"

Delaney was silent, thinking it over. "No," he said finally, "not so crazy. In fact, it may make a lot of sense. Can you have lunch today?"

"You paying?"

"Sure."

"Then I can have lunch today. Where and when?"

"How about that chophouse where we ate before?"

"Sure. Fine. Great ale."

"About twelve-thirty? In the bar?"

"I'll be there."

The Captain went to shave. As he scraped his jaw, he thought that Handry's impression might possibly be correct. Blank's little hobby could be affecting his efficiency during office hours; that wasn't hard to understand. He had been the corporation's fairhaired boy when that Fink File release was sent out. But now they weren't happy about his being interviewed by the press. Interesting.

Wiping away excess lather and splashing after-shave lotion on his face, Delaney decided he better brief Handry on the upcoming interview during lunch. The interview was scheduled for the day after Christmas. By that time Handry might be reporting the results to Broughton, if he wanted to. But Delaney was determined to do everything he possibly could right up to that 24-hour deadline Alinski had promised which, when the Captain left the house, was now only six hours away.

Handry ordered a broiled veal chop and draft ale. Delaney had a rye highball and steak-and-kidney pie.

"Listen," the Captain said to the reporter, "we've got a lot to get through, so let's get started on it right away."

Handry stared at him. "What's up?" he asked.

"What's up?" Delaney repeated, puzzled. "What do you mean, 'What's up'?"

"We've been sitting here five minutes at the most. You've already looked at your watch twice, and you keep fiddling with the silverware. You never did that before."

"You should be a detective," Delaney growled, "and go looking for clues."

"No, thanks. Detectives lie too much, and they always answer a question with a question. Right?"

"When did I ever answer a question with a question?"

Handry shook with laughter, spluttering. Finally, when he calmed down, he said: "On the way over, just before I left the office. I met a guy at the water cooler. He's on the political side. City. He says there was a big meeting at the Mansion last night. Heavy brass. He says the rumor is that Deputy Commissioner Broughton is on the skids. Because of his flop with Operation Lombard. You know anything about that?"

"No."

"Doesn't affect you one way or another?"

"No."

"All right," Handry sighed. "Have it your own way. So, like you said, let's get started."

"Look," Delaney said earnestly, leaning forward across the table on his elbows. "I'm not conning you. Sure, there are some things I'm not telling you, but they're not mine to tell. You've been a great help to me. This interview with Blank is important. I don't want you to think I'm deliberately lying to you."

"All right, all right," Handry said, holding up a hand. "I believe you. Now, what I'd guess you'd like to know most from this Blank interview is whether or not he's a mountain climber, and if he owns an ice ax. Right?"

"Right," the Captain said promptly, not bothering to mention that he had already established these facts. It was necessary that Handry continue to believe that his interview was important. "Sure, I want to know what he does at Javis-Bircham, what his job is, how many people work for him, and so on. That has to be the bulk of the interview or he'll get suspicious. But what I *really* want is his personal record, his history, his background, the man himself. Can you get that?"

"Sure."

"You can? All right, let's suppose I'm Blank. You're interviewing me. How do you go about it?"

Handry thought a moment, then: "Could you tell me something about your personal life, Mr. Blank? Where you were born, schools you attended—things like that."

"What for? I thought this interview was about the installation of AMROK II and the possibilities for the computer in business?"

"Oh, it is, it is. But in these executive interviews, Mr. Blank, we always try to include a few personal items. It adds to the readability of the article and to make the man interviewed a real person."

"Good, good," Delaney nodded. "You've got the right idea. Play up to his ego. There are millions of readers out there who want to know about *him*, not just the job he does."

Their food and drinks arrived, and they dug in, but Delaney wouldn't pause.

"Here's what I need about him," he said, and took a deep swallow from his glass. "Where and when he was born, schools, military service, previous jobs, marital status. All right—let's take marital status. I'm Blank again. You ask questions."

"Are you married, Mr. Blank?" Handry asked.

"Is that important to the article?"

"Well, if you'd rather not . . ."

"I'm divorced. I guess it's no secret."

"I see. Any children?"

"No."

"Any plans for marriage in the near future?"

"I really don't think that has any place in your article, Mr. Handry."

"No. You're right. I guess not. But we have a lot of women readers, Mr. Blank—more than you'd guess—and things like that interest them."

"You're doing great," Delaney said approvingly. "Actually, he's got a girl friend, but I doubt if he'll mention her. Now let's rehearse the mountain climbing thing. How will you go about that?"

"Do you have any hobbies, Mr. Blank? Stamp collecting, skiing, boating, bird watching—anything like that?"

"Well . . . as a matter of fact, I'm a mountain climber. An amateur one, I assure you."

"Mountain climbing? That *is* interesting. Where do you do that?"

"Oh . . . here, in the States. And in Europe."

"Where in Europe?"

"France, Switzerland, Italy, Austria. I don't travel as much as I'd like to, but I try to include some climbing wherever I go."

"Fascinating sport—but expensive, isn't it, Mr. Blank? I mean, outside the travel. I'm just asking out of personal curiosity, but don't you need a lot of equipment?"

"Oh . . . not so much. Outdoor winter wear, of course. A rucksack. Crampons. Nylon rope."

"And an ice ax?"

"No," Delaney said definitely. "Don't say that. If Blank doesn't mention it, don't you suggest it. If he's guilty, I don't want to alert him. Handry, this stuff could be important, very important, but don't say anything or suggest anything that might make him think your conversation is anything but what it's supposed to be—an interview with a young executive who works with a computer."

"You mean if he suspects it's not what it seems, I may be in danger."

"Oh yes," the Captain nodded, digging into his meat pie. "You may be."

"Thanks a whole hell of a lot," Handry said, trying to keep his voice light. "You're making me feel much better about the whole thing."

"You'll do all right," Delaney assured him. "You take shorthand on these interviews?"

"My own kind. Very short notes. Single words. No one else can read it. I transcribe as soon as I get home or back to the office."

"Good. Just take it easy. From what you've said, I don't think you'll have any trouble with the personal history, the background. Or with the hobby of mountain climbing. But on the ice ax and his romantic affairs, don't push. If he wants to tell you, fine. If not, drop it. I'll get it some other way."

They each had another drink, finished their food. Neither wanted dessert, but Captain Delaney insisted they have espresso and brandy.

"That's a great flavor," Handry said, having taken a sip of his cognac. "You're spoiling me. I'm used to a tuna fish sandwich for lunch."

"Yes," Delaney smiled. 'Me, too. Oh, by the way, a couple of other little things."

Handry put down his brandy snifter, looked at him with wonderment, shaking his head. "You're incredible," he said. "Now I understand why you insisted on the cognac. "A couple of little things?" Like asking Blank if he's the killer, or putting my head in the lion's mouth at the zoo?"

"No, no," Delaney protested. "Really little things. First of all, see if you can spot any injury to his left hand. Or wrist, arm or elbow. It might be bandaged or in a sling."

"I don't get it."

"Just take a look, that's all. See if he uses his left arm normally. Can he grip anything in his left hand? Does he hide it beneath his desk? Just observe—that's all."

"All right," Handry sighed. "I'll observe. What's the other 'little thing'?"

"Try to get a sample of his handwriting."

Handry looked at him in astonishment. "You *are* incredible," he said. "How in Christ's name am I supposed to do that?"

"I have no idea," Delaney confessed. "Maybe you can swipe something he signed. No, that's no good. I don't know. You think about it. You've got a good imagination. Just some words he's written and his signature. That's all I need. If you can manage it."

Handry didn't answer. They finished their brandy and coffee. The Captain paid the check, and they left. Outside on the sidewalk, they turned coat collars up against the winter wind. Delaney put his hand on Handry's arm.

"I want the stuff we talked about," he said in a low voice. "I really do. But what I want most of all are your *impressions* of the man. You're sensitive to people; I know you are. How could you want to be a poet and not be sensitive to people, what they are, what they think, what they feel, who they hate, who they love? That's what I want you to do. Talk to this man. Observe him. Notice all the little things he does—bites his fingernails, picks his nose, strokes his hair, fidgets, crosses his legs back and forth—anything and everything. Watch him. And absorb him. Let him seep into you. Who is he and what is he? Would you like to know him better? Does he frighten you, disgust you, amuse you? That's really what I want—your *feeling* about him. All right?"

"All right," Thomas Handry said.

As soon as he got home, Delaney called Barbara at the hospital. She said she had had a very good night's sleep and was feeling much better. Monica Gilbert was there, they were having a nice visit, she liked Monica very much. The Captain said he was glad, and would come over to see her in the evening, no matter what.

"I send you a kiss," Barbara said, and made a kissing sound on the phone.

"And I send you one," Captain Edward X. Delaney said, and repeated the sound. What he had always considered silly sentimentality now didn't seem silly to him at all, but meaningful and so touching he could hardly endure it.

He called Charles Lipsky. The doorman was low-voiced and cautious.

"Find anything?" he whispered.

For a moment, Delaney didn't know what he was talking about, then realized Lipsky was referring to the previous afternoon's search.

"No," the Captain said. "Nothing. The girl friend been around?"

"Haven't seen her."

"Remember what I said; you get the license number and—"

"I remember," Lipsky said hurriedly. "Twenty. Right?"

"Yes," Delaney said. "One other thing, is anything wrong with Blank's left arm? Is it hurt?"

"He was carrying it in a sling for a couple of days."

"Was he?"

"Yeah. I asked him. He said he slipped on a little rug in his living room. His floors were just waxed. He landed on his elbow. And he hit his face on the edge of a glass table, so it was scratched up."

"Well," the Captain said, "they say most accidents happen in the home."

"Yeah. But the scratches are gone and he ain't wearing the sling no more. That worth anything?"

"Don't get greedy," Delaney said coldly.

"Greedy?" Lipsky said indignantly. "Who's greedy? But one hand washes the other—right?"

"I'll call you tomorrow," the Captain said. "You still on days?'

"Yeah. Until Christmas. Jesus, you know you was up there over an hour, and I buzzed you, and you—"

The Captain hung up. A little of Charles Lipsky went a long, long way.

He wrote up reports of his meeting with Thomas Handry and his conversation with the doorman. The only thing he deliberately omitted was his final talk with Handry on the sidewalk outside the restaurant. That exchange would mean nothing to Broughton.

It was past 4.00 p.m. when he finished putting it all down on paper. The reports were added to the Daniel G. Blank file. He wondered if he'd ever see that plump folder again. Alinski and the Anti-Group had about two more hours. Delaney didn't want to think of what would happen if he didn't hear from them. He'd have to deliver Blank's file to Broughton, of course, but *how* he'd deliver it was something he wouldn't consider until the crunch.

He went into the living room, slipped off his shoes, lay down on the couch, intending only to relax, rest his eyes, think of happier times. But the weariness he hadn't yet slept off, the two drinks and brandy at lunch—all caught up with him; he slept lightly and dreamed of the wife of a homicide victim he had interrogated years and years ago. "He was asking for it," she said, and no matter what questions he put to her, that's all she'd say: "He was asking for it, he was asking for it."

When he awoke, the room was dark. He laced on his shoes, walked through to the kitchen before he put on a light. The wall clock showed almost 7.00 p.m. Well, it was time . . . Delaney opened the refrigerator door, looked for a cold can of beer to cleanse his palate and his dreams. He found it, was just peeling back the tab when the phone rang.

He walked back into the study, let the phone ring while he finished opening the beer and taking a deep swallow. Then:

"Captain Edward X. Delaney here."

There was no answer. He could hear loud conversation of several men, laughter, an occasional shout, the clink of bottles and glasses. It sounded like a drunken party.

"Delaney here," he repeated.

"Edward?" It was Thorsen's voice, slurred with drink, weariness, happiness.

"Yes. I'm here."

"Edward, we did it. Broughton is out. We pooped him."

"Congratulations," Delaney said tonelessly.

"Edward, you've got to return to active duty. Take over Operation Lombard. Whatever you want—men, equipment, money. You name it, you've got it. Right?" Thorsen shouted; Delaney grimaced, held the phone away from his ear. He heard two or three voices shout, "Right!" in reply to Thorsen's question.

"Edward? You still there?"

"I'm still here."

"You understand? You back on active duty. Head of Operation Lombard. Whatever you need. What do you say?"

"Yes," Captain X. Delaney said promptly.

"Yes? You said yes?"

"That's what I said."

"He said yes!" Thorsen screamed. Again Delaney held the phone away, hearing the loud gabble of many voices. This was fraternity house stuff, and it displeased him.

"My God, that's great," the Deputy Inspector said in what Delaney was sure Thorsen thought was a sober and solemn voice.

"But I want complete control," the Captain said stonily. "Over the whole operation. No written reports. Verbal reports to you only. And—"

"Whatever you want, Edward."

"And no press conferences, no press releases, no publicity from anyone but me."

"Anything, Edward, anything. Just wrap it up fast. You understand? Show Broughton up for the stupid *schmuck* he is. He gets canned and three days later you've solved it. Right? Shows up the bastard."

"Canned?" the Captain asked. "Broughton?"

"'mounts to the same thing," Thorsen giggled. "Filed for retirement. Stupid sonofabitch. Says he's going to run for mayor next year."

"Is he?" Delaney said, still speaking in a dull, toneless voice. "Ivar, are you certain you've got this straight? I'll take it on, but only on the conditions that I have complete control, verbal reports only to you, pick my own men, handle all the publicity personally. Is that understood?"

"Captain Delaney," a quiet voice said, "this is Deputy Mayor Herman Alinski. I apologize, but I have been listening in on an extension. There is a certain celebration going on here."

"I can hear it."

"But I assure you, your conditions will be met. You will have complete control. Whatever you need. And nothing in the press or TV on Operation Lombard will come from anyone but you. Satisfactory?"

"Yes."

"Great!" Deputy Inspector Thorsen burbled. "The Telex will go out immediately. We'll get out a press release right away—just so we can make the late editions—that Broughton has put in for retirement and you're taking over Operation Lombard. Is that all right, Edward? Just a short, one-paragraph release. Okay?"

"Yes. All right."

"Your personal orders have already been cut. The Commissioner will sign them tonight."

"You must have been very sure of me," Delaney said.

"I wasn't," Thorsen laughed, "and Johnson wasn't. But Alinski was."

"Oh?" Delaney said coldly. "Are you there, Alinski?"

"I am here, Captain," the soft voice came back.

"You were sure of me? That I'd take this on?"

"Yes," Alinski said. "I was sure."

"Why?"

"You don't have any choice, do you, Captain?" the Deputy Mayor asked gently.

Delaney hung up, just as gently.

The first thing the Captain did was finish his beer. It helped. Not only the tang of it, the shock of coldness in his throat, but it stimulated the sudden realization of the magnitude of the job he had agreed to, the priorities, big responsibilities and small details, and the fact that "first things first" would be the only guide that might see him through. Right now, the first thing was finishing a cold beer.

"You don't have any choice, do you, Captain?" the Deputy Mayor had asked gently.

What had he meant by that?

He switched on the desk lamp, sat down, put on his glasses, pulled the yellow, legal-lined pad toward him, began to doodle—squares, circles, lines. Rough diagrams, very rough, and random ideas expressed in arrowheads, lightning bolts, spirals.

First things first. First of the first was around-the-clock surveillance of Daniel G. Blank. Three plainclothesmen on foot and two unmarked cars of two men each should do it. Seven men. Working eight-hour shifts. That was 21 men. But a police commander with any experience at all didn't multiply his personnel requirements by three; he multiplied by four, at least. Because men are entitled to days off, vacations, sick leave, family emergencies, etc. So the basic force watching Danny Boy was 28, and Delaney wondered if he had been too optimistic in thinking he could reduce the 500 detectives assigned to Operation Lombard by two-thirds.

That was one division: the outside force shadowing Blank. A second division would be inside, keeping records, monitoring walkie-talkie reports from the Blank guards. That meant a communications set-up. Receivers and transmitters. Somewhere. Not in the 251st Precinct house. Delaney owed Lt. Dorfman that one. He'd get Operation Lombard out of there, establish his command post somewhere else, anywhere. Isolate his men. That would help cut down leaks to the press.

A third division would be research: the suspect's history, background, credit rating, bank accounts, tax returns, military record—anything and everything that had ever been recorded about the man. Plus interviews with friends, relatives, acquaintances, business associates. Cover stories could be concocted so Blank wasn't alerted.

(But what if he was? That blurry idea in the back of Delaney's mind began to take on a definite outline.)

A possible fourth division might investigate the dark, skinny girl friend, the boy Tony, the friends—what was their name? Morton. That was it. They owned the Erotica. All that might take another squad.

It was all very crude, very tentative. Just a sketching-in. But it was a beginning. He doodled on for almost an hour, starting to firm it up, thinking of what men he wanted where, who he owed favors to, Favors. "I owe you one." "That's one you owe me." The lifeblood of the Department. Of politics. Of business. Of the thrusting, scheming, rude world. Wasn't that the rough cement that kept the whole rickety machine from falling apart? You be nice to me and I'll be nice to you. Charles Lipsky: "One hand washes the other—right?"

It was an hour—more than that—since his conversation with Thorsen. The Telex would now be clicked out in every precinct house, detective division, and special unit in the city. Captain Delaney went up to his bedroom, stripped down to his underwear and took a "whore's bath," soaping hands, face and armpits with a washcloth, then drying, powdering, combing his hair carefully.

He put on his Number Ones, his newest uniform, used, so far, only for ceremonies and funerals. He squared his shoulders, pulled the blouse down tautly, made certain his decorations were aligned. He took a new cap from a plastic bag on the closet shelf, wiped the shield bright on his sleeve, set the cap squarely atop his head, the short beak pulled down almost over his eyes.

The uniform was a brutal one: choker collar, shielded eyes, wide shoulders, tapered waist. Menace there.

He inspected himself in the downstairs mirror. It was not egotism. If you had never belonged to church, synagogue or mosque, you might think so. But the costume was continuing tradition, symbol, myth—whatever you like. The clothing, decorations, insignia went beyond clothing, decorations, insignia. They were, to those of the faith, belief.

He decided against an overcoat; he wouldn't be going far. He went into the study just long enough to take the photo of Daniel G. Blank from the file and scrawl the man's address, but not his name, on the back. He slipped the photo into his hip pocket. He left his glasses on the desk. If possible, you did not wear eyeglasses when you exercised command, or exhibit any other signs of physical infirmity. It was ridiculous, but it was so.

He locked up, marched next door to the 251st Precinct house. The Telex had obviously come through; Dorfman was standing near the sergeant's desk, his arms folded, waiting. When he saw Delaney, he came forward at once, his long, ugly face relaxing into a grin. He held out a hand eagerly.

"Congratulations, Captain."

"Thank you," Delaney said, shaking his hand. "Lieutenant, I'll have this gang out of your hair as soon as possible. A day or two at the most. Then you'll have your house back."

"Thank you, Captain," Dorfman said gratefully.

"Where are they?" Delaney asked.

"Detectives' squad room."

"How many?"

"Thirty, forty—around there. They got the word, but they don't know what to do."

Delaney nodded. He walked up the old creaking stairway, past the commander's office. The frosted glass door of the detectives' squad room was closed. There was noise from inside, a lot of men talking at once, a buzz of confused sound, angry turbulence. The Captain opened the door, and stood there.

The majority were in plainclothes, a few in uniform. Heads turned to look at him, then more. All. The talk died down. He just stood there, looking coldly out from under the beak of his cap. They all stared at him. A few men rose grudgingly to their feet. Then a few more. Then more. He waited unmoving, watching them. He recognized a few, but his aloof expression didn't change. He waited until they were all standing, and silent.

"I am Captain Edward X. Delaney," he said crisply. "I am now in command. Are there any lieutenants here?"

Some of the men looked around uneasily. Finally, from the back, a voice called, "No, Captain, no lieutenants."

"Any detective sergeants?"

A hand went up, a black hand. Delaney walked toward the raised hand, men stepping aside to let him through. He walked to the back of the room until he was facing the black sergeant, a short, heavyset man with sculpted features and what appeared to be a closely-fitted knitted cap of white wool. He was, Delaney knew, called "Pops," and he looked like a professor of Middle English literature. Strangely enough, he had professorial talents.

"Detective sergeant Thomas MacDonald," Captain Delaney said loudly, so everyone could hear him.

"That's right, Captain."

"I remember. We worked together. A warehouse job over on the west side. About ten years ago."

"More like fifteen, Captain."

"Was it? You took one in the hip."

"In the ass, Captain."

There were a few snickers. Delaney knew what MacDonald was trying to do, and fed him his lines.

"In the ass?" he said. "I trust it healed, sergeant?"

The black professor shrugged. "Just one more crease, Captain," he said. The listening men broke up, laughing and relaxing.

Delaney motioned to MacDonald. "Come with me." The sergeant followed him out into the hallway. The Captain closed the door, shutting off most of the laughter and noise. He looked at MacDonald. MacDonald looked at him.

"It really was the hip," Delaney said softly.

"Sure, Captain," the sergeant agreed. "But I figured—"

"I know what you figured," the Captain said, "and you figured right. Can you work till eight tomorrow morning?"

"If I have to."

"You have to," Delaney said. He drew Blank's photo from his pocket, handed it to MacDonald. "This is the man," he said tonelessly. "His address is on the back. You don't have to know his name—now. It's a block-size apartment building. Entrance and exit through a lobby on east Eighty-third. One doorman this time of night. I want three men, plain, covering the lobby. If this man comes out, I want them close to him."

"How close?"

"Close enough."

"So if he farts, they can smell it?"

"Not that close. But don't let this guy out of their sight. Not for a second. If he spots them, all right. But I wouldn't like it."

"I understand, Captain. A crazy?"

"Something like that. Just don't play him for laughs. He's not a nice boy."

The sergeant nodded.

"And two cars. Two men each, in plain. At both ends of the block. In case he takes off. He's got a black Chevy Stingray in the underground garage, or he might take a cab. Got all that?"

"Sure, Captain."

"You know Shakespeare and Lauder?"

"The 'Gold Dust Twins?' I know Lauder."

"I'd like them in one of the cars. If they're not on duty, any good men will do. That makes seven men. You pick six more, three in plain and three in uniform, and have them stand by here until eight tomorrow morning. Everyone else can go home. But everyone back by eight tomorrow, and anyone else you can reach by phone or who calls in. Got it?"

"Where do you want me, Captain?"

"Right here. I've got to go out for an hour or so, but I'll be back. We'll have some coffee together and talk about that extra crease in your ass."

"Sounds like a jolly night."

Delaney looked at him a long time. They had started in the Department the same year, had been in the same Academy class. Now Delaney was a captain, and MacDonald was a sergeant. It wasn't a question of ability. Delaney wouldn't mention what it was, and MacDonald never would either.

"What's Broughton had you on?" he asked the sergeant finally.

"Roasting street freaks," MacDonald said.

"Shit," Delaney said disgustedly.

"My sentiments exactly, Captain," the sergeant said.

"Well, lay it all on," the Captain said. "I'll be back in an hour or so. Your men should be in position by then. The sooner, the better. Show them that photo, but you hang onto it. It's the only one I've got. I'll have copies run off tomorrow."

"Is he it, Captain?" Detective sergeant MacDonald asked.

Delaney shrugged. "Who knows?" he said.

He turned, walked away. He was at the staircase when the sergeant called softly: "Captain." He turned around.

"Good to be working with you again, sir," MacDonald said.

Delaney smiled faintly but didn't answer. He walked down the stairway thinking of Broughton's stupidity in using MacDonald to pull in street freaks. MacDonald! One of the best professors in the Department. No wonder those forty men had been sour and grumbling. It wasn't that Broughton hadn't kept them busy, but he had misused their individual abilities and talents. No one could take that for long without losing drive, ambition, even interest in what he was doing. And what was he, Delaney? What were his abilities and talents? He waved a hand in answer to the desk sergeant's salute as he walked out. He knew what he was. He was a cop.

He would have commandeered a squad car, but there was none around. So he walked over to Second Avenue, got a cab heading downtown. He walked into the hospital and, for once, the white tiled walls and the smell couldn't depress him. Wait until Barbara heard!

Then he pushed open the door of her room. There was a nurses' aide sitting alongside the bed. Barbara appeared to be sleeping. The aide motioned to him, beckoning him outside into the corridor.

"She's had a bad evening," she whispered. "Earlier it took two of us to hold her down, and we had to give her something. Doctor said it would be all right."

"Why?" the Captain demanded. "What is it? Is it the new drug?"

"You'll have to ask doctor," the aide said primly. Delaney wondered again, in despair, why they always just said "doctor." Never "the doctor." "You have to consult engineer." "You'll have to talk to architect." "You'll have to discuss that with lawyer." It made the same sense, and it all made no sense whatever.

"I'll sit with her awhile," Delaney told the aide. She was so young; he couldn't blame her. Who could he blame?

She nodded brightly. "Tell me when you leave. Unless she's asleep by then."

"She's not asleep now?"

"No. Her eyes are closed, but she's awake. If you need any help, ring the bell or call."

She walked away quickly, leaving him wondering what help he might need. He went softly back into the hospital room, still wearing his uniform cap. He pulled a chair over to Barbara's bedside, sat looking at her. She did seem to be sleeping; her eyes were shut tight, she was breathing deeply and regularly. But, while he watched, her eyelids flicked open, she stared at the ceiling.

"Barbara?" he called gently. "Darling?"

Her eyes moved, but her head didn't turn. Her eyes moved to look at him, into him, through him, not seeing him.

"Barbara, it's Edward. I'm here. I have so much to tell you, dear. So much has happened."

"Honey Bunch?" she said.

"It's Edward, dear. I have a lot to tell you. A lot has happened."

"Honey Bunch?" she said.

He found the books in the metal taboret alongside her bed. He took the top one, not even glancing at the title, and opened it at random. Not having his glasses, he had to hold the book almost at arm's length. But the type was large, there was good white space between the lines.

Sitting upright in his Number One uniform, gleaming cap squarely atop his head, the commander of Operation Lombard began reading:

"Honey Bunch picked her nasturtiums that morning and she gave away her first bouquet. That is always a lovely garden experience—to give away your first bouquet. Of course Honey Bunch gave hers to Mrs. Lancaster and the little old lady said that she would take the flowers home and put them in water and make them last as long as possible.

"'Haven't you any garden at all' asked Honey Bunch. 'Just a little one?'

"'No garden at all,' replied the old lady sadly. 'This is the first year I can remember that I haven't had a piece of ground to do with as . . .'"

5

HE SLEPT when he could, but it wasn't much; perhaps four or five hours a night. But, to his surprise and pleasure, it didn't slow him down. Within three days he had it all organized. It was functioning.

He took Lt. Jeri Fernandez out of the Garment Center division he hated, put him in command of the squad shadowing Daniel Blank. Delaney let him select his own spooks; the "Invisible Man" almost wept with gratitude. It was exactly the kind of job he loved, that he did best. It was his idea to borrow a Consolidated Edison van and tear up a section of East 83rd Street near the driveway leading to Blank's apartment house. Fernandez' men wore Con Ed uniforms and hard hats, and worked slowly on the hole they dug in the pavement. It played hell with traffic, but the van was filled with communication gear and weapons, and served as Fernandez' command post. Delaney was delighted. Fuck the traffic jams.

For "Mr Inside," the Captain requisitioned Detective first grade Ronald Blankenship, the man who had handled the two original beefs on Daniel Blank. Working together closely, Delaney and Blankenship transferred the command post of Operation Lombard from the 251st Precinct house to the living room of Delaney's house, next door. It wasn't as spacious as they would have liked, but it had its advantages; the communications men could run wires out the window, up to Delaney's roof, then across to tie in with the antennae on the precinct house roof.

Detective sergeant Thomas MacDonald, "Pops," was Delaney's choice to head up the research squad, and MacDonald was happy. He got as much pleasure from an afternoon of sifting through dusty documents as another man might get in an Eighth Avenue massage parlor. Within 24 hours his men had compiled a growing dossier on Daniel G. Blank, taking him apart, piece by piece.

Captain Delaney appreciated the unpaid labors of his amateurs, but he couldn't deny the advantages and privileges of being on active duty, in official command, with all the resources of the Department behind him, and a promise of unlimited men, equipment, funds.

Item: A tap was put on the home telephone of Daniel Blank. It was installed in the central telephone office servicing his number.

Item: The next day's call to Charles Lipsky had resulted in the time of departure and license number of a cab picking up Blank's dark-haired girl friend at his apartment house. Delaney told Blankenship what he wanted. Within three hours the license number had been traced, the fleet identified, and a dick was waiting in the garage for the driver to return. His trip sheet was checked, and the Captain had the address where the cab had dropped her off. One of Fernandez' boys went over to check it; it turned out to be a townhouse on East End Avenue. After consultation with the lieutenant, Delaney decided to establish surveillance, one plainclothesman around-the-clock. Fernandez suggested detailing a two-man team to comb the neighborhood, to learn what they could about that house.

"It's an expensive section," Delaney said thoughtfully, "Lots of VIP's around there. Tell them to walk softly."

"Sure, Captain."

"And lots of servants. You got a good-looking black who could cuddle up to some of the maids and cooks on the street?"

"Just the man!" Fernandez said triumphantly. "A big, handsome stud. He don' walk, he glides. And smart as a whip. We call him 'Mr. Clean.'"

"Sounds good," the Captain nodded. "Turn him loose and see what he can come up with."

He then put on his civilian clothes, went over to Blank's apartment house to slip Lipsky his twenty dollars. The doorman thanked him gratefully.

Item: An hour later, Blankenship handed him the trace on Charles Lipsky. As Delaney had suspected, the man had a sheet. As a matter of fact, he was on probation, having been found guilty of committing a public nuisance, in that he did "with deliberate and malicious intent," urinate on the hood of a parked Bentley on East 59th Street.

Item: Christopher Langley called to report he had completed a list of all retail outlets of the West German ice ax in the U.S. With his new authority, Delaney was able to dispatch a squad car to go up to Langley's, pick up the list, bring it back to the command post. The list was assigned to one of Detective sergeant MacDonald's research men and, on the phone, he struck gold with his first call. Daniel G. Blank had purchased such an ax five years ago from Alpine Haven, a mail order house in Stamford, Conn., that specialized in mountaineering gear. A man was immediately sent to Stamford to bring back a photostatic copy of the sales check made out to Daniel G. Blank.

Item: Fernandez' men, particularly "Mr. Clean," made progress on that East End Avenue townhouse. At least, they now had the names of the residents: Celia Montfort, Blank's dark, thin girl friend; her young brother Anthony; a houseman named Valenter; and a middle-aged housekeeper. The names were turned over to MacDonald; the professor set up a separate staff to check them out.

During these days and nights of frantic activity, in the week before Christmas, Captain Delaney took time out to perform several personal chores. He gave Mary her Christmas gift early and, in addition, two weeks' vacation. Then he brought in an old uniformed patrolman, on limited duty, waiting for retirement, and told him to buy a 20-cup coffee urn and keep it going 24 hours a day in the kitchen; to keep the refrigerator filled with beer, cold cuts, cheese; and have enough bread and rolls on hand so anyone in Operation Lombard coming off a cold night's watch, or just stopping by during the day to report, would be assured of a sandwich and a drink.

He ordered folding cots, pillows and blankets brought in, and they were set up in the living room, hallway, kitchen, dining room—any place except in his study. They were in use almost constantly. Men who lived out on Long Island or up in Westchester sometimes preferred to sleep in, rather than make the long trip home, eat, sleep a few hours, turn around and come right back again.

He also found time to call his amateurs, wish them a Merry Christmas, thank them, for their help and support and tell them as gently as he could, that their efforts were no longer needed. He assured them their aid had been of invaluable assistance in developing a "very promising lead."

He did this on the phone to Christopher Langley and Calvin Case. He took Monica Gilbert to lunch and told her as much as he felt she should know: that partly through her efforts, he had a good chance to nail the killer but, because of the press of work, he wouldn't be able to call her or see her as often as he'd like. She was understanding and sympathetic.

"But take care of yourself," she entreated. "You look so tired."

"I feel great," he protested. "Sleep like a baby."

"How many hours?"

"Well . . . as much as I can."

"And you have regular, nourishing meals, I'm sure," she said sardonically.

He laughed. "I'm not starving," he assured her. "With luck, this may be over soon. One way or another. Are you still visiting Barbara?"

"Almost every day. You know, we're so dissimilar, but we have so much in common."

"Do you? That's good. I feel so guilty about Barbara. I dash in and dash out. Just stay long enough to say hello. But she's been through this before. She's a cop's wife."

"Yes. She told me."

Her sad voice gave him a sudden, vague ache, of something he should have done but did not do. But he couldn't think about it now.

"Thank you for visiting Barbara and liking her," he said. "Did I tell you we're now grandparents?"

"Barbara did. *Mazeltov.*"

"Thank you. An ugly little boy."

"Barbara told me," she repeated. "But don't worry, within six months he'll be a beautiful little boy."

"Sure."

"Did you send a gift?"

"Well . . . I really didn't have time. But I did talk to Liza and her husband on the phone."

"It's all right. Barbara sent things. I picked them out for her and had them sent."

"That was very kind of you." He rubbed his chin, felt the bristle, realized he had neglected to shave that morning. That was no good. He had to present the image of a well-groomed, crisply uniformed, confident commander to his men. It was important.

"Edward," she said, in a low voice, with real concern, "are you all right?"

"Of course I'm all right," he said stonily. "I've been through things like this before."

"Please don't be angry with me."

"I'm not angry. Monica. I'm all right. I swear it. I could be sleeping more and eating better, but it's not going to kill me."

"You seem so—so wound up. This is important to you, isn't it?"

"Important? That I nail this guy? Of course it's important to me. Isn't it to you? He killed your husband."

She flinched at his brutality. "Yes," she said faintly, "it's important to me. But I don't like what it's doing to you."

He wouldn't think of what she had said, or what she had meant. First things first.

"I've got to get back," he said, and signaled for a check.

During that wild week he found time for two more personal jobs. Still not certain in his mind why he was doing it, he selected the business card of a certain J. David McCann, representative of something called the Universal Credit Union. Wearing his stiff Homburg and floppy civilian overcoat, he walked into the effete, scented showroom of the Erotica on Madison Avenue and asked to speak to Mr. or Mrs. Morton, hoping neither would recognize him as the former commander of the precinct in which they lived and worked.

He spoke to both in their backroom office. Neither glommed him; he realized that except for members of business associations, VIPs, community groups and social activists, the average New Yorker hadn't the slightest idea of the name or appearance of the man who commanded the forces of law and order in his precinct. An ego-deflating thought.

Delaney took off his hat, bowed, presented his phony business card, did everything but tug his forelock.

"I'm not selling anything," he said ingratiatingly. "Just a routine credit investigation. Mr. Daniel G. Blank has applied for a loan and given us your names as references. We just want to make sure you actually do know him."

Flo looked at Sam. Sam looked at Flo.

"Of course we know him," Sam said, almost angrily. "A very good friend."

"Known him for years," Flo affirmed. "Lives in the same apartment house we do."

"Mm-hmm," Delaney nodded. "A man of good character, you'd say? Dependable? Honest? Trustworthy?"

"A Boy Scout," Sam assured him. "What the hell's this all about?"

"You mentioned a loan," Flo said. "What kind of a loan? How big?"

"Well . . . I really shouldn't reveal these details," Delaney said in soft confidential tones, "but Mr. Blank has applied for a rather large mortgage covering the purchase of a townhouse on East End Avenue."

The Mortons looked at each other in astonishment. Then to Delaney's interest, they broke into pleased smiles.

"Celia's house!" Sam shouted, smacking his thighs. "He's buying her place!"

"It's on!" Flo screamed, hugging her arms. "They're really getting together!"

Captain Delaney nodded at both, snatched his business card back from Sam's fingers, replaced his Homburg, started from the office.

"Wait, wait, wait," Sam called. "You don't mind if we tell him you were here?"

"That you were checking up?" Flo asked. "You don't mind if we kid him about it?"

"Of course not," Captain Delaney smiled. "Please do."

On the second call he wore the same clothes, used the same business card. But this time he had to sit on his butt in an overheated outer office for almost a half-hour before he was allowed to see Mr. René Horvath, Personnel Director of the Javis-Bircham Corp. Eventually he was ushered into the inner sanctum where Mr. Horvath inspected the Captain's clothing with some distaste. As well he might, he himself was wearing a black raw silk suit, a red gingham plaid shirt with stiff white collar and cuffs, a black knitted tie. What Delaney liked most, he decided, were the black crinkle-patent leather moccasins with bright copper pennies inserted into openings on the top flaps. Exquisite.

Delaney went through the same routine he used with the Mortons, varying it to leave out any mention of a mortgage on a townhouse, saying only that Mr. Daniel G. Blank had applied for a loan, and that he, Mr. J.

David McCann—"My card, sir"—and the Universal Credit Union were simply interested in verifying that Mr. Blank was indeed, as he claimed to be, employed by Javis-Bircham Corp.

"He is," the elegant Mr. Horvath said, handing back the soiled business card with a look that suggested it might be a carrier of VD. "Mr. Daniel Blank is presently employed by this company."

"In a responsible capacity?"

"Very responsible."

"I suppose you'd object to giving me a rough idea of Mr. Blank's annual income?"

"You suppose correctly."

"Mr. Horvath, I assure you that anything you tell me will be held in strictest confidence. Would you say that Mr. Blank is honest, dependable, and trustworthy?"

Horvath's pinched face closed up even more. "Mr. McClosky—"

"McCann."

"Mr. McCann, all J-B executives are honest, dependable and trustworthy."

Delaney nodded, replaced the Homburg on his big head.

"Thank you for your time, sir. I certainly do appreciate it. Just doing my job—I hope you realize that."

"Naturally."

Delaney turned away, but suddenly a squid hand was on his arm, gripping limply.

"Mr. McCann . . ."

"Yes?"

"You said Mr. Blank has applied for a loan?"

"Yes, sir."

"How large a loan?"

"That I am not allowed to say sir. But you've been so cooperative that I can tell you it's a very large loan."

"Oh?" said Mr. Horvath. "Hmmm," said Mr. Horvath, staring at the bright pennies inserted into his moccasin tongues. "That's very odd. Javis-Bircham, Mr. McCann, has its own loan program for all employees, from cafeteria busboy to Chairman of the Board. They can draw up to five thousand dollars, interest-free, and pay it back by salary deductions over a period of several years. Why didn't Mr. Blank apply for a company loan?"

"Oh well," Delaney laughed merrily, "you know how it is, everyone gets caught by the shorts sooner or later—right? And I guess he wanted to keep it private."

He left a very perturbed Mr. René Horvath behind him, and he thought, if Handry's impression was right and Blank's position with the company was shaky, it was shakier now.

In that week before Christmas, while the Delaney's living room furniture was being pushed back to the walls, deal tables and folding chairs brought in, cots set up, and communications men were still fiddling with their equipment, including three extra telephone lines, a "council of war" was scheduled every afternoon at 3.00 p.m. It was held in the Captain's study where the doors could be closed and locked. Attending were Captain Delaney, Lt. Jeri Fernandez, Detective first grade Ronald Blankenship, and Detective sergeant Thomas MacDonald. Delaney's liquor cabinet was open or, if they preferred, there was cold beer or hot coffee from the kitchen.

The first few meetings were concerned mostly with planning, organization, division of responsibility, choice of personnel, chain of command. Then, as information began to come in, they spent part of their time discussing the "Time-Habit Charts" compiled by Blankenship's squad. They were extremely detailed tabulations of Daniel Blank's daily routine: the time he left for work, his route, time of arrival at the Javis-Bircham Building, when he left for lunch, where he usually went, time of arrival back at the office, departure time, arrival at home, when he departed in the evening, where he went, how long he stayed. By the end of the fourth day, his patterns were pretty well established. Daniel Blank appeared to be a disciplined and orderly man.

Problems came up, were hashed out. Delaney listened to everyone's opinion. Then, after the discussion, he made the final decision.

Question: Should an undercover cop, with the cooperation of the management, be placed in Daniel Blank's apartment house as a porter, doorman, or whatever? Delaney's decision. No.

Question: Should an undercover cop be placed in Javis-Bircham, as close to Blank's department as he could get? Delaney's decision: Yes. It was assigned to Fernandez to work out as best he could a cover story that might seem plausible to the J-B executives he'd be dealing with.

Question: Should a Time-Habit Chart be set up for the residents of that townhouse on East End Avenue? Delaney's decision: No, with the concurring opinions of all three assistants.

"It's a screwy household," MacDonald admitted. "We can't get a line on them. This Valenter, the butler—or whatever you want to call him—has a sheet on molesting juvenile males. But no convictions. But that's all I've got so far."

"I don't have much more," Fernandez confessed. "The dame—this Celia Montfort—was admitted twice to Mother of Mercy Hospital for suicide attempts. Slashed wrists, and once her stomach had to be pumped out. We're checking other hospitals, but nothing definite yet."

"The kid seems to be a young fag," Blankenship said, "but no one's given me anything yet that makes a pattern. Like Pops said, it's a weird set-up. I don't think anyone knows what's going on over there. Nothing we can chart, anyway. She's in, she's out, at all hours of the day and night. She was gone for two days. Where was she? We don't know and won't until we put a special tail on her. Captain?"

"No," Delaney said. "Not yet. Keep at it."

Keep at it. Keep at it. That's all they heard from him, and they did because he seemed to know what he was doing, radiated an aura of confidence, never appeared to doubt that if they all kept at it, they'd nail this psycho and the killings would stop.

Daniel G. Blank. Captain Delaney knew his name, and now the others did, too. Had to. The men on the street, in the Con Ed van, in the unmarked cars adopted, by common consent, the code name "Danny Boy" for the man they watched. They had his photo now, reprinted by the hundreds, they knew his home address and shadowed his comings and goings. But they were told only that he was a "suspect."

Sometime during that week, Captain Delaney could never recall later exactly when, he scheduled his first press conference. It was held in the now empty detectives' squad room of the 251st Precinct house. There were reporters from newspapers, magazines, local TV news programs. The cameras were there, too, and the lights were hot. Captain Delaney wore his Number Ones and delivered, from memory, a brief statement he had labored over a long time the previous evening.

"My name is Captain Edward X. Delaney," he started, standing erect, staring into the TV cameras, hoping the sweat on his face didn't show. "I have been assigned command of Operation Lombard. This case, as you all know, involves the apparently unconnected homicides of four men: Frank Lombard, Bernard Gilbert, Detective Roger Kope, and Albert Feinberg. I have spent several days going through the records of Operation Lombard during the time it was commanded by former Deputy Commissioner Broughton. There is nothing in that record that might possibly lead to the indictment, conviction, or even identification of a suspect. It is a record of complete and utter failure."

There was a gasp from the assembled reporters; they scribbled furiously. Delaney didn't change expression, but he was grinning inwardly. Did Broughton really think he could talk to Delaney the way he had and not pay for it, eventually? The Department functioned on favors. It also functioned on vengeance. Run for mayor, would he? Lots of luck, Broughton!

"So," Captain Delaney continued, "because there is such a complete lack of evidence in the files of Operation Lombard while it was under the command of former Deputy Commissioner Broughton, I am starting from the beginning, with the death of Frank Lombard, and intend to conduct a totally new investigation into the homicides of all four men. I promise you nothing. I prefer to be judged by my acts rather than by my words. This is the first and last press conference I intend to hold until I either have the killer or am relieved of command. I will not answer any questions."

An hour after this brief interview, shown in its entirety, appeared on local TV news programs, Captain Delaney received a package at his home. It was brought into his study by one of the uniformed patrolmen on guard duty at the outside door—a 24-hour watch. No one went in or out without showing a special pass Delaney had printed up, issued only to bona fide members of *his* Operation Lombard. The patrolman placed the package on Delaney's desk.

"Couldn't be a bomb, could it, Captain?" he asked anxiously. "You was on TV tonight, you know."

"I know," the Captain nodded. He inspected the package, then picked it up gingerly. He tilted it gently, back and forth. Something sloshed.

"No," he said to the nervous officer. "I don't think it's a bomb. But you did well to suggest it. You can return to your post."

"Yes, sir," the young patrolman said, saluted and left.

Handsome, Delaney thought, but those sideburns were too goddamned long.

He opened the package. It was a bottle of 25-year-old brandy with a little envelope taped to the side. Delaney opened the bottle and sniffed; first things first. He wanted to taste it immediately. Then he opened the sealed envelope. A stiff card. Two words: "Beautiful" and "Alinski."

The mood of the "war councils' changed imperceptibly in the three days before Christmas. It was obvious they now had a working, efficient organization. Danny Boy was blanketed by spooks every time he stepped outside home or office. Blankenship's bookkeeping and communications were beyond reproach. Detective sergeant MacDonald's snoops had built up a file on Blank that took up three drawers of a locked cabinet in Delaney's study. It included the story of his refusal to attend his parents' funeral and a revealing interview with a married woman in Boston who agreed to give her impressions of Daniel Blank while he was in college, under the cover story that Blank was being considered for a high-level security government job. Her comments were damning, but nothing that could be presented to a grand jury. Blank's ex-wife had remarried and was presently on an around-the-world honeymoon cruise.

During those last three days before Christmas, the impression was growing amongst Delaney's assistants—he could *feel* the mood—that they were amassing a great deal of information about Daniel G. Blank—a lot of it fascinating and libidinous reading—but it amounted to a very small hill of beans. The man had a girl friend. So? Maybe he was or was not sleeping with her brother, Tony. So? He came out occasionally at odd hours, wandered about the streets, looked in shop windows, stopped in at The Parrot for a drink. So?

"Maybe he's on to us," Blankenship. "Maybe he knows the decoys are out every night, and he's being tailed."

"Can't be," Fernandez growled angrily. "No way. He don' even *see* my boys. As far as he's concerned, we don' exist."

"I don't know what else we can do," MacDonald confessed. "We've got him sliced up so thin I can see right through him. Birth certificate, diplomas, passport, bank statements—everything. You've seen the file. The man's laid out there, bareassed naked. Read the file and you've got him. Sure, maybe he's a psychopath, capable of killing I guess. He's a cold, smart, slick sonofabitch. But take him into court on what we've got? Uh-uh. Never. That's my guess."

"Keep at it," Captain Edward X. Delaney said.

Things slowed down on Christmas Eve. That was natural; men wanted to be home with their families. Squads were cut to a minimum (mostly bachelors or volunteers), and men sent home early. Delaney spent that quiet afternoon in his study, reading once again through his original Daniel G. Blank file and the great mass of material assembled by Pops and his squad who seemed to get their kicks sifting through dusty documents, military records, tax returns.

He read it all once more, sipping slowly from a balloon glass of that marvelous brandy Alinski had sent. He would have to call the Deputy Mayor to thank him, or perhaps mail a thank-you note, but meanwhile Alinski's envelope was added to the stack of unopened Christmas cards and presents that had accumulated in a corner of the study. He'd get to them, eventually, or take them over to Barbara when she was well enough to open them and enjoy them.

So he sipped brandy through a long Christmas Eve afternoon (the usual conference had been cancelled). As he read, the belief grew in him that the chilling of Danny Boy would come about through the man's personality, not by any clever police work, the discovery of a "clue," or by a sudden revelation of friend or lover.

Who was Daniel G. Blank? Who *was* he? MacDonald had said he was sliced thin, that he was laid out in that file bareassed naked. No, Delaney thought, just the facts of the man's life were there. But no one is a simple compilation of official documents, of interviews with friends and acquaintances, of Time-Habit schedules. The essential question remained: Who *was* Daniel G. Blank?

Delaney was fascinated by him because he seemed to be two men. He had been a cold, lonely boy who grew up in what apparently had been a loveless home. No record of juvenile delinquency. He was quiet, collected rocks and, until college, didn't show any particular interest in girls. Then he refused to attend his parents' funeral. That seemed significant to Delaney. How could anyone, no matter how young, do a thing like that? There was a callous brutality about it that was frightening.

Then there was his marriage—what was it Lipsky had called her? A big *zoftig* blonde—the divorce, the girl friend with a boy's body, then possibly the boy himself, Tony. And meanwhile the sterile apartment with mirrors, the antiseptic apartment with silk bikini underwear and scented toilet paper. And according to one of MacDonald's beautifully composed and sardonic reports, a fast climb up the corporate ladder.

Delaney went back to an interview one of MacDonald's snoops had with a man named Robert White who had been Blank's immediate superior at Javis-Bircham. He had, from all the evidence and statements available, been knifed and ousted by Daniel Blank. The interview with White had been made under the cover story that Blank was being considered for a high executive position with a corporation competing with J-B.

"He's a nice lad," Bob White had stated ("Possibly under the influence of alcohol," the interrogating detective had noted carefully in his report). "He's talented. Lots of imagination. Too much maybe. But he gets the job done: I'll say that for him. But no blood. You understand? No fucking blood."

Captain Delaney stared up at the ceiling. "No fucking blood." What did that mean? Who *was* Daniel G. Blank? Of such complexity . . . Disgusting and fascinating. Courage—no doubt about that; he climbed mountains and he killed. Kind? Of course. He objected when he saw a man hit a dog, and he kept sentimental souvenirs of the men he murdered. Talented and imaginative? Well, his previous boss had said so. Talented and imaginative enough to fuck a 30-year-old woman and her 12-year-old brother, but Delaney didn't suppose Bob White knew anything about *that!*

Who *was* Dan?

Captain Delaney rose to his feet, brandy glass in hand, about to propose a toast: "Here's to you, Danny Boy," when there was a knock on his study door. He sat down sedately behind his desk.

"Come in," he called.

Lt. Jeri Fernandez stuck his head through the opened door.

"Busy, Captain?" he asked. "Got a few minutes?"

"Of course, of course," Delaney gestured. "Come on in. Got some fine brandy here. How about it?"

"Ever know me to refuse?" Fernandez asked in mock seriousness, and they both laughed.

Then Delaney was in his swivel chair, swinging back and forth gently, holding his glass, and Fernandez was in the leather club chair. The lieutenant sipped the brandy, said nothing, but his eyes rolled to Heaven in appreciation.

"Thought you'd be home by now," the Captain said.

"On my way. Just making sure everything's copasetic."

"I know I've told you this before, lieutenant, but I'll say it again; tell your boys not to relax, not for a second. This monkey is fast."

Fernandez hunched over in the club chair, leaning forward, head lowered, moving the brandy snifter between his palms.

"Faster than a thirty-eight, Captain?" he asked in a voice so low that Delaney wasn't sure he heard him.

"What?" he demanded.

"Is this freak faster than a thirty-eight?" Fernandez repeated. This time he raised his head, looked directly into Delaney's eyes.

The Captain rose immediately, went to the study doors, closed them and locked them, then came back to sit behind his desk again.

"What's on your mind?" he asked quietly, looking directly at Fernandez.

"Captain, we been at this for—how long? Over a week now. Almost ten days. We got this Danny Boy covered six ways from Sunday. You keep calling him a 'suspect.' But I notice we're not out looking for other suspects, digging into anyone else. Everything we do is about this guy Blank."

"So?" Delaney said coldly.

"So," Fernandez sighed, looking down at his glass, "I figure maybe you know something we don' know, something you're not telling us." He held up a hand hastily, palm out. "This isn't a beef, Captain. If there's something we don' have to know, that's your right and privilege. Just thought—maybe— you might be sure of this guy but can't collar him. For some reason. No witnesses. No evidence that'll hold up. Whatever. But I figure you know it's him. *Know* it!"

The Captain resumed his slow swinging back and forth in his swivel chair. "Supposing," he said, "just *supposing*, mind you, that you're right, that I know as sure as God made little green apples that Blank is our pigeon, but we can't touch him. What do you suggest then?'

Fernandez shrugged. "Supposing,' he said, "just *supposing* that's the situation, then I can't see us collaring Danny Boy unless we grab him in the act. And if he's as fast as you say he is, we'll have another stiff before we can do that. Right?"

Delaney nodded. "Yes," he said, "I've thought of that. So what's your answer?"

Fernandez took a sip of brandy, then looked up.

"Let me take him, Captain," he said softly.

Delaney set his brandy glass on the desk blotter, poured himself another small portion of that ambrosia, then carried the bottle over to Fernandez and added to his snifter. He returned to his swivel chair, set the bottle down, began to drum gently on his desk top with one hand, watching the moving fingers.

"You?" he asked Fernandez. "You alone?"

"No. I got a friend. The two—"

"A friend?" Delaney said sharply, looking up. "In the Department?"

The lieutenant was astonished. "Of course in the Department. Who's got any friends outside the Department?"

"All right," Delaney nodded. "How would you handle it?"

"The usual," Fernandez shrugged. "We go up to his apartment and roust him. He resists arrest and tries to escape, so we ice him. Clean and simple and neat."

The Captain sighed, shook his head. "It doesn't listen," he said.

"Captain, it's been done before."

"Goddam it, don't try to tell me my business," Delaney shouted furiously. "I know it's been done before. But we do it your way, and we all get pooped."

He jerked to his feet, unbuttoned his uniform jacket, jammed his hands in his hip pockets. He began to pace about the study, not glancing at Fernandez as he talked.

"Look, lieutenant," he said patiently, "this guy is no alley cat with a snoot full of shit, that no one cares if he lives or dies. Burn a guy like that, and he's just a number in a potter's field. But Danny Boy is *somebody*. He's rich, he lives in a luxury apartment house, drives an expensive car, works for a big corporation. He's got friends, influential friends. Chill him, and people are going to ask questions. And we better have the answers. If it's done at all, it's got to be done *right*."

Fernandez opened his mouth to speak, but Delaney held up a hand. "Wait a minute. Let me finish. Now let's take your plan. You and your friend go up to brace him. How you going to get inside his apartment? I happen to know that guy's got more locks on his door than you'll find in a Tomb's cellblock. You think you'll knock, say, "Police officers," and he'll open up and let you in? The hell he will; he's too smart for that. He'll look at you through the peephole and talk to you through the locked door."

"Search warrant?" Fernandez suggested.

"Not a chance," Delaney shook his head. "Forget it."

"Then how about this: One of us goes up and waits outside his door, before he gets home from work. The other guy waits in the lobby until he comes in and rides up in the elevator with him. Then we got him in his hallway between us."

"And then what?" the Captain demanded. "You weight him right there in the corridor, while he's between you, and then claim he was trying to escape or resisting arrest? Who'd buy that?"

"Well . . . " Fernandez said doubtfully, "I guess you're right. But there's got to—"

"Shut up a minute and let me think," Delaney said. "Maybe we can work this out."

The lieutenant was silent then, sipping a little brandy, his bright eyes following the Captain aas he lumbered about the room.

"Look," Delaney said, "there's a doorman over there. Guy named Charles Lipsky. He's got access to duplicate keys to every apartment in the building. They hang on a board outside the assistant manager's office. This Lipsky's got a sheet. As a matter of fact, he's on probation, so you can lean on him. Now . . . you hear on the radio that Danny Boy has left work and is heading home. You and your friend get the keys from Lipsky, go upstairs and get inside Blank's apartment. Then you relock the door from the inside. So when he comes home, unlocks his door and marches in, you're already in there."

"I like it," Fernandez grinned.

"When the time comes I'll draw you a floor plan so you'll know where to be when he comes in. Then you—"

"A floor plan?" the lieutenant interrupted. "But how—"

"Just don't worry about it. Don't even think about it. When the time comes, you'll have a floor plan. But you give him time to get inside before you show yourselves. Maybe even give him time to relock his door so he can't make a fast run for it. He's sure to relock once he's inside his apartment; that's the kind of a guy he is. *Then* you show yourselves. Now here's where it begins to get cute. Can you get hold of a piece that can't be traced?"

"Oh sure. No trouble."

"What is it?"

"A Saturday-night special."

The Captain took a deep breath, blew it out in an audible sigh.

"Lieutenant," he said gently, "Danny Boy makes fifty-five big ones a year, drives a Stingray, and wears silk underwear. Do you really think he's the kind of guy who'd own a piece of crap like that? What else can you get?"

The "Invisible Man" thought for a moment, his teeth clenched.

"A nine-millimeter Luger," he said finally. "Brand-new. Right off the docks. Never been used. Still in the oiled envelope."

"What kind of grips."

"Wood."

"Yesss . . . " Delaney said thoughtfully. "He might own a gun like that. But the brand-new part is no good. It'll have to have at least three magazines fired through with a complete breakdown and cleaning between firings. Can you manage that?"

"No sweat, Captain."

"And it's got to be banged up a little. Not a lot. A few nicks on the grips. A little scratch here and there. You understand?"

"Like he's owned it for a long time?"

"Right. And took it on those mountain climbing trips of his to plink at tin cans or some such shit. Now here's something else: keep the box or envelope it came in, get the right cleaning tools and some oil-soaked rags. You know, the usual crap. This stuff you turn over to me."

"To *you*, Captain?"

"Yes, to me. All right, now you and your buddy are inside the apartment, and the door is locked. You've both got your service revolvers, and one of you has also got the used Luger. It's loaded. Full magazine. As soon as Danny Boy is inside his apartment, and has locked the door, you show. And for God's sake, have your sticks out. Don't relax for a second. Keep this guy covered."

"Don' worry, he'll be covered."

"Don't say a word to him, not a word. Just back him toward the bedroom door. You'll see where it is on that floor plan I'll draw for you. Now this is where you've got to work fast. As soon as he's in the bedroom doorway, or near it, facing you, weight him. Make it fast, and—this is important—make certain you both ice him. I don't know how good a friend this pal of yours is, but you've *both* got to do it. You understand?"

Fernandez smiled slyly. "You're a smart man, Captain."

"Yes. Now you're working fast. He's down, and for Christ's sake make certain he's gone."

"He'll have enough weight in him to sink him," the lieutenant assured him. "He'll be a clunk before he hits the floor."

"I'll take your word for it," Delaney grunted. "Now, the moment he's down, one of you—I don't care who it is—straddles his body, facing in the direction he was facing just before he bought it. And then—"

"And then we fire two or three shots from the Luger into the opposite wall," Fernandez said rapidly. "Where the two of us was just standing."

"Now you're catching it," the Captain said approvingly. "But it's got to be done fast—so that if anyone hears the shots, it's just a lot of shots, no pauses. No witness is going to remember how many shots were fired, when, or in what order. But just to play safe, the Luger should be fired into the opposite wall as soon as possible after you've iced him."

"I've got it," Fernandez smiled. "Two or three shots into the wall. Not too high. Like he really was firing at us."

"Right. Splinter a couple of mirrors if you can. That opposite wall is full of mirrors. Then what do you do?"

"Easy," Fernandez said. "Wipe the Luger clean. Put it in his hand and—"

"His *right* hand," Delaney cautioned. "He's right-handed. Don't forget it."

"I won't forget it. The Luger gets wiped clean and put in his right hand."

"Try it," Delaney said, "but don't get spooked if it doesn't work. It's tougher than you think to get a clunk's hand to grip a gun—even a fresh clunk. Just make sure you get a couple of good prints on it. They probably won't show on the wood grips, especially if they're checkered, but put them on the metal. Anywhere. The gun can even be on the floor, near his right hand. But a couple of good prints are what we need. What do you do next?"

"Let's see . . . " Fernandez thought deeply. He took a sip of his brandy. "Well, we've still got the keys to the guy's apartment."

"Right," Delaney said promptly. "So your friend has got to go down to the lobby and slip the keys back to Lipsky. Tell him to leave Danny Boy's apartment door open on the way out. Not open, but unlocked. And while he's doing that, what are you doing?"

"Me? Well, I guess I could start tossing—"

"Forget it," the Captain said, "Don't touch a goddam thing. The first thing you do is call me on Blank's phone. I'll be waiting for your call. I'll collect a squad and be right over. But don't do a thing until I get there. Don't even sit down in a chair. Just stand there. If you get any flak from neighbors, just identify yourself, tell them more cops are on the way, and keep them out in the corridor. All right, I come in with a squad. You tell us what happened, and keep it as short as possible. I make the calls I have to make—the ME, lab, and so forth. *Then* we start a search, and *then* I'll plant the oily rag, the cleaning tools, the extra Luger magazines, and so forth. I don't know how I'll carry them up there, but I'll—"

"But why should *you* do it, Captain?" Fernandez protested. "We could take that stuff up there with us."

Delaney grinned cynically. "In case like this, it's best that everyone be involved, as equally as possible. It's insurance. That's why I want you to make certain that both you and your friend feed Danny Boy the pills."

The lieutenant puzzled over this. Then his face cleared.

"Smart," he nodded. "So no one talks ever, and knows none of the others is going to spill."

"Something like that," Delaney agreed, not smiling. "Mutual trust. Now here's the cover story: Operation Lombard determined that the weapon used in the four homicides was an ice ax. That's a tool used by mountain climbers. Danny Boy is a mountain climber. There's hard evidence for all this. We checked into purchasers of ice axes in the Two-five-one Precinct, where all the killings occurred, and you and your friend were given a list of ice ax owners to question. Just to put the icing on the cake, I'll give you two or three names and addresses to check out before you get to Danny Boy. Then you say you identified yourselves as police officers, he let you in, and you asked to examine his ice ax. He said it was in his bedroom and went in there to get it. It's really in the outside hall closet, but he went into the bedroom and came out with the Luger, blasting. But he missed. The two of you went for your sticks and iced him. How does it sound?"

The lieutenant shook his head admiringly. "You're a wonder, Captain," he said. "It sounds great, just great."

"And, with any luck, while I'm planting the Luger equipment, I'll turn up the evidence that will put the finger on Danny Boy but good. It was there a few weeks ago. If it's still there, believe me, no one will ask any questions. But even if he's destroyed it by now, it won't make any difference. He'll be wasted, and it'll all be over."

"Sounds perfect, Captain."

"No," Delaney said, "it's not perfect. There are some loose ends we'll have to take care of. For instance, this friend of yours—I'll have to meet him."

"You already know him."

"He's in Operation Lombard?"

"Yes."

"Good. That makes it easier. This was just a quick outline, lieutenant. The three of us will have to go over it again and again and again until we've got it just right and our timing set. Maybe we could even have a dry-run to work out any bugs, but essentially I think it's a logical and workable plan."

"I think it's a winner, Captain. Can't miss."

"It can miss," Delaney said grimly. "Anything can miss. But I think it's worth a chance."

"Then it's on, Captain? Definitely?"

Delaney took a deep breath, came back to sit behind his desk again. He sat erect in his swivel chair, put his big hands flat on the desk top.

"Well . . . maybe not definitely," he said finally. "I like it because it gives me another option, and I'm practically running out of those. I've got just one other idea that's been percolating in my brain. I tell you what: Go ahead and get the Luger. Fire it, clean it, and bang it up a little. But don't mention a word to your friend. If I decide to go ahead, I'll let you know. Got it?"

"Sure," Fernandez nodded. "I do what you said about the Luger but hold up on anything else until I get the word from you."

"Exactly."

They both rose to their feet. The lieutenant put out his hand; Delaney grasped it.

"Captain," Lt. Fernandez said seriously, "I want to wish a Merry Christmas and a very happy New Year to you and yours. I hope Mrs. Delaney is feeling much better real soon."

"Thank you, lieutenant," Delaney said. "The very merriest of Christmases to you and your family, and I hope the New Year brings you everything you want. It's a real pleasure working with you."

"Thank you, Captain," Fernandez said. "Likewise."

Delaney closed the door, came back into the study.

He sat down at his desk, wished he had a fresh Cuban cigar, and considered the plan he had discussed with Lt. Fernandez. It wasn't foolproof; such plans never were. There was always the possibility of the unexpected, the unimagined: a scream from somewhere, a sudden visitor, a phone call. Danny Boy might even charge the two police officers, going right into their naked guns. He was capable of such insanity.

But essentially, Delaney decided, it was a logical and workable program. It was a solution. There were a lot of loose ends: how would he carry the Luger tools and cleaning equipment up to the apartment when he answered Fernandez' call, where would he plant them (in the bedroom, obviously), what if the souvenirs were no longer taped to the bottom of the dresser drawer? A hundred questions would be asked, by newsmen and by his superiors. How had Operation Lombard determined that an ice ax was the weapon used in the four homicides? How had they latched onto Daniel Blank? There would be many, many such questions; he would have to anticipate them all and have his answers ready.

He looked at his watch. Almost 4:15; it was a long afternoon. He sighed, pulled himself to his feet, unlocked the study door to the living room, wandered in.

The two big transceivers were on plain pine planks, placed across sawhorses. A uniformed officer was seated in front of each instrument, hunched over a table microphone. A separate table, not as large, held the three new telephones. There was a uniformed officer on duty there, reading a paperback novel. Two men, stripped to their scivvies, were sleeping on cots alongside the wall. One was snoring audibly. Detective second grade Samuel Wilding—he was one of Blankenship's assistants—was seated at a card table making notes on a chart. Delaney raised a hand to him.

He stood a moment near the radios, hands clasped behind his back. He was probably, he thought regretfully, making the operators nervous. But there was no answer for that.

The room was quiet. No, not quiet; except for the low snoring, it was absolutely silent. Late afternoon darkness crept through open drapes, and with it came a—what? A sweetness, Captain Delaney admitted, laughing at himself, but it was a kind of sweetness.

The uniformed men had taken off their blouses. They were working at their desks in sweaters or T-shirts, but still wearing gun belts. Only Detective Wilding wore a jacket, and his was summer-weight, with lapels. So what was it? Delaney wondered. Why the sweetness? It came, he decided, from men on duty, doing their incredibly boring jobs, enduring. The fraternity. Of what? (Delaney: "A friend? In the Department?"

Fernandez: (astonished): "Of course in the Department. Who's got any friends outside the Department?") A kind of brotherhood.

"A phone rang on the deal desk. The officer on duty put aside his paperback, picked up the ringing phone. "Barbara," he said.

They had devised a radio and telephone code as simple and brief as they could make it. Not because Danny Boy might be listening in, but to keep away the short-wave nuts who tuned to police frequencies.

"Danny Boy"—Daniel G. Blank.

"Barbara"—the command post in Delaney's home.

"White House"—Blank's apartment house.

"Factory"—the Javis-Bircham Building.

"Castle"—the East End Avenue townhouse.

"Bulldog One"—the phony Con Ed van on the street outside the White House. It was Lt. Fernandez' command post.

"Bulldog Two, Three, Four, etc"—code names for Fernandez' unmarked cars and spooks on foot.

"Tiger One"—the man watching the Montfort townhouse. "Tiger Two" and "Tiger Three" were the street men sweeping the neighborhood.

Other than that, the Operation Lombard investigators used their actual names in transmissions, keeping their calls, in compliance with frequently repeated orders, informal and laconic.

When the phone rang, the officer who answered it said "Barbara." Then he listened awhile, turned to look at Detective Wilding. "Stryker at the Factory," he reported. "Danny Boy has his coat and hat on, looks like he's ready to leave." Stryker was the undercover man planted at Javis-Bircham. He was a tabulating clerk—and a good one—in Blank's department.

Detective Wilding nodded. He turned to a man at the radio. "Alert Bulldog Three." He looked at Delaney. "Okay for Stryker to cut out?"

The Captain nodded. The detective called to the man on the phone, "Tell Stryker he can take off. Report back the day after Christmas."

The officer spoke into the phone, then grinned. "That Stryker," he said to everyone listening. "He doesn't want to take off. He says they've got an office party going, and he ain't going to miss it."

"The great cocksman in the Department," someone said.

The listening men broke up. Captain Delaney smiled thinly. He leaned forward to hear one of the radio operators say, "Bulldog Three from Barbara. Got me?"

"Yes. Very nice." It was a bored voice.

"Danny Boy on his way down."

"Okay."

There was a quiet wait of about five minutes. Then: "Barbara from Bulldog Three. We've got him. Heading east on Forty-sixth Street. A yellow cab. License XB sixty-one—dash—forty-nine—dash—three—dash—one. Got it?"

"XB sixty-one—dash—forty-nine—dash—three—dash—one."

"Right on."

It was all low key; it was routine. The logs were kept carefully, and the 24-hour Time-Habit Charts were marked in. But nothing was happening.

Delaney stalked back into his study, put on his glasses, drew his yellow pad toward him. He jotted two lists. The first consisted of five numbered items:

1. Garage attendant.
2. Bartender at Parrot.
3. Lipsky.
4. Mortons.

5. Horvath at J-B.

The second list came slower, over a period of almost an hour. It finally consisted of four numbered items.

Delaney put it aside, rose, lumbered back into the living room. He went directly to Detective Samuel Wilding.

"When's Blankenship coming back on?" he demanded.

"Tomorrow at noon. Captain. We're splitting up because of Christmas."

Delaney nodded. "Tell him, or leave a note for him, that I want to be informed immediately of any change in Danny Boy's Time-Habit pattern. Got that?"

"Yes, sir."

"Informed immediately," the Captain repeated.

He marched through to his dining room and up to the lone man of Detective sergeant MacDonald's squad on duty. The man looked up, startled.

"When's MacDonald due back?" Delaney asked.

"Tomorrow at four in the afternoon, Captain. We're splitting—"

"I know, I know," Delaney said testily, "Christmas. I want to leave a message for him." The duty officer took up a pad and waited, pencil in hand. "Tell him I want a photograph of Detective Kope."

The officer's pencil hesitated.

"Kope? The guy who got chilled?"

"Detective third grade Roger Kope, homicide victim," Delaney said grimly. "I need a photograph of him. Preferably with his family. A photograph of the entire Kope family. Got that?"

He looked down at the officer's pad. It was covered with squiggles.

"You know shorthand?" he asked.

"Yes, sir. I took a course."

"Very good. It's valuable. I wish I knew it. But I guess I'm too old to learn now."

He started to explain to the officer that MacDonald would do best to send a man for the photo who had known Kope, who had been a friend of the family. But he stopped. The sergeant was an old cop: he'd know how to handle it.

He tramped back into his study, closed the doors. He looked at his watch. Almost 7:00 p.m. It was time. He looked at the list on his desk, then dialed the number of Daniel G. Blank. The phone rang and rang. No one answered. He walked back into the living room, over to the radio operator keeping the log.

"Danny Boy in the White House?" he asked.

"Yes, sir. No departure. About half an hour ago Tiger One called in. Princess left the Castle in a cab." ("Princess" was the code name for Celia Montfort.) "About ten minutes later Bulldog One reported her arrival at the White House. They're both still in there, as far as we know."

Delaney nodded, went back into his study, closing the door. He called Blank's number again. No answer. Maybe Danny Boy and the Princess were having a sex scene and weren't anwering the phone. Maybe. And maybe they were at a Christmas Eve Party. At the Mortons, possibly? Possibly. He went to the file cabinet, took out the thin folder on the Mortons that MacDonald's snoops had assembled. Their home phone number was there.

Delaney came back to his desk, dialed the number.

"Mortons' residence," a female voice answered, after the seventh ring.

In the background Delaney could hear the loud voices of several people, shouts, laughter. A party. He didn't grin.

"I'm trying to reach Mr. Daniel Blank," he said slowly, distinctly, "and I was given this number to call. Is he there?"

"Yes, he is. Just a minute, please."

He heard her call, "Mr Blank! Phone!" Then that familiar voice was there, curious and cautious. Delaney knew what Danny Boy was wondering: how had anyone traced him to the Morton's Christmas Eve party?

"Hello?"

"Mr. Daniel G. Blank?"

"Yes. Who is this?"

"Frank Lombard."

There was a sound at the other end of the phone: part moan, part groan, part gasp—something sick and unbelieving.

"Who?"

"Frank Lombard," Delaney said in a low, soft voice. "You know me. We've met before. I just wanted to wish you—"

But the connection went dead. Delaney hung up gently, smiling now. Then he put on overcoat and cap and went out into the dark night to find a drugstore that was still open so he could buy a bottle of perfume and take it to the hospital. A Christmas gift for his wife.

PART EIGHT

1

SOMETHING WAS happening. What was happening? Something . . .

Daniel Blank thought it had started two weeks ago. Or perhaps it was three; it was difficult to remember. But the garage attendant in his apartment house casually mentioned that an insurance examiner had been around, asking about Blank's car.

"He thought you had been in some kind of accident," the man said. "But he took one look at your car and knew you wasn't. I told him so. I told him you ain't had that car out in momths."

Blank nodded and asked the man to wash the Stingray, check the battery, oil, gas. He thought no more about the insurance examiner. It had nothing to do with him.

But then, one night, he stopped in at The Parrot. The bartender served him his brandy, then asked if his name was Blank. When Daniel acknowledged it—a tickle of agitation there—the bartender told him a private detective had been in, asking questions about him. He couldn't recall the man's name, but he described him. Troubled now, Blank went back to the garage attendant; his description of the "insurance examiner" tallied with that of the bartender's "private detective."

Not two days later, doorman Charles Lipsky reported that a man had been around asking "very personal questions" about Daniel Blank. The man, Lipsky said, had not stated his name or occupation, but Lipsky could describe him, and did.

From these three descriptions Blank began to form a picture of the man dogging him. Not so much a picture as a silhouette. A dark, hulking figure, rough as a woodcut. Big, with stooped shoulders. Massive. Wearing a stiff Homburg set squarely atop his head, an old-fashioned, double-breasted, shapeless overcoat.

Then, with great glee, Flo and Sam Morton told him of the visit of the credit investigator, and Dan—you devil!—why hadn't you told your best friends about your plans to marry Celia Montfort and purchase her townhouse? He grinned bleakly.

Then that humbling, mumbling meeting with René Horvath, Javis-Bircham's Director of Personnel. Blank finally got it straight that a credit investigator had been making inquiries; apparently Blank had applied for a "very large loan"—much larger than that offered by the J-B employees' loan program. Horvath had felt it his duty to report the investigator's visit to his superiors, and he had been assigned to ask Daniel Blank the purpose of the loan.

Blank finally got rid of the disgusting little creep, but not before eliciting a physical description of the "credit investigator." Same man.

He knew now his days at Javis-Bircham were numbered, but it wasn't

481

important. The phony credit investigation would just be the last straw. But it wasn't important. He'd be fired, or allowed to resign, and given a generous severance payment. It wasn't important. He knew that during the last few months he simply hadn't been doing his job. He wasn't interested. It wasn't important.

What was important, right now, was the insurance examiner-private detective-credit investigator—a composite man who had become more than a silhouette, a vague image, but was now assuming a rotundity, a solidity, with heavy features and gross gestures, a shambling walk and eyes that never stopped looking. Who was he? God in a stiff Homburg and floppy overcoat?

Blank looked for him wherever he went, on the street, in bars and restaurants, at night, alone in his apartment. On the streets he would search the faces of approaching strangers, then whirl suddenly to see if that big, huddled man was lumbering along behind him. In restaurants, he strolled to the men's room, looking casually at patrons, walking into the kitchen "by accident," glancing into occupied phone booths, inspecting toilet cubicles. Where was he? At home, at night, the door locked, bolted, jammed tight, he would lie awake in the darkness and suddenly hear night noises: thumpings, creakings, a short snap. Then he would rise, put on all the lights, stalk through the apartment, wanting to meet him face to face. But he was not there.

Then, finally, it was Christmas Eve. Javis-Bircham would not fire him until after the holidays; he knew that. So he could accept happily an invitation to the Mortons' Christmas Eve party and ask Celia to join him. He would drink a little, laugh, put his arm around Celia's slender, hard waist, and surely the dark, thrusting shadow could not be there.

The call shattered him. For how could anyone know he was at the Mortons'? He approached the phone cautiously, picked it up as if expecting it to explode in his hand. Then that soft, insinuating voice said: "Frank Lombard. You know me. We've met before. I just wanted—"

Then he was out of there, leaving Celia behind him, saying goodnight to no one. The elevator took a decade; it was a generation before he got his door unlocked and locked again; it was a century before he had the drawer out, turned upside down on his bed. He inspected the taped envelope carefully but, as far as he could see, it had not been touched. He opened it; everything was there. He sat on his bed, fingering his mementoes, and became aware that he had wet his pants. Not a lot. But a few drops. It was degrading.

He stuffed the black velvet suit, white cashmere turtleneck sweater, and flowered panties into the bathroom laundry hamper. He peeled off the Via Veneto wig before getting under a shower as hot as he could stand it. When he soaped his bare skull, he felt the light fuzz and knew he'd soon need another shave.

He dried, smoothed on cologne, powdered, stuck the wig firmly back into place. Then he put on one of his silk robes, the crane design, and padded barefoot into the living room to pour himself a warm vodka and light one of his dried lettuce cigarettes.

Then he realized the apartment doorbell was chiming, had been for several rings. He stubbed his cigarette out carefully and drained his vodka before going into the hallway to peer at Celia Montfort through the peephole. He unlocked the door to let her in, bolted it again behind her.

"You're not ill, are you, Dan?"

"You don't talk in your sleep, do you?" he asked. Even in his own ears his laugh sounded wild and forced.

She stared at him, expressionless.

She sat on the living room couch, waited patiently while he opened a bottle of bordeaux, poured her a stemmed glass and for himself the glass still wet from the vodka he had finished. She sipped the wine cautiously.

"Good," she nodded. "Dry as dust."

"What? Oh, yes. I should have bought more. The price has almost doubled. Did you tell anyone about me?"

"What are you talking about, Dan?"

"What I've done. Did you tell anyone?"

Her answer was prompt, but it was no answer at all: "Why should I do a thing like that?"

She was wearing a tube of black jersey, high at the neck, long-sleeved, hanging to her dull black satin evening pumps. About her neck was what appeared to be a six-foot rope of cultured pearls, wound tightly, around and around, so it formed a gleaming collar that kept her head erect, chin raised.

He had the sense—as he had at their first meeting—of never being able to recognize her, of forgetting what she looked like when she was out of his sight. The long, black, almost purple hair; drawn, witch-like face; slender, tapering hands; but the eyes—were they grey or blue? Were the lips full or flat? Was the nose Egyptian—or merely pinched? And the pallid complexion, bruised weariness, aura of corruption, of white flesh punished to a puddle—where did those fantasies come from? She was as much a mystery to him now as at their first meeting. Was it a thousand years ago?

She sat on the couch, composed, withdrawn, sipping her wine as he passed back and forth. He never took his eyes from her as he told her about the man who had been dogging him—the insurance examiner-private detective-credit investigator man—and the people this man had seen, the questions he had asked, what he had said.

As he talked, words spilling out so fast that he spluttered a few times and white spittle gathered in the corners of his mouth—well, as he chattered, he saw her cross her legs slowly, high up, at her thighs, hidden by her long dress. But from the bent knee, one ankle showed, a satin evening pump hung down. As he told her what had happened, that loose foot, that black shoe, began to bob up and down, lower leg swinging from the hidden knee, slow at first, nodding in a graceful rhythm, then moving faster in stronger jerks. Her face was still expressionless.

Watching Celia's bobbing foot, the leg from the knee down swinging faster under her long dress, he thought she must be masturbating, sitting there on his couch, naked thighs presssed tightly together beneath her gown. The rhythm of that jerking foot became faster and faster until when he told her about the telephone call he had just received at the Mortons, she began to pant, her eyes glazed, pearls of sweat to match her necklace formed on brow and upper lip. Then, eyes closed now, her entire body stiffened for a moment. He stopped talking to watch her. When she finally relaxed, shuddering, looked about with vacant eyes, uncrossed her legs, he thought she must have been sexually excited by his danger, but for what reason did he not know, could not guess.

"Could the man be Valenter?" he asked her.

"Valenter?" She took a deep sip of wine. "How could he know? Besides, Valenter is skinny, a scarecrow. You said this man following you about is heavy, lumbering. It couldn't be Valenter."

"No, I suppose not."

"How could this man—the one on the phone—know about Frank Lombard?"

"I don't know. Perhaps there was an eyewitness—to Lombard or one of the others—and he followed me home and got my address and then my name."

"For what reasons?"

"It's obvious, isn't it? He didn't go to the police, so it must be blackmail."

"Mmm, possibly. Are you frightened?"

"Well . . . disturbed." Then he told her about what he had been doing since he left the Mortons' apartment so abruptly: trying to make his mind into a blank blackboard, erasing thoughts as quickly as they appeared in chalk script.

"Oh no," she shook her head, and in her voice was an imploring tone he had never heard her use before, "you shouldn't do that. Open your mind wide. Let it expand. Let it shatter into a million thoughts, sensations, memories, fears. That's how you'll find perception. Don't erase your consciousness. Let it flower as it will. Anything is possible. Remember that: anything is possible. Something will come to you, something that will explain the man following you and the phone call. Open your mind; don't close it down. Logic won't help. You must become increasingly aware, increasingly sensitive. I have a drug at home. Do you want to use it?"

"No."

"All right. But don't shut yourself in, inside yourself. Be open to everything."

She stood, picked up the remainder of the wine.

"Let's go to your bedroom," she said. "I'll stay the night."

"I won't be any good."

Her free hand slid inside the opening of his robe. He felt her slim, cool fingers drift across his nakedness to find him, to hold him.

"We'll play with each other," she murmured.

And so they did.

2

On the day following Christmas, Captain Delaney worked all morning in his study, in his shirtsleeves—it was unseasonably warm, the house overheated—trying to prepare estimates of his manpower and vehicle requirements for the coming week. The holiday season complicated things; men wanted to spend time at home with their families. That was understandable, but it meant schedules had to be reshuffled, and it was impossible to satisfy everyone.

Delaney's three commanders—Fernandez, MacDonald, and Blankenship—had prepared tentative schedules for their squads, but had appended suggestions, questions, requests. From this tangled mess of men available for duty, men on vacation or about to go, sick leave, hardship cases, special pleadings (one of Fernandez' spooks had an appointment with a podiatrist to have his bunions trimmed), Delaney tried to construct a master schedule for Operation Lombard that would, at least, have every important post covered 24 hours a day but still leave enough "wiggle room" so last-minute substitutions could be made, and there would always be a few men playing poker for matchsticks in the radio room, available for emergency duty if needed.

By noon he had a rough timetable worked out; he was shocked at the number of men it required. The City of New York was spending a great deal of money to monitor the activities of Daniel G. Blank. That didn't bother

Delaney; the City spent more money for more frivolous projects. But the Captain was concerned about how long Thorsen, Johnson, *et al.*, would give him a free hand and a limitless budget before screaming for results. Not too long, he thought grimly; perhaps another week.

He pulled on jacket, civilian overcoat and hat, and checked out with the uniformed patrolman keeping an entrance-exit log at a card table set up just inside the outer door. Delaney gave him destination and phone number where he could be reached. Then he had one of the unmarked cars parked outside drive him over to the hospital. Another breach of regulations, but at least it gave the two dicks in the car a few minutes' relief from the boredom of their job: sitting and waiting.

Barbara seemed in a subdued mood, and answered his conversational offerings with a few words, a wan smile. He helped her with her noon meal and, that finished, just sat with her for another hour. He asked if she'd like him to read to her, but when she shook her head, he just sat stolidly, in silence, hoping his presence might be of some comfort, not daring to think of how long her illness would endure, or how it might end.

He returned home by cab, dutifully showed his Operation Lombard pass for entrance, even though the uniformed outside guard recognized him immediately and saluted. He was hungry for a sandwich and a cold beer, but the kitchen was crowded with at least a dozen noisy men taking a lunch-hour break for coffee, beer, or some of the cheese and cold cuts for which they all contributed, a dollar a day per man.

The old uniformed patrolman on kitchen duty saw the Captain walk through to his study. A few minutes later he knocked on the door to bring Delaney a beer and ham-and-Swiss on rye. The Captain smiled his thanks; it was just what he wanted.

About an hour later a patrolman knocked and came in to relay a request from Detective first grade Blankenship; could the Captain come into the living room for a minute? Delaney hauled himself to his feet, followed the officer out. Blankenship was standing behind the radio operators, bending over the day's Time-Habit log of Daniel Blank's activities. He swung around when Delaney came up.

"Captain, you asked to be informed of any erratic change in Danny Boy's Time-Habit Pattern. Take a look at this." Delaney leaned forward to follow Blankenship's finger pointing out entries in the log. "This morning Danny Boy comes outside the White House at ten minutes after nine. Spotted by Bulldog One. Nine-ten is normal; he's been leaving for work every day around nine-fifteen, give or take a few minutes. But this morning he doesn't leave. According to Bulldog One, he turns around and goes right back into the White House. He comes out again almost an hour later. That means he just didn't forget something—right? Okay . . . he gets a cab. Here it is: at almost ten a.m. Bulldog Two tails him. But he doesn't go right to the Factory. His cab goes around and around Central Park for almost forty-five minutes. What a meter tab he must have had! Then, finally, he gets to his office. It's close to eleven o'clock when Stryker calls to clock him in, almost two hours late. Captain, I realize this all might be a lot of crap. After all, it's the day after Christmas, and Danny Boy might just be unwinding. But I thought you better know."

"Glad you did," Delaney nodded thoughtfully. "Glad you did. It's interesting."

"All right, now come over here and listen to this. It's a tape from Stryker, recorded about a half-hour ago. I wasn't here then so I couldn't talk to him. He asked the operator to put it on tape for me. Spin it, will you, Al?"

One of the operators at the telephone table started his deck recorder. The other men in the room quieted to listen to the tape.

"Ronnie, this is Stryker, at the Factory. How you doing? Ronnie, I just came back from lunch with the cunt I been pushing down here. A little bony, but a wild piece. At lunch I got the talk around to Danny Boy. He was almost two hours late getting to work. This cunt of mine—she's the outside receptionist in Danny Boy's department—she told me that just before I met her for lunch, she was in the ladies' john talking to Mrs. Cleek. That's C-l-e-e-k. She's Danny Boy's personal secretary. A widow. First name Martha or Margaret. White, female, middle thirties, five-three, one-ten or thereabouts, dark brown hair, fair complexion, no visible scars, wears glasses all the time. Well, anyway, in the can, this Mrs. Cleek tells my cunt that Danny Boy was acting real queer this morning. Wouldn't dictate or sign any letters. Wouldn't read anything. Wouldn't even answer any important phone calls. Probably a sack of shit, Ronnie—but I figured I better report it. If you think it's important, I can cozy up to this Cleek dame and see what else I can find out. No problem; she's hungry I can tell. Nice ass. Let me know if you want me to follow up on this. Stryker at the Factory, off."

There was silence in the radio room after the tape was stopped. Then someone laughed. "That Stryker," someone said softly, "all he thinks about is pussy."

"Maybe," Captain Delaney said coldly, speaking to no one man, speaking to them all, "but he's doing a good job." He turned to Blankenship. "Call Stryker. Tell him to cozy up to the Cleek woman and keep us informed—of anything."

"Will do, Captain."

Delaney walked slowly back into his study, heavy head bowed, hands shoved into his hip pockets. The altered Time-Habit Pattern and Danny Boy's strange behavior in his office: the best news he'd had all day. It might be working. It just might be working.

He searched for the sheet of yellow paper on which he had jotted his nine-point plan. It wasn't in his locked top desk drawer. It wasn't in the file. Where was it? His memory was really getting bad. He finally found the plan under his desk blotter, alongside the plus-minus list he used to evaluate the performance of men under his command. Before looking at the plan, he added the name of Stryker to the plus column of the performance list.

Peering at the plan closely through his reading glasses, he checked off the first six items: Garage attendant, Parrot bartender, Lipsky, the Mortons at Erotica, Visit to Factory, Lombard Christmas Eve call to Blank. The seventh item was: "Monica's call to Blank." He sat back in his swivel chair, stared at the ceiling, tried to think out the best way to handle *that*.

He was still pondering his options—what *he* would say and what *she* would say—when the outside guard knocked on his study door and didn't enter until he heard Delaney's shouted, "Come in!" The officer said a reporter named Thomas Handry was on the sidewalk and claimed he had an appointment with the Captain.

"Sure," Delaney nodded. "Let him in. Tell the man at the desk to make certain he's logged in and out."

He went into the kitchen for some ice cubes. When he came back Handry was standing in front of the desk.

"Thanks for coming," Delaney smiled genially. "I had it marked down: 'Day after Christmas, Handry interviews Blank.'"

Handry sat in the leather club chair, then rose immediately, took two folded sheets from his inside breast pocket, tossed them onto Delaney's desk.

"Background stuff on this guy," he said, slumping back into his soft chair. "His job, views on the importance of the computer in industry, biography, personal life. But I imagine you've got all this by now."

The Captain took a quick look at the two typed pages. "Got most of it," he acknowledged. "But you've got a few things here we'll follow up on—a few leads."

"So my interview was just wasted time?"

"Oh, Handry," Delaney sighed. "At the time I asked you to do this, I was on my own. I had no idea I'd be back on active duty with enough dicks to run all this down. Besides, all this background shit isn't so important. I told you that at the restaurant. I wanted your personal impressions of the man. You're sensitive, intelligent. Since I couldn't interview him myself, I wanted you to meet him and tell me what your reactions were. That *is* important. Now give me the whole thing, how it went, what you said and what he said."

Thomas Handry took a deep breath, blew it out. Then he began talking. Delaney never interrupted once, but leaned forward, cupping one ear, the better to hear Handry's low-voiced recital.

The newspaperman's report was fluid and concise. He had arrived precisely at 1:30 p.m., the time previously arranged for the interview by Javis-Bircham's Director of Public Relations. But Blank had kept him waiting almost a half-hour. It was only after two requests to Blank's secretary that Handry had been allowed into the inner office.

Daniel G. Blank had been polite, but cold and withdrawn. Also, somewhat suspicious. He had asked to inspect Handry's press card—an odd act for a business executive giving an interview arranged by his own PR man. But Blank had spoken lucidly and at length about the role played by AMROK II in the activities of Javis-Bircham. About his personal background, he had been cautious, uncommunicative, and frequently asked Handry what his questions had to do with the interview in progress. As far as the reporter could determine, Blank was divorced, had no children, had no plans to marry again. He lived a bachelor's life, found it enjoyable, had no ambitions other than to serve J-B as best he might.

"Very pretty," Delaney nodded. "You said he was 'withdrawn.' Your word. What did you mean by that?"

"Were you in the military, Captain?"

"Yes. Five years U.S. Army."

"I did four with the Marines. You know the expression 'a thousand-yard stare'?"

"Oh yes. On the range. For an unfocused vision."

"Right. That's what Blank has. Or had a few hours ago during the interview. He was looking at me, in me, through me, and somewhere beyond. I don't know what the hell he was focussing on. Most of these high-pressure business executives are all teeth, hearty handshake, sincere smile, focussing between your eyes, over the bridge of your nose, so it looks like they're returning your stare frankly, without blinking. But this guy was gone somewhere, off somewhere. I don't know where the hell he was."

"Good, good," Delaney muttered, taking quick notes. "Anything else? Physical peculiarities? Habits? Bite his nails?"

"No . . . But he wears a wig. Did you know that?"

"No," the Captain said in apparent astonishment. "A wig? He's only in his middle- thirties. Are you sure?"

"Positive," Handry said, enjoying the surprise. "It wasn't even on straight. And he didn't give a goddam if I knew. He kept poking a finger up under the edge of the rug and scratching his scalp. Anything?"

"Mmmm. Maybe. How was he dressed?"

"Conservative elegance" is the phrase. Black suit well-cut. White shirt, starched collar. Striped tie. Black shoes with a dull gloss, not shiny."

"You'd make a hell of a detective."

"You told me that before."

"Smell any booze on his breath?"

"No. But a high-powered cologne or after-shave lotion."

"That figures. Scratch his balls?"

"*What?*"

"Did he play with himself?"

"Jesus, no! Captain, you're wild."

"Yes. Did he look drawn, thin, emaciated? Like he hasn't been eating well lately?"

"Not that I could see. Well . . ."

"What?" Delaney demanded quickly.

"Shadows under his eyes. Puffy bags. Like he hasn't been sleeping so well lately. But all the rest of his face was tight. He's really a good-looking guy. And his handshake was firm and dry. He looked to be in good physical shape. Just before I left, when we were both standing, he handed me a promotion booklet Javis-Bircham got out on AMROK II. It slipped out of my hand. It was my fault; I dropped it. But Blank stooped and caught it before it hit the floor. The guy's quick."

"Oh yes," Delaney nodded grimly, "he's quick. All right, this is all interesting and valuable. Now tell me what you think about him, what you *feel* about him."

"A drink?"

"Of course. Help yourself."

"Well . . ." Thomas Handry said, pouring Scotch over ice cubes, "he's a puzzle. He's not one thing and he's not another. He's a between-man, going from A to B. Or maybe from A to Z. I guess that doesn't make much sense."

"Go on."

"He's just not *with* it. He's not *there*. The impression I got was of a guy floating. He's out there somewhere. Who the hell knows where? That thousand-yard stare. And it was obvious he couldn't care less about Javis-Bircham and AMROK II. He was just going through the motions; a published interview couldn't interest him less. I don't know what's on his mind. He's lost and floating, like I said. Captain, the guy's a balloon! He's got no anchor. He puzzles me and he interests me. I can't solve him." A long pause. "Can you?"

"Getting there," Captain Delaney said slowly. "Just beginning to get there."

There was a lengthy silence, while Handry sipped his drink and Delaney stared at a damp spot on the opposing wall.

"It's him, isn't it?" Handry said finally. "No doubt about it."

Delaney sighed. "That's right. It's him. No doubt about it."

"Okay," the reporter said, surprisingly chipper. He drained his glass, rose, walked toward the hallway door. Then, knob in hand, he turned to stare at the Captain. "I want to be in on the kill," he stated flatly.

"All right."

Handry nodded, turned away, then turned back again. "Oh," he said nonchalantly, "one more thing . . . I got a sample of his handwriting."

He marched back to Delaney's desk, tossed a photo onto the blotter. Delaney picked it up slowly, stared. Daniel G. Blank: a copy of the photo taken from the "Fink File," the same photo that was now copied in the hundreds and in the hands of every man assigned to Operation Lombard.

Delaney turned it over. On the back, written with a felt-tipped pen, was: "With all best wishes. Daniel G. Blank."

"How did you get this?"

"The ego-trip. I told him I kept a scrapbook of photos and autographs of famous people I interviewed. He went for it."

"Beautiful. Thank you for your help."

After Handry left, Delaney kept staring at that inscription: "With all best wishes. Daniel G. Blank." He rubbed his fingers lightly over the signature. It seemed to bring him closer to the man.

He was still staring at the handwriting, trying to see beyond it, when Detective sergeant Thomas MacDonald came in sideways, slipping his bulk neatly through the hallway door, left partly open by Handry.

The black moved a step into the study, then stopped.

"Interrupting you, Captain?"

"No, no. Come on in. What's up?"

The short, squat detective came over to Delaney's desk.

"You wanted a photo of Roger Kope, the cop who got wasted. Will this do?"

He handed Delaney a crisp white cardboard folder, opening sideways. On the front it said, in gold script, "Holiday Greetings." Inside, on the left, in the same gold script, it read: "From the Kope family." On the right side was pasted a color photo of Roger Kope, his wife, three little children. They were posed, grinning self-consciously, before a decorated Christmas tree. The dead detective had his arm about his wife's shoulders. It wasn't a good photo: obviously an amateur job taken a year ago and poorly copied. The colors were washed out, the face of one of the children was blurred. But they were all there.

"It was all we could get," MacDonald said tonelessly. "They had about a hundred made up a month ago, but I guess Mrs. Kope won't send them this year. Will it do?"

"Yes," Delaney nodded. "Just fine." Then, as MacDonald turned to go, he said, "Sergeant, a couple of other things . . . Who's the best handwriting man in the Department?"

MacDonald thought a moment, his sculpted features calm, carved: a Congo mask or a a Picasso sketch. "Handwriting," he repeated, "That would be Willow, William T., Detective lieutenant. He works out of a broom- closet office downtown."

"Ever had any dealings with him?"

"About two years ago. It was a forged lottery ticket ring. He's a nice guy. Prickly, but okay. He sure knows his stuff."

"Could you get him up here? No rush. Whenever he can make it."

"I'll give him a call."

"Good. The next day or so will be fine."

"All right, Captain. What's the other thing?"

"What?"

"You said you had a couple of things."

"Oh. Yes. Who's controlling the men on the tap on Danny Boy's home phone?"

"I am, Captain. Fernandez set it up: technically they're his boys. But he asked me to take over. He's got enough on his plate. Besides, these guys are just sitting on their ass. They've come up with zilch. Danny Boy makes one or two calls a week, usually to the Princess in the Castle. Maybe to the Mortons. And he gets fewer calls. So far it's nothing."

"Uh-huh," Delaney nodded. "Listen, sergeant, would it be possible to make some clicks or buzzes the next time Danny Boy makes or gets a call?"

MacDonald picked up on it instantly. "So he thinks or knows his phone is tapped?"

"Right."

"Sure. No sweat; we could do that. Clicks, buzzes, hisses, an echo—something. He'll get the idea."

"Fine."

MacDonald stared at him a long time, putting things together. Finally: "Spooking him, Captain?" he asked softly.

Captain Delaney put out his hands, palms down on his desk blotter, lowered his massive head to stare at them.

"Not spooking," he said in a gentle voice. "I mean to split him. To crack him open. Wide. Until he's in pieces and bleeding. And it's working. I know it is. Sergeant, how do *you* know when you're close?"

"My mouth goes dry."

Delaney nodded. "My armpits begin to sweat something awful. Right now they're dripping like old faucets. I'm going to push this guy right over the edge, right off, and watch him fall."

MacDonald's smooth expression didn't change. "You figure he'll suicide, Captain?"

"Will he suicide . . ." Delaney said thoughtfully. Suddenly, that moment, something began that he had been hoping for. *He* was Daniel G. Blank, penetrating deep into the man, smoothing his body with perfumed oils, dribbling on scented powders, wearing silk bikini underwear and a fashionable wig, living in sterile loneliness, fucking a boy-shaped woman, buggering a real boy, and venturing out at night to find loves who would help him to break out, to feel, to discover what he was, and meaning.

"Suicide?" Delaney repeated, so quietly that MacDonald could hardly hear him. "No. Not by gunshot, pills or defenestration." He smiled slightly when he pronounced the last word, knowing the sergeant would pick up the mild humor. Defenestration: throwing yourself out a window to smash to jelly on the concrete below. "No, he won't suicide, no matter how hard the pressure. Not his style. He likes risk. He climbs mountains. He's at his best when he's in danger. It's like champagne."

"Then what will he do, Captain?"

"I'm going to run," Delaney said in a strange, pleading voice. "I've *got* to run."

3

THE SECOND day after Christmas, Daniel Blank decided the worst thing—the *worst* thing—was committing these irrational acts, and *knowing* they were irrational, and not being able to stop.

For instance, this morning, completely unable to get to work at his usual hour, he sat stiffly in his living room, dressed for a normal day at Javis-Bircham. And between 9:00 and 11:00 a.m., he rose from his chair at least three times to check the locks and bolts on the front door. They were fastened—he *knew* they were fastened—but he had to check. Three times.

Then suddenly he darted through the apartment, flinging open closet doors, thrusting an arm between hanging clothes. No one there. He knew it was wrong to be acting the way he was.

He mixed a drink, a morning drink, thinking it might help. He picked up a knife to slice a wedge of lime, looked at the blade, let it clatter into the sink. No temptation there, none, but he didn't want the thing in his hand. He might reach up to wipe his eyes and . . .

What about the sandals? That was odd. He owned a pair of leather strap-sandals, custom-made. He still remembered the shop in Greenwich Village, the cool hands of the young Chinese girl tracing his bare feet on a sheet of white paper. He frequently wore the sandals at night, when he was home alone. The straps were loose enough so that he could slip the sandals onto his feet without unbuckling and buckling. He had been doing it for years. But this morning the straps had been unbuckled, the sandals there beside his bed with straps flapping wide. Who had done that?

And time—what was happening to his sense of time? He thought ten minutes had elapsed, but it turned out to be an hour. He guessed an hour, and it was 20 minutes. What was happening?

And what was happening to his penis? It was his imagination, of course, but it seemed to be shrinking, withdrawing into his scrotum. Ridiculous. And he no longer had his regular bowel movement a half-hour after he awoke. He felt stuffed and blocked.

Other things . . . Little things . . .

Going from one room to another and, when he got there, forgetting why he had made the trip.

Hearing a phone ring on a television program and leaping up to answer his own phone.

Finally, when he got to the office, things didn't go well at all. Not that he couldn't have handled it; he was thinking logically, he was lucid. But what was the point?

Near noon, Mrs. Cleek came in and found him weeping at his desk, head bent forward, palms gripping his temples. Her eyes blurred immediately with sympathy.

"Mr. Blank," she said, "what *is* it?"

"I'm sorry," he gasped, and then, saying the first thing that came into his mind: "A death in the family."

What caused his tears was this: do mad people know they are mad? That is, do they know they are acting abnormally but cannot help it? That was why he wept.

"Oh," Mrs. Cleek mourned, "I'm so sorry."

He got home, finally. He was as proud as a drunk who walks out of a bar without upsetting anything, steadfast, steps slowly through the doorway without brushing the frame, follows a sidewalk seam slowly and carefully homeward, never wavering.

It was early in the evening. Was it 6:00 p.m.? It might be eight. He didn't want to look at his watch bracelet. He wasn't sure he could trust it. Perhaps it might not be his own faulty time sense; it might be his wristwatch running wild. Or time itself running wild.

He picked up his phone. There was a curious, empty echo before he got a dial tone. He heard it ring. Someone picked up the phone. Then Blank heard two sharp clicks.

"Mith Montforth rethidenth," he heard Valenter say.

"This is Daniel Blank. Is Miss Montfort in?"

"Yeth, thir. I'll call—"

But then Daniel Blank heard a few more soft clicks, a strange hissing on the line. He hung up abruptly. Jesus! He should have known. He left the apartment immediately. What time *was* it? It didn't matter.

"He's tapping my phone," he said to Celia indignantly. "I definitely heard it. Definitely."

They were in that tainted room at the top of the house; city sounds came faintly. He told her he had followed her advice, had opened his mind to instinct, to all the primitive fears and passions that had come flooding in. He told her how he had been acting, the irrational fits and starts of his daily activities, and he told her about the clicks, hisses, and echo on the phone when he had called her.

"Do you think I'm going mad?" he demanded.

"No," she said slowly, almost judiciously, "I don't think so. I think that in the time I have known you, you have been moving from the man you were to the man you are to be. What that is, I don't believe either of us know for sure. But it's understandable that this growth be painful, perhaps even frightening. You're leaving everything familiar behind you and setting out on a journey, a search, a climb, that's leading . . . somewhere. Forget for a moment the man who has been following you and the phone call you received. These pains and dislocations have nothing to do with that. Dan, you're being born again, and you're feeling all the anguish of birth, being yanked from the safety of a warm womb into a foreign world. The wonder is that you've endured it as well as you have."

As usual, her flood of murmured words soothed and assured him; he felt as relaxed as if she was stroking his brow. She *did* make sense; it *was* true that he had changed since he met her, and was changing. The murders were part of it, of course—she was wrong to deny that—but they were not the cause but just one effect of the monumental upheaval inside him, something hot and bubbling there thrusting to the surface.

They made love slowly then, with more tenderness than passion, more sweetness than joy. In the eerie light of that single orange bulb he leaned closer to see her for the first time, microscopically.

Her nipples, under his tongue's urging, engorged and, peering close, he saw the flattened tops with ravines and gorges, tiny, tiny, a topographic map. And threaded through the small breasts a network of bluish veins, tangled as a silken skein.

Along the line of curved hips sprouted a Lilliputian wheatfield of surprisingly golden hairs, and more at the dimpled small of her back. These tender sprouts tickled dry and dusty on his tongue. The convoluted navel returned his stare in a lascivious wink. Inside, prying, he found a sharp bitterness that tingled.

Far up beneath her long hair, at nape of neck, was swamp dampness and scent of pond lilies. He stared at flesh of leg and groin, so close his eyelashes brushed and she made a small sound. There was hard, shiny skin on her soles, a crumbling softness between her toes. It all became clear to him, and dear, and sad.

They fenced with tongues—thrust, parry, cut—and then he was tasting creamy wax from her ear and in her armpits a sweet liquor that bit and melted on his lips like snow. Behind her knees more blue veins meandered, close to a skin that felt like suede and twitched faintly when he touched.

He spread her buttocks; the rosebud glared at him, withdrawing and expanding—a time-motion film of a flower reacting to light and darkness. He put his erect penis in her soft palm, slowly guided her fingers to stroke, circle, gently probe the opening, their hands clasped so they might share. He touched his lips to her closed eyes, thought he might suck them out and gulp them down like oysters, seasoned with her tears.

"I want you inside me," she said suddenly, lay on her back, spread her knees wide, guided his cock up into her. She wrapped arms and legs about him and moaned softly, as if they were making love for the first time.

But there was no love. Only a sweetness so sad it was almost unendurable.

Even as they fucked he knew it was the sadness of departure; they would never fuck again; both knew it.

She was quickly slick, inside and out; they grappled to hold tight. He spurted with a series of great, painful lunges and, stunned, he continued to make the motions long after he was drained and surfeited. He could not stop his spasm, had no desire to, and felt her come again.

She looked at him through half-opened eyes, glazed; he thought she felt what he did: the defeat of departure. In that moment he knew she had told. She had betrayed him.

But he smiled, smiled, smiled, kissed her closed mouth, went home early. He took a cab because the darkness frightened him.

If it was a day of departure and defeat for Daniel Blank, it was a day of arrival and triumph for Captain Edward X. Delaney. He dared not feel confident, lest he put the whammy on it, but it did seem to be coming together.

Paper work in the morning: requisitions, reports, vouchers—the whole schmear. Then over to the hospital to sit awhile with Barbara, reading to her from "Honey Bunch: Her First Little Garden." Then he treated himself to a decent meal in one of those west side French restaurants: *coq au vin* with a half-bottle of a heavy burgundy to help it along. He paid his bill and then, on the way out, stopped at the bar for a Kirsch. He felt good.

It was good; everything was good. He had no sooner returned to his home when Blankenship came in to display Danny Boy's Time-Habit Pattern. It was very erratic indeed: Arrived at the Factory at 11:30 a.m. Skipped lunch completely. Took a long zigzag walk along the docks. Sat on a wharf for almost an hour—"Just watching the turds float by" according to the man tailing him. Report from Stryker: Hs had taken Mrs. Cleek to lunch, and she told him she had found Danny Boy weeping in his office, and he had told her there had been a death in the family. Danny Boy returned to the White House at 2:03 p.m.

"Fine," the Captain nodded, handling the log back to Blankenship. "Keep at it. Is Fernandez on?"

"Comes on at four, Captain."

"Ask him to stop by to see me, will you?"

After Blankenship left, Delaney closed all the doors to his study, paced slowly around the room, head bowed. "A death in the family." That was nice. He paused to call Monica Gilbert and ask if he could come over to see her that evening. She invited him for dinner but he begged off; they arranged that he would come over at 7:00 p.m. He told her it would only be for a few minutes; she didn't ask the reason. Her girls were home from school during the holiday week so, she explained, she hadn't been able to visit Barbara as much as she wanted to, but would try to get there the following afternoon. He thanked her.

More pacing, figuring out options and possibilities. He walked into the radio room to tell Blankenship to requisition four more cars, two squads and two unmarked, and keep them parked on the street outside, two men in each. He didn't want to think of the increase in manpower that entailed, and went back into his study to resume his pacing. Was there anything he should have done that he had not? He couldn't think of anything, but he was certain there would be problems he hadn't considered. No help for that.

He took out his plan and, alongside the final three items, worked out a rough time schedule. He was still fiddling with it when Lt. Jeri Fernandez knocked and looked in.

"Want me, Captain?"

"Just for a minute, lieutenant. Won't take long. How's it going?"

"Okay. I got a feeling things are beginning to move. Don' ask me how I know. Just a feeling."

"I hope you're right. I've got another job for you. You'll have to draw more men. Get them from wherever you can. If you have any shit with their commanders, tell them to call me. It's a woman—Monica Gilbert. Here's her address and telephone number. She's the widow of Bernard Gilbert, the second victim. There was a guard on her right after he was iced, so there may be a photo of her in the files and some Time-Habit reports. I want a twenty-four hour tap on her phone, two men in an unmarked car outside her house, and two uniformed men outside her apartment door. She's got two little girls. If she goes out with the girls, both the buttons stick with them, and I mean close. If she goes out alone, one man on her and one on the kids. Got all that?"

"Sure, Captain. A tight tail?"

"But I mean *tight*. Close enough to touch."

"You think Danny Boy'll try something?"

"No. I don't. But I want her and her children covered, around the clock. Can you set it up?"

"No sweat, Captain. I'll get on it right away."

"Good. Put your men on at eight tonight. Not before."

Fernandez nodded. "Captain . . ."

"Yes?"

"The Luger's almost ready."

"Fine. Any problems?"

"Nope. Not a one."

"You spending any money on this?"

"Money?" Fernandez looked at him incredulously. "What money? Some guys owed me some favors."

Delaney nodded. Fernandez opened the hallway door to depart, and there was a man standing there, his arm bent, knuckles raised, about to knock on the Captain's door.

"Captain Delaney?" the man asked Fernandez.

The lieutenant shook his head, jerked a thumb over his shoulder at the Captain, stepped around the newcomer and disappeared.

"I'm Captain Edward X. Delaney."

"My name is William T. Willow, Detective lieutenant. I believe you wanted to consult me."

"Oh yes," Delaney said, rising from his chair. "Please come in, lieutenant, and close the door behind you. Thank you for coming up. Please sit down over there. Sergeant MacDonald tells me you're the best man in your field."

"I agree," Willow said, with a sweet smile.

Delaney laughed. "How about a drink?" he asked. "Anything?"

"You don't happen to have a glass of sherry, do you, Captain?"

"Yes, I do. Medium dry. Will that be all right?"

"Excellent, thank you."

The Captain walked over to his liquor cabinet, and while he poured the drink, he inspected the handwriting expert. A queer bird. The skin and frame of a plucked chicken, and clad in a hairy tweed suit so heavy Delaney wondered how the man's frail shoulders could support it. On his lap was a plaid cap, and his shoes were over-the-ankle boots in a dark brown suede. Argyle socks, wool Tattersall shirt, woven linen tie secured with a horse's head clasp. Quite a sight.

But Willow's eyes were washed blue, lively and alert, and his movements, when he took the glass of sherry from Delaney, were crisp and steady.

"Your health, sir," the lieutenant said, raising his glass. He sipped. "Harvey's," he said.

"Yes."

"And very good, too. I would have been up sooner, Captain, but I've been in court."

"That's all right. No rush about this."

"What is it?"

Delaney searched in his top desk drawer, then handed Willow the photo Thomas Handry had delivered, with the inscription on the back: "With all best wishes. Daniel G. Blank."

"What can you tell me about the man who wrote this?"

Detective lieutenant William T. Willow didn't even glance at it. Instead, he looked at the Captain with astonishment.

"Oh dear," he said, "I'm afraid there's been a frightful misunderstanding. Captain, I'm a QD man, not a graphologist."

Pause.

"What's a QD man?" Delaney asked.

"Questioned Documents. All my work is with forgeries or suspected forgeries, comparing one specimen with another."

"I see. And what is a graphologist?"

"A man who allegedly is able to determine character, personality, and even physical and mental illness from a man's handwriting."

"'Allegedly'," Delaney repeated. "I gather you don't agree with graphologists?"

"Let's just say I'm an agnostic on the matter," Willow smiled his sweet smile. "I don't agree and I don't disagree."

The Captain saw the sherry glass was empty. He rose to refill it, and left the bottle on the little table alongside Willow's elbow. Then the Captain sat down behind his desk again, regarded the other man gravely.

"But you're familiar with the theories and practice of graphology?"

"Oh my yes, Captain. I read everything on the subject of handwriting analysis, from whatever source, good and bad."

Delaney nodded, laced his fingers across his stomach, leaned back in his swivel chair.

"Lieutenant Willow," he said dreamily, "I am going to ask a very special favor of you. I am going to ask you to pretend you are a graphologist and not a QD man. I am going to ask you to inspect this specimen of handwriting and analyze it as a graphologist would. What I want is your opinion. I do not want a signed statement from you. You will not be called upon to testify. This is completely unofficial. I just want to know what you think—putting yourself in the place of a graphologist, of course. It will go no further than this room."

"Of course," Willow said promptly. "Delighted."

From an inner pocket he whipped out an unusual pair of glasses: prescription spectacles with an additional pair of magnifying glasses hinged to the top edge. The lieutenant shoved on the glasses, flipped down the extra lenses. He held the Daniel Blank inscription so close it was almost touching his nose.

"Felt-tipped pen," he said immediately. "Too bad. You lose the nuances. Mmm. Uh-huh. Mmm. Interesting, very interesting. Captain, does this man suffer from constipation?"

"I have no idea," Delaney said.

"Oh, my, look at this," Willow said, still peering closely at Blank's handwriting. "Would you believe . . . Sick, sick, sick. And this . . . Beautiful capitals, just beautiful." He looked up at the Captain. "He grew up in a small town in middle America—Ohio, Indiana, Iowa—around there?"

"Yes."

"He's about forty, or older?"

"Middle-thirties."

"Well . . . yes, that could be. Palmer Method. They still teach it in some schools. Goodness, look at that. This is interesting."

Suddenly he jerked off his glasses, tucked them away, half-rose to his feet to flip the photo of Blank onto Delaney's desk, then settled back to pour himself another glass of sherry.

"Schizoid," he said, beginning to speak rapidly. "On one side, artistic, sensitive, imaginative, gentle, perceptive, outgoing, striving, sympathetic, generous. The capitals are works of art. Flowing. Just blooming. On the other side, lower case now, tight, very cold, perfectly aligned: the mechanical mind, ordered, disciplined, ruthless, without emotion, inhuman, dead. It's very difficult to reconcile."

"Yes," Delaney said. "Is the man insane?"

"No. But he's breaking up."

"Why do you say that?"

"His handwriting is breaking up. Even with the felt-tipped pen you can see it. The connections between letters are faint. Between some there are no connections at all. And in his signature, that should be the most fluid and assured of anyone's handwriting, he's beginning to waver. He doesn't know who he is."

"Thank you very much, Lieutenant Willow," Captain Delaney said genially. "Please stay and finish your drink. Tell me more about handwriting analysis—from a graphologist's point of view, of course. It sounds fascinating."

"Oh yes," the bird-man said, "it is."

Later that evening Delaney went into the living room to inspect the log. Danny Boy had returned to the White House at 2:03 p.m. At 5:28 p.m., he had called the Princess in the Castle, hung up abruptly after speaking only a few minutes and then, at 5:47 p.m., had taken a cab to the Castle. He was still inside as of that moment, reported by Bulldog Three.

Delaney went over to the telephone desk.

"Did you get a tape of Danny Boy's call to the Castle at five twenty-eight?"

"Yes, sir. The man on the tap gave it to us over the phone. Spin it?"

"Please."

He listened to Daniel Blank talking to the lisping Valenter. He heard the clicks, hisses, and echo they were feeding onto the tapped line. He smiled when Blank slammed down his phone in the middle of the conversation.

"Perfect," Delaney said to no one in particular.

He had planned his meeting with Monica Gilbert with his usual meticulous attention to detail, even to the extent of deciding to keep on his overcoat. It would make her think he could only stay a moment, he was rushed, working hard to convict her husband's killer.

But when he arrived at 7:00 p.m., the children were still awake, but in their nightgowns, and he had to play with them, inspect their Christmas gifts, accept a cup of coffee. The atmosphere was relaxed, warm, pleasant, domestic—all wrong for his purpose. He was glad when Monica packed the girls off to bed.

Delaney went back to the living room, sat down on the couch, took out the single sheet of paper he had prepared, with the speech he wanted her to deliver.

She came in, looking at him anxiously.

"What is it, Edward? You seem—well, tense."

"The killer is Daniel Blank. There's no doubt about it. He killed your husband, and Lombard, Kope, and Feinberg. He's a psycho, a crazy."

"When are you going to arrest him?"

"I'm not going to arrest him. There's no evidence I can take into court. He'd walk away a free man an hour after I collared him."

"I can't believe it."

"It's true. We're watching him, every minute, and maybe we can prevent another killing or catch him in the act. But I can't take the chance."

Then he told her of what he had been doing to smash Daniel Blank. When he described the Christmas Eve call as Frank Lombard, her face went white.

"Edward, you didn't," she gasped.

"Oh yes. I did. And it worked. The man is breaking apart. I know he is. A couple of more days, if I keep the pressure on, he's going to crack wide open. Now here's what I want you to do."

He handed her the sheet of dialogue he had written out. "I want you to call him, now, at his home, identify yourself and ask him why he killed your husband."

She looked at him with shock and horror. "Edward," she choked, "I can't do that."

"Sure you can," he urged softly. "It's just a few words. I've got them all written down for you. All you've got to do is read them. I'll be right here when you call. I'll even hold your hand, if you want me to. It'll just take a minute or so. Then it'll all be over. You can do it."

"I can't, I *can't*!" She turned her head away, put her hands to her face. "Please don't ask me to," she said, her voice muffled. "Please don't. Please."

"He murdered your husband," he said stonily.

"But even if—"

"And three other innocent strangers. Cracked their skulls with his trusty little ice ax and left them on the sidewalk with their brains spilling out."

"Edward, please . . ."

"You're the woman who wanted revenge, aren't you? 'Vengeance", you said. 'I'll do anything to help,' you said. 'Type, run errands, make coffee.' That's what you told me. A few words is all I want, spoken on the phone to the man who slaughtered your husband."

"He'll come after me. He'll hurt the children."

"No. He doesn't hurt women and children. Besides, you'll be tightly guarded. He couldn't get close even if he tried. But he won't. Monica? Will you do it?"

"Why me? Why must I do it? Can't you get a policewoman—"

"To call him and say it's you? That wouldn't lessen any possible danger to you and the girls. And I don't want any more people in the Department to know about this."

She shook her head, knuckles clenched to her mouth. Her eyes were wet.

"Anything but this," she said faintly. "I just can't do it. I *can't*."

He stood, looked down at her, his face pulled into an ugly smile.

"Leave it to the cops, eh?" he said in a voice he scarcely recognized as his own. "Leave it to the cops to clean up the world's shit, and vomit, and blood. Keep your own hands clean. Leave it all to the cops. Just so long as you don't know what they're doing."

"Edward, it's so cruel. Can't you see that? What you're doing is worse than what he did. He killed bcause he's sick and can't help himself. But you're killing him slowly and deliberately, knowing exactly what you're doing, everything planned and—"

Suddenly he was sitting close beside her, an arm about her shoulders, his lips at her ear.

"Listen," he whispered, "your husband was Jewish and you're Jewish—right? And Feinberg, that last guy he chilled, was a Jew. Four victims; two Jews. Fifty percent. You want this guy running loose, killing more of your people? You want—"

She jerked away from under his arm, swung from the waist, and slapped his face, an open-handed smack that knocked his head aside and made him blink.

"Despicable!" she spat at him. "The most despicable man I've ever met!"

He stood suddenly, looming over her.

"Oh yes," he said, tasting the bile bubbling up. "Despicable. Oh yes. But Blank, he's a poor, sick lad—right? Right? Smashed your husband's skull in, but it's Be Nice to Blank Week. Right? Let me tell you—let me tell you—" He was stuttering now in his passion to get it out. "He's dead. You understand that? Daniel G. Blank is a dead man. Right now. You think—you think I'm going to let him walk away from this just because the law . . . You think I'm going to shrug, turn away, and give up? I tell you, he's *dead*! There's no way, *no* way, he can get away from me. If I have to blow his brains out with my service revolver at high noon on Fifth Avenue, I'll do it. Do it! And wait right there for them to come and take me away. I don't care. The man is *dead*! Can't you get that through your skull? If you won't help me, I'll do it another way. No matter what you do, it doesn't matter, doesn't matter. He's gone. He's just gone."

He stood there quivering with his anger, trying to draw deep breaths through his open mouth.

She looked at him timidly. "What do you want me to say?" she asked in a small voice.

He sat beside her on the couch, holding her free hand, his ear pressed close to the phone she held so he could overhear the conversation. The script he had composed lay on her lap.

Blank's phone rang seven times before he picked it up.

"Hello?" he said cautiously.

"Daniel Blank?" Monica asked, reading her lines. There was a slight quaver in her voice.

"Yes. Who is this?"

"My name is Monica Gilbert. I'm the widow of Bernard Gilbert. Mr. Blank, why did you kill Bernie? My children and I want—"

But she was interrupted by a wild scream, a cry of panic and despair that frightened both of them. It came wailing over the wire, loud enough to be painful in their ears, shrill enough to pierce into their hearts and souls and set them quivering. Then there was the heavy bumping of a dropped phone, a thick clatter.

Delaney took the phone from Monica's trembling hand, hung it up gently. He stood, buttoned his overcoat, reached for his hat.

"Fine," he said softly. "You did just fine."

She looked at him.

"You're a dreadful man," she whispered. "The most dreadful man I've ever met."

"Am I?" he asked. "Dreadful and despicable, all in one evening. Well . . . I'm a cop."

"I never want to see you again, ever."

"All right," he said, saddened. "Good-night, and thank you."

There were two uniformed men outside her apartment door. He showed them his identification, made certain they had their orders straight. Both had been given copies of Daniel Blank's photo. Outside the house, two plainclothesmen sat in an unmarked car. One of them recognized Delaney, raised a hand in greeting. Fernandez had done an efficient job; he was good on this kind of thing.

The Captain shoved his hands into his overcoat pockets and, trying not to think of what he had done to Monica Gilbert, walked resolutely over to Blank's apartment house and into the lobby. Thank God Lipsky wasn't on duty.

"I have a letter for Daniel Blank," he told the doorman. "Could you put it in his box? No rush. If he gets it tomorrow, it'll be okay."

Delaney gave him two quarters and handed over the Holiday Greetings from Roger Kope and Family, sealed in a white envelope addressed to Mr. Daniel G. Blank.

4

AFTER THAT call from Monica Gilbert, Daniel Blank had dropped the phone and gone trotting through the rooms of his apartment, mouth open, scream caught in his throat; he could not end it. Finally, it dribbled away to moans, heaves, gulps, coughs, tears. Then he was in the bathroom, forehead against the full-length mirror, staring at his strange, contorted face, torn apart.

When he quieted, fearful that his shriek had been heard by neighbors, he went directly to the bedroom phone extension, intending to call Celia Montfort and ask one question: "Why did you betray me?" But there was an odd-sounding dial tone, and he remembered he had dropped the living room handset. He hung up, went back into the living room, hung up that phone, too. He decided not to call Celia. What could she possibly say?

He had never felt such a sense of dissolution and, in self-preservation, undressed, checked window and door locks, turned out the lights and slid into bed naked. He rolled back and forth until silk sheet and wool blanket were wrapped about him tightly, mummifying him, holding him together.

He thought, his mind churning, that he might be awake forever, staring at the darkness and wondering. But curiously, he fell asleep almost instantly: a deep, dreamless slumber, more coma than sleep, heavy and depressing. He awoke at 7:18 a.m. the next morning, sodden with weariness. His eyelids were stuck shut; he realized he had wept during the night.

But the panic of the previous day had been replaced by a lethargy, a non-thinking state. Even after going through the motions of bathing, shaving, dressing, breakfasting, he found himself in a thoughtless world, as if his overworked brain had said, "All right! Enough already!" and doughtily rejected all fears, hopes, passions, visions, ardors. Even his body was subdued; his pulse seemed to beat patiently at a reduced rate, his limbs were slack. Dressed for work, like an actor waiting for his cue, he sat quietly in his living room, staring at the mirrored wall, content merely to exist, breathing.

His phone rang twice, at an hour's interval, but he did not answer. It could be his office calling. Or Celia Montfort. Or . . . or anyone. But he did not answer, but sat rigidly in a kind of catalepsy, only his eyes wandering across his mirrored wall. He needed this time of peace, quiet, non-thinking. He might even have dozed off, there in his Eames chair, but it wasn't important.

He roused early in the afternoon, looked at his watch; it seemed to be 2:18 p.m. That was possible; he was willing to accept it. He thought vaguely that he should get out, take a walk, get some fresh air.

But he only got as far as the lobby. He walked past the locked mail boxes. The mail had been delivered, but he just didn't care. Late Christmas cards, probably. And bills. And . . . well, it wasn't worth thinking about. Had Gilda sent him a Christmas card this year? He couldn't remember. He hadn't sent her one; of that he was certain.

Charles Lipsky stopped him.

"Message for you, Mr. Blank," he said brightly. "In your box." And he stepped behind the counter.

Blank suddenly realized he hadn't given the doormen anything for Christmas, nor the garage attendant, nor his cleaning woman. Or had he? Had he bought a Christmas gift for Celia? He couldn't remember. Why did she betray him?

He looked at the plain white envelope Lipsky thrust into his hand. "Mr. Daniel G. Blank." That was his name. He knew that. He suddenly realized he better not take that short walk—not right now. He'd never make it. He knew he'd never make it.

"Thank you," he said to Lipsky. That was a funny name—Lipsky. Then he turned around, took the elevator back up to his apartment, still moving in that slow, lethargic dream, his knees water, his body ready to melt into a dark, scummed puddle on the lobby carpet if an elevator didn't come soon. He took a deep breath. He'd make it.

When the door was bolted, he leaned back against it and slowly opened the white envelope. Holiday greetings from the Kope Family. Ah well. Why had she betrayed him? What possible reason could she have, since everything he had done had been at her gentle urging and wise tutelage?

He went directly to the bedroom, took out the drawer, turned it upside down on the bed, scattering the contents. He ripped the sealed envelope free. The souvenirs had been a foolish mistake, he thought lazily, but no harm had been done. There they were. No one had taken them. No one had seen them.

He brought in a pair of heavy shears from the kitchen and chopped Lombard's license, Gilbert's ID card, Kope's identification and leatherette holder, and Feinberg's rose petals into small bits, cutting, cutting, cutting. Then he flushed the whole mess down the toilet, watching to make sure it disappeared, then flushing twice more.

That left only Detective third grade Roger Kope's shield. Blank sat on the edge of the bed, bouncing the metal on his palm, wondering dreamily how to get rid of it. He could drop it down the incinerator, but it might endure, charred but legible enough to start someone thinking. Throw it out the window? Ridiculous. Into the river would be best—but could he walk that far and risk someone seeing? The most obvious was best. He would put the shield in a small brown paper bag, walk no more than two blocks or so, and push it down into a corner litter basket. Picked up by the Sanitation Department, dumped into the back of one of those monster trucks, squashed in with coffee grounds and grape fruit rinds, and eventually disgorged onto a dump or landfill in Brooklyn. Perfect. He giggled softly.

He pulled on gloves, wiped the shield with an oily rag, then dropped it into a small brown paper bag. He put on his topcoat; the bag went into the righthand pocket. Through the lefthand pocket he carried his ice ax, beneath the coat, though for what reason he could not say.

He walked over to Third Avenue, turned south. He paused halfway down the block, spotting a litter basket on the next corner. He paused to look in a shop window, inspecting an horrendous display of canes, walkers, wheel-chairs, prosthetic devices, trusses, pads and bandages, emergency oxygen bottles, do-it-yourself urinalysis kits. He turned casually away from the window and inspected the block. No uniformed cops. No squad cars or anything that looked like an unmarked police car. No one who could be a plainclothes detective. Just the usual detritus of a Manhattan street—housewifes and executives, hippies and hookers, pushers and priests: the swarm of the city, swimming in the street current.

He walked quickly to the litter basket at the corner, took out the small brown paper bag with the shield of Detective Kope inside, thrust it down into the accumulated trash: brown paper bags just like his, discarded newspapers, a dead rat, all the raw garbage of a living city. He looked about quickly. No one was watching him; everyone was busy with his own agonies.

He turned and walked home quickly, smiling. The simplest and most obvious was best.

The phone was ringing when he entered his apartment. He let it ring, not answering. He hung away his topcoat, put the ice ax in its place. Then he mixed a lovely vodka martini, stirring endlessly to get it as chilled as possible and, humming, took it into the living room where he lay full-length upon the couch, balanced his drink on his chest, and wondered why she had betrayed him.

After awhile, after he had taken a few sips of his drink, still coming out of his trance, rising to the surface like something long drowned and hidden, rising on a tide or cannon shot or storm to show itself, the phone rang again. He got up immediately, set his drink carefully and steadily on the glass cocktail table, went into the kitchen and selected a knife, a razor-sharp seven-inch blade with a comfortable handle.

Strange, but knives didn't bother him anymore; they felt good. He walked back into the living room, almost prancing, stooped, and with his sharp, comfortable knife, sawed through the coiled cord holding the handset to the telephone body. He put the severed part gently aside, intestine dangling.

With that severance, he cut himself loose. He felt it. Free from events, the world, all reality.

Captain Delaney awoke with a feeling of nagging unease. He fretted that he had neglected something, overlooked some obvious detail that would enable Danny Boy to escape the vigil, fly off to Europe, slide into anonymity in the city streets, or even murder once again. The Captain brooded over the organization of the guard, but could not see how the net could be drawn tighter.

But he was in a grumpy mood when he went down for breakfast. He drew a cup of coffee in the kitchen, wandered back through the radio room, dining room, hallways, and he did become aware of something. There were no night men sleeping on the cots in their underwear. Everyone was awake and dressed; even as he looked about, he saw three men strapping on their guns.

Most of the cops in Operation Lombard were detectives and carried the standard .38 Police Special. A few lucky ones had .357 Magnums or .45 automatics. Some men had two weapons. Some holstered on the hip; some in front, at the waist. One man carried an extra holster and a small .32 at his back. One man carried an even smaller .22 strapped to his calf, under his trouser leg.

Delaney had no objection to this display of unofficial hardware. A dick carried what gave him most comfort on a job in which the next opened door might mean death. The Captain knew some carried saps, brass knuckles, switch-blade knives. That was all right. They were entitled to anything that might give them that extra edge of confidence and see them through.

But what was unusual was to see them make these preparations now, as if they sensed their long watch was drawing to a close. Delaney could guess what they were thinking, what they were discussing in low voices, looking up at him nervously as he stalked by.

First of all, they were not unintelligent men; you were not promoted from patrolman to detective by passing a "stupid test." When Captain Delaney took over command of Operation Lombard, all their efforts were concentrated on Daniel G. Blank, with investigations of other suspects halted. The dicks realized the Captain knew something they didn't know: Danny Boy was their pigeon. Delaney was too old and experienced a cop to put his cock on the line if he wasn't sure, of that they were certain.

Then the word got around that he had requested the Kope photo. Then the telephone men heard the taped replay, from the man tapping Danny Boy's phone, of the phone call from Monica Gilbert. Then the special guard was placed on the Gilbert widow and her children. All that was chewed over in radio room and squad car, on lonely night watches and long hours of patrol. They knew now, or guessed, what he was up to. It was a wonder, Delaney realized, he had been able to keep it private as long as he had. Well, at least it was his responsibility. His alone. If it failed, no one else would suffer from it. If it failed . . .

There was no report of any activity from Danny Boy at 9:00 a.m., 9:15, 9:30, 9:45, 10:00. Early on when the vigil was first established, they had discovered a back entrance to Blank's apartment house, a seldom-used service door that opened onto a walk leading to 82nd Street. An unmarked car, with one man, was positioned there, in full view of this back exit, with orders to report in every fifteen minutes. This unit was coded Bulldog 10, but was familiarly known as Ten-O. Now, as Delaney passed back and forth through the radio room, he heard the reports from Ten-O and from Bulldog One, the Con Ed van parked on the street in front of the White House.

10:15, nothing. 10:30, nothing. No report of Danny Boy at 10:45, 11:00, 11:15, 11:30. Shortly before 12:00, Delaney went into his study and called Blank's apartment. The phone rang and rang, but there was no answer. He hung up; he was worried.

He took a cab over to the hospital. Barbara seemed in a semi-comatose state and refused to eat her meal. So he sat helplessly alongside her bed, holding her limp hand, pondering his options if Blank didn't appear for the rest of the day.

It might be that he was up there, just not answering his phone. It might be that he had slipped through their net, was long gone. And it might be that he had slit his throat after receiving the Kope photo, and was up there all right, leaking blood all over his polished floor. Delaney had told Sergeant MacDonald that Danny Boy wouldn't suicide, but he was going by patterns, by percentages. No one knew better than he that percentages weren't certainties.

He got back to his brownstone a little after 1:00 p.m. Ten-O and Bulldog One had just reported in. No sign of Danny Boy. Delaney had Stryker called at the Factory. Blank hadn't arrived at the office. The Captain went back into his study and called Blank's apartment again. Again the phone rang and rang. No answer.

By this time, without intending to, he had communicated his mood to his men; now he wasn't the only one pacing through the rooms, hands in pockets, head lowered. The men, he noticed, were keeping their faces deliberately expressionless, but he knew they feared what he feared: the pigeon had flown.

By two o'clock he had worked out a contingency plan. If Danny Boy didn't show within another hour, at 3:00 p.m., he'd send a uniformed officer over to the White House with a trumped-up story that the Department had received an anonymous threat against Daniel Blank. The patrolman would go up to Blank's apartment with the doorman, and listen. If they heard Blank moving about, or if he answered his bell, they would say it was a mistake and come away. If they heard nothing, and if Blank didn't answer his bell, then the officer would request the doorman or manager to open Blank's apartment with the pass-keys "just to make certain everything is all right."

It was a sleazy plan, the Captain acknowledged. There were a hundred holes in it; it might endanger the whole operation. But it was the best he could come up with; it had to be done. If Danny Boy was long gone, or dead, they couldn't sit around watching an empty hole. He'd order it at exactly 3:00 p.m.

He was in the radio room, and at 2:48 p.m. there was a burst of static from one of the radio speakers, then it cleared.

"Barbara from Bulldog One."

"Got you, Bulldog One."

"Fernandez," the voice said triumphantly. "Danny Boy just came out."

There was a sigh in the radio room; Captain Delaney realized part of it was his.

"What's he wearing?" he asked the radioman.

The operator started to repeat the question into his mike, but Fernandez had heard the Captain's loud voice.

"Black topcoat," he reported. "No hat. Hands in pockets. He's not waiting for a cab. Walking west. Looks like he's out for a stroll. I'll put Bulldog Three on him, far back, and two sneaks on foot. Officer LeMolle, designated Bulldog Twenty. Officer Sanchez, designated Bulldog Forty. Got that?"

"LeMolle is Bulldog Twenty, Sanchez is Forty."

"Right. You'll get radio checks from them as soon as possible. Danny Boy is nearing Second Avenue now, still heading west. I'm out."

Delaney stood next to the radio table. The other men in the room closed in, heads turned, ears to the loudspeaker.

Silence for almost five minutes. One man coughed, looked apologetically at the others.

Then, almost a whisper: "Barbara from Bulldog Twenty. Read me?"

"Soft but good, Twenty."

"Danny Boy between Second and Third on Eighty-third, heading west. Out." It was a woman's voice.

"Who's Lemolle?" Delaney asked Blankenship.

"Policewoman Martha LeMolle. Her cover is a housewife—shopping bag, the whole bit."

Delaney opened his mouth to speak, but the radio crackled again.

"Barbara from Bulldog Forty. Make me?"

"Yes. Forty. Good. Where is he?"

"Turning south on Third. Out."

Blankenship turned to Delaney without waiting for his question. "Forty is

Detective second grade Ramon Sanchez. Dressed like an orthodox Jewish rabbi."

So when Daniel G. Blank deposited the brown paper bag in the litter basket, the housewife was less than twenty feet behind him and saw him do it, and the rabbi was across the avenue and saw him do it. They both shadowed Danny Boy back to his apartment house, but by the time he arrived they had both reported he had discarded something in a litter basket, they had given the exact location (northeast corner, Third and 82nd; and, at Delaney's command, Blankenship had an unmarked car on the way with orders to pick up the entire basket and bring it back to the brownstone. Delaney thought it might be the ice ax.

At least twenty men crowded into the kitchen when the two plainclothesmen carried in the garbage basket and set it on the linoleum.

"I always knew you'd end up in Sanitation, Tommy," someone called. There were a few nervous laughs.

"Empty it," Delaney ordered. "Slowly. Put the crap on the floor. Shake out every newspaper. Look into every bag."

The two detectives pulled on their gloves. They began to snake out the sodden packages, the neatly wrapped bags, the dead rat (handled by the tip of its tail), loose garbage, a blood-soaked towel. The stench filled the room, but no one left; they had all smelled worse odors than that.

It went slowly, for almost ten minutes, as bags were pulled out, emptied onto the floor, and tied packages were cut open and unrolled. Then one of the dicks reached in, came out with a small brown paper bag, opened it, looked inside.

"Jesus Christ!"

The waiting men said nothing, but there was a tightening of the circle; Captain Delaney felt himself pressed closer until his thighs were tight against the kitchen table. Holding the bag by the bottom, the detective slowly slid the contents out onto the tabletop. Cop's shield.

There was something: a collective moan, a gasp, something of anguish and fear. The men peered closer.

"That's Kope's tin," someone cried, voice crackling with fury. "I worked with him. That's Kope's number. I know it."

Someone said: "Oh, that dirty cocksucker."

Someone said, over and over: "Motherfucker, motherfucker, motherfucker . . ."

Someone said: "Let's get him right now. Let's waste him."

Delaney had been bending over, staring at the buzzer. It wasn't hard to imagine what had happened; Daniel G. Blank had destroyed the evidence, the ID cards and rose petals flushed down the toilet or thrown into the incinerator. But this was good metal, so he figured he better ditch it. Not smart, Danny Boy.

"Let's waste him," someone repeated, in a louder voice.

And here was another problem, one he had hoped to avoid by keeping his knowledge of Daniel Blank's definite guilt to himself. He knew that when a cop was killed, all cops became Sicilians. He had seen it happen; a patrolman shot down, and immediately his precinct house was flooded with cops from all over the city, wearing plaid windbreakers and business suits, shields pinned to lapels, offering to work on their own time. Was there anything they could do? Anything?

It was a mixture of fear, anguish, sorrow. You couldn't possibly understand it unless you belonged. Because it was a brotherhood, and corrupt cops, stupid cops, cowardly cops had nothing to do with it. If you were a cop, then *any* cop's murder diminished you. You could not endure that.

The trouble was, Captain Edward X. Delaney acknowledged to himself, the trouble was that he could understand all this on an intellectual level without feeling the emotional involvement these men were feeling now, staring at a murdered cop's tin. It wasn't so much a lack in him, he assured himself, as that he looked at things differently from these furious men. To him *all* murders, in sanity and without conscience, demanded judgment, whether assassinated President, child thrown from rooftop, drunk knifed to death in a tavern brawl, whatever, wherever, whomever. His brotherhood was wider, larger, broader, and encompassed all, all, all . . .

But meanwhile, he was surrounded by a ring of bloodcharged men. He knew he had only to say, "All right, let's take him," and they would be with him, surging, breaking down doors. Daniel G. Blank would dissolve in a million plucking bullets, torn and falling into darkness.

Captain Delaney raised his head slowly, looked around at those faces: stony, twisted, blazing.

"We'll do it my way," he said, keeping his voice as toneless as he could. "Blankenship, have the shield dusted. Get this mess cleaned up. Return the basket to the street corner. The rest of you men get back to your posts."

He strode into his study, closed all the doors. He sat stolidly at his desk and listened. He heard the mutterings, shufflings of feet. He figured he had another 24 hours, no more. Then some hothead would get to Blank and gun him down. Exactly what he told Monica Gilbert he would do. But for different reasons.

About 7.30 p.m., he dressed warmly and left the house, telling the log-man he was going to the hospital. But instead, he went on his daily unannounced inspection. He knew the men on duty were aware of these unscheduled tours; he wanted them to know. He decided to walk—he had been inside, sitting, for too many hours—and he marched vigorously over to East End Avenue. He made certain Tiger One—the man watching the Castle—was in position and not goofing off. It was a game with him to spot Tiger One without being spotted. This night he won, bowing his shoulders, staring at the sidewalk, limping by Tiger One with no sign of recognition. Well, at least the kid was on duty, walking a beat across from the Castle and, Delaney hoped, not spending too much time grabbing a hot coffee somewhere or a shot of something stronger.

He walked briskly back to the White House and stood across the street, staring up at Blank's apartment house. Hopefully, Danny Boy was tucked in for the night. Captain Delaney stared and stared. Once again he had the irrational urge to go up there and ring the bell.

"My name is Captain Edward X. Delaney, New York Police Department. I'd like to talk to you."

Crazy. Blank wouldn't let him in. But that's all Delaney really wanted—just to talk. He didn't want to collar Blank or injure him. Just talk, and maybe understand. But it was hopeless; he'd have to imagine.

He knocked on the door of the Con Ed van; it was unlocked and opened cautiously. The man at the door recognized him and swung the door wide, throwing a half-assed salute. Delaney stepped inside; the door was locked behind him. There was one man with binoculars at the concealed flap, another man at the radio desk. Three men, three shifts; counting the guy in the hole and extras, there were about 20 men assigned to Bulldog One.

"How's it going?" he asked.

They assured him it was going fine. He looked around at the hot plate they had rigged up, the coffee percolator, a miniature refrigerator they had scrounged from somewhere.

"All the comforts of home," he nodded.

They nodded in return, and he wished them a Happy New Year. Outside again, he paused at the hole they had dug through the pavement of East 83rd Street, exposing steam pipes, sewer lines, telephone conduits. There was one man down there, dressed like a Con Ed repairman, holding a transistor radio to his ear under his hardhat. He took it away when he recognized Delaney.

"Get to China yet?" the Captain asked, gesturing toward the shovel leaning against the side of the excavation.

The officer was black.

"Getting there, Captain," he said solemnly. "Getting there. Slowly."

"Many complaints from residents?"

"Oh, we got plenty of those, Captain. No shortage."

Delaney smiled. "Keep at it. Happy New Year."

"Same to you, sir. Many of them."

He walked away westward, disgusted with himself. He did this sort of thing badly, he knew; talking informally with men under his command. He tried to be easy, relaxed, jovial. It just didn't work.

One of his problems was his reputation. "Iron Balls." But it wasn't only his record; they sensed something in him. Every cop had to draw his own boundaries of heroism, reality, stupidity, cowardice. In a dicey situation, you could go strictly by the book and get an inspector's funeral. Captain Edward X. Delaney would be there, wearing his Number Ones and white gloves. But all situations didn't call for sacrifice. Some called for a reasoned response. Some called for surrender. Each man had his own limits, set his own boundaries.

But what the men sensed was that Delaney's boundaries were narrower, stricter than theirs. Too bad there wasn't a word for it: coppishness, copicity, copanity—something like that. "Soldiership" came close, but didn't tell the whole story. What was needed was a special word for the special quality of being a cop.

What his men sensed, why he could never communicate with them on equal terms, was that he had this quality to a frightening degree. He was the quintessential cop, and they didn't need any words to know it. They understood that he would throw them into the grinder as fast as he would throw himself.

He got to the florist's shop just as it was closing. They didn't want to let him in, but he assured them it was an order for the following day. He described exactly what he wanted: a single longstem rose to be placed, no greenery, in a long, white florists' box and delivered at 9.00 a.m. the next morning.

"Deliver one rose?" the clerk asked in astonishment. "Oh, sir, we'll have to charge extra for that."

"Of course," Delaney nodded. "I understand, I'll pay whatever's necessary. Just make certain it gets there first thing tomorrow morning."

"Would you like to enclose a card, sir?"

"I would."

He wrote out the small white card: "Dear Dan, here's a fresh rose for the one you destroyed." He signed the card "Albert Feinberg," then slid the card in the little envelope, sealed the flap, addressed the envelope to Daniel G. Blank, including his street address and apartment number.

"You're certain it will get there by nine tomorrow morning?"

"Yes, sir. We'll take care of it. That's a lot of money to spend on one flower, sir. A sentimental occasion?"

"Yes," Captain Edward X. Delaney smiled. "Something like that."

5

THE NEXT morning Delaney awoke, lay staring somberly at the ceiling. Then, for the first time in a long time, he got out of bed, kneeled, and thought a prayer for Barbara, for his own dead parents, for all the dead, the weak, the afflicted. He did not ask that he be allowed to kill Daniel Blank. It was not the sort of thing you asked of God.

Then he showered, shaved, donned an old uniform, so aged it was shiny enough to reflect light. He also loaded his .38 revolver, strapped on his gunbelt and holster. It was not with the certainty that this would be the day he'd need it, but it was another of his odd superstitions: if you prepared carefully for an event, it helped hasten it.

Then he went downstairs for coffee. The men on duty noted his uniform, the bulge of his gun. Of course, no one commented on it, but a few men did check their own weapons, and one pulled on an elaborate shoulder holster that buckled across his chest.

Fernandez was in the kitchen, having a coffee and Danish. Delaney drew him aside.

"Lieutenant, when you're finished here, I want you to go to Bulldog One and stay there until relieved. Got that?"

"Sure, Captain."

"Tell your lookout to watch for a delivery by a florist. Let me know the minute he arrives."

"Okay," Fernandez nodded cheerfully. "You'll know as soon as we spot him. Something cooking, Captain?"

Delaney didn't answer, but carried his coffee back into the radio room. He set it down on the long table, then went back into his study and wheeled in his swivel chair. He positioned it to the right of the radio table, facing the operators.

He sat there all morning, sipping three black coffees, munching on the dry, stale heel of a loaf of Italian bread. Calls came in at fifteen-minute intervals from Bulldog One and Ten-O. No sign of Danny Boy. At 9:20, Stryker called from the Factory to report that Blank hadn't shown up for work. A few minutes later, Bulldog One was back on the radio.

Fernandez: "Tell Captain Delaney a boy carrying a long, white florist's box just went into the White House lobby."

Delaney heard it. Leaving as little as possible to chance, he went into his study, looked up the florist's number called, and asked if his single red rose had been delivered. He was assured the messenger had been sent and was probably there right now. Satisfied, the Captain went back to his chair at the radio table. The waiting men had heard Fernandez' report but what it meant, they did not know.

Sergeant MacDonald leaned over Delaney's chair.

"He's freaking, Captain?" he whispered.

"We'll see. We'll see. Pull up a chair, sergeant. Stay close to me for a few hours."

"Sure, Captain."

The black sergeant pulled over a wooden, straight-backed chair, sat at Delaney's right, slightly behind him. He sat as solidly as the Captain, wearing steel-rimmed spectacles, carved face immobile.

So they sat and waited. So everyone sat and waited. Quiet enough to hear a Sanitation truck grinding by, an airliner overhead, a far-off siren, hoot of tugboat, the bored fifteen-minute calls from Ten-0 and Bulldog One. Still no sign of Danny Boy. Delaney wondered if he could risk a quick trip to the hospital.

507

Then, shortly before noon, a click loud enough to galvanize them, and Bulldog One was on:

"He's coming out! He's carrying stuff. A doorman behind him carrying stuff. What? A jacket, knapsack. What? What else? A coil of rope. Boots. What?"

Delaney: "Jesus Christ. Get Fernandez on."

Fernandez: "Fernandez here. Wearing black topcoat, no hat, left hand in coat pocket, right hand free. No glove. Knapsack, coil of rope, some steel things with spikes, jacket, heavy boots, knitted cap."

Delaney: "Ice ax?"

Barbara: "Bulldog One, ice ax?"

Fernandez: "No sign. Car coming up from garage. Black Chevy Corvette. His car."

Captain Delaney turned slightly to look at Sergeant MacDonald. "Got him," he said.

"Yes," MacDonald nodded. "He's running."

Fernandez: "They're pushing his stuff into the car. Left hand still in coat pocket, right hand free."

Delaney (to MacDonald): "Two unmarked cars, three men each. Start the engines and wait. You come back in here."

Fernandez: "He's loaded. Getting into the driver's seat. Orders?"

Delaney: "Fernandez to trail in Bulldog Two. Keep in touch."

Fernandez: "Got it. Out."

Captain Delaney looked around. Sergeant MacDonald was just coming back into the room.

MacDonald: "Cars are ready, Captain."

Delaney: "Designated Searcher One and Searcher Two. If we both go, I'll take One, you take Two. If I stay, you take both."

MacDonald nodded. He had taken off his glasses.

Fernandez: "Barbara from Bulldog Two. He's circling the block. I think he's heading for the Castle. Out."

Delaney: "Alert Tiger One. Send Bulldog Three to Castle."

Fernandez: "Bulldog Two. It's the Castle all right. He's pulling up in front. We're back at the corner, the south corner. Danny Boy's parked in front of the Castle. He's getting out. Left hand in pocket, right hand free. Luggage still in car."

Bulldog Three: "Barbara from Bulldog Three."

Barbara: "Got you."

Bulldog Three: "We're in position. He's walking up to the Castle door. He's knocking at the door."

Delaney: "Where's Tiger One?"

Fernandez: "He's here in Bulldog Two with me. Danny Boy is parked on the wrong side of the street. We can plaster him."

Delaney: "Negative."

Barbara: "Negative, Bulldog Two."

Fernandez (laughing): "Thought it would be. Shit. Look at that . . . Barbara from Bulldog Two."

Barbara: "You're still on, Bulldog Two."

Fernandez: "Something don' smell right. Danny Boy knocked at the door of the Castle. It was opened. He went inside. But the door is still open. We can see it from here. Maybe I should take a walk up there and look."

Delaney: "Tell him to hold it."

Barbara: "Hold it, Bulldog Two."

Delaney: "Ask Bulldog Three if they're receiving our transcriptions to Bulldog Two."

Barbara: "Bulldog Three from Barbara. Are you monitoring our conversation with Bulldog Two?"

Bulldog Three: "Affirmative."

Delaney: "To Bulldog Two. Affirmative for a walk past Castle but put Tiger One with walkie-talkie on the other side of the street. Radio can be showing."

Fernandez: "Bulldog Two here. Got it. We're starting."

Bulldog Three: "Bulldog Three here. Got it. Fernandez is getting out of Bulldog Two. Tiger One is getting out, crossing to the other side of the street."

Delaney: "Hold it. Check out Tiger One's radio."

Barbara: "Tiger One from Barbara. How do you read?"

Tiger One: "T-One here. Lots of interference but I can read."

Delaney: "Tell him to cover. Understood?"

Barbara: "Tiger One, cover Lieutenant Fernandez on the other side of the street. *Coppish?*"

Tiger One: "Right on."

Delaney: "Bring in Bulldog Three."

Bulldog Three: "They're both walking toward us, slowly. Fernandez is passing the Castle, turning his head, looking at it. Tiger One is right across the street. No action. They're coming toward us. Walking slowly. No sweat. Fernandez is crossing the street toward us. He'll probably want to use our mike. Ladies and gentlemen, the next voice you hear will be that of Lieutenant Jeri Fernandez."

Delaney (stonily): "Get that man's name."

Fernandez: "Fernandez in Bulldog Three. Is the Captain there?"

Delaney bent over the desk mike.

Delaney: "Here. What is it, lieutenant?"

Fernandez: "It smells, Captain. The door to the Castle is half-open. Something's propping it open. Looks like a man's leg to me."

Delaney: "A leg?"

Fernandez: "From the knee down. A leg and a foot propping the door open. How about I take a closer look?"

Delaney: "Where's Tiger One?"

Fernandez: "Right here with me."

Delaney: "Both of you go back to Bulldog Two. Tiger One across the street, covering again. You take a closer look. Tell Tiger One to give us a continuous. Got that?"

Fernandez: "Sure."

Delaney: "Lieutenant . . ."

Fernandez: "Yeah?"

Delaney: "He's fast."

Fernandez (chuckling): "Don' give it a second thought, Captain."

Tiger One: "We're walking south. Slowly. Fernandez is across the street.

Delaney: "Gun out?"

Barbara: "Is your gun out, Tiger One?"

Tiger One: "Oh Jesus, it's been out for the last fifteen minutes. He's coming up to the Castle. He's slowing, stopping. Now Fernandez is kneeling on one knee. He's pretending to tie his shoelace. He's looking toward the Castle door. He's—Oh my God!"

Daniel Blank awoke in an antic mood, laughing at a joke he had dreamed but could not remember. He looked to the windows; it promised to be a glorious day. He thought he might go over to Celia Montfort's house and kill

her. He might kill Charles Lipsky, Valenter, the bartender at The Parrot.
He might kill a lot of people, depending on how he felt. It was that kind
of a day.

It took off like a rocket: hesitating, almost motionless, moving, then
spurting into the sky. That's the way the morning went, until he'd be out
of the earth's pull, and free. There was nothing he might not do. He
remembered that mood, when he was atop Devil's Needle, weeks,
months, years ago.

Well, he would go back to Devil's Needle and know that rapture again.
The park was closed for the winter, but it was just a chain-link fence, the
gate closed with a rusty padlock. He could smash it open easily with his
ice ax. He could smash anything with his ice ax.

He bathed and dressed carefully, still in that euphoria he knew would
last forever.

So the chime at his outside door didn't disturb him at all.

"Who is it?" he called.

"Package for you, Mr. Blank."

He heard retreating footsteps, waited a few moments, then unbolted
his door. He brought the long, white florist's box inside, relocked the
door. He took the box to the living room and stared at it, not understanding.

Nor did he comprehend the single red rose inside. Nor the card. Albert
Feinberg? Feinberg? Who was Albert Feinberg? Then he remembered
that last death with longing; the close embrace, warm breath in his face,
their passionate grunts. He wished they could do it again. And Feinberg
had sent him another rose! Wasn't that sweet. He sniffed the fragrance,
stroked the velvety petals against his cheek, then suddenly crushed the
whole flower in his fist. When he opened his hand, the petals slowly came
back to shape, moving as he watched, forming again the whole exquisitely
shaped blossom, as lovely as it had been before.

He drifted about the apartment, dreaming, nibbling at the rose. He ate
the petals, one by one; they were soft, hard, moist, dry on his tongue,
with a tang and flavor all their own. He ate the flower down to the stem,
grinning and nodding, swallowing it all.

He took his gear from the hallway closet; ice ax, rucksack, nylon line,
boots, crampons, jacket, knitted watch cap. He wondered about sandwiches and a thermos—but what did he need with food and drink? He
was beyond all that, outside the world's pull and the hunger to exist.

It was remarkable, he thought happily, how efficiently he was operating; the call to the garage to bring his car around, the call to a
doorman—who turned out to be Charles Lipsky—to help him down with
his gear. He moved through it all smiling. The day was sharp, clear,
brisk, open, and so was he. He was in the lemon sun, in the thin blue sac
filled with amniotic fluid. He was one with it all. He hummed a merry
tune.

When Valenter opened the door and said, "I'm thorry, thir, but Mith
Montfort ith not—" he smashed his fist into Valenter's face, feeling the
nose crunch under his blow, seeing the blood, feeling the blood slippery
between his knuckles. Then, stepping farther inside, he hit the shocked
Valenter again, his fist going into the man's throat, crushing that jutting
Adam's apple. Valenter's eyes rolled up into his skull and he went down.

So Daniel Blank walked easily across the entrance hall, still humming
his merry tune. What was it? Some early American folksong; he couldn't
remember the title. He climbed the stairs steadily, the ice ax out now,
transferred to his right hand. He remembered the first time he had

followed her up these stairs to the room on the fifth floor. She had paused, turned, and he had kissed her, between navel and groin, somewhere on the yielding softness, somewhere . . . Why had she betrayed him?

But even before he came to that splintered door, a naked Anthony Montfort darted out, gave Daniel one mad, frantic glance over his shoulder, then dashed down the hall, arms flinging. Watching that young, bare, unformed body run, all Blank could think of was the naked Vietnamese girl, burned by napalm, running, running, caught in pain and terror.

Celia was standing. She, too, was bare.

"Well," she said, her face a curious mixture of fear and triumph. "Well . . ."

He struck her again and again. But after the first blow, the fear faded from her face; only the triumph was left. The certitude. Was this what she wanted? He wondered, hacking away. Was this her reason? Why she had manipulated him. Why she had betrayed him. He would have to think about it. He hit her long after she was dead, and the sound of the ice ax ceased to be crisp and became sodden.

Then, hearing screams from somewhere, he transferred the ice ax to his left hand, under the coat, hidden again, and rushed out. Down the stairs. Over the fallen Valenter. Out into the bright, sharp, clear day. The screams pursued him: screams, screams, screams.

They were all on their feet in the radio room, listening white-faced to Tiger One's furious shouts, a scream from somewhere, "Fernandez is—", shots, roar of a car engine, squeal of tires, metallic clatter. Tiger One's radio went dead.

Captain Delaney stood stock-still for almost 30 seconds, hands on hips, head lowered, blinking slowly, licking his lips. The men in the room looked to him, waiting.

He was not hesitating as much as deliberating. He had been through situations as fucked-up as this in the past. Instinct and experience might see him through, but he knew a few seconds of consideration would help establish the proper sequence of orders. First things first.

He raised his head, caught MacDonald's eye.

"Sergeant," he said tonelessly, raised a hand, jerked a thumb over his shoulder, "on your way. Take both cars. Sirens. I'll stay here. Report as soon as possible."

MacDonald started out. Delaney caught up with him before he reached the hallway door, took his arm.

"In the outside toilet," he whispered, "in the cabinet under the sink. A pile of clean white towels. Take a handful with you."

The sergeant nodded, and was gone.

The Captain came back into the middle of the room. He began to dictate orders to the two radiomen and the two telephone men.

"To Bulldog Two, remain on station and assist."

"To Bulldog Three, take Danny Boy. Extreme caution."

Both cars cut in to answer; the waiting men heard more shots, curses, shouts.

"To downtown Communications. Operation Lombard top priority. Four cars New York entrance to George Washington Bridge. Detain black Chevy Corvette. Given them license number, description of Danny Boy. Extreme caution. Armed and dangerous."

"You and you. Take a squad. Up to George Washington Bridge. Siren and flasher. Grab a handful of those photos of Danny Boy and distribute them."

"To Communications. Officer in need of assistance. Ambulance. Urgent. Give address of Castle."

"To Deputy Inspector Thorsen: ' He's running. Will keep you informed. Delaney.'"

"To Assault-Homicide Division. Crime in progress at Castle. Give address. Urgent. Please assist Operation Lombard."

"To Bulldog Ten. Recall to Barbara with car."

"To Bulldog One. Seal Danny Boy's apartment in White House. Twenty-one H. No one in, no one out."

"To Stryker. Seal Danny Boy's office. No one in, no one out."

"You and you, down to the Factory to help Stryker. Take Ten-0's car when he arrives."

"To Special Operations. Urgently need three heavy cars. Six men with vests, shotguns, gas grenades, subs, the works. Three snipers, completely equipped, one in each car. Up here as soon as possible. Oh yes . . . cars equipped with light bars, if possible."

"You and you, pick up the Mortons, at the Erotica on Madison Avenue, for questioning."

"You, pick up Mrs. Cleek at the Factory. You, pick up the owner of The Parrot on Third Avenue. You, pick up Charles Lipsky, doorman at the White House. Hold all of them for questioning."

"To Communications. All-precinct alert. Give description of car and Danny Boy. Photos to come. Wanted for multiple homicide. Extreme caution. Dangerous and armed. Inform chief inspector."

Delaney paused, drew a deep breath, looked about dazedly. The room was emptying out now as he pointed at men, gave orders, and they hitched up their guns, donned coats and hats, started out.

The radio crackled.

"Barbara from Searcher One."

"Got you, Searcher One."

"MacDonald. Outside the Castle. Fernandez down and bleeding badly. Tiger One down. Unconscious. At least a broken leg. Bulldog Three gone after Danny Boy. Bulldog Two and Searcher Two blocking off the street. Send assistance. Am now entering Castle."

Delaney heard, began speaking again.

"To Communications. Repeat urgent ambulance. Two officers wounded."

"To Assault-Homicide Division. Repeat urgent assistance needed. Two officers wounded."

"Sir, Deputy Inspector Thorsen is on the line," one of the telephone operators interrupted.

"Tell him two officers wounded. I'll get back to him. Recall guard on Monica Gilbert and get men and car over here. Recall taps on Danny Boy's phone and Monica Gilbert's phone. Tell them to remove all equipment, clean up, no sign."

"Barbara from Searcher One."

"Come in, Searcher One."

"MacDonald here. We have one homicide female, white, black hair, early thirties, five-four or five, a hundred and ten, slender, skull crushed, answering description of the Princess. White, male boy, about twelve, naked and hysterical, answering description of Anthony Montfort. One white male, six-three or four, about one-sixty or sixty-five, unconscious, answering description of houseman Valenter, broken nose, facial injuries, bad breathing. Need two ambulances and doctors. Fernandez is alive but still bleeding. We can't stop it. Ambulance? Soon, please. Tiger One had broken right leg, arm, bruises, scrapes. Ambulances and doctors, please."

Delaney took a deep breath, started again.

"To Communications. Second repeat urgent ambulance. One homicide victim, four serious injuries, one hysteria victim. Need two ambulances and doctors soonest."

"To Assault-Homicide. Second repeat urgent assistance. Anything on those cars Communications sent to block the George Washington Bridge?"

"Cars in position, sir. No sign of Danny Boy."

"Our men there with photos?"

"Not yet, sir."

"Anything from Bulldog Three?"

"Can't raise them, sir."

"Keep trying."

Blankenship came over to the Captain, looking down at a wooden board with a spring clamp at the top. He had been making notes. Delaney noted the man's hands were trembling slightly but his voice was steady.

"Want a recap, sir?" he asked softly.

"A tally?" Delaney said thankfully. "I could use that. What have we got left?"

"One car, unmarked, and four men. But the recalls should be here soon, and Lieutenant Dorfman next door sent over two men in uniform to stand by. He also says he's holding a squad car outside the precinct house in case we need it. The three cars from Special Operations are on the way."

"No sign of Danny Boy at the Bridge, sir. Traffic beginning to back up."

"What?" the other radio operator said sharply. "Louder. Louder! I'm not making you."

Then they heard the hoarse, agonized whisper:

"Barbara . . . Bulldog Three . . . cracked up . . . lost him . . ."

"Where?" Delaney roared into the mike. "God damn you, stay on your feet? Where are you? Where did you lose him?"

". . . north . . . Broadway . . . Broadway . . . Ninety-fifth . . . hurt . . ."

"You and you," Delaney said, pointing. "Take the car outside. Over to Broadway and Ninety-fifth. Report in as soon as possible. You, get on to Communications. Nearest cars and ambulance. Officers injured in accident. Son of a bitch!"

"Barbara from Searcher One."

"Got you, Searcher One."

"MacDonald. One ambulance here. Fernandez is all right. Lost a lot of blood but he's going to make it. The doc gave him a shot. Thanks for the towels. Another ambulance pulling up. Cars from Assault-Homicide. Mobile lab . . ."

"Hold it a minute, sergeant," Delaney turned to the other radio operator. "Did you check the cars on the Bridge?"

"Yes, sir. The photos got there, but no sign of Danny Boy."

Delaney turned back to the first radio. "Go on, sergeant."

"Things are getting sorted out. Fernandez and Tiger One (what the hell *is* his name?) on their way to the hospital. The way I make it, Danny Boy came running out of the Castle and caught Fernandez just as he was straightening up, beginning his draw. Swung his ax at the lieutenant's skull. Fernandez moved and turned to take it on his left shoulder, back, high up, curving in near the neck. Danny Boy pulled the ax free, jumped into his car. Tiger One rushed the car from across the street, firing as he ran. He got off there. Two hits on the car, he says, with one through the front left window. But Danny

Boy apparently unhurt. He got started fast, pulled away, sideswiped Tiger One, knocked him down and out. The whole goddamned thing happened so *fast*. The men in Bulldog Two and Three were left with their mouths open."

"I know," Delaney sighed. "Remain on station. Assist Assault-Homicide. Guards on the kid and Valenter until we can get statements."

"Understood. Searcher One out."

"Any word from the Bridge?" Delaney asked the radio operator.

"No, sir. Traffic backing up."

"Captain Delaney, the three cars from Special Operations are outside."

"Good. Hold them. Blankenship, come into the study with me."

They went in; Delaney closed all the doors. He searched a moment, pulled from the bookshelves a folded road map of New York City and one of New York State. He spread the city map out on his desk, snapped on the table lamp. The two men bent over the desk. Delaney jabbed his finger at East End Avenue.

"He started here," he said. "Went north and made a left onto Eighty-sixth Street. That's what I figure. Went right past Bulldog Three who still had their thumbs up their asses. Oh hell, maybe I'm being too hard on them."

"We heard a second series of shots and shouts when we alerted Bulldog Three," Blankenship reminded him.

"Yes. Maybe they got some off. Anyway, Danny Boy headed west."

"To the George Washington Bridge?"

"Yes," the Captain said, and paused. If Blankenship wanted to ask any questions about why Delaney had sent blocking cars to the Bridge, now would be the time to ask them. But the detective had too much sense for that, and was silent.

"So now he's at Central Park," Delaney went on, his blunt finger tracing the path on the map. "I figure he turned south for Traverse Three and crossed to the west side at Eighty-sixth, went over to Broadway, and turned north. Bulldog Three said he was heading north. He probably turned left onto Ninety-sixth to get on the West Side Drive."

"He could have continued north and got on the Drive farther up. Or taken Broadway or Riverside Drive all the way to the Bridge."

"Oh shit," Captain Delaney said disgustedly, "he could have done a million things."

Like all cops, he was dogged by the unpredictable. Chance hung like a black cloud that soured his waking hours and defiled his dreams. Every cop lived with it: the meek, humble prisoner who suddenly pulls a knife, a shotgun blast that answers a knock on a door during a routine search, a rifle shot from a rooftop. The unexpected. The only way to beat it was to live by percentages, trust in luck, and—if you needed it—pray.

"We have a basic choice," Delaney said dully, and Blankenship was intelligent to note the Captain had said, "We have . . ." not "I have . . ." He was getting sucked in. This man, the detective reflected, didn't miss a trick. "We can send out a five-state alarm, then sit here on our keisters and wait for someone else to take him, or we can go get him and clean up our own shit."

"Where do you think he's heading, Captain?"

"Chilton," Delaney said promptly. "It's a little town in Orange County. Not ten miles from the river. Let me show you."

He opened the map of New York State, spread it over the back of the club chair, tilted the lampshade to spread more light.

"There it is," he pointed out, "just south of Mountainville, west of the Military Academy. See that little patch of green? It's Chilton State Park. Blank goes up there to climb. He's a mountain climber." He closed his eyes a moment, trying to remember details of that marked map he had found in Danny Boy's car a million years ago. Once again Blankenship was silent and asked no questions. Delaney opened his eyes, stared at the detective. "Across the George Washington Bridge," he recited, delighted with his memory. "Into New Jersey. Onto Four. Then onto Seventeen. Over into New York near Mahwah and Suffern. Then onto the Thruway, and turn off on Thirty-two to Mountainville. Then south to Chilton. The Park's a few miles out of town."

"New Jersey?" Blankenship cried, "Jesus Christ, Captain, maybe we better alert them."

Delaney shook his head. "No use. The Bridge was blocked before he got there. He couldn't possibly have beat that block. No way, city traffic being what it is. No, he by-passed the Bridge. If he hadn't he'd have been spotted by now. But he's still heading for Chilton. I've got to believe that. How can he get across the river north of the George Washington Bridge?"

They bent over the state map again. Blankenship's unexpectedly elegant forefinger traced a course.

"He gets on the Henry Hudson Parkway, say at Ninety-sixth. Okay, Captain?"

"Sure."

"He gets up to the George Washington Bridge, but maybe he sees the block."

"Or the traffic backing up because of the search."

"Or the traffic. So he sticks on the Henry Hudson Parkway, going north. My God, he can't be far along right now. He may be across this bridge here and into Spuyten Duyvil. Or maybe he's in Yonkers, still heading north."

"What's the next crossing?"

"The Tappan Zee Bridge. Here. Tarrytown to South Nyack."

"What if we closed that off?"

"And he kept going north, trying to get across? Bear Mountain Bridge is next. He's still south of Chilton."

"And if we blocked the Bear Mountain Bridge?"

"Then he's got to go up to the Newburgh-Beacon Bridge. Now he's north of Chilton."

Delaney took a deep breath, put his hands on his waist. He began to pace about the study.

"We could block every goddammed bridge up to Albany," he said, speaking to himself as much as to Blankenship. "Keep him on the east side of the river. What the hell for? I want him to go to his hole. He's heading for Chilton. He feels safe there. He's alone there. If we block him, he'll just keep running, and God alone knows what he'll do."

Blankenship said, almost timidly, "There's always the possibility he might have made it across the George Washington Bridge, sir. Shouldn't we alert Jersey? Just in case."

"The hell with them."

"And the FBI?"

"Fuck 'em."

"And the New York State cops?"

"Those shitheads? With their sombreros. You think I'm going to let those apple-knockers waltz in and grab the headlines? Fat chance! This boy is mine. You got your pad?"

"Yes, sir. Right here."

"Take some notes. No . . . wait a minute."

Captain Delaney strode to the door of the radio room, yanked it open. There were more men; the recalls were coming in. Delaney pointed at the first man he saw. "You. Come here."

"Me, sir?"

The Captain grabbed him by the arm, pulled him inside the study, slammed the door behind him.

"What's your name?"

"Javis, John J. Detective second grade."

"Detective Javis, I am about to give orders to Detective first grade Ronald Blankenship. I want you to do nothing but listen and, in case of a Departmental hearing, testify honestly as to what you heard."

Javis' face went white.

"It's not necessary, sir," Blankenship said.

Delaney gave him a particularly sweet smile. "I know it isn't," he said softly. "But I'm cutting corners. If it works, fine. If not, it's my ass. It's been in a sling before. All right, let's go. Take notes on this. You listen carefully, Javis."

"Do all this through Communications. To New Jersey State Police, to the FBI, to New York State Police, a fugitive alert on Danny Boy. Complete description of him and car. Photos to follow. Apprehend and hold for questioning. Exercise extreme caution. Wanted for multiple homicide. Armed and dangerous. Got that?"

"Yes, sir."

"A *general* alert. The fugitive can be anywhere. You understand?"

"Yes, sir. I understand."

"Phone calls from here to police in Tarrytown, Bear Mountain, Beacon. Same alert. But tell them, do not stop or interfere with suspect. Let him run. If he crosses their bridge, call us. Let him get across the river but inform us immediately. Tell them he's a cop-killer. Got that?"

"Yes, sir," Blankenship nodded, writing busily. "If he tries to cross at the Tappan Zee, Bear Mountain, or Newburgh-Beacon Bridges, they are to let him cross but observe and call us. Correct?"

"Correct." Delaney said definitely. He looked at Javis. "You heard all that?"

"Yes, sir," the man faltered.

"Good," Delaney nodded. "Outside and stand by."

When the door closed behind the detective, Blankenship repeated, "You didn't have to do that, Captain."

"Screw it."

"You're going after him?"

"Yes."

"Can I come?"

"No. I need you here. Get those alerts off. I"ll take the three cars from Special Operations and more men. I don't know the range of the radios. If they fade, I'll check by phone. I'll call on my private line here." He put his hand on his desk phone. "Put a man in here. No out-going calls. Keep it clear. I'll keep calling. You keep checking with Tarrytown, Bear Mountain and Beacon, to see where he goes across. You got all this?"

"Yes," Blankenship said, still jotting notes. "I'm caught up."

"Bring MacDonald back to Barbara. The two of you start on the paperwork. You handle the relief end: schedules, manpower, cars, and so forth. MacDonald is to get the statements, the questioning of everyone we took in. Clean up all the crap. He'll know what to do."

"Yes, sir."

"If Deputy Inspector Thorsen calls, just tell him I'm following and will contact him as soon as possible."

Blankenship looked up. "Should I call the hospital, sir?" he asked. "About your wife?"

Delaney looked at him, shocked. How long had it been?

"Yes," he said softly. "Thank you. And about Fernandez, Tiger One, and Bulldog Three. I'd appreciate that. I'll check with you when I call in. Let's see . . . is there anything else? Any questions?"

"Can I come with you, sir?"

"Next time," Captain Edward X. Delaney said. "Get on those alerts right now."

The moment the door closed behind Blankenship, Delaney was on the phone. He got information, asking for police headquarters in Chilton, N.Y. It took time for the call to go through, but he wasn't impatient. If he was right, time didn't matter. And if he was wrong, time didn't matter.

Finally, he heard the clicks, the pauses, the buzzing, then the final regular ring.

"Chilton Police Department. Help you?"

"Could I speak to the commanding officer, please?"

A throaty chuckle. "Commanding Officer? Guess that's me. Chief Forrest. What can I do you for?"

"Chief, this is Captain Edward X. Delaney, New York Police Department. New York *City*. I've got—"

"Well!" the Chief said. "This *is* nice. How's the weather down there?"

"Fine," Delaney said. "No complaints. A little nippy, but the sun's out and the sky's blue."

"Same here," the voice rumbled, "and the radio feller says it's going to stay just like this for another week. Hope he's right."

"Chief," Delaney said, "I've got a favor I'd like to ask of you."

"Why yes," Forrest said, "Thought you might."

Delaney was caught up short. This was no country bumpkin.

"Got a man on the run," he said rapidly. "Five homicides known, including a cop. Ice ax. In a Chevy Corvette. Heading—"

"Whoa, whoa," the chief said. "You city fellers talk so fast I can't hardly make sense. Just slow down a mite and spell it out."

"I've got a fugitive on the run," Delaney said slowly, obediently. "He's killed five people, including a New York City detective. He crushed their skulls with an ice ax."

"Mountain climber?"

"Yes," the Captain said, beginning to appreciate Chief Forrest. "It's just a slim chance, but I think he may be heading for the Chilton State Park. That's near you, isn't it?"

"Was the last time I looked. About two miles out of town. What makes you think he's heading there?"

"Well . . . it's a long story. But he's been up there to climb. There's some rock—I forget the name—but apparently he—"

"Devil's Needle," Forrest said.

"Yes, that's it. He's been up there before, and I figured—"

"Park closed for the winter."

"If he wanted to get in, how would he do it, Chief?"

"It's a small park. Not like the Adirondacks. Nothing like that. Chain-link fence all around. One gate with a padlock. I reckon he could smash the gate or climb the fence. No big problem. This fugitive of yours—he a crazy?"

"Yes."

"Probably smash the gate. Well, Captain, what can I do you for?"

"Chief, I was wondering if you could send one of your men out there. Just to watch. You understand? If this nut shows up, I just want him observed. What he does. Where he goes. I don't want anyone trying to take him. I'm on my way with ten men. All I want is him holed up."

"Uh-huh," Chief Forrest said. "I think I got the picture. You call the State boys?"

"Alert going out right now."

"Uh-huh. Kinda out of your territory, isn't it, Captain?"

Shrewd bastard, Delaney thought desperately.

"Yes, it is," he confessed.

"But you're bringing up ten men?"

"Well . . . yes. If we can be of any help . . ."

"Uh-huh. And you just want a watch on the Park gate. Out of sight naturally. Just to see where this crazy goes and what he does. Have I got it right?"

"Exactly right," Delaney said thankfully. "If you could just send one of your men out . . ."

There was a silence that extended so long that finally Captain Delaney said, "Hello? Hello? Are you there?"

"Oh, I'm here, I'm here. But when you talk about sending out one of my men, I got to tell you, Captain: there ain't no men. I'm it. Chief Forrest. The Chilton Police Department. I suppose you think that's funny, a one-man po-*leece* department calling hisself "Chief." I know what a big-city "Chief" means."

"I don't think it's funny," Delaney said. "Different places have different titles and different customs. That doesn't mean one is any better or any worse than another."

"Sonny," Chief Forrest rumbled, "I'm looking forward to meeting you. You sound like a real bright boy. Now you get up here with your ten men. Meanwhile, I'll mosey out to the Park and see what I can see. It's been a slow day."

"Thank you, Chief," Delaney said gratefully. "But it may take some time."

"Time?" the deep voice laughed. "Captain, we got plenty of that around here."

Delaney made one more call, to Thomas Handry. But the reporter wasn't in, so he left a message. "Break it. Blank running. After him. Call Thorsen. Delaney." Having paid his debt, he hitched up his gun belt, hooked his choker collar. He went into the radio room, pointed at three men; they all headed out to the heavy, armed cars waiting at the curb.

Still high, the air in his lungs as sharp and dry as good gin, Daniel Blank came dashing down the inside staircase of Celia Montfort's home, leaped over the fallen Valenter, went sailing out into the thin winter sunlight, those distant screams pursuing him.

There was a man kneeling on the sidewalk between Blank and his car. This man saw Blank coming; his face twisted into an expression of wicked menace. He began to rise from his knee, one hand snaked beneath his jacket; Blank understood this man hated him and meant to kill him.

He performed his ax-transferring act as he rushed. He struck the man who was very quick and jerked aside so that the ax point did not enter his skull but crunched in behind his shoulder. But he went down. Daniel wrenched the ice ax free, ran to his car, conscious of shouts from across the avenue. Another man came dodging through traffic, pointing his finger at Blank. Then there were light, sharp explosions—snaps, really—and something smacked into and through the car body. Then there was a hole in the left window, another in the windshield, and he felt a stroke of air across his cheek, light as an angel's kiss.

The man was front left and seemed determined to yank open the door or point his finger again. Blank caught a confused impression of black features contorted in fear and fury. There was nothing to do but accelerate, knock the man aside. So he did that, heard the thud as the body went flying, but he didn't look back.

He turned west onto 86th Street, saw a double-parked car with three men scrambling to get out. More shouts, more explosions, but then he was moving fast down 86th Street, hearing the rising and dwindling blare of horns, the squeal of brakes as he breezed through red lights, cut to the wrong side of the street to avoid a pile-up, cut back in, increasing his speed, hearing a far-off siren, enjoying all this, loving it, because he had cut that telephone line that held him to the world, and now he was alone, all alone, no one could touch him. Ever again.

He took Traverse No. 3 across Central Park, turned right on Broadway, went north to 96th Street, made a left to get onto the Henry Hudson Parkway, which everyone called the West Side Drive. He went humming north on the Drive, keeping up with the traffic, no faster, no slower, and laughed because it had all been such a piece of cake. No one could touch him; not even the two police squads screaming by him, sirens open, could bring him down or spoil the zest of this bright, lively, *new* day.

But there was some kind of hassle at the Bridge—maybe an accident—and traffic was backing up. So he just stayed on the Parkway, went winging north as traffic thinned out and he could sing a little song—what was it? That same folksong he had been crooning earlier—and tap his hands in time on the steering wheel.

North of Yonkers he pulled onto the verge, stopped, unfolded his map. He could take the Parkway to the Thruway, cross the Tappan Zee Bridge to South Nyack. Around Palisades Interstate Park to 32, take that to Mountainville. Then south to Chilton. Simple . . . and beautiful. Everything was like that today.

He was folding up his map when a police car pulled alongside on the Parkway. The officer in the passenger's seat jerked his thumb north. Blank nodded, pulled off the verge, fell in behind the squad car, but kept his speed down until the cops were far ahead, out of sight. They hadn't even noticed the holes in window, windshield, car body.

He had no trouble at all. Not even any toll to pay going west on the Tappan Zee. If he returned eastward, of course, he'd have to pay a toll. But he didn't think he'd be returning. He drove steadily, a mile or two above the limit, and almost before he knew it, he was in and out of Chilton, heading for the Park. Now his was the only car on the gravel road. No else anywhere. Wonderful.

He turned into the dirt road leading to the Chilton State Park, saw the locked gate ahead of him. It seemed silly to stop and hack off the padlock with his ice ax, so he simply accelerated, going at almost 50 miles an hour at the moment of impact. He threw his forearm across his eyes when he hit, but the car slammed through the fence easily, the two wings of the gate flinging back. Daniel Blank braked suddenly and stopped. He was inside. He got out of the car and stretched, looking about. Not a soul. Just a winter landscape: naked black trees against a light blue sky. Clean and austere. The breeze was wine, the sun a tarnished coin that glowed softly.

Taking his time, he changed to climbing boots and lined canvas jacket. He threw his black moccasins and topcoat inside the car; he wouldn't need those anymore. At the last minute he also peeled off his formal "Ivy League" wig and left that in the car too. He pulled the knitted watch cap over his shaved scalp.

He carried his gear to Devil's Needle, a walking climb of less than ten minutes, over a forest trail and rock outcrops. It was good to feel stone beneath his feet again. It was different from city cement. The pavement was a layer, insulating from the real world. But here you were on bare rock, the spine of the earth; you could feel the planet turning beneath your feet. You were close.

At the entrance to the chimney, he put on his webbed belt, attached one end of the nylon line, shook out the coils of rope carefully, attached the other end to all his gear; rucksack, crampons, extra sweater, his ice ax. He put on his rough gloves.

He began to climb slowly, wondering if his muscles had gone slack. But the climb went smoothly; he gained confidence as he hunched and wiggled upward. Then he reached to grasp the embedded pitons, pulled himself onto the flat. He rested a moment, breathing deeply, then rose and hauled up his gear. He unbuckled his belt, dumped everything in a heap. He straightened, put his hands on his waist, inhaled deeply, forcing his shoulders back. He looked around.

It was a different scene, a winter scene, one he had never witnessed before from this elevation. It was a steel etching down there: black trees spidery, occasional patches of unmelted snow, shadows and glints, all blacks, greys, browns, the flash of white. He could see the roofs of Chilton and, beyond, the mirror river, seemingly a pond, but moving, he knew, slowly to the sea, to the wide world, to everywhere.

He lighted one of his lettuce cigarettes, watched the smoke swirl away, enter into, disappear. The river became one with the sea, the smoke one with the air. All things became one with another, entered into and merged, until water was land, land water, and smoke was air, air smoke. Why had she smiled in triumph? Now he could think about it.

He sat on the bare stone, bent his legs, rested one cheek on his knee. He unbuttoned canvas jacket, suit jacket, shirt, and slid an ungloved hand inside to feel his own breast, not much flatter than hers. He worked the nipple slowly and thought she had been happy when her eyes turned upward to focus on that shining point of steel rushing downwards to mark a period in her brain. She had been happy. She wanted the certitude. Everything she had told him testified to her anguished search for an absolute. And then, wearied of the endless squigglings of her quick and sensitive intelligence—so naked and aware it must have been as painful as an open wound—she had involved him in her plan, urging him on, then betraying him. Knowing what the end would be, wanting it. Yes, he thought, that was what happened.

He sat there a long time—the sky dulling to late afternoon—dreaming over what had happened. Not sorry for what had happened, but feeling a kind of sad joy, because he knew she had found her ultimate truth, and he would find his. So they both—but then he heard the sound of car engines, slam of car doors, and crawled slowly to the edge of Devil's Needle to peer down.

They came down the gravel road from Chilton, saw the sign: "One mile to Chilton State Park," then made their turn onto the dirt road. They pulled up outside the fence. The wings of the gate were leaning crazily. Inside was Daniel Blank's car. A big man, clad in a brown canvas windbreaker with a dirty sheepskin collar, was leaning against the car and watched them as they stopped. There was a six-pack of beer on the hood of the car; the man was sipping slowly from an opened can.

Captain Delaney got out, adjusted his cap, tugged down his jacket. He walked through the ruined gate towards Blank's car, taking out identification. He inspected the big man as he advanced. Six-four, at least: maybe five or six if he straightened up. At least 250, maybe more, mostly in the belly. Had to be pushing 65. Wearing the worn windbreaker, stained corduroy pants, yellow, rubber-soled work shoes laced up over his ankles, a trooper's cap of some kind of black fur. Around his neck the leather cord of what appeared to be Army surplus field glasses from World War I. About his waist, a leather belt blotched with the sweat of a lifetime, supporting one of the biggest dogleg holsters Delaney had ever seen, flap buttoned. On the man's chest, some kind of a shield, star or sunburst: it was difficult to make out.

"Chief Forrest?" Delaney asked, coming up.

"Yep."

"Captain Edward X. Delaney, New York Police Department." He flipped open his identification, held it out.

The Chief took it in a hand not quite the size and color of a picnic ham, and inspected it thoroughly. He passed it back, then held a hand out to Delaney.

"Chief Evelyn F. Forrest," he rumbled. "Pleased to make your acquaintance, Captain. I suppose you think "Evelyn" is a funny name for a man."

"No, I don't think that. My father's name was Marion. Not so important, is it?"

"Nooo . . . unless you've got it."

"I see our boy got here," Delaney said, patting the fender of the parked car.

"Uh-huh," Forrest nodded. "He arrived, Captain, I've got a cold six-pack here. Would you like . . ."

"Sure. Thank you. Go good right now."

The Chief selected a can, pulled the tab, handed over the beer. They both raised their drinks to each other, then sipped. The Captain inspected the label.

"Never had this brand before," he confessed. "Good. Almost like ale."

"Uh-huh," Chief Forrest nodded. "Local brewery. They don't go into the New York City area, but they sell all they can make."

He had, Delaney decided, the face of an old bloodhound, the skin a dark purplish-brown, hanging in wrinkles and folds; bags, jowls, wattles. But the eyes were unexpectedly young, mild, open; the whites were clear. Must have been quite a boy about 40 years ago, the Captain thought, before the beer got to him, ballooned his gut, slowed him up.

"Look here, Captain," Forrest said. "One of your men got some into him."

The Chief pointed out a bullet hole in the body of the car and another through the left front window.

"Come out here," he continued, pointing to a star-cracked hole in the windshield.

Delaney stooped to sight through the entrance hole in the window and the exit hole in the windshield.

"My God," he said, "by rights it should have taken his brains right along with it, if he was in the driver's seat. The man's got the luck of the Devil."

"Uh-huh," Chief Forrest nodded. "Some of 'em do. Well, here's what happened . . . I get here about an hour before he does, pull off the gravel road into the trees, opposite to the turnoff to the Park. Not such good concealment, but I figure he'll be looking to his right for the Park entrance and won't spot me."

"That makes sense."

"Yep. Well, I'm out of my station wagon, enjoying a brew, when he comes barreling along, pretty as you please. Turns into this here dirt road, sees the locked gate, speeds up, and just cuts right through; hot knife through butter. Then he gets out of the car, stretches, and looks around. I got him in my glasses by now. Handsome lad."

"Yes, he is."

"He starts changing to his outdoor duds: a jacket, boots, and so forth. I got a turn when he ducks into the car with a full head of hair and comes out balder'n a peeled egg."

"He wears a wig."

"Uh-huh. I found it, back there in the car. Looks like a dead muskrat. Also his coat and city shoes. Then he pulls on a cap, packs up his gear, and starts for Devil's Needle. I come across the road then and into the Park."

"Did he spot you?"

"Spot me?" the Chief said in some amazement. "Why no. I still move pretty good, and I know the land around here like the palm of my hand. No, he didn't spot me. Anyways, he gets there, attaches a line to his belt and to his gear, and goes into the chimney. Makes the climb in pretty good time. After awhile I see his line going out, and he pulls up his gear. Then I see him standing on top of Devil's Needle. I see him for just a few seconds, but he's up there all right, Captain; no doubt about that."

"Did you see any food in his gear? Or a canteen? Anything like that?"

"Nope. Nothing like that. But he had a rucksack. Might have had food and drink in that."

"Maybe."

"Captain . . ."

"Yes, Chief?"

"That alert you phoned to the State boys . . . You know, they pass it on to all us local chiefs and sheriffs by radio. I was on my way out here when I heard the call. Didn't mention nothing about Chilton."

"Uh . . . well, I didn't mention Chilton to them. It was just a hunch, and I didn't want them charging out here on what might have been a wild-goose chase."

The Chief looked at him steadily a long moment. "Sonny," he said softly, "I don't know what your beef is with the State boys, and I don't want to know. I admit they can be a stiff-necked lot. But Captain, when this here is cleaned up, you're going back home. This is my home, and I got to deal with the State boys every day in the week. Now if they find out I knew a homicidal maniac was holed up on State property and didn't let them know, they'll be a mite put out, Captain, just a mite put out."

Delaney scuffed at the dirt with the toe of his city shoe, looking down. "Guess you're right," he muttered finally. "It's just . . ." He looked up at the Chief; his voice trailed away.

"Sonny," Forrest said in a kindly voice, "I been in this business a lot longer'n you, and I know what it means to be after a man, to track him for a long time, and to corner him. Then the idea of anyone but you takin' him is enough to drive you right up into the rafters."

"Yes," Delaney nodded miserably. "Something like that."

"But you see my side of it, don't you. Captain? I got to call them. I'll do it anyway, but I'd rather you say, 'All right.'"

"All right. I can understand it. How do you get them?"

"Radio in my wagon. I can reach the troop. I'll be right back."

The Chief moved off, up the dirt road, with a remarkably light stride for a man his age and weight. Captain Delaney stood by Blank's car, looking through the window at the coat, the shoes, the wig. They already had the shapeless, dusty look of possessions of a man long dead.

He should be feeling an exultation, he knew, at having snubbed Daniel Blank. But instead he felt a sense of dread. Reaction to the excitement of the morning, he supposed, but there seemed to be more to it than that. The dread was for the future, for what lay ahead. "Finish the job," he told himself, "finish the job." He refused to imagine what the finish might be. He remembered what his Army colonel had told him. "The best soldiers have no imagination."

He turned as Chief Forrest came driving through the sprung gate in an old, dilapidated station wagon with "Chilton Police Department" painted on the side in flaking red letters. He pulled up alongside Blank's car. "On their way," he called to Delaney. "About twenty minutes or so, I reckon."

He got from behind the wheel with some difficulty, grunting and puffing, then reached back inside to haul out two more six-packs of beer. He held them out to Delaney.

"For your boys," he said. "While they're waiting."

"Why, thank you, Chief. That's kind of you. Hope it's not leaving you short."

Forrest's big belly shook with laughter. "That'll be the day," he rumbled.

The Captain smiled, took the six-packs over to his cars.

"Better get out and stretch your legs," he advised his men. "Looks like we'll be here awhile. The State boys are on their way. Here's some beer, compliments of Chief Forrest of the Chilton Police Department."

The men got out of the cars happily, headed for the beer. Delaney went back to the Chief.

"Could we take a close look at Devil's Needle?" he asked.

"Why sure."

"I've got three snipers with me, and I'd like to locate a spot where they could cover the entrance to the chimney and the top of the rock. Just in case."

"Uh-huh. This fugitive of yours armed, Captain?"

"Just the ice ax, as far as I know. As for a gun, I can't guarantee either way. Chief, you don't have to come with me. Just point out the way, and I'll get there."

"Shit," Chief Forrest said disgustedly, "that's the first dumb thing you've said, sonny."

He started off with his light, flat-footed stride; Captain Delaney stumbled after him. They made their way down a faint dirt path winding through the skeleton trees.

Then they came to the out-crops. Captain Delaney's soles slipped on the shiny rocks while Chief Forrest stepped confidently, never missing his footing, not looking down, but striding and moving like a gargantuan ballet dancer to the base of Devil's Needle. When Delaney came up, breathing heavily, the Chief had opened his holster flap and was bending it back, tucking it under that sweat-stained belt.

Delaney jerked his chin toward the dogleg holster. "What do you carry, Chief?" he asked, one professional to another.

"Colt forty-four. Nine-inch barrel. It belonged to my daddy. He was a lawman, too. Replaced the pin and one of the grips, but otherwise it's in prime condition. A nice piece."

The Captain nodded and turned his eyes, unwilling, to Devil's Needle. He raised his head slowly. The granite shaft poked into the sky, tapering slightly as it rose. There were mica glints that caught the late afternoon sunlight, and patches of dampness. A blotter of moss here and there. The surface was generally smooth and wind-worn, but there was a network of small cracks: a veiny stone torso.

He squinted at the top. It was strange to think of Daniel G. Blank up there. Near and far. Far.

"About eighty feet?" he guessed aloud.

"Closer to sixty-five, seventy, I reckon," Chief Forrest rumbled.

Up and down. They were separated. Captain Delaney had never felt so keenly the madness of the world. For some reason, he thought of lovers separated by glass or a fence, or a man and woman, strangers, exchanging an eye-to-eye stare on the street, on a bus, in a restaurant, a wall of convention or fear between them, yet unbearably close in that look and never to be closer.

"Inside," he said in a clogged voice, and stepped carefully into the opening of the vertical cleft, the chimney. He smelled the rank dampness, felt the chill of stone shadow. He tilted his head back. Far above, in the gloom, was a wedge of pale blue sky.

"A one-man climb," Chief Forrest said, his voice unexpectedly loud in the cavern. "You wiggle your way up, using your back and feet, then your hands and knees as the rock squeezes in. He's up there with an ice ax, ain't no man getting up there now unless he says so. You've got to use both hands."

"You've made the climb, Chief?"

Forrest grunted shortly. "Uh-huh. Many, many times. But that was years ago, before my belly got in the way."

"What's it like up there?"

"Oh, about the size of a double bedsheet. Flat, but sloping some to the south. Pitted and shiny. Some shallow rock hollows. Right nice view."

They came outside, Delaney looked up again.

"You figure sixty-five, seventy feet?"

"About."

"We could get a cherry-picker from the Highway Department, or I could bring up a ladder truck from the New York Fire Department. They can go up a hundred feet. But there's no way to get a truck close enough; not down that path and across the rocks. Unless we build a road. And that would take a month."

They were silent then.

"Helicopter?" Delaney said finally.

"Yes," Forrest acknowledged. "They could blast him from that. Tricky in these downdrafts and cross-currents, but I reckon it could be done."

"It could be done," Captain Delaney agreed tonelessly. "Or we could bring in a fighter plane to blow him away with rockets and machineguns."

Silence again.

"Don't set right with you, does it, sonny?" the Chief asked softly.

"No, it doesn't. To you?"

"No. I never did hanker to shoot fish in a barrel."

"Let's get back."

On the way, they selected a tentative site for the snipers. It was back in a clump of firs, offering some concealment but providing a clear field of fire covering the entrance to the chimney and the top of Devil's Needle.

The State police had not yet arrived. Delaney's men were lounging in and out of the cars, nursing their beers. The three pale snipers stood a little apart from the others, talking quietly, hugging their rifles in canvas cases.

"Chief, I've got to make some phone calls. Do I go into Chilton?"

"No need. Right there." Forrest waved his hand toward the gate-keeper's cottage. He pointed out the telephone wire that ran on wooden poles back to the gravel road. "They keep that line open all winter. Highway crews plowing snow use it, and Park people who come in for early spring planting."

They walked over to the weathered wooden shack, stepped up onto the porch. Delaney inspected the hasp closed with a heavy iron padlock.

"Got a key?" he asked.

"Sure," the Chief said, pulling the massive revolver out of his holster. "Step back a mite, sonny."

The Captain backed away hastily, and Chief Forrest negligently shot the lock away. Delaney noted he aimed at the shackle, not the body of the lock where a bullet might do nothing but jam the works. He was beginning to admire the old man. The explosion was unexpectedly loud; echoes banged back and forth; Delaney's men rose uneasily to their feet. Two brown birds took off from the dry underbrush alongside the dirt road, went whirring off with raucous cries.

The Chief pushed the door open. The cabin smelled dusty and stale. An old, wood-based "cookie-cutter" phone was attached to the wall, operated by a little hand crank.

"Haven't seen one of those in years," Delaney observed.

"We still got a few around. The operator's name is Muriel. You might tell her I'm out here, in case she's got any words for me." He left Delaney alone in the shack.

The Captain spun the crank; Muriel came on with pleasing promptness. Delaney identified himself, and gave her the Chief's message.

"Well, his wife wants to know if she should hold supper," she said. "You tell him that."

"I will."

"You got the killer out there?" she asked sternly.

"Something like that. Can I get through to New York City?"

"Of course. What do you think?"

He called Blankenship first and reported the situation as briefly as he could. He told the detective to call Deputy Inspector Thorsen and repeat Delaney's message.

Then he called Barbara at the hospital. It was a harrowing call; his wife was weeping, and he couldn't find out the cause. Finally a nurse came on the phone and told the Captain his wife was hysterical; she didn't think the call should be continued. He hung up, bewildered and frightened.

Then he called Dr. Sanford Ferguson, and got him in his office.

"Captain Edward X. Delaney here."

"Edward! Congratulations! I hear you got him."

"Not exactly. He's on top of a rock, and we can't get to him."

"On top of a rock?"

"High. Sixty-five, seventy feet. Doctor, how long can a man live without food and water?"

"Food *or* water? About ten days, I'd guess. Maybe less."

"Ten days? That's all?"

"Sure. The food isn't so important. The water is. Dehydration is the problem."

"How long does it take to get to him?"

"Oh . . . twenty-four hours."

"Then what?"

"What you might expect. Tissue shrinks, strength goes, the kidneys fail. Joints ache. But by that time, the victim doesn't care. One of the first psychological symptoms is loss of will, a lassitude. Something like freezing to death. He'll lose from one-fifth to one-quarter of his body weight in fluids.

Dizziness. Loss of voluntary muscles. Weakness. Can't see. Blurry images. Probably begin to hallucinate after the third day. The bladder goes. Just before death, the belly swells up. Not a pleasant way to die—but what is? Edward, is that what's going to happen?"

"I don't know. Thank you for your help."

He broke the connection, put in a call to Monica Gilbert. But when she recognized his voice, she hung up; he didn't try to call her again.

He came out onto the cottage porch and said to Forrest: "Your wife wants to know if she should hold supper."

"Uh-huh," the Chief nodded. "I'll let her know when I know. Captain, why don't—" He stopped suddenly, tilted his head. "Sireens," he said. "Coming fast. That'll be the troopers."

It was five seconds before Captain Delaney heard them. Finally, two cars careened around the curve into the Park entrance, skidded to a stop outside the fence, their sirens sighing slowly down. Four men in each car and, bringing up the rear, a beat-up Ford sedan with "Orange County Clarion" lettered on the side. One man in that.

Delaney came down off the porch and watched as the eight troopers piled out of their cars, put their hands on their polished holsters.

"Beautiful," he said aloud.

Then one man, not too tall, wider in the hips than the shoulders, stalked through the gate toward them.

"Oh-oh," Chief Forrest murmured. "Here comes Smokey the Bear."

The Captain took out his identification, watching the approaching officer. He was wearing the grey woolen winter uniform of the New York State Police, leather belt and holster gleaming wickedly. Squarely atop his head was the broad-brimmed, straight-brimmed, stiff-brimmed Stetson. He carried his chin out in front of him, a bare elbow, with narrow shoulders back, pigeon breast thrust. He marched up to them, stood vacant-faced. He glanced at Chief Forrest and nodded slightly, then stared at Delaney.

"Who are you?" he demanded.

The Captain looked at him a moment, then proffered his identification. "Captain Edward X. Delaney, New York Police Department. Who are you?"

"Captain Bertram Sneed, New York State Police."

"How do I know that?"

"Jesus Christ. What do I look like?"

"Oh, you look like a cop. No doubt about it; you're wearing a cop's uniform. But four men in cops' uniforms pulled the St. Valentine's Day Massacre. You just can't be too sure. Here's my ID. Where's yours?"

Sneed opened his trap mouth, then shut it suddenly with a snap of teeth. He opened one button of his woolen jacket, tugged out his identification. They exchanged.

As they examined each other's credentials, Delaney was conscious of men moving in, his men and Sneed's men. They sensed a confrontation of brass, and they wouldn't miss it for the world.

Sneed and Delaney took back their ID cards.

"Captain," Sneed said harshly, "we got a jurisdiction problem here."

"Oh?" Delaney said. "Is that our problem?"

"Yes. This here Park is State property, under the protection of the New York State Police Organization. You're out of your territory."

Captain Delaney put away his identification, tugged down his jacket, squared his cap away.

"You're right," he smiled genially. "I'll just take my men and get out. Nice to have met you, captain. Chief. Goodby."

He was turning away when Sneed said, "Hey, wait a minute."
Delaney paused. "Yes?"

"What's the problem here?"

"Why," Delaney said blandly, "it's a problem of jurisdiction. Just like you said."

"No, no. I mean what have we got? Where's this here fugitive?"

"Oh . . . him. Well, he's sitting on top of Devil's Needle."

Chief Forrest had fished a wooden match from his side pocket and inserted the bare end into the corner of his mouth. He appeared to be sucking on it, watching the two captains with a benign smile on his droopy features.

"Sitting on top of the rock?" Sneed said. "Shit, is that all? We got some good climbers in our outfit. I'll send a couple of men up there and we'll take him."

Delaney had turned away again, taken a few steps. His back was to Sneed when he halted, put his hands on his waist, then turned back again. He came close to Sneed.

"You shit-headed, wet-brained sonofabitch," he said pleasantly. "By all rights, I should take my men and go and leave you to stew in your own juice, you fucking idiot. But when you talk about sending a brave man to his death because of your stupidity, I got to speak my piece. You haven't even made a physical reconnaissance, for Christ's sake. That's a one-man climb, captain, and every man you send up there will get his skull crushed in. Is that what you want?"

Sneed's puppet face had gone white under the lash of Delaney's invective. Then red blotches appeared on his cheeks, discs of rouge, and his hands worked convulsively. Everyone stood in silence, frozen. But there was an interruption. A heavy white van turned into the entrance from the gravel road; heads turned to look at it. It was a mobile TV van from one of the national networks. They watched it park outside the gate. Men got out and began unloading equipment. Sneed turned back to Delaney.

"Well . . . hell," he said, smiling triumphantly, "so I won't send a man up. But the first thing tomorrow morning, I'll have a helicopter up there and we'll pick him off. Make a great TV picture."

"Oh yes," Delaney agreed. "A great TV picture. Of course, this man is just a suspect right now. He hasn't been convicted of *anything*. Hasn't even been tried. But you send your chopper up and grease him. I can see the headlines now: 'State Cops Machine-gun Suspect on Mountaintop.' Good publicity for your outfit. Good public relations. Especially after Attica."

The last word stiffened Captain Bertram Sneed. He didn't breathe, his arms hanging like fluked anchors at his side.

"Another thing," Delaney went on. "See that TV truck out there? By dawn, there'll be two more. And reporters and photographers from newspapers and magazines. It's already been on radio. If you don't get the roads around here closed off in a hell of a hurry, by morning you'll have a hundred thousand creeps and nuts with their wives and kiddies and picnic baskets of fried chicken, all hurrying to be in on the kill. Just like Floyd Collins in the cave."

"I got to make a phone call," Captain Sneed said hoarsely. He looked around frantically. Chief Forrest jerked a thumb toward the gate-keeper's cottage. Sneed hurried toward it. "You stay here a minute," he called back to Delaney. "Please," he added.

He got up on the porch, saw the smashed lock.

"Who blew open this door?" he cried.

"I did," Chief Forrest said equably.

"State property," Sneed said indignantly, and disappeared inside.

"O Lord, will my afflictions never cease?" the Chief asked.

"I shouldn't have talked to him like that," Delaney said in a low voice, his head bowed. "Especially in front of his men."

"Oh, I don't know, Captain," the Chief said, still sucking on his matchstick. "I've heard better cussing-outs than that. Besides, you didn't say nothing his men haven't been saying for years. Amongst theirselves, of course."

"Who do you think he's calling?"

"I know exactly who he's calling: Major Samuel Barnes. He's in command of Sneed's troop."

"What's he like?"

"Sam? Cut from a different piece of cloth. A hard little man, smart as a whip. Knows his business. Sam comes from up near Woodstock. I knew his daddy. Hy Barnes made the best applejack in these parts, but Sam don't like to be reminded of that. Smokey the Bear will explain the situation, and Major Sam will listen carefully. Sneed will complain about you being here, and he'll tell Sneed what you said about machinegunning that man from a chopper, and what you said about a mob of nuts descending on us tomorrow. Sneed will tell the Mayor *you* said those things, because he's too damned dumb to take credit for them hisself. Sam Barnes will think a few seconds, then he'll say, 'Sneed, you turd-kicking nincompoop, you get your fat ass out there and ask that New York City cop, just as polite as you can, if he'll stick around and tell you what to do until I can get on the scene. And if you haven't fucked things up too bad by the time I get there, you might—you just might—live to collect your pension, you asshole.' Now you stick around a few minutes, sonny, and see if I ain't exactly right."

A few moments later Captain Sneed came out of the cottage, pulling on his gloves. His face was still white, and he moved like a man who has just been kneed in the groin. He came over to them with a ghastly smile.

"Captain," he said. "I don't see why we can't cooperate on this."

"Cooperation!" the Chilton Chief cried unexpectedly. "That's what makes the world go round!"

They went to work, and by midnight they had it pretty well squared away, although many of the men and much of the equipment they had requisitioned had not yet arrived. But at least they had a tentative plan, filled it in and revised it as they went along.

The first thing they did was to establish a four-man walking patrol around the base of Devil's Needle, the sentries carrying shotguns and sidearms. The walkers did four hours on, and eight off.

Delaney's snipers established their blind in the fir copse, sitting crossed-legged atop folded blankets. They had mounted their scopes, donned black sweaters and pants, socks and shoes, jackets and tight black gloves. Each wore a flak vest on watch.

Squad cars were driven in as close as possible; their headlights and searchlights were used to illuminate the scene. Portable battery lanterns were set out to open up the shadows. Captain Delaney had called Special Operations and requisitioned a generator truck and a flatbed of heavy searchlights with cables long enough so the lights could be set up completely around Devil's Needle.

Captain Bertram Sneed was bringing in a field radio receiver-transmitter; the local power company was running in a temporary line. The local telephone company was bringing in extra lines and setting up pay phones for the press.

Major Samuel Barnes had not yet put in an appearance, but Delaney spoke to him on the phone. Barnes was snappish and all business. He promised to reshuffle his patrol schedules and send another twenty troopers over by bus as soon as possible. He was also working on the road blocks, and expected to have the Chilton area sealed off by dawn.

He and Delaney agreed on some ground rules. Delaney would be the on-the-spot commander with Sneed acting as his deputy. But Major Barnes would be nominal commander when the first report to the press was made, calling the siege of Devil's Needle a "joint operation" of New York State and New York City police. All press releases were to be okayed by both sides; no press conferences were to be held or interviews granted without representatives of both sides present.

Before agreeing, Captain Delaney called Deputy Inspector Thorsen to explain the situation and outline the terms of the oral agreement with the State. Thorsen said he'd call back; Delaney suspected he was checking with Deputy Mayor Alinksi. In any event, Thorsen called back shortly and gave him the okay.

Little of what they accomplished would have been possible without the aid of Chief Evelyn Forrest. Laconic, unflappable, never rushing, the man was a miracle of efficiency, joshing the executives of the local power and telephone companies to get their men cracking.

It was Forrest who brought out a highway crew to open up the shut-off water fountains in the Park and set up two portable chemical toilets. The Chief also got the Chilton High School, closed for the Christmas holiday, to open up the gymnasium, to be used as a dormitory for the officers assigned to Devil's Needle. Cots, mattresses, pillows and blankets were brought in from the county National Guard armory. Forrest even remembered to alert the Chilton disaster unit; they provided a van with sides that folded down to form counters. They served hot coffee and doughnuts in the Park around the clock, the van staffed by lady volunteers.

Chief Forrest had offered Captain Delaney the hospitality of his home, but the Captain opted for a National Guard cot set up in the gate-keeper's cottage. But, the night being unexpectedly chill, he did accept the Chief's loan of a coat. What a garment it was! Made of grey herringbone tweed, it was lined with raccoon fur with a wide collar of beaver. It came to Delaney's ankles, the cuffs to his knuckles. The weight of it bowed his shoulders, but it was undeniably warm.

"My daddy's coat," Chief Forrest said proudly. "Made in Philadelphia in Nineteen-and-one. Can't buy a coat like that these days."

So they all worked hard, and Delaney had one moment of laughing fear when he thought of what fools they'd all look if it turned out that somehow Daniel G. Blank had already climbed down off his perch and escaped into the night. But he put that thought away from him.

Shortly after dark they started bullhorn appeals to the fugitive, to be repeated every hour on the hour:

"Daniel Blank, this is the police. You are surrounded and have no chance of escape. Come down and you will not be hurt. You will be given a fair trial, represented by legal counsel. Come down now and save yourself a lot of trouble. Daniel Blank, you will not be injured in any way if you come down now. You have no chance of escape."

"Do any good, you think?" Forrest asked Delaney.

"No."

"Well," the Chief sighed, "at least it'll make it harder for him to get some sleep."

By 11:30 p.m., Delaney felt bone-weary and cruddy, wanted nothing more than a hot bath and eight hours of sleep. Yet when he lay down on his cold cot without undressing, just to rest for a few moments, he could not close his eyes, but lay stiffly awake, brain churning, nerves jangling. He rose, pulled on that marvelous coat, walked out onto the porch.

There were a lot of men still about—detectives and troopers, power and telephone repairmen, highway crews, reporters, television technicians. Delaney leaned against the railing, observed that all of them, sooner or later, went wandering off, affecting nonchalance, but looking back in guilt, anxious to see if anyone had noted their departure, half-ashamed of what they were doing. He knew what they were doing; they were going to Devil's Needle to stand, stare up and wonder.

He did the same thing himself, drawn against his will. He went as far as the rock outcrops, then stepped back into the shadow of a huge, leafless sugar maple. From there he could see the slowly circling sentries, the sniper sitting patiently on his blanket, rifle cradled on one arm. And there were all the men who had come to watch, standing with heads thrown back, mouths open, eyes turned upward.

Then there was the palely illuminated bulk of Devil's Needle itself, looming like a veined apparition in the night. Captain Delaney, too, lifted his head, opened his mouth, turned his eyes upward. Above the stone, dimly, he could see stars whirling their courses in a black vault that went on forever.

He felt a vertigo, not so much of the body as of the spirit. He had never been so unsure of himself. His life seemed giddy and without purpose. Everything was toppling. His wife was dying and Devil's Needle was falling. Monica Gilbert hated him and that man up there, that man . . . he knew it all. Yes, Captain Edward X. Delaney decided, that man now knew it all, or was moving toward it with purpose and delight.

He became conscious of someone standing near him. Then he heard the words.

". . . soon as I could," Thomas Handry was saying. "Thanks for the tip. I filed a background story and then drove up. I'm staying at a motel just north of Chilton."

Delaney nodded.

"You all right, Captain?"

"Yes. I'm all right."

Handry turned to look at Devil's Needle. Like the others, his head went back, mouth opened, eyes rolled up.

Suddenly they heard the bullhorn boom. It was midnight.

The bullhorn clicked off. The watching men strained their eyes upward. There was no movement atop Devil's Needle.

"He's not coming down, is he, Captain?" Handry asked softly.

"No," Captain Delaney said wonderingly. "He's not coming down."

6

HE AWOKE the first morning on Devil's Needle, and it seemed to him he had been dreaming. He remembered a voice calling, "Daniel Blank . . . Daniel Blank . . . " That could have been his mother because she always used his full name. "Daniel Blank, have you done your homework? Daniel Blank, I want you to go to the store for me. Daniel Blank, did you wash your hands?" That was strange, he realized for the first time—she never called him Daniel or Dan or son.

He looked at his watch; it showed 11:43. But that was absurd, he knew;

the sun was just rising. He peered closer and saw the sweep second hand had stopped; he had forgotten to wind it. Well, he could wind it now, set it approximately, but time really didn't matter. He slipped the gold expansion band off his wrist, tossed the watch over the side.

He rummaged through his rucksack. When he found he had neglected to pack sandwiches and a thermos, he was not perturbed. It was not important.

He had slept fully clothed, crampons wedged under his ribs, spikes up, so he wouldn't roll off Devil's Needle in his sleep. Now he climbed shakily to his feet, feeling stiffness in shoulders and hips, and stood in the center of the little rock plateau where he could not be seen from the ground. He did stretching exercises, bending sideways at the waist, hands on hips; then bending down, knees locked, to place his palms flat on the chill stone; then jogging in place while he counted off five minutes.

He was gasping for breath when he finished, and his knees were trembling; he really wasn't in very good condition, he acknowledged, and resolved to spend at least an hour a day in stretching and deep-breathing exercises. But then he heard his name being called again. Lying on his stomach, he inched cautiously to the edge of Devil's Needle.

Yes, they were calling his name, asking him to come down, promising he wouldn't be hurt. He wasn't interested in that, but he was surprised by the number of men and vehicles down there. The packed dirt compound around the gate-keeper's cottage was crowded; everyone seemed very busy with some job they were all doing. When he looked directly downward, he could see armed men circling the base of Devil's Needle, but whether they were protecting the others from him or him from the others, he could not say and didn't care.

He felt a need to urinate, and did so, lying on his side, peeing so the stream went over the edge of the rock. There wasn't very much, and it seemed to him of a milky whiteness, not golden at all. There was a clogged heaviness in his bowels, but the difficulties of defecating up there, what he would do with the excrement, how he would wipe himself clean, were such that he resisted the urge, rolled back to the center of the stone, lay on his back, stared at the new sun.

At no time had he debated with himself and come to a conscious decision to stay up there, to die up there. It was just something his mind grasped instinctively and accepted. He was not driven to it; even now he could descend if he wanted to. But he didn't. He was content where he was, in a condition of almost drowsy ease. And he was safe; that was important. He had his ice ax and could easily smash the skull of any climber who came after him. But what if one should come in the dark, wiggling his way silently upward to kill Daniel G. Blank as he slept?

He didn't think it likely that anyone would attempt a night climb, but just to make it more difficult, he took his ice ax and using it as a hammer, knocked loose the two pitons that aided the final crawl from the chimney to the top of Devil's Needle. The task took a long time; he had to rest awhile after the pitons were free. Then he slid them skittering across the stone, watched them disappear over the side.

Then they were calling his name again, a great mechanical booming: "Daniel Blank . . . Daniel Blank . . . " He wished they wouldn't do that. For a moment he thought of shouting down and telling them to stop. But they probably wouldn't. The thing was, it was disturbing his reverie, intruding on his isolation. He was enjoying his solitude, but it should have been a silent separateness.

He rolled over on his face, warming now as the watery sun rose higher. Beneath his eyes, close, close, he saw the rock itself, its texture. In all his years of mountain climbing and rock collecting, he had never looked at stone in that manner, seeing beneath the worn surface gloss, penetrating to the deep heart. He saw then what the stone was, and his own body, and the winter trees and glazed sun: infinite millions of bits, multicolored, in chance motion, a wild dance that went on and on to some silent tune.

He thought, for awhile, that these bits might be similar to the "bits" stored by a computer, recalled when needed to form a pattern, solve a problem, produce a meaningful answer. But this seemed to him too easy a solution, for if a cosmic computer did exist, who had programmed it, who would pose the questions and demand the answers? What answers? What questions?

He dozed off for awhile, awoke with that steel voice echoing, "Daniel Blank . . .Daniel Blank . . . " and was forced to remember who he was.

Celia had found her certitude—whatever it was—and he supposed everyone in the world was searching for his own, and perhaps finding it, or settling, disappointed, for something less. But what was important, what was important was . . . What was important? It had been right there, he had been thinking of it, and then it went away.

There was a sudden griping in his bowels, a sharp pain that brought him sitting upright, gasping and frightened. He massaged his abdomen gently. Eventually the pain went away, leaving a leaden stuffiness. There was something in there, something in him . . . He fell asleep finally, dimly hearing the ghost voice calling, "Daniel Blank . . . Daniel Blank . . . " It might be his imagination, he admitted, but it seemed to him the voice was higher in pitch now, almost feminine in timbre, dawdling lovingly over the syllables of his name. Someone who loved him was calling.

Was it the second day or the third? Well . . . no matter. Anyway, a helicopter came over, dipped, circled his castle, tilted. He had been sitting with his knees drawn up, head down on folded arms, and he raised his head to stare at it. He thought they might shoot him or drop a bomb on him. He waited patiently, dreaming. But they just circled him, low, three or four times; he could see pale faces at the windows, peering down at him. He lowered his head again.

They came back, every day, and he tried to pay no attention to them, but the heavy throbbing of the rotor was annoying. It was slow enough to have a discernible rhythm, a heartbeat in the sky. Once they came so low over him that the downdraft blew his knitted watch cap off the stone. It went sailing out into space, then fell into the reaching spines of winter trees. He watched it go.

One morning—when was it?—he knew he was going to defecate and could not control himself. He fumbled at his belt with weak fingers, got it unbuckled and his pants down, but was too late to pull down his flowered bikini panties, and had to void. It was painful. Later he got his pants off his feet—he had to take his boots off first—then pulled down the panties and shook them out.

He looked at his feces curiously. They were small black balls, hard and round as marbles. He flicked them, one by one, with his forefinger; they rolled across the stone, over the edge. He knew he no longer had the strength to dress, but he could tug off socks, jacket, and shirt. Then he was naked, baring his shrunken body to pale sun.

He was no longer thirsty, no longer hungry. Most amazing, he was not cold, but suffused with a sleepy warmth that tingled his limbs. He was, he knew, sleeping more and more until on the fourth day—or perhaps it was the fifth—he was not conscious of sleep as a separate state. Sleep and wakefulness became so thin that they were no longer oil and water, but one fluid, grey and without flavor, that ebbed and flowed.

The days passed, he supposed, and so did the nights. But where one ended and the other began, he did not know. Days and darkness, all boundaries lost, became part of that grey, flavorless tide, warm, milky at times, without odor now. It was a great placid sea, endless; he wished he had the strength to stand and see just once more that silver river that flowed to everywhere.

But he could not stand, could not even make the effort to wipe away a thin, viscous liquid leaking from eyes, nose, mouth. When he moved his hand upon himself, he felt pulped nipples, knobbed joints, wrinkles, folds of scratchy skin. Pain had gone; will was going. But he held it tight, to think awhile longer with a slow, numbed brain.

"Daniel Blank . . . Daniel Blank . . ." the voice called seductively. He knew who it was who called.

On the second day, an enterprising New York City newspaper hired a commercial helicopter; they flew over Devil's Needle and took a series of photos of Daniel Blank sitting on the rock, knees drawn up. The photograph featured on the newspaper's front page showed him with head raised, pale face turned to the circling 'copter.

Delaney was chagrined that he hadn't thought of aerial reconnaissance first and, after consultation with Major Samuel Barnes, all commercial flights over Devil's Needle were banned. The reason given to the press was that a light plane or helicopter approach might drive Blank to a suicide plunge, or the chopper's downdraft might blow him off the edge.

Actually, Captain Delaney was relieved by the publication of that famous photo; Danny Boy was up there, no doubt about it. At the same time, with the cooperation of Barnes, he initiated thrice-daily flights of a New York State Police helicopter over the scene. Aerial photographs were taken, portions greatly enlarged and analyzed by Air Force technicians. No signs of food or drink were found. As the days wore away and Blank spent more and more time on his back, staring at the sky, his physical deterioration became obvious.

Delaney went along on the first flight, taking a car north with Chief Forrest and Captain Sneed to meet Barnes at an Air Force field near Newburgh. It was his first face-to-face meeting with Sam Barnes. The Major was like his voice: hard, tight, peppery. His manner was cold, withdrawn, his gestures quick and short. He wasted little time on formalities, but hustled them aboard the waiting helicopter.

On the short flight south, he spoke only to Delaney. The Captain learned the State officer had consulted his departmental surgeon and was aware of what Delaney already knew: without food or liquid, Blank had about ten days to live, give or take a day or two. It depended on his physical condition prior to his climb, and to the nature and extent of his exposure to the elements. The Major, like Delaney, was monitoring the long-range weather forecasts daily. Generally, fair weather was expected to continue with gradually lowering temperatures. But there was a low-pressure system building up in northwest Canada that would bear watching.

They were all discussing their options when the 'copter came in view of Devil's Needle, then tilted to circle lower. Their talk died away; they stared out their windows at the rock. The cabin was suddenly cold as a crewman slid open the cargo door, and a police photographer positioned his long-lensed camera.

Captain Delaney's first reaction was one of shock at the small size of Daniel Blank's aerie. Chief Forrest had said it was "double bedsheet size," but from the air it was difficult to understand how Blank could exist up there for an hour without rolling or stumbling off the edge.

As the 'copter circled lower, the photographer snapping busily, Delaney felt a sense of awe and, looking at the other officers, suspected they were experiencing the same emotion. From this elevation, seeing Blank on his stone perch and the white, upturned faces of the men surrounding Devil's Needle on the ground, the Captain knew a dreadful wonder at the man's austere isolation and could not understand how he endured it.

It was not only the dangerous height at which he had sought refuge, lying atop a rock pillar that thrust into the sky, it was the absolute solitude of the man, deliberately cutting himself off from life and the living. Blank seemed, not on stone, but somehow floating in the air, not anchored, but adrift.

Only a few times before in his life had Delaney felt what he felt now. Once was when he forced his way into that concentration camp and saw the stickmen. Once was when he had taken a kitchen knife gently from the nerveless fingers of a man, soaked in blood, who had just murdered his mother, his wife, his three children, and then called the cops. The final time Delaney had helped subdue a mad woman attempting to crunch her skull against a wall. And now Blank . . .

It was the madness that was frightening, the loss of anchor, the float. It was a primitive terror that struck deep, plunged to something papered over by civilization and culture. It stripped away millions of years and said, "Look." It was the darkness.

Later, when copies of the aerial photos were delivered to him, along with brief analyses by the Air Force technicians, he took one of the photos and thumb-tacked it to the outside wall of the gate-keeper's cottage. He was not surprised by the attention it attracted, having guessed that the men shared his own uncertainty that their quarry was actually up there, that any man would deliberately seek and accept this kind of immolation.

Captain Delaney also noted a few other unusual characteristics of the men on duty: They were unaccountably quiet, with none of the loud talk, boasting and bantering that usually accompanied a job of this type. And they were in no hurry, when relieved, to return to their warm dormitory in the high school gymnasium. Invariably, they hesitated, then wandered once again to the base of Devil's Needle, to stare upward, mouths open, at the unseen man who lay alone.

He discussed this with Thomas Handry. The reporter had gone out to the roadblocks to interview some of the people being turned back by the troopers.

"You wouldn't believe it," Handry said, shaking his head. "Hundreds and hundreds of cars. From all over the country. I talked to a family from Ohio and asked them why they drove so far, what they expected to see."

"What did they say?"

"The man said he had a week off, and it wasn't long enough to go to Disneyworld, so they decided to bring the kids here."

They were organized now: regular shifts with schedules mimeographed daily. There were enough men assigned to cover all the posts around the clock, and the big searchlights and generator truck were up from New York City so Devil's Needle was washed in light 24 hours a day.

Captain Delaney had a propane stove in his cottage now, and a heavy radio had been installed on the gate-keeper's counter. The radiomen had little to do and so, to occupy their time, had rigged up a loudspeaker, a timer, and a loop tape, so that every hour on the hour, the message went booming out mechanically: "Daniel Blank . . . Daniel Blank . . . come down . . . come down . . ." It did no good. By now no one expected it would.

Every morning Chief Forrest brought out bags of mail received at the Chilton Post Office, and Captain Delaney spent hours reading the letters. A few of them contained money sent to Daniel Blank, for what reason he could not guess. Blank also received a surprisingly large number of proposals of marriage from women; some included nude photos of the sender. But most of the letters, from all over the world, were suggestions of how to take Daniel Blank. Get four helicopters, each supporting the corner of a heavy cargo net, and drop the net over the top of Devil's Needle. Bring in a large group of "sincere religious people" and pray him down. Set up a giant electric fan and blow him off his rock. Most proposed a solution they had already rejected: send up a fighter plane or helicopter and kill him. One suggestion intrigued Captain Delaney: fire gas grenades onto the top of Devil's Needle and when Daniel Blank was unconscious, send up a climber in a gas mask to bring him down.

Captain Delaney wandered out that evening, telling himself he wanted to discuss the gas grenade proposal with one of the snipers. He walked down the worn path toward Devil's Needle, turned aside at the sniper's post. The three pale-faced men had improved their blind. They had dragged over a picnic table with attached benches. From somewhere, they had scrounged three burlap bags of sand—Chief Forrest had helped with that, Delaney guessed—and the bags were used as a bench rest for their rifles. The sniper could sit and be protected from the wind by canvas tarps tied to nearby trees.

The man on duty looked up as Delaney approached.

"Evening, Captain."

"Evening. How's it going?"

"Quiet."

Delaney knew that the three snipers didn't mix much with the other men. They were pariahs, as much as hangmen or executioners, but apparently it did not affect them, if they were aware of it. All three were tall, thin men, two from Kentucky, one from North Carolina. If Delaney felt any uneasiness with them, it was their laconism rather than their chosen occupation.

"Happy New Year," the sniper said unexpectedly.

Delaney stared at him. "My God, is it?"

"Uh-huh. New Year's Eve."

"Well . . . Happy New Year to you. Forgot all about it."

The man was silent. The Captain glanced at the scope-fitted rifle resting on the sandbags.

"Springfield Oh-three," Delaney said. "Haven't seen one in years."

"Bought it from Army surplus," the man said, never taking his eyes from Devil's Needle.

"Sure," the Captain nodded. "Just like I bought my Colt Forty-five."

The man made a sound; the Captain hoped it was a laugh.

"Listen," Delaney said, "we got a suggestion, in the mail. You think there's any chance of putting a gas grenade up there?"

The sniper raised his eyes to the top of Devil's Needle. "Rifle or mortar?"

"Either."

"Not mortar. Rifle maybe. But it wouldn't stick. Skitter off or he'd kick it off."

"I guess so," Captain Delaney sighed. "We could clear the area and blanket it with gas, but the wind's too tricky."

"Uh-huh."

The Captain strolled away and only glanced once at that cathedral rock. Was he *really* up there? He had seen the day's photos—but could he trust them? The uneasiness returned.

He went back to the cottage, found a heavy envelope of reports a man coming on duty from Chilton had dropped off for him. They were from

Sergeant MacDonald, copies of all the interrogations and statements of the people picked up in the continuing investigation. Delaney walked out to the van, got a paper cup of black coffee, brought it back. Then he sat down at his makeshift desk, pulled the gooseneck lamp closer, put on his heavy glasses, began reading the reports slowly.

He was looking for . . . what? Some explanation or lead or hint. What had turned Daniel G. Blank into a killer? Where and when did it begin? It was the motive he wanted, he needed. It wasn't good enough to use words like nut, crazy, insane, homosexual, psychopath. Just labels. There had to be more to it than that. There had to be something that could be comprehended, that might explain why this young man had deliberately murdered five people. And four of them strangers.

Because, Delaney thought angrily, if there was no explanation for it, then there was no explanation for anything.

It was almost two in the morning when he pulled on that crazy coat and wandered out again. The compound around the cottage was brilliantly lighted. So was the packed path through the black trees; so was the bleak column of Devil's Needle. As usual, there were men standing about, heads back, mouths gaping, eyes turned upward. Captain Delaney joined them without shame.

He opened himself to the crisp night, lightly moaning wind, stars that seemed holes punched in a black curtain beyond which shone a dazzling radiance. The shaft of Devil's Needle rose shimmering in light, smoothed by the glare. Was he up there? Was he *really* up there?

There came to Captain Edward X. Delaney such a compassion that he must close his mouth, bite his lower lip to keep from wailing aloud. Unbidden, unwanted even, he shared that man's passion, entered into him, knew his suffering. It was an unwelcome bond, but he could not deny it. The crime, the motive, the reason—all seemed unimportant now. What racked him was that lonely man, torn adrift. He wondered if that was why they all gathered there, at all hours, day and night. Was it to comfort the afflicted as best they might?

A few days later—was it three? It could have been four—late in the afternoon, the daily envelope of aerial photos was delivered to Captain Delaney. Daniel G. Blank was lying naked on his rock, spread-eagled to the sky. The Captain looked, took a deep breath, turned his gaze away. Then, without looking again, he put the photos back into the envelope. He did not post one outside on the cottage wall.

Soon after, Major Samuel Barnes called.

"Delaney?"

"Yes."

"Barnes here. See the photos?"

"Yes."

"I don't think he can last much longer."

"No. Want to go up?"

"Not immediately. We'll check by air another day or so. Temperature's dropping."

"I know."

"No rush. We're getting a good press. Those bullhorn appeals are doing it. Everyone says we're doing all we can."

"Yes. All we can."

"Sure. But the weather's turning bad. A front moving in from the Great Lakes. Cloudy, windy, snow. Freezing. If we're socked in, we'll look like fools. I say January the sixth. In the morning. No matter what. How do you feel about it?"

"All right with me. The sooner the better. How do you want to do it: climber or 'copter?'

"'Copter. Agreed?"

"Yes. That'll be best."

"All right. I'll start laying it on. I'll be over tomorrow and we'll talk. Shit, he's probably dead right now."

"Yes," Captain Delaney said. "Probably."

The world had become a song for Daniel Blank. A song. Soonngg . . . Everything was singing. Not words, or even a tune. But an endless hum that filled his ears, vibrated so deep inside him that cells and particles of cells jiggled to that pleasant purr.

There was no thirst, no hunger and, best of all, there was no pain, none at all. For that he was thankful. He stared at a milky sky through filmed eyes almost closed by scratchy lids. The whiteness and the tuneless drone became one: a great oneness that went on forever, stretched him with a dreamy content.

He was happy he no longer heard his name shouted, happy he no longer saw a helicopter dipping and circling above his rock. But perhaps he had imagined those things, he had imagined so much: Celia Montfort was there once, wearing an African mask. Once he spoke to Tony. Once he saw a hunched, massive silhouette, lumbering away from him, dwindling. And once he embraced a man in a slow-motion dance that faded into milkiness before the ice ax struck, although he saw it raised.

But even these visions, all visions, disappeared; he was left only with an empty screen. Occasionally discs, whiter than white, floated into view, drifted, then went off, out of sight. They were nice to watch, but he was glad when they were gone.

He had a slowly diminishing apprehension of reality, but before weakness subdued his mind utterly, he felt his perception growing even as his senses faded. It seemed to him he had passed through the feel-taste-touch-smell-hear world and had emerged to this gentle purity with its celestial thrum, a world where everything was true and nothing was false.

There was, he now recognized with thanksgiving and delight, a logic to life, and this logic was beautiful. It was not the orderly logic of the computer, but was the unpredictable logic of birth, living, death. It was the mortality of one, and the immortality of all. It was all things, animate and inanimate, bound together in a humming whiteness.

It was an ecstasy to know that oneness, to understand, finally, that he was part of the slime and part of the stars. There was no Daniel Blank, no Devil's Needle, and never had been. There was only the continuum of life in which men and rocks, slime and stars, appear as seeds, grow a moment, and then are drawn back again into that timeless whole, continually beginning, continually ending.

He was saddened that he could not bring this final comprehension to others, describe to them the awful majesty of the certitude he had found: a universe of accident and possibility where a drop of water is no less than a moon, a passion no more than a grain of sand. All things are nothing, but all things are all. In his delirium, he could clutch that paradox to his heart, hug it, know it for truth.

He could feel life ebbing in him—*feel* it! It oozed away softly, no more than an invisible vapor rising from his wasted flesh, becoming part again of that oneness from whence it came. He died slowly, with love, for he was passing into another form: the process so gentle that he could wonder why men cried out and fought.

Those discs of white on white appeared again to drift across his vision. He thought dimly there was a moisture on his face, a momentary tingle; he wondered if he might be weeping with joy.

It was only snow, but he did not know it. It covered him slowly, soothing the roughened skin, filling out the shrunken hollows of his body, hiding the seized joints and staring eyes.

Before the snow ended at dawn, he was a gently sculpted mound atop Devil's Needle. His shroud was white and without stain.

Late on the night of January 5th, Captain Delaney met with Major Samuel Barnes, Chief Forrest, Captain Sneed, the crew of the State Police helicopter, and the chief radioman. They all crowded into the gate-keeper's cottage; a uniformed guard was posted outside the door to keep curious reporters away.

Major Barnes had prepared a schedule, and handed around carbon copies.

"Before we get down to nuts-and-bolts," he said rapidly, "the latest weather advisory is this: Snow beginning at midnight, tapering off at dawn. Total accumulation about an inch and a half or two. Temperatures in the low thirties to upper twenties. Then, tomorrow morning, it should clear with temperatures rising to the middle thirties. Around noon, give or take an hour, the shit will really hit the fan, with a dropping barometer, temperature going way down, snow mixed with rain, hail, and sleet, and winds of twenty-five gusting to fifty.

"Beautiful," one of the pilots said. "I love it."

"So," Barnes went on, disregarding the interruption, "we have five or six hours to get him down. If we don't, the weather will murder us, maybe for days. This is a massive storm front moving in. All right, now look at your schedules. Take-off from the Newburgh field at nine ayem. I'll be aboard the 'copter. The flight down and the final aerial reconnaissance completed by nine-thirty ayem, approximate. Lower a man to the top of Devil's Needle via cable and horse collar by ten ayem. Captain Delaney, you will be in command of ground operations here. This shack will be home base, radio coded Chilton One. The 'copter will be Chilton Two. The man going down will be Chilton Three. Everyone clear on that? Sneed, have your surgeon here at nine ayem. Forrest, can you bring out a local ambulance with attendants and a body bag?"

"Sure."

"I think Blank is dead, or at least unconcious. But if he's not, the man going down on the cable will be armed."

Captain Delaney looked up. "Who's Chilton Three?" he asked. "Who's going down on the cable?"

The three-man helicopter crew looked at each other. They were all young men, wearing sheepskin jackets over suntan uniforms, their feet in fleece-lined boots.

Finally the smallest man shrugged. "Shit, I'll go down," he said, rabbity face twisted into a tight grin. "I'm the lightest. I'll get the fucker."

"What's your name?" Delaney asked him.

"Farber, Robert H."

"You heard what the Major said. Farber. Blank is probably dead or unconscious. But there's no guarantee. He's already killed five people. If you get down there, and he makes any threatening movement—anything at all—grease him."

"Don't worry, Captain. If he as much as sneezes, he's a dead fucker."

"What will you carry?"

"What? Oh, you mean guns. My thirty-eight, I guess. Side holster. And I got a carbine."

Captain Delaney looked directly at Major Barnes. "I'd feel better if he carried more weight," he said. He turned back to Farber. "Can you handle a forty-five?" he asked.

"Sure, Captain. I was in the fuckin' Marine Corps."

"You can borrow mine, Bobby," one of the other pilots offered.

"And a shotgun rather than the carbine," Delaney said. "Loaded with buck."

"No problem," Major Barnes said.

"You really think I'll need all that fuckin' artillery?" Farber asked the Captain.

"No, I don't," Delaney said. "But the man was fast. So fast I can't tell you. Fast enough to take out one of my best men. But he's been up there a week now without food or water. If he's still alive, he won't be fast anymore. The heavy guns are just insurance. Don't hesitate to use them if you have to. Is that an order, Major Barnes?"

"Yes," Barnes nodded. "That's an order, Farber."

They discussed a few more details: briefing of the press, positioning of still and TV cameramen, parking of the ambulance, selection of men to stand by when Blank was brought down.

Finally, near midnight, the meeting broke up. Men shook hands, drifted away in silence. Only Delaney and the radioman were left in the cabin. The Captain wanted to call Barbara, but thought it too late; she'd probably be sleeping. He wanted very much to talk to her.

He spent a few minutes getting his gear together, stuffing reports, schedules, and memos into manila envelopes. If all went well in the morning, he'd be back in Manhattan by noon, leading his little squad of cops home again.

He hadn't realized how tired he was, how he longed for his own bed. Some of it was physical weariness: too many hours on his feet, muscles punished, nerves pulled and strained. But he also felt a spiritual exhaustion. This thing with Blank had gone on too long, had done too much to him.

Now, the last night, he pulled on cap and fur-lined greatcoat, plodded down to Devil's Needle for a final look. It was colder, no doubt of that, and the smell of snow was in the air. The sentries circling the base of the rock wore rubber ponchos over their sheepskin jackets: the sniper was huddled under a blanket, only the glowing end of a cigarette showing in black shadow. Captain Delaney stood a little apart from the few gawkers still there, still staring upward.

The gleaming pillar of Devil's Needle rose above him, probing the night sky, ghostly in the searchlight glare. About it, he thought he heard a faintly ululant wind, no louder than the cry of a distant child. He shivered inside his greatcoat: a chill of despair, a fear of something. It would have been easy, at that moment, to weep, but for what he could not have said.

It might, he thought dully, be despair for his own sins, for he suddenly knew he had sinned grievously, and the sin was pride. It was surely the most deadly; compared to pride, the other six seemed little more than physical excesses. But pride was a spiritual corruption and, worse, it had no boundaries, no limits, but could consume a man utterly.

In him, he knew, pride was not merely self-esteem, not just egotism. He knew his shortcomings better than anyone except, perhaps, his wife. His pride went beyond a satisfied self-respect; it was an arrogance, a presumption of moral superiority he brought to events, to people and, he supposed wryly, to God.

But now his pride was corroded by doubt. As usual, he had made a moral judgment—was that unforgivable for a cop?—and had brought Daniel G. Blank to this lonely death atop a cold rock. But what else could he have done?

There were, he now acknowledged sadly, several other courses that had been open to him if there had been a human softness in him, a sympathy for others, weaker than he, challenged by forces beyond their strength or control. He could have, for instance, sought a confrontation with Daniel Blank after he had discovered that damning evidence in the illegal search. Perhaps he could have convinced Blank to confess; if he had, Celia Montfort would be alive tonight, and Blank would probably be in an asylum. The story this revealed would have meant the end of Captain Delaney's career, he supposed, but that no longer seemed of overwhelming importance.

Or he could have admitted the illegal search and at least attempted to obtain a search warrant. Or he could have resigned the job completely and left Blank's punishment to a younger, less introspective cop.

"Punishment." That was the key word. His damnable pride had driven him to making a moral judgment, and, having made it, he had to be cop, judge, jury. He had to play God; that's where his arrogance had led him.

Too many years as a cop. You started on the street, settling family squabbles, a Solomon in uniform; you ended hounding a man to his death because you knew him guilty and wanted him to suffer for his guilt. It was all pride, nothing but pride. Not the understandable, human pride of doing a difficult job well, but an overweening that led to judging him, then to condemning, then to executing. Who would judge, condemn, and execute Captain Edward X. Delaney?

Something in his life had gone wrong, he now saw. He was not born with it. It did not come from genes, education, or environment, any more than Blank's homicidal mania had sprung from genes, education, or environment. But circumstances and chance had conspired to debase him, even as Daniel Blank had been perverted.

He did not know all things and would never know them; he saw that now. There were trends, currents, tides, accidents of such complexity that only an unthinking fool would say, "I am the master of my fate." Victim, Delaney thought. We are all victims, one way or another.

But, surprisingly, he did not feel this to be a gloomy concept, nor an excuse for licentious behavior. We are each dealt a hand at birth and play our cards as cleverly as we can, wasting no time lamenting that we received only one pair instead of a straight flush. The best man plays a successful game with a weak hand—bluffing, perhaps, when he has to—but staking everything, eventually, on what he's holding.

Captain Delaney thought now he had been playing a poor hand. His marriage had been a success, and so had his career. But he knew his failures . . . he knew. Somewhere along the way humanity had leaked out of him, compassion drained, pity became dry and withered. Whether it was too late to become something other than what he was, he did not know. He might try—but there were circumstances and chance to cope with and, as difficult, the habits and prejudices of more years than he cared to remember.

Uncertain, shaken, he stared upward at Devil's Needle, shaft toppling, world tilting beneath his tread. He was anxious and confused, sensing he had lost a certitude, wandered from a faith that, right or wrong, had supported him.

He felt something on his upturned face: a light, cold tingle of moisture. Tears? Just the first frail snowflakes. He could see them against the light: a fragile lacework. At that moment, almost hearing it, he knew the soul of Daniel Blank had escaped the flesh and gone winging away into the darkness, taking with it Captain Delaney's pride.

Shortly before dawn the snowfall dissolved into a freezing rain. Then that too ceased. When Captain Delaney came out on the porch at 8.30 a.m., the ground was a blinding diamond pavé; every black branch in sight was gloved with ice sparkling in the new sun.

He wore his greatcoat when he walked over to the van for black coffee and a doughnut. The air was clear, chill, almost unbearably sharp—like breathing ether. There was a chiselled quality to the day, and yet the world was not clear; a thin white scrim hung between sun and earth; the light was muted.

He went back to the shack and instructed the radioman to plug in an auxiliary microphone, and a hand-held model with an extension cord so he could stand out in the porch, see the top of Devil's Needle above the skeleton trees, and communicate with Chilton Two and Chilton Three.

The ambulance rolled slowly into the compound. Chief Forrest climbed out, puffing, to direct its parking. A stretcher and body bag were removed; the two attendants went back into the warmth of the cab, smoking cigarettes. Captain Sneed showed a squad of ten men where they were to take up their positions, handling his duties with the solemnity of an officer arranging the defense of the Alamo. But Delaney didn't interfere; it made no difference. Finally Forrest and Sneed came up to join the Captain on the porch. They exchanged nods. Sneed looked at his watch. "Take-off about now," he said portentously.

Chief Forrest was the first to hear it. "Coming," he said, raised his old field glasses to his eyes, searched northward. A few minutes later Captain Delaney heard the fluttering throb of the helicopter and, shortly afterward, looking where Forrest was pointing, saw it descending slowly, beginning a tilted circle about Devil's Needle.

The radio crackled.

"Chilton One from Chilton Two. Do you read me?" It was Major Samuel Barnes' tight, rapid voice, partly muffled by the throb of rotors in the background.

"Loud and clear, Chilton Two," the radioman replied.

"Beginning descent and reconnaissance. Where is Captain Delaney?"

"Standing by with hand-held mike. On the porch. He can hear you."

"Top of rock covered with snow. Higher mound in the middle. I guess that's Blank. No movement. We're going down."

The men on the porch shielded their eyes from sun glare to stare upward. The 'copter, a noisy dragonfly, circled lower, then slowed, slipping sideways, hovered directly over the top of the rock.

"Chilton One from Chilton Two."

"We got you, Chilton Two."

"No sign of life. No sign of anything. Our downdraft isn't moving the snow cover. Probably frozen over. We'll start the descent."

"Roger."

They watched the chopper hanging almost motionless in the air. They saw the wide cargo door open. It seemed a long time before a small figure appeared at the open door and stepped out into space, dangling from the cable, a padded leather horse collar around his chest, under his arms. The shotgun was held in his right hand; his left was on the radio strapped to his chest.

"Chilton One from Chilton Two. Chilton Three is now going down. We will stop at six feet for a radio check."

"Chilton Two from Chilton One. Delaney here. We can see you. Any movement on top of the rock?"

"None at all, Captain. Just an outline of a body. He's under the snow. Radio check now. Chilton Three from Chilton Two: How do you read?"

They watched the man dangling on the cable beneath the 'copter. He swung lazily in slow circles.

"Chilton Two from Chilton Three. I'm getting you loud and clear." Farber's voice was breathless, almost drowned in the rotor noise.

"Chilton Three from Chilton Two. Repeat, how do you read me?"

"Chilton Two, I said I was getting you loud and clear."

"Chilton Three from Chilton Two. Repeat, are you receiving me?"

Captain Delaney swore softly, moved his hand-held mike closer to his lips.

"Chilton Three from Chilton One. Do you read me?"

"Christ, yes, Chilton One. Loud and Clear. What the hell's going on? Do you hear me?"

"Loud and clear, Chilton Three. I'll get right back to you. Chilton Two from Chilton One."

"Chilton Two here. Barnes speaking."

"Delaney here. Major, we're in communication with Chilton Three. He can read us and we're reading him. He can hear you, but apparently you're not getting him."

"Son of a bitch," Barnes said bitterly. "Let me try once more. Chilton Three from Chilton Two, do you read me? Acknowledge."

"Yes, I read you, Chilton Two, and I'm getting fuckin' cold."

"Chilton Two from Chilton One. We heard Chilton Three acknowledge. Did you get it?"

"Not a word," Barnes said grimly. "Well, we haven't got time to pull him back up and check out the goddamn radios. I'll relay all orders through you. Understood?"

"Understood," Delaney repeated. "Chilton Three from Chilton One. You are not being read by Chilton Two. But they read us. We'll relay all orders through Chilton One. Understood?"

"Understood, Chilton One. Who's this?"

"Captain Delaney."

"Captain, tell them to lower me down onto the fuckin' rock. I'm freezing my ass off up here."

"Chilton Two from Chilton One. Lower away."

They watched the swinging figure hanging from the cable. Suddenly it dropped almost three feet, then brought up with a jerk, Farber swinging wildly.

"Goddamn it!" he screamed. "Tell 'em to take it fuckin' easy up there. They almost jerked my fuckin' arms off."

Delaney didn't bother relaying that. He watched, and in a few minutes the cable began to run out slowly and smoothly. Farber came closer to the top of Devil's Needle.

"Chilton Three from Chilton One. Any movement?"

"No. Not a thing. Just snow. Mound in the middle. Snow drifted up along one side. I'm coming down. About ten feet. Tell them to slow. Slow the fuckin' winch, goddam it!"

"Chilton Two from Chilton One. Farber is close. Slow the winch. Slow, slow."

"Roger, Chilton One. We see him. He's almost there. A little more. A little more. . .

"Chilton Three here. I'm down. Feet are down."

"How much snow?"

"About an inch to three inches where it's drifted. I need more fuckin' cable slack to unshackle the horse collar."

"Chilton Two, Farber needs more cable slack."

"Roger."

"Okay, Chilton One. I've got it unsnapped. Tell them to get the fuck out of here; they're damn near blowing me off."

"Chilton Two, collar unshackled. You can take off."

The 'copter tilted and circled away, the cable slanting back beneath it. It began to make wide rings about Devil's Needle.

"Chilton Three, you there?" Delaney asked.

"I'm here. Where else?"

"Any sign of life?"

"Nothing. He's under the snow. Wait'll I get this fuckin' collar off."

"Is he breathing? Is the snow over his mouth melted? Is there a hole?"

"Don't see anything. He's covered completely with the fuckin' snow."

"Brush it off."

"What?"

"Brush the snow away. Brush all the snow off him."

"With what, Captain? I got no gloves."

"With your hands—what do you think? Use your hands. Scrape the snow and ice away."

They heard Farber's heavy breathing, the clang of shotgun on rock, some muffled curses.

"Chilton One from Chilton Two. What's going on?"

"He's brushing the snow away. Farber? Farber, how's it coming?"

"Captain, he's naked!"

Delaney took a deep breath and stared at Forrest and Sneed. But their eyes were on Devil's Needle.

"Yes, he's naked," he spoke into the mike as patiently as he could. "You knew that; you saw the photos. Now clean him off."

"Jesus he's cold. And hard. So fuckin' hard. God, is he white."

"You got him cleaned off?"

"I—I'm—"

"What the hell's wrong?"

"I think I'm going to be sick."

"So be sick, you shithead!" Delaney roared. "Haven't you ever seen a dead man before?"

"Well . . . sure, Captain," the shaky voice came hesitantly, "but I never touched one."

"Well, touch him," Delaney shouted. "He's not going to bite you, for Chrissakes. Get his face cleaned off first."

"Yeah . . . face . . . sure . . . Jesus Christ."

"Now what?"

"His fuckin' eyes are open. He's looking right at me."

"You stupid sonofabitch," Delaney thundered into the mike. "Will you stop acting like an idiot slob and do your job like a man?"

"Chilton One from Chilton Two. Barnes here. What's the problem?"

"Farber's acting up," Delaney growled. "He doesn't enjoy touching the corpse."

"Do you have to rough him?"

'No, I don't," Delaney said. "I could sing lullabies to him. Do you want that stiff down or don't you?"

Silence.

"All right," Barnes said finally. "Do it your way. When I get down, you and I will have a talk."

"Any time, anywhere," Delaney said loudly, and saw that Forrest and Sneed were staring at him. "Now get off my back and let me talk to this infant. Farber, are you there? Farber?"

"Here," the voice came weakly.

"Have you got him brushed off?"

"Yes."

"Put your fingers on his chest. Lightly. See if you can pick up a heartbeat or feel any breathing. Well . . .?"

After a moment: "No. Nothing, Captain."

"Put your cheek close to his lips."

"What?"

"Put. Your. Cheek. Close. To. His. Lips. Got that?"

"Well . . . sure . . ."

"See if you can feel any breath coming out."

"Jesus . . ."

"Well?"

"Nothing. Captain, this guy is dead, he's fuckin' *dead*."

"All right. Get the horse collar on him, up around his chest, under his arms. Make sure the shackle connection is upward."

They waited, all of them on the porch now straining their eyes to the top of Devil's Needle. So were all the men in the compound, sentries, snipers, reporters. Still and TV cameras were trained on the rock. There was remarkably little noise, Delaney noted, and little movement. Everyone was caught in the moment, waiting . . .

"Farber?" Delaney called into his mike. "Farber, are you getting the collar on him?"

"I can't," the voice came wavering. "I just can't."

"What's wrong now?"

"Well . . . he's all spread out, Captain. His arms are out wide to his sides, and his legs are spread apart. Jesus, he's got no cock at all."

"Screw his cock!" Delaney shouted furiously. "Forget his cock. Forget his arms. Just get his feet together and slip the collar over them and up his body."

"I can't," the voice came back, and they caught the note of panic. "I just can't."

Delaney took a deep breath. "Listen, you shit-gutted bastard, you volunteered for this job. 'I'll bring the fucker down,' you said. All right, you're up there. Now bring the fucker down. Get his ankles together."

"Captain, he's cold and stiff as a board."

"Oh no," Captain Edward X. Delaney said. "Cold and stiff as a board, is he? Isn't it a shame this isn't the middle of July and you could pick him up with a shovel and a blotter. You're a cop, aren't you? What the hell you think they pay you for? To clean up the world's garbage—right? Now listen, you milk-livered sonofabitch, you get working on those legs and get them together."

There was silence for a few moments. Delaney saw that Captain Bertram

Sneed had turned away, walked to the other end of the porch. He was gripping the railing tightly, staring off in the opposite direction.

"Captain?" Farber's voice came faintly.

"I'm here. How you coming with the legs?"

"Not so good, Captain. I can move the legs a little, but I think he's stuck. His skin is stuck to the fuckin' rock."

"Sure it is," Delaney said, his voice suddenly soft and encouraging now. "It's frozen to the rock. Of course it would be. Just pull the legs together slowly, son. Don't think about the skin. Work the legs back and forth."

"Well . . . all right . . . Oh God."

They waited. Delaney took advantage of the pause to pull off his coat. He looked around, then Chief Forrest took it from him. The Captain realized he was soaked with sweat; he could feel it running down his ribs.

"Captain?"

"I'm here, son."

"Some of the skin on his legs and ass came off. Patches stuck to the fuckin' rock."

"Don't worry about it. He didn't feel a thing. Got his ankles together?"

"Yes. Pretty good. Close enough to get through the collar."

"Fine. You're doing just fine. Now move his whole body back and forth, side to side. Rock him so his body comes free from the stone."

"Oh Jesus . . ." Farber gasped, and they knew he was weeping now. They didn't look at each other.

"He's all shrunk," Farber moaned. "All shrunk and his belly is puffed up."

"Don't look at him," Delaney said. "Just keep working. Keep moving him. Get him loose."

"Yes. All right. He's loose now. He didn't lose much skin."

"Good. You're doing great. Now get that horse collar on him. Can you lift his legs?"

"Oh sure. Christ he don't weigh a thing. He's a skeleton. His arms are still out straight to the sides."

"That's all right. No problem there. Where's the collar?"

"Working it upward. Wait a minute . . . Okay. There. It's in position. Under his arms."

"He won't slip through?"

"No chance. His fuckin' arms go straight out."

"Ready for the 'copter?"

"Jesus, yes!"

"Chilton Two from Chilton One."

"Chilton Two. Loud and clear. Barnes here."

"The collar is on the body. You can pick up."

"Roger. Going in."

"Farber? Farber, are you there?"

"I'm still here, Captain."

"The 'copter is coming over for the pickup. Do me a favor, will you?"

"What's that, Captain?"

"Feel around under the snow and see if you can find an ice ax. It's about the size of a hammer, but it has a long pick on one side of the head. I'd like to have it."

"I'll take a look. And do me a favor, Captain."

"What?"

"After they pick him up and land him, make sure they come back for me. I don't like this fuckin' place."

"Don't worry," Delaney assured him. "They'll come back for you. I promise."

He watched until he saw the helicopter throttling down, moving slowly toward the top of Devil's Needle. He walked back inside to place his microphone on the radioman's counter. Then he took a deep breath, looked with wonder at his trembling hands. He went outside again, down the steps, into the compound. The photographers were busy now, lens turned to the 'copter hovering over Devil's Needle.

Delaney stood in the snow, his cap squarely atop his head, choker collar hooked up. Like the others, his head was tilted back, eyes turned upward, mouth agape. They waited. Then they heard the powered roar of the rotors as the 'copter rose swiftly, tilted, circled, came heading toward them.

At the end of the swinging cable, Daniel Blank hung in the horse collar. It was snug under his outstretched arms. His head was flung back in a position of agony. His ankles were close together. His shrunken body was water-white, all knobs and bruises.

The helicopter came lower. They saw the shaved skull, the purpled wounds where skin had torn away. The strange bird floated, dangling. Then, suddenly, caught against the low sun, there was a nimbus about the flesh, a luminous radiation that flared briefly and died as the body came back to earth.

Delaney turned, walked away. He felt a hand on his shoulder, stopped, turned to see Smokey the Bear.

"Well," Captain Sneed grinned, "we got him, didn't we?"

Delaney shrugged off that heavy hand and continued to walk, his back to the thunder of the descending 'copter.

"God help us all," Captain Edward X. Delaney said aloud. But no one heard him.

EPILOGUE

IN THE months after the events recounted here, the following occurred:

Christopher Langley and the Widow Zimmerman were wed, in a ceremony attended with great pleasure by Captain Delaney. The happy newlyweds moved to Sarasota, Florida.

Calvin Case, with the assistance of a professional writer, produced a book called "Basic Climbing Techniques." It had a modest but encouraging sale, and seems on its way to becoming a manual of Alpinism. Case is currently working on a second book: "The World's Ten Toughest Climbs."

Anthony (Tony) Montfort rejoined his parents in Europe. The whereabouts of Valenter is presently unknown.

Charles Lipsky became involved in a criminal ring forging welfare checks and is currently being held for trial.

Samuel and Florence Morton opened the first of a chain of "health clubs" featuring mixed nude swimming. They are under indictment for "maintaining a public nuisance," but are free on bail pending trial.

Former Deputy Commissioner Broughton was defeated in the primary to select his party's candidate for mayor of New York City. He is attempting to form a new political party based on the promise of "law and order."

Former Lt. Marty Dorfman passed the examination for captain, and was appointed Legal Officer of the Patrol Division.

Lt. Jeri Fernandez, Sergeant MacDonald, and Detective Blankenship received commendations.

Reporter Thomas Handry apparently giving up hopes of becoming a poet, has been reassigned to his newspaper's Washington Bureau.

Dr. Sanford Ferguson was killed in an automobile accident early one morning when returning to his home from a visit to his mistress.

Deputy Mayor Alinski is still Deputy Mayor. Former Inspector Johnson and former Deputy Inspector Thorsen have both been promoted one rank.

Captain Edward X. Delaney was jumped to Inspector and made Chief of the Detective Division. About a month after the death of Daniel Blank, Barbara Delaney died from Proteus infection. After a year's period of mourning, Inspector Delaney married the former Monica Gilbert. Mrs. Delaney is pregnant.

The Sixth Commandment

LATE NOVEMBER, and the world was dying. A wild wind hooted faintly outside the windows. Inside, the air had been breathed too many times.

"It's got nothing to do with your age," I said.

"Liar," she said.

I tried to groan. Swung my legs out of bed and lighted a cigarette. Sat there smoking, hunched over. She fumbled with my spine.

"Poor baby," she said.

I wouldn't look at her. I knew what I'd see: a small body so supple it twanged. Short brown hair cut like a boy's. All of her sleek. She had me in thrall. Soft swell to her abdomen. A little brown mole on the inside of her left thigh. Her ass was smooth and tight.

"All I'm saying," I said, "is that I've got to go away on a business trip. A week, two weeks, a month—who knows? I've *got* to; it's my job."

"I've got five weeks' vacation coming," she said. "I could get a leave of absence. I could quit. No problem."

I didn't answer.

Her squid arm slid around my neck. Even when she was coming, her flesh was cool. Did she ever sweat? Her skin was glass. But I could never break her.

"It's impossible," I said. "It wouldn't work."

She kneeled on the bed behind me. Put her arms about my neck. Pressed. Pointy little breasts. Very elegant. Pink bosses. All of her elegant. She worked at it: jogging, yoga, dance. I told her once that she even had muscles in her crap, and she said I was vulgar, and I said that was true.

"I'll be back," I said.

"No you won't," she said, and that was true, too.

I leaned forward to stub my cigarette in the ashtray on the floor. She leaned with me. For a moment I was supporting her naked weight on my back. Her warm breath was in my ear. I straightened slowly, pushing her back.

"At least," she said, "let's end things with a bang."

"You're outrageous," I said.

"Am I not?" she said.

See her in one of her tailored Abercrombie & Fitch suits, and you'd never guess. The Gucci brogues. Benjamin Franklin spectacles. Minimal makeup. Crisp. Aloof. All business. But naked, the woman was a goddamned tiger. Joan Powell. How I hated her. How I loved her. She taught me so much. Well, what the hell, I taught her a few things, too. I must have; why else had she endured my infidelities and shitty moods for three years?

"You'll call?" she said, and when I didn't answer, she said forlornly, "You'll write?"

551

It wasn't her pleading that disgusted me so much as my own weakness. I wanted her so much, right then, that moment. After psyching myself for weeks, preparing for this break. If she had made the right gesture just then, the right touch, I'd have caved. But she didn't. Which meant she didn't want to, because she knew what the right gesture was, the right touch. She had invented it.

So I shrugged her off, got up, started to dress. She lay back on the rumpled sheets, watching me with hard eyes.

"The best you'll ever get," she said.

"I agree," I said. "Wholeheartedly."

She said she was forty-four, and I believed her. I said I was thirty-two, and she believed me. We didn't lie to each other about things like that. About facts. We lied about important things. It wasn't so much the difference in our ages that bothered me; it was the thralldom. I was addicted. She had me hooked.

I knotted my tie, looking at her in the mirror. Now she had one arm over her eyes. Her upper torso was supine, then, at the waist, her body curved over onto a hip. One knee drawn up. All of her in a sweet S curve, tapering. She kept a year-round tan. Milkier to mark the straps and little triangles of her string bikini. She liked me to shave her. I liked it, too.

"I'm going now," I said.

"Go," she said.

The Bingham Foundation wasn't the Ford or the Rockefeller, but it wasn't peanuts either. We gave away about ten million a year, mostly for scientific research. This was because the original Silas Bingham had been an ironmonger who had invented a new casting process. And his son, Caleb Bingham, had invented a cash register that kept a running total. *His* son, Jeremiah Bingham, had been a surgeon who invented a whole toolbox of clamps, saws, chisels, files, pliers, mallets, etc., for the repair of the human carcass.

Mrs. Cynthia, widow of Jeremiah, ran the Bingham Foundation. She looked like a little old man. The executive director was Stacy Besant. He looked like a little old woman. My name is Samuel Todd. I was one of several field investigators. The Bingham Foundation does not disburse its funds casually.

I was sitting in Besant's office on Friday morning, watching him twist a benzedrine inhaler up one hairy nostril. Fascinating. He unplugged it, with some difficulty, then sniffed, blinked, sneezed. He slid the inhaler into a vest pocket.

"A cold, sir?" I asked.

"Not yet," he said. "But you never know. You've reviewed the Thorndecker file?"

I flipped a palm back and forth.

"Briefly," I said. "I'll take it with me for closer study."

Actually, I had spent the previous night saying goodby to Joan Powell. I hadn't cracked the file. I didn't know who Thorndecker was. Moral: Ignorance really is bliss.

"What do you think?" Besant asked.

"Hard to say," I said. "The application sounds impressive, but all applications sound impressive."

"Of course, of course," he said.

Out came the inhaler again. Into the other nostril this time. Sniff. Blink. Sneeze.

"He's asking for a million," he said.

"Is he sir?" I said. "They always double it, knowing we'll cut it in half, at least. It's a game."

"Usually," he said. "But in this case, I'm not so sure. He comes highly recommended. His work, I mean. Won a third of a Nobel at the age of thirty-eight."

"What was that for, sir?"

His eyes glazed over. Hunching across the desk toward me, he looked like a Galapagos tortoise clad in Harris tweed.

"Uh, it's all in the file," he said. "The science people are very high on him. Very high indeed." Pause. "His first wife was my niece."

"Oh?"

"Dead now. Drowned in the surf on the Cape. Terrible tragedy. Lovely girl."

I was silent.

The inhaler appeared again, but he didn't use it. Just fondled it. It looked like an oversize bullet. Something for big game.

"Go along then," he said. "Take as much time as you need. Keep in touch."

He held out his hand, and I moved it up and down. I thought again of a turtle. His flipper was dry and scaly.

Out in the gloomy corridor I met old Mrs. Cynthia. She was moving slowly along, leaning heavily on a polished cane. It had a silver head shaped like a toucan's bill. Handsome.

"Samuel," she said, "you're going up to see Doctor Thorndecker?"

"Yes, ma'am."

"I knew his father," she said. "Knew him well."

"Did you?"

"A sweet man," she said, and something that might have been pain pinched her eyes. "It was all so—so sad."

I stared at her.

"Does that mean you'd like me to approve the grant, Mrs. Cynthia?" I asked bluntly.

Her eyes cleared. She reached out a veined hand and tapped my cheek. Not quite a slap.

"Sometimes, Samuel," she said, "you carry lovable irascibility a little too far. I know you won't let my friendship with Doctor Thorndecker's father affect your judgment. If I thought that, I would never have mentioned it."

There didn't seem to be anything more to say. I went back to my broom-closet office, slid the Thorndecker file into my battered briefcase, and went home to pack. I planned to go over the research on Sunday night, and get an early start the next morning.

I should have slit my wrists instead.

Over the years the Bingham Foundation had developed a reasonably efficient method of processing grant applications. Unless they were obviously from nut cases ("I am on the verge of inventing perpetual motion!"), requests went to three independent investigative organizations and, occasionally, the federal government.

The firm of Donner & Stern, older even than Pinkertons, was too discreet to call their operatives "private detectives." They preferred "inquiry agents," and they provided personal background material on grant applicants. This included family history, education, professional employment record, personal habits (drinking? drug addiction?), and anything else of an intimate nature Donner & Stern felt would assist the Bingham Foundation in forming an opinion on the applicant's merit.

Lifschultz Associates conducted an inquiry into the applicant's financial status, his credit rating, banking history, investments, tax record, current assets, and so forth. The purpose here was to determine the applicant's honesty and trustworthiness, and to insure, as certainly as possible, that upon receipt of a Bingham Foundation grant, he wouldn't immediately depart for Pago Pago with his nubile secretary.

Finally, Scientific Research Records provided an unbiased analysis of the value, or lack of it, of the applicant's proposals: the reasons for which the subsidy was sought. The SRR report usually included a brief summary of similar work being conducted elsewhere, the chances for success, and a compilation of professional judgments on the applicant's intelligence and expertise by associates, colleagues, and rivals.

These three preliminary investigations eliminated about 90 percent of the hopeful scientists who approached the Bingham Foundation, hat in hand. The remaining applications were then handed over to Bingham's own field investigators.

Our job was to make an assessment of what Stacy Besant liked to call "the intangibles, human relations, and things known only to the applicant's priest, psychiatrist, or mistress."

First of all, we tried to discover if his family life was reasonably happy, if his relations with assistants and employees was troublefree, and if he enjoyed a good reputation in his neighborhood and community. If he was himself employed in a university or research facility, it was necessary to make certain the applicant had the confidence and respect of his superiors.

All this was fairly cut-and-dried, necessitating nothing more than talking informally to a great number of people and assuring them their comments would be off the record. But sometimes the results were surprising.

I remember the case of one renowned scientist, happily married, father of four, who applied for a grant for a research project into the nature and origins of homosexuality. During the final interview, the Bingham field investigator discovered the applicant himself was gay. His request was denied, not on moral grounds but because it was feared his predilection would prejudice his research.

In another case, a criminologist's request for funds was rejected when it was learned that he was an avid hunter and gun collector. It was a damaging revelation only because he had asked for the subsidy to make an in-depth analysis of "The Roots of Violence." Bingham decided to let some other foundation have the honor of financing the gunslinger's research.

"Field investigators" may have been our title, but "snoops" was more accurate. I had been doing it for almost five years, and if I was growing increasingly suspicious and cynical, it was because those were exactly the qualities the job required. It gave me no particular pleasure to uncover a weakness or ancient misstep that might mean the end of a man's dreams. But that was what I was being paid for, and paid well.

At least so I told myself. But occasionally, in moments of drunken enlightenment, I wondered if I enjoyed prying into other men's lives because my own was so empty.

The file on the application of Dr. Thorndecker was a fat one. Before I settled down with it, I put out a bottle of Glenlivet Scotch, pitcher of water, bucket of ice cubes. And two packs of cigarettes. I started something on the hi-fi—I think it was Vivaldi—the volume turned down so low the music was only a murmur. Then I started . . .

THORNDECKER, Telford Gordon, 54, BSCh, MD, MSc, PhD, etc., etc., member of this, fellow of that, Nobel Prize Winner for research in the pathology of mammalian cells. Father of daughter Mary, 27, and son Edward, 17. Presently married to second wife Julie, 23.

I took a swallow of Scotch at that. His second wife was four years younger than his daughter. Interesting, but not too unusual. About as interesting as the ten years difference in the ages of his two children.

I sat staring a few moments at the photograph of Dr. Thorndecker included in the file. It was an 8 x 10 glossy, apparently intended for publication; it had that professional type of pose and lighting. It was a head-and-shoulders shot, eyes looking into the camera lens, mouth smiling faintly, chin raised.

He was a handsome man; no doubt of that. Thick shock of dark, wavy hair; heavy, masculine features; surprisingly sensitive lips. Eyes large and widely spaced. High brow, a jaw that was solid without being massive. Smallish ears set close to the skull. Strong, straight nose, somewhat hard and hawkish.

In the photo, the fine lips were smiling, but the eyes were grave, almost moody. I wondered how his voice would sound. I set great store by the timbre of a man's voice. I guessed Thorndecker's would be a rumbling baritone, with deep resonance.

I read on . . . about his brilliant teaching career, and even more brilliant research into the pathology of mammalian cells. I am not a trained scientist, but I've read a great deal of chemistry and physics, and learned more on my job at Bingham. I gathered, from the SRR report, that Thorndecker was especially interested in the biology of aging, and particularly the senescence of normal mammalian cells. He had made a significant contribution to a research project that produced a statistical study of the reproduction (doublings) of human embryo cells *in vitro*.

After this pioneer work, Thorndecker, on his own, had followed up with a study of the reproduction of human cells *in vitro* from donors of various ages. His findings suggested that the older the donor, the fewer times the donated cells could be induced to reproduce (double). Thorndecker concluded that mammalian cells had a built-in clock. Aging and death were not so much the result of genetic direction or of disease and decay, but were due to the inherent nature of our cells. A time for living, and a time for dying. And all the improved medical skills, diet, and health care in the world could not affect longevity except within very definite natural parameters.

A jolly thought. I had another drink of Glenlivet on that. Then I turned to the report of Lifschultz Associates on the good doctor's finances. It was revealing . . .

Prior to the death of his first wife by drowning, Dr. Telford Thorndecker apparently had been a man of moderate means, supporting his family on his professor's salary, fees from speaking engagements, the Nobel Prize award, and royalty income from two college textbooks he had written: "Human Cells" and "The Pathology of Human Cells."

He had been sole beneficiary of his wife's estate, and I blinked my eyes when I saw the amount: almost a million dollars. I made a mental note to ask Stacy Besant the source of this inherited wealth. As the first Mrs. Thorndecker's uncle, he should certainly know. And while I was at it, I might as well ask Mrs. Cynthia what she had meant by her lament: "It was all so—so sad," when she mentioned knowing Thorndecker's father.

Shortly after the will was probated, Dr. Thorndecker resigned all his teaching, research, and advisory positions. He purchased Crittenden Hall, a 90-bed nursing and convalescent home located near the village of Coburn, south of Albany, N.Y. The Crittenden grounds and buildings were extensive, but the nursing home had been operating at a loss for several years prior to Thorndecker's purchase. This may have been due to its isolated location, or perhaps simply to bad management.

In any event, Thorndecker showed an unexpected talent for business administration. Within two years, a refurbishing program was completed, a new, younger staff recruited, and Crittenden Hall was showing a modest profit. All this had been accomplished in spite of reducing occupancy to fifty beds and converting one of the buildings to a research laboratory that operated independently of the nursing facility.

Thorndecker managed this by creating a haven for the alcoholic, mentally disturbed, and terminally ill members of wealthy families. The daily rates were among the highest in the country for similar asylums. The kitchen was supervised by a Swiss cordon bleu chef, the staff was large enough to provide a one-to-one relationship with patients, and a wide variety of social activities was available, including first-run movies, TV sets in every room, dances, costume balls, and live entertainment by visiting theatrical troupes. No basket weaving or finger painting at Crittenden Hall.

As chief executive of this thriving enterprise, Dr. Thorndecker paid himself the relatively modest salary of $50,000 a year. All profits of the nursing facility went to the Crittenden Research Laboratory which was, according to the prospectus distributed to potential donors, "Devoted to a continuing inquiry into the biology of aging, with particular attention to cellular morphology and the role it plays in productive longevity."

The Lifschultz Associates' report concluded by stating that the Crittenden Research Laboratory was supported by the profits of the nursing home, by grants and contributions from outside donors, and by bequests, many of them sizable and some of them willed to the laboratory by former patients of Crittenden Hall.

Dr. Thorndecker, I decided, had a nice thing going. Not illegal certainly. Probably not even immoral or unethical. Just nice.

I flipped the stack of records on the hi-fi, visited the can, mixed a fresh highball, lighted the last cigarette in pack No. 1, and settled down to read the original application submitted to the Bingham Foundation by the Crittenden Research Laboratory.

The petition was succinct and well-organized. It made it clear from the outset that despite similar names, the connection between Crittenden Hall, the nursing home, and the Crittenden Research Laboratory was kept deliberately distant. Each facility had its own building, each its own staff. Lab employees were not encouraged to associate with those of the nursing home; they even lunched in separate chambers. What the application was emphasizing was that no Bingham Foundation funds, if granted, would be used in support of Crittenden Hall, a profit-making institution. All monies would go to Crittenden Research Laboratory, a non-profit organization performing original and valuable investigation into the basic constitution of mammalian cells.

The specific purpose for which a million dollars was requested was a three-year study on the effects of the entire spectrum of electromagnetic radiation on human embryo cells *in vitro*. This would include everything from radio waves and visible light to infrared, X rays, ultraviolet, and gamma rays. In addition, the cells' reaction to ultrasound would be explored, as well as laser and maser emissions.

Preliminary experiments, the application stated, indicated that under prolonged exposure to certain wavelengths of electromagnetic radiation, human cells underwent fundamental alterations of their reproductive capabilities, the nature of which the basic research had not clearly revealed. But, it was suggested, the thorough study for which funds were requested could conceivably lead to a fuller understanding of the cause of senescence in mammalian cells. In effect, what the project was designed to discover was the cellular clock that determined the normal life span of human beings.

It was an ambitious proposal. The money requested would be used to pay the salaries of an enlarged staff and to purchase the expensive equipment and instruments needed. A detailed budget was submitted.

I shuffled the file back to the report of Scientific Research Records. It stated that while a great deal of work in this field had already been done by research facilities around the world, the information available was fragmented; no single study of this nature had ever been made, and no researchers, to the knowledge of SRR, had set out with this particular aim: to uncover exactly what it was in human cells that, within a finite time, made our eyesight dim, muscles weaken, organs deteriorate, and brought about aging and death.

That was the stated objective of Dr. Telford Gordon Thorndecker. I didn't believe it for a minute. Here was this brilliant, imaginative, and innovative scientist requesting funds to replicate the experiments of other men and perhaps identify the primary cause of senescence in mammalian cells. I just couldn't see Thorndecker limiting himself to such a goal. The man was a genius; even his rivals and opponents admitted that. Geniuses don't follow; they lead.

I thought I knew the secret ambition of Dr. Telford Thorndecker. It followed the usual pattern of research in the biological sciences: discover, analyze, manipulate. He could never be content with merely identifying and describing the factor in mammalian cells that caused aging and death. He had a hidden desire to control that factor, to stretch our three-score-and-ten, or whatever, and push back the natural limits of human growth.

I grinned, convinced that I had guessed the real motives of Thorndecker in applying for a Bingham Foundation grant. Which only proves how stupid I can be when I set my mind to it.

I took Thorndecker's photograph, and stared at it again.

"Hello, Ponce de Leon," I said aloud.

Then I finished the whiskey. My own Fountain of Youth.

THE FIRST DAY

WHEN THE alarm chattered at 7:00 A.M. on Monday, I poked an arm out from my warm cocoon of blankets and let my hand fall limply on the shut-off button. When I awoke the second time, I looked blearily at the bedside clock. Almost eleven. So much for my early start.

Thirty-two is hardly a ripe old age, but I had recently noticed it was taking me longer and longer to put it together and get going in the morning. Ten years previously, even five years, I could splurge a rough night on the town, maybe including a bit of rub-the-bacon, get home in the wee hours, catch some sleep, bounce out of bed at seven, take a cold shower and quick shave, and go whistling off to face the day's challenges.

That morning I moved slowly, balancing my head carefully atop my neck. I climbed shakily out of my warm bed with a grumbled curse. I stared at myself in the bathroom mirror, shuddering. I took a long, hot shower, but the cobwebs were made of stainless steel. Brushing my teeth didn't eliminate the stale taste of all those cigarettes the night before. I didn't even try to shave; I can't stand the sight of blood.

In the kitchen, I closed my eyes and gulped down a glass of tomato juice. It didn't soothe the bubbling in my stomach from all that whiskey I had consumed while reviewing the Thorndecker file. Two cups of black coffee didn't help much either.

Finally, while I was dressing, I said aloud, "Screw it," went back into the kitchen and mixed an enormous Bloody Mary, with salt, pepper, Tabasco, Worcestershire, and horse radish. I got that down, gasping. In about ten minutes I felt like I might live—but still wasn't certain I wanted to.

I looked out the window. It was gray out there, sky lowery, a hard wind blowing debris and pedestrians along West 71st Street. This was in Manhattan, in case you haven't guessed.

A sickeningly cheerful radio voice reported a storm front moving in from the west, with a dropping barometer and plunging thermometer. Snow flurries or a freezing rain predicted; driving conditions hazardous by late afternoon. It all sounded so *good*.

I pulled on whipcord slacks, black turtleneck sweater, tweed jacket, ankle-high boots. I owned a leather trenchcoat. It was a cheapie, and the last rainstorm had left it stiff as a board. But I struggled into it, pulled on a floppy Irish hat, and carried my packed bags down to my Pontiac Grand Prix.

Someone had written in the dust on the hood: "I am dirty. Please wash me." I scrawled underneath, "Why the hell should I?" I got started a little after twelve o'clock. I wouldn't say my mood was depressed. Just sadly thoughtful. I resolved to stop smoking, stop drinking, stop mistreating my holy body. I resolved to—ahh, what was the use? It was *my* holy body, envelope of my immortal soul, and if I wanted to kick hell out of it, who was there to care?

I stopped somewhere near Newburgh for a lunch of steak and eggs, with a couple of ales. There was a liquor store next to the diner, and I bought a pint of Courvoisier cognac. I didn't open it, but it was a comforting feeling knowing it was there in the glove compartment. My security blanket.

Driving up the Hudson Valley was like going into a tunnel. Greasy fog swirled; a heavy sky pressed down between the hills. There was a spatter of hail against the windshield. It turned to rain, then to sleet. I started the wipers, slowed, and got a local radio station that was warning of worse to come.

There wasn't much traffic. The few cars and trucks were moving steadily but cautiously, lights on in the gloom. No one even thought of trying to pass on that slick highway, at least until the sand spreaders got to work. I drove hunched forward, peering into the blackness. I wasn't thinking about the storm. I wasn't even brooding about Dr. Telford Thorndecker. I was remembering Joan Powell.

I had met her three years ago, and there was a storm then much like this one. I wish I could tell you that we met like that couple in the TV commercial, on a hazy, sunlit terrace. We are sipping wine at separate tables, me red, her white. I raise my glass to her. She smiles faintly. The next thing you know, we're sharing the same table, our wine bottles nestling side by side. Don't like that? How about this one, from an old Irene Dunne-Cary Grant movie. We both run for the same cab, get in opposite sides. Big argument. Then the bent-nosed driver (Allen Jenkins) persuades us to share the cab, and we discover we're both going to the same party. You know how *that* turns out.

It wasn't like that at all. On a blowy, rancorous day, I had a late-afternoon appointment with my dentist, Dr. Hockheimer, in a medical building on West 57th Street. It was only for a checkup and cleaning, but I'm terrified of dentists. The fact that Dr. Hockheimer gave all his patients a lollipop after treatment didn't help much.

Hockheimer shared a suite with two other dentists. The waiting room was crowded. I hung up my wet trenchcoat, put my dripping umbrella in the corner rack. I sat down next to a nice looking woman. Early forties, I guessed. She was holding a two-year-old copy of the *National Geographic* in shaking hands. The magazine was upside down. I knew exactly how she felt.

I sat there for almost five minutes, embarrassed to discover I had a lighted cigarette in each hand. I was tapping one out when a god-awful scream of pain came from one of the dentists' offices.

That was all I needed. I jerked to my feet, grabbed up trenchcoat and umbrella, headed for the door. The nice looking lady beat me out by two steps. At the elevator, we smiled wanly at each other.

"I'm a coward," she said.

"Welcome to the club," I said. "Need a drink?"

"Do I ever!" she said.

We dashed across Sixth Avenue, both of us huddling under my umbrella, buffeted by the driving rain. We ran into a dim hotel bar, laughing and feeling better already. We sat at a front table, about as big as a diaper, and ordered martinis.

"Was that a man or a woman who screamed?" I asked.

"Don't talk about it. Joan Powell," she said, offering a firm hand.

"Samuel Todd," I said, shaking it. "You a patient of Hockheimer's?"

She nodded.

"We won't get our lollipops today."

"These are better," she said, sipping her drink.

She stared out the front window. Cold rain was driving in gusts. There was a flash of lightning, a crack of thunder.

She was a severely dressed, no-nonsense, executive-type lady. Sensible shoes. Tailored suit. High-collared blouse. Those crazy half-glasses. Good complexion. Marvelous complexion. Crisp features. A small, graceful, cool lady.

"You're a literary agent," I said. "An executive assistant to a big-shot lawyer. Editor of a women's magazine. Bank officer."

"No," she said. "A department store buyer. Housewares. You're a newspaper reporter. A computer programmer. An undercover cop. A shoe salesman."

"A shoe salesman?" I said. "Jesus! No, I'm with the Bingham Foundation. Field investigator."

"I knew it," she said, and I laughed.

The storm showed no signs of letting up, but I didn't care. It was pleasant in there with her, just talking, having another round. I never made a pass at her, nor she at me. It was all very civilized.

I figured her about ten years older than I. What I liked most about her was that she was obviously content with her age, made no effort to appear younger by dress, makeup, or manner. As I said, a very cool lady. Self-possessed.

After the second martini, she stared at me and said, "You're not the handsomest man I've ever met."

"Oh, I don't know," I said. "Last year I was runner-up in the Miss King of Prussia contest."

She looked down at her drink, expressionless.

"King of Prussia," I said. "A town in Pennsylvania."

"I know where it is," she said. "It wasn't a bad joke, but I very rarely laugh aloud. I chuckle inwardly."

"How will I know when you're chuckling inwardly?"

"Put your hand on my stomach. It flutters. Listen," she went on before I had a chance to react to that, "I didn't mean to insult you. About not being the handsomest man I've ever met. I don't particularly like handsome men. They're always looking in mirrors and combing their hair. You have a nice, plain, rugged face. Very masculine."

"Thank you,"

"And you're polite. I like that."

"Good," I said. "Tell me more."

"You're eyes are good," she said. "Greenish-brown, aren't they?"

"Sort of."

"Was your nose broken?"

"A long time ago," I said. "I didn't think it showed."

"It does," she said. "Do people call you Sam?"

"They do. I don't like it."

"All right," she said equably. "Todd, may we have another drink? I'm going to split the check with you. Are you married?"

"No, Powell," I said. "Are you?"

"Not now. I was. Years ago. It was a mistake. Have you ever been married?"

"No," I said. "I was madly in love with my childhood sweetheart, but she ran off with a lion tamer."

"My childhood sweetheart *was* a lion tamer," she said. "Isn't that odd? You don't suppose . . . ?"

The rain had turned to sleet; the streets and sidewalks were layered with slush. There didn't seem much point in trying to get anywhere. So we had dinner right there in the hotel dining room. The food wasn't the greatest, but it was edible. Barely.

We talked lazily of this and that. She was from Virginia. I was from Ohio. She had come directly to New York after graduation from some girls' school. I had come to New York after a two-year detour in Vietnam.

"Army?" she asked.

"Not infantry," I said hastily. "No frontline action or anything like that. Criminal investigation. And there was plenty to investigate."

"I can imagine," she said. She stared down at her plate. "Tom, my younger brother, was killed over there. Marine Corps. I hate violence. *Hate* it."

I didn't say anything.

We had wine during the meal and vodka stingers afterward. I guess we were both more than a little zonked. We started chivying each other, neither of us laughing or even smiling. Very solemn. I don't know if she was chuckling inwardly—I didn't feel her stomach—but I was. What a nice, nice lady.

"Do you have a pet?" she asked. "Dog? Cat?"

"I have this very affectionate oryx," I said. "Name of Cynthia. I've trained her to sit up and beg. You have a pet?"

"A lemur named Pete," she said. "He can roll over and play dead. He's been doing it for a week now."

"Did you ever smoke any pot?"

"All the time. Takes me hours to scrub it clean with Brillo. You're not gay, are you?"

"Usually I'm morose."

And so on, and so on. I suppose it sounds silly. Maybe it was. But it was a pleasant evening. In today's world, "pleasant" is good enough.

After awhile we settled our bill—she insisted on paying half—and staggered out of there. We stood on the wind-whipped sidewalk for half an hour trying to get a taxi. But when a storm like that hits New York, empty cabs drive down into the subways and disappear.

We were both shivering under the hotel marquee, feet cold and wet. We watched the umpteenth occupied cab splash by. Then Joan Powell turned, looked into my eyes.

"The hell with this, Todd," she said firmly. "Let's get a room here for the night."

I stared at her, wondering again if she was chuckling inwardly.

"We've got no luggage," I pointed out.

"So?" she said. "We're a couple in from the suburbs. We've been to the theatre. Now we can't get home because the trains aren't running. Try it. It'll go like a dream."

It did.

I looked at her admiringly in the elevator. The bellhop, key in hand, was examining the ceiling.

"Call the babysitter the moment we get in the room, dear," I said. "Ask her to stay over with the children. I'm sure she'll oblige."

"Oh, she's obliging," Joan Powell said bitterly. "I'm sure you find that out when you drive her home."

The bellhop had a coughing fit.

The room was like our dinner: endurable, but just. A high-ceilinged, drafty barn of a place. A fake gas fireplace that wasn't burning. But a big radiator in the corner hissed steadily. Crackled enamel fixtures in the old-fashioned bathroom. One huge bed that sloped down to the center.

I gave the bellhop a five, and he was so grateful he didn't wink. He closed the door behind him, and I locked it. I turned to Joan Powell.

"Well, here we are, dear," I said. "Just married."

We could hear the world outside. Lash of hard rain against glass. Wail of wind. Thunder clap. Window panes rattled; the air seemed to flutter. But we were sealed off, protected. Warm and dry. Just the two of us in our secret, tawdry place. I didn't want to be anywhere else.

She undressed like an actress changing costumes. Off came the steel-rimmed spectacles, tailored suit, Gucci brogues, opaque pantyhose. A bra so small it looked like two miniature half-moons.

"What size?" I asked hoarsely, staring at her elegant breasts.

"T-cup," she said.

She kept making sounds of deep satisfaction, "Mmm, mmm," when I put my lips and teeth to her. She was so complete and full. Not a dimple. All of her taut. Bulging hard. Trig, definitely trig. With strength and energy to challenge. I thought this was the real her. The other was role-playing. She was waiting to be free of the pretend.

What did we do? What did we not do? Our howls muffled the wind; our cries silenced the hissing radiator. She didn't give a damn, and after awhile I didn't either.

I topped her by a head, at least, but that can be interesting, too. I could look down with wonder at this cool, intent woman. She was very serious. It wasn't a your-place-or-mine thing. It had meaning for her. It was significant, I knew. And responded.

Sinuous legs came around my waist. Ankles locked. She pulled me deeper, fingernails digging. Her eyes were open, but glazed.

"Samuel," she said. "Samuel Todd."

"That's me," I said, and gave it my best shot.

I think it was enough. I hope it was enough. But it was difficult to tell. For a woman who hated violence, she was something.

The best part was when, sated, we lay slackly in each other's arms. Half-asleep. Murmuring and moaning nothing. That was nice, being warm and close, kissing now and then, rubbing. The storm was outside, growling, howling, but we were totally gone. Everything was quiet and smelled good.

Three years later I remembered that first night with Joan Powell. The storm was still howling and growling outside, but now I was alone. Well, that's the way I wanted it. Wasn't it?

My headlights picked up a sign through the snow's swirl: COBURN—1 MILE. I leaned forward to the windshield, peering into the darkness, searching for the turnoff. I found it, came down a long, winding ramp. There was a steel sign that had several holes blown through it, like someone had blasted away with a shotgun at close range. The sign said: WELCOME TO COBURN.

I was in the village before I knew it. An hour previously, I later learned, there had been a power failure; Coburn was completely without electricity; all street lamps and traffic signals were out. I glimpsed a few flickering candles and kerosene lanterns inside stores and houses, but this deserted place was mostly black. I drove slowly, and when I saw a muffled pedestrian lumping along with a flashlight for company, I pulled up alongside him and cranked down the window.

"The Coburn Inn?" I yelled.

He motioned forward, in the direction I was heading. I nodded my thanks, sealed myself in, and started up again. For a few moments I thought I was stuck; my wheels spun. But I rocked the Grand Prix back and forth, and after awhile I got traction again and plowed ahead. I found the Coburn Inn dimly lighted with propane lamps. There were a lot of cars parked every which way in the courtyard: tourists who had decided to postpone their trips, to spend this broken night in the nearest warm, dry haven.

In the lobby it looked like most of the stranded travelers had decided to wait out the storm in the restaurant-bar. The flickering lamps gave enough light so I could see crowded tables and stand-up drinkers keeping two bartenders hustling.

There was a kerosene lantern on the front desk.

"Sorry," the bald clerk grinned cheerfully, "we're full up for tonight. The storm, y'know. But you can sit up in the lobby if you like. Plenty to eat and drink. Make a party of it."

"My name's Samuel Todd," I explained patiently. "My office called for a reservation."

"Sorry," he grinned. "No reservations for tonight. We're taking them first-come, first-served."

"I'm here at Dr. Thorndecker's request," I said desperately. "Dr. Telford Thorndecker of Crittenden Hall. He recommended this place. I'm meeting with him tomorrow."

Something happened to the grin. It remained painted on his face, mouth spread, teeth showing, but all the cheer went out of it. The eyes changed focus. I had the feeling that he wasn't seeing me anymore, that he was looking through me to something else. A thousand-yard stare.

"Samuel Todd," I repeated, to shake him out of his reverie. "Reservation. Friend of Dr. Thorndecker."

He shook his head in a kind of shudder, a brief, whiplike motion. His eyes slid down to the big register on the desk.

"Why didn't you say so?" he said in a low voice. "Samuel Todd, sure. Nice, big corner room. Sign here please. You got luggage?"

"Out in my car."

"You'll have to bring it in yourself. Half my people didn't show up tonight."

"I'll manage," I said.

He turned to a small bank of cubbyholes, took an old-fashioned skeleton key from 3-F. The key was attached to a brass medallion. He handed it to me, along with a sealed white envelope that had been in the box.

"Message for you," he said importantly. "See, it's got your name on it, and 'Hold for arrival.' "

"Who left it?"

"That I couldn't say."

"Well, when was it left here?"

"Beats me. It was in the box when I came on duty tonight. You might ask the day man tomorrow."

I nodded, and stuffed the envelope into my trenchcoat pocket. I went out into the storm again, and brought in my two suitcases and the briefcase containing the Thorndecker file. And the pint of brandy from the glove compartment.

The single elevator wasn't working. The bald clerk gestured toward the steep staircase. I went clumping slowly up, pausing on the landings to catch my breath. Kerosene lanterns had been set out in all the corridors. I found Room 3-F, and took one of the lanterns with me. As far as I could see in the wavery light, it was a big corner room, just as the clerk had promised. Nothing palatial, but it seemed reasonably clean. It would do; I wasn't planning to settle permanently in Coburn.

I was peeling off my wet trenchcoat when I found the note that had been left for me. I took the envelope to the yellowish lantern light to examine it. "Mr. Samuel Todd. Please hold for arrival." Neatly typed.

I opened the flap. A single sheet of white typing paper. I unfolded that. Two words:

"Thorndecker kills."

THE SECOND DAY

THE STORM passed over sometime during the night and went whining off to New England. When I awoke Tuesday at 7:30, power had been restored; I was able to use the electric shaver I carry in my travel kit. I noticed I had left about three fingers in the brandy bottle, demonstrating massive strength of character.

In daylight, my room looked old-fashioned, but okay. Lofty ceiling, raddled rug, sprung but comfortable armchairs. A small desk, the top tattooed with cigarette burns. Two dressers. The bed was flinty, but that's the way I like it. Biggest bathroom I had ever seen in a hotel, with a crackled pedestal sink, a yellowed tub on clawed legs, a toilet that flushed by pulling a tarnished brass chain hanging from an overhead tank. A

Holiday Inn it wasn't, but there were plenty of towels, and the steam radiators were clanking away busily.

I took a peek outside. Instant depression. The sky was slate. Patches of sooty snow were melting; there wasn't a bright color in sight. No pedestrians. No life anywhere. Two of my five windows faced on what I guessed was Coburn's main street. I made a bet with myself that it was called Broadway. (It wasn't; it was called Main Street.) I saw the usual collection of small town stores and shops: Ideal Bootery, Samson's Drugs, E-zee Super-Mart, Bill's 5-and-10, Knowlton's Ladies and Gents Apparel, the Coburn *Sentinel*, Sandy's Liquors and Fine Wines.

Before sallying forth to take a closer look at this teeming metropolis, I spent a few minutes considering what to do about that anonymous billet-doux: "Thorndecker kills."

I was born a nosy bastard, and all my life I've been less interested in the how of things than in the why of people. I've had formal training in investigation, but you can't learn snoopery from books, any more than swimming, love making, or how to build the Eiffel Tower out of old Popsicle sticks.

Experience is what an investigator needs most. That, plus a jaundiced view of human nature, plus a willingness to listen to the palaver of old cops and learn by *their* experience.

Also, I have one other attribute of an effective shamus: I can't endure the thought of being scammed and made a fool of. I don't have that much self-respect that I can afford to let it be chipped away by some smart-ass con man. Con woman. Con person.

That dramatic note—"Thorndecker kills."—smelled of con to me.

In the groves of academe there's just as much envy, spite, deceit, connivery, and backbiting as in Hackensack politics. The upper echelons of scientific research are just as snaky a pit. The competition for private and federal funding is ruthless. Research scientists rush to publication, sometimes on the strength of palsied evidence. There's no substitute for being first. Either you're a discoverer, and your name goes into text-books, or you're a plodding replicator, and the Nobel Committee couldn't care less.

So the chances were good that the author of "Thorndecker kills." was a jealous rival or disgruntled aide who felt he wasn't getting sufficient credit. I had seen it happen before: anonymous letters, slanderous rumors slyly spread, even sabotage and deliberate falsification of test results.

And the accusation—"Thorndecker kills."—wasn't all that shocking. All research biologists kill—everything from paramecia to chimpanzees. That's what the job requires. If the note had said: "Thorndecker murders," my hackles might have twitched a bit more. But all I did was slide the letter into an envelope addressed to Donner & Stern, along with a personal note to Nate Stern requesting a make on the typewriter used. I added the phone number of the Coburn Inn, and asked him to call when he had identified the machine. I doubted the information would have any effect on the Thorndecker inquiry.

That was my second mistake of that miserable day. The first was getting out of bed.

I waited and waited and waited for the rackety elevator, watching the brass dial move like it was lubricated with Elmer's Glue-All. When the open cage finally came wheezing down from the top (sixth) floor, the operator turned out to be a wizened colored gentleman one year younger than God. He was wearing a shiny, black alpaca jacket and a little skullcap something like a yarmulke. He was sitting on a wooden kitchen stool. He stopped the elevator five inches below floor level, creaked open the gate slowly. I stepped down and in.

"Close," I said, "but no cigar. How's life treating you this bright, sparkling morning?"

"It's hard but it's fair," he said, closing the gate and shoving the lever forward. "You checking out?"

"I just checked in."

"I thought you was one of those drummers the storm drove in."

"Not me," I said. "I'm here for a few days. Or maybe a few weeks."

"Glad to hear it," he said. "We can use all the customers we gets. My name's Sam. Sam Livingston."

"Sam's my name, too," I said. "Sam Todd. Glad to meet you, Sam."

"Likewise, Sam," he said.

We shook hands solemnly. About this time we were inching past the second floor.

"We'll get there," he said encouragingly. "I hop bells and hump bags and gets you room service, if you want. Like a jug late at night. A sandwich. I can provide."

"That's good to know," I said. "What hours do you work?"

"All hours," he said. "I live here. I got me a nice little place in the basement."

"Where were you last night when I needed you?"

"Hustling drinks in the saloon, I reckon."

"You busy, Sam?" I asked. "Many guests?"

"You," he said, "and half a dozen permanents. It's not our season."

"When is your season?"

He showed me a keyboard of strong, yellow teeth.

"We ain't got a season," he said.

We both laughed, and I looked down into the lobby as we slowly descended.

The floor was a checkerboard of greasy black and white tiles. There were a few small oriental rugs, so tatty the brown backing showed through. The couches and club chairs had once been sleek leather; now they were crackled, cushions lumped with loose springs. Alongside some of the chairs were round rubber mats with ancient brass cuspidors that had been planted with plastic ferns.

Fat wooden pillars, painted to imitate marble, rose from floor to vaulted ceiling. There was ornate iron grillwork around the elevator shaft and cashier's cage. Tucked in one corner was a glass cigar counter, presided over by a shimmering blonde wearing a tight turtleneck sweater punctuated by two Saturn nose cones.

The elevator bobbed to a stop. The gate squeaked open. I moved out. I had the feeling of stepping into the past, a scene of fifty years ago, caught and frozen. Old men slumped in dusty chairs, stared at me over the tops of newspapers. The clerk behind the desk, another baldy, looked up from sorting letters into cubbyholes. The creampuff behind the counter paused in the act of opening a carton of cigarettes and raised her shadowed eyes.

It was not a memory, since I was too young to recall an ancient hotel lobby like that, smelling of disinfectant and a thousand dead cigars. I could only guess I remembered the set from an old movie, and any moment Humphrey Bogart was going to shamble over to the enameled blonde, buy a pack of Fatimas, and lisp, "Keep the change, thweetheart."

I shook my head. The vertigo vanished. I was staring at a shabby hotel lobby in a small town that had seen better days none of the citizens could recall. I went to the front desk . . .

"My name's Samuel Todd."

"Yes, Mr. Todd," the clerk said. "Room 3-F. Everything all right?"

He resembled the night clerk, but all bald men look like relatives.

"Everything's fine," I told him. "There was a letter waiting for me when I checked in last night. Could you tell me who left it?"

He shook his head.

"Can't say. I went back in the office for a few minutes. When I came out, the letter was laying right there on the register. Wasn't it signed?"

"Didn't recognize the name," I lied. "Where can I buy a stamp?"

"Machine over there on the cigar counter. Mailing slot's next to the door. Or you can take it to the post office if you like. That's around the corner on River Street. Go out a lot faster if you mail it from there. We don't get a pickup till three, four this afternoon."

I nodded my thanks, and walked over to the cigar counter. The machine sold me a 15-cent stamp for 20 cents. Nice business.

"Good morning, sir," brass head said throatily. "You're staying with us?"

She was something, a dazzle of wet colors: metallic hair, clouded eyes with lashes like inky centipedes, an enormous blooded mouth, pancaked cheeks. The red sweater was cinched with a studded belt wide enough for a motorcycle ride. Her skirt of purple plaid was so tight that in silhouette she looked like a map of Africa. Knee-high boots of white plastic. Tangerine-colored fingernails somewhere between claws and talons. A walking Picasso.

"Good morning," I said. "Yes, I'm staying with you."

I came down hard on the *you*, and she giggled and took a deep breath. It would have been cruel to ignore that. It would have been impossible to ignore that. I bought a candy bar I didn't want.

"Keep the change, sweetheart," I said.

The seediness was getting to me. All I needed was a toothpick in the corner of my mouth, and an unsmoked cigarette behind my ear.

I started for the doorway under the neon Restaurant-Bar sign.

"My name's Millie," the cigar counter girl called after me.

I waved a hand and kept going. Women like that scare me. I have visions of them cracking my bones and sucking the marrow.

One look at the Restaurant-Bar and I understood how the Coburn Inn survived without a season. There were customers at all twenty tables, and only two empty stools at the long counter. There were even three guys bellying up to the bar in an adjoining room, starting their day with a horn of the ox that gored them.

A few women, but mostly men. All locals, I figured: merchants, insurance salesmen, clerks, some blue-collar types, farmers in rubber boots and wool plaid shirts. They all seemed to know each other: a lot of loud talk, hoots of laughter. This had to be the *in* place in Coburn for a scoff or a tipple. More likely, it was the *only* place.

The menu was encouraging: heavy, country breakfasts with things like pork sausages, grits, scrapple, ham steaks, home fries, and so forth. I glanced around, and it looked like no one in Coburn ever heard of cholesterol. I had a glass of orange juice (which turned out to be freshly squeezed), a western omelette, hash browns, hot Danish, and coffee. When in Rome . . .

As I ate, the room gradually emptied out. It was getting on to 9:00 A.M., time to open all those swell stores I had seen, to start the business day thrumming. I figured that in Coburn, the sale of a second-hand manure spreader qualified as a thrum.

I was starting on my second cup of coffee when I realized someone was standing at my shoulder. I glanced around. A cop in khaki uniform under a canvas ranchers' jacket with a shearling collar. His star was on his lapel, his gun belt was buckled tightly. A long, tight man.

"Mr. Samuel Todd?" he asked. His voice was a flat monotone, hard. A pavement voice.

"That's right," I said. "I'm parked in a towaway zone?"

"No, sir," he said, not smiling. "I'm Constable Ronnie Goodfellow." He didn't offer to shake hands. "Mind if I join you?"

"Pull up a stool," I said. "How about a coffee?"

"No, sir. Thank you."

"No drinking on duty, eh?" I said. Still no smile. I gave up.

He took off his fur trooper's hat, opened the gun belt, took off his jacket. Then he buckled the gun belt about his waist again. He hung up hat and jacket, swung onto the stool alongside me.

While he was going through this slow, thoughtful ballet, I was watching him in the mirror behind the counter. I figured him for Indian blood. He was sword-thin, with dark skin, jetty hair, a nose that could slice cheese. He moved with a relaxed grace, but he didn't fool me. I saw the thin lips, squinny eyes. And his holster was oiled and polished.

I had known men like that before: so much pride they shivered with it. You see it mostly in blacks, Chicanos, and all the other put-downs. But some whites have it, too. Country whites or slum whites or mountain whites. Men so sensitive to a slight that they'll kill if they're insulted, derided, or even accidentally jostled. Temper isn't the reason, or merely conceit. It's a hubris that becomes violent when self-esteem is threatened. The image cannot be scorned. You don't chivy men like that; you cross to the other side of the street.

"Reason I'm here," he said in that stony voice, "is Dr. Telford Thorndecker asked me to stop by. Check to see you got settled in all right. See if there's anything you're wanting."

"That's very nice of you and Dr. Thorndecker," I said. "I appreciate your interest. But I'm settled in just dandy. No problems. And the western omelette was the best I've ever tasted."

"Introduce you to folks in Coburn, if you like," he said. "I know them all."

I blew across my coffee to cool it.

"Thorndecker tell you why I'm here?" I asked casually.

Then I turned to look at him. No expression in those tarry eyes.

"About the grant, you mean?" he said.

"The application for the grant," I said.

"He told me."

"That's surprising," I said. "Usually applicants like to keep it quiet. So if they're turned down, which they usually are, there's no public loss of face."

He looked down at his hands, twisted his thin wedding band slowly.

"Mr. Todd," he said, "Crittenden Hall is big business in Coburn. About a hundred people work out there, including the folks in the research lab. Biggest employer around here. They all live hereabouts, take home good paychecks, buy their needs from local stores. It's important to us—you know?"

"Sure," I said. "I understand."

"And with so many local people working out there, it would be pretty hard for Dr. Thorndecker to keep this grant business a secret. He didn't even try. There was a front-page story in the Coburn *Sentinel* a month ago. Everyone in town knows about it. Everyone's hoping it comes through. A million dollars. That would mean a lot to this town."

"Everyone's cheering for Thorndecker?" I said. "Is that it?"

"Just about everyone," he said carefully. "The best people. We're all hoping you give him a good report, and he gets the money. It would mean a lot to Coburn."

"I don't make the decision," I told him. "I just turn in a recommendation, one way or another. There are a lot of other factors involved. My bosses say Yes or No."

"We understand all that," he said patiently. "We just want to make sure you know how the people around here feel about Dr. Thorndecker and his work."

"The best people," I said.

"That's right," he said earnestly. "We're all for him. Dr. Thorndecker is a great man."

"Did he tell you that?" I said, finishing my coffee.

Those dark eyes turned slowly to mine. It wasn't a kindly look he gave me. No amusement at all.

"No," he said. "He didn't tell me. I'm saying it. Dr. Thorndecker is a great man doing fine work."

"Opinion received and noted," I said. "Now if you'll excuse me, Constable Goodfellow, I've got to go mail a letter."

"The post office is around the corner on River Street."

"I know."

"I'll be happy to show you the way."

"All right," I sighed. "Show me the way."

Goodfellow hadn't been exaggerating when he claimed to know all of Coburn. He exchanged greetings with everyone we met, usually on a first-name basis. We stopped a half-dozen times while I was introduced to Leading Citizens. After the Constable carefully identified me and explained what I was doing in Coburn, I was immediately assured that Dr. Telford Gordon Thorndecker was a prince, a cross between Jesus Christ and Albert Schweitzer—with maybe a little Abner Doubleday thrown in.

We mailed my letter. I had hopes then of ditching my police escort. It wasn't that he was *bad* company; he was no company at all. But I had underestimated him.

"Got a few minutes?" he asked. "Something I want to show you."

"Sure," I said, trying to sound enthusiastic. "I'm not on any schedule."

River Street was exactly that. It intersected Main Street, then ran downhill to the Hudson River. We stood at the top, before the street made its snaky descent to the water. The road was potholed, and bordering it were deserted homes and shops; crumbling warehouses, falling-down sheds, and sodden vacant lots littered with rubbish.

The slate sky still pressed down; God had abolished the sun. The air was shivery, wet, and smelled of ash. There was a greasy mist on the river. A current was running, I guess, but all I could see was floating debris, garbage, and patches of glinting oil. Empty crates, grapefruit rinds, dead fish. I don't think travel agents would push Coburn as "two weeks of fun-filled days and glamorous, romance-laden nights."

Constable Ronnie Goodfellow stood there, hands on hips, smoky eyes brooding from under the fur cap pulled low on his forehead.

"My folks lived here for two hundred years," he said. "This was a sweet river once. All the jumping fish you could catch. Salmon, bass, perch. Everything. The river was alive. Boats moving up and down. I mean there was commerce. Busy. Everyone worked hard and made a living. New York people, they wanted to go to Albany, they took the paddlewheel up. This was before trains and buses and airplanes. I mean the river was *important*.

We shipped food down to the city by boat and barge. It all moves by truck now, of course. What there is of it. There were big wharves here. You can still see the stubs of the pilings over there. This town was *something*. It's all gone now. All different. Even the weather. My daddy used to tell me the winters were so hard that the river froze deep, and you could walk across the ice to Harrick. Or skate across. Hell, Harrick doesn't even *exist* anymore. Lots of small farms around here then. Good apples. Good grapes. Small manufacturing, like furniture, silverware, glassware. Did you know there was a special color called Coburn Blue? Something to do with the sand around here. They put it into vases and plates. Known all over the country, it was. Coburn Blue. That must have been something. The population was about five times what it is now. The young people stayed right here. This was their home. But now . . . This place . . ."

His voice got choky. I began to like him.

"I'll tell you what," I said, "it's not only Coburn. It's New York City. It's the United States of America. It's the world. Everything changes. You, me, and the universe. It's the only thing you can depend on—change."

"Yes," he said, "You're right. And I'm a fool."

"You're not a fool," I told him. "A romantic maybe, but there's no law against that."

"A fool," he insisted, and I didn't argue.

We walked slowly back to Main Street.

"You're married?" I said.

He didn't answer.

"Children?"

"No," he said. "No kids."

"Does your wife like Coburn?" I asked him.

"Hates it," he said in that hollow voice of his. "Can't wait to get out."

"Well . . . ?"

"No," he said. "We'll stay."

We didn't talk anymore until we were standing outside the Coburn Inn.

"Maybe you met my wife," he said, looking over my head. "Works right here in the hotel. Behind the cigar counter. Name's Millie."

I nodded goodby, and marched into the Inn. I considered calling Dr. Thorndecker, but I figured Constable Goodfellow would let him know I was in town. To tell you the truth, I was miffed at the doctor. Not only had he made his Bingham Foundation grant application a matter of public knowledge—something that just isn't done—but he had sent an emissary to greet me. Ordinarily I wouldn't have objected to that, but this agent carried a .38 Police Special. I had a feeling I was being leaned on. I didn't like it.

At this hour in the morning, getting on to eleven o'clock, there was only one customer in the hotel bar. He was a gaffer wearing a checked hunting cap, stained canvas jacket, and old-fashioned leather boots laced to the knees. We used to call them "hightops" where I came from. You bought a pair at Sears after your feet stopped growing, and they lasted for the rest of your life, with occasional half-soling and a liberal application of saddle soap or goose grease before you put them away in the spring. The codger was hunched over a draft beer. He didn't look up when I came in.

The bartender was another baldy, just like the desk clerks. A lot of bald men in one small town. Maybe it was something in the water. I ordered a vodka gimlet on the rocks. He knew what it was, and mixed a fine one, shaking it the way it should be made, not stirred. Most bartenders follow the recipe on the bottle, and make a gimlet tart enough to pucker your asshole. But this one was mostly vodka, with just a flavoring of the lime juice. Drink gimlets and you'll never get scurvy—right? That's my excuse.

The bartender was wearing a lapel badge that read: "Call me Jimmy."
"Good drink, Jimmy," I said.
"Thank you, sir," he said. "I usually have some fresh lime to put in, but that crowd last night cleaned me out. Maybe I'll have some more by tomorrow, if you're still here."
"I'll be here," I said.
"Oh?" he said. "Staying in Coburn?"
"For awhile," I said.
The old character swung around on his barstool and almost fell off.
"What the hell for?" he demanded in a cracked, screaky voice. "Why would anyone in his right mind want to stay in this piss-ass town?"
"Now, Mr. Coburn," the bartender soothed.
"Don't you 'Now, Mr. Coburn' me," the ancient grumbled. "I knowed you when you was sloppin' hogs, and here you are still in the same line of work."
I turned to look at him.
"Mr. *Coburn?*" I said. "Original settlers?"
"From the poor side of the family," he said with a harsh laugh. "The others had the money and sense to get out."
"Now, Mr. Coburn," Jimmy said, again, nervously.
I saw the beer glass was almost empty.
"Buy you a drink, Mr. Coburn?" I asked respectfully.
"Why the hell not?" he said, and shoved the glass across the bar. "And this time go easy on the head," he told the bartender. "When I want a glass of froth, I'll tell you."
Jimmy sighed, and drew the brew.
"Mind if I join you, Mr. Coburn?" I asked.
"Come ahead," he said, motioning to the stool next to him.
When I moved over, I noticed he had a long gun case, an old, leather-trimmed canvas bag, propped against the bar on his far side.
"Hunting?" I said, nodding toward the case.
"Was," he said, "but it's too damned wet after that storm. Ain't a damned thing left worth shooting around here anyways. Except a few two-legged creatures I could mention but won't. What you doing in town, sonny?"
There was no point in trying to keep it a secret, not after that tour of the village with Constable Goodfellow.
"I'm here to see Dr. Thorndecker," I said. "Of Crittenden Hall."
He didn't say anything, but something happened to that seamed face. Caterpillar brows came down. Bloodless lips pressed. Seared cheeks fell in. The elbow-chin jutted, and I thought I saw a sudden flare in those washed-blue eyes.
Then he lifted his glass of beer and drained it off, just drank it down in steady gulps, the wrinkled Adam's apple pumping away. He slammed the empty glass back down on the bar.
"Do me again, Jimmy," he gasped.
I nodded at the bartender, and motioned toward my own empty glass. We sat in silence. When our drinks were served, I glanced around. The bar was still empty. There were small tables for two set back in the gloom, and a few high-sided booths that could seat four.
"Why don't we make ourselves comfortable?" I suggested. "Stretch out and take it easy."
"Suits me," he grunted.
He picked up his beer and gun case, and led the way. I noticed his limp, a dragging of the right leg. He seemed active enough, but slow. He picked

a booth for four, and slid onto one of the worn benches. I sat opposite him. I held out my hand.

"Samuel Todd," I said.

"Al Coburn," he said. His handshake was dry, and not too firm. "No relation to the Todds around here, are you?"

"Don't think so, sir," I said. "I'm from Ohio."

"Never been there," he said. "Never been out of New York State, to tell the truth. Went down to the City once."

"Like it?" I asked.

"No," he said. He glanced toward the bar where Jimmy was studiously polishing glasses, not looking in our direction. "What the hell you want with Thorndecker?"

I told him what I was doing in Coburn. He nodded.

"Read about it in the papers," he said. It was almost a Bostonian accent: "pay-puh." "Think he'll get the money?"

"Not for me to say," I said, shrugging. "You know him?"

"Oh, I know him," he said bitterly. "He's living on my land."

"*Your* land?"

"Coburn land," he said. "Originally. Was still in the family when my daddy died. He left me the farm and my sister the hill." Something happened to his eyes again: that flare of fury. "I thought I got the best of the deal. It was a working farm, and all she got was uncleared woods and a stretch of swamp."

"And then?" I prompted him.

"She married a dude from Albany. Some kind of a foreigner. His name ended in 'i' or 'o'. I forget."

I looked at him. He hadn't forgotten. Would never forget.

"He talked her into selling her parcels off. To a developer. I mean, she sold the *land*. Land that daddy left her."

I watched him raise his beer to his thin lips with a shaking hand. It means that much to some of the old-timers—land. It's not the money value they cherish. It's a piece of the world.

"Then what happened?" I asked him.

"The developer drained the swamp and cleared out most of the trees. Built houses. Sold the hill to a fellow named Crittenden who built the sick place."

"Crittenden Hall," I said.

"This was in the Twenties," he said. "Before the Great Depression. Before your time, sonny. Land was selling good then. My sister did all right. Then she and her foreigner upped and moved away."

"Where are they now?"

"Who the hell knows?" he rasped. "Or cares?"

"And what happened to your farm?"

"Ahh, hell," he said heavily. "My sons didn't take to farming. They moved away. Florida, California. Then I busted up my leg and couldn't get around so good. The old woman died of the cancer. I got tenants on the land now. I get by. But that Thorndecker, he's living on Coburn land. I ain't saying it's not perfectly legal and aboveboard. I'm just saying it's Coburn land."

I nodded, and signaled Jimmy for another round. But a waitress brought our drinks. There were three customers at the bar now, and from outside, in the restaurant, I could hear the sounds of the crank-up for the luncheon rush.

"You know Dr. Thorndecker, Mr. Coburn?" I asked him. "Personally?"

"I've met him," he said shortly.

"What do you think of him?"

His flaky eyelids rose slowly. He stared at me. But he didn't answer.

"Constable Goodfellow tells me all the best people in town are behind him one hundred percent," I said, pressing him. "That's Goodfellow's phrase: 'the best people'."

"Well, I ain't one of the best people," he said, "and I wouldn't trust that quack to cut my toenails."

He was silent a moment, then said sharply, "Goodfellow? How did you meet the Indian? My great-grandpa shot Indians hereabouts."

"He says Thorndecker sent him around. To see if I was settled in, if there was anything I needed, if I wanted to meet anyone in town."

Al Coburn stared down at what was left in his glass of beer. He was quiet a long time. Then he drained his glass, climbed laboriously to his feet, picked up his gun case. I stayed where I was. He stood alongside the table, looking down at me.

"You watch your step, Sam Todd," he said in that hard, creaking, old man's voice.

"Always do," I said.

He nodded and limped away a few steps. Then he stopped, turned, came back.

"Besides," he said, "I'm guessing it wasn't Thorndecker who sent Constable Goodfellow to see you. Thorndecker may be a fraud, but he ain't stupid."

"If not Thorndecker," I asked him, "then who?"

He stared at me.

"I reckon it was that hot-pants wife of his," he said grimly.

He was silent then, just standing there staring at me. It seemed to me he was trying to decide whether or not to say more. I waited. Finally he made up his mind . . .

"You know what they're doing out there?" he demanded. "In that laboratory of theirs?"

He pronounced it almost in the British manner: la*bor*atory.

I shrugged. "Biological research," I said. "Something to do with human cells."

"Devil's work!" he burst out, so forcibly I felt the spittle on my face. "It's the devil's work!"

I sat up straight.

"What are you talking about?" I said harshly. "What does that mean—devil's work?"

"That's for me to know," he said, "and you to find out. Thank you kindly for the drinks."

He actually tipped that checked hunting cap to me. I watched him drag away.

I finished my drink, paid my tab, stalked out of the bar. That country breakfast had been enough; I didn't feel up to lunch. Went into the hotel lobby. Thumbed through magazines in a rack near the cigar counter. Waited until there were no customers. I wanted to talk to her alone.

"Hello, Millie," I said.

"Hi there!" she said, flapping her lashes like feather dusters. "Enjoying your visit to Coburn, Mr. Todd?"

So she had asked the desk clerk my name. I wondered if she had asked my room number, too.

"Lousy town," I said, watching her.

"You can say that again," she said, eyes dulling. "It died fifty years ago,

but no one has enough money to give it a decent burial. Can I help you?
Cigarettes? A magazine? *Anything?*"

She gave that "anything" the husky, Marilyn Monroe exhalation,
arching her back, pouting. God help Constable Ronnie Goodfellow.

"Just information," I told her hastily. "How do I get to Dr. Thorndecker's place? Crittenden Hall?"

I tried to listen and remember as she told me how to drive east on Main
Street, turn north on Oakland Drive, make a turn at Mike's Service Station
onto Fort Peabody Drive, etc., etc. But I was looking at her and trying to
figure why a hard, young Indian cop had married a used woman about five
years older than he, and whose idea of bliss was probably a pound box of
chocolate bonbons and the tenth rerun of "I Love Lucy."

When she ran down, I said, foolishly, "I met your husband this
morning."

"I meet him every morning," she said. Then she added, "Almost."

She stared at me, suddenly very sober, very serious. Challenging.

I tried to smile. I turned around and walked away. I didn't know if it was
good sense or cowardice. I did know I had misjudged this lady. Her idea of
bliss wasn't the boob tube and bonbons. Far from it.

I found my car in the parking area, and while it was warming up, I
scraped the ice off the windshield. Then I headed out of town.

I remember an instructor down in Ft. Benning telling us:

"You can stare at maps and aerial photos until your eyeballs are coming
out your ass. But nothing can take the place of physical reconnaissance.
Maps and photos are okay, but seeing the terrain and, if possible, walking
over it, is a thousand times better. *Learn the terrain.* Know what the hell
you're getting into. If you can walk over it before a firefight, maybe you'll
walk out of it after."

So I decided to go have a look at Dr. Telford Thorndecker's terrain.

By following Millie Goodfellow's directions, with a little surly assistance
at Mike's Service Station, I found Crittenden Hall without too much
difficulty. The grounds were less than a mile east of the river, the main
buildings on the hill that had once belonged to Al Coburn's daddy.

The approach was through an area of small farms: stubbled land and
beaten houses. Some of the barns and outbuildings showed light between
warped siding; tarpaper roofing flapped forlornly; sprained doors hung
open on rusty hinges. I saw farm machinery parked unprotected, and more
than one field unpicked, the produce left to rot. It was cold, wet, desolate.
Even more disturbing, there was no one around. I didn't see a pedestrian,
pass another car, or glimpse anyone working the land or even taking out
the garbage. The whole area seemed deserted. Like a plague had struck, or
a neutron bomb dropped. The empty, weathered buildings leaned. Stripped trees cut blackly across the pewter sky. But the people were gone. No
life. I ached to hear a dog bark.

The big sign read Crittenden Hall, and below was a small brass plaque:
Crittenden Research Laboratory. There was a handsome cast iron fence at
least six feet tall, with two ornate gates that opened inward. Inside was a
guard hut just large enough for one man to sit comfortably, feet on a gas
heater.

I drove slowly past. The ornamental iron fence became chain link, but it
entirely enclosed the Thorndecker property. Using single-lane back roads,
I was able to make a complete circuit. A lot of heavily wooded land. Some
meadows. A brook. A tennis court. A surprisingly large cemetery, well-
tended, rather attractive. People were dying to get in there. I finally saw
someone: a burly guy in black oilskins with a broken shotgun over one

arm. In his other hand was a leash. At the end of the leash, a straining German shepherd.

I came back to the two-lane macadam that ran in front of the main gate. I parked off the verge where I couldn't be seen from the guard hut. I got out, shivering, found my 7×50 field glasses in the messy trunk, got back in the car and lowered the window just enough. I had a reasonably good view of the buildings and grounds. The light was slaty, and the lens kept misting up, but I could see what I wanted to see.

I wasn't looking for anything menacing or suspicious. I just wanted to get a quick first impression. Did the buildings look in good repair? Were the grounds reasonably well-groomed? Was there an air of prosperity and good management—or was the place a dump, run-down and awaiting foreclosure?

Dr. Thorndecker's place got high marks. Not a broken window that I could see. Sashes and wooden trim smartly painted. Lawn trimmed, and dead leaves gathered. Trees obviously cared for, brick walks swept clean. Bushes and garden had been prepared for the coming winter. Storm windows were up.

All this spelled care and efficiency. It looked like a prosperous, functioning set-up with strong management that paid attention to maintenance and appearance even in this lousy weather at this time of year.

The main building, the largest building, was also, obviously, the oldest. Probably the original nursing home, Crittenden Hall. It was a three-story brick structure sited on the crest of the hill. The two-story wings were built on a slightly lower level. All outside walls were covered with ivy, still green. Roofs were tarnished copper. Windows were fitted with ornamental iron grilles, not unusual in buildings designed for the ill, infirm, aged, and/ or loony.

About halfway down the hill was a newer building. Also red brick, but no ivy. And the roof was slated. The windows were also guarded, but with no-nonsense vertical iron bars. This building, which I assumed to be the Crittenden Research Laboratory, was not as gracefully designed as Crittenden Hall; it was merely a two-story box, with mean windows and a half-hearted attempt at an attractive Georgian portico and main entrance. Between nursing home and laboratory was an outdoor walk and stairway, a roofed port set on iron pillars, without walls.

There were several smaller outbuildings which could have been kitchens, labs, storehouses, supply sheds, whatever; I couldn't even guess. But everything seemed precise, trim, clean and well-preserved.

Then why did I get such a feeling of desolation?

It might have been that joyless day, the earth still sodden, the sky pressing down. It might have been that disconsolate light. Not light at all, really, but just moist steel. Or maybe it was Coburn and my mood.

All I know is that when I put down the binoculars, I had seen nothing that could possibly count against Dr. Telford Gordon Thorndecker and his grant application to the Bingham Foundation. Yet I felt something I struggled to analyze and name.

I stared at those winter-stark buildings on the worn hill, striving to grasp what it was I felt. It came to me on the trip back to Coburn. It wasn't fear. Exactly. It was dread.

After that little jaunt to the hinterland, Coburn seemed positively sparkling. I counted at least four pedestrians on Main Street. And look! There was a dog lifting his leg at a hydrant. Marvelous!

I parked and locked the car. What I wanted right then was—oh, I could think of a lot of things I wanted: vodka gimlet. Straight cognac. Coffee and

Danish. Club sandwich and ale. Hot pastrami and Celery Tonic. Joan Powell. On rye. So I walked across Main Street to the office of the Coburn *Sentinel*.

It was a storefront with a chipped gold legend on the plate glass window: "Biggest little weekly in the State!" Just inside the door was a stained wooden counter where you could subscribe or buy a want-ad or complain your name was spelled wrong in that front-page story they did on the anniversary party at the Gulek Fat Processing Plant.

Behind the counter were a few exhausted desks, typewriters, swivel chairs. There was a small private office enclosed by frosted glass partitions. And in the rear was the printing area. Everything was ancient. Hand-set type, flatbed press. I guessed they did business cards, stationery, and fliers to pay the rent.

The place was not exactly a humming beehive of activity. There was a superannuated lady behind the counter. She was sitting on a high stool, clipping ads from old *Sentinels* with long shears. She had a bun of iron-gray hair with two pencils stuck into it. And she wore a cameo brooch at the ruffled neck of her shirtwaist blouse. She had just stepped off a *Saturday Evening Post* cover by Norman Rockwell.

Behind her, sitting at one of the weary desks, was a lissome wench. All of 18, I figured. The cheerleader type: so blond, so buxom, so healthy, so glowing that I immediately straightened my shoulders and sucked in my gut. Vanity, thy name is man. Miss Dimples was pecking away at an old Underwood standard, the tip of a pink tongue poked from one corner of her mouth. I'd have traded my Grand Prix for one—Enough. That way lies madness.

Farther to the rear, standing in front of fonts in the press section, a stringy character was setting type with all the blinding speed of a sloth on Librium. He was wearing an ink-smeared apron and one of those square caps printers fold out of newsprint. He was also wearing glasses with lenses like the bottoms of coke bottles. I wondered about the *Sentinel*'s typos per running inch . . .

That whole damned place belonged in the Smithsonian, with a neat label: "American newspaper office, circa 1930." Actually, all of Coburn belonged in the same Institution, with a similar label. Time had stopped in Coburn. I had stepped into a warp, and any minute someone was going to turn on an Atwater Kent radio, and I'd hear Gene Austin singing "My Blue Heaven."

"May I help you?" the old lady said, looking up from her clipping.

"Is the editor in, please?" I asked. "I'd like to see him."

"Her," she said. "Our editor is female. Agatha Binder."

"Pardon me," I said humbly. "Might I see Miss, Mrs., or Ms. Binder?"

"About what?" she said suspiciously. "You selling something? Or got a complaint?"

I figured the Coburn *Sentinel* got a lot of complaints.

"No, no complaints," I said. I gave her my most winning smile, with no effect whatsoever. "My name is Samuel Todd. I'm with the Bingham Foundation. I'd like to talk to your editor about Dr. Telford Thorndecker."

"Oh," she said, "*that*. Wait right here."

She slid off the stool and went trotting back into the gloomy shop. She went into the closed office. She was out in a minute, beckoning me with an imperious forefinger. I pushed through the swinging gate. On the way back, I passed the desk of the nubile cheerleader. She was still pecking away at the Underwood, tongue still poked from her mouth.

"I love you," I whispered, and she looked up in alarm.

The woman sprawled behind the littered desk in the jumbled office was about my age, and fifty pounds heavier. She was wearing ink-stained painter's overalls over a red checkerboard shirt that looked like it was made from an Italian restaurant tablecloth. Her feet were parked on the desk, in unbuckled combat boots of World War II. There was a cardboard container of black coffee on the floor alongside her, and she was working on the biggest submarine sandwich I've ever seen. Meatballs.

Everything about her was massive: head, nose, jaw, shoulders, bosom, hips, thighs. The hands that held the sub looked like picnic hams, and her wrists were as thick as my ankles. But no ogre she. It all went together, and was even pleasing in a monumental way. If they had a foothill left over from Mt. Rushmore, they could have used it for her: rugged, craggy. Even the eyes were granite, with little sparkling lights of mica.

"Miss Binder," I said.

"Todd," she said, "sit down."

I sat.

Her voice was like her body: heavy, with an almost masculine rumble. She never stopped munching away at that damned hoagie while we talked, and never stopped swilling coffee. But it didn't slow her down, and the meatballs didn't affect her diction. Much.

"Thorndecker getting his dough?" she demanded.

"That's not for me to say," I told her. How many times would I have to repeat that in Coburn? "I'm just here to do some poking. You know Thorndecker? Personally?"

"Sure, I know him. I know everyone in Coburn. He's a conceited, opinionated, sanctimonious, pompous ass. He's also the greatest brain I've ever met. So smart it scares you. He's a genius; no doubt about that."

"Ever hear any gossip about that nursing home of his? Patients mistreated? Lousy food? Things like that?"

"You kidding?" she said. "Listen, buster, I should live like Thorndecker's patients. Caviar for breakfast. First-run movies. He's got the best wine cellar in the county. And why not? They're paying for it. Listen, Todd, there are lots and lots of people in this country with lots and lots of money. The sick ones and the old ones go to Crittenden Hall to die in style—and that's what they get. I know most of the locals working up there—the aides, cooks, waitresses, and so forth. They all say the same thing: the place is a palace. If you've got to go, that's the way to do it. And when they conk off, as most of them eventually do, he even buries them, or has them cremated. At an added cost, of course."

"Yeah," I said, "I noticed the cemetery. Nice place."

"Oh?" she said. "You've visited Crittenden Hall?"

"Just a quick look," I said vaguely. "What about the research lab?"

"What about it?"

"Know anything about what they're doing up there?"

She kept masticating a meatball, but her expression changed. I mean the focus of her eyes changed, to what I call a "thousand-yard stare." Meaning she was looking at me, through me, and beyond. The same look I had seen in the eyes of the night clerk at the Coburn Inn when I had checked in and mentioned Thorndecker's name.

I had interrogated enough suspects in criminal cases in the army to know what that stare meant. It didn't necessarily mean they were lying or guilty. It usually meant they were making a decision on what and how much to reveal, and what and how much to hide. It was a signal of deep thought, calculating their own interests and culpability.

"No," she said finally. "I don't know what they're doing in the lab. Something to do with human cells and longevity. But all that scientific bullshit is beyond me."

She selected that moment to lean over and pick up her coffee cup. So I couldn't see her face, and maybe guess that she was lying?

"You know Thorndecker's family?" I asked her. "Wife? Daughter? The Son? Can you tell me anything about them?"

"The wife's less than half his age," she said. "A real beauty. She's his second wife, you know. Julie comes into town occasionally. She dresses fancy. Buys her clothes on Fifth Avenue. Not your typical Coburn housewife."

"Thinks she's superior?"

"I didn't say that," she said swiftly. "She's just not a mixer, that's all."

"She and the doctor happy?"

Again she leaned away from me. This time to set the coffee container back on the floor.

"As far as I know," she said in that deep, rumbling voice. "You really dig, don't you?"

I ignored the question.

"What about the daughter?" I asked. "Does she mix in Coburn's social life?"

"What social life?" she jeered. "Two beers at the Coburn Inn? No, I don't see much of Mary either. It's not that the Thorndeckers are standoffish, you understand, but they keep pretty much to themselves. Why the hell shouldn't they? What the fuck is there to do in this shithole?"

She peered at me, hoping I had been shocked by her language. But I had heard those words before.

"And the son?" I asked. "Edward?"

"No secret about him," she said. "He's been bounced from a couple of prep schools. Lousy grades, I understand. Now he's living at home with a private tutor to get him ready for Yale or Harvard or wherever. I met him a few times. Nice kid. Very handsome. Like his pa. But shy, I thought. Doesn't say much."

"But generally, you'd say the Thorndeckers are a close, loving American family?"

She looked at me suspiciously, wondering if I was putting her on. I was, of course, but she'd never see it in my expression.

"Well . . . sure," she said. "I suppose they've got their problems like everyone else, but there's never been any gossip or scandal, if that's what you mean."

"Julie Thorndecker," I said, "the wife . . . she's a good friend of Constable Ronnie Goodfellow?"

The combat boots came off the desk onto the floor with a crash. Agatha Binder jerked toward me. Her mouth was open wide enough so I could see a chunk of half-chewed meatball.

"Where the hell did you hear that?" she demanded.

"Around," I shrugged.

"Shit," she said, "that's just vicious gossip."

"You just said there's never been any gossip about the Thorndeckers."

She sat back, finished chewing and swallowing.

"You're a smartass, aren't you, Todd?"

I didn't answer.

She pushed the remnants of her sandwich aside. She leaned across the desk to me, ham-hands clasped. Her manner was very earnest, very sincere. Apparently she was staring directly into my eyes. But it's difficult to look steadily into someone else's eyes, even when you're telling the truth. The trick is to stare at the bridge of the nose, between the eyes. The effect is the same. I figured that's what she was doing.

"Look, buster," she said in a basso profundo rumble, "you're going to hear a lot of nasty remarks about the Thorndeckers. They're not the richest people hereabouts, but they ain't hurting. Anytime there's money, you'll hear mean, jealous gossip. Take it for what it's worth."

"All right," I said agreeably, "I will. Now how about Thorndecker's staff? I mean the top people. Know any of them?"

"I know Stella Beecham. She's an RN, supervisor of nurses and aides in Crittenden Hall. She practically runs the place. A good friend of mine. And I've met Dr. Draper. He's Thorndecker's Chief of Staff or Executive Assistant or whatever, in the research lab. I've met some of the others, but their names didn't register."

"Competent people?"

"Beecham certainly is. She's a jewel. Draper is the studious, scientific type. I've got nothing in common with him, but he's supposed to be a whiz. I guess the others in the lab are just as smart. Listen, I told you Thorndecker is a genius. He's a good administrator, too. He wouldn't hire dingbats. And the staff in the nursing home, mostly locals, do their jobs. They work hard."

"So Thorndecker's got no labor problems?"

"No way! Jobs are scarce around here, and he pays top dollar. Sick leave, pensions, paid vacation . . . the works. I'd like to work there myself."

"The hell you would," I said.

"Yeah," she said, grinning weakly. "The hell I would."

"You know Al Coburn?"

"That old fart?" she burst out. "He's been crazy as a loon since his wife died. Don't listen to anything *he* says."

"Well, I've got to listen to *someone*," I said. "Preferably someone who knows Thorndecker. Where does he bank?"

"Locally?" she said. "That would have to be the First Farmers & Merchants. The only bank in town. Around the corner on River Street. Next to the post office. The man to see is Arthur Merchant. He's president. That really is his name—Merchant. But the 'Merchants' in the bank's name has nothing to do with his. That means the bank was—"

"I get it, I get it," I assured her. "Just a fiendish coincidence. Life is full of them. Church? Is Thorndecker a church-goer?"

"He and his wife are registered Episcopalians, but they don't work at it."

"You're a walking encyclopedia of Coburn lore," I said admiringly. "You said, 'He and his wife.' What about the daughter? And the son?"

"I don't know what the hell Eddie is. A Boy Scout, I suspect."

"And the daughter? Mary?"

"Well . . ." she said cautiously. "Uh . . ."

"Uh?" I said. "What does 'Uh' mean?"

She punched gently at the tip of her nose with a knuckle.

"What the hell has that got to do with whether or not Dr. Thorndecker gets a grant from the Bingham Foundation?"

"Probably not a thing," I admitted. "But I'm a nosy bastard."

"You sure as hell are," she grumbled. "Well, if you must know, I heard Mary Thorndecker goes to a little church about five miles south of here. It's fundamentalist. Evangelical. You know—being born again, and all that crap. They wave their arms and shout, 'Yes, Lord!' "

"And speak in tongues," I said.

She looked at me curiously.

"You're not so dumb, are you?" she said.

"Dumb," I said, "but not so." I paused a moment, pondering. "Well, I can't think of anything else to ask. I want to thank you for your kind cooperation. You've been a big help."

"I have?" she said, surprised. "That's nice. I hope I've helped Thorndecker get his bread. He deserves it, and it would be a great help to this town."

"So I've heard," I said. "Listen, if I come up with any more questions, can I come around again?"

"Often as you like," she said, rising. I stood up too, and saw she was almost as tall as I am. A *big* woman. "Go see Art Merchant at the bank. He'll tell you anything you want to know. By the way, he's also mayor of Coburn."

"Fantastic," I said.

We were standing there, shaking hands and smiling idiotically at each other, when there was a timid knock on the door.

"Come in," Agatha Binder roared, dropping my hand.

The door opened hesitantly. There was my very own Miss Dimples. She looked even better standing up. Miniskirt. Yummy knees. Black plastic boots. A buttery angora sweater. I remembered an old army expression: "All you need with a dame like that is a spoon and a straw." She was holding a sheaf of yellow copy paper.

"Yes, Sue Ann?" the *Sentinel* editor said.

"I've finished the Kenner funeral story, Miss Binder," the girl faltered.

"Very good, Sue Ann. Just leave it. I'll get to it this afternoon."

The cheerleader dropped the copy on the desk and exited hastily, closing the door behind her. She hadn't glanced at me, but Agatha Binder was staring at me shrewdly.

"Like that?" she asked softly.

"It's okay," I said, flipping a palm back and forth. "Not sensational, but okay."

"Hands off, kiddo," she said in a harder voice, eyes glittering. "It's mine."

I was glad to hear it. I felt better immediately. The sensation of Coburn being in a time warp disappeared. I was back in the 1970s, and I walked out of there with my spirit leaping like a demented hart.

When I strolled into the lobby of the Coburn Inn, the baldy behind the desk signaled frantically.

"Where have you been?" he said in an aggrieved tone.

"Sorry I didn't check in," I said. "Next time I'll bring a note from home."

But he wasn't listening.

"Dr. Thorndecker has called you *three* times," he said. "He wants you to call him back as soon as possible. Here's the number."

Upstairs in my room, I peeled off the trenchcoat, kicked off the boots. I lay back on the hard bed. The telephone was on the rickety bedside table. Calls went through the hotel switchboard. I gave the number and waited.

"Crittenden Hall."

"Dr. Thorndecker, please. Samuel Todd calling."

"Just a moment, please."

Click, click, click.

"Crittenden Research Laboratory."

"Dr. Thorndecker, please. Samuel Todd calling."

"Just a moment, please."

Click, click, click.

"Lab."

"Dr. Thorndecker, please. Samuel Todd calling."

No clicks this time; just, "Hang on."

"Mr. Todd?"

"Yes, Dr. Thorndecker?"

"No. I'm sorry, Mr. Todd, but Dr. Thorndecker can't come to the phone at the moment. I'm Dr. Kenneth Draper, Dr. Thorndecker's assistant. How are you, sir?"

It was a postnasal-drip kind of voice: stuffed, whiny, without resonance.

"If I felt any better I'd be unconscious, thank you. I have a message to call Dr. Thorndecker."

"I know, sir. He's been trying to reach you all afternoon, but at the moment he's involved in a critical experiment."

I was trying to take my socks off with my toes.

"So am I," I said.

"Pardon, sir?"

"Childish humor. Forget it."

"Dr. Thorndecker asks if you can join the family for dinner tonight. Here at Crittenden Hall. Cocktails at six, dinner at seven."

"Be delighted," I said. "Thank you."

"Do you know how to get here, Mr. Todd? You drive east on Main Street, then—"

"I'll find it," I said hastily. "See you tonight. Thank you, Dr. Draper."

I hung up, and took off my socks the conventional way. I lay back on the bed, figuring to grab a nap for an hour or so, then get up and shower, shave, dress. But sleep wouldn't come. My mind was churning.

You've probably heard the following exchange on a TV detective drama, or read it in a detective novel:

Police Sergeant: "That guy is guilty as hell."

Police Officer: "Why do you say that?"

Police Sergeant: "Gut instinct."

Sometimes the sergeant says, "Gut feeling" or "A hunch." But the implication is that he's had an intuitive feeling, almost a subconscious inspiration, that has revealed the truth.

I asked an old precinct dick about this, and he said: "Bullshit."

Then he said: "Look, I don't deny that you get a gut feeling or a hunch about some cases, but it doesn't just appear out of nowhere. You get a hunch, and if you sit down and analyze it, you discover that what it is, is a logical deduction based on things you know, things you've heard, things you've seen. I mean that 'gut feeling' they're always talking about is really based on hard evidence. Instinct has got nothing to do with it."

I didn't have a gut feeling or a hunch about this Thorndecker investigation. What I had was more like a vague unease. So I started to analyze it, trying to discover what hard evidence had triggered it, and why it was spoiling my nap. My list went like this:

1. When a poor wife is killed accidentally, people cluck twice and say, "What a shame." When a rich wife is killed accidentally, people cluck once, say "What a shame," and raise an eyebrow. Thorndecker's first wife left him a mil and turned his life around.

2. Thorndecker had released the story of his application for a Bingham Foundation grant to the local press. It wasn't unethical, but it was certainly unusual. I didn't buy Constable Goodfellow's story that it was impossible to keep a secret like that in a small town. Thorndecker could have prepared the application himself, or with the help of a single discreet aide,

and no one in Coburn would have known a thing about it. So he had a motive for giving the story to the Coburn *Sentinel*. To rally the town on his side, knowing there'd be a field investigation?

3. Someone dispatched an armed cop to welcome me to Coburn. That was a dumb thing to do. Why not greet me in person or send an assistant? I didn't understand Goodfellow's role at all.

4. Al Coburn might have been an "old fart" to Agatha Binder but I thought he was a crusty old geezer with all his marbles. So why had he said, "You watch your step, Sam Todd?" Watch my step for *what?* And what the hell was that "devil's work" he claimed they were doing in the research lab?

5. Agatha Binder had called Thorndecker a "pompous ass" and put on a great show of being a tough, cynical newspaper editor. But she had been careful not to say a thing that might endanger the Bingham grant. Her answers to my questions were a beautiful example of manipulation, except when she blew her cool at my mention of the Julie Thorndecker-Ronnie Goodfellow connection. What the hell was going on *there?*

6. And while I was what-the-helling, just what the hell were Crittenden Hall (a nursing home) and the research laboratory doing with an armed guard and an attack dog patrolling the grounds? To make sure no one escaped from the cemetery?

7. That anonymous note: "Thorndecker kills."

Those were most of the reasons I could list for my "gut instinct" that all was not kosher with Dr. Thorndecker's application. There were a few other little odds and ends. Like Mrs. Cynthia's comment in the corridor of the Bingham Foundation: "I knew his father . . . it was all so sad . . . A sweet man." And the fact that the Crittenden Research Laboratory was supported, in part, by bequests from deceased patients of Crittenden Hall.

I agree that any or all of these questions might have had a completely innocent explanation. But they nagged, and kept me from sleeping. Finally, I got up, dug my case notebook from my suitcase, and jotted them all down, more or less in the form you just read.

They were even more disturbing when I saw them in writing. Something about this whole business reeketh in the nostrils of a righteous man (me), and I didn't have a clue to what it was. So I solved the whole problem in my usual decisive, determined manner.

I shaved, showered, dressed, went down to the bar, and had two vodka gimlets.

I started out for Crittenden Hall about five-thirty. At that time of year it was already dark, and once I got beyond the misty, haloed street lights on Coburn, the blackness closed in. I was falling down a pit, and my low beams couldn't show the end of it. Naked tree trunks whipped by, a stone embankment, culvert, a plank bridge. But I kept falling, leaning forward over the steering wheel and bracing for the moment when I hit bottom.

I never did, of course. Instead of the bottom of the pit, I found Crittenden Hall, and pulled up to those ornate gates. The guard came ambling out of his hut and put a flashlight on me. I shouted my name, he swung the gates open, I drove in. The iron clanged shut behind me.

I followed the graveled roadway. It curved slowly through lawn that was black on this moonless night. The road ended in a generous parking area in front of Crittenden Hall. As I was getting out of the car, I saw portico lights come on. The door opened, someone stepped out.

I paused a moment. I was in front of the center portion of the main building, the old building. The two wings stretched away in the darkness. At close range, the Hall was larger than I expected: a high three stories,

mullioned windows, cornices of carved stone. The style was vaguely
Georgian, with faint touches—like narrow embrasures—of a castle to
withstand Saracen archers.

A lady came forward as I trudged up to the porch. She was holding out a
white hand, almost covered by the ruffled lace cuff of her gown.

"Welcome to Crittenden, Mr. Todd," she said, smiling stiffly. "I'm Mary
Thorndecker."

While I was shaking the daughter's cold hand and murmuring something
I forget, I was taking her in. She was Alice in Wonderland's maiden aunt in
a daisied gown designed by Tenniel. I mean it billowed to her ankles, all
ribbons and bows. The high, ruffled collar matched the lace cuffs. The
waist was loosely crumpled with a wide velvet ribbon belt. If Mary
Thorndecker had breasts, hips, ass, they were effectively concealed.

Inside the Hall, an attendant came forward to take my hat and coat. He
was wearing a short, white medical jacket and black trousers. He might
have been a butler, but he was built like a linebacker. When he turned
away from me, I caught the bulge in his hip pocket. This bucko was
carrying a sap. All right, I'll go along with that in an establishment where
some of the guests were not too tightly wrapped.

"Now this is the main floor," Mary Thorndecker was babbling away,
"and in the rear are the dining room, kitchen, social rooms, and so forth.
The library, card room, and indoor recreational area. All used by our
guests. Their private suites, the medical rooms, the doctors' offices and
nurses' lounges, and so forth, are in the wings. We're going up to the
second floor. That's where we live. Our private home. Living room, dining
room, our own kitchen, daddy's study, sitting room . . . all that."

"And the third floor?" I inquired politely.

"Bedrooms," she said, frowning, as if someone had uttered a dirty word.

It was a handsome staircase, curving gracefully, with a gleaming carved
oak balustrade. The walls were covered with ivory linen. I expected
portraits of ancestors in heavy gilt frames. At least a likeness of the original
Mr. Crittenden. But instead, the wall alongside the stairway was hung with
paintings of flowers in thin black frames. All kinds of flowers: peonies,
roses, poppies, geraniums, lilies . . . everything.

The paintings blazed with fervor. I paused to examine an oil of lilac
branches in a clear vase.

"The paintings are beautiful," I said, and I meant it.

Mary Thorndecker was a few steps ahead of me, higher than me. She
stopped suddenly, whirled to look down.

"Do you think so?" she said breathlessly. "Do you *really* think so?
They're mine. I mean I painted them. You *do* like them?"

"Magnificent," I assured her. "Bursting with life."

Her long, saturnine face came alive. Cheeks flushed. Thin lips curved in
a warm smile. The dark eyes caught fire behind steel-rimmed granny
glasses.

"Thank you," she said tremulously. "Oh, thank you. Some people . . ."

She left that unfinished, and we continued our climb in silence. On the
second floor landing, a man stumbled forward, hand outstretched. His
expression was wary and hunted.

"Yes, Mary," he said automatically. Then: "Samuel Todd? I'm Kenneth
Draper, Dr. Thorndecker's assistant. This is a . . ."

He left that sentence unfinished, too. I wondered if that was the
conversational style in Crittenden Hall: half-sentences, unfinished
thoughts, implied opinions.

Agatha Binder had said Draper was a "studious, scientific type . . .

supposed to be a whiz." He might have been. He was also a nervous, jerky type . . . supposed to be a nut. He shook hands and wouldn't let go; he giggled inanely when I said, "Happy to meet you," and he succeeded in walking up my heels when he ushered me into the living room of the Thorndeckers' private suite.

I got a quick impression of a high vaulted room richly furnished, lots of brocades and porcelains, a huge marble-framed fireplace with a blaze crackling. And I was ankledeep in a buttery rug. That's all I had a chance to catch before Draper was nudging me forward to the two people seated on a tobacco-brown suede couch facing the fireplace.

Edward Thorndecker lunged to his feet to be introduced. He was 17, and looked 12, a young Botticelli prince. He was all blue eyes and crisp black curls, with a complexion so enameled I could not believe he had ever shaved. The hand he proffered was soft as a girl's, and about as strong. There was something in his voice that was not quite a lisp. He did not say, "Pleathed to meet you, Mithter Todd," it was not that obvious, but he did have trouble with his sibilants. It made no difference. He could have been a mute, and still stagger you with his physical beauty.

His stepmother was beautiful, too, but in a different way. Edward had the beauty of youth; nothing in his smooth, flawless face marked experience or the passage of years. Julie Thorndecker had stronger features, and part of her attraction was due to artifice. If Mary Thorndecker found inspiration for her art in flowers, Julie found it in herself.

I remember well that first meeting. Initially, all I could see were the satin evening pajamas, the color of fresh mushrooms. Full trousers and a tunic cinched with a mocha sash. The neckline plunged, and there was something in that glittery, slithery costume that convinced me she was naked beneath, and if I listened intently I might hear the whispery slide of soft satin on softer flesh. She was wearing high-heeled evening sandals, thin ribbons of silver leather. Her bare toes were long, the nails painted a crimson as dark as old blood. There was a slave bracelet of fine gold links around one slender ankle.

I was ushered to an armchair so deep I felt swallowed. Mary Thorndecker and Dr. Draper found chairs—close to each other, I noted—and there was a spate of fast, almost feverish small talk. Most of it consisted of questions directed at me. Yes, I had driven up from New York. Yes, Coburn seemed a quiet, attractive village. No, I had no idea how long I'd stay—a few days perhaps. My accommodations at the Inn were certainly not luxurious, but they were adequate. Yes, the food was exceptionally good. No, I had not yet met Art Merchant. Yes, it had certainly been a terrible storm, with all the lights off and power lost. I said:

"But I suppose you have emergency generators, don't you, Dr. Draper?"

"What?" he said, startled at being addressed. "Oh, yes, of course we do."

"Naturally," I nodded. "I imagine you have valuable cultures in the lab under very precise temperature control."

"We certainly do," he said enthusiastically. "Why, if we lost refrigeration even for—"

"Oh, Kenneth, please," Julie Thorndecker said lazily. "No shop talk tonight. Just a social evening. Wouldn't you prefer that, Mr. Todd?"

I remember bobbing my head violently in assent, but I was too stunned by her voice to make any sensible reply.

It was a husky voice, throaty, almost tremulous, with a kind of crack as if it was changing. It was a different voice, a stirring voice, an adorable voice.

It made me want to hear her murmur and whisper. Just the thought of it rattled my vertebrae.

Before I had a chance to make a fool of myself by asking her to read aloud from the Coburn telephone directory, I was saved by the entrance of the gorilla who had taken my hat and coat. He was pushing a wheeled cart laden with ice bucket, bottles, mixes, glasses.

"Daddy will be along in a few minutes," Mary Thorndecker told us all. "He said to start without him."

That was fine with me; I needed something. Preferably two somethings. I was conscious of currents in that room: loves, animosities, personal conflicts that I could only guess from glances, tones of voice, turned shoulders, and sudden changes of expression I could not fathom.

Julie and Edward Thorndecker each took a glass of white wine. Mary had a cola drink. Dr. Draper asked for a straight bourbon, which brought a look of sad reproof from Mary. Not seeing any lime juice on the cart, I opted for a vodka martini and watched the attendant mix it. He slugged me—a double, at least—and I wondered if those were his instructions.

While drinks were being served, I had a chance to make a closer inspection of the room from the depths of my feather bed. My first impression was reinforced: it was a glorious chamber. The overstuffed furniture was covered with brown leather, beige linen, chocolate velvet. Straight chairs and tables were blond French provincial, and looked to me to be antiques of museum quality. There was a cocktail table of brass and smoked glass, the draperies were batik, and the unframed paintings on the walls were abstracts in brilliant primary colors.

In the hands of a decorator of glitchy taste, this eclecticism would have been a disaster. But it all came together; it pleased the eye and was comfortable to a sinful degree. Part of the appeal, I decided, was due to the noble proportions of the room itself, with its high ceiling and the perfect ratio between length and width. There are some rooms that would satisfy even if they were empty, and this was one of them.

I said something to this effect, and Julie and Edward exchanged congratulatory smiles. If it was their taste reflected here, their gratification was warranted. But I saw Mary Thorndecker's lips tighten slightly—just a prim pressing together—and I began to glimpse the outlines of the family feuds.

We were on our second round—the talk louder now, the laughs more frequent—when the hall door banged open, and Dr. Telford Gordon Thorndecker swept into the room. There's no other phrase for it: he swept in, the President arriving at the Oval Office. Dr. Kenneth Draper jerked to his feet. Edward stood up slowly. I struggled out of my down cocoon, and even Mary Thorndecker rose to greet her father. Only Julie remained seated.

"Hello, hello, hello, all," he said briskly, and I was happy to note I had been correct: it was a rumbling baritone, with deep resonance. "Sorry I'm late. A minor crisis. Very minor! Darling . . ." He swooped to kiss his young wife's cheek. "And you must be Samuel Todd of the Bingham Foundation. Welcome to Crittenden. This *is* a pleasure. Forgive me for not greeting you personally, but I see you've been well taken care of. Excellent! Excellent! How are you, Mr. Todd? A small scotch for me, John. Well, here we are! This *is* nice."

I've seen newsreels of President Franklin Roosevelt, and this big man had the same grinning vitality, the energy, and raw exuberance of Roosevelt. I've met politicians, generals, and business executives, and I don't impress easily. But Thorndecker overwhelmed me. When he spoke to you, he gave the impression of speaking only to *you*, and not talking just to hear the sound of his own voice. When he asked a question, he made you feel he was genuinely interested in your opinion, he was hanging on your every word, and if he disagreed, he still respected your intelligence and sincerity.

The photograph I had seen of him was a good likeness; he was a handsome man. But the black-and-white glossy hadn't prepared me for the physical presence. All I could think of was that he was smarter, better looking, and stronger than I was. But I didn't resent it. That was his peculiar gift: your admiration was never soured with envy. How could you envy or be jealous of an elemental force?

He took command immediately. We were to finish our drinks at once, and file into the dining room. This is how we'd be seated, this is what we'd eat, these were the wines we'd find superb, and so forth. And all this without the touch of the Obersturmführer. He commanded with humor, a self-deprecating wit, and a cheerful willingness to bend to anyone's whims, no matter how eccentric he found them.

If the table in the rather gloomy dining room had been set to make an impression on me, it did. Pewter serving plates, four crystal wine glasses and goblets at each setting, a baroque silver service, fresh flowers, slender white tapers in a cast iron candelabrum.

I sat on Thorndecker's right. Next to me was Dr. Draper. Julie was at the foot of the table. On her right was Edward, and across from me was Mary, on Thorndecker's left. Cozy.

The moment we were seated, two waitresses with starched white aprons over staid black dresses appeared and began serving. We had smoked salmon with chopped onion and capers; a lobster bisque; an enormous Beef Wellington carved at the table; a potato dish that seemed to be mixed tiny balls of white and sweet potatoes, boiled and then sautéed in seasoned butter; fresh green beans; buttered baby carrots; endive salad with hearts of palm; raspberry sherbet; espresso or regular coffee.

I've had better meals, but never in a private home. If the beans were overcooked and the crust of the Wellington a bit soggy, it could be forgiven or forgotten for the sake of the wines Thorndecker uncorked and the efficiency of the service. Every time my wine glass got down to the panic level, one of the waitresses or the gorilla-butler was at my elbow to refill it. Hot rolls and sweet butter were passed incessantly. It seemed to me that I had only to wish another spoonful of those succulent potatoes, when presto! they appeared on my plate.

"Do your patients eat as well?" I asked Thorndecker.

"Better," he assured me, smiling. "We have one old lady who regularly imports truffles from the south of France. Two years ago we had an old gentleman who brought along his private chef. That man—the chef, I mean—was a genius. A genius! I tried to hire him, but he refused to cook for more than four at a time."

"What happened to him?" I asked. "Not the chef, the old gentleman."

"Deceased," Thorndecker said easily. "Are you enjoying the dinner?"

"Very much so," I said.

"Really?" he said, looking into my eyes. "I thought the beans over-cooked and the Wellington crust a bit soggy. Delighted to hear I was wrong."

The conversation was dominated by Dr. Thorndecker. Maybe "directed" is a better word, because he spoke very little himself. But he questioned his children and wife about their activities during the day, made several wry comments on their reports, asked them about their plans for the following day. I had a sense of custom being honored, a nightly interrogation. If Thorndecker had planned to present a portrait of domestic felicity, he succeeded admirably.

Between courses, and during Thorndecker's quizzing, I had an opportunity to observe the ménage more closely. I picked up some interesting impressions to store away, for mulling later.

Edward Thorndecker had been reasonably alert and cheerful prior to his father's appearance; after, he became subdued, somewhat sullen.

Julie wore her hair cut quite short. It was fine, silvered, brushed close to her skull. It appeared to be an extension of her satin pajamas, as if she was wearing a helmet of the same material.

Dr. Kenneth Draper drank too much wine too rapidly, looking up frequently to Mary Thorndecker to see if she was noticing.

Thorndecker himself had a remarkably tanned face. At that time of year, it was either pancake makeup or regular use of a suntan lamp. When I caught him in profile, it suddenly occurred to me he might have had a face-lifting.

The servants were efficient, but unsmiling. Conversations between servants and family were kept to a minimum. Instructions for serving were given by Mary Thorndecker. I had the oddest notion that she was mistress of the house. In fact, on appearance alone, she could have been Thorndecker's wife, and Julie and Edward their children.

Thorndecker's pleasantness had its limits; his elbow was joggled by one of the waitresses, and I caught the flash of anger in his eyes. I didn't hear what he muttered to her.

After his fourth glass of wine, Dr. Draper stared at Mary Thorndecker with what I can only describe as hopeless passion. I was convinced the poor mutt was smitten by her charms. What they were escaped me.

I wondered if Julie and Edward Thorndecker were holding hands under the tablecloth, improbable as that seemed.

Dr. Thorndecker was wearing a cologne or after-shave lotion that I found fruity and slightly sickening.

Mary Thorndecker, with her thin, censorious lips, seemed disapproving of this flagrant display of rich food and strong drink. She ate sparingly, drank nothing but mineral water. Very admirable, even if it was imported water.

Julie was a gamine, with an inexhaustible supply of expressions: pouts, smiles, moues, frowns, grins, leers. In repose, her face was a beautifully tinted mask, triangular, with high cheekbones and stung lips. Occasionally she bit the full lower lip with her sharp upper teeth, a stimulating sight.

Never once during the meal did Mary address Julie directly, or vice versa. In fact, they both seemed to avoid looking at each other.

That was about all I was able to observe and remember. It was enough.

I was on my second cup of espresso, replete and wondering how I might cadge a brandy, when the butler-gorilla entered hurriedly. He went directly to Dr. Kenneth Draper, leaned down, whispered in his ear. I saw this happen. I saw Draper's Bordeaux-flushed cheeks go suddenly white. He looked to Dr. Thorndecker. If a signal passed between them, I didn't catch it. But Draper rose immediately, weaving slightly. He excused himself, thanking the Thorndeckers for the "'nificent dinner," addressing himself to Mary. Then he was gone, and no one commented on it.

"A brandy, Mr. Todd?" Telford Thorndecker sang out. "Cognac? Armagnac? I have a calvados I think you'll like. Let's all move back to the living room and give them a chance to clean up in here and get home at a reasonable hour. All right, everyone . . . up and out!"

We straggled back into the living room: Julie, Edward, Thorndecker, me. Mary stayed behind, for housewifely chores I suppose. Maybe to make sure that no one swagged a slice of that soggy Beef Wellington.

The calvados was good. Not great, but good. Julie took a thimbleful of green Chartreuse. Edward got a stick in the eye.

"Don't you have homework to do, young man?" Thorndecker demanded sternly.

"Yes, father," the youth said. A crabbed voice, surly manner.

But he said his goodnights politely enough, kissing his stepmother and father, on their cheeks, offering me his limp hand again. We watched him leave.

"Good-looking boy," I offered.

"Yes," Thorndecker said shortly. "Now take a look at this, Mr. Todd. I think you'll be interested."

We left Julie curved felinely in a corner of the suede couch, running a tongue tip around the rim of her liqueur glass. Thorndecker showed me a small collection of eighteenth-century miniatures, portraits painted on thin slices of ivory. I admired those, and Sevres porcelains, a beautifully crafted antique microscope in gleaming brass, a set of silver-mounted flintlock duelling pistols, an ornate Italian mantel clock that showed the time of day, date, phases of the moon, constellations, tides and, for all I know, when to take the meatloaf out of the oven.

Thorndecker's attitude toward these treasures was curious. He knew the provenance of everything he owned. He was proud of them. But I don't think he really *liked* them. They were valuable possessions, and fulfilled some desire he had to surround himself with beautiful things of value. He could have collected Duesenbergs or rare Phoenician coins. It would be all the same to him.

"It's a magnificent room," I told him.

"Yes," he said, nodding, looking about, "yes, it is. A few pieces I inherited. But Julie selected most of them. She decorated this room. She and Edward. It's what I've wanted all my life. A room like this."

I said nothing.

We strolled back to his wife. She rose as we approached, finishing her Chartreuse, set the empty glass on the serving cart. Then she did an incredible thing.

She lifted her slender arms high above her head and stretched wide, yawning. I looked at her with amazement. She was a small, perfectly formed woman: a cameo body. She stood there, weight on one leg, hip-sprung, her feet apart. Her head was back, throat taut, mouth yawned open, lips wet and glistening.

Thorndecker and I stood there, frozen, staring at the strained torso, hard nipples poking the shining stuff. Then she relaxed, smiling at me.

"Please forgive me," she said in that throaty voice. "The wine . . . I think I'll run along to bed."

We exchanged pleasantries. I briefly held the sinewy hand she offered.

"Don't be long, darling," she said to her husband, drawing fingertips down his cheek.

"I—I—I won't," he stammered, completely undone.

We watched her sway from the room. The gleaming satin rippled.

"Another calvados?" Thorndecker said hoarsely.

"Another drink, thank you," I said. "But I see you have cognac there. I'd prefer that, if I may, sir."

"Of course, of course," he muttered.

"Then I'll be on my way," I promised him. "I'm sure you have a full day tomorrow."

"Not at all," he said dully, and poured us drinks.

We sat on the suede couch, staring into dying embers.

"I suppose you'll want to see the place?" he said.

"I would, yes," I acknowledged. "The nursing home and the lab."

"Tomorrow morning? And stay for lunch?"

"Oh no," I said. "Not after that dinner! I'll skip lunch tomorrow. Would—oh, say about one o'clock be convenient? I have things to do in the morning."

"One o'clock would be fine," he said. "I may not be able to show you around myself, but I'll tell Draper to be available. He'll show you everything. I'll make that very clear. Anything and everything you want to see."

"Thank you, sir," I said.

We were turned half-sideways to converse. Now his heavy eyes rose to lock with mine.

"You don't have to call me 'sir'," he said.

"All right," I said equably.

"If you have any questions, Draper will answer them. If he can't, I will."

"Fine."

Pause, while we both sipped our drinks daintily.

"Of course," he said, "you may have some personal questions for me."

I considered a moment.

"No," I said, "I don't think so."

He seemed surprised at that. And maybe a little disappointed.

"I mean about my personal life," he explained. "I know how these grant investigations work. You want to know all about me."

"We know a great deal about you now, Dr. Thorndecker," I said, as gently as I could.

He sighed, and seemed to shrivel, hunching down on the couch. He looked every one of his 54 years. Suddenly I realized what it was: this man was physically tired. He was bone-weary. All the youthful vigor had leaked out of him. He had put in a strenuous, stressful day, and he wanted nothing more at this point than to crawl into bed next to his warm, young wife, melt down beneath the covers, and sleep. To tell you the truth, I felt much the same myself.

"I suppose," he said, ruminating in a low voice, "I suppose you find it odd that a man my age would have a wife young enough to be my daughter. Younger than my daughter."

"Not odd," I said. "Understandable. Maybe fifty, or even thirty or twenty years ago, it would have been considered odd. But not today. New forms of relationships. The old prejudices out the window. It's a whole new ballgame."

But he wasn't listening to my cracker-barrel philosophy.

"She means so much to me," he said wonderingly. "So much. You have no idea how she has made—"

His confessions disturbed me and embarrassed me. I drained my drink and stood up.

"Dr. Thorndecker," I said formally, "I want to thank you and your wife and your family for your gracious hospitality. A very pleasant evening, and I hope we—"

But at that precise instant the hall door was flung open. Dr. Kenneth Draper stood rooted. He was wearing a stained white lab coat. He had jerked his tie loose and opened his collar. His eyes were blinking furiously, and I wondered if he was about to cry.

"Dr. Thorndecker," he said desperately, "please, can you come? At once? It's Petersen."

Thorndecker finished his drink slowly, set the glass slowly aside. Now he looked older than his 54 years. He looked defeated.

"Do you mind?" he asked me. "A patient with problems. I'm afraid he won't last the night. We'll do what we can."

"Of course," I said. "You go ahead. I can find my way out. Thank you again, doctor."

We shook hands. He smiled stiffly, moved brokenly to the door. He and Draper disappeared. I was alone. So, what the hell, I poured myself another small brandy and slugged it down. I took a final look around that splendid room and then wandered out onto the second floor landing. In truth, I was feeling no pain.

I had taken one step down the stairway when I heard the sound of running feet behind me. I turned. Mary Thorndecker came dashing up.

"Take this," she said breathlessly. "Don't look at it now. Read it later."

She thrust a folded paper into my hand, whirled, darted away, the long calico gown snapping about her ankles. I wondered if she was heading for a brisk run through the heather, shouting, "Heathcliff! Heathcliff!"

I stuffed the folded paper into my side pocket. I walked down that long, long stairway as erect and dignified as I could make it. The butler-gorilla was waiting below with my coat and hat.

"Nighty-night," I said.

"Yeah," he said.

I drove slowly, very, very slowly, around the graveled road to the gates. They opened magically for me. I turned onto the paved road, went a few hundred yards, then pulled off onto the verge. I switched off engine and lights. It was raw as hell, and I huddled down inside my leather trenchcoat and wished I had a small jug of brandy to keep me alive. But all I could do was wait. So I waited. Don't ask me what I was waiting for; I didn't know. Maybe I figured it was best not to drive on unfamiliar roads in my condition. Maybe I was just sleepy. I don't know what my motives were; I'm just telling you what happened.

The cold woke me up. I snapped out of my daze, shivering. I glanced at the luminous dial of my watch; it was almost 2:00 A.M. I had left Crittenden Hall before midnight. Now I was sober, with a headache that threatened to break down the battlements of my skull. I lighted a cigarette and tried to remember if I had misbehaved during the evening, insulted anyone, done anything to besmirch the Bingham Foundation escutcheon. I couldn't think of a thing. Other than developing an enormous lech for Julie Thorndecker—which no one could possibly be aware of, except, perhaps, Julie Thorndecker—I had conducted myself in exemplary fashion as far as I could recall.

I was leaning forward to snub out my cigarette when I saw the lights. One, two, three of them, bobbing in line from the rear of Crittenden Hall, heading out into the pitchy grounds.

I slid from the car, leaving the door open. I went loping along outside the chain-link fence, trying to keep the lights in view. They moved up and down in a regular rhythm: marching men carrying flashlights or battery lanterns.

The fence curved around. I ran faster to catch up, happy that whoever had planned the security of Crittenden had cleared the land immediately outside the fence. No bushes, no trees. I was running on half-frozen stubble, the ground resisting, then squishing beneath my feet.

I came up to them, raised a hand to shield my mouth so they might not spot the white vapor of my breath. Another light came on, a more powerful lantern. I moved along with them, hanging back a little, the fence between us, and the bare trees on the Crittenden grounds.

Four men, at least. Then, in the lantern's beam, I saw more. Six men, heavily muffled against the cold. Three of them were hauling a wheeled cart. And on the cart, a black burden, a bulk, a box, a coffin.

When they stopped, I stopped. Crouched down. Lay down on the frost-silvered grass. The beams of flashlights and lanterns concentrated. I could see an open grave. A mound of loose earth at one side. I had not seen that during my afternoon reconnaissance.

The load was taken off the cart. A plain box. I could hear the grunts of the lifting men from where I lay. The coffin was slid into the open hole. One end first, and then it was dropped and allowed to thump to the bottom. Shovels had been brought. Two men attacked the mound of loose dirt, working slowly but steadily. The first few shovelfuls rattled on the coffin lid. Then, as the grave filled, they worked in silence. All I could see were the steady beams of light, the lifting, swinging, dumping shovels. Then the flash of empty shovel blades.

The grave was filled, the loose earth smacked down and rounded. Squares of sod were placed over the raw dirt. Then the procession, still silent, turned back to Crittenden Hall. I watched them go, knowing a chill without, a chill within. The lights bobbed slowly away. They went out, one by one.

I lay there as long as I could endure it, teeth making like castanets, feet and hands lumpy and dull. Then I made a run for my car, hobbling along as fast as I could, trying to flex my fingers, afraid to feel my nose in case it had dropped off.

I got the heater going, held my hands in front of the vents, and in a few minutes reckoned I'd live to play the violin again. I drove away from there at a modest speed, hoping the gate guard and roving night sentinel (if there was one) wouldn't spot my lights.

I told myself that both Thorndecker and Draper were licensed MD's, and could sign a death certificate. I told myself that one of the shrouded figures with flashlight or lantern could have been a licensed mortician. I told myself all sorts of nonsense. The cadaver was infected with a deadly plague and had to be put underground immediately. Or, all burials were made at this hour so as not to disturb the other withering guests at Crittenden Hall. Or, the dead man or woman was without funds, without family, without friends, and this surreptitious entombment was a discreet way of putting a pauper to rest.

I didn't believe a word of it. Of any of it. That slow procession of shadowed figures and bobbing lights scared the hell out of me. I had a wild notion of giving Dr. Telford Gordon Thorndecker an A-plus rating and, as quickly as possible, getting my ass back to the familiar violence of New York City. A dreadful place with one saving grace: the dead were buried during daylight hours.

The lobby of the Coburn Inn did nothing to lift my spirits or inspire confidence in a better tomorrow. It was almost three in the morning; only a night light on the desk shed a ghastly, orange-tinted glow. The place was totally empty. I guessed the night clerk was snoozing in the back office, and Sam Livingston was corking off in his basement hideaway.

I looked around at the slimy tiled floor, the shabby rugs, the tattered couches and armchairs. Even the plastic ferns in the old brass spittoons seemed wilted. And over all, the smell of must and ash, the stink of age and decay. The Coburn Inn: Reasonable Rates and Instant Senescence.

I didn't have the heart to wake Sam Livingston to run me up, so I trudged the stairway, still bone-chilled, muscle-sore, brain-dulled. I got to room 3-F all right, seeing not a soul in the shadowed corridors. But there was enough illumination to see that the door of my room was open a few inches. I had left it locked.

Adrenaline flowed; I moved cautiously. The room was dark. I kicked the door open wider, reached around, flicked the light switch. Someone had paid me a visit. My suitcases and briefcase had been upended, contents dumped on the floor. The few things I had stowed away in closet and bureaus had been pulled out and trashed. Even my toilet articles had been pawed over. The mattress on that hard bed had been lifted and tipped. Chairs were lying on their sides, the bottom coverings slit, and the few miserable prints on the walls had been taken off their hooks and the paper backing ripped away.

I made a quick check. As far as I could see, nothing was missing. Even my case notebook was intact. My wallet of credit cards was untouched. So why the toss? I gave up trying to figure it, or anything else that had happened that black night. All I wanted was sleep.

I restored the bed to reasonable order, but left all the rest of the stuff exactly where it was, on the floor. I started undressing then, so weary that I was tempted to flop down with my boots on. It was when I was taking off my jacket that I found, in the side pocket, the folded paper that Mary Thorndecker had slipped me just before I left Crittenden Hall.

I unfolded it gingerly, like it might be a letter bomb. But it was only a badly printed religious tract, one of those things handed out on street corners by itinerant preachers. This one was headed: WHERE WILL YOU SPEND ETERNITY?

Not, I hoped, at the Coburn Inn.

THE THIRD DAY

CONSTABLE RONNIE Goodfellow stood with arms akimbo, surveying the wreckage of my hotel room.

"Shit," he said.

"My sentiments exactly," I said. "But look, it's no big deal. Nothing was stolen. The only reason I wanted you to know was if it fits a pattern of hotel room break-ins. You've had them before?"

Sleek head turned slowly, dark eyes observed me thoughtfully. Finally . . .

"You a cop?" he said.

"No, but I've had some training. Army CID."

"Well, there's no pattern. Some petty pilferage in the kitchen maybe, but there hasn't been a break-in here since I've been on the force. Why should there be? What is there to steal in this bag of bones? The regulars who live here are all on Social Security. Most of the time they haven't got two nickels to rub together."

He took slow steps into the room, looking about.

"The bed tossed?" he asked.

"That's right. I put it straight so I could get some sleep last night."

He nodded, still looking around with squinty eyes. Suddenly he swooped, picked up one of those vomit-tinted prints that had hung on the tenement-green wall. He inspected the torn paper backing.

"Looking for something special," he said. "Something small and flat that could be slid between the backing and the picture. Like a photo, a sheet of paper, a document, a letter. Something like that."

I looked at him with new respect. He was no stupe.

"Got any idea what it could be?" he asked casually.

"Not a clue," I said, just as off-handedly. "I haven't got a thing like that worth hiding."

He nodded again, and there was nothing in that smooth, saturnine face to show if he believed me or not.

"Well . . ." he said, "maybe I'll go down and have a few words with Sam Livingston."

"You don't think—" I began.

"Of course not," he said sharply. "Sam's as honest as the day is long. But maybe he saw someone prowling around late last night. He's up all hours. You say you got in late?"

I hadn't said. I hoped he didn't catch the brief pause before I answered.

"A little after midnight," I lied. "I had dinner with the Thorndeckers."

"Oh?" he said. "Have a good time?"

"Sure did. Great food. Good company." Then I added, somewhat maliciously: "Mrs. Thorndecker is a beauty."

"Yes," he said, almost absently, "a very attractive woman. Well, I'll see what I can do about this, Mr. Todd. Sorry it had to happen to a visitor to our town."

"Happens everywhere," I shrugged. "No real harm done."

I closed and locked the door behind him. He hadn't inspected that lock, but I had. No sign of forced entry. That was one for me. But he had seen that the object of the search had been something small and flat, something that could be concealed in a picture frame. That was one for him.

I knew what it was, of course. My visitor had been trying to recover that anonymous note. The one that read: "Thorndecker kills."

With only half-dozen regulars and me staying at the Coburn Inn, the management didn't think it necessary to employ a chambermaid. Old Sam Livingston did the chores: changing linen, emptying wastebaskets, throwing out "dead soldiers," vacuuming when the dust got ankle-deep.

I was still trying to set my room to rights when he knocked. I let him in.

"I'll straighten up here," he told me. "You go get your morning coffee."

"Thanks, Sam," I said gratefully.

I handed him a five-dollar bill. He stared at it.

"Abraham Lincoln," he said. "Fine-looking man. Good beard." He held the bill out to me. "Take it back, Mr. Todd. I'd clean up anyways. You don't have to do that."

"I know I don't *have* to do it," I said. "All I *have* to do is pay taxes and die. I *want* to do it."

"That's different," he said, pocketing the bill. "I thank you kindly."

I took another look at him: an independent old cuss in his black alpaca jacket and skullcap. He had a scrubby head of greyish curls and a face as gnarled as a hardwood burl. All of him looked like dark hardwood: chiseled, carved, sanded, oiled, and then worked for so many years that the polish on face and hands had a deep glow that could only come from hard use.

"Live in Coburn all your life?" I asked him.

"Most of it," he said.

"Seventy-five years?" I guessed.

"Eighty-three," he said.

"I'll never make it," I said.

"Sure you will," he said, "you lay off the sauce and the women."

"In that case," I said, "I don't want to make it. Sam, I want to come down to your place sometime, maybe have a little visit with you."

"Anytime," he said. "I ain't going anywhere. The French toast is nice this morning."

I can take a hint. I left him to his cleaning and went down for breakfast. But I skipped the French toast. Juice, unbuttered toast, black coffee. Very virtuous. On my way out, I looked in at the bar but Al Coburn wasn't there. Just Jimmy the bartender reading the *Sentinel*. I waved at him and went out to the lobby. I stopped for cigarettes. I really did need cigarettes. Honest.

"Good morning, Millie," I said.

"Oh, Mr. Todd," she said excitedly, "I heard about your trouble. I'm so sorry."

I stared at her glassily, trying to figure which trouble she meant.

She was wearing the same makeup, probably marketed under the trade name "Picasso's Clown." But the costume was different. This morning it was a voluminous shift, a kind of muumuu, in an orange foliage print. It had a high, drawstring neckline, long sleeves, tight cuffs. The yards and yards of sleazy synthetic fell to her ankles. Hamlet's uncle could have hidden behind that arras.

Strange, but it was sexier than the tight sweater and skirt she had worn the day before. The cloth, gathered at the neck, jutted out over her glorious appendages, then fell straight down in folds, billows, pleats. She was completely covered, concealed. It was inflammatory.

"Your trouble," she repeated. "You know—the robbery."

"Burglary," I said automatically. "But the door didn't seem to be jimmied."

"That's what Ronnie said. He thinks whoever did it had a key."

So the Indian had caught it after all. That pesky redskin kept surprising me. I resolved never to underestimate him again.

Millie Goodfellow crooked a long, slender forefinger, beckoning me closer. Since the glass cigar counter was between us, I had to bend forward in a ridiculous posture. I found myself focusing on the nail of that summoning finger. Dark brown polish.

"A passkey," she whispered. "I told Ronnie it was probably a passkey. There's a million of them floating around. Everyone has one." Suddenly she giggled. "I even have one myself. Isn't that awful?"

I was in cloud-cuckoo land.

"*You* have a hotel passkey, Millie?" I asked. "Whatever for?"

"It gets me in the little girls' room," she said primly. Then she was back in her Cleopatra role. "And a lot of other places, too!"

I think I managed a half-ass grin before I stumbled away. My initial reaction had been correct: this lady was scary.

Wednesday morning in Coburn, N. Y. . . .

At least the sun was shining. Maybe not exactly shining, but it was there. You could see it, dull and tarnished, glowing dimly behind a cloud cover. It put a leaden light on everything: illumination but no shadows. People moved sluggishly, the air was cold without being invigorating, and I kept hoping I'd hear someone laugh aloud. No one did.

Around to River Street and the First Farmers & Merchants Bank. It had the flashiest storefront in Coburn, with panels of gray marble between gleaming plateglass windows, and lots of vinyl tile and mirrors inside. The foreclosure business must be good.

There were two tellers' windows and a small bullpen with three desks occupied by New Accounts, Personal Loans, and Mortgages. There was one guard who could have been Constable Ronnie Goodfellow fifty years older and fifty pounds heavier. I went to him. His side-holstered revolver had a greenish tinge, as if moss was growing on it.

I gave my name and explained that I'd like to see the president, Mr. Arthur Merchant, although I didn't have an appointment. He nodded gravely and disappeared for about five minutes, during which time two members of the Junior Mafia could have waltzed in and cleaned out the place.

But finally he returned and ushered me to a back office, enclosed, walled with a good grade of polished plywood. A toothy lady relieved me of hat and trenchcoat, which she hung on a rack. She handled my garments with her fingertips; I couldn't blame her. Finally, finally, I was led into the inner sanctum, and Arthur Merchant, bank president and Coburn mayor, rose to greet me. He shook my hand enthusiastically with a fevered palm and insisted I sit in a leather club chair alongside his desk. When we were standing, I was six inches taller than he. When we sat down, he in his swivel chair, he was six inches taller. That chair must have had 12-inch casters.

He was a surprisingly young man for a bank president and mayor. He was also short, plump, florid, and sweatier than the room temperature could account for. Young as he was, the big skull was showing the scants; strands of thin, black hair were brushed sideways to hide the divot. The face bulged. You've seen faces that bulge, haven't you? They seem to protrude. As if an amateur sculptor started out with an ostrich egg as a head form, and then added squares and strips of modeling clay: forehead, nose, cheeks, mouth, chin. I mean everything seems to hang out there, and all that clay just might dry and drop off. Leaving the blank ostrich egg.

We exchanged the usual pleasantries: the weather, my reaction to Coburn, my accommodations at the Inn, places of interest I should see while in the vicinity: the place where a British spy was hanged in 1777; Lovers' Leap on the Hudson River, scene of nineteen authenticated suicides; and the very spot where, only last summer, a bear had come out of the woods and badly mauled, and allegedly attempted to rape, a 68-year-old lady gathering wild strawberries.

I said it all sounded pretty exciting to me, but as Mr. Merchant was undoubtedly aware, I was not in Coburn to sightsee or visit tourist attractions; I had come to garner information about Dr. Telford Gordon Thorndecker. That's when I learned that Arthur Merchant was a compulsive fusser.

The pudgy hands went stealing out to straighten desk blotter, pencils, calendar pad. He tightened his tie, smoothed the hair at his temples, examined his fingernails. He crossed and recrossed his knees, tugged down the points of his vest, brushed nonexistent lint from his sleeve. He leaped to his feet, strode across the room, closed a bookcase door that had been open about a quarter-inch. Then he came back to his desk, sat down, and began rearranging blotter, pencils, and pad, aligning their edges with quick, nervous twitches of those pinkish squid hands.

And all during this *a cappella* ballet he was explaining to me what a splendid fellow Thorndecker was. Salt of the earth. Everything the Boy Scout oath demanded. Absolutely straight-up in his financial dealings. A loyal contributor to local charities. And what a boon to Coburn! Not only as the biggest employer in the village, but as a citizen, bringing to Coburn renown as the home of one of the world's greatest scientists.

"One of the *greatest*, Mr. Todd," Art Merchant concluded, somewhat winded, as well he should have been after that ten-minute monologue.

"Very impressive," I said, as coldly as I could. "You know what he's doing at Crittenden?"

It was a small sneak punch, but Merchant reacted like I had slammed a knee into his groin.

"What? Why . . . ah . . ." he stammered. Then: "The nursing home," he burst out. "Surely you know about that. Beds for fifty patients. A program of social—"

"I know about Crittenden Hall," I interrupted. "I want to know about the Crittenden Research Laboratory. What's going on in the lab?"

"Well, ah, you know," he said desperately, limp hands flailing. "Scientific stuff. Don't ask me to understand; I'm just a small-town banker. But valuable things—I'm sure of that. The man's a genius! Everyone says so. And still young. Relatively. He's going to do great work. No doubt about that. You'll see."

He maundered on and on, turning now to what an excellent business manager Thorndecker was, what a fine executive, and how rare it was to find that acumen in a doctor, a professor, a man of science. But I wasn't listening.

I was beginning to feel slight twinges of paranoia. I am not ordinarily a subscriber to the conspiracy theory of history. For instance, I do not believe an evil cabal engineered the deaths of the Kennedys and Martin Luther King, the disappearance of Jimmy Hoffa, or even the lousy weather we've been having.

I believe in the Single Nut theory of history, holding that one goofy individual can change the course of human affairs by a well-placed bomb or a well-aimed rifle shot. I don't believe in conspiracies because they require the concerted efforts of two or more people. In other words, a committee. And I've never known a committee that achieved anything but endless bickering and the piling up of Minutes of the Last Meeting that serve no useful purpose except being recycled for the production of Mother's Day cards.

Still, as I said, I was beginning to feel twinges. I thought Agatha Binder had lied to me. I thought Art Merchant was lying to me. These two, along with the Thorndeckers, Dr. Draper, and maybe Ronnie Goodfellow and a few other of the best people of Coburn, all knew something I didn't know, and wasn't being told. I didn't like that. I told you, I don't like being conned.

I realized Arthur Merchant had stopped talking and was staring at me, expecting some kind of response.

"Well," I said, rising to my feet, "that's certainly an enthusiastic endorsement, Mr. Merchant. I'd say Dr. Thorndecker is fortunate in having you and the other citizens of Coburn as friends and neighbors."

I must have said the right thing, because the fear went out of his eyes, and some color came back into those clayey cheeks.

"And we are fortunate," he sang out, "in having Dr. Thorndecker as a friend and neighbor. You bet your life! Mr. Todd, you stop by again if you have any more questions, any questions at all, concerning Dr. Thorndecker's financial affairs. He's instructed me to throw his books open to you, as it were. Anything you want to know. Anything at all."

"I've seen the report of Lifschultz Associates," I said, moving toward the door. "It appears Dr. Thorndecker is in a very healthy financial position."

"Healthy?" Art Merchant cried, and did everything but leap into the air and click his heels together. "I should say so! The man is a fantastic money manager. Fan-tas-tic! In addition to being one of the world's greatest scientists, of course."

"Of course," I said. "By the way, Mr. Merchant, I understand you're the mayor of Coburn?"

"Oh . . ." he said, shrugging and spreading his plump hands deprecatingly, "I guess I got the job because no one else wanted it. It's unpaid, you know. About what it's worth."

"The reason I mention it," I said, "is that I haven't seen any public buildings around town. No courthouse, no city hall, no jail."

"Well, we have what we call the Civic Building, put up by the WPA back in 1936. We've got our fire department in there—it's just one old pumper and a hose cart—the police station, a two-cell jail, and our city hall, which is really just one big office. We have a JP in town, but if we get a serious charge or trial, we move it over to the courthouse at the county seat."

"The Civic Building?" I said. "I'd like to see that. How do I find it?"

"Just go out Main Street to Oakland Drive. It's one block south, right next to the boarded-up A&P; you can't miss it. Not much to look at, to tell you the truth. There's been some talk of replacing it with a modern building, but the way things are . . ."

He let that sentence trail off, the way so many Coburnites did. It gave their talk an effect of helpless futility. Hell, what's the point of finishing a sentence when the world's coming to an end?

I thanked him for his kind cooperation and shook that popover with fingers. I claimed hat and trenchcoat, and got out of there. No customers in the bank, and the people at the desks marked New Accounts, Personal Loans, and Mortgages didn't seem to have much to do. I began to appreciate how much a big, active account like Thorndecker's meant to First Farmers & Merchants, and to Mayor Art Merchant.

Having time to kill before my visit to Crittenden at 1:00 P.M., I spent an hour wandering about Coburn. If I had walked at a faster clip, I could have seen the entire village in thirty minutes. I made a complete tour of the business section—about four blocks—featuring boarded-up stores and Going Out of Business sales. Then I meandered through residential districts, and located the Civic Building. I kept walking until vacant lots became more numerous and finally merged with farms and wooded tracts.

When I had seen all there was to see, I retraced my steps, heading back to the Coburn Inn. I had my ungloved hands shoved into my trenchcoat pockets, and I hunched my shoulders against a whetted wind blowing from the river. I was thinking about what I had just seen, about Coburn.

The town was dying—but what of that? A lot of villages, towns, and cities have died since the world began. People move away, buildings crumble, and the grass or the forest or the jungle or the desert moves back in. As I told Constable Goodfellow, history is change. You can't stop it; all you can do is try to keep from getting run over by it.

It wasn't the decay of Coburn that depressed me so much as the layout of the residential neighborhoods. I saw three-story Victorian mansions right next to leaky shacks with a scratchy yard and tin garage. Judging by homes, Coburn's well-to-do didn't congregate in a special, exclusive neighborhood; they lived cheek-by-jowl with their underprivileged brethren.

You might find that egalitarian and admirable. I found it unbelievable. There isn't a village, town, or city on earth where the rich don't huddle in their own enclave, forcing the poor into theirs. I suppose this has a certain social value: it gives the poor a *place* to aspire to. What's the point of striving for what the sociologists call upward mobility if you have to stay in the ghetto?

The problem was solved when I spotted a sign in a ground-floor window of one of those big Victorian mansions. It read: "Rooms to let. Day, week, month." Then I understood. *All* of the Incorporated Village of Coburn was on the wrong side of the tracks. As I trudged back to the Inn, the sky darkening, the smell of snow in the air, I thought this place could have been the capital city of Gloom.

I went into the bar and asked the spavined water for a club sandwich and a bottle of beer. While I waited, I looked idly around. It was getting on to noon; the lunch crowd was beginning to straggle in. Then I became aware of something else about Coburn, something I had observed but that hadn't really registered until now.

There were no young people in town. I had seen a few schoolkids on the streets, but no one in the, oh, say 18-to-25 age bracket. There was Miss Dimples in the *Sentinel* office, but except for her, Coburn seemed devoid of young people. Even the gas jockeys at Mike's Service Station looked like they were pulling down Spanish-American War pensions.

The reason was obvious, of course. If you were an eager, curious, reasonably brainy 20-year-old with worlds to conquer, would you stay in Coburn? Not me. I'd shake the place. And that's what Coburn's young people had done. For Albany, New York, Miami, Los Angeles. Or maybe Paris, Rome, Amsterdam, Karachi. *Any*place was better than home.

On my way out, I stopped at the bar for a quick vodka gimlet. I know it was a poor choice on top of my luncheon beer. But after the realization, "*Any*place was better than home," I needed it.

Once again I drove to Crittenden through that blasted landscape, and was admitted by the gate guard. He was pressing a transistor radio against his skull. There was a look of ineffable joy on his face, as if he had just heard his number pulled in the Irish Sweeps. I don't think he even saw me, but he let me in; I followed the graveled road to the front of Crittenden Hall.

Dr. Kenneth Draper came out to greet me. I took a closer look at him. You know the grave, white-coated, eye-glassed guy in the TV commercials who looks earnestly at the camera and says, "Have you ever suffered from irregularity?" That was Draper. As a matter of fact, he looked like he was suffering himself: forehead washboarded, deep lines from nose to corners of mouth, bleached complexion, and a furtive, over-the-shoulder glance, wondering when the knout would fall.

"Well!" Draper said brightly. "Now what we've planned is the grand tour. The nursing home first. Look around. Anything you want to see. Meet the head staff. Then to the lab. Ditto there. Take a look at our setup, what we're doing. Meet some of our people. Then Dr. Thorndecker would like to speak with you when we're finished. How does that sound?"

"Sounds fine," I assured him. The poor simp looked so apprehensive that I think if I had said, "Sounds lousy," he would have burst into tears.

We turned to the left, and Draper hauled a ring of keys from his pocket.

"The wings are practically identical," he explained. "We didn't want to waste your time by dragging you through both, so we'll take a look at the west wing. We keep the door locked for security. Some of our patients are mentals, and we try to keep access doors locked for their protection."

"And yours?" I asked.

"What?" he said. "Oh yes, I suppose that's true, although the few violent cases we have are kept pretty, uh, content."

There was a wide, tiled, institutional corridor with doors on both sides.

"Main floor": Dr. Draper recited, "Doctors' and nurses' offices and lounges. Records and admitting room. X ray and therapy. Clinic and dispensary. Everything here is duplicated in the east wing."

"Expensive setup, isn't it?" I said. "For fifty patients?"

"They can afford it," he said tonelessly. "Now I'm going to introduce you to Nurse Stella Beecham. She's an RN, head nurse in Crittenden Hall. She'll show you through the nursing home, then bring you over to the lab. I'll leave you in her hands, and then take you through the Crittenden Research Laboratory myself."

"Sounds fine," I said again, trying to get some enthusiasm into my voice.

Stella Beecham looked like a white stump: squat, straight up and down. She was wearing a short-sleeved nurse's uniform, and I caught the biceps and muscles in her forearms and thick wrists. But nurses are usually strong; they have to be to turn a two-hundred-pound patient in his bed, or lift a deadweight from stretcher to wheelchair.

Beecham wasn't the prettiest angel of mercy I've ever seen. She had gross, thrusting, almost masculine features. No makeup. Her complexion was rough, ruddy, with the beginnings of burst capillaries in nose and cheeks. To me, that signals a heavy drinker. She had a faint mustache. On the left side of her chin, just below the corner of her pale mouth, was a silvery wen with two short, black hairs sticking out. It looked for all the world like a transistor, and I consciously avoided staring at it when I talked to her.

Dr. Kenneth Draper cut out, and Nurse Beecham took me in tow, spouting staccato statistics. It went like this, in her hard, drillmaster's voice:

"Fifty beds. Today's occupancy rate: forty-nine. We have a waiting list of thirty-eight to get in. Seven addicts at present: five alcoholics, two hard drugs. Six mentals. Prognosis: negative. All the others are terminals. Cancer, MS, emphysema, myasthenia gravis, cardiacs, and so forth. Their doctors have given up. About all we can do is try to keep them pain-free. A hundred and fifty meals prepared each day in the main kitchen, not counting those for staff, maintenance personnel, and security guards. Plus special meals. Some of our guests like afternoon tea or a late-night snack. We have a chef on duty around-the-clock. These are the nurses' offices and lounges. The doctors' are across the hall."

"You have MD's in residence?" I asked—not that I was so interested, but just to let her know I was listening.

"Two assigned to each wing. Plus, of course, Dr. Thorndecker and Dr. Draper. They're both MD's. Two RN's around-the-clock in each wing. Plus a pharmaceutical nurse for each wing. Three shifts of aides and orderlies. Our total staff provides a better than one-to-one ratio with our guests. Here's the X-ray room. We have a resident radiologist. Therapy in here. Our resident therapist deals mostly with the addiction cases, particularly the alcoholics. Spiritual therapy, if desired, is provided by the Reverend Peter Koukla of the First Episcopal Church. We also have an Albany rabbi on call, when needed. Examination room here, dispensary here. Combined barber and beauty shop. This is handled by a concession. Dietician's office here. We send out all our laundry and drycleaning. I think that about completes the main floor of this wing."

"What's in the basement?" I asked, in the friendliest tone possible.

"Storage," she said. "Want to see it?"

"No," I said, "that won't be necessary."

It was a short, brusque exchange—brusque on her part. She had the palest blue eyes I've ever seen, almost as colorless as water, and showing about as much. All they did was glitter; I could read nothing there. So why did I have the feeling that my mention of the cellar had flicked a nerve? Just a tensing, almost a bristling of her powerful body.

"Now we'll go upstairs," she said. "The vacant suite is in this wing, so I'll be able to show it to you."

We had passed a few aides, a few orderlies. But I hadn't seen anyone who looked like a patient.

"Where is everyone?" I asked. "The place seems deserted."

She gave me a reasonable explanation:

"It's lunchtime. The dining room is in the rear of the main entrance hall. Most of our guests are there now, except for those who dine in their rooms. The aides and doctors usually eat in the dining room also. Dr. Thorndecker feels it helps maintain rapport with our patients."

"I hope I haven't interrupted *your* luncheon," I said.

"Not at all," she said. "I'm on a diet. I skip lunch."

That sounded like a friendly, personal comment—a welcome relief from the officialese she had been spouting—so I followed up on it.

"I met an acquaintance of yours," I said. "Agatha Binder. I had a talk with her yesterday."

"Did you?" she said. "Now you'll notice that we have no elevators. But during Dr. Thorndecker's refurbishing program, the stairways at the ends of the corridors were made much narrower, and the ramps were installed. So we're able to move wheeled stretchers and wheelchairs up to the top floors without too much trouble. Actually, there's very little traffic. Non-ambulatory guests are encouraged to remain in their suites. What do you think of Crittenden Hall so far?"

The question came so abruptly that it confused me.

"Well . . . uh," I said. "I'll tell you," I said. "I'm impressed," I said, "by how neat and immaculate and sparkling everything is. I almost suspect you prepared for my visit—like sailors getting ready for a white-glove inspection on a U.S. Navy ship."

I said it in a bantering tone, keeping it light, but she had no humor whatsoever—except, possibly, bad.

"Oh no," she said, "it's like this all the time. Dr. Thorndecker insists on absolutely hygienic conditions. Our cleaning staff has been specially trained. We've gotten highest ratings in the New York State inspections, and I mean to keep it that way."

It was a grim declaration. But she was a grim woman. And, as I followed her up the narrow staircase to the second floor, I reflected that even her legs were grim: heavy, thick, with clumped muscles under the white cotton stockings. I wouldn't, I thought, care to be given a needle by Nurse Stella Beecham. She was liable to pin me to the goddamned bed.

"I won't show you any of the occupied suites," she said. "Dr. Thorndecker felt it might disturb our guests unnecessarily."

"Of course."

"But he wanted you to see the one vacant suite. We have a guest arriving for it tomorrow morning."

"Was it occupied by a man—or maybe it was a woman—named Petersen?" I asked.

I don't know why I said that. My tongue was ahead of my brain. I just said it idly. Nurse Beecham's reaction was astonishing. She was standing on the second-floor landing, three steps above me. When I said, "Petersen," she whirled, then went suddenly rigid, her lumpy features set in an ugly expression that was half fear, half cunning, and all fury.

"Why did you say that?" she demanded, the "say" hissed so that it came out "ssssay."

"I don't know," I told her honestly, staring up at her transistor-wen. "But I was at the Thorndeckers for dinner last night, and late in the evening Dr. Thorndecker was called away by Dr. Draper. I got the impression it involved some crisis in the condition of a patient named Petersen. Dr. Thorndecker said he was afraid Petersen wouldn't last the night."

The gorgon's face relaxed, wax flowing. She took a deep breath. She had an awesome bosom.

"He didn't," she said. "He passed. The empty suite is just down the corridor here. Follow me, please."

She unlocked the door, and stood aside. I walked in ahead of her. It was a suite all right: sitting room, bedroom, bathroom. There was even a little kitchenette, with a waist-high refrigerator. But no stove. The windows faced the sere fields of Crittenden.

The rooms were clean and cheerfully decorated: chintz drapes and slipcovers. Bright, innocuous paintings on the warm beige walls. A new, oval-shaped rag rug. Windows were washed, floor polished, upholstery spotless, small desk set neatly with blotter, stationery, ballpoint pen, Bible. The bed had been freshly made. Spotless white towels hung in the bathroom. The closet door was open. It was empty of clothes, but wooden hangers were precisely arranged along the rod.

Nurse Beecham stood patiently at the hallway door while I prowled around. A quiet, impersonal suite of rooms. Nothing of Petersen showed, nor any of the others who had gone before. No cigarette butts, worn slippers, rumpled pillows. No initials carved in the desk top. There was a faint scent of disinfectant in the air.

I stood at the window, staring down at the withered fields. It was a comfortable place to die, I supposed. Warm. Lighted. And he had been well cared for. Pain-free. Still, the place had all the ambience of a motel suite in Scranton, Pa. It had that hard, machine look, everything clean enough, but aseptic and chilling.

I turned back to Stella Beecham.

"What did he die of?" I asked. "Petersen?"

"Pelvic cancer," she said. "Inoperable. He didn't respond to chemotherapy. Shall we go now?"

I followed her in silence down the stairway to the main floor. We stopped three times while she introduced me to staff: one of the resident MD's, the radiologist, and another RN. We all smiled and said things. I don't remember their names.

Nurse Beecham paused outside the back door of the west wing.

"It's a few steps to the lab," she said. "Would you like your coat?"

"No, I'll leave it here," I said. "Thank you for showing me around. It must be very boring for you."

"I don't mind," she said gruffly.

We walked out to that roofed port that led down the hill to the Crittenden Research Laboratory. It was a miserably rude day, the sun completely hidden now, air biting, wind slicing. But I didn't see Beecham hurry her deliberate tread or hug her bare arms. She just trundled steadily along, a boulder rolling downhill.

The side door of the lab was locked. Nurse Beecham had the key on an enormous ring she hauled from her side pocket. When we were inside, she double-locked the door.

"Wait here, please," she said, and went thumping down a wide, waxed linoleum corridor. I waited, looking around. Nothing of interest to see, unless closed doors excite you. In a few minutes, Dr. Kenneth Draper came bustling down the hall, rubbing his palms together and trying hard to look relaxed and genial.

"Well!" he said again. "Here we are! See everything you wanted in the Hall?"

"I think so," I said. "It appears to be a very efficient operation."

"Oh, it is, it is," he assured me. "Quality care. If you'd care to test the patients' food, just drop in unexpectedly, for any meal. I think you'll be pleasantly surprised."

"I'm sure I would be," I said. "But that won't be necessary, Dr. Draper. By the way, Nurse Beecham strikes me as being a very valuable member of your staff. How long has she been with you?"

"From the start," he said. "When Dr. Thorndecker took over. He brought her in. I understand she was the first Mrs. Thorndecker's nurse during a long illness prior to her—her accident. I don't know what we'd do without Beecham. Perhaps not the most personable, outgoing woman in the world, but she certainly does a job running the Hall. Keeps problems to a minimum so Dr. Thorndecker and I can devote more time to the lab."

"Where your real interests lie?" I suggested.

"Well . . . uh, yes," he said hesitantly, as if afraid of saying too much. "The nursing home is our first responsibility, of course, but we are doing some exciting things here, and I suppose it's natural . . ."

Another Coburnite who couldn't finish his sentences. I wondered how these people expressed love for one another. Did they just say, "I love . . ." and let it go at that?

"Now this is our main floor," Dr. Draper was saying. "Here you'll find our offices, records room, reference library, a small lounge, a locker and dressing room, showers, and a room we've equipped with cots for researchers who might want to sleep here after a long day's work or during a prolonged project. Do you want to see any of these rooms?"

"I'd like to glance at the reference library, if I may," I said. "Just for a moment."

"Of course, of course. Along here, please."

This place was certainly livelier than the nursing home. As we walked along the corridor, I heard voices from behind closed door, hoots of laughter, and once a shouted argument in which I could distinguish one screamed statement: "You're full of shit!"

We stopped several times for Dr. Draper to introduce me to the staff members hustling by. They all seemed to know who I was, and shook my hand with what appeared to be genuine enthusiasm. There were almost as many women as men, and all of them seemed young and—well, I think "keen" would describe them best. I said something about this to Draper.

"Oh, they're top-notch," he said proudly. "The best. Dr. Thorndecker recruited them from all over: Harvard, Duke, Berkeley, Johns Hopkins, Chicago, MIT. We have two Japanese, one Swede, and a kid from Mali you wouldn't believe, he's so smart. We pay them half of what they would be making with any of the big drug companies."

"Then why . . . ?" I said. I was beginning to suffer from the Coburn Syndrome.

"Thorndecker!" Dr. Draper cried. "It's Thorndecker. The opportunity of working with him. Learning from him. They're very highly motivated."

"Or he's charmed them," I said, smiling.

Suddenly he was sober.

"Yes," he said in a low voice. "That, too. Here's our library. Small, but sufficient."

We stepped inside. A room about twenty by forty feet, lined with bookcases. Several small oak tables with a single chair at each, and one long conference table with twelve captain's chairs. A Xerox machine. The shelves were jammed with books on end and periodicals lying flat. It wasn't too orderly: the ashtrays filled, wastebaskets overflowing, books and magazines lined up raggedly. But after a visit to the late Mr. Petersen's abode, it was a pleasure to see human mess.

"Looks like it's used," I commented, wandering around.

"All the time," he told me. "Sometimes the researchers will get caught up in something, read all night, and then flop into one of those cots I told you about. Very irregular hours. No one punches a time clock. But if they do their jobs, they can work any hours they please. A very relaxed atmosphere. Dr. Thorndecker feels it pays off in productivity."

Meanwhile I was inspecting the titles of the books and periodicals on the shelves. If I had hoped they'd give me a clue to what was going on at the Crittenden Research Laboratory, I was disappointed. They appeared to me to be standard scientific reference texts, with heavy emphasis on human biology and the morphology of mammalian cells. A thick stack of recent oncological papers. One shelf of US Government publications dealing with demography, census, and public health statistics. I didn't see a single volume I'd care to curl up with on a cold winter night.

"Very nice," I said, turning to Draper. "Where do we go now—the labs?"

"Fine," he said. "They're on the second floor. On each side of the corridor is a large general lab used by the researchers. And then a smaller private lab used by the supervising staffers."

"How many supervisors do you have?"

"Well . . ." he said, blushing, "actually just Dr. Thorndecker and me. But when the grant—*if* the grant comes through, we hope to expand. We have the space and facilities to do it. Well, you'll see. Let's go up."

Unlike nursing homes and hospitals, research laboratories don't necessarily have to be sterile, efficient, and as cozy as a subway station. True, I've been in labs that look like operating rooms: all shiny white tile and equipment right out of *The Bride of Frankenstein*. I've also been in research labs not much larger than a walk-in closet and equipped with not much more than a stained sink and a Bunsen burner.

When it comes to scientific research, there's no guarantee. A million dollars sunk into a palace of a lab with all the latest and most exotic stainless steel doodads can result in the earth-shaking discovery that when soft cheese is exposed to the open air, mold results. And from that little closet lab with roaches fornicating in unwashed flasks can come a discovery that remakes the world.

The second-floor working quarters of the Crittenden Research Laboratory fell about halfway between palace and closet. The space was ample enough; the entire floor was divided in two by a wide corridor, and on each side was a huge laboratory. Each had, at its end, a small, private laboratory enclosed by frosted glass panels. These two small supervisors' labs had private entrances from the corridor, and also etched glass doors leading into the main labs. All these doors, I noted, could be locked.

The main laboratories were lighted with overhead fluorescent fixtures, plus high-intensity lamps mounted near microscopes. Workbenches ran around the walls, with additional work tables in the center areas. Plenty of sinks, garbage disposal units, lab stools, metal and glass welding torches and tanks—from which I guessed they had occasional need to fabricate their own equipment.

But it was the profusion of big, complex, obviously store-bought hardware that bewildered me.

"I can recognize an oscilloscope when I see one," I told Draper. "And that thing's a gas diffusion analyzer, and that's a scanning electron microscope. But what's all this other stuff?"

"Oh . . . various things," he said vaguely. "The big control board is for an automated cell culture, blood and tissue analyzer. Very complete readings, in less time than it would take to do it by hand. Incidentally, in addition to our own work, we do all the tests needed by the nursing home. That includes blood, urine, sputum, stools, biopsies—whatever. We have pathologists on staff."

There had been half a dozen researchers working in the first lab we visited, and I saw about the same number when we walked into the lab across the hall. A few of them looked up when we entered, but most didn't give us a glance.

The second lab had workbenches along three walls. The fourth, a long one, was lined with stainless steel refrigerators and climate-controlled cabinets. Through the front glass panels I could see racks and racks of flasks and tubes of all sizes and shapes.

"Cell cultures?" I asked Dr. Draper.

"Mostly," he nodded. "And some specimens. Organ and tumor slices. Things of that sort. We have some very old, very valuable cultures here. A few originals. We're continually getting requests from all over the world."

"You give the stuff away?"

"Sometimes, but we prefer to trade," he said, laughing shortly. " 'Here's what we've got; what have you got?' Research laboratories do a lot of horse-trading like that."

"You have bacteria?" I asked.

"Some."

"Viruses?"

"Some."

"Lethal?"

"Oh yes," he nodded. "Including a few rare ones from Africa. They're in those cabinets with the padlocks. Only Dr. Thorndecker and I have the key."

"What are they all doing?" I said, motioning toward the researchers bent over their workbenches. "What's your current project?"

"Well, ah," he said, "I'd prefer you direct that question to Dr. Thorndecker. He specifically said he wished to brief you personally on our current activities. After we've finished up here."

"Good enough," I said. Just seeing the Crittenden Research Laboratory in action revealed nothing. If they were brewing up a bubonic plague and told me they were making chicken noodle Cup-a-Soup, I wouldn't have known the difference.

"The only thing left to see is the basement," Draper said.

"What's down there?"

"Mostly our experimental animals. A dissection room. Mainly for animals," he added hastily. "We don't do any human PM's unless it's requested by relatives of the deceased."

"Why would they request it?"

"For various reasons. Usually to determine the exact cause of death. We had a case last year in which a widow authorized an autopsy of her deceased husband, a mental who had been at Crittenden Hall for two years. She was afraid of a genetic brain disorder that might be inherited by their son."

"Did you find it?"

"Yes," he said. "And there have been some postmortems authorized by the subjects themselves, prior to their death. These were people who wished to donate organs: kidneys, corneas, hearts, and so forth. But these cases have been few, considering the advanced age of most of the patients in the nursing home. Their organs are rarely, ah, desirable."

And on that cheery note, we descended the stairway to the basement of the Crittenden Research Laboratory. Dr. Kenneth Draper paused with his hand on the knob of a heavy, padded steel door. He turned to me.

He seemed suddenly overcome by embarrassment. Spots of color appeared high on his cheeks. His forehead was pearled with sweat. Wet teeth appeared in a hokey grin.

"We have mostly mice, dogs, cats, chimps, and guinea pigs," he said.

"Yes?" I said encouragingly. "And . . . ?"

"Well," he said, tittering nervously, "you are not, by any chance, an anti-vivisectionist, are you, Mr. Todd?"

"Rather them than me," I said, and looked at him. But he had turned away; I couldn't see his face.

When we stepped inside, I heard immediately the reason for that outside door being padded. The big basement room was an audiophile's nightmare: chirps, squeals, barks, hisses, honks, roars, howls. I looked around, dazed.

"You'll get used to it," Draper shouted in my ear.

"Never," I shouted back.

We made a quick tour of the cages. I didn't mind the smell so much as that cacophony. I really am a sentimental slob, and I kept thinking the imprisoned beasts were making all that racket because they were suffering and wanted out. Not a very objective reaction, I admit; most of them looked sleek and well-fed. It's just that I hate to see an animal in a cage. I hate zoos. I see myself behind those bars, with a neat label: "Samuel Todd, Homus Americanus, habitat New York City. A rare species that feeds on vodka gimlet and celery stalks stuffed with anchovy paste."

There were a few aproned attendants around who grinned at us. One of them was wearing a set of heavy earphones. Maybe he was just blocking out that noise, or maybe he was listening to Mahler's Fifth.

After inspecting the spitting cats, howling dogs, barking chimps, and squealing mice, it was a relief to get into a smaller room closed off by another of those padded steel doors.

This one was also lined with cages. But the occupants were those animals being used in current experiments and were reasonably quiet. Some of them lay on their sides, in what appeared to be a comatose state. Some were bandaged. Some had sensors taped to heads and bodies, the wires leading out to a battery of recording machines.

And some of them—one young chimpanzee in particular—were covered with tumors. Great, monstrous growths. Blossoms of wild flesh. Red and blue and yellow. A flowering of raw tissue. The smell in there was something.

The young chimp was almost hidden by the deadly blooms. The eruptions covered his head, body, limbs. He lay on his back, spreadeagled, breathing shallowly. I could see his black, glittering eyes staring at the cage above him.

"Carcinosarcoma," Dr. Draper said. "He's lasted longer than any other in this particular series of tests."

"You infected him?" I asked, knowing the answer.

"Yes," Draper said. "To test the efficacy of a drug we had high hopes for."

"Your hopes aren't so high now?"

"No," he said, shrinking.

I felt like shit.

"Forgive me, doctor," I said. "I know in my mind this kind of thing has to be done. I know it's valuable. I'd just prefer not to see it."

"I understand," he said. "Actually, we all try to be objective. I mean all of us—attendants, researchers. But sometimes we don't succeed. We give them names. Al, Tony, Happy Boy, Sue. When they die, or have to be destroyed, we feel it, I assure you."

"I believe you," I said.

I took a quick look at the dissecting room. Just two stainless steel tables, sinks, pots and pans for excised organs. Choppers. Slicers. Shredders. Something like a kitchen in a gourmet restaurant.

We walked back through the animal room. I was happy to get out of there. The stairway up to the main floor was blessedly quiet.

"Thank you, Dr. Draper," I said. "I'm sure you're a busy man, and you'll probably have to work late to catch up. But I appreciate your showing me around."

"My pleasure," he said.

Of course I didn't believe him.

"And now," I said, "I understand a meeting with Dr. Thorndecker is planned?"

"Correct," he said, obviously pleased that everything had gone so well, and one of his wild, young researchers hadn't dropped a diseased guinea pig's spleen down my neck. "I'll call Crittenden Hall from here. Then I'll unlock the back door, and if you'll just go back the way you came, someone will be at the Hall to let you in."

"Thanks again," I said, shaking his damp hand.

I figured him for a good second-level man: plenty of brains, but without the energy, ambition, and obsessive drive to make it to the top level. His attitude toward Thorndecker seemed ambivalent; I couldn't figure it. But he seemed enthusiastic enough about his work and the Crittenden Research Laboratory.

He made his phone call and was unlocking the back door when suddenly, on impulse, I asked him, "Are you married, Dr. Draper?"

His reaction reminded me of that analyzing computer I had just seen. Lights flashing, bubbles bubbling, bleeps bleeping; I could almost *see* him computing, wondering how his answer might affect a grant from the Bingham Foundation to the Crittenden Research Laboratory. Finally . . .

"Why no," he said. "I'm not."

"I'm not either," I said, hoping it might make him feel better. He might even get to like me, and start calling me Sam, or Happy Boy, like one of his experimental animals in that room of the doomed I had just seen.

Turned out into the cold, I trudged determinedly up the steps, back to Crittenden Hall. But then I realized how pleasant it was to be alone, even for a moment or two. It seemed to me I had been accompanied almost every minute I had been on the grounds. And it was possible I had been under observation for the few seconds I had been alone when Nurse Beecham went to fetch Dr. Draper.

I shook my head. Those paranoiac twinges again. But, looking around at the ruined day, the decayed fields of Crittenden, I figured they came with the territory.

A little, snub-nosed nurse's aide had the back door of Crittenden Hall open for me when I arrived. She escorted me down the corridor and delivered me to the white-jacketed goon in the entrance hall. He told me Dr. Thorndecker was awaiting me in his second-floor study, and waved me up the wide staircase. I went about halfway up, raised my eyes, and saw an aproned maid waiting for me on the second-floor landing. I glanced down to see the goon still watching me from the main floor entrance hall.

Then I was certain; it wasn't paranoia at all. They were keeping me in sight. Every minute. They didn't want me wandering around by myself. Who knew what closed door I might open?

Dr. Thorndecker's study was a rumpled warehouse of a room. It looked like an attic for furniture that wasn't good enough for the other rooms in Crittenden Hall, but was too good to give to the Salvation Army. No two chairs, styles, or colors matched. The desk was a scarred and battered rolltop. The lamps had silk shades with beaded fringe. The couch was one big, lumpy stain, and books and periodicals were stacked higgledy-piggledy on the floor. Some of the stacks had collapsed; there were puddles of magazines, scientific papers, spiral-bound notebooks. I had to step over them to get in.

Thorndecker made no apology for this mess, for which I admired him. He got me seated in a cretonne-covered armchair that had stuffing coming out one arm. I wriggled around cautiously until I could sit comfortably without being goosed by a loose spring. The doctor slumped in a swivel chair swung around from his desk.

"Your wife decorate this room?" I asked politely.

He laughed. "To tell you the truth, I like it just the way it is. It's my private place. A hideaway. No one ever comes in here except the cleaning woman."

"Once every five years?" I suggested. "Whether it needs it or not?"

He laughed again. He seemed to enjoy my chivying. He had whipped off his glasses the moment I entered, but not before I had noted they made him look older. Not older than his 54 years, but just as old. He certainly looked younger without them.

The tanned complexion helped. Perfect teeth that I guessed were capped, not store-bought. Thick billows of dark hair; not a smidgen of gray. No jowls. No sagging of neck flesh. The skin was ruddy and tight, eyes clear and alert. He moved lithely, with an energetic bounce. If he had told me he was 40 years old, I might have thought he was shaving five years. But 54? Imfuckingpossible.

The clothes helped. Beige doeskin slacks, sports jacket of yummy tweed, open-collar shirt with a paisley ascot. Glittering, tasseled moccasins on his small feet. A very spiffy gentleman. When he spoke in that rich, fruity baritone, I could understand how he could woo whiz-kids away from drug cartels at half the salary. He had charm, and even the realization that it was contrived was no defense against it.

Suddenly I had a suspicion that not only the charm, but the man himself might be contrived. The artfully youthful look of bronzed skin, California whites, and hair unblemished by a speck of gray. That appearance might have been a perfectly natural bounty but was, more likely, the result of sunlamp, expensive dental work, facials, and hair dye. And those too-young clothes. I didn't expect Dr. Telford Gordon Thorndecker to dress like a mortician, but I didn't expect him to dress like a juvenile lead either.

Supposing my suspicions correct, what could possibly be his motive? The first one that occurred to me—the *only* one that occurred to me—was that this Nobel winner, this gifted scientist, this *genius* was trying to keep himself attractive and exciting to his young wife. The pampered body was for her. The elegant duds were for her. Even this mess of a room was to prove to her that disorder didn't faze him, that he was capable of whim and youthful nuttiness. He might be an amusing character, an original personality. But he was not a fuddy-duddy; *he was not.*

Irrational? No, just human. I don't mean my own suspicions; I mean Thorndecker's conduct. I had seen how swiftly his vigorous exuberance collapsed the night before when his wife was not present. I began to feel sorry for the man, and like him more.

He looked at me narrowly.

"The animals shake you up?" he asked.

"How did you know that?" I said.

"They usually do. But it must be done."

"I know."

"I have some brandy here. Join me?"

I nodded. He poured us small drinks from a bottle he took from a file drawer in his desk. He used plastic throwaway cups, and again made no apology or excuse. He took one of my cigarettes, and we lighted up.

"I'd be interested in hearing your reactions, Mr. Todd," he said. "On or off the record."

"Oh, on," I said. "I won't try to mislead you. I thought the nursing home a very efficient operation. Of course, it only has a peripheral bearing on your application, but it's nice to know you run a clean, classy institution. Good food, good care, pleasant surroundings, sufficient staff, planned social activities and all that stuff."

"Yes," he said, not changing expression, "all that stuff."

"From what I've read of our preliminary investigation reports, Crittenden Hall makes a modest profit. Which goes to the Crittenden Research Laboratory. Correct?"

He gestured toward the stacks of papers on his desk.

"Correct," he said. "And that's what I've been doing this afternoon, and why I couldn't show you around personally; I've been shuffling papers: bills, checks, requisitions, budgets, vouchers, salaries, and so forth. We have an accountant, of course; he comes in once a month. But I do the day-to-day management. It's my own fault; I could delegate the responsibility to Draper or Beecham—or hire a smart bookkeeper to do it. But I prefer doing it myself. I want to know where every penny comes from and where it goes. And you know, Mr. Todd, I hate it. Hate every minute of it. This paper shuffling, I mean. I'd much rather be in the lab with Dr. Draper and the others. Hard at work. The kind of work I enjoy."

It sounded swell: gifted scientist not interested in the vulgar details of making money, but only in pure research. For the benefit of mankind. What a cynical bastard I am! I said:

"That's a natural lead-in to my next question, Dr. Thorndecker. What kind of work? Everyone I saw in the lab seemed gung-ho and busy as hell. What's going on? What are you doing in the lab? I mean right now. Not if you get the grant, but what's going on *now?*"

He leaned back in his swivel chair, clasped his hands behind his head. He stared at plaster peeling off the high ceiling. His face suddenly contorted in a quick grimace, a tic that lasted no more than a second.

"Know anything about science?" he said. "Human biology in particular? Cells?"

"Some," I said. "Not much. I read your application and the report by our research specialists. But I'm not a trained scientist."

"An informed layman?"

"I guess you could say that."

"Anything in the application or report you didn't understand?"

"I caught the gist of it. I gather you're interested in why people get old."

His ceiling-aimed stare came slowly down. He looked directly into my eyes.

"Exactly," he said. "That's it in a nutshell. Why do people get old? Why does the skin lose its elasticity at the age of thirty-five? Why, at a later age, do muscles grow slack and eyesight dim? Why does hearing fail? Why should a man's cock shrink and his ass sink, or maybe shrivel up until there's nothing there but a crack on a spotted board? Why do a woman's breasts sag and wrinkle? Why does her pubic hair become sparse and scraggly? Why does a man go bald, a woman get puckered thighs? Why do lines appear? What happens to muscle tone and skin color? Did you know that some people actually shrink? They do, Mr. Todd, they *shrink*. Not only in body weight, but in their bone structure. Not to mention teeth falling out, a hawking of phlegm, an odor of the flesh like ash or foam, a tightening of the bowels."

"Jesus," I gasped, "I can hardly wait. Could I have a little more brandy, please?"

He laughed, and filled up my plastic cup. And his own, I noted. Once again I noted that sudden, brief twitching of his features. Almost a spasm of pain.

"I'm not telling you anything you didn't know," he said. "You just don't want to think about it. No one does. Mortality. A hard concept to grasp. Maybe even impossible. But the interesting thing about senescence, Mr. Todd, is that science was hardly aware of it as a biological phenomenon until the last—oh, let's say fifty years. Back in the Middle Ages, if you lived to the ripe old age of thirty or forty, you were doing well. Oh sure, there were a few oldsters of fifty or sixty, but most humans died in childbirth or soon after. If they survived a few years, disease, accidents, pestilence, or wars took them off before they really achieved maturity. Now, quite suddenly, with the marvelous advances in medical science, public health, hygiene, improved diet, and so forth, we have more and more people living into their sixties, seventies, eighties, nineties, and no one thinks it remarkable. It isn't. What is remarkable is that, in spite of medical care, diet, exercise, and sanitary toilets, very few humans make it to a hundred. Why is that, Mr. Todd?"

"Have no idea."

"Sure you do," he said gently. "They don't necessarily sicken. They don't get typhoid, the plague, smallpox, or TB. They just decay. They degenerate. The body not only stops growing, it simply stops. It's not a sudden thing; in a healthy human it takes place over a period of thirty or forty years. But we can see it happening, all those awful things I mentioned to you, and there's no way we can stop it. The human body declines. Heart, liver, stomach, bowels, brain, circulation, nervous system: all subject to degenerative disorders. The body begins to waste away. And if you study actuarial tables, you'll see there's a very definite mathematical progression. The likelihood of dying doubles every seven years after the age of thirty. How does that grab you? But it's only been in the past fifty years that science has started asking Why? Why should the human body decay? Why should hair fall out and skin become shrunken and crepey? We've extended longevity, yes. Meaning most people live longer than they did in the Middle Ages. But now we find ourselves up against a barrier, a wall. Why don't people live to be a hundred, two hundred, three hundred? We can't figure it out. No matter how good our diet, how efficient our sewers, how pure our air, there seems to be something in the human body, in our species, Mr. Todd, that decrees: Thus far, but no farther. We just can't seem to get beyond that one-hundred-year limit. Oh, maybe a few go a couple of years over, but generally a hundred years seems to be the limit for *Homo sapiens*. Why? Who or what set that limit? Is it something in *us*?

Something in our physical makeup? Something that decrees the time for dying? What is it? What the hell *is* it? And that, Mr. Todd, is what those gung-ho, busy-as-hell young researchers you just saw in the Crittenden Research Laboratory are trying to find."

I must admit, he had me. He spoke with such earnestness, such fervor, leaning toward me with hands clasped, that I couldn't take my eyes from him, couldn't stop listening because I was afraid that in the next sentence he might reveal the miracle of creation, and if I wasn't paying attention, I might miss it.

When he paused, I sat back, took a deep breath, and drank half my brandy.

I stared at him over the rim of my plastic cup. This time the contraction that wrenched his features was more violent than the two I had previously noted. This one not only twisted his face but wracked his body: he stiffened for an instant, then shuddered as his limbs relaxed. I don't think he was aware that it was evident. When it passed, his expression was unchanged, and he made no reference to it.

"Wow," I said. "Heady stuff, even for an informed layman. And I don't mean the brandy. Are you saying that the Biblical three-score-and ten don't necessarily have to be that? But could be more?"

He looked at me strangely.

"You're very quick," he said. "That's exactly what I'm saying. It doesn't *have* to be three-score-and-ten. Not if we can find what determines that span. If we can isolate it, we can manipulate it. Then it could become five-score-and-ten, or ten-score-and-ten. Or more. Whatever we want."

I was staggered. Almost literally. If that spring-sprung armchair hadn't clasped me close, I might have trembled. After reading his application, I had suspected Thorndecker wanted Bingham Foundation to finance a search for the Fountain of Youth. Everything I had seen of him up to that moment reinforced that suspicion. Older man-youthful wife. Cosseted body and the threads of a swinger. Contrived enthusiasm and the energy of a spark. It all made a kind of very human sense.

But now, if I understood him, he wasn't talking about the Fountain of Youth, of keeping smooth-skinned and romping all the days of our lives; he was talking about immortality—or something pretty close to it. I couldn't believe it.

"Dr. Thorndecker," I said, "let me get this straight . . . Are you saying there is a factor in human biology, in our bodies, that causes aging? And that once this agent—let's call it the X Factor—can be discovered and isolated, then the chances are that it can be manipulated, modified, changed— whatever—so that the natural span of a man's years could be increased without limit?"

He put his feet up on his desk. He sipped his brandy. Then he nodded. "That's exactly what I'm saying."

I leaned back, lighted another cigarette, crossed my legs. I couldn't look at him. I was afraid that if I did, and he said, "Now jump out of the window," out I'd go.

Because I can't tell you how convincing the man was. It wasn't only the manner: the passionate voice, the deep, unblinking gaze. But it was the impression of personal confession he gave, as if he were revealing the secret closest to his heart, a secret he had never revealed to anyone but me, because he knew I would understand and be sympathetic. It was as moving as a murmured, "I love you," and could no more be withstood.

"All right," I said finally, "supposing—just supposing—I go along with your theory that there is something in human biology, in the human body, that determines our lifespan—it is just a theory, isn't it?"

"Of course. With some hard statistical evidence to back it up."

"Assuming I agree with you that we all have something inside us that dictates when the cock shrinks and the ass sinks, what is it? What is the X Factor?"

"You read my application, and my professional record?"

"Yes."

"Then you must know that I believe the X Factor—as you call it—is to be found in the cell. The human cell."

"Germ cells? Sex cells?"

"No, we're working with body cells. Heart, skin, lung."

"Why cells at all? Couldn't the X Factor, the aging factor, be a genetic property?"

He gave me a glassy smile.

"You *are* an informed layman," he said. "Yes, I admit many good men working in this field believe senescence has a genetic origin. That the lifespan of our species, of all species, is determined by a genetic clock."

"It makes sense," I argued. "If my parents and grandparents live into their eighties and nineties, chances are pretty good that, barring a fatal accident or illness, I'll live into my eighties or nineties, too. At least, the insurance companies are betting on it."

"You may," he acknowledged. "And the geneticists make a great point of that. Perhaps the X Factor exists in DNA, and determines the lifespan of every human born. And perhaps the X Factor in DNA could be isolated. Then what?"

I shook my head. "You've lost me. You speak of manipulating the X Factor in human cells, if and when it can be isolated. So . . . ? Why couldn't it be manipulated if found in the genetic code? I understand gene splicing is all the rage these days."

"Oh, it's all the rage," he said, not laughing. "But recombination with *what?* If you isolated the senescence gene, what would you combine it with—the tortoise gene? They grow to a hundred and fifty, you know. As my son Edward might say, 'Big deal!' What I'm trying to say, Mr. Todd, is that, in this case, gene splicing does not offer anything but the possibility of extending the human lifespan by fifty years. I happen to believe that my cellular theory offers more than that. Much more. You ask if it's a theory, I reply that it is. You ask if I have any proof that the cellular approach to senescence is viable, I reply that there is much proof that the X Factor exists in human cells, but it has not been isolated. As of this date. You ask if I have anything to go on, other than my own conviction, that the X Factor can be isolated and manipulated, and I must reply in all honesty: no, nothing but my own conviction."

I took a deep breath.

"All right, Dr. Thorndecker," I said, "I appreciate your honesty. But why in hell didn't you spell all this out in your application? Why did you base it all on that crap about exposing human embryo cells to electromagnetic radiation?"

"First of all, that was accurate. We intend to do exactly that, in our effort to isolate the X Factor. Second of all, if I had stated in the application that my ultimate aim was to make humans immortal, would the Bingham Foundation even have bothered to process the application, or would it have been immediately consigned to deep six?"

"You know the answer to that," I said. "If you had stated your true reason for requesting the subsidy, I wouldn't be here now."

"Of course not," he said.

I looked at him in wonderment.

"So why are you telling me now?" I asked him. "Aren't you afraid I'll roll up my tent and go home?"

"It's a possibility," he acknowledged. "You could tell your superiors I misled the Bingham Foundation. I didn't, of course. But I admit I was not as totally forthright as I might have been. Still, my application is entirely truthful. It is not dishonest."

"You draw a fine line," I told him. I stared at that handsome, brooding face a long time. "And you're confessing," I said, still marveling. "Are you that sure of me?"

"I'm not sure of you at all," he said, somewhat testily. "But I think you're a shrewd man. I'm paying you the compliment of not trying to deceive you. You can report this conversation to your superiors or not, as you please. The decision is yours."

"You don't care?"

"Mr. Todd, I care a great deal. That grant is important to me. It's essential I get it. And it's vital, as I'm sure you're aware, to all of Coburn. But as I say, the decision is yours."

I drained my plastic cup, struggled out of that creaking armchair.

"You're certain," I said, "that the X Factor, the aging factor, will be found in human body cells and not in the genetic code?"

He grinned at me. "I'm certain. No one else is."

"Dr. Thorndecker, you stated there is hard statistical evidence to back up your belief in the existence of the X Factor in human body cells."

"That's correct; there is."

"Could I take a look at it?"

"Of course," he said promptly. "It consists not only of my work, but the work of others in this field. I'll have it collected and prepared for you. It will be ready in a day or so."

"Fine," I said. "Let's let it go until then. You've given me enough to think about for one day."

He walked me out onto the second-floor landing, chatting amiably, hand on my shoulder. He held me fast, went on and on about this and that, and I wondered—why the stall? Then I saw his eyes flickering to the lobby below. Sure enough, when the white-jacketed goon-doorman appeared, Thorndecker released my shoulder, shook my hand, told me how much he had enjoyed our palaver—his word: "palaver"—and gave me a smile of super-charm. I was becoming impervious to it. You can endure just so much charm in a given period. After that, it's like being force-fed a pound of chocolate macaroons.

I ambled slowly down that sweeping staircase. I was handed my coat and hat. I was ushered out the front door of Crittenden Hall.

I stood on the graveled driveway a moment, belting my trenchcoat, turning up the collar. Something odd was happening to that day: it was going ghostly on me. There was a cold mist in the air. At the same time, a whitish fog was rolling down.

Everything was silvered, swathed in the finest chain mail imaginable. It was a metallic mesh, wrapped around the physical world. I could see my car looming, but dimly, dimly, all glitter and glint. Beyond, even dimmer, the bare trunks of trees appeared, disappeared, appeared again, wavery in the hazy light. I could feel the wet on my face, and see it on my black leather coat.

I heard a weird chonking sound, and turned toward it. Then it became clopping. I heard the whinny of a horse, and out of the shivery mist, coming at a fast trot, rode Julie Thorndecker, sitting astride a big bay gelding. She pulled up alongside me. I stepped back hastily as the horse took a few skittering steps on the gravel, his eyes stretched. Then she quieted him, stroking his neck, whispering to him. I moved closer.

They had obviously been on a gallop. Steam came drifting from the beast's flanks and haunches; its breath was one long plume of white. It still seemed excited from the run: pawed the driveway, moved about restlessly, tossed its head. But Mrs. Thorndecker continued her ministering, solid in the English saddle. That was one hell of a horse. From my point of view, it seemed enormous, with a neck that was all glistening muscle, and a mouthful of teeth as big as piano keys.

Julie was wearing brown boots, whipcord jodhpurs, a creamy flannel shirt, suede jacket, gloves. There was a red silk scarf about her throat: the only splash of color in that somber scene. Her head was not covered, and the mist had matted down her fine hair so that it clung to her skull.

Before I could say, "Hi," or "Hello," or "Does he bite?" she had slipped from the saddle and landed lightly on her feet alongside me. She flipped the reins over the horse's head, then wrapped them around her hand.

"You always ride in the rain?" I asked her.

"It isn't raining," she said. "Just dampish. When the ground freezes, and the snow comes, I don't ride at all. Today was super."

"Glad to hear it."

"I have to cool him off," she said. "Take a little walk?"

"Sure," I said. "You walk between me and the horse."

"Are you afraid of horses?"

"Lady," I said, "I'm afraid of cocker spaniels."

So off we went, strolling slowly, that great beast following us like an equine chaperon.

"Have a nice visit?" she asked.

I hadn't forgotten that husky voice, that throaty, almost tremulous voice. It still seemed to promise everything a man might desire, and more. I began to warm under my trenchcoat.

"I like your hat," she said suddenly.

"Thanks," I said, flipping the limp brim at her. "It was made in Ireland, so I suppose it loves weather like this. Might even begin to grow. How long do we walk before that monster cools off?"

"A few minutes," she said. "Bored with me already?"

"No," I said. "Never," I vowed.

She laughed, a deep, shirred chuckle.

"Aren't you sweet," she said.

"I am," I acknowledged.

It seemed to me we were walking down a narrow road of packed earth. On both sides, indistinct in the fog, were the black trunks of winter-stripped trees, with spidery branches almost meeting overhead. It was like walking into a tunnel of smoke: everything gray and swirling. Even the light seemed to pulse: patches of pearl, patches of sweat.

"Did you have a good visit?" she asked again.

"Very good."

"And did you like what you saw?"

"Oh yes."

"Glad to hear it. You had a talk with my husband?"

"I did. A long talk. A long, interesting talk."

"Good," she said. "Perhaps he'll forgive me."

I turned to look at her. "Oh? For what?"

"For sending Ronnie Goodfellow to see you. I did that, you know. From the best motives in the world."

"I'm sure they were," I said.

"You aren't angry, are you?"

She stopped, I stopped, the horse stopped. She put a hand on my arm. She came a half-step closer, looked up at me.

"It won't hurt Telford, will it?" she breathed. "My sending Ronnie to see if you were settled in? It won't hurt our chances of getting the grant?"

That young face was as damp as mine. I remember seeing tiny silver beads of moisture on her long, black lashes. Her cheeks were still flushed from the gallop, and those ripe lips seemed perpetually parted, waiting. Everything about her seemed complaisant and yearning. Except the eyes. The eyes were wet stones.

Why, I wondered, with hard eyes like that, should she seem so peculiarly vulnerable to me? It was her crackly voice, I decided, and the little boy's hair-do, and the warmth of her hand on my arm, and the loose, free way she moved. The giving way.

"Of course not," I said. "You didn't do anything so awful. As a matter of fact, I liked Goodfellow. No harm done."

"Thank you," she said faintly. "You've made me feel a lot better." She came another half-step closer. "It's so important, you see. To Telford. To me. To all of us."

If, at that moment, she had looked into my eyes, batted her lashes, and murmured, "I'll do anything to get my husband that grant—*anything*," I think I would have burst out laughing. But she wasn't that obvious. There was just the warm hand on my arm, the two half-steps toward me, the implied intimacy in that furry scene of smoke, lustrous mist, shadowy trees, and a steaming horse making snorting noises behind us and beginning to paw impatiently at the earth.

We turned back, slowly. We walked a few minutes in silence. She hauled on the reins with both hands until the gelding's head was practically over her shoulder. She reached up to stroke that velvety nose.

"You darling," she said. "Darling."

I didn't know if she meant the horse or me. But then, at that moment, I suspected I might be happy.

We were about halfway back to the Hall when faintly, from far off, I heard the cry, "Julie! Julie!" Dimmed by distance, muffled by fog, that wailed cry stopped us dead in our tracks. It seemed to come from everywhere, almost howled, distorted: "Joo-lee! Joo-lee!" We looked around in the tunnel, trying to determine the direction. "Joo-lee! Joo-lee!" Louder now.

Then, first a drifting shade, then a dark presence, and then a figure wavering in the putty light, came running Edward Thorndecker. He pounded up to us, stood accusingly, hands on waist, chest heaving.

"Where *were* you?" he demanded of his stepmother. "You didn't come back from your ride and, my God, I was so worried! I thought you might have been thrown. Hurt. Killed! Julie, you've got to—"

"Edward," she interrupted sweetly, putting a hand on his arm (the same goddamned hand that had been on *my* arm!), "say hello to Mr. Todd."

"Hello, Mr. Todd," he said, not bothering to look at me. "Julie, you have no idea how frantic I was. My God, I was ready to call the cops."

"Were you, dear?" she said with that throaty chuckle. "You *must* have been upset if you were ready to call the cops."

I guessed it was an inside joke, because they both started laughing, he hesitantly at first, then without restraint. I didn't catch the enormous humor of it all, but it gave me a chance to take a closer look at him.

He was wearing a prep school uniform: dark blue blazer, gray flannel slacks, black shoes, black knitted tie. No coat, no hat. He was a beautiful, beautiful boy, clear cheeks flushed from running, red lips open, blue eyes clear and sparkling. And those crisp black curls, glittering with the wet.

"Julie," he said, "I've got to talk to you. Do you know what father—"

She leaned forward and pressed a gloved forefinger softly to his lips, silencing him. If she had done that to me, I'd have—ahh, the hell with it.

"Shh, Edward," she said, smiling with her mouth but not with her eyes. "We have a guest, and I'm sure Mr. Todd is not interested at all in a minor family disagreement. Mr. Todd, will you excuse us, please?"

Both looked at me, he for the first time. Since neither showed any indication of moving, I gathered I was being given the bum's rush.

"Of course," I said. I removed my sodden tweed hat and held it aloft. "Mrs. Thorndecker," I said. "Edward," I said.

I replaced the lid, turned, and plodded away from them. I trudged back to my car, resolved that I absolutely would not turn around to look back at them. I did about twenty steps before I turned around to look back at them.

I could see them glimmering through that scrim of fine chain mail. They were framed in the billowing fog between the rows of black trees and veiny, arching branches. Their figures wavered. I wiped a hand across my eyes, hoping to get a clearer look. But it was not clear. It was all smoke and shadow. Still, it seemed to me they were in each other's arms. Close. Close.

Somewhere, on the way back to Coburn, I pulled off the road. I left the motor running, the heater on. I lowered the window a bit so I wouldn't take the long, long sleep. I lighted a cigarette, and I pondered. I'm good at that. Not concluding, just pondering. In this case, my reflections were a mishmash: objective judgments of things I had observed that afternoon interspersed with subjective memories of parted lips, silvered hair plastered flat, husky laughs, and a loose, yielding way of moving.

Conclusions? You'll never guess. The only hard fact I came up with was that Al Coburn was a wise old owl. He had guessed Julie Thorndecker had sicced Constable Goodfellow onto me, and he had been right. Decision: cultivate Al Coburn and see what other insights the old fart might reveal.

As for the rest: all was confusion. But if you can't endure that, you shouldn't be in the snooping business. Sooner or later (if your're lucky), actions, relationships, and motives get sorted out and begin to make sense. It might not be rational sense, but I was dealing with human beings—and who says people have to be logical? Not me. And I speak from self-knowledge.

But there was one thing I could nail down, and had to. So I finished my cigarette, flicked the butt into what was now a freezing rain, and completed my drive into Coburn. It was about four-thirty, and I hoped I'd get there before the place closed for the day.

I made it—but not by much. Art Merchant had been right: the Coburn Civic Building was definitely not a tourist attraction. It was a two-story structure of crumbling red brick, designed along the general lines of an egg crate. The fire department occupied the ground level in front, the police department the ground level in back. The second floor was the City Hall: one big, hollow room. A bronze plaque on the outside wall stated: "This building erected by the Works Progress Administration, 1936; Franklin D. Roosevelt, President." Some loyal Democrat should have destroyed that.

I tramped up a wooden stairway, steps dusty and sagging. The wall was broken by tall, narrow windows affording a splendid view of the boarded-up A&P. At the top of the stairs were frosted glass doors bearing the legend: "oburn ity all." The lettering was in black paint, which had lasted. I figured the capital letters had been in gilt which had flaked off years ago and had never been replaced.

In all that cavernous room there was one middle-aged lady spraying her blue hair with a long aerosol can that could have been "Sparkle-Clear" or "Roach-Ded," for all I knew. She looked at me disapprovingly.

"We're closed," she yelled at me from across the room.

I made a big business of looking at my watch.

"Nah," I called, smiling winsomely, "you wouldn't do that to me—would you? You've got to finish spraying your lovely hair, and then the nails to touch up, and a few phone calls to your girlfriends, and it's only fifteen minutes to five, and I swear what I want won't take more than two minutes. Three maybe. Five at the most. Look at me—a poor traveler from out of town, come to your fair city seeking help in my hour of need. Can you turn me away? In your heart of hearts, can you really reject me?"

I don't apologize for this shit.

"Real estate?" she guessed. "The plats are over on the left, and if you—"

"No, no," I said. "Something much sadder. An uncle of mine passed away in Coburn only last night. Poor man. I need copies of the death certificate. You know—for insurance, bank accounts, the IRS and so forth. I need about ten copies."

"Sorry," she sang out. We were shouting at each other across at least fifty feet of empty office. "Death certificates go to the county seat. The Health Department. They have fire-proof files."

"Oh," I said, deflated. "Well, thanks, anyway."

"Of course, we keep photocopies of Coburn deaths," she said. "They're in the Deceased file on your right, between Bankruptcies and Defaults."

"May I take a quick look, ma'm?" I asked politely. "Just to make sure there is a certificate filed on my uncle?"

"Help yourself," she called. "I have to make a phone call. Then I'm locking up, so don't be long."

"Won't take a minute," I promised.

She got busy on the phone. I got busy on the Deceased file. The photocopy of Petersen's certificate was easy to find; it was in front, the most recent Coburn death. Chester K. Petersen, 72, resident of Crittenden Hall. The certificate was signed by Dr. Kenneth Draper.

But that wasn't what I was looking for. My eyes raced to find Cause of Death. There it was:

Congestive heart failure.

I glanced at the blue-haired lady. She was still giggling on the phone. I fumbled through the file as quickly as I could. I managed to go back through the previous two years. There had been twenty-three death certificates filed that listed Crittenden Hall as place of residence. The certificates were signed by Dr. Kenneth Draper and several other doctors. I guessed they were the resident MD's in Crittenden Hall.

Item: Two years ago, there had been six certificates filed, signed by four different MD's, including Draper. There had been a variety of causes of death.

Item: During the past year, there had been eighteen certificates filed, including Petersen's. Of these, fourteen had been signed by Draper, the others by residents.

Item: Of the fourteen death certificates in the past year signed by Dr. Kenneth Draper, eleven listed congestive heart failure as cause of death. The other three noted acute alcoholism, emphysema, and leukemia.

Nowhere, on any of the death certificates, did the name Dr. Telford Gordon Thorndecker appear.

"Finished?" the blue-haired lady called.

"Yes, thank you."

"Find what you wanted?" she yelled.

I smiled, waved, and got out of there. Did I find what I wanted? What did I want?

Driving back to the Coburn Inn, I recalled the exact conversation:

Me: "What did he die of? Petersen?"

Nurse Stella Beecham: "Pelvic cancer. Inoperable. He didn't respond to chemotherapy."

Someone was lying. Beecham or Draper, who had signed the certificate stating congestive heart failure was the cause of death.

And all those other puzzling statistics . . .

I needed a drink.

So, apparently, did half of Coburn. The bar at the Inn was two-deep with stand-up drinkers, and all of the booths were occupied. I took a small table, and grabbed the harried waiter long enough to order a vodka gimlet and a bag of potato chips with a bowl of taco-flavored cheese dip. My brain was whirling—why not my stomach?

I was working on drink and dip, using both hands, when I heard a breathless . . .

"Hi! Buy a thirsty girl a drink?"

I lurched to my feet.

"Hello, Millie," I said, gagging on a chip. "Sure, sit down. What'll you have?"

"My usual," she said. "Chivas Regal and 7-Up."

I don't think she saw me wince. I shouted the order at the passing waiter, then looked around nervously; I don't enjoy being seen in public with a cop's wife. It's not a matter of morality; it's a matter of survival. But fortunately, there was an old John Wayne movie on the bar's seven-foot TV screen, and most of the patrons were staring at that.

"Don't worry," Millie laughed. "Ronnie's working a twelve-hour shift tonight: four to four."

I looked at her with respect, and began to revise my opinion. I pushed the dip toward her, and she dug in.

"Besides," she said, spraying me with little bits of potato chip, "he doesn't give a damn who I drink with."

"Besides," I added, "he'd be happy to know you're helping make my stay in Coburn a pleasant one. He wants me to be happy."

"Yeah," she said, brightening, "that's right. Am I really helping?"

"You bet your sweet patootie," I said. "Love that tent you're wearing."

She looked down at the flowered muumuu.

"Really?" she said doubtfully. "This old thing? It doesn't show much."

"That's what makes it so exciting," I told her. "It leaves everything to the imagination."

She leaned forward and whispered:

"Know what I've got on underneath?"

I knew the answer to that one, but I couldn't spoil her big yock.

"What?" I asked.

"Just perfume?" she shouted, leaned back and laughed like a maniac.

Her drink arrived, and she took a big gulp, still spluttering with mirth. It gave me a chance to take a closer look at her.

The face was older than the body. There were lines at the corners of eyes and mouth. Beneath the heavy makeup, the skin was beginning to look pouchy and tired. And there was something in her expression perilously close to defeat. But the neck was strong and smooth, firm breasts poked, the backs of her hands were unblemished. Nothing defeated about that body.

"Where do you and Ronnie live, Millie?" I asked idly.

"Way to hell and gone," she said sullenly. "Out on Fort Peabody Drive." I thought for a moment.

"Near Crittenden Hall?"

"Yeah," she said sourly, "right *near* it. Their fence runs along the back line of our property."

"What have you got—a house, farm, mobile home?"

"A dump," she said. "We got a dump. Could I have another one of these?"

I ordered another round of drinks.

"Tell me, Millie," I said, "where do the good citizens of Coburn go when they want to cut loose? Don't tell me they all come in here and watch television?"

"Oh, there's a few places," she said, coming alive. "Roadhouses. Out on the Albany post road. Nothing fancy, but they have jukes and dancing. Sometimes Red Dog Betty's has a trio on Saturday night."

"Red Dog Betty's?"

"Yeah. There's a big poodle in red neon outside the place. It's kind of a rough joint. A lot of truckers stop there. But loads of fun."

She looked at me hopefully, but I wasn't having any. I wasn't drunk enough for Red Dog Betty's and loads of fun.

"Tell me about the places you go to in New York," she said.

I didn't tell her about the places I go to; she'd have been bored silly. But I told her what I thought she wanted to hear, describing fancy restaurants, swinging bars, discos, outdoor cafes, beaches, pick-up joints and make-out joints.

Her face became younger and wistful. She asked eager questions. She wanted to know how the women dressed, how they acted, what it cost to live in New York, could she get an apartment, could she get a job.

"Could I have fun there?" she asked.

I felt like weeping.

"Sure, you could," I said. "Maybe not every minute. It can be the loneliest place in the world. But yes, you could have fun."

She thought about that for a moment. Then the defeat came back in her eyes.

"Nah," she said mournfully. "I'd end up peddling my tail on the street."

It was another revelation. No dumbbell she. I had underestimated her. The clown makeup and the tart's costume she was wearing the first time I saw her had misled me. Maybe she wasn't intelligent, but she was shrewd enough to know who she was and what she was.

She knew that in Coburn she was *somebody*. Men came to the Inn lobby to buy their cigars and cigarettes and magazines and newspapers, just to wisecrack with her, to get a look at the finest lungs west of the Hudson River, to flirt, to dream. The femme fatale of Coburn, N.Y. As much a tourist attraction as Lovers' Leap and the place where the British spy was hanged. And in New York City, she'd end up hawking her ass on Eighth Avenue, competing with 15-year-old hookers from Minneapolis, and she knew it.

She knew it in her mind, but knowing couldn't entirely kill the dream, end the fantasy. The wild, crazy, raucous, violent city drew her, beckoned, lured, seduced. Loads of fun down there. *Loads* of fun.

The bar was emptying, the patrons going off grumbling to farms, homes, wherever. There were several empty booths.

"Have dinner with me, Millie," I said impulsively. "You'd be doing me a favor. I get tired of eating alone, and I'd—"

"Sure," she said promptly. "We'll eat right here. Okay? I hear the meat loaf is very good tonight."

It was good, as a matter of fact. I think it was a mixture of beef, pork, and lamb, very juicy and nicely seasoned. With it, they served thick slices of potato that had been baked, then browned and crusted in a skillet. Creamed spinach. We both had warm apple pie a la mode for dessert. I figured if this Thorndecker investigation went on much longer, I was going to need a new wardrobe, three sizes larger.

We had a bottle of New York State red with the meal, and brandy stingers with our coffee. Millie Goodfellow sat there, chin propped on her hand, a benign smile on her face, and I admit I was feeling the way she looked: slack, satisfied, and grinny. The memory of those eleven congestive heart failures in the past year at Crittenden Hall slid briefly into my mind, and slid right out again.

"You were talking about going to New York," I said. "Just you? Or you and your husband?"

"What do you think?" she said scornfully. "He'll never leave this turd-kicking town. He *likes* it here, for God's sake."

"Well . . ." I said, "it's his home. I understand his family have lived here for years and years."

"That's not the reason," she said darkly. "The reason he won't get out."

"Oh?" I said. "What is the reason?"

She put her two forefingers together and her two thumbs together, and made an elongated spade-shaped opening. She looked down at it, then up at me.

"Know what I mean?" she said.

"Yes," I said, "I think I know what you mean."

We were sitting across from each other in a highbacked booth. The checkered tablecloth hung almost to the floor. Millie Goodfellow squirmed around a bit, and before I knew it, she had a stockinged foot in my groin, tapping gently.

"Hi there!" she said brightly.

"Uh . . . hi," I said, sliding a hand below the tablecloth to grip her ankle. It wasn't passion on my part; it was fear. One sharp kick would have me singing soprano.

"Sex is keeping him in Coburn?" I asked.

She winked at me.

"You said it, I didn't," she said.

"Let me guess," I said. "Julie Thorndecker."

She winked again.

"You catch on fast," she said. "She's got him hypnotized. He's in heat for her all the time. Walks around with his tongue hanging out. And other things a lady can't mention. He can't think straight. He runs errands for her. If she told him to, he'd jump in the river. He's gone nuts. He's out there all the time. I think they're making it in the back seat of his cruiser. Hell, maybe they're making it in our place while I'm working. She'd get a charge out of that: screwing my husband in my bed."

"Are you sure, Millie?"

"Sure, I'm sure," she said roughly. "But you think I give a damn? I don't give a damn. Because you know what the funny thing is?"

"What's the funny thing?"

"He thinks he's the only one, but he's only one of many, son. She's laying everything in pants. Maybe even that bull dyke Agatha Binder. Maybe even that sissy stepson of hers, that kid Edward. I wouldn't be a bit surprised. I'm telling you, Constable Ronald H. Goodfellow is in for a rude awakening one of these days. Oh yes. And I couldn't care less. But you know what burns my ass?"

"A flame about this high?" I asked, holding my palm at table level.

She was drunk enough to think that funny.

"What burns me," she said, still giggling, "is that I've got the reputation for being the fast one. Always playing around—you know? Cheating on my husband with every drummer and trucker who comes to town. That's what people think. And she's the re-*feened* Mrs. Lah-de-dah, wife of the big scientist, the first lady of Coburn. And she's just a randy bitch. She out-fucks me three to one. But I get the reputation. Is that fair? You know what I'm going to do? I'm going to hire a private detective and get pictures of them together. You know—naked as jaybirds and banging away. Then I'm going to sue Ronnie for divorce and smear her name and the pictures all over the place."

"No, Millie," I said, "you're not going to do that."

"No," she said dully, "I won't. I can't. Because Ronnie knows about me. Names, dates, places. He's got it all in that little goddamned notebook of his. He knows about me, and I know about him. Hey!" she said brightly. 'What happened to our happy little party?" Her stockinged toes beat a rapid tattoo on my cringing testicles. "Let's you and me go up to your room. You show me the New York way, and I'll show you the Coburn way."

"What's the Coburn way?"

"Standing up in a hammock."

"Hell," I said laughing, "I don't even know the New York way. Unless it's impotence. I'm going to beg off, Millie. I appreciate your kind offer, but I'm somewhat weary and I'm somewhat drunk, and I wouldn't want to disappoint you. Another time. When I'm in tip-top condition."

The toes dug deeper.

"Promise?" she breathed.

"Promise," I nodded.

I paid the tab, we collected hats and coats, and I walked her out to her Ford Pinto in the parking lot. She was feeling no pain, but she was talking lucidly and wasn't staggering or anything. I believed her when she said she could get home all right.

"As a matter of fact," she said, "I'm practically stone cold sober. I might even stop by Red Dog Betty's and see if there's any action tonight."

"Don't do that, Millie," I urged. "Go home, go to bed, and dream of me. I'll go upstairs, go to bed, and dream of you. We'll have a marvelous dream together."

"Okay," she said, "that's what we'll do. You're so sweet, I could eat you up. Come in and sit with me a minute while the car warms up."

She pulled me into the car with her, started the engine, turned on the heater. I fumbled for a cigarette, but before I knew what was happening, she was all over me like a wet sheet. Her mouth was slammed against mine, a frantic tongue was exploring my fillings.

I knew it wasn't my manly charm. It wasn't even her physical wanting. It was misery and loneliness and hurt. It was despair. And the only way she could exorcise that was to cleave to a warm bod, any bod. I just happened to be the nearest.

She pulled her mouth away.

"Hold me," she gasped. "Please. Just hold me."

I held her, and hoped it was comfort. She took my hand and thrust it under her coat, under that long, voluminous skirt. She had been truthful: all she had on beneath the shift was perfume. She pressed my palm against a long, cool thigh. She just held it there and closed her eyes.

"Sweet," she whispered. "So sweet. Isn't it sweet?"

"Yes," I said. "Millie, I've—"

"I know," she said, releasing my hand and smiling bravely, "you've got to go. Okay. You'll be in town awhile?"

"Another few days at least," I said.

"We'll get together?" she asked anxiously.

"Sure we will."

"Listen, all that stuff I said about Julie Thorndecker—I shouldn't have said all that. It's all bullshit. None of it's true. I'm just jealous, that's all. She's so beautiful."

"And young," I said, like an idiot.

"Yes," she said in a low voice. "She's young."

I kissed her cheek and got out of there. I watched her drive away. When she turned onto Main Street, I waved, but I don't think she saw me. I hoped she wasn't going to Red Dog Betty's. I hoped nothing bad would happen to her. I hoped she'd be happy. I hoped I'd wake in the morning without a hangover. I hoped I'd go to Heaven when I died.

I knew none of these things was going to happen.

I went back into the bar. I had two straight brandies, figuring they'd settle the old tum-tum, and I'd be able to sleep without pills. Something was nagging at me. A memory was nagging, and I couldn't recall, couldn't define, couldn't pin it down. It had nothing to do with the Thorndecker investigation. It was a memory revived by something that had happened in the past hour, something that had happened with Millie Goodfellow.

It was more than an hour before I grabbed it. I was up in my room, hunched over on a bed, two boots and one sock off, when it came to me. I sat there, stunned, a wilted sock dangling in my fingers. The memory stunned me. Not the memory itself, but the fact that when it happened, I was convinced it would turn my life around, and I'd never forget it. Now it took me an hour to dredge it out of the past. So much for the woes of yesteryear.

What happened was this . . .

About two years previously—Joan Powell and I enjoying a sharp, hard, bright, and loving relationship—I was assigned a field investigation in Gary, Indiana: not *quite* the gardenspot of America.

An assistant professor in a second-rate engineering school had submitted an application for a modest grant. His specialty was solar energy, and he had been doing independent research on methods to increase the efficiency of solar cells. They're squares of gallium arsenide that convert sunlight directly to electricity. Even the types used in the space program were horribly expensive and not all that efficient.

The professor had developed, he said, a method of electronic amplification that boosted the energy output above that of fossil fuels at half the cost. Not only did I not know what the hell his diagrams and equations meant, but Scientific Research Records, who analyzed his proposals, more or less admitted they were stumped: "The claims made herein represent a totally new and unique approach to this particular problem, and there is nothing in current research to substantiate or refute the applicant's proposals." In other words: "We just don't know."

Lifschultz Associates reported the professor was small potatoes, financially speaking. He had a mortgage, a car loan, two kids in college, and a few bucks in the bank. Small insurance, small investments, small everything. Mr. Everyman.

Donner & Stern didn't have much to add of a personal nature. The professor had been married to the same woman for twenty-six years, had those two kids, drove a five-year-old car, didn't drink, gamble, or carouse, was something of an enigma to neighbors and colleagues. He was polite, quiet, withdrawn, didn't seem to have any close friends, and apparently his only vice was playing viola in a local amateur string quartet.

I went out to Gary to see him, and it was pretty awful. He had fixed up a basement lab in his home, but it looked like a tinkerer's workshop to me. He didn't talk much, and his dumpy wife was even quieter. I remember they served me a glass of cranberry juice, and put out a plate of Milky Ways cut into little cubes.

I thought he was a loser—the whole family were losers—and I guess some of this crept into my report. Anyway, his application was denied, and he got one of our courteous goodby letters.

A few days later he tried to swallow a shotgun and blew his brains all over his basement workshop.

I don't know why it hit me so hard. The professor wasn't rejected just on the basis of my report; the special investigators had been as unenthusiastic as I was. But I couldn't get rid of the notion that his suicide was my fault; I had done him in. If I had been a little kinder, more sympathetic, more understanding, maybe he'd have gotten his ridiculously small grant, and maybe his cockamamie invention would have proved out. Maybe the guy was another Edison. We'll never know, will we?

The night after I heard of his death, I had dinner with Joan Powell. We ate at a restaurant on West 55th Street that specialized in North Italian cooking. Usually I thought the food was great. That night the pasta tasted like excelsior. Powell knew my moods better than her own, and asked me what was wrong. I told her about the suicidal professor in Gary, Indiana.

"And don't tell me it wasn't my fault," I warned her. "Don't tell me that logically I have no business blaming myself. I don't want to listen to any logic."

"I wasn't going to serve you any," she said quietly.

"It goes beyond logic," I said. "It's irrational, I know. I just feel like shit, that's all."

"*Must* you use words like that?"

"You do," I reminded her.

"Not at the dinner table," she said loftily. "There is a time and place for everything."

I poked at my food, and she stared at me.

"Todd, you're really hurting, aren't you?"

"He was such a sad schlumpf," I groaned. "A little guy. And plain. His wife was plain, too. I mean they had nothing: no wit, no personality, and they weren't even physically attractive. Do you think that affected my judgment?"

"Probably," she said.

"You're a big help."

"Do you want advice or sympathy?"

"Neither," I said. "But five minutes of silence would be nice."

"Fuck you," she said.

"*Must* you use words like that?"

"I told you, there's a time and place for everything."

"Powell, what am I going to *do?*"

"Do? You can't do anything, can you? It's done, isn't it?"

"How long am I going to feel this lousy? The rest of my life?"

"Nooo," she said wisely, "I don't think so. A week. A month maybe. It'll pass."

"The hell you say," I growled. "Let's go."

"Go? Where?"

"Anywhere. I've got to get out of here."

"All right," she said equably. "You owe me half a veal cutlet Parmesan."

"Put it on my bill," I said.

"You're running up a big tab, buster," she said. "I'm not sure you're good for it."

If I had been in a better mood, I would have enjoyed that night: late September, with balm in the air over a little nip that warned of what was coming. I don't know how long we drove—an hour maybe. No, it was longer than that. We went up to the George Washington Bridge, turned around, and drove back down to the Battery. Not what you'd call a restful, bucolic drive. But working the traffic helped keep my mind off my misery. I don't think Joan Powell and I exchanged a dozen words during that trip. But she was there beside me, silent. It helped.

After we watched a Staten Island ferry pull in and pull out—about as exciting as watching grass grow—I drove back up the east side to Powell's home. She lived in one of those enormous high-rise luxury apartment houses that have an institutional look: hospitals, office buildings, or just a forty-story file cabinet.

There were two below-ground parking levels. Powell didn't own a car— didn't drive, as a matter of fact—but after I started seeing her, dating her, spending time in her apartment, including weekends, I persuaded her to rent a parking space. It cost fifty a month, and I paid it gladly. A lot easier than trying to find parking space on the street in that neighborhood. Plus the fact that my hubcaps were relatively secure.

Our parking space was down on the second level. A little like parking in the Lincoln Tunnel. It was a scary place: pools of harsh light and puddles of black darkness. Silent cars, heavy and gleaming. Concrete pillars and oil stains. I parked, switched off the motor. We lighted cigarettes, and were very alone.

I went through it all again. The schlumpfy professor, his crazy scheme, his mousy wife. The glass of cranberry juice and cubes of cut-up Milky Ways. The amateurish home laboratory, and how I couldn't understand what the hell he was mumbling about when he showed me his equations, demonstrated his equipment, and made an electric fan run on the power of a 100-watt lightbulb shining on a chip of white, glassy stuff.

Joan Powell let me gabble. She sat apart, hugging herself against the basement chill. A cigarette burned down in her lips. Her sleek head was tilted to keep the smoke from her eyes. She didn't say a word while I spun out my litany of woe and declaimed my guilt.

I ended my soliloquy and waited for a reaction. Nothing.

"Well?" I demanded.

"You know what I think you need right now?" she said.

"What?"

"A good fuck."

"Oh my," I said. "Listen to the lady."

We put out our cigarettes, turned to stare at each other. Powell was looking at me steadily, and there was something in her fine features I had never seen before: strength and knowing and calm acceptance. Maybe we're all created equal, in the sight of God and under the law, but there is quality in people. I mean human character runs the gamut from slug to saint. I realized, maybe for the first time, that this was one superior human.

And because I was feeling so deeply it embarrassed me, I had to say something brittle and smart-alecky. But I never did get it out. I choked on the words, and just came apart. I don't apologize for it; it had been coming on since I heard of the professor's messy death. But I wasn't mourning just for him; I was crying for all the sad, little schlumpfs in the world. For all of us. The losers.

Powell was holding me in her arms then, and I was gasping and moaning and trying to tell her all those things.

"Shh," she kept saying. "Shh. Shh."

I remembered she stroked my hair, kissed my fingers, touched my lips. She held me until I stopped shivering, pulling my head down to her warm breast. She rocked a little, back and forth, like a mother holding an infant. She smelled good to me, warm and fragrant, and I nuzzled my nose down into her neckline and kissed the soft skin.

It all went so slowly. After awhile it went in silence. I had the feeling, and I think she did too, that we were alone on earth. We were locked in a car, in an underground garage, the weight of an enormous building above, the whole earth below. We were in a coffin in a cavern in a mine. I had never known such sweet solitude, closed around like that.

And I had never known such intimacy, such closeness, not even naked on a sweated sheet. Without speaking, we opened to each other. I could feel it, feel the flow between us. My anguish was diluted by her strength; I suppose she took some of my hurt into her. Sharing eased the pain. When I kissed her, it was almost like kissing myself. A strange experience, but there it was. She was me, and I was her. It was peace. That's the only way I can describe it: it was total peace.

Well . . . that happened two years previously. I was convinced that night was going to remake my life, that I would suddenly become saintly and good, full of kindness and understanding. I didn't change, of course. The next day I was my normal shitty self, and a week later I had forgotten all about the dead professor, and a week after that I had forgotten all about an hour of total peace in an underground garage with Joan Powell when we had done nothing but hold each other and share. If I remembered it at all, it was to wonder why we hadn't screwed.

Now, two years later, sitting in a lonely room in Coburn, N.Y., the memory of that night came back. I knew what had triggered it: those few moments alone in the car with Millie Goodfellow. I had felt the stirring of the same emotion, the feeling of closed-in intimacy, of being the only survivors in the world, everything blocked out but the two of us, comforting, consoling.

I had been deceiving myself to think I was the only comforter, the lone consoler. She had given warm assurance to me as well, and when I waved goodby, the lights of her car fading into the black night, I was sorry to see her go. Because then I was really alone. And I was afraid.

I knew what it was. It all came back to Thorndecker. I could hear the name itself, boomed out by the Voice of Doom, with deep organ chords in the background: "Thooorn-deck-er. Thoorn-deck-er." It was like the tolling of a mournful bell. And even when I was in bed, covers pulled up, anxious for sleep to come, in my fear I heard that slow dirge and saw a dark funeral procession moving across frozen ground.

THE FOURTH DAY

I woke suddenly, tasting my tongue, smelling my breath. I stared at the crackled ceiling and wondered how long I had been buried in Coburn, N.Y.

I had been through that mid-case syndrome before. In any investigation, the disparate facts and observations pile up, a jumble, and you'd like nothing better than to walk away whistling, tossing a live grenade over your shoulder as you go. Then you close the door carefully and —*boom!*—all gone.

I think, in my case, the discouragement comes from a hopeless romanticism. I want people to be nice. Everyone should be sweet-tempered, polite, considerate, and brush their teeth twice a day. There should be no stale breaths and furry tongues in the world. I like happy endings.

I stared morosely at my sallow face in the mirror of the bathroom medicine cabinet, and I knew the Thorndecker investigation wasn't going to have a happy ending. It saddened me, because I didn't dislike any of the people involved. Some, like Stella Beecham and banker Art Merchant, left me indifferent. But most of the others I liked, or recognized as fallible human beings caught up in fates they could not captain.

Except Dr. Telford Gordon Thorndecker. I couldn't see him as a willy-nilly victim. The man was master of his soul; that much was obvious. But his motives were wrapped around. At that dinner party—his youthful vigor and raw exuberance. A part he was playing? And then, in his study, another role: the serious, intent man of science, with a politician's use of charm and a secret delight in the manipulation of others. Which man was Thorndecker? Or was there another, another, another? A whole deck of Thorndeckers: Jack, Queen, King, and finally . . . the Joker?

I showered, shaved, dressed, and had a terrible desire to telephone Joan Powell, that complete woman. Not even to talk. Just to hear her say, "Hello?" Then I'd hang up. I didn't call, of course. I just mention it here to illustrate my state of mind. I wasn't *quite* out of the tree but I was swinging.

Sam Livingston took me down in the ramshackle elevator. We exchanged mumbles. We both seemed to be in the same surly mood. If I had given him a bright, "Good morning, Sam!" he'd have kicked me in the jewels, and if he had sung out, "Nice, sunny morning," I'd have delivered a sharp karate chop behind his left ear. So we both just mumbled. It was that kind of a morning.

I saw Millie Goodfellow behind the cigar counter, and was pleased to know she was still alive. She was in one of her biddy's costumes again: a ruffled blouse cut down to the pipik, wide black leather belt, short denim skirt with rawhide lacing down the front, like a man's fly. She was also wearing dark, dark sunglasses.

I bought another pack of cigarettes I didn't need.

"Incognito this morning, Millie?" I inquired casually.

She lifted those dark cheaters, and I saw the mouse: a beauty. She had tried to cover it with pancake makeup, but the colors came through: glistening black, purple, yellow. The whole eye was puffed and bulging.

"Nice," I said. "Did you collect that at Red Dog Betty's?"

"No," she said, replacing the glasses, "this one was home-grown. I told him what I thought about him and his fancy lady."

I really didn't want to hear it. I didn't know if she was lying. I didn't know what the truth was. And on that feckless morning, I didn't care.

"See you around," I said, and started away.

A hand shot out, grabbed my arm.

"Remember what you promised last night?" she whispered.

That was last night, in another mood, another world, and before I knew her husband got physical.

"What?" I said. "Oh. Sure."

I stared at blank glass, not seeing her eyes.

"I remember," I said with a sleazy grin, more determined than ever to get my ass back to civilization as soon as possible.

I had another of those big, bulky country breakfasts. This one involved pancakes and pork sausages. I don't know what it did for my cholesterol count, but at least it took my mind off such topics as hanging, cyanide, and a long walk off a short pier. When I returned to the city, I decided, I'd diet, join a health club, exercise regularly, manufacture a hard stomach, and put the roses back in my cheeks. Is there no end to self-delusion?

On the way out, I detoured through the bar. Jimmy was behind the taps. I nodded at him. I didn't see anyone else, until I heard a rasped, "Todd. You there." I turned, and there was old Al Coburn sitting alone in a booth. He had a beer in front of him. I walked over.

"May I join you, Mr. Coburn?" I asked.

"No law against it," he said—as gracious an invitation as I've ever had.

I slid in opposite, called to Jimmy, pointed to Coburn's beer, and held up two fingers.

While we waited for our drinks to come, I said to him, "What's it like outside? Is the sun shining?"

"Somewhere," he said.

That seemed to take care of that. I stared at him. Have you ever seen bald land after a bad drought? Say the banks of a drained reservoir, or a parched river bed? That's the way Al Coburn's face looked. All cracks and lines, cut up like a knife had been drawn deep, the flesh without juice, squares and diamonds of dry skin.

But there was nothing juiceless about those washed-blue eyes. Looking into those was like staring into the Caribbean off one of the Bahamian cays. You stared and stared, seeing deep, deep. Moving things there, shifting shadows, sudden shapes, and then the clean, cool bottom. A few shells. Hard coral.

Maybe it was those pork sausages bubbling in my gut, but I felt uneasy. I felt there was more to Al Coburn than I had reckoned. I had misread Millie Goodfellow; there was more to her than the frustrated wife, the Emma Bovary of Coburn, N.Y. There was more to Al Coburn. If that was true, then it might be true of Agatha Binder, Art Merchant, Constable Goodfellow, Stella Beecham, Dr. Kenneth Draper—for the whole lot of them.

Maybe I was making an awful mistake. I was seeing them all (except Dr. Thorndecker) as two-dimensional cutouts. Types. Cardboard characters. But the longer I stayed around, the deeper I dug, the more they sprouted a third dimension. I was beginning to glimpse hidden motives and secret passions. It was like picking up Horatio Alger and finding William Faulkner. In *Coburn, N.Y.!?* A boggling thought, that in this brackish backwater there were characters who, if they didn't qualify for a Greek tragedy, were at least a few steps above, or deeper, than a TV sitcom.

We sipped our beers and looked vaguely at each other.

"How you coming?" Al Coburn asked in his scrawly voice.

"Coming?" I said. "On what?"

He looked at me with disgust.

"Don't play smarty with me, sonny," he said. "This Thorndecker thing. That's what I mean."

"Oh," I said. "That. Well, I'm making progress. Talking to people. Learning things."

He grunted, finished his old beer, started on the new.

"He's doing all right, ain't he," he said. "On Coburn land. Got a nice business going."

"It appears to be prosperous," I said cautiously. "Yes. I looked it over."

"That's what you think," he said darkly.

"What's that supposed to mean, Mr. Coburn?"

"The death of a man?" he said. "The world's heart don't skip a beat."

I shook my head, bewildered. I grabbed at a straw, and came up with nothing.

"Are you talking about Petersen?" I asked.

"Who?"

"Chester K. Petersen."

"Never heard of him."

"All right," I sighed. "You've lost me completely."

We drank awhile in silence. He glowered at his glass of beer, almost snarling at it. What a cantankerous old geezer he was. I watched him, damned if I'd give him another opening. If he had something to say, let him say it. Finally:

"Was he another?" he said.

"Petersen? I don't know. Another *what?*"

"Heart attack?"

"He died of congestive heart failure."

"Who says?"

"The death certificate says."

He smiled at me. I hope I never see another smile like it. It was all store teeth and blanched lips. A skeleton could smile with more warmth than that.

"The death certificate says," he repeated. "You believe *that?*"

This isn't original with me; I remember reading somewhere that the worst American insult, absolutely the *worst*, is to say, "Do you believe everything you read in the papers?" Al Coburn's last question had the same effect. I immediately went on the defensive.

"Well, uh, of course not," I stammered. "Not necessarily."

"Tell you a story," he said. More of a statement than a question.

I nodded, waved for two more beers, and settled back. I had nothing to lose but my sanity.

"Feller I knew name of Scoggins," he started. "Ernie Scoggins. We was friends from way back. Grew up together, Ernie and me. His folks had a sawmill on the river, but that went. They had an ice house, too. That was before refrigerators, you know, and them with all that sawdust to pack it in. Cut it on Loon Lake in the winter, and cover it over with burlap and sawdust in the ice house. Ernie and me used to sneak in there in the summer and suck on slivers of ice. I guess we was two crazy kids."

I could feel my eyeballs beginning to harden, and I knew I was getting a glassy stare. I wanted to yelp, "Get on with it, for God's sake!" But Al Coburn wasn't the kind of man you could hurry. He'd just shutter on me, and I'd never learn what he had on his mind. So I let him yabber.

"Bad luck," Coburn said. "Ernie sure had bad luck. His son got killed in Korea, and his two daughters just up and moved on. His wife died the same year my Martha went, and that brought us closer together, Ernie and me. Something in common—you know? Anyway, the sawmill went, and the ice house, of course. Ernie tried this and that, but nothing come out good for him. He took a lick at farming, and lost his crop in a hailstorm. Tried a hardware store, and that went bust. Put some money in a Florida land swindle, and lost that."

"Bad luck," I said sympathetically, repeating what he had said. But now he disagreed.

"Mebbe," he said. "But Ernie wasn't all that smart. I knew it, and I think sometimes he knew it. He just didn't have much above the eyebrows, Ernie didn't. Throwing his money around. But I'll tell you this: he was the best friend a man could have. Shirt off his back. Always cheerful. Could he tell a joke? Land! And a good word for everyone. Wasn't a soul in Coburn who didn't like Ernie Scoggins. Ask anyone; they'll tell you. Old Ernie Scoggins . . ."

He fell silent then, staring at his empty beer glass, ruminating. I took it for a hint, and signaled Jimmy for two more.

"What happened to him?" I asked Al Coburn. "Old Ernie Scoggins—is he still around?"

He didn't answer until Jimmy brought over our beers, collected the empty glasses, and went back behind the bar again.

"No, he ain't around," Coburn said in a low voice. "Not for almost a month now."

"Dead?"

He glanced at Jimmy, then leaned across the table to me.

"No one knows," he whispered. "Mebbe dead, mebbe not. He just disappeared."

"Disappeared?" I said incredulously. "You mean one fine day he just turned up missing?"

"That's right."

"Didn't anyone try to find him? His family?"

"Ernie didn't have no family," Coburn said, "rightly speaking. No one even knows where his two daughters are, if *they're* still alive. No brothers or sisters. I reckon you could say I was Ernie Scoggins' family. So after he didn't show up for a few days, I asked around. No one knew a thing."

"Did you report his disappearance to the police?"

Coburn snorted disdainfully, then took a long swallow of beer.

"To that Indian," he nodded. "Ronnie Goodfellow. The two of us went out to Ernie's place. He was living in a beat-up trailer out on Cypress Road. Goodfellow tried the door, it was open, and we went in. Everything looked all right. I mean the place wasn't broken up or anything like that. But most of Ernie's clothes was gone, including his Sunday-go-to-meeting suit, and a battered old suitcase I knew he owned. Goodfellow said it looked to him like Ernie just took off of his own free will. Just packed up and left."

"Sounds like it," I said. "Did he have any debts in town?"

"Oh hell, Ernie *always* had debts. All his life."

"Well then? He just flew the coop. Got fed up and decided to try his luck somewhere else."

Al Coburn looked at me with a twisted face. I couldn't read it. Contempt there for me, and something else: indecision, and something else. Fear maybe.

"I'll tell you," he said. "The debts wasn't all that big. And for about two years before he disappeared, Ernie Scoggins had been working for Thorndecker out in Crittenden Hall."

"Oh," I said.

"It wasn't much of a job," Coburn said. " 'Maintenance personnel' was what they called it. Raking leaves, cutting down dead branches, taking care of the wife's bay gelding. Like that. But Ernie said it wasn't too hard, he was outside most of the time, you know, and the pay was good. I don't figure he ever paid a penny to Social Security in his life, and he needed that job. I can't see him just walking away from it. He wasn't any spring chicken, you know. My age."

I moved my beer glass around, making interlocking rings on the tabletop.

"What do you think happened?" I asked him. "Why did he leave?"

His answer was so faint I had to lean forward to hear his scratchy voice.

"I don't think Ernie Scoggins did leave," he said. "First of all, if he was taking off, he'd have stopped by to say so-long to me. I *know* that. Second of all, Ernie was in World War One, with the Marines. And he still had his helmet. You know, one of those pie-shaped hats with a brim. The old hunk of rusty tin was the one thing Ernie treasured. It was valuable to him. He never would have moved on without taking it with him. But when Goodfellow and I went into his place, the helmet was still there, setting on his little TV set."

"But his clothes were gone?"

"Most of them."

"And a suitcase?"

"Yes."

"And the door was open?"

He nodded.

I sat back, propped myself against the wall, put my feet up on the booth bench, sitting sideways to Coburn. I watched Jimmy polishing glasses behind the bar.

"I don't know," I said slowly. "I'll have to go along with Goodfellow. Ernie Scoggins packed some clothes and walked away. And left the door open because he wasn't coming back. He didn't take the helmet because there was no room for it in the valise. What's he going to do—wear it?"

He stared at me.

"Don't be a wisenheimer," he said.

I took a deep breath, blew it out, brought my feet down with a thump, and faced him.

"All right," I said, "you've obviously got more. What is it?"

"His car. It was still parked outside his trailer."

"So he took a bus, a train, a plane."

"He didn't," Al Coburn said. "I checked."

"*You* checked? Didn't Constable Goodfellow check?"

"Not so's you know it."

"Scoggins could have walked, or hitched a ride."

"With his car there? Gas in the tank? You believe that?"

"No," I said unhappily. "All right, let's have it: what happened to Ernie Scoggins?"

When he didn't answer, I said:

"Look, Mr. Coburn, I've listened patiently to this sad story. You apparently think it's important enough for me to know about it. So I guess it's got something to do with Thorndecker. So why are you holding back? Is that all there is to the whole thing? An old boyhood pal of yours disappeared? What's the *point*?"

"Finish your beer," he said, finishing his.

I finished my beer. He jerked a thumb, got up, hobbled toward the exit. I paid Jimmy, then hurried after Coburn. He stumped his way through the lobby, out to the parking lot. We got in the cab of his dented Chevy pickup. I had time to note that it was a phlegmy day again, the sun hidden, an iron sky pressing down. And rawly cold.

"I think he's dead," Al Coburn said. "Ernie Scoggins. Dead and buried somewheres around here. I think they took some of his clothes and his suitcase to make it look like he just took off."

"*They?*" I cried. "Who's *they?*"

He wouldn't answer that.

"Besides . . ." he said. "Besides . . ."

I held my breath. I had a feeling we had finally come to it. Coburn was gripping the steering wheel with bleached knuckles, leaning forward, staring unseeingly through the splattered windshield.

"Besides," he said, "about six months or so before he disappeared, Ernie gives me something to hold for him. A letter, in an envelope. If anything happens to me, he says, you open this and read it. Otherwise you just leave it sealed. He knew he could trust me, you see."

The old man had gotten to me. It was damned cold in that pickup cab, but I could feel sweat trickling down my spine, a pressure under the sternum.

"All right, all right," I said tersely. "So something happened to him, and you opened it—right?"

He nodded.

"You read it?"

He nodded.

"Well, goddammit!" I exploded. "What the hell *was* it?"

He hunched forward a little further, still staring out that stupid windshield. I saw him in profile, saw what an ancient man he was: wattled and mottled, the jowls hanging slack, face cut and pitted deep. He looked terribly frail and vulnerable then. A strong wind might blow him away, a push crack a hip, a blow puddle the white, fragile skull showing through wisps of hair fine as corn silk.

"I haven't made up my mind," he said heavily. "Haven't decided."

"Is it a police matter?" I asked. "Should the cops know?"

"I can't," he said dully.

"Then show it to me, Mr. Coburn. Or tell me what it's all about. Maybe I can help. I think you need help."

"I've got notes at the bank," he said suddenly.

"What?" I said, bewildered by this new tack. "What are you talking about?"

"Notes," he said. "Loans with Art Merchant. He's given me one extension. I need another."

I caught on.

"And you think if you talk about what's in Ernie Scoggins' letter, you won't get your extension?"

"They'll crucify me."

"*They?*" I shouted again. "*They?* Who in God's name is *they?*"

"All of them," he said.

"Thorndecker?" I demanded.

But I couldn't get any more information out of him. All he'd say was that he had some thinking to do. The stubborn old coot! I slammed out of the cab and went back into the Inn, furious with him and furious with myself for listening to him. He didn't even thank me for the beers.

As usual, the lobby looked like the showroom of an undertaking parlor. The only thing lacking was a selection of caskets, lids open and waiting. I went over to the desk where one of the baldies was slowly turning the pages of *Hustler*, making "Tch, tch" sounds with tongue and teeth.

"I hate to interrupt your studies," I said, taking out my peevishness on him, "but I'd like to visit your local Episcopal Church. You got one?"

"Sure do," he said proudly. "First Episcopal Church of Coburn. My church. Nice place. The Reverend Peter Koukla. A marvelous preacher."

"How do I find it?"

"Easy as pie," he said happily. "East on Main Street to Cypress. Make a left, and there you are. You an Episcopalian?"

"Today I am," I said. "Thanks for the directions."

I started away.

"Mr. Todd," he said.

I turned back. He was looking somewhere over my head.

"Can I give you some advice, Mr. Todd?" he said in a low voice, in a rush.

"Sure. Everyone else does."

"I seed you with Al Coburn. You being a stranger in town and all, I got to tell you: Al Coburn is a nut. Always has been, always will be. I wouldn't pay no attention to anything he says, if I was you."

"Thank you," I said.

"A nut," he repeated. "He just shoots off his mouth. Everyone in town knows it. Senile, I guess. You know how they get."

"Sure," I said. "Thanks for the tip."

"Craperoo," he called after me. "He just talks craperoo."

I drove slowly east on Main Street, watching the rusted street signs for Cypress Road. Old Ernie Scoggins had lived on Cypress Road, I recalled. And the First Episcopal Church of Coburn was on Cypress Road. A coincidence that meant precisely nothing.

I was certain that sometime during the year, on favored days, blessed weeks, the sun shone on Coburn, N.Y. But I couldn't testify to it personally. It was now Thursday, and as far as I knew, there was a permanent shroud over the village. It seemed to have its own cloud cover. Sometimes, around the horizon, I could see a thin strip of blue sky and the sun shining on someone else. But an inverted bowl hung over Coburn. When it wasn't drizzling, it was misting, raining, snowing, sleeting. Or, as it was that day, just growly and frowning. It was only early December. What it might be like in January and February, I hated to think.

But the Episcopal Church was cheerful enough. Not a new building, but the weathered brick was warm and solid, wood trim white and freshly painted. A sign on the lawn gave the times for Sunday services, Sunday school, luncheon of the women's club, trustees' meeting, young folks' hootenanny, and so forth. Also, the subject of next Sunday's sermon: LOVE IS THE ANSWER. I wondered what the question was.

The wide front door was unlocked, and I walked into a big, pleasant nave. The most prosperous public setting I had seen in Coburn. Polished floor. Glistening pews. Well-designed altar and choir stall. Handsome organ. Everything clean and shipshape. A well-tended House of God, smelling faintly of Lemon Pledge.

I don't care how cynical you are, a church—any church—has a chastening effect. You find yourself speaking in whispers, walking on tiptoe, and trying very hard not to fart. Anyway, that's what church-going does to me. Religion is a language I don't understand, but I'm prepared to accept the fact that people communicate in it. Like Sanskrit.

I had the whole place to myself. If I knew how to fence new hymnals, I could have made a fine haul. I stepped gently up the center aisle, then heard the sound of hammering coming from somewhere. Bang, bang, bang. Pause. Bang, bang, bang. I followed the sound, through a side door, down a wide flight of iron steps. Bang, bang, bang. Louder now. There was a recreation room in the basement. Two Ping-Pong tables, and a sign on the wall: TRUST IN JESUS. Rather than a good backhand.

I walked down a cement corridor, and the banging stopped. He must have heard me coming because when I entered a small storage-workshop area, a man was facing the door with a hammer in his hand, raised.

"Beg your pardon," I said, "but I'm looking for the Reverend Peter Koukla."

"That's me," he smiled with relief, putting aside his weapon. "How may I be of service?"

"Samuel Todd," I said. "I'm here in—"

"Mr. Todd!" he cried enthusiastically, rushing forward to pump my hand. "Of course, of course! The Thorndecker grant! I heard you were in town. A pleasure. This *is* a pleasure!"

I don't know what I expected. A moth-eaten Moses, I suppose. But this Man of God was about my own age, or maybe a few years younger. He was shorter than me, and skinny as a fencer, nervy as an actor. Black hair covered his ears. Very long. Prince Valiant. A precisely trimmed black mustache and Vandyke beard. A white T-shirt that had IT'S FUN TO BE A CHRISTIAN printed on the front. Tailored, hand-stitched jeans that must have set him back a C-note, and Gucci loafers. But he wasn't wearing earrings; I'll say that for him.

We chatted of this and that for openers. Or rather, he chatted, and I listened, grinned, and nodded like one of those crazy dogs in the rear window of a car with Georgia license plates. The Reverend Peter Koukla was sure a talker.

He mentioned Dr. Thorndecker, Agatha Binder, and Art Merchant—all in one sentence. He commented on the weather, and assured me such muck was unusual, unique; usually Coburn, N.Y. enjoyed a blazing tropical sun cooled by the trade winds. He showed me what he had been hammering on: a miniature stable that was to become part of a crèche for the church's Christmas celebration.

"Ping-Pong is all very well," he informed me gravely, "but traditions cannot be slighted. No indeed! The golden generation is heartened by this remembrance of the rituals of their youth, and the youngsters are introduced to the most sacred rites of their church."

Beautiful. I noted he had not repeated himself, using the words celebration, traditions, rituals, and rites. Guys who deliver a sermon every Sunday can do that: the Bible on their right hand, Roget's Thesaurus on their left.

"Do you have many youngsters in your congregation, Father?" I asked, a trifle nastily. "Pardon me, I'm not up on correct usage. Do I call you Father, Pastor, Padre, Reverend—or what?"

"Oh, call me anything you like," he laughed merrily. "But don't call me late for supper!"

He looked at me, suddenly stern, and didn't relax until I laughed dutifully.

"No," he said, "frankly, we don't have too many youngsters. Simply because Coburn is not a young community. Not too many young married couples. Ergo, not too many children. That is not to say the problems of our senior citizens are not of equal importance. Oh, I *am* enjoying this talk, and the opportunity to exchange opinions."

I wasn't aware that I had voiced any opinions, but I was willing to go along with him. He dusted off a shop stool, and made me sit down. He took a little leap and ended up sitting on his workbench, his legs dangling. I was bemused to note that he was wearing no socks inside those Gucci loafers. Very *in*. In Antibes and Southampton. A little uncomfortable, I guessed, in Coburn, N.Y., in early December.

"It's a challenge," he was saying. "The average age of our population increases every year. More and more of those over sixty-five. Can we ignore them? Discard them? Cut them off from the mainstream of American thought and culture? I say no! What do you think?"

"Very interesting," I said. "Your ideas. Refreshing."

"Refreshing," he repeated. "I like that. No, please, don't light a cigarette. We voted last year to ban the smoking of cigarettes, cigars, and pipes on church grounds. Sorry."

"My fault," I said, putting the pack back in my pocket. "It'll do me good to go without."

"Of course it will," he caroled, throwing back his head and shouting at Heaven. "Of course, of course!"

I don't know . . . maybe he was just high on God. If he had been a theatrical agent, I would have suspected cocaine, and if he had been an advertising copywriter, I would have suspected grass. But this guy was high on ideas. Loony ideas, possibly, but they were enough to keep him floating.

At the moment, the Reverend Peter Koukla was expounding on how the steady increase in the median age of the American population would affect national political attitudes. I was getting woozy with his machine-gun delivery: spouted words accompanied by a fine spray of saliva.

"Very interesting," I broke in. "A challenging concept. But I really came to talk to you about Dr. Thorndecker."

"Of course, of course!" he yelped, and changed gears in mid-course without a pause.

What followed were the same panegyrics I had heard from Ronnie Goodfellow, Agatha Binder, Art Merchant: that is, Dr. Telford Gordon Thorndecker was a prince of princes, one of God's noblemen. They were spreading it on thickly. Didn't the man have any warts? Koukla obviously didn't think so; he told me the doctor was a "great friend" of the church, lent his name and time to special activities, and made frequent and sizable contributions.

"I only mention this," the Reverend added, "to give credit where credit is due. The man is much too modest to tell you himself. I really don't know what we'd do without him."

"Attends services regularly, does he?"

"Frequently," Koukla said—which, I reflected, is a little different from "regularly."

"His wife and son, also?"

"They are members, yes."

"But not his daughter?"

"Ah . . . no. She has her own religious preferences, I understand. Somewhat more fundamental than our teachings."

"Is Draper one of your members? Dr. Kenneth Draper?"

"He was," Koukla said shortly. "I have not seen him at services recently. But we get many staff members from the Hall and the research laboratory."

All his answers were bright, swift, delivered with every appearance of openness and honesty. It was hard to default this perky little man. I went at him from another direction . . .

"Nurse Beecham told me that occasionally you are called to Crittenden Hall to provide spiritual comfort for some of the patients?"

"When they request it, yes. I had a discussion with Dr. Thorndecker about the possibility of providing a regular Sunday afternoon service, after my duties here are completed. But so many of the guests are bedridden, it probably wouldn't be a satisfactory arrangement. I do conduct a service in the Hall on Christmas and Easter, however."

"Reverend, I was surprised to learn that Crittenden has its own cemetery. When a patient dies, isn't the body usually claimed by his family? I mean, isn't he returned to his home for burial?"

"Usually," he said, "but not always. Sometimes the family of the deceased prefer burial on the Crittenden grounds. It's very convenient. Sometimes the deceased request it in their wills."

"Do you ever, ah, officiate at these burials?"

"Of course, of course! Several times. Sometimes the final service is held here at the church, and the casket returned to Crittenden for interment."

I nodded, wondering how far I might go without having my interest reported back to Dr. Thorndecker. The hell with it, I decided. Let Koukla report it. It just might stir things up. So I asked my question:

"Didn't attend the burial of a man named Petersen, did you? Chester K. Petersen?"

"Petersen?" he said. "No, I don't think so. When did he pass?"

"Two nights ago."

"Oh, no," he said, "definitely not. My last funeral service for a Crittenden guest was about a month ago. But if the deceased was of another faith—Catholic, perhaps, or Jewish—naturally I wouldn't be . . ."

His sentence trailed off, in the approved Coburn manner. He had started his last speech with a confident rush, then slowed, slowed, until his final words were a doubtful drawl. I could almost see him begin to wonder if he wasn't talking too much, revealing something (in all innocence) that the church's "great friend" wouldn't want revealed.

I rose quickly to my feet, before he got the notion of asking what the death of Chester K. Petersen had to do with the Thorndecker grant.

"Thank you very much, sir," I said briskly, holding out my hand. "You've been very cooperative, and I appreciate it."

He hopped spryly off the workbench, and clasped my proffered hand in both of his.

"Of course, of course!" he said. "Happy to oblige. If you're still in town on Sunday morning, it would give me great pleasure to welcome you to our Sabbath services. I believe and preach the religion of joy. I think you'll find it invigorating."

"I might do just that," I nodded. "Well, I'm sure you're anxious to get back to your carpentry. Don't bother showing me out; I can find my way. Thanks again for your trouble."

"No trouble, no trouble!" he shouted, and waved a farewell.

I walked noisily down the cement corridor, then tramped heavily up the iron steps. At the top, I opened and slammed shut the side door leading to the church nave. But I remained inside, on the stairway landing, standing, listening, wondering if the hammering would commence again. It didn't. But I figured it wouldn't. I had seen the telephone in the Reverend Peter Koukla's workshop.

I went slowly down those iron steps again, moving as quietly as I could. I didn't have to go far along the cement corridor before I heard him speaking:

"This is Reverend Koukla," he was saying. "Could I talk to Dr. Thorndecker, please?"

I slipped silently away, and went out the side entrance into the church nave, easing the door shut behind me. I didn't have to listen to the rest of Koukla's conversation. I knew what he was going to say.

Walked out to my car, lighted a cigarette, took three fast, greedy drags. Nasty habit, smoking. So is drinking. So is burying dead men at two in the morning.

I felt I was running one of those Victorian garden mazes, my movements all false starts and retracings. The box hedges walled me around, higher than my head, and all I could do was wander, trying to find the center where I might be rewarded with a candy apple, or the hand of a princess and half the kingdom. I told you I was a closet romantic.

I was floundering and thinking crazy; I knew it. All I had was a hatful of suspicions, and there wasn't one of them I couldn't demolish with a reasonable, acceptable, *legal* explanation. I tried to convince myself that my mistrust was all smoke, and the smart thing for me to do was to stamp Thorndecker's application A-OK, and say, "Goom-by" to Coburn, N.Y.

So why did I sit in my car shivering, and not only from the cold? The hand holding the cigarette trembled. I had never felt so hollow in my life. It was a presentiment of being in over my head, up against something I couldn't handle, wrestling with a force I couldn't define and was powerless to stop.

I started the car and drove along Cypress Road, away from the business section. I left the heater off and cranked the window down a few inches, hoping the cutting air might blow through my skull and take the jimjams along with it. I drove slowly until the houses became fewer and fewer. Then I was in a section of scrabby wooded plots and open fields that looked like they had been shaved a week ago.

I drove past a sign that read: NEW FRONTIER TRAILER COURT, and kept on going. Then I braked hard, backed up, and read the smaller print: "Trailer parking by day, week, or month. All conveniences. Reasonable rates." In Coburn, N.Y., they still called it a "trailer court." The rest of the country called them "mobile home communities."

But it was on Cypress Road, and Al Coburn had said his old buddy, Ernie Scoggins, had lived in a trailer on Cypress Road. So I followed the bent tin arrow nailed to a pine stump, and rattled and jounced down a rutted dirt road to a clearing where maybe twenty trailers, camper vans, and mobile homes were drawn up in a rough circle. Maybe they were expecting an attack by Mohawks on the New Frontier.

I parked, got out of the car, looked around. God, it was sad. There wasn't a soul to be seen, and under that mean sky the place looked crumbling and abandoned. Maybe the Mohawks really had come through, scalped all the men, carried off the women and kids. Fantasy time. There were overflowing garbage cans, and lights on in some of the vans. People lived there; no doubt about it. Although "lived" might be an exaggeration. It looked like the kind of place where, if all the TV sets konked out simultaneously, they'd go for each other's throats. Nothing else to do.

I wandered around and finally found a mobile home that had a MANAGER sign spiked into the hard-scrabble front yard. There was another sign over the door with two painted dice showing seven, and the legend: PAIR-O-DICE. Those dice should have shown crap.

The steps were rough planks laid across piled bricks; they swayed when I stepped cautiously up. I knocked on the door. From inside I could hear the sound of gunfire, horses' hooves, wild screams. If it wasn't a TV western, I was going to skedaddle the hell out of there.

I knocked again. The guy who answered the door looked familiar. I had never met him, but I knew him. You'd have known him, too. Soiled undershirt showing a sagging beer belly. Dirty chinos. Unlaced work shoes over gray wool socks. A fat head with a cigar sprouting from the middle. An open can of local brew in his hand. He wasn't happy about being dragged away from the boob tube. It was filling the room behind him with flickering, blue-tinted light, and the gunfire sounded like thunder.

"Yeah?" he said, glowering at me.

"Who is it, Morty?" a woman shrieked from inside the room.

"You shut your mouth," he screamed, not bothering to turn his head, so for a moment I thought he was yelling at me.

"I understand there's a trailer out here for sale," I began my scam, "and I was—"

"What?" he roared. "Iola, will you turn that goddamned thing down? I can't hear what the man is saying."

We waited. The gunfire was reduced to a grumble.

"Now," he said, "you want a place to park? We got all modern conveniences. You can hitch up to—"

"No, no," I said hastily. "I understand there's a trailer out here for sale."

His piggy eyes got smaller, if possible, and he removed the sodden cigar from his mouth with an audible *plop!*

"Who told you that?" Morty demanded.

"Fellow I met in the bar at the Coburn Inn. Name of Al Coburn. He says a friend of his, name of Ernie Scoggins, lived out here. That right?"

"Well . . . yeah," he said mistrustfully. "He did."

"I understand this Scoggins took off, and his rig's up for sale."

He rubbed his chin with the back of his beer-can hand. I could hear the rasp of the stubble.

"I don't know about that," he said. "I ain't even sure he owned the thing. He's got debts all over town. He took off owing me a month's rent. I'm holding the rig and his car until I get mine."

"Maybe we can work something out," I said. "The bank's holding the title. Al Merchant's willing to work a deal if I decide to buy. All I want to do is take a look at the thing."

"Well . . ." He couldn't decide. "What the hell you want Scoggins's pisspot for? It ain't worth a damn."

"Just for summer," I said hurriedly. "You know—holidays and weekends in the good weather. I figure it would be cheaper than buying a cottage."

"Oh, hell," he said heavily, "it'd be cheaper than buying an outhouse. Well . . . it's your money. It's that gray job over there. The one with the beat-up VW parked alongside. Take a look if you want to; the door ain't locked."

"Thank you very much," I said, turned carefully on those rickety steps, started down.

"Hey, listen," he called after me, "if you decide to buy, I got to get that month's rent he owes me."

"Off the top," I promised him, and he seemed satisfied. He went back in, slammed the door, and in a few seconds I heard the thunder of gunfire again.

I took a look at the VW first. Either Scoggins had been a lousy driver, or he had bought it fourth-hand after it had endured a series of horrendous accidents. You could see the geography of its history: dents, scars, scrapes, nicks, cuts, patches of several-colored paints, rust spots, places where bare metal showed through. All the hubcaps were missing. The front trunk lid was wired shut to the bumper with a twisted coat hanger.

I looked through one of the dirty windows. Nothing to see but torn upholstery, rags on the floor, some greasy road maps, and a heap of empty Copenhagen snuff tins. I would have liked to unbend that coat hanger and take a look in the trunk, but I was afraid Morty might be watching me from one of his windows.

Scoggins's trailer was exactly that: a trailer, not a mobile home. It was an old, *old* model, a box on wheels, narrow enough and light enough to be towed by a passenger car on turnpikes, highways, or secondary roads. It was a plywood job, with one side door and two windows that were broken and covered with tacked shirt cardboards.

It had been propped up on cement blocks; the wheels were missing. A tank of propane was still connected, and a wire led to an electrical outlet in a pipe that poked above the ground at every parking space. There was a hose hookup to another underground pipe, for water.

There were no stairs; it was a long step up from ground to doorway. The door was not only unlocked, it was ajar an inch or so. I pushed it open, stepped up and in. A cold, damp, musty odor: unwashed linen and mouldering furniture. There was a wall switch (bare, no plate), and when I flicked it, what I got was a single 60-watt bulb hanging limply from the center of the room.

And it was really one room. There was a small alcove with waist-high refrigerator, small sink, a grill over propane gas ring, plywood cupboard. No toilet or shower. I hoped the New Frontier offered public facilities. The bed folded up against the wall. Mercifully, it was up. Judging by the rest of the interior, I really didn't want to see that bed. One upholstered armchair, torn and molting. A twelve-inch, portable TV set on a rusted tubular stand. A varnished maple table with two straight-back kitchen chairs. An open closet with a few scraps of clothing hanging from wall hooks. A scarred dresser with drawer knobs missing.

That was about all. The World War I helmet was still where Al Coburn had said it was, atop the TV set. There were some unwashed dishes in the sink, clotted and crusted. Brownish water dripped from the tap. The plywood floor squeaked underfoot. The only decoration was last year's calendar from Mike's Service Station, showing a stumpy blonde in a pink bikini. She was standing on a beach, one knee coyly bent, with palm trees in the background. She had an unbelievable mouthful of teeth, and was holding a beachball over her head.

"A little chilly in here, honey?" I asked her.

Compared to that place, my room at the Coburn Inn was the Taj Mahal. I looked around, trying to imagine what it was like for old Ernie Scoggins—wife dead, son dead, daughters moved away—to do a hard day's work in Crittenden Hall, and then to lump home to this burrow in his falling-apart VW. Take off his shoes, fry a hamburger, open a beer. Collapse into the sprung armchair in front of the little black-and-white screen. Drink his beer, munch his hamburger, and watch people sing and dance and laugh.

I tried to imagine all that, but it didn't work. It was like trying to imagine what war was like if you had never been there.

I went through the Grand Rapids dresser but found nothing of interest. A pair of torn longjohns, some gray, unpressed handkerchiefs, a blue workshirt, wool socks that needed toes, junk. I figured Constable Goodfellow or Al Coburn had taken the old man's papers away, if there were any. I found nothing.

I poked around in the cabinet over the sink. All I found were a few cockroaches who stared at me, annoyed at being interrupted. One interesting thing: there was an eight-ounce jar of instant coffee, practically new, with no more than one or two teaspoonsful taken out. The jar still bore the supermarket pricetag: $5.45. Odd that a poor old man would take off for parts unknown and leave that treasure behind.

I didn't unlatch the bed, let it down, and paw through it. I just couldn't.

So that was that, I figured. Nothing plus nothing equals nothing. I stood in the doorway, my finger on the lightswitch, taking a final look around. My God, that must have been a cold place to live. There was a small electric heater set into one wall, and I suppose he used the propane stove for added warmth, but still . . . The chill came right up through that bare, sagging plywood floor and stiffened my toes inside my boots.

Maybe the trailer had been carpeted when it was new. But now the only piece of rug was under the old man's armchair. It was about a three-foot square, with ravelled edges. It looked like a remnant someone had thrown out, a piece left over after a cheap wall-to-wall carpeting job had been completed.

I stared at it, wondering why I was staring. Just a ragged piece of rug in a shit-brown color. It was under the armchair and stuck out in front where his feet would rest when he gummed his hamburger and watched TV. Keep his tootsies relatively warm while he stared at young, handsome people winning Cadillacs and trips to Bermuda on the game shows.

It made sense; that's why the rug was there. So far so good. But why wasn't the rug scarred and scuffed and stained in front of the armchair, where his feet rested and he dribbled food while guffawing at the funny, funny Master of Ceremonies? It wasn't scarred or scuffed or stained. It looked new.

I took my finger off the light switch. I went back to the armchair, got down on my knees, peered underneath. The portion of the rug *under* the chair was scarred and scuffed and stained.

"Shit," I said aloud.

I stood, lifted the armchair, set it aside. He could have turned the rug, I acknowledged. Shortly before he departed, he noticed the rug under his feet was getting worn and spotted. So he just turned it around. Then the worn part would be under the chair, and he'd have a nice, new, thick pile under his feet in front of the chair.

Except . . . Except . . .

There were special stains on the portion of the rug that had been under the armchair. I got down on my knees again, put my nose right down to them. They didn't look like food stains to me. They were reddish-brown, crusted. There were several heavy blobs with crowns of smaller stains radiating around them. Like the heavy blobs had fallen from a distance and splashed.

I smelled the stains. It wasn't a scientific test, I admit, but it was good enough for me. I knew what those stains were. They weren't Aunt Millie's Spaghetti Sauce.

I replaced the armchair in its original position, switched off the light, got out of there. I didn't look toward the manager's mobile home. I slid into the Grand Prix, jazzed it, spun away.

They didn't have much time: that's what I was thinking as I drove back to the Coburn Inn. They were in a hurry, frantic, afraid of being seen by Manager Morty or some other denizen of the New Frontier Trailer Court. So they did what they had come to do. And then they got him out of there— what was left of him—with some clothes thrown hastily into his old suitcase, trying to make it look like he had scampered of his own free will. And because the blood was ripe and thick and glistening in front of the armchair, they had turned the rug around so the stains would be hidden under the chair.

Time! Time! They were working so fast, so anxiously. Maybe even desperately. They just wanted him snuffed and out of there. What about his car? Maybe it was one killer, and he couldn't handle the VW and the car he came in. Maybe it was two killers, and one couldn't drive. Fuck the car. And fuck the helmet; they didn't know it was his most prized possession. And they didn't have time to search the place and find that almost-full jar of coffee. They didn't have time, they didn't plan it well, they weren't thinking. Amateurs.

I went at it over and over again. The final thought as I pulled into the parking lot of the Coburn Inn: they couldn't have known that he had written a letter, or they would have tossed the place to find it. And Al Coburn had said, ". . . the place wasn't broken up, or anything like that."

I felt so goddamned smug with my brilliant ratiocination. My depression was gone. I walked into the lobby humming a merry tune. I should have been droning a dirge. I was so wrong, so *wrong!*

But at the moment I was in an euphoric mood, bouncing and admiring the way the overhead fluorescent lights gleamed off the nude pate of the guy behind the desk. *Another* baldy!

"Oh, Mr. Todd," he called in a lilting, chirpy voice, and held up one manicured finger.

In my new humor, I was willing to accommodate; I walked over for my message.

"The Reverend Koukla has called you *twice*," he breathed, in hushed and humble tones. "Such a *fine* man. Could you call him at once, *please?*"

"I'm going in for lunch," I said. "I'll call him as soon as I'm finished."

"Please, *please*," he said. "It sounded so *urgent*. You can talk to him right here on the desk phone. I'll put it through for you."

"Okay," I said, shrugging, "if it's so important."

"I'm not supposed to let people use the desk phone for personal calls," he whispered. "But it's the *Reverend Koukla!*"

"Have you caught his walking-on-the-water act?" I asked him. "A smash."

But he was already inside the office, where the switchboard was located, and I don't think he heard me.

Koukla came on immediately.

"Mr. Todd," he said briskly, "I owe you an apology."

"Oh?"

"Yes, indeedy!" he said, then went on with a rush: "I'm afraid I was not as hospitable as I should have been to a visitor to Coburn, a stranger in our midst. As a matter of fact, I'm having some people in this evening for good talk and a buffet supper. No occasion; very informal. Just a friendly get-together. The Thorndeckers will be here, and Art Merchant, Agatha Binder, others you've met, and people who would like to meet *you*. Could you possibly join us? About sixish? For refreshements and talk and then a cold supper later? It should be fun."

That had to be the most quickly arranged buffet supper in the annals of Coburn's social life. I figured Dr. Thorndecker had put the Reverend up to it, and sometime during the evening I'd get a casual explanation of what happened to Chester K. Petersen.

"Sounds good to me," I said. "Thank you for the invitation. I'll be there."

"Good, good, good," he gurgled, making it sound like, "Googoogoo."

"I'm in the Victorian monstrosity just west of the church. You can't miss it; the porch light will be on."

"See you at six," I said, and hung up.

I went into the bar a little subdued, a little thoughtful. It seemed to me Thorndecker was over-reacting. If there was nothing fishy about Petersen's death and burial, he didn't have to do a thing until I inquired, and then he could set me straight. If it was a juggle, then he had to go on the con, preferably in an atmosphere of good cheer, of bonhomie. That's the way I figured he figured it, and I resented it. They were taking me for an idiot.

The bar was full, and the restaurant was crowded: all seats taken. I gave up, came back to the lobby, and asked Sam Livingston if he could get me a club sandwich and a bottle of Heineken, and bring it up to my room. He said it might take half an hour, and I said no problem. He went immediately to the kitchen, and I tramped up the stairs to Room 3-F.

Skinned off damp hat, damp trenchcoat, damp boots. Lighted another cigarette. Stood in my stockinged feet at the window, staring down at Main Street but not seeing it. Thinking. I wish I could tell you my thoughts came in a neat, logical order. They didn't; I was all over the place. Something like this:

1. Maybe they tried to take Scoggins's car, but it was locked.

2. Why didn't they roll up the blood-stained rug and take it with them? I could brainstorm a lot of reasons for that. Maybe Al Coburn and other friends had seen that cheap scrap of carpet many times, and would wonder at its absence. Maybe it was just easier and faster to turn the carpet front to back. They figured no one would notice, and no one did. Not investigating officer Constable Ronnie Goodfellow, not best friend Al Coburn.

3. Why was I using the mysterious pronoun "they," when I had become so furious when Al Coburn used it?

4. Those debts of Al Coburn at the bank . . . Was he afraid of Art Merchant? Or was it Thorndecker, working through Merchant?

5. How could Nurse Beecham tell me Petersen died of cancer when the death certificate, signed by Dr. Draper, listed congestive heart failure as cause of death? Was one of them innocent, and one of them lying? Or were they both in on it, and just got their signals crossed?

6. What color were Julie Thorndecker's eyes?

At this point Sam Livingston knocked and came in with my club sandwich and Heineken. I signed, slipped Livingston a buck, and locked the door behind him. I went back to my station at the window, chomping ravenously at a quarter-wedge of sandwich and swilling the beer. The rambling went on . . .

7. If Al Coburn was right, and Ernie Scoggins was "buried somewheres around here," where would be the logical place to put him under? Easy answer: in the Crittenden cemetery. Who'd go digging there?

8. Something's going on in that lab that's not quite kosher, and Scoggins tumbled to it.

9. Just what in hell was in that letter Scoggins left with Al Coburn? It couldn't be a vague accusation; it had to be hard evidence of some kind if it had that effect on Coburn. A photograph? Something lifted from the Crittenden Research Laboratory? A photocopy of someone else's letter? A microfilm? What?

10. Was Julie Thorndecker really making it with her stepson?

11. How was I going to get out of my promise to Millie Goodfellow?

12. Who killed Cock Robin?

I had finished the beer and sandwich, and was licking mayonnaise off my fingers, when the phone rang. I wiped my hands on the back of an armchair slipcover and picked up the handset.

"Todd," I said.

"Nate Stern," the voice said.

"Nate. Good to hear from you. How're the wife, kids, grandchildren?"

"Fine," he said. "You?"

Nate Stern, a man of few words, was boss of Donner & Stern. Lou Donner had been shot dead by a bank officer who had been dipping in the till. Lou made the mistake of trying to get back some of the loot before turning the guy over to the blues.

"I'm surviving, Nate," I said.

"Switchboard?" he asked.

"Yes," I said, beginning to talk just like him.

"That sample . . ."

"Yes?"

"Olympia Standard, about five years old."

"Thanks."

"Any help?"

"Not much. Be talking."

"Sure."

We both rang off.

In case you forgot, we were talking about that anonymous note: "Thorndecker kills." I had tried to get a look at the typewriters out at Crittenden. I hadn't seen any in the nursing home. The two I saw in the research lab were both IBM electrics. So? So nothing.

There was a telephone call of my own I had to make. I admitted that maybe I had been putting it off because I was afraid it might cause pain to the people I had to talk to. But I couldn't postpone it any longer. It couldn't go through the hotel switchboard, where the desk baldy might be listening in, nodding, and busily taking notes.

So I pulled on damp boots, damp trenchcoat, damp hat again. I crossed Main Street to Samson's Drugs, and crowded myself into an old wooden phone booth. I made a person-to-person call, collect, to Mr. Stacy Besant at the Bingham Foundation in New York City. I knew he'd be in; he never went out to lunch. He always brought a peanut butter sandwich from home in a Mark Cross attaché case.

"Samuel," he said, "how are matters progressing?"

"Slowly," I said, "but surely."

Something in my voice must have alerted him.

"Problems?" he asked.

Problems! The man asked if I had problems! I was *selling* problems.

"Some," I said, "yes, sir."

I heard a long, sniffing wheeze, and figured he had jammed the inhaler up his nose again.

"Anything we can do at this end?"

"Yes, Mr. Besant," I said. "I have a few questions. You said the first Mrs. Thorndecker was your niece. Was she older than Thorndecker?"

There was a silence a moment. Then, quietly:

"Does that have a bearing on your investigation?"

"Yes, sir, it does."

"I see. Well, the first Mrs. Thorndecker, Betty, was approximately ten years older than her husband."

It was my turn to say, "I see." I thought a moment, then asked Besant: "Thorndecker inherited a great deal. Could you tell me the source of the first Mrs. Thorndecker's wealth?"

"Old money," he said. "Pharmaceuticals. That's how Thorndecker met Betty. He was running a research project for her company."

"That takes care of that. Could you tell me a little more about the circumstances of her death?"

Again I heard the sniffing wheeze.

"Well . . ." he said finally, "Betty had a drinking problem, and—"

"Pardon the interruption, sir," I said, "but did she have the problem before she married Thorndecker, or did it develop afterward."

Silence.

"Sir," I said. "Are you there?"

"I'm here," he said in a low voice. "I had never considered that aspect before, and I am attempting to search my memory."

"Take your time, Mr. Besant," I said cheerily.

"Do not be insolent, Samuel," he said sharply. "I am not as senile as you sometimes seem to think. I would say that prior to her marriage, Betty was an active social drinker. Her marriage appears to me now to have exacerbated her problem."

"She became an alcoholic?"

The old man sighed. "Yes. She did."

"And exactly how did she die?"

"It was summer. The family went to the Cape. She had the habit, Betty did, when she was, ah, in her cups, so to speak, to take midnight swims. Or in the early hours of the morning."

"Cold sea at the Cape. Even during the day."

"Oh yes," the old man mourned. "Everyone warned her. Husband, daughter, son—everyone. But they couldn't lock her up, could they? When possible, someone went with her. No matter what the hour. But she would sneak away, go off by herself."

"Asking for it?"

"What?"

"Was she courting death, sir? Seeking it? Did she want to die?"

Silence again. Then a heavy sigh.

"Samuel," he said, "you are a very *old* young man. The thought had never occurred to me. But perhaps you're right, perhaps she was courting death. In any event, it came. One morning she wasn't there when the household awoke. Her body was found in the surf."

"Uh," I said, "any signs of—you know?"

"Just minor bruises and scrapes. Things to be expected in such a death. No unusual wounds, no abnormalities. Salt water in the lungs."

"Was she a good swimmer?"

"An excellent swimmer. When sober."

"How about Thorndecker?" I asked. "A good swimmer?"

"Samuel, Samuel," he groaned. "I have no idea. *Must* you be so suspicious?"

"Yes, sir," I said, "I must. Any evidence of his having something on the side? You know—mistress? Girlfriend? Anything like that?"

He cleared his throat.

"No," he said.

"You're sure?"

"As a matter of fact," he said, and I could almost see that tortoise head ducking defensively, "I made a few discreet inquiries of my own."

"Oh-ho," I said. "And he was pure?"

"Absolutely."

"Where was he the night his wife died? Home in bed?"

"No," he said. "At a medical conference in Boston. He had departed that evening. His presence in Boston that night was verified."

"Oh," I said, deflated. "I guess he *was* pure. Unless . . ."

"Unless what, Samuel?"

"Nothing, sir. You're right; I *am* very suspicious. I was just imagining a way he could have jiggered it."

The old man shocked me.

"I know," he said. "A drug in her bottle. He had easy access to drugs."

I sucked in my breath.

"You're right again, sir," I said. "I do tend to underestimate you, and I apologize for it. Were the contents of her bottle analyzed?"

"Oh yes," he said. "Everything was done properly; I saw to that. The contents were just gin; no foreign substances. But, of course, by the time the body was found, the authorities called, and the investigation started, Thorndecker had been summoned back to the Cape from Boston."

"What you're saying is that he could have switched bottles, or replaced the contents?"

"There is that remote possibility, yes."

"Do you think he did?"

The silence lasted a long time. It was finally ended by another deep sniff, then another: a two-nostril job.

"I would not care to venture an opinion," Mr. Stacy Besant said gravely.

"All right," I said. "It's a moot point anyway. Barring a confession, we'll never know, will we?"

"No," he said, "we never will."

"One final question, sir. I'm puzzled by the dates and ages involved. Particularly the ten-year difference between Mary and Edward, Thorndecker's two children. A little unusual, isn't it?"

"A simple explanation," he said. "Betty was a widow when Thorndecker married her. Mary is her daughter by her first husband. Edward is the son of Betty and Telford Thorndecker. So Mary and Edward are really half-brother and half-sister."

"Thank you, sir," I said. "That explains a great deal."

"Does it?" he said surprised.

"Mr. Besant," I said, "I wonder if you'd be kind enough to switch me to Mrs. Cynthia, if she's available."

"Of course," he said. "At once. Hang on."

I'll say this for the old boy: he wouldn't dream of asking why I wanted to talk to the boss-lady of the Bingham Foundation. If she wanted him to know about her conversation with me, she'd tell him.

He had my call switched, and in a few seconds I was talking to Mrs. Cynthia. We exchanged news about the states of our health (good), and the weather (miserable), and then I said:

"Ma'am, just before I came up here, I met you in the corridor, and you mentioned you had known Dr. Thorndecker's father."

"Yes," she said, "so I did."

"You also said he was a sweet man—those are your words, ma'am—and then you added, 'It was all so sad.' What did you mean by that?"

"Samuel," she said, "I wish I had your memory."

"Mrs. Cynthia," I said, "I wish I had your brains and beauty."

She laughed.

"You scamp," she said. "If I was only fifty years younger . . ."

"If I was only fifty years older," I said.

"You will be, soon enough. Yes, I knew Dr. Thorndecker's father. Gerald Thorndecker. Gerry. I knew him quite well."

She didn't add to that, and I didn't pry any deeper. The statement just lay there, given and accepted.

"And what was so sad, Mrs. Cynthia?"

"The manner of his death," she said. "Gerald Thorndecker was killed in a hunting accident. Shocking."

"A hunting accident?" I repeated. "Where was this?"

"In Maine. Up near the border."

"How old was his son at the time?"

"Telford? Thirteen perhaps. Fourteen. Around there."

"Thank you," I said, ready to say goodby.

"He was with him when it happened."

It took me a second to comprehend that sentence.

"The son?" I asked. "Telford Thorndecker? He was there when his father was killed in a hunting accident?"

"That is correct," she said crisply.

"Do you recall the details, Mrs. Cynthia?"

"Of course I recall the details," she said sharply. "I'm not likely to forget them. They had flushed a buck, and—"

"They?" I said. "Gerald Thorndecker and his son?"

"Samuel," she said, sighing, "either you let me tell this story in my own, old woman's way, or I shall ring off this instant."

"Sorry, ma'am," I said humbly. "I promise not to interrupt again."

"The hunting party consisted of Gerald Thorndecker, his young son Telford, and four friends and neighbors. Six in all. They flushed a buck, spread out on a line, and pressed forward. Later, at the coroner's inquest, it was stated that Gerald Thorndecker walked faster than the rest of them. Trotting, moving out ahead of them. I believe it. He was that kind of man. Eager. In any event, the others were behind him. They heard a crashing in the brush, saw what they thought was the buck doubling back, and they fired. They killed Gerald. Now you may ask your questions."

"Thank you," I said, without irony. "How many of the hunters fired at Gerald?"

"Three, I believe."

"Including the son, Telford?"

"Yes."

"Were ballistics tests made?"

"Yes. He had been hit twice."

"Including a bullet from his son's rifle?"

"Yes. And another."

I should have known. You think that in any investigation, criminal or otherwise, you get the facts, put them together, and the whole thing opens up like one of those crazy Chinese lumps you drop in water and a gorgeous blossom unfolds? Not so. Because you rarely deal with facts. You deal with half-facts, or quarter-, eighth-, or sixteenth-facts. Little bitty things that you can't prove or disprove. Nothing is ever sure or complete.

"All right," I said to Mrs. Cynthia, "Gerald Thorndecker was killed by two bullets, one fired by his son. What about the mother?"

"Her name was Grace. She died of breast cancer when Telford was just a child. I think he was three. Or four. His father raised him."

"Money?"

"Not much," she said regretfully. "Gerald was foolish that way. He squandered. He had a standard of living and was determined to maintain it. He inherited a good income, but it goes fast when nothing new is coming in."

"What did he do? Did he have a job or profession?"

"Gerald Thorndecker," she said severely, "was a poet."

"A poet? Oh my God. I can understand why the money went. Was he published?"

"Privately. By himself." Then she added softly, "I still have his books."
"Was he any good?" I asked.
"No," she said. "His genius was for living."
"Telford was an only child."
"How did you know?"
"He *looks* like an only child. He *acts* like an only child. Mrs. Cynthia, just let me recap a moment to see if I've got this straight. Dr. Thorndecker is an only child. His mother dies when he's three or four. He's brought up by his father, a failed poet rapidly squandering his inheritance. The father is killed accidently when the boy is thirteen."
"Or fourteen," she said.
"Or fourteen," I agreed. "Around there. Now, what happened to the boy? Who took him in?"
"An aunt. His father's sister."
"She put him through medical school?"
"Oh no," Mrs. Cynthia said. "She was poor as a church mouse. Telford never would have made it without his father's insurance. That's all he had. The insurance saw him through medical school and his post-graduate work."
"Wow," I said.
"Wow?" she said.
"He wanted to be a doctor all along?" I asked.
"Oh yes. For as long as I can remember. Since he was just a little boy."
"Mrs. Cynthia, I thank you," I said. "Sorry to take up so much of your time."
"That's quite all right, Samuel," she said. "I hope what I've told you may be of some help in your inquiry. If you see Dr. Thorndecker, please give him my love. He may remember me."
"How could he forget you?" I said gallantly.
She made a humphing sound, but I knew she was pleased. She really was a grand old dame, and I loved her and didn't want to hurt her. Which is why I didn't make a snide comment about the extraordinary coincidence of two violent deaths in the life of Dr. Telford Thorndecker, both of which he might possibly have caused, and from both of which he had profited handsomely. But maybe it wasn't an extraordinary coincidence; maybe it was just a plain coincidence, and I was seeing contrivance where only accident existed.
I walked slowly back to the Inn. One good thing about Coburn: you didn't have to look about fearfully for traffic when you crossed the street.
Stacy Besant and Mrs. Cynthia had given me a lot to think about. Now I knew much more; my plate was full. A full plate, hell; my platter was overflowing. The investigation was slowly becoming two: the history, character, personality, and ambitions of Dr. Telford Gordon Thorndecker; and the strange events that had taken place in and around Crittenden during the past month. That the two would eventually come together, merge, and make some kind of goofy sense, I had no doubt. But meanwhile I didn't know what the hell to do next.
What I did was to go back across Main Street to Sandy's Liquors and Fine Wines. I bought a fifth of a twelve-year-old Scotch. It came all gussied up in a flashy box. Carrying that in a brown paper sack, I returned to the Coburn Inn. I looked around for Sam Livingston, but he was nowhere to be seen. The lobby was enjoying its early afternoon siesta. Even Millie Goodfellow was somnolent, filing slowly at her talons behind the cigar counter.
I walked down the stairway into the basement, pushed through a fire

door, and wandered along a cement corridor lined with steam and water pipes. I found a door with a neat sign that read : SAMUEL LIVINGSTON. PLEASE KNOCK BEFORE ENTERING. I knocked, but I didn't enter; I waited.

He came to the door wearing his usual shiny, black alpaca jacket and little skullcap. He also had on half-glasses and was carrying a closed paperback novel, a forefinger marking his place. I took the bottle of Scotch from the sack and thrust it at him.

"Greeks bearing gifts," I said. "Beware."

His basalt face warmed in a slow smile.

"For me?" he said. "Now I take that kindly of you. Come in, get comfy, and we'll sample a taste of this fine sippin' whiskey."

He had a snug little place down there. One low-ceilinged room with kitchenette, and a small bathroom. Everything neat as a pin. A sleeping sofa, two overstuffed armchairs, a table with ice cream parlor chairs. A chest of drawers. No TV set, but a big bookcase of paperbacks. I took a quick look. Barbara Cartland. Frank Yerby. Daphne du Maurier. Elsie Lee. Like that. Romantic novels. Gothics. Edwardians. Regencies. Women with long, glittering, low-cut gowns. Men with mustaches, wearing open, ruffled shirts and carrying swords. Castles in dark mountains with one light burning in a high window. Well . . . what the hell; I read H. Rider Haggard.

He had me sit in one of the soft armchairs, and he brought us each a small glass of the Scotch.

"We don't want to hurt this with water," he said.

"Straight is fine," I agreed.

He lowered himself slowly into the other armchair, lifted his glass to me, then took a small sip. His eyes closed.

"Yes," he breathed. "Oh my yes." He opened his eyes, passed the glass back and forth under his nose, inhaling with pleasure. "How you finding Coburn, Sam? Slow and quiet enough for you?"

"You'd think so," I said, "judging from the surface. But I'm getting the feeling that underneath, things might be faster and noisier."

"Could be," he said noncommittally. "I hear you been doing some digging?"

"Just talking to people," I said. "I figured you might be able to help me."

"How might I do that?"

"Well, you've lived here a long time, haven't you?"

"Thirty years," he said. "And I figure to live out the rest of it right here. So you, being a smart man, won't expect me to bad-mouth any of the people I got to live with."

"Of course not," I said. "It's just that I've picked up some conflicting opinions, and I thought you could straighten me out."

He stared at me over the rim of his glass. It was a dried apple of a face: lines and creases and a crinkly network of wrinkles. Black and gleaming. The teeth were big and yellow. His ears stuck out like flags, and his eyes had seen everything.

"Tell you what," he said. "Supposin' you asks your questions. If I want to answer, I will. If I don't, I won't. If I don't know, I'll tell you so."

"Fair enough," I said. "My first question is about Al Coburn. You know him?"

"Sure, I know him. Everyone in town knows Al Coburn. His people *started* this place."

"You think he's a nut?"

He showed me that keyboard of teeth.

"Mr. Coburn?" he said. "A nut? Nah. Sly as a fox, that man. Good brain on him."

"Okay," I said. "That was my take, too. Art Merchant?"

"The banker man? He's just a banker. What do you expect?"

"You think that newspaper, the *Sentinel*, is making money?"

He took a sip of his drink, then looked at me reflectively.

"Just," he said.

"You think they've got loans from the bank?"

"Now how would I know a thing like that?"

"Sam," I said, "I got the feeling that there's not much going on in Coburn that you don't know about."

"Agatha Binder could have some notes at the bank," he acknowledged. "Most business folks in Coburn do."

"You know the Thorndeckers?"

"I've seen them," he said cautiously.

"To speak to?"

"Only Miz Mary. We're friends."

"Constable Goodfellow? You know him?"

"Oh sure."

I threw my curve.

"Anything between him and Dr. Thorndecker's wife?"

The curtain came down.

"I wouldn't know," he said.

"Ever hear any gossip about what's going on at the Crittenden Research Laboratory?"

"I never believe in gossip."

"But you listen to it?"

"Some."

"Ever hear about a man named Petersen? Chester K. Petersen?"

"Petersen? Can't say that I have."

"Scoggins? Ernie Scoggins?"

"Oh my yes, I knew Ernie Scoggins. He sat right where you're sitting many's a time. Stop by here to chew the fat. Bring me a jug sometimes. Sometimes he was broke, and I'd make him a little something to eat. Nice, cheerful man. Always joking."

"They say he just took off," I said.

"So they say," he nodded.

"Do you think he did?" I asked him.

He thought a long moment. Finally . . .

"I don't know what happened to Ernie Scoggins," he said.

"What do you *think* happened?"

"I just don't know."

"When was the last time you saw him?"

"Couple of days before he disappeared."

"He came here?"

"That's right."

"When? What time of day?"

"In the evening. When he got off work."

"Anything unusual about him?"

"Like what?"

"What was his mood? Was he in a good mood?"

"Yeah, he was in a good mood. Said he was going to get some money pretty soon, and him and me would go up to Albany and have a steak dinner and see the sights."

"Did you tell Constable Goodfellow this?"

"No."

"Why not?"

"He didn't ask."

"Did Scoggins tell you how much money he'd be getting?"

"No."

"But could you guess from what he said how much it'd be? A lot of money?"

"Anything over a five-dollar bill would be a lot of money to Ernie Scoggins."

"Did he tell you where the money would be coming from?"

"No, and I didn't ask."

"Could you make a guess where it was coming from?"

"I just don't know."

I went along like that, with his "I don't know's" getting more frequent. I couldn't blame him. As he said, he had to survive in Coburn; I was going home one blessed day. I knew he wouldn't reveal the town's secrets—until thumbscrews come back in fashion.

I ran out of questions, and accepted another small Scotch. Then we just sat there sipping, talking of this and that. I discovered he had a deadpan sense of humor so subtle, so hidden, that you could easily miss it if you weren't watching for it. For instance:

"Are you a church-going man?" I asked him.

"I certainly am," he said. "Every Saturday—that's my afternoon off here—I sweep and dust the Episcopalian Church."

Said with no smile, no lifted eyebrow, no irony, no bitterness. Apparently just an ingenuous statement of fact. Ingenuous, my ass! This gaffer was *deep*. He was laughing, or weeping, far down inside himself. If you caught it, fine. If it went over your head, that was also fine. He didn't give a damn.

But he could say profound things, too.

"What do you think of Millie Goodfellow?" I inquired.

He said: "She's lonely with too many men."

I asked him if he was the only black in town. He said no, there were two families, a total of nine men, women, and children. The men farmed, the women worked as domestics, the kids went to a good school.

"They doin' all right," Sam Livingston said. "I don't mess with them much."

"Why is that?"

"I don't mess with *anyone* much."

"No family of your own, Sam?"

"No," he said. "They all gone."

Whether that meant they were dead or had deserted Coburn, I didn't know, and didn't ask.

"Sam," I said, "you say you and Mary Thorndecker are friends. How is that? I mean, does she visit you here? What opportunity do you have to talk to her?"

"Oh . . ." he said vaguely. "Here and there."

I stared at him, remembering what Agatha Binder had said about Mary Thorndecker going to an evangelist church about five miles south of Coburn. A fundamentalist church. The Reverend Peter Koukla had said something similar.

"Your church?" I asked Livingston. "You and Mary Thorndecker go to the same church? A born-again place about five miles south of here?"

The glaze came down over his ocherous eyes again.

"Sam," he said, "you do get around."

"I'd like to visit that church," I said. "How do I get there?"

"Like you said: five miles south. Take the river route, then make a left. You'll see the signs."

"You drive there?"

"No," he said, "I don't drive. Miz Mary, she stops by for me."

"When are services?" I asked. "Sunday?"

"Sunday, and every other night of the week. Every night at eight."

"I think I'll go," I said. "Good minister?"

"Puts on a good show," he said, grinning. "A joy to hear."

The Scotch was making me drowsy. I thanked him for his hospitality, and stood up to leave. He thanked me for the whiskey, and offered to take me up in the elevator. It came down into the basement, alongside his little apartment, and he could hear the bell from inside his room. I told him I'd walk up, the exercise would do me good.

I started down the cement corridor. He was still standing at his open door. A small, wizened figure, a frail antique. I had walked perhaps five steps when he called my name. I stopped, turned around. He didn't say anything more.

"What is it, Sam?" I asked him.

"It's worse than you think," he said, moved inside his room, and closed the door.

I stood there, surrounded by cement and iron, trying to decipher: "It's worse than you think." What did he mean by that? Coburn? The Thorndecker investigation? Or maybe life itself?

I just didn't know.

Not then I didn't.

I trudged slowly up the stairway to Room 3-F. I was pondering the sad fate of Ernie Scoggins. Thought he was coming into some money, did he? The hopeful slob. As Al Coburn had said, he just didn't have much above the eyebrows. After what Sam Livingston had told me, this was the scenario I put together:

Scoggins had seen something or heard something. Or both. Probably on his job at Crittenden Hall. If Constable Ronnie and Julie Thorndecker really did have the hots for each other, maybe Scoggins walked in on them while they were rubbing the bacon. Somewhere. In the woods. In the stall of that big bay gelding. In the back seat of Goodfellow's cruiser. Anywhere.

So Scoggins, having watched plenty of *Kojack*, *Baretta*, and *Police Woman*, thinks he knows just how to profit from this unexpected opportunity, the poor sod. He tries a little cut-rate blackmail (which in Coburn, N.Y., would be on the order of $9.95). If they don't pay up, Scoggins threatens to report their hanky-panky to Dr. Thorndecker. Who knows—maybe he's got some hard evidence: a tape recording, photograph, love letter—something like that.

But the lovers, realizing like all blackmail victims that the first demand is just a down payment, decided that Ernie Scoggins had to be scrubbed. I figured Goodfellow did it himself, driving his cruiser; he had the balls for it. And the Constable working alone would explain why Scoggins's car hadn't been taken away, and why Goodfellow had said nothing about the blood-stained rug when he "investigated" Scoggins's disappearance. It would also explain what was in that letter left with Al Coburn: the hard evidence of Julie and Ronnie putting horns on the head of the august Dr. Telford Gordon Thorndecker—photograph, love letter, tape recording, whatever.

That scenario sounded good to me. I could buy it.

And tomorrow, I reflected sourly, I would solve the riddle of Chester K. Petersen's death and burial, on Saturday I would discover what was meant by that note: "Thorndecker kills," and on Sunday I would rest.

Ordinarily I keep a case notebook during an investigation, filling it with observations, bits of dialogue, suggestions for further inquiries. The notebook is a big help when it comes time to write my final report.

But after the tossing of my room at the Coburn Inn, I hadn't put anything on paper. I kept it all in my pointy little head. It was a mess up there. Nothing seemed neat.

I couldn't get a handle on what the hell was going on. Or even know positively that anything *was* going on.

I sprawled on the hard bed, boots off, hands clasped behind my head. I tried to find a thread, an element, a theme that might pull it all together. I had been flummoxed like this on other investigations, and had devised a trick that sometimes worked for me.

What I did was try my damndest to stop *thinking* about the case. I mean, try to ignore who did what, who said what, and the things I had seen, done, guessed. Just wash the whole shmear out of my consciousness and leave myself open to emotions, sensations, instincts. It was an attempt to get down to a very primitive level. Reasoning was out; *feeling* was in.

When I tried to determine what I felt about the Thorndecker inquiry, what my subjective reactions were, I came up with an odd one: I suddenly realized how much this case was dominated by the conflicts of youth and age, the problems of senescence, the puzzles of natural and perverse death.

Start with the Thorndecker application. That was for a grant to investigate and, hopefully, isolate and manipulate the X Factor in mammalian cells that causes aging and the end of life.

Add a nursing home with a high death rate: normal for institutions that provided care of the terminally ill.

Add a middle-aged doctor married to a very young wife who, possibly, was finding her jollies elsewhere with, amongst others, a macho Indian cop and, maybe, a stepson younger than she.

Add a bedraggled covey of old, old men: Scoggins, Petersen, Al Coburn. Even Sam Livingston.

Add a staff of very young, whiz-kid researchers who might be long on talent and short on ethics.

Add a village that was a necropolis of fractured dreams. A village that seemed to be stumbling toward oblivion, that was not merely old but obsolete, showing its toothless mouth and sounding its creaks.

All these were notes in a player piano roll: holes punches in thin paper. And the discordant melody I heard was all about age, the enigma of age. I could understand Thorndecker's passion to solve it. Compared to what he hoped to do, a walk on the moon was a stroll to the corner drugstore. I mean the man wanted it *all*.

One other factor crept into my merry-go-round brain . . . Maybe *I* was obsessed with youth and age, their mysteries and collisions. I had rejected Joan Powell for what I imagined was a good and logical reason: the difference in our years. But was that really a rational reaction, or had I demonstrated an inherited response I was not even aware of? Something in my cells, or genes, that forced me to discard that good woman? Something to do with the preservation of my species?

I didn't, I decided, understand *anything*. All I knew was that right then, I wanted her, needed her. Loved her? Who said that?

I spent the late afternoon that way: stewing. It had been a yo-yo day: I was up, I was down, I was up, I was down. When it came time to shower and dress, preparing for the Reverend Peter Koukla's "friendly get-together," I had resolved to put in a token appearance, split as quickly as I reasonably could, and return to the sanctuary of Room 3-F with a jug of comfort provided by Sandy's Liquors and Fine Wines.

So much for high hopes and good intentions . . .

Koukla had been right; his place was easy to find. Not only was the porch light on, but the front door was open and there were guests standing outside, drinks in hand, even though it was a sharp night. Cars were parked in Koukla's driveway, and on both sides of the street. I took my place at the tail end of the line, about a block away, left coat and hat in my locked car, walked back to the party.

If he had organized that bash on short notice, the Reverend had done one hell of a job. I reckoned there were forty or fifty people milling about, drinking up a storm. But after I plunged into the throng, shaking hands and grinning like an idiot, I saw that most of the guests were researchers from the lab and off-duty staff from Crittenden Hall. In other words, Thorndecker had called out the troops.

Most of them were in civvies, but a few were wearing white trousers and short white jackets, as if they had just rushed over from nursing home or laboratory. I didn't see Mary Thorndecker, but the rest of the clan was there. And Agatha Binder, Art Merchant, Dr. Kenneth Draper, and Ronnie Goodfellow, self-conscious in his uniform. There were others whose names I had forgotten but whose faces were vaguely familiar: the "best people" Goodfellow had introduced on my first morning in Coburn.

There was a punch bowl, and white wine was available. No hard booze. But the kids out on the porch were puffing away like mad, and even inside the house the smell of grass was sweet and thick. Include me out. I had tried pot twice, with Joan Powell, and each time, at the crucial moment, I fell asleep. I'd rather have a hangover.

It was all genial enough, everyone talking, laughing, mixing. No one leaned on me, and Koukla didn't try to introduce me to everyone; just left me free to roam. I met some of the kid researchers and listened to their patter. The fact that I couldn't understand their sentences didn't bother me so much as the fact that I couldn't understand their *words*. I had a hazy notion of what "endocrinology" meant, but when they moved down the dictionary to "endocytosis," they lost me.

"Do you understand what they're talking about?" I asked Julie Thorndecker.

"Not me," she said, rewarding me with a throaty chuckle. "I leave all that to my husband. I prefer words of one syllable."

"Me, too," I said. "Four-letter words." Then, when she froze, I added, "Like 'love' and 'kiss'. I laughed heartily, signifying it was all a big yuck, and after awhile her lips smiled.

"Enjoying your stay in Coburn, Mr. Todd?" she asked me.

"Not really. Quiet place. Lonely place."

"My, my." she said mockingly. She put a hand on my arm again. She seemed to have a need to touch. "We'll have to do something about that."

She was wearing a pantsuit of black velvet. Stud earrings of small diamonds. The gold-link ankle bracelet. She looked smashing. But she could have made a grease monkey's coveralls look chic.

In that crush, in the jabber of voices around us, it would have been possible to say the most outrageous things—make an assignation: "You do this to me, and I'll do that to you."—and no one would have heard. But actually we talked inconsequentialities: her horse, my car, her home, my job. All innocent enough.

Except that as we said nothing memorable, we were jammed up against each other by the mob. I could feel her heat. She made no effort to pull away. And while we yakked, our eyes were locked—and it was like being goosed with an icicle: painful, shivery, pleasurable, frightening, mind-blowing. The look in her eyes wasn't flirty or seductive; it was elemental, primeval. It was raw sex, stripped of subterfuge. No game-player she. My scenario sounded better to me; I could understand how a man could kill for such a woman.

"There you are!" Dr. Thorndecker said, slipping an arm about his wife's shoulders. "Entertaining our guest, are you? Splendid! Suppose we get a cup of that excellent punch?"

We worked our way over to the punch bowl. In the process, Julie Thorndecker moved away. If a signal had passed between the doctor and her, I hadn't caught it.

"A lot of your people here tonight," I mentioned, sampling a plastic cup of the punch and setting it carefully aside.

Later, thinking about it, I had only admiration for the way he used that offhand comment to lead into exactly what *he* wanted to say. I think if I had offered, "The price of soybeans in China is going up," he would have done the same thing. The man was masterful.

"Oh yes," he said, looking around, suddenly serious. "We should plan more social activities like this. These people work very hard; they not only deserve a break, they *need* it. It's not the happiest place to work. I refer to the nursing home, of course, not the lab."

"I can imagine," I murmured, pouring myself a paper cup of the white wine. That was a *little* better.

"Can you?" he said. "I'm not sure anyone not intimately associated with such an institution can even guess the emotional stress involved. We try to remain objective, to refrain from becoming personally involved. But it's impossible. We *do* become involved, intimately involved. Even with those we know have only a week, a month, a year to live. Some of them are such marvelous human beings."

"Of course," I said. "Maybe, when they accept their fate, know their days are numbered, maybe then they become superior human beings. More understanding. Kinder."

"You think so?" he asked. His dark eyes came down from the ceiling to focus on me. "Maybe. Although I'm not certain any of us is capable of believing in our own mortality. One effect I have noted, though: the closer to death our patients grow, the more exaggerated their eccentricities become. That's odd, isn't it? A man who might have sung aloud occasionally, just sung for his own amusement with no one else present, begins to sing constantly as death approaches. A vain woman becomes vainer, spending all her waking hours making-up and doing her hair. Whatever weakness or whim they might have, intensifies as death approaches."

"Yes," I agreed, "that *is* odd."

"For instance . . ." he said, almost dreamily.

No, not dreamily. But he was away from me, disconnected from his surroundings, off someplace I couldn't reach. It was not just that he was lying; I knew he was. But, while lying, he had retreated deep within himself, to a secret dream. I was seeing another facet of this many-sided man. Now there was almost a stillness in him, a certainty. His stare turned inward, and he seemed to be listening to his own falsehoods, with approval. He was so *sure*, so sure that what he was doing was right, that the splendid end justified any sordid means.

"He came to us a few years ago," he said, speaking in a steady voice, but so low that I had to bend close to hear him in that hubbub. Finally, he was almost whispering in my ear. "A man named Petersen. Chester K. Petersen. Pelvic cancer. Terminal. Inoperable. I talked to his personal physician. Petersen had always been a solitary. Almost a recluse. A wealthy man, unmarried, who had let his family ties dwindle. And as his illness worsened, his craving for solitude intensified. Meals were left outside his door. He refused to submit to medical examinations. He seemed anxious to end all human contact. It was as I told you: in the last stages, the eccentricity becomes a dreadful obsession. We've seen it—all of us who serve in this field—happen again and again."

I knew it was a fairy tale, beautifully spun, but I had to hear it out. The man had me locked. I could not resist his certitude.

But in spite of my fascination with what he was saying, I have to tell you this: I was observing him. What I mean is that I was two people. I was a witness, spellbound by his resonant voice and intriguing story. I don't deny it. But at the same time I was an investigator, searching. What I was looking for was evidence of what I had seen in our previous meetings: the weariness that concluded the first, those racking spasms of pain I had noted during our second interview.

On that night, at that moment, I saw no indication of either: no weariness, no pain.

What I did see were preternaturally bright eyes, that secretive expression, and movements, gestures, that were slowed and glazed. It hit me: this man was drugged. Somehow. On something. He was so drawled out, so spaced and deliberate. He was functioning; no doubt about that. And functioning efficiently. But he was gone. That's the only way I can express it: he was gone. Off somewhere. Maybe he was dulling the weariness, the pain. I just didn't know.

"What became of him?" I asked. "This Petersen?"

"He left a will," Thorndecker said, smiling faintly. "Quite legal. Drawn by a local attorney. Signed and witnessed. In the event of his death, he desired to be buried late at night, or in the early morning hours. Between midnight and dawn. The wording of the will was quite specific. He was to be buried in the Crittenden cemetery. No religious service, no mourners, no funeral. With as little fuss as possible. He just didn't want the world to note his passing."

"Weird," I said.

"Wasn't it?" he nodded.

"And you respected his wishes?"

"Of course."

"He died of cancer?"

"Well . . ." Thorndecker said, pulling gently at the lobe of one ear, "the immediate cause of death was congestive heart failure. But, of course, it was the cancer that brought it on."

He looked at me narrowly, tilting his head to one side. He had me, and I knew it. Try to fight that diagnosis and that death certificate in a court of law, and see how far you'd get.

He must have glimpsed confusion and surrender in my eyes, for he suddenly slapped me on the shoulder.

"Good Heavens!" he cried. "Enough of this morbidity! Let's enjoy this evening. Now I'll leave you to your own devices, and let you meet and talk with some of these fine young people. I'm happy you could attend the Reverend Koukla's party, Mr. Todd."

I put a hand on his arm to stop him.

"Before you go," I said, "I must tell you. Mrs. Cynthia Bingham asked me to give you her regards. Her love."

The change in him was startling. He froze. His face congealed. Suddenly he was looking back, remembering. He was alone in that crowded room.

"Cynthia Bingham," he repeated. I couldn't hear him, but I saw his lips move.

His features became so suddenly tragic that I thought he might burst out weeping.

"Can we ever escape the past, Mr. Todd?" he asked me.

I mean he really *asked* me. It wasn't a rhetorical question. He was confounded, and wanted an answer.

"No, sir," I told him. "I don't think we can."

He nodded sadly.

He disappeared into the crowd. What a great performance that had been. A bravura! The man had missed his calling; he should have been an actor, playing only Hamlet. Or Lear. He left me stunned, shaken, and almost convinced.

"Mr. Todd," Dr. Kenneth Draper said, with his nervous smile, "enjoying the party?"

"Beginning to," I said, pouring myself another cup of white wine. "I haven't seen Mary Thorndecker this evening. Is she around?"

"Ah, regretfully no," he said, wiping a palm across a forehead that as far as I could see was completely dry. "I understand she had a previous engagement."

"Lovely young woman," I said. "And talented. I liked her paintings."

He came alive.

"Oh yes!" he said. "She does beautiful things. Beautiful! And she's such a help to us."

"A help?"

"In Crittenden Hall. She visits our guests, talks to them for hours, brings them flowers. Things of that sort. She's very people-oriented."

"People-oriented'," I repeated, nodding solemnly. "Well, I guess that's better than being horse-oriented."

He didn't pick up on that at all, so I let it slide.

"By the way," he said, looking about, searching for someone, "Dr. Thorndecker asked us to prepare a report for you. A precis of the research that's been done to date on aging and its relationship to human cells."

"Yes, he said he'd get something together for me."

"Well, we've completed it. Mostly photocopies of papers and some original things we've been doing in the lab. Are you familiar with the term *in vitro?*"

"Means 'In glass,' doesn't it?"

"Specifically, yes. Generally, it means under laboratory conditions. That is, in test tubes, dishes, flasks—whatever. In an artificial environment. As opposed to *in vivo*, which means in the body, in living tissue."

"I understand."

"Most of the papers you'll receive report on experiments with mammalian cells *in vitro.*"

"But you have experimented on living tissue, haven't you?" I said. "I saw your animals."

Also, at that moment, I saw the sudden sweat on his forehead.

"Of course," he said. "Rats, guinea pigs, chimps, dogs. It's all there. My assistant has the package for you. Linda Cunningham. She's around here somewhere."

He looked about wildly.

"I'll bump into her," I soothed him. "And if we don't get together, you can always drop the package off at the Coburn Inn."

"I suppose so," he said doubtfully, "but Dr. Thorndecker was most explicit about getting it to you tonight."

I nodded, and wandered away. Geniuses might be great guys: fun to read about, fun to know. But I'm not sure I'd care to work for one.

"*So* glad you could make it, Mr. Todd," the Reverend Peter Koukla said, clasping my hand in both of his. "You have a drink? Good. It's a *nice* white wine, isn't it?"

"Very nice."

"Excuse me, please. I must see to the chow."

I hadn't heard food called "chow" since Boy Scout camp. Unless, I reflected idly, Koukla was referring to his dog—the kind with a black tongue.

I worked my way across the room to where Agatha Binder and Nurse Stella Beecham were standing stolidly, close together, backs against the wall. They looked like a bas relief in mahogany.

"Ladies," I greeted them.

"Watch your language, buster," Agatha Binder said, grinning. "So you made it, did you? Well, what would a party be without a guest of honor?"

"Is that what I am?" I asked, smiling with all my boyish charm at Nurse Beecham.

If looks could kill, I'd have been bundling with Chester K. Petersen.

"Mr. Todd!" Art Merchant caroled, twitching. "Nice to see you again. How is your investigation progressing?"

"Leaps and bounds," I said, turning to him. "Tell me something, Mr. Merchant . . . Do you ever lend money on trailers?"

"Trailers?"

"Mobile homes."

"Oh," he said. "Well . . . it depends."

"Thank you," I said.

I moved away. I'm tall enough to see over heads. I saw Dr. Telford Thorndecker crowding his wife into a corner. He was all over her, not caring. His hands were on her shoulders, arms, stroking her hip, touching her hair. Once he put a finger to her lips. Once he leaned down to kiss her ear. Another role: Dr. Telford Thorndecker, sex fiend.

"They seem very happy," I said to Constable Ronnie Goodfellow, who was watching the same scene. "Not drinking? Oh . . . on duty, are you?"

"Yes," he said, staring at the Thorndeckers. "Just stopped in to say hello."

"Something I've been meaning to ask you," I said. "You're not the only cop in town, are you?"

He turned those black eyes to look at me. Finally . . .

"Of course not," he said. "We've got the country sheriff's deputies and the state troopers."

"No," I said, "I mean here in Coburn. Are you the only constable?"

"No, sir," he said. "Four constables. I work mostly nights."

"Who's top man?"

"Chief Constable? That's Anson Merchant."

"Merchant?" I said. "Related to Art Merchant, the banker?"

"Yes," Ronnie Goodfellow said shortly, turning his eyes back to the Thorndeckers loving it up in the corner. "The chief is the mayor's brother."

"Are you Mr. Todd?" she asked breathlessly.

A plump, little butterball. A Kewpie doll. She was holding out a sealed manila envelope.

"And you must be Linda Cunningham," I said. "Dr. Draper's assistant."

"Right on!" she cried, slapping the envelope into my hand. "And here's your report. Now you tell Kenneth you got it, y'hear? He was so *nervous!*"

"I'll tell him," I promised. "But what if I have questions about it? Who do I contact?"

"Me," she said, giggling. "My name, address, and phone number are on the report."

"Super," I said, getting high on her breath. "You may be hearing from me."

"Super," she said, still giggling.

I folded the heavy envelope lengthwise and jammed it into my jacket pocket. I was prepared to talk nonsense to her a little longer, just to hear her giggle, but a long drink of water in a lab coat dragged her away. I looked around the crowded room. Most of the guests were straggling into the dining room where I could see a table laid with cold meats, potato salad, dishes of this and that. I saw Thorndecker talking to the Reverend Koukla. I turned back to Constable Goodfellow, but he was gone.

"Hello, Mr. Todd," Edward Thorndecker said in his half-lisp. "Going to get something to eat?"

"Soon," I said. "How are you, Edward?"

"Okay, sir," he said politely. "I wanted to get Julie a plate. Have you seen her?"

"Not recently." I said.

"She's around here somewhere," he said fretfully, his beautiful eyes anxious. "I saw her, and then she just disappeared."

"You'll find her," I said.

He moved away without replying. I watched the mob at the buffet, and decided I wasn't all that hungry. I wandered out onto the porch to smoke a cigarette. The tobacco kind. But a flock of chattering guests came after me, juggling filled paper plates and plastic cups of coffee. I didn't want noisy company; I wanted quiet, solitude, and the chance to sort things out.

I stepped down from the porch. Cigarette in my lips, hands jammed into pockets, shoulders hunched against the cold, I sauntered slowly down the deserted street.

What happened next was a scene from an Italian movie: as wildly improbable.

There were street lights on both corners: orange globes with dim and flickering halos. But mid-block, sidewalks and street were shadowed, black as sin and not half as inviting. I was moving toward my parked Grand Prix. Across the street I could see, dimly, the official cruiser of Constable Ronnie Goodfellow. In 1976, it had been painted in a gaudy Bicentennial design. Now the bold stars were faded, the brave stripes mud-encrusted and indistinct.

It seemed to me, as I glanced at the cruiser, that slender white arms were beckoning me from the back seat. I spat out my cigarette, ground it out quickly. I slipped farther back into the gloom, behind a tree. I waited until my eyes became accustomed to the dark. I peered cautiously around. I saw . . .

Not slender white arms, but bare feet, ankles, calves. The window frame cut off the legs at mid-thigh. A woman's legs, waving in the air as languidly as a butterfly's wings. A slave bracelet glinted about one ankle. I watched without shame. I could make out a man's shirted back bent between those stroking legs. The image, in that somber light, had the eerie and stirring quality of a remembered dream.

I glanced back toward Koukla's house. I saw the lights, the guests on the porch. I heard faintly the tinkle of talk and laughter. But the two in the car were oblivious to everything but their own need. The broad back rose and fell, faster and faster. The slender white legs stretched and flexed in response.

I caught something in peripheral vision: the brief flare of a lighted match. I turned slowly . . .

I was not the only silent stalker, the only bemused witness. Halfway between me and the lighted Koukla home, Dr. Telford Gordon Thorndecker stood back from the sidewalk, observing the scene in the cruiser, quiet and contemplative while his wife was being done. There was no mistaking his massive frame, his leonine head. He smoked his cigarette with care and deliberation. Nothing in his manner or posture showed anger or defeat. Resignation, possibly.

Then I moved, as silently and stealthily as I could. I slid down the row of trees to my car. I unlocked the door, pulled it quietly shut behind me. I started the engine, but didn't turn on the lights. I backed up to the corner, so I wouldn't have to pass that busy official cruiser of the Coburn constabulary.

On my way back to the Inn, I did not reflect on Thorndecker's hurt or on the lovers' scorn. All I could think was that if they had dared it, in such a place, at such a time, then they knew he was aware. And his knowledge had no significance for them. They just didn't care.

And if he knew, and they didn't care, then why was Ernie Scoggins snuffed? My beautiful scenario evaporated.

It was not until I had parked in the lot of the Coburn Inn, and was stumbling across Main Street to Sandy's Liquors and Fine Wines, that the squalidness of the scene I had just witnessed bludgeoned me. I saw again that calm, silent husband watching his wife getting it off with a man half his age. I saw again the frantically pounding back, the jerking, naked legs.

Did he love her that much? Did they both love her that much?

I wanted to weep. For their misery and doomed hopes. For the splintered dreams of all of us.

I had no desire for food, wasn't sure I ever wanted to eat again. But I did want to numb my dread. I drank warm vodka from a bathroom glass caked with Pepsodent around the rim.

I sat in one of the gimpy armchairs, pulled a spindle lamp close. I began going through the report Linda Cunningham had delivered. I think I mentioned that I've had no formal education or training in science, so most of the research papers meant little to me. But I could grasp, hazily, the conclusions.

They weren't very startling, because I had read much the same in the preliminary investigation of Dr. Thorndecker's work by Scientific Research Records for the Bingham Foundation. It had been found that normal human body cells reproduced (doubled) a finite number of times *in vitro*. There seemed to be a significant correlation between the number of doublings and the age of the donor.

When normal human embryo cells were nurtured and reproduced *in vitro*, about fifty doublings could be expected. As donor age increased, the number of doublings decreased. The normal cultured cells did not die, exactly, but after each doubling became less differentiated and simpler, until they bore little resemblance to the original normal cells.

All this argued forcibly, as Dr. Thorndecker had said, for a "cellular clock," an X Factor that determined how long a normal human cell remained viable. When I read the reports on reproduction *in vitro* of normal mammalian cells other than human, the same apparently held true. So, obviously, each species had a built-in lifespan that was reflected in the lifespan of each body cell of which it was composed. When the cells completed their allotted number of doublings and died, the organism died.

"I'll drink to that," I said aloud, and took another hefty belt of Pepsodent-flavored vodka.

One thing bothered me here. It concerned a paper on original research done by the Crittenden lab on the morphology of normal chimpanzee cells. The conclusions were consistent with the research on normal body cells of other species.

But there was nothing in the report concerning the testing of an experimental cancer drug on chimps. Yet I had seen that young, comatose specimen in the basement of the Crittenden Research Laboratory. He had been a mass of putrescent, cancerous tumors, and Dr. Draper had stated that the animal had been deliberately infected, then treated, and the experimental drug had failed.

There was nothing of this in the report I received. But after thinking about it awhile, I could understand why it might not be mentioned. The lab was undoubtedly engaged in several research projects. One of them might be the development of drugs efficacious against sarcomas and carcinomas. But information on this project was not included in the report prepared for me simply because it was extraneous. It had nothing to do with Dr. Thorndecker's application for funds to investigate the cause of aging. It had nothing to do with my inquiry.

That made sense, I told myself.

Finally, the report tossed aside, vodka in the bottle getting down to the panic level, I closed my eyes, stretched out my legs, and tried to determine exactly what it was in that report that was nagging at me. There was a question I wanted answered, and for the life of me I couldn't determine what it was.

Sighing, I picked up the report and skimmed it through again. It told me nothing more, but the feeling persisted that I was missing something. It was something that wasn't stated in the report, but was implied.

I gave up. I capped the vodka bottle. I went into the bathroom. I peed. I washed hands and face in cold water. I combed my hair. I slapped cologne on my jaw. I decided to go down to the bar. Maybe Millie Goodfellow was lounging about, and I could buy her a drink. After all, it was only what any other normal, red-blooded American would—

I stopped. "Normal, red-blooded American boy." The key word was "normal." I rushed back to the living room. I grabbed up the research report from the floor. I flipped through it wildly.

It was as I remembered. *Now* I remembered. It was all about *normal* body cells, *normal* mammalian cells, *normal* human embryo cells, *normal* chimpanzee cells. In every instance, in every report on reproduction, doubling, aging, the qualifying adjective "normal" had been used to describe the cells *in vitro*.

I took a deep breath. I didn't know what the hell it meant, but I thought it had to mean something. I found the phone number of Linda Cunningham.

"Hi!" she said, and giggled. "Whoever you are."

"Samuel Todd," I said. "How're you doing?"

"Super!" she said, and I believed her. I could hear punk rock blaring in the background—it sounded like the Sex Pistols—and there was a lot of loud talk, yells, groans, screams of laughter. I figured she had invited a few friends to her home, for something a little stronger than fruit punch and white wine.

"Sorry to interrupt your party," I said, "but this will just take a minute. Linda? Linda, are you there?"

"Super!" she said.

"Linda, in that report—you know what report I'm talking about, don't you?"

"Report?" she said. "Oh sure. Report. Who is this?"

"Samuel Todd," I repeated patiently. "I'm the guy you gave the report to earlier tonight at the Reverend Koukla's party."

"Oh wow!" she cried. "Harry, don't you *ever* do that again! That *hurt*."

"Linda," I said desperately, "this is Sam Todd."

"Super!" she said.

There was a louder blast of music, then the sound of scuffling. A male voice came on the phone.

"Are you an obscene phone caller?" he asked drunkenly. "I can breathe heavier than you."

More scuffling sounds. Crash of dropped phone. I heard Linda say, "Now stop it. You're just *awful*."

"Linda!" I yelled. "Linda? Are you there?"

She came back on the line.

"Who is this?" she said. "Who—whom are you calling?"

"This is Samuel Todd. I am calling Linda Cunningham, that's whom."

"Mr. Todd?" she cried. "Really? Super! Come on right over. We have a marvelous party all our—"

"No, no," I said hastily. "Thanks very much, but I can't come over. Linda, I have a question about the report. You said I could contact you if I had a question about the report."

"Report? What report?"

"Linda," I said as calmly as I could, "tonight at Koukla's party you gave me a report. Dr. Draper prepared it on orders of Dr. Thorndecker."

"Oh," she said, suddenly sober. "*That* report. Well, yes, sure, I remember. This is Mr. Todd?"

"Right," I said gratefully. "Just one little question about the report, and then I'll let you get back to your party."

"Super party," she said, giggling.

"Sounds like it," I said, hearing glass smashing in the background. "Sounds like a jim-dandy party. I wish I could join you, I really do. Linda, in that report you keep talking about normal cells. Normal embryo cells, and normal mammalian cells, and so forth. All the statistics have to do with normal cells—right?"

"Right," she said, and it came out "Ri." She giggled. "All normal cells. Normal body cells."

"Now my question is this:" I said. "Do all those statistics hold true for *ab*normal cells, too? Do abnormal cells decay or die after a limited number of reproductions?"

"Abnormal cells?" she said, beginning to slur. "What kind of abnormal cells?"

"Well, say cancer cells."

"Oh no," she said. "No no no no. Cancer cells go on forever. *In vitro*, that is. They never die. Harry, I *told* you not to *do* that again. It's really very embarrassing."

"Cancer cells never die?" I repeated dully.

"Didn't you know?" she said, giggling. "Cancer cells are immortal. Oh wow, Harry, do *that* again. That's super!"

I hung up softly.

I didn't go down to the bar that night. I didn't finish the quart of vodka either, though I put a hell of a dent in it. But the more I drank, the more sober I became. Finally I undressed and got into bed. I didn't know when sleep would come. Maybe in about ten years.

Didn't you know? Cancer cells are immortal.

I had a vision of a pinhead of pulsing jelly. Becoming something about as large as a dried pea. Discolored and wrinkled. Growing. Swelling. Expanding. The tiny wrinkles becoming folds and valleys. The discolorations becoming blobs of corruption. Larger and larger. A tumor as big as the Ritz. Taking over. Something monstrous. Blooming in wild colors. Runny tissue. The stink of old gardenias. Spreading, oozing, engulfing. And never dying. Never, never, never. But conquering, filling a slimed universe.

Immortal.

THE FIFTH DAY

I DON'T know what your life is like, but sometimes, in mine, I just don't want to get out of bed. It's not a big thing, like I've suddenly come to the conclusion that life is a scam. It's a lot of little things: Con Edison just sent me a monthly bill for $3,472.69.; a new shirt was missing when my laundry was returned; a crazy woman on the bus asked me why my nose was so long; a check from a friend, in repayment of a loan, promptly bounced. *Little* things. Maybe you could cope with them one at a time. But suddenly they pile up, and you don't want to get out of bed; it just isn't worth it.

That's how I felt on Friday morning. I looked toward the light coming through the window. It was the color of snot; I knew the sun wasn't shining. I wasn't hung over. I mean my head didn't ache, my stomach didn't bubble. But I felt disoriented. And I had all these problems. It seemed easier to stay exactly where I was, under warm blankets, and forget about "taking arms against a sea of troubles." Hamlet's soliloquy. Hamlet should have spent a week in Coburn, N. Y. He'd have found a use for that bare bodkin.

But why the hassle? There was no reason, I told myself, why I *should* get out of bed. What for? No one I wanted to see. No one I wanted to talk to. Events were moving smoothly along without my intervention. Corpses were getting shoveled into the ground at two in the morning, old geezers were disappearing, young wives were cuckolding their husbands in the back seats of police cars, cancer cells were reproducing like mad. God's in His Heaven; all's right with the world. What could I do?

It went on like that until about ten in the morning. Then I got out of bed. I wish I could tell you it was from stern resolve, a conviction that I owed myself, my employers, and the human race one more effort to tidy up the Thorndecker mess. It wasn't that at all. I got out of bed because I had to pee.

This led to the reflection that maybe the memorable acts of great men were impelled by similarly basic drives. Maybe Einstein came up with E= MC^2 while suffering from insomnia. Maybe Keats dashed off "Ode on a Grecian Urn" while he was constipated. Maybe Carnot jotted down the second law of thermodynamics while enduring an attack of dyspepsia and awaiting the arrival of Mother Tums. It was all possible.

I record this nonsense to illustrate my state of mind on that Friday morning. I may not have been hung over, but I wasn't certain I was completely sober.

Breakfast helped bring me back to reality. A calorie omelette, with a side order of cholesterol. Delicious. Three cups of black coffee.

"*Another?*" the foot-sore waitress asked when I ordered the third.

"Another," I nodded. "And a warm Danish. Buttered."

"It's your stomach," she said.

But it wasn't. It belonged to someone else, thank God. And my brain was also up for grabs.

I came down to earth during that final black coffee. Then I knew who I was, where I was, and what I was doing. Or trying to do. Caffeine restored my anxieties; I was my usual paranoiac self. Stunned by what I had seen and heard the previous evening. Wanting to put the jigsaw together, and looking frantically for those easy corner pieces.

I sighed my breakfast tab, then wandered through the bar on my way to nowhere.

"Hey you, Todd," Al Coburn called in his raspy voice. "Over here."

He was seated alone in one of the high-backed booths. I slid in opposite, and before I looked at him, I glanced around. Jimmy was behind the bar, as usual. Two guys in plaid lumberjackets were drinking beer and arguing about something. I turned back to Al Coburn. He was drinking whiskey, neat, with a beer wash.

I jerked my chin at the booze.

"Taking your flu shot?" I asked.

"They killed my dog last night," he said hoarsely. "Poisoned her."

"Who's 'they?' Who poisoned your dog?"

"I come out this morning, and there she was. Stiff. Tongue hanging out."

"You call a vet?"

"What the hell for?" he said angrily. "Any fool could see she was dead."

"How old a dog?"

"Thirteen," he said.

"Maybe she died of natural causes," I said. "Thirteen's a good age for a dog. What makes you think she was poisoned?"

He tried to get the full shot glass up to his lips, but his hand was trembling too much. Finally, he bent over it and slurped. When he straightened up, whiskey dripped from his chin. He hadn't shaved for a few days; I watched drops run down through white stubble.

"Two nights ago," he said, "someone fired off a rifle, through my windows."

"Joy-riding kids," I said.

"That hound," he said, choking. "The best."

This time he got the shot glass to his mouth, and drained it. I went over to the bar and bought him another, and a beer for me. I carried the drinks back to the booth.

Grief must have mellowed him; this time he thanked me.

"You tell Goodfellow about this?" I asked him.

He shook his head. His rough, liver-spotted hands were still trembling; he gripped the edge of the table to steady himself.

"You tell any cop about it?"

"What's the use?" he said despairingly. "They're all in on it."

"In on what?"

He wouldn't answer, and we were back on the merry-go-round: vague hints, intimation, accusations—and no answers.

"Mr. Coburn," I said, "why would anyone want to poison your dog?"

He leaned across the table. Those washed-blue eyes were dulled and rheumy.

"That's simple, ain't it? A warning to me to keep my trap shut. A sign of what might happen to me."

"Why you?" I asked him. "Because you were Ernie Scoggins's best friend?"

"Maybe just that," he said. "Or maybe they looked for that letter, couldn't find it, and figured Ernie give it to me. Listen, maybe they *hurt* him, and he *told* them he give me the goddamned letter. Ernie, he wouldn't do anything to cause me harm, but maybe he told them I had the letter, hoping it would keep them from killing him. But it didn't. Now they're after me."

"What are you going to do?"

He sat back, folded his twitchy hands in his lap, stared down at them.

"I don't know," he muttered. "Killed my dog. Shot out my windows. I don't know what to do."

"Mr. Coburn," I said, as patiently as I could, "if you feel your life's threatened because of the Scoggins letter, why don't you do this: put the letter in a safe deposit box at the bank. Then tell it around town how Scoggins gave you that letter, and it's in a safe place, and it will only be opened in the event of your death. That's a good insurance policy."

"No," he said, "I don't trust the bank. That Art Merchant. How do I know them boxes are safe?"

"They can't open the box without your key."

He laughed scornfully. "That's what *they* say."

I didn't try to argue. He was so spooked, so irrational, that compared to him, my paranoia seemed like a mild whim.

"All right," I said, "then show me the letter. Let me read it. Tell everyone in town I've seen it. They're not going to kill both of us."

"What makes you think so?" he said.

I didn't even have sense enough to be frightened. All I could think of was that I was drinking beer with a psychotic old man who kept talking about how "they" poisoned his dog, shot holes in his windows, and wanted to kill him. And I was going right along with him as if what he was saying was real, logical, believable.

"The hell with it," I said suddenly.

"What?" he said.

"Mr. Coburn, I've had it. I've enjoyed our little chats. Interesting and instructive. But I've gone as far as I can go. Either you tell me more, or I'm cutting loose. I can't go stumbling along in the dark like this."

"Yeah," he said unexpectedly, "I can see that."

He took his upper denture from his mouth, wiped it carefully on a cocktail napkin, slipped in back in. A jolly sight to see.

"Tell you what," he said. Then he stopped.

"What?" I asked. "Tell me what?"

He went through the same act with the lower plate. His way of gaining time, I suppose. I would have preferred finger-drumming or a trip to the loo.

"Maybe I can get this whole thing stopped," he said. "If I can, then there's no need to worry."

"And if you can't?"

He looked up sharply. Bleached lips pressed tighter. That elbow chin jutted. Resolve seemed to be returning.

"You figuring on being here tomorrow?" he asked.

"Sure. I guess so. Another day at least."

"I'll see you. Here at the Inn."

"I may not be in."

"I'll leave a message."

"All right. Are you sure you don't want to tell me now what this is all about?"

"Maybe tomorrow," he said evasively. "I'll know by tomorrow."

I wanted to nail it down. "And if you don't get the whole thing stopped, like you said, then you'll show me Ernie Scoggins's letter?"

"You'll see it," he said grimly.

Later, when it was all over, I realized I should have leaned on him harder. I should have leaned on all of them harder, bulldozing my way to the truth. But hindsight is always 20-20 vision. And at the time, I was afraid that if I came on too strong, they'd all clam, and I'd have nothing.

Besides, I doubt if what I did or did not do had much effect on what happened. Events had already been set in motion before I arrived in Coburn and visited Crittenden Hall. Perhaps my presence acted as a catalyst, and the Thorndecker affair rushed to its climax faster simply because I was there. But the final outcome was always inevitable.

Al Coburn went stumping off, and I went thoughtfully out into the hotel lobby. Millie Goodfellow beckoned me over to the cigar counter. She was wearing a tight T-shirt with a road sign printed on the front: SLIPPERY WHEN WET.

"How do you like it?" she said, arching her back. "Cute?"

"Cute as all get out," I said, nodding.

The dark glasses were still in place, the black eye effectively concealed.

"I know something you don't," she said, making it sound like a 6-year-old girl taunting her 8-year-old brother.

"Millie," I said, sighing, "*everyone* knows something I don't know."

"What will you give me if I tell you?", she asked.

"What do you want—a five-pound box of money?"

"I could use it," she giggled. "But I want you to keep your promise, that's all."

"I would have done that anyway," I lied. "What do you know that I don't know?"

She glanced casually about. The lobby was in its usual state of somnolence. A few of the permanent residents were reading Albany newspapers in the sagging armchairs. The baldy behind the desk was busy with scraps of paper and an old adding machine.

Millie Goodfellow beckoned me closer. I leaned across the counter, which put my face close to that damned road sign. I felt like an idiot, and undoubtedly looked like one.

"You remember when someone broke into your room?" she said in a low voice, still watching the lobby.

"Of course I remember."

"You won't tell anyone will you?"

"Tell anyone what?"

"Tell anyone that I told you."

It would have been laughable if it wasn't so goddamned maddening.

"Told me *what*?" I said angrily.

"My husband," she whispered. "I think it was Ronnie who did it."

I stared at her, blinking. If she was right, that Indian cop had done a hell of an acting job when he came up to "investigate" the break-in.

"Why do you think that, Millie?"

"He took my keys that night. He thinks I didn't notice, but I did. I told you I've got a passkey. And the next morning my keys were back."

"Why didn't you tell me this before?"

She lifted the black glasses. The mouse under her eye was a rainbow.

"I didn't have *this* before," she said. "You won't tell him I told you, will you? I mean about the keys?"

"Of course I won't tell him," I said. "Or anyone else. Thank you, Millie."

"Remember your promise," she called after me.

The elevator door bore a hand-printed sign: NOT WORKING. That would do for me, too, I thought glumly, walking up the stairs. Oh, I was working—but nothing was getting done. Bits and pieces—that's what I was collecting: bits and pieces. I wondered, if Constable Goodfellow *had* been my midnight caller, how he had learned of that anonymous note and why he was so anxious to recover it. Every time I got the answer to one question, it led to at least two more. The whole damn thing kept growing, spreading. Of course I made the comparison to cancerous cells *in vitro*. No end to it.

When I got to my room, the door was open, and I discovered why the elevator was out of operation: Sam Livingston was in 3-F, sweeping up, making the bed, setting out a clean drinking glass and fresh towels.

"Morning, Sam," I said grumpily.

"Morning, Sam," he said. He held up the quart vodka bottle. Maybe two drinks were left. "You have friends in?" he asked.

"No, I did that myself."

"My, my. Someone must have been thirsty."

"Someone must have been disgusted. Have a belt, if you like."

"A little early in the morning for me," he said, "but I thank you kindly. What you disgusted about?"

He kept moving around the room, emptying ashtrays, rearranging the dust."

"You want a complete list?" I asked him. "The weather, for starters. With this lousy town running a close second."

"Nothing you can do about the weather," he said. "God sends it; you take it."

"That doesn't mean I can't bitch about it."

"As for this town, I don't reckon it's much worse than any other place. Trouble is, it's so small, you see it clearer."

"I'm not tracking, Sam."

"Well, like in New York City. Now, you got a lot of rich, powerful people running that town—right?"

"Well . . . sure."

"And maybe some of them, you don't even know their names. Like bankers maybe, newspaper editors, preachers, union people, big property owners, businessmen. They really run the town, don't they? I mean, they got the muscle."

"I suppose so."

"I know so. And you don't even know who they are, because that city is so big, and they like to keep their names out of the papers and their faces off the TV. They want to be invisible. They can do that in a great big city. But in Coburn, now, we're small. Everyone knows everyone else. No one can keep invisible. But otherwise it's the same."

"You mean a small group of movers and shakers who run things?"

"Pretty much," he said. "Also, this town's in such a bad money way—no jobs around, the young folks moving out, property values dropping—that these here people they got to stick together. They can't go fighting amongst theirselves."

I stared at him, saw that old, black face deliberately expressionless. It was a mask that had been crumpled up, then partly smoothed out. But the wrinkles were still there, the scars and wounds of age.

"Sam," I said softly to him, "I think you're trying to tell me something."

"Nah," he said, "I'm just blabbing to pass the time whilst I tidy up in here. Now you get a lot of people in a lifeboat, and they all got to keep rowing and bailing, bailing and rowing. If they don't want the whole damn boat to go down."

I thought about that pearl of wisdom for a moment of two.

"Sam, are you hinting that there's a conspiracy? Amongst the movers and shakers of Coburn? About this Thorndecker grant?"

"Conspiracy?" he said. "What does that mean—a bunch of folks get together and make a plan? Nah. They don't have to do that. They all know what they got to do to keep that lifeboat floating."

"Rowing and bailing," I said.

"Now you got it," he said. "These people, they don't want to get wet, floating around out there in the ocean, boat gone, not a prayer. So they go along, no matter what they hear or what they guess. They *gotta* go along. They got no choice, do they?"

"Self-preservation," I said.

"Sure," he said cheerfully. "That's why you finding it so tough to get people to talk to you. No one wants to kick holes in the boat."

"Are things really that bad in Coburn?" I asked.

"They ain't good," he said shortly.

"Well, let me ask you this: would the 'best people' of Coburn, the ones who run the town, would they go along with something illegal, something criminal or evil, just to keep the boat floating?"

"You said it yourself," he said. "Self-preservation. Mighty powerful. Can make a man do things he wouldn't do if he don't have to. Just to hang onto what he's got, you understand."

"Yes, I do understand," I said slowly. "Thank you, Sam. You've given me something else to think about."

"Aw hell," he said, gathering up broom, mop, pail and rags, "I'd have thought you'd have figured that out for yourself."

"I was getting to it," I said. "I think. But you spelled it out for me."

He turned suddenly, looked at me with something like alarm in his face.

"What did I say?" he demanded. "I didn't say nothing."

I turned my eyes away. It was embarrassing to see that fear.

"You didn't say anything, Sam," I assured him. "You didn't tell me word one."

He grunted, satisfied.

"I got a message for you," he said. "From Miz Thorndecker."

"Mary?"

"No," he said, "the married one."

I couldn't tell if his "Miz" meant "Miss" or "Mrs."

"Mrs. Julie Thorndecker?" I asked.

"That's the one," he said. "She wants to meet with you."

"She does? When did she tell you this?"

"She got the word to me," he said vaguely.

"Where does she want to meet?"

"There's a place out on the Albany post road. It's—"

"Don't tell me," I said. "A roadhouse. Red Dog Betty's."

"You know it?" he said, surprised. "Yeah, that's the place. It's got a big parking lot. That's where she'll meet you. She don't want to go inside."

"When?"

"Noon today," he said. "She drives one of these sporty little foreign cars."

"She would," I said. "All right, I'll meet her. Thanks again, Sam."

He told me how to get to Red Dog Betty's. I gave him five dollars, which he accepted gratefully and with dignity.

I had more than an hour to kill before my meeting with Julie Thorndecker. There was only one thing I wanted to do: I got into the Grand Prix and drove out to Crittenden. I didn't have anything planned; I just wanted to look at the place again. It drew me.

It was another lost day: someone had destroyed the sun and thrown a gauzy sheet across the world. The sky came right down—you wanted to duck your head—and the light seemed to be coming through a wire strainer, and a rusty one at that. Damp wood smell, and the river, and frosted fields. The melancholy of that place seeped into my bones. The marrow shriveled, and if someone had tapped my tibia, I'd have gone *ting!* Like a crystal goblet.

Nearing Crittenden, I passed a Village of Coburn cruiser going the other way. The constable driving wasn't Ronnie Goodfellow, but he raised a hand in greeting as we passed, and I waved back. I was happy to see another officer. I was getting the idea that the Indian worked a twenty-four-hour shift.

I drove slowly around the Crittenden grounds. The buildings looked silent and deserted. I had the fantasy that if I broke in, I'd hear a radio playing, see hot food on the tables, smell hamburgers sizzling on the grill—and not a soul to be found. A new *Marie Celeste* mystery. All the signs of life, but no life.

I saw a blue MGB parked on the gravel before the main entrance of Crittenden Hall, and figured it was Julie's "sporty little foreign car" that Sam Livingston had mentioned. But I didn't see her, or anyone else.

I drove around the fenced estate. Fields and woods dark and empty under the flat sky. No guard with shotgun and attack dog. Just a vacant landscape. I came up to the cemetery, still rolling gently, and then I saw someone. A black figure moving quietly among the tombstones, not quite sauntering.

There was no mistaking that massive, almost monumental bulk: Dr Telford Gordon Thorndecker surveying his domain, a shadow across the land. He was overcoated, hatless; heavy brown hair fluffed in gusts of wind. He walked with hands clasped behind him, in the European fashion. His head was slightly bowed, as if he was reading the tombstones as he passed.

Something in that wavery air, that tainted light, magnified his size, so that I imagined I was seeing a giant stalking the earth. He tramped the world as if he owned it, as indeed he did—at least that patch of it.

He was doing nothing suspicious. He was doing nothing at all. Apparently just out for a morning stroll. But his posture—bowed head, slumped shoulders, hands clasped in back—spoke of deep, deep thoughts, heavy pondering, dense reflection. A ruminative figure.

Even at a distance, seeing him as a silhouette cut from black paper and pasted against a frosty scene, the man dominated. I thought of how we all revolved around him, whirling our crazy, uncertain courses. But he was the eye of the storm, the sure calm, and everyone looked to him for answers.

I had a wild desire to walk alongside him through that home of the dead and ask him all the questions that were troubling me:

Did you shoot your father deliberately, Dr. Thorndecker?

Did you contrive your first wife's death?

Why did you marry such a young second wife, and how are you able to endure her infidelities?

Why are you obsessed with the problems of aging, and do you really hope to unlock the secret of immortality?

He might, I dreamed, tell me the whole story: father, wife, love, dream—everything. In grave, measured tones, that resonant baritone booming, he would tell me the complete story, leaving nothing out, and the tale would be so wondrous that all I'd be able to say would be, "And then what happened?"

And nothing in his story would be vile or ugly. I wanted it all to be the chronicle of a hero, moving from triumph to triumph. I wanted him to succeed, I really did, and hoped all my doubts and suspicions were due to envy, because I could never be the man he was, never be as handsome, know as much, or have the ability to win a woman as beautiful as Julie.

I had spent only a few hours in the man's company, but I had come under his spell. I admit it. Because he was endless. I could not get to his limits, couldn't even glimpse them. The first colossus I had ever met, and it was a chastening experience.

I didn't want to stop the car to watch him, and after a while he and the graveyard were hidden behind a copse of bare, black trees stuck in the hard ground like grease pencils. I completed the circuit of Crittenden. As I headed for the Albany post road, the Coburn constabulary cruiser passed me again.

This time the officer didn't wave.

The place wasn't hard to find. There was a big red neon poodle out in front, and underneath was the legend: RED DOG BETTY'S. Even at noontime the sign was flashing on and off, and there were three semitrailers and a score of private cars parked in the wide blacktop lot. I made a complete circle, and then selected a deserted spot as far from the roadhouse as I could get. I parked where I had a good view of arrivals and departures. I switched off, opened the window a bit, lighted a cigarette.

It was larger than I had imagined: a three-story clapboard building with a shingled mansard roof and dormer windows on the top floor. I couldn't figure what they needed all that space for, unless they were running games upstairs or providing hot-pillow bedrooms for lonely truckers and traveling salesmen. But maybe those upper floors were something as innocent as the owner's living quarters.

There were neon beer signs in the ground floor windows, and I could hear a juke box blaring from where I sat. As I watched, another semi pulled into the lot, and two more private cars. That place must have been a gold mine. Over the entrance was a painted sign: STEAKS, CHOPS, BAR-B-QUE. I wondered how good the food was. The presence of truckers was no indication; most of those guys will eat slop as long as the beer is cold and the coffee hot.

I sat there for two cigarettes before the blue MGB turned off the road and came nosing slowly around. I rolled down the window, stuck out my arm, and waved. She pulled up alongside, and looked at me without expression.

"Your place or mine?" she called.

Funny lady.

"Why don't you join me?" I said. "More room in here."

She came sliding out of her car, feet first. Her skirt rode up, and I caught a quick flash of bare legs. If she wanted to catch my attention, she succeeded. She took the bucket seat next to me, and slammed the door. I lighted her cigarette. Her hands weren't shaking, but her movements were brittle, almost jerky.

"Mrs. Thorndecker," I said, "nice to see you again."

"Julie," she said mechanically.

"Julie," I said, "nice to see you again."

She tried a small laugh, but it didn't work.

She was wearing a white corduroy suit. Underneath was a white turtleneck sweater, a heavy Irish fisherman's sweater. Her fine, silvered hair was brushed tight to the scalp. No jewelry. Very little makeup. Maybe something around the eyes to make them look big and luminous. But the lips were pale, the face ivory.

She was one beautiful woman. All of her features were crisp and defined. That heavy suit and bulky sweater made her look fragile. But there was nothing vulnerable in the eyes. They were knowing and, looking at her, all I could see was a gold slave bracelet glittering on a naked ankle high in the back seat of a cop's car.

"Been here before?" she said absently.

"No, never," I said. "Looks like an okay place. How's the food?"

She flipped a palm back and forth.

"So-so," she said. "The simple stuff is good. Steaks, stews—things like that. When they try fancy, it's lousy."

I wasn't really hearing her words. I was hearing that marvelous, husky voice. I had to stop that, I decided. I had to listen to this lady's words, and not get carried away by her laughing growls, murmurs, throaty chuckles.

I didn't give her any help. I didn't say, "Well?" Or, "You wanted to see me?" Or, "You have something to say?" I just waited.

"I like Coburn," she said suddenly. "I know you don't, but I do."

"It's your home," I observed.

"That's part of it," she agreed. "I never had much of a home until I married. Also, I think part of it is that in Coburn I'm a big frog in a little pond. I don't think I could live in, say, Boston or New York. Or even Albany. I know. I've tried. I was lost."

"Where are you from, Julie? Originally?"

"A little town in Iowa. You never heard of it."

"Try me."

"Eagle Grove."

"You're right," I said. "I never heard of it. You don't speak like a midwesterner."

"I've been away a long time," she said. "A long, *long* time. I wanted to be a dancer. Ballet."

"Oh?" I said. "Were you any good?"

"Good enough," she said. "But I didn't have the discipline. Talent's never enough."

"How did you meet your husband?"

"At a party," she said. "He saved my life."

She said that very simply, a statement of absolute fact. So, of course, I had to joke about it because I was embarrassed.

"Choking on a fishbone, were you?" I said lightly.

"No, nothing like that. It was the last party I was going to go to. I had been to too many parties. I was going to have a good time, then go back to my fleabag and eat a bottle of pills."

I couldn't believe it. She was young, young, young. And beautiful. I just couldn't make the connection between suicide and this woman with the cameo face and limpid body who sat beside me, filling the car with her very personal fragrance, a scent of warm breath and fresh skin.

All I could think of to say was: "Where was it? This party?"

"Cambridge. Then Telford came over to me. He had been staring at me all evening. He took me aside and told me who he was, how old he was, what he did, how much money he had, how his wife had died a few months before. He told me everything. Then he asked me to marry him."

"Just like that?"

"Just like that," she said, nodding. "And I said yes—just like that. The shortest courtship on record."

"You think he knew?" I asked her. "What you intended to do?"

"Oh yes," she said in a low voice. "I didn't tell him, but he knew. I didn't tell him a thing about myself, but he knew. And asked me to marry him."

"And you've never regretted it?"

"Never," she said firmly. "Never for a minute. Do you have any idea of what kind of man he is?"

"I've been told he's a genius."

"Not his work," she said impatiently. "I mean *him*?"

"Very intelligent," I said cautiously. "Very charming."

"He's a great man," she said definitely. "A *great* man. But I have a problem."

Sure you do, I thought cynically; you fuck Indian cops: that's your problem.

"His daughter," she went on, leaning forward to peer out the fogged windshield. "Mary. She's really his stepdaughter. His first wife was a widow when she married Telford."

I didn't tell her this was old news to me. I lighted cigarettes for us again. She was slowly calming, her movements and gestures becoming easier, more fluid as she talked. I wanted to keep her talking. I was conscious of that suggestive voice, but I was listening to her words now.

"Mary is older than me," she said. "Four years older. She loves her stepfather very much."

She suddenly turned sideways on the seat. She drew up her legs so those bare knees were staring at me. They were round, smooth, hairless as breasts.

"*Very* much," she repeated, staring into my eyes. "Mary loves her stepfather *very* much. So she resents me. She hates me."

I made a sound. I waved a hand.

"Surely it's not that bad," I said.

"It's that bad," she said solemnly. "And also—I don't know whether you know this or not—Mary is a very, uh, disturbed woman. She's into this religious thing. Goes to some outhouse church. Shouts. Reads the Bible. Born again. The whole bit."

"Maybe she's sincere," I said.

She put a soft hand on my arm, leaned closer.

"Of *course* she's sincere," she whispered. "Believes every word of that shit. That's one of the reasons she hates me. Because I took her mother's place. She thinks I'm committing adultery with her father."

I was bewildered.

"But Thorndecker isn't her father," I said.

"*I* know that. *You* know that. But Mary is so mixed up, she thinks of Telford as her father. She thinks I stole her father from her and her dead mother. It's very complex."

"The understatement of the year."

"Sex," Julie Thorndecker said. "Sex has got a lot to do with it. Mary is so in love with Telford, she can't think straight. She thinks we—she and I—are competing for the love of the same man. That's why she hates me."

"What about Dr. Draper? Where does he fit into all this?"

"He'd marry Mary tomorrow if she'd have him. She never will. She wants Telford. But Draper keeps tagging after her like a puppy, hoping she'll suddenly see the light. I feel sorry for him."

"And for Mary?"

"Well . . . yes. I feel sorry for Mary, too. She's so mixed up. But also, I'm scared of her."

"Scared?" I said. "I can't picture you being frightened of anything or anyone."

"I thank you, kind sir," she said, tilting her head, giving me a big smile, tightening her grip on my arm.

She shouldn't have said that. It was a false note. She was not the flirty, girlish type of woman who says, "I thank you, kind sir." I began to get the idea that I was witnessing a performance, and when she finished, the audience would rise, applauding, and roses would be tossed.

"Why are you frightened of Mary?" I asked her.

She shrugged. "She's so—so unbalanced. Who knows what she might do? Or say? Oh, don't get me wrong. I'm not frightened of what she might say about me. That's of no importance. But I'm afraid for my husband. I'm afraid crazy Mary might endanger his career, his plans. That's really why I asked you to meet me here today, to have this talk."

"You're afraid Mary might—well, let's say slander her stepfather?"

If she had said, "Yes," then I was going to say, "But why should Mary endanger Thorndecker's career and his plans if she loves him as much as you say?"

But Julie didn't fall into that trap.

"Oh, she'd never do or say anything against Telford. Not directly. She loves him too much for that. But she might slander *me*. Say things. Spread stories. Because she hates me so much. Not realizing how it might reflect on Telford, how it might affect the grand dreams he has."

I leaned forward to stub out my cigarette. The movement had the added advantages of removing my arm from Julie's distracting grasp and tearing my eyes away from those shiny knees.

"What you're saying," I said slowly, "is that you hope whatever Mary might say about you will not affect Dr. Thorndecker's application for a Bingham Foundation grant. Isn't that it?"

"Yes," she said, "that's it. I just wanted you to know what a disturbed woman she is. Whatever she might say has absolutely nothing to do with my husband's application or his work."

Then we sat without speaking. I became more conscious of her scent. I'm sensitive to odors, and it seemed to me she was exuding a tantalizing perfume that was light, fragrant, with an after-scent, the way some wines have an after-taste. Julie's after-scent was deep, rich, musky. Very stirring. I thought of rumpled sheets, howls, and wet teeth.

I came back to this world to see the Coburn constabulary cruiser move slowly by. It drove up behind us, passed, made the turn behind the roadhouse, and disappeared. The officer driving, the same one I had twice met near Crittenden, didn't turn his head as he drove by. I don't know if he saw us sitting together or not. It didn't seem important. But we both watched him as he went by.

"I love my husband," Julie Thorndecker said thoughtfully.

I was silent. I hadn't even asked her.

"Still . . ." she said.

I said nothing.

"You're not giving me much encouragement," she said.

"When did you ever need encouragement?" I asked her.

"Never," she said. "You're right. Could I have a cigarette, please?"

We lighted up again. I ran the window down to get rid of the smoke.

"Too cold for you?" I said.

"Yes," she said, "too cold. But not the weather. Leave the window down. The trouble is . . ."

Another Coburnite. The unfinished sentence.

"What's the trouble?" I said.

She turned her head slowly to stare at me. I could read nothing in her eyes. Just eyes.

"I'd like to fuck you," she said steadily. "I really would. The trouble is, you'd think I was flopping so you'd give Telford a good report."

I don't care how much experience you've had, what a hot-shot cocksman you are. You're still going to feel fear when a woman says, "Yes."

"That's exactly what I'd think," I said. "What I'm thinking."

"Too bad," she said. "It's not like that at all. If you picked me up in a bar . . .?"

"Or met you at a party? A different can of worms."

"A lovely figure of speech. Thank you."

"You know what I mean," I said. "In another place, another time."

She looked at me shrewdly.

"You're sure you're not making excuses?" she said.

"I'm not sure," I said. "I'm not sure of anything. I'm especially not sure of a woman who makes an offer like that right after she's told me she loves her husband."

She looked at me in astonishment.

"What has one got to do with the other?" she asked.

She wasn't dissembling. She meant it. There's so much about living I don't understand.

"Mrs. Thorndecker," I said. "Julie. I'm not making any value judgment. I'm just saying it's impossible. For me."

"All right," she said equably. "I can live with it. What about Millie Goodfellow?"

"What about her?"

"She's married. Is your fine sense of propriety working there?"

"Not much point to this conversation," I said. "Is there?"

"You're something of a prig, aren't you?" she said.

"Yes," I said. "Something. I'll just have to live with it."

She opened her door, then turned back.

"About Mary," she said. "She *is* disturbed. Please remember what I told you."

"I'll remember," I said.

She gave me a brief smile. Very brief. I watched her drive away. I took a deep breath and blew it out slowly. I felt like a fool. But I've felt like that before, and will again.

I put up the window. I scootched far down on the seat. I tilted my lumpy tweed hat over my closed eyes. I wasn't dreaming of my lost chance with Julie Thorndecker; I was remembering a somewhat similar incident with Joan Powell. It had started similarly; it had ended differently.

We had spent a whole Saturday together, doing everything required of an unmarried couple on the loose in Manhattan: wandering about Bloomingdale's for an hour, lunch at Maxwell's Plum, a long walk over to the Central Park Zoo to say hello to Patty Cake, then a French movie in which the actors spent most of their time climbing sand dunes, dinner at an Italian place in the Village, and back to Powell's apartment.

It should have been a great day. The sun was shining. Garbage had been collected; the city looked neat and clean. I think Joan enjoyed the day. She acted like she did. She said she did. But sometime during the afternoon, it began going sour for me. It wasn't the movie or the restaurants. It wasn't Joan. It was just a mood, a foul mood, without reason. I couldn't account for it; I just knew I had it.

Powell assumed we'd end our busy day in bed. A reasonable assumption based on past experience. When we got back to her place, she went into the bathroom for a quick shower. She came out bareass naked, rubbing her damp hair with a big pink towel.

Jean Powell is something to see naked. She really fits together. Nothing extra, nothing superfluous. She's just there, complete. She's a small woman, but so perfectly proportioned that she could be tarnishing in the garden of the Museum of Modern Art.

I was sitting on the edge of her Scarpa sofa, leaning over, hands clasped between my knees.

"How about mixing us something?" she suggested.

"No," I said. "Thanks. I think I better take off."

She looked at me.

"Sick?" she said.

"No," I said, "just lousy. I don't know what it is. Instant depression. I think I better be alone. I don't want to bore you."

"That's what I want you to do," she said. "Bore me."

"When you get out of those Gucci loafers," I said, "you can be incredibly vulgar."

"Can't I though?" she said cheerfully. "Take off your clothes."

"Oh God," I groaned, "haven't you understood a thing I've said? I just don't *feel* like it."

She tossed the towel aside. She moved naked about the room. Lighted her own cigarette. Mixed her own Cutty and soda.

"You don't feel like it," she repeated. "So what?"

"So what?" I said, outraged. "I've just said I don't feel like fun and games tonight. What are you going to do—rape me? For God's sake, it's got nothing to do with you. I just don't feel like a toss, so I'm taking off."

"Go ahead," she said. "Take off. But don't come back."

This was during a time when the last thing in the world I wanted was to lose her. We were just in the process of working out a sweet, easy, take-it-as-it-comes relationship, and I thought I could be completely honest with her.

"I can't believe you," I said. "One night—*one* night; the first time—I don't want to rub the bacon, and you're ready to call it quits."

She looked at me narrowly.

"It's been more than one time for me, kiddo," she said.

Then she may have seen in my face what that did to my ego, because she came over to sit beside me and slid a cool arm around my neck.

"Look, Todd," she said, "there have been times when I've climbed between the sheets with you when I didn't feel like it. Because you wanted to. Because I love you. And doing something you wanted to do, and I didn't want to, was a sacrifice that proved that love. More important, it turned out to be the best sex we've ever had—for me. Because I was proving my love. And in addition to the physical thing, I was feeling so warm and tender and giving. Try it; you'll like it."

She was right. It was the best sex we ever had—for me. I told you she taught me a lot.

But I didn't think it would work that way with Julie Thorndecker. There was no love between us; I wasn't ready to make a willing sacrifice so she could be happy. And something else kept me away from her. Maybe she was right; I was a prig. Maybe I was just a hopeless romantic. It had to do with Thorndecker. Screwing his wife would be like throwing mud at a statue.

Just to complicate matters further, there was an additional factor involved in my rejection of Julie Thorndecker.

As you've probably gathered by now, I'm a fantasist. I could get twenty years in the pokey for what I dream in one day. For instance, I've had a lot of sexual daydreams about Joan Powell. Some I told her about; some I didn't. I even had some recent fantasies about Millie Goodfellow.

But I found myself totally incapable of fantasizing about Julie Thorndecker. God knows I tried. But the dreams just slid away and dissolved. It wasn't all due to the fact that she was married to a man I admired. It was that she was so beautiful, the body so young and tender, that I couldn't dream about her.

Fantasies, to be pleasurable, must have *some* relation to reality. Even daydreams must be *possible* to be stirring. You can't, for instance, successfuly fantasize about hitting the sheets with Cleopatra because a part of your brain keeps telling you that she was smooched by an asp centuries ago, and any fantasy involving her would be a waste of time.

I could fantasize about Joan Powell and Millie Goodfellow because those daydreams were possible. But when I attempted a sexual fancy involving Julie Thorndecker . . . nothing. I told myself it was because of her husband and her superbeauty.

But there was another reason. Powell and Goodfellow were living, breathing, warm, eager women. Julie Thorndecker was not. She was, I thought, a dead lady.

After all that heavy thinking, I decided that if I didn't get a drink immediately I might shuffle off to Buffalo from a hyperactive cerebellum. So I got out off to Buffalo from a hyperactive cerebellum. So I got out of the car, locked up, stomped over to Red Dog Betty's.

Inside, the place looked like it had originally been a private home: a dozen connecting rooms. The doors had been removed, but the hinge butt plates were still there, painted over. The wall between what I guessed were the original living room and parlor had been knocked down to make a long barroom. The other rooms, smaller, were used for dining. It was an attractive arrangement: a lot of intimate nooks; you didn't feel like you were eating in a barn, and the jukebox in the barroom was muffled to an endurable decibel level.

The barroom itself wasn't fake English pub, or fake fishermen's shanty, or fake anything. The decorations didn't looked planned; just accumulated. A few Tiffany lamps shed a pleasantly mellow glow. The long, scarred mahogany bar was set with stools upholstered in black vinyl. There were a few battered oak tables with captain's chairs. A wall of booths had table candles stuck in empty whiskey bottles covered with wax drippings.

The light was dim, the air redolent of stale beer. There was no chrome or plastic. A snug place, with no cutesy signs. In fact, the only sign I saw bore the stern admonition: BE GOOD OR BE GONE. There was a big array of liquor bottles behind the bar—much larger than the selection at the Coburn Inn—and I was happy to see they kept their "garbage" on the bar, in plain view.

"Garbage" is what bartenders call their little containers of cherries, olives, onions, lemon peel, lime wedges, and orange slices. Keeping these ganishes atop the bar is a tip-off to a quality joint; you know you're getting fresh fixings in your drinks. When the "garbage" is kept below the bar, out of sight, that olive in your martini was probably the property of a previous martini drinker who either forgot to eat it, ignored it, or tasted it and spit it back into his empty glass. A schlock bar can keep one olive going a week that way.

I hung up my coat and hat on a brass tree, gratified to note the absence of a hatcheck attendant. I swung onto one of the barstools and looked around. Sitting near me were three guys who looked like traveling salesmen. They were working on double martinis and exchanging business cards. Down the other end were two truckers in windbreakers, wearing caps decorated with all kinds of metal badges. They had boilermakers on the bar in front of them, and were already shaking dice in a cup to see who'd pay for the next round.

There were no other customers in the barroom; all the action was in the dining areas. They were crowded, and there was a crew of young, fresh-faced waitresses serving drinks, taking orders, lugging in trays of food from the kitchen in the rear.

There was one black bartender doing nothing but working the service section of the bar, preparing drinks for the diners as the waitresses rushed up with their orders. The other bartender, the one who waited on me, was a heavy woman of 50-55, around there. She was comfortably upholstered, wearing a black silk dress two sizes too tight for her. She had a ring on every finger—and she hadn't found those in Crackerjack boxes. Her face was at once doughy and tough. A lot of good beef and bourbon had gone into that complexion.

She flashed diamond earrings, and a doubled strand of pearls. A brooch of what looked to me like rubies in the shape of a rose bloomed on her awesome bosom. Her black wig went up two feet into the air, and was pierced with long, jeweled pins. As the ad says: if you got it, flaunt it.

Like a lot of heavy people, she was light on her feet, and worked with a skillful economy of movement that was a joy to watch. When I ordered Cutty and soda, she slid a napkin in front of me, poured an honest shotglass to the brim, uncapped a nip of soda, placed a clean twelve-ounce glass on the napkin, and half-filled it with ice from a little scoop. All this in one continuous, flowing motion. If I owned a bar, I'd like to have her working for me.

"Mix?" she asked, looking at me.

"Please," I said.

She dumped the Scotch into the tall glass without spilling a drop, added an inch of soda, then waited until I took a sip.

"Okay?" she asked. Her voice was a growl, low and burred.

"Just what the doctor ordered," I said.

"What doctor is that?" she said. "I'd like to send him a few of my customers. You passing through?"

"Staying a few days in Coburn," I told her.

"We all got troubles," she said philosophically, then went down the bar to the truckers to pour them another round. A chubby little waitress came up to the bar to whisper something to her. She walked back to the three salesmen. "Your table's ready, boys," she rasped. "The waitress will bring your drinks."

"Thanks, Betty," one of them said.

I waited until they disappeared into one of the dining rooms. The diamond-studded barmaid began washing and rinsing glasses near me.

"Your name's Betty?" I asked.

"That's right."

"*The* Betty? You own the place?"

"Me and the bank," she growled. She dried her hand carefully and stuck it over the bar. I shook a fistful of silver, gold, and assorted stones. And not, I bet, a hunk of glass in the lot. "Betty Hanrahan," she said. "You?"

"Samuel Todd."

"A pleasure. I don't want to hustle you, Mr. Todd, take your time, but I just wanted you to know that if you're alone and thinking of eating, we can serve you right here at the bar."

"Thanks," I said. "I might do that. But maybe I'll have another first."

"Sure," she said, and refilled the shotglass with one swift, precise motion. She also gave me a fresh highball glass and fresh ice. I was beginning to like this place.

"What's with the red dog?" I asked her.

"I had a poodle once," she said. "Reddish brown. A mean, miserable bitch. When I took this place over, I thought it would be like a trademark. Something different."

"Looks like it worked out just fine," I said, nodding toward the crowded dining rooms.

"I do all right," she acknowledged. "You should stop in some night, if you're looking for action."

"What kind of action?" I said cautiously.

She polished glasses for a few moments.

"Nothing heavy," she said. "Nothing rough. I run a clean joint. But at night, after the dinner crowd clears out, we get a real friendly drinking bunch. A lot of local girls from the farms and small towns around here. Not hookers; nothing like that. Just out for a good time. Have a few drinks, dance a little. Like that."

"And sometimes a trio on Saturday nights?" I asked.

She stopped polishing glasses long enough to look up at me.

"Who told you that?" she asked curiously.

"A loyal customer of yours," I said. "Millie Goodfellow. Know her?"

"Oh hell yes, I know her. Millie's a lot of woman. Life of the party."

"I figured," I said. "Can I buy you a drink?"

"Not till the sun goes down," she said.

"It's been down for the past five days," I said.

She considered that thoughtfully.

"You got something there," she said. "I'll have a short beer, and thank you."

"My pleasure."

She drew herself a small brew from the Michelob tap. She planted herself in front of me and lifted her glass.

"Health," she said, drained off the glass, and went back to her washing, drying, and polishing chores.

"How well do you know Millie?" she asked casually.

"Not very well. Just to talk to. I'm staying at the Coburn Inn."

She nodded.

"I know she's married to a cop," I added. "Ronnie Goodfellow."

Betty Hanrahan looked relieved.

"Good," she said. "As long as you know it."

"I'm not likely to forget it."

"Millie does," she said. "Frequently."

"It doesn't seem to bother him," I said.

"Uh-huh," she said. "Now I'll tell you a story. The same story I told Millie Goodfellow. Thirty years ago I was married—for the first and last time. His name was Patrick Hanrahan. My unmarried name is Dubcek, Betty Dubcek from Hamtramck, Michigan. Anyway, Pat turned out to be a lush, and I turned out to be Miss Roundheels of Detroit. I was a wild one in those days; I admit it. Pat knew about it, and didn't seem to mind. It went on like that for almost two years, with him trying to drink the breweries dry, and me making it with anyone who had a Tootsie Roll between his legs. I thought Pat just didn't care. Then one night he came home stone-cold sober and gave me this . . ."

She lifted a corner of that heavy wig. I saw a deep, angry scar that seemed to run across the top of her skull down to her left ear.

"He damned near killed me," she said. "After two years of taking it, and telling himself it didn't matter, and he couldn't care less, he blew up and damned near killed me. I should have known it would get to him eventually; he was a prideful man. They're like that. It may bubble along inside them for a long while, but sooner or later . . ."

"What happened to him?" I asked.

"Pat? He just took off. I didn't try to find him. Didn't even make a complaint to the cops; I had it coming. After ten years I got a legal divorce. But the reason I'm telling you this is because that Ronnie Goodfellow is the same kind of prideful man as Pat was. Millie thinks he doesn't care. Maybe he doesn't—now. Some day he will, mark my words, and then biff, bam, and pow."

"Thanks for the warning," I said. "Maybe I'll have some lunch now. What's good?"

"Try the broiled liver and bacon," she said. "Home fries on the side."

It was served to me right there on the bar, with slices of pumpernickel and sweet butter, and a small bowl of salad. It wasn't a great meal, but for a roadhouse like that, in the middle of nowhere, it was a pleasant surprise. I had a Ballantine ale, and that helped. And Betty Hanrahan mixed me some fresh Colman's mustard to smear on the liver. It was hot enough to bring the sweat popping out on my scalp. That's the way to eat broiled liver, all right.

I was on my second black coffee, wondering if I wanted a brandy or something else. Betty Hanrahan was down at the end of the bar near the door, checking her bottled beer supply. A guy came in wearing a fleece-collared trucker's jacket. He was still wearing his gloves, and didn't bother removing his badge-encrusted cap. He spoke to Betty for a few minutes, and I could see him gesturing toward the outside, toward the parking lot. Then the owner turned and stared at me. She came slowly down the bar.

"Mr. Todd," she said, "you don't, by any chance, drive a Grand Prix, do you?"

"Sure, I do," I said. "A dusty black job. Why?"

"You got trouble," she said. "Someone slashed your tires. All four tires."

"Son of a bitch!" I said bitterly.

Betty Hanrahan said she'd call the cops. I walked out to the parking lot with the trucker, and he told me what had happened. He had pulled his semitrailer onto the lot, and parked three spaces from my Pontiac. He and his mate got down from the cab, locked up, started for the roadhouse. They had to walk by the Grand Prix, and the mate was the first to see the tires had been slashed.

When we reached my car, the mate was hunkering down, examining one of the tires. He looked up at me.

"Your car?"

I nodded.

"Someone did a job on you," he said in a gravelly voice. "Looks to me like a hatchet, but it could have been a heavy hunting knife—something like that. One deep cut in every tire, except the left rear. That has two cuts, like the guy who did it started there, didn't cut deep enough on the first slash and had to swing again."

"How long do you figure it took?" I asked him.

The two truckers looked at each other.

"A couple of minutes, Bernie?" the mate asked.

"No more than that," the other said. "Just walked around the car hacking. The balls of the guy! In broad daylight yet. You got any enemies, mister?"

"Not that I know of."

"Haven't been sleeping in any strange beds, have you?" Bernie asked, and they both laughed.

I moved slowly around the Grand Prix. The car wasn't exactly on its rims, but it had settled wearily and was listing.

We heard the growl of a siren, and looked up. The Coburn constabulary cruiser, the same car I had seen thrice before, was pulling into the parking lot. One of the truckers waved his arms; the cruiser turned away from the roadhouse, came cutting across the lot toward us, pulled to a stop about ten feet away. The constable cut his flashing light and got out, tugging on his cap. He strutted toward us.

"What have we got here?" he demanded.

"Someone did a hatchet job on this man's tires," Bernie said. "All four of them."

The constable circled the Grand Prix. He was a short, hard bantam with a slit mouth and eyes like licked stones. He came back to join us and stood staring at the car, hands on his hips.

"Jesus," he said disgustedly, "ain't that a kick in the ass."

"I figure a hatchet," the mate said. "Hell, maybe it was an ax."

The constable stooped, fingered one of the cuts.

"Could be," he said. "Or a heavy knife. But I'd say you're right: a hatchet. No sign of sawing with a knife. Just one deep slash. Who discovered it?"

"We did," the mate said. "Pulled in, locked up, and started for the roadhouse. Then I seen it, and Bernie went on ahead to tell Betty, and I stayed here."

"How long ago was this?"

"Not more'n ten minutes. Right, Bernie?"

"About that. Fifteen tops."

The constable turned to me.

"Your car?"

"Yes, it's mine."

"How long you been parked here?"

I looked at my watch.

"Two hours," I said. "Give or take ten minutes."

"You were inside all that time? In the restaurant?"

He stared at me, waiting. The son of a bitch, he *had* seen Julie Thorndecker and me.

"Not all the time," I said. "I smoked a cigarette out here first, then went in. I'd say I was in the bar about an hour and fifteen minutes. Something like that."

He kept staring at me, eyes squinted. But he didn't ask why it took me forty-five minutes to smoke a cigarette or why I hadn't gone into the roadhouse right after I parked.

"See anyone hanging around?" he asked me. "Anyone acting suspicious?"

"No," I said. "No one."

"I came through here a little after noon," he said, "just on routine patrol, you understand, and I didn't see anyone either." He paused thoughtfully. "Come to think of it, I don't recollect seeing your car."

"I was here," I said.

"Well," he said, "what the hell. A lot of cars here; I can't be expected to remember everyone I seen." He sighed deeply. "Crazy kids, I expect. Just doing something wild. We've had a lot of vandalism lately." He paused again, looking at me without expression. "Unless you got some idea of who'd do a thing like this to you?"

"No," I said. "No idea at all."

"Well, I'm sorry this had to happen, Mr. Todd," he said briskly. "It's a damned shame. I'll have to make out a report. Could I see your license and registration, please?"

"We'll be in the bar if you need us," Bernie said.

The constable waved a hand.

"Sure, boys, you go along. I'll drop by in a few minutes to get your names and addresses."

He used the hood of the Pontiac as a desk to copy information into a small notebook he took from a leather pouch strapped to his gunbelt.

"Some of these rotten kids," he said as he wrote, "you wouldn't believe the things they do. Smash windshields, rip off radio antennas, sometimes run a nail down a car they're walking by. Just to ruin the finish, you understand. No rhyme or reason to it. Damned troublemakers."

He replaced the notebook in his gunbelt, handed the license and registration back to me. We started walking toward the roadhouse.

"New York City—huh?" he said. "I guess you're used to shit like this. I hear the place is a jungle."

"Oh, I don't know," I said. "There are places just as bad. Maybe worse."

"Yeah," he said in a flat, toneless voice, "ain't it the truth? Well, you'll be needing a wrecker, I expect. Know any garages around here?"

"How about Mike's Service Station?" I asked. "Could they handle the job?"

"Oh hell, yes. They got a tow car. A job like this, I figure you won't get it today. Maybe tomorrow, if they put a rush on it. My name's Constable Fred Aikens. Mike knows me. Mention my name, and maybe he'll shave the price a little. But I doubt it," he added with a dry laugh.

We paused just inside the entrance of the roadhouse.

"We'll do what we can, Mr. Todd," Constable Aikens said, "but don't get your hopes up. A malicious mischief job like this, probably we'll never catch who done it unless they pull it again, and we get something to go on."

"I understand," I said.

"Besides," he said, "you got insurance—right?"

"I have insurance," I said, "but I'm not sure it covers malicious mischief. I'll have to call my agent."

"Well, I'm sorry it happened, Mr. Todd," he said again. "But at least no one got hurt—right? I mean, no bodily harm done. That's something to be thankful for, ain't it?" He smiled coldly. "Well, I got to find those truckers and get their names and addresses. You'll be hearing from us if we come up with anything."

He waved a hand, started toward the back of the bar where Bernie and his mate had joined the two truckers who had been there since I had first entered. All four of them were drinking boilermakers.

The black bartender was alone, and motioned me over.

"Miss Betty is upstairs in the office," he told me. "She'd like to see you up there, if you got a minute. Take that door over there, and it's at the head of the stairs."

"Thanks," I said. "I'll go up."

"She says maybe you better bring your hat and coat with you."

"Yeah," I said sourly, "maybe I better."

The door of the office was open. Betty Hanrahan was on the phone. She motioned me to come in, and pointed to a wooden armchair alongside her cluttered desk. I sat down, took out my cigarettes, offered the pack to Betty. She took one, and I lighted it for her as she was saying, "Yes, Dave . . . Yes . . . I understand, but I've never made a single claim before . . ."

I lighted my own cigarette and looked around. It was about as big as a walk-in closet, with just enough room for a desk, two chairs, a scarred metal file cabinet, and a small, old-fashioned safe shoved into one corner: a waist-high job on big casters with a single dial and brass handles.

Betty Hanrahan leaned back in her oak swivel chair and parked her feet up on the desk. Good legs. Her rhinestone-trimmed shoes had heels at least four inches high, and I wondered how she could wait bar on those spikes. I also realized that in her stockinged feet she'd be a small one. In length, not in width.

"Okay, David love," she was saying, "do what you can . . . Fine . . . Let me know as soon as you hear."

She leaned forward to hang up the phone. As she did, she looked at her skirt and tugged it down a bit over her knees.

"Nothing showing, is there?" she said.

"I didn't see a thing," I assured her.

"Well, what the hell, I'm wearing pants"

She opened a side drawer and pulled out a half-full bottle of Wild Turkey. She also set out a stack of paper cups.

"Build us a couple," she said.

I rose and began pouring the bourbon into two cups.

"I'll get you some water," she said, "if you want it."

"This'll do fine."

"I need a shot," she said. "I don't like rough stuff on my property. It scares me, and gives the joint a bad name. That was my insurance agent I was talking to. He thinks I'm covered against malicious mischief. But even if I'm not, I want you to know I'm picking up the tab."

"I appreciate that, Betty," I said. "But I may be covered myself. I'll wait till I get back to New York, and check it out."

"New York," she said, shaking her head. "That's funny. I had you pegged for Chicago. You don't talk like a New Yorker."

"Transplanted," I said. "Ohio originally. Could I use your phone? I want to call Mike's Service Station and see what they can do about my car."

"Let me call Mike," she said. "I know how to handle that old crook."

She took her feet off the desk, rummaged through a drawer, came up with a dog-eared business card. She had to put on a pair of glasses to read the number. The frames of the spectacles were sparkling with little rhinestones and seed pearls.

I listened to her explain to Mike what had happened. She told him she wanted the car picked up immediately, and new tires installed by 5:00 P.M. I heard an angry crackle on the phone. She screamed back, and finally agreed on the job being finished before noon on Saturday. Then they started talking cost, and another argument erupted. I didn't catch what the final figure was, but I do know she beat him down, and concluded by yelling, "And you make sure I get the bill, you goddamned pirate."

She slammed down the phone and grinned at me. She took off her glasses and put her feet back on the desk again. This time she didn't bother tugging down her skirt. She was right; she was wearing pants.

"They'll pick it up right away," she told me. "He claims he just can't get to it today. But they'll have it ready for you by noon tomorrow. They'll deliver it to the Coburn Inn. Okay?"

"Thanks, Betty," I said gratefully. "But you don't have to pay the bill. It wasn't your fault."

"It happened on my property, didn't it?" she said. "I'm responsible for the safety of my customers' cars."

"I'm not sure you are," I said. "Under the law."

"Fuck the law," she said roughly. "I feel responsible, and that makes it so. Got any idea who did it?"

I had a lot of ideas.

"I have no idea," I said.

"Haven't been leaving your shoes under a strange bed, have you?"

"That's what one of the truckers suggested. But it just isn't so. As far as I know, I have no enemies in these parts. Maybe it was an accident. I mean that my car was hit. Maybe some joy-riding kids just picked on me because my heap was parked by itself, way down at the end of the lot."

"Maybe," she said doubtfully.

"That's what Constable Fred Aikens thinks. Claims you've had a lot of vandalism by wild kids lately."

"Constable Fred Aikens," she said with great disgust. "He couldn't find his ass with a boxing glove."

"Betty," I said, "tell me something . . . When you called the cops, when I went out to look at my car, did you tell them my name? Did you say the car was owned by Samuel Todd?"

She thought a moment, frowning.

"No," she said definitely. "I just told them a customer had gotten his tires slashed. I didn't mention your name."

"When Aikens showed up and was inspecting the car—this was before he checked my license and registration—he called me Mr. Todd. I just wondered how he knew who I was."

"Maybe he saw you around Coburn and asked who you were. Or maybe someone pointed you out to him."

"That's probably what it was," I said casually. "Someone pointed me out to him."

"Ready for another?" she asked, nodding toward the bottle.

"Sure."

"Use fresh cups. They begin to leak if you use them too long."

I poured us two more drinks in fresh cups. She drank hers with no gasps, coughs, or changes of expression. I hardly saw her throat move; she just tilted it down. No way was I going to try keeping up with this lady.

"You're in Coburn on business, Mr. Todd? If you don't mind my asking?"

"I don't mind," I said, and I told her, briefly, about the Bingham Foundation, the Thorndecker application, and how I had come to Crittenden to make a field investigation.

"I know that Crittenden bunch," she said. "The Thorndeckers have been over two or three times for dinner. That wife is a doll, isn't she?"

"Yes," I said. "A doll."

"And we get staff from the nursing home, and a lot of the young kids from the lab. Usually on Saturday and Sunday nights. A noisy bunch, but they mean no harm. Drink up a storm. Mostly beer or wine."

"Mary Thorndecker ever show up?"

"Never heard of her. Who is she?"

"Thorndecker's daughter. Stepdaughter actually. Twenty-seven. Spinsterish looking."

"I don't think I've ever seen her."

"How about Draper? Dr. Kenneth Draper?"

"Him I know. A loner. He comes in two or three nights a week. Late. Sits by himself. Drinks until he's got a load on. A couple of times he got a crying jag."

"Oh?" I said. "That's interesting. How about Stella Beecham? She's chief nurse at Crittenden Hall."

"Yeah," Betty Hanrahan said scornfully, "I know that one. I had to kick her ass out of here. She was hustling one of my young waitresses. Listen, I'm strictly live and let live. I don't care who screws who. Or how. But not on my premises. I got a license to think about. Also, this waitress's folks are friends of mine, and I promised to keep an eye on the kid. So I had to give that nurse the heave-ho. That's one tough bimbo."

"Yes," I agreed, "she is. Betty, I don't want you telling any tales out of school, but did Julie Thorndecker, the doll, ever come in with any man but her husband?"

"No," she said promptly. "At least not while I was working, and I usually am. You want me to ask around?"

"No, thanks. You've done plenty for me already, and I appreciate it. Could I call a cab—if there is such a thing around here? I've got to get back to the Inn."

"I'll do better than that," she said. "You need wheels until Mike fixes up your car. I can take care of that. Not a car exactly. I drive a Mark Five; you can't have that, but we got a wreck, an old Ford pickup. We use it for shopping and put a plow on it to clear snow off the parking lot. It's not much to look at, but it goes. You're welcome to use it until you get your own car back."

I didn't want to do it, but she wouldn't take No for an answer. I kissed her thankfully. Much woman.

So there I was, twenty minutes later, rattling back to Coburn in the unheated cab of an ancient pickup truck that seemed to be held together with Dentyne and Dill's pipe cleaners. But it rolled, and I was so busy figuring out its temperamental gearbox, trying to coax it to do over thirty-five, and mastering its tendencey to turn to the right, that I was back at the Coburn Inn before I remembered that I had forgotten to pay my lunch tab at Red Dog Betty's. When I returned to New York, I resolved, I would send Betty Hanrahan a handsome gift.

Something encrusted with rhinestones, seed pearls, and sequins. She'd like that.

Up in my room, I glared balefully at those two drinks lying quietly in the bottom of the quart vodka bottle, not doing anyone any harm. Not doing anyone any good either. I got my fresh bathroom glass and emptied the bottle. I flopped down and took a sip. So far that day I had swilled beer, Scotch, ale, bourbon and vodka. How had I managed to miss ouzo, sangria, and hard cider?

I drank morosely. I was not feeling gruntled. The slashing of my tires seemed such a childish thing to do. I knew it was intended as a warning—but how juvenile can you get?

I figured it had to be Constable Fred Aikens, acting on orders from Ronnie Goodfellow. I could even imagine how it went:

Aikens makes a routine patrol of the parking lot at Red Dog Betty's. Or maybe he's been tailing me since he saw me nosing around Crittenden Hall. Anyway, he spots me parked outside the roadhouse, thigh-to-thigh with Julie Thorndecker. If Aikens didn't actually see her face, he sure as hell recognized her blue MGB nuzzling my Grand Prix. So he hightails it to the nearest public phone. It must have gone something like this:

"Ronnie? Fred. Did I wake you up?"

"That's okay. What's going on?"

"I just spotted your girlfriend's car. Parked in the lot at Red Dog Betty's."

"So?"

"Right next to a black Grand Prix. She's sitting in the front seat of the Pontiac with this tall dude. Thought you might want to know."

Silence.

"Ronnie? You there?"

"I'm here. That son of a bitch!"

"You know him?"

"A snoop from the City. A guy named Todd. He's here to investigate Thorndecker about that grant."

"Oh. It's okay then? Them being together?"

Silence.

"I just thought you might want to know, Ronnie."

"Yeah. Thanks. Listen, Fred. Could you fix that smartass bastard?"

"Fix him?"

"Just his car. Don't touch him. But if you get the chance, you could do a job on the car."

"What for, Ronnie?"

"Just to give him something to think about."

"Oh, yeah, I get it. You know that hatchet you took away from Abe Tompkins when he was going to brain his missus?"

"I remember."

"The hatchet's still in the trunk. If I get the chance, maybe I can chop down that Grand Prix."

"Thanks, Fred. I won't forget it."

"You'd do the same for me—right?"

"Right."

I figured it went something like that. But solving the Mystery of the Slashed Tires gave me no satisfaction. Small mystery; small solution. It had nothing to do with the Thorndecker investigation.

I thought.

I sat there, trying to make the vodka last, glowering at nothing. In any inquiry there is an initial period during which the investigator asks, listens, observes, collects, accumulates, and generally lets things happen to him, with no control.

Then, when certain networks are established, relationships glimpsed, the investigator must start flexing his biceps and make things happen. This is the Opening Phase, when all those sealed cans get their lids peeled off, you lean close to peer in—and usually turn away when the stench flops your stomach.

It was time, I decided, to get started. One thing at a time. I chose the first puzzle of the Thorndecker inquiry. It turned out to be ridiculously easy.

But the simple ones sometimes take the most time to unravel. I remember working a pilferage case in a two-story Saigon warehouse. This place stored drugs for front-line medical units and base hospitals. An inventory turned up horrendous shortages.

The warehouse had three entrances. I had two of them sealed up; all military and civilian personnel had to enter and exit from one door. I doubled the guards, and everyone leaving the place had to undergo a complete body search. The thefts continued. I checked for secret interior caches, for tunnels. I even had a metal detector set up, the kind airports use, in case someone was swallowing the drugs in small metal containers, or getting them out in capsules up the rectum.

Nothing worked. We were still losing drugs in hefty amounts, and I was going nuts trying to figure how they were getting the stuff out of the place.

Know how I solved it? One day I was sitting at my desk in the security office. I took the last cigarette out of a pack. I crumpled the empty pack in my fist and tossed it negligently out an open window. I then leapt to my feet and shouted something a little stronger than "Eureka!"

That's how they were doing it, all right. A bad guy was dropping the stuff out a second-story window, right into the arms of a pal standing in an alley below. Simple? Sure it was. All the good scams are. Took me three weeks to break it.

But finding the author of the note, "Thorndecker kills," wasn't going to take me that long. I hoped.

I grabbed up my hat and trenchcoat, and went back down to the lobby, using the stairs. Twice as fast, I had learned, as waiting for Sam Livingston's rheumatic elevator.

I glanced toward the cigar counter, but Millie Goodfellow had a customer, one of the antediluvian permanent residents. He was leaning over the counter, practically falling, trying to read the sign on the front of her tight T-shirt.

"What?" I heard his querulous voice. "What does it say? I left my reading glasses upstairs."

I went to the desk, and the baldy on duty looked up, irritated at being interrupted in his contemplation of the *Playboy* centerfold.

"Yes?" he said testily.

"I need a new typewriter ribbon," I said. "You got any place in town that sells office supplies?"

"Of course we do," he said in an aggrieved tone, angry because he thought I doubted Coburn could provide such an amenity.

He told me how to find Coburn Office Supplies, a store located one block north of the post office.

"I'm sure they'll have everything you need," he said stiffly.

I thanked him, and started away. Then my eyes were caught by the right shoulder of his blue serge suit. He saw me staring, and twisted his head and looked down, trying to see what I was looking at. I reached out and brushed his shoulder twice with the edge of my hand.

"There," I said. "That looks much better."

"Thank you, Mr. Todd," he said, humble and abashed.

There was nothing on his shoulder, of course. God, I can be a nasty son of a bitch.

I found Coburn Office Supplies, a hole in-the-wall with a dusty window and a sad display of pencils, erasers, faded stationery, and office gadgets already beginning to rust. The opening door hit a suspended bell that jangled in the quiet of the deserted store. I looked around. The place was a natural for a Going-Out-of-Business Sale.

And the little guy who came dragging out of the back room was perfectly suited to be custodian of this mausoleum. All I remember about him was that he wore shredded carpet slippers and had six long strands of hair (I counted them) brushed sideways across his pale, freckled skull.

"Yew, sir," he sighed. "Can I help?"

That last word came out "hep." In fact, he said, "Kin ah hep?" Southern, I thought, but I couldn't place it exactly. Hardscrabble land somewhere.

I had intended to waltz him around, but he was so beaten, so defeated, I had no desire to make a fool of him. Life had anticipated me. So I just said:

"I want to bribe you."

The pale, watery eyes blinked.

"Bribe me?"

I took out my wallet, extracted a ten-dollar bill. I dangled it, flipping it with my fingers.

"This is the only office supply store in town?"

"Wull . . . sure," he said, eyeing that sawbuck like it was a passport to Heaven, or at least out of Coburn.

"Good," I said. "The ten is yours for a simple answer to a simple question."

"I don' know . . . ." he said, anxious and cautious at the same time.

"You can always deny you talked to me," I told him. "No one here but us chickens. Your word against mine."

"Yeah," he said slowly, brightening, "thass right, ain't it? Whut's the question?"

"Anyone in town buy ribbons for an Olympia Standard typewriter?"

"Olympia Standard?" he said, licking his dry lips. "Only one machine like that in town as I know of."

"Who?"

"Mary Thorndecker. She comes in ever' so often to buy—"

I handed him the ten.

"Thanks," I said.

"Mebbe ever' two months or so," he droned on, staring down at the bill in his hand. "She always asks—"

The bell over the door jangled as I went out.

I strutted back to the Coburn Inn, so pleased with myself it was sickening. As a reward for my triumph, I stopped off at Sandy's and bought another quart of Popov, a fine Russian-sounding vodka distilled in Hartford, Conn. But by the time I entered Room 3-F, my euphoria had evaporated; I didn't even open the bottle.

I lowered myself gingerly into one of those grasping armchairs and sat sprawled, staring at nothing. All the big problems were still there. Mary Thorndecker may have written the note, and Ronnie Goodfellow may have tried to recover it. An interesting combo. Tinker to Evers to Chance. But who was Chance?

How's this?

Mary Thorndecker types out a note, "Thorndecker kills," and leaves it for me. What's her motive? Well, maybe she's driven by something as innocent as outrage at the vivisection being practiced at the Crittenden Research Laboratory. If she's a deeply religious woman, a fundamentalist, as everyone claims, she could be goaded to write, "Thorndecker kills." Anyway, she writes the note, for whatever reason.

Now, who might Mary tell what she had done? She could tell Dr. Kenneth Draper. But I doubted that; he was deeply involved in the activities of the research lab. She might tell her half-brother, Edward Thorndecker. That made more sense to me. She wants to protect Edward from what she conceives to be an evil existing in Crittenden.

Let's say she does tell Edward, and hints to him that she intends to end what she sees as wickedness pervading the tiled corridors of Crittenden. But Edward, smitten by Julie's beauty and sexuality—I had observed this; it was more than a crush—tells his stepmother what Mary is up to. Especially the note left in my box at the Coburn Inn.

Julie, wanting to protect her husband, the "great man," before the letter can be used as evidence to deny Thorndecker's application for a grant, asks Constable Ronnie Goodfellow to recover the damned, and damning thing. For all Julie knows, it could be a long bill of particulars signed by Thorndecker's stepdaughter.

And because he is so pussy-whipped, Goodfellow gives it the old college try (using his wife's passkey), and strikes out. Only because I had already mailed the note to Donner & Stern for typewriter analysis.

All right, I admit it: the whole thing was smoke. A scenario based on what I knew of the people involved and how they might react if their self-interest was threatened. But it all made sense to me. As a matter of fact, it turned out to be about 80 percent accurate.

But it was that incorrect 20 percent that almost got me killed.

I had something to eat that evening. I think it was a tunafish salad and a glass of milk; the size of my gut was beginning to embarrass me. Anyway, I dined lightly and had only two vodka gimlets for dessert at the Coburn Inn bar before I climbed into Betty Hanrahan's pickup truck, drove happily out of Coburn, and rattled south on the river road. I was heading for Mary Thorndecker's church. It wasn't that I was looking for salvation, although I could have used a small dollop. I just wanted to touch all bases. I wanted to find out why a young, intelligent woman seemed intent on destroying a man she reportedly loved.

I've attended revival meetings in various parts of the country, including a snake-handling session in a tent pitched on the outskirts of Macon, Georgia. I've heard members of fundamentalist churches speak in tongues, and I've seen apparent cripples throw away their crutches or rise from wheelchairs to dance a jig. I'm familiar with the oratorical style of backwoods evangelists and the fervor of their congregations. This kind of down-home religion is not my cup of vodka, but I can't see where they're hurting anyone—except possibly themselves, and you won't find anything in the Constitution denying a citizen the right to make a fool of himself.

So I thought I knew what to expect: a mob of farmers, rednecks, and assorted blue-collar types shouting up a storm, clapping their hands, and stomping their feet as they confessed their piddling sins and came forward to be saved. All this orchestrated by a leather-lunged preacher man who knew all the buzzwords and phrases to lash his audience to a religious frenzy.

I was in for a surprise.

The First Fundamentalist Church of Lord Jesus was housed not in a tent or ramshackle barn, but in a neat, white clapboard building with well-kept grounds, a lighted parking area, and a general appearance of modest prosperity. The windows were washed, there were bright boxes of ivy, and the cross atop the small steeple was gilded and illuminated with a spotlight.

I had expected a junkyard collection of battered sedans, pickup trucks, rusted vans, and maybe a few motorcycles. But the cars I saw gave added evidence of the economic well-being of the congregation: plenty of Fords, Chevys, VW's, and Toyotas, but also a goodly sprinkling of imported sports cars, Cadillacs, Mercedes-Benzes, and one magnificent maroon Bentley. I parked Betty Hanrahan's heap amongst all that polished splendor, feeling like a poor relation.

They were signing "Jesus, Lover of My Soul" when I entered. I slid into an empty rear pew, opened a hymnal, and looked around. A simple interior painted an off-white, polished walnut pews, a handsome altar covered with a richly brocaded cloth, an enormous painting of the crucifixion on the wall behind the altar. It was no better and no worse than the usual church painting. Lots of blood. The seated congregation was singing along with music from an electronic organ up front against the left wall. There was a door set into the opposite wall. I assumed it led to the vestry.

There wasn't any one thing about the place that I could label as definitely fake or phony. But I began to get the damndest feeling that I had wandered into a movie or TV set, put together for a big climactic scene like a wedding or funeral, or maybe the church into which the bullet-riddled hero staggers to cough his last on the altar, reaching for the cross.

Trying to analyze this odd impression, I decided that maybe the *newness* of the place had something to do with it. Churches usually looked used, worn, comfortably shabby. This one looked like it had been put up that morning; there wasn't a nick, stain, or scratch that I could see. It even smelled of paint and fresh plaster.

Maybe the congregation had something to do with my itchy feeling that the whole thing was a scam. There were a few blacks, but most of them were whites in their twenties and thirties. The men favored beards, the women either pigtails or hair combed loosely to their waist. Both sexes sported chain necklaces and medallions. Most of them, men and women, wore jeans. But they were French jeans, tailored jeans, or jeans with silver studs, appliques, or designs traced with bugle beads and seed pearls.

All I could do was guess, but I guessed there was a good assortment of academics, writers, artists, musicians, poets, and owners of antique shops. They looked to be the kind of people who had worked their way through Freudian-analysis, high colonics, est, Yoga, TM, primal scream, communal tub bathing, and cocaine. Not because they particularly needed any of these things, but because they had been the *in* things to do. I'd make book that the First Fundamentalist Church of Lord Jesus was only the latest brief enthusiasm in their fad-filled lives, and as soon as they all got "born again," the whole crowd would decamp for the nearest disco, with shouts of loud laughter and a great blaring of horns.

The hymn came to an end. The congregation put their hymnals in the racks on the pew backs in front of them. A young man in the front pew stood up and faced us. "Faced" is an exaggeration; he had so much hair, beard, and mustache, all I could see were two blinking eyes.

"Welcome to the First Fundamentalist Church of Lord Jesus. My name is Irving Peacock, and I am first vestryperson of your church. Most of you I know, and most of you know each other. But I do see a few brothers and sisters who, I believe, are here for the first time. To these newcomers, may I say, 'Welcome! Welcome to our family!' It is our custom, at the beginning of the service, for each sister and brother to turn to the right and left and kiss their neighbors as a symbol of our devotion to the love and passion of Lord Jesus. Now, please, all kiss. On the lips now! On the lips!"

The congregation stood. I rose along with them, wondering what kind of a nuthouse I had strayed into. I watched, fascinated, as men and women turned right and left, embracing and kissing their neighbors. A great smacking of lips filled the room.

I was alone in the rear pew and figured I was safe. But no, a grizzly bear of a man in the pew in front of me kissed right and left, then turned suddenly and held out his arms to me.

"Brother!" he said.

What could I do—say, "Please, not on the first date?" So I kissed him, or let him kiss me. He had a walrus mustache. It tickled. Also, he had just eaten an Italian dinner. A cheap Italian dinner.

After this orgy of osculation, the congregation sat down, and Irving Peacock announced the offertory. Contributions would be accepted by vestrypersons John Millhouse and Mary Thorndecker, and we were urged to give generously to "support the splendid work of Father Michael Bellamy and to signify our faith in and love for our Lord Jesus."

The two vestrypersons started down the center aisle. Brass trays, velvet-lined to eliminate the vulgar sound of shekels clinking, were passed along each pew, hand-to-hand, then returned to the aisle. I saw that Mary Thorndecker was collecting on the other side. I slipped across the aisle, into the empty rear pew on her side. I watched her approach, features still and expressionless.

She was wearing an earth-colored tweed suit over a death-gray sweater. Opaque hose and flat-heeled brogues. Her hair was drawn back tightly, pinned back with a barrette. No jewelry. No makeup. I wondered if she was making herself as unattractive as possible in reaction to Julie's obvious charms.

She moved slowly down the aisle toward me, not looking up. Even when she took the brass tray from the pew in front of me, she still hadn't seen me. I had time to note the plate contained a nifty pile of coins and folding money. Father Michael Bellamy was doing all right.

Then she was at my pew. Her eyes rose as she proffered the tray.

"Why . . . Mr. Todd!" she said, not quite gasping, her face flushing.

I looked at her. I may have smiled pleasantly.

"Thorndecker kills?" I said.

Down went the brass tray. Coins clanged, bounced, rolled. Bills fluttered to the floor. For a moment I thought she was going to cave. Her face went putty-white, then greenish. A pale hand fluttered up to her hair, and just hung there, waving futilely.

Then she was gone, dashing out the double-door. I thought I heard a sound: a sob, a moan. I let her go. I helped others gather up the spilled coins, the scattered bills. I added a fin of my own. Atonement.

The collection plates were returned to the first vestryperson; everyone setttled down. A few moments passed while the congregation gradually quieted. Nothing happened. But I felt the expectation, saw heads turning toward the vestry door. Still nothing. A very professionally calculated stage wait. Tension grew.

Then the effete lad at the Hammond organ played something that sounded suspiciously like a fanfare. The vestry door was flung open. Father Michael Bellamy, clad in flowing white robes, swept into the nave, arms outstretched to embrace his followers.

"Blessings on my children!" he intoned.

"Blessings on our father!" they shouted back.

He stood before the altar, arms wide, head thrown back, eyes turned heavenward.

"Let us pray together a moment in silence," he declaimed. "Let our souls' voices merge and rise to Lord Jesus, asking love, understanding, and redemption for our sins."

All heads bowed. Except mine. I was too busy studying Father Michael Bellamy.

A big man, maybe six-four. Broad shoulders and chest. I couldn't see much more because of those robes, but got an impression of a comfortable corporation. A marvelous head of wavy, snow-white hair. If it wasn't a carpet, it had enjoyed the attentions of an artful coiffeur. No one's hair could be that white or that billowy without aid.

The hair was long enough and full enough to cover what I guessed were big, meaty ears. I reckoned that from the rest of his face, also big and meaty. A nose like a sausage, a brow like a rare roast, chin and jowls like beef liver. The man was positively appetizing. Stuck in all this rosy suet were glistening eyes, round and hard as black marbles.

The voice was something; it made the electronic organ sound like a twopenny whistle. Orotund, booming, it not only filled the church but rattled the windows and, for all I knew, browned the ivy in the outside window boxes. That voice conquered me; it was an instrument, and if a good soprano can shatter a wine glass, this guy should have been able to bring down the Brooklyn Bridge.

"Children," he said, and his praying family looked up, "tonight we shall speak of sin and forgiveness. We shall speak of the unutterable lusts that corrupt the human heart and soul; and how we may all be washed clean in the blood of our Redemptor, Lord Jesus Christ of Nazareth."

Then he was off. I had heard the sermon before, but never so well delivered. The man was a natural, or practiced preacher. His magnificent voice roared, whispered, entreated, scorned, laughed, hissed, wailed. There was nothing he could not do with that voice. And the gesturings and posturings! Waves, flappings, pointings, clenched fists, pleading palms, stoopings, leaps, stridings from one side of the platform to the other. And tears. Oh yes. The eyes moist and brimming on demand.

Did they listen to his words? I wasn't sure. I found it difficult to listen, so overwhelming was his physical performance. He was a whirlwind, white robes streaming in the tempest, and what he said seemed of less importance than the presence of the man himself. Behind him, on the wall, Christ bled and died on the cross. And Father Michael Bellamy, the white-haired prophet incarnate, stamped the boards before this image and mesmerized his trendy flock with a performance worth four Oscars, three Emmys, two Grammys, one Ike, and a platinum record. The man was a master.

As I said, the sermon was familiar. He told us that the human heart was a fetid swamp, filled with nasty crawling things. We were all sinners, in thought or in deed. We betrayed the best impulses of our souls, and turned instead to lechery, lust, and lasciviousness. (The Father was big on alliteration.)

He gave a fifteen-minute catalogue of human sins of the flesh, listened to attentively by the congregation who, I figured, wanted to find out if they had missed any. This portion of the sermon was all stern denunciation, a jeremiad against the permissiveness of our society which condoned conduct that in happier times would have earned burning at the stake, or at least a holiday weekend in the stocks.

And where was such lewdness and licentiousness leading us? To eternal damnation, that's where. To a hell which, according to Father Bellamy's description, was something like a Finnish sauna without the snowbanks.

But all was not lost. There was a way to redeem our wasted lives. That was to pledge our remaining days to the service of Lord Jesus, following in His footsteps. It was being born again, finding the love and forgiveness of the Father of Us All, and dedicating our lives to walking the path of righteousness.

Up to this point, the sermon had followed the standard revivalist pattern: scare 'em, then save 'em. But then Bellamy got into an area that made me a little queasy.

He said there was only one way to prove sincere relinquishment of a wicked life. That was by full public confession, acknowledgement of past sins, and whole-hearted and soul-felt determination to make a complete break with the past, to seek the comforting embrace of Lord Jesus and be saved.

"O, my children!" cried Father Bellamy, throwing his gowned arms wide like a great white bat. "Is there not one among ye willing to stand now, this moment, and confess your most secret vices openly and honestly in the presence of Lord Jesus and these witnesses?"

As a matter of fact, there was more than one amongst us; several leaped to their feet and clamored for attention. What followed convinced me that this mob had come to church directly from a grass-uppers-LSD buffet, or was on leave from a local acorn academy.

A young woman, tears streaming down her cheeks, described, graphically, how she had been unfaithful to her husband on "myriad occasions," and how she was tortured by the memories. During this titillating recital, her hand was held by the young man seated beside her. He was, I presumed, the betrayed husband. Or he could have been one of the tortured memories.

A young man, twisting his fingers nervously, told how he had been seduced by his aunt when he was wearing his Boy Scout uniform, and how the relationship continued until he was wearing a U.S. Army uniform, at which time the aunt deserted him, leaving him with a seared psyche and a feeling of guilt that frequently resulted in nocturnal emissions.

Three witnesses, in rapid succession, testified to how much they hated their mother/father/brother/sister, and wished them dead.

A woman confessed to unnatural sex acts with a dalmatian owned by her local fire company.

A stuttering lad, desperately sincere, confessed to a secret passion for Madame Ernestine Schumann-Heink, who died in 1936. He had come across her photograph in an old magazine, and her image had haunted his waking hours and dreams ever since.

A wispy blond girl, eyes glazed and enormously swollen, said she had this "thing." She could never get rid of this "thing." She thought about it constantly and she wanted Lord Jesus, or at least Father Michael Bellamy, to exorcise this "thing."

It went on and on like that: a litany of personal confessions that had me squirming with shame and embarrassment. I am, by nature, a private man. I could match anyone of them sin for sin, depravity for depravity, in dream or in deed, but I'd be damned if I'd stand voluntarily before a jury of my peers and spill my guts. It was just none of their business. I don't think I could do it in a confessional booth either. I can't even watch TV talk shows. Listen, if we all told one another what we really did, thought, and dreamed, the world would dissolve into mad laughter, helpless with despair, and then who would have the strength and resolve to plan wars?

So I rose quietly from the rear pew and slipped out the church door, just as an older, bearded man was describing how he had been abusing himself ever since he picked up a weight-lifting magazine in a barber shop and, as a consequence, had become a chronic bed-wetter.

I climbed into the dank cab of the pickup. I turned up the collar of my trenchcoat and slouched down. I lighted a cigarette and waited. I wasn't bored; I had a lot of questions to ponder.

Like: were those idiots inside who were stripping themselves naked in front of friends and strangers really sincere about this confession and redemption jazz? Or was it just another kick like Zen or rolfing?

Like: had any bright young sociologist ever written a PhD thesis on the remarkable similarities between bucolic American revival meetings and sophisticated American group therapy sessions? Both had a father-leader (preacher/psychiatrist). Both demanded public confession. Both promised salvation.

Like: where did Mary Thorndecker run after I jolted her? I figured she'd have to call me, that night or Saturday morning. I put my money on a morning call, after she had a desperate night wondering how I had fingered her as the author of the anonymous note.

Three cigarettes later, the service ended. The congregation of the First Fundamentalist Church of Lord Jesus streamed forth into the cold night air, presumably cleansed and rejuvenated. I had been right: there were bursts of raucous laughter and a great tooting of horns as they roared away from the parking lot. Kids let out of school.

Still I sat there in Betty Hanrahan's broken wreck. The spotlight illuminating the steeple cross went out. The interior lights of the church went out. Only one car remained in the parking area: that impressive maroon Bentley. Of course, it would be his.

I got out of the truck slowly, being careful not to slam that tinny door. I made a slow circuit of the church building. Lights still burned in a side extension of the nave: the vestry. I went back to the main entrance. The double-door was still unlocked. I slid in, tiptoed up the aisle. Even in broad daylight a church is a ghostly place. At night, in almost total darkness, it can spook you. Don't ask me why.

The only illumination was a thin bar of light coming from the interior door of the vestry. I heard laughter, the clink of glasses. I pulled down my tweed hat to shadow my eyes, stuck my hands deep in the trenchcoat pockets. All I needed was a Lone Ranger mask.

I shoved the door open with my foot and stalked in. I was thinking of a joke a cop had told me: this nervous robber goes into a bank on his first job and pulls out a gun. "All right, you mother-stickers," he snarls. "This is a fuck-up."

There were two of them in there. Father Michael Bellamy had doffed his pristine robes. Now he was wearing a beautifully tailored suit of soft, gray doeskin with a Norfolk jacket, lavender shirt, knitted black silk tie. I had time to eyeball his jeweled cufflinks: twin Kohinoors. He was seated behind a desk, counting the night's collection. Piling the coins in neat columns, tapping the bills into square stacks.

The other gink was the limp young man I had seen playing the organ. He was a washed-out lad with strands of lank blond hair falling across his acned forehead. The acne was hard to spot under the pancake makeup. He was wearing a ranch suit: faded blue jeans and jacket. With high-heeled western boots yet. He looked as much like a Wyoming cowpoke as Joan Powell looks like Sophie Tucker.

There was a bottle of Remy Martin on the desk. Bellamy was taking his straight in a little balloon glass. The organist was diluting his cognac with a can of Pepsi, which is like blowing your nose in a Gobelin tapestry.

The effete youth was first to react to my entrance. He jerked to his feet and glared at me, not knowing whether to shit, go blind, or wind his watch.

Bellamy didn't pop a capillary.

"Easy, Dicky," he said soothingly. "Easy now." Then to me, brightly: "Yes, sir, and how may I be of service?"

I gave them the silent treatment, looking at them, one to the other, back and forth.

"Well?" Bellamy said. "If it's spiritual advice you're seeking, my son, I must tell you I conduct personal sessions only on Tuesdays and Thursdays, beginning at twelve noon."

I said nothing. He leaned forward a little to stare at my shadowed face.

"At the service tonight, weren't you?" he said in that rich, rolling voice. "In the rear pew, left side?"

"Keen eyes," I said. "What were you doing, counting the house?"

I had been keeping watch on nervous Dicky. But as I spoke, he relaxed back in his chair, apparently reassured. But he never took his glittering eyes off me.

"If this is a robbery," Father Bellamy said steadily, "you're welcome to everything you see before you. Just don't hurt us."

"It isn't a robbery," I told him, "and why should I want to hurt you?"

That Bellamy was one cool cat. He sat back comfortably, took out a pigskin cigar case, and went through all the business of selecting, cutting off the tip, and lighting it with a wooden match. The whole ceremony took about two minutes. I waited patiently. He took an experimental puff to see if it was drawing satisfactorily. Then he blew a plume of blued smoke at me.

"All right," he said, "what's this all about?"

"It's a grift, isn't it?" I asked him.

"Grift?" he said perplexedly. "I don't believe I'm familiar with that term."

"Bullshit," I said. "You're in the game. It's all a con."

"A con?" he said. "Could you possibly be implying trickery? That I, as an ordained minister of the First Fundamentalist Church of Lord Jesus, am running a confidence game designed to deceive and defraud my parishioners?"

"Tell you what," I said, "you call the cops and tell them I'm threatening you. I'll wait right here until they come. No rough stuff, I promise you. Then, when they take me in, I'll ask them to run a trace. The Feds should have you in their files. Or someone, somewhere. They'll find out about the outstanding warrants, skips, and like that. Well? How about it?"

He looked at me with a beatific smile, rolling the cigar around in his plump lips.

"Mike, for Christ's sake!" Dicky cried. "Let's throw this turd out on his ass."

"Now, sonny," I said, "be nice. Have a little respect for a seeker of the truth. How about it, Mr. Bellamy?"

He sighed deeply, running a palm lightly over his billowy white hair.

"How did you tumble?" he asked me curiously.

"You're too good," I said. "Too good for the come-to-Jesus scam. With your looks and voice and delivery, I figure you for Palm Beach or Palm Springs, peddling cheesy oil stock. Or maybe in a Wall Street boardroom, trading conglomerates. You don't belong in the boon-docks, Mr. Bellamy."

The Father smiled with great satisfaction. He raised his brandy snifter to me.

"Thank you for those kind words, sir," he said. "Did you hear that, Dicky? Haven't I told you the same thing?"

"Lots of times," Dicky grumbled.

"But I haven't asked your name, sir," Bellamy said to me.

"Jones," I said.

"To be sure," he said. "Very well, Mr. Jones. Assuming—just assuming, mind you—that your false and malicious allegations are correct, where do we go from here?"

"Mike, what are you doing?" the organist yelled. "Can't you see that this crud—"

Bellamy whirled on him.

"Shut your trap!" he said in a steely voice, the black eyes hard. "Just sit there and drink that loathsome mixture and don't say word one. Understand?"

"Yes, Mike," the youth said meekly.

"As I was saying," Bellamy went on blandly, turning back to me, "where do we go from here?"

I was still standing. There were two empty chairs in the room, but he didn't ask me to sit down. That was okay. Oneupsmanship. You keep a guy standing in front of your desk, he becomes the inferior, the supplicant.

"I don't want to blow the whistle on you," I assured him. "You got a nice thing going here, and as far as I'm concerned, you can milk it until you run out of sinners. I just want a little information. Whatever you can tell me about one of your vestrypersons."

He took a sip of cognac, a puff of his cigar. Then he dipped the mouth of the cigar in the brandy and took a pull on that. He looked at me narrowly through the smoke.

"Are you heat?"

"No. Just a concerned citizen."

"Aren't we all?" he said, smiling again. "Who do you want?"

"Mary Thorndecker."

"Mike, will you stop it?" the damp youth agonized. "You don't have to tell this creep anything, except to get lost."

"Sonny, sonny," I groaned, "can't you be civilized? The Father and I have reached a cordial understanding. Can't you see that? Now just let us get on with our business, and then I'll climb out of your hair, and you can go back to counting the take. Won't that be nice?"

"Listen to the gentleman, Dicky," Bellamy rumbled. "He is obviously a man of breeding and a rough but nimble wit. Mary Thorndecker, you said? Ah, yes. A plain jane. And yet I have the feeling that with the advice and assistance of a clever hairdresser, corsetiere, and dress designer, our dull, drab Mary might blossom into quite a swan indeed. Do you share that dream, Mr. Jones?"

"Could be," I said. "But what I really came to find out is anything you know about her private life, especially her family. Has she ever had one of those private consultations with you on Tuesdays and Thursdays, beginning at noon?"

"On occasion."

"And?"

"A very troubled young woman," he said promptly, staring over my head. "A difficult family situation. A stepmother who is younger and apparently much prettier than Mary. A man who wishes to marry her and who, for some reason she has not revealed to me, she both loves and loathes."

"And?" I said.

"And what?"

"That's it? That's all she talked about in those private sessions?"

"Well . . ." he said, waving a hand negligently, "she did confess to a few personal peccadilloes, a few minor misdeeds that could hardly be dignified as sins. Would you care to hear them?"

"No," I said. "And that's all there is?"

He smoked slowly, frowning in an effort to remember conversations in which, I was sure, he had no interest whatsoever. He leaned forward to pour himself another cognac. I licked my lips as obviously as I could. It won me an amused smile, but no invitation.

"Mike," Dicky said loudly, "you've told this jerk enough. Let's bounce him."

"Sonny," I said, "I'm trying very hard to ignore you, but it's a losing battle. If you'd like to—"

"Now, now," Bellamy interrupted smoothly, raising a palm. "There is no room for animosity and ill-feeling in God's house. Calm down, you two; I detest scenes." He took another sip of brandy, closing his eyes, smacking his wet lips. Then he opened his eyes again and looked at me thoughtfully. "She did say something else. Ask something else. In the nature of a hypothetical question. To wit: what is the proper course of conduct for a child of Lord Jesus who becomes aware that her loved ones are involved in something illegal? They are, in fact, not only sinning but engaged in a criminal activity."

"Did she tell you who the loved ones are?"

"No."

"Did she tell you the nature of the criminal activity?"

"No."

"What did you tell her to do?"

"I suggested that she report the entire matter to the police," he said virtuously. "I happen to be a very law-abiding man."

"I'm sure you are," I said.

I decided not to push it any further; he was obviously tiring. After his physical performance at the church service that evening, considering his age it was a wonder he wasn't in intensive care.

"Nice doing business with you, Father," I said. "Keep up the good work. By the way, I put a finif in the plate tonight. You and sonny have a drink on me."

"Don't call me sonny!" the infuriated youth screamed at me.

"Why not!" I said innocently. "If I had a son, I'd want him to be just like you." I paused at the door, turned back. "Father, just out of curiosity, is Mary Thorndecker a heavy mark?"

"She is generous in contributing to God's work on earth," he said sonorously, rolling his eyes to heaven.

"Could you give me a ballpark figure?" I asked him.

He inspected the soaked stump of his cigar closely.

"It is a very large ballpark," he said.

I laughed and left the two of them together. They deserved each other.

I chugged back to Coburn, glad I couldn't coax any more speed out of that groaning heap, because I had some thinking to do. Up to that moment I had vaguely suspected Dr. Telford Gordon Thorndecker might be cutting corners in that combined nursing home-research-lab organization of his. I was thinking along the lines of unethical conduct: not an indictable offense but serious enough to put the kibosh on his application for a grant. Something like trying out new drugs without an informed consent agreement. Or maybe persuading doomed patients to include a plump bequest to the Crittenden Research Laboratory in their wills. Nasty stuff, but difficult, if not impossible, to prosecute.

But Mary Thorndecker hinted at something illegal. A criminal activity. I couldn't guess what it was. I did know it was heavy enough to get Ernie Scoggins chilled when he found out about it. And heavy enough to give Al Coburn the shakes when *he* found out about it.

I must have dreamed up a dozen ugly plots on my way back to Coburn. I had Thorndecker rifling the bank accounts of guests, hypnotizing them into signing over their estates, working on biological warfare for the U.S. Army, trying to determine safe radiation dosages with human subjects, even raping sedated female patients. I went wild, but nothing I imagined really made sense.

I pulled into the parking lot at the Coburn Inn. It was a paved area, lighted with two floods on short poles. They cast puddles of weak yellowish illumination, but most of the lot was either in gloom or lost in black shadow. Still, that was no excuse for what happened next. After the Great Slashed Tire Caper, I should have been more alert.

I parked, got out of the truck, turned to struggle with a balky door lock. The next thing I knew, I was face down on cold cement. That was the sequence: I went down first, and *then* I felt the punch that did it, a slam in the kidneys that spun me around and dumped me. Strange, but even as I realized what had happened, I remember thinking, "That wasn't so bad. It hurt like hell, but this guy is no pro." Probably the last thoughts of every man who's been killed by an amateur.

On the ground, I went into the approved drill: draw up the knees to protect the family jewels, bend neck, cover face and head with folded arms, make yourself into a tight, hard ball. And this to endure the boot you've got to figure is coming. It came, in the short ribs mostly. And though it banged me something fierce, there wasn't any crushing force, and I never came close to losing consciousness. I remember the other guy breathing in wheezing sobs, and thinking he was as much out of condition as I was.

So there I was, lying on my side on a hard bed, curled into a knot. After a few ineffectual kicks to my crossed arms, thighs, and spine, I began to get annoyed. At myself, not the guy who was trying so hard and doing such a lousy job of messing me up.

I recalled an army instructor I had who specialized in unarmed combat. His lecture went something like this:

"Forget about trying to fight with your fists. Forget about those roundhouse swings and uppercuts you see in the movies and on TV. All that'll get you is a fistful of broken knuckles. While you're trying the Fancy Dan stuff, an experienced attacker will be cutting you to ribbons, even if you're a Golden Gloves champ. Rule Number One: hug him. If he's a karate or judo man, and you stand back, he'll kill you. So get in close where he can't swing his arms or legs. Rule Number Two: there are no rules. Forget about fair play and the Marquis of Queensberry. A guy is trying to murder you. Murder him first. Or at least break him. A knee in the nuts is very effective, but if he's fast enough, he'll turn to take it on his thigh. A punch to the balls is better. A hack at the Adam's apple gets good results. If you can get behind him, put two fingers up his nostrils and yank up. The nose rips. Very nice. Also the eyes. Put in a stiff thumb and roll outward. The eyeball pops out like a pit from a ripe peach. And don't forget your teeth. The human jaw can exert at least two hundred pounds of pressure—enough to take off an ear or nose. Shin kicks are fine, and if you can stomp down on the kneecap, you can get his legs to bend the wrong way. Pretty. Pulling hair comes in handy at times, and fingers bent backward make a nice snapping sound."

He went on and on like that, telling us what we could do to stay alive. So after taking a series of nondisabling kicks, I peeked out from under my folded arms, and the next time I saw a stylish black moccasin flashing for my ribs, I reached out, grabbed an ankle, and pulled hard. He landed on his coccyx, and his sharp yelp of pain was music to my ears.

Then I swarmed all over him. A hard knee into the testicles. A knuckled chop at his throat. I stiffened my thumb and started for the eyes when I suddenly saw that if I carried through, Edward Thorndecker would need a cane and tin cup.

"Oh for God's sake," I said disgustedly.

I dragged myself to my feet, tried to catch my breath. I dusted myself off. I left him lying there, weeping and puking. After my breathing returned to normal, and I had satisfied myself that I had no broken bones or cracked ribs, just bruises and wounded pride, I dug the toe of my boot into his ass.

"Get up," I told him.

"You keep away from her," he croaked, in rage and frustration. "If you go near my stepmother again, I'll kill you. I swear to God I'll kill you!"

All in that half-lisp of his, sobbed out, coughed out, spluttered out. All in a cracked voice after that hack on his voice box.

I reached down, got a good grip on his collar, hauled him to his feet. I propped him back against the door of the pickup and patted him down. Just in case he was carrying a lethal weapon, like a Ping-Pong paddle or a lime Popsicle. Then I opened the door, shoved him inside, and climbed in after him. I rolled down the windows because he had upchucked all over himself. I lighted a cigarette to help defuse the stench.

I smoked patiently, waiting for his snuffling and whimpering to fade away. I wasn't as calm as it sounds. Every time I thought of how close I came to wasting that young idiot, I'd get the shakes and have to go to deep breathing to get rid of them. I handed over my handkerchief to help him clean himself. But he was one sad looking dude, hanging onto his balls and bending far over to cushion the hurt.

We must have sat there in the damp cold for at least fifteen minutes before he was able to straighten up. He didn't know which part of his anatomy to massage first. I was glad he was aching; his attack had scared me witless. I had thought it was Ronnie Goodfellow, of course. But if *he* had punched me in the kidneys, I'd have been peeing blood for three weeks. After I came to.

"All right," I said, "let's get to it. What makes you think I'm annoying your stepmother?"

"I don't want to talk about it," he said sullenly.

I turned sideways, and laid an open palm against his chops. His head snapped around, and he began crying again.

"Sure you want to talk about it," I said stonily. "Unless you want another knock on the cojones that'll have you singing soprano for the rest of your life."

"She said so," he mumbled.

"Julie told you I made a pass at her?"

"She didn't tell me. She told father. I heard her."

I didn't doubt him.

We sat there in silence. I gave him a cigarette and lighted another for myself. He began to feel a little better; his nerve came back.

"I'm going to tell my father that you beat me up," he said angrily.

"Do that," I told him. "Tell your father that we met by accident in the parking lot of the Coburn Inn, at an hour when you should be home studying, and I suddenly attacked you for no reason at all. Your father is sure to believe it."

"Julie will believe me," he said hotly.

"No one will believe you," I said cruelly. "Everyone knows you're a sack of shit. The only thing you've got going for you is that you're young enough to outgrow it. Possibly."

"Oh God," he said hollowly, "I want to die."

"Love her that much, do you?" I said.

"I saw her naked once," he said, in the same tone of wonderment someone might use to say, "I saw a flying saucer."

"Good on you," I said, "but she happens to be your father's wife."

"He doesn't appreciate her," he said.

What's the use? You can't talk to snotty kids. They know it all.

"All right, Edward," I said, sighing. "I could tell you that I never propositioned your stepmother, but I know you wouldn't believe me. Now you tell me something: what's going on in the research lab?"

"Going on?" he said, puzzled. "Well, you know, they do experiments. I don't understand that stuff. I'm not into science."

"Oh? What are you into?"

"I like poetry. I write poems. Julie says they're very good."

Full circle. Thorndecker's father was a poet. Thorndecker's son was a poet. I hoped the son wouldn't die as his grandfather had.

"And you've got no idea of anything strange going on out there?"

"I don't know what you're talking about."

I believed him.

He said he had "borrowed" Julie's sports car and parked it a block away. I told him that if he was smart, he'd drive directly home, soak in a hot tub, and keep his mouth shut about what had happened.

"I'm here to check on your father's qualifications for a grant," I said. "I don't think he or Julie would be happy to hear you tried to dent my head tonight."

I don't believe he had thought of that. It sobered him. He got out of the truck, then turned back to stick his head through the open window.

"Listen," he said, "my father's a great man."

"I know," I said. "Everyone tells me so."

"He wouldn't do anything wrong," he said, then walked away into the shadows. I watched him go. After awhile I got out, locked up, trotted to the Inn.

I'd had my fill of parking lots for one day.

Up in Room 3-F, I stripped down and inspected the damage. Not too bad. Some scrapings, bruises, minor contusions. I took a shower as hot as I could stand it, and that helped. Then I cracked that bottle of vodka I had purchased ten years ago and bought myself a princely snort.

I sat there in my skin, sipping warm Popov, and wondering why Julie Thorndecker had done it. Why she had told her husband that I had, ah, taken liberties. I couldn't blame it on the "woman scorned" motive; she was more complex than that.

This is what I came up with:

She was preparing ammunition in case I gave Thorndecker a negative report, as she feared I might. Then, having reported my churlish behavior to her husband, she might prevail upon him to write the Bingham Foundation claiming that my reactions were hardly objective, but had been colored by my unsuccessful attempt to seduce his wife.

I could imagine the response of Stacy Besant and Mrs. Cynthia to such an allegation. They might not believe it entirely; they'd tell me they didn't believe it. But they might think it wise to send a second field investigator to check out the Thorndecker application. An older investigator. More mature. Less impetuous. And on the strength of *his* report, Thorndecker might squeak through.

I believed Julie was capable of such a Byzantine plot. Not entirely for her husband; self-interest was at work here. In Coburn, she had said, I'm a big frog in a little pond—and that was true. Most women are conservative by nature; she, in addition, was conservative by circumstance. The little she had let drop about the rackety life she led before she met Thorndecker convinced me that she enjoyed and cherished the status quo, didn't want it to change. She had found a home.

Having settled the motives of Julie Thorndecker, and resolving to meet with her husband as soon as possible to see how much damage she had done, I got back to my favorite topic: what was going on at the Crittenden Research Laboratory? I came up with another choice assortment of wild and improbable scenarios:

Thorndecker was developing a new nerve gas. Thorndecker was a Frankenstein, putting together a monster from parts of deceased patients. Thorndecker was engaged in recombinant genetic research, combining the DNA of a parrot with that of a dog, and trying to breed a schnauzer who talked. The more Popov I inhaled, the sappier my fantasies became.

What gave me nightmares for months afterward was that I had already come up with the solution and didn't know it.

THE SIXTH DAY

THE PHONE woke me up the next morning. I have a thing about phones. I claim that when I'm calling someone who isn't at home, dialing a number that no one will answer, I can tell after the second ring. It has a hollow, empty sound. Also, I think I can judge the mood of anyone who calls me by *their* ring: angry, loving, good or bad news. Tell me, doctor, do you think I . . .?

In this case, coming out of a deep, dreamless sleep, the ring of the phone sounded desperate, even relayed through the hotel switchboard. I was right. It was Mary Thorndecker, and she had to see me as soon as possible. It couldn't be at the Coburn Inn. It couldn't be at Crittenden Hall. It couldn't be anywhere in public. I figured that left the Carlsbad Caverns, but she insisted on the road that led around the Crittenden grounds, in the rear, past the cemetery. She said eleven o'clock, and I agreed.

I got out of bed feeling remarkably chipper. Unhungover. You can usually trust vodka for that. After all, it's just grain alcohol and water. Very few congeners. Drink vodka all your life, and everything will be hunky–dory— except you may end up with a liver that extends from clavicle to patella.

A shower, a shave, a fresh turtleneck—and I was ready for a fight or a frolic. When I went out into the hall, the brass indicator showed the elevator was coming down. I rang the bell, waited, watched Sam Livingston come slowly into view in his cage: feet, ankles, knees, hips, waist, shoulders, head. A revelation. The elevator shuddered to a stop. I stepped in.

"Sam," I said, "you suckered me."

He knew immediately what I meant.

"Nah," he said, with almost a smile, "I just told you he puts on a good show."

"The guy's a phonus-balonus," I said.

"So? He gives the folks what they want."

"Aren't you ashamed of yourself? You got Mary Thorndecker driving you out there. She thinks she's bringing in another convert, and all the time you're laughing up your sleeve."

"Well . . ." he said solemnly, "it's better'n TV. Hear you had a little trouble with your car."

"Good gracious me," I said, "word does get around. Mike's is delivering it with new tires, I hope, at noon today. If I'm not here, will you ask them to leave the keys at the desk? No, scratch that. Will you keep the keys for me?"

He explained that he expected to leave by 1:00 P.M., to take care of his cleaning chores at the Episcopal church. He'd keep my car keys until then. If

I hadn't returned by one o'clock, he'd leave the keys on the dresser in my room. I said that would be fine.

We descended slowly past the second floor. In the old Greek plays, the gods must have come down out of heaven in their basket at about our speed.

"Sam," I said, "you know Fred Aikens? The constable?"

"Seen him around," he said cautiously.

"What's your take?"

He didn't answer.

"I wouldn't want to stroll down a dark alley with him," I offered.

"No," he said thoughtfully, "don't do that."

"Is he buddy-buddy with Ronnie Goodfellow?"

The old man turned to stare at me with his yellowish eyes.

"You ever know two cops who weren't?" he asked. "And they don't even have to *like* each other."

We inched our way down to the lobby. Millie was chatting it up with two customers at the cigar counter, and didn't notice me as I sneaked into the restaurant. It was practically empty, which surprised me until I remembered it was Saturday morning. I assumed the bank and a lot of offices and maybe some stores were closed. Anyway, I was able to get a table to myself and spread out.

After that tunafish salad for dinner the night before, I was ravenous. I shot the works with an Australian breakfast: steak and eggs, with a side order of American home-fries and a sliced tomato that tasted like a tomato. First one like that I had eaten in years.

I started my second cup of black coffee, and looked up to see Constable Ronnie Goodfellow standing opposite. From where I sat, he looked like he was on stilts. Did I tell you what a handsome guy he was? A young Clark Gable, before he grew a mustache. Goodfellow was as lean and beautiful, in a tight, chiseled way. I'm a het, and have every intention of staying that way. But even the straightest guy occasionally meets a man who makes him wonder. This is what I call the "What-if-we-were-marooned-on-a-desert-island Test." I don't think there's a man alive who could pass it.

"Morning," I said to him. "Join me for a cup?"

"I'd like to join you," he said, "but I'll skip the coffee, thanks. Four cups this morning, so far."

He took of his trooper's hat, and sat down across from me. He removed his gloves, folded them neatly inside the hat on an empty chair. Then he put his elbows on the table, scrubbed his face with his palms. He may have sighed.

"Heavy night?" I asked him.

"Trouble sleeping," he said. "I don't want to start on pills."

"No," I said, "don't do that. Try a shot of brandy or a glass of port wine."

"I don't drink," he said.

"One before you go to sleep isn't going to hurt you."

"My father died a rummy," he said, with no expression whatsoever in his voice. "I don't want to get started. Listen, Mr. Todd, I'm sorry about your car."

I shrugged. "Probably some wild kids."

"Probably. Still, it doesn't look good when it happens to a visitor. I stopped by Mike's Service Station. You'll have your car by noon."

"Good."

Then we sat in silence. It seemed to me we had nothing to say to each other. I know I didn't; he'd never tell me what I wanted to know. So I waited, figuring he had a message to deliver. If he did, he was having a hard time getting it out. He was looking down at his tanned hands, inspecting every finger like he was seeing it for the first time, massaging each knuckle, clenching a fist, then stretching palms wide.

"Mr. Todd," he said in a low voice, not looking at me, "I really think you're prying into things that are none of your business, that have nothing to do with your investigation."

Then he raised those dark eyes to stare at me. It was like being jabbed with an icepick.

I took a sip of coffee that scalded my lips. I moved back from the table, fished for my cigarettes. I lighted one. I didn't offer the pack to him.

"Let me guess," I said. "That would be the Reverend Father Michael Bellamy reporting in. Sure. How could a grifter like him operate around here without official connivance? Tell you about our little conversation, did he?"

"I don't know what you're talking about," he said, face impassive.

"Then what are *you* talking about?"

"As I understand it, you came up here to take a look around, inspect Dr. Thorndecker's setup, make sure it was what he claimed it was. Is that right?"

"That's about it."

"Well? You've looked over the place. It's what he said it was, isn't it?"

"Yes."

"So? Why are you poking into things that have nothing to do with your job? Private matters. You get some kind of a kick trying to turn up dirt? You really shouldn't do that, Mr. Todd. It could be dangerous."

What I said next I know I shouldn't have said. I knew it while I was saying it. But I was so frustrated, so maddened by hints, and eyebrow-liftings, and vague suggestions, and now so infuriated by this cop's implied threat, that I slapped cards on the table I should have been pressing to my chest.

I made a great show of sangfroid, old nonchalant me: sipped coffee, puffed cigarette, stared at him with what I hoped was amusement, insolence, secret knowing—the whole bit.

"I get kicks out of a lot of things," I told him. "Of seeing a guy named Chester K. Petersen being stuck in the Crittenden cemetery at two in the morning. Of being told by one person that he died of internal cancer, and by another person that he died of congestive heart failure. Of discovering that a remarkable number of patients at Crittenden Hall have died of congestive heart failure, with most of the death certificates signed by the same doctor. Let's see—what else? Oh yes—the mysterious disappearance of one Ernie Scoggins, a Crittenden employee. With blood stains on the rug in his trailer. Did you spot those during your investigation, *Constable* Goodfellow? Anything more? not much—except rumors and hints and insinuations that something unethical, illegal, and probably criminal is going on out at Crittenden. I suppose I could add a few things, but they're mostly supposition. Like Dr. Thorndecker owns this village and every soul in it. I use the word 'soul' loosely. That Thorndecker has a finger in every pie in town. That this place is dying, and if he goes down, you all go down. That's about all I've got. Private matters? Nothing to do with my job? You don't really believe that, do you?"

I'll say this for him: he didn't break, or gulp, or give any indication that what I was saying was getting to him. He just got harder and harder, turned to stone, those black eyes glittering. Maybe he got a little paler. Maybe the hands spread out on the table trembled a little.

But he made no reply, no threat. Just stood, pulled on gloves and hat with precise movements, staring at me all the time.

"Goodby, Mr. Todd," he said tonelessly.

And that was enough to set my nerve ends flapping. "Goodby." No So-long, or See you around, or *Ciao*, baby. Just "Goodby." Final.

I was glad I hadn't mentioned anything about Al Coburn. That was the only thing I was glad about. It didn't help. I had talked too much, and knew it. I tried to persuade myself that I had told Goodfellow all that stuff deliberately, to let everyone know what I knew, to stir them up, spook them into making some foolish move.

But I couldn't quite convince myself that I had just engineered an extremely clever ploy. All I had done was blab. I got up, signed my check, and strolled into the bar whistling. Like a frightened kid walking through a graveyard on his way home.

The restaurant may have been dying, but that bar was doing jim-dandy business for an early Saturday morning. Most of the stools were taken; three of the booths were occupied. The customers looked like farmers killing time while their wives shopped, had their hair done, or whatever wives did in Coburn on a Saturday morning. I finally caught Jimmy's eye, ordered a stein of beer, took it over to a small table away from the babble at the bar.

I had started the day in a hell-for-leather mood, but my little confabulation with Constable Goodfellow had brought that to a screeching halt. A new Samuel Todd record: one hour from manic to depressive. I sipped my beer and reflected that Coburn and the Coburnites had that effect: they doused the jollies, and nudged you mournfully into the Slough of Despond. I think I've already reported that I heard no laughter on the streets. Maybe, I thought, the Board of Selectmen had passed an anti-giggling ordinance. "Warning! Levity is punishable by a fine, imprisonment, or both."

I watched one of the customers climb down from his bar stool, waddle over to the door of the Men's Room, and try to get in. But the room was occupied; the door was locked. The guy rattled the knob angrily a few times, then went growling back to the bar. A very ordinary incident. Happens all the time. The only reason I mention it is that seeing the customer rattle the knob on the locked door inspired, by some loony chain of thought, a magnificent idea: I would break into Crittenden Hall and the Crittenden Research Laboratory late at night and look around.

My first reaction to that brainstorm was a firm conviction that I was over the edge, around the bend, and down the tube. First of all, if I got caught, it would mean my job, even if I was able to weasel out of a stay in the slammer. Second, how could I get over that high fence, avoid the armed guards, and gain entrance to the locked buildings? Finally, what could I possibly hope to find that I hadn't been shown on my tour of the premises?

Still, it was an enticing prospect, just the thing to keep me awake and functioning until it was time to drive out for my meet with Mary Thorndecker.

The more I chewed on it, the more reasonable the project seemed to me. I could get over the fence with the aid of a short ladder. There were only three guards I knew of: the rover with shotgun and attack dog, the guy on the gate, and the bentnose inside the nursing home. A sneaky type like me shouldn't find it too difficult to duck all three.

The stickler was how to get inside the locked buildings without smashing windows or breaking down doors. That business of opening a lock with a plastic credit car—beloved by every private eye on TV—works only when there's no dead bolt. And, I had noted on my visit, the doors at Crittenden had them. I'm no good at picking a lock, even if I owned a set of picks, which I don't. Also, I don't wear hairpins. That left only one impossible solution: keys.

But even assuming I got inside undetected, what did I expect to find? The answer to that was easy: if I knew what I'd find, a break-in wouldn't be necessary. This would be what the sawbones call an exploratory operation. It really was the only way, I acknowledged. Waiting for one of the cast of characters to reveal all was getting me nowhere.

I bought myself another beer, and went into the campaign a little deeper. Dr. Kenneth Draper had mentioned that his eager, young research assistants sometimes worked right through till dawn. But surely there wouldn't be many in the labs on Saturday or Sunday night. Even whiz-kids like to relax on weekends, or so Betty Hanrahan had said. As for the nursing home, it would probably be quiet at, say, two in the morning, with a skeleton night staff drinking coffee in offices and labs when they weren't making their rounds.

See how easy it is to talk youself into a course of action you know in your heart of hearts is dangerous, sappy, and unlikely to succeed? Talk about Father Bellamy being a grifter! His talents were nothing compared to the skills we all have in conning ourselves. Self-delusion is still the biggest scam of all.

I know it now, I knew it on that Saturday morning in Coburn. I told myself to forget the whole cockamamie scheme.

But all I could think about was how I could get the keys to those locked Crittenden doors.

"Hey, Todd," Al Coburn said in his cracked voice, kicking gently at my ankle. "You dreaming or something?"

"Or something," I said. "Pull up a chair, Mr. Coburn."

He was carrying his own beer, and when I pushed a chair toward him, he flopped down heavily. His hands were trembling. He wrapped them around his beer glass and held on for dear life.

"*Mister* Coburn," he said, musing. "You got manners on you for a young whipper."

"Sure," I said. "I'm also trustworthy, loyal, friendly, brave, clean, and reverent. Boy Scout oath."

"Yeah," he said, looking around absently. "Well, you remember what we were talking about before?"

"The letter from Ernie Scoggins?"

"What happened was this: I got in touch with the, uh, party concerned, and maybe it was all like a misunderstanding."

I looked at him, but he wouldn't meet my eyes. His vacant stare was over my head, around the walls, across the ceiling.

"You're a lousy liar," I said.

"No, no," he said seriously. "I just gabbed more than I should. That Ernie Scoggins—a crazy feller. I told you that. He blew it all up. Know what I mean? So I'm having a meeting late this afternoon, and we'll straighten the whole thing out. Everything's going to be fine. Yes. Fine."

I felt sick. I leaned across the table to him, tried to hold his gaze in mine. But he just wouldn't lock eyes.

"Your notes at the bank?" I said. "They got to you?"

I was doing it: using the word "they." Who? The CIA, the FBI, the KGB, the Gold Star Mothers, the Association for the Investigation of Paranormal Phenomena? Who?

"Oh no," he said, very solemn now. "No no no. This has nothing to do with my notes. Just a friendly discussion. To come to an agreement for our mutual benefit."

That wasn't Al Coburn talking. "An agreement for our mutual benefit." I knew he was quoting someone. It smelled of con.

"Mr. Coburn," I said slowly and carefully, "let's see if I've got it right. You're going to meet someone late this afternoon and talk about whatever is in that letter Ernie Scoggins left you? Is that it?"

"Well . . . yeah," he said, looking down into his beer. "It'll all get straightened out. You'll see."

"Want me to come along?" I asked him. "Maybe it would be better if you had—you know, like a witness. I won't say a word. I won't do anything. I'll just *be* there."

He bristled.

"Listen, sonny," he said, "I can take care of myself."

"Sure you can," I said hastily. "But what's wrong with having a third party present?"

"It's confidential," he said. "That was the agreement. Just him and me."

I grabbed that.

"Him?" I said. "So you're meeting just one man?"

"I didn't say that."

"No, you didn't. I guessed it. Am I wrong?"

"I'm tired," he said fretfully.

I looked at him, and I knew he was telling the truth: he *was* tired. The head was bowed, shoulders slumped, all of him collapsed. Tired or defeated.

"I don't want no trouble," he mumbled.

What was I to do—hassle a weary old man? The years had rubbed away at him. As they do at all of us. Will slackens. Resolve fuzzes. Worst of all, physical energy leaks out. We just don't have the verve to cope. A good bowel movement becomes life's highest pleasure, and we see a tanned teenager in a bikini and think bitterly, "Little do you know!"

I wanted to take his stingy craw in my fists and choke the truth from him. Who was the guy he was going to meet? What was in Scoggins's letter? What were they going to agree about? But what the hell could I do—stomp it out of him?

I'm pretty good at self-control. I mean I don't rant and rave. The stomach may be bubbling, but the voice is low, level, contained.

"Look, Mr. Coburn," I said, "this meeting of yours—I hope it comes out just the way you want it. That everything is solved to your satisfaction. But just in case—in *case,* you understand—things don't turn out to be nice-nice, don't you think you should have an insurance policy? An ace in the hole?"

Then, finally, he looked at me. Those washed-out eyes focused on my stare, and I knew I had him hooked.

"Like what?" he said.

I shrugged. "A copy of Scoggins's letter. Left some place only you and I know about. Doesn't that make sense? Gives you a bargaining point, doesn't it? With the guy you're meeting? A copy of the letter, or the original, left in someone else's hands. In case . . ."

True to the Coburn tradition, I didn't finish that sentence. I didn't have to. He understood, and it shook him. I started from the table to buy him another beer, but he wagged his head and waved me back. All he wanted to do was think, ponder, figure, reckon. He may have been an old man, but he wasn't an old dummy.

"Yes," he said at last. "All right. I'll go along with that. It'll be in the glove compartment of my pickup. In case. But I won't need to use it; you'll see. I'll call you right after the meeting. You'll be here?"

"What time are you talking about?"

"Five, six this evening. Around there."

"Sure," I said, "I'll be here. If not, you can always leave a message. Just tell me everything's okay."

He nodded, nodded, like one of those Hong Kong dolls, the spineless head bobbing up and down.

"That's a good way," he said. "I'll call you to tell you everything's okay. Hey, maybe we can eat together tonight. Listen, Todd, I made a good stew last night. You come out and eat with me. I'll tell you about stew: you cook it, and then you let it cool, and you eat it the next day, after it's got twenty-four hours of soaking. Tastes better that way."

"Sounds good to me," I said. "I'll wait for your call. Then I'll come out, and we'll have the stew. What's in it?"

"This and that," he said.

I began to have second thoughts. Not about the stew, but about the arrangements we had made. Too many things could go wrong. Murphy's Law.

"Well, look," I said, "I expect to be in and out all day, so maybe you'll call and I won't be here, and those nut-boys at the desk will forget to deliver your message. So why don't you give me your phone number now, and tell me how to locate your place?"

He wasn't exactly happy about that, but I finally got his phone number and directions on how to find his home. He said he lived in a farmhouse not too far from the foot of Crittenden Hill, and if I looked for a clumsy clapboard house set on cinder blocks, that was it. I'd know it by a steel flagpole set in cement in the front yard. He flew Old Glory day and night, no matter what the weather. When the flag got shagged to ribbons, he bought a new one.

"If I get six months out of a flag," Al Coburn said, "I figure I'm lucky. But I don't care. I'm patriotic, and I don't give a damn who knows it."

"Good for you," I said.

I watched him stumble out of there. He was trying to keep his shoulders back, chest inflated. I wanted to be like that when I was his age: cocky and hopeful. None of us can win the final decision. But, with luck, we can pick up a few rounds. I hoped old Al Coburn would pick up this round.

That blighted week . . . The sharpest memory I have is my Saturday morning phone call to Dr Telford Thorndecker. I planned it: what I would say, what he might say, what I would reply.

I got through to Crittenden Hall with no trouble, but it took them almost five munutes to locate Thorndecker. Then I was told he was in his private office at the Crittenden Research Labortatory, and didn't wish to be disturbed except in case of emergency. I said it was an emergency. A string of clicks, and he finally came on the line. Angry.

"Who is this?" he demanded.

I told him.

"Oh yes," he said. "Mr. Todd. Did you get that report I promised you?"

"I did," I said, "and I want to—"

"Good," he said. "Then I presume the grant will be forthcoming shortly."

"Well, not exactly. What I really—"

"The skeptics," he said disgustedly. "The nay-sayers. Don't listen to them. We're on the right track now."

"Dr. Thorndecker," I said, "I was wondering if—"

"Of course there's a lot to be done. We've just scratched the surface. No one knows. No one can possibly guess."

"If you could—"

"I don't know when I've been so optimistic about a research project. I mean that sincerely. It just seems like everything is falling into place. The Thorndecker Theory. That's what they'll call it: the Thorndecker Theory."

All this in his booming baritone. But I missed the conviction the words should have conveyed. The man was remote: that's the only way I can describe it. I didn't know if he was trying to convince me or himself. But I had a sense of him being way up there in the wild blue yonder, repeating dreams.

"Dr. Thorndecker," I said, trying again, "I have some questions only you can answer, and I was hoping you might be able to spare me a few moments this afternoon."

"Julie," he said. "She'll be so proud of me. Of course. What is it you wanted?"

"If we could meet," I said. "For a short time. This afternoon."

"Delighted," he shouted. "Absolutely delighted, Now? This minute? Are you at the gate? I'm in my lab."

"Well . . . no, sir," I said. "I was thinking about this afternoon. Maybe three o'clock. Around there. Would that be all right?"

There was silence.

"Hello?" I said. "Dr. Thorndecker? Are you there?"

"What's this about?" he said suspiciously. "Who is this?"

Once more it occurred to me that he might be on something. In never-never land. He wasn't slurring; his speech was distinct. But he wasn't tracking. He wasn't going from A to B to C; he was going from K to R to F.

I tried again.

"Dr. Thorndecker," I said formally, "this is Samuel Todd. I have a few more questions I'd like to ask you regarding your application to the Bingham Foundation for a grant. Could I see you at three this afternoon?"

"But of course!" he said heartily. Pause. "Perhaps two o'clock would be better. Would that inconvenience you?"

"Not at all," I said. "I'll be out there at two."

"Excellent!" he said. "I'll leave word at the gate. You come directly to the lab. I'll be here."

"Fine," I said. "See you then."

"And Mary and Edward," he said, and hung up.

It was Loony Tunes time. I figured I might as well be equipped. I found a hardware store that was open, and bought a three-cell flashlight with batteries, a short stepladder, 50 feet of cheap clothesline, and a lead sash weight. They didn't have any ski masks. I stowed my new possessions in Betty Hanrahan's pickup and headed out to Crittenden to meet Mary Thorndecker. If she had showed up in a Batman cape, I wouldn't have been a bit surprised. The whole world had gone lunatic. Including me.

She wasn't hard to find. Parked off the road in a black car long enough to be a hearse. I pulled up ahead of her, figuring I might want to get away in a hurry and wouldn't want to be boxed in. I got out of the pickup, ready to sit in her limousine. It had to be warmer in there. The Yukon would be warmer than Betty Hanrahan's pickup.

But Mary Thorndecker got out of her car, too. Slammed the door: a solid *chunk* muffled in the thicker air. Maybe she didn't want to be alone with me in a closed space. Maybe she didn't trust me. I don't know. Anyway, we were both out in the open, stalking toward each other warily. High Noon at Crittenden.

But we waded, actually. Because there was a morning ground fog still swirling. It covered our legs, and we pushed through it. It was white smoke, billowing. The earth was dry ice. And as we breathed, long plumes of vapor went out. I glanced around that chill, deserted landscape. Bleak trees and frosted stubble. A blurred etching: fog, vapor, my slick trenchcoat and her heavy, old-fashioned wrap of Persian lamb. I hadn't seen one of those in years.

She wore a knitted black cloche, pulled down to her eyes. Her face was white, pinched, frightened. Everything that had seemed to me mildly curious and faintly amusing about the Thorndecker affair suddenly sank to depression, dread, and inevitability. Her demonic look. Bleached lips. Her hands were thrust deep into her pockets, and I wondered if she had brought a gun and planned to shoot me dead. In that lost landscape it was possible. Any cold violence was possible.

"Miss Thorndecker," I said. "Mary. Would you—"

"How did you know?" she demanded. Her voice was dry and gaspy. "About the note? That I wrote the note?"

"What difference does it make?" I said. I stamped my feet. "Listen, can we walk? Just walk up and down? If we stand here without moving for fifteen minutes, we'll never dance the gavotte again."

She didn't say anything, but dug her chin down into her collar, hunched her shoulders, tramped beside me up the graveled road and back. Behind the fence was the Crittenden cemetery. On the other side were the winter-shredded trees. Not another car, a sound, a color. We could have been alone on earth, the last, the only. Smoke swirled about us, and I wanted a quart of brandy.

"Why did you write it?" I asked her. "I thought you loved your father. Stepfather."

She tried to laugh scornfully.

"*She* told you that," she said. "I hate the man. *Hate* him! He killed my mother."

"Can you prove that?"

"No," she said, "but I *know*."

I wondered if she was out to lunch, if her fury had corroded her so deeply that she was lost. To me, herself, everyone.

"Is that why you wrote: 'Thorndecker kills'? Because you think he murdered your mother?"

"And his father," she said. "I know that, too. No, that's not why. Because he's killing, now, in that lab of his."

"Scoggins?" I suggested. "Thorndecker killed him?"

"Who?"

"Scoggins. Ernie Scoggins. He used to work at Crittenden. A maintenance man."

"Maybe," she said dully. "The man who disappeared? I don't know anything about him. But there were others."

"Petersen?" I asked. "Chester K. Petersen? They buried him a few days ago. Pelvic cancer."

"No," she said, "he was a heart patient. That's why he came to Crittenden Hall. I saw his file. Angina. No close relatives. A sweet old man. Just a sweet old man. Then, about three months ago, he began to develop tumors. Sarcomas, carcinomas, melanomas. All over his body. On his scalp, his face, hands, arms, legs. I saw him. I visited him. He rotted away. He smelled."

"Jesus," I said, looking away, remembering the dying chimp.

"But he was only the latest," she said. "There were others. Many, many others."

"How long?" I demanded. "How long has this been going on?"

She thought a moment.

"Eighteen months," she said. "But mostly in the past year. Patients with no medical record of cancer. Cardiacs, mentals, alcoholics, addicts. Then they developed horrible cancers. They decayed. He's doing it to them. Thorndecker is. I *know* it!"

"And Draper?" I said softly. "Dr. Kenneth Draper?"

A hand came swiftly out of her coat pocket. She gnawed on a chalky knuckle.

"I don't know," she said. "I ask him. I plead with him. But he won't *tell* me. He cries. He worships Thorndecker. He'll do anything Thorndecker says."

"Draper is in on it," I told her flatly. "He's the physician in attendance. He signs the death certificates. But *why* are they doing it? For the bequests? For the money the dead patients leave to the lab?"

The question troubled her.

"I don't know," she said. "That's what I thought at first, but that can't be right. Some of them didn't leave the lab anything. Most of them didn't. I don't know. Oh my God . . ."

She began weeping. I put an uncomfortable arm about her shoulders. We leaned together. Still stamping back and forth, wading through that twisting fog.

"All right," I said, "let's go over it . . . A patient checks in. A cardiac case, or a mental, drugs, alcoholic, whatever. Young or old?"

"Mostly old."

"Then after awhile they develop cancer and die of that?"

"Yes."

"The same way Petersen died? Or internal cancer, too? Lung cancer? Stomach? Spleen? Liver?"

"All ways," she said in a low voice.

"In how long a time? How long does it take them to die of the cancer?"

"At first, when I became aware of what was going on, it was very quick. A few weeks. Lately it's been longer, Petersen was the most recent. He lasted almost three months."

"And they're all buried here on the grounds?"

"Or shipped home in a sealed coffin."

"But all of them tumorous?"

"Yes. Decayed."

"And no complaints from relatives? No questions asked?"

"I don't know," she said. "Probably not. People are like that. People are secretly relieved when a sick relative dies. A problem relative. They wouldn't ask questions."

"You're probably right," I said sadly. "Especially if they're inheriting. And Draper hasn't told you a thing about what's going on?"

"He just claims Thorndecker is a genius on the verge of a great discovery. That's all he'll say."

"He loves you."

"He says," she said bitterly, "but he won't tell me anything."

We paced back and forth in silence. It was the pits, absolutely the pits.

"What will you do to find out?" I asked her finally.

"What? I don't understand."

"How far will you go to discover what's going on? How important is it to you to stop Thorndecker?"

Suddenly she came apart. Just splintered. She stopped, jerked away from my shielding arm, turned to face me.

"That cocksucker!" she howled. Her spittle stung. I took a step back, shocked, bewildered. "That murderer!" she screamed. "Turdy toad! Wife killer! You think I don't— And he—with that slimy wife of his rubbing up against everything in sight. He has no right. No right! He must suffer. Oh yes! Skin flayed away. Flesh from his bones. Rot in the deepest, hottest hell. Vengeance is mine, sayeth the Lord! Naked! The way she dresses! Licking up to every male she meets. Edward! Oh my God, poor, young, innocent Edward. Yes, even him. What does she *do* to them? And he, *he*, lets her go her way, his life destroyed by that wanton with her filthy ways. Ruining him. Her body there. For everyone! Oh yes, I know. Everyone knows. The whore! The smirking whore! Den of iniquity. That house of wickedness. Oh God, strike down the evil. Lord Jesus. I beg you! Smite this filth. Root out—"

She went on and on, using words I could hardly believe she knew. The schoolteacher gone berserk. The spinster wrung by an orgasm. Obscenity, jealousy, sexual frustration, religious frenzy: it was all in her inchoate shouts, words tumbling, white stuff gathering in the corners of her mouth, something leaking from her eyes.

And love there. Oh yes: love. Julie hadn't been so wrong. This woman had to love Thorndecker to damn him so viciously, to want him so utterly destroyed. Every woman deserves one shot at the man she loves, and this was Mary's, this wailed revilement, this hysterical abuse that frightened me with its intensity. The vapor of her screams came at me in spouts of steam smelling of acid and ash.

I wondered if I might shake her, slap her, or take her in my arms and say, "There, there," and commiserate over her wounded soul, lost hopes, wasted life. Finally, I did nothing but let her rant, rave, wind down, lose energy, becoming eventually silent, just standing there, mouth open, trembling. And not from cold, I knew, but from pain and shame. Pain of her hurts, shame for having revealed it to another.

I put a hand on her arm as gently as I could, and led her back to her car. She came willingly enough, and let me get her seated behind the wheel. I pulled up her collar, folded the coat carefully over her knees, did everything but tuck her in. I offered her a cigarette, but I don't think she saw it. I lighted up, with shaking fingers, smoked like a maniac. I finally had to open the window on my side just a crack.

When, after a few moments, I turned to look at her, I saw her eyes were closed, her lips were moving. She was praying, but to whom or for what, I did not know.

"Mary?" I said softly. "Mary, can you hear me? Are you listening to me?"

Lips stopped moving, eyes opened. Head turned, and she looked at me. The focus of her eyes gradually shortened until she saw me.

"I can help you, Mary," I whispered. "But you must help me do it."

"How?" she said, in a voice less than a whisper.

I laid it out for her:

I wanted to know the number of exterior and interior security guards on duty Sunday night. I wanted to know their schedules, when the shift changed, their routines, where they stayed when they weren't patrolling.

I wanted to know everything she could find out about alarms, electric and electronic, and where the on-off switch or fuse box was located. Also, the location of the main power switches for the nursing home and the research laboratory.

I wanted to know the number of medical staff on duty Sunday night in Crittenden Hall and who, if anyone, might be working in the laboratories.

Finally, most important, I wanted that big ring of keys that Nurse Stella Beecham carried. If she wasn't on duty late Sunday night—say from midnight till eight Monday morning—she probably left the keys in her office. I wanted them. If Beecham was on duty, or if she handed over her keys to a night supervisor, then I needed at least two keys: to the Hall and to the research lab. If those were impossible to obtain, then Mary Thorndecker would have to let me in from the inside of the nursing home, and I'd have to get into the lab by myself, somehow.

It took me a long time to detail all this, and I wondered if she was listening. She was. She said dully: "You're going to break in?"

"Yes. I'm going to find out about those cancer deaths."

"You're going to get the evidence?"

I felt like weeping. But I had no compunction, none whatsoever, about using this poor, disturbed woman.

"Yes," I said, "I'm going to get the evidence."

In my own ears, it sounded as gamy and cornball as if I had said, "I'm going to grab the boodle and take it on the lam."

"All right," she said firmly. "I'll help you."

We went over it again in more detail: what I wanted, what she could get, what we might have to improvise.

"How will you get over the fence?" she asked.

"Leave that to me."

"You won't hurt anyone, will you?"

"Of course not. I don't carry a gun or a knife or any other weapon. I'm not a violent man, Mary."

"All you want is information?"

"Exactly," I said, nodding virtuously. "Just information. Part of my investigation of Thorndecker's application for a grant."

That seemed to satisfy her. Made the whole scam sound more legal.

We left it like this: she was to collect as much of what I wanted as she could, and on Sunday she was to call me at the Coburn Inn.

"Don't give your real name to the switchboard," I warned her. "Just in case they ask who's calling. Use a phony name."

"What name?"

"Joan Powell," I said instantly, without thinking. "Say your name is Joan Powell. If I'm at the Inn, don't mention any of this over the phone. Just laugh and joke and make a date to meet me somewhere. Anywhere. Right here would be fine; it's deserted enough. Then we'll meet, and you can tell me what you've found out. And give me the keys if you've been able to get them."

"What if I call the Coburn Inn, and you're not there?"

"Call every hour on the hour. Sooner or later I'll be there. Any time before midnight on Sunday. Okay?"

We went over the whole thing once more. I wasn't sure she was getting it. She was still white as paper, and every once in a while her whole body would shudder in a hard fit of trembling. But I spoke as quietly and confidently as I could. And I kept touching her. Her hand, arm, shoulder. I think I made contact.

Just before I got out of the car, I leaned forward to kiss her smooth, chill cheek.

"Tell me everything's going to be all right," she said faintly.

"Everything's going to be all right," I said.

I knew it wasn't.

I drove back to Coburn as fast as Hanrahan's rattletrap would take me. I kept watching for a public phone booth. I had a call to make, and didn't want it to go through the hotel switchboard. My paranoia was growing like "The Blob."

I found a booth on Main Street, just before the business section started. I knew the offices of the Bingham Foundation were closed on Saturday, so I called Stacy Besant at his home, collect. He lived in a cavernous nine-room apartment on Central Park West with an unmarried sister older than he, three cats, a moth-eaten poodle, and a whacking great tank of tropical fish.

Edith Besant, the sister, answered the phone and agreed to accept the call.

"Samuel!" she caroled. "This *is* nice. Stacy and I were speaking of you just last night, and agreed you must come to us for dinner as soon as you return to New York. You and that lovely lady of yours."

"Well, ah, yes, Miss Edith," I said. "I certainly would enjoy that. Especially if you promise to make that carrot soup again."

"Carrot vichyssoise, Samuel," she said gently. "Not soup."

"Of course," I said. "Carrot vichyssoise. I remember it well."

I did, too. Loathsome. But what the hell, she was proud of it.

We chatted of this and that. It was impossible to hurry her, and I didn't try. So we discussed her health, mine, her brother's, the cats', the poodle's, the fishes'. Then we agreed the weather had been miserable.

"Well, my goodness, Samuel," she said gaily, "here we are gossiping away, and I imagine you really want a word with Stacy."

"Yes, ma'am, if I could. Is he there?"

"Of course he is. Just a minute."

He came on so quickly he must have been listening on the extension.

"Yes, Samuel?" he said. "Trouble?"

"Sir," I said, "there are some questions I need answers to. Medical questions. I'd like to call Scientific Research Records and speak to one of the men who worked on the Thorndecker investigation."

"Now?" he asked. "This minute? Can't it go over to Monday?"

"No, sir," I said. "I don't think it can. Things are moving rather rapidly here."

There was a moment of silence.

"I see," he said finally. "Very well. Wait just a few minutes; I have the number somewhere about."

I waited in the closed phone booth. It was an iced coffin, and I should have been shivering. I wasn't. I was sweating.

He came back on the phone. He gave me the number of SRR, and the name of the man to talk to, Dr. Evan Blomberg. If SRR was closed on Saturday, as it probably was, I could call Dr. Blomberg at his home. The number there was—

"Mr. Besant," I interrupted, "I know this is an imposition, but I'm calling from a public phone booth for security reasons, and I just don't have phone credit cards, although I have suggested several times that it would make your field investigators' jobs a lot easier if you—"

"All right, Samuel," he said testily, "all right. You want me to locate Dr. Blomberg and ask him to call you at your phone booth. Is that it?"

"If you would, sir. Please."

"It's that important?"

"Yes," I said. "It is."

"Let me have the number."

I read it off the phone. He told me it would take five minutes. It took more than ten. I was still sweating. Finally the phone shrilled, and I grabbed it off the hook.

"Hello?" I said. "Dr. Evan Blomberg?"

"To whom am I speaking?" this deep, pontifical voice inquired. I loved that "To whom." Much more elegant than, "Who the hell is this?"

I identified myself to his satisfaction and apologized for calling him away from his Saturday relaxation.

"Quite all right," Dr. Blomberg said stiffly. "I understand you have some questions regarding our investigation of the application of Dr. Telford Gordon Thorndecker?"

"Well, ah, in a peripheral way, doctor," I said cautiously. "It's just a general question. A general medical question."

"Oh?" he said, obviously puzzled. "Well, what is it?"

I didn't want to say it. It was like asking an astronomer, "Is the moon *really* made of green cheese?" But finally I nerved myself and said:

"Is it possible to infect a human being with cancer? That is, could you, uh, take cancerous cells from one human being who is suffering from some form of the disease and inject them into a healthy human being, and would the person injected then develop cancer?"

His silence sounded more shocked than any exclamation.

"Good God!" he said finally. "Who would want to do a thing like that? For what reason?"

"Sir," I said desperately, "I'm just trying to get an answer to a what-if question. Is it possible?"

Silence again. Then:

"To my knowledge," Dr. Evan Blomberg said in his orotund voice, "it has never been done. For obvious reasons. Unethical, illegal, criminal. And I can't see any possible value to any facet of cancer research. I suppose it might be theoretically possible."

Try to get a Yes or No out of a scientist. Hah! They're as bad as lawyers. Almost.

"Then you could infect someone with cancer cells, and that person would develop cancer?"

"I said theoretically," he said sharply. "As you are undoubtedly aware, experimental animals are frequently injected with cancer cells. Some host animals reject the cells completely. Others accept them, the cells flourish, the host animal dies. In other words, *some* animals have an immunity to *some* forms of cancer. By extension, I suppose you could speculate that *some* humans might have or develop an immunity to *some* forms of cancer. By extension, I suppose you could speculate that *some* humans might have or develop an immunity to *some* forms of cancer. It is not a chance I'd care to take."

"I can understand that, Dr. Blomberg, but—"

"Different species of animals are used for different kinds of cancer research, depending on how similar they are to humans insofar as the way they react to specific types of cancer. Rats, for instance, are used in leukemia research."

"Yes, Dr. Blomberg," I said frantically, "I can appreciate all that. Let's just call this speculation. That's all it is: speculation. What I'm asking is if healthy humans are infected with cancer cells from a diseased human, will the healthy host develop cancer?"

"Speculation?" he asked carefully.

"Just speculation," I assured him.

"I'd say the possibility exists."

"Possibility?" I repeated. "Would you go so far as to say 'probability'?"

"All right," he said resignedly. "Since we're talking in theoretical terms, I'm willing to say it's probable the host human will develop cancer."

"One final question," I said. "We have been talking about injecting a healthy human host with cancerous cells from a live but diseased human donor. You've said it's probable the host would develop cancer. Does the same hold true of abnormal cells that have been cultivated *in vitro*?"

"Good God!" he burst out again. "What kind of a nightmare are you talking about?"

I wouldn't let him off the hook. "Would it be possible to infect a healthy human being with cancerous cells that have been grown *in vitro*?"

"Yes, goddammit," he said furiously, "it would be possible."

"In fact—probable?" I asked softly. "That you could infect a healthy human being with cancerous cells grown in a lab?"

"Yes," he said, in such a low voice that I could hardly hear him. "Probable."

"Thank you, Dr. Blomberg," I said, hung up gently and wondered if I had spoiled his weekend. The hell with him. Mine was already shot.

I drove the rest of the way into Coburn, reflecting that now I knew it could be done, what Mary Thorndecker feared. But why? *Why?* As Blomberg had said, who would want to do a thing like that? For what reason?

The Grand Prix was waiting for me in the parking lot of the Coburn Inn. Not only had it been equipped with new radials, but the car had been washed and waxed. I walked around it, kicking the tires with delight. But gently! Then I transferred my new purchases from the pickup to the trunk of the Pontiac.

In the lobby, a tall, skinny gink with "Mike's Service Station" stitched on the back of his coveralls was leaning over the cigar counter, inspecting Millie Goodfellow's cleavage with a glazed stare. He had a droopy nose and looked like a pointer on scent. Any minute I expected him to raise a paw and freeze.

I interrupted their tête-à-tête—and guessing the subject of their conversation, that's the only phrase for it. I asked the garageman about the bill for the tires and wax job. He said Betty Hanrahan had picked up the tab; I didn't owe a cent. I handed him a ten for his trouble, and he looked at it.

"Jesus, Mr. Todd," he said, "Betty told me I wasn't to take any money from you *a*-tall. She find out about this, she'll bite my ass."

He and Millie laughed uproariously. At last—Coburn humor. The hell with the quality; people were laughing, and after the way I had spent the last two hours, that was enough for me.

"I won't tell Betty if you don't," I said. "Can you get her pickup back to the Red Dog?"

"Sure," he said happily. "No problem. Hey, Millie, I'm a rich man now. Buy you a drink tonight?"

"I'll be there," she nodded. "For the ten, you can look but don't touch."

He said something equally as inane, and they gassed awhile. It was that kind of raunchy sexual chivying you hear between a man and woman who have been friends a long time and know they'll never go to bed together. I listened, smiling and nodding like an idiot.

Because I can't tell you how comforting it was. Their smutty jokes were so *normal*. There was nothing deep, devious, or depraved about it. It had nothing to do with cancerous cells and fluorescent tumors. No one dying in agony and pushed into frosted ground. That stupid conversation restored a kind of tranquillity in me; that's the only way I can describe it. I felt like an infantryman coming off the front line and being handed a fresh orange. Fondling it, smelling it, tasting it. Life.

I waved goodby and went up to my room. I had an hour to kill before my meeting with Dr. Thorndecker. I didn't want to eat or drink. I just wanted to flop on my bed, dressed and booted, and think about the man and wonder why he was doing what he was.

I think that investigators work on the premise that most people act out of self-interest. The kicker is that a lot of us don't know, or can't see, our true self-interest. Case in point: my breaking up with Joan Powell. I thought I acted out of concern for my own well-being. All I got was a galloping attack of the guilts and a growing realization that I had tossed away a relationship that was holding me together.

What was Telford Gordon Thorndecker's self-interest—or what did he *think* it was? Not merely avarice, since Mary had said the lab didn't profit from the deaths of many of the victims. Then it had to be some kind of human experimentation that might result in professional glory. A different kind of greed.

I tried that on for motive. Mary had reported that Dr. Draper had said Thorndecker was a genius on the verge of a great discovery. Thorndecker himself had admitted to me that human immortality was his true goal. So far the glory theory made sense. Until I asked myself why he was injecting cancer-free patients with abnormal cells. Then the whole thing fell apart. The only fame you achieve by that is on the wall of a post office.

The man was such a fucking enigma to me. Inspired scientist. Paterfamilias. Skilled business administrator. Handsome. Charming. Energetic. And remote. Not only from me, I was convinced, but from wife, children, friends, staff, Coburn, the world. Either he had something everyone else was lacking, or he lacked something everyone else had. Or perhaps both.

Have you ever seen one of those intricately carved balls of ivory turned out by Oriental craftsmen? It only takes about ten years to make. The artist starts with a solid sphere of polished ivory. The outer shell is carved with fanciful open designs, and within a smaller sphere is cut free to revolve easily. That second ball is also carved with a complex open design, and a third smaller ball cut free to revolve. And so on. Until, at the center, is a ball no larger than a pea, also intricately incised. Spheres within spheres. Designs within designs. Worlds within worlds. The carving so marvelously complicated that it's almost impossible to make out the inscription on that pea in the center.

That was Dr. Telford Gordon Thorndecker.

Who had carved him?

But all that was purple thinking, ripe fancy. When I came back to earth, all I saw was a big man standing in the shadows, watching his young wife's bangled ankle flashing in the back of a cop's cruiser. And the man's face showing no defeat.

An hour later I was on my way out to Crittenden again. The only pleasure I had in going was being behind the wheel of the Grand Prix. After bruising my kidneys in Betty Hanrahan's junk heap, the Pontiac's ride felt like a wallow in a feather bed. I took it up to seventy for a minute or two, just to remind myself what was under the hood. The car even smelled good to me. More important, the heater worked.

I had no trouble at the gate. The guard came out of his hut when I gave the horn a little *beep*. Apparently he recognized the car; he didn't ask for identification. I watched his routine carefully. He had a single key attached by a chain to a length of wood. He opened the tumbler lock. The gates swung inward. After I drove through, I glanced in my rearview mirror. He swung the gates back into place, locked up, went back into his hut. He was a slow-moving older man wearing a pea jacket. No gun that I could see. But of course it could have been under the jacket or in the hut.

I didn't like the idea of those iron gates opening inward. I would have preferred they swung outward, in case I had to bust through in a hasty exit. But you can't have everything. Some days you can't have *anything*.

The gate guard must have called, because when I got to the front door of the Crittenden Research Laboratory, Dr. Kenneth Draper was waiting for me. He looked like a stunned survivor. He was staring at me, but I wasn't sure he saw me.

"Dr. Draper," I said, "you all right?"

He came out of his trance with a slight shake of his head, like someone trying to banish an ugly dream. Then he gave me a glassy smile and held out his hand.

He was wearing a white laboratory coat. There were dark brown stains down the front. I didn't even want to wonder about those. His hand, when I clasped it, was cold, damp, boneless. I think he tried to press my fingers, but there was no strength in him. His face was white as chalk, and as dusty. When he led me inside, his walk was stumbling and uncertain. I thought the man was close to collapse. I didn't think he'd suddenly fall over, but I had an awful vision of him going down slowly, melting, joints loose and limbs rubber. Then he'd end up sitting on the floor, knees drawn up, head down on his folded arms, and weeping softly.

But he made it up to the second floor, painfully, dragging himself hand over hand on the banister. I asked him if many staff were working on Saturday. I asked him if his research assistants worked through the weekend. I asked him if lab employees worked only daylight hours, or was there a night shift. I don't think he heard a word I said. I know he didn't answer.

So I looked around, peeked into the big laboratories. There were a few people at the workbenches, a few peering through microscopes. But not more than a half-dozen. The entire building had the tired silence of a Saturday afternoon, everything winding down and ready to end.

Draper led me to the frosted glass door of one of the small private labs. He knocked. No answer. He knocked again, louder this time, and called, "Dr. Thorndecker. Mr. Todd is here." Still no reply.

"Maybe he fell asleep," I said, as cheerfully as I could. "Or stepped out."

"No, no," Dr. Draper said. "He's in there. But he's very, uh, busy, and sometimes he . . . Dr. Thorndecker! Mr. Todd is here."

No one answered from inside the room. It was getting embarrassing, and just a little spooky. We could see lights burning through the frosted glass door, and I thought I heard the sounds of small movements.

Finally Draper hiked the skirt of his lab coat, fished in his pants pocket, and came out with a ring of keys which he promptly dropped on the floor. He stooped awkwardly, recovered them, and pawed them nervously, trying to find the one he wanted. He unlocked the door, pushed it open cautiously, peeked in. My view was blocked.

"Wait here," Draper said. "Please. Just for a moment."

He slipped in, closed the door behind him. I was left standing alone in the corridor. I didn't know what was going on. I couldn't even guess. I didn't think about it.

Draper came out in a minute. He gave me a ghastly smile.

"Dr. Thorndecker will see you now," he said.

He brushed closely past me. I caught an odor coming from him, and wondered if it was possible to smell of guilt.

The laboratory was small, with minimal equipment: a blackboard, workbench, a fine compound microscope, stacks of books and papers, a slide projector and screen, a TV monitor.

Dr. Telford Gordon Thorndecker was seated in a metal swivel chair behind a steel desk. He didn't rise when I entered, nor did he smile or offer to shake hands. He was wearing a laboratory coat like Draper's, but his was starched and spotless. In addition, he was wearing white cloth gloves with long, elasticized gauntlets that came to his elbows.

I did not think the man looked well. His face was pallid, but with circles of hectic flush high on his cheeks, and lips almost a rosy red. I think what startled me most was that his head was covered with a circular white cloth cap, similar to the type worn by surgeons. But the cap did not cover his temples, and it was apparent that Thorndecker was losing his hair in patches; the sideburns I remembered as full and glossy were almost totally gone.

But that resonant baritone voice still had its familiar boom.

"What is of paramount importance," he said sternly, "is the keeping of careful, accurate, and detailed records. That is what I have been doing: bringing my journal up to the present, to this very minute."

"Yes," I said. "May I sit down, Dr. Thorndecker?"

He gestured toward the book in which he had been writing. It was a handsome volume bound in buckram.

"More than two hundred of these," he said. "Covering every facet of my professional career from the day I entered medical school."

I slid quietly into the tubular chair alongside his desk. He was looking down at the journal, and I couldn't see his eyes. But his voice was steady, and his hands weren't trembling.

"Dr. Thorndecker," I said, "I have a few questions concerning your work here at the research lab."

"Two hundred personal diaries," he mused. "A lifetime. I remember a professor—who was he?—telling us how important it was to keep precise notes. So that if something should happen, an accident, the work could be continued. Nothing would be lost."

Then he raised his eyes to look at me. I saw nothing unusual in the pupils but it seemed to me the whites were clouded, with a slight bluish cast, like spoiled milk.

"Mr. Todd," he said, "I appreciate your coming by. I regret I have not been able to spend more time with you during your visit, but I have been very involved with projects here at the lab. Plus the day-to-day routine of Crittenden Hall, of course."

"Dr. Thorndecker, when I spoke to you on the phone this morning, you seemed excited about a potential breakthrough in your work, a development of considerable importance."

He continued to stare at me. His face was totally without expression.

"A temporary setback," he said. "These things happen. Anyone in scientific research learns to live with disappointment. But we are moving in the right direction; I am convinced of that. So we will pick ourselves up and try a new approach, a different approach. I have several ideas. They are all here." He tapped the open pages of his journal. "Everything is here."

"Does this concern the X Factor, Dr. Thorndecker? Isolating whatever it is in mammalian cells that causes aging and determines longevity?"

"Aging . . ." he said.

He swung slowly in his swivel chair and stared at the blackboard across the room. My eyes followed his gaze. The board had been recently erased. I could see, dimly, the ghost of a long algebraic equation and what appeared to be a few words in German.

"Of course," he said, "we begin dying at birth. A difficult concept to grasp perhaps, but physiologically sound. I always wanted to be a doctor.

Always, for as long as I can remember. Not necessarily to help people. Individually, that is. But to spend my life in medical research. I have never regretted it. Never."

This was beginning to sound like a valedictory, if not a eulogy. I knew I was not going to get answers to specific questions from this obviously troubled man, so I thought it best to let him ramble.

"Aging," he was saying again. "Perhaps rather than study the nature of senescence, we should study the nature of youth. My wife is a very young woman."

I wondered if he would now mention what his wife had told him about my alleged advances. But he made no reference to it. Perhaps he was inured to his wife's infidelities, real or fancied. Anyway, he kept staring at the erased blackboard.

"Are you a religious man, Mr. Todd?"

"No, sir. Not very."

"Nor I. But I do believe in the immortality of the human race."

"The *race*, Dr. Thorndecker? Not the individual?"

But he wasn't listening to me. Or if he was, he disregarded my question.

"Sacrifices must be made," he said quietly. "There can be no progress without pain."

He had me. I knew he was maundering, but the shields were coming down; he was revealing himself to me. I wanted to hear more of the aphorisms by which he lived.

"Did I do wrong to dream?" he asked the air. "You must dare all."

I waited patiently, staring at him. I had an odd impression that the man had shrunk, become physically smaller. He was effectively concealed by the lab coat and long gloves, of course, but the shoulders seemed narrower, the torso less massive. The back was bowed; arms and legs thinner. Perhaps his movements gave the effect of shriveled senescence. They had slowed, stiffened. The exuberant energy, so evident at our first meeting, had vanished. Thorndecker appeared drained. All his life force had leaked out, leaving only a scaly husk and dry memories.

He said nothing for several minutes. Finally I tried to provoke him . . .

"I hope, Dr. Thorndecker, you have no more surprises for me. Like admitting your application to the Bingham Foundation was not as complete as it should have been. I haven't yet decided what to do about that, but I wouldn't care to discover we have been misled in other things as well."

Still he sat in silence, brooding. He looked down at his closed journal, touched the cover with his gloved fingertips.

"I could never take direction," he said. "Never work under another man's command. They were so slow, so cautious. Plodders. They couldn't fly. That's the expression. None of them could fly. I had to be my own man, follow my instincts. What an age to live in. What an age!"

"The past, sir?" I asked. "The present?"

"The future!" he said, brightening for the first time since I had entered the room. "The next fifty years. Oh! Oh! It's all opening up. We're on the edge of so much. We are close. You'll see it all within fifty years. Human cloning. Gene splicing and complete manipulation of DNA. New species. Synthesis of human blood and all the enzymes. Solution of the brain's mysteries, and mastery of immunology. And here, in my notebooks, the ultimate secret revealed, human life extended—"

But as suddenly as he had become fervent, he dimmed again, seemed to dwindle, retreat, lose his glowing vision of tomorrow.

"Youth," he said, and his voice no longer boomed. "The beauty of youth. She made me so happy and so wretched. On our wedding night we . . . The body. The youthful human body. The design. The way it moves. Its gloss and sweet perfume. A man could spend his life in . . . The taste. Did you know, Draper, that a—"

"Todd, sir," I said. "Samuel Todd."

"A proved diagnostic technique," he said. "Oh yes. Taste the skin. Acidity and—and—all that. So near. So close. Another year perhaps. Two, at most. And then . . ."

"You think it will be that soon, sir?"

"Please let me," he said. "Please."

I had a sudden feeling of shame listening to him. Watching the statue crumble. Nothing was worth witnessing that destruction. I stood abruptly. He looked up at me in surprise.

"Finished?" he said. "Well, I'm glad we've had this little chat, and I'm happy I've been able to answer your questions and clear up your doubts. Could you give me some idea of when the grant might be made?"

He was serious. I couldn't believe it.

"Difficult to say, sir. I turn in my report, and then the final decision is with my superiors."

"Of course, of course. I understand how these things work. Channels, eh? Everything must go through channels. That's why I . . . Forgive me for not seeing you out, Mr. Todd, but—"

"That's perfectly all right."

"So much to do. Every minute of my time."

"I understand. Thank you for all your help."

Again he failed to rise or offer to shake hands. I left him sitting there, staring at an erased blackboard.

I had hoped I might have the chance to snoop around the labs unattended, but Linda Cunningham, Draper's chubby assistant, was waiting for me in the corridor.

"Hi, Mr. Todd," she said brightly, "I'm supposed to show you the way out."

So that was that. I was in the Pontiac, warming the engine, when suddenly Julie Thorndecker was standing alongside the window. I don't know where she came from; she was just there. She was wearing jodhpurs, tweed hacking jacket, a white shirt, ascot, a V-necked sweater. I turned off the ignition, lowered the window.

"Mrs. Thorndecker," I said.

Her face was tight, drawn. Gone were the pouts and moues, the sensuous licking of lips. I glimpsed the woman underneath: hard, wary, merciless.

"We're not getting the grant, are we?" she said.

"For God's sake," I said roughly, "get your husband to a doctor."

"For God's sake," she replied mockingly, "my husband *is* a doctor."

I was in such a somber mood, so confused and saddened, that I didn't trust myself to speak. I watched her put a thumb to her mouth and bite rapidly at the nail, spitting little pieces of matter onto the gravel. I had the feeling that if I could look into her brain, it would not be a cold, gray, convoluted structure; it would be a live lava bed, bubbling and boiling, with puffs of live steam.

"Well," she said finally, "it was nice while it lasted. But all good things must come to an end."

"Also," I said, "a stitch in time saves nine, and a rolling stone gathers no moss."

She looked at me with loathing.

"You're a smarmy bastard," she said, her face ugly. "When are you leaving?"

"Soon. Probably Monday."

"Not soon enough," she said, turning away.

I was less than a mile outside the gates when I passed a Coburn police cruiser heading toward Crittenden. Constable Ronnie Goodfellow was driving. He didn't look at me.

When I got back to Coburn I realized that on the big things, my mind wasn't working. It wouldn't turn over. But on the little things, it was ticking right along. It knew that the next day was Sunday, and liquor stores would be closed. So off I went to Sandy's to pick up a quart of vodka, a fifth of Italian brandy, and a fifth of sour mash bourbon. The vodka and brandy were for me. The sour mash was for Al Coburn. Somehow I figured him for a bourbon man, and I saw us having a few slugs together before digging into that stew he promised. And a few shots after. I also picked up two cold six-packs of Ballantine ale. I reckoned I might need them early Sunday morning.

I carted all these provisions back to the Coburn Inn. I stopped at the desk long enough to ask if there were any messages for me. There weren't, but then I didn't expect any; it was barely 3:30, too early to expect Al Coburn to call. So up I went to 3-F. I put the six-packs out on the windowsill. If they didn't slide off and brain a passing pedestrian, I could count on cold ale for Sunday breakfast. I opened the brandy, and had a small belt with water from the bathroom tap. It tasted so good that I had another to keep it company. Then I fell asleep.

It wasn't that I was tired; it was emotional exhaustion. If I've given you the impression that investigative work is a lark, I've misled you. The physical labor is minimal, the danger is infinitesimal. But what gets you—or rather, what gets *me*—is the agitation of dealing with people. I don't think this is a unique reaction. Doctors, lawyers, psychiatrists, waiters, cab drivers, and shoe clerks suffer from the same syndrome. Anyone who deals with the public.

People exert a pressure, deliberately or unconsciously. They force their wills. Their passion, wants, angers, lies, and fears come on like strong winds. Deal with people, and inevitably you feel you're being buffeted. No, that's no good. You feel like you're in a blender, being sliced, chopped, minced, ground, and pureed.

The problem for me was that I could appreciate the hopes and anxieties of everyone in Coburn I had interviewed. I could understand why they acted the way they did. I could *be* them. And everyone of them made sense to me, in a very human way. They weren't monsters. Cut anyone of them, and they'd bleed. They were sad, deluded shits, and I had such empathy that I just couldn't take any more pain. So I fell asleep. It's the organism's self-defense mechanism: when stress becomes overwhelming, go unconscious. It's the only way to cope.

I awoke, startled, a little after five. It took me a moment to get oriented. It was early December. I was in Coburn, N.Y. I was staying at the Coburn Inn, Room 3-F. My name was Samuel Todd. After that, everything came flooding back. I grabbed up the phone. The desk reported no messages. Al Coburn hadn't called.

I splashed cold water on my face, dried, looked at my image in the bathroom mirror. Forget it. The Monster Who Ate Cleveland. I went downstairs and told the baldy on duty that I'd be in the bar if I got a call. He promised to switch it.

The bar was almost empty. But Millie Goodfellow was sitting alone at one end.

"Join you?" I asked.

"Be my guest," she said, patting the stool alongside her.

She was wearing a white blouse with a ruffled neckline cut down to her two charlotte russe. She had obviously gussied up after getting off work; her hair looked like it had been worked on by a crew of carpenters, and the perfume was strong enough to fumigate a rice warehouse. She was trying.

She drank crazy things like Grasshoppers, Black Russians, and Rusty Nails. That night she was nibbling on something called a Nantucket Sleighride. I don't know exactly what it was, except that it had cranberry juice in it and enough *spiritus frumentum* to give the 2nd Airborne Division a monumental hangover.

I ordered her a new one, and a vodka gimlet for me.

"Millie," I said, gesturing toward her tall glass, "I hope you know what you're doing."

"I don't know," she said, "and I don't care."

"Oh-ho," I said. "It's like that, is it?"

"What are you doing tonight?" she asked.

I took out my cigarettes and offered her one. She shook her head. She waited until I lighted up, then took out her own pack of mentholated filtertips. She put one between her lacquered lips and bent close to me.

"Light my cold one with your hot one," she said.

It was so awful, so *awful*. But obediently, I lighted her cigarette from mine.

"How can you drink those things?" I asked, when Jimmy brought our drinks.

"One is an eye-opener," she said, swinging around to face me, putting a warm hand on my knee. "Two is a fly-opener. Three is a thigh-opener."

Oh God, it was getting worse. But I laughed dutifully.

"You didn't answer my question," she said. "What are you doing tonight?"

"Right now? Waiting for a phone call. Haven't seen Al Coburn around, have you?"

"Not since this morning. You're waiting for a phone call from *him*?"

"That's right. I'm supposed to have dinner with him."

"Instead of *me*?"

"It's business," I said. "I'd rather have dinner with you."

She wasn't mollified.

"*You* say," she sniffed. "What if he doesn't call?"

"Then I guess I better call him. Right now, in fact. Excuse me a minute."

I used the bar phone. It went through the hotel switchboard, but I couldn't see any danger. Anyway, Al Coburn didn't answer. No one answered.

I sat at the bar with Millie Goodfellow for another hour and two more drinks. I called Coburn, and I called him, and I called him. No answer. I was surprised that I wasn't alarmed, until I realized that I never did expect to hear from him.

"Millie," I said, "let's have dinner together. But I've got an errand to run first. Take me maybe an hour. If I can't get back, I'll call you here at the bar. You'll be here?"

"I may be," she said stiffly, "and I may not."

I nodded and turned away. She grabbed my arm.

"You won't stand me up, will you?"

"I wouldn't do that."

"And if you can't make it, you'll call?"

"I promise."

"You promise a lot of things," she said sadly.

That was true.

So there I was, back in the Grand Prix, heading out toward Crittenden for the third time that day. I felt like a commuter. My low beams were on, and I drove slowly and carefully, avoiding potholes and bumps. I had the bottle of bourbon on the seat beside me.

It was a sharp, black night, and when I thought of complaisant Millie Goodfellow waiting for me back in that warm bar, I wondered just what the hell I thought I was doing. I knew what I'd find at Al Coburn's place.

I've read as many detective-mystery-suspense paperbacks as you have —probably more—and there was only one ending to a situation like this:

I'd walk into Coburn's house and find him dead. Bloodily dead. Horribly mutilated maybe, or swinging on a rope from a rafter in a faked suicide. His home would be turned upside down because his killer would have tossed the place for that letter left by Ernie Scoggins.

I knew that was what I'd find. The only reason I was going out was the skinny hope that the old man had done what he promised: left the Scoggins letter or a copy in the glove compartment of his pickup. If he had the strength to withstand the vicious torture he had undergone.

Dramatic? You bet. Maybe I was disappointed, because it wasn't like that at all.

I could have driven past Al Coburn's farmhouse a dozen times without picking it out of the gloom if it hadn't been for that flagpole in the frontyard. Old Glory was hanging listlessly, barely stirring. I pulled into a gravel driveway and looked around. No lights anywhere. And no pickup truck.

I left my headlights beamed against the front door and got out of the car, taking the bourbon with me. I found my new flashlight, switched it on, started toward the house. I got within a few yards before I noticed the door was open. Not yawning wide, but open a few inches.

I pushed the door wider, went in, switched on the lights. It was a surprisingly neat home, everything clean and dusted. Not luxurious, but comfortable and tidy. And no one had turned it upside down in a futile search.

I didn't find the Scoggins letter. I didn't find evidence of murder most foul. I didn't find Al Coburn either. I found nothing. Just a warm, snug home with an unlocked door. I went through it slowly and carefully, room to room. I looked in every closet and cupboard. I poked behind drapes and got down on my knees to peer under beds and couches. I opened the trap to the unfinished attic and beamed my flashlight around in there. Ditto the half-basement.

Nothing.

No, not quite nothing. In the kitchen, on an electric range, a big cast-iron pot of stew was simmering. It smelled great. I turned off the light.

I went outside and made three circuits of the house, each one a little farther out. I found nothing. I saw nothing that might indicate what had happened to Al Coburn. He was just gone, vanished, disappeared. I came back into the house and lifted his phone. It was working normally. I called the Coburn Inn, identified myself, asking if anyone had called me. No one had.

I stood there, in the middle of the silent living room, looking around dazedly at the maple furniture with the cretonne-covered cushions. "Al Coburn!" I yelled. "Al Coburn!" I screamed. "Al Coburn!" I howled.

Nothing.

I think the quiet of that empty house spooked me more than a crumpled corpse. It was so like what had happened to Ernie Scoggins: now you see him, now you don't. Only in this case there wasn't even a blood-stained rug as a tip-off. There was nothing but a pot of stew simmering on a lighted range.

What could I do—call the cops and tell them a man hadn't phoned me as he promised? Ask for a search, an investigation? And then have Al Coburn waltz in with two quarts of beer he had gone to buy for our dinner?

But I knew, I *knew*, Al Coburn was never going to waltz in on me or anyone else, that night or any night. He was gone. He was just gone. How it had been managed I couldn't figure. It had to be some kind of a scam to get him out of the house. To get rid of him and his pickup truck. If the man he met had threatened, Al Coburn would have fought; I was convinced of that. And I would have found evidence of violence instead of just a pot of simmering stew. So he had been tricked. Maybe he had been conned to drive his truck himself to some other meeting place, some deserted place. And there . . .

I left the unopened bottle of bourbon in the kitchen. To propitiate the Gods? I turned off the lights inside the house. I closed the door carefully. I looked up at the flag still drooping from the staff. Patriotic Al Coburn. His folks had founded the town.

Then I drove slowly back into Coburn.

When I entered the lobby of the Inn, a gaggle of permanent residents was clustered about the desk, chattering excitedly. As I walked by, the clerk called out, "Hey, Mr. Todd, hear the news? They just found Al Coburn and his truck in the river. He's deader'n a doornail."

They had heard about it in the bar. "You won't be having dinner with Al Coburn," Millie Goodfellow said. "No," I said. "He probably had one too many and just drove in," Jimmy said. "Yes," I said. "Another gimlet?" he asked. "Make it a double," I said. "Just vodka. On the rocks."

That's where I was—on the rocks. I won't pretend to remember all the details of that Walpurgisnacht. But that's how it began—on the rocks. Millie and I drank at the Coburn Inn for another hour or two. I wanted her husband to come in and catch us together. I don't know why. I think I had some childish desire to bend his nose.

"Why don't we go out to Red Dog Betty's for dinner?" Millie suggested. "Splendid idea."

I drove, and not too badly. I mean I wasn't swarming all over the road, and I didn't exceed the limit by more than five or ten. Millie snuggled against me, singing, "You Light Up My Life." That was okay with me. I might even have joined in. Anything to keep from thinking.

Betty's joint was crowded, but she took one look at us, and hastily shoved us into a booth in a far dining area.

"Get your car all right?" she asked me.

"Did indeed," I said. "For which much thanks."

I leaned forward to kiss her.

"If you can ditch Miss Tits," she said, "I'll be around."

"Hey, wait a minute," Millie protested, "I saw him first."

Betty Hanrahan goosed her, and went back to the bar. Millie and I ordered something: skirt steaks I think they were. And we drank. And we danced. I saw people from Crittenden, including Linda Cunningham. I waved at her. She stuck her tongue out at me. I like to think it was more invitation than insult.

We kept chomping a few bites, finishing our drinks, then rushing back to the dance floor when someone played something we liked on the juke. Millie was a close-up dancer. I mean she was *close*.

"Carry a Coke bottle in your pocket?" she asked.

"Something like that."

"Come on," she yelled gaily in my ear. "Have fun!"

"Sure," I said.

So I had fun. I really did. I drank up a storm. Told hilariously funny stories. Asked Betty Hanrahan to marry me. Sang the opening verse of "Sitting One Night in Murphy's Bar." Bought drinks for Linda Cunningham's table. And threw up twice in the men's room. Quite a night.

Millie Goodfellow must have seen worse. Anyway, she stuck with me: conduct above and beyond the call of duty. She'd leave occasionally to dance with a trucker she knew, or with the tall, skinny gink from Mike's Service Station. But she always came back to me.

"You're so good to me," I told her, wiping my brimming eyes.

"You're not going to pass out on me, are you?" she said anxiously.

Betty Hanrahan came back to persuade me to switch to beer. I agreed, but only, I told her, because she had bought me four "radical" tires. I may have kissed her again. I was in a kissing mood. I kissed Millie Goodfellow. I kissed Linda Cunningham. I wanted to kiss the black bartender, but he said he was busy.

Millie drove us back to Coburn.

"What a super car," she said.

"Super," I said.

"You need some black coffee," she said.

"Super," I said. "Millie, you drop me at the Inn, and then you go home."

"You really want me to go home?"

"No," I said.

"Super," she said.

It was then, I estimate, about 2:00 A.M. The lobby of the Coburn Inn was deserted, but the bar was still open. Millie sat me down in one of the spavined armchairs and disappeared. I sat there, content and giggling, until she returned with a cardboard container of black coffee. She helped me to my feet.

"Up we go," she said.

"Up we go," I said.

We took the stairs. It didn't take long, no more than a month or so, but eventually we arrived in Room 3-F. Millie locked the door behind us.

"Madam," I said haughtily, "do you intend to seduce me?"

"Yes," he said.

"Excuse me," I said suddenly, grabbed the black coffee, ran for the bathroom, and just did make it. I had let myself think about Al Coburn. So I threw up for the third time that night. Brushed my teeth. Showered. For some reason I'll never know, washed my hair and shaved. Finished the coffee. Put on a towel. Came out feeling mildly human. Millie Goodfellow was still there.

"You're very patient," I told her. "For a seductress."

"I found the brandy," she said cheerfully. "It's very good. Want one?"

"Do I ever!" I said.

She was using my sole glass, so I drank from the bottle. Not elegant, but effective.

"I'm sorry," I told her.

"What for? You weren't so bad."

"Bad enough. Did I pay the tab at Betty's?"

"Of course you did. And left too much tip."

"It couldn't have been too much," I groaned. "Betty and I are still friends?"

"She loves you."

"And I love her. Nice lady."

"Who was the little butterball you were slobbering over?"

"Linda Cunningham? She works at the Crittenden lab."

"You like her?"

"Sure. She's nice."

"You love her?"

"Come on, Millie. Tonight was the third time I've seen her. Just an acquaintance."

"I'm jealous."

I picked up her hand and kissed her fingertips.

"I like that," I said, grinning. "You jealous! You've got every guy in Coburn popping his suspenders."

"It's just a game," she said. "You play the game, and you get the name."

"And don't do the crime if you can't do the time."

"That's very true," she said seriously.

There I was in my towel. She was still fully clothed, sitting rather distantly in one of the sprung armchairs. I poured her another brandy.

"I talked to Al Coburn just this morning," I said. "Hearing he was dead hit me hard."

"I figured," she said. "You okay now?"

"Oh sure. I'm even sober. Sort of."

"I am, too," she said. "Sort of. I think Ronnie's going to leave me."

I tilted the brandy bottle again. I wasn't gulping. I was tonguing the opening. Little sips. It was helping.

"What makes you think that?" I asked her.

"I just know," she said. "A woman's instinct," she said virtuously.

"Well . . . if he does, how do you feel about it?"

"It's that chippy," she burst out. "It's because of her."

"Julie? Julie Thorndecker?"

"She'll be the end of him." Millie Goodfellow said. "He's pussy-whipped. If he wanted to leave me for some nice, sweet homebody who likes to cook, I could understand it, and wish him the best. But that hoor? She'll finish him."

I looked at her with awe. You never know people. Never. You think you've got them analyzed and tagged. You think you know their limits. Then they surprise you. They stagger you and stun you. They have depths, complexities you never even imagined. Here was this nutty broad mourning her husband's infidelity, not for her own injury, but because of the pain he would suffer. I admired her.

"Well, Millie," I said, "I don't think there's a thing you can do about it. He's got to make his own mistakes."

"I suppose so," she said, staring into her glass of brandy. "If I come to New York, could you do anything for me? I don't mean money—nothing like that. I mean introduce me to people. Tell me how to go about getting a job. Would you do that?"

"Of course," I said bravely.

"Oh hell," she said, shaking her head. "Who am I kidding? I'll never leave Coburn. You know why?"

"Why?"

"Because I'm scared. I watch television. I see all these young, pretty, bright girls. I'm not like that. I sell cigarettes at the Coburn Inn. They could put in a coin machine, but I bring guys around to eat in the restaurant and drink at the bar. Think I don't know it? But I'm safe here.

I'll never leave. I might dream about it, but I know I'll never leave. I'll die in Coburn."

I groaned. I went down on my knees, put my head in her lap. I took up her hand again, kissed her palm.

"You'll be nice to me, won't you?" she asked anxiously. It was a pleading, little girl's voice. "Please be nice."

I nodded.

From the way she dressed and the way she came on, I expected her to be sex with four-wheel drive, a heaving, panting combination of Cleopatra, Catherine the Great, and the Dragon Lady. But she undressed with maidenly modesty, switching off all the bedroom lamps first, leaving only the bathroom light burning with the door open just wide enough to cast long shadows across the softly illuminated bed.

She turned her back to me when she took off her clothes. I think she was humming faintly. I watched her in amazement. She didn't come diving eagerly between the sheets like a chilled swimmer entering a heated pool. She slid in next to me demurely, her back still turned. All cool indifference.

I pulled her over to face me.

"Be nice," she kept murmuring. "Please be nice."

That Picasso clown makeup ended at her neck. On almost a straight line. Above was the painted, weathered, used face of a woman who's been through the mill twice: seams and wrinkles, crow's feet and puckers, worried eyes and a swollen, hungry mouth. She looked like she had been picked up by the heels and dipped in age.

But below the pancake makeup line, from neck to toes, her body was fruit, as fresh and as juicy. It was a revelation. She was made of peach skin and plum pulp: a goddamned virgin.

"Millie," I said. "Oh Millie . . ."

"Please be nice," she said.

Nice? I was in bed with a white marble Aphrodite, a faintly veined Venus. Having sex with her was like slashing a Rubens or taking a sledge to a Michelangelo. Screwing that woman was sheer vandalism.

I made lover to her like an archeologist, being ever so careful. I didn't want to break or mar anything. After awhile she lay on her back, closed her eyes, and stopped saying, "Be nice," for which I was thankful. But she gave me no hint, no clue as to what I might do that would bring her pleasure. She made small sounds and small movements. If she felt anything, it was deep, deep, and there were few outer indications that she might not be falling asleep.

It became evident that I could do anything to her or with her, and she would slackly submit. Not from desire or unendurable passion, but simply because this was what one did on Saturday night in Coburn, N.Y., after a drunken dinner at Red Dog Betty's. It was ritual.

But something happened to me. I think it was caused by the texture of her skin: fine-pored, tight and soft, firm and yielding. Joan Powell had skin like that, and holding a naked Millie Goodfellow in my arms, putting lips and tongue to her warm breast, I thought of Powell.

"Aren't you going to *do* anything?" she breathed finally.

So I knew that if I did not *do* something, Europe would be the less. She expected tribute; denial would have demolished what little ego survived. Almost experimentally, and certainly deliberately, I began a long, whispered hymn of love.

"Oh Millie," I declaimed into her ear, "I've never seen a woman like you. Your body is so beautiful, so beautiful. Your breasts are lovely, and here, and here. I want to eat your sweetness, take all of you into me. This waist! Legs! And here behind your knees. So soft, so tender. This calf. These toes . . ."

On and on. And as I reassured her, she came alive. Her magnificent body warmed, began to twist and writhe. Her sounds became stronger, her pulse beat more powerfully, and she pressed to me.

"How lovely," I carried on, "how wonderful. You have a perfect body. Perfect! Never have I seen nipples so long. And this slender waist! Look, I can almost put my hands around it. And down here. So warm, so warm and loving."

It wasn't my caresses, I knew. It was the con, the scam. Is it so awful to be wanted? She awoke as if my words were feathers between her thighs. Her eyes opened just a bit, wetly, and I thought she might be weeping from happiness.

"Don't stop," she told me. "Please don't stop."

So I continued my sexual gibberish as she became fevered and bursting beneath me. In all things I was gentle, and hoped it was what she meant by, "Be nice." And all the time, delivering my cocksman's spiel, I was remembering Joan Powell, tasting *her* skin, kissing *her* skin, biting *her* skin. I loved Millie Goodfellow, and loving her, loved Joan Powell more. I'll never understand what it's all about.

THE SEVENTH DAY

I GUESS it was the clanking of the radiator that woke me up Sunday morning. Of course it might have been the clanking in my head, but I didn't think so; I wasn't hissing and spitting.

It was nice in that cocoon of warmed sheets and wool blankets. For the second time since I arrived in Coburn, I debated the wisdom of staying there for the rest of my life. I could pay Sam Livingston to bring me bologna sandwiches and take away the bedpan. What I had to do that day offered no hope of jollity. Maybe it's a sign of age (maturity?) when the future holds less than the past.

I turned to look at the other pillow, still bearing the dent of Millie Goodfellow's architectural hairdo. I leaned across to sniff. It still smelled of her scent but, faded, it didn't seem as awful as it had the night before. Now it seemed warm, fragrant, and very, very intimate. I kissed the pillow like a demented poet.

We had dressed shortly before what laughingly passes for dawn in Coburn, N.Y., and I had escorted Millie down to her car in the parking lot. An affecting parting. We clung to each other and said sappy things. It wasn't the world's greatest love affair—just a vigorous one-night stand—but we liked each other and had a few laughs.

Then I had returned to my nest for five good hours of dreamless sleep. When I awoke, other than that crown of thorns (pointed inward) I was wearing, the carcass seemed in reasonably efficient condition: heart pumping, lungs billowing, all joints bending in the proper direction. Bladder working A-OK; I tested it. Then I rescued a cold ale from the windowsill. See how rewarding careful planning can be?

Sat sprawled naked, sipping my breakfast calories, and tried to remember what goofy things I had done the night before. But then I gave up on the self-recriminations. I've played the fool before, and will again. You'd be surprised at how comforting that acknowledgment can be.

Finished the ale, went in to shave and discovered I had shaved the night before. In fact, at about two in the morning. Beautiful. So I showered and dressed, happy to feel the headache fading to a light throb. Went to the window again, not expecting to see the sun, and didn't. Had another chilled ale while planning the day's program. I didn't want to stray too far from the hotel in case Mary Thorndecker called. But there was one thing I decided I had to do: try to convince the local cops to let me take a look at Al Coburn's pickup truck, especially the glove compartment. It wasn't a job I was looking forward to, but I figured I had to make the try.

Went down to the lobby to discover the restaurant and bar didn't open until 1:00 P.M. I decided that a day-long fast wouldn't hurt me. After my behavior the night before, maybe a week-long penance would be more appropriate.

Sam Livingston came to my rescue. He found me in the lobby, trying to get a newspaper out of a coin machine. Sam showed me where to kick it. Not only did you get your newspaper, but your money came back. Then I accepted his invitation to join him in his basement apartment for coffee and a hunk of Danish.

It was snug in that warm burrow, and the coffee was strong and hot. We sat at the little table with the ice cream parlor chairs, drank our coffee, chewed Danish, and grunted at each other. It wasn't till the second cup and second cigarette that we started talking. That may have been because this wise old man was putting a dollop of the 12-year-old Scotch in the drip brew. Coffee royal. Nothing like it to unglue the tongue on a frosty Sunday morning.

"I keep hearing things," he told me.

"Voices?" I asked idly.

"Nah. Well . . . . them too. I was talking about gossip."

"Thought you didn't believe in gossip?"

"Don't," he said stoutly. "But this was about something you asked me, so I listened."

"What did you hear?"

He poured us each a little more coffee, a little more whiskey. It was warming, definitely warming. The headache was gone. I began to expand.

"I should have been a detective," he said. "Like you."

"I'm not a detective; I'm an investigator."

"There's a difference?"

"Sometimes. Sometimes they're the same. But why should you have been a detective?"

"Well, you've got to know that in a place small like this, we ain't got too much to talk about. Small town; small talk. Like Mrs. Cimenti had her hair dyed red. Aldo Bates bought a new snow shovel. Fred Aikens bounced a bad check at Red Dog Betty's. Little things like that."

"So? What did you hear?"

"On Friday, one of the regulars here told me he stood behind Constable Ronnie Goodfellow at the bank, and Goodfellow closed out his account. More'n three hundred dollars. Then that fellow from Mike's Service Station, he told Millie Goodfellow that her husband had brought in their car for a tune-up. Then one of the clerks from Bill's Five-and-Dime happened to mention that Ronnie Goodfellow stopped in and bought the biggest cardboard suitcase they got. Now you put all those things together, and what do you get?"

I grinned at him.

"A trip," I said. "Constable Goodfellow is cutting loose."

"Yeah," he said with satisfaction, taking a sip of the coffee royal, "that's what I figured."

"Thanks for telling me," I said. "Any idea where he's going?"

"Nope."

"Any idea who he's going *with*?"

"Nope, except I know it ain't his wife."

"Sam," I said, "why would Goodfellow go about planning this trip so openly? He must know how people talk in this town. Is it that he just doesn't give a damn?"

That seamed basalt face turned to me. He showed the big, yellowed teeth in what I supposed was intended as a smile. The old eyes stared, then lost their focus, looking inward.

"You know what I figure?" he said. "I figure it's part what you say: he don't give a damn. But why don't he? I tell you, I think since he took up with that woman—or she took up with him—he ain't been thinking straight. I figure that woman scrambled his brains. Just stirred him up to such a hot-pants state, he don't know if he's coming or going. I hear tell of them two . . ."

"All right," I said, "that fits in with what I've heard. Sam, you think he'd kill for her? You think he'd do murder for a woman he loves?"

He reflected a moment.

"I reckon he would," he said finally. Then he added softly, "I did."

I froze, not certain I had heard him aright.

"You killed for a woman?"

He nodded.

I glanced briefly at his bookcase of romantic novels. I wondered if what he was telling me was fact or fiction. But when I looked at him again, I recognized something I had never before put a name to. That unreadable, inward look. Speaking with a minimum of lip movement. The ability to turn a question. The coldly suspicious, standoffish manner. Friendly enough, genial enough. To a point. Then the steel shutter came rattling down.

"You've done time," I told him.

"Oh yes," he said. "Eleven years."

"Couldn't have been manslaughter. Murder two?"

He sighed. "My woman's husband. He was a no-good. She wanted him gone. After awhile, I wanted him gone, too. I'd have done anything to keep her. Anything. Murder? Sheesh, that wasn't nothing. I'd have cut my own throat to make her happy. Some women can do that to you."

"I guess," I said. "Did she wait for you?"

"Not exactly," he said. "She took up with others. Got killed when a dancehall burned down in Chicago. This happened a long time ago, whilst I was inside."

He just said it, without rancor. It was something that had happened a long time back, and he had learned to live with it. Memories blur. Pain becomes a twinge. Can you remember the troubles you had five years ago?

"So you think Goodfellow would do it?"

"Oh, he'd do it; no doubt about that. If she said, 'Jump,' he'd just say, 'How high?' You think he did?"

I started to say yes, started to say I thought Ronnie Goodfellow had murdered both Ernie Scoggins and Al Coburn. But I shut my mouth. I had nothing to take to a D.A. Nothing but the sad knowledge of how a tall, proud Indian cop might become so impassioned by sleek, soft Julie Thorndecker that the only question he'd ask would be, "How high?"

We finished our coffee. I thanked Sam Livingston and left. He didn't rise to see me out. Just waved a hand slowly. When I closed the door, he was still seated at the table with empty cups and a full ashtray. He was an old, old man trying vainly to recall a dim time of passion and resolve.

When I got up to the lobby, the desk clerk motioned me over and said I had a call at ten o'clock. A Miss Joan Powell had called.

I was discombobulated. Then insanely happy. Joan Powell? How had she learned where I was? What could she—? Then I remembered: it was the name Mary Thorndecker was to use.

"Did she say she'd call again?"

"Yes, sir, Mr. Todd. At eleven." He glanced at the wood-cased regulator clock on the wall behind him. "That'll be about twenty minutes or so."

I told him I'd be in my room, and asked him to switch the call. Upstairs, I sat patiently, flipping the pages of my Sunday newspaper, not really reading it or even seeing it. Just turning pages and wondering if I'd ever meet a woman I'd kill for. I didn't think so. But I don't suppose Sam Livingston or Ronnie Goodfellow ever anticipated doing what they had done.

I remember meeting a grunt in Vietnam, a very shy, religious guy who told me that during training he had given the matter a great deal of painful thought, and had decided that if he got in a firefight, he'd shoot over the heads of the enemy. He just believed it was morally wrong to kill another human being.

Then, less than a week after he arrived in Nam, his platoon got caught in an ambush.

"How long did it take you to change your mind?" I asked him. "Five minutes?"

"About five seconds," he said sadly.

I grabbed up the phone after the first ring. I might have had my fingers crossed.

"Samuel Todd," I said.

"This is Joan Powell," Mary Thorndecker said faintly. "How are you, Mr. Todd?"

"Very well, thanks. And you, Miss Powell?"

"What? Oh yes. Fine. I'm going to church this morning. The Episcopal church. The noon service, and I was wondering if you were planning to attend?"

"As a matter of fact, I am. The noon service at the Episcopal church. Yes, I'll be there."

"Then maybe I'll see you."

"I certainly hope so. Thank you, Miss Powell."

I hung up slowly, and thought about it. I decided she was a brainy woman. A crowded church service would offer a good opportunity to talk. There's always privacy in mobs. I glanced at my watch and figured I had about forty-five minutes to kill.

I wandered out to the vacant streets of Coburn. A drizzle was beginning to slant down from a choked sky. I turned up my collar, turned down the hat brim. It seemed to me that my boots had been damp for a week, and soggy pant and sleeve cuffs rubbed rawly. I passed a few other Sunday morning pedestrians, hunched beneath black umbrellas. I didn't see any cars moving. The deserted village.

I walked over to River Street, stood at the spot where Ronnie Goodfellow and I had paused a week ago to watch the garbage-clogged water slide greasily by. Then I turned away and went prowling through the empty streets. There were some good storefronts beneath the grime. A few bore the date of construction: 1886, 1912, 1924.

A paint job and clean-up drive would have done wonders for Coburn.

Like putting cosmetics on a corpse. I had told Goodfellow that if history teaches anything, it teaches change. That people, cities, nations, civilizations are born, flourish, die. How fatuous can you get? That may be the way things are, but knowing it doesn't make it any easier to accept. Especially when you're a witness to the senescence of what had once been a vital, thriving organism.

Coburn was dying. Unless I had misread the signs, Dr. Telford Gordon Thorndecker was dying. If he went, the village would surely go, for so much of the town's hopes seemed built on his money, his energy, his dreams. They would vanish together, Thorndecker and his Troy.

I shouldn't have felt anything. This place meant nothing to me. It was just a mouldering crossroad on the way to Albany. But once, I suppose, it had been a busy, humming community with brawls and parades, good times, laughter, a sense of growth, and a belief it would last forever. We all think that. And here was Coburn now, the damp and the rot crumbling away brave storefronts and streaking dusty glass.

If this necropolis and the sordid Thorndecker affair meant anything, they persuaded me to feel deeply, cherish more, smell the blooms, see the colors, love, laugh at pinpricks and shrug off the blows. What do the Hungarian's say? "Before you have time to look around, the picnic is over." The picnic was ending for Coburn. For Thorndecker. Nothing but litter left to the ants.

I plodded back to the Coburn Inn. I had a sudden vision of this place in twenty years, or fifty. A lost town. No movement. No lights. No voices. Dried leaves and yellowed newspapers blowing down cracked pavements. Signs fading, names growing dim. Everyone moved away or dead. Nothing but the rain, wind, and maybe, by then, a blank and searing sun.

You're as old as you feel? Bullshit. You're as old as you look. And you can't fake youth, not really. The pain is in seeing it go, grabbing, trying to hold it back. No way. Therefore, do not send to ask for whom the ass sinks; it sinks for thee. Forgive me, Joan Powell, I cast you aside not from want of affection, but from fear. I thought by rejecting an older mate I might stay young forever: the Peter Pan of the Western World. Why do we think of the aged as lepers when we are all registered for that drear colony?

So much for Sunday morning thoughts in Coburn, N.Y. Gloomsville-on-the-Hudson. But I met this emotional wrench with my usual courage and steadfastness. I rushed up to Room 3-F and had a stiff belt of vodka before setting out for the noon service at the Episcopal church.

My nutty fantasy of the morning had been the right one: I should have stood in bed.

I was a few minutes late getting to the church. But I wasn't the only one; others were hurrying up the steps, collapsing their umbrellas, taking seats in the rear pews. I stood a moment at the back of the nave, trying to spot Mary Thorndecker. A robed choir was singing "My Faith Is a Mountain," and not badly.

I finally saw her, sitting about halfway down on the aisle. Next to her were Dr. Kenneth Draper, Edward Thorndecker, and Julie. *Julie?!* I couldn't figure out what she was doing there, unless she was screwing the choir.

I noticed Mary was turning her head occasionally, glancing toward the rear of the church, searching for me. I moved over to one side, and the next time she looked in my direction, I raised a hand and jerked a thumb over my shoulder. I thought she nodded slightly. I went back outside. I wasn't about to sit through the service. If Mary could get out while it was going on, so much the better. If not, I'd wait outside until it was over.

I stood on the pillared porch, protected from the rain. I lighted a cigarette. The Reverend Peter Koukla had practically said it was a sin to smoke on church grounds. But it wasn't a 100 mm. cigarette, so it was really a *small* sin.

I was leaning against a pillar watching the rain come down—almost as exciting as watching paint dry—when an old guy came around the corner of the church. Another of Coburn's gnarled gaffers. He had to be 70, going on 80. Coburn, I decided, had to be the geriatric capital of the U.S.

This ancient was wearing a black leather cap, rubberized poncho, and black rubber boots. He was carrying a rake and dragging a bushel basket at the end of a piece of soggy rope. He was raking up broken twigs, sodden leaves, refuse, and dumping all the slop in his basket.

When he came close to me, I said pleasantly, "Working on Sunday?"

"What the hell does it look like I'm doing?" he snarled.

It was a stupid question I had asked, so I was willing to endure his ill-humor. I pulled out my pack of cigarettes and held it out to him. He shook his head, but he dropped rake and rope, and climbed the steps to join me on the porch. He fished under his poncho and brought out a blunt little pipe. The shank was wound with dirty adhesive tape. The pipe was already loaded. He lighted it with a wooden kitchen match and blew out an explosion of blue smoke. It smelled like he had filled it with a piece of the wet rope tied to his bushel basket.

"No church service for you?" I said.

"Naw," he said. "I been. See one, you seen 'em all."

"You're not a religious man?" I asked.

"The hell I'm not," he said. He cackled suddenly. "What the hell, it don't cost nothing."

I looked at him with interest. All young people look different; all old people look alike. You see the bony nose, wrinkled lips, burst capillaries. The geezer sucked on his pipe with great enjoyment, looking out at the wet world.

"How come you ain't inside?" he asked.

"Like you," I said, "I been."

"I got no cause to go," he said. "I'm too old to sin. You been sinning lately?"

"Not as much as I want to."

He grunted, and I hoped it was with amusement. At that moment, a religious nut I didn't need.

"You the sexton?" I asked.

"How?"

"Sexton. Church handyman."

"Yeah," he said, "I guess you could say that. Ben Faber."

"Samuel Todd," I said.

His hands were under his poncho. He didn't offer to shake, so I lighted another cigarette and dug my chilled hands back into my trenchcoat pockets.

"You don't live hereabouts?" he said.

"No."

"Just passing through?"

"I hope so."

He grunted again, and then I was certain it was his way of expressing amusement.

"Yeah," he said, "it's a pisser, ain't it? Going down the drain, this town is. Well, I won't be here to see it."

"You're moving?"

"Hell, no," he said, astonished. "But I figure I'll be six feet under before it goes. I'm eighty-four."

"You look younger," I said dutifully.

"Yeah," he said, puffing away. "Eighty-two."

I was amazed at how this chance conversation was going, how it seemed a continuation of my melancholy musings of the morning.

"It doesn't scare you?" I asked him. "The idea of dying?"

He took the pipe out of his mouth long enough to spit off the porch into a border of shrubs tied up in burlap sacks.

"I'll tell you, sonny," he said, "when I was your age, it scared me plenty. But don't worry it; as you get along in years, the idea of croaking gets easier to live with. You see so many people go. Family. Friends. It gets familiar-like. And then, so many of them are shitheads, you figure if they can do it, you can do it. Then too, you just get tired. Nothing new ever happens. You've seen it all before. Wars and accidents. Floods and fires. Marriages. Murders. People dying by the billions, and billions of babies getting born. Nothing new. So just slipping away seems like the most natural thing in the world. Naw, it don't scare me. Pain, maybe. I don't like that. Bad pain, I mean. But as for dying, it's got to be done, don't it?"

"Yes," I said faintly, "it surely does."

He knocked the dottle from his pipe against the heel of his rubber boot. It made a nice mess on the porch, but that didn't seem to bother him. He took out an oilskin pouch, unrolled it, began to load the pipe again, poking the black, rough-cut tobacco into the bowl with a grimy forefinger.

"Want some advice, sonny?" he said.

"Well . . . yeah, sure."

"Do what you want to do," he said between puffs, as he lighted his pipe. "That's my advice to you."

I thought that over a moment, then shook my head, flummoxed.

"I don't get it," I told him. "I always do what I want to do."

The grunts came again. But this time he showed me a mouthful of browned, stumpy teeth.

"The hell you do," he said. "Don't tell me there ain't been things you wanted to do, but then you got to thinking about it. What would this one say? What would that one say? What if this happened? What if that happened? So what you wanted to do in the first place never got done. Ain't that right?"

"Well . . . I guess so. There have been things I wanted to do, and never did for one reason or another."

"I'm telling you," he said patiently. "I'm giving you the secret, and not charging for it neither. What it took me eight-four years to learn. I ain't got a single regret for what I done in this life. But I'll go to my grave with a whole lot of regrets for things I wanted to do and never did. For one reason or another. Now you remember that, sonny."

"I surely will," I said. "Tell me, Mr. Faber, how long do you figure this service will last?"

"What time you got?"

I glanced at my watch. "About ten to one."

"Should be breaking up any minute now. The Ladies' Auxiliary, they're serving coffee and doughnuts in the basement. Think I'll get me some right now. You coming?"

"No, thanks. I'll stay here."

"Waiting for someone?"

"Yes."

"A woman?"

I nodded.

He cackled again, then clumped down the steps to pick up his rake and rope tow to the wet bushel basket.

"A woman," he repeated. "I don't have to fret about *that* no more. But you remember what I said: you want to do something, you just *do* it."

"I'll remember," I said. "Thanks again."

He grunted, and trudged away in the rain. I watched him go. I wasn't sure what the hell he had been talking about, but somehow I felt better. He had found a kind of peace, and if that's what age brought, it might be a little easier to endure varicose veins, dentures, and a truss.

I moved back toward the doors and heard the swelling sonority of the church organ. A few people came out, buttoning up coats and opening umbrellas. I stood to one side and waited. In a few minutes Mary Thorndecker came flying out, face flushed. The long Persian lamb coat was flapping around her ankles. She was gripping a black umbrella. She grabbed my arm.

"The others are having coffee," she said breathlessly. "I don't think they saw you. I only have a minute."

"All right," I said, taking the umbrella from her and opening it. "Let's go to my car."

"Oh no," she cried. "They may come out and see us."

"This was your idea," I said. "What do you want to do?"

"Let's walk across the street," she said nervously. "Away from the church. Just a block or two. It won't take long."

I took her arm. I held the big umbrella over both of us. We crossed the street and walked away from the church on the opposite sidewalk.

"There are three guards," she said rapidly. "The gate guard, one on duty in the nursing home, and a man with a dog who patrols outside. They come on at midnight. A day shift takes over at eight in the morning."

"No guard in the lab?"

"No. Each building has its own power switches and alarm switches. In the basements of both buildings. The switch boxes are kept locked."

"Shit," I said. "I beg your pardon."

"I can't get Nurse Beecham's keys," she went on. "She hands them over to the night supervisor, a male nurse. He carries them around with him."

"Listen," I said, "I've narrowed it down. There's only one place I want to go, one thing I want to see. Your stepfather's private office. On the second floor of the research laboratory."

"I can't get the keys."

"Sure you can," I said gently. "Dr. Draper has keys to the main lab building and to your stepfather's private lab. Get the keys from Draper."

"But how?" she burst out desperately. "I can't just ask him for them."

"Lie," I told her. "Where does Draper live?"

"In Crittenden Hall. He has a little apartment. Bedroom, sitting room, bathroom."

"Good," I said. "Wake him up about two o'clock tomorrow morning. Tell him Thorndecker is working late in Crittenden Hall and wants his journal from the lab. Tell him anything. You're a clever woman. Make up some excuse, but get the keys."

"He'll want to get the journal himself."

"Not if you handle it right. Just get the keys. By fifteen minutes after two, I'll be inside the fence. I'll be waiting at the back entrance to the research lab. The door at the end of that covered walk that comes down the hill from the nursing home."

She didn't say anything, but I felt her shiver under my hand. I thought I might have thrown it at her too fast, so I slowed down and went over it once again. Get the keys from Draper at 2:00 A.M. Let me into the lab at 2:15.

"I'm not going to steal anything," I told her. "You'll be with me; you'll see. I just want to look in Thorndecker's journal."

"What for?"

"To see what he's been doing, and why. He said he keeps very precise, complete notes. It should all be there."

She was silent awhile, then . . .

"Do I have to be with you?" she asked. "Can't I just give you the keys?"

I stopped and turned her toward me. There we stood under that big, black umbrella, the rain sliding off it in a circular curtain. She wouldn't meet my eyes.

"You don't really want to know, do you?" I asked softly.

She shook her head dumbly, teeth biting down into her lower lip.

"Mary, I *need* you there. I need a witness. And maybe you can help me with the scientific stuff. You must know more of that than I do. Anyone would!"

She smiled wanly.

"And also," I said, "I need you with me for a very selfish reason. If we're caught, it'll be impossible to charge me with breaking-and-entering if I'm with a member of the family."

She nodded, lifted her chin.

"All right," she said. "I'll get the keys. Somehow. I'll let you in. I'll go with you. We'll read the journal together. I don't care how awful it is. I do want to know."

I pressed her arm. We started walking back toward the church. Her stride seemed more confident now. She was leading the way. I had to hurry to keep up with her. We stopped across the street from the church. We faced each other again.

"I know how to get the keys from Kenneth," she said, looking into my eyes.

"Good," I said. "How?"

"I'll go to bed with him," she said, plucked the umbrella from my hand, dashed across the street.

I just stood there, hearing the faint hiss of rain, watching her run up the church steps and disappear. And I had thought her prissy.

It was a few minutes before I could move. I felt the drops pelt my sodden tweed hat. I saw the rain run down my trenchcoat in wavy rivulets. I knew my boots were leaking and my feet were wet.

Simple solution: "I'll go to bed with him." Just like that. Maybe old Ben Faber was right. You want to do something, then *do* it.

I got back in my car, still in a state of bemused wonderment. I drove around awhile, trying to make sense of what was going on, of what people were doing, of what I was doing. What amazed me most was how Telford Gordon Thorndecker, unknowingly, was impinging on the lives of so many. Mary. Dr. Draper. Julie. Edward. Ronnie and Millie Goodfellow. The "best people" of Coburn. And me. Thorndecker was changing us. Nudging our lives, for better or for worse. None of us would ever be the same.

The man was a force. It went out in waves, affecting people he didn't even know. Joan Powell, for example. Thorndecker was the reason I had come to Coburn. Coburn was changing the way I felt about Joan Powell. Her life might be turned around, or at least altered, by the influence of a man she had never met.

I wondered if all life was like this: a series of interlocking concentric circles, everything connected to everything else in some mad scheme that the greatest computer in the world would digest and then type out on its TV monitor: "Insufficient data."

It was a humbling thought, that we are all pushed and pulled by influences that we are not even aware of. Life is not a bowl of cherries. Life is a bowl of linguine with clam sauce, everything intertangled and slithery. No end to it.

Maybe that was the job of the investigators. We're the guys with the fork and the soup spoon, lifting high a tangle of the strands, twirling fork tines in the bowl of the spoon, and producing a neat, palatable ball.

It made me hungry just to think of it.

The Coburn Civic Building looked like it had shrunk in the rain. I didn't expect bustling activity on a Sunday afternoon, but I thought *someone* would be on duty in the city hall, minding the store. I finally found a few real, live human beings by peering through the dirty glass window in the wide door of the firehouse. Inside, four guys in coveralls sat around a wooden table playing cards. I would have bet my last kopeck it was pinochle. I also got a view of their equipment: an antique pumper and a hose truck that looked like a converted Eskimo Pie van. Neither vehicle looked especially clean.

I walked around the building to the police station in the rear. It was open, desolate, deserted. It smelled like every police station in the world: an awful amalgam of eye-stinging disinfectant, vintage urine, mold, dust, vomit, and several other odors of interest only to a pathologist.

There was a waist-high railing enclosing three desks. A frosted glass door led away to inner offices. This splintered room was tastefully decorated with *Wanted* posters and a calendar displaying a lady in a gaping black lace negligee. I thought her proportions highly improbable. She may have been one of those life-size inflatable rubber dolls Japanese sailors take along on lengthy cruises.

From somewhere beneath my feet, a guy was singing—sort of. He was bellowing. "Oh Dolly, oh Dolly, how you can love." That's all. Over and over. "Oh Dolly, oh Dolly, how you can love." From this, I deduced that the drunk tank was in the basement.

"Hello?" I called. "Anyone home?"

No answer. One of these days, some smart, big-city gonnif was going to drop by and steal the Coburn police station.

"Hello?" I yelled again, louder. Same result: none.

I pushed open the railing gate, went over to the frosted glass door, opened that, stepped into a narrow corridor with four doors. Three were unmarked; one bore the legend: Chief. One of the unmarked doors was open. I peeked in.

My old friend, Constable Fred Aikens. He was sprawled in a wood swivel chair, feet parked up on the desk. His hands were clasped across his hard, little pot belly. His head was thrown back, mouth sagging, and he was fast asleep. I could hear him. It wasn't exactly a snore. More like a regular, "Aaagh. Aaagh. Aaagh." There was a sheaf of pornographic photos spread out on his desk blotter.

I stared at Coburn's first line of defense against criminal wrongdoing. I had forgotten what a nasty little toad he was, with his squinchy features and a hairline that seemed anxious to tangle with his eyebrows. I had an insane impulse. I'd very carefully, very quietly tiptoe into the office and very slowly, very easily slide his service revolver from his holster. Then I'd tiptoe from the room, from the building, and drive back to the Coburn Inn where I'd finish the vodka while laughing my head off as I thought of Fred Aikens explaining to the Chief Constable how he happened to lose his gun.

I didn't do it, of course. Instead, I went back to the main room. I slammed the gate of the railing a few times, and I really screamed, "Hello? Hello? Anyone here?"

That did the trick. In a few minutes Aiken came strolling out, uniform cap squared away, tunic smoothed down, every inch the alert police officer.

"Todd," he said. "No need to bellow. How you doing?"

"Okay," I said. "How *you* doing?"

"Quiet," he said. "Just the way I like it. If you came to ask about those slashed tires of yours, we haven't been able to come up with—"

"No, no," I said. "This is about something else. Could I please talk to you for a couple of minutes?"

I said it very humbly. Some cops you can handle just like anyone else. Some you can manipulate better if you start out crawling. Fred Aikens was one of those.

"Why, sure," he said genially. "Come on into my private office where we can sit."

I followed him through the frosted glass door into his room. He jerked open the top desk drawer and swept the pornographic photos out of sight.

"Evidence," he said.

"Yes," I said. "Terrible what's going down these days."

"Sure is," he said. "You park there and tell me what's on your mind."

I sat in a scarred armchair alongside his desk, and gave him my best wide-eyed, sincere look.

"I heard about Al Coburn," I said. "That's a hell of a thing."

"Ain't it though?" he said. "You knew him?"

Those mean, little eyes never blinked.

"Well . . . sure," I said. "Met him two or three times. Had a few drinks with him at the Coburn Inn."

"Yeah," he said, "old Al like the sauce. That's what killed him. The nutty coot must have had a snootful. Just drove right off the bluff into the river."

"The bluff?"

"A place we call Lovers' Leap. Out of town a ways."

"How did you spot the truck? Someone call it in?"

"Hell, no," he said. "Goodfellow saw him go over. Had been tailing him, see. Coburn was driving like a maniac, all over the road, and Ronnie was trying to catch up, figuring to pull him over. Had the siren and lights going: everything. But before he could stop him, Al Coburn drives right off the edge. There's been talk of putting a guard rail up there, but no one's got around to it."

I shook my head sadly. "Hell of a thing. Where is he now? The body, I mean."

"Oh, he's on ice at Markham's funeral parlor. We're trying to locate next of kin."

"You do an autopsy in cases like that?" I asked him casually.

"Well, hell yes," he said indignantly. "What do you think? Bobby Markham is our local coroner. He's a good old boy."

"Coburn drowned?"

"Oh sure. Lungs full of water."

"Was he banged up?"

"Plenty. Listen, that's more'n a fifty-foot drop from Lovers' Leap. He was a mess. Head all mashed in. Well, you'd expect that. Probably hit it on the wheel or windshield when he smacked the water."

I didn't say anything. He looked at me curiously. Something wary came into those hard eyes. I knew he was wondering if he had said too much.

"What's your interest in this, Todd?"

"Well, like I said, I knew the guy. So when I heard he was dead, it really shook me."

"Uh-huh," he said.

"Also," I said, "something silly. I'm embarrassed to mention it."

He leaned back in his swivel chair, clasped his hands across his belly. He regarded me gravely.

"Why, you go right ahead," he said. "No need to be embarrassed. I hear a lot of things right here in this office, and it never gets past these walls."

I bet.

"Well," I said hesitantly, "I had a drink with Al Coburn yesterday morning. A beer or two. Then afterward, he wanted me to see where he lived. The flagpole and all."

"Oh yeah," he laughed. "Old Al's flagpole. That's a joke."

"Yes," I said. "Anyway, I own a gold cigarette lighter. Not very valuable. Cost maybe twenty, thirty bucks. But it's got a sentimental value—you know?"

"Woman give it to you?" he said, winking.

I tried a short laugh.

"Well . . . yeah. You know how it is. Anyhow, I remember using it while I was in Al Coburn's pickup. And then, a few hours later, after I got back to the Inn, it was missing. So I figure I dropped it in Coburn's truck. Maybe on the floor or back between the cushions. I was wondering where Coburn's pickup is now?"

"The truck?" he said, surprised. "Right now? Why it's out back in our garage. We're holding it until everything gets straightened out on his estate and will and all. You think your gold cigarette lighter is in the truck?"

"I figured it might be."

"I doubt it," he said, staring at me. "When we went down to get Coburn out, we had to pry open the doors, and the river just swept through. Then we winched the truck out of the water. Nothing in it by then. Hell, even the back seat cushion was gone."

"Well," I said haltingly, "I was hoping you'd let me take a quick look . . ."

"Why not?" he said cheerily, jerking to his feet. "Never can tell, can you? Maybe your gold cigarette lighter got caught in a corner somewhere. Let's go see."

"Oh, don't bother yourself," I said hastily. "Just tell me where it is. I'll take a quick look and be on my way. I imagine you have to stick close to the phones and all."

"No bother," he said, his mouth smiling but not his eyes. "Nothing happens in Coburn on a Sunday. Let's go."

I had pushed it as far as I thought I could. So I had to follow him out of the station house, around to a corrugated steel garage. He unlocked the padlock, and we went in.

Al Coburn's pickup truck was a sad-looking mess. Front end crumpled, windshield starred with cracks, doors sprung, seat cushion soaked, steering column bent.

And the glove compartment open and empty.

"Stinks, don't it?" Aikens said.

"Sure does," I said.

I made a show of searching for a cigarette lighter. The constable leaned against the wall of the garage and watched me with iron eyes.

I crawled out of the sodden wreck, rubbing my palms.

"Ahh, the hell with it," I said. "It's not here."

"I told you," he said. "Nothing's there. The river got it all."

"I suppose," I said dolefully. "Well, thanks very much for your trouble."

"No trouble," he said. "I'm just sorry you didn't find what you were looking for."

"Yes," I said, "too bad. Well, I guess I'll be on my way."

"Leaving Coburn soon?"

That's what Julie Thorndecker had asked me. And in the same hopeful tone.

"Probably tomorrow morning," I said

"Stop by and see us again. Happy to have you."

"Thanks. I might do just that."

We grinned at each other. A brace of liars.

Nothing's ever neat. The investigator who's supposed to twirl a tight ball of linguine with fork and spoon usually ends up with a ragged clump with loose ends. That's what I had: loose ends.

I didn't know how it was managed, but I knew Al Coburn never drove off that cliff deliberately. His truck was nudged over, or driven over with a live driver leaping out at the last second, leaving an unconscious or dead Al Coburn in the cab. An experienced medical examiner could have proved those head injuries were inflicted before drowning, but not Good Old Boy Bobby Markham.

Maybe the glove compartment had been searched before the truck was pushed over. Maybe after it was hauled out. Or maybe the river really did sweep it clean. It didn't make any difference. I knew I'd never see the letter Ernie Scoggins had left with Al Coburn.

I could guess what was in the letter. I could guess at a lot of things. Loose ends. But in any kind of investigative work, you've got to live with that. If you're the tidy type, take up bookkeeping. Business ledgers have to balance. Nothing balances in a criminal investigation. You never learn it all. There's always something missing.

I got out to Red Dog Betty's about 3:30 in the afternoon. That crawl through Al Coburn's death truck had affected me more than I anticipated. When I held out a hand, the fingertips vibrated like tuning forks. So I went to Betty's, for a drink, something to eat, just to sit quietly awhile and cure the shakes.

This time I parked as close to the entrance to the roadhouse as I could get, hoping it would discourage the Mad Tire Slasher from striking again. I hung up hat and coat, sat at the bar, ordered a vodka gimlet. I asked for Betty, but the black bartender said she wouldn't be in until the evening.

The barroom and dining areas had that peaceful, dimmed, hushed atmosphere of most watering places on a Sunday afternoon. No one was playing the juke. No voices were raised. The laughter was low-pitched and rueful. Everyone ruminating on their excesses of the night before. I knew that Sunday afternoon mood; you move carefully and slowly, abjure loud sounds and unseemly mirth. The ambience is almost church-like.

I must have been wearing my head hanging low, because I saw them for the first time when I straightened up and looked in the big, misty mirror behind the bar. Sitting in an upholstered banquette on the other side of the room were Nurse Stella Beecham, editor Agatha Binder, and the cheerleader type from the *Sentinel* office, Sue Ann. Miss Dimples was seated between the two big women. They looked like massive walnut bookends pressing one slim volume of fairy tales.

If they had noticed me come in, they gave no sign. They might have been ignoring me, but it seemed more likely they were too busy with their own affairs to pay any attention to anyone else. Beecham was wearing her nurse's uniform, without cap. Binder had a clean pair of painters' overalls over a black turtleneck. The lollipop between them had on a pink angora sweater with a long rope of pearls. She kept nibbling on the pearls as the two gorgons kept up a running conversation across her. The older women were drinking beer from bottles, scorning their glasses. The young girl had an orange-colored concoction, with a lot of fruit and two long straws.

I stole a glance now and then, wondering what the relationship of that trio was, and who did what to whom. About 3:45, Nurse Beecham lurched to her feet and moved out from behind the table. She smoothed down her skirt. That was one hefty bimbo. Get an injection in the rump from her, and the needle was likely to go in the right buttock and come out the left.

She said something to the other women, bent to kiss them both. She took a plastic raincoat and hat from the rack, waved once, and was gone. I figured she was heading for Crittenden Hall, for the four-to-midnight shift.

The moment the nurse disappeared, Agatha Binder turned slightly sideways and slid one meaty arm across Sue Ann's shoulders. She leaned forward and whispered something in the girl's ear. They both laughed. Chums.

I saw Miss Dimples' drink was getting low, and the editor was tilting her beer bottle high to drain the last few drops. I got off my barstool and went smiling toward them.

"Hi!" I said brightly. "How are you ladies?"

They looked up in surprise. The nubile one with some interest, Agatha Binder with something less than delight.

"Well, well," the editor said, "if it isn't supersnoop. What are you doing here, Todd?"

"Recovering," I said. "May I buy you two a drink?"

"I guess so," she said slowly. "Why not?"

"Won't you join us?" Sue Ann piped up, and I could have kissed her.

I moved onto the seat vacated by Stella Beecham, ignoring Binder's frown. I signaled the waitress for another round, and offered cigarettes. We all lighted up, and chatted animatedly about the weather until the drinks arrived.

"When are you planning on leaving Coburn?" Agatha asked. Same question. Same hopeful tone. It's so nice to be well-liked.

"Probably tomorrow morning."

"Find out all you need to know about Thorndecker?"

"More," I said.

We sampled our drinks. Sue Ann said, "Oh, wow," and blushed. She was so fresh, so limpid and juicy, that I think if you embraced her tightly, she'd squirt mead.

"Well, he's quite a man, Thorndecker," the editor said. "Very convincing."

"Oh yes," I said. "Very. I'll bet he could get away with murder."

She looked at me sharply. "What's that supposed to mean?"

"Figure of speech," I said.

She continued to stare at me. Something came into her eyes, something knowing.

"This is yummy," Miss Dimples said, sucking happily at her straws. Lucky straws.

"He's not going to get the grant, is he?" Binder demanded.

"When is your next edition coming out?" I asked her.

"We just closed. Next edition is next week."

"Then I can tell you," I said. "No, he's not going to get the grant. Not if I have anything to do with it, he isn't."

"Well . . . what the hell," she said. "I figured you'd find out."

"You mean you knew?"

"Oh Christ, Todd, everyone in Coburn knows."

I took a deep breath, sat back, stared into the air.

"You're incredible," I said. "You and everyone else in Coburn. Something like this going on under your noses, and you just shrug it off. I don't understand you people."

"Sometimes I have a Tom Collins," the creampuff giggled, "but I really like this better."

"You know, Todd, you're an obnoxious bastard," the editor said. "You come up here with your snobbish, big-city, sharper-than-thou attitude. You stick your beezer in matters that don't concern you. And then you condemn Thorndecker because of the way his wife acts. Now I ask you: is that fair?"

My stomach flopped over. Then I just spun away. My hand stopped halfway to my glass. I tried to slow my whirling thoughts. I had a sense of total disorientation. It took awhile. A minute or two. Then things began to harden, come into focus again. I understood: Agatha Binder and I had been talking about two different things.

"I tried beer a few times," Miss Dimples volunteered, "but I really didn't like it. Too bitter."

I drained my glass, motioned toward their glasses.

"Ready for another?" I asked hoarsely.

"Hell, yes," the editor said roughly.

Sue Ann said, "Whee!"

By the time my fresh gimlet arrived, I had it organized: how I would handle it.

"You think Thorndecker knows about it?" I asked cautiously.

"Oh hell," she said, "he has to know. Those trips to Albany and Boston and New York. Once to Washington. To talk to potential sponsors. Big-money guys who might dip into their wallets for the Crittenden Research Laboratory. Then Thorndecker would come back alone. Julie would return a day or two or a week later. And a day or two after *that*, the contribution would come in. It wasn't hard to figure out what was going on."

I nodded as if I was aware of this all along.

"I knew you'd catch on," Agatha Binder said morosely. "Listen, is what they do so bad? It's in a good cause. You talk like it's a federal case or something."

"No," I said thoughtfully, "it's not so bad. Maybe a little shabby, but I suppose it's done in other businesses every day in the week."

"You better believe it," she said, nodding violently.

"I'm hungry," Sue Ann said.

I mulled over this new information. An angle I hadn't even considered. Was this the "conspiracy" that all the Coburnites shared? Pretty sleazy stuff.

"A very complex woman, our Julie," I said wonderingly. "I'm just beginning to appreciate her. My first take was of a bitch with a libido bigger than all outdoors. But now it seems there's more to her than that. Why does she do it, Agatha? Is it the sex? Or just the money to keep her lifestyle intact?"

Binder punched gently at the tip of her nose with one knuckle. Then she took a deep swig from her beer bottle.

"When are we going to eat?" Sue Ann asked plaintively.

"A little of both," the big woman said. "But mostly because she loves Thorndecker. *Loves* him! And believes in him, in his work. She worships him, thinks he's a saint. She's really a very loving, sacrificing woman."

I literally threw up my hands.

"It's a masquerade," I said hopelessly. "Everyone wearing masks. Do you all take them off at midnight?"

"You come up here from the big city and think you're dealing with simple country bumpkins. It's obvious in your attitude, in your sneers and jokes. Then you act like we've been misleading you when it turns out that we're not cardboard cutouts, that we're as screwed-up as everyone else."

I thought about that for a few moments.

"You may be right," I admitted. "To some extent. I've underestimated most of the people here I've met; that's true. But not Thorndecker. I never sold him short."

"Oh, he's one of a kind," Agatha Binder said. "You can't judge him by ordinary standards."

"I don't," I said. "I just wonder what kind of a man would endure what his wife is doing. Encourage her to do it. Or at least accept it without objection."

"His work comes first," the editor told me. "That's his only test. Is it good or bad for his work?"

"A monomaniac?" I suggested

"Or a genius," she said.

"Obsessed?" I said.

"Or committed," she said.

"Insensitive?" I said.

"Or totally dedicated," she said.

Then we were both silent, neither of us certain.

"Maybe a hamburger," Sue Ann said dreamily. "A cheeseburger. With relish."

I sighed and stood up.

"Feed the child," I told Agatha Binder, "before she collapses. Thanks for the talk."

"Thanks for the drinks."

Unexpectedly, she thrust out a hand, hard and horny. I shook it. I won't say we parted friends, but I think there was some respect.

I went back to the bar. I had intended to have something to eat there, but I decided to return to the Coburn Inn. I didn't want to look into a misty bar mirror and see Agatha Binder sticking her tongue in Sue Ann's ear. Then I knew I was getting old. It upset me to see things in public that people used to do only in bedrooms after the lights were out and the kids were asleep.

On the drive back to the Coburn Inn, I tried not to think of what the editor had told me about Julie Thorndecker. But it bothered me that what she had revealed came as such an unexpected shock. The whole Thorndecker business had been like that: unfolding slowly and painfully. I wondered if I stayed in Coburn another week, a month, a year, if it would all be disclosed to me, right down to the final surprise.

Agatha Binder's accusation rankled because it was true. Partly true. I *had* assumed that these one-horse-town denizens were a different species, made of simpler, evident stuff, their motives easily perceived, their passions casually analyzed. There was hardly one of them who hadn't proved my snobbery just by being human, displaying all the mysterious, inexplicable quirks of which humans are capable. I should have known better.

The dining room at the Coburn Inn was moderately crowded; I ate in the bar. Had two musty ales with broiled porkchops, apple sauce, a baked potato, green beans with a bacon sauce, and rum cake for dessert. Well, listen, the fast I vowed that morning had lasted almost nine hours. After all, I *am* a growing boy.

Went up to my room and began packing. I wasn't planning to leave until the following morning, but I was nagged by the feeling that after my criminal enterprise scheduled for 2:00 A.M., I might want to make a quick getaway. So I packed, leaving the two suitcases and briefcase open.

Then, using hotel stationery, I wrote out a precis of the Thorndecker affair. I tried to keep it brief and succinct, but included everything I had discovered, and what I hadn't discovered: Thorndecker's motive for infecting his nursing home patients with cancer.

It ran to five pages, front and back, before I had finished. I read it over, made a few minor corrections, then sealed it in an envelope addressed to myself at the address of the Bingham Foundation in New York. I remembered what Thorndecker had said about keeping precise, complete notes "in case of an accident." Then someone else could carry on the work.

If there was no "accident" (like driving off Lovers' Leap), I could destroy the manuscript when I got back to the office on Tuesday. If, for some reason, I didn't return, someone at the ofice would open the letter. And know.

Put on coat and hat again, went down to the lobby, bought stamps at the machine on the cigar counter.

"Mail that for you, Mr. Todd?" the baldy behind the desk sang out.

"No, thanks," I said. "I'll take a walk and drop it in the slot at the post office."

"Wet walking," he said.

"The farmers need it," I said.

I liked saying that. A Coburn tradition. A hurricane could hit, decimating Coburn and half of New York State, and someone was sure to crawl painfully from the wreckage, look up at the slashing, ripping sky, and croak, "Well, the farmers need it."

When I got back to Room 3-F, I shucked off wet coat, wet hat, wet boots, and fell into bed. I had heard that if you fall asleep concentrating on the hour you want to awake, you'll get up on the dot. So I tried it, thinking "Get up at midnight, get up at midnight, get up at midnight." Then I conked off.

I awoke at 1:15, which isn't bad, considering it was my first try. But I did have to rush, making sure I was dressed completely in black, sneaking down the stairs, waiting until the lobby was deserted and the desk clerk was in the back office. Then I strode swiftly out to the parking lot. Still raining. I figured that was a plus. That roaming shotgun-armed guard with the attack dog would probably be inside someplace dry and warm, reading *Penthouse* or *The Wall Street Journal*. Something like that.

I drove out to Crittenden at a moderate speed. I didn't want to be late for my rendezvous with Mary Thorndecker—I doubted if her nerves would endure the wait—but I didn't want to be too early either, chancing discovery by one of the guards.

I cruised slowly by the gate. There were outside lights burning on the portico of Crittenden Hall, and I could see Julie Thorndecker's blue MGB parked on the gravel driveway. It seemed odd that the car wasn't garaged on a night like that.

There were a few lights burning on the main floor of the nursing home, none on the second and third floors. No lights in the laboratory. There was a dim bluish glow (TV?) coming from the gatekeeper's hut.

I passed the gate, followed the fence until it began to curve around toward the cemetery. Then I pulled well off the road, doused my lights, waited until my eyes became accustomed to the dark. I opened the car door cautiously, stepped out, closed the door but left it unlatched.

Gathered my equipment: stepladder, clothesline, sash weight, flashlight. I stuck the flash and weight in my hip pockets. My pants almost fell down.

Carried ladder and rope across the road to the fence. Still raining. Not hard, but steadily. Straight down. A rain that soaked and chilled.

Tied one end of the rope to the top of the aluminum stepladder. Threw the loose coils over the fence. Then I set up the ladder carefully, making sure the braces were locked. I climbed up.

You've seen movies where James Bond or one of his imitators goes over a high fence by leaping, grabbing the top, pulling himself up and over. Try that little trick some time. Instant hernia. It's a lot easier to carry your own stepladder.

I stood on the top rung, swung one leg over the fence, straddled, swung the other leg over and jumped, remembering to land with flexed knees. Then I pulled my rope, and the ladder came up the outside of the fence. It took me a few minutes to jiggle it over, but eventually it dropped down inside. I caught it, and set it up against the inside of the fence, ready for a quick escape.

Now I was inside the grounds. I had selected a spot where the bulk of Crittenden Hall came between me and the gate guard. I hoped I was right about the roving sentry keeping out of the rain. But just in case, I crouched a few moments in the absolute dark and strained to hear. A silence like thunder. No, not quite. I heard the rain hitting my hat, coat, the ground. But other than that—nothing.

Moved warily toward the nursing home and its outbuildings. Didn't use my flash, so twice I blundered into trees. Didn't even curse. Did when I tripped over a fallen branch and fell to my hands and knees.

Figure it took me at least fifteen minutes to work my way slowly around Crittenden Hall. A light came on briefly on the second floor, then went out. I hoped that was Mary Thorndecker with the keys, leaving the apartment of Dr. Kenneth Draper, starting down to meet me.

Sudden angry barking of a dog. I froze. The barking continued for a minute or two, then ended as abruptly as it began. I moved again. Slowly, slowly. Trying to peer through the black, through the rain. Nightglow was practically nonexistent. I was in a tunnel. Down a well. Buried.

Came up to Crittenden Hall. Eased around it as noiselessly as I could, fingertips lightly brushing the brick. Reflected that I was no outdoorsman. Not trained for this open-country stuff. I could navigate a Ninth Avenue tenement better than I could a copse, stubbled field, meadowland, or hills.

Found the covered steps leading down from the nursing home to the back door of the Crittenden Research Laboratory. Kept off the paved walk, but moved in a crouch alongside it. Tried to avoid crashing through shrubbery or kicking the slate border.

Finally, at the door. No Mary. I hunkered down. Put flashlight under the skirt of my trenchcoat. Risked quick look at my wristwatch. About 2:20. Sudden fear that I had missed her at 2:15, and she, spooked, had gone back to Draper's bed.

Waited. Hoping.

Heard something. Creak of door opening. Pause. Soft thud as it closed. Wiped my eyes continually, peering up the hill. Saw something lighter than the night floating down. Tensed. Watched it draw closer.

Mary Thorndecker. In white nightgown partly covered by old-fashioned flannel bathrobe cinched with a cord. Heavy brogues on bare feet. She was carrying the big umbrella, open. Beautiful. But I didn't feel like laughing.

She almost fell over me. I straightened up. She jerked back. I grabbed her, palm over her mouth. Then she steadied. I released her. Shoved my face close to hers under the umbrella.

"The keys?" I whispered.

Felt rather than saw her nod. Rings of keys pressed into my hand. I put my lips close to her ear.

"I'm going to give you the flashlight. Before you switch it on, put your fingers across the lens. We just want a dim light. A glimmer. Just enough to show the lock. Understand?"

She did just fine. We stood huddled at the door, blocking what we were doing with our bodies. She held the light, her fingers reducing the beam to a reddish glow. I tried three keys before the fourth slid in. I was about to turn it, then stopped. Still.

"What is it?" she said.

There had to be an alarm.

I left the keys in the lock. Took her hands in mine, turned the flashlight slowly upward along the jamb of the door. There, at the top, another lock taking a barrel key.

"Alarm," I breathed in her ear. "Got to be turned off first before we open the door. There's a barrel key on the ring. Let's hope it—"

At that moment. Precisely. Two sounds. Muffled. Indoors. From the nursing home. They were not snaps. More like dulled booms.

"What—?" Mary said.

I put a hand on her arm. We waited. In a few seconds, four more hard sounds in rapid succession. These were louder, more like cracks. They sounded closer.

"Handgun," I said in my normal voice, knowing it had all come apart. "Heavy caliber. You stay here."

"No," she said, "I'm going with you."

I grabbed the flashlight from her. Took her hand. We went stumbling up the walk, the open umbrella ballooning behind us, a puddle of light jerking along at our feet.

Reached the back door of Crittenden Hall. Both of us panting.

The door was locked.

"The keys," I said.

"You left them in the door of the lab."

"What a swell burglar I am," I said bitterly.

I took out the sash weight, smashed the pane of glass closest to the lock. Hammered the shards away from the frame so I wouldn't slit my wrists. Then reached in, opened the door.

We ran into a brightly lighted corridor. Chaos. Alarms and excursions. Shouts and screams. People in white running, running. All toward the main entrance hall.

And a shriek that shivered me. A wailing shriek, on and on. Man or woman? I couldn't tell.

"That's Edward," Mary Thorndecker gasped. "Edward!"

We dashed like the others. Debouched into the lobby. Joined the jostling mob. All circling. Looking down.

The shriek was all wail now. A weeping siren. It rose and fell in hysterical ululation.

"Shut him up!" someone yelled. "Slap him!"

I pushed roughly through, Mary following. No one saw us. Everyone was looking at what lay on the marble floor, at the foot of the wide staircase.

They must have been shot while coming down the stairs. Then they fell the rest of the way. Ronnie Goodfellow, clad in mufti, hit first. He was prone, face turned to one side. His right leg snapped under him when he hit. A jagged splinter of bone stuck out through the cloth.

Julie Thorndecker had landed near him, on her back. One side of her head was gone. Her arms were thrown wide. Her coat was flung open, skirt hiked up. One naked, pale, smooth, beautiful leg was lying across Goodfellow's neck.

Two pigskin suitcases had fallen with them. One had snapped open on impact, the contents cascading across the floor. Blue panties, brassieres, a small jewel case, negligees, the silver evening pajamas and sandals she had been wearing the night I met her.

I don't think the first two shots killed them. But then he followed them down and emptied his gun. The blood was pooling, beginning to merge, his and hers, and trickle across the marble tiles.

Like the others, I stared at the still, smashed dolls. Dr. Draper knelt alongside, wearing a raincoat, bare shins sticking out. He fumbled for a pulse at their throats, but it was hopeless. Everyone knew it. He knew it. But his trembling fingers still searched.

When I first glimpsed them, Edward Thorndecker was sitting cross-legged on the floor, his stepmother's torn head in his lap. His head was back, face wrung, and that shrieking wail came out of his open mouth continuously, as if he needed no breath but only grief to produce that terrifying scream. Finally, hands reached down, pulled him away, took him off somewhere. They half-carried him, his toes dragging on the marble. The shriek faded, faded, then stopped suddenly.

Surprisingly, Mary Thorndecker took charge.

"Don't touch anything," she commanded in a loud, sharp voice. "Kenneth, you call the police. At once. Did anyone see where he went?"

Where he went. There was no doubt in her mind, nor in anyone else's, who had done this slaughter.

The gorilla-butler, with a shoulder holster and gun strapped across a soiled T-shirt, pushed forward.

"Out the back door, Miss Thorndecker," he said. "I heard the shots and come running. I seen him. Out the back door and onto the grounds."

Mary Thorndecker nodded. "Alma, you and Fred see to the patients. Some of them may have heard the commotion. Calm them down. Sedation, if needed. The rest of you get your hats and coats. Bring flashlights and lanterns. We must find him. He is not a well man."

I pondered that: "He is not a well man." And Hitler was "disturbed."

It took us maybe ten minutes to get organized. Mary Thorndecker ordered us around like a master sergeant. I couldn't fault her. She got us spread out on a ragged line, at about fifteen-foot intervals. Most of the beaters had flashlights or lanterns. One guy had a kerosene lamp. And all the interior lights of Crittenden Hall were switched on, cutting the gloom in the immediate vicinity.

At a command from Mary, we started moving forward, trying to keep the line intact. Once we were out of the Hall's glow, the dark night closed in. Then all I could see was a bobbing, wavering necklace of weak lights, shimmering in the rain.

"Thorndecker!" someone called in a quavery voice, and the others took up the cry.

"Thorndecker!"

"Thorndecker!"

"Thorndecker!"

Then it became a long, wailing moan: "Thorndecker!" And we all, scarcely sane, went stumbling across the slick, frosted fields, lights jerking up and down, calling his name again and again, echoing his name, while the cold rain pelted a black and ruined world.

Oh yes, we found him. We had passed through the cemetery and were slowly, fearfully working the stand of bare trees on the far side. There was a shout, the wild swinging of a lantern in wide circles. We all ran, breathless and blundering, to the spot. We clustered.

He lay on his back, spreadeagled, face turned to the falling sky. He wore only pajama pants. He was almost completely bald; only a few wet tufts of hair were left. Bare feet were bruised and bleeding. His eyes were open. He was dead.

Arms, shoulders, torso, neck, face, scalp—all of him exposed to view was studded with suppurating tumors. Great blooms of red and yellow and purple. Rotting excrescences that seemed to have a vigorous life of their own, immortal, sprouting from his cooling flesh. They had soft, dough-like centers, and browned, crusted petals.

There was hardly an inch of him not choked by cancerous growths. Eyes bulging with necrosis, mouth twisted, nose lumped, the limbs swollen with decay, trunk gnarled with great chunks of putrescent matter. The smell was of deep earth, swamp, and the grave.

The trembling circles of light exposed the horror he had become. I heard a sobbing, was conscious of people turning away to retch. Someone began to murmur a prayer. But I was stone, transfixed, looking down at what was left of Dr. Telford Gordon Thorndecker, wanting desperately to find meaning, and finding nothing.

The butler-thug volunteered to remain with the body. The rest of us wandered back to Crittenden Hall. We moved, I noted, in a tight group, seeking the close presence of others to help hold back the darkness, to prove that live warmth still existed in the world. No one spoke. Silently we filed through the cemetery, gravestones glistening in our lights, and straggled across the stubbled fields to the brightness of Crittenden Hall, a beacon in the black.

A half-hour later I was seated with Dr. Kenneth Draper in Thorndecker's private office in the Crittenden Research Laboratory. I had left Mary Thorndecker to deal with the police. I had latched onto Draper—literally. I took him by the arm and would not let him go, not for an instant, I am not certain if any of us were acting rationally that night.

I marched Draper upstairs to his apartment and let him dress. Then I pulled him into that marvelous Thorndecker sitting room where I swiped a bottle of brandy, and thought nothing of it. I made Draper gulp a mouthful, because his face was melting white wax, and he was moving like an invalid. I took him and the brandy back to the research lab. Found the keys, turned off the alarm, opened the door, turned on the lights.

In Thorndecker's private lab, I pushed Draper into the chair behind the desk. I peeled off my soaked hat and coat. I found paper cups, and poured us each a deep shot of brandy. Some color came back into his face, but he was racked with sudden shivers, and once his teeth chattered.

Thorndecker's journal, the one he had been working on the last time I saw him alive, still lay open on the desk. I shoved it toward Draper.

"When did it start?" I asked him.

"What will they do to me?" he said in a dulled voice. "Will I go to jail?"

I could have told him that if he kept his mouth shut, probably nothing would happen to him. How could they prove all those Crittenden Hall patients had died other than natural deaths? I figured the Coburn cops would be satisfied that Thorndecker had killed his wife and her lover, then died himself from terminal cancer. It was neat, and it closed out a file. They wouldn't go digging any deeper.

But I wanted to keep Draper guilty and quivering.

"It depends," I told him stolidly, "on how willing you are to cooperate. If you spell it out for me, I'll put in a good word for you."

I didn't tell him that I had about as much clout with the Coburn cops as I do with the Joint Chiefs of Staff.

"All right," I said, in the hardest voice I could manage, "when did it start?"

He raised a tear-streaked face. I poured him another brandy, and he choked it down. He stared at the ledger, then began turning the pages listlessly.

"You mean the—the experiments?"

"Yes," I said, trying not to yell at him, "the experiments."

"A long time ago," he said, in a voice so low I had to crane forward to hear him. "Before we came to Crittenden. We started with normal mammalian cells. Then concentrated only on normal human cells. We were looking for the cellular clock that causes aging and death. Dr. Thorndecker believed that—"

"I know what Thorndecker believed," I interrupted him. "Did you believe in the cellular clock theory?"

He looked at me in astonishment.

"Of course," he said. "If Dr. Thorndecker believed in it, I *had* to believe. He was a great man. He was—"

"I know," I said, "a genius. But you didn't find it? The cellular clock?"

"No. Hundreds of experiments. Thousands of man-hours. It's extremely difficult, working with normal human cells *in vitro*. Limited doublings. The cells become less differentiated, useless for our research. We confirmed conclusively that the cell determines longevity, but we couldn't isolate the factor. It was—well, frustrating. During that period, Dr. Thorndecker became very demanding, very insistent. Hard to deal with. He could not endure failure."

"This was before you came to Crittenden?"

"Yes. Dr. Thorndecker's first wife was still alive. Most of our research was being done on small grants. But we had no exciting results to publish. The grant money ran out. But then Dr. Thorndecker's first wife was killed in an accident, and he was able to buy Crittenden and establish this laboratory."

"Yes," I said, "I know. And then?"

"We had been here only a short time, when one night he woke me up. Very excited. Laughing and happy. He said he had solved our basic problem. He said he knew now what our approach should be. It was an inspiration. Only a genius could have thought of it. A quantum leap of pure reason."

"And what was that?" I asked.

"We couldn't keep normal cells viable *in vitro*. Not for long. But cancer cells flourished, reproduced endlessly. Apparently they were immortal. Dr. Thorndecker's idea was to forget about finding the factor in normal cells that caused senescence and death, and concentrate on finding the factor in abnormal cells that caused such wild proliferation."

"The factor that made cancer cells immortal *in vitro*?"

"Yes."

I took a deep breath. There it was.

I knew what was coming. I could have stopped right there. But I wanted him to spell it out. Maybe I wanted to rub his nose in it.

"And you found the factor?"

He nodded. "But the problem was how to separate the longevity effect from the fatal effect. You understand? The cancer cells themselves simply grew and grew—forever, if you allowed them to. But they killed the host organism. So all our research turned to filtering out the immortality factor, purifying it in effect, so that the host's normal cells could absorb it and continue to grow indefinitely without harm. Very complex chemistry."

"It didn't work?" I said.

"It did, it did!" he cried, with the first flash of spirit he had exhibited. "I can show you mice and guinea pigs in the basement that have lived three times as long as they would normally. And they're absolutely cancer-free. And we have one dog that, in human terms, is almost two hundred years old."

"But no success with chimps?"

"No. None."

"So this essence of yours, this injection, wasn't always successful?"

"No, it wasn't. But animals are notoriously difficult to work with. Sometimes they reject the most virulent cancer cells. Sometimes a strain of rats supposed to be leukemia-prone will prove to be immune. Animals do not always give conclusive results, insofar as their reactions can be applied to humans. And animal experimentation is expensive, and takes time."

I leaned back and lighted a cigarette. Like most specialists, he tended to lecture when riding his own hobbyhorse. I probably knew as much about nuclear physics as he did, but bio-medicine was his world; he was confident there.

"Animal experimentation is expensive," I said, repeating his last words, "and it takes time. And Thorndecker never had enough money for what he wanted to do. But more than that, he didn't have the time. He was a man in a hurry, wasn't he? Impatient? Anxious for the fame the published discovery would bring?"

"He was convinced we were on the right track," Dr. Draper said. "I was, too. We were so close, so close. We had those animals in the basement to prove it—the ones who had doubled and tripled their normal life spans."

I rose and began to pace back and forth in front of the desk. Somehow I found myself with a lighted cigarette in each hand, and stubbed one out.

"All right," I said, "now we come to the worm in the apple. Whose idea was it to try the stuff on humans?"

He lowered his head and wouldn't answer.

"You don't have to tell me," I said. "I know it was Thorndecker's idea; you don't have the balls for it. I'll bet I even know how he convinced you. 'Look, Draper,' he said, 'there can be no progress without pain. Sacrifices must be made. We must dare all. Those patients in Crittenden Hall are terminal cases. How long do they have—weeks, months, a year? If we are unsuccessful, we'll only be shortening slightly their life span. And think of what they will be contributing! We can give their remaining days meaning. Think of that, Draper. We can make their deaths meaningful!' Isn't that what Thorndecker told you? Something like that?"

He nodded slowly. "Yes. Something like that."

"So you selected the ones you thought were terminal?"

"They were, they were!"

"You *thought* they were. You weren't sure. Doctors can never be sure; you know that. There are unexpected remissions. The patient recovers for no explainable reason. One day he wakes up cured. It happens. You know it happens."

He poured himself another cup of brandy, raised it to his pale lips with a shaking hand. Some of the brandy spilled down his chin, dripped onto his shirtfront.

"How many?" I demanded. "How many did you kill?"

"I don't know," he muttered. "We didn't keep—"

"Don't give me that shit!" I screamed at him. "Thorndecker kept very complete, precise records, and you know it. You want me to grab up this journal and all the others for the past three years, and take them to the cops? You think you can stop me? Try it! Just try it! How many?"

"Eleven," he said in a choked voice.

"And none survived?"

"No," he said. Then, brightly: "But the survival time was lengthening. We were certain we were on the right track. Dr. Thorndecker was convinced of it. I was, too. We had purified the extract. A week ago we were absolutely certain we had made the breakthrough."

"Why didn't you try it on another patient?"

Draper groaned.

"Don't you understand? If it had succeeded, how could Thorndecker publish the results? Admit experiments on humans? Fatal experiments? With no informed consent agreements? They'd have crucified him. The only way was to inject himself. He was so sure, so sure. He laughed about it. 'The elixir of life, Draper,' he told me. 'I'll live forever!' That's what he told me."

I marveled at the man, at Thorndecker. To have such confidence, such absolute faith in your own destiny, such pride in your own skill. To dare death to prove it.

"What went wrong?" I asked Draper.

"I don't know," he said, shaking his head. "Initially, everything was fine. Then, in a short time, the first symptoms appeared. Hair falling out, skin blotches that signaled the beginning of tumors, sudden loss of weight, loss of appetite, other things . . ."

"Thorndecker knew?"

"Oh yes. He knew."

"How did he react?"

"We've spent the last few days working around the clock, trying to discover what went wrong, why the final essence not only didn't extend life but produced such rapid tumor germination."

"Did you find out what it was?"

"No, not definitely. It may have been in the purifying process. It may have been something else. It could have been Dr. Thorndecker's personal immunochemistry. I just don't know."

"Julie Thorndecker was aware of this?"

"She was aware that her husband was fatally ill, yes."

"Was she aware of the experiments you two ghouls were carrying out?"

"No. Yes. I don't know."

I sat down again. I slumped, so exhausted that I could have slept just by closing my eyes.

Dazed, not thinking straight, I wondered what I could do about this guy. I could have him racked up on charges, but I knew a smart lawyer could easily get him off. Do what? Exhume the corpses and find they had died of cancer? He'd never spend a day in jail. There might be a professional inquiry, and his career would be ruined. But so what? I wanted this prick to *suffer*.

"What about Ernie Scoggins?" I asked him dully. "Was Scoggins blackmailing Thorndecker?"

"I don't know anything about that," he mumbled.

"You goddamned shitwit!" I yelled at him. "You were Thorndecker's righthand man. You know about it all right."

"He got a letter from Scoggins," Draper said hastily, frightened. "Not mailed. A note shoved under his door. Scoggins was working here at the time. He helped out with the animals occasionally. And when we had burials in the cemetery. He guessed something was wrong. All those tumorous corpses . . ."

"Did he have any hard evidence of what was going down?"

"He stole one of Dr. Thorndecker's journals. It was—ah—incriminating."

"Then what happened?"

"I don't know. Dr. Thorndecker said he'd take care of it, not to worry."

"And he got the journal back?"

"Yes."

"And Ernie Scoggins disappeared."

"Dr. Thorndecker had nothing to do with that," he said hotly.

"Maybe not personally," I said. "But he had his wife persuade Constable Ronnie Goodfellow to take care of it. She persuaded him all right. It wasn't too difficult. She could be a very persuasive lady. And I suppose the same thing happened when it turned out that old Al Coburn had a letter from Scoggins recounting what was in Thorndecker's journal. So Al Coburn had to be eliminated, and the letter recovered. Constable Goodfellow went to work again, and did his usual efficient job."

"I don't know anything about Al Coburn," Draper insisted, in such an aggrieved tone that he might have been telling the truth.

I couldn't think of anything else to ask. Not only was my body weary, but my brain felt flogged. Too many strong sensations for one night. Too many electric images. The circuits were overloaded.

I stood up, pulled on my sodden coat and hat, preparing to leave. I had a sudden love for that bed in Room 3-F.

"What's going to happen to me?" Dr. Kenneth Draper asked.

"Keep your mouth shut," I advised him resignedly. "Tell no one what you've told me. Except Mary Thorndecker."

"I can't tell her," he groaned.

"If you don't," I said, "I will. Besides, she's already guessed most of it."

"She'll hate me," he said.

"Oh, I think she'll find it in her heart to forgive you," I told him. "Just like Lord Jesus. Also, she'll probably inherit, and she'll need someone to help her run Crittenden Hall and the lab."

He brightened a little at that.

"Maybe she will forgive me," he said, almost to himself. "After all, I just did what Dr. Thorndecker told me to."

"I know," I said. "You just obeyed orders. Now where have I heard that before? Goodnight, Dr. Draper. I hope you and Mary Thorndecker get married and live happily ever after."

There were two Coburn police cruisers, a car from the sheriff's office, and an ambulance in the driveway when I went outside. The gates were wide open. I just walked out, and no one made any effort to stop me.

Thirty minutes later I was snuggling deep in bed, purring with content. The last thing I thought of before I dropped off to sleep was that I had forgotten to pick up my aluminum stepladder before I left Crittenden. I was more convinced than ever that I just wasn't cut out for a life of crime.

THE EIGHTH DAY

I AWOKE about eleven Monday morning. I got out of bed immediately. Showered, shaved, dressed. Finished packing and snapped the cases shut. Took a final look around Room 3-F to make certain I wasn't forgetting anything. Then I rang for Sam Livingston, and asked him to take the luggage down to my car. I told him he could have what was left of the ale and vodka. I took the remainder of the brandy with me.

The desk clerk wanted to talk about the terrible tragedy out at Crittenden. That was his label: "Terrible tragedy." I cut him short and asked for my bill. While he was totaling it, I glanced over toward the locked cigar stand. There was a sign propped on the counter. I went over to read it.

"Closed because of death in the family."

I think that sad, stupid sign hit me harder than anything I had seen the night before.

I paid my bill with a credit card, and said goodby to the clerk. Went into the bar to shake Jimmy's hand, pass him a five and say goodby. Went out to the parking lot and helped Sam Livingston stow the suitcases and briefcase in the trunk. Put my hat, coat, and brandy bottle in the back seat.

I gave Sam a twenty. He took it with thanks.

"Take care," I said, as lightly as I could.

That ancient black face showed nothing—no distress, sadness, sorrow. Why should it? He had seen everything twice. Like Ben Faber, the old sexton, had said: nothing new ever happens.

I got in the Grand Prix, slammed the door. I stuck my hand out through the open window. The mummy shook it briefly.

"Sam," he said, "you ain't going to change this world."

"I never thought I could," I told him.

"Um . . ." he said. "Well, if you ever get up this way . . ."

I drove away. It seemed only right that the last words I heard in Coburn were an unfinished sentence.

It was a long, brooding drive back to New York. I wish I could tell you that once Coburn was behind me, the sky cleared, the sun came out, the world was born again. It would have been a nice literary touch. But nothing like that happened. The weather was almost as miserable as it had been a week ago, when I drove north. A wild west wind scattered snow flurries across the road. Dark clouds whipped in a grim sky.

I stopped for breakfast at the first fast-food joint I came to. Tomato juice, pancakes, bacon, three cups of black coffee. Nothing tasted of anything. Sawdust maybe. Wet wallboard. Paste. The fault may have been mine. Back in the car, I cleansed my palate with a belt of brandy.

I hit the road again, driving faster than I should have. It was all automatic: steering, shifting, braking. Because I was busy trying to understand.

I started with Julie Thorndecker. Maybe, as Agatha Binder said, she was a loving, sacrificing wife. But deserting a fatally ill husband to run away with a young lover is not the act of a loving, sacrificing wife. I thought that in all Julie's actions there was a strain of sexual excitement. I do not mean to imply she was a nymphomaniac—whatever that is. I just believe she was addicted to illicit sex, especially when it included an element of risk. Some people, men and women, are like that. They cannot feel pleasure without guilt. And they cannot feel guilt unless there is a possibility of punishment.

I think Julie Thorndecker had the instincts of a survivor. If Thorndecker hadn't saved her at that Cambridge party, someone else would have. She was too young, too beautiful to perish. Her reactions were elemental. When she saw her husband dying, she thought simply: the game is up. And so she planned to move on. She may have loved him and respected him—I think she did—but she just didn't know how to grieve. Life was too strong in her. So she made ready to take off with a hot, willing stud. I'm sure she loved him, too. Goodfellow, that is. She would love any man who worshipped her, since he was just giving her back a mirror image of her own infatuation with herself, her body, her beauty. A man's love confirmed her good taste.

Telford Gordon Thorndecker offered a more puzzling enigma. I could not doubt his expertise in his profession. I'd agree with everyone else and say he was a genius—if I was certain what a genius was. But I think he was driven by more than scientific curiosity and a desire for fame. I think his choice of his particular field of research—senescence, death; youth, immortality—was a vital clue to his character.

Few of us act from the motive we profess. The worm is always there, deep and squirming. A man might say he wishes to work with and counsel young boys, to give them the benefit of his knowledge and experience, to keep them from delinquency, to help them through the agonies of adolescence. That may all be true. It may also be true that he simply loves young boys.

In Thorndecker's case, I think he was motivated by an incredible seductive, sexually active young wife as much as he was by the desire to pioneer in the biology of aging. I think, perhaps unconsciously, the disparity in their ages was constantly on his mind. He saw her almost every day: youthful, live, energetic, vibrant, physically beautiful and sexually eager. He recognized how he himself, more than twice her age, had slowed, bent, become sluggish, his blood cooling, all the portents of old age becoming evident.

The search for immortality was as much, or more, for himself as it was for the benefit of mankind. He was in a hurry to stop the clock. Because in another ten years, even another five, his last chance would be gone. There could be no reversal; he knew that. He dreamt that, with hard work and good fortune, he might never grow older while she aged to his level and beyond.

You see, he loved her.

Although he could understand the rational need for her infidelity with Goodfellow—his work must not be delayed!—jealousy and hatred cankered his ego. In the end, he could not endure the thought of those two young bodies continuing to exist, rubbing in lubricious heat, swollen with life, while he was cold mould.

So he took them with him.

Wild supposition, I know. All of it was. So I came to the dismal conclusion: how could I hope to understand others when I was a mystery to myself. I wanted desperately to tell the saga of Dr. Telford Gordon Thorndecker to Joan Powell. That brainy lady had the ability to thread her way through the tangles of the human heart and make very human sense.

It was raining in New York, too. I found a parking space only a half-block away from my apartment, and wrestled my luggage into the lobby in a single, shin-bumping trip. I collected my mail, and banged my way up the narrow staircase. Inside, door locked and chained, I made myself a dark

Scotch highball and took it into the bathroom with me while I soaked in a hot tub. My feet had been wet and cold for a week; I was delighted to see the toes bend and the arches flex.

Came back into the living room, dressed casually, and went through the accumulated mail. Bills. Junk. Nothing from Joan Powell. I unpacked, put dirty laundry in the hamper, restored my toilet articles to the medicine cabinet.

Put something low and mournful on the hi-fi, and sat down to prepare an official report on the Thorndecker affair. The Bingham Foundation supplied its field investigators with a five-page printed form for such reports. It had spaces for Personal Habits, Financial Status, Religious Affiliation, Neighbors' comments, etc., etc. I stared at the form a few minutes, then printed APPLICANT DECEASED in big block letters across the top page, and let it go at that.

There was a can of sardines in the refrigerator, and I finished that with soda crackers. I also ate a few olives, a slice of dill pickle, a small wedge of stale cheddar, and a spoonful of orange marmalade. But that was all right; I wasn't hungry.

I watched the news on TV. All bad. I tried reading three different paperbacks, and tossed them all aside. I piled my outstanding bills neatly for payment. I sharpened two pencils. I smoked almost half a pack of cigarettes. I found a tin of rolled anchovies in the kitchen cupboard, opened it, and wolfed them down. And got thirsty, naturally.

About 9:30 P.M., on my third highball, I gave up, and sat down near the phone, trying to plan how to handle it. I brought over several sheets of paper and the sharpened pencils. I started making notes.

"Hello?" she would say.

"Powell," I'd say, "please don't hang up. This is Samuel Todd. I want to apologize to you for the way I acted. There is nothing you can call me as bad as what I've called myself. I'm phoning now to ask if there is any way we can get together again. To beg you. I will accept any conditions, endure any restraints, suffer any ignominy, do anything you demand, if you'll only let me see you again."

It went on and on like that. Abject surrender. I made copious notes. I imagined objections she might have, and I jotted down what my answer should be. I covered three pages with humility, crawling, total submission. I thought sure that, if she didn't hang up immediately, I could weasel my way back into her favor, or at least persuade her to give me a chance to prove how much I loved her and needed her.

And if she brought up the difference in our ages again, I prepared a special speech on that:

"Powell, the past week has taught me what a lot of bullshit the whole business of age can be. What's important is enjoying each other's company, having interests in common, loving, and keeping sympathy and understanding on the front burner, warm and ready when needed."

I read over everything I had written. I thought I had a real lawyer's brief, ready for any eventuality. I couldn't think of a single way she might react, from hot curses to cold silence, that I wasn't prepared to answer.

I mixed a fresh drink, drained half of it, picked up the phone. I arranged my speeches in front of me. I took a deep breath. I dialed her number.

She picked it up on the third ring.

"Hello?" she said.

"Powell," I said, "please don't hang—"

"Todd?" she said. "Get your ass over here."

I ran.

The Marlow Chronicles

ACT I

SCENE ONE

HE SAT on the edge of the receptionist's desk, leaned over, peered down her neckline.

"I once knew a mountain range that looked like you," he said. "The Grand Tetons."

"Oh Mr. Marlow!" She giggled.

"Are you really a widow, Suzy?" he asked.

"Twice," she said. "Both my husbands are deceased."

"What from—exhaustion?"

He swung off the desk, tried to straighten up, clasped a hand to his ribs.

"Are you all right?" she asked anxiously. "Maybe you should be home in bed."

"Splendid idea," he said. "Let's go."

He stalked around the office, trying to draw deep breaths. It hurt.

"I was sorry to hear you were in the hospital, Mr. Marlow," she said. "I hope it wasn't anything serious."

"I was being examined for the Guinness Book of World Records," he said. "They just wouldn't believe. Where *is* that man?"

"He should be here any minute. He knew you were coming today."

"Then he's one up on my wife. I'm going into his office and make a phone call."

"Mr. Ostretter doesn't like the phone being used for personal calls."

"I know, Suzy," Toby Marlow said. "He's so mean he farts in elevators. I'll leave you a dime on the way out."

He went into Julius Ostretter's private office, sat in his swivel chair, put his feet up on the polished desk. He called Hollywood, then held his ribs with one hand. The phone was answered on the third ring.

"Hi ya, baby," Marlow said, "I love you, too. . . . Who is this? . . . Who? . . . The *bookie?* Leo's got a bookie who makes house calls? Now I know where his ten percent goes. Put him on, will you? . . . Leo? Hiya, baby . . . I love you, too . . . Leo, what's with Universal? . . . Who got the job? . . . You gotta be kidding! Isn't he the guy with a gold ring in his nose? . . . I know, Leo, but for *Martin Luther?* . . . Okay, forget it. Who's playing Queen Elizabeth? . . . Listen, Leo, Harry just hasn't got the panache . . . I know he does that, but I said *panache.* It's French for chutzpah . . . Oh? He does that, too?"

Julius Ostretter came striding into the office, carrying a black attaché case. He glared angrily at the man behind this desk.

"Okay, Leo, I've got to run; I'm double-parked. Tell everyone out there I'm in perfect health and ready to get back to work. . . . Right. . . . Will do. . . . Love you too, baby."

He hung up and glared back at Ostretter.

"Where were you calling?" the lawyer demanded.

"Hong Kong," Marlow said. "Where the hell have you been?"

"So I'm a little late," Ostretter said. "I was watching the Hungarians parade."

"How much did they charge?" Toby Marlow asked.

"So what's so important it can't wait a few minutes? Get out of my chair."

"Julius, for God's sake, I'm practically an invalid, and you'd make me move?"

Grumbling, Ostretter took the leather club chair alongside the desk.

"All right," he said, "so what's the emergency?"

"I got a nasty letter from the government."

"Where is it?"

"In Washington, D.C."

"Come on, Toby, the letter . . . where is the letter?"

"I tore it up and flushed it down the kazoo. From the IRS, the bastards. They claim I owe more taxes. Julius, what does the government *do* with all my money?"

"The FBI . . ."

"I got mugged twice this year."

"The armed forces . . ."

"Last night a sailor propositioned me."

"Aid to underdeveloped nations . . ."

"Hah! Last week the ambassador from Nigeria got *my* table at the Chantilly. I tell you, Julius, the government lives in luxury and I live in squalor."

"Last year you tried to deduct fifty percent of your rent as a business expense."

"Fifty percent! That doesn't even pay for my vodka."

"I told you it wouldn't work. How are you feeling?"

"Lousy. Your brother is coming over this afternoon to—"

"Stop!" Ostretter shouted, holding up a hand. "Don't mention that creature's name! I don't want to hear a word about him!"

"All right, already. Calm down. I swear I won't mention the name of Jacob Ostretter."

Julius Ostretter groaned.

"So what should I do? About the letter?"

"Pay them what you owe, Toby. So the government can buy another destroyer."

"A destroyer I wouldn't mind. But the Sixth Fleet? Ah, screw it. I'll fight it. Let them take me to court."

"You'll lose," Julius Ostretter said.

"Then I'll appeal and appeal and appeal. I'll take it to the highest court!"

"That'll be some vote," the lawyer said. "Nine to nothing."

"Not the Supreme Court, dummy," Toby Marlow said. He rolled his eyes heavenward. "The *highest* court."

In the outer office, the receptionist said, "The phone call, Mr. Marlow."

He fished a dime from his jacket pocket and pressed it into her soft hand.

"There's plenty more where that came from," he whispered.

He had to wait a long time for a cab. He had trouble folding himself into the back seat. In truth, he wasn't feeling so good.

"Where to, pop?" the driver asked.

That didn't help.

SCENE TWO

THE APARTMENT house on Central Park West was called The Montana. Butte should have sued. But rents were low, ceilings were high, and sometimes the elevator worked. The Marlows' apartment was on the top floor. It had four bedrooms, three baths, and closets large enough for assignations. The apartment hadn't been painted in six years; some of the walls were molting.

The cavernous living room looked like a Bolivian designer's concept of a Bavarian brauhaus. The walls were whitewashed plaster, jaundiced by age, cigar smoke, and bad jokes. Blackened beams crisscrossed the walls and ribbed the lofty ceiling. Suspended overhead was an old-fashioned, wood-bladed electric fan that turned lazily with a thoughtful hum, hardly stirring the soupy air.

At the rear was a brick fireplace, large enough to roast a cocker spaniel. There was a yellowed marble mantel, and over it hung a framed theatrical poster of Toby Marlow in the costume and makeup of Falstaff. A door at the left opened to the dining room, pantry, kitchen. The door at the right led to the entrance hall and bedrooms.

There were high windows on both sides of the fireplace. The one on the right was a bow window with a cushioned window seat. The curved bow window was fitted with leaded colored glass. Several of the small panes were broken; cardboard squares had been Scotchtaped over most of them. From one, a stuffed rag protruded.

The furniture, scaled for this barnlike room, was big, old, worn. There was an enormous couch, originally of good lines, now lumpy and sagging wearily. The velvet covering was shiny, stained, pocked with cigarette burns. Chairs were everywhere. No two matched; they all had the transient look of having come from a theatrical warehouse. They had. One had lost a leg and was propped on a tilting pile of old playscripts.

There were rickety end tables, a liquor bar on wheels, a long cocktail table in front of the couch, an old, scarred upright piano against one wall. The sheet music on the stand was "Just a Song at Twilight."

The room was further cluttered with a numbing profusion of theatrical props: a tarnished halberd with a bent blade, a plastic skull, a devil's mask, a large brass tray set with glass jewels, two burlesque bladders, a bass drum with a torn skin, fake feathers and rubber fronds, and more swell stuff. Everywhere were framed autographed photographs of obscure actors with whom Marlow had played—and some famous ones with whom he had not.

Toby Marlow, clad in a shabby, brocaded dressing gown, frayed carpet slippers, and a silk ascot of hellish design knotted awry, knelt on the window seat. He was leaning out an opened section of the bow window, screaming imprecations and flapping his arms wildly at pigeons despoiling a small terrace. Dr. Jacob Ostretter was repacking a black gripsack at the cocktail table. Blanche, the Marlows' maid, housekeeper, cook, and sergeant major, was making futile gestures at dusting and straightening the living-room thrift shop.

"Get the fuck out of here!" Marlow screamed. "Go on! Beat it!" He waved his arms, muttering. Then he closed the window, came back into the room. "Goddamn birds! They're diseased, aren't they?"

"I don't know," Dr. Ostretter said. "I've never treated a pigeon."

"Wise-ass," Marlow said. "I make all the jokes in this house. I saw your brother a few hours ago. He said—"

Jacob Ostretter threw up his hands.

"Don't tell!" he yelled. "Don't mention that man's name!"

"Julius Ostretter?" Marlow said innocently. "Nice name. It flows trippingly off the tongue."

"A gonif!" Dr. Jacob shouted. "A Fiend in human form!"

Marlow laughed. "You two guys remind me of that pair from the Bible. You know . . ."

"Cain and Abel?" Ostretter asked.

"Don't cue me, kiddo," Marlow said. "I was thinking of Sodom and Gomorrah." He scratched his ribs and stomach. "Jesus Christ, Jake, what did you do—sprinkle itching powder under that bandage?"

"That's the incision healing."

"Healing? The hell you say. It looks like a clown's mouth."

Dr. Jacob Ostretter snapped shut his case, placed his black bowler squarely atop his pear-shaped head. But he fussed about, seemed reluctant to leave. He was a roly-poly, scarcely five-feet four with built-up heels. He lifted his plump chin and rose to his toes while speaking. He imagined it gave him a manner of stern authority. But his soft, sympathetic voice usually betrayed him. He was almost kicked out of medical school for weeping while dissecting a frog.

"Toby," he said gently, "I've got to talk to you."

"So talk."

Dr. Ostretter looked at Blanche, morosely dusting a papier-mâché owl.

"In private," he said.

Blanche started for the kitchen door.

"Horsey," Marlow said, "you take one more step and I'll give you a curettage with a Popsicle stick. Jake, whatever you've got to say, you say it in front of Blanche. I haven't had any secrets from her in thirty years, and I'm not about to start now."

Dr. Ostretter shrugged. "All right. Toby, how long have you been bleeding?"

"All my life," Marlow said.

"Don't give me any of your fancy-pantsy actors' talk. You know what I mean. How long?"

"A few years."

"How many years?"

"Four. Five. Something like that."

"Five years bleeding and you didn't come to see me?"

"I had more important things to do," Marlow said.

"More important?" Dr. Jake was shocked. "What? Tell me what?"

"Well, when it started, I was going to see you, but then I got the lead in *The Idiot.*"

"Typecasting," Blanche said.

Marlow whirled on her.

"It talks!" he cried. "Jake, did you hear that? It actually talks! You get one silver star on your report card this month, honey."

"So just because you got a job, you didn't come see me?"

Marlow wandered about the room, picking things up, inspecting them, putting them down.

"*The Idiot,*" he mused. "I was great in it, but it closed in Boston the first week. Lousy sets. The story of my life. When my time comes, I want to be taken there so they can put on my tombstone, 'He closed in Boston.'"

Dr. Ostretter shook his head in disgust.

"Can't you be serious for a minute?"

"No," Toby Marlow said.

"Well, this *is* serious. Malignant, Toby. It started in your colon. Now it's spread to the pancreas. They took one look and sewed you up. Toby, I was *there*. There's nothing that can be done."

There was silence then. The three were caught in an awkward tableau. Jake and Blanche stared at Marlow. He closed his eyes slowly. Only the derisive whir of the overhead electric fan could be heard. The moment swelled, swelled. . . . Then Toby opened his eyes, too much the trouper to let a stage quiet become an embarrassment.

"So much for dramatic pauses," he said. "Nothing that can be done, Jake? That's keen."

"*Keen?*" Blanche said. "I haven't heard that word in twenty years."

"Of course you haven't," Marlow said. "Because nothing's been keen in the last twenty years. So I'm shuffling off this mortal coil—right, Jake?"

Ostretter made a gesture.

"Yes," he said, voice breaking. "I'm sorry, Toby."

"Go to hell," Marlow said. He resumed his wandering, and Blanche resumed her halfhearted dusting. "How long do I have, Jake?"

Dr. Ostretter shrugged. "Maybe six months," he said. "Tops."

"Much pain?" Marlow said.

"Yes," Ostretter said. "A lot. But we can help control it. You want to go into the hospital again?"

"Christ no! All those nurses had mustaches. I'll stay right here and drive everyone up the wall. I might even fuck myself to death before those six months are up."

"Wouldn't surprise me a bit," Ostretter said. "You want to consult another doctor?"

"What the hell for? I trust you. The villains with the long knives were good men, weren't they?"

"Yes, they were good men. There's no way out, Toby."

"Never has been, has there? Okay, Jake; you better send me your bill before those six months are up."

Dr. Ostretter took off his horn-rimmed glasses, wiped them carefully with his handkerchief. And with his head still lowered, he dabbed hastily at his eyes.

"I'll stop by tomorrow, Toby, and talk to you some more—about what to expect."

"I know what to expect."

The doctor moved toward the door, shoulders bowed. Then he stopped, turned back.

"Toby, have you talked to Miss Evings?"

"Barbara? Sure, I talked to her last night. Every night. She practically lives here. Why?"

"Did she tell you?"

"Tell me what?"

"I'd rather she told you."

"Tell me *what*, goddamn it? What's this all about?"

"I'll let her tell you."

"Ahh, go screw yourself. Jake . . . a lot of pain?"

"Yes. A lot of pain."

"I can stand anything but pain, hunger, and poverty."

Blanche said, "That's what makes you so different from everyone else."

"See Jake?" Toby said. "She never says anything clever. I've played a hundred drawing-room comedies, and in every one of them the maid is funny as hell. But what do I get? A maid who's been playing Lady Macbeth all her life."

"I'm not your maid," Blanche said.

"Then what are you?"

"Your keeper."

"Not bad," Marlow acknowledged. "Another silver star."

"Keep on the pills, Toby," Dr. Ostretter said. "Every three hours. No drinking, no smoking, no sex. You can have sponge baths."

"Listen, Blanche," Marlow said, "maybe instead of the silver star, I'll let you give me a sponge bath."

"No, thanks," she said. "I've seen you naked before. Two prunes and a noodle."

"There you are, Jake," Marlow said. "The moment they know you're dying, the wolves close in."

The doctor shook his head dolefully, and departed through the hallway door. The moment he was gone, Toby Marlow rushed to the liquor cart and poured two whiskies. He handed one to Blanche, and set his on the cocktail table.

He then took a fat cigar from the breast pocket of his robe. He peeled off the cellophane wrapper and dropped it on the floor. He took a wooden kitchen match from a box on the table and held it high—a nonchalant Statue of Liberty. A blade of the ceiling electric fan came around, scratched across the match head and ignited it. Toby lighted his cigar, waved out the match, dropped it on the floor.

He lowered himself cautiously onto the couch, picked up his whiskey. Blanche came over to stand in front of him. They raised their glasses in a silent toast, gulped greedily. After Marlow got his cigar drawing well, he took a deep puff, blew a series of perfect rings, handed the cigar up to Blanche. She took a deep puff, with pleasure, and handed the cigar back to him.

She was from a Nebraska farm family, and looked it. She was a big woman, with the physical presence and aggressive posture of a bordello bouncer. She was five-feet nine, weighed 158, was raw-boned, massive through the shoulders and hips, with an awesome bosom. Her wiry grey hair was pulled back tightly and tied with a girlish pink ribbon. She was pushing 60, and her features were heavy, masculine, almost equine. But the skin was unwrinkled, the complexion peachlike, even to the golden fuzz. The single gulp of whiskey had blushed not only her face, but her bare arms as well. Probably her entire strong body.

"Jake said no drinking and no smoking," she reminded Marlow.

"And no sex." He nodded. "But dying is okay."

She took another sip of the whiskey and looked at him over the glass. Their eyes locked; they stared at each other a long moment in silence.

"Scared?" she asked softly.

He took a deep breath. "'Each plays his part and has his day. What ho! The world's all right, I say.' Know who wrote that?"

"Shakespeare?"

"Jesus Christ, Blanche, he didn't write *everything!* No, it wasn't Will. I forget who the hell it was. My memory is a laundry bag of other men's words. What's for dinner?"

"Lamb stew," she said.

"Again?"

"What do you mean—again?" she demanded angrily. "We haven't had lamb stew for a month."

"That's what I mean—*again?*"

She snorted, finished off her drink, helped herself to more from the liquor cart. He held out his empty glass with an expression of such piteous pleading that she laughed, and poured him more, too.

"Toby," she said, "you want me to keep it quiet?"

"The lamb stew?" he said. "Yes, I'm no prouder of it than you are. But I suppose—"

"You know what I mean," she said. "What Jake said. You going to tell the others?"

He stared at her, aghast. . . .

"Are you out of your tiny, tiny mind? Of course I'm going to tell the others. You never supposed I'd suffer nobly and in silence, did you? Listen, sweetie, this is the fattest part I've had in five years. I'm going to pull out all the stops. I'll be magnificent: all smiling bravura on the outside, all lightness and careless gaiety that'll tear your fucking heart out. Because you'll know that deep down, inside, I'm suffering. I'll do that mostly with gestures: little controlled John Gielgud movements that will convey my unbearable anguish. God, what a performance this is going to be! How I wish the critics could catch it. I can hardly wait to get started."

"You already have," she said.

He handed her the cigar again, so she could take another puff. He inspected her through the smoke, his head tilted, eyes narrowed . . .

"You know, darling, you *do* look like a horse. Did I ever tell you that? Withers, fetlocks, haunch, and shank. If some day you whinnied at me, I wouldn't be a bit surprised. And yet . . . And yet . . ."

"And yet *what*, Godzilla?"

"Oh shit . . . I don't know. Sometimes I think that in another world, another life, another time, you and I might have been something. Something together. Something fine and beautiful. Did you ever dream of that?"

"Ohh," she whispered, "you're a devil, you are. A devil!"

He laughed and started to speak: "I suppose I—"

Suddenly he clutched his abdomen. Pain wrenched his features. His eyes rolled up into his skull.

"My God," he gasped. "Oh my God . . . Oh Blanche . . ."

She was terrified. "What is it? What is it, Toby? Should I get the pills Should I call—"

"I'm rehearsing, for Chrissake," he said cheerfully, straightening up. "But I had you, didn't I? See how good I'm going to be when I get this part moving?" Blanche glared at him angrily. She drained her whiskey, then began again her ineffectual housecleaning. She wielded a feather duster furiously but futilely, not neglecting to dust Toby Marlow's bald head from behind, an attack he accepted with a benign smile.

For this fustian fellow was completely hairless—not even a horseshoe fringe. But his shining crown was of noble dimensions, looking like a limitlessly high brow. Far from being embarrassed by this naked pate, he gloried in its nudity, and was not above anointing it occasionally with baby oil to heighten its sheen. "This pristine globe," he called it proudly.

He had lied so often about his age that no one, including wife and son, was *quite* certain. One said 60, one said 65. *He* said 53. His complexion was ruddy, with the roadmap capillaries of a heavy drinker and the course skin texture resulting from too many years of wearing stage makeup. His nose was meaty, lips large and full, eyes wide and despicably innocent.

His voice was magnificent: deep, resonant, with a velvety vibrato—a theatre-trained voice, so even his whispers carried to peanut heaven. In spite of his age, he moved lightly, with an almost feline grace. His hands and feet were unexpectedly dainty.

Like most actors offstage, he had the appearance of unwashed seediness. His clothes were costumes; his gestures had the outsize flamboyance of a man living his life in an arena. His favorite work of art was a mirror; if he could achieve complete androgyny, he would marry himself. Now, he sat calmly, condemned to death, lord of all he surveyed, and more, and with monumental self-assurance sipped his whiskey and puffed his cigar. His reverie was interrupted by the arrival of Barbara Evings. She floated into the room, a voluptuous wraith, bearing a nosegay of drooping violets. She embraced Blanche, kissed her cheek. Then she trotted over to the couch with bitty steps, bent to kiss Toby's bald head. She melted onto the floor at his feet, looked up, offered him the flowers.

He accepted them grandly, as his due, plucked one from the bunch to put behind his ear. He leaned forward to pull Barbara's neckline away from her body, and stared therein with a burlesque leer and a great smacking of lips. He then inserted the remaining violets between Barbara's unbra-ed breasts.

"'Weep no more,'" he recited. "'Nor sigh, nor groan,
"'Sorrow calls no time that's gone;
"'Violets plucked, the sweetest rain
"'Makes not fresh nor grow again.'"

"How do you feel today, Toby?" she asked.

"Like I've been born again."

"How wonderful!" she said. "I met Doctor Ostretter on the street. He said he had been to see you. Good news?"

Marlow turned his head away slowly, chin rising. A lofty smile curved his lips. St. Sebastian awaiting the next arrow.

"Oh, that's all right, dear," he said sadly. "Let's just talk about you."

"But, Toby, what did Jake say about you—about your condition? Are you going to be all right?"

He disengaged her arms from about his legs. He rose to his feet with some difficulty, tottered to the nearest wall. He faced it closely, pressed his forehead against it. After a two-count, he beat the wall gently with a tight fist.

"'There is no death,'" he said hollowly. "'What seems so is mere transition.'"

"Jesus Christ!" Blanche said disgustedly.

"Toby," Barbara faltered, "what are you saying?"

Marlow turned from the wall, straightened to a grand posture. With heroic gestures, he began declaiming:

"'Cowards die many times before their death; the valiant never taste of death but once. Of all the wonders that I yet have heard, it seems to me most strange that men should fear; seeing that death, a necessary end, will come when it will come.'"

Barbara, bewildered, rose to her feet. She looked to Blanche, who nodded her head. Barbara made a cry—a sob, a groan, a moan. She rushed to Toby and embraced him.

"Oh Toby, Toby, no, no! Say you're just joking."

"There, there, little one," he said sweetly, patting her head. "This too shall pass."

"Is it true, Toby? Are you dying?"

"It is true, dear," he said cheerily. "They cut me open and within they found such a turmoil, such a bustle of comings and goings, and little animals without number, and tissue grievously bitten. So they thought it best to sew me up again and send me home with their blessing. Go forth, they said, and sin no more. The shitheads!"

"Oh God . . . oh Toby . . . oh my God. . . ."

His orotund voice rolled out, filling the room like a Moog synthesizer:

"'There is no God stronger than death,'" he boomed, "'and death is a sleep.'"

"When?" she asked frantically. "How long do you have?"

"The end may come at any moment," he said in sepulchral tones.

Blanche headed for the door to the kitchen.

"I can't take any more of this," she said. "No bone, no fat, no water added. Just pure ham."

"Go dress like Lady Windermere," he yelled angrily after her. "Come to my bedroom at midnight and beat me off with your fan."

She thumbed her nose at him, then slammed the door behind her. Toby went over to the liquor cart, poured more whiskey, filled a glass of wine for Barbara.

"Enough of fun and games, child," he said. "Dry your tears and have a glass of sherry. 'Twill put the dimples back in your ass."

He handed Barbara the wine glass, then returned to the couch where he sat and sipped his drink, regarding her with some amusement. She stood leaning at the mantel, forehead laid upon her raised arm. With her draped dress, violets at her bosom, long black hair hanging halfway down her back, she resembled a portrait by Burne-Jones. But he would never have painted her in sneakers.

Barbara Evings hovered between girlhood and womanhood. There was something in her physical appearance that suggested she might continue to hover for the rest of her life. She was tall, thin as a breadstick, with attenuated hands and feet. Apostolic toes. Her willowy body, pliant as a stem, was usually swathed in ankle-length dresses of printed chiffon: sheer, floating stuff with ruffles, tucks, flounces—gowns that might be displayed in a museum of couturier design, hung on a mannequin of the 1920's with marcelled hair and a star-shaped mouche.

Barbara's face was smooth, untouched by age or pain. Her light blue eyes were without guile. It was a sweet, open face, tremulous, halfway between spirituality and insipidity. A poet might believe there was something in those sensuous lips and that clearly defined chin that hinted of passion and will. Something that might one day ignite and consume her.

There was a dreaminess in her movements, a delicacy in her manner. Naturally, she adored flowers, birds, kittens, walking in the rain, the poetry of Indian mystics, health food, beaded headbands, antique jewelry, and pink babies. It was difficult to believe she had ever been constipated.

"Barbara," Toby said, "do you have something to tell me?"

"It isn't important."

"Doctor Jake acted like it was. So say it. Have I ever held anything back from you?"

"No," she acknowledged, "but you're different."

"Different?" he shouted. "I'm unique! But tell me, sweet; what's the problem?"

"I'm pregnant," she said.

"Mazeltov," he said. "But what's the problem?"

"Toby, I'm *pregnant*!"

"Thank God," he said fervently. "I was afraid it might be an ingrown toenail. Who's the father? David—right? My son, the actor. The actor who can't pick his nose without asking, 'What's my motivation?' David knocked you up?"

"Yes," she said faintly.

"It figures," Marlow said. "The clumsy oaf! The night I went to see him in *Philadelphia Story* he knocked over an end table. All right, honey, sit down and let's talk about it. It's really not the end of the world."

She returned to the couch and started to sit next to him. But he pulled her up to him so she ended up sitting on his lap, her arm about his neck. He nuzzled his big nose into the violets in her bodice.

"Am I hurting you, Toby?" she asked innocently, moving about on his lap.

"Ooh yes!" he breathed. "It hurts so good."

"You're a dirty old man."

"Is there a better kind? So what do you want to do? Get a free abortion?"

"They're not free, Toby. They're legal now, but not free."

"Really? I don't remember reading that in *Variety*. So you need the money—right, kid? You can't afford Doc Ostretter's fee—right? Don't worry, I'll give you the money. No problem. What will it cost?"

"Jake wants five hundred."

"Five hundred?" he screamed. "That filthy abortionist! I'll talk to him, Barbara, and for the same five hundred he'll give you a high colonic and shave your armpits. Is that what had you worried? The money? Consider the problem solved."

"No, Toby," she said. "It isn't solved. I don't want an abortion."

"Then you want to marry David?"

"No, I don't want that either."

"Whee!" he yelled.

He slid her off his lap. He staggered to his feet, pulled the robe belt tighter, fluffed his ascot. He went over to the bow window, opened a section and leaned out, looking up at the sky. Then he turned back into the room leaving the window open.

"Pardon me for about ten minutes, luv," he said. "I think I'll take a flight around the park with the other cuckoos." He stopped suddenly, put his hands on his hips. He stared down at her, frowning. "How come you're pregnant, Barbara? Aren't you on the pill?"

"No."

"Why not?"

"It seemed so—so mechanical."

"I know. Like breathing. Didn't he use anything?"

"No. I asked him not to. It seemed so—so—"

"I know—mechanical. Everything is mechanical except getting knocked up."

"Well, I believed if I thought about it, really concentrated, telling myself, 'You will *not* get pregnant, you will *not* get pregnant,' everything would be all right. I thought it was all in the mind."

"Where did he screw you—in the left ear?"

"Oh Toby," she said, "don't be so vulgar."

"One of the few advantages of growing old, baby. You can be as vulgar as you like. Belch or fart, and never say, 'Excuse me.' It's beautiful. The golden years. All right, you don't want an abortion and you don't want to marry David. What *do* you want?"

She rose and came over to stand directly in front of him. She took him by the elbows and moved her face close. She stared directly into his eyes.

"I want to have the baby, Toby. I've never had anything of my own—nothing I could really love and treasure. I'll be a good mother, really I will, Toby. I'll love the baby and take care of it and protect it. I'll read books and go to classes. I *will* be a good mother, honest I will."

He took her into his arms.

"I believe you, sweetie," he said tenderly. "But I'm not sure they'll let you keep it. There may be legal complications. I'll have to talk to Julius

Ostretter about that. But look, little mother, you could marry David, just temporarily, and have the baby. That would take care of the legal end. Then you could divorce him, and he'd have to provide support. How about that?"

"No, Toby. I don't want to marry David—even for one day."

"I don't blame you," he said. "But what are *your* reasons?"

She pulled from him, turned away so he couldn't see her face.

"Well. . . . David's very nice," she said in a low voice. "I like David. I love David."

"Well then . . . ?"

"Toby, it's just that I don't want to be—to be caged! I don't want to be any man's wife. I just want to be free to be myself, to own my own life."

He took her by the shoulders, turned her to him. He lifted her chin gently so she had to look into his eyes.

"You're shitting me, baby," he said.

"Yes." She nodded miserably. "I am."

"I thought you and I could talk to each other straight out, no faking."

"We can, Toby," she pleaded, "we can. But I can't talk about this. Not now."

He was silent a moment.

"Okay, kiddo," he said finally. "Whenever you're ready, I'll be here. For a while."

"Promise me you won't say anything to David about my being pregnant?"

"I promise," he said. "I won't say a word."

They heard a loud rumble of running in the hallway. The door burst open. An excited David Marlow rushed into the room.

"I got it!" he shouted. "I got it! I got it!"

"Barbara's pregnant," Toby Marlow said.

"Oh Toby," she said sorrowfully. "You promised."

"I lied," he said.

"You're looking at the world's newest Hamlet!" David Marlow laughed. "I got the job! How about that!"

"Barbara's knocked up," Toby said.

"What? What?"

"Your little Ophelia here, Hamlet. She's pregnant."

"Jesus Christ!" David cried.

"No, its yours," his father told him.

David shook himself, a pup doused. He looked wildly about. The opened bow window appeared his only means of escape. But he was not enamored of the nine-story drop. He didn't object to the fall so much as the landing. So in his manly way, he addressed the cause of his misfortune:

"Barbara," he demanded sternly, "is this true?"

"I didn't want you to know," she said, suddenly tearful. "Toby promised he wouldn't tell."

The hallway door opened again. Cynthia Marlow came sweeping grandly into the room, arms laden with packages. She dumped them on the couch, removed her hat, shook her hair free. She went directly to Toby and kissed his bald head.

"How do you feel, Toby?"

"I'm dying," he said.

"That's nice. I'm so glad, dear. Barbara, you have new sneakers. So pretty. And clean. David, tell me—how did you make out?"

"Oh, he made out great," Toby said. "He knocked up the Bird Girl."

"I got it," David said. "We go into rehearsal on Friday. We open in six months. And Barbara's pregnant. By me. Right, Bobbie?"

"No, Judge Crater did it," Toby said.

"Toby, what do you mean you're dying?" Cynthia Marlow said. "When I came in and asked you how you were, you said you were dying. Just what did you mean by that?"

Blanche entered from the kitchen. She stood in the doorway, feet planted, balled fists at her waist, challenging. . . .

"How many for dinner?" she asked. "It's lamb stew, and I don't want to hear another word about it."

"Doc Ostretter gives me six months," Toby said.

"We'll have to get married," David said to Barbara.

"And fresh spinach salad," Blanche added.

"Toby, you must be joking," Cynthia said.

"I don't want to marry you," Barbara sobbed.

"No no no," Cynthia said, embracing Toby. "I don't believe it. I won't believe it."

"Will you listen to reason?" David said. "Either marry me or have an abortion. One or the other."

"And a nice honeydew melon for dessert." Blanchs nodded.

"What did you read for them?" Toby asked David over Cynthia's shoulder.

"'Alas, poor Yorick . . .'" David said.

"I *won't* marry you," Barbara said, "and I *won't* have an abortion. I'm going to have the baby—*my* baby."

Cynthia pulled away from Toby, looked at the others, appealed to the virago in the doorway:

"Blanche, is Toby telling the truth? Is that what Doctor Jake said?"

"That's what he said." Blanche nodded. "Six months."

"Oh my God," Cynthia said.

"What?" David said. "Toby dead? Six months?"

Suddenly they were all silent, staring at Toby Marlow with horror, disbelief, pity. At last, at last, he was the center of attention. He raised two fingers slowly: the Pope blessing the multitudes in St. Peter's Square. He bestowed upon them all an odiously gallant smile and whispered his benediction:

"'Weep not for me; be blithe as wont, nor tinge with the gloom the stream of love that circles home, light hearts and free! Joy in the gifts Heaven's bounty lends, nor miss my face, dear friends! I am still near.'"

"I can't stand any more of this!" David Marlow shouted. "I just can't stand it!"

He rushed from the room, slamming the door behind him.

"Go to him, Barbara," Cynthia said. "He's upset about his father."

"The hell he is," Toby said. "He's upset about *becoming* a father."

"A father?" Cynthia said. "Our David?"

"Cyn, where have you been?" Toby said. "Didn't you hear us talking? Barbara's got one in the oven, and David put it there."

"Barbara pregnant?" Cynthia Marlow said. She moved to embrace the girl. "Oh, how nice! Dear, I'm so happy for you. You're going to have it, of course?"

"Oh, she's going to have it," Toby said, "but she doesn't want to marry David."

"Why ever not, dear?"

"She's afraid he'll lock her up in a cage, or some such shit."

"What a strange idea," Cynthia said. "David would *never* do a thing like that; he's a very sweet, sensitive boy. When is the baby due, Barbara?"

"In about six months," Barbara muttered.

"Holy Christ!" Toby Marlow cried. "This house is going to be hell on wheels in six months."

"It's not doing bad right now," Blanche said. "Should I get dinner ready?"

"Might as well," Toby said. "It can't make matters any worse. Barbara, go to David's room and see if you can talk him into coming to the table. Assure him the lamb stew isn't punishment for what he's done."

"Hah!" Blanche said. "I notice you always take second helpings."

"I am your employer," Toby Marlow said loftily. "Noblesse oblige. What you don't notice, Ms. Frankenstein, is that I vomit immediately after leaving the dining room."

"You go to hell," she said hotly.

"Up yours," Marlow said.

Blanche and Barbara left the living room. Toby, finally alone with Cynthia, poured each of them a small drink.

"First today," he assured her, and she smiled wanly.

Then she slumped in a corner of the couch, leaned forward, elbows on knees. She hid her face in her hands. Toby Marlow sat beside her. He gently pried loose one of her hands, clamped her fingers around the glass.

"Over the river and through the woods," he said, holding up his glass.

She dropped her other hand, looked at him with glistening eyes.

"To grandfather's house we go," she faltered.

They simultaneously drained their shots of whiskey—a familiar ceremony—and set their empty glasses on the cocktail table. They rose, and with arms about each other's waists, moved slowly toward the door.

"I suppose we should dress for dinner," Cynthia said.

"For lamb stew?" Toby asked. "What do you suggest—sackcloth and ashes?"

He had her laughing as they went out. . . .

SCENE THREE

THE DRESSING room in the Marlow apartment was actually a wide passageway between master bedroom and bathroom. One side of this rectangular chamber was wholly taken up by folding doors leading to high, walk-in closets in which Cynthia and Toby's outer clothing and shoes were stored.

The opposite wall was almost covered by the mirror of an enormous vanity table, bearing an apothecary's stock of oils, lotions, brushes, perfumes, powders, unguents, hand mirrors, colognes, combs, and makeup aids of all kinds. The table was long enough to accommodate two benches, side by side, so the mirrored table could be used simultaneously by both Marlows.

The mirror itself was a handsome sheet of beveled glass, badly in need of resilvering. Along both ends and across top and bottom ran a wooden channel in which bare electric bulbs were spaced at six-inch intervals. It was, indeed, the type of brightly lighted mirror used in theatrical dressing rooms. Even with several bulbs burned out, as they inevitably were, this blazing border provided so much illumination that further lighting of the dressing room was not needed. Not needed, but desired. Lamps shaped like spotlights were attached to the ceiling in each of the four corners. their bright beams were aimed at the stars' benches.

Taped to the streaked mirror were withered telegrams, fan letters, photographs, jotted telephone numbers, a dried cornflower, the cover of a playbill, yellowed newspaper clippings, and similarly aged mementos of Toby Marlow's stage career. In fact, the mirror was so heavily layered with this memorabilia that only two open spaces, like portholes, remained in which Cynthia and Toby could inspect their images, an activity of which they were fond, and presently engaged.

Toby was stripped to the waist. His heavy torso was muffled in bandages, from armpits to the waist of his trousers. He looked like a wounded Buddha. Cynthia was wearing a slip, leaning forward to inspect her reflection intently as she applied makeup. Toby's study of his own phiz was no less engrossed. He stared, and sighed. . . .

" 'His life was gentle, and the elements so mix'd in him that Nature might stand up and say to all the world, "This was a man!" ' "

Cynthia put aside her eyebrow pencil, turned to look at him sorrowfully.

"Poor, poor Toby," she said sadly.

"Just an average day, old girl." He shrugged. "It's the Curse of the Marlows."

"Toby, what *are* we going to do? Everything's just falling apart."

"Hang in there, kiddo," he said. "Leave everything to King Toby the First, Last, and Always. Oh, by the way—I love you, Cyn."

She smiled and reached out to stroke his bare shoulder.

"I know you do, dear—in your own strange way. You always came back to me."

"Didn't I though?" he said proudly. "Always. But of course I didn't leave you all that often."

"Often enough," she said, "often enough. . . ."

They fell silent then, and as often happens with two people whose lives are so intertwined, their remembrance was the same. Staring at the bright lights of the dressing table, they recalled the total, hard brilliance of a Mediterranean sun. . . .

They were on the beach at St. Tropez. The year was 1938, and bathing suits were funny. Cynthia, swaddled in something voluminous and filmy, was sitting on the sands, knees drawn up, hugging her bare feet. She was staring dreamily out to sea from under the enormous brim of a straw hat banded with a blue ribbon.

From far down the beach approached the jaunty figure of Toby Marlow. He was fully dressed in white flannels, white shirt, white cravat, white socks, white shoes, white Panama. He shone! He swung a careless Malacca, stabbing it into the sand, twirling it in complete circles, even tossing it into the air to catch adroitly and spin between his fingers.

He came up to Cynthia, quite close, and leaned on his cane, ankles crossed. He looked down at her gravely.

"I'm back," he said.

"And who might you be?" Cynthia asked coldly, not looking at him.

"I am the man with whom you are intimate."

"Oh no," she said. "No no no. The man with whom I *was* intimate— swore undying love."

"And meant it," Toby said.

They were both, in 1938, beautiful people, with the terrified self-assurance that only stage training can create. Like the well-rehearsed actors they were, they knew how this scene would end. But they had to play it out as if its climax would come as as great a surprise to them as to the audience.

"You might have written to tell me you were alive," Cynthia said. "Although I preferred to think not."

"Didn't you get the checks I sent?" he asked.

"Checks!" She laughed scornfully. "You think money absolved you of guilt?"

"Guilt?" he said. "Guilt? Guilt? What's that? The shiny stuff dancers in the Folies put on their nipples?"

"I hope she kicked you out," Cynthia said savagely.

"You know better than that. I walked away laughing.

"How old was she?"

"Nine."

"Toby, how old was she?"

"She was eighteen, but acted like nine."

"I suppose she worshiped you."

"Of course."

Cynthia made a twist of distaste, and moved so her back was to him. But he circled so he could see the tip of her nose, the point of her chin beneath the broad-brimmed hat.

"Eighteen," she repeated. "And all she wanted out of life was to be screwed by the famous Toby Marlow. That's all any of them want."

"They really don't want to be screwed by me. But they want to be able to say they have. It nourishes their egos."

"But you do it anyway."

"Why should I deny them a chance to be happy? It's such a small sacrifice to make."

"*Small* indeed!" she cried. "Undoubtedly *small!*"

"No need to get nasty about it," he said. "I did come back, you know. I always come back to you."

"Because I love you so much. Love you for what you are, with all your dirty language and evil tempers and rotten infidelities. That's why you come back to me. Not because you love me, but because you can't resist the love I have for you. I'm the only human being in the world who loves you more than you love yourself."

He was shocked by her insight. He had sensed the truth of what she said. But hearing his frailty exposed so pitilessly in words disturbed him. There were, after all, certain things a gentleman did not discuss: venereal disease, God, and the sexual proclivities of ballet dancers were three of them. His dependence on her was another.

"You know not whereof you speak," he said haughtily.

"Oh yes," she said. A derisive laugh here. "You don't love me, but only the love I have for you. I've always known it. I'm not as sexy or pretty or young as your little girls, but I love you in a way they can't. It's my only weapon."

"Well, babe," he said lamely, "it's really not such a bad life, is it? A lot of laughs to get us over the rough spots. A few little bits of happiness— enough to keep us going. Some marvelous brawls. Do you remember the time you brained me with a flowerpot?"

"Oh yes," she said. "The moment I did it I could have killed myself. It was my best African violet."

Toby laughed aloud, and Cynthia could not refrain from smiling. Finally, finally, she looked up at him. Interpreting this as a thaw, he immediately folded onto the sand alongside her and removed his Panama. He was wearing a wig of luxuriant brown hair, quite long for male styles of that day.

She inspected him critically, reached to feel his ribs.

"You're thinner," she said.

"I haven't been sleeping much."

"No, I don't suppose you have. Was she pretty?"

"In a vacuous sort of way. When she drank a cup of tea, she held up her little finger."

"Toby, she didn't."

"She did—until one night I hung my hat on it. The tea spilled into her lap."

"You're such a brute."

"Yes. And in bed she wanted to talk baby talk. I damned soon put a stop to *that*, I can tell you."

He hitched a bit closer to her on the sand. He reached up and gently removed her hat. Then he could see her classically crisp features in profile, chiseled against an impossibly blue sky. She was aware of his stare and posed for him, lifting her chin, smoothing the long hair away from her ear.

"Oh Toby," she sighed. "*Why* do you do it? Will you tell me why? Is it *your* ego that needs young girls?"

"*My* ego doesn't need nourishing; you know that. It's because—well, I think it's because it gives me a fresh audience. You know all my lines, all my moods, tempers, passions, furies, jokes, melancholies. Cyn, you *know* me. You can't react any more. You've seen the play too often. I'm not blaming you for that. But you must understand that occasionally I need someone who doesn't know me, to whom I'm totally new, someone I can play to who *does* react, who laughs or frowns or weeps. It's like a new role for me. Does that make sense?"

"Not much," she said. "You don't have to be on *all* the time, do you?"

"Yes," he said. "I do. All the time. Then, after I've conquered this new audience of one—not in bed; that's not significant—but convinced her by my performance, made her admire me and love me, well then—then I come back to you."

"To the old, familiar audience."

"That's right. But, my God, Cyn, I'm a player. You knew that from the start. Onstage or offstage, I'm a player."

"How I wish you were a dentist."

"No, you don't. You'd be bored to tears."

"I suppose so," she sighed.

He inched closer. Tentatively he slid an arm lightly about her waist. When she didn't object, he moved a little closer. He put his lips to her ear.

"Miss me?" he whispered.

"No."

"Liar!"

He rose from the sand, walked on his knees until he was directly behind her. Then gently, he began to massage her neck and shoulder muscles, softly soothing. Gradually her head dropped forward; she sighed with contentment.

"Still at the villa?" he asked.

"Mmm-hmm."

"Rent paid for the month?"

"Mmm-hmm."

"I bumped into Mike Spigelow in Nice. He's doing a new thing for the fall season. They go into rehearsal next month. Mike thinks there's a part that's right for me. Second lead—very strong character. Lots of makeup and a heavy death scene."

"Sounds good."

"Oh yes," he said. "I think we better get back to London."

"All right," she said equably. "Anything in it for me?"

"Ahh, no," he said. "Unfortunately."

"Mike's wife going to be in it?" she asked casually.

"I believe he mentioned she is. A few lines."

"You had a thing going with her once, didn't you?"

"That was before I met you, dear."

"My, my," she said. "You were certainly a busy little boy before you met me. And you haven't slowed down noticeably *since* you met me."

"But I always—" he started.

"I know," she said. "You always come back. Just like my heat rash. . . ."

And there they were, both remembering, back in the dressing room, older now, and both reflecting, "But no wiser." Toby was standing behind Cynthia, gently massaging the muscles of her bare neck and shoulders. Finally he left off, and went into the bathroom. He came back with a glass, holding it up to the light.

"If you don't mind toothpaste-flavored Scotch," he said, "we can share a wee bit of the old nasty."

"Did Doctor Jake say you could drink?" she asked anxiously.

"Oh sure," Toby said. "And smoke. It doesn't make any difference now."

He took a bottle of whiskey from the dresser cupboard, poured half a glass. He handed it to Cynthia who took a small, ladylike sip, and handed it back. Toby sat down heavily on his bench, took a deep swallow, stared at his image in the fogged mirror.

"Mirror, mirror, on the wall," he said, "who's the biggest schmuck of all?"

"Toby, do you think you should see another doctor?"

"No, I do not think I should see another doctor. What the hell's the point? If Jake's wrong, I'll be alive six months from now and can tell him to fuck off. But I don't think he's wrong. I saw the surgeons' reports, and—"

"Toby, you didn't tell me that."

"I didn't tell Jake that, either. You were both so happy I came out of surgery okay, I didn't want to spoil things for you. But I bribed a nurse with a kiss and found out what the score was. Nothing to nothing. The sawbones said it had spread too much, too far . . ."

She reached quickly for the glass of whiskey, took a much larger gulp, shuddered, handed it back to him.

"Tastes awful," she gasped.

"I know," he said. "But it'll prevent cavities."

She turned sideways to lean on him, put her head on his shoulder, grip his arm.

"Frightened, darling?"

"Of course not. That's one advantage of being an old actor. By the time you've reached my age, you've played so many death scenes you know how it's done. I can handle it."

"*We* can handle it, love," she said.

As the many years passed, Cynthia Marlow bloomed from a rather large, plump, obviously attractive girl into a composed and tranquil woman who spoke in a musical, somewhat flutey voice in which syllable emphasis seemed to be by change of pitch rather than force of breath.

She was undeniably handsome, with splendid posture and the carriage of a minor duchess. Her fine blond hair had become more silvered than white. Combed back from a high, broad forehead, and usually gathered in a chignon, it revealed a long, soft neck. She favored collarless dresses, robes, and coats. It pleased her to accentuate Toby's raffish appearance by close attention to her own personal cleanliness and grooming. There was a warm, sweet, womanly glow to her that attracted both males and females, but especially incestuous young men searching for a mother.

Her smile was particularly radiant, and her angers rarely displayed. From her long association with Toby Marlow, she had developed the serene manner of a practical nurse dealing with a nonviolent and frequently amusing maniac. Her eyes were an unusual greenish brown, her nose patrician, her complexion unmarked except for fine smile lines at the corners of her mouth. Her body, unnecessarily girdled, was still yielding. The plumpness of youth had become the ripeness of middle age. She was pleased with this change, and so was Toby.

The man himself leaned over to kiss her bare arm. . . .

"*We* can handle it," he agreed. "Sweet Cyn, the most unsinful woman who ever lived. Well, luv, we have a lot to do in the next six months. First of all, we must get David through his rehearsals and see him open. It's just a university theatre, but it's a marvelous chance. Maybe a scout for porn movies will see him."

"Oh Toby," she protested, "you know you're proud of him."

"He'll be a disaster."

"Toby, that's not fair! David shows a lot of promise."

"I wish he'd show talent."

"You can coach him, dear."

"If he'll let me," Toby said. " 'How sharper than a serpent's tooth it is to have a thankless child.' And there's the business of Barbara's child. She wants to have it and keep it as her very own, like some kind of teddy bear. Just wait until she changes her first diaper and gets crap under her fingernails. She'll change her mind about the joys of motherhood."

"Toby, can Barbara keep the baby? Legally, I mean?"

"I don't know. I'll have to talk to Julius about it. But in any event, she'll need help and money. I think she should move in here until the baby arrives—and afterwards, too, if she likes. I don't fancy the idea of her being alone in that Parisian garret she lives in."

"Oh Toby," she said lovingly, "you're so *kind.*"

"Goddamned right," he said.

"She must move in," Cynthia said firmly. "I can make your study into a nursery."

"Screw that!" Toby shouted. "Make over David's study. He put the loaf in the stove."

"Well, we have plenty of room." She soothed him. "And Barbara will be warm and get regular meals."

"She's a health-food nut," Toby warned. "She won't eat anything that isn't grown in horseshit."

"Oh Toby!"

"It's the truth. Besides, Blanche's cooking will stunt the baby's growth."

"How can you say a thing like that?" Cynthia asked. "Blanche is a very good cook. She may not be fancy, but she has a way with plain, wholesome food like pork butts and cauliflower. And she—"

But during this encomium to Blanche's culinary skills, Toby rose and went into the bedroom. He returned in a moment, shrugging slowly and laboriously into a clean white shirt. He held out his cuffs, and Cynthia obediently put in the links.

"Now about us," he said, interrupting her monologue.

"What about us?"

"Cyn, I think we ought to get married."

"Toby!" she cried, shocked and pleased. "You're proposing!"

"Against my better judgment," he said. "Remember when Kellerman talked me into a run-of-the-play contract? I thought the damned thing was a turkey, but it ran for two years. After a while I could walk through that part dead drunk—and frequently did. I swore then—no more long-run contracts. But now I'm willing to risk it for six months. As things stand, you're my common-law wife, and I don't think there will be any trouble with inheriting. But I'd feel better if we made it all legal and nice and tidy. I know Julius Östretter will feel better, too—bless his gnarled legal heart. Cynthia, will you marry me?"

"Well . . ." she said thoughtfully, "this isn't *quite* the way I dreamed it might happen, but the answer, darling, is yes, yes, yes!"

"I was afraid you'd say that, damn it. All right, that's settled. Now I've got to make out a will."

"Who's going to tell David?"

"That he's a bastard? I guess I'll have to. I'm not looking forward to it. 'Son, you're a bastard.' He'll probably say, 'Father, so are you.' It'll rupture my wit explaining why we never married."

"We started to a few times," she said.

"I know—but something always came up. Once I got the lead in *Much Ado*—"

"And once I got the measles."

"And once I got drunk."

"And once I lost the license."

"And once the war started."

"Yes," she said reproachfully. "And once you ran off with the belly dancer at your bachelor party."

"That diamond in her navel was a fake," Toby Marlow said.

"How do you know?"

"I tried to scratch a window with her. Well, anyway, we never got married. But better late than never. You know who said that?"

"You just did."

"If there's anything I can't stand, it's a smart-ass. For your information, my illiterate concubine, it was John Heywood who wrote 'Better late than never.' And he swiped it from Livy. Listen, Cyn, we'll have a beautiful wedding. Maybe David will be my best man."

"And Blanche can be my maid of honor," she said.

"And Barbara can be the flower girl," he said, "festooning our nuptial bed with rose petals."

"Oh yes!" she cried. "Yes! Yes!"

Toby, tucking his shirt into his pants, went into the bedroom again. Cynthia sat for a moment, chin on hand, dreaming and smiling. Not seeing her image in the aged mirror. Then she called into the bedroom, voice raised:

"Toby, did you ask Doctor Jake about sex?"

The answering shout came back:

"I asked him—but he wasn't interested."

SCENE FOUR

THE SIDEWALK along the west border of Manhattan's Central Park is paved with hexagonal slates. Some sections of the walk tilt crazily; in some, the stones are loose, cracked, or missing. Then you have your everyday, run-of-the-mill stretches where hopeful moss and stunted grass poke up between the stones. It is a city walk, demanding a wary eye for obstacles and a keen eye for dog droppings.

A stone parapet prevents pedestrians from falling into the park itself, which in several sections slopes off sharply eastward. But park trees project branches over the sidewalk, as do a line of trees set between walk and street. The result is faintly bucolic, not unlike a stage set that has become worn and somewhat tattered during the original production, and has then been taken on the road to end its days in Keokuk.

On this night the sidewalk stones were greasy with fog. Occasionally, when the clouds parted, they reflected dimly the silver paring of a quarter-moon.

The air was damp, pleasantly redolent of city smells. The wind was strong without being sharp. David Marlow wore a cardigan under his tweed jacket. Toby Marlow wore a stained trench coat and battered deerstalker cap. He was smoking an enormous cigar. After inhaling the fumes for several paces, David moved around to the upwind side for the remainder of their postprandial stroll.

Toby belched loudly.

"That lamb wasn't led to slaughter," he said. "It was chased for five miles."

David said, "You shouldn't have screamed at Blanche like that."

"And why the hell not?" Toby demanded. "I happen to love Blanche. If you can't scream at people you love, who can you scream at?"

"One of these days she'll get fed up with your tantrums and walk out on us."

"Not Blanche," Toby said. "Not a chance. She worships me. She sticks around in the hope that one of these nights I might dip Cecil in the hot grease."

"You bastard!" David said.

"You took the words right out of my mouth."

"What? What are you talking about?"

Toby turned his head and held up his hand as if he was whispering an aside to an audience. "Not yet," he said. "Not yet. The time is not ripe."

He paused under a streetlight, and David waited patiently. Toby fumbled inside his trench coat, brought out a long hammered silver flask (U.S., circa 1927). He unscrewed the top, took a deep swallow, then offered the flask to David.

"Want a douche?" he asked. "Oh, I keep forgetting your perversion: you don't touch the stuff."

"No, I don't," David said.

"No, you don't," Toby repeated. "You have other, more unnatural vices—like impregnating young girls, thou hungry, lean-faced villain."

"I offered to marry her, but she doesn't want to."

"Thus proving her intelligence and good sense."

"Dad," David sighed, "do we have to argue about this?"

"I have asked you—asked? Nay, demanded!—a million times not to call me 'Dad' or 'Pop' or 'Old Man' or 'Dad-dums' or anything but 'Toby.' My name is Tobias, of which the affectionate diminutive is 'Toby.' And everyone—relatives, friends, and fans without number—is affectionate toward me and calls me 'Toby.' I extend that same right to my pigeon-livered son who has more hair than wit, and who was born under a caul when the moon was hidden, there was a weeping in the sky, and the earth trembled."

"Just what the hell are you maundering about?"

"And what's so terrible about arguing?" his father asked. "It cools the blood, cleanses the stuffed bosom of that perilous stuff which weights upon the heart, thins the bile, and clears the air. Thou clam! Thou oyster! You're so closed up that one of these days you're going to explode and splatter yourself all over the landscape."

David, convinced that his old man was finally over the edge, around the bend, and down the drain, said: "Maybe I will have a drink. A small one."

They paused again. Passersby glanced curiously as Toby took out the flask, unscrewed the cap, wiped the mouth on his sleeve, handed it over to David.

"'Wonder of Wonders, a miracle, a miracle,' " he said. "Sip it slowly and with respect: the first big step for mankind, the first small step on the road to perdition."

David wet his tongue cautiously from the flask.

"God!" he said. "That's awful!"

"Of course it's awful," Toby said. "Did you think I've been enjoying myself all these years?"

He reclaimed the flask, took a deep swallow. They resumed their walk in silence. Occasionally they passed other strollers, dogwalkers, young couples with arms about each other's shoulders.

David Marlow was a bit over six feet tall, weighed 163. He was erect, slim, athletic, with a lightness that was part his parents' grace, part his natural musculature, and part a disciplined regimen of Yoga and dancing exercises. He had more than his father's rugged good looks, but it was an elegant beauty; his face, in repose, was almost feminine.

His hair was dark brown, silky, worn long but brushed and neatly trimmed. Brows were heavy. He shaved twice a day. This very young man had a very young mustache sprouting from his upper lip like a child's toothbrush. He had extraordinarily light blue eyes, sculpted lips, small ears set flat to the skull, teeth white and sharp. Fifty years ago he would have qualified as a "matinee idol." But he was too serious about his art to believe physical beauty an advantage; he was convinced that even if he looked like Quasimodo, he would still be destined to become the world's greatest actor.

This solemnity—about himself, his craft, his future—was reflected in the way he usually dressed: sober business suits worn with vests, white shirts, conservative ties, unwrinkled socks, and polished shoes. Verve disappeared when he stepped off the stage. Only occasionally did a warm, uninhibited laugh suggest there might be more to him than cold ambition.

His trained voice was far from being the splendid diapason of his father's, but there was good resonance to it. On occasion, it suffered from a kind of self-satisfied sonority: a corporation lawyer reading a tax brief. His gestures were artful, most of them involving the heavy black-rimmed glasses he wore offstage: whipping them off (anger), shoving them atop his head (perplexity), peering over them (disbelief), gnawing the earpiece (ratiocination). Without his glasses, he seemed ingenuous, without cunning.

"Toby . . ." he said.

"What?"

"Toby . . ."

"Are you drunk already?" his father demanded. "Instead of loosening your tongue, has that half-gram of alcohol frozen it? Now say 'Toby' just once more, and off you go to a giggle factory or dry out."

"I just wanted to tell you I'm sorry."

"Sorry?" Toby said. "About what?"

"About—about what Doctor Jake told you."

"You mean croaking? Don't by shy, thou mongrel, beef-witted loon. You won't offend me. I'm going to croak in six months. I'm going to die. Death. See? I can say it. It doesn't hurt. I've said it a hundred times in a hundred good parts, and it doesn't bother me a bit. I'm going to die."

"Well . . . I'm sorry."

"You know," Toby said, "you're a lousy player. Did anyone ever tell you that besides me? You-are-one-lousy-player. This is how you express sympathy—'I'm sorry'? Let me give you a short lesson, m'lad. Now you're Toby. I'm David, your son. I have just learned you're going to be dead in six months. Now get this—and *listen*, for God's sake."

The two men halted under a streetlight. Toby stepped briefly outside the circle of light, into the gloom. When he stepped back into the weak orange illumination, the transformation was startling. He seemed to have aged physically. His shoulders slumped, arms dangled helplessly, fingers trembled, knees sagged. His whole posture was one of shock and despair. When he began to speak directly to David, his gestures were more than theatrical; they were the exaggerated, distraught movements of a man staggered by an emotional cataclysm he cannot fully comprehend. His voice, ordinarily booming, had become hesitant, almost cracked with hysteria, draining away to a scratchy whisper at the end of each sentence.

"Toby . . . Toby . . . I just heard. Six months? Oh my God! I wanted to die when I heard. I wanted the earth to split beneath my feet, the whole world to crack apart. Life without you? Not life, Toby, but a kind of living death for all of us. I won't—I can't—please God, say it isn't so! Toby, when you go, something will go out of my life as well, something from the lives of all of us—light and laughter and wonder and joy. We'll all die a little with you. Don't leave us, Toby. I beg of you, don't leave us!"

Almost against his will, David was conquered by this performance, fascinated by his father's technical skill, deeply moved by the emotional appeal of Toby's words.

"My God," he breathed.

"Got you, didn't I?" Toby said complacently. "As Oscar said, when it comes to sincerity, style is everything."

"Well, it's not *my* style."

Furious at himself for having been bamboozled by Toby's demonstration, David turned and began walking again, a little faster. His father hurried to catch up.

"No, it's not your style. I know your style. The method, the motivation, the introspection."

"It isn't a 'method,'" David said angrily. "Can't you get that through your marinated brain?"

"Maybe not, but it's an approach—and the wrong approach. I never went to acting school a day in my life. I had my first walk-on at the age of six in *A Midsummer Night's Dream*. We learned from each other. We lived, ate, and slept theatre. We—"

"Oh lord, Toby," David begged piteously, "not again!"

"Yes, goddamn it, again! Walk-ons and carrying spears. Prop man and stage manager. Selling tickets and handing out programs. Burlesque and flea-bag hotels. Getting stranded and swindled on contracts. Coming into hotels through the service entrance, and what decent woman would be seen with an actor? We were rogues and renegades, thieves and seducers, whores and pimps. But now we go on TV talk shows and get knighted by the Queen. But when I started, you waded through shit to learn your art. But you *learned*. Not in any crap-ass school, but by doing! You swiped tricks from everyone you could. And you watched people, studied them. How a young boy laughed. How an old man blew his nose. How a man stabbed to death fell to the ground. How a politician swallowed his words. You learned from life. From *life*, thou arrant knave! And you learned the theatre doesn't hold a mirror up to life. Yes, it does, but it's a magnifying mirror, and everything on stage should be twice the size of life. How else can you show the wonder and sadness and humor and cruelty and madness of it? And so we, the players, must be twice the size, must be superhumans. With outsize passions and lusts and laughter. You can't walk off the stage, cold cream your face, buckle your braces, and take the midnight train to New Rochelle. Impossible! Because it's in your gut. If you have any talent at all—and I have a lot more than you give me credit for—then you're never off. Never! You're on every minute you're awake. Your life becomes the best part you ever played."

"My God, what a gassy old windbag you are!" David said. "What a diarrhea of words! What a constipation of ideas! 'The best part you ever played.' For you, acting is playing, and actors are players. *Play*. You make it sound like a sport or diversion, a recreation or game. To you, the stage is no more than an amusement. Entertainment. Equal to baseball, backgammon, and Ring-Around-the-Rosie. And so, like the mean-souled yahoo you are, you corrupt to a craft what should be an art."

"'Mend your speed a little,'" Toby said, "'lest you mar your fortunes.'"

"'Great wits are sure to madness near allied,'" David retorted, "'and thin partitions do their bounds divide.'"

"Hmm," Toby said. "Not bad—for a wet-nosed dunderpate."

"And having debased acting from a talent to a knack, you think to master it with tricks. You very words: 'You swiped tricks from everyone you could.' As if acting was nothing but that; the more tricks, the better actor. With your tearful winks and snuffles and shuffles and flapping eyebrows and twitches and completely irrelevant gestures and body movements. Yes, I *am* a lousy player—thank God! I cannot *play* at acting, croquet, ticktacktoe, or professional football. But I *am* an actor who respects his art and means to use it to reveal the truth."

"The truth? What truth?"

"The truth in me. But this you cannot do with your bag of superficial tricks—except to reveal your own shallowness and false pretense. Toby, you're not an actor, you're a mummer. The art of the theatre has passed you by. Most of the actors you knew and worked with would be laughed off the stage today if they appeared and ripped a passion to tatters. The theatre—"

"*Tear* a passion to tatters."

"The theatre began in great open-air arenas, and actors had to wear grotesque masks and use grand gestures to be seen and understood. Even Will's plays were done out-of-doors, the actors competing with street noise. But then the theatre moved indoors, the stage became smaller. The movie screen made it even smaller, and the TV screen smaller yet. Today acting must be closer, tighter, more disciplined, and more controlled. Not as—as *gross* as it was in your day."

"My day!" Toby shouted furiously. "My day! You whey-faced whelp!"

"In your day," David repeated inexorably. "Now we look for the motivation of a character; the appearance is not enough. We search for the significance of the speeches; the words are not enough. We're digging, digging, digging, to reveal new truths through the art of acting."

"'Young men think old men are fools; but old men *know* young men are fools.' So you're not a player, you scurvy milksop? Hah! You are, and so am I, and your mother, and Barbara, and Blanche, and so is every human being who screws and farts his hour upon the stage and then is heard no more. All you know of me and all I know of you are those 'grotesque masks' we turn to each other, the manner, the gestures, and all the little tricks of speech and movement you claim to despise. And you present a different mask, a different manner, a different character to every person you meet, and so do I, and so do we all."

David halted, drew a deep breath, whipped off his horn-rimmed glasses. "I think I'll have another drink," he said.

"That's one trick you've swiped from me," Toby jeered.

They handed the flask back and forth. David's swallow went down easier this time. He replaced his glasses, and they resumed their walk and argument.

"Listen, you senile anachronism," David said, "are you saying we all put on an act for each other?"

"Of course, loon-boy. With everyone. And each performance is different and unique. We're all players, and we adjust to the other players, even if it's a cast of two."

"That's unadulterated bullshit! I don't play a part with you."

"The hell you don't. You've been playing Spencer Tracy when I happen to know you're Ben Turpin. I'm not accusing you of fraud or insincerity. It's just that in this lousy world, honesty would be unendurable, the final outrage. So we all try to be the player we feel the other player wants and will respond to."

"Ah, the Hero of the Geritol Generation speaks! Don't credit everyone with your hypocrisy. We're all false—is that what you're trying to say?"

"No more false than any good stage performance is false. The point I'm trying to get into your Roquefort brain is this: we all adjust the roles we play in private life to the other players in order to gain maximum response. We do this instinctively, not with malice aforethought, knowing that life, as well as the theatre, depends on communication. And that's where all your fancy theories on method acting and searching for truth fall apart. You ignore the other players, to say nothing of the audience, and make your playing a futile exercise in selfishness. Futile because all you're doing is tickling your ego. But you're not communicating. Your so-called 'acting' compares to real playing as masturbating compares to fucking. If you want to flip your daisy onstage for the rest of your life, that's your business—but don't imagine it's giving pleasure to others or opening their eyes to any great truth. Just think of how many parts you play in your private life—hundreds! thousands!—and how each role is determined by the person you're playing to, and you'll see how right I am."

"Will said it better," David grumbled.

"'All the world's a stage'? Well, Will said everything better—that son of a bitch! God, I would love to have known that man. Just to drink with him. And when he was in his cups—just tipsy, you know, but not falling-down drunk—why then he might babble. I mean, if he could write like that to make money, that commercial writing with the discipline it demands, then think of what he might say when the drink was in him, when there was no need for discipline, when he might just babble on and on, wonderful babble, whatever floated to the surface of that incredible, frightening mind. Oh, how I would have loved to share a jug with William Shakespeare and listen to him babble, the sweet, sweet man."

"I think I'll have another little drink," David said.

"Ah-ha! Getting to you, is it?"

Again they paused under a streetlight. Toby took a swallow, then handed the flask to his son. David stood a moment, holding it.

"No, it's not getting to me—and neither are you. Toby, you're living in yesterday. You're an antique."

"And you're a bastard," Toby said.

"A bastard? Because of what I said? Was that so frightening to you?"

"What you said? Oh, that was drivel. No, I mean it literally. You *are* a bastard. Your mother and I aren't married."

There was silence a moment. Then David took an enormous gulp from the opened flask. He gasped, sucked in his breath, took another deep swallow, and coughed, coughed, coughed. Toby pounded him enthusiastically on the back, and finally David recovered, shaking his head, wiping his mouth on his sleeve.

"Wow!" he said.

"Wow?" Toby asked. "Would you explain the motivation of that 'Wow' to me? The hidden significance? The real truth?"

"Why didn't you get married?" David demanded.

"Oh . . ." Toby said casually, "we never got around to it."

"Why are you telling me now?"

"We've decided to get married before I die. I'd like you to be my best man."

David stared at him, about to explode and splatter himself all over the landscape. But finally he removed his glasses again and collapsed in helpless laughter, ending with what sounded suspiciously like a drunken giggle. Finally, when he was able to speak . . .

"I like you, sir. I do indeed. You are an original, sir. An original!"

"Who the hell is that supposed to be?" Toby asked.

"Sydney Greenstreet in *The Maltese Falcon*."

"It stinks. Here's the way it should be done: 'I like you, sir. Mmm, you are an original. You are that, sir.'"

And in truth, his impersonation was much better than David's.

"So . . ." David said, drawing a deep breath. "Going to make an honest man out of me, are you?"

"Something like that."

"How does it feel to be the father of a bastard?"

Toby looked at him a long moment. "You should know. How *does* it feel to be the father of a bastard?"

Realization was slow in coming. Then . . .

"Oh Jesus!" David said in a shocked voice. "I forgot about Barbara. What are we going to do about that?"

"Oh-ho, now it's 'we,' is it? 'What are *we* going to do about that?' Well, issue of my loins, I will make you a very generous offer. I will either marry your mother or the mother of your child. Is that not a fair offer? Can I possibly do more?"

"Yes," David said. "Go fuck yourself."

"Good," Toby nodded. "Excellent. I'm beginning to think there may be more than Drano surging through those clogged arteries of your."

David was still disbelieving. "I'm really a bastard?"

"I've been telling you that for years."

"And you're really going to marry Mother before you—before you—"

"Before I croak?"

"Yes. Before you croak."

"I am indeed," Toby said. "A marvelous ceremony. In Technicolor, wide-screen, with a cast of thousands. You may invite as many as you wish—especially from your acting class. Let them get a final look at what it means to be a player."

"Don't start that again."

"Not only will I start it," Toby said, "but I shall continue it until I pry some sense into that mass of Play-Doh you call your brain. When do your read-throughs begin?"

"On Friday."

"Got the lines?" Toby asked.

"Not too well."

"Get the lines. The lines! Then we'll start working."

"You never played Hamlet, did you?"

"No, but I did Claudius twice and Polonius three times. I know that script better than you'll ever know it."

"I've got some great ideas for it," David said.

"Forget your ideas," Toby advised. "Will had them long before you did, and his are better."

"How come you never played Hamlet?"

Toby Marlow was silent a moment, then said, "It's getting late. We'll go back now."

David upended the flask and drained it. Then, giggling, he shook it upside down to prove it empty. He handed it back to Toby, who also shook it upside down, looking at it sorrowfully.

"Oh, what a generous slob art thou!" he said. " 'A woman would run through fire and water for such a kind heart.' "

They turned about and began to retrace their steps. But David was staggering a bit, stumbling, making heavy going of it. Finally Toby put an arm about his son's shoulders, half supporting him.

"Lissen, Toby . . ." David said. "Lissen . . .'s wise son knows his own father."

"Thank you, Henry Wadsworth Longfellow. Ask Barbara to stay with us. To move in. She shouldn't be alone, and we have plenty of room. Your mother and I want her to stay. And Blanche loves her."

"All ri'." David nodded wildly. "I'll tell her."

"Don't tell her, ask her."

"All ri', all ri', I'll ask her. Toby . . . Toby, I'd marry that woman tomorrow if she'd jus' say yes."

"Forget it. She won't."

"Jus' say yes. One little yes."

"Are you drunk?" Toby asked incredulously. "On what must be at least two ounces of blended Scotch?"

"Not drunk," David protested vehemently. "Not drunk 'tall. Feel li'l—li'l light-headed."

"And tomorrow, after you sober up, you'll still be light-headed. I can see your reviews now: 'David Marlow played Hamlet. Hamlet lost.' "

The two, father and son, linked together and sharing their staggers, dwindled away through the gloom, lurching from side to side, occasionally trading insults, spouting quotations of no particular relevance, and sometimes breaking into fragments of song. Their voices were surprisingly harmonious, but passing pedestrians were careful to give these roistering clowns a wide berth. Eventually, they disappeared in the fog. . . .

SCENE FIVE

THE MARLOWS' bedroom was a high-ceilinged, squarish chamber dominated by an enormous four-poster bed, complete with fringed canopy. The entrance was from the left. An archway at right led to the mirrored dressing room and bathroom (decorated with circus posters).

This room was large enough to accommodate four chests of drawers placed between five curtained, floor-to-ceiling windows.

There was an oval, glass-topped table set around with chairs, used for breakfasts and occasional late suppers. A damask-covered chaise longue was positioned near the windows. There was a heavy leather club chair with a drum table alongside. The table bore a green-shaded student lamp on its scarred and pitted top. Concealed within the cabinet was a small cellaret. A marble-topped commode and a bedside table, with telephone, completed the room's heavier furnishings.

But like the living room, this sleeping chamber was a hodgepodge of theatrical props, mementos, framed photographs, souvenirs, and, oddest of all, a little one-word sign of red neon tubing set on a special stand. At the moment, this sign was switched on and was flashing "Marlow . . . Marlow . . . Marlow . . ." at regular and hypnotic intervals

Toby Marlow was properly costumed for sleep, wearing a long linen nightshirt and nightcap with a tassel ball hanging rakishly over his left ear. His feet were bare. He stood near the oval dining table. There was a bowl of fresh fruit on the table, and Toby was dexterously juggling three oranges and an apple. He was glancing about indifferently—but really waiting for the applause to start.

Cynthia, in flowing nightgown and negligee, was stretched out on her side of the chaise longue. She was engaged in a complex series of languid, preslumber exercises that included patting gently beneath her chin with the back of her hand, moving her head slowly about on her neck, opening her mouth wide in a strained and frightening grimace, etc.

Blanche, wearing an old flannel robe over her flannel nightgown, her hair in curlers, was engaged in a housekeeping chore: changing the linen on the Marlows' bed. Neither she nor Cynthia glanced at Toby's juggling feat; they had seen it many times before. Finally, unappreciated, Toby replaced the oranges in the fruit bowl and began wandering about the room, munching on the apple.

"Well," he said, "I told him."

"That's nice, dear," Cynthia said.

"How did he take it?" Blanche asked curiously.

"All right," Toby said shortly. "The kid's all right." Then he turned, threatening: "But don't tell him I said so."

Blanche laughed. "God forbid that anyone might think you were human."

Still wandering, still gnawing on his apple, Toby stopped at the bedside phone and pointed.

"Look at that goddamn phone. It never rings. It just *never* rings. I've been in plays where the phone rings every ten minutes. That's how you learn your rich uncle just died and left you a million dollars, or your wife ran away with the butler, or with your mistress—or whatever. But our phone never rings. Damn it, doesn't *anything* work in this house?"

"You sure as hell don't," Blanche said.

"You're really asking for it, kiddo," Toby said. "Keep on like that, and you'll earn a swift kick in the cruller. I'm bigger than you are."

"The bigger they are, the harder they fall," said Blanche.

"Don't you believe it," Toby said. "The bigger they are, the harder they kick. Listen, will you stop caressing my sheets and get the hell out of here? I want to seduce my wife."

"She's not your wife," Blanche said, turning down the comforter and patting it.

"Perhaps not at this point in time," Toby said, all haughty dignity. "But she is the woman with whom I share connubial bliss."

Both women had a fit of the giggles, and Toby looked at them suspiciously.

"I don't like the way you two witches have been acting lately," he said. "There's something going on. A conspiracy. Against me."

"Oh Toby!" Cynthia said.

"It's true. Two witches. If there was one more of you, you could play *Macbeth*."

"And if you weren't so bald," Blanche said, "you could star in *The Hairy Ape*."

"And you could star at Epsom Downs just the way you are," Toby retorted. "Don't ever try to stop me, horsey. It can't be done."

Blanche made a lewd gesture toward him, middle finger extended. And then laughing inaudibly, she exited and closed the door behind her. Toby finished his apple, tossed the core into the bowl of fresh fruit. Then he shuffled over to the freshly made bed and sat down heavily. Cynthia looked at him anxiously.

"How do you feel, Toby? Truly."

"Truly? Not so good. A little weary. It's been a heavy day. I think I'll lie down and take a little nap till morning."

"A very good idea," Cynthia nodded approvingly. "I'll be along in a minute."

"I don't think I'll be able to get it up tonight."

"You always say that, but you always do."

"With a little help from my friends."

Toby slowly straightened out on his side of the bed, pulled the comforter over his legs. Cynthia rose and moved about the room, taking his apple core from the bowl of fresh fruit and dropping it into a waste basket, opening windows, adjusting curtains, etc. Toby's eyes followed her as she moved.

"Cyn, did I tell you I loved you?"

"Yes, you did." She smiled. "That's twice in one day."

"I might even say it again. That'll be three times—a new world's record."

"In one day!" Cynthia exclaimed.

She came over to the bed, sat near him. He moved over a bit to make room for her. She took up his hand, kissed the fingertips.

"Tastes of apple," she said. "Toby . . ."

"What?"

"Will everything be all right? Tell me everything will be all right."

"Stick with me, kid, and you'll be wearing diamonds."

They smiled, looking at each other, remembering the first time he had told her that. The first time they met . . .

It was a cramped, rather ratty backstage dressing room. The ceiling was low, the paint on the walls leprous, the furnishings old without being quaint. The light came from a single naked bulb hanging from an overhead wire and from a border of low-wattage bulbs surrounding a dressing table much smaller and infinitely more tatty than the grand mirror in the Marlows' present dressing room.

The year was 1932. Toby Marlow was scoring a personal success as the leading juvenile in a dreadful musical comedy called *Please Don't, Sophie*! It had already played two nights and would play two more before dying a merciful death, hurried along by a respected critic who wrote, among other things, "The sex in this alleged 'comedy' makes me want to set fire to every bed in the world."

But Toby's notices had been very good indeed, and he had every right to the complacent smile he exchanged with his reflection in the dressing-table mirror as he removed his stage makeup. He was stripped to the waist, his torso still sweated from the final frantic and hopeless dance scene. Even his bald pate gleamed with moisture. Toby wiped it dry with a distressingly soiled towel.

Suddenly there was a sharp, peremptory knock on the dressing-room door. . . .

A male voice shouted, "Mr. Marlow! Someone to see you. Are you decent?"

"Just a minute," Toby yelled.

Hastily he pulled on a wig, adjusted it carefully, patted it smooth.

"Entrez vous!" he caroled. Then, when there was no answer, no reaction, he screamed, "Come in, come in, goddamn it!"

As he spoke the last line, Toby rose to his feet, took two strides to the door, yanked it open angrily. He thawed immediately when he saw what fortune had brought him: a soft, uncorseted, pretty young woman. She was trembling with nervousness, holding a single red rose awkwardly.

"Well well well," Toby said. "What have we here?"

Faltering at first, then in a rush to recite the speech she had obviously rehearsed, the young woman said, "Mr. Marlow, I just wanted to tell you I think you're the greatest actor ever, and I've seen the play both nights, and it's a terrible play, and the only reason I went was to see you, and I wanted you to know and to have this."

She thrust the rose at him. He accepted it gracefully with a tender smile.

"Bless you, child—son of a *bitch*!"

He shook his hand furiously, then sucked at his thumb.

"Oh dear!" she said. "I guess I should have removed the thorns."

Toby smiled bravely.

"'The heart that is soonest awake to the flowers is always the first to be touched by the thorns.' Do come in, darling. It was very sweet of you to visit me."

He ushered her into the dressing room, closed the door and, while she was looking about, locked it furtively.

"Not very palatial, is it?" he asked cheerily. "Sit over here in this chair. But do be careful of that right rear leg; it has a tendency to collapse. How did you manage to get past the stage door? Bribe?"

"Oh no. Mac and I are old friends. I played this theatre once."

"Did you now? In what?"

"Well . . . it was just a Christmas pantomime. I played a cantaloupe."

"A cantaloupe? Juicy part!"

They both laughed. Toby was excited by the way she laughed: head thrown back, throat strong and full. He pulled his wire-back chair over to face her. He sat down, still holding the rose gingerly. He moved his chair so close their knees were almost touching.

"What is your name, dear?"

"Cynthia Seidensticker. But I use the name Cynthia Blake."

"I should think so! Cynthia is a beautiful name. I love the sound of it. I could do a lot with 'Cynthia.' For instance: Angry: 'Cynthia!' Imploring: 'Cynthia?' Passionate: 'Sss-Cyn-the-aaah.'"

"You're just marvelous!"

"Oh yes," he said. "And what else have you done—on the stage, I mean?"

"Well—uh—I did a season of summer stock in the States."

"You're lying, of course?"

"Of course."

Again they both laughed, and Toby hitched his chair even closer to her. Cynthia couldn't seem to take her eyes from his wet torso.

"You're all perspired," she said faintly.

"Sweaty. Lords perspire; actors sweat. Be a luv and wipe me down, will you?"

He stood, tossed the rose aside. He held the soiled towel out to her. Hesitantly she stood up, took the towel, began to wipe his turned back gently.

"I'm really not a very good actress," she confessed. "I'd like to be, but I'm not."

"Then forget about the theatre," Toby advised. "It's no place for doubt."

"But I love it," she said, wiping away busily.

"Good. Buy tickets then. Married?"

"No."

"Lover?"

"No."

"Boy friend—or friends?"

"A few," she said hesitantly. "Nothing serious. But I don't know why I'm telling you all this. You can't be interested."

Toby turned to face her. She continued wiping his neck, shoulders, chest, and ribs with the sodden towel, engrossed in her work. Young Toby had an impressive torso, firm and gracefully muscled. He took the towel from her trembling fingers, dropped it to the floor. He clasped her upper arms softly.

"Of course I'm interested," he said. "You're very lovely, Cynthia."

"Thank you."

"'Cynthia, fair regent of the night.'"

"What's that from?" she asked.

"I don't know. Something that sticks in my mind." Gently, hands still on her upper arms, he pulled her toward him until she was pressed against him. Her head bent back fearfully.

"Cynthia," he whispered. "Do you know what the name 'Cynthia' means?"

"What?" she said, breathless now.

"She who seeks love."

"You're—you're making that up . . . aren't you?"

"Yes, but that doesn't make it a lie. Does it?"

She was silent.

"It's not a lie, is it?"

"No," she said faintly.

He moved a hand behind her head, pressed her face close to his.

"'Then come kiss me, sweet and twenty;
"'Youth's a stuff will not endure.'"

"Oh, I couldn't, Mr. Marlow," she said. "I just *couldn't!*"

"'They do not love that do not show their love.'"

He pushed his mouth against her closed lips. She stared at him with widened, shocked eyes. He withdrew his opened mouth.

"'The kiss you take is better than you give.'"

"Please don't, Mr. Marlow. I didn't—I just—this is all wrong."

"'To do a great right,'" he quoted, "'do a little wrong.'"

He kissed her again. This time she melted against him, her mouth open. But her eyes compensated for it by closing. Then, breathing heavily, she pulled away. A little.

"'Love goes toward love,'" he whispered.

"I want to leave here this instant," she said loudly. "I want—"

"'Speak low,'" he urged, "'if you speak love.'"

"What makes you think I want you to make love to me? How dare you—"

"'I dare do all that may become a man; who dares do more is none.'"

"You're the most conceited person I've ever met. Just because I—"

Again he kissed her, and again she melted. His slow hands moved over her shoulders, down her back, across her ass. Then, with tender fingers, he touched her face.

"'There's language in her eyes, her cheek, her lip.'"

"Please don't, Mr. Marlow, I beg of you. I've never done anything like this before. I will *not* do it. I shall scream for help."

"'The brain may devise laws for the blood.'"

"'But a hot temper o'er leaps a cold decree.'"

"Have you no shame, sir? No shame at all?"

"'The lady doth protest too much, me-thinks.'"

"And me-thinks you are a cad and a—uh—bounder. You are certainly no gentleman. Doesn't my virtue mean anything to you?"

"'Some rise by sin, and some by virtue fall.'"

Again they kissed, more warmly this time. Their arms curved about each other, pulled sweetly close.

"I'm going to cry," she said.

"'Love comforteth like sunshine after rain.'"

"No no no! Can't you understand what 'no' means?"

"'Have you heard it fully oft,

"'A woman's nay does stand for naught.'"

He took up one of her hands, pressed the opened palm to his mouth.

"What are you doing?" she cried.

"'To kiss the tender inward of thy hand.'"

"Oh . . ." she said dreamily. "Oh . . . Your tongue drives me wild."

"'Her voice was ever soft, gentle, and low, an excellent thing in woman.'"

He fumbled at the top button of her blouse, but so intense was his excitement that he made a sorry job of it. She attempted to help him, but their fingers became entangled as their efforts grew increasingly frantic.

Toby was furious. "'The attempt and not the deed confounds us!'"

"Here," she directed, "take your hands away and let me do it. There's a button *and* a snap."

Obediently he dropped his hands to her waist. After a moment she succeeded in opening the top fastening.

"'Let me take you a buttonhole lower,'" he said eagerly.

He unbuttoned the front of her blouse and spread it wide. He caressed the tops of her breasts bulging from her chemise.

"Oh . . . Oh, Toby . . ."

"'A dish fit for the gods!'"

"Where can we . . . ? Is there a . . . ?"

He kicked a chair out of the way, sank to his knees on the dusty floor, reached up for her.

"'Come unto these yellow sands and then take hands.'" She sank down alongside him. They kissed again, only their lips touching as their maddened fingers ripped at buttons, hooks, belts. They paused a moment, half-naked, to catch their breath.

"'Give me your hand,'" he said, "'and let me feel your pulse.'"

"Oh Toby, you skin's so smooth. You're so beautiful."

"'Love looks not with the eyes but with the mind,

"'And therefore is winged Cupid painted blind.'"

He slipped the straps of her chemise from her shoulders, tugged it gently down to her waist. In the fashion of that day, she was wearing a bandeau, and reached around to her back to unbutton it. Unfettered, her naked breasts swelled out, nipples already engorged. Toby swooped . . .

"'Where the bee sucks, there suck I.'"

He lipped and tongued her faintly veined breasts, then drew his mouth away with a soft plopping sound. He touched the tumescent flesh.

"'As smooth as monumental alabaster.'"

"We must undress," she gasped. "We must be completely *bare*!"

"'I never knew so young a body with so old a head.'"

They disrobed each other, not in frenzied haste, but not wasting any time either. Then they were both nude, lying on their sides atop their crumpled clothing. They stroked, almost timorously.

"'The naked truth,'" Toby said.

"How lovely!" she breathed. "How delightful! Why have I been denying myself?"

"'Lady, you are the cruellest she alive

"'If you will lead these graces to the grave

"'And leave the world no copy.'"

"Oh heavens! How silky his ass is!"

"'There's a divinity that shapes our ends

"'Rough-hew them how we will.'"

They explored each other's bodies with hungry mouths, grapsing hands, prying fingers. Cynthia ran her lips across Toby's ribs.

He said: "'Love's best habit is a soothing tongue.'"

She blew warm breath upon his belly and groin, then fluttered her eyelashes lightly over his skin.

"'The fringed curtain of thy eye advance!'"

She grasped his penis in her hot fist.

"What a glorious twitcher!" she exclaimed.

"'A very gentle beast, and of good conscience.'"

She moved it to her mouth and sucked thoughtfully.

"'O! that way madness lies; let me shun that.'"

"Don't you like me to do it?"

Toby stroked her hair tenderly.

"'What's mine is yours, and what is yours is mine.'"

Promptly he moved around until his face was at her feet. He inspected closely.

"'Toes unplagu'd with corns.'"

He popped her toes into his mouth. She squirmed with pleasure.

"We are mad! Toby, we are mad!"

"'If this were played upon a stage now, I could condemn it as an improbable fiction.'"

His nibbling mouth moved over her naked calves, behind her knees, up her soft thighs.

"Oh . . ." she moaned. "Oh . . ."

"'As chaste as unsunn'd snow.'"

"Oh my dear, I think I shall die. Or at least faint. What are you going to do next?"

"'I'll tickle your catastrophe,'" he said.

"Heavens, I'm all wet."

Toby turned her onto her back, lifted her knees high and spread them. His face delved between her thighs, and he peered at her softly furred vulva.

"'Tis not so deep as a well, nor so wide as a church door; but 'tis enough; 'twill serve.'"

He buried his face in her, his lips, tongue, yea, even his teeth busy with his passion.

He gasped: "'A very ancient and fish-like smell.'"

"Brute!" she said. "Can we do it now? Please, Toby, do it now. Any way you like. How shall we do it?"

"'Commit the oldest sins the newest kind of ways.'"

Toby rose to his knees, Cynthia to hers. Both kneeling, backs straight, they faced each other and embraced. They kissed, mouths wide and working.

"What fun!" she cried.

"'Keep a good tongue in your head.'"

Cynthia drew away, sat back on her heels, regarded him gravely. She drew smooth palms down his torso, encircled his stiffening halberd with gentle fingers.

"There is something I must tell you, dear Toby. I am a virgin. I've never done it before. Does that spoil everything?"

"'An unlesson'd girl, unschool'd, unpractised,

"'Happy in this, she is not so old but she may learn.'"

"Will it hurt?" she asked anxiously.

"'The pleasing punishment that women bear.'"

"Oh darling, darling . . ."

"'When love speaks, the voice of all the gods

"'Makes heaven drowsy with the harmony.'"

"Do you love me, Toby?"

"'Talkers are no good doers.'"

"Can't you say you love me—just once?"

"'Men of few words are the best men.'"

"All right," she said, "I'll twist it off,"

She mangled his poniard dreadfully, flicking it, snapping it, threading it through her fingers. Then she leaned forward to munch on it hungrily. He groaned . . .

"'Do you think I am easier to be played on than a pipe?'"

"I'll bite it off!" she vowed.

He panted: "'Do not give dalliance too much rein!'"

She dropped her hands and watched with wonder and delight as his stiletto became a scimitar, swelling and throbbing, empurpled and nodding at her.

"Heavens," she said, "how it's changed!"

"'This is the short and long of it.'"

"Oh Toby, do it now. *Now*, Toby!"

She leaned forward on her knees again, pressed close, hugged him tightly.

"'Eyes, look your last!'" he shouted. "'Arms, take your last embrace!'" She reached up to stroke his hair. Before she could touch it, he cried . . . "'If you have tears, prepare to shed them now!'"

. . . and snatched off his wig. He tossed it onto the dressing table, a dead pelt. Cynthia laughed and caressed his bald pate, then pulled it down to kiss it. Toby arranged her, and she docilely allowed herself to be moved into position on her spread knees, forearms flat on the floor, head down between her hands, rump up and sprung. Her cheek was on the floor, her hair flung wide. Toby knelt behind her. His hands followed her narrow waist, the mellow flare of her hips. Then his fingers sought and found the opening to her purse. He rubbed swiftly.

"Don't tease," she begged. "Please don't tease!"

"'I must be cruel, only to be kind.'"

"I want you *in* me!"

He looked down at himself with astonishment . . .

"'Is this a dagger I see before me, the handle toward my hand?'"

He grasped his rigid bilbo. He leaned forward. He thrust it home.

"Ahh!" she wailed. "Ahh! Ahh!"

"'A hit!'" he screamed. "'A very palpable hit!'"

"How sweet! How glorious! How lovely! How sublime! What must I do, Toby? Tell me what to do."

Toby: "'Play out the play!'"

He pressed tightly to her. Imprisoned, he put his hands upon her hips and moved them about. In circles, squares, heptagons, quattuordecillions, and other geometric forms. Including spirals.

"Oh . . ." she moaned. "Oh . . . I am burning up."

"'A little pot and soon hot.'"

Cynthia's gyrations became more excited. Now her entire body was caught up in the rhythm of her pleasure. She no longer needed his professorial hands.

"'Though she be little,'" he said. "'she is fierce.'"

"Must you make jokes about it?" she demanded.

"'How oft when men are at the point of death, have they been merry.'"

Cynthia. carried away by her quick mastery of this new art, became too ferocious in her efforts, and Toby was dislocated.

"Sorry, dear," she said.

"'The course of true love never did run smooth.'"

"I'll go slower."

"'More matter and less art.'" he urged.

Cynthia's movements became more subtle, and the two worked away with a right good will, giving each other gladness and exchanging such pleasantries as moans, groans, gasps, and expiring sighs.

"Don't leave me now!" she entreated.

"'I'll not budge an inch!'"

"Faster! Deeper!"

He puffed: "'Can one decree too much of a good thing?'"

"I feel . . . I feel . . . Don't stop! Toby, I beg you, don't stop!"

"'A man can die but once.'"

Their joy became more intense until, bursting, a final jolt exploded them both.

"Bliss!" she expired. "Bliss!"

"'O, amiable, lovely death!'"

Still joined, the two-backed beast, they coupled compulsively in diminishing rhythm.

"I come, I come," she said dreamily. "I drown, I drown."

"'Great floods have flown from simple sources.'"

Their bodies shuddered to a halt. Without strength, without sense, they collapsed, stretched out flat. Both were face down, Toby lying on Cynthia's back. He was still within her. Just. Their breathing eased, heartbeats slowed.

"I never knew," she murmured. "I never knew. Perfection."

Toby: "'I'll tell the world.'"

Cynthia fumbled between her legs, then looked at her fingers. . . .

"And I'm not even bleeding!"

"'All's well that ends well,'" he said.

"Let's do it again!"

"'What?'" He laughed. "'Wouldst thou have a serpent sting thee twice?'"

Gently he disengaged himself from her, rolled off, sat on the floor. She too sat up, close to him. They looked down sadly at his blunted lance.

"Oh dear . . ." she mourned. "Did I do that?"

"'O, withered is the garland of the war!

"'The soldier's pole is fallen.'"

"But you liked it, didn't you, Toby?"

"'I may justly say, with the hook-nosed fellow of Rome, I came, I saw, I overcame.'"

Lying on the dusty floor, they embraced and spent a time kissing quietly and whispering nonsense. Then there was a hard, demanding knock on the dressing-room door.

"Mr. Marlow," a voice demanded, "are you decent?"

Toby looked questioningly at Cynthia. She nodded happily. He swooped to bestow a kiss of benediction on her thicket.

"We're locking up, Mr. Marlow," the offstage voice continued. "You've got to leave now."

Toby grumbled. . . .

"'Cursed be he that moves my bones.'"

Cynthia and Toby Marlow, smiling and nodding, were back in their bedroom in the apartment on Central Park West. There was faint illumination from the five tall windows. The chandelier and lamp had been turned off, but the red neon sign flashed endlessly "Marlow . . . Marlow . . . Marlow . . ." The forms of Cynthia and Toby were dimly apparent in their canopied bed.

"I remember," Toby said. "And then I took you to the Savoy for supper."

"Where I paid the bill," Cynthia said.

"Did you?" Toby said. "Well, it was the least you could do after what I had done for you."

"I agreed completely—at the time. And it was after supper that you said, 'Stick with me, kid, and you'll be wearing diamonds.' I didn't know then it was a joke; you were just quoting from some awful book or movie."

"Well, it was a joke and it wasn't. It was a half-joke."

"And you half-meant it," she said. "Then we walked home to that dreadful hotel where I was staying."

"And you wouldn't let me come up," he recalled.

"That's right. I said it was too late at night, and do you remember what you said then?"

"What did I say?"

"It was your last quotation of the evening. You said, 'It is not night when I do see your face.' That was so dear, so dear."

"That's true." He nodded.

"You meant *that*, didn't you, Toby? Are you falling asleep, darling?"

"Mmm . . . getting there. Hold me."

"Like this?"

"Yes. Good night, dear love."

"Good night," she said tenderly. "Good night, good night . . ."

There were a few moments of silence, dim movement on the bed, then springs creaking . . .

"Cyn . . ."

"What is it, darling?"

"Cyn, I forgot to say my prayers."

"Oh Toby, you haven't said your prayers in forty years."

"Well, I want to say them now."

"Then *say* them, dear."

Silence again; a short pause.

"Cyn . . ."

"What is it now?"

"Will you say my prayers for me?"

"Whatever for?"

"Well . . . I think they'll carry more weight coming from you."

"All right, Toby. I'll say your prayers for you."

He was satisfied, and snuggled down, hugging her.

"Thank you, Cyn. Give a good performance, will you?"

Finally, they slept. But the neon sign continued to blink: "Marlow . . . Marlow . . . Marlow . . ."

ACT II

Scene One

The office of Julius Ostretter was on 58th Street, opposite the Plaza. Julius was the Marlows' attorney and brother of their family doctor, Jacob Ostretter. His chambers would serve as a stage set for any successful lawyer's office: couch and chairs of mahogany, with dark green leather and brass nailheads. There were framed diplomas and licenses on the walls, a worn but good Oriental rug on the parquet floor. There were glass-fronted cases of law books, an enormous but faded globe within a walnut stand, a small table bearing a thermos of ice water and four glasses (turned down) on a silver tray.

On Attorney Ostretter's imposing desk was a tinted photograph of his wife; phone and intercom; sharpened pencils arranged precisely along the edge of an oversized desk blotter with corners of black alligator, the same leather that adorned a rocker blotter, the handle of a letter knife, and a heavy penholder.

At the moment, this neat, organized desk was littered with stacks of dog-eared papers, some yellowed with age; an ancient ledger, the binding broken and mended with tape; several smaller notebooks; bankbooks; bond and stock certificates; and the like. . . .

Cynthia Marlow was seated comfortably in a club chair in front of the desk. She was knitting placidly on what appeared to be a 40-foot scarf of fire engine red, the wool coming from a shopping bag at her feet.

Toby Marlow, clad in grey flannel slacks, an open-necked shirt with carelessly tied cravat, and a sport jacket of shocking plaid, was, unaccountably, practicing dance steps. He was moving about the room in slow pirouettes and crouches, the aged ballet dancer, arms waving languorously, legs lifting and drifting downward. He was making no sound, moving to a music that only he could hear. But there was a pleased smile on his face and, indeed, there was grace and happiness in his solo dance.

The only sounds, other than the click of Cynthia's knitting needles, came from Julius Ostretter, seated in the heavy swivel chair behind the desk. Funereally dressed, steel-rimmed spectacles set firmly in place, he was reading slowly through some of the tattered papers on his desk blotter. He refused to look at Toby's ridiculous antics.

"Mm-hmm," he mm-hmmed. "Mm-hmm. Mm-*hmm*."

"Cynthia, luv," said Toby, "have you ever heard more meaningful dialogue in your life? 'Mm-hmmm. Mm-hmm. Mm-*hmm*.' David could do wonders with that—if someone told him his motivation."

Julius finally looked up and slapped the pile of papers with his palm.

"Mr. Marlow, I must—"

"Your brother Jake calls me Toby."

"Please don't mention that disgusting creature's name in my presence!"

"I beg your pardon," Toby said humbly, "A certain physician, who shall be nameless here, addresses me as Toby. He has ministered to the physical needs of my family for many years. You have devoted your considerable legal talents on our behalf for a similar number of years. Could you not—in the kindness of your shrunken, juridical heart—address me as Toby? I, in grateful return, shall call you Julie."

"It's not professional," the attorney said. "I prefer 'Mr. Ostretter.' "

Toby sighed heavily.

" 'The first thing we do,' " he said to Cynthia, " 'let's kill all the lawyers.' King Henry the Sixth, Part Two, Act Four, Scene One."

"Scene Two, dear," she said placidly.

"Tell me, Mr. Marlow," Ostretter said, "this is a complete declaration of all your assets?"

"Except for my genius," Toby said. "Yesterday Cynthia and I made the perilous journey to our safe deposit box in a downtown bank. There we retrieved all that crap on your desk."

"And I typed out the inventory on David's typewriter," Cynthia said brightly. "With two carbons. Messy job. I just *can't* get the black off my fingers."

"Tell me, Julie," Toby said, "have you ever been in a safe deposit vault?"

"I have. Of course I have."

"Those little rooms they give you, where you take your box. And you can lock the door from the inside. Cynthia and I thought we might screw in there."

"I beg your pardon?" the lawyer said.

"That cute little room," Toby said. "With a small glass-topped table, scissors, rubber bands, paper clips, and a wastebasket. You could fuck in there, and no one would know the difference. Absolute privacy. Cheaper than a motel. I'll bet a lot of business executives have done it during their lunch hour. With their secretaries ending up with the imprint of scissors and paper clips on their backsides."

"I don't understand," Ostretter said, bewildered.

"On the glass-topped table," Toby explained patiently. "We didn't, of course."

"Pity," Cynthia said.

"We talked of doing it in an airliner," Toby said dreamily. "At thirty-five thousand feet. Oh darling, there's so much we've negelcted. I'm dying much too soon."

"Yes, dear, you are."

"Um—ah—well . . ." the attorney said.

"Julie, I don't wish to be critical, but who writes your dialogue? 'Um—ah—well . . .' I think it needs work."

Julius Ostretter was a lawyerish lawyer: tall, deliberately solemn, cold-mannered. His speech was pedantic, though there was no denying his cleverness. If he was a lawyerish lawyer, he was also a priggish prig, the features of his coffin face pinched with self-satisfaction. He affected a round-shouldered posture, a brooding, enigmatic smile, an annoying habit of grasping his own lapels. Toby Marlow once remarked: "Julie Ostretter says 'Hello' like Abe Lincoln delivering the Second Inaugural Address."

He made a church of his fingers, tapped the tips together importantly . . .

"Mr. Marlow, if this inventory is accurate—and I must assume it is—you have fourteen savings accounts in banks all over the country, the sums generally between fifty and five hundred dollars. Is that assumption correct?"

Toby made a church of his fingers, tapped his tips together importantly . . .

"I can attest to the veracity of your statement, counselor."

"Why?" Ostretter asked.

"Why what?"

"Why do you maintain savings accounts in such places as Peoria, Illinois, and Salt Lake City, Utah—and have maintained them since the late nineteen-thirties and early nineteen-forties? Can you explain that?"

"With pleasure," Toby said. He left off mimicking the attorney and took up his dancing again. "Lawyer Ostretter, have you spoken to Jake lately?"

"Do not mention that name!" Ostretter thundered.

Toby laughed softly. "Very well. Now about the savings accounts. . . . In the early days of my career, when I toured the United States in various stock companies, I soon learned that most theatrical promoters and producers are direct lineal descendants of Jack the Ripper. And, having been stranded without pay and without hope of being paid in a number of cities, towns, and villages—oh God, darling, do you remember that week in Duluth?"

"Do I ever?" Cynthia exclaimed. "If it hadn't been for sex, we'd have frozen to death."

"Well, then, Lawyer Ostretter of the nameless brother, it became our habit whenever we were booked into a city or small town, to take whatever money we could spare and open an account at a local bank. In case we should ever return and be temporarily without funds—robbed again!—we would have no need to exist on peanut butter sandwiches and potato chips but could, at least, afford a bottle of Piper-Heidsieck and a train ticket to more salubrious climes."

"But some of these bankbooks go back almost forty years!"

"So? After I made it, and the movie and TV work came along, we had no need for the money. But old habits die hard, and who knows—some day I may be reduced to playing *The Drunkard* in Oshkosh, Wisconsin. Then, being hissed off the stage by those good Oshkoshians, or Osh-koshers, or Oshkoshniks, or whatever they call themselves, I could immediately repair to the local bank where I had squirreled away a goodly sum in the event of such an emergency. I still have some money in Oshkosh, don't I?"

"What? Hmm . . . Oh yes . . . here it is: more than two hundred dollars in the First Farmers Bank of Oshkosh."

"Well, there you are!" Toby said triumphantly. "Cynthia, sweet, if we ever get stranded in Oshkosh, we'll have a marvelous meal of broiled Malemute meat, or perhaps a stewed wolf."

Julius Ostretter shook his head in wonder.

"But these old accounts have increased tremendously in value. I trust you have been paying income tax on the interest earned?"

"Well—ah—the President of the United States and I have an understanding. I promised not to pay any income tax on these accounts, and he promised not to play King Lear."

"Oh my. Oh my. And I see no mention here of any life insurance policies, Mr. Marlow. Do you have any insurance at all?"

"No. None."

"A man of your means? Why, may I ask, is that?"

"What was the point of life insurance?" Toby asked. "Cynthia and I agreed quite early in our relationship that if I should die before she did, she'd have no reason to go on living. Correct, Cyn?"

"Absolutely, darling."

"Oh my, oh my, oh my. But I seem to recall a conversation we once had during which you recounted your adventures aboard a submarine with the United States Navy in World War Two. Surely you must have had service insurance?"

"Let it lapse, unfortunately, after I was honorably discharged because of wounds suffered in action. But it wasn't the Navy. I served with the U.S. Army Air Force."

"The Air Force?"

"Oh yes. Fighter pilot."

"Strange . . . I distinctly remember your telling me you were the executive officer of a submarine, and took command after the captain was incapacitated with a bad case of sunburn. You told me you sank a Japanese battleship."

"Oh no, sir," Toby laughed lightly. "I am afraid you have my military career confused with that of someone else. No, I definitely was a fighter pilot. In the European theatre. An ace, in fact. Twenty-four German fighters, twelve bombers, nine barrage balloons and, of course, locomotives, troop trains, ammunition dumps—things of that sort. But I don't like to talk about it."

"Oh . . . of course."

"How I recall those days! Waking up at dawn, wondering whether or not you were fated to see another sunrise. A quick breakfast—usually just a glass of chilled chablis and a smoked kipper. Then into your flying togs, silk scarf about your throat, and off you went into the wild blue yonder. But it all brings back too many unhappy memories—of those who didn't return. They were so young, laughing and gay. I can't talk about it."

"I under—"

"I remember once I was flying a Spitfire, and we—"

"Wasn't the Spitfire a British plane?"

"Of course. But I was testing one, you see, because they were so far superior to anything we were flying, and I had been ordered to test its flight capabilities and submit a report. A written report, directly to the White House. Well, there I was at ten thousand feet, looking for an enemy target, when suddenly I spotted a flight of three German fighters above me. I knew at once they were from Baron von Richthofen's Flying Circus. I knew that, you see, because on their wings they had this red checker-board pattern and—"

"The Red Baron's Flying Circus was in World War One."

"Of course it was! But you know how the Germans worship military tradition, and they had named one of their squadrons after the Red Baron—hero worship all down the line with those caps—and there they were, six of them, thirsting for blood. And there I was, alone and apparently a sitting duck. Well, I sized up the situation at a glance and went into an immediate power dive. Zoooommmm! And when I came down to—"

"Dear," Cynthia interrupted softly. "Weren't you supposed to meet David at the university theatre?"

"What? What? Oh yes. Well, I'm afraid we'll have to leave those Messerschmidts for another time, Julie. But remind me to tell you about the dogfight; I think you'll be interested."

"Oh I will, I will. Very interested. Now, to get back to your assets. These fifty shares of Intel-Extra. When did you buy those, Mr. Marlow?"

"Buy what?"

"Intel-Extra, Incorporated. Fifty shares of common stock. Do you recall what you paid for them?"

"Cynthia, what's that all about?"

"You remember, darling. That funny little man—the friend of Sam Beaver—was starting this company and he asked you to buy some stock and you were drunk and we wanted to help him out because he was such a *nice* little man. They send us those silly checks all the time. You cash them at the liquor store, dear."

"So I do, so I do. God takes care of fools, drunks, and actors. I think we paid a dollar a share for that stock, Lawyer Ostretter. Was that a wise investment?"

"Wise? Good gracious me! I can see you don't follow the stock reports."

"I certainly do!" Toby said indignantly. "Who they've hired, what companies are on the road, what plays they're planning. I follow the stock reports very carefully, I can tell you."

"No, no. I meant—well, let it go, Mr. Marlow. I'll have to study these documents and the inventory you've submitted. First of all, you want a will drawn. Is that correct?"

"Right"

"Now let me make a few notes here . . . Who is to be the executor?"

"Who else but sweet Cynthia."

"Thank you, darling."

"You'll make a beautiful executor," Toby said fondly.

"Execu*trix*," the lawyer said.

"Better yet," Toby said. "Cyn knows so many wonderful tricks."

"I love you, too," she said.

"Any other beneficiaries besides your executrix?"

"Oh yes," Toby said. "A certain amount to our son, David, to our faithful retainer, Blanche, to our lovely and almost-daughter, Barbara Evings. And a few small stipends to ex-burlesque bananas currently living in abject poverty, some actors' charities, a few shekels to various friends, and memorabilia: gold cuff links, a semen-stained bedsheet from Lisbon, annotated scripts, a diary I kept for three days until the pages began to scorch, a toenail that came off after kicking an idiot who upstaged me during a performance of *Life with Father*, and several other sentimental bequests of a like nature."

Julius Ostretter sighed and began shuffling the papers and records into stacks. . . .

"Well, first let me pull all this in order and try to make some sense out of it. I will strike an approximate value to your total estate, and we can then sit down and plan specific bequests. A paid-up annuity for your wife might be best, for instance, but—"

"Oh, that's another thing," Toby said. "She's not my wife."

"Who's not your wife?" Ostretter asked.

"My wife."

"I beg your pardon?"

"Cynthia here," Toby explained. "She's not my wife. We're living in sin."

Cynthia shivered with delight.

" 'Living in sin,' " she repeated. "How delicious that sounds!"

Attorney Ostretter took a deep breath.

"Perhaps I do not comprehend the situation, and if I do not, I apologize most humbly, madam. But am I to understand that you two are not legally married?"

"Good show!" Toby cried. "Now you've got it. But we've been living together for almost forty years. That gives us some points, doesn't it?"

"Forty wonderful years!" Cynthia added.

Ostretter shook his head in stupefied wonder.

"Irregular," he mumbled. "Highly irregular."

"As a matter of fact they were," Toby said cheerfully. "I'd go away for months at a time. But I always came back, didn't I, dear?"

"Always," Cynthia affirmed. "No woman could have wished for a more faithful husband."

"But I wasn't, you see," Toby said to Julius. "Not really. Her husband, I mean. In any event, now that I'm about to shuffle off to Buffalo, we thought it best, Cynthia and I, that we be wed so that we may enjoy legally what we have for so many years enjoyed clandestinely. How did you like that speech, luv?"

"Very nice indeed," Cynthia approved. "Balanced, formal, and yet feeling, with a rolling rhythm to it."

"I rather fancied it myself," Toby said, preening. "Naturally, you are invited to the ceremony, Lawyer Ostretter—you and your charming spouse. You will, in due course, receive an official invitation, possibly engraved on the head of a pin."

"Awk!" the attorney said, disbelieving. "Awk!"

"So please make application for the proper license and necessary papers and so forth, and inform us of our duties and obligations, one of which, I understand, involves offering a libation of our royal blood to the civic authorities. Is that correct?"

"Hmm?" Ostretter said, completely rattled now. "Yes! Mm-hmm. What? Yes, oh yes! Forty years? Shocking! Must . . . Oh yes, *must*! Of course. Naturally. Yes, blood samples. Oh my, yes. And things . . . things to do. YOU—YOU ANIMALS!"

He screamed this last imprecation at them as he rose to his feet and rushed from the room, waving his arms wildly. He slammed the door behind him. Cynthia and Toby gazed after him in astonishment.

"Poor man," Cynthia said, shaking her head sadly. "He seemed quite upset. I wonder what on earth is bothering him?"

Toby shrugged. . . .

"Overindulging in torts, no doubt."

Scene Two

ONE OF those premature days in early spring: dark green buds poking, sun flexing its muscle, summer nuzzling around the edges with a warm breeze that smelled of July. The earth itself seemed to be thawing, giving up winter's heavy odor; the city stretched and sighed under a blue sky with small clouds that had been washed and hung up to dry.

Toby Marlow had insisted on hiring a victoria at the Plaza for a long ride through Central Park to David's university theatre. Cynthia had protested this extravagance, but not too vehemently; she knew the memory that inspired the decision: years ago she and Toby had intercourse, strenuously, in a London hansom. That success had resulted in what Toby called Marlow's First Law of Sexual Bliss—"Copulation without locomotion is tyranny."

Today the victoria driver was moribund, the horse feeblish; their journey was necessarily slow and wheezy. But the day was all youth and hope, the sun a glory as they wended northward on the twisty drive, surrounded by walking trees. They lolled comfortably, held hands, beamed approvingly at the beauty of this brave emerald patch set down on the steel and concrete city.

"'. . . So bedazzled with the sun that everything I look on seemeth green,'" Toby sighed. "And everything seemeth to be moving along in excellent fashion. We shall be married to the clarion of triumphant bells, a perfectly legal will shall be drawn, and now I may turn my full attention to making an acceptable player of our beef-witted son."

"And Barbara's problem," Cynthia reminded him. "Don't forget that. You must promise to fix that too, Toby."

"So I shall, luv, so I shall. Little Felix Fixit will put a Band-Aid on the world and make it well. But first, a small toast to the discomfiture of Lawyer Ostretter . . ."

He withdrew the hammered silver flask from his inside jacket pocket and proffered it to Cynthia. She shook her head, smiling. So Toby treated himself, closing his eyes in ecstasy as he swallowed.

"Ahhh!" he sighed. "'I drink no more than a sponge.' Nothing like geneva to cleanse the nasal passages of the stench of lawyers."

"Toby, why do Jacob and Julius refuse to speak to each other?"

"An argument they had, years and years ago."

"An argument? About what?"

"Neither can remember, but neither can ever forget."

"And what possessed you to tell Julie that ridiculous war story?"

"It amused me." He shrugged.

"But you're such a bad liar, Toby."

"You're wrong," he said. "I'm a very good liar."

"But it was such a silly story," she protested, "and you made so many mistakes."

"Deliberate mistakes, dear Cynthia," he said complacently. "All deliberate. Any fool can be an amateur liar and concoct a believable falsehood and tell it with a straight face. But to the professional, prevarication is a fine art—and I am a professional liar, if nothing else. What sets the professional off from the amateur is that the falsehood you relate must be intellectually unacceptable—so shot through with outrageous mistakes and exaggerations that the listener cannot possibly believe it. The lie must then succeed by its dramatic content and emotional appeal. The listener knows in his mind it's all a crock of shit, but he becomes so interested, so moved,

794

so involved that he's willing to trust, to follow what he feels rather than what he thinks."

The dreaming horse plodded, the victoria creaked, and Cynthia puzzled over this paradox. Toby took another sip from the flask and looked about grandly, owning the world.

"Why, Toby," Cynthia said finally, "you're talking about the theatre, aren't you?"

He laughed, pressed her gloved fingertips to his lips. Then he slid an arm about her shoulders, hugged her close

"Why in God's name couldn't David have inherited your brains as well as your looks?"

She patted his cheek lovingly.

"That's one of the nicest things you've ever said to me."

"Gin always makes me nice. Of course it's the theatre. Professional lying at its best. When that audience shows up for David's *Hamlet*, they'll be sitting on hard seats in an overheated theatre. They'll know they're not really in Elsinore, that David is not really the Prince of Denmark, that Ophelia doesn't really do a swan dive into a nearby puddle. They'll *know* those things in their minds, but they'll be willing—willing? Nay, eager!—to suppress their knowledge, and swallow the lie if it interests them, moves them, involves them. That's what playing is all about— professional lying. If I could only get David to see it!"

"Do you think you could have convinced Julie Ostretter with that awful story?"

"I could," he said. "Of course I could—if you hadn't cut me short."

She looked at him coldly.

"Perhaps I cut you short because I know the true story of your war record."

"Oh God, Cyn," he groaned. "Can't you ever forgive and forget?"

"I forgave you a long time ago," she said sternly. "But no, I cannot forget. You shouldn't expect me to."

"Why the hell not?" he demanded. "You forget to tell the Chinaman not to starch my collars."

Then both were silent, sharing another memory. The spangled park disappeared. In its place appeared the squeezed, shabby kitchen of a dilapidated London flat. The year was 1941, and Britain had been under bombardment for several weeks. But age rather than bombs had crumbled this sad and seedy room.

The coin-operated gas meter was the newest furnishing. The old table and chairs were sprung, zinc sink discolored, sagging wall shelves filled with a disheartening assortment of chipped dishes, dented pots, mismatched sets of empty jam jars. Blackout curtains hung across the narrow windows.

But despite this shoddy, the room was made bearably cheerful by what appeared to be preparations for a small celebration. The table had been spread with a reasonably clean bedsheet; an oddly assorted setting for two had been laid out. There was a loaf of greyish bread, an opened tin of meatballs and one of sardines, a box of biscuits, a jar of marmalade, a half-filled bottle of Scotch whiskey.

Cynthia, wearing the uniform of a nurse's aide, was moving about the table, inspecting her handiwork, making infinitesimal adjustments. She heard the sound of running feet pounding up the outside stairs. She started for the kitchen door. But before she reached it, it was flung back. Toby raced in, slammed the door behind him, lunged to grasp Cynthia into his arms. They exchanged passionate kisses, hugs, strokings, more kisses. . . .

"Love!" she cried. "Lover! Lover!"

"Sweet!" he cried. "Precious! Divine!"

They separated far enough to inspect each other, smiling. Toby was perfectly costumed to play the soldier returning from the wars, even though his khaki uniform was without insignia and his boots were most unmilitarily scruffy. About his shoulders hung gas mask and musette bag. And about his head was entwined a bandage, an impressive turban suitably stained.

"Oh Toby, Toby, Toby,' Cynthia sighed. "How wonderful to have you home safe and sound! How long has it been?"

"Almost a week."

"Seems like two. I was so lonely and—"

Suddenly she noticed the bandage swaddling his crown. Her jaw dropped, eyes widened; she reached out timorously to touch the bandage gently.

"Oh, you poor, poor dear," she groaned. "You're wounded! Does it hurt?"

"'He jests at scars, that never felt a wound.'"

"The bombing? Oh Toby, why *didn't* you take shelter? You might have been killed!"

"Ah . . . well . . . no, not the bombing. I'll tell you later, Cyn; it's a long, long story. How are things at the hospital?"

"Dreadful," she said.

"I can imagine," he said sympathetically.

"We've been going all hours. It never lets up. I'm weary inside my bones."

"Ah-ha!" he exclaimed. "I have just the thing for inside-the-bone weariness. Take a look at this!"

He unstrapped his musette bag, carefully withdrew a bottle swathed in blue underpants. He unwrapped it with caution, then displayed it proudly to Cynthia. . . .

"Chateau Rothschild, 1932!"

"How *nice!*" she said. "Was '32 a good year?"

"It was for me—the year I met you."

"Darling!"

She embraced him again. They kissed a very long time, and only stopped when the wail of the sirens started. They stood a moment, listening to the high-pitched warble.

"Damn, damn, damn!" he said. "The fucking alert."

"Oh, not again! I suppose we should go to the shelter?"

"The hell with it! Not before we have a glass of wine to celebrate my return from the horrors of war."

He took off his tunic, busied himself with the wine bottle and corkscrew. Cynthia sat down at the kitchen table, put chin in hand, regarded him fondly.

"How did the show go, Toby?"

"Just incredible. Max and I were *the* hit. They wouldn't let us off. What a success! It was at a big camp in Liverpool."

"I didn't know Liverpool had been bombed."

"It hasn't. But of course, we weren't *in* Liverpool. Outside, it was. Big army camp. Wonderful audience. How they laughed! We did the Flugle Street routine."

"How did you get wounded?" she asked quietly.

"Damn . . ." he said, "this cork is tight. If they had allowed encores, we'd have been there yet. You never heard such applause."

"How did you get hurt, Toby?"

"Here we go! Just let me try a sip. Oooh! Marvelous! Let me fill your jam jar, dear."

"Was the camp bombed?"

"Did you taste it? What flavor! What bouquet!"

"Toby, please tell me."

"Later."

"Now."

"It was sort of an accident," he said.

"A *sort* of an accident?"

"Well, if you must know, I fell out of a truck."

"I see," she said slowly. "Were you drunk?"

"Before I fell. Not after."

"Too bad you're not in the American army. You'd have gotten a Purple Heart."

"Have you heard that joke?" he inquired eagerly. "This maid in a bordello says to the madam, 'There's a soldier outside with a Purple Heart on.' And the madam says, 'I don't care what color—'"

"I heard it, Toby. What were you doing in the truck? Drunk in the truck?"

"Well, you see, after the show was such a success, some of us and some young officers went into Liverpool to celebrate. Damn it, Cyn, there's a war on! A man's got to make every minute count and grab his fun while he can."

"Oh, I agree, Toby. There *is* a war on. And who knows—your next show may be a dud. But that's a danger you must face during wartime."

"No need to get snotty about it," he said stiffly. "This was supposed to be a celebration."

"It hasn't turned out quite the way I hoped it would."

"I've been drunk before, and I'll be drunk again."

"I know, I know," she said. "It's just that I've been slaving away in that horrible hospital, seeing absolutely dreadful things, and worrying my head off about you. And now I find you've been getting drunk and falling out of trucks. Oh Toby, I don't blame you for having fun, it's just that I've had a bad week, and I'm in a vile mood. You must be extra nice and extra understanding to me tonight."

"Oh, I will, dear," he said, gulping wine. "I will indeed."

"We'll have this funny supper, and then we'll go to bed and make love, and then I'll be all right again."

"Well—ah—" he said, gulping wine. "I don't think we better do that, dear."

"But, Toby, we have all this food. It was very hard to come by. I had to beg or borrow most of it."

"No, no, it's not the supper," he said, gulping wine. "We'll definitely have the supper. Oh yes, definitely. I could eat a horse. A mare, of course. Hah!"

"We can have the supper," she said quietly, "but we can't make love. Is that what you're trying to tell me?"

"Well—ah—I don't think it would be wise."

"Why? Did you hurt something besides your head when you fell out of the truck?"

The air-raid sirens began again. And now, far off, they could hear the low, sodden crump of bombs falling.

"Second alert!" Toby said gaily. "Everyone off to the shelter!"

He smiled winningly at Cynthia, but it didn't do him a damn bit of good.

"Why can't we make love, Toby?" she asked.

"Oh . . . hell!" He shrugged. "It's just a precaution. Probably nothing. We'll just have to put it off for a bit, that's all."

"What have you done, Toby?"

"The shelter?" he asked hopefully.

"Toby, what have you done?"

"Well, you see, we went into Liverpool for this party. Marvelous party, really. To celebrate the success of the show, you understand. Well, then, later we went to this incredible place down near the docks. A home, really. Well, a private house. And—and . . ."

"And there were women there?"

"Well . . . yes. And whiskey, too, of course."

"Whores?"

"Oh no! No. I don't think so. Well . . . maybe. But very intelligent and jolly. They loved my jokes. But I really wasn't functioning too well by then, dear. The excitement and all. But it's possible they were ladies of loose virtue. Yes, that's entirely possible. And I'm not sure—I'm not completely certain—but there *is* a possibility I may have picked up something I didn't bargain for. A little extra, you might say. Nothing serious, mind you. Definitely not serious. But the doctor did say that—"

"You bastard!" she screamed. You *bastard*!"

"Now, Cyn . . ."

"How dare you? How *dare* you?"

The sirens were louder now, building to an ear-piercing crescendo. And the sound of exploding bombs was louder. Anti-aircraft guns were also starting up nearby, and Toby found he needed to shout to make himself heard. Cynthia would be shouting even if the outside night were silent.

"You filthy scoundrel!" she shrieked.

She stood suddenly, upsetting her chair. She grabbed up the half-empty wine bottle from the table.

"Cynthia!" he wailed, anguished. "It was a good year!"

She hurled the wine bottle at his bandaged head. He ducked. The bottle smashed against the opposite wall; wine stained slowly downward.

"Now, Cyn . . ."

"Viper!"

She flung bread, tins of meatballs and sardines, jar of marmalade, whiskey bottle. Toby danced about frantically, trying to avoid the missiles.

"Now, Cyn . . ."

"Toad! Crawling thing!"

Toby cringed under a hail of thrown plates, pots, pans. Cynthia wrenched wooden shelves from the walls to fling them, followed by a clock, a porcelain goose in flight, and framed lithograph of Loch Lomond. All, all were hurled at the cowering Toby. The room became a shambles, and Cynthia looked about wildly for something else to throw. She leaped at the gas meter and strove mightily to wrest it from the wall, but it resisted her most strenuous efforts. Finally she desisted and stood quivering with rage, too furious to weep, too breathless to scream. Toby emerged cautiously from behind the stove.

"You're upset, aren't you?" he said.

"Upset!"

"You have me?"

"No. Not hate you. Deceived. Betrayed."

"But I—"

"Now I know what you think of me. What you *really* think of me. Just another woman to oil your ego. I come in handy—sewing your buttons, toasting your muffins, nursing your rotten hangovers."

"There's more—"

"Don't you realize I now know what you think of me? That I'm a lump, a post, a stupid fool of a woman who gives and gives and gives, and needs nothing in return? That's how you think of me. Admit it!"

"I swear I—"

"Toby, I exist. Can't you get that through your head? *I do exist!* I am a person, a human being, and I breathe, and think, and feel. I think things and feel things you are quite incapable of understanding. I assure you."

"When did I—"

"You think I don't know how you use me? Nurse, housekeeper, and cook. Audience for your terrible jokes, and butt of your mean and childish tricks. In that burlesque skit where you hit the other comic with a bladder—well, in our little skit, I'm the one who gets hit."

"I never—"

"I'm a woman, you brainless idiot! I'm not just a something—a something that's always there to cheat and deceive, and to hell with her. Kick her and she smiles. Hurt her and she holds out loving arms."

"But I—"

"And another thing . . . If I ever—"

"Goddammit!" he screamed. "Will you never let me finish a sentence?"

"You just did," she said coldly. "If I ever—"

Again she halted. They both looked instinctively upward. They heard the scream of falling bombs, muffled explosions, the wail of fire engines. Their house was shaken; somewhere glass shattered and tinkled down to the street.

"If I ever did love you—" Cynthia went on, "for what reason I no longer know—you have succeeded in killing that love. Poor, tender little thing. It might have taken root and bloomed, but you put your great, cruel heel on it and ground it and ground it until it was nothing, *is* nothing. I hope you're proud of that."

They were silent then, glaring at each other, oblivious to the pandemonium in the city around them. Finally . . .

"Are you finished?" Toby asked.

"Yes."

"*Quite* finished?"

"Yes. Oh no—just one more thing. You're a shithead. Now I'm finished."

"You always were a lousy player," he said. "That could have been a great scene, and you muffed it."

"I wasn't playing," Cynthia said with grand dignity.

"You were speaking from the heart?"

"I was," she said.

"Too bad you lack the training and experience to be sincere. Look, Cynthia, I admit I am not the easiest man in the world to live with."

"Hah!"

"I admit I lie, cheat, and even, on occasion, steal. I admit I deceive you and betray you."

"Hah!"

"I admit I take advantage of your sweet good nature, and that, infrequently, I have not given proper consideration to your needs and wishes and hopes."

"Hah!"

"But I *am* capable of forgiving a woman who shouts 'Hah!' to everything I say. I forgive you a great many things, Cynthia, most of which you probably are not aware of. But I don't think of it as forgiving because I love you, for who you are and what you are. I know you are not a lump, a post, a foolish woman. And I know I am egotistical, self-centered, and rarely do anything I don't want to do. But have I ever denied what I am? Have I ever tried to conceal from you my true nature? You know I haven't."

"But you never—"

"No, now stop. You did your turn; I'm on now. I've always shown myself to you with all my warts, pimples, scars, and bald head. No makeup. I've hidden nothing from you. And I've always assumed that if you didn't like what you saw, you had the intelligence and courage to walk away from me. But you've stayed."

"I've stayed because I thought I could change you."

"I never want to change *you*."

There was a pause. . . .

"Thank you," she said faintly.

There was a heavy crump of exploding bombs, closer now. The lights flickered wildly. They heard the wail of sirens, shouts in the street, the continuous barking of anti-aircraft guns. . . .

"Cynthia," Toby said tenderly, "you're deluding yourself if you think you want me different from what I am. In your heart of hearts, you're content with what I am—or at least with the image you have of me. Occasionally, only occasionally, you are so horrified by what I do that you cry, 'Why can't Toby be like other men?' But you know, don't you, Cyn, that if I was like other men, I'd feel very differently about you, and you about me. We make a marvelous cast, you and I, the way we are. Let's stick to our parts and not try to rewrite the lines. Our life together *plays*, darling. I feel it, and I think you feel it, too. Don't you?"

No answer.

"Don't you feel it, Cyn?"

"Yes," she sighed. "It's just . . ."

"I know, I know," he said. "I've been a bastard. Again. And you were disappointed in me. Again. That's why you said those silly things and threw stuff and tore up the place."

"I suppose."

"Oh darling, darling . . ."

He moved to her swiftly and embraced her, clasping her waist, stroking her hair. Finally, finally, she relaxed into his arms, hugged him fiercely.

"Cynthia, promise me you'll never again attack me in that vulgar and primitive fashion."

"I promise, Toby."

"Promise you'll never, as long as you live, throw another dinner plate, soup kettle, or salt shaker at me."

"I promise. Oh, I promise, dear!"

They were embracing again when a stick of bombs fell across their square of flats. There was a tremendous crash. The lights flickered, went off, came back on again to show the ceiling had fallen, the outside wall had been blown away to reveal London burning. The air was filled with smoke and plaster dust.

Cynthia and Toby had been knocked off their feet. They crawled shakily from under the rubble, staggered upright. They brushed debris and plaster chunks from their heads and clothes.

"Goddammit, Cyn." Toby coughed. "You *promised*!"

•   •   •

But now the sun was shining. Central Park was greening. It was another world, another spring. They listened to the clop of the horse's hooves, creak of the victoria's wheels. Cynthia and Toby were carried in a new dream up to the university theatre. Toby took out his flask again, held it up so it glinted flashing in the sunlight.

"To wedded bliss!" he toasted.

"I must drink to that!" Cynthia said.

They each took a sip from the flask. Then Toby returned it to his pocket and resumed his former position, his arm about Cynthia's shoulders.

"Glad we're getting married, Cyn?"

"We've always been married."

"I know," he said. "But now you'll have a piece of paper signed by the Commissioner of Sanitation—or *someone*. As for me, I'm all choked up and giggly and nervous. You *will* be kind to me on our wedding night, won't you?"

"I'll be ever so gentle and understanding."

"I can see it now," Toby said dreamily. "After the sumptuous wedding feast, we shall be blessed by the assembled company and then, in a rain of flowers, we shall retire to the nuptial chamber. And then you will coyly excuse yourself to go into the dressing room and change into a negligee."

"And you'll be right in there with me."

"Of course," he agreed. "I must buy you a special negligee for the wedding night. Something in black lace with pink ribbons and a badge that says 'Garter Inspector.' As for myself, I intend to wear a new pair of tweed pajamas with the pins still in them, cuffs over my knuckles, and a drawstring that goes around me three times. Oh Cyn, we're going to be so happy together!"

Suddenly she broke and began weeping. She turned to bury her face against his chest, clutching him to her.

"What's this, what's this?" he said. "Come on, darling. What happened to all your brave promises? No tears and no regrets. Remember? That's what we agreed."

"I lied," she sobbed. "I lied!"

"No fair. That's my line."

"I don't want to live without you," she said dully.

"Very understandable, luv; I don't want to live without me either. But I'm hanging on. You can, too. You've never failed me yet. Don't start now."

She straightened, sniffed, took a tissue from her bag and dabbed at her eyes.

"I'm sorry, Toby," she said, biting her lower lip.

"You plenty woman," he said tenderly. "You cook good, give me man-child, keep house, work hard, smell nice. I tell chief; he give me you. You be my number-one wife."

"I've never been unfaithful to you, Toby. Never! In my whole life."

"I know you haven't, baby. And it was a dirty trick. Just to make me feel guiltier."

"I didn't mind. Truly I didn't. As long as you came back."

"Why do you endure me, Cyn?"

"Because you're the only man who makes me feel alive. I'm dead without you, Toby. Oh, I might breathe and move around and talk and smile. But inside I'm just dead and nothing counts. Without you . . ."

He embraced her.

"Beautiful, beautiful words, darling. Will couldn't have said it half as well. Cyn . . . ."

"Yes, Toby?"

"Our wedding night. In bed together. I want it to be something special."

"I do too, dear."

"Do you think you could manage to get the hiccups?"

SCENE THREE

AT FIRST glance the stage of the university theatre appeared bare, empty, unset. A brick wall was at the rear. Above, the fly was cluttered with dead lights, hoists, pulleys, sandbags, a catwalk, etc. The wings were a jumble of scenery flats: sections of a stone fence, library paneling, a false door that would never open, painted fireplace, a net of foliage, etc.

But on closer examination, it became evident this empty stage was actually set; the setting was that of a bare stage. That brick wall in the rear was a canvas drop. The overhead lights, catwalk, scenery flats in the wings—all dummies, artfully designed and arranged to give the illusion of a vacant stage.

There was not much on the apron, but a few props enhanced the impression of an undecorated stage being used for early rehearsals. There was a rickety kitchen table, four plain wooden chairs. Upstage, beyond the proscenium arch, was a rough wooden box, actually a large packing crate. This was plainly labeled "Property of Costume Department." It was filled with a variety of hats.

The only illumination in this hollow and echoing place came from a single electric bulb fastened atop an eye-level pipe extending from a metal base.

David Marlow was seated at the kitchen table. He was wearing a dark, vested business suit. Heavy eyeglasses in place, he was studying a playscript. His father was bent over the crate of hats in the rear, rummaging. . . .

"Where's Mother?" David asked, not looking up from his script. "I thought she was coming with you."

Toby Marlow straightened up, faced the missing audience. He was wearing the cocked hat of an eighteenth-century admiral. He stalked forward majestically and, in pompous bearing and rolling gait, he *was* an admiral. He slowly raised a nonexistent telescope to his eye, slowly scanned a nonexistent horizon for a nonexistent enemy.

"She took the carriage back to Saks," he said. "She wants to buy favors for the wedding."

Still paying no attention to his father's antics, David said absently, "I suppose she's all excited and fluttery about getting married."

"Let me tell you something about your mother, m'lad. She's been playing Spring Byington all her life, but deep down inside she's Norma Shearer, and don't you ever forget it. Where's Barbara?"

"She'll be along later," David said. "Right now she's over at the Fine Arts Center doing those silly little drawings of hers."

Toby had exchanged the admiral's hat for the high, hard bowler of a Victorian detective or thug. Now his hunched walk was menacing, his manner brutal.

"Well, let's get at your silly little performance. Three more weeks and you'll be exhibiting your ineptitude to the world."

"I know," David said, "I know. You don't have to remind me."

"Butterflies, kiddo?" Toby jeered. "Sweat beginning to crawl down the spine? A weakness in the knees and a looseness in the bowels? The lines disappearing from your memory overnight and a wild desire to take a rocket to the moon?"

David looked up then and glared at his father.

"Just shut up, will you?" he said fiercely. "I'll be all right."

"The hell you will—unless you show me more than you have so far. How did the rehearsal go?"

"Not so good. I've got to come back tonight. Just Watkins—he's the director—and me. I think he's worried."

"Worried? If I was him I'd be hysterical, and you'd be out on your ass. All right, what do you want to do?"

David rose and held the playscript out to Toby . . .

" 'Oh that this too too solid flesh . . .' "

Toby waved the book away.

"I don't need it. I knew that speech before I knew 'There was a young man from Racine . . .' All right, let's hear it. Take it from the top."

" 'Oh that—' "

"Stop," Toby said immediately. "Do me a favor, will you? Take off those cheaters. Playing Hamlet in hornrims is like making love in hip boots."

David removed the glasses. He stood in front of the table, facing upstage. Toby wandered about behind him, rummaging again through the crate of hats.

" 'Oh that this too too solid flesh would—' "

"Stop," Toby said again. "Look at your script. That first word. It's not 'Oh'—O-h; it's the single capital letter 'O' followed by an exclamation point. Right?"

"David flipped through pages of the script, looking for the speech.

"Well . . . yes," he said finally. "But what difference does it make?"

Toby came out of the crate wearing a cardinal's biretta. He moved upstage with great, slow dignity, a soft, forgiving smile on his face. He swept imaginary robes about him and made the sign of the Cross in an elegant blessing over all the empty seats in the darkened theatre.

"No difference at all," he told David. "Just whether the lady comes or doesn't come. Will you listen to me, for God's sake? Hamlet is making a cry of despair. So Will has him shout 'O!' Single letter 'O' followed by exclamation point. Will knew what he was doing—which is more than I can say for you, Count Dreckela. You give this cry as 'Oh'—O-h. Now listen to the difference. 'O!' Hear how short and full of pain that single letter is? It's Hamlet's despair, coming right out of his gonads. Now here's the way you do it: 'Oh.' You're getting that o-h sound in there. It's like you said, 'Ohhh!' You're drawing it out and making it soft, like a constipated moan. But it's a fucking cry, a sharp cry of pain. 'O!' Can't you hear it? One letter, one syllable, one emotion that tears your goddamn heart out. Try it again."

" 'O!' " David cried.

"Well . . ." Toby sighed. "Where there's an oi, there's a vay. It's better. Lousy, but better. All right, start again.'

" 'O! that this is too too solid—' "

"Stop again. Tutu? What the hell are you talking about—ballet skirts? It's two separate words: too and too, 'O! that this *too too* solid flesh would melt . . .' Will didn't use just a single 'too,' he used a couple of them. Trust his instinct. And enunciate, for Chrissake. The peasants in the balcony want to hear you. They paid less for their tickets, but it means more to them. Play to the peanut gallery, you creep! Take it again."

"'O! that this too too solid flesh would melt, thaw and resolve itself into a dew; or that the Everlasting—'"

"Stop," Toby said. "Please stop," he pleaded. "Stop, stop, stop! I can't bear to hear the mighty Will scorned and brought so low."

Now Toby was wearing a cowboy's sombrero, strutting with exaggeratedly bowed legs. His hands hovered near imaginary guns. He took a few steps away from David, then whirled suddenly, his face contorted and mean. Thumbs in the air, his extended forefingers jerked at David.

"Pow!" Toby shouted. "Pow! Pow! Pow! Look, sonny, you want a pause after the word 'dew.' Hamlet wants his body dissolved; he doesn't want to exist. Then he gets another idea; he could commit suicide if God had not said that suicide is a no-no. But it takes him a moment to get this idea. He's thinking all the time, you see. Even while he's talking. So you pause a bit. Take a beat of one or two, and then you deliver this near idea. Try it again."

"'O! that this too too solid flesh would melt, thaw and resolve itself into a dew . . . Or that the Everlasting had not fixed his canon 'gainst self-slaughter. O God! O God! How weary, stale, flat and unprofitable seem to me all the uses of this world.'"

Toby Marlow was silent a moment, staring at his son. Then he sighed deeply.

"Did you ever consider pimping or basket-weaving as a career?" he inquired. "Look, you're coming up on that final line when you should be going down. It's not a cry of exultation, for God's sake! Hamlet's already said he wants his flesh to melt. But he knows that isn't possible. And he can't slit his own throat because God says that's naughty. So the final line is a summing-up; a dull, sad realization that he can't win. 'How weary, stale, flat and unprofitable seem to me all the uses of this world.' You make it sound like The Battle Cry of Freedom! Can't you understand what Hamlet is saying, thou lily-liver'd boy? Suddenly Hamlet is old. He's an old, old man, long before his time. He's lived too much. Nothing has flavor any more. Nothing has meaning. That line is a lament, the lament of an old man."

"You should know," David said furiously. "How to grow old disgracefully—you're an expert at that!"

"Old?" Toby shouted. "Yes, goddamn it, I'm old. And shall I tell you what it's like? The cock shrinks and the ass sinks. You wake up in the morning belching and farting. Your breath is a terror and all you can remember is childhood. You dream more than you do. And then, one day, little animals get in your gut and eat you up. But of course you'll never know all that. You'll be young forever. Peter Pan! Hello, Peter Pan!"

"You got to hell!" David screamed.

"I did," Toby said. "Years ago. It's something like Yonkers."

They were silent then, glaring at each other, quivering with their fury. Toby turned away first. He went back to the costume crate, dug out a high silk topper. He walked about the dusty stage with belly thrust out, a bloated capitalist. He doffed his fine hat right and left to the admiring multitudes.

"All right," he said finally, "take it from the top."

"Again?" David asked despairingly.

"Yes, again, you—you *mechanic!* And try to give it something this time."

"'O! that this too too solid flesh would melt, thaw and resolved itself into a dew. Or that the Everlasting had not fix'd his canon 'gainst self-slaughter. O God! O God! How weary, stale, flat and unprofitable seem to me all the uses of this world.'"

David turned to look at his father, awaiting his judgment. Toby paced back and forth, top hat pushed to the back of his head. He took out his flask, helped himself to a deep swallow while continuing to pace.

"Not bad," he muttered. "Not bad."

"I thought you said I was lousy."

"I changed my mind."

"It's got to be an improvement!"

"I didn't say you were good," Toby said. "Just not bad. Not *too* bad. There's something there. Something. But it's not coming through. Block. There's a block there. Listen, Mandrake the Magician, what do you think about when you deliver that speech? What's your motivation? Come on, don't be ashamed. You can tell your dear old daddy."

"Well," David said, putting on his glasses, "as you—"

"Take off those damned specs!" Toby roared. 'Don't hide from me, thou jelly-eyed knave!"

David compromised; he shoved the glasses atop his head.

"As you said, that speech is a lament. I think of how difficult it is to live—just to live! All the things that go wrong . . . It's hard enough just to exist and earn a living, but life closes in. You and Mother aren't married, so I'm a bastard. I've knocked up Barbara, and she won't marry me. You're dying, and there's nothing I can do about it. I've got this great chance, but I'm insecure. All that's my motivation."

"Gee," Toby said, "that's swell."

He went back to the box of hats, selected a guardsman's busby. Stiffly erect, swinging his arms in the British fashion, he began a kind of military drill. He paced up and down, stamped his foot, did a sharp about-face, etc.

"Got it all cut down to size, haven't you?" he sneered. "*Your* size. Hamlet happens to be a prince of Denmark. A *prince!* And his father was the king. A *king!* And his mother has married his murdering uncle in 'most unseemly haste.' But all this—having to do with big people of dignity and importance and outsize passions—you reduce to your bastardy and your piddling little ambitions and the fact that the woman you've inflated with your reckless gism is now—"

"Oh my God, can you never understand? I have nothing to do with princes and kings of Denmark who lived a thousand years ago. I've got to have motives I can understand and feel, I am *not* Hamlet; I am *not* the Prince of Denmark, I am *me*. And all I can express is what I am. Don't expect any more of me than that. I will not *play* at acting. I will not assume emotions I do not feel. I do not want to be Hamlet or Captain Brassbound or the Great White Hope. If I'm going to be anything at all, I must be *myself*, what I am and what I feel. Everything else is faking."

"You think I'm a faker?" Toby demanded.

"Yes!" David said, nodding wildly. "Yes! You're a faker. A con man. A pretender. A player!"

His father stared at him.

"If you had a brain," he said, "you'd be dangerous."

Barbara Evings entered, drifting in quietly from the wings. She was wearing something earth-colored and flowing. She heard the last shouted exchange, but neither man noticed her. She floated down onto the dusty stage, sitting silently, watching father and son intently.

"A faker, eh?" Toby said. "Well, I've already told you what you are—

so enamored of your own ego that you can't communicate, onstage or off. You just can't open up. There's no passion in you."

"You're referring to that conversation we had along the park, I presume?"

"'I presume, I presume,'" Toby mimicked. "You're beginning to talk like a ruptured bookkeeper. Yes, you presume correctly."

"Well, I've been thinking—"

"I thought I smelled rubber burning."

"Ho ho, Dad, that's rich. I've been thinking about your ridiculous claim that we all play roles constantly, not only onstage but in our relations with other people. And that an individual is nothing but the sum of the parts he plays."

"Well . . . yes," Toby said warily. "That's about what I said."

"Don't weasel, you weasel," David said scornfully. "That's *exactly* what you said. And what you believe?"

"Yes."

"You're sure of that?"

"Who the hell are you playing now—Perry Mason? I'm not on trial, for God's sake."

"I just want to make sure I've understood you."

Toby donned a beret, cocked it over one eye. He shoved hands into pockets, hunched his shoulders, pouted his lower lip. He slouched about the stage, creating a Parisian Apache.

"Merde!" he rasped. "Get on with it, espece de dingue!"

"If you believe all that," David said triumphantly, "then how do you account for the fact that good actors—I mean the great ones, the stars—how do you account for the fact that they project their own personalities no matter what roles they play?"

"What?" Toby said, confused. "What? I don't follow you."

"The hell you don't," David cried delightedly. "You're demolished and stalling for time to think of an answer. You yourself have told me a dozen times that Hampden was Hampden no matter what part he played. And so, reportedly, was Henry Irving. And so was Barrymore. And so is Olivier and Richardson and Gielgud. No matter what parts they played—king or commoner, lover or clown—the essential personality of the man comes through. His performance in a role is unique, different from the performance of another great actor in the same part."

"So? So?" Toby demanded, agitated now. "What's the point? What are you saying?"

"You know damned well what I'm saying. That actors, great actors, are not merely players. They are artists. They bring something extra to their work—their ego or soul or whatever the hell you want to call it. But the fact that this very personal quality they have comes through—no matter what the makeup or costume or lines they speak—this proves there is an essence, a unique essence, that goes beyond merely 'playing a part' and triumphs over it. That's why you're not a great actor and never have been. That's why no one ever wanted you to do Hamlet. Because you are what you said— merely the sum of the parts you've played. You've never made that final step to greatness because you have no unique essence. You don't know who you are."

Toby was plainly rattled. He tossed the beret back into the crate, fumbled about for a new hat, then turned away. He uncapped his flask again and took a deep swallow, then left the opened flask on the kitchen table.

David defiantly slid his glasses into place and stared owl-eyed at his father.

"Well?" he asked. "What have you to say to that?"

"If I had my wits about me, I'd iambic you to death or annihilate you with a trochee."

"If you had your usual half-measure of wits about you, you'd admit the truth of what I just said, that—"

"I admit nothing!" Toby thundered. "I am not now nor have I ever been a member of the wrinkled-assed school of acting."

"That there is a unique essence in each of us," David went on inexorably, "that good actors express creatively on the stage. And, with enough talent and the right technique—no tricks!—that ego is revealed as something splendid and moving, A piece of the truth. When I look for my motivation, Toby, I'm just trying to discover who I am, *what* I am. It's not easy. Sometimes it's painful. But it's what I want to do. I want to be a great actor. I want to create on the stage the same moments of truth you know when you look at an El Greco or read Shelley or hear Bach. What's so awful about that?"

Toby went over to his son and unexpectedly stroked his head. His hand remained on the back of David's hair.

"My sweet, sweet bastard," Toby said tenderly. "I love you. Do you know that?"

David couldn't raise his eyes, couldn't look at him.

"Yes," he said in a low voice. "I know."

"Good. And I'm going to make a great player—all right, all right, a great *actor*—out of you before I die."

"I have to do it my own way."

"There's nothing wrong with you that time and an enema won't cure. Can't we keep working together?"

"Of course," David said.

"Keep on the lines. If nothing else, speak in a loud, clear voice. Speak to the balcony and beyond."

"Beyond?"

"God deserves a good laugh."

"Go fuck yourself," David said.

"Don't think I haven't tried," Toby said. He turned away to leave. He saw Barbara Evings curled up on the stage. He went over to her. "Ahh, Rima, the Cat Girl. How long have you been there?"

"Not very long," Barbara said. "You were arguing when I came in, but then you ended up loving."

"Yes," Toby said, touching her cheek. "We ended up loving. That's the way to end up, baby. Would you like to come home and tickle me off with feathers?"

"If you want me to, Toby. I love feathers."

He laughed and started to stoop, to kiss her. But his features wrenched with pain, he clapped a hand to his ribs. He stood bent over a moment, eyes closed, waiting for the spasm to pass. Then he straightened slowly, smiled wanly at Barbara.

"Something that ate me," he said. "Ta-ta, luv."

He flipped a hand casually at David and walked off the stage steadily.

David had been silent and brooding during this exchange. After Toby had departed, David saw the flask on the table. He made a movement toward the wings, to call Toby back. Then he checked himself and picked up the flask.

"I think I'll have a small drink," he said loudly. "I'm beginning to like it."

"I know," Barbara said.

"Would you like a sip?"

"No, thank you."

"Well, get off the floor and come sit over here. You'll catch a cold in your ass."

Barbara rose awkwardly and moved over to the table. She lowered herself into one of the plain wooden chairs. David took off his glasses, rubbed his eyes wearily. He started to replace his spectacles, then folded them and slid them into his jacket pocket. He stood up, began to pace about the stage, mostly behind Barbara. His head was down. He stared at the bare boards.

"Oh wow," he said. "What a session that was! You wouldn't believe the screamings."

"But you ended friends?"

"Of course. But . . ."

"But what?"

"Bobbie, his ideas are so old-fashioned, so out-of-date. The old fart!"

"But you love him, David?"

"Oh sure. The monster! He knows so much."

"About what?"

"The stage. Theatre. Tricks. Lighting. Makeup. Audiences. All the techniques. Fantasy. He's always on, you know. The curtain went up when he was born, and it's never come down . . . yet."

"He's always performing? Is that what you mean?"

"Oh yes. Lights in his face, embracing the audience, bellowing to the gallery. But I don't know who he is. And he doesn't either."

In his wanderings, David came abreast of the wooden crate. He stopped and turned over a few of the hats. He selected a steel helmet of World War I vintage, a doughboy's helmet. He strapped it on. Crouching, he began to search about warily, grasping an imaginary rifle, a soldier on patrol.

"David, he's *Toby*."

"Who is Toby Marlow?" David demanded. "He's played a million parts. He knows five languages, ten accents, twenty dialects. Better than any actor I've ever heard. His philosphy is a stew of playwright's ideas, and his conversation is bits and pieces of other men's words. But who the hell is *he*?"

David traded the helmet for a fez and began to do a greasy headwaiter or Cairo guide, bowing and scraping, a horribly oily smile on his face.

"David, Toby is your *father*."

"Oh, yes," David said gloomily. "My unmarried father. And I'm his 'sweet, sweet bastard.' What hurts is that he gets to me, he *gets* to me! He's such a player. He can make me laugh and he can make me cry. Against my will, mind you. But I don't know where the greasepaint ends and he begins. Can't you understand? I don't know who he *is*."

"Is it important?"

"Of course it's important. I don't want my father to be a clown in a fright wig and a painted mask."

"Aren't we all?" she said.

"What the hell is that supposed to mean?"

"I don't know." She shrugged. "It seemed very profound to me, so I said it."

"Well, it's not profound."

"Yes, David."

He tossed the fez back into the crate and came over to the table where Barbara was sitting. He pulled up a chair and sat down across from her, leaning forward onto the table.

"He's still a burlesque banana," he grumbled. "With a putty nose. Hitting people with bladders and making dirty jokes. He's *playing* at living."

"Yes, David."

"Will you stop saying, 'Yes, David'? I will not be patted on the head and humored."

"Yes, David."

"One last time—will you marry me?"

"One last time—no."

He stared at her, drew a deep breath.

"Why not?" he asked.

"You're not Toby," she said.

He tried to laugh.

"Sorry. My mother got there first. He's going to marry her."

"You know that's not what I meant."

"I know what you meant—that I'm not the man my father is."

"Yes," she said determinedly. "That's what I meant. You're not the man your father is."

"I thank you very much."

He tilted back his head, took a long swig from the flask. He coughed, spluttered, wiped the back of his hand across his eyes. Then he took a deep breath. He wouldn't look at her.

"Now you're angry with me, aren't you?" she said.

"You, Toby, myself," he said. "I don't know who. Or what. Oh God, Babara, what *am* I going to do?"

"Are you frightened?"

"No. Yes. I don't know."

"Frightened about playing Hamlet?"

"*Acting* Hamlet. That, and you, and Toby dying. Suddenly I'm not sure. Suddenly I realize I can't control things. My confidence is just *oozing* away. What a sensation! Like watching your blood flow out, and you can't stop it."

"You were confident enough the night we met. You were so sure of yourself, so sure."

"That night!" he cried. "If I could only feel again what I felt that night!"

"As I recall," she said, "you felt me."

He laughed ruefully.

"You—amongst other things . . ."

They both smiled gently, remembering. . . . They stared at the bare electric bulb atop the pipe stand. It began to grow in size—a grapefruit, a melon, a pumpkin. It became huge, softly luminous, and floated up higher, higher into the darkness. Then it was a full moon, plump and juicy, hanging over a splashing sea. The Cape Cod beach was etched into white dunes, black shadows.

The year was 1973. Toby Marlow was playing summer stock in Provincetown, and David had come up from Manhattan to catch his father in *The Man Who Came to Dinner*. Toby had been at his outrageous best: snarling, hacking, wind-milling, belching, 'catching flies,' and interpolating whispered asides that would have enraged the playwrights, but convulsed the audience.

At midnight, leaving his father to the sickening adulation of the dressing-room mob, David Marlow went strolling slowly along the shore. He breathed deeply, surrendering to the seductive night. He looked up at the sky dreamily, eyeglasses glittering. His hands were clasped behind him as he paced, and quoted . . .

"'How sweet the moonlight sleeps upon this bank! Here will we sit and let the sounds of music creep in our ears: soft stillness and—'"

But suddenly his recital was interrupted by a series of loud female screams coming from seaward. David halted, trembled, stared fearfully.

"My God!" he said aloud.

The screams concluded with a trill, then changed to words:

"Au secours! Au secours! Aidez-moi! Aidez-moi!"

David giggled nervously. "She's either French or a fearful snob."

He whipped off his glasses, set them carefully aside in the sand. He backed off two steps, set himself—and after a moment's hesitation (only a moment) dashed bravely into the mild surf. He paused when the sea reached his knees.

"Halloo?" he yelled. "Halloo?"

"Halloo!" the call came back. "Halloo!"

David turned toward the voice, waded out farther until the water was lapping at his thighs. He looked about frantically.

"Halloo? Halloo?"

"Halloo! Halloo!"

Manfully he struggled out deeper. The ocean was up to his waist now. He realized it had filled his pockets: his trousers were beginning to droop.

"Halloo?" he screamed desperately.

"Halloo!"

"Where are you?" he shouted.

"Here! I'm here!"

"Where the goddamn hell is *here*?"

There was a short pause. Then a feminine voice said firmly, "There is no need for profanity."

A slim white arm came out of the sea, just a few yards beyond David. He strove forward mightily, waves up to his chest now. He leaned ahead to grasp a hand, a wrist, an arm.

"All right," he said loudly. "Don't fight me. You're safe now. I have you."

"I have no clothes on."

"Shall I turn my back?" he asked bitterly.

Without waiting for an answer, he swooped, picked up the young woman in his arms, began staggering back toward shore. She tilted her head back over his arm, stared upward.

"Courage," he gasped. "Just a little further now."

"What a glorious night!" she said. "Have you ever seen such stars?"

He regained the beach, breathing heavily. The sea streamed from his sodden clothes. He stumbled up onto dry sand. Then he stood, chest heaving, suddenly conscious that he was holding something that felt like a peeled snake.

"You may put me down now, thank you," she said.

"Shouldn't I do something?" he asked.

"Like what?"

"Well . . . like roll you over a barrel?"

"Do you have a barrel?"

"Unfortunately not."

"Well then?"

"How about mouth-to-mouth resuscitation?"

"No, thank you," she said stiffly. "I don't wish to become involved. *Will* you put me down please?"

"I would, but I left my eyeglasses in the sand somewhere, and I don't want you stepping on them."

"Well, look for them."

"Yes. All right."

Still carrying her, he shuffled damply down the beach a few steps, both of them searching the sand.

"No," he said, "this doesn't look familiar. Must be the other way."

He turned around, the dripping burden in his arms gaining weight every moment. He lurched in the opposite direction, hearing himself slosh.

"What do your glasses look like?" she asked.

"Well—you know—glasses. Black horn-rims. Rather handsome, actually. You can't miss them."

"There!" she said. "Over there. Toward the water."

"No, that's a beer can. Oh . . . there they are."

He carried her a bit farther inland, across the beach. He was bent almost double, panting and wheezing with his exertions. Her wet flesh was slowly slipping from his grasp.

"I'm going to set you down now," he said. "Please don't step on the glasses."

"I won't."

Carefully, with a final effort, he set her slowly down on her feet. Then he straightened up with a sigh of relief. But he had released her too soon; her knees buckled, she sat suddenly on the sand.

"My God!" he groaned, anguished. "You sat on my glasses!"

"I didn't."

"You did, you did! You sat down on top of them."

She rolled sideways onto one hip. She explored the sand beneath her. She came up with the glasses, examined them, blew sand away. Then she handed them up to David.

"There you are," she said. "Good as new."

David put them on immediately, stared up at the moon.

"Loose," he said angrily. "The right earpiece is definitely loose."

"I'm sorry," she said in a small voice.

He stared down at her, took an involuntary step backward.

"My God," he gasped, "you're naked!"

"I told you I was."

"I know, but I didn't think you'd be so—so *bare*. Is that an appendicitis scar?"

"Yes."

"It's charming."

"Thank you. Might I borrow your jacket? The wind is chilly."

"Oh . . . of course. I should have thought of that. It's soaked, I'm afraid."

"That's all right. So am I."

David peeled off his wet jacket. He tried to squeeze out excess moisture, then flapped it a few times in the breeze. He draped it tenderly about her shoulders, helping her to turn up the collar, tuck the tails in snugly. Then he sat down on the sand alongside her, hugging his drawn-up knees.

"Where are your clothes?" he asked her.

"I took them off."

"Oh? Were they dragging you down?"

"Oh no," she said. "They're down the beach somewhere. I was committing suicide, and I wanted to be naked. Just as I came into the world."

He was so horrified, so pained by what she said that he wanted to weep.

"Suicide! My God! But if—if—"

"If I was committing suicide, why did I cry out?"

"Yes," he nodded. "Why did you?"

"I changed my mind."

"I see."

She turned to stare at him.

"Do you? Do you really?"

"Not really," he confessed. "My name is David Marlow."

"Mine is Barbara Evings," she said. "I'm very glad to meet you. I suppose if you hadn't come along, I'd be dead this very minute."

"I suppose so," he agreed. "I was going straight home tonight—I have some very important reading to do—but then I decided to take a walk along the shore; the night is so beautiful. I was going to walk only a few minutes and go home. But then I heard you scream. It's all chance, isn't it?"

"What is?"

"Well, I mean my suddenly deciding to walk along the shore and your deciding that you didn't want to drown. All chance."

"Well . . . yes," she said doubtfully. "Unless . . ."

"Unless what?"

"Nothing. Really nothing . . ."

They were silent then, sitting with shoulders touching in identical positions: knees bent and clasped. Now they carefully avoided looking at each other. They carefully inspected the moon, stars, scudding clouds. It was all there—but it was beginning to tilt.

"Why did you shout in French?" he asked curiously.

"I'm studying it," she told him. "It's a lovely language, but I have trouble with the genders."

"Everyone does," he assured her. "Especially the French. If it's not too painful to discuss, could you tell me why you wanted to kill yourself?"

"Because I decided that life has no value."

"And why did you decide *not* to kill yourself?"

"Because, when I was going down for the fourth time, I realized that if life has no value, then suicide is meaningless."

Then he looked at her. Admiringly.

"You're very deep," he said.

"I almost was," she said.

"What? Oh yes! But why do you feel life has no value?"

She squirmed on the sand, turning to face him. She thrust her head forward until their noses were quite close. She stared intently into his eyes.

"Do you know how many people in this world die of starvation every day?" she demanded.

It was almost an accusation; he felt uneasy.

"Not exactly," he said. "Hundreds, I suppose."

"Thousands!" she assured him. "And I'm sure you read about that earthquake in Tibet?"

"Oh yes. I read about it. Terrible."

"Horrible," she nodded. "And off the coast of Peru, all the anchovies are dying."

"Is that why you feel life has no value?"

"Yes. But then I discovered death doesn't either. There's really *nothing* for us, is there?"

"You mustn't feel that way," he said earnestly. "People have things."

"Ho!" she said. "What do you have?"

"Ambition. Dreams."

"About what?"

"Being a great actor. Some day . . ."

She turned her head sideways, laid her cheek on her clasped knees. He couldn't see her eyes, but he was certain they were sad and defeated.

"I don't have any ambition," she said in a low voice. "Or dreams about anything. I'm just empty."

"Barbara, don't say that!"

"It's true, David. I have absolutely no future. None at all. And my past has been rather uneventful, too. Would you believe that the most exciting thing that ever happened to me was winning a contest where you had to guess how many aspirins were in a big jar in a druggist's window?"

"What did you win?"

"The aspirins," she said. "That's not very exciting, is it?"

"No," he admitted, "not very. But my God, you've got so much going for you! You're a beuatiful woman."

"I'm not," she said, lifting her chin, wetting her lips with her tongue. "I'm not beautiful."

"You are, you really are. Your hair is gorgeous."

"Oh this old thing," she said, trying to comb out tangles with her fingers. "It's all wet and matted and smells of carp."

He leaned to her, thrust his nose into the tangles, inhaled deeply.

"Not carp," he breathed. "It smells of the salt sea. Wild. And you have great eyes."

She rolled them to the moon.

"They're too close together," she said.

"No, no!" he protested. "Just the right distance. Also, your mouth is lovely."

She pouted slightly, and made little guppy movements.

"Aren't my lips too thin?" she said.

"I should say not! Your lips are full and beautifully shaped."

She lifted her head, turned it slowly back and forth.

"My neck is too long?" she suggested.

"Absolutely not!" he said firmly. "Slender and swanlike. Definitely swanlike."

She looked down at herself sorrowfully.

"I have no breasts," she said.

"You do, too! Elegant and exciting."

"Elegant?"

"Really."

"Exciting?"

"Scout's honor."

But then she shook her head dolefully.

"My hips are too wide," she said

"How can you say that?" he demanded. "Your hips are very womanly and feminine."

"Womanly and feminine?"

"No doubt about it."

"The thighs?" she asked.

"In excellent taste," he assured her.

She sighed.

"Big ass, though," she said. "I sat on your glasses."

"Yes," he said eagerly, "but you didn't *break* them. And your calves and ankles are fantastic. I even like your feet."

She brightened.

"I admit my feet are good. Everyone likes my feet." Then she collapsed, fell to brooding. "But that's all I've got—feet. Everything else is—well, nothing. You're just trying to make me feel better about myself."

"I'm not," he said. "I swear I'm not."

Then his actor's instinct telling him the moment called for it, he struggled to his feet. He stood apart from her, legs planted solidly, hands thrust into his wet pockets. He lifted his chin, stared sternly out to sea.

"No, that's not true," he said. "I *was* trying to make you feel better. By telling you the truth. By telling you what you don't realize. That you're a very beautiful woman. Haven't other men told you that?"

"Yes," she said in a faint voice. "But only so they could fuck me."

"Oh."

"Do *you* want to fuck me?"

"I wish you wouldn't use that word," he said.

"Why not?"

"The night's too lovely."

"Oh yes," she breathed. "Yes. I understand exactly what you mean. I'm sorry."

"Oh, that's all right," he said cheerfully. He sat down again at her side. "The night's so incredible—that's all."

"I understand." She nodded.

"So incredible—that I want to fuck you."

"I want to fuck you, too. I belong to you; you saved my life."

"Oh no . . ."

"You did, you did!"

"Oh, just because I know a little French . . ." He shrugged modestly. "Don't feel you owe me anything. You don't."

"My life belongs to you," she said solemnly.

"You told me that was worthless."

"That was before you told me how beautiful I am. My nose. You didn't mention my nose."

"Your nose is divine," he said.

She sniffed, wiped her nose with the sleeve of his jacket.

"Right now it's running," she said.

"Running divinely," he said.

He slid an arm across her shoulders. He pulled her close, experimentally. She did not object.

"Do you really want to?" he asked. "Make love, I mean?"

She hesitated a moment, considering.

"Yes, I believe I do," she said finally. "I'm not certain, you understand, but I think I do."

"You don't have to, you know. I'm not a mad rapist."

"I know that, silly. I could run back into the ocean."

"Oh God, not again. But *why*? Do you want to make love, I mean? Or think perhaps you want to make love even if you're not absolutely certain?"

"Because you have ambition," she said.

"I do."

"And dreams."

"Plenty of those."

"I don't, you see," she said sorrowfully. But then she brightened. "But maybe, just maybe, if we make love, I'll catch it from you."

"Catch what?"

"Well . . . you know who you are, what you want. Maybe I'll catch that if we make love. Through osmosis or something. Then I'll know who I am and what I want."

"Well . . ." he said doubtfully. "There's no guarantee, you know."

"I'm willing to take the chance. I *must* take the chance. Please?"

He was horrified, and looked at her sternly.

"Don't *ever* say 'Please' to me or any other man. You're too much of a woman to say 'Please.' "

"It's working!" she cried. "It's working!"

She wrestled out of David's jacket, tossed it aside. She rolled over atop him, pressing him back onto the sand. Crazed with lust, she began fumbling at his trousers.

"My glasses are steaming up," he told her.

"Damn, damn, damn!" she said furiously.

"What's wrong?"

"Your zipper is stuck. I think there's a piece of seaweed caught in it."

They both bent their heads over his stubborn fly, and eventually got it open. Then, with much awkwardness and flopping about, he grew naked also. In white moonlight and black shadow, they became part of the etched beach. They embraced, shivering, and kissed, kissed, kissed.

"The sand may hurt," he warned her. "It irritates, you know."

"I don't care."

"Let me spread out my jacket. We'll lie on that."

"It'll get all wrinkled."

"Who cares? I love you."

"It's a very nice tweed. I love you too."

"Actually, the sleeves are a quarter-inch too long. You're so beautiful."

"I love tweed," she said. "It's so—so tweedy. Isn't that a funny word— tweedy? Say it three times."

"Tweedy, tweedy, tweedy," he said. "Yes, it is strange."

"Darling, are you cold?"

"Cold?" he said. "Me? Oh no. No."

"I thought you shivered."

"With delight. When you ran your fingernails down my back. The books say it takes time for a man and a woman to become sexually accustomed to each other."

"The books," she scoffed. "What do they know about it? I mean, if they *knew* about it, the writers, they'd be doing it instead of writing about it, wouldn't they? May I touch you?"

"If you wish."

"It's so strange," she said wonderingly.

He propped himself on his elbows and they both stared down at him. In truth, it looked a bit odd, throbbing in the moonlight.

"How can men go through life with this hanging from them?" she asked. "It's really incredible."

"No more incredible than a woman's breasts. They hang too. Sometimes."

"Well, doesn't it get in the way? Doesn't it annoy you?"

"Not really. You get used to it."

"I suppose so," she said doubtfully. "What do you do with it when you sleep?"

"I mail it to Boston."

"Seriously," she insisted.

"Seriously, it's not a problem," he assured her. "What do women do with their breasts when they sleep?"

"Still . . . Look at it, David, It *is* strange."

"Like a turkey's neck?"

"Oh no. More like a sausage."

"A Vienna sausage?"

"Heavens, no!"

"Thank you," he said. "But it's not a salami, either."

"Look, David!" she cried. "it's growing!"

"I know," he said happily. "Perhaps it will become a kielbasy."

"What's that?"

"A hot Polish sausage."

"Yummy!" she said. "Still, when you think of it, David, if you were God and creating men and women, it would be very difficult to think of a better design."

"I can't think of one," he acknowledged.

"It's getting bigger, David!"

"Perhaps it's trying for a bologna. Does it frighten you?"

"No, not frighten . . . but it awes me. I'm very impressed."

"Thank you."

"Can you walk when it's like that?" she asked.

"Must I?"

"Of course not. I was just asking a question."

"Yes, I can walk. But I'd prefer not to. It looks silly."

"It doesn't look silly at all. It's sweet. Besides, it's for me, isn't it?"

"Oh yes," he vowed, "yes. It is yours. I hope you like it."

"I'm sure I shall," she said. "You know what I think we should do now?"

"I hope I guess right," he said.

"I think I should lie on my back," she said thoughtfully. "With my knees spread and lifted. And you must lie on top of me between my legs."

"I think that's a splendid idea," he said. "As soon as possible."

Not without difficulty, they rolled, lifted, and plunged into the position she had prescribed. She stared at the moon over his left shoulder and winked at the man.

"Yes, David," she murmured. "That's just right . . . just right . . ."

"Am I too heavy on you?" he inquired solicitously.

"Gloriously heavy."

"You must never do that again," he said severely.

"I thought you liked it?"

"Suicide, I mean."

"Oh," she said. "Well . . . it brought us together."

"Enchanting suicide!" he said.

"Marvelous suicide!" she said. "David . . . my ears. You didn't mention my ears."

"I worship your ears," he gasped. "Fabulous, sexy ears," he grunted. "I think I'm ready," he groaned.

"I know you're ready."

"Are you ready?"

"Oh so ready," she breathed.

"Well then . . . 'soft stillness and the night become the touches of sweet harmony.' "

"What is that?"

"*Merchant of Venice*. I was reciting it when I heard you cry out."

"David . . ."

"What?"

"Au secours!" she cried out. "Au secours! Aidez-moi! Aidez-moi!"

"I'll save you," he said, proving it.

"Oh yes!" She wept with bliss. "Oh yes! Save me, dear David, save me, save me . . ."

The bloated moon dwindled, dwindled, and lowered in the sky. It became no larger than an electric bulb illuminating the bare stage of the university theatre. Barbara Evings and David Marlow sat across the table from each other. His arm was extended, his hand covered one of hers.

"I remember, I remember." He smiled. "It was a wonderful night—a night full of wonders."

"We never had a night like that again," she said sadly.

"We had others just as good."

"Just as good," she said. "But—different."

He looked at her, the smile going from his eyes.

"Did it work, Barbara? Did you find out who you were that night?"

"Oh yes," She nodded. "I found out. That I loved you. I thought that would be enough for me."

He drew his hands away, sat back in his chair. He began to fiddle with the capped flask, spinning it on the tabletop. He stared down at the flashing silver.

"But it wasn't?" he asked. "Isn't?"

"Wasn't," she agreed gravely. "Isn't. Loving you isn't enough. I want more."

"You have all I have to give," he told her.

"I don't believe that."

"It's the truth."

"David, if I believed that, I'd walk back into the ocean, baby and all."

"Don't say that!" he cried.

"That *is* the truth. But don't worry. I won't do it. I have faith in you."

He glanced at her swiftly, then looked down again. He tried a short laugh, but it came out as a snort.

"I'm glad one of us does," he said.

"I do."

"You pretend you do," he told her.

"Can't you pretend?"

Now it was so complicated, they were both lost.

What did she want him to pretend—faith in himself? Or . . .? He guessed correctly.

"Play at love?" he asked.

"Yes," she said promptly. "All right. Play the lover. Tell me I mean more to you than you do to yourself. Open up. Give yourself to me. Can't you do that?"

"Jesus Christ!" he said angrily. "You're as bad as Toby."

"Is it really so awful, David? To pretend, I mean? To play at loving me?"

"What would that accomplish—if we both knew I was playing a part?"

"It might become second nature to you," she said. "And then first nature."

"I don't believe that," he said, his voice echoing around the empty theatre. "Essence is created from within, not by outside influence. I cannot act what I cannot feel. That would be faking. And if I play a role with you, why not with everyone? Then Toby would be right, and Toby is not right. I proved that to him an hour ago. The essence of a man exists beyond playing parts. The ego is what makes a great creative actor.'

"Toby says—" she started.

But she stopped when he slammed his fist down on the table. Then he grabbed up the flask, opened it, tilted his head backward. He drained it, then threw it skittering across the table to fall to the stage. Barbara bent slowly to pick it up.

"Toby, Toby, Toby!" he shouted furiously. "That's all I hear. The man is all old stories, dirty jokes, misquoted lines, fake angers, simulated loves, fictitious passions, and imagined memories. Everyone listens to Toby Marlow. Everyone believes Toby Marlow. But *he* is nothing. He doesn't exist."

Barbara continued calmly . . .

"Toby says players who feel as you do ignore communication just to massage their own egos. That you give pleasure to no one but yourself."

"I know what Toby thinks. I don't want to hear any more about it. I know what is true."

"Do you? Is that why you're frightened? David, I know now who I am. Do you know who you are?"

He folded his arms on the tabletop, leaned forward to hide his face. He and Barbara sat long moments in silence. Finally . . .

"What did you say?" she asked.

"Nothing," he said, his voice muffled. "I said nothing."

"Strange," she said. "I could have sworn I heard someone cry ever so faintly. 'Au secours! Au secours!'"

SCENE FOUR

THE MARLOW living room, almost dusted, was decorated for the wedding of Cynthia and Toby. A small, square pavilion had been erected in front of the fireplace. The fluttering walls were white nylon curtains, overhead was suspended an enormous white paper bell.

The remainder of the room was adorned with Japanese paper doves, paper fish, paper animals, and streamers hanging from beams, the ceiling electric fan, and lighting fixtures. Behind the couch, a rough table had been fashioned of planks laid across sawhorses. The surface had been covered with sheets, and on display were bottles of beer, wine, and whiskey, buckets of ice, trays of food, baskets of fruit, a whole sliced ham, turkey, smoked trout, glasses, plates, cutlery, platters of bread, side dishs, desserts, pastries, etc. While not exactly groaning, this board was certainly whimpering softly.

Also prominent in this festive room were twenty (20! Count them! 20!) cardboard cutouts, five to six feet tall, standing upright on splayed wooden bases. They were the type of photographic cutouts (nauseously tinted) exhibited outside theatres, nightclubs, and burlesque houses. These two-dimensional statues were of actors and dancers, clowns and kings, whores, villains, saints and comics. Showing more teeth than seemed humanly possible, standing immobile in exaggerated postures—but bobbing slightly in the wind of a live celebrant passing by—the cutouts gave the impression of a crowded room, a "cast of thousands," the hurly-burly of a jammed, excited scene.

Actually, as a keen-eye spectator would soon discern, the wedding congregation was a very small multitude. Present in the flesh were the bride and groom, Cynthia and Toby, standing in the pavilion hand in hand before the minister, who was nondenominational and nondescript. Also present were Jacob and Julius Ostretter, keeping as far apart as possible, and their practically identical wives—plump, jolly women with granite corsets, behived hairdos, and plenty of sequins. David Marlow and Barbara Evings stood close to the pavilion, dressed to the nines and solemn. In the background, a beaming Blanche, dressed to the tens, wept genially from much happiness and one small whiskey.

If the evening had been scored, it would have been marked con brio.

"And now," the minister intoned. "I pronounce you husband and wife. You may kiss the bride."

"Goddamn right!" Toby Marlow shouted.

He immediately embraced Cynthia passionately, bent her backward in a theatrical hug, and pressed his lips to hers like Rudolph Valentino giving the business to Nita Naldi. When he let her up for air, the eager minister rushed forward to kiss a surprised Cynthia on the lips. The others clustered about—David and Barbara, the Ostretters, and Blanche—to salute bride and groom with handshakes, hugs, kisses. And shouts and laughter . . .

"Bravo!"

"Congratulations!"

"Mazeltov!"

"May all your troubles be little ones!"

"Hapiness forever!"

"Well done, well done!"

In the confusion, the minister sneaked to the end of the kissing line and was about to claim seconds. Toby pushed him away.

"Enough of sex!" he cried. "Now all I want to hear is the popping of corks! David, thou legal son, wilt thou do the honors?"

David and Blanche moved to the table behind the couch. Champagne bottles were taken from ice buckets, corks were extracted, goblets were filled and passed around in a buzz of excited chatter.

"Silence!" David shouted. "Silencio!"

When he had their attention, he raised his glass high.

"A toast!" Toby crowed. "A royal toast!"

"How *nice!*" Cynthia said.

"Ladies and gentlemen," David said, "I give you Mr. and Mrs. Toby Marlow, of whom I have the honor of being the fruit."

"Hear, hear!" Toby shouted.

"To my mother and father," said David. "Long may they wave!"

"Long may they wave!" came the answering roar, and glasses were drained, including those of Cynthia and Toby's. The latter immediately whirled and smashed his glass into the fireplace.

"Oh Toby!" Cynthia said. "Our best Waterford crystal!"

"The hell it was!" he said. "Just a five-and-ten glass—something I keep handy for dramatic gestures."

David and Blanche refilled the empty goblets.

Suddenly Dr. Ostretter's wife rushed to the tinny upright piano, seated herself, and began to bang out the wedding march, the recessional from the altar. Toby, champagne glass in hand, took Cynthia's hand under his arm, and the two, raising wine to the assembled company, made a grand parade about the room.

"Dear friends, dear friends," Toby caroled, "drink deep the nuptial cup and give us your blessings all! Let wassail proceed and joy be unrefined!"

Cynthia and Toby continued their tour, queen and king, bowing to the felicitations of their subjects and pausing to embrace and kiss, once more, David, Barbara, and Blanche.

"I beg you all," Toby shouted, "eat, drink, and make merry. For such a union as this was made in heaven, and tickets to witness the wild revelry of the marriage bed will go on sale shortly. It is, regrettably, a limited engagement."

Mrs. Ostretter, at the piano, launched into an enthusiastic but barely recognizable rendition of "Oh, how we danced on the night we were wed . . ." and Toby and Cynthia began waltzing about the room, soon to be joined by David and Barbara, Julius Ostretter and his wife, Dr. Jake and Blanche. The minister, smiling and nodding approvingly, made himself an enormous sandwich and filled a highball glass with champagne. He then moved over to the piano bench where his attentions to Mrs. Jacob Ostretter were something more (or less) than ecclesiastical.

Toby suddenly stopped dancing, withdrew from Cynthia's arms. He faced the carousing company, held up a hand for silence.

"Wait!" he yelled. "Wait! Stop the goddamned music! Listen to me!" Then, when they had quieted and looked at him expectantly, "Ladies and gentlemen—ruffians all!—in the excitement of this celebration and in my feverish hunger for what is to come, I almost forgot an important ceremony. Since I anticipate my wife's enthusiastic cooperation on our nuptial cot, I can safely term what I shall now display as this evening's piece de resistance. Ladies and gentlemen, my wedding gift to darling Cynthia!"

There was laughter, chatter, a spattering of applause as Toby darted from the room into the entrance hall. In the few moments he was gone, there were excited guesses as to what the gift would be.

Cynthia: "A black lace negligee!"

David: "An autographed photograph of himself!"

Barbara: "A collection of obscene limericks!"

Jacob: "A mink-covered pessary!"

Julius: "Last year's calendar!"

Blanche: "Six months' supply of horehound candy!"

But Toby ended their speculation by dashing back into the rowdy scene. He was carrying a gilded bird cage. Within was perched a rather scuffy mynah bird, squawking irritably at his treatment. Toby held up the cage before Cynthia.

"For you, darling," he said. "With everlasting devotion."

"Oh," she said, somewhat startled, "oh Toby, how nice. He—she—it's lovely. Thank you so much, dear."

"Now talk," Toby said.

"What shall I say?"

"No, no, not you," Toby said. "The bird. All right, now talk."

The bird squawked indignantly.

"'Speak the speech, I pray you,'" Toby entreated, "'as I pronounced it to you, trippingly on the tongue.'"

"Squawk!"

"Goddman it," Toby said, "we rehearsed for hours! Will you, for Chrissake, say *something*? Anything!"

"Squawk!"

"Ahh, go fuck yourself," Toby said disgustedly.

"I love you, Cyn," the bird said clearly.

The company broke into cheers and loud applause, although David Marlow could be heard to mutter, "No motivation."

"Oh Toby," Cynthia said, "how truly *nice!*"

"I love you, Cyn," the bird said.

"What power!" Toby said proudly. "What feeling! What presence! What deep, heartfelt passion!"

"I love you, Cyn," the bird said. "I love you, Cyn. I love you, Cyn. I love—"

"All right already!" Toby yelled. "Shut up and eat a seed. It's my wedding gift to you, darling. The birds of the sky—and even of the cage—know and respect and echo my emotions. I love you, Cyn."

There were more laughs, cheers, and applause from the miniature mob. The cardboard cutouts bobbed approvingly.

"And I love you, Toby," Cynthia said. "And here is my wedding gift to you."

She lifted the lid of the upright piano, extracted a small package wrapped in white tissue paper and tied with a blue ribbon. She presented it to Toby and kissed his bald head. The guests watched expectantly as he tore the paper away frantically.

"What is it, what is it?" he said. "It's heavy! Maybe it's a five-pound box of money!"

He discarded the wrappings on the floor. In his hands, revealed, was an ornately carved wooden box, a music box. Toby looked up at Cyn a moment, looked down again, and slowly raised the lid. The silent, entranced audience heard a low whir of machinery, and then the plinked melody of what sounded like a hopelessly old-fashioned, sentimental, rinky-tink vaudeville tune. Toby roared with laughter, and shouting, "You remembered, you remembered!" clasped Cynthia to him and kissed lips, cheeks, eyes, hair, and whatever additional morsels came within reach.

Finally, gasping from his efforts, he held her away and gazed fondly into her eyes.

"How wonderful! Cyn, it must have cost a fortune!"

"What is it?"

"What is it?"

"What's playing?"

"What the hell is that?"

"I don't recognize it."

"What's the song?"

Toby held up both palms and patted them toward his audience, shushing them.

"Lydies and gents, you are hearing a tender work of musical art I had the honor of singing before the crowned heads of Europe and the bald heads of America on the vaudeville stage more years ago than I care to remember. It's called 'Go Into the Roundhouse, Nellie; He'll Never Corner You There,' and as soon as the melody comes around again, I will be pleased to favor you with one stanza and one refrain."

The company waited happily; Toby set the opened music box on the table. He then assumed an exaggerated posture of fear and despair, the back of one hand pressed to his brow, the other arm extended, palm held up beseechingly. He awaited his musical cue; the others were silent and attentive. Then he began singing.

"At last the mother saw her child
"Flee thru the stormy night;
"And close behind her ran the fiend
"Who gave her such a fright.
"The mother cried aloud in pain,
"And prayed with all her might."
(Refrain)
"Go into the roundhouse, Nellie;
"He'll never corner you there.
"Go into the roundhouse, Nellie,
"And put your faith in prayer.
"The world is cruel and heartless,
"But keep your virtue fair-r-r.
"Go into the roundhouse, Nellie;
"He'll nev-v-ver co-o-o-or-r-rner you there!"

Toby bowed low after this touching rendition, which had been complete with broad expressions and elocutionary gestures. His audience broke into wild applause.

"Bravo!"

"Encore!"

"More! More!"

"Marvelous!"

"What a performance!"

"Bravissimo!"

Toby held up a hand modestly.

"Enough, dear friends. Always leave them laughing when you say good-by."

"Oh, I want to get married again and again and again!" Cynthia exclaimed. "It's so much *fun!*"

"And so we shall, luv!" Toby shouted, to be heard above the hubbub. "A Jewish wedding, and a Catholic wedding, and a Buddhist wedding, and a Cherokee wedding. As long as weddings and our days shall last. Every day a new marriage, a new ceremony, and one more orgy until the wine runs dry!"

The jollity resumed. People ate, people drank; there was purposeless movement; groups formed and disbanded, conversations ended as quickly as they began; Laughter, shouting, kisses, spilled drinks, and broken glasses.

The minister wandered over to the mynah's cage, Looking about slyly to make certain he was unobserved, he poured whiskey into the bird's drinking cup. Then he watched, nodding approvingly as the bird poked its beak experimentally into the liquid.

The rhinestoned lady at the piano launched into a Greek-inspired tune ("Never on a Sunday . . ."). Toby immediately shook out a handkerchief, held one corner, handed the other to David. Father and son did a slow, graceful Greek dance, bobbing and dipping. Occasionally they slapped their thighs and shouted. "Yah!"

"What a pleasure to watch!" Dr. Jacob Ostretter said.

"Two grown men dancing together?" Lawyer Julius Ostretter demanded. "That's a pleasure to you?"

"Who asked you, moron?" Jacob said.

"Who are you calling moron?" Julius said. "You idiot—which happens to be worse than a moron."

"I don't like your tone," Jacob said.

"I don't like your manner," Julius said.

"With your taste," Jacob said, "that's a compliment."

"Quack!" Julius said.

"Shyster!" Jacob said.

"I warn you," Julius said, "you go too far!"

"You can't go far enough!" Jacob said.

"I dare you to strike me!" said Julius.

"I double-dare *you!*" said Jacob.

The Greek dance of Toby and David had stopped. The music had stopped. The guests had quieted and were now watching this confrontation with fascination. As Jacob and Julius bristled, moved closer to each other, butted their paunches, the others, including their delighted wives, formed a circle about the increasingly red-faced combatants.

"I slap your face!" Julius shouted.

He did so.

"I slap yours!" Jacob shouted.

He did so.

"I twist your nose!" Julius screamed.

He did so.

"I twist yours!" Jacob screamed.

He did so.

Puffing furiously, tears in their eyes from their wrenched proboscises, the brothers jammed closer to each other, their arms cocked, hands clenched and held up awkwardly.

"I'll demolish you!" Julius shrieked.

"I'll destroy you!" Jacob shrieked.

They swung simultaneously, thumping each other ineffectually on the upper arms. Then suddenly they were grappling, roaring with anger, huffing, groaning. They came down with a heavy thud, clasped in each other's arms, trying to strike blows. They rolled about, dust rising, and a chair, end table, and several cardboard cutouts went over with a crash.

Suddenly galvanized, but almost helpless with laughter, the remainder of the company pounced on the panting pugilists and pried them apart. Jacob and Julius were hauled protesting to their feet, soothed, patted, hair and clothing straightened. Then they were led away to opposite corners of the room, still glaring at each other, shaking fists, yelling blood-curdling Yiddish curses.

"Wonderful!" Toby cried, wiping his eyes. "How wonderful! Darling, our wedding bash is a success. A fight!"

"Oh Toby!" Cynthia said. "Please, please, all of you! No fights and no arguments on this of all nights."

Toby embraced her.

"You're right, Cyn—as usual. No fights, no disagreements, no deep, deep thoughts on this, the happiest of all occasions, thou fairest of the fair!"

The party regained its festive spirit. The minister interrupted his gorging long enough to replenish the whiskey in the bird's emptied water cup (thereby contributing to the delinquency of a mynah). David and Barbara fed each other tidbits from the wedding feast. Blanche and Mrs. Julius Ostretter arm-wrestled on the cocktail table. The Ostretter brothers, keeping carefully apart, wandered about, morosely munching on sandwiches.

Mrs. Jacob Ostretter, back at the piano, began playing a lively Irish jig. Blanche left off arm-wrestling, leapt to her feet and, champagne goblet in hand, began to dance, capering, skirt held high. The others circled around her, laughing, drinking, eating, a few clapping in time to the music.

"Higher!" Cynthia called. "Higher!"

"Take it off!" the minister yelled. "Take it off!"

"Put it on!" David yelled. "Put it on!"

"Pink drawers!" Toby marveled, watching Blanche cavort. "I swear to God, pink drawers! Oh Cyn, dear Cyn, let me marry this marvelous woman too. Canst thou not share me?"

"Of course, sweet Toby," she said. "Whomever your loving heart desires."

"Barbara, too," Toby said. "And every woman and man in this room and in the whole wide world. I wish to wed you all and bed you all and enter into all of you, and you shall enter into me!"

"I love sin!" the mynah squawked, obviously inebriated. "I love sin!"

Silenced for a moment by this shocking outburst, the guests soon responded with laughter and applause. The bird was fed crumbs from the table, his drinking cup replenished with champagne, his cage decorated with paper streamers.

The lady at the piano began something slow and sentimental.

David put his arms about Barbara's swollen waist, his fingers dangling on her ass. She clasped her hands behind his neck. They shuffled their feet in time to the music, moving in a very small circle.

"Love me?" he asked.

"Hate you," she said.

"I hate you, too. For the last time, will you marry me?"

"For the last time, no."

"Because I'm me?"

"Because you're not you," she said.

"I'm all there is," he said. "There isn't any more."

"There is!" she insisted. "There is!"

"Dreamer!" he scoffed.

"You taught me that," she told him.

They stopped dancing and drew apart a little, staring bravely into each other's eyes. Slowly their hands unclasped, fell to their sides. They moved farther apart, still staring. Toby, rushing by with a slice of naked ham in one hand, an opened bottle of beer in the other, saw their solemn estrangement. He skidded to a halt, looked from one to the other.

"What's this, kids?" he demanded. "What's this? Where is the bloom of roses in those happy cheeks? Where is the gleam of California whites in those delighted smiles? What the fuck is going on?"

David said, "The lady said no—again."

"I told you you were a lousy player," Toby said. "How did you ask her?"

"I said, 'Barbara will you marry me?'"

"Barbara, is that what he said?" Toby asked her in disbelief.

"Yes."

"Nothing more?" he persisted.

"Nothing more."

"Dolt!" Toby said to David. "Must I play Cyrano to your Christian? Tell Barbara you love her. Go ahead—tell her!"

"Barbara, I love you."

"Barbara, I love you," Toby mimicked. "Ye gods and little fishes! Have you learned nothing from me? Nothing at all? Now listen to this . . . Barbara, darling . . . I know better than you what I am, and how far short I fall from the man you dreamed you might love and hoped you might marry. I know only too well that I am dull and withdrawn and locked up in my own ego. I know I have little capacity for joy. I don't have any small talk, and I have moods of gloom when there is no living with me. I know that I am opinionated and frequently pompous. But I—"

"Hey, wait a minute!" David said. "You can't—"

"But Barbara," Toby continued without a pause, "there is one thing I do have, overflowing and without end. And that is my love for you. That love makes up for all my faults, those I know and those I don't. It is a love so enormous, so overwhelming, that it carries the power to correct my faults, to teach me passion, to make me a new man and make you a new life. I beg you to be blinded by the love I have for you. As a brilliant sun casts everything in a golden radiance, so my love for you will make our life together warm and glowing. Barbara, wilt thou marry me?"

"Yes," she said promptly, "I will."

"And that, my imbecile son," Toby said to David, "is how it's done. Now get on the goddamn ball, prune-wit!"

Toby trotted away to join the gaiety. Barbara and David were left alone, still staring at each other sadly. They turned, busied themselves at the table, selecting food, mixing drinks.

"You can't say that, can you?" she asked. "What Toby said?"

"No, I can't," he said coldly. "I told you; I won't pretend. I won't be a player."

"Have you tried the smoked trout?" she asked.

The music increased, in tempo and volume; the party whirled on with laughter, bursts of song, solo dances, increasingly amorous embraces. Then Toby mounted a chair, held up a commanding hand. When the piano and company fell silent, he declaimed:

"'If music be the food of love, play on! Give me excess of it, that, surfeiting, the appetite may sicken, and so die. That strain again! It had a dying fall; O! it came o'er my ear like the sweet sound that breathes upon a bank of violets, stealing and giving odour!'"

All entranced and then applauding.

"Bravo! Bravo!"

"Well done!"

"Beuatiful, just beautiful!"

"There's no one like Toby Marlow!"

"More! More!"

"Encore!"

The mad music, the dancing, the eating, the drinking—all took up again. It was Breughel's 'The Wedding Feast'—without codpieces. Toby was dancing by himself now, caught up in some secret dream that only he could recognize. Cynthia and Blanche danced together in a formal, faintly smiling and faintly drunken delight. The minister sat alongside Mrs. Jacob Ostretter on the piano bench, rubbing his wine-stained lips along her bare shoulders. More glasses had been spilled, more food dropped. Barbara and David circled each other aimlessly, waiting . . . Jacob and Julius advanced and retreated, wary cocks looking for an opening to strike.

"A reel!" Toby shouted suddenly. "A reel! Musician, I will have a reel! King Toby commands a reel!"

Obediently the pianist launched into a spirited, if off-key version of 'Turkey in the Straw.' The entire company, with fumblings and stumblings and lurchings, joined hands and began gamboling in a rough circle about the couch and dining table. They shouted, 'Da-da-diddle-diddle-da; da-da-diddle-diddle-da,' and similar nonsense just to keep time to the raw music. It grew faster and louder, all caught up in a joy too frantic to contain, until . . .

. . . until Toby Marlow stopped dancing, dropped hands, uttered a scream of such pain and anguish that the others shivered and were brought to a halt. The music ended on a crushing cord. They all turned to stare at Toby as, clutching a chair arm, he slid slowly, tragically to the floor. They were too shocked, too stunned to come to his aid. He was obviously in pain he could hardly endure, but he could not—*could not*—pass up the opportunity for a theatrical gesture. His arm rose slowly from his side; a trembling finger pointed at a startled Dr. Jacob Ostretter.

"Goddamn you, Jake!" Toby gasped. "You promised me a run of six months, and now you're sending me out on the road, and I don't want to go. Wait till Equity hears about this!"

ACT THREE

SCENE ONE

THE MARLOW'S bedroom had undergone changes and taken on the appearance of a sickroom. Extra bolsters had been added to the unmade bed, and the churned blankets and rumpled sheets were littered with books, magazines, an opened box of candy, a torn bag of popcorn, etc. Next to the bed was a tall tank of oxygen, with attached tube and mask. Alongside the oxygen tank, on the floor, was a half-empty bottle of whiskey.

The shades were drawn; the chandelier and lamp were lighted. There were several bouquets in the room, in vases, in various stages of decay. On a small table was a collection of medical supplies: bottles of pills, towels, basins, a plastic container of ice, a hot-water bottle, etc. Also a decanter of wine and a box of cigars.

Toby Marlow was seated in a wheelchair near the drum table. He was covered to the waist with a plaid comforter. He was paler, drawn, and his speech had become somewhat slurred. But he hadn't lost any of his defiance, and talked as rapidly and loudly as ever. But now he had a tendency to splutter, and wiped his lips frequently with tissues plucked from a box he held on his lap. He dropped the used tissues onto the floor; they surrounded him like a snowfall. A heavy cane was hooked over the arm of his wheelchair.

David Marlow was seated in the leather club chair on the other side of the drum table. He wore his usual conservative business suit, with vest, and the hornrimmed spectacles. He was consulting his playscript, leafing through it to find the speech he wanted. He too seemed thinner, tense, paler.

"Toby, are you sure you're up to this?" he asked.

"Yes. I'm up to this, sonny boy," Toby snarled. "There's nothing wrong with me a little death won't cure. So what's eating your director?"

"I don't know," David said. "I honestly don't know. He keeps saying, 'You're fine, David; you're doing fine.' But I get a take on him, and I don't think he thinks I'm doing fine. I think he thinks I'm a one-man catastrophe. But he can't verbalize it. He can't tell me what I'm doing wrong."

"Goddamn it," Toby said disgustedly. "I know I suffer from verbal diarrhea, but do you think still water runs deep? The hell it does! Still water runs stupid. Your director can't say what he wants because he doesn't *know* what he wants. He may feel it, but he can't put it into words? So what good is it? Words are everything. They're beautiful. Sublime. Where the fuck would we be without lovely words? Unexpressed ideas and emotions last as long as a fart in a keg of nails. What words have you been working on?"

"The big soliloquy," David told him. "'To be or not to be.' Toby, that's a bitch."

"I know, I know." His father nodded. "In a speech as long as that, the first thing you've got to do is get your breathing right. Unless you've got the breathing and timing and pauses, you've got nothing. After you learn to get through it without panting like you've been running a four-minute mile, then you can start thinking about what the hell you're talking about. Have you got the breathing?"

"Yes, I've got the breathing and the timing and the beats. But I can't get a hook on it. I don't know what's going on. There's no logic to that speech."

"No logic?" Toby shouted. "Thou devil's spawn! Listen, Will was a poet before he was a playwright. Since when do you expect logic from a poet? You're lucky if you get decent table manners. I know about these things. I'm something of a poet myself."

"I know," David said resignedly. "I've heard your limericks."

"I'd call you a son of a bitch if I didn't respect your mother so much. Get me a big Scotch on ice."

"Toby, you're drinking too much."

"Balls."

"How many drinks do you have a day?"

"Who the hell counts?"

"Come on Toby—how many?"

"Ten. Twelve. Something like that."

"Can't you cut that in half?" David asked earnestly.

" All right," Toby said. "I will."

"You will?" David said, astonished. "Five or six drinks a day?"

"Sure," Toby cackled. "All doubles."

"Doctor Jake said—"

"Fuck Doctor Jake!" Toby said furiously. "It's my goddamn pancreas! 'Pancreas.' Jesus Christ, what a word to do in a king. It's as humiliating as choking to death on a toothpick. Now get me that drink or I'll crawl across the floor on my belly and die at your feet like Leslie Howard in *The Petrified Forest*."

Sighing, David put his playscript aside and retrieved the bottle of Scotch next to the oxygen tank. He poured a dollop into a medicine glass, added ice and a little water. He stirred the drink with a thermometer, wondering which type it was and not really caring. He brought the whiskey to Toby.

"Go ahead, kill yourself," he said. "I don't care if you live or not."

Toby took a deep swallow. Then, trembling with clawed hands, he began to play an old codger.

"Oh God bless you, boy, God bless you! You warm the heartles of my cock. Oh, you're so kind to your feeble old father."

"You're not the easiest father in the world to live with."

"So?" Toby said, straightening up. "Who gave you guarantees? The Declaration of Independence says you can *pursue* happiness; it doesn't say anything about catching it."

"I think I'll have a little drink," David said.

"Smartest thing you've done all day."

David went back to the medicine table and began busying himself with Scotch and water.

"I owe you an apology," he mumbled.

"What?" Toby said. "Speak up, for Chrissake."

"I owe you an apology!" David roared.

"So does God," Toby said. "What's yours for?"

"When I said I don't care if you live or not. I do care."

Toby didn't say anything. He watched David move across the room back to the club chair. David sat on the edge of the chair, hunched over, his glass held between his knees. The playscript was on the floor. David nudged it with his toe.

"I just don't feel it," he said miserably. "The soliloquy, I mean."

"I know that. And your director knows it."

"Well . . . what's my motivation?"

Toby sighed wearily, took a mouthful of his drink, put his head back, gargled a moment, then swallowed it.

"I don't know what your motivation is, muttonhead. For that speech or for wanting to be a player."

"An actor," David said mechanically. "I don't play at it."

"You sure as hell don't."

There were several moments of silence while they nibbled slowly at their drinks. They didn't look at each other. Occasionally Toby's eyes closed, but only for an instant. He seemed to force them open by conscious will.

"Listen, Toby," David said hesitantly. "I have a wonderful idea on how that 'To be or not to be' speech should be given."

"Oh? What's that?"

"I want to deliver it with my back to the audience."

"Your back to the audience?"

"Yes. It's obviously a very intellectual, introspective contemplative speech, and the actor should do nothing by expression or gesture to detract from the words.'

"Uh-huh."Toby nodded. "And what does your director think of this wonderful idea?"

"Well, ah, I haven't told him yet."

"Before you do, I have an even better idea for you. Why appear onstage at all? Why not record the speech on tape, and all the stage manager has to do is turn it on. You could be out having a beer and a giant McDonald's hamburger."

"You don't have to get snotty about it."

"I knew you were an imbecile, but I didn't think you were a coward. Turn your back on the audience for that speech? Heavens to Betsy, you poor little bantling, that's a cop-out. You're scared shitless of this one, aren't you?"

"I don't know," David muttered. "That's the problem. I don't know what I'm supposed to do. What I'm supposed to feel."

"What *you* feel?" Toby hooted. "Triple-damned egotist!"

"You're the biggest egotist of all!" David yelled at him.

"The hell I am! I gave myself as much as I can, and give and give and give, and screw my motivation and diddling my ego; it doesn't mean a thing to me." He stopped suddenly, took a deep swallow of his drink, chewed a few fragments of ice. Then he drew a deep breath. "All right. Let's calm down. Let me try once more—just once more. David, you've got to admit we're all sad shits. Ninety-nine percent of all the people in the world are sad, sad shits. We're all failures in one way or another. We lie and we cheat and we rob and we betray, and we act in a million other awful ways. God, we're such small, crawling things! We're not even animals! Animals don't do the things we do. What animals torture and kill for kicks? So fucking *awful*! But occasionally someone like Willie Shakespeare comes along and shows us what we might be. And not only poets and playwrights, but novelists and artists, and sculptors and musicians, and scholars and saints—and maybe a few raggedy-assed players in there. Not showing us what we *are*, but what we might be. What in God's name do you think art is all about? It shows us what we could be: princes and kings, princesses and queens, nobles and courtiers, beautiful people of dignity and resolve. Heroes! Jesus Christ, we can be heroes! Do you know what that means? Do you realize what hope that offers? That we can all, each of us, aspire to something we know we are not. That's why Will wrote that long soliloquy, why he opened up Hamlet's mind and showed us his deepest thoughts—to link Hamlet with humanity, to make everyone who reads or hears those words feel an affinity for the Prince of Denmark, and so feel larger and better and grander, and forget, for a few minutes, that he's a sad, sad shit who cheats on his wife and betrays his best friend, or sells out his dreams, and he's going to die no smarter than he was born, never knowing what it was all about. So when you deliver that speech, you've got to open up. You've got to rip yourself open, split yourself wide. You're not only the Prince of Denmark; you're Everyman. And you've got to give everyone in the audience a sense of the possibility of dignity and meaning in life."

"Does it exist?" David said wonderingly.

"Does what exist?"

"Does life have dignity and meaning?"

"You infant!" Toby said pityingly. "Did you have your pap this morning? Of course life doesn't have dignity and meaning, you witless wonder. But you've got to pretend that it does. How else can you endure?"

"I want to be an actor. But I don't want to pretend."

"I've been pretending all my life," Toby said, "but I've just come to realize it. Nothing like a death sentence to make a man a philosopher. And while I'm giving your so-called brain the massage it needs, there's something else I want to straighten you out on. But first build me a drink. And take it easy on the ice: I'm not a corpse—yet."

Obediently, David took Toby's glass back to the medicine table. There was a moment of panic when both realized the whiskey bottle was empty. But terror was averted when a new bottle was discovered in the cellaret of the drum table. David poured their drinks with a heavy hand.

"Water?" he asked.

"Not too much. Peeing isn't one of my favorite pastimes these days."

They sat back, relaxed and smiling, holding their glasses up to each other a brief moment before taking the first swallow.

"I've decided what I want on my tombstone," Toby announced.

"What's that?"

"Here lies Toby Marlow, stiff at last."

"Not bad." David laughed. "But how about: 'I'm only pretending'?"

"Bravo!" Toby said. "Every now and then I think there may be some hope for you."

"What did you want to tell me?" David said.

"About what?"

"I don't know. But you said there was something you wanted to straighten me out on."

"I did? Now what the hell was it . . . ?"

"About Barbara?"

"Don't prompt me, goddamn it," Toby snarled. "No, Barbara wasn't involved. Now—oh, I've got it. See—the famous Marlow memory is still working; it's just slowing down, that's all. It's about what we talked about before. When—"

"We talked about a lot of things," David said.

"Will you stop flapping your flatulent mouth and let me finish? I said— that night we took a walk along the park—I said all of us—not only players but *everyone*—plays many, many roles in a lifetime, suiting the part to the other performer, whether it be onstage or off. And that good playing was a matter of style which, essentially, is having a good bag of tricks. Then, at the theatre, when we were rehearsing the 'O! that this too too solid flesh . . .' speech, you said I was wrong because the good players are—"

"The great actors," David interrupted.

"All right, the great actors. You said, in effect, that there was—there was . . . What the hell's wrong with me? I can't remember what I wanted to say."

"Probably the Scotch," David said casually.

"Never affected me like this before," Toby said, troubled. "I played a year of *Rain* dead drunk and never missed a cue. Where was I?"

David wanted to end this, seeing his father's tiredness, but could think of no graceful or easy way to withdraw. He took a gulp of his drink and plunged ahead. . . .

"I said, when we were rehearsing that speech, that you were wrong in believing that life is all pretending and great acting just a matter of tricks. I said you were wrong because great actors remain themselves no matter what part they're playing. With Olivier, Robards, Richardson, Scott, Gielgud, or any other star, we never forget who they are no matter what role they play. In other words, their ego and essence come across, come through the lines and action of the play. And the proof of that is that

Olivier's Hamlet would be different from Richardson's, just as Garrick's Othello would be different from Irving's. So there's more to it than just tricks; it's the truth of the man that commands our respect. He knows who he is, and he projects that on the stage and by so doing, moves us and convinces us and reveals to us his truth. That's what I said."

"So you said, so you said." Toby nodded, obviously weary now. "And I've been thinking about it. I really have. And . . ."

"Toby, maybe we better cut this short. I've got to get to the theatre."

"No, no, don't go yet. I've got to tell you this while it's on my mind. No good on my mind. Words are everything. The beautiful words. The sound of them! The taste of them! Because you're wrong, you see. I've been thinking about it, and I know now why you're wrong. Because those great players are not revealing to us what you call their ego and essence. On no. Now each of us has an image of himself—who he is and what he is. I, for instance, think I'm the greatest player who ever lived. Another man might fancy himself as a great lover, or a great statesman, or a great general, who is only prevented by chance, bad luck, or circumstance from revealing his genius to the world. We all have this self-image, and we try to play the part as best we can. You get it? We pretend we are the man we'd like to be. All of us. Everyone. We've got this illusion of who we are, and we act the part. Sometimes we even dress the part. The closer reality comes to our dream, the happier we are. But no one totally succeeds. It is still pretend. It is all playing."

"I don't get it," David said. "What's that got to do with great actors? With the stars?"

"Everything. It's got everything to do with them. Because what you call their ego and essence, the truth they reveal on the boards, is the part they are playing for themselves! Now do you get it? What they project on the stage is not their ego and essence; it's their vision of themselves, a part they've been playing all their lives and play so well that it convinces everyone. But it's still all illusion. *Their* illusion."

"Wait a minute," David said slowly. "Are they convinced that the part they're playing is actually them?"

"No," Toby said. "Well . . . maybe. The stupid ones might convince themselves that they're genuine and not playing. But the smart ones, like me, lie awake at three in the morning and know who they are. They know then they're not the greatest players in the world, and the face they present to the public is as false as if they were wearing makeup and a nylon beard."

"Are you telling me that all great actors are playing a part *in addition* to the role they're playing onstage?"

"Right!" Toby shouted, nodding like a madman. "Now you've got it! They're so good at pretending, at *playing*, that they've created a part of their own, what you call their ego and essence. And not only great players. But everyone. Everyone does it. But it's all illusion, all dreaming. And the smart ones know it."

"Do you know it? About yourself?"

"Sure," Toby said genially. "I'm smart."

"All right," David said. "If you're not the greatest actor—or player— in the world, who are you?"

"Who am I? Who am I? I'll tell you who I am."

"That's what I want to hear," David said. "Tell me."

Toby began his next speech haltingly, almost diffidently. But his voice gained strength and resolution as he proceeded, the marvelous organ tones booming out. Finally he was speaking with fervor, as if shucking off a burden he had carried along too long and was now happy to be rid of, knowing how it freed him. His physical actions enforced his words. He began the speech seated in the wheelchair. He rose, let the plaid comforter fall to the floor. He used the cane to stalk about the room, keeping his face turned to David, never taking his eyes from him. When he reached his peroration, he threw the cane from him and ended with arms flung wide, standing triumphant, feet braced, chest outthrust, head up. It was a bravura.

"I," he began, "I am a—a charming buffoon. But there is a—a self-assurance about me that convinces. Yes. You may begin by laughing at me, but you end up impressed. I *convince*. Yes, I am a 'character' and glory in it. And if you don't like it, fuck you! Constantly drinking, constantly smoking, constantly flirting, I succeed at once in exemplifying and caricaturing a 'dirty old man,' As if there was any other kind!

"Every conversation, every gesture, every body movement, every expression, every action and reaction is not so much calculated as practiced. I am a natural player, my instincts sharpened by more than forty years of stage experience. Everything from Shakespeare to burlesque and back again. I have little knowledge of or interest in abstract ideas, except as they affect the theatre. But I have the gut aptitudes and the understanding of human frailties of the born survivor.

"I am shrewd rather than intelligent. But there is a streak of meanness in me. I come perilously close to being a grotesque. I am given to sudden furies, over as quickly as they begin. I am a poseur. I have played so many roles that I have never quite decided if I prefer playing hero or villain.

"I cheerfully insult family and friends. I fight with acquaintances and strangers, bullying, shouting, screaming, shouldering my way through life, striking before I can be struck. But if I must take blows, I give them back trebled. I enjoy being ribald. Maybe vulgar. Sometimes obscene.

"I am larger than life, but there is a little boy's swagger about me. Perhaps you have glimpsed something uncertain and fearful beneath my braggadocio. I know you have to work at liking me—I can be wearing, I suppose—but I can be so inimitable and charming, when I want to be, that all are my slaves. Do they recognize something in me, perhaps a heroic quality, they cannot find in themselves?

"Finally, I am a physical coward with a terror of death that no one knows except myself. And I will die nobly without revealing it, so fearful am I of being scorned or, worse yet, ignored. I know I am not a giant theatrical talent. But surely, after my passing, there is one person in the world, somewhere, who might one day say, 'He did very well with what he had.' "

As this speech progressed, David had been impressed, then shocked by Toby's apparent honesty. Toward the end, he rose to his feet in unconscious homage, surrendering completely to Toby's skill and intensity.

Toby concluded with a rather hokey shtick of letting his arms fall limply at his sides, bowing his head, allowing his entire frame to slump in resignation and defeat. Then, in the unendurable silence, David made a choked cry deep in his throat. He gathered up his playscript, rushed from the room. Toby remained in his 'defeated' position until the door slammed behind his son.

Then Toby slowly raised his head, looked about cautiously. He stretched, smiled mysteriously. He moved to the medicine table, mixed a heavy drink. He shook two pills from a bottle onto his palm, popped them into his mouth, washed them down with a swallow of Scotch. He returned to the wheelchair, sat down, pulled up the comforter, tucked himself in. He was sitting serenely, sipping his drink, when Blanche entered without knocking.

"Ah, Ma Barker!" Toby said. "Just in time. Light me a cigar."

"You know what the doctor—" she started.

"I know what the goddamn doctor said, Madame LaFarge. Would you deny a dying man his last request?"

"Seems to me you have these 'last requests' every hour on the hour."

"Cut the shit and pour yourself a drink," he told her. "And light us a cigar."

Blanche mixed a highball for herself. Then she lighted a cigar, taking it from the box on the drum table. After she got it drawing smoothly, she handed it over to Toby, standing before him.

"Now what?" she asked. "Sure you don't want a Welsh rarebit or pickled onions as a last request? Maybe you're as pregnant as Barbara."

"You go to hell," he said affably. "Babe, tell me something honestly, will you?"

"Have I ever faked you?" she asked.

"No, God bless you, you never have. Tell me—who am I?"

She looked at him, bewildered.

"You're Toby Marlow," she said.

"Toby Marlow?" he cried. "By God, I'll pretend I am! It's a marvelous part!"

She still looked at him, then shrugged, but finally smiled at his obvious good spirits. They raised their glasses in an unspoken toast. They handed the cigar back and forth.

SCENE TWO

THE MARLOW'S living room had also taken on the appearance of a sickroom. Medical supplies and pill bottles were set out on the cocktail table. A small tank of oxygen, with mask, stood near the couch. Toby's wheelchair, with cane hooked over one arm, was nearby. A battered guitar with a broken and coiled string leaned against the liquor cart.

Toby Marlow was, apparently, asleep on the couch. At least he was stretched out, covered with a throw quilt. And yet, during the following conversation, his eyes opened on occasion, he winced, grimaced, made certain small gestures with his hands atop the coverlet. In other words, the old bastard was faking his sleep, eavesdropping on the talk of the two women in the room.

Cynthia was in her armchair, patiently doing needlework by the light of a gooseneck floor lamp. Barbara Evings, mostly in shadow, sat on the floor, knees drawn up and spread to accommodate her swollen belly. Occasionally she turned her head sideways to rest her cheek on a knee, looking more than ever like a dreamy Burne-Jones portrait.

It was early evening. The light from the windows was soft, violet, at once melancholy and restful. It was a time for quiet talk and sweet remembrances. Voices were low; the rhythm of conversation was slowed, almost contemplative. . . .

"Oh . . ." Cynthia said regretfully. "I do believe I've dropped a stitch."

"Is it serious?" Barbara Evings asked.

"Oh no. Just a row. I'm so bad at counting. Did you see Doctor Jake today, dear?"

"Yes, I saw him."

"And what did he say?"

"I'm too skinny. I'm supposed to take vitamins and drink eggnog and eat regular meals."

"Very good." Cynthia nodded approvingly. "Toby has an excellent recipe for eggnog. It has rum and whiskey and brandy in it. It's delicious."

"I don't know," Barbara said doubtfully. "I think Doctor Jake meant just plain eggnog, without any alcohol in it."

"Really, dear? I'm not sure you can make it without whiskey. I must ask Blanche; she'll know. What else did he say?"

"Oh . . . nothing much. I'm a little run-down but generally in good shape. And I have an unexpectedly wide pelvis. I never knew that."

Cynthia looked up, concerned.

"It doesn't bother you, does it?"

"Of course not, Cynthia. Why should it?"

"Well, I once knew a woman who had three kidneys, and it bothered *her*; I don't know why. I thought it was rather a mark of distinction."

"Tomorrow I got to the obstetrician. Jake says he's very young and wealthy."

"That's nice, dear," Cynthia said, comforted. "I wouldn't want you going to a *poor* obstetrician. Did you see David today?"

"Cynthia, is Toby really asleep?"

"Of course he is, dear; can't you see? There are little bubbles on his lips. That means he's asleep."

"He's probably pretending."

"He may very well be. But it's not important, is it? Well, did you?"

"Did I what?"

"See David today."

"Oh. No. I've been sleeping so much lately, and he had gone to rehearsal when I got up. Then he came home for lunch while I was at the doctor's. And now I'm here, and he's gone again. But he left me a note."

Cynthia left off her sewing and looked up with interest, peering at Barbara over her spectacles.

"A note? Oh, I'm so glad, dear. What did it say?"

Barbara took a folded piece of paper from her bodice, opened it, craned to read it by the dim light from Cynthia's lamp.

"It says: 'Got to run. Rehearsal till late. Wait up if you can. Marry me. David.'"

"Isn't that *nice!* Such a *loving* note! Are you going to?"

"Wait up for him?" Barbara said. "I might."

"No, dear. Marry him."

"No," Barbara said determinedly. "I've made up my mind. I'm not going to."

"But you *love* him!"

"I don't. I *don't!*"

Cynthia's steadily moving hands came to rest. She disentangled her fingers. She leaned forward to stroke the girl's hair.

"Oh dear, dear, I may not be a very intelligent women, but I do *feel* things, you know. And I feel you love David."

Suddenly Barbara began to weep audibly. She bent forward, buried her face in her hands, and sobbed, sobbed, sobbed. Cynthia made a sudden, impulsive, sympathetic movement toward her, then drew back and resumed her knitting. After a moment Barbara's crying eased; she raised her face and sniffed a few times. Cynthia handed her a tissue from Toby's box on the cocktail table.

"Blow," Cynthia said.

Obediently Barbara blew her nose a few times, then wiped her wet eyes with the heel of her hand.

"Oh Cynthia, why can't everything be—be *nice?*"

"I know just what you mean, dear." Cynthia nodded, busily knitting. "Sometimes it's very difficult to understand why the world doesn't devote itself to making us happy. But that's not the way things work. And we must understand it and get on with the business of living."

"Well, even supposing I did—love David. I mean—what difference would that make?"

"What difference?" Cynthia cried, as aghast as she was capable of being. "Good gracious! All the difference in the world!"

"But David doesn't love me," Barbara mourned.

"What difference does that make?"

"What difference?" Barbara cried. "All the difference in the world! Why should I love him, and he not me? I might marry him if he loved me like Toby loves you."

"Oh child," Cynthia said, smiling sweetly. "Toby doesn't love me."

"What?" Barbara whispered, horrified. "Cynthia, what are you saying? Toby not love you? That's nonsense. He'd be lost without you. He may not love you as much as you love him, but he does love you."

"Oh no," Cynthia said serenely. "Toby has a very great affection for me; I know that. But he doesn't love me. He just loves the idea of my worshiping him."

"And you've settled for that?"

(It was a good day for aghastness in the Marlow manse.)

"I've settled for that," Cynthia agreed.

"All your life?"

"All my life. It *has* been my life—my love for Toby. That's all I've ever asked, that he allow me to love him."

"Well, that's not enough for me," Barbara said definitely.

"Mmm," Cynthia said, peering down at her work and counting stitches. "It's your decision, dear."

There was silence a long moment while Barbara considered what she had just heard. Then . . .

"I think I'd like a glass of wine," she said. "Would you like something?"

"That would be nice. A little Scotch for me, dear."

Barbara rose from the floor with some difficulty. First she rolled onto one hip, then bent her legs, then used the couch to lean on, then straightened her legs slowly, hauling herself erect. Cynthia watched these panting efforts closely, but made no effort to help. Barbara, finally standing, bent slightly backward, duck-footed to the liquor cart, and began pouring drinks.

That was when an invisible observer would become absolutely certain that Toby was awake and listening to the conversation. For as Barbara was filling the glasses, his hand rose from the coverlet and reached piteously in her direction. But she didn't notice him; she took her own and Cynthia's glass back to the couch. Toby's hand and arm fell back sadly, forlornly.

"Oh my," Cynthia said after the first sip. "That *is* good. I'm sure it will help me count stitches. Toby taught me how to appreciate good liquor, you know. He taught me so many things."

"What kind of things?" Barbara asked, easing herself down backward onto the couch.

"Oh . . . how to play billiards and gamble at chemin de fer and how to faint—how to *pretend* to faint—and fall to the floor without bruising yourself, and how to use makeup, and what to do if someone insults you."

"What do you do if someone insults you?" Barbara asked, fascinated.

"Spit in his eye," Cynthia said sweetly.

"Oh well . . ." Barbara laughed. "That's Toby. But David isn't the man Toby is."

"He might be, dear—some day."

"Oh . . . maybe. But I doubt it. Toby is so open, so outgoing. He says exactly what he feels. He's not afraid to expose himself."

Cynthia dropped her needlework. Her head went back in great guffaws of laughter. She found it difficult to stop. Even Toby's chest could be seen heaving silently under the coverlet.

"Expose himself?" Cynthia gasped. "Expose himself? Well, he has done that on *very* rare occasions. But I really do think you mean Toby is willing to *reveal* his feelings."

"Oh," Barbara said. "Of course. Toby's not afraid to reveal himself."

"He enjoys it," Cynthia said. "The skunk!"

"But David isn't like that at all. He's so withdrawn, so involved in himself. He's such an egotist."

"You think Toby isn't?"

"But in a different way," Barbara argued. "Toby plays at it. It's a part he's acting. But with David, the egotism is real. 'What's my motivation?' That's all he's interested in. He's so wound up in himself, so tight. Even in bed—he's very good in bed, Cynthia—he—"

"That's nice, dear."

"But even in bed he never forgets himself, never really lets himself go. He's removed from me, apart from me. Cynthia, he's just not *passionate*. He's saying to himself, 'Now I must be passionate. Now I must be tender. Now I must be brutal.' He's playing a part, but he doesn't realize it. Toby isn't just playing like that, is he?"

"If he is"—Cynthia smiled—"he's awfully good at it."

On the couch, under the throw quilt, eyes closed, Toby Marlow nodded approvingly.

"Cynthia, I want something too," Barbara said earnestly. "It's not enough for me to sit in the audience and worship David. I want to be loved in return. I'm ready for it. Really I am. I can respond, honest I can. But just loving and not being loved in return isn't enough. Maybe you can do it, but I can't."

"It's better than nothing, dear," Cynthia said placidly.

"Oh God, is it? I don't think so. I couldn't take it for a lifetime, the way you have."

Cynthia sighed deeply and put aside her needles and yarn. She took off her glasses to stare long and thoughtfully at Barbara Evings.

"Take what?" she asked softly. "Do you think I've been punished, that I've been suffering for a lifetime? I don't want you to think as I do, you very foolish young girl, but I assure you I have no feeling of suffering or punishment. I am grateful to Toby for having given me so much happiness, and I know he feels the same way toward me. He may not love me—at least, not the way I love him—but I know, I *know* I am very dear to him. Yes. There is a tenderness. I remember I went on a tour with him once. We were in—where was it? Chicago, I think. Or perhaps Santa Fe. Some place like that. Toby had the lead in *Man and Superman*, and it was a very great success. Marvelous reviews. Worshipping audiences. Then I got sick. In Chicago or Sante Fe. Toby let the company go on without him. They flew in a replacement from New York. But Toby stayed with me and nursed me. His replacement was very, very good, and Toby didn't rejoin the company. But I never heard a word of complaint from him. Never! I knew that it hurt him to give up the tour, but he knew what he had to do. Through affection for me. Just affection. But it was enough. He nursed me until I was well. I think it was hepatitis, or perhaps it was hemorrhoids; goodness, I've had so *many* things. And then, when I was well enough to travel, we came back to New York, and he was out of work for more than a year. But he never reproached me, never regretted what he had done, never mentioned it again. So you see, dear, loving with no hope of love in return can have its rewards—unexpected rewards."

Barbara was depressed; eyes lowered, head bowed, shoulders slumped.

"I don't think David would ever nurse me," she said mournfully. "He'd just go on with the tour and leave me there."

"David is a very young man, dear."

"I don't mind that. But what scares me, why I don't want to marry him, is that I'm afraid he'll never grow up."

Cynthia put her spectacles back on, began to gather up her knitting and stuff it into a paper shopping bag from Zabar's Delicatessen.

"Well, you must make up your mind, Barbara. I try never to advise people. When your advice is bad, and they take it, they never forgive you. And when your advice is good, and they take it, they never forgive you. Oh my! That was witty, wasn't it?"

"Yes," Barbara laughed. "It was."

"Well, dear," Cynthia said, finishing her drink, "you do what you want to do. You know this is your home as long as you want it to be. Just remember that Toby and David are players, in spite of what David thinks. And players need special understanding."

"Special"

"Oh yes." Cynthia nodded. "For instance, Toby and I never had sex when he was in rehearsal. But then after opening night, everything was all right again. Better, if the show was a hit."

"That's odd."

"Is it? Have you and David had sex since he's been in rehearsal?"

"No."

"Well, there you are!" Cynthia said triumphantly. "And it bothered you, didn't it?"

"Yes, if did."

"I know. You thought that just because you were pregnant, he didn't want anything to do with you."

"Yes, that's what I thought."

Cynthia leaned forward, a soft smile lighting her face, recalling another time, another place . . .

"I remember I thought the same thing. Toby was doing Iago when I was carrying David, and I thought he didn't like me any more because he wouldn't come near me. I thought he hated me because I was pregnant and had trapped him. But it wasn't that at all. It was because he was in rehearsal."

"I don't understand that," Barbara said, shaking her head.

"I'm sure I don't either, my dear. I'm just passing along a very odd fact: if you're married to or sleeping with an actor, you must be prepared for an absolute *dry* spell if he's in rehearsal."

"Oh Cynthia, you know so much."

"I know very little, darling. But whatever perception I do have, Toby has given me. Will you think about that?"

"Oh yes . . . yes . . ."

"Now let's go in the kitchen and help Blanche. I think she's making lamb stew. It's Toby's favorite, you know."

The two women left the room. The moment the door closed behind them, Toby Marlow threw the coverlet aside, stumbled to his feet, staggered to the liquor cart. He poured himself a heavy whiskey with a shaking hand, took a deep gulp gratefully.

"JAYSUS H. KEE-RIST!"

He took another swallow, smaller, then drained the glass.

"Mommy," he said aloud, "can I lick the spoon?"

Then he poured another drink, added ice and a little water, and carried the glass as he stalked about the room somewhat weakly, unsteadily. He picked up the cane hanging from the wheelchair, took a few hesitant steps with it, leaning on it. Then he threw it from him angrily and paced unaided.

"'She's making lamb stew,'" he mimicked. "'It's Toby's favorite, you know.' Oh God, oh God, how long must Thou forsake me? Lamb stew, for Chrissake, and she who just said, 'Whatever perception I do have, Toby has given me.' Well, I failed miserably on the subject of lamb stew, luv!"

He laughed, freshened his drink, sat on the edge of the couch. He sipped with one hand, caressed his shiny pate with the other. The room was darkening now, but he made no effort to turn on more lights. The shadows were lengthening. Occasionally he heard muted kitchen sounds and faraway laughter. But Toby was alone, and savoring it. Finally he placed his whiskey glass on the cocktail table and reached for the guitar leaning against the liquor cart. He spread his knees, placed the guitar flat across them. He made a few experimental thrums, paused to tighten a few strings. Then he strummed chords as he sang in a strong, resonant, and not unmusical voice.

"'He that has and a tiny little wit,

"'With a hey, ho, the wind and the rain,

"'Must make content with his fortunes fit,

"'Though the rain it raineth every day . . .'"

He stopped singing but continued to flick the guitar softly, making a rhythm by thudding the box softly with the heel of his hand. Finally he put it aside, stood, and began to wander again. He moved about the room, picking up photos and theatrical memorabilia to inspect them and then put them away gently, remembering and smiling. Then, hands in the pockets of his robe, head lowered, he prowled the room at a faster pace. He stopped once to pick up his glass of whiskey and sip. His speed increased, arms and hands swinging free in wide gestures. He began muttering—nothing intelligible. But as he paced, pausing frequently to sip from his glass, then resuming his prowl, gesturing, his voice became gradually louder with words, disjointed phrases. Finally he nodded . . .

"Got it!" he said, with satisfaction.

He adjusted the gooseneck lamp under which Cynthia had been knitting. The beam of light was now cast upward. Toby took his position in the glare; the effect was of a spotlight. He began to declaim his "big soliloquy," an impromptu speech the scamp had just composed. It was roguish enough to entrance and serious enough to make any listener believe he was speaking the truth. He delivered this rip-off of the big soliloquy from *Hamlet* in the grand manner. It was heroic playing, with broad gestures, obvious expressions, coarse body movements, etc.—just the way he wanted David to deliver the real thing. Now the words were nothing, but he overcame them by his craft. He relished the put-on—knowing the speech was not worth the effort, but his expertise making it convincing. . . .

"To love, or to be loved; that is the question.

"Whether 'tis nobler in the heart to suffer

"The slings and arrows of unrequited lust

"Or to accept with grace and dignity
"Another's sweet devotion and, by accepting,
"Give it life. To love, to hope, and by that hope
"To charge with meaning this life's hopeless days.
"To love, to hope—to dream. Ay, there's the rub!
"For in that dream of lovers what . . ."

His voice faltered, then faded, then stopped. It was silent then; even sounds from the kitchen were stilled. Toby Marlow stared at the lamp/spotlight, far away and remembering . . .

The illumination that suddenly brightened the room was daylight, flooding through three tall windows skimpily covered with torn gauze curtains. It was a hotel room in "Chicago or Santa Fe—some place like that." It was a hotel in the grimy downtown section, close to the theatres, and if it once knew glory, you'd never know it. It had that dented, dusty, worn, splintered, sheepish look of hotel rooms that offer mattresses shared by ten thousand strangers.

The furniture was stained veneer, the wallpaper stained roses, the small rugs merely stains with fringe. There was an entrance from the hotel corridor at right. The door at left led to the bathroom. There were two beds, two chests of drawers, two chairs, two tables, two luggage racks, two lamps, two coat trees, and one awful smell.

Open valises were on the luggage racks. Coats, jackets, trousers, dresses, underwear, shoes were scattered about. There was the expected bottle of whiskey on one of the tables, with two sticky glasses. There were the remains of a breakfast on the other table; clotted coffee cups, an ashtray with a cold cigar butt, crusted dishes, half-eaten rolls, a single apple with one bite experimentally removed, then laid carefully alongside the mother.

Cynthia was in one of the beds, a sheet and thin blanket pulled up to her waist. She was younger, in her late 30s, but now pale, fragile, and moving with the deliberate slowness of the ill. She was reading a novel, pausing occasionally to take a sip of a dark brown liquid from a small medicine bottle. On the floor alongside her bed were more bottles of medicine, tissues, boxes of pills, comb, brush, mirror, makeup, etc.

Cynthia heard a key fumble in the lock and stopped her reading to look up. A younger Toby slammed the door behind him. He strode directly to the whiskey bottle, poured himself half a glass, and downed it. Then he yanked off his hat and scaled it into one corner of the room, peeled off his wig and hurled it into another corner.

"Damn! Damn! Damn!"

"Was he that good, dear?" Cynthia asked sympathetically.

"The son of a bitch was great."

"But he's your friend, Toby."

"So? That makes it all the worse. Who the hell wants to see his friends succeed? He's set for the rest of the tour. Goddamn it, Cyn, why the hell did you have to go and get the bug right now? My notices were marvelous."

"I told you to go on without me, Toby. I wouldn't mind. Truly I wouldn't."

"Ahh . . . screw it!" he said angrily. "I'm out, and Jack's in. Even my costumes fit him—the bastard!"

"Did you tell him how good he was?"

"Oh sure," Toby sighed. "I smiled sincerely and shook his hand. Then I tried to nudge him into the orchestra pit, but he wasn't having any. Damn it to hell, Cyn, I think you got sick deliberately."

"Of course I did, dear. I love this room; it's so comfy. I want to stay here for years and years."

Toby slumped disconsolately in one of the rickety chairs at the table. He began to examine the label on the whiskey bottle as if he had never seen it before. He didn't look at Cynthia when he spoke.

"No. I know what it was. You thought there was something between me and that kid with the balloon tits, and you wanted to break it up, so you pretended to get sick so I'd have to leave the company."

"Now you're being ridiculous," she said coldly. "I never even thought of that. Toby, I am ill. I really am."

"Oh sure," he scoffed.

"Besides, there isn't, is there?"

"Isn't what?"

"Anything between you and that girl?"

"There!" he shouted. "You see? That proves it. It's enough to drive a man to drink."

To prove it, he poured another heavy shot and drained it off as quickly as the first. Then he took a deep breath.

"Well," he said tragically, "there goes my career."

"Oh Toby, don't be so—so dramatic."

"So *dramatic?* My God, that's what I'm supposed to be. That's my job. What did the doctor say?"

"Another week. Then maybe I'll be well enough to travel."

"Another week?" he said gloomily. "Might as well be another year."

"He said my—"

"Stop right there!" Toby cried, holding up a hand. "Women's plumbing is a mystery to me, and I want it to remain a mystery."

"Toby, I'm *suffering!*"

"Well, what the hell do you think I'm doing—flipping my wick? The first good job I've had in three years, and you ruin it."

"I'm sorry," she said faintly.

"Sorry. Fat lot of good that does."

"You needn't be so nasty about it."

"You have no idea how nasty I can be if I put my mind to it."

"I have an inkling, dear," she told him. "I have an inkling. May I have a whiskey, please? The doctor said it would be good for me."

Toby grudgingly poured her a thimbleful of whiskey, barely dampening the inside of the sticky glass. He brought it over to her.

"Oh thank you so much," she said. "I'll sip it slowly so I don't choke on it."

"Well, we've got to go easy on that stuff," Toby said, returning to the table and slouching down again. "I'm off the payroll, you know. If we're lucky, we'll just make it back to New York. But we've got to cut expenses to the bone."

Whereupon he poured himself a huge dollop from the same bottle.

"That's what I like most about you, dear," she said sweetly. "Your self-sacrifice."

"Shut up and heal your ass so we can get out of this hellhole."

They were silent then, shocked to quiet by his snarl. Toby, seated at one of the small tables, had his back half-turned to Cynthia's bed. She knew better than to expect him to make the first tentative offer at reconciliation.

"I really am sorry, Toby," she said softly. "About your losing the job."

He grunted.

"I know how much it meant to you."

He grunted.

"I think it was a sweet and loving thing for you to do, to stay and nurse me."

Then he turned to face her, shaking his head in wild disbelief.

"I must be out of my ever-loving mind. I could have hired a nurse for you, or asked a bellhop to look in occasionally, or *something*."

"But you didn't. Because you love me."

He grunted.

"You love me, don't you?"

"Sure."

"Can't you say it like you mean it?"

He stared at her, all cold hauteur, the Abominable Snowman attacked by swans. In his reply, his rich voice came to life. He pulled out all the stops—a full diapason. He delivered his lines for an audience of two thousand. It was a sincere boom that carried to the balcony, and every syllable was choked with deep, heartfelt emotion.

"Cynthia, I love you. I love you more than any woman I've ever known."

"Much better," she said approvingly.

"What do you want to eat?" he said.

"You."

"Don't be silly. I might catch what you've got. There's a Chinese place around the corner. Do you feel like some fantail shrimp?"

"After what the doctor did to me today," she said, "I feel *exactly* like some fantail shrimp."

"Not bad." He smiled.

"You're not angry with me any more?"

"Would it do me any good?"

"But you'll never let me forget it, will you?" she mourned. "I mean getting sick and making you leave the company. You'll keep reminding me of the sacrifice you made for me, won't you?"

"Of course."

"For years and years."

"As long as we both shall live." He nodded.

"And you're not joking. Because from now on, every time I catch you doing something dreadful, you'll weasel out of it by reminding me of the time I cost you your job."

"So?" he said. "That's normal, adult human behavior."

"Oh God, why must I love you so much?"

"Who can resist me?"

"I wish I could." She sighed. "But I can't. Toby, please don't stop letting me love you. I would die, just die."

"Love away, dear," he said cheerily. "Love away."

"And tell me again you had nothing to do with that girl."

"What girl?"

"The one with the pumpkins."

"I swear I had nothing to do with the girl with the pumpkins."

"Besides," Cynthia said, "her body isn't all that great. I saw her in the dressing room, and she has this great horrible appendicitis scar that looks like you could mail letters in it."

"What appendicitis scar?" he said. "I didn't see—"

His mouth clamped shut—too late, he had been trapped.

"You bastard!" Cynthia gasped.

She collapsed down into her bed, face in hands, weeping bitterly. Toby immediately rushed to her side. He sat on the bed, gathered her into his arms. He pressed her to him, her face against his chest. He stroked her hair, stroking, stroking . . .

"Love me, Cyn," he whispered. "Love me, love me, love me . . ."

But then the light from the gooseneck lamp in the Marlow living room on Central Park West was there. It glowed, it shone, it beamed, haloing an exultant Toby Marlow as he concluded his grand soliloquy triumphantly, arms flung wide . . .

"To love, or to be loved: which is the better fate?
"For rarely do the two find a happy junction,
"But each must waste of talent and desire
"On a partner not his natural mate.
"But what care I for this philosophy?
"I love myself—and Cynthia loves me!"

Scene Three

TEN DAYS later, again in the Marlows' living room, dimly lighted by flickering flames in the brick fireplace . . . It was almost midnight. Barbara Evings was alone, moving slowly about in the dimness, almost drifting. She was softly crooning a folksong to herself: "Black is the color of my true love's hair . . ." or "I know who I love and I know where I'm going . . ." or something like that. Alone, enormously pregnant, singing to herself, she seemed particularly young and vulnerable.

Suddenly the hallway door banged open; David Marlow strode in. He slammed the door behind him, rushed directly to the liquor cart. Barbara lowered herself cautiously onto the couch and watched him pour a large glass of whiskey. He demolished almost half of it in one gargantuan swallow. He gagged on it, gasped, coughed. Then he took another small sip, quieted down, took a deep breath. He flopped on the couch, away from Barbara. He hunched over, head down, hands and drink between his spread knees.

"Bad?" she asked sympathetically.

"A disaster," he said dully. "Everything went wrong that could possibly go wrong."

"Isn't that what a dress rehearsal is for—to find out what can go wrong, what *is* wrong, and fix it?"

"Supposed to be." He nodded. "But it's too late to fix this performance."

"David, what *is* it?"

He sighed, took another sip of his drink. He straightened up, then slid down to a slumped position. His head was pressed against the back of the couch; he stared at the ceiling.

"It was me. I was a stick. I know it. No fire, no passion, no guts. The words came out like lumps. Cinders. Forgot my lines a dozen times. Stumbled twice. Knocked over a prop. Dropped my sword in the dueling scene. Oh, I was beautiful."

"Just nerves," she comforted him.

"Nerves? Why should I have nerves at a dress rehearsal? No, it was more than that. I was halfway through the 'What a piece of work is man' speech, and suddenly I realized I just didn't have it. No confidence. I should never have taken the part, never have tried out for it. Maybe I'm too young, too inexperienced. I'm just not ready for it. Maybe someday I will be. Maybe.

Someday. But not now, not for tomorrow night. And everyone knew it. I could see it in their looks—those damned, happy, triumphant looks. The play will go down, but they'll salvage some pleasure from my failure. That's the way people are."

"Are they?"

"Sure," he said bitterly. "If they could think of any reason to cancel, it would be off the boards right now. Well . . . maybe I'll be lucky and lose my voice before tomorrow night, or step in front of a gypsy cab—or *something*."

He sighed again, finished his drink. He rose, started for the liquor cart. Then he stopped, stared around, became aware for the first time of the quietness and emptiness of the room.

"Where is everyone?" he asked Barbara.

"Gone to bed. Toby is very bad. He threw up right after dinner."

"Lamb stew?"

"No, just the soft things he's been eating lately—the cottage cheese and custard. But he couldn't keep it down. Cynthia was frightened and called Doctor Jake. He came over, and finally they got Toby to sleep. He was in awful pain."

"Moaning and groaning, I suppose?"

"Oh yes," Barbara said. "He wouldn't let a chance like that go by. He insisted on kissing us all good-by, and he left a message for you."

"Oh God, did he? The old ham! All right, what was the message?"

"He said to tell you to stop masturbating."

"Stop masturbating? What the hell's with him? I don't masturbate. Haven't since I got out of the Coast Guard. Was he delirious?"

"With Toby, it's hard to tell."

"It sure as hell is," he agreed. "Want a drink?"

"A little glass of port, please."

David replenished his own glass, poured Barbara a small glass of wine. He brought it to her, and sat closer to her this time.

"Mother with him now?" he asked.

"Yes. She and Blanche and I are going to take turns sitting up all night with him. I go on in an hour, but I couldn't sleep so I decided to wait up for you."

David was shocked.

"Sitting up with him all night? The three of you? Jesus Christ, that doesn't sound good."

"No, it isn't," she said sadly. "He's going, David. Doctor Jake told Cynthia it could be any time, and not more than a week."

"Oh God," David groaned. "That means he won't be able to see me open tomorrow night."

"No."

"Well, maybe that's for the best. That would kill him if anything would. But shouldn't he be in the hospital?"

"He won't go."

"The hell with what he wants! We'll make him go."

"Make Toby do something he doesn't want to do?"

"Jake can give him a shot, knock him out, and we'll get him over there before he knows what's happening."

"David, would you do that to Toby?"

"If it'll save his life."

"It won't. Doctor Jake says they couldn't do anything for him. He says let the man die in peace in his own home if that's what he wants."

"Die in peace?" David repeated incredulously. "That's a laugh. Toby never did anything in peace in his whole life, and he's not about to start now. He'll go kicking and screaming, in the greatest display of histrionics you've ever seen. Oh God, what an ugly, depressing, fucked-up, senseless world this is."

"Didn't Will say that better?" she mocked him.

"You mean, 'O God! O God! how weary, stale, flat, and unprofitable seem to me all the uses of this world'! Act One, Scene Two. See, I do know my lines. Yes, Will said everything better. And he deserves a better actor than me."

They were silent a long moment. Then she moved clumsily along the couch, sliding closer to him. She put a hand on his arm.

"Are you hungry, David? I can make you a sandwich. There's some cold roast beef."

"No, thanks. My stomach's a knot. I couldn't swallow. I'm all wound up."

"Do you want me to sleep with you tonight?" she asked softly. "I will, if you want me to."

He touched her face tenderly.

"No, luv. I want you, but not out of pity."

"We can't *do* anything," she said. "Well . . . maybe I could do something. Or we could just lie there. I don't think you should be alone tonight."

"I appreciate it," he said, somewhat formally, "but no, thanks. I'll be all right. I'll get through this by myself."

"You won't give and you won't take," she said angrily.

He pulled away from her and stared.

"What the hell is that supposed to mean? Come on—let's have it. It won't make this night any worse than it's been. Nothing can do that."

"Oh . . . what's the use, David?" she said wearily. "We've been through all this before. Let's just try to stay friends. Can't we do that?"

"Jesus Christ, you're a walking soap opera! 'No, David, I will not marry you. But can't we still be friends! I'll cherish the memory of you forever.' What shit!"

"Toby would have played those lines better," she said.

He rose in a fury and began stalking about the room, his voice growing louder. . . .

"Toby, Toby, Toby!" he cried. "That's all I've been hearing all my life. 'Toby can do it better. You'll never be the player Toby is. Go ask Toby how to do it.' Goddamn it, I'm grown up and I'm my own man. I don't care how Toby would deliver those lines or how Toby would play that scene. I'm me—*David* Marlow! I'll never be Toby, and thank God for that! Don't any of you realize what a ridiculous clown he is? With his posturings and grand manner and heroic acting and gestures and a style that were hilarious thirty years ago? The man's a silly old fossil! Can't you see that? He's living in a never-never land of Duse and Barrymore and W. C. Fields. Gone, all gone. You can't act that way any more. You'd be laughed off the stage. People want to think, to know . . . You've got to go deeper, down, down, within yourself, to reveal the truth."

"What truth?" she asked quietly.

"What?" he cried, still excited. "What?"

"What truth must you reveal, David?"

"Well . . . the truth, just the truth. Is there more than one truth?"

"Isn't there? For Hamlet and for Othello? For Duke Mantee and for Billy Budd. For Stanley Kowalski and for King Arthur? They're all truths, aren't they? Different, but true."

"I won't play at them," he shouted stubbornly. "I won't pretend."
"You can," she said. "I know you can."
"I can't."
"Remember that Sunday morning the baby was born?"
He looked at her, flummoxed.
"Born?"
"Well . . . conceived."
"How can you know?" he scoffed.
"I *do!* I do know. *That* morning you pretended. And it was beautiful.
Beautiful. . . ."

They gazed at each other, remembering, and suddenly the Marlows' living
room was wiped out by a sudden torrent of white light as if a master
electrician had thrown the switch of floods, spots, foots, borders. It was a
milky glare blazing Barbara Evings' former loft apartment. A single long
room dwindling to a blur. The furnishings were minimal, all painted white.
Even the few framed graphics on the walls seemed to be hidden behind
white silk gauze, or perhaps the viewer's eyeballs had been lightly smeared
with Vaseline.
    It was a lazy Sunday morning in this out-of-focus scene. Barbara and
David were seated at a small white bistro table, on white wire ice-cream
parlor chairs. Both were barefoot, wearing white terry-cloth robes. On the
table was a white pitcher of coffee and a white china platter of croissants.
Farther back in the hazy room, drenched with light, was a folding bed—
really a wire cot with a thin mattress; the type of bed that can be doubled
up and wheeled into a closet.
    The entire room had a pleasing simplicity, a peaceful emptiness, a
kind of vacant charm. And over all hung the quiet languor of Sunday
morning.
    David selected a croissant from the platter and held it up near his mouth
and ear, like a French telephone.
    "Hello?" he said. "Tom?"
    Barbara looked at him a moment, puzzled. Then her face cleared, she
selected a croissant daintily, and held it to her ear and mouth.
    "I'm sorry," she said. "I think you have the wrong number."
    "Isn't this 555–1212?"
    "No, it's 4X7–G9T3–19678326–K."
    "I beg your pardon, I must have dialed the wrong number."
    "That's all right," Barbara said. "Could have happened to anyone. It's
nice to hear a wrong number apologize."
    "Yes. Well, good-by now."
    "Good-bye," she said.
    They paused, looked speculatively at each other. After a moment
Barbara ate a bit of her croissant, crunching off the tip. David did the same
with his croissant, then moved it closer to his mouth to speak.
    "Hello?" Barbara said eagerly.
    "Look," David said. "I called last night. I asked for a man named Tom.
Or perhaps Bernie. You answered. I had dialed the wrong number, and I
apologized."
    "I remember," Barbara said. "And . . .?"
    "Well . . . I'm not an obscene phone caller or anything like that.
Except . . ."
    "Except what?"
    "I like your voice," he said with a rush. "Look, if I'm annoying you or

offending you, please tell me and I'll hang up, and I swear I'll never call you again."

"Why are you calling me now?"

"Well . . . as I said, I like your voice. And . . ."

"And?"

"And I just wanted to say hello."

"Oh," she said. "Well . . . hello."

"You won't be offended if I call again?" he asked.

"No. I won't be offended."

During this exchange, each nibbled on his croissant while the other spoke. Now, pastries reduced to crumbs, each selected a new croissant from the platter, took a sip of coffee, and the dialogue continued as before. Both were deliberately solemn, deadpan, but as the exchange progressed, a certain tension began to build; the "play acting" began to cut close to the bone, and what began as fantasy and sleepy Sunday-morning nuttiness started to take on a significance neither had anticipated. David raised his croissant. . . .

"Good evening!" he said cheerfully.

"Hello!" she caroled into her croissant.

"How are you?"

"I've got a little cold. Can't you hear?"

"What are you taking for it?"

"What are you offering?"

"Ho ho. Look, I said it last night: if you don't want me to call, if I'm bothering you, for God's sake tell me. I'm not a fiend, really I'm not."

"If you are, you're a very *nice* fiend."

"Then I can call you again?"

"If you like . . ."

Their fantasy had begun lazily, drawled. But now the tempo began to pick up; they spoke faster and, curiously, they no longer looked at each other, but peered intently at their coffee cups or croissant phones. Nibbling, of course.

"Hello?" Barbara said.

"Hi," David said. "It's me again. How's the cold?"

"Better, thank you. I was afraid it might be the flu or a virus. But now I think it's just the sniffles. May I ask you a personal question?"

"Must I answer?"

"No. Of course not."

"Sure, go ahead—ask."

"What's your name?"

David paused a moment.

"Romeo," he said finally.

"That's a nice name," she said. "Polish?"

"Swedish, ekshully. What's yours?"

"Juliet."

"Oh? French?"

"Assyrian, ekshully. On my mother's side. The left one. My father is an Irish setter."

"My father is a paranoid," David said.

"Lovely country that."

"Oh yes," he agreed. "Especially in the spring."

"How old are you, Romeo?" she asked.

"I'm fifteen."

"And what do you want to be when you grow up?"

"Sixteen. How old are you?"

"Thirteen," she said, "going on twelve."

"Strange," he said. "I had pictured you as a much younger woman. Do you work?"

"What else?"

"What do you do?"

"I'm an opera singer. Contralto. But I moonlight as a stewardess on a ferry boat."

"They have their own boats now?"

"What do you do?"

"I'm a brain surgeon," he said. "But I moonlight as a short-order cook. My limit is two eggs. Got anyone? A man. I mean?"

"A few," she said. "Nothing serious. Do you have a woman?"

"Yes. I've been seeing her for years. Since I was six."

"Going to marry her?"

"I suppose so," he said. "Eventually. Life isn't all bubble gum, is it?"

"No," she said, picking up on his sudden seriousness. "It isn't."

"You sound down tonight."

"I am . . . down."

"I guess I shouldn't have called."

"No, no. I'm glad you did. It's hearing a human voice. You know?"

"Oh God, do I ever know!" he said. "Will you call me—some time?"

"I may."

"Please do. I want you to. If I'm not in, please try again. I have crazy hours."

"How tall are you?"

"I'm almost four feet."

"Goodness. I'll have to wear heels. Good night, Romeo."

"Are you really glad I called?"

"Yes, I'm really glad."

"That's nice. Good night, Juliet."

They both reached for new croissants. They were becoming troubled—well, perhaps not troubled but stirred by their manic dialogue. Maybe they sensed their pretense had taken on a life of its own; they could not control how it might develop. Their make-believe had suddenly assumed a stature and dignity they had not intended. My God, it was *significant!* And who knew where or how it might end? Still, they were too involved and too curious to get off.

"Hello," Barbara said.

"Oh! *You* called *me!*"

"I surely did."

"Loverly," he gurgled. "How's the cold?"

"Much better, thank you. And I bought a new hat today, and that helped."

"What's it like?"

"The hat? Like a man's fedora. Wide, slouch brim. Makes me look like Ava Gardner in that African picture with Clark Gable."

"I look a little like Clark Gable," he said. "Around the knees. What color is the hat?"

"A deep red."

"Sounds marvelous."

"It does wonders for me. I wore it home and bookkeepers whistled at me. Great for my bedraggled ego."

"Listen . . ." he said hesitantly, "do you think we should see each other? You know—meet?"

"No," she said firmly. "I don't. Do you?"

"I guess not. Let's keep it like this."

"No disappointments this way."

"Right," he said stiffly. "No disappointments. How's the job?"

"Shitty. And yours?"

"Shitty. Anything doing in the romance department?"

"Very quiet. And you?"

"The usual," he said. "More of the same. No problems, but boring, boring, boring."

"Are you angry with me?" she asked.

"Angry? Of course not. Why should I be angry?"

"I don't know. But there's something in your voice. You think we should see each other?"

"Oh no. No. You were absolutely right. Avoid disappointments. Yes, that's the right thing to do."

"Will you call me tomorrow night?"

"Sure."

"Promise?"

"Of course," he said, somewhat coldly. "I promise. I'll call tomorrow night. I'll make a note of it."

They were tense now, gobbling up their croissants. It teetered, the scene, and they sensed it could go either way. One wrong word, a tonal quality. . . . But neither had the courage to end it. The risk was exciting. They plugged their pastries into their ears.

"Hi, Juliet," he sang.

"You didn't call me last night," she said stonily.

"I know," he said softly. "Not that I didn't want to. But I got involved in a kind of a party."

"Your woman?" she said coldly.

"Yes."

"Is she nice?"

"Of course she's nice. Unexciting but nice."

"Did you have fun?"

"Not much. What did you do?"

"I had a date," she said firmly.

"Fun?"

"Oh . . . I guess. Dinner at a new Italian restaurant. It was so-so. Then we went to one of those Greek places where everyone throws soup plates at the dancers. He saw me home to my door, and that was that. I didn't ask him in, in case you're wondering."

"Yes, I was."

"So was I," she said, "about an hour later. Then I took a pill and went to sleep. Do you take sleeping pills?"

"Doesn't everyone?"

"Oh God, Romeo," she said, thawing, "there's got to be more to it than this. Listen . . ."

"What?"

"Don't stop calling me. Please."

"You!" he cried exultantly. "*You!* Don't *you* stop calling *me!* I need it."

"I know, I know," she said. "How awful."

"Isn't it."

"Romeo."

"Juliet."

They sensed they had successfully skirted some horrible chasm, some terrible fate. Now they could look directly at each other and smile, gnawing their pastries and waiting to see how the play ended. They leaned toward each other across the little bistro table, excited and anticipating. The croissants were held in trembling hands. . . .

"Hello?" Barbara said nervously.

"Hi, Juliet."

"Romeo! I'm *so* happy you called."

"What are you doing?"

"Counting the walls. I'm so fucking bored." She paused a moment, then: "Do you mind my using words like that?"

"Words like 'bored'?"

"Smart-ass. You know what I mean. Do you mind?"

"Four-letter words?" he asked.

"That's right," she said. "Like 'love.' Do you mind?"

"Of course I don't mind. How are you?"

"I am very well, thank you. And how are you?"

"I am very well, thank you," he answered. "Well, now that we've got all the polite shit out of the way, I want to tell you about an article I read. It was about some survey they made about how bachelors live and their life expectancy and all that."

"Are you a bachelor, Romeo?"

"No, I'm married and have ten children and I'm calling from home."

"I wouldn't be a bit surprised."

"Yes, you silly dear. I'm a bachelor."

"Good on you."

"Are you married?"

"I was. I'm not now."

"What happened?" he asked.

"That was the problem," she replied. "Nothing happened. What about this article you read about bachelors?"

"Well, it said bachelors die off faster than married men. They commit suicide more often, they have a higher percentage of mental disorders, and they end up doing swell things like lifting little girls' skirts and watching apartments across the way through telescopes."

"Does that scare you—lifting my skirt?"

"Strange, but that doesn't scare me."

"Did this article say anything about women bachelors?"

"No."

"Double it in spades. Fun it ain't."

"I know. Do you ever see your ex husband?"

"Occasionally. We're still friends."

"Any children?"

"No," she said.

"That's lucky."

"Yes. Lucky. Are you really four feet tall?"

"Almost."

"What color hair?" she asked.

"Green. What color is yours?"

"Blue. And I work very hard to keep it that way. Listen, Romeo, I have a very personal question to ask you."

"Ask away."

"Do you play Scrabble?"

"No."

"Well . . . no one's perfect."

"You are," David said. "I love you, Juliet."

"Do you?" she said wonderingly.

"I'm beginning to think so. What are you doing this weekend?"

"Going away. Up to the lake. A married couple I know."

"Will they have a man for you?"

"Of course. They always do. A man with nostrils. Do you have nostrils?"

"Naturally."

"That flutter?"

"No, my nostrils don't flutter. I'm going away, too. A dude ranch."

"With your woman?"

"Yes."

"That article about bachelors really scared you, didn't it?"

"It surely did."

"Going to propose?" she asked.

"It didn't scare me that much," he said.

"It only hurts when you laugh," she advised.

"I know. Can I call you on Monday?"

"Do you have to ask?"

"I'll tell you all about the dude ranch, and you tell me about the guy with the fluttering nostrils."

"I could tell you all about him right now, and I haven't even met him yet. A blank."

"That's what the dude ranch will be. A blank. I hate horses. They're so fucking superior."

"Why are you going?"

"She promised a mare."

"How's the sex?"

"Well . . ." he said. "You know. Comme ci, comme ça."

"The story of my life," she said. "Are you in bed right now?"

"Yes."

"Naked?"

"Yes," he said in a low voice. "Are you?"

"Yes. Let's breathe heavily at each other for a while."

"Don't joke about it," he said, hurt.

"I'm sorry," she said. "I shouldn't have. Please forgive me."

"Sure."

"I joke about things too much, I know. I joke because . . . well, you know. I *have* to joke."

"I know, Juliet."

"Do you really love me?"

"I really do."

"I love you, Romeo. Can you take that?"

"Can I ever! Say it again."

"I love you, Romeo."

Suddenly, inexplicably excited by their sappy dialogue, Barbara and David rose simultaneously to their feet and moved toward the bed, turning their backs on the croissant crumbs. They didn't rush, but they didn't dawdle either. Their white robes dropped magically away; their movements seemed to slow as they swam gracefully naked through the aquarium of light. The bed loomed hazily out of the glare, as through a white scrim, and the room and time had the elusive quality of a vaguely remembered dream.

David lay on the bed, on his back, his engorged cudgel pointing accusingly at God. Barbara stood at the bedside, then leaned forward to touch him lightly, lovingly. . . .

"Romeo, Romeo," she murmured, "what a big little boy you are."

The white glare sheened their flesh, made faint lilac shadows in the hollows of their bodies when they moved. . . .

"Horses are so fucking superior," he repeated in a whisper.

Obediently, with more crave than grace, she swung one leg wide across him and, with a minimum of fuss, impaled herself, sitting atop him, knees drawn up alongside his waist. Hands on his shoulders, she leaned forward so her long hair enveloped their faces. Unseen by bachelors with telescopes, they kissed and kissed. . . .

His hands sought the long muscles of her hard back, swoop of waist, flare of ass. They pulled her to him with slowly increasing urgency. She straightened up astride him, pushed her hair back with both hands, a movement she knew would please him, and hopefully inflame. . . .

It did! His eyes were half shut now, his mouth half open, and she began to move, fitting her gait to his. Their groans were soft and dignified, almost lost in the not unmusical squeaks and twangs of the wire cot. . . .

Here their dialogue was improvised, consisting of equal measures of passion and gibberish. The names David, Barbara, Romeo, and Juliet were heard frequently. along with reiterated protestations of love and undying allegiance, interspersed by increasing sobs of pleasure, moans of delight, and similar stuff. Experienced players know how to do this sort of thing well.

Their litany was suddenly interrupted by a loud metallic *crack*! clearly heard but, understandably, disregarded by the players. A cold-eyed critic would have soon become aware that an important part of the bed—a rigid strut that held it in its unfolded position—had broken under the unusual strains placed upon it. Before the horrified stare of such a critic, the bed, with most of the weight and now violent shocks concentrated in the middle, began to fold up like a giant clam shell lined with mattress and sheets.

Slowly the head section and the foot section lifted their legs from the floor. The two halves wavered in the air, then paused a brief moment. But the players, now locked in the final anguish of their desire, were oblivious to their danger. If anything, their labors increased, in tempo and fury, and so intense was their concentration that their howls of bliss drowned out the cracking that resumed beneath them.

David's head, shoulders, and upper torso rose slowly, mysteriously, from his waist, as his legs did from his hips. As the bed inexorably folded up, so did he, and Barbara was forced to sit erect, her nose elevated, to escape suffocation.

But they were determined not to be halted short of their goal by accident, war, or Act of Princes. Their final scream of triumph rang out, somewhat muffled, even as the perfidious bed completed its closing with a *chwung*!, entrapping them in closer embrace than ever lovers dreamt.

The room and memories went dark, to be replaced by the dimness and flickering flames in the fireplace of the Marlows' living room. David and the pregnant Barbara were back in their original positions: she sitting on the couch, he standing nearby.

'That Sunday morning the baby was made," she said dreamily. "I know it."

"How do you know?" he asked.

"I just do."

"Well . . . maybe." He shrugged. "We were lucky to get out of that damned thing alive."

"I just wanted you to remember that you *can* pretend. You did that morning. And you can again."

"That morning was—well, just between us. It has nothing to do with my job, with acting. I won't pretend at that."

"Oh no," she said. "You'll be yourself, won't you? Your own sweet self. You'll go deeper, down, down, within yourself to reveal 'the truth.' *Your* truth. And just what is that? Something I wouldn't marry in a million years. So locked up inside yourself, closed off to me, so conscious of your own thoughts and motivations that you lose all conception of what the playwright is trying to say. The writer—that poor man! At least he's *trying* to create something, to open a window, to make the world a little wider, a little bigger." (*Hear, hear!—Author.*) "But you take what he's done and sqeeze it down so it reflects only *you* and has no more meaning than *you* can bring to it."

She hauled herself to her feet with difficulty, shaking off his proffered hand angrily. She waddled to the door, yanked it open. Then she turned to glare at him. . . .

Toby was right," she yelled. "Why don't you stop masturbating, you—you *organist!*"

He looked at her in astonishment, shaking his head.

"What?" he said. "What was that? Why am I an organist?"

"An organist is a man who spills his seed upon the ground. It's in the bible."

"Oh Jesus," he said, "you mean *onanist*, not organist."

"Well, what the hell's the difference?" she shouted, slamming out.

SCENE FOUR

TOBY MARLOW was dying—and didn't care who knew it. He lay propped up on bolsters, glaring indignantly at the world, in his own bed, in the Marlows' bedroom. Cynthia, Blanche, and Barbara hovered nearby. David stood helplessly to one side. The scene was as artfully composed as a crèche. The room was brilliantly illuminated with chandelier, lamps, the red neon sign flashing 'Marlow . . . Marlow . . .'

"Turn on the goddam lights!" Toby cried petulantly. "Why is it so dark in here?"

"The lights are on, dear," Cynthia said softly. "All the lights."

"Then brings some candles," Toby insisted. "For the love of God, give me some light."

Blanche went over to the commode, lighted tapers in twin candelabra. She placed one on the table next to Toby's bed. She held the other close to his face.

"Light, Toby," she said.

"Who's that? Who's that?"

"Blanche, Toby."

"Blanche, the horse. We never did fuck, did we, babe?"

"No, Toby. We never did."

"In the next world, I promise. Where's David?"

"I'm here, Father," he said, stepping forward.

"'Father.' That's the first you've called me that."

"Yes. The first time."

"Soon enough. Soon enough. Why aren't you at the theatre?"

"There's time Toby. There's time."

"No, no. You can't be late. Not professional. Makeup and costume. Do you have a dresser?"

"No, no dressers. We help each other."

"I had a dresser," Toby said. "Once. Blanche was a dresser, weren't you, Blanche?"

"Yes, I—"

"Cyn?" he cried out. "Cyn? Are you there? Where the hell is Cyn?"

"I'm here, Toby."

"Hold my hand," he said, and she took his hand and continued to hold it to the end. "Cyn. Dear Cynthia. Cyn, Cyn, Cyn. That's how you caught me. Captured me. By sin! You grabbed me by the balls, hung on, and never would let go."

"Yes, Toby. That's how I did it."

"Barbara?" he asked. "She here?"

"I'm here, Toby."

"I met you too late, sweet. Too late. What a brangle-buttock game we could have had. And rub the bacon . . . 'Ring down the curtain, the farce is over.' Who wrote that, shithead?"

"I don't know, Toby," David said.

"Someone did," Toby murmured. " 'Ring down the curtain, the farce is over.' Bad line. But there are no bad parts, just . . . How many sides do you have, David?"

"What? I don't understand."

"In the old days . . . in the old days . . ."

"Shh, dear," Cynthia soothed. "Just lie quietly. Try not to talk."

"Not talk? Why don't you tell me not to breathe? 'Give sorrow words; the grief that does not speak whispers the o'er-fraught heart and bids it break.' David? What?"

"*Macbeth*," David said.

"Yes. Will again. Oh how lovely! The dear, dear man. I'm going to be in hell with Will. They'd never let him into heaven, he who knew so much of vice and lechery. 'All in all, I'd rather be in Philadelphia.' That was W. C. Fields. I knew him, you know. His epitaph. He called Chaplin a goddamn ballet dancer. Sides. When we didn't have mimeograph or Xerox machines, David, that was how you got your part. Not the entire script, but just the pages that had your lines and cues. So you judged the importance of the part by the number of sides you got."

"But not always," Blanche said.

"Right," Toby said faintly. "Not always. You might be a butler and have forty-five sides, but each typed sheet would only have your 'Yes, milord' or 'No, milord' and your cues on it. The trick was getting a big number of sides in sequence, a real scene. Right, Blanche?"

"Right."

"Right, Cynthia?"

"Right, Toby. The most number of sides I ever had was nine."

"Once . . ." he said, "once I had three thousand, four hundred and eighty-nine in one play."

"Oh Toby . . ." Cynthia said.

"I did! I did! Four thousand, three hundred, and ninety-eight. Sides. How many sides have I had in my lifetime . . . how many sides . . .?"

"Do you want to sleep now, dear?" she said gently.

"No, I do not—*Oh Jesus!*"

He groaned in agony, jerked halfway up, hugging his midsection.

"Squeeze my hand," Cynthia said. "Is the pain bad?"

"Screw the pain," he gasped, falling back. "I was hissed off the stage at the Palladium. Is there any pain worse than that? Cynthia. . . ."

"I'm here, Toby."

"We're married now, aren't we, Cyn?"

"Yes, Toby, we're married."

"And my bastard shithead is now my own dear, sweet shithead. Is he at the theatre?"

"No, Father. I'm here. There's time, there's time."

"No. No time, no time. Barbara? Are you there? I can't see you."

"Here, Toby."

"Kiss me, luv," he murmured. "On the lips." She leaned over and kissed him on the lips. "Oh," he breathed. "Oh, Cyn, I may go away for a little while. With Barbara."

"But you'll come back to me," she said.

"Oh yes. Oh yes. I always come back . . . to you. . . ."

There was no more talk, for a while. The door opened slowly, and Jacob Ostretter and Julius Ostretter, both clad in black, entered quietly with their identical wives, in their gold lamé dresses and high, teased beehive hairdoos. The four took up stations at the corners of Toby's bed, standing erect with hands folded in front, shockingly similar to the honor guard at the bier of an important personage.

"Who's there?" Toby cried. "Who's there?"

"Friends, Toby," Jacob Ostretter said.

"Friends," he repeated. "Friends and lovers. Oh, what a life that was! 'Think only this when I have gone: that there was laughter, love, and tears as sweet as wine.' Who wrote that, David?"

"I don't know, Father."

"I wrote that. *I*. Toby Marlow. A player. I wrote that. Yes . . . I did . . . just now . . ."

The lights were gradually dimming now, from the rear of the room forward, all growing darker, darker . . .

"Get thee to a theatre, go!" Toby shouted.

"There is time," David repeated.

"No time. No time. Shuck off your husk, my legal and passionless son. Throw off that shell that—Cynthia, what is that fish that has a shell?"

"Shrimp?"

"No. Blanche?"

"Lobster?"

"No. Barbara?"

"A kind of crustacean?"

"Crustacean! Beautiful word. Why must you be a crustacean, blood of my blood and seed of my seed? Open yourself and throw off your crust, you sweet, sweet shithead. Give. Please give. You have it; I know you have it. Are you not my legal and devoted heir? I am in you, and all you must learn is to give and spend. Give all and spend all, and never fear the well runs dry because . . . because . . . Cynthia, what do I want to say?"

"You've said it, Toby"

"Have I? Have I said it all? Thank God for that. It was a good run, a good run. And they applauded. Most of the time. I wouldn't change . . . Remember, in . . . in some place . . . She came to my dressing room with a single rose. Was that you, Cyn?"

"Yes, Toby. I did that."

"You were a lousy player, Cyn."

"I know Toby."

"But a marvelous fuck. You were always a marvelous fuck, Cynthia."

"Thank you, Toby," she said, quite sincerely.

"Is that your hand?" he asked.

"Yes, it is my hand."

"Good. Good. You know when Barrymore—that was John. Yes, John.

Not Lionel or Ethel. Well, someone said to John, 'Did Hamlet really seduce Ophelia?' And John said, 'Well . . . maybe in the Chicago company.' No, no. That's not the story. Oh . . . Now . . . When John Barrymore was going down, defeated by the demon rum and his own terror, he saw a very young and pretty girl—Barbara, are you listening?"

"I'm listening, Toby."

"It was a good run, a good run. He said—John Barrymore said—'So much to do, so little time.' Yes. I could have . . . I might have . . . Ahh, the hell with it. It's getting late."

"Hang on, you son of a bitch,"Blanche said, weeping.

"O!" he said, "I can't! I can't any more. Hoc in Spiritum sed non in corpore. That's Latin. I know a little bit of Latin. I know a little bit of everything. Cynthia?"

"I'm here, Toby."

"I loved you all the time." he said. "All the time."

"I knew that, Toby," she said, not weeping. "I knew it."

"Good. Good. David, open yourself to . . ."

The lights had gradually dimmed until there was now just a circle of soft radiance about the bed. There was no more talk. Toby Marlow, player, had died. Barbara dropped heavily to her knees and took his other hand to kiss it. The Ostretters were immobile. Blanche was weeping silently, making no effort to cover her face. Cynthia, still clutching Toby's dead hand, did not move.

"'Now cracks a noble heart,' " David said. " 'Goodnight . . .' "

But he could not finish Horatio's speech. He began sobbing and fell to his knees at his father's bedside, embracing the dead man. As he wept uncontrollably, footlights came on, a spotlight glared, and when the still weeping David stood and faced the audience, he was the only one seen clearly; the others, in postures of grief, were in semidarkness. David strode to the footlights, challenging the audience. He flung his arms wide and began the big soliloquy from *Hamlet*, with grand gestures, in the heroic manner, opening himself to the world. . . .

" 'To be, or not to be: that is the question.

" 'Whether 'tis nobler in the mind to suffer the . . .' "

He continued declaiming, *playing* the role, as . . .

. . . the curtain falls.